DIAMOND
GERMAN
DICTIONARY

GERMAN · ENGLISH   ENGLISH · GERMAN

Leona Robertson

This edition published 1994 by
Diamond Books
77–85 Fulham Palace Road
Hammersmith, London W6 8JB

Reprinted 1992

Latest reprint 1994

---

contributors
Veronika Schnorr, Ute Nicol, Peter Terrell

assistant editor
Anne Dickinson

Printed in Great Britain

VORWORT

Der Wörterbuchbenutzer, dem es darum geht, Englisch zu lesen und zu verstehen, findet in diesem Wörterbuch eine ausführliche Erfassung der englischen Gegenwartssprache mit zahlreichen gebräuchlichen Wendungen und Anwendungsbeispielen. Er findet in alphabetischen Listen auch die häufigsten geläufigen Abkürzungen, Kurzwörter und Ortsnamen.

Der Benutzer, der sich verständigen, also auf Englisch ausdrücken will, findet eine klare und ausführliche Behandlung aller Grundwörter mit zahlreichen Hinweisen für eine angebrachte Übersetzung und den korrekten Gebrauch.

INTRODUCTION

The user whose aim is to read and understand German will find a comprehensive and up-to-date wordlist including numerous phrases in current use. He will also find listed alphabetically the main irregular forms with a cross-reference to the basic form where a translation is given, as well as some of the most common abbreviations, acronyms and geographical names in separate alphabetical lists.

The user who wishes to communicate and to express himself in the foreign language will find clear and detailed treatment of all the basic words, with numerous indicators pointing to the appropriate translation, and helping him to use it correctly.

Adjektiv	a	adjective
Abkürzung	abbr	abbreviation
Akkusativ	acc	accusative
Adverb	ad	adverb
Landwirtschaft	Agr	agriculture
Anatomie	Anat	anatomy
Architektur	Archit	architecture
Artikel	art	article
Kunst	Art	art
Astrologie	Astrol	astrology
Astronomie	Astron	astronomy
attributiv	attr	attributive
Kraftfahrzeuge	Aut	automobiles
Hilfsverb	aux	auxiliary
Luftfahrt	Aviat	aviation
Biologie	Biol	biology
Botanik	Bot	botany
britisch	Brit	British
Kartenspiel	Cards	
Chemie	Chem	chemistry
Film	Cine	cinema
Konjunktion	cj	conjunction
umgangssprachlich	col	colloquial
Handel	Comm	commerce
Komparativ	comp	comparative
Kochen und Backen	Cook	cooking
zusammengesetztes Wort	cpd	compound
Dativ	dat	dative
kirchlich	Eccl	ecclesiastical
Elektrizität	Elec	electricity
besonders	esp	especially
und so weiter	etc	et cetera
etwas	etw	something
Euphemismus, Hüllwort	euph	euphemism
Femininum	f	feminine
übertragen	fig	figurative
Finanzwesen	Fin	finance
Genitiv	gen	genitive
Geographie	Geog	geography
Grammatik	Gram	grammar
Geschichte	Hist	history
unpersönlich	impers	impersonal
unbestimmt	indef	indefinite
nicht getrennt gebraucht	insep	inseparable
Interjektion, Ausruf	interj	interjection
interrogativ, fragend	interrog	interrogative
unveränderlich	inv	invariable
unregelmäßig	irreg	irregular
jemand	jd	somebody
jemandem	jdm	(to) somebody
jemanden	jdn	somebody
jemandes	jds	somebody's
Rechtswesen	Jur	law
Sprachwissenschaft	Ling	linguistics
wörtlich	lit	literal
literarisch	liter	literary

Literatur	Liter	of literature
Maskulinum	m	masculine
Mathematik	Math	mathematics
Medizin	Med	medicine
Meteorologie	Met	meteorology
militärisch	Mil	military
Bergbau	Min	mining
Musik	Mus	music
Substantiv, Hauptwort	n	noun
nautisch, Seefahrt	Naut	nautical, naval
Nominativ	nom	nominative
Neutrum	nt	neuter
Zahlwort	num	numeral
Objekt	obj	object
veraltet	old	
sich	o.s.	oneself
Parlament	Parl	parliament
abschätzig	pej	pejorative
Photographie	Phot	photography
Physik	Phys	physics
Plural	pl	plural
Politik	Pol	politics
besitzanzeigend	poss	possessive
Präfix, Vorsilbe	pref	prefix
Präposition	prep	preposition
Presse	Press	
Typographie	Print	printing
Pronomen, Fürwort	pron	pronoun
Psychologie	Psych	psychology
1. Vergangenheit, Imperfekt	pt	past
Partizip Perfekt	ptp	past participle
Radio	Rad	radio
Eisenbahn	Rail	railways
Relativ-	rel	relative
Religion	Rel	religion
jemand (—en, —em)	sb	someone, somebody
Schulwesen	Sch	school
Naturwissenschaft	Sci	science
schottisch	Scot	Scottish
Singular, Einzahl	sing	singular
Skisport	Ski	skiing
etwas	sth	something
Suffix, Nachsilbe	suff	suffix
Superlativ	superl	superlative
Technik	Tech	technology
Nachrichtentechnik	Tel	telecommunications
Theater	Theat	theatre
Fernsehen	TV	television
Hochschulwesen	Univ	university
(nord)amerikanisch	US	(North) America
gewöhnlich	usu	usually
Verb	v	verb
intransitives Verb	vi	intransitive verb
reflexives Verb	vr	reflexive verb
transitives Verb	vt	transitive verb
Zoologie	Zool	zoology
zwischen zwei Sprechern	~	change of speaker
ungefähre Entsprechung	≈	cultural equivalent
eingetragenes Warenzeichen	®	registered trademark

Regular German noun endings

nom		gen	pl	nom		gen	pl
-ant	m	-anten	-anten	-ion	f	-ion	-ionen
-anz	f	-anz	-anzen	-ist	m	-isten	-isten
-ar	m	-ar(e)s	-are	-ium	nt	-iums	-ien
-chen	nt	-chens	-chen	-ius	m	-ius	-iusse
-ei	f	-ei	-eien	-ive	f	-ive	-iven
-elle	f	-elle	-ellen	-keit	f	-keit	-keiten
-ent	m	-enten	-enten	-lein	nt	-leins	-lein
-enz	f	-enz	-enzen	-ling	m	-lings	-linge
-ette	f	-ette	-etten	-ment	nt	-ments	-mente
-eur	m	-eurs	-eure	-mus	m	-mus	-men
-euse	f	-euse	-eusen	-schaft	f	-schaft	-schaften
-heit	f	-heit	-heiten	-tät	f	-tät	-täten
-ie	f	-ie	-ien	-tor	m	-tors	-toren
-ik	f	-ik	-iken	-ung	f	-ung	-ungen
-in	f	-in	-innen	-ur	f	-ur	-uren
-ine	f	-ine	-inen				

Phonetic symbols
Lautschrift

[:] length mark Längezeichen   ['] stress mark Betonung
[ˀ] glottal stop Knacklaut

all vowel sounds are approximate only
alle Vokallaute sind nur ungefähre Entsprechungen

lie	[aɪ]	weit	day	[eɪ]		
now	[au]	Haut	girl	[ɜː]		
above	[ə]	bitte	board	[ɔː]		
green	[iː]	viel	root	[uː]	Hut	
pity	[ɪ]	Bischof	come	[ʌ]	Butler	
rot	[ɒ,ɔ]	Post	salon	[ɔ̃]	Champignon	
full	[ʊ]	Pult	avant (garde)	[ũ]	Ensemble	
			fair	[ɛə]	mehr	
bet	[b]	Ball	beer	[ɪə]	Bier	
dim	[d]	dann	toy	[ɔɪ]	Heu	
face	[f]	Faß	pure	[ʊə]		
go	[g]	Gast	wine	[w]		
hit	[h]	Herr	thin	[θ]		
you	[j]	ja	this	[ð]		
cat	[k]	kalt				
lick	[l]	Last	Hast	[a]	mash	
must	[m]	Mast	Ensemble	[ã]	avant (garde)	
nut	[n]	Nuß	Metall	[e]	meths	
bang	[ŋ]	lang	häßlich	[ɛ]		
pepper	[p]	Pakt	Cousin	[ɛ̃]		
sit	[s]	Rasse	vital	[i]		
shame	[ʃ]	Schal	Moral	[o]		
tell	[t]	Tal	Champignon	[õ]	salon	
vine	[v]	was	ökonomisch	[ø]		
loch	[x]	Bach	gönnen	[œ]		
zero	[z]	Hase	Heu	[ɔy]	toy	
leisure	[ʒ]	Genie	kulant	[u]		
			physisch	[y]		
bat	[æ]		Müll	[ʏ]		
farm	[ɑː]	Bahn	ich	[ç]		
set	[e]	Kette				

[ˀ] r can be pronounced before a vowel; Bindungs-R

DEUTSCH - ENGLISCH
GERMAN - ENGLISH

A

A, a [aː] *nt* A, a.

Aal [aːl] *m* -(e)s, -e eel.

Aas [aːs] *nt* -es, -e *or* **Äser** carrion; **~geier** *m* vulture.

ab [ap] *prep* +*dat* from; *ad* off; **links ~** to the left; **~ und zu** *or* **an** now and then *or* again; **von da ~** from then on; **der Knopf ist ~** the button has come off.

Abänderung ['ap'ɛndəruŋ] *f* alteration.

abarbeiten ['ap'arbaɪtən] *vr* wear o.s. out, slave away.

Abart ['ap'aːrt] *f* (*Biol*) variety; **a~ig** *a* abnormal.

Abbau ['apbaʊ] *m* -(e)s dismantling; (*Verminderung*) reduction (*gen* in); (*Verfall*) decline (*gen* in); (*Min*) mining; quarrying; (*Chem*) decomposition; **a~en** *vt* dismantle; (*Min*) mine; quarry; (*verringern*) reduce; (*Chem*) break down.

abbeißen ['apbaɪsən] *vt irreg* bite off.

abberufen ['apbəruːfən] *vt irreg* recall.

Abberufung *f* recall.

abbestellen ['apbəʃtɛlən] *vt* cancel.

abbezahlen ['apbətsaːlən] *vt* pay off.

abbiegen ['apbiːgən] *irreg vi* turn off; (*Straße*) bend; *vt* bend; (*verhindern*) ward off.

Abbild ['apbɪlt] *nt* portrayal; (*einer Person*) image, likeness; **a~en** ['apbɪldən] *vt* portray; **~ung** *f* illustration.

Abbitte ['apbɪtə] *f*: **~ leisten** *or* **tun** make one's apologies (*bei* to).

abblasen ['apblaːzən] *vt irreg* blow off; (*fig*) call off.

abblenden ['apblɛndən] *vti* (*Aut*) dip, dim (*US*).

Abblendlicht *nt* dipped *or* dimmed (*US*) headlights *pl*.

abbrechen ['apbrɛçən] *vti irreg* break off; (*Gebäude*) pull down; *Zelt* take down; (*aufhören*) stop.

abbrennen ['apbrɛnən] *irreg vt* burn off; *Feuerwerk* let off; *vi* (*aux sein*) burn down; **abgebrannt sein** (*col*) be broke.

abbringen ['apbrɪŋən] *vt irreg*: **jdn von etw ~** dissuade sb from sth; **jdn vom Weg ~** divert sb; **ich bringe den Verschluß nicht ab** (*col*) I can't get the top off.

abbröckeln ['apbrœkəln] *vti* crumble off *or* away.

Abbruch ['apbrʊx] *m* (*von Verhandlungen etc*) breaking off; (*von Haus*) demolition; **jdm/etw ~ tun** harm sb/sth; **a~reif** *a* only fit for demolition.

abbrühen ['apbryːən] *vt* scald; **abgebrüht** (*col*) hard-boiled.

abbuchen ['apbuːxən] *vt* debit.

abbürsten ['apbyrstən] *vt* brush off.

abdanken ['apdaŋkən] *vi* resign; (*König*) abdicate.

Abdankung *f* resignation; abdication.

abdecken ['apdɛkən] *vt* uncover; *Tisch* clear; *Loch* cover.

abdichten ['apdɪçtən] *vt* seal; (*Naut*) caulk.

abdrängen ['apdrɛŋən] *vt* push off.

abdrehen ['apdreːən] *vt Gas* turn off; *Licht* switch off; *Film* shoot; **jdm den Hals ~** wring sb's neck; *vi* (*Schiff*) change course.

abdrosseln ['apdrɔsəln] *vt* throttle; (*Aut*) stall; *Produktion* cut back.

Abdruck ['apdrʊk] *m* (*Nachdrucken*) reprinting; (*Gedrucktes*) reprint; (*Gips~, Wachs~*) impression; (*Finger~*) print; **a~en** *vt* print, publish.

abdrücken ['apdrʏkən] *vt* make an impression of; *Waffe* fire; *Person* hug, squeeze; **jdm die Luft ~** squeeze all the breath out of sb; *vr* leave imprints; (*abstoßen*) push o.s. away.

abebben ['ap'ɛbən] *vi* ebb away.

Abend ['aːbənt] *m* -s, -e evening; **zu ~ essen** have dinner *or* supper; **a~** *ad* evening; **~brot** *nt*, **~essen** *nt* supper; **a~füllend** taking up the whole evening; **~kurs** *m* evening classes *pl*; **~land** *nt* West; **a~lich** *a* evening; **~mahl** *nt* Holy Communion; **~rot** *nt* sunset; **a~s** *ad* in the evening.

Abenteuer ['aːbəntɔʏər] *nt* -s, - adventure; **a~lich** *a* adventurous.

Abenteurer *m* -s, - adventurer; **~in** *f* adventuress.

aber ['aːbər] *cj* but; (*jedoch*) however; **das ist ~ schön** that's really nice; **nun ist ~ Schluß!** now that's enough!; **ad tausend und ~ tausend** thousands upon thousands; **A~** *nt* but; **A~glaube** *m* superstition; **~gläubisch** *a* superstitious.

aberkennen ['ap'ɛrkɛnən] *vt irreg*: **jdm etw ~** deprive sb of sth, take sth (away) from sb.

Aberkennung *f* taking away.

aber- cpd: **~malig** *a* repeated; **~mals** *ad* once again.

abfahren ['apfaːrən] *irreg vi* leave, depart; *vt* take *or* cart away; *Strecke* drive; *Reifen* wear; *Fahrkarte* use.

Abfahrt ['apfaːrt] *f* departure; (*Ski*) descent; (*Piste*) run; **~slauf** *m* (*Ski*) descent, run down; **~s-tag** *m* day of departure; **~szeit** *f* departure time.

Abfall ['apfal] *m* waste; (*von Speisen etc*) rubbish, garbage (*US*); (*Neigung*) slope; (*Verschlechterung*) decline; **~eimer** *m* rubbish bin, garbage can (*US*); **a~en** *vti irreg* (*lit, fig*) fall *or* drop off; (*Pol, vom*

Glauben) break away; (*sich neigen*) fall *or* drop away.

abfällig ['ap-fɛlıç] *a* disparaging, deprecatory.

abfangen ['ap-faŋən] *vt irreg* intercept; *Person* catch; (*unter Kontrolle bringen*) check.

abfärben ['ap-fɛrbən] *vi* (*lit*) lose its colour; (*Wäsche*) run; (*fig*) rub off.

abfassen ['ap-fasən] *vt* write, draft.

abfertigen ['ap-fɛrtıgən] *vt* prepare for dispatch, process; (*an der Grenze*) clear; *Kundschaft* attend to; **jdn kurz ~** give sb short shrift.

Abfertigung *f* preparing for dispatch, processing; clearance.

abfeuern ['ap-fɔyərn] *vt* fire.

abfinden ['ap-fındən] *irreg vt* pay off; *vr* come to terms; **sich mit jdm ~/nicht ~** put up with/not get on with sb.

Abfindung *f* (*von Gläubigern*) payment; (*Geld*) sum in settlement.

abflauen ['ap-flauən] *vi* (*Wind, Erregung*) die away, subside; (*Nachfrage, Geschäft*) fall *or* drop off.

abfliegen ['ap-fli:gən] *irreg vi* (*Flugzeug*) take off; (*Passagier auch*) fly; *vt Gebiet* fly over.

abfließen ['ap-fli:sən] *vi irreg* drain away.

Abflug ['ap-flu:k] *m* departure; (*Start*) take-off; **~zeit** *f* departure time.

Abfluß ['ap-flus] *m* draining away; (*Öffnung*) outlet.

abfragen ['ap-fra:gən] *vt* test; **jdn** *or* **jdm etw ~** question sb on sth.

Abfuhr ['ap-fu:r] *f* -, **-en** removal; (*fig*) snub, rebuff.

Abführ- ['ap-fy:r] *cpd*: **a~en** *vt* lead away; *Gelder, Steuern* pay; *vi* (*Med*) have a laxative effect; **~mittel** *nt* laxative, purgative.

abfüllen ['ap-fylən] *vt* draw off; (*in Flaschen*) bottle.

Abgabe ['apga:bə] *f* handing in; (*von Ball*) pass; (*Steuer*) tax; (*eines Amtes*) giving up; (*einer Erklärung*) giving; **a~nfrei** *a* tax-free; **a~npflichtig** *a* liable to tax.

Abgang ['apgaŋ] *m* (*von Schule*) leaving; (*Theat*) exit; (*Med: Ausscheiden*) passing; (*Fehlgeburt*) miscarriage; (*Abfahrt*) departure; (*der Post, von Waren*) dispatch.

Abgas ['apga:s] *nt* waste gas; (*Aut*) exhaust.

abgeben ['apge:bən] *irreg vt Gegenstand* hand *or* give in; *Ball* pass; *Wärme* give off; *Amt* hand over; *Schuß* fire; *Erklärung, Urteil* give; (*darstellen, sein*) make; **jdm etw ~** (*überlassen*) let sb have sth; *vr*: **sich mit jdm/etw ~** associate with sb/bother with sth.

abgedroschen ['apgədrɔʃən] *a* hackneyed; *Witz* corny.

abgefeimt ['apgəfaımt] *a* cunning.

abgegriffen ['apgəgrıfən] *a Buch* well-thumbed; *Redensart* hackneyed.

abgehen ['apge:ən] *irreg vi* go away, leave; (*Theat*) exit; (*Post*) go; (*Med*) be passed; (*Baby*) die; (*Knopf etc*) come off; (*abgezogen werden*) be taken off; (*Straße*) branch off; **etw geht jdm ab** (*fehlt*) sb

lacks sth; *vt Strecke* go *or* walk along.

abgelegen ['apgəle:gən] *a* remote.

abgemacht ['apgəmaxt] *a* fixed; **~!** done.

abgeneigt ['apgənaıkt] *a* averse to, disinclined.

Abgeordnete(r) ['apgə'ɔrdnətə(r)] *mf* member of parliament; elected representative.

Abgesandte(r) ['apgəzantə(r)] *mf* delegate; (*Pol*) envoy.

abgeschmackt ['apgəʃmakt] *a* tasteless; **A~heit** *f* lack of taste; (*Bemerkung*) tasteless remark.

abgesehen ['apgəze:ən] *a*: **es auf jdn/etw ~ haben** be after sb/sth; **~ von...** apart from...

abgespannt ['apgəʃpant] *a* tired out.

abgestanden ['apgəʃtandən] *a* stale; *Bier auch* flat.

abgestorben ['apgəʃtɔrbən] *a* numb; (*Biol, Med*) dead.

abgetakelt ['apgəta:kəlt] *a* (*col*) decrepit, past it.

abgetragen ['apgətra:gən] *a* shabby, worn out.

abgewinnen ['apgəvınən] *vt irreg*: **jdm Geld ~** win money from sb; **einer Sache etw/Geschmack ~** get sth/pleasure from sth.

abgewöhnen ['apgəvø:nən] *vt*: **jdm/sich etw ~** cure sb of sth/give sth up.

abgleiten ['apglaıtən] *vi irreg* slip, slide.

Abgott ['apgɔt] *m* idol.

abgöttisch ['apgœtıʃ] *a*: **~ lieben** idolize.

abgrenzen ['apgrɛntsən] *vt* (*lit, fig*) mark off; fence off.

Abgrund ['apgrunt] *m* (*lit, fig*) abyss.

abgründig ['apgryndıç] *a* unfathomable; *Lächeln* cryptic.

abhacken ['aphakən] *vt* chop off.

abhaken ['apha:kən] *vt* tick off.

abhalten ['aphaltən] *vt irreg Versammlung* hold; **jdn von etw ~** (*fernhalten*) keep sb away from sth; (*hindern*) keep sb from sth.

abhandeln ['aphandəln] *vt Thema* deal with; **jdm die Waren/8 Mark ~** do a deal with sb for the goods/beat sb down 8 marks.

abhanden [ap'handən] *a*: **~ kommen** get lost.

Abhandlung ['aphandluŋ] *f* treatise, discourse.

Abhang ['aphaŋ] *m* slope.

abhängen ['aphɛŋən] *irreg vt Bild* take down; *Anhänger* uncouple; *Verfolger* shake off; *vi* (*Fleisch*) hang; **von jdm/etw ~** depend on sb/sth.

abhängig ['aphɛŋıç] *a* dependent (*von* on); **A~keit** *f* dependence (*von* on).

abhärten ['aphɛrtən] *vtr* toughen (o.s.) up; **sich gegen etw ~** inure o.s. to sth.

abhauen ['aphauən] *irreg vt* cut off; *Baum* cut down; *vi* (*col*) clear off *or* out.

abheben ['aphe:bən] *irreg vt* lift (up); *Karten* cut; *Masche* slip; *Geld* withdraw, take out; *vi* (*Flugzeug*) take off; (*Rakete*) lift off; (*Cards*) cut; *vr* stand out (*von* from), contrast (*von* with).

abhelfen ['aphɛlfən] vi irreg (+dat) remedy.

abhetzen ['aphɛtsən] vr wear or tire o.s. out.

Abhilfe ['aphilfə] f remedy; ~ **schaffen** put things right.

abholen ['aphoːlən] vt Gegenstand fetch, collect; Person call for; (am Bahnhof etc) pick up, meet.

abhorchen ['aphɔrçən] vt (Med) auscultate, sound.

abhören ['aphøːrən] vt Vokabeln test; Telefongespräch tap; Tonband etc listen to.

Abhörgerät nt bug.

Abitur [abi'tuːr] nt -s, -e German school leaving examination; ~**i'ent(in** f) m candidate for school leaving certificate.

abkämmen ['apkɛmən] vt Gegend comb, scour.

abkanzeln ['apkantsəln] vt (col) bawl out.

abkapseln ['apkapsəln] vr shut or cut o.s. off.

abkaufen ['apkaufən] vt: jdm etw ~ buy sth from sb.

abkehren ['apkeːrən] vt Blick avert, turn away; vr turn away.

Abklatsch ['apklatʃ] m -es, -e (fig) (poor) copy.

abklingen ['apklɪŋən] vi irreg die away; (Radio) fade out.

abknöpfen ['apknœpfən] vt unbutton; jdm etw ~ (col) get sth off sb.

abkochen ['apkɔxən] vt boil.

abkommen ['apkɔmən] vi irreg get away; **von der Straße/von einem Plan ~** leave the road/give up a plan; **A~** nt -s, - agreement.

abkömmlich ['apkœmlɪç] a available, free.

abkratzen ['apkratsən] vt scrape off; vi (col) kick the bucket.

abkühlen ['apkyːlən] vt cool down; vr (Mensch) cool down or off; (Wetter) get cool; (Zuneigung) cool.

Abkunft ['apkʊnft] f - origin, birth.

abkürzen ['apkyrtsən] vt shorten; Wort auch abbreviate; **den Weg ~** take a short cut.

Abkürzung f (Wort) abbreviation; (Weg) short cut.

abladen ['aplaːdən] vt irreg unload.

Ablage ['aplaːgə] f -, -n (für Akten) tray; (für Kleider) cloakroom; **a~rn** vt deposit; vr be deposited; vi mature.

ablassen ['aplasən] irreg vt Wasser, Dampf let off; (vom Preis) knock off; vi: **von etw ~** give sth up, abandon sth.

Ablauf ['aplauf] m (Abfluß) drain; (von Ereignissen) course; (einer Frist, Zeit) expiry; **a~en** irreg vi (abfließen) drain away; (Ereignisse) happen; (Frist, Zeit, Paß) expire; vt Sohlen wear (down or out); **jdm den Rang a~en** steal a march on sb.

ablegen ['apleːgən] vt put or lay down; Kleider take off; Gewohnheit get rid of; Prüfung take, sit; Zeugnis give.

Ableger m -s, - layer; (fig) branch, offshoot.

ablehnen ['apleːnən] vt reject; Einladung decline, refuse; vi decline, refuse.

Ablehnung f rejection; refusal.

ableiten ['aplaɪtən] vt Wasser divert; (deduzieren) deduce; Wort derive.

Ableitung f diversion; deduction; derivation; (Wort) derivative.

ablenken ['aplɛŋkən] vt turn away, deflect; (zerstreuen) distract; vi change the subject.

Ablenkung f distraction.

ablesen ['apleːzən] vt irreg read out; Meßgeräte read.

ableugnen ['aplɔygnən] vt deny.

ablichten ['aplɪçtən] vt photocopy; photograph.

abliefern ['apliːfərn] vt deliver; **etw bei jdm/einer Dienststelle ~** hand sth over to sb/in at an office.

Ablieferung f delivery; ~**sschein** m delivery note.

abliegen ['apliːgən] vi irreg be some distance away; (fig) be far removed.

ablisten ['aplɪstən] vt: **jdm etw ~** trick or con sb out of sth.

ablösen ['apløːzən] vt (abtrennen) take off, remove; (in Amt) take over from; Wache relieve.

Ablösung f removal; relieving.

abmachen ['apmaxən] vt take off; (vereinbaren) agree.

Abmachung f agreement.

abmagern ['apmaːgərn] vi get thinner.

Abmagerungskur f diet; **eine ~ machen** go on a diet.

Abmarsch ['apmarʃ] m departure; **a~bereit** a ready to start; **a~ieren** vi march off.

abmelden ['apmɛldən] vt Zeitungen cancel; Auto take off the road; **jdn bei der Polizei ~** register sb's departure with the police; vr give notice of one's departure; (im Hotel) check out.

abmessen ['apmɛsən] vt irreg measure.

Abmessung f measurement.

abmontieren ['apmɔntiːrən] vt take off.

abmühen ['apmyːən] vr wear o.s. out.

Abnäher ['apnɛːər] m -s, - dart.

Abnahme ['apnaːmə] f -, -n removal; (Comm) buying; (Verringerung) decrease (gen in).

abnehmen ['apneːmən] irreg vt take off, remove; Führerschein take away; Geld get (jdm out of sb); (kaufen, col: glauben) buy (jdm from sb); Prüfung hold; Maschen decrease; **jdm Arbeit ~** take work off sb's shoulders; vi decrease; (schlanker werden) lose weight.

Abnehmer m -s, - purchaser, customer.

Abneigung ['apnaɪgʊŋ] f aversion, dislike.

abnorm [ap'nɔrm] a abnormal.

abnötigen ['apnøːtɪgən] vt: **jdm etw/Respekt ~** force sth from sb/gain sb's respect.

abnutzen ['apnʊtsən] vt wear out.

Abnutzung f wear (and tear).

Abonnement [abɔn(e)'mãː] nt -s, -s subscription.

Abonnent(in *f)* [abɔ'nɛnt(ɪn)] *m* subscriber.

abonnieren [abɔ'niːrən] *vt* subscribe to.

abordnen ['apˈɔrdnən] *vt* delegate.

Abordnung *f* delegation.

Abort [a'bɔrt] *m* -(e)s, -e lavatory.

abpacken ['appakən] *vt* pack.

abpassen ['appasən] *vt Person, Gelegenheit* wait for; (*in Größe*) *Stoff etc* adjust.

abpfeifen ['appfaɪfən] *vti irreg (Sport)* **(das Spiel)** ~ blow the whistle (for the end of the game).

Abpfiff ['appfɪf] *m* final whistle.

abplagen ['applaːgən] *vr* wear o.s. out.

Abprall ['appral] *m* rebound; (*von Kugel*) ricochet; **a~en** *vi* bounce off; ricochet.

abputzen ['apputsən] *vt* clean.

abquälen ['apˈkvɛːlən] *vr* drive o.s. frantic; **sich mit etw** ~ struggle with sth.

abraten ['apraːtən] *vt irreg* advise, warn (*jdm von etw* sb against sth).

abräumen ['aprɔʏmən] *vt* clear up *or* away.

abreagieren ['apreagiːrən] *vt Zorn* work off (*an +dat* on); *vr* calm down.

abrechnen ['aprɛçnən] *vt* deduct, take off; *vi (lit)* settle up; *(fig)* get even.

Abrechnung *f* settlement; (*Rechnung*) bill.

Abrede ['apreːdə] *f:* etw in ~ **stellen** deny *or* dispute sth.

abregen ['apreːgən] *vr (col)* calm *or* cool down.

abreiben ['apraɪbən] *vtr irreg* rub off; (*säubern*) wipe; **jdn mit einem Handtuch** ~ towel sb down.

Abreise ['apraɪzə] *f* departure; **a~n** *vi* leave, set off.

abreißen ['apraɪsən] *vt irreg Haus* tear down; *Blatt* tear off.

abrichten ['aprɪçtən] *vt* train.

abriegeln ['apriːgəln] *vt Tür* bolt; *Straße, Gebiet* seal off.

Abriß ['aprɪs] *m* -sses, -sse (*Übersicht*) outline.

Abruf ['apruːf] *m:* auf ~ on call; **a~en** *vt irreg Mensch* call away; (*Comm*) *Ware* request delivery of.

abrunden ['aprundən] *vt* round off.

abrüsten ['aprystən] *vi* disarm.

Abrüstung *f* disarmament.

abrutschen ['aprutʃən] *vi* slip; (*Aviat*) sideslip.

Absage ['apzaːgə] *f* -, -n refusal; **a~n** *vt* cancel, call off; *Einladung* turn down; *vi* crv off; (*ablehnen*) decline.

absägen ['apzɛːgən] *vt* saw off.

absahnen ['apzaːnən] *vt (lit)* skim; **das beste für sich** ~ take the cream.

Absatz ['apzats] *m* (*Comm*) sales *pl*; (*Bodensatz*) deposit; (*neuer Abschnitt*) paragraph; (*Treppen~*) landing; (*Schuh~*) heel; **~flaute** *f* slump in the market; **~gebiet** *nt* (*Comm*) market.

abschaben ['ap-ʃaːbən] *vt* scrape off; *Möhren* scrape.

abschaffen ['ap-ʃafən] *vt* abolish, do away with.

Abschaffung *f* abolition.

abschalten ['ap-ʃaltən] *vti (lit, col)* switch off.

abschattieren ['ap-ʃatiːrən] *vt* shade.

abschätzen ['ap-ʃɛtsən] *vt* estimate; *Lage* assess; *Person* size up.

abschätzig ['ap-ʃɛtsɪç] *a* disparaging, derogatory.

Abschaum ['ap-ʃaum] *m* -(e)s scum.

Abscheu ['ap-ʃɔʏ] *m* -(e)s loathing, repugnance; **a~erregend** *a* repulsive, loathsome; **a~lich** [ap'ʃɔʏlɪç] *a* abominable.

abschicken ['ap-ʃɪkən] *vt* send off.

abschieben ['ap-ʃiːbən] *vt irreg* push away; *Person* pack off.

Abschied ['ap-ʃiːt] *m* -(e)s, -e parting; (*von Armee*) discharge; ~ **nehmen** say good-bye (*von jdm* to sb), take one's leave (*von jdm of* sb); **seinen** ~ **nehmen** (*Mil*) apply for discharge; **zum** ~ on parting; **~sbrief** *m* farewell letter; **~sfeier** *f* farewell party.

abschießen [ap-ʃiːsən] *vt irreg Flugzeug* shoot down; *Geschoß* fire; (*col*) *Minister* get rid of.

abschirmen ['ap-ʃɪrmən] *vt* screen.

abschlagen ['ap-ʃlaːgən] *vt irreg* (*abhacken, Comm*) knock off; (*ablehnen*) refuse; (*Mil*) repel.

abschlägig ['ap-ʃlɛːgɪç] *a* negative.

Abschlagszahlung *f* interim payment.

abschleifen ['ap-ʃlaɪfən] *irreg vt* grind down; *Rost* polish off; *vr* wear off.

Abschlepp- ['ap-ʃlɛp] *cpd:* **~dienst** *m* (*Aut*) breakdown service; **a~en** *vt* take in tow; **~seil** *nt* towrope.

abschließen ['ap-ʃliːsən] *irreg vt Tür* lock; (*beenden*) conclude, finish; *Vertrag, Handel* conclude; *vr* (*sich isolieren*) cut o.s. off.

Abschluß ['ap-ʃlus] *m* (*Beendigung*) close, conclusion; (*Comm: Bilanz*) balancing; (*von Vertrag, Handel*) conclusion; **zum** ~ in conclusion; **~feier** *f* end-of-term party; **~rechnung** *f* final account.

abschmieren ['ap-ʃmiːrən] *vt* (*Aut*) grease, lubricate.

abschneiden ['ap-ʃnaɪdən] *irreg vt* cut off; *vi* do, come off.

Abschnitt ['ap-ʃnɪt] *m* section; (*Mil*) sector; (*Kontroll~*) counterfoil; (*Math*) segment; (*Zeit~*) period.

abschnüren ['ap-ʃnyːrən] *vt* constrict.

abschöpfen ['ap-ʃœpfən] *vt* skim off.

abschrauben ['ap-ʃraubən] *vt* unscrew.

abschrecken ['ap-ʃrɛkən] *vt* deter, put off; (*mit kaltem Wasser*) plunge in cold water; **~d** *a* deterrent; **~des Beispiel** warning.

abschreiben ['ap-ʃraɪbən] *vt irreg* copy; (*verlorengeben*) write off; (*Comm*) deduct.

Abschreibung *f* (*Comm*) deduction; (*Wertverminderung*) depreciation.

Abschrift ['ap-ʃrɪft] *f* copy.

abschürfen ['ap-ʃʏrfən] *vt* graze.

Abschuß ['ap-ʃus] *m* (*eines Geschützes*) firing; (*Herunterschießen*) shooting down; (*Tötung*) shooting.

abschüssig ['ap-ʃʏsɪç] *a* steep.

abschütteln ['ap-ʃʏtəln] *vt* shake off.

abschwächen ['ap-ʃvɛçən] *vt* lessen;

Behauptung, Kritik tone down; *vr* lessen.
abschweifen ['apʃvaifən] *vi* wander.
Abschweifung *f* digression.
abschwellen ['apʃvɛlən] *vi irreg* (*Geschwulst*) go down; (*Lärm*) die down.
abschwenken ['apʃvɛŋkən] *vi* turn away.
abschwören ['apʃvøːrən] *vi irreg* (+*dat*) renounce.
abseh- ['apze:] *cpd*: ~**bar** a foreseeable; **in ~barer Zeit** in the foreseeable future; **das Ende ist ~bar** the end is in sight; ~**en** *irreg vt* Ende, Folgen foresee; **jdm etw ~en** (*erlernen*) copy sth from sb; *vi*: **von etw ~en** refrain from sth; (*nicht berücksichtigen*) leave sth out of consideration.
abseits ['apzaits] *ad* out of the way; *prep* +*gen* away from; **A~** *nt* (*Sport*) offside; **im A~ stehen** be offside.
Absend- ['apzɛnd] *cpd*: **a~en** *vt irreg* send off, dispatch; ~**er** *m* -**s**, - sender; ~**ung** *f* dispatch.
absetz- ['apzɛts] *cpd*: ~**bar** a Beamter dismissible; Waren saleable; (*von Steuer*) deductible; ~**en** *vt* (*niederstellen, aussteigen lassen*) put down; (*abnehmen*) take off; (*Comm: verkaufen*) sell; (*Fin: abziehen*) deduct; (*entlassen*) dismiss; König depose; (*streichen*) drop; (*hervorheben*) pick out; *vr* (*sich entfernen*) clear off; (*sich ablagern*) be deposited; **A~ung** *f* (*Fin: Abzug*) deduction; (*Entlassung*) dismissal; (*von König*) deposing; (*Streichung*) dropping.
absichern ['apziçərn] *vtr* make safe; (*schützen*) safeguard.
Absicht ['apzıçt] *f* intention; **mit ~** on purpose; **a~lich** a intentional, deliberate; **a~slos** a unintentional.
absinken ['apzıŋkən] *vi irreg* sink; (*Temperatur, Geschwindigkeit*) decrease.
absitzen ['apzıtsən] *irreg vi* dismount; *vt* Strafe serve.
absolut [apzo'lu:t] a absolute; **A~ismus** ['-tısmus] *m* absolutism.
absolvieren [apzɔl'vi:rən] *vt* (*Sch*) complete.
absonder- ['apzɔndər] *cpd*: ~**lich** [ap'zɔndərlıç] a odd, strange; ~**n** *vt* separate; (*ausscheiden*) give off, secrete; *vr* cut o.s. off; **A~ung** *f* separation; (*Med*) secretion.
abspalten ['apʃpaltən] *vt* split off.
Abspannung ['apʃpanʊŋ] *f* (*Ermüdung*) exhaustion.
absparen ['apʃpa:rən] *vt*: **sich** (*dat*) **etw ~** scrimp and save for sth.
abspeisen ['apʃpaizən] *vt* (*fig*) fob off.
abspenstig ['apʃpɛnstıç] ~ **machen** lure away (*jdm* from sb).
absperren ['apʃpɛrən] *vt* block or close off; Tür lock.
Absperrung *f* (*Vorgang*) blocking or closing off; (*Sperre*) barricade.
abspielen ['apʃpi:lən] *vt* Platte, Tonband play; (*Sport*) Ball pass; **vom Blatt ~** (*Mus*) sight-read; *vr* happen.
absplittern ['apʃplıtərn] *vti* chip off.
Absprache ['apʃpra:xə] *f* arrangement.
absprechen ['apʃprɛçən] *vt irreg* (*vereinbaren*) arrange; **jdm etw ~** deny sb sth.

abspringen ['apʃprıŋən] *vi irreg* jump down/off; (*Farbe, Lack*) flake off; (*Aviat*) bale out; (*sich distanzieren*) back out.
Absprung ['apʃprʊŋ] *m* jump.
abspülen ['apʃpy:lən] *vt* rinse; Geschirr wash up.
abstammen ['apʃtamən] *vi* be descended; (*Wort*) be derived.
Abstammung *f* descent; derivation.
Abstand ['apʃtant] *m* distance; (*zeitlich*) interval; **davon ~ nehmen, etw zu tun** refrain from doing sth; ~ **halten** (*Aut*) keep one's distance; **mit ~ der beste** by far the best; ~**ssumme** *f* compensation.
abstatten ['apʃtatən] *vt* Dank give; Besuch pay.
abstauben ['apʃtaubən] *vti* dust; (*col: stehlen*) pinch; (**den Ball**) ~ (*Sport*) tuck the ball away.
abstechen ['apʃtɛçən] *irreg vt* cut; Tier cut the throat of; *vi* contrast (*gegen, von* with).
Abstecher *m* -**s**, - detour.
abstecken ['apʃtɛkən] *vt* (*losmachen*) unpin; Fläche mark out.
abstehen ['apʃte:ən] *vi irreg* (*Ohren, Haare*) stick out; (*entfernt sein*) stand away.
absteigen ['apʃtaigən] *vi irreg* (*vom Rad etc*) get off, dismount; (*in Gasthof*) put up (*in* +*dat* at); (*Sport*) be relegated (*in* +*acc* to).
abstellen ['apʃtɛlən] *vt* (*niederstellen*) put down; (*entfernt stellen*) pull out; (*hinstellen*) Auto park; (*ausschalten*) turn or switch off; Mißstand, Unsitte stop; (*ausrichten*) gear (*auf* +*acc* to).
Abstellgleis *nt* siding.
abstempeln ['apʃtɛmpəln] *vt* stamp.
absterben ['apʃtɛrbən] *vi irreg* die; (*Körperteil*) go numb.
Abstieg ['apʃti:k] *m* -(**e**)**s**, -**e** descent; (*Sport*) relegation; (*fig*) decline.
abstimmen ['apʃtımən] *vi* vote; *vt* Instrument tune (*auf* +*acc* to); Interessen match (*auf* +*acc* with); Termine, Ziele fit in (*auf* +*acc* with); *vr* agree.
Abstimmung *f* vote.
abstinent [apstı'nɛnt] a abstemious; (*von Alkohol*) teetotal.
Abstinenz [apstı'nɛnts] *f* abstinence; teetotalism; ~**ler** *m* -**s**, - teetotaller.
abstoßen ['apʃto:sən] *vt irreg* push off or away; (*verkaufen*) unload; (*anekeln*) repel, repulse; ~**d** a repulsive.
abstrahieren [apstra'hi:rən] *vti* abstract.
abstrakt [ap'strakt] a abstract; *ad* abstractly, in the abstract; **A~ion** [apstraktsi'o:n] *f* abstraction; **A~um** *nt* -**s**, -**kta** abstract concept/noun.
abstreiten ['apʃtraitən] *vt irreg* deny.
Abstrich ['apʃtrıç] *m* (*Abzug*) cut; (*Med*) smear; ~**e machen** lower one's sights.
abstufen ['apʃtu:fən] *vt* Hang terrace; Farben shade; Gehälter grade.
abstumpfen ['apʃtʊmpfən] *vt* (*lit, fig*) dull, blunt; *vi* (*lit, fig*) become dulled.
Absturz ['apʃtʊrts] *m* fall; (*Aviat*) crash.
abstürzen ['apʃtyrtsən] *vi* fall; (*Aviat*) crash.

absuchen ['apzuːxən] *vt* scour, search.

absurd [ap'zurt] *a* absurd.

Abszeß [aps'tsɛs] *m* **-sses, -sse** abscess.

Abt [apt] *m* **-(e)s, ˙e** abbot.

abtasten ['aptastən] *vt* feel, probe.

abtauen ['aptauən] *vti* thaw.

Abtei [ap'tai] *f* **-, -en** abbey.

Abteil [ap'tail] *nt* **-(e)s, -e** compartment; **'a ~ en** *vt* divide up; (*abtrennen*) divide off; **~ung** *f* (*in Firma, Kaufhaus*) department; (*Mil*) unit; **~ungsleiter** *m* head of department.

abtönen ['aptøːnən] *vt* (*Phot*) tone down.

abtragen ['aptraːgən] *vt irreg* Hügel, Erde level down; *Essen* clear away; *Kleider* wear out; *Schulden* pay off.

abträglich ['aptrɛːklɪç] *a* harmful (*dat* to).

abtransportieren ['aptranspɔrtiːrən] *vt* take away, remove.

abtreiben ['aptraibən] *irreg vt* Boot, Flugzeug drive off course; *Kind* abort; *vi* be driven off course; abort.

Abtreibung *f* abortion; **~sversuch** *m* attempted abortion.

abtrennen ['aptrɛnən] *vt* (*lostrennen*) detach; (*entfernen*) take off; (*abteilen*) separate off.

abtreten ['aptreːtən] *irreg vt* wear out; (*überlassen*) hand over, cede (*jdm* to sb); *vi* go off; (*zurücktreten*) step down.

Abtritt ['aptrɪt] *m* resignation.

abtrocknen ['aptrɔknən] *vti* dry.

abtrünnig ['aptrʏnɪç] *a* renegade.

abtun ['aptuːn] *vt irreg* take off; (*fig*) dismiss.

aburteilen ['ap'urtailən] *vt* condemn.

abverlangen ['ap-fɛrlaŋən] *vt*: **jdm etw ~** demand sth from sb.

abwägen ['apvɛːgən] *vt irreg* weigh up.

abwählen ['apvɛːlən] *vt* vote out (of office).

abwandeln ['apvandəln] *vt* adapt.

abwandern ['apvandərn] *vi* move away.

abwarten ['apvartən] *vt* wait for; *vi* wait.

abwärts ['apvɛrts] *ad* down.

Abwasch ['apvaʃ] *m* **-(e)s** washing-up; **a ~ en** *vt irreg* Schmutz wash off; *Geschirr* wash (up).

Abwasser ['apvasər] *nt* **-s, -wässer** sewage.

abwechseln ['apvɛksəln] *vir* alternate; (*Personen*) take turns; **~d** *a* alternate.

Abweg ['apveːk] *m*: **auf ~e geraten/führen** go/lead astray; **a ~ig** ['apveːgɪç] *a* wrong.

Abwehr ['apveːr] *f* **-** defence; (*Schutz*) protection; (*—dienst*) counter-intelligence (service); **a ~ en** *vt* ward off; *Ball* stop; **a ~ende Geste** dismissive gesture.

abweichen ['apvaiçən] *vi irreg* deviate; (*Meinung*) differ; **~d** *a* deviant; differing.

abweisen ['apvaizən] *vt irreg* turn away; *Antrag* turn down; **~d** *a* Haltung cold.

abwenden ['apvɛndən] *irreg vt* avert; *vr* turn away.

abwerben ['apvɛrbən] *vt irreg* woo away (*jdm* from sb).

abwerfen ['apvɛrfən] *vt irreg* throw off; *Profit* yield; (*aus Flugzeug*) drop; *Spielkarte* discard.

abwerten ['apvɛrtən] *vt* (*Fin*) devalue.

abwesend ['apveːzənt] *a* absent.

Abwesenheit ['apveːzənhait] *f* absence.

abwickeln ['apvɪkəln] *vt* unwind; *Geschäft* wind up.

abwiegen ['apviːgən] *vt irreg* weigh out.

abwimmeln ['apvɪməln] *vt* (*col*) Person get rid of; *Auftrag* get out of.

abwinken ['apvɪŋkən] *vi* wave it/him *etc* aside.

abwirtschaften ['apvɪrt-ʃaftən] *vi* go downhill.

abwischen ['apvɪʃən] *vt* wipe off or away; (*putzen*) wipe.

abwracken ['apvrakən] *vt* Schiff break (up); **abgewrackter Mensch** wreck of a person.

Abwurf ['apvurf] *m* throwing off; (*von Bomben etc*) dropping; (*von Reiter, Sport*) throw.

abwürgen ['apvʏrgən] *vt* (*col*) scotch; *Motor* stall.

abzahlen ['aptsaːlən] *vt* pay off.

abzählen ['aptsɛːlən] *vti* count (up).

Abzahlung *f* repayment; **auf ~ kaufen** buy on hire purchase.

abzapfen ['aptsapfən] *vt* draw off; **jdm Blut/Geld ~** take blood from sb/bleed sb.

abzäunen ['aptsɔynən] *vt* fence off.

Abzeichen ['aptsaiçən] *nt* badge; (*Orden*) decoration.

abzeichnen ['aptsaiçnən] *vt* draw, copy; *Dokument* initial; *vr* stand out; (*fig: bevorstehen*) loom.

Abziehbild *nt* transfer.

abziehen ['aptsiːən] *irreg vt* take off; *Tier* skin; *Bett* strip; *Truppen* withdraw; (*subtrahieren*) take away, subtract; (*kopieren*) run off; *vi* go away; (*Truppen*) withdraw.

abzielen ['aptsiːlən] *vi* be aimed (*auf +acc* at).

Abzug ['aptsuːk] *m* departure; (*von Truppen*) withdrawal; (*Kopie*) copy; (*Subtraktion*) subtraction; (*Betrag*) deduction; (*Rauch—*) flue; (*von Waffen*) trigger.

abzüglich ['aptsyːklɪç] *prep +gen* less.

abzweigen ['aptsvaigən] *vi* branch off; *vt* set aside.

Abzweigung *f* junction.

Accessoires [akseso'aːrs] *pl* accessories *pl*.

ach [ax] *interj* oh; **mit A ~ und Krach** by the skin of one's teeth.

Achse ['aksə] *f* **-, -n** axis; (*Aut*) axle; **auf ~ sein** be on the move.

Achsel ['aksəl] *f* **-, -n** shoulder; **~höhle** *f* armpit; **~zucken** *nt* shrug (of one's shoulders).

Achsenbruch *m* (*Aut*) broken axle.

Acht [axt] *f* **-** attention; (*Hist*) proscription; **sich in ~ nehmen** be careful (*vor +dat* of), watch out (*vor +dat* for); **etw außer a ~ lassen** disregard sth; **~ f -, -en, a ~ num** eight; **a ~ Tage** a week; **a ~ bar** *a* worthy; **a ~ e(r,s)** *a* eighth; **~el** *num* eighth; **a ~ en** *vt* respect; *vi* pay attention (auf +acc to); **darauf a~en, daß . . .** be careful that . . .

ächten ['εçtən] vt outlaw, ban.

Achter- cpd: **~bahn** f big dipper, roller coaster; **~deck** nt (Naut) afterdeck.

acht- cpd: **~fach** a eightfold; **~geben** vi irreg take care (auf +acc of); **~los** a careless; **~mal** ad eight times; **~sam** a attentive.

Achtung ['axtuŋ] f attention; (Ehrfurcht) respect; interj look out!; (Mil) attention!; **~ Lebensgefahr/Stufe!** danger/mind the step!

acht- cpd: **~zehn** num eighteen; **~zig** num eighty; **A~ziger(in** f) m -s, - octogenarian; **A~zigerjahre** pl eighties pl.

ächzen ['εçtsən] vi groan (vor +dat with).

Acker ['akər] m -s, ¨ field; **~bau** m agriculture; **a~n** vti plough; (col) slog away.

addieren [a'di:rən] vt add (up).

Addition [aditsi'o:n] f addition.

Ade [a'de:] nt -s, -s, **a~** interj farewell, adieu.

Adel ['a:dəl] m -s nobility; **a~ig,** **adlig** a noble.

Ader ['a:dər] f -, -n vein.

Adjektiv ['atjεkti:f] nt -s, -e adjective.

Adler ['a:dlər] m -s, - eagle.

Admiral [atmi'ra:l] m -s, -e admiral; **~i-** **'tät** f admiralty.

adopt- cpd: **~ieren** [adɔp'ti:rən] vt adopt; **A~ion** [adɔptsi'o:n] f adoption; **A~iveltern** [adɔp'ti:f-] pl adoptive parents pl; **A~ivkind** nt adopted child.

Adress- cpd: **~ant** [adrε'sant] m sender; **~at** [adrε'sa:t] m -en, -en addressee; **~e** [a'drεsə] f -, -n address; **a~ieren** [adrε'si:rən] vt address (an +acc to).

Advent [at'vεnt] m -(e)s, -e Advent; **~skranz** m Advent wreath.

Adverb [at'vεrp] nt adverb; **a~ial** [atvεrbi'a:l] a adverbial.

aero- [aero] pref aero-.

Affäre [a'fε:rə] f -, -n affair.

Affe ['afə] m -n, -n monkey.

affektiert [afεk'ti:rt] a affected.

Affen- cpd: **a~artig** a like a monkey; **mit a~artiger Geschwindigkeit** like a flash; **~hitze** f (col) incredible heat; **~schande** f (col) crying shame.

affig ['afiç] a affected.

After ['aftər] m -s, - anus.

Agent [a'gεnt] m agent; **~ur** [-'tu:r] f agency.

Aggregat [agre'ga:t] nt -(e)s, -e aggregate; (Tech) unit; **~zustand** m (Phys) state.

Aggress- cpd: **~ion** [agrεsi'o:n] f aggression; **a~iv** [agrε'si:f] a aggressive; **~ivität** [agrεsivi'tε:t] f aggressiveness.

Agitation [agitatsi'o:n] f agitation.

Agrar- [a'gra:r] cpd: **~politik** f agricultural policy; **~staat** m agrarian state.

aha [a'ha:] interj aha.

Ahn [a:n] m -en, -en forebear.

ähneln ['ε:nəln] vi (+dat) be like, resemble; vr be alike or similar.

ahnen ['a:nən] vt suspect; Tod, Gefahr have a presentiment of; **du ahnst es nicht** you have no idea.

ähnlich ['ε:nliç] a similar (dat to); **Ä~keit** f similarity.

Ahnung ['a:nuŋ] f idea, suspicion; presentiment; **a~slos** a unsuspecting.

Ahorn ['a:hɔrn] m -s, -e maple.

Ähre ['ε:rə] f -, -n ear.

Akademie [akade'mi:] f academy.

Akademiker(in f) [aka'de:mikər(in)] m -s, - university graduate.

akademisch [aditsi'o:n] a academic.

akklimatisieren [aklimati'zi:rən] vr become acclimatized.

Akkord [a'kɔrt] m -(e)s, -e (Mus) chord; **im ~ arbeiten** do piecework; **~arbeit** f piecework; **~eon** [a'kɔrdeɔn] nt -s, -s accordion.

Akkusativ ['akuzati:f] m -s, -e accusative (case).

Akrobat(in f) [akro'ba:t(in)] m -en, -en acrobat.

Akt [akt] m -(e)s, -e act; (Art) nude.

Akte ['aktə] f -, -n file; **etw zu den ~n legen** (lit, fig) file sth away; **a~nkundig** a on the files; **~nschrank** m filing cabinet; **~ntasche** f briefcase.

Aktie ['aktsiə] f -, -n share; **~ngesell-** **schaft** f joint-stock company; **~nkurs** m share price.

Aktion [aktsi'o:n] f campaign; (Polizei-, Such-) action; **~är** ['nε:r] m -s, -e share-holder.

aktiv [ak'ti:f] a active; (Mil) regular; **A~** nt -s (Gram) active (voice); **A~a** [ak'ti:va] pl assets pl; **a~ieren** [-'vi:rən] vt activate; **A~i'tät** f activity; **A~saldo** m (Comm) credit balance.

Aktualität [aktuali'tε:t] f topicality; (einer Mode) up-to-dateness.

aktuell [aktu'εl] a topical; up-to-date.

Akustik [a'kustik] f acoustics pl.

akut [a'ku:t] a acute.

Akzent [ak'tsεnt] m accent; (Betonung) stress.

akzeptieren [aktsεp'ti:rən] vt accept.

Alarm [a'larm] m -(e)s, -e alarm; **a~bereit** a standing by; **~bereitschaft** f stand-by; **a~ieren** [-'mi:rən] vt alarm.

albern ['albərn] a silly.

Album ['album] nt -s, **Alben** album.

Algebra ['algebra] f - algebra.

alias ['a:lias] ad alias.

Alibi ['a:libi] nt -s, -s alibi.

Alimente [ali'mεntə] pl alimony.

Alkohol ['alkohɔl] m -s, -e alcohol **a~frei** a non-alcoholic; **~iker(in** f) [alko'ho:likər(in)] m -s, - alcoholic; **a~isch** a alcoholic; **~verbot** nt ban on alcohol.

All [al] nt -s universe; **a~'abendlich** a every evening; **a~bekannt** a universally known; **a~e(r,s)** a all; **wir a~e** all of us; **a~e beide** both of us/you etc; **a~e vier Jahre** every four years; ad (col: zu Ende) finished; **etw a~e machen** finish sth up.

Allee [a'le:] f -, -n avenue.

allein [a'lain] ad alone; (ohne Hilfe) on

one's own, by oneself; **nicht** ~ (*nicht nur*) not only; *cj* but, only; **A~gang** *m*: **im A~gang** on one's own; **A~herrscher** *m* autocrat; **A~hersteller** *m* sole manufacturer; ~**stehend** a single.

alle- *cpd*: ~**mal** *ad* (*jedesmal*) always; (*ohne weiteres*) with no bother; **ein für** ~**mal** once and for all; ~**nfalls** *ad* at all events; (*höchstens*) at most; ~**rbeste(r,s)** a very best; ~**rdings** *ad* (*zwar*) admittedly; (*gewiß*) certainly.

allerg- *cpd*: ~**isch** [a'lɛrgɪʃ] a allergic; **A~ie** [-'gi:] *f* allergy.

aller- ['alər] *cpd*: ~**hand** a *inv* (*col*) all sorts of; **das ist doch ~hand!** that's a bit thick; ~**hand!** (*lobend*) good show!; **A~-'heiligen** *nt* All Saints' Day; ~**höchste(r,s)** a very highest; ~**höchstens** *ad* at the very most; ~**lei** a *inv* all sorts of; ~**letzte(r,s)** a very last; ~**seits** *ad* on all sides; **prost ~seits!** cheers everyone!; ~**wenigste(r,s)** a very least.

alles *pron* everything; ~ **in allem** all in all.

allgemein ['algə'maɪn] a general; ~**gültig** a generally accepted; **A~heit** *f* (*Menschen*) general public; (*pl: Redensarten*) general remarks *pl*.

Alliierte(r) [ali'i:rtə(r)] *f* *m* ally.

all- *cpd*: ~**jährlich** a annual; ~**mählich** a gradual; **A~tag** *m* everyday life; ~**täglich** a,ad daily; (*gewöhnlich*) commonplace; ~**tags** *ad* on weekdays; ~'**wissend** a omniscient; ~**zu** *ad* all too; ~**zuoft** *ad* all too often; ~**zuviel** *ad* too much.

Almosen ['almo:zən] *nt* **-s**, - alms *pl*.

Alpen ['alpən] *pl* Alps *pl*; ~**blume** *f* alpine flower.

Alphabet [alfa'be:t] *nt* **-(e)s**, **-e** alphabet; **a~isch** a alphabetical.

Alptraum ['alptraum] *m* nightmare.

als [als] *cj* (*zeitlich*) when; (*comp*) than; (*Gleichheit*) as; **nichts ~** nothing but; ~ **ob** as if.

also ['alzo:] *cj* so; (*folglich*) therefore; **ich komme ~ morgen** so I'll come tomorrow; ~ **gut or schön!** okay then; ~, **so was!** well really!; **na ~!** there you are then!

alt [alt] a old; **ich bin nicht mehr der ~e** I am not the man I was; **alles beim ~en lassen** leave everything as it was; **A~** *m* **-s**, **-e** (*Mus*) alto; **A~ar** [al'ta:r] *m* **-(e)s**, **-äre** altar; ~**bekannt** a long-known; **A~'eisen** *nt* scrap iron.

Alter ['altər] *nt* **-s**, - age; (*hohes*) old age; **im** ~ **von** at the age of; **a~n** *vi* grow old, age; ~**na'tive** *f* alternative; ~**sgrenze** *f* age limit; ~**sheim** *nt* old people's home; ~**sversorgung** *f* old age pension; ~**tum** *nt* antiquity.

alt- *cpd*: ~'**hergebracht** a traditional; ~**klug** a precocious; ~**modisch** a old-fashioned; **A~papier** *nt* waste paper; **A~stadt** *f* old town; **A~stimme** *f* alto; **A~'weibersommer** *m* Indian summer.

Aluminium [alu'mi:nium]   *nt*   **-s**

aluminium, aluminum (*US*); ~**folie** *f* tinfoil.

am [am] = **an dem**; ~ **Sterben** on the point of dying; ~ **15. März** on March 15th; ~ **besten/schönsten** best/most beautiful.

Amalgam [amal'ga:m] *nt* **-s**, **-e** amalgam.

Amateur [ama'tø:r] *m* amateur.

Amboß ['ambɔs] *m* **-sses**, **-sse** anvil.

ambulant [ambu'lant] a outpatient.

Ameise ['a:maɪzə] *f* -, **-n** ant.

Ampel ['ampəl] *f* -, **-n** traffic lights *pl*.

amphibisch [am'fi:bɪʃ] a amphibious.

amputieren [ampu'ti:rən] *vt* amputate.

Amsel ['amzəl] *f* -, **-n** blackbird.

Amt [amt] *nt* **-(e)s**, **-er** office; (*Pflicht*) duty; (*Tel*) exchange; **a~ieren** [am'ti:rən] *vi* hold office; **a~lich** a official; ~**sperson** *f* official; ~**srichter** *m* district judge; ~**sstunden** *pl* office hours *pl*; ~**szeit** *f* period of office.

amüsant [amy'zant] a amusing.

Amüsement [amyzə'mã:] *nt* amusement.

amüsieren [amy'zi:rən] *vt* amuse; *vr* enjoy o.s.

an [an] *prep* +*dat* (*räumlich*) at; (*auf, bei*) on; (*nahe bei*) near; (*zeitlich*) on; +*acc* (*räumlich*) on) to; ~ **Ostern** at Easter; ~ **diesem Ort/Tag** at this place/on this day; ~ **und für sich** actually; *ad*: **von** ... ~ **from** ... **on**; ~ **die 5 DM** around 5 marks; **das Licht ist** ~ the light is on.

analog [ana'lo:k] a analogous; **A~ie** [-'gi:] *f* analogy.

Analyse [ana'ly:zə] *f* -, **-n** analysis.

analysieren [analy'zi:rən] *vt* analyse.

Ananas ['ananas] *f* -, - or **-se** pineapple.

Anarchie [anar'çi:] *f* anarchy.

Anatomie [anato'mi:] *f* anatomy.

anbahnen ['anba:nən] *vtr* open up.

anbändeln ['anbɛndəln] *vi* (*col*) flirt.

Anbau ['anbau] *m* (*Agr*) cultivation; (*Gebäude*) extension; **a~en** *vt* (*Agr*) cultivate; *Gebäudeteil* build on.

anbehalten ['anbəhaltən] *vt* *irreg* keep on.

anbei [an'baɪ] *ad* enclosed.

anbeißen ['anbaɪsən] *irreg* *vt* bite into; *vi* (*lit*) bite; (*fig*) swallow the bait; **zum A~** (*col*) good enough to eat.

anbelangen ['anbəlaŋən] *vt* concern; **was mich anbelangt** as far as I am concerned.

anberaumen ['anbəraumən] *vt* fix.

anbeten ['anbe:tən] *vt* worship.

Anbetracht ['anbətraxt] *m*: **in** ~ (+*gen*) in view of.

Anbetung *f* worship.

anbiedern ['anbi:dərn] *vr* make up (*bei* to).

anbieten ['anbi:tən] *irreg* *vt* offer; *vr* volunteer.

anbinden ['anbɪndən] *irreg* *vt* tie up; *vi*: **mit jdm** ~ start something with sb; **kurz angebunden** (*fig*) curt.

Anblick ['anblɪk] *m* sight; **a~en** *vt* look at.

anbrechen ['anbrɛçən] *irreg* *vt* start; *Vorräte* break into; *vi* start; (*Tag*) break; (*Nacht*) fall.

anbrennen ['anbrɛnən] vi irreg catch fire; (Cook) burn.

anbringen ['anbrɪŋən] vt irreg bring; Ware sell; (festmachen) fasten.

Anbruch ['anbrʊx] m beginning; ~ des Tages/der Nacht dawn/nightfall.

anbrüllen ['anbrʏlən] vt roar at.

Andacht ['andaxt] f -, -en devotion; (Gottesdienst) prayers pl.

andächtig ['andɛçtɪç] a devout.

andauern ['andaʊərn] vi last, go on; ~d a continual.

Andenken ['andɛŋkən] nt -s, - memory; souvenir.

andere(r,s) ['andərə(r,z)] a other; (verschieden) different; am ~n Tage the next day; ein ~s Mal another time; kein ~r nobody else; von etw ~m sprechen talk about sth else; ~nteils, ~rseits ad on the other hand.

ändern ['ɛndərn] vt alter, change; vr change.

ander- cpd: ~nfalls ad otherwise; ~s ad differently (als from); wer ~s? who else?; jd/irgendwo ~s sb/somewhere else; ~s aussehen/klingen look/sound different; ~sartig a different; ~seits ad on the other hand; ~sfarbig a of a different colour; ~gläubig a of a different faith; ~sherum ad the other way round; ~swo ad elsewhere; ~swoher ad from elsewhere; ~swohin ad elsewhere.

anderthalb ['andərt'halp] a one and a half.

Änderung ['ɛndərʊŋ] f alteration, change.

anderweitig ['andər'vaɪtɪç] a other; ad otherwise; (anderswo) elsewhere.

andeuten ['andɔytən] vt indicate; (Wink geben) hint at.

Andeutung f indication; hint.

Andrang ['andraŋ] m crush.

andrehen ['andreːən] vt turn or switch on; (col) jdm etw ~ unload sth onto sb.

androhen ['androːən] vt: jdm etw ~ threaten sb with sth.

aneignen ['an'aɪgnən] vt: sich (dat) etw ~ acquire sth; (widerrechtlich) appropriate sth.

aneinander [an'aɪ'nandər] ad at/on/to etc one another or each other; ~fügen vt put together; ~geraten vi irreg clash; ~legen vt put together.

anekeln ['an'eːkəln] vt disgust.

Anemone [ane'moːnə] f -, -n anemone.

anerkannt ['an'ɛrkant] a recognized, acknowledged.

anerkennen ['an'ɛrkɛnən] vt irreg recognize, acknowledge; (würdigen) appreciate; ~d a appreciative; ~swert a praiseworthy.

Anerkennung f recognition, acknowledgement; appreciation.

anfachen ['anfaxən] vt (lit) fan into flame; (fig) kindle.

anfahren ['anfaːrən] irreg vt deliver; (fahren gegen) hit; Hafen put into; (fig) bawl out; vi drive up; (losfahren) drive off.

Anfall ['anfal] m (Med) attack; a~en irreg vt attack; (fig) overcome; vi (Arbeit) come up; (Produkt) be obtained.

anfällig ['anfɛlɪç] a delicate; ~ für etw prone to sth.

Anfang ['anfaŋ] m -(e)s, -fänge beginning, start; von ~ an right from the beginning; zu ~ at the beginning; ~ Mai at the beginning of May; a~en vti irreg begin, start; (machen) do.

Anfänger(in f) ['anfɛŋər(ɪn)] m -s, - beginner.

anfänglich ['anfɛŋlɪç] a initial.

anfangs ad at first; A~buchstabe m initial or first letter; A~stadium nt initial stages pl.

anfassen ['anfasən] vt handle; (berühren) touch; vi lend a hand; vr feel.

anfechten ['anfɛçtən] vt irreg dispute; (beunruhigen) trouble.

anfertigen ['anfɛrtɪgən] vt make.

anfeuern ['anfɔyərn] vt (fig) spur on.

anflehen ['anfleːən] vt implore.

anfliegen ['anfliːgən] irreg vt fly to; vi fly up.

Anflug ['anfluːk] m (Aviat) approach; (Spur) trace.

anfordern ['anfɔrdərn] vt demand.

Anforderung f demand (gen for).

Anfrage ['anfraːgə] f inquiry; a~n vi inquire.

anfreunden ['anfrɔyndən] vr make friends.

anfügen ['anfyːgən] vt add; (beifügen) enclose.

anfühlen ['anfyːlən] vtr feel.

anführen ['anfyːrən] vt lead; (zitieren) quote; (col: betrügen) lead up the garden path.

Anführer m leader.

Anführung f leadership; (Zitat) quotation; ~striche, ~zeichen pl quotation marks pl, inverted commas pl.

Angabe ['angaːbə] f statement; (Tech) specification; (col: Prahlerei) boasting; (Sport) service; ~n pl (Auskunft) particulars pl.

angeben ['angeːbən] irreg vt give; (anzeigen) inform on; (bestimmen) set; vi (col) boast; (Sport) serve.

Angeber m -s, - (col) show-off; ~ei [-'raɪ] f (col) showing off.

angeblich ['angeːplɪç] a alleged.

angeboren ['angəboːrən] a inborn, innate (jdm in sb).

Angebot ['angəboːt] nt offer; (Comm) supply (an +dat of).

angebracht ['angəbraxt] a appropriate, in order.

angegriffen ['angəgrɪfən] a exhausted.

angeheitert ['angəhaɪtərt] a tipsy.

angehen ['angeːən] irreg vt concern; (angreifen) attack; (bitten) approach (um for); vi (Feuer) light; (col: beginnen) begin; ~d a prospective; er ist ein ~der Vierziger he is approaching forty.

angehören ['angəhøːrən] vi belong (dat to).

Angehörige(r) ['angəhøːrɪgə(r)] mf relative.

Angeklagte(r) ['angəklaːkta(r)] mf accused.

Angel ['aŋəl] f -, -n fishing rod; (*Tür*—) hinge.

Angelegenheit ['angəle:gənhait] f affair, matter.

Angel- cpd: ~**haken** m fish hook; **a**~**n** vt catch; vi fish; ~**n** nt -s angling, fishing; ~**rute** f fishing rod.

angemessen ['angəmɛsən] a appropriate, suitable.

angenehm ['angəne:m] a pleasant, ~**!** (*bei Vorstellung*) pleased to meet you; **jdm** ~ **sein** be welcome.

angenommen ['angənomən] a assumed; ~, **wir** ... assuming we....

angesehen ['angəze:ən] a respected.

angesichts ['angəziçts] prep +gen in view of, considering.

angespannt ['angəʃpant] a *Aufmerksamkeit* close; *Arbeit* hard.

Angestellte(r) ['angəʃtɛltə(r)] mf employee.

angetan ['angəta:n] a: **von jdm/etw** ~ **sein** be impressed by sb/sth; **es jdm** ~ **haben** appeal to sb.

angewiesen ['angəvi:zən] a: **auf jdn/etw** ~ **sein** be dependent on sb/sth.

angewöhnen ['angəvø:nən] vt: **jdm/sich etw** ~ get sb/become accustomed to sth.

Angewohnheit ['angəvo:nhait] f habit.

angleichen ['anglaiçən] vtr irreg adjust (*dat* to).

Angler ['aŋlər] m -s, - angler.

angreifen ['angraifən] vt irreg attack; (*anfassen*) touch; *Arbeit* tackle; (*beschädigen*) damage.

Angreifer m -s, - attacker.

Angriff ['angrif] m attack; **etw in** ~ **nehmen** make a start on sth.

Angst [aŋst] f -, ⁻e fear; ~ **haben** be afraid or scared (*vor* +dat of); ~ **haben um jdn/etw** be worried about sb/sth; **nur keine** ~**!** I don't be scared; **a**~ a: **jdm ist a**~ sb is afraid or scared; **jdm a**~ **machen** scare sb; ~**hase** m (*col*) chicken, scaredy-cat.

ängst- [ɛŋst] cpd: ~**igen** vt frighten; vr worry (o.s.) (*vor* +dat, um about); ~**lich** a nervous; (*besorgt*) worried; Ä~**lichkeit** f nervousness.

anhaben ['anha:bən] vt irreg have on; **er kann mir nichts** ~ he can't hurt me.

anhalt- ['anhalt] cpd: ~**en** irreg vt stop; (*gegen etw halten*) hold up (*jdm against sth*); **jdn zur Arbeit/Höflichkeit** ~**en** make sb work/be polite; vi stop; (*andauern*) persist; ~**end** a persistent; A~**er** m -s, - hitch-hiker; **per** A~**er fahren** hitch-hike; A~**spunkt** m clue.

anhand [an'hant] prep +gen with.

Anhang ['anhaŋ] m appendix; (*Leute*) family; supporters pl.

anhäng- ['anhɛŋ] cpd: ~**en** vt irreg hang up; *Wagen* couple up; *Zusatz* add (on); **sich an jdn** ~**en** attach o.s. to sb; A~**er** m -s, - supporter; (*Aut*) trailer; (*am Koffer*) tag; (*Schmuck*) pendant; A~**erschaft** f supporters pl; A~**eschloß** nt padlock; ~**ig** a (*Jur*) sub judice; ~**ig machen** *Prozeß* bring; ~**lich** a devoted; A~**lichkeit** f devotion; A~**sel** nt -s, - appendage.

Anhäufung ['anhɔyfuŋ] f accumulation.

anheben ['anhe:bən] vt irreg lift up; *Preise* raise.

anheimelnd ['anhaiməlnt] a comfortable, cosy.

anheimstellen [an'haimʃtɛlən] vt: **jdm etw** ~ leave sth up to sb.

Anhieb ['anhi:b] m: **auf** ~ at the very first go; (*kurz entschlossen*) on the spur of the moment.

Anhöhe ['anhø:ə] f hill.

anhören ['anhø:rən] vt listen to; (*anmerken*) hear; vr sound.

animieren [ani'mi:rən] vt encourage, urge on.

Anis [a'ni:s] m -es, -e aniseed.

ankaufen ['ankaufən] vt purchase, buy.

Anker ['aŋkər] m -s, - anchor; **vor** ~ **gehen** drop anchor; **a**~**n** vti anchor; ~**platz** m anchorage.

Anklage ['ankla:gə] f accusation; (*Jur*) charge; ~**bank** f dock; **a**~**n** vt accuse; (*Jur*) charge (*gen* with).

Ankläger ['anklɛ:gər] m accuser.

Anklang ['anklaŋ] m: **bei jdm** ~ **finden** meet with sb's approval.

Ankleide- ['anklaidə] cpd: ~**kabine** f changing cubicle; **a**~**n** vtr dress.

anklopfen ['anklɔpfən] vi knock.

anknüpfen ['anknypfən] vt fasten or tie on; (*fig*) start; vi (*anschließen*) refer (*an* +acc to).

ankommen ['ankomən] vi irreg arrive; (*näherkommen*) approach; (*Anklang finden*) go down (*bei* with); **es kommt darauf an** it depends; (*wichtig sein*) that (is what) matters; **es kommt auf ihn an** it depends on him; **es darauf** ~ **lassen** let things take their course; **gegen jdn/etw** ~ cope with sb/sth.

ankündigen ['ankyndigən] vt announce.

Ankündigung f announcement.

Ankunft ['ankunft] f -, -**künfte** arrival; ~**szeit** f time of arrival.

ankurbeln ['ankurbəln] vt (*Aut*) crank; (*fig*) boost.

Anlage ['anla:gə] f disposition; (*Begabung*) talent; (*Park*) gardens pl; (*Beilage*) enclosure; (*Tech*) plant; (*Fin*) investment; (*Entwurf*) layout.

anlangen ['anlaŋən] vi arrive.

Anlaß ['anlas] m -**sses**, -**lässe** cause (*zu* for); (*Ereignis*) occasion; **aus** ~ (+gen) on the occasion of; ~ **zu etw geben** give rise to sth; **etw zum** ~ **nehmen** take the opportunity of sth.

anlassen irreg vt leave on; *Motor* start; vr (*col*) start off.

Anlasser m -s, - (*Aut*) starter.

anläßlich ['anlɛslıç] prep +gen on the occasion of.

Anlauf ['anlauf] m run-up; **a**~**en** irreg vi begin; (*Film*) show; (*Sport*) run up; (*Fenster*) mist up; (*Metall*) tarnish; **rot a**~**en** colour; **gegen etw a**~**en** run into or up against sth; **angelaufen kommen** come running up; vt call at.

anläuten ['anlɔytən] vi ring.

anlegen ['anle:gən] vt put (*an* +acc

against/on); (*anziehen*) put on; (*gestalten*) lay out; *Geld* invest; *Gewehr* aim (*auf* +*acc* at); **es auf etw** (*acc*) ~ **be** out for sth/to do sth; **sich mit jdm** ~ (*col*) quarrel with sb; *vi* dock.

Anlegestelle *f*, **Anlegeplatz** *m* landing place.

anlehnen ['anle:nən] *vt* lean (*an* +*acc* against); *Tür* leave ajar; *vr* lean (*an* +*acc* on).

anleiten ['anlaɪtən] *vt* instruct.

Anleitung *f* instructions *pl*.

anlernen ['anlɛrnən] *vt* teach, instruct.

anliegen ['anli:gən] *vi irreg* (*Kleidung*) cling; **A**~ *nt* -**s**, - matter; (*Wunsch*) wish; ~ **d** *a* adjacent; (*beigefügt*) enclosed.

Anlieger *m* -**s**, - resident.

anlügen ['anly:gən] *vt irreg* lie to.

anmachen ['anmaxən] *vt* attach; *Elektrisches* put on; *Salat* dress.

anmaßen ['anma:sən] *vt*: **sich** (*dat*) **etw** ~ lay claim to sth; ~ **d** *a* arrogant.

Anmaßung *f* presumption.

Anmeld- ['anmɛld] *cpd*: ~**eformular** *nt* registration form; **a**~**en** *vt* announce; *vr* (*sich ankündigen*) make an appointment; (*polizeilich, für Kurs etc*) register; ~**ung** *f* announcement; appointment; registration.

anmerken ['anmɛrkən] *vt* observe; (*anstreichen*) mark; **jdm etw** ~ notice sb's sth; **sich** (*dat*) **nichts** ~ **lassen** not give anything away.

Anmerkung *f* note.

Anmut ['anmu:t] *f* - grace; **a**~**en** *vt* give a feeling; **a**~**ig** *a* charming.

annähen ['annɛ:ən] *vt* sew on.

annähern ['annɛ:ərn] *vr* get closer; ~ **d** *a* approximate.

Annäherung *f* approach; ~**sversuch** *m* advances *pl*.

Annahme ['anna:mə] *f* -, -**n** acceptance; (*Vermutung*) assumption.

annehm- ['anne:m] *cpd*: ~**bar** *a* acceptable; ~**en** *irreg vt* accept; *Namen* take; *Kind* adopt; (*vermuten*) suppose, assume; **angenommen, das ist so** assuming that is so; *vr* take care (*gen* of); **A**~**lichkeit** *f* comfort.

annektieren [anɛk'ti:rən] *vt* annex.

Annonce [a'nõ:sə] *f* -, -**n** advertisement.

annoncieren [anõ'si:rən] *vti* advertise.

annullieren [anu'li:rən] *vt* annul.

Anode [a'no:də] *f* -, -**n** anode.

anöden ['anˈø:dən] *vt* (*col*) bore stiff.

anonym [ano'ny:m] *a* anonymous.

Anorak ['anorak] *m* -**s**, -**s** anorak.

anordnen ['anˈɔrdnən] *vt* arrange; (*befehlen*) order.

Anordnung *f* arrangement; order.

anorganisch ['anˈɔrganɪʃ] *a* inorganic.

anpacken ['anpakən] *vt* grasp; (*fig*) tackle; **mit** ~ lend a hand.

anpassen ['anpasən] *vt* fit (*jdm* on sb); (*fig*) adapt (*dat* to); *vr* adapt.

Anpassung *f* fitting; adaptation; **a**~**sfähig** *a* adaptable.

Anpfiff ['anpfɪf] *m* (*Sport*) (starting) whistle; kick-off; (*col*) rocket.

anpöbeln ['anpø:bəln] *vt* abuse.

Anprall ['anpral] *m* collision (*gegen, an* +*acc* with).

anprangern ['anpraŋərn] *vt* denounce.

anpreisen ['anpraɪzən] *vt irreg* extol.

Anprobe ['anpro:bə] *f* trying on.

anprobieren ['anprobi:rən] *vt* try on.

anrechnen ['anrɛçnən] *vt* charge; (*fig*) count; **jdm etw hoch** ~ value sb's sth greatly.

Anrecht ['anrɛçt] *nt* right (*auf* +*acc* to).

Anrede ['anre:də] *f* form of address; **a**~**n** *vt* address; (*belästigen*) accost.

anregen ['anre:gən] *vt* stimulate; **angeregte Unterhaltung** lively discussion; ~**d** *a* stimulating.

Anregung *f* stimulation; (*Vorschlag*) suggestion.

anreichern ['anraɪçərn] *vt* enrich.

Anreise ['anraɪzə] *f* journey; **a**~**n** *vi* arrive.

Anreiz ['anraɪts] *m* incentive.

Anrichte ['anrɪçtə] *f* -, -**n** sideboard; **a**~**n** *vt* serve up; *Unheil* **a**~**n** make mischief.

anrüchig ['anryçɪç] *a* dubious.

anrücken ['anrykən] *vi* approach; (*Mil*) advance.

Anruf ['anru:f] *m* call; **a**~**en** *vt irreg* call out to; (*bitten*) call on; (*Tel*) ring up, phone, call.

anrühren ['anry:rən] *vt* touch; (*mischen*) mix.

ans [ans] = **an das**.

Ansage ['anza:gə] *f* -, -**n** announcement; **a**~**n** *vt* announce; *vr* say one will come; ~**r(in** *f*) *m* -**s**, - announcer.

ansammeln ['anzaməln] *vtr* collect.

Ansammlung *f* collection; (*Leute*) crowd.

ansässig ['anzɛsɪç] *a* resident.

Ansatz ['anzats] *m* start; (*Haar*—) hairline; (*Hals*—) base; (*Verlängerungsstück*) extension; (*Veranschlagung*) estimate; **die ersten Ansätze zu etw** the beginnings of sth; ~**punkt** *m* starting point.

anschaffen ['anʃafən] *vt* buy, purchase.

Anschaffung *f* purchase.

anschalten ['anʃaltən] *vt* switch on.

anschau- ['anʃau] *cpd*: ~**en** *vt* look at; ~**lich** *a* illustrative; **A**~**ung** *f* (*Meinung*) view; **aus eigener A**~**ung** from one's own experience; **A**~**ungsmaterial** *nt* illustrative material.

Anschein ['anʃaɪn] *m* appearance; **allem** ~ **nach** to all appearances; **den** ~ **haben** seem, appear; **a**~**end** *a* apparent.

Anschlag ['anʃla:k] *m* notice; (*Attentat*) attack; (*Comm*) estimate; (*auf Klavier*) touch; (*Schreibmaschine*) character; **a**~**en** ['anʃla:gən] *irreg vt* put up; (*beschädigen*) chip; *Akkord* strike; *Kosten* estimate; *vi* hit (*an* +*acc* against); (*wirken*) have an effect; (*Glocke*) ring; (*Hund*) bark; ~**zettel** *m* notice.

anschließen ['anʃli:sən] *irreg vt* connect up; *Sender* link up; *vir*: (**sich**) **an etw** (*acc*) ~ adjoin sth; (*zeitlich*) follow sth; *vr* join (*jdm/etw* sb/sth); (*beipflichten*) agree (*jdm/etw* with sb/sth); ~**d** *a* adjacent; (*zeitlich*) subsequent; *ad* afterwards; ~**d an** (+*acc*) following.

Anschluß ['anʃlʊs] m (Elec, Rail) connection; (von Wasser etc) supply; **im ~ an** (+acc) following; **~ finden** make friends.

anschmiegsam ['anʃmiːkzaːm] a affectionate.

anschmieren ['anʃmiːrən] vt smear; (col) take in.

anschnallen ['anʃnalən] vt buckle on; vr fasten one's seat belt.

anschneiden ['anʃnaɪdən] vt irreg cut into; Thema broach.

Anschnitt ['anʃnɪt] m first slice.

anschreiben ['anʃraɪbən] vt irreg write (up); (Comm) charge up; (benachrichtigen) write to; **bei jdm gut/schlecht angeschrieben sein** be well/badly thought of by sb, be in sb's good/bad books.

anschreien ['anʃraɪən] vt irreg shout at.

Anschrift ['anʃrɪft] f address.

Anschuldigung ['anʃʊldɪgʊŋ] f accusation.

anschwellen ['anʃvɛlən] vi irreg swell (up).

anschwemmen ['anʃvɛmən] vt wash ashore.

anschwindeln ['anʃvɪndəln] vt lie to.

ansehen ['anzeːən] vt irreg look at; **jdm etw ~ see** sth (from sb's face); **jdm als etw ~** look on sb/sth as sth; **~ für** consider; **A~** nt -s respect; (Ruf) reputation.

ansehnlich ['anzeːnlɪç] a fine-looking; (beträchtlich) considerable.

ansein ['anzaɪn] vi irreg (col) be on.

ansetzen ['anzɛtsən] vt (anfügen) fix on (an +acc to); (anlegen, an Mund etc) put (an +acc to); (festlegen) fix; (entwickeln) develop; Fett put on; Blätter grow; (zubereiten) prepare; **jdn/etw auf jdn/etw ~** set sb/sth on sb/sth; vi (anfangen) start, begin; (Entwicklung) set in; (dick werden) put on weight; **zu etw ~** prepare to do sth; vr (Rost etc) start to develop.

Ansicht ['anzɪçt] f (Anblick) sight; (Meinung) view, opinion; **zur ~** on approval; **meiner ~ nach** in my opinion; **~skarte** f picture postcard; **~ssache** f matter of opinion.

anspannen ['anʃpanən] vt harness; Muskel strain.

Anspannung f strain.

Anspiel ['anʃpiːl] nt (Sport) start; **a~en** vi (Sport) start play; **auf etw** (acc) **a~en** refer or allude to sth; **~ung** f reference, allusion (auf +acc to).

Ansporn ['anʃpɔrn] m -(e)s incentive.

Ansprache ['anʃpraːxə] f address.

ansprechen ['anʃprɛçən] irreg vt speak to; (bitten, gefallen) appeal to; **jdn auf etw** (acc) **(hin) ~** ask sb about sth; **etw als etw ~** regard sth as sth; vi react (auf +acc to); **~d** a attractive.

anspringen ['anʃprɪŋən] vi irreg (Aut) start.

Anspruch ['anʃprʊx] m (Recht) claim (auf +acc to); **hohe Ansprüche stellen/haben** demand/ expect a lot; **jdn/etw in ~ nehmen** occupy sb/take

up sth; **a~slos** a undemanding; **a~svoll** a demanding.

anspucken ['anʃpʊkən] vt spit at.

anstacheln ['anʃtaxəln] vt spur on.

Anstalt ['anʃtalt] f -, -en institution; **~en machen, etw zu tun** prepare to do sth.

Anstand ['anʃtant] m decency.

anständig ['anʃtɛndɪç] a decent; (col) proper; (groß) considerable; **A~keit** f propriety, decency.

anstandslos ad without any ado.

anstarren ['anʃtarən] vt stare at.

anstatt [an'ʃtat] prep +gen instead of; cj: **~ etw zu tun** instead of doing sth.

anstechen ['anʃtɛçən] vt irreg prick; Faß tap.

Ansteck- ['anʃtɛk] cpd: **a~en** vt pin on; (Med) infect; Pfeife light; Haus set fire to; vr: **ich habe mich bei ihm angesteckt** I caught it from him; vi (fig) be infectious; **a~end** a infectious; **~ung** f infection.

anstehen ['anʃteːən] vi irreg queue (up), line up (US).

anstelle [an'ʃtɛlə] prep +gen in place of; **~n** ['an-] vt (einschalten) turn on; (Arbeit geben) employ; (machen) do; vr queue (up), line up (US); (col) act.

Anstellung f employment; (Posten) post, position.

Anstieg ['anʃtiːk] m -(e)s, -e climb; (fig: von Preisen etc) increase (gen in).

anstift- ['anʃtɪft] cpd: **~en** vt Unglück cause; **jdn zu etw ~en** put sb up to sth; **A~er** m -s, instigator.

anstimmen ['anʃtɪmən] vt Lied strike up with; Geschrei set up; vi strike up.

Anstoß ['anʃtoːs] m impetus; (Ärgernis) offence; (Sport) kick-off; **der erste ~** the initiative; **~ nehmen an** (+dat) take offence at; **a~en** irreg vt push; (mit Fuß) kick; vi knock, bump; (mit der Zunge) lisp; (mit Gläsern) drink (a toast) (auf +acc to); **an etw** (acc) **a~en** (angrenzen) adjoin sth.

anstößig ['anʃtøːsɪç] a offensive, indecent; **A~keit** f indecency, offensiveness.

anstreben ['anʃtreːbən] vt strive for.

anstreichen ['anʃtraɪçən] vt irreg paint.

Anstreicher m -s, - painter.

anstrengen ['anʃtrɛŋən] vt strain; (Jur) bring; vr make an effort; **angestrengt** ad as hard as one can; **~d** a tiring.

Anstrengung f effort.

Anstrich ['anʃtrɪç] m coat of paint.

Ansturm ['anʃtʊrm] m rush; (Mil) attack.

ansuchen ['anzuːxən] vi: **um etw ~** apply for sth; **A~** nt -s, - request.

Antagonismus [antago'nɪsmʊs] m antagonism.

antasten ['antastən] vt touch; Recht infringe upon; Ehre question.

Anteil ['antaɪl] m -s, -e share (an +dat in); (Mitgefühl) sympathy; **~ nehmen an** (+dat) share in; (sich interessieren) take an interest in; **~nahme** f - sympathy.

Antenne [an'tɛnə] f -, -n aerial; (Zool) antenna.

Anthrazit [antra'tsiːt] m -s, -e anthracite.

Anti- ['anti] in cpds anti; **~alkoholiker** m

teetotaller; **a~autori'tär** a anti-authoritarian; **~biotikum** [antibi'o:tikom] nt -s, -ka antibiotic.

antik [an'ti:k] a antique; **A~e** f -, -n (Zeitalter) ancient world; (Kunstgegenstand) antique.

Antikörper m antibody.

Antilope [anti'lo:pə] f -, -n antelope.

Antipathie [antipa'ti:] f antipathy.

Antiquariat [antikvari'a:t] nt -(e)s, -e secondhand bookshop.

Antiquitäten [antikvi'tɛ:tən] pl antiques pl; **~handel** m antique business; **~händler** m antique dealer.

Antrag ['antra:k] m -(e)s, -träge proposal; (Parl) motion; (Gesuch) application.

antreffen ['antrɛfən] vt irreg meet.

antreiben ['antraıbən] irreg vt drive on; Motor drive; (anschwemmen) wash up; vi be washed up.

antreten ['antre:tən] irreg vt Amt take up; Erbschaft come into; Beweis offer; Reise start, begin; vi (Mil) fall in; (Sport) line up; **gegen jdn ~** play/fight against sb.

Antrieb ['antri:p] m (lit,fig) drive; **aus eigenem ~** of one's own accord.

antrinken ['antrɪŋkən] vt irreg Flasche, Glas start to drink from; **sich** (dat) **Mut/einen Rausch ~** give oneself Dutch courage/get drunk; **angetrunken sein** be tipsy.

Antritt ['antrɪt] m beginning, commencement; (eines Amts) taking up.

antun ['antu:n] vt irreg: **jdm etw ~** do sth to sb; **sich** (dat) **Zwang ~** force o.s.

Antwort ['antvɔrt] f -, -en answer, reply; **um ~ wird gebeten** RSVP; **a~en** vi answer, reply.

anvertrauen ['anfɛrtrauən] vt: **jdm etw ~** entrust sb with sth; **sich jdm ~** confide in sb.

anwachsen ['anvaksən] vi irreg grow; (Pflanze) take root.

Anwalt ['anvalt] m -(e)s, -wälte, **Anwältin** ['anvɛltɪn] f solicitor; lawyer; (fig) champion.

Anwandlung ['anvandluŋ] f caprice; **eine ~ von etw** a fit of sth.

Anwärter ['anvɛrtər] m candidate.

anweisen ['anvaızən] vt irreg instruct; (zuteilen) assign (jdm etw sth to sb).

Anweisung ['anvaızuŋ] f instruction; (Comm) remittance; (Post—, Zahlungs—) money order.

anwend- ['anvɛnd] cpd: **~bar** ['anvɛnt-] a practicable, applicable; **~en** vt irreg use, employ; Gesetz, Regel apply; **A~ung** f use; application.

Anwesen- ['anve:zən] cpd: **a~d** a present; **die ~den** those present; **~heit** f presence; **~heitsliste** f attendance register.

anwidern ['anvi:dərn] vt disgust.

Anwuchs ['anvu:ks] m growth.

Anzahl ['antsa:l] f number (an +dat of); **a~en** vt pay on account; **~ung** f deposit, payment on account.

anzapfen ['antsapfən] vt tap; Person (um Geld) touch.

Anzeichen ['antsaıçən] nt sign, indication.

Anzeige ['antsaıgə] f -, -n (Zeitungs—) announcement; (Werbung) advertisement; (bei Polizei) report; **~ erstatten gegen jdn** report sb (to the police); **a~n** vt (zu erkennen geben) show; (bekanntgeben) announce; (bei Polizei) report; **~nteil** m advertisements pl; **~r** m indicator.

anzetteln ['antsɛtəln] vt (col) instigate.

anziehen ['antsi:ən] irreg vt attract; Kleidung put on; Mensch dress; Schraube, Seil pull tight; Knie draw up; Feuchtigkeit absorb; vr get dressed; **~d** a attractive.

Anziehung f (Reiz) attraction; **~skraft** f power of attraction; (Phys) force of gravitation.

Anzug ['antsu:k] m suit; **im ~ sein** be approaching.

anzüglich ['antsy:klıç] a personal; (anstößig) offensive; **A~keit** f offensiveness; (Bemerkung) personal remark.

anzünden ['antsyndən] vt light.

Anzünder m lighter.

anzweifeln ['antsvaıfəln] vt doubt.

apart [a'part] a distinctive.

Apathie [apa'ti:] f apathy.

apathisch [a'pa:tıʃ] a apathetic.

Apfel ['apfəl] m -s, ⁼ apple; **~saft** m apple juice; **~sine** [apfəl'zi:nə] f -, -n orange; **~wein** m cider.

Apostel [a'pɔstəl] m -s, - apostle.

Apostroph [apo'stro:f] m -s, -e apostrophe.

Apotheke [apo'te:kə] f -, -n chemist's (shop), drugstore (US); **~r(in** f) m -s,- chemist, druggist (US).

Apparat [apa'ra:t] m -(e)s, -e piece of apparatus; camera; telephone; (Rad, TV) set; **am ~ bleiben** hold the line; **~ur** [-'tu:r] f apparatus.

Appartement [apart(ə)'mã:] nt -s, -s flat.

Appell [a'pɛl] m -s, -e (Mil) muster, parade; (fig) appeal; **a~ieren** [apɛ'li:rən] vi appeal (an +acc to).

Appetit [ape'ti:t] m -(e)s, -e appetite; **guten ~** enjoy your meal; **a~lich** a appetizing; **~losigkeit** f lack of appetite.

Applaus [a'plaus] m -es, -e applause.

Appretur [apre'tu:r] f finish.

Aprikose [apri'ko:zə] f -, -n apricot.

April [a'prıl] m -(s), -e April; **~wetter** nt April showers pl.

Aquaplaning [akva'pla:nıŋ] nt -(s) aquaplaning.

Aquarell [akva'rɛl] nt -s, -e watercolour.

Aquarium [a'kva:rium] nt aquarium.

Äquator [ɛ'kva:tɔr] m -s equator.

Arbeit ['arbaıt] f -, -en work (no art); (Stelle) job; (Erzeugnis) piece of work; (wissenschaftliche) dissertation; (Klassen—) test; **das war eine ~** that was a hard job; **a~en** vi work; vt work, make; **~er(in** f) m -s, - worker; (ungelernt) labourer; **~erschaft** f workers pl, labour force; **~geber** m -s, - employer; **~nehmer** m -s, - employee; **a~sam** a industrious.

Arbeits- in cpds labour; **~amt** nt employment exchange; **a~fähig** a fit for work;

able-bodied; ~**gang** m operation;
~**gemeinschaft** f study group; ~**kräfte**
pl workers pl, labour; **a**~**los** a
unemployed, out-of-work; ~**losigkeit** f
unemployment; ~**platz** m job; place of
work; **a**~**scheu** a work-shy; ~**tag** m
work(ing) day; ~**teilung** f division of
labour; **a**~**unfähig** a unfit for work;
~**zeit** f working hours pl.

Archäologe [arçɛo'lo:gə] m -n, -n
archaeologist.

Architekt(in f) [arçi'tɛkt(ɪn)] m -en, -en
architect; ~**ur** [-'tu:r] f architecture.

Archiv [ar'çi:f] nt -s, -e archive.

arg [ark] a bad, awful; ad awfully, very.

Ärger ['ɛrgər] m -s (Wut) anger;
(Unannehmlichkeit) trouble; **ä**~**lich** a
(zornig) angry; (lästig) annoying,
aggravating; **ä**~**n** vt annoy; vr get
annoyed; ~**nis** nt -ses, -se annoyance;
öffentliches ~**nis erregen** be a public
nuisance.

arg- cpd: ~**listig** a cunning, insidious;
~**los** a guileless, innocent; **A**~**losigkeit** f
guilelessness, innocence; **A**~**ument**
[argu'mɛnt] nt argument; **A**~**wohn** m
suspicion; ~**wöhnisch** a suspicious.

Arie ['a:riə] f -, -n aria.

Aristokrat [aristo'kra:t] m -en, -en aristocrat; ~**ie** [-'ti:] f aristocracy; **a**~**isch** a
aristocratic.

arithmetisch [arɪt'me:tɪʃ] a arithmetical.

arm [arm] a poor; **A**~ m -(e)s, -e arm;
(Fluß—) branch; **A**~**a'tur** f (Elec) arma-
ture; **A**~**a'turenbrett** nt instrument
panel; (Aut) dashboard; **A**~**band** nt
bracelet; **A**~**banduhr** f (wrist) watch;
A~**e(r)** mf poor man/woman; **die A**~**en**
the poor; **A**~**ee** [ar'me:] f -, -n army;
A~**eekorps** nt army corps.

Ärmel ['ɛrməl] m -s, - sleeve; **etw aus**
dem ~ **schütteln** (fig) produce sth just
like that.

ärmlich ['ɛrmlɪç] a poor.

armselig a wretched, miserable.

Armut ['armu:t] f - poverty.

Aroma [a'ro:ma] nt -s, **Aromen** aroma;
a~**tisch** [aro'ma:tɪʃ] a aromatic.

arrangieren [arã'ʒi:rən] vt arrange; vr
come to an arrangement.

Arrest [a'rɛst] m -(e)s, -e detention.

arrogant [aro'gant] a arrogant.

Arroganz f arrogance.

Arsch [arʃ] m -es, **-e** (col) arse, bum.

Art [a:rt] f -, -en (Weise) way; (Sorte) kind,
sort; (Biol) species; **eine** ~ **(von) Frucht**
a kind of fruit; **Häuser aller** ~ houses of
all kinds; **es ist nicht seine** ~, **das zu**
tun it's not like him to do that; **ich mache**
das auf meine ~ I do that my (own)
way; **nach** ~ **des Hauses** à la maison;
a~**en** vi: **nach jdm** **a**~**en** take after sb;
der Mensch ist so geartet, daß . . .
human nature is such that . . .

Arterie [ar'te:riə] f artery; ~**nverkal-**
kung f arteriosclerosis.

artig ['a:rtɪç] a good, well-behaved.

Artikel [ar'ti:kəl] m -s, - article.

Artillerie [artɪlə'ri:] f artillery.

Arznei [a:rts'nai] f medicine; ~**mittel** nt
medicine, medicament.

Arzt [a:rtst] m -es, **-e**, **Ärztin** ['ɛ:rtstɪn] f
doctor.

ärztlich ['ɛ:rtstlɪç] a medical.

As [as] nt -ses, -se ace.

Asbest [as'bɛst] m -(e)s, -e asbestos.

Asche ['aʃə] f -, -n ash, cinder; ~**nbahn** f
cinder track; ~**nbecher** m ashtray;
~**nbrödel** nt Cinderella; ~**rmittwoch** m
Ash Wednesday.

asozial ['azotsia:l] a antisocial; **Familien**
asocial.

Aspekt [as'pɛkt] m -(e)s, -e aspect.

Asphalt [as'falt] m -(e)s, -e asphalt;
a~**ieren** [-'ti:rən] vt asphalt; ~**straße** f
asphalt road.

Assistent(in f) [asɪs'tɛnt(ɪn)] m assistant.

Assoziation [asotsiatsi'o:n] f association.

Ast [ast] m -(e)s, **-e** bough, branch; ~**er** f
-, -n aster.

ästhetisch [ɛs'te:tɪʃ] a aesthetic.

Asthma ['astma] nt -s asthma; ~**tiker(in**
f) [ast'ma:tikər(ɪn)] m -s, - asthmatic.

Astro- [astro] cpd: ~**loge** m -n, -n astrologer; ~**lo'gie** f astrology; ~'**naut** m
-en, -en astronaut; ~'**nautik** f astro-
nautics; ~'**nom** m -en, -en astronomer;
~**no'mie** f astronomy.

Asyl [a'zy:l] nt -s, -e asylum; (Heim) home;
(Obdachlosen—) shelter.

Atelier [atəli'e:] nt -s, -s studio.

Atem ['a:təm] m -s breath; **den** ~
anhalten hold one's breath; **außer** ~ out
of breath; **a**~**beraubend** a breath-taking;
a~**los** a breathless; ~**pause** f breather;
~**zug** m breath.

Atheismus [ate'ɪsmʊs] m atheism.

Atheist m atheist; **a**~**isch** a atheistic.

Äther ['ɛ:tər] m -s, - ether.

Athlet [at'le:t] m -en, -en athlete; ~**ik** f
athletics.

Atlas ['atlas] m - or -ses, -se or **At-**
lanten atlas.

atmen ['a:tmən] vti breathe.

Atmosphäre [atmo'sfɛ:rə] f -, -n
atmosphere.

atmosphärisch a atmospheric.

Atmung ['a:tmʊŋ] f respiration.

Atom [a'to:m] nt -s, -e atom; **a**~**ar**
[ato'ma:r] a atomic; ~**bombe** f atom
bomb; ~**energie** f atomic or nuclear
energy; ~**kern** m atomic nucleus;
~**kernforschung** f nuclear research;
~**kraftwerk** nt nuclear power station;
~**krieg** m nuclear or atomic war;
~**macht** f nuclear or atomic power;
~**müll** m atomic waste; ~**sperrvertrag**
m (Pol) nuclear non-proliferation treaty;
~**versuch** m atomic test; ~**waffen** pl
atomic weapons pl; ~**zeitalter** nt atomic
age.

Attentat [atɛn'ta:t] nt -(e)s, -e
(attempted) assassination (auf +acc of).

Attentäter [atɛn'tɛ:tər] m (would-be)
assassin.

Attest [a'tɛst] nt -(e)s, -e certificate.

attraktiv [atrak'ti:f] a attractive.

Attrappe [a'trapə] f -, -n dummy.

Attribut [atri'bu:t] *nt* -(e)s, -e (*Gram*) attribute.

ätzen ['ɛtsən] *vi* be caustic.

auch [aux] *cj* also, too, as well; (*selbst, sogar*) even; (*wirklich*) really; **oder ~** or; **~ das ist schön** that's nice too *or* as well; **das habe ich ~ nicht gemacht** I didn't do it either; **ich ~ nicht** nor I, me neither; **~ wenn das Wetter schlecht ist** even if the weather is bad; **wer/was ~** whoever/whatever; **so sieht es ~ aus** it looks like it too; **~ das noch!** not that as well!

auf [auf] *prep* +*acc or dat* (*räumlich*) on; (*hinauf*: +*acc*) up; (*in Richtung*: +*acc*) to; (*nach*) after; **~ der Reise** on the way; **~ der Post/dem Fest** at the post office/party; **~ das Land** into the country; **~ der Straße** on the road; **~ dem Land/der ganzen Welt** in the country/the whole world; **~ deutsch** in German; **~ Lebenszeit** for sb's lifetime; **bis ~ ihn** except for him; **~ einmal** at once; *ad*: **~ und ab up and down; ~ und davon** up and away; **~! (***los***)** come on!; **~ sein** (*col*) (*Person*) be up; (*Tür*) be open; **von Kindheit ~** from childhood onwards; **~ daß** so that.

aufatmen ['auf'a:tmən] *vi* heave a sigh of relief.

aufbahren ['aufba:rən] *vt* lay out.

Aufbau ['aufbau] *m* (*Bauen*) building, construction; (*Struktur*) structure; (*aufgebautes Teil*) superstructure; **a~en** *vt* erect, build (up); *Existenz* make; (*gestalten*) construct; (*gründen*) found, base (*auf* +*dat* on).

aufbäumen ['aufbɔʏmən] *vr* rear; (*fig*) revolt, rebel.

aufbauschen ['aufbauʃən] *vt* puff out; (*fig*) exaggerate.

aufbehalten ['aufbəhaltən] *vt irreg* keep on.

aufbekommen ['aufbəkɔmən] *vt irreg* (*öffnen*) get open; *Hausaufgaben* be given.

aufbessern ['aufbɛsərn] *vt Gehalt* increase.

aufbewahren ['aufbəva:rən] *vt* keep; *Gepäck* put in the left-luggage office.

Aufbewahrung *f* (safe)keeping; (*Gepäck*—) left-luggage office; **jdm etw zur ~ geben** give sb sth for safekeeping; **~sort** *m* storage place.

aufbieten ['aufbi:tən] *vt irreg Kraft* summon (up), exert; *Armee, Polizei* mobilize; *Brautpaar* publish the banns of.

aufblasen ['aufbla:zən] *irreg vt* blow up, inflate; *vr* (*col*) become big-headed.

aufbleiben ['aufblaibən] *vi irreg* (*Laden*) remain open; (*Person*) stay up.

aufblenden ['aufblɛndən] *vt Scheinwerfer* turn on full beam.

aufblicken ['aufblikən] *vi* (*lit, fig*) look up (*zu* (*lit*) at, (*fig*) to).

aufblühen ['aufbly:ən] *vi* blossom, flourish.

aufbrauchen ['aufbrauxən] *vt* use up.

aufbrausen ['aufbrauzən] *vi* (*fig*) flare up; **~d** *a* hot-tempered.

aufbrechen ['aufbrɛçən] *irreg vt* break *or* prize open; *vi* burst open; (*gehen*) start, set off.

aufbringen ['aufbriŋən] *vt irreg* (*öffnen*) open; (*in Mode*) bring into fashion; (*beschaffen*) procure; (*Fin*) raise; (*ärgern*) irritate; **Verständnis für etw ~** be able to understand sth.

Aufbruch ['aufbrux] *m* departure.

aufbrühen ['aufbry:ən] *vt Tee* make.

aufbürden ['aufbyrdən] *vt* burden (*jdm etw* sb with sth).

aufdecken ['aufdɛkən] *vt* uncover.

aufdrängen ['aufdrɛŋən] *vt* force (*jdm* on sb); *vr* intrude (*jdm* on sb).

aufdringlich ['aufdrɪŋlɪç] *a* pushy.

aufeinander [auf'ai'nandər] *ad* **achten** after each other; **schießen** at each other; **vertrauen** each other; **A~folge** *f* succession, series; **~folgen** *vi* follow one another; **~folgend** *a* consecutive; **~legen** *vt* lay on top of one another; **~prallen** *vi* hit one another.

Aufenthalt ['auf'ɛnthalt] *m* stay; (*Verzögerung*) delay; (*Rail*: *Halten*) stop; (*Ort*) haunt; **~sgenehmigung** *f* residence permit.

auferlegen ['auf'ɛrle:gən] *vt* impose (*jdm etw* sth upon sb).

Auferstehung ['auf'ɛrʃte:uŋ] *f* resurrection.

aufessen ['auf'ɛsən] *vt irreg* eat up.

auffahr- ['auffa:r] *cpd*: **~en** *irreg vi* (*Auto*) run, crash (*auf* +*acc* into); (*herankommen*) draw up; (*hochfahren*) jump up; (*wütend werden*) flare up; (*in den Himmel*) ascend; *vt Kanonen, Geschütz* bring up; **~end** *a* hot-tempered; **A~t** *f* (*Haus*—) drive; (*Autobahn*—) slip road; **A~unfall** *m* pile-up.

auffallen ['auffalən] *vi irreg* be noticeable; **jdm ~** strike sb; **~d** *a* striking.

auffällig ['auffɛlɪç] *a* conspicuous, striking.

auffang- ['auffaŋ] *cpd*: **~en** *vt irreg* catch; *Funkspruch* intercept; *Preise* peg; **A~lager** *nt* refugee camp.

auffassen ['auffasən] *vt* understand, comprehend; (*auslegen*) see, view.

Auffassung *f* (*Meinung*) opinion; (*Auslegung*) view, concept; (*also* **~sgabe**) grasp.

auffindbar ['auffɪntba:r] *a* to be found.

auffordern ['auffɔrdərn] *vt* (*befehlen*) call upon, order; (*bitten*) ask.

Aufforderung *f* (*Befehl*) order; (*Einladung*) invitation.

auffrischen ['auffrɪʃən] *vt* freshen up; *Kenntnisse* brush up; *Erinnerungen* reawaken; *vi* (*Wind*) freshen.

aufführen ['auffy:rən] *vt* (*Theat*) perform; (*in einem Verzeichnis*) list, specify; *vr* (*sich benehmen*) behave.

Aufführung *f* (*Theat*) performance; (*Liste*) specification.

Aufgabe ['aufga:bə] *f* -, -n task; (*Sch*) exercise; (*Haus*—) homework; (*Verzicht*) giving up; (*von Gepäck*) registration; (*von Post*) posting; (*von Inserat*) insertion.

Aufgang ['aufgaŋ] *m* ascent; (*Sonnen*—) rise; (*Treppe*) staircase.

aufgeben ['aufge:bən] *irreg vt* (*verzichten*) give up; *Paket* send, post; *Gepäck* register;

Bestellung give; *Inserat* insert; *Rätsel, Problem* set; *vi* give up.

Aufgebot ['aufgəbo:t] *nt* supply; (*von Kräften*) utilization; (*Ehe—*) banns *pl*.

aufgedreht ['aufgədre:t] *a* (col) excited.

aufgedunsen ['aufgədunzən] *a* swollen, puffed up.

aufgehen ['aufge:ən] *vi irreg* (*Sonne, Teig*) rise; (*sich öffnen*) open; (*klarwerden*) become clear (*jdm to sb*); (*Math*) come out exactly; (*sich widmen*) be absorbed (*in +dat in*); **in Rauch/Flammen ~** go up in smoke/flames.

aufgeklärt ['aufgəklɛ:rt] *a* enlightened; (*sexuell*) knowing the facts of life.

aufgelegt ['aufgəle:kt] *a:* **gut/schlecht ~ sein** be in a good/bad mood; **zu etw ~ sein** be in the mood for sth.

aufgeregt ['aufgəre:kt] *a* excited.

aufgeschlossen ['aufgəʃlɔsən] *a* open, open-minded.

aufgeweckt ['aufgəvɛkt] *a* bright, intelligent.

aufgießen ['aufgi:sən] *vt irreg Wasser* pour over; *Tee* infuse.

aufgreifen ['aufgraifən] *vt irreg Thema* take up; *Verdächtige* pick up, seize.

aufgrund [auf'grunt] *prep +gen* on the basis of; (*wegen*) because of.

aufhaben ['aufha:bən] *vt irreg* have on; *Arbeit* have to do.

aufhalsen ['aufhalzən] *vt* (col) **jdm etw ~** saddle *or* lumber sb with sth.

aufhalten ['aufhaltən] *irreg vt Person* detain; *Entwicklung* check; *Tür, Hand* hold open; *Augen* keep open; *vr* (*wohnen*) live; (*bleiben*) stay; **sich über etw/jdn ~** go on about sth/sb; **sich mit etw ~** waste time over.

aufhängen ['aufhɛŋən] *irreg vt Wäsche* hang up; *Menschen* hang; *vr* hang o.s.

Aufhänger *m* **-s, -** (*am Mantel*) hook; (*fig*) peg.

aufheben ['aufhe:bən] *irreg vt* (*hochheben*) raise, lift; *Sitzung* wind up; *Urteil* annul; *Gesetz* repeal, abolish; (*aufbewahren*) keep; **bei jdm gut aufgehoben sein** be well looked after at sb's; *vr* cancel o.s. out; **viel A~(s) machen make a fuss** (*von* about).

aufheitern ['aufhaitərn] *vtr* (*Himmel, Miene*) brighten; *Mensch* cheer up.

aufhellen ['aufhɛlən] *vtr* clear up; *Farbe, Haare* lighten.

aufhetzen ['aufhɛtsən] *vt* stir up (*gegen* against).

aufholen ['aufho:lən] *vt* make up; *vi* catch up.

aufhorchen ['aufhɔrçən] *vi* prick up one's ears.

aufhören ['aufhø:rən] *vi* stop; **~ etw zu tun** stop doing sth.

aufklappen ['aufklapən] *vt* open.

aufklären ['aufklɛ:rən] *vt Geheimnis etc* clear up; *Person* enlighten; (*sexuell*) tell the facts of life to; (*Mil*) reconnoitre; *vr* clear up.

Aufklärung *f* (*von Geheimnis*) clearing up; (*Unterrichtung, Zeitalter*) enlightenment; (*sexuell*) sex education; (*Mil, Aviat*) reconnaissance.

aufkleben ['aufkle:bən] *vt* stick on.

Aufkleber *m* **-s, -** sticker.

aufknöpfen ['aufknœpfən] *vt* unbutton.

aufkommen ['aufkɔmən] *vi irreg* (*Wind*) come up; (*Zweifel, Gefühl*) arise; (*Mode*) start; **für jdn/etw ~** be liable *or* responsible for sb/sth.

aufladen ['aufla:dən] *vt irreg* load.

Auflage ['aufla:gə] *f* edition; (*Zeitung*) circulation; (*Bedingung*) condition; **jdm etw zur ~ machen** make sth a condition for sb.

auflassen ['auflasən] *vt irreg* (*offen*) leave open; (*aufgesetzt*) leave on.

auflauern ['auflauərn] *vi:* **jdm ~** lie in wait for sb.

Auflauf ['auflauf] *m* (*Cook*) pudding; (*Menschen—*) crowd.

aufleben ['aufle:bən] *vi* revive.

auflegen ['aufle:gən] *vt* put on; *Telefon* hang up; (*Print*) print.

auflehnen ['aufle:nən] *vt* lean on; *vr* rebel (*gegen* against).

Auflehnung *f* rebellion.

auflesen ['aufle:zən] *vt irreg* pick up.

aufleuchten ['auflɔyçtən] *vi* light up.

aufliegen ['aufli:gən] *vi irreg* lie on; (*Comm*) be available.

auflockern ['auflɔkərn] *vt* loosen; (*fig*) *Eintönigkeit etc* liven up.

auflösen ['auflø:zən] *vtr* dissolve; *Haare etc* loosen; *Mißverständnis* sort out; (**in Tränen**) **aufgelöst sein** be in tears.

Auflösung *f* dissolving; (*fig*) solution.

aufmachen ['aufmaxən] *vt* open; *Kleidung* undo; (*zurechtmachen*) do up; *vr* set out.

Aufmachung *f* (*Kleidung*) outfit, get-up; (*Gestaltung*) format.

aufmerksam ['aufmɛrkza:m] *a* attentive; **jdn auf etw** (*acc*) **~ machen** point sth out to sb; **A~keit** *f* attention, attentiveness.

aufmuntern ['aufmuntərn] *vt* (*ermutigen*) encourage; (*erheitern*) cheer up.

Aufnahme ['aufna:mə] *f* **-, -n** reception; (*Beginn*) beginning; (*in Verein etc*) admission; (*in Liste etc*) inclusion; (*Notieren*) taking down; (*Phot*) shot; (*auf Tonband etc*) recording; **a~fähig** *a* receptive; **~prüfung** *f* entrance test.

aufnehmen ['aufne:mən] *vt irreg* receive; (*hochheben*) pick up; (*beginnen*) take up; (*in Verein etc*) admit; (*in Liste etc*) include; (*fassen*) hold; (*notieren*) take down; (*photographieren*) photograph; (*auf Tonband, Platte*) record; (*Fin: leihen*) take out; **es mit jdm ~ können** be able to compete with sb.

aufopfern ['aufɔpfərn] *vtr* sacrifice; **~d** *a* selfless.

aufpassen ['aufpasən] *vi* (*aufmerksam sein*) pay attention; **auf jdn/etw ~** look after *or* watch sb/sth; **aufgepaßt!** look out!

Aufprall ['aufpral] *m* **-s, -e** impact; **a~en** *vi* hit, strike.

Aufpreis ['aufprais] *m* extra charge.

aufpumpen ['aufpumpən] *vt* pump up.

aufputschen ['aufputʃən] *vt* (*aufhetzen*)

inflame; (*erregen*) stimulate.

aufraffen ['aʊfrafən] *vr* rouse o.s.

aufräumen ['aʊfrɔʏmən] *vti* Dinge clear away; *Zimmer* tidy up.

aufrecht ['aʊfrɛçt] *a* (*lit, fig*) upright; **~erhalten** *vt irreg* maintain.

aufreg- ['aʊfre:g] *cpd*: **~en** *vt* excite; *vr* get excited; **~end** *a* exciting; **A~ung** *f* excitement.

aufreiben ['aʊfraɪbən] *vt irreg Haut* rub open; (*erschöpfen*) exhaust; **~d** *a* strenuous.

aufreißen ['aʊfraɪsən] *vt irreg Umschlag* tear open; *Augen* open wide; *Tür* throw open; *Straße* take up.

aufreizen ['aʊfraɪtsən] *vt* incite, stir up; **~d** *a* exciting, stimulating.

aufrichten ['aʊfrɪçtən] *vt* put up, erect; (*moralisch*) console; *vr* rise; (*moralisch*) take heart (*an +dat* from).

aufrichtig ['aʊfrɪçtɪç] *a* sincere, honest; **A~keit** *f* sincerity.

aufrücken ['aʊfrʏkən] *vi* move up; (*beruflich*) be promoted.

Aufruf ['aʊfru:f] *m* summons; (*zur Hilfe*) call; (*des Namens*) calling out; **a~en** *vt irreg* (*auffordern*) call upon (*zu* for); *Namen* call out.

Aufruhr ['aʊfru:r] *m* **-(e)s, -e** uprising, revolt; **in ~ sein** be in uproar.

aufrührerisch ['aʊfry:rərɪʃ] *a* rebellious.

aufrunden ['aʊfrʊndən] *vt Summe* round up.

Aufrüstung ['aʊfrʏstʊŋ] *f* rearmament.

aufrütteln ['aʊfrʏtəln] *vt* (*lit, fig*) shake up.

aufs [aʊfs] = **auf das**.

aufsagen ['aʊfza:gən] *vt Gedicht* recite; *Freundschaft* put an end to.

aufsammeln ['aʊfzaməln] *vt* gather up.

aufsässig ['aʊfzɛsɪç] *a* rebellious.

Aufsatz ['aʊfzats] *m* (*Geschriebenes*) essay; (*auf Schrank etc*) top.

aufsaugen ['aʊfzaʊgən] *vt irreg* soak up.

aufschauen ['aʊfʃaʊən] *vi* look up.

aufscheuchen ['aʊfʃɔʏçən] *vt* scare or frighten away.

aufschieben ['aʊfʃi:bən] *vt irreg* push open; (*verzögern*) put off, postpone.

Aufschlag ['aʊfʃla:k] *m* (*Ärmel~*) cuff; (*Jacken~*) lapel; (*Hosen~*) turn-up; (*Aufprall*) impact; (*Preis~*) surcharge; (*Tennis*) service; **a~en** *irreg vt* (*öffnen*) open; (*verwunden*) cut; (*hochschlagen*) turn up; (*aufbauen*) Zelt, Lager pitch, erect; *Wohnsitz* take up; *vi* (*aufprallen*) hit; (*teurer werden*) go up; (*Tennis*) serve.

aufschließen ['aʊfʃli:sən] *irreg vt* open up, unlock; *vi* (*aufrücken*) close up.

Aufschluß ['aʊfʃlʊs] *m* information; **a~reich** *a* informative, illuminating.

aufschnappen ['aʊfʃnapən] *vt* (*col*) pick up; *vi* fly open.

aufschneiden ['aʊfʃnaɪdən] *irreg vt Geschwür* cut open; *Brot* cut up; (*Med*) lance; *vi* brag.

Aufschneider *m* **-s, -** boaster, braggart.

Aufschnitt ['aʊfʃnɪt] *m* (slices of) cold meat.

aufschnüren ['aʊfʃny:rən] *vt* unlace; *Paket* untie.

aufschrauben ['aʊfʃraʊbən] *vt* (*fest—*) screw on; (*lösen*) unscrew.

aufschrecken ['aʊfʃrɛkən] *vt* startle; *vi irreg* start up.

Aufschrei ['aʊfʃraɪ] *m* cry; **a~en** *vi irreg* cry out.

aufschreiben ['aʊfʃraɪbən] *vt irreg* write down.

Aufschrift ['aʊfʃrɪft] *f* (*Inschrift*) inscription; (*auf Etikett*) label.

Aufschub ['aʊfʃu:p] *m* **-(e)s, -schübe** delay, postponement.

aufschwatzen ['aʊfʃvatsən] *vt*: **jdm etw ~** talk sb into (getting/having *etc*) sth.

Aufschwung ['aʊfʃvʊŋ] *m* (*Elan*) boost; (*wirtschaftlich*) upturn, boom; (*Sport*) circle.

aufsehen ['aʊfze:ən] *vi irreg* (*lit, fig*) look up (*zu* (*lit*) at, (*fig*) to); **A~** *nt* **-s** sensation, stir; **~erregend** *a* sensational.

Aufseher(in *f*) *m* **-s, -** guard; (*im Betrieb*) supervisor; (*Museums—*) attendant; (*Park—*) keeper.

aufsein ['aʊfzaɪn] *vi irreg* (*col*) be open; (*Person*) be up.

aufsetzen ['aʊfzɛtsən] *vt* put on; *Flugzeug* put down; *Dokument* draw up; *vr* sit upright; *vi* (*Flugzeug*) touch down.

Aufsicht ['aʊfzɪçt] *f* supervision; **die ~ haben** be in charge.

aufsitzen ['aʊfzɪtsən] *vi irreg* (*aufrecht hinsitzen*) sit up; (*aufs Pferd, Motorrad*) mount, get on; (*Schiff*) run aground; **jdn ~ lassen** (*col*) stand sb up; **jdm ~** (*col*) be taken in by sb.

aufspalten ['aʊfʃpaltən] *vt* split.

aufsparen ['aʊfʃpa:rən] *vt* save (up).

aufsperren ['aʊfʃpɛrən] *vt* unlock; *Mund* open wide.

aufspielen ['aʊfʃpi:lən] *vr* show off; **sich als etw ~** try to come on as sth.

aufspießen ['aʊfʃpi:sən] *vt* spear.

aufspringen ['aʊfʃprɪŋən] *vi irreg* jump (*auf +acc* onto); (*hochspringen*) jump up; (*sich öffnen*) spring open; (*Hände, Lippen*) become chapped.

aufspüren ['aʊfʃpy:rən] *vt* track down, trace.

aufstacheln ['aʊfʃtaxəln] *vt* incite.

Aufstand ['aʊfʃtant] *m* insurrection, rebellion.

aufständisch ['aʊfʃtɛndɪʃ] *a* rebellious, mutinous.

aufstechen ['aʊfʃtɛçən] *vt irreg* prick open, puncture.

aufstecken ['aʊfʃtɛkən] *vt* stick on, pin up; (*col*) give up.

aufstehen ['aʊfʃte:ən] *vi irreg* get up; (*Tür*) be open.

aufsteigen ['aʊfʃtaɪgən] *vi irreg* (*auf etw*) get onto; (*hochsteigen*) climb; (*Rauch*) rise.

aufstellen ['aʊfʃtɛlən] *vt* (*aufrecht stellen*) put up; (*aufreihen*) line up; (*nominieren*) put up; (*formulieren*) Programm *etc* draw up; (*leisten*) Rekord set up.

Aufstellung *f* (*Sport*) line-up; (*Liste*) list.

Aufstieg ['aʊfʃti:k] *m* **-(e)s, -e** (*auf Berg*)

ascent; (Fortschritt) rise; (beruflich, Sport) promotion.

aufstoßen ['aufʃtoːsən] irreg vt push open; vi belch.

aufstrebend ['aufʃtreːbənd] a ambitious; Land up-and-coming.

Aufstrich ['aufʃtrɪç] m spread.

aufstülpen ['aufʃtʏlpən] vt Ärmel turn up; Hut put on.

aufstützen ['aufʃtʏtsən] vr lean (auf +acc on); vt Körperteil prop, lean; Person prop up.

aufsuchen ['aufzuːxən] vt (besuchen) visit; (konsultieren) consult.

auftakeln ['auftaːkəln] vt (Naut) rig (out); vr (col) deck o.s. out.

Auftakt ['auftakt] m (Mus) upbeat; (fig) prelude.

auftanken ['auftaŋkən] vi get petrol; vt refuel.

auftauchen ['auftauxən] vi appear; (aus Wasser etc) emerge; (U-Boot) surface; (Zweifel) arise.

auftauen ['auftauən] vti thaw; (fig) relax.

aufteilen ['auftailən] vt divide up; Raum partition.

Aufteilung f division; partition.

auftischen ['auftɪʃən] vt serve (up); (fig) tell.

Auftrag ['auftraːk] m -(e)s, -träge order; (Anweisung) commission; (Aufgabe) mission; im ~ von on behalf of; a~en [-gən] irreg vt Essen serve; Farbe put on; Kleidung wear out; jdm etw a~en tell sb sth; vi (dick machen) make you/me etc look fat; dick a~en (fig) exaggerate; ~geber m -s, - (Comm) purchaser, customer.

auftreiben ['auftraibən] vt irreg (col: beschaffen) raise.

auftreten ['auftreːtən] irreg vt kick open; vi appear; (mit Füßen) tread; (sich verhalten) behave; A~ nt -s (Vorkommen) appearance; (Benehmen) behaviour.

Auftrieb ['auftriːp] m (Phys) buoyancy, lift; (fig) impetus.

Auftritt ['auftrɪt] m (des Schauspielers) entrance; (lit, fig: Szene) scene.

auftun ['auftuːn] irreg vt open; vr open up.

aufwachen ['aufvaxən] vi wake up.

aufwachsen ['aufvaksən] vi irreg grow up.

Aufwand ['aufvant] m -(e)s expenditure; (Kosten auch) expense; (Luxus) show; bitte, keinen ~! please don't go out of your way.

aufwärmen ['aufvɛrmən] vt warm up; alte Geschichten rake up.

aufwärts ['aufvɛrts] ad upwards; A~entwicklung f upward trend; ~gehen vi irreg look up.

aufwecken ['aufvɛkən] vt wake(n) up.

aufweichen ['aufvaiçən] vt soften, soak.

aufweisen ['aufvaizən] vt irreg show.

aufwenden ['aufvɛndən] vt irreg expend; Geld spend; Sorgfalt devote.

aufwendig a costly.

aufwerfen ['aufvɛrfən] irreg vt Fenster etc throw open; Probleme throw up, raise; vr: sich zu etw ~ make o.s. out to be sth.

aufwerten ['aufvɛrtən] vt (Fin) revalue; (fig) raise in value.

aufwiegeln ['aufviːgəln] vt stir up, incite.

aufwiegen ['aufviːgən] vt irreg make up for.

Aufwind ['aufvɪnt] m up-current.

aufwirbeln ['aufvɪrbəln] vt whirl up; Staub ~ (fig) create a stir.

aufwischen ['aufvɪʃən] vt wipe up.

aufzählen ['auftsɛːlən] vt count out.

aufzeichnen ['auftsaiçnən] vt sketch; (schriftlich) jot down; (auf Band) record.

Aufzeichnung f (schriftlich) note; (Tonband—) recording; (Film—) record.

aufzeigen ['auftsaigən] vt show, demonstrate.

aufziehen ['auftsiːən] vt irreg (hochziehen) raise, draw up; (öffnen) pull open; Uhr wind; (col: necken) tease; (großziehen) Kinder raise, bring up; Tiere rear.

Aufzug ['auftsuːk] m (Fahrstuhl) lift, elevator; (Aufmarsch) procession, parade; (Kleidung) get-up; (Theat) act.

aufzwingen ['auftsvɪŋən] vt irreg: jdm etw ~ force sth upon sb.

Aug- ['auk] cpd: ~apfel m eyeball; (fig) apple of one's eye; ~e nt -s, -n eye; (Fett—) globule of fat; unter vier ~en in private; ~enblick m moment; im ~enblick at the moment; a~enblicklich a (sofort) instantaneous; (gegenwärtig) present; ~enbraue f eyebrow; a~enscheinlich a obvious; ~enweide f sight for sore eyes; ~enzeuge m eye witness.

August [au'gust] m -(e)s or -, -e August.

Auktion [auktsi'oːn] f auction; ~ator [-'aːtɔr] m auctioneer.

Aula ['aula] f -, Aulen or -s assembly hall.

aus [aus] prep +dat out of; (von . . . her) from; (Material) made of; ~ ihr wird nie etwas she'll never get anywhere; ad out; (beendet) finished, over; (ausgezogen) off; ~ und ein gehen come and go; (bei jdm) visit frequently; weder ~ noch ein wissen be at sixes and sevens; auf etw (acc) ~ sein be after sth; vom Fenster ~ out of the window; von Rom ~ from Rome; von sich ~ of one's own accord; A~ nt - outfield; ins A~ gehen go out.

ausarbeiten ['ausʔarbaitən] vt work out.

ausarten ['ausʔartən] vi degenerate; (Kind) become overexcited.

ausatmen ['ausʔaːtmən] vi breathe out.

ausbaden ['ausbaːdən] vt: etw ~ müssen (col) carry the can for sth.

Ausbau ['ausbau] m extension, expansion; removal; a~en vt extend, expand; (herausnehmen) take out, remove; a~fähig a (fig) worth developing.

ausbedingen ['ausbədɪŋən] vt irreg: sich (dat) etw ~ insist on sth.

ausbessern ['ausbɛsərn] vt mend, repair.

ausbeulen ['ausbɔylən] vt beat out.

Ausbeute ['ausbɔytə] f yield; (Fische) catch; a~n vt exploit; (Min) work.

ausbild- ['ausbɪld] cpd: ~en vt educate; Lehrling, Soldat instruct, train; Fähigkeiten develop; Geschmack cultivate; A~er m -s, - instructor; A~ung f education; training, instruction; development, cultivation.

ausbitten ['ausbɪtən] vt irreg: **sich** (dat) **etw ~** (erbitten) ask for sth; (verlangen) insist on sth.

ausbleiben ['ausblaɪbən] vi irreg (Personen) stay away, not come; (Ereignisse) fail to happen, not happen.

Ausblick ['ausblɪk] m (lit, fig) prospect, outlook, view.

ausbomben ['ausbɔmbən] vt bomb out.

ausbrechen ['ausbrɛçən] irreg vi break out; **in Tränen/Gelächter ~** burst into tears/out laughing; vt break off.

ausbreiten ['ausbraɪtən] vt spread (out); Arme stretch out; vr spread; (über Thema) expand, enlarge (über +acc on).

ausbrennen ['ausbrɛnən] irreg vt scorch; Wunde cauterize; vi burn out.

ausbringen ['ausbrɪŋən] vt irreg ein Hoch propose.

Ausbruch ['ausbrux] m outbreak; (von Vulkan) eruption; (Gefühls—) outburst; (von Gefangenen) escape.

ausbrüten ['ausbry:tən] vt (lit, fig) hatch.

Ausbuchtung ['ausbuxtʊŋ] f bulge; (Küste) projection, protuberance.

ausbuhen ['ausbu:ən] vt boo.

ausbürsten ['ausbʏrstən] vt brush out.

Ausdauer ['ausdauər] f perseverance, stamina; a~nd a persevering.

ausdehnen ['ausde:nən] vtr (räumlich) expand; Gummi stretch; (Nebel) extend; (zeitlich) stretch; (fig) Macht extend.

ausdenken ['ausdɛŋkən] vt irreg (zu Ende denken) think through; **sich** (dat) **etw ~** think sth up.

ausdiskutieren ['ausdɪskuti:rən] vt talk out.

ausdrehen ['ausdre:ən] vt turn or switch off; Licht auch turn out.

Ausdruck ['ausdrʊk] m expression, phrase; (Kundgabe, Gesichts—) expression.

ausdrücken ['ausdrʏkən] vt (also vr: formulieren, zeigen) express; Zigarette put out; Zitrone squeeze.

ausdrücklich a express, explicit.

ausdrucks- cpd: **~los** a expressionless, blank; **~voll** a expressive; **A~weise** f mode of expression.

auseinander [ausʔaɪˈnandər] ad (getrennt) apart; **~ schreiben** write as separate words; **~bringen** vt irreg separate; **~fallen** vi irreg fall apart; **~gehen** vi irreg (Menschen) separate; (Meinungen) differ; (Gegenstand) fall apart; (col: dick werden) put on weight; **~halten** vt irreg tell apart; **~nehmen** vt irreg take to pieces, dismantle; **~setzen** vt (erklären) set forth, explain; vr (sich verständigen) come to terms, settle; (sich befassen) concern o.s.; **A~setzung** f argument.

auserlesen ['ausʔɛrle:zən] a select, choice.

ausfahren ['ausfa:rən] irreg vi drive out; (Naut) put out (to sea); vt take out; (Tech) Fahrwerk drive out; **ausgefahrene Wege** rutted roads.

Ausfahrt f (des Zuges etc) leaving, departure; (Autobahn—, Garagen—) exit, way out; (Spazierfahrt) drive, excursion.

Ausfall ['ausfal] m loss; (Nichtstattfinden

cancellation; (Mil) sortie; (Fechten) lunge; (radioaktiv) fall-out; **a~en** vi irreg (Zähne, Haare) fall or come out; (nicht stattfinden) be cancelled; (wegbleiben) be omitted; (Person) drop out; (Lohn) be stopped; (nicht funktionieren) break down; (Resultat haben) turn out; **wie ist das Spiel ausgefallen?** what was the result of the game?; **a~end** a impertinent; **~straße** f arterial road.

ausfegen ['ausfe:gən] vt sweep out.

ausfeilen ['ausfaɪlən] vt file out; Stil polish up.

ausfertigen ['ausfɛrtɪgən] vt draw up; Rechnung make out; **doppelt ~** duplicate.

Ausfertigung f drawing up; making out; (Exemplar) copy.

ausfindig machen ['ausfɪndɪç maxən] vt discover.

ausfliegen ['ausfli:gən] vti irreg fly away; **sie sind ausgeflogen** they're out.

ausflippen ['ausflɪpən] vi (col) freak out.

Ausflucht ['ausflʊxt] f -, **-flüchte** excuse.

Ausflug ['ausflu:k] m excursion, outing.

Ausflügler ['ausfly:klər] m -s, - tripper.

Ausfluß ['ausflʊs] m outlet; (Med) discharge.

ausfragen ['ausfra:gən] vt interrogate, question.

ausfransen ['ausfranzən] vi fray.

ausfressen ['ausfrɛsən] vt irreg eat up; (aushöhlen) corrode; (col: anstellen) be up to.

Ausfuhr ['ausfu:r] f -, **-en** export, exportation; in cpds export.

ausführ- ['ausfy:r] cpd: **~bar** a feasible; (Comm) exportable; **~en** vt (verwirklichen) carry out; Person take out; Hund take for a walk; (Comm) export; (erklären) give details of; **~lich** a detailed; ad in detail; **A~lichkeit** f detail; **A~ung** f execution, performance; (Durchführung) completion; (Herstellungsart) version; (Erklärung) explanation.

ausfüllen ['ausfʏlən] vt fill up; Fragebogen etc fill in; (Beruf) be fulfilling for.

Ausgabe ['ausga:bə] f (Geld) expenditure, outlay; (Aushändigung) giving out; (Gepäck—) left-luggage office; (Buch) edition; (Nummer) issue.

Ausgang ['ausgaŋ] m way out, exit; (Ende) end; (Ausgangspunkt) starting point; (Ergebnis) result; (Ausgehtag) free time, time off; **kein ~** no exit; **~sbasis** f, **~spunkt** m starting point; **~ssperre** f curfew.

ausgeben ['ausge:bən] irreg vt Geld spend; (austeilen) issue, distribute; vr: **sich für etw/jdn ~** pass o.s. off as sth/sb.

ausgebucht ['ausgəbu:xt] a fully booked.

ausgedient ['ausgədi:nt] a Soldat discharged; (verbraucht) no longer in use; **~ haben** have done good service.

ausgefallen ['ausgəfalən] a (ungewöhnlich) exceptional.

ausgeglichen ['ausgəglɪçən] a (well-)balanced; **A~heit** f balance; (von Mensch) even-temperedness.

Ausgeh- ['ausge:] cpd: **~anzug** m good suit; **a~en** vi irreg go out; (zu Ende gehen) come to an end; (*Benzin*) run out; (*Haare, Zähne*) fall *or* come out; (*Feuer, Ofen, Licht*) go out; (*Strom*) go off; (*Resultat haben*) turn out; **mir ging das Benzin aus** I ran out of petrol; **auf etw** (*acc*) **a~en** aim at sth; **von etw a~en** (*wegführen*) lead away from sth; (*herrühren*) come from sth; (*zugrunde legen*) proceed from sth; **wir können davon a~en, daß . . .** we can take as our starting point that . . .; **leer a~en** get nothing; **schlecht a~en** turn out badly; **~verbot** *nt* curfew.

ausgelassen ['ausgəlasən] *a* boisterous, high-spirited; **A~heit** *f* boisterousness, high spirits *pl*, exuberance.

ausgelastet ['ausgəlastət] *a* fully occupied.

ausgelernt ['ausgəlɛrnt] *a* trained, qualified.

ausgemacht ['ausgəmaxt] *a* (*col*) settled; *Dummkopf etc* out-and-out, downright; **es gilt als ~, daß . . .** it is settled that . . .; **es war eine ~e Sache, daß . . .** it was a foregone conclusion that . . .

ausgenommen ['ausgənɔmən] *prep +gen or dat, cj* except; **Anwesende sind ~** present company excepted.

ausgeprägt ['ausgəprɛ:kt] *a* prominent.

ausgerechnet ['ausgərɛçnət] *ad* just, precisely; **~ du/heute** you of all people/today of all days.

ausgeschlossen ['ausgəʃlɔsən] *a* (*unmöglich*) impossible, out of the question; **es ist nicht ~, daß . . .** it cannot be ruled out that . . .

ausgeschnitten ['ausgəʃnɪtən] *a Kleid* low-necked.

ausgesprochen ['ausgəʃprɔxən] *a Faulheit, Lüge etc* out-and-out; (*unverkennbar*) marked; *ad* decidedly.

ausgezeichnet ['ausgətsaɪçnət] *a* excellent.

ausgiebig ['ausgi:bɪç] *a Gebrauch* thorough, good; *Essen* generous, lavish; **~ schlafen** have a good sleep.

Ausgleich ['ausglaɪç] *m* -(e)s, -e balance; (*Vermittlung*) reconciliation; (*Sport*) equalization; **zum ~** (*+gen*) in order to offset; **das ist ein guter ~** that's very relaxing; **a~en** *irreg vt* balance (out); reconcile; *Höhe* even up; *vi* (*Sport*) equalize; **~stor** *nt* equalizer.

ausgraben ['ausgra:bən] *vt irreg* dig up; *Leichen* exhume; (*fig*) unearth.

Ausgrabung *f* excavation; (*Ausgraben auch*) digging up.

Ausguß ['ausgus] *m* (*Spüle*) sink; (*Abfluß*) outlet; (*Tülle*) spout.

aushaben ['ausha:bən] *vt irreg* (*col*) *Kleidung* have taken off; *Buch* have finished.

aushalten ['aushaltən] *irreg vt* bear, stand; *Geliebte* keep; *vi* hold out; **das ist nicht zum A~** that is unbearable.

aushandeln ['aushandəln] *vt* negotiate.

aushändigen ['aushɛndɪgən] *vt:* **jdm etw ~** hand sth over to sb.

Aushang ['aushaŋ] *m* notice.

aushängen ['aushɛŋən] *irreg vt Meldung* put up; *Fenster* take off its hinges; *vi* be displayed; *vr* hang out.

Aushängeschild *nt* (shop) sign.

ausharren ['ausharən] *vi* hold out.

ausheben ['aushe:bən] *vt irreg Erde* lift out; *Grube* hollow out; *Tür* take off its hinges; *Diebesnest* clear out; (*Mil*) enlist.

aushecken ['aushɛkən] *vt* (*col*) concoct, think up.

aushelfen ['aushɛlfən] *vi irreg:* **jdm ~** help sb out.

Aushilfe ['aushɪlfə] *f* help, assistance; (*Person*) (temporary) worker.

Aushilfs- *cpd:* **~kraft** *f* temporary worker; **a~weise** *ad* temporarily, as a stopgap.

ausholen ['ausho:lən] *vi* swing one's arm back; (*zur Ohrfeige*) raise one's hand; (*beim Gehen*) take long strides; **weit ~** (*fig*) be expansive.

aushorchen ['aushɔrçən] *vt* sound out, pump.

aushungern ['aushuŋərn] *vt* starve out.

auskennen ['auskɛnən] *vr irreg* know thoroughly; (*an einem Ort*) know one's way about; (*in Fragen etc*) be knowledgeable.

auskippen ['auskɪpən] *vt* empty.

ausklammern ['ausklamərn] *vt Thema* exclude, leave out.

Ausklang ['ausklaŋ] *m* end.

auskleiden ['ausklaɪdən] *vr* undress; *vt Wand* line.

ausklingen ['ausklɪŋən] *vi irreg* (*Ton, Lied*) die away; (*Fest*) peter out.

ausklopfen ['ausklɔpfən] *vt Teppich* beat; *Pfeife* knock out.

auskochen ['auskɔxən] *vt* boil; (*Med*) sterilize; **ausgekocht** (*fig*) out-and-out.

auskommen ['auskɔmən] *vi irreg:* **mit jdm ~** get on with sb; **mit etw ~** get by with sth; **A~** *nt* **-s: sein A~ haben** get by.

auskosten ['auskɔstən] *vt* enjoy to the full.

auskugeln ['ausku:gəln] *vt* (*col*) *Arm* dislocate.

auskundschaften ['auskuntʃaftən] *vt* spy out; *Gebiet* reconnoitre.

Auskunft ['auskunft] *f* **-, -künfte** information; (*nähere*) details *pl*, particulars *pl*; (*Stelle*) information office; (*Tel*) inquiries; **jdm ~ erteilen** give sb information.

auskuppeln ['auskupəln] *vi* disengage the clutch.

auslachen ['auslaxən] *vt* laugh at, mock.

ausladen ['ausla:dən] *irreg vt* unload; (*col*) *Gäste* cancel an invitation to; *vi* stick out.

Auslage ['ausla:gə] *f* shop window (display); **~n** *pl* outlay, expenditure.

Ausland ['auslant] *nt* foreign countries *pl*; **im/ins ~** abroad.

Ausländer(in *f*) ['auslɛndər(ɪn)] *m* **-s, -** foreigner.

ausländisch *a* foreign.

Auslands- *cpd:* **~gespräch** *nt* international call; **~korrespondent(in** *f*) *m* foreign correspondent; **~reise** *f* trip abroad.

auslassen ['auslasən] *irreg vt* leave out;

Wort etc auch om|it; *Fett* melt; *Kleidungsstück* let out; *Wut, Ärger* vent (*an* +*dat* on); *vr:* **sich über etw** (*acc*) ~ speak one's mind about sth.

Auslassung *f* omission; ~**zeichen** *nt* apostrophe.

Auslauf ['auslauf] *m* (*für Tiere*) run; (*Ausfluß*) outflow, outlet; **a~en** *vi irreg* run out; (*Behälter*) leak; (*Naut*) put out (to sea); (*langsam aufhören*) run down.

Ausläufer ['auslɔYfər] *m* (*von Gebirge*) spur; (*Pflanze*) runner; (*Met*) (*von Hoch*) ridge; (*von Tief*) trough.

ausleeren ['auslerən] *vt* empty.

auslegen ['auslegən] *vt Waren* lay out; *Köder* put down; *Geld* lend; (*bedecken*) cover; *Text etc* interpret.

Auslegung *f* interpretation.

Ausleihe ['auslaiə] *f* -, -n issuing; (*Stelle*) issue desk; **a~n** *vt irreg* (*verleihen*) lend; **sich** (*dat*) **etw a~n** borrow sth.

Auslese ['ausleːzə] *f* -, -n selection; (*Elite*) elite; (*Wein*) choice wine; **a~n** *vt irreg* select; (*col: zu Ende lesen*) finish.

ausliefern ['auslifərn] *vt* deliver (up), hand over; (*Comm*) deliver; **jdm/etw ausgeliefert sein** be at the mercy of sb/sth; *vr:* **sich jdm** ~ give o.s. up to sb.

auslöschen ['auslœʃən] *vt* extinguish; (*fig*) wipe out, obliterate.

auslosen ['auslozən] *vt* draw lots for.

auslösen ['auslœːzən] *vt Explosion, Schuß* set off; (*hervorrufen*) cause, produce; *Gefangene* ransom; *Pfand* redeem.

Auslöser *m* -s, - (*Phot*) release.

ausmachen ['ausmaxən] *vt Licht, Radio* turn off; *Feuer* put out; (*entdecken*) make out; (*vereinbaren*) agree; (*beilegen*) settle; (*Anteil darstellen, betragen*) represent; (*bedeuten*) matter; **das macht ihm nichts aus** it doesn't matter to him; **macht es Ihnen etwas aus, wenn . . .?** would you mind if . . .?

ausmalen ['ausmaːlən] *vt* paint; (*fig*) describe; **sich** (*dat*) **etw** ~ imagine sth.

Ausmaß ['ausmaːs] *nt* dimension; (*fig auch*) scale.

ausmerzen ['ausmɛrtsən] *vt* eliminate.

ausmessen ['ausmɛsən] *vt irreg* measure.

Ausnahme ['ausnaːmə] *f* -, -n exception; **eine** ~ **machen** make an exception; ~**fall** *m* exceptional case; ~**zustand** *m* state of emergency.

ausnahms- *cpd:* ~**los** *ad* without exception; ~**weise** *ad* by way of exception, for once.

ausnehmen ['ausneːmən] *irreg vt* take out, remove; *Tier* gut; *Nest* rob; (*col: Geld abnehmen*) clean out; (*ausschließen*) make an exception of; *vr* look, appear; ~**d** *a* exceptional.

ausnützen ['ausnʏtsən] *vt Zeit, Gelegenheit* use, turn to good account; *Einfluß* use; *Mensch, Gutmütigkeit* exploit.

auspacken ['auspakən] *vt* unpack.

auspfeifen ['auspfaifən] *vt irreg* hiss/boo at.

ausplaudern ['ausplaudərn] *vt Geheimnis* blab.

ausprobieren ['ausprobiːrən] *vt* try (out).

Auspuff ['auspuf] *m* -(e)s, -e (*Tech*) exhaust; ~**rohr** *nt* exhaust (pipe); ~**topf** *m* (*Aut*) silencer.

ausradieren ['ausradiːrən] *vt* erase, rub out.

ausrangieren ['ausrãʒiːrən] *vt* (*col*) chuck out.

ausrauben ['ausraubən] *vt* rob.

ausräumen ['ausrɔYmən] *vt Dinge* clear away; *Schrank, Zimmer* empty; *Bedenken* put aside.

ausrechnen ['ausrɛçnən] *vt* calculate, reckon.

Ausrechnung *f* calculation, reckoning.

Ausrede ['ausreːdə] *f* excuse; **a~n** *vi* have one's say; *vt:* **jdm etw a~n** talk sb out of sth.

ausreichen ['ausraiçən] *vi* suffice, be enough; ~**d** *a* sufficient, adequate; (*Sch*) adequate.

Ausreise ['ausraizə] *f* departure; **bei der** ~ when leaving the country; ~**erlaubnis** *f* exit visa; **a~n** *vi* leave the country.

ausreißen ['ausraisən] *irreg vt* tear or pull out; *vi* (*Riß bekommen*) tear; (*col*) make off, scram.

ausrenken ['ausrɛŋkən] *vt* dislocate.

ausrichten ['ausrɪçtən] *vt Botschaft* deliver; *Gruß* pass on; *Hochzeit etc* arrange; (*erreichen*) get anywhere (*bei* with); (*in gerade Linie bringen*) get in a straight line; (*angleichen*) bring into line; **jdm etw** ~ take a message for sb; **ich werde es ihm** ~ I'll tell him.

ausrotten ['ausrɔtən] *vt* stamp out, exterminate.

ausrücken ['ausrʏkən] *vi* (*Mil*) move off; (*Feuerwehr, Polizei*) be called out; (*col: weglaufen*) run away.

Ausruf ['ausruf] *m* (*Schrei*) cry, exclamation; (*Verkünden*) proclamation; **a~en** *vt irreg* cry out, exclaim; call out; ~**zeichen** *nt* exclamation mark.

ausruhen ['ausruːən] *vtr* rest.

ausrüsten ['ausrʏstən] *vt* equip, fit out.

Ausrüstung *f* equipment.

ausrutschen ['ausrutʃən] *vi* slip.

Aussage ['auszaːgə] *f* -, -n (*Jur*) statement; **a~n** *vt* say, state; *vi* (*Jur*) give evidence.

ausschalten ['ausʃaltən] *vt* switch off; (*fig*) eliminate.

Ausschank ['ausʃaŋk] *m* -(e)s, -schänke dispensing, giving out; (*Comm*) selling; (*Theke*) bar.

Ausschau ['ausʃau] *f:* ~ **halten** look out, watch (*nach* for); **a~en** *vi* look out (*nach* for), be on the look-out.

ausscheiden ['ausʃaidən] *irreg vt* separate; (*Med*) give off, secrete; *vi* leave (*aus etw* sth); (*Sport*) be eliminated or knocked out; **er scheidet für den Posten aus** he can't be considered for the job.

Ausscheidung *f* separation; retiral; elimination.

ausschenken ['ausʃɛŋkən] *vt* pour out; (*Comm*) sell.

ausschimpfen ['aʊsʃɪmpfən] vt scold, tell off.

ausschlachten ['aʊsʃlaxtən] vt Auto cannibalize; (fig) make a meal of.

ausschlafen ['aʊsʃlaːfən] irreg vir have a long lie (in); vt sleep off; **ich bin nicht ausgeschlafen** I didn't have or get enough sleep.

Ausschlag ['aʊsʃlaːk] m (Med) rash; (Pendel—) swing; (Nadel) deflection; **den ~ geben** (fig) tip the balance; **a~en** [-gən] irreg vt knock out; (auskleiden) deck out; (verweigern) decline; vi (Pferd) kick out; (Bot) sprout; (Zeiger) be deflected; **a~gebend** a decisive.

ausschließen ['aʊsʃliːsən] vt irreg shut or lock out; (fig) exclude; **ich will mich nicht ~** myself not excepted.

ausschließlich a, ad exclusive(ly); prep +gen excluding, exclusive of.

Ausschluß ['aʊsʃlʊs] m exclusion.

ausschmücken ['aʊsʃmʏkən] vt decorate; (fig) embellish.

ausschneiden ['aʊsʃnaɪdən] vt irreg cut out; Büsche trim.

Ausschnitt ['aʊsʃnɪt] m (Teil) section; (von Kleid) neckline; (Zeitungs—) cutting; (aus Film etc) excerpt.

ausschreiben ['aʊsʃraɪbən] vt irreg (ganz schreiben) write out (in full); (ausstellen) write (out); Stelle, Wettbewerb etc announce, advertise.

Ausschreitung ['aʊsʃraɪtʊŋ] f excess.

Ausschuß ['aʊsʃʊs] m committee, board; (Abfall) waste, scraps pl; (Comm: also ~ware f) reject.

ausschütten ['aʊsʃʏtən] vt pour out; Eimer empty; Geld pay; vr shake (with laughter).

ausschweifend ['aʊsʃvaɪfənt] a Leben dissipated, debauched; Phantasie extravagant.

Ausschweifung f excess.

ausschweigen ['aʊsʃvaɪgən] vr irreg keep silent.

ausschwitzen ['aʊsʃvɪtsən] vt exude; (Mensch) sweat out.

aussehen ['aʊszeːən] vi irreg look; **das sieht nach nichts aus** that doesn't look anything special; **es sieht nach Regen aus** it looks like rain; **es sieht schlecht aus** things look bad; **A~** nt -s appearance.

aussein ['aʊszaɪn] vi irreg (col) be out; (zu Ende) be over.

außen ['aʊsən] ad outside; (nach —) outwards; **~ ist es rot** it's red (on the) outside; **A~antenne** f outside aerial; **A~bordmotor** m outboard motor.

aussenden ['aʊszɛndən] vt irreg send out, emit.

Außen- cpd: **~dienst** m outside or field service; (von Diplomat) foreign service; **~handel** m foreign trade; **~minister** m foreign minister; **~ministerium** nt foreign office; **~politik** f foreign policy; **~seite** f outside; **~seiter** m -s, -, **~stehende(r)** mf outsider; **~welt** f outside world.

außer ['aʊsər] prep +dat (räumlich) out of; (abgesehen von) except; **~ Gefahr sein** be out of danger; **~ Zweifel** beyond any doubt; **~ Betrieb** out of order; **~ sich** (dat) **sein/geraten** be beside o.s.; **~ Dienst** retired; **~ Landes** abroad; cj (ausgenommen) except; **~ wenn** unless; **~ daß** except; **~amtlich** a unofficial, private; **~dem** cj besides, in addition; **~dienstlich** a unofficial.

äußere(r,s) ['ɔʏsərə(r,z)] a outer, external.

außer- cpd: **~ehelich** a extramarital; **~gewöhnlich** a unusual; **~halb** prep +gen, ad outside; **A~kraftsetzung** f putting out of action.

äußer- cpd: **~lich** a, ad external; **~n** vt utter, express; (zeigen) show; vr give one's opinion; (sich zeigen) show itself.

außer- cpd: **~ordentlich** a extraordinary; **~planmäßig** a unscheduled; **~'stande** ad not in a position, unable.

äußerst ['ɔʏsərst] ad extremely, most; **~e(r,s)** a utmost; (räumlich) farthest; Termin last possible; Preis highest; **~enfalls** ad if the worst comes to the worst.

aussetzen ['aʊszɛtsən] vt Kind, Tier abandon; Boote lower; Belohnung offer; Urteil, Verfahren postpone; **jdn/sich etw** (dat) **~** lay sb/o.s. open to sth; **jdm/etw ausgesetzt sein** be exposed to sth/sb; **an jdm/etw etwas ~** find fault with sb/sth; vi (aufhören) stop; (Pause machen) drop out.

Aussicht ['aʊszɪçt] f view; (in Zukunft) prospect; **in ~ sein** be in view; **etw in ~ haben** have sth in view; **a~slos** a hopeless; **~spunkt** m viewpoint; **a~sreich** a promising; **~sturm** m observation tower.

aussöhnen ['aʊszøːnən] vt reconcile; vr reconcile o.s., become reconciled.

Aussöhnung f reconciliation.

aussondern ['aʊszɔndərn] vt separate, select.

aussortieren ['aʊszɔrtiːrən] vt sort out.

ausspannen ['aʊsʃpanən] vt spread or stretch out; Pferd unharness; (col) Mädchen steal (jdm from sb); vi relax.

aussparen ['aʊsʃpaːrən] vt leave open.

aussperren ['aʊsʃpɛrən] vt lock out.

ausspielen ['aʊsʃpiːlən] vt Karte lead; Geldprämie offer as a prize; **jdn gegen jdn ~** play sb off against sb; vi (Cards) lead; **ausgespielt haben** be finished.

Aussprache ['aʊsʃpraːxə] f pronunciation; (Unterredung) (frank) discussion.

aussprechen ['aʊsʃprɛçən] irreg vt pronounce; (zu Ende sprechen) speak; (äußern) say, express; vr (sich äußern) speak (über +acc about); (sich anvertrauen) unburden o.s.; (diskutieren) discuss; vi (zu Ende sprechen) finish speaking.

Ausspruch ['aʊsʃprux] m saying, remark.

ausspülen ['aʊsʃpyːlən] vt wash out; Mund rinse.

ausstaffieren ['aʊsʃtafiːrən] vt equip, kit out; Zimmer furnish.

Ausstand ['aʊsʃtant] m strike; **in den ~ treten** go on strike.

ausstatten ['aʊsʃtatən] vt Zimmer etc

furnish; **jdn mit etw** ~ equip sb or kit sb out with sth.

Ausstattung f (Ausstatten) provision; (Kleidung) outfit; (Aussteuer) dowry; (Aufmachung) make-up; (Einrichtung) furnishing.

ausstechen ['aʊsʃtɛçən] vt irreg Augen, Rasen, Graben dig out; Kekse cut out; (Übertreffen) outshine.

ausstehen ['aʊsʃteːən] irreg vt stand, endure; vi (noch nicht dasein) be outstanding.

aussteigen ['aʊsʃtaɪgən] vi irreg get out, alight.

ausstellen ['aʊsʃtɛlən] vt exhibit, display; (col: ausschalten) switch off; Rechnung etc make out; Paß, Zeugnis issue.

Ausstellung f exhibition; (Fin) drawing up; (einer Rechnung) making out; (eines Passes etc) issuing.

aussterben ['aʊsʃtɛrbən] vi irreg die out.

Aussteuer ['aʊsʃtɔʏər] f dowry.

ausstopfen ['aʊsʃtɔpfən] vt stuff.

ausstoßen ['aʊsʃtoːsən] vt irreg Luft, Rauch give off, emit; (aus Verein etc) expel, exclude; Auge poke out.

ausstrahlen ['aʊsʃtraːlən] vti radiate; (Rad) broadcast.

Ausstrahlung f radiation; (fig) charisma.

ausstrecken ['aʊsʃtrɛkən] vtr stretch out.

ausstreichen ['aʊsʃtraɪçən] vt irreg cross out; (glätten) smooth out.

ausströmen ['aʊsʃtrøːmən] vi (Gas) pour out, escape; vt give off; (fig) radiate.

aussuchen ['aʊszuːxən] vt select, pick out.

Austausch ['aʊstaʊʃ] m exchange; a~bar a exchangeable; a~en vt exchange, swop; ~motor m reconditioned engine.

austeilen ['aʊstaɪlən] vt distribute, give out.

Auster ['aʊstər] f -, -n oyster.

austoben ['aʊstoːbən] vr (Kind) run wild; (Erwachsene) sow one's wild oats.

austragen ['aʊstraːgən] vt irreg Post deliver; Streit etc decide; Wettkämpfe hold.

Austräger ['aʊstrɛːgər] m delivery boy; (Zeitungs~) newspaper boy.

austreiben ['aʊstraɪbən] vt irreg drive out, expel; Geister exorcize.

austreten ['aʊstreːtən] irreg vi (zur Toilette) be excused; **aus etw** ~ leave sth; vt Feuer tread out, trample; Schuhe wear out; Treppe wear down.

austrinken ['aʊstrɪŋkən] irreg vt Glas drain; Getränk drink up; vi finish one's drink, drink up.

Austritt ['aʊstrɪt] m emission; (aus Verein, Partei etc) retirement, withdrawal.

austrocknen ['aʊstrɔknən] vti dry up.

ausüben ['aʊsʔyːbən] vt Beruf practise, carry out; Funktion perform; Einfluß exert; Reiz, Wirkung exercise, have (auf jdn on sb).

Ausübung f practice, exercise.

Ausverkauf ['aʊsfɛrkaʊf] m sale; a~en vt sell out; Geschäft sell up; a~t a Karten, Artikel sold out; (Theat) Haus full.

Auswahl ['aʊsvaːl] f selection, choice (an +dat of).

auswählen ['aʊsvɛːlən] vt select, choose.

Auswander- ['aʊsvandər] cpd: **~er** m emigrant; **a~n** vi emigrate; **~ung** f emigration.

auswärtig ['aʊsvɛrtɪç] a (nicht am/vom Ort) out-of-town; (ausländisch) foreign; **A~e(s) Amt** nt Foreign Office, State Department (US).

auswärts ['aʊsvɛrts] ad outside; (nach außen) outwards; ~ **essen** eat out; **A~spiel** nt away game.

auswechseln ['aʊsvɛksəln] vt change, substitute.

Ausweg ['aʊsveːk] m way out; **a~los** a hopeless.

ausweichen ['aʊsvaɪçən] vi irreg: **jdm/etw** ~ (lit) move aside or make way for sb/sth; (fig) side-step sb/sth; **~d** a evasive.

ausweinen ['aʊsvaɪnən] vr have a (good) cry.

Ausweis ['aʊsvaɪs] m -es, -e identity card, passport; (Mitglieds~, Bibliotheks~ etc) card; **a~en** [-zən] irreg vt expel, banish; vr prove one's identity; **~karte** f, **~papiere** pl identity papers pl; **~ung** f expulsion.

ausweiten ['aʊsvaɪtən] vt stretch.

auswendig ['aʊsvɛndɪç] ad by heart; ~ **lernen** vt learn by heart.

auswert- ['aʊsveːrt] cpd: **~en** vt evaluate; **A~ung** f evaluation, analysis; (Nutzung) utilization.

auswirk- ['aʊsvɪrk] cpd: **~en** vr have an effect; **A~ung** f effect.

auswischen ['aʊsvɪʃən] vt wipe out; **jdm eins** ~ (col) put one over on sb.

Auswuchs ['aʊsvuːks] m (out)growth; (fig) product.

auswuchten ['aʊsvʊxtən] vt (Aut) balance.

auszacken ['aʊstsakən] vt Stoff etc pink.

auszahlen ['aʊstsaːlən] vt Lohn, Summe pay out; Arbeiter pay off; Miterbe buy out; vr (sich lohnen) pay.

auszählen ['aʊstsɛːlən] vt Stimmen count; (Boxen) count out.

auszeichnen ['aʊstsaɪçnən] vt honour; (Mil) decorate; (Comm) price; vr distinguish o.s.

Auszeichnung f distinction; (Comm) pricing; (Ehrung) awarding of decoration; (Ehre) honour; (Orden) decoration; **mit** ~ with distinction.

ausziehen ['aʊstsiːən] irreg vt Kleidung take off; Haare, Zähne, Tisch etc pull out; (nachmalen) trace; vr undress; vi (aufbrechen) leave; (aus Wohnung) move out.

Auszug ['aʊstsuːk] m (aus Wohnung) removal; (aus Buch etc) extract; (Konto~) statement; (Ausmarsch) departure.

Auto ['aʊto] nt -s, -s (motor-)car; ~ **fahren** drive; **~bahn** f motorway; **~fahrer(in** f) m motorist, driver; **~fahrt** f drive; **a~gen** [-'geːn] a autogenous; **~gramm** nt autograph; **~mat** m -en, -en machine; **a~matisch** a automatic; **a~nom** [-'noːm] a autonomous.

Autopsie [aʊtɔ'psiː] f post-mortem, autopsy.

Autor ['autɔr] *m* **-s, -en, Autorin** ['baldiç] *a* early, speedy; **~möglichst** *ad*
[au'to:rin] *f* author.   as soon as possible.
Auto- *cpd:* **~radio** *nt* car radio; **~reifen**   Baldrian ['baldria:n] *m* **-s, -e** valerian.
   m car tyre; **~rennen** *nt* motor racing.   Balken ['balkən] *m* **-s, -** beam; (*Trag*—)
autoritär [autori'tɛ:r] *a* authoritarian.   girder; (*Stütz*—) prop.
Autorität *f* authority.   Balkon [bal'kõ:] *m* **-s, -s** *or* **-e** balcony;
Auto- *cpd:* **~unfall** *m* car *or* motor   (*Theat*) (dress) circle.
   accident; **~verleih** *m* car hire.   Ball [bal] *m* **-(e)s, ˆe** ball; (*Tanz*) dance,
Axt [akst] *f* **-, ˆe** axe.   ball.
                                                        Ballade [ba'la:də] *f* **-, -n** ballad.
                                                        Ballast ['balast] *m* **-(e)s, -e** ballast; (*fig*)
                      B   weight, burden.
                                                        Ballen ['balən] *m* **-s, -** bale; (*Anat*) ball;
B, b [be:] *nt* B, b.   b~ *vt* (*formen*) make into a ball; *Faust*
Baby ['be:bi] *nt* **-s, -s** baby;   clench; *vr* build up; (*Menschen*) gather.
   ~ausstattung *f* layette; **~sitter**   Ballett [ba'let] *nt* **-(e)s, -e** ballet;
   ['be:bizitər] *m* **-s, -** baby-sitter.   **~(t)änzer(in** *f*) *m* ballet dancer.
Bach [bax] *m* **-(e)s, ˆe** stream, brook.   Ball- *cpd:* **~junge** *m* ball boy; **~kleid** *nt*
Back- [bak] *cpd:* **~blech** *nt* baking tray;   evening dress.
   ~bord *nt* **-(e)s, -e** (*Naut*) port; **~e** *f* **-, -n**   Ballon [ba'lõ:] *m* **-s, -s** *or* **-e** balloon.
   cheek; **b~en** *vti irreg* bake; **~enbart**   Ballspiel *nt* ball game.
   m sideboards *pl*; **~enzahn** *m* molar.   Ballung ['baluŋ] *f* concentration; (*von*
Bäcker ['bɛkər] *m* **-s, -** baker; **~ei** ['-'rai] *f*   *Energie*) build-up; **~sgebiet** *nt* conur-
   bakery; (*—laden*) baker's (shop).   bation.
Back- *cpd:* **~form** *f* baking tin;   Bambus ['bambus] *m* **-ses, -se** bamboo;
   ~hähnchen *nt* roast chicken; **~obst** *nt*   **~rohr** *nt* bamboo cane.
   dried fruit; **~ofen** *m* oven; **~pflaume** *f*   Bammel ['baməl] *m* **-s** (*col*) (**einen**) **~**
   prune; **~pulver** *nt* baking powder;   haben vor jdm/etw be scared of sb/sth.
   ~stein *m* brick.   banal [ba'na:l] *a* banal; **B~ität**
Bad [ba:t] *nt* **-(e)s, ˆer** bath; (*Schwimmen*)   [banali'tɛ:t] *f* banality.
   bathe; (*Ort*) spa.   Banane [ba'na:nə] *f* **-, -n** banana.
Bade- ['ba:də] *cpd:* **~anstalt** *f* (swim-   Banause [ba'nauzə] *m* **-n, -n** philistine.
   ming) baths *pl*; **~anzug** *m* bathing suit;   Band [bant] *m* **-(e)s, ˆe** (*Buch*—) volume;
   ~hose *f* bathing *or* swimming trunks *pl*;   *nt* **-(e)s, ˆer** (*Stoff*—) ribbon, tape;
   ~kappe *f* bathing cap; **~mantel** *m* bath-   (*Fließ*—) production line; (*Faß*—) hoop;
   (ing) robe; **~meister** *m* baths attendant;   (*Ton*—) tape; (*Anat*) ligament; etw **auf** ~
   b~n *vi* bathe, have a bath; *vt* bath; **~ort**   **aufnehmen** tape sth; **am laufenden** ~
   m spa; **~tuch** *nt* bath towel; **~wanne** *f*   (*col*) non-stop; *nt* **-(e)s, -e** (*Freund-
   bath (tub); **~zimmer** *nt* bathroom.   schafts*— *etc*) bond; [bent] *f* **-, -s** band,
baff [baf] *a:* **~ sein** (*col*) be flabber-   group.
   gasted.   Bandage [ban'da:ʒə] *f* **-, -n** bandage.
Bagatelle [baga'tɛlə] *f* **-, -n** trifle.   banda'gieren *vt* bandage.
Bagger ['bagər] *m* **-s, -** excavator; (*Naut*)   Bande ['bandə] *f* **-, -n** band; (*Straßen*—)
   dredger; **b~n** *vti* excavate; (*Naut*)   gang.
   dredge.   bändigen ['bɛndigən] *vt Tier* tame; *Trieb,
Bahn [ba:n] *f* **-, -en** railway, railroad (*US*);   *Leidenschaft* control, restrain.
   (*Weg*) road, way; (*Spur*) lane; (*Renn*—)   Bandit [ban'di:t] *m* **-en, -en** bandit.
   track; (*Astron*) orbit; (*Stoff*—) length;   Band- *cpd:* **~maß** *nt* tape measure;
   b~brechend *a* pioneering; **~damm** *m*   **~säge** *f* band saw; **~scheibe** *f* (*Anat*)
   railway embankment; **b~en** *vt:*   disc; **~wurm** *m* tapeworm.
   sich/jdm einen Weg b~en clear a   bange ['baŋə] *a* scared; (*besorgt*) anxious;
   way/a way for sb; **~fahrt** *f* railway   jdm wird es ~ sb is becoming scared;
   journey; **~hof** *m* station; **auf dem ~hof**   jdm ~ machen scare sb; B~macher *m*
   at the station; **~hof station con-**   **-s, -** scaremonger; **~n** *vi:* **um jdn/etw**
   course; **-hofsvorsteher** *m* station-master;   **~n** be anxious *or* worried about sb/sth.
   ~hofswirtschaft *f* station restaurant;   Banjo ['banjo, 'bɛndʒo] *nt* **-s, -s** banjo.
   ~linie *f* (railway) line; **~steig** *m* plat-   Bank [baŋk] *f* **-, ˆe** (*Sitz*—) bench; (*Sand*—
   form; **~steigkarte** *f* platform ticket;   *etc*) (sand)bank *or* -bar; *f* **-, -en** (*Geld*—)
   ~strecke *f* (railway) line; **~übergang**   bank; **~anweisung** *f* banker's order;
   m level crossing, grade crossing (*US*);   **~beamte(r)** *m* bank clerk.
   ~wärter *m* signalman.   Bankett [ban'ket] *nt* **-(e)s, -e** (*Essen*) ban-
Bahre ['ba:rə] *f* **-, -n** stretcher.   quet; (*Straßenrand*) verge.
Bajonett [bajo'net] *nt* **-(e)s, -e** bayonett.   Bankier [baŋki'e:] *m* **-s, -s** banker.
Bakelit® [bake'li:t] *nt* **-s** Bakelite®.   Bank- *cpd:* **~konto** *nt* bank account;
Bakterien [bak'te:riən] *pl* bacteria *pl*.   **~note** *f* banknote; **~raub** *m* bank
Balance [ba'lã:sə] *f* **-, -n** balance, equilib-   robbery.
   rium.   Bankrott [baŋ'krɔt] *m* **-(e)s, -e** bank-
balan'cieren *vti* balance.   ruptcy; ~ **machen** go bankrupt; **b~** *a*
bald [balt] *ad* (*zeitlich*) soon; (*beinahe*)   bankrupt.
   almost; **~...~...** now... now...; **~ig**

Bann [ban] m -(e)s, -e (Hist) ban; (Kirchen—) excommunication; (fig: Zauber) spell; b~en vt Geister exorcise; Gefahr avert; (bezaubern) enchant; (Hist) banish; ~er nt -s, - banner, flag.

bar [ba:r] a (unbedeckt) bare; (frei von) lacking (gen in); (offenkundig) utter, sheer; ~e(s) Geld cash; etw (in) ~ bezahlen pay sth (in) cash; etw für ~e Münze nehmen (fig) take sth at its face value; B~ f~, -s bar.

Bär [bε:r] m -en, -en bear.

Baracke [ba'rakə] f~, -n hut, barrack.

barbarisch [bar'ba:rɪʃ] a barbaric, barbarous.

Bar- cpd: ~bestand m money in hand; b~fuß a barefoot; ~geld nt cash, ready money; b~geldlos a non-cash; b~häuptig a bareheaded; ~hocker m bar stool; ~kauf m cash purchase; ~keeper ['ba:rki:pər] m -s, -, ~mann m barman, bartender.

barmherzig [barm'hεrtsɪç] a merciful, compassionate; B~keit f mercy, compassion.

Barometer [baro'me:tər] nt -s, - barometer.

Baron [ba'ro:n] m -s, -e baron; ~esse [baro'nεsə] f~, -n, ~in f baroness.

Barren ['barən] m -s, - parallel bars pl; (Gold—) ingot.

Barriere [bari'ε:rə] f~, -n barrier.

Barrikade [bari'ka:də] f~, -n barricade.

Barsch [barʃ] m -(e)s, -e perch; b~ [barʃ] a brusque, gruff.

Bar- cpd: ~schaft f ready money; ~scheck m open or uncrossed cheque.

Bart [ba:rt] m -(e)s, -e beard; (Schlüssel—) bit.

bärtig ['bε:rtɪç] a bearded.

Barzahlung f cash payment.

Base ['ba:zə] f~, -n (Chem) base; (Kusine) cousin.

basieren [ba'zi:rən] vt base; vi be based.

Basis ['ba:zɪs] f~, Basen basis.

basisch ['ba:zɪʃ] a (Chem) alkaline.

Baß [bas] m Basses, Bässe bass; ~schlüssel m bass clef; ~stimme f bass voice.

Bassin [ba'sε:] nt -s, -s pool.

Bassist [ba'sɪst] m bass.

Bast [bast] m -(e)s, -e raffia; b~eln vt make; vi do handicrafts.

Bataillon [batal'jo:n] nt -s, -e battalion.

Batist [ba'tɪst] m -(e)s, -e batiste.

Batterie [batə'ri:] f battery.

Bau [bau] m -(e)s (Bauen) building, construction; (Aufbau) structure; (Körper—) frame; (Baustelle) building site; pl ~e (Tier—) hole, burrow; (Min) working(s); pl ~ten (Gebäude) building; sich im ~ befinden be under construction; ~arbeiter m building worker.

Bauch [baux] m -(e)s, Bäuche belly; (Anat auch) stomach, abdomen; ~fell nt peritoneum; b~ig a bulging; ~muskel m abdominal muscle; ~redner m ventriloquist; ~tanz m belly dance; belly dancing; ~schmerzen pl, ~weh nt stomach-ache.

bauen ['bauən] vti build; (Tech) construct; auf jdn/etw ~ depend or count upon sb/sth.

Bauer ['bauər] m -n or -s, -n farmer; (Schach) pawn; nt or m -s, - (Vogel—) cage.

Bäuerin ['bɔyərɪn] f farmer; (Frau des Bauers) farmer's wife.

bäuerlich a rustic.

Bauern- cpd: ~brot nt black bread; ~fänge'rei f deception; ~haus nt farmhouse; ~hof m farm(yard); ~schaft f farming community.

Bau- cpd: b~fällig a dilapidated; ~fälligkeit f dilapidation; ~firma f construction firm; ~führer m site foreman; ~gelände f building site; ~genehmigung f building permit; ~herr m purchaser; ~kasten m box of bricks; ~kosten pl construction costs pl; ~land nt building land; ~leute pl building workers pl; b~lich a structural.

Baum [baum] m -(e)s, Bäume tree.

baumeln ['bauməln] vi dangle.

bäumen ['bɔymən] vr rear (up).

Baum- cpd: ~schule f nursery; ~stamm m tree trunk; ~stumpf m tree stump; ~wolle f cotton.

Bau- cpd: ~plan m architect's plan; ~platz m building site.

Bausch [bauʃ] m -(e)s, Bäusche (Watte—) ball, wad; in ~ und Bogen (fig) lock, stock and barrel; b~en vtir puff out; b~ig a baggy, wide.

Bau- cpd: b~sparen vi insep save with a building society; ~sparkasse f building society; ~stein m building stone, freestone; ~stelle f building site; ~teil nt prefabricated part (of building); ~unternehmer m contractor, builder; ~weise f (method of) construction; ~werk nt building; ~zaun m hoarding.

Bazillus [ba'tsɪlus] m -, Bazillen bacillus.

beabsichtigen [bə'apzɪçtɪgən] vt intend.

beachten [bə'axtən] vt take note of; Vorschrift obey; Vorfahrt observe; ~swert a noteworthy.

beachtlich a considerable.

Beachtung f notice, attention, observation.

Beamte(r) [bə'amtə(r)] m -n, -n, **Beamtin** f official, civil servant; (Bank—etc) employee.

beängstigend [bə'εŋstɪgənt] a alarming.

beanspruchen [bə'anʃpruxən] vt claim; Zeit, Platz take up, occupy; Mensch take up sb's time.

beanstanden [bə'anʃtandən] vt complain about, object to.

Beanstandung f complaint.

beantragen [bə'antra:gən] vt apply for, ask for.

beantworten [bə'antvɔrtən] vt answer.

Beantwortung f reply (gen to).

bearbeiten [bə'arbaitən] vt work; Material process; Thema deal with; Land cultivate; (Chem) treat; Buch revise; (col: beeinflussen wollen) work on.

Bearbeitung f processing; treatment; cultivation; revision.

Beatmung [bə'ʔaːtmʊŋ] f respiration.
beaufsichtigen [bə'ʔaʊfzɪçtɪgən] vt supervise.
Beaufsichtigung f supervision.
beauftragen [bə'ʔaʊftraːgən] vt instruct; **jdn mit etw ~ entrust** sb with sth.
bebauen [bə'baʊən] vt build on; (Agr) cultivate.
beben ['beːbən] vi tremble, shake; **B~** nt **-s -** earthquake.
bebildern [bə'bɪldərn] vt illustrate.
Becher ['bɛçər] nt **-s, -** mug; (ohne Henkel) tumbler.
Becken ['bɛkən] nt **-s, -** basin; (Mus) cymbal; (Anat) pelvis.
bedacht [bə'daxt] a thoughtful, careful; **auf etw** (acc) **~ sein** be concerned about sth.
bedächtig [bə'dɛçtɪç] a (umsichtig) thoughtful, reflective; (langsam) slow, deliberate.
bedanken [bə'daŋkən] vr say thank you (bei jdm to sb).
Bedarf [bə'darf] m **-(e)s** need, requirement; (Comm) demand; supply; **je nach ~** according to demand; **bei ~** if necessary; **~ an etw** (dat) **haben** be in need of sth; **~sartikel** m requisite; **~sfall** m case of need; **~shaltestelle** f request stop.
bedauerlich [bə'daʊərlɪç] a regrettable.
bedauern [bə'daʊərn] vt be sorry for; (bemitleiden) pity; **B~** nt **-s** regret; **~swert** a Zustände regrettable; Mensch pitiable, unfortunate.
bedecken [bə'dɛkən] vt cover.
bedeckt a covered; Himmel overcast.
bedenken [bə'dɛŋkən] vt irreg think (over), consider; **B~** nt **-s, -** (Überlegen) consideration; (Zweifel) doubt; (Skrupel) scruple.
bedenklich a doubtful; (bedrohlich) dangerous, risky.
Bedenkzeit f time for reflection.
bedeuten [bə'dɔʏtən] vt mean; signify; (wichtig sein) be of importance; **~d** a important; (beträchtlich) considerable.
Bedeutung f meaning; significance; (Wichtigkeit) importance; **b~slos** a insignificant, unimportant; **b~svoll** a momentous, significant.
bedienen [bə'diːnən] vt serve; Maschine work, operate; vr (beim Essen) help o.s.; (gebrauchen) make use (gen of).
Bedienung f service; (Kellnerin) waitress; (Verkäuferin) shop assistant; (Zuschlag) service (charge).
bedingen [bə'dɪŋən] vt (voraussetzen) demand, involve; (verursachen) cause, occasion.
bedingt a limited, conditional; Reflex conditioned.
Bedingung f condition; (Voraussetzung) stipulation; **~sform** f (Gram) conditional; **b~slos** a unconditional.
bedrängen [bə'drɛŋən] vt pester, harass.
Bedrängung f trouble.
bedrohen [bə'droːən] vt threaten.
bedrohlich a ominous, threatening.

Bedrohung f threat, menace.
bedrucken [bə'drʊkən] vt print on.
bedrücken [bə'drʏkən] vt oppress, trouble.
bedürf- [bə'dʏrf] cpd: **~en** vi irreg +gen need, require; **B~nis** nt **-ses, -se** need; **B~nis nach etw haben** need sth; **B~nisanstalt** f public convenience, comfort station (US); **~nislos** a frugal, modest; **~tig** a in need (gen of), poor, needy.
beehren [bə'eːrən] vt honour; **wir ~ uns** we have pleasure in.
beeilen [bə'aɪlən] vr hurry.
beeindrucken [bə'aɪndrʊkən] vt impress, make an impression on.
beeinflussen [bə'aɪnflʊsən] vt influence.
Beeinflussung f influence.
beeinträchtigen [bə'aɪntrɛçtɪgən] vt affect adversely; Freiheit infringe upon.
beend(ig)en [bə'ɛnd(ɪg)ən] vt end, finish, terminate.
Beend(ig)ung f end(ing), finish(ing).
beengen [bə'ɛŋən] vt cramp; (fig) hamper, oppress.
beerben [bə'ɛrbən] vt inherit from.
beerdigen [bə'eːrdɪgən] vt bury.
Beerdigung f funeral, burial; **~sunternehmer** m undertaker.
Beere ['beːrə] f **-, -n** berry; (Trauben—) grape.
Beet [beːt] nt **-(e)s, -e** bed.
befähigen [bə'fɛːɪgən] vt enable.
befähigt a (begabt) talented; (fähig) capable (für of).
Befähigung f capability; (Begabung) talent, aptitude.
befahrbar [bə'faːrbaːr] a passable; (Naut) navigable.
befahren [bə'faːrən] vt irreg use, drive over; (Naut) navigate; a used.
befallen [bə'falən] vt irreg come over.
befangen [bə'faŋən] a (schüchtern) shy, self-conscious; (voreingenommen) biased; **B~heit** f shyness; bias.
befassen [bə'fasən] vr concern o.s.
Befehl [bə'feːl] m **-(e)s, -e** command, order; **b~en** irreg vt order; **jdm etw b~en** order sb to do sth; vi give orders; **b~igen** vt be in command of; **~sempfänger** m subordinate; **~sform** f (Gram) imperative; **~shaber** m **-s, -** commanding officer; **~sverweigerung** f insubordination.
befestigen [bə'fɛstɪgən] vt fasten (an +dat to); (stärken) strengthen; (Mil) fortify.
Befestigung f fastening; strengthening; (Mil) fortification.
befeuchten [bə'fɔʏçtən] vt damp(en), moisten.
befinden [bə'fɪndən] irreg vr be; (sich fühlen) feel; vt: **jdn/etw für** or **als etw ~** deem sb/sth to be sth; vi decide (über +acc on), adjudicate; **B~** nt **-s** health, condition; (Meinung) view, opinion.
befliegen [bə'fliːgən] vt irreg fly to.
befolgen [bə'fɔlgən] vt comply with, follow.
befördern [bə'fœrdərn] vt (senden) transport, send; (beruflich) promote.

Beförderung f transport, conveyance; promotion; ~skosten pl transport costs pl.

befragen [bə'fra:gən] vt question.

befreien [bə'fraiən] vt set free; (erlassen) exempt.

Befreier m -s, - liberator.

Befreiung f liberation, release; (Erlassen) exemption.

befremden [bə'frɛmdən] vt surprise, disturb; B~ nt -s surprise, astonishment.

befreunden [bə'frɔyndən] vr make friends; (mit Idee etc) acquaint o.s.

befreundet a friendly.

befriedigen [bə'fri:digən] vt satisfy; ~d a satisfactory.

Befriedigung f satisfaction, gratification.

befristet [bə'fristət] a limited.

befruchten [bə'fruxtən] vt fertilize; (fig) stimulate.

Befugnis [bə'fu:knis] f -, -se authorization, powers pl.

befugt a authorized, entitled.

befühlen [bə'fy:lən] vt feel, touch.

Befund [bə'funt] m -(e)s, -e findings pl; (Med) diagnosis.

befürchten [bə'fyrçtən] vt fear.

Befürchtung f fear, apprehension.

befürwort- [bə'fy:rvɔrt] cpd: ~en vt support, speak in favour of; B~er m -s, - supporter, advocate; B~ung f support(ing), favouring.

begabt [bə'ga:pt] a gifted.

Begabung [bə'ga:buŋ] f talent, gift.

begatten [bə'gatən] vr mate; vt mate or pair (with).

begeben [bə'ge:bən] vr irreg (gehen) proceed (zu, nach to); (geschehen) occur; B~heit f occurrence.

begegnen [bə'ge:gnən] vi meet (jdm sb); meet with (etw (dat) sth); (behandeln) treat (jdm sb); Blicke ~ sich eyes meet.

Begegnung f meeting.

begehen [bə'ge:ən] vt irreg Straftat commit; (abschreiten) cover; Straße etc use, negotiate; Feier celebrate.

begehren [bə'ge:rən] vt desire; ~swert a desirable.

begehrt a in demand; Junggeselle eligible.

begeistern [bə'gaistərn] vt fill with enthusiasm, inspire; vr: sich für etw ~ get enthusiastic about sth.

begeistert a enthusiastic.

Begeisterung f enthusiasm.

Begierde [bə'gi:rdə] f -, -n desire, passion.

begierig [bə'gi:riç] a eager, keen.

begießen [bə'gi:sən] vt irreg water; (mit Alkohol) drink to.

Beginn [bə'gin] m -(e)s beginning; zu ~ at the beginning; b~en vti irreg start, begin.

beglaubigen [bə'glaubigən] vt countersign.

Beglaubigung f countersignature; ~sschreiben nt credentials pl.

begleichen [bə'glaiçən] vt irreg settle, pay.

Begleit- [bə'glait] cpd: b~en vt accompany; (Mil) escort; ~er m -s, -

companion; (Freund) escort; (Mus) accompanist; ~erscheinung f concomitant (occurrence); ~musik f accompaniment; ~schiff nt escort vessel; ~schreiben nt covering letter; ~umstände pl concomitant circumstances pl; ~ung f company; (Mil) escort; (Mus) accompaniment.

beglücken [bə'glykən] vt make happy, delight.

beglückwünschen [bə'glykvynʃən] vt congratulate (zu on).

Beglückwünschung f congratulation, good wishes pl.

begnadigen [bə'gna:digən] vt pardon.

Begnadigung f pardon, amnesty.

begnügen [bə'gny:gən] vr be satisfied, content o.s.

Begonie [bə'go:niə] f begonia.

begraben [bə'gra:bən] vt irreg bury.

Begräbnis [bə'grɛ:pnis] nt -ses, -se burial, funeral.

begradigen [bə'gra:digən] vt straighten (out).

begreifen [bə'graifən] vt irreg understand, comprehend.

begreiflich [bə'graifliç] a understandable.

Begrenztheit [bə'grɛntsthait] f limitation, restriction; (fig) narrowness.

Begriff [bə'grif] m -(e)s, -e concept, idea; im ~ sein, etw zu tun be about to do sth; schwer von ~ (col) slow, dense; ~sbestimmung f definition; b~sstutzig a dense, slow.

begründ- [bə'grynd] cpd: ~en vt (Gründe geben) justify; ~et a well-founded, justified; B~ung f justification, reason.

begrüßen [bə'gry:sən] vt greet, welcome; ~swert a welcome.

Begrüßung f greeting, welcome.

begünstigen [bə'gynstigən] vt Person favour; Sache further, promote.

begutachten [bə'gu:t'axtən] vt assess.

begütert [bə'gy:tərt] a wealthy, well-to-do.

behaart [bə'ha:rt] a hairy.

behäbig [bə'hɛ:biç] a (dick) portly, stout; (geruhsam) comfortable.

behaftet [bə'haftət] a: mit etw ~ sein be afflicted by sth.

behagen [bə'ha:gən] vi: das behagt ihm nicht he does not like it; B~ nt -s comfort, ease.

behaglich [bə'ha:kliç] a comfortable, cosy; B~keit f comfort, cosiness.

behalten [bə'haltən] vt irreg keep, retain; (im Gedächtnis) remember.

Behälter [bə'hɛltər] m -s, - container, receptacle.

behandeln [bə'handəln] vt treat; Thema deal with; Maschine handle.

Behandlung f treatment; (von Maschine) handling.

beharren [bə'harən] vi: auf etw (dat) ~ stick or keep to sth.

beharrlich [bə'harliç] a (ausdauernd) steadfast, unwavering; (hartnäckig) tenacious, dogged; B~keit f steadfastness; tenacity.

behaupten [bə'hauptən] vt claim, assert,

maintain; *sein Recht* defend; *vr* assert o.s.

Behauptung *f* claim, assertion.

Behausung [bə'hauzuŋ] *f* dwelling, abode; (*armselig*) hovel.

beheimatet [bə'haima:tət] *a* domiciled; *Tier, Pflanze* with its habitat in.

beheizen [bə'haitsən] *vt* heat.

Behelf [bə'hɛlf] *m* -(e)s, -e expedient, makeshift; **b~en** *vr irreg*: **sich mit etw b~en** make do with sth; **b~smäßig** *a* improvised, makeshift; (*vorübergehend*) temporary.

behelligen [bə'hɛligən] *vt* trouble, bother.

Behendigkeit [bə'hɛndiçkait] *f* agility, quickness.

beherbergen [bə'hɛrbɛrgən] *vt* put up, house.

beherrschen [bə'hɛrʃən] *vt Volk* rule, govern; *Situation* control; *Sprache, Gefühle* master; *vr* control o.s.

beherrscht *a* controlled; **B~heit** *f* self-control.

Beherrschung *f* rule; control; mastery.

beherzigen [bə'hɛrtsigən] *vt* take to heart.

beherzt *a* spirited, brave.

behilflich [bə'hilfliç] *a* helpful; **jdm ~ sein** help sb (*bei* with).

behindern [bə'hindərn] *vt* hinder, impede.

Behinderte(r) *mf* disabled person.

Behinderung *f* hindrance; (*Körper—*) handicap.

Behörde [bə'hø:rdə] *f* -, -n authorities *pl*.

behördlich [bə'hø:rtliç] *a* official.

behüten [bə'hy:tən] *vt* guard; **jdn vor etw** (*dat*) ~ preserve sb from sth.

behutsam [bə'hu:tza:m] *a* cautious, careful; **B~keit** *f* caution, carefulness.

bei [bai] *prep* +*dat* (*örtlich*) near, by; (*zeitlich*) at, on; (*während*) during; ~ **m Friseur** at the hairdresser's; ~ **uns** at our place; ~ **einer Firma arbeiten** work for a firm; ~ **Nacht** at night; ~ **Nebel** in fog; ~ **Regen** if it rains; **etw ~ sich haben** have sth on one; **jdn ~ sich haben** have sb with one; ~ **Goethe** in Goethe; ~**m Militär** in the army; ~**m Fahren** while driving.

beibehalten ['baibəhaltən] *vt irreg* keep, retain.

Beibehaltung *f* keeping, retaining.

Beiblatt ['baiblat] *nt* supplement.

beibringen ['baibriŋən] *vt irreg Beweis, Zeugen* bring forward; *Gründe* adduce; **jdm etw ~** (*zufügen*) inflict sth on sb; (*zu verstehen geben*) make sb understand sth; (*lehren*) teach sb sth.

Beichte ['baiçtə] *f* -, -n confession; **b~n** *vt* confess; *vi* go to confession.

Beicht- *cpd*: ~**geheimnis** *nt* secret of the confessional; ~**stuhl** *m* confessional.

beide(s) ['baidə(z)] *pron, a* both; **meine ~n Brüder** my two brothers, both my brothers; **die ersten ~n** the first two; **wir ~** we two; **einer von ~n** one of the two; **alles ~s** both (of them); ~**mal** *ad* both times; ~**rlei** *a* of both; ~**rseitig** *a* mutual, reciprocal; ~**rseits** *ad* mutually; *prep* +*gen* on both sides of.

beidrehen ['baidre:ən] *vi* heave to.

beieinander [bai'ai'nandər] *ad* together.

Beifahrer ['baifa:rər] *m* passenger; ~**sitz** *m* passenger seat.

Beifall ['baifal] *m* -(e)s applause; (*Zustimmung*) approval.

beifällig ['baifɛliç] *a* approving; *Kommentar* favourable.

Beifilm ['baifilm] *m* supporting film.

beifügen ['baify:gən] *vt* enclose.

beige ['be:ʒə] *a* beige, fawn.

beigeben ['baige:bən] *irreg vt* (*zufügen*) add; (*mitgeben*) give; *vi* (*nachgeben*) give in (*dat* to).

Beigeschmack ['baigəʃmak] *m* aftertaste.

Beihilfe ['baihilfə] *f* aid, assistance; (*Studien—*) grant; (*Jur*) aiding and abetting.

beikommen ['baikɔmən] *vi irreg* (+*dat*) get at; (*einem Problem*) deal with.

Beil [bail] *nt* -(e)s, -e axe, hatchet.

Beilage [baila:gə] *f* (*Buch— etc*) supplement; (*Cook*) vegetables and potatoes *pl*.

beiläufig ['bailɔyfiç] *a* casual, incidental; *ad* casually, by the way.

beilegen ['baile:gən] *vt* (*hinzufügen*) enclose, add; (*beimessen*) attribute, ascribe; *Streit* settle.

beileibe [bai'laibə] : ~ **nicht** *ad* by no means.

Beileid ['bailait] *nt* condolence, sympathy; **herzliches ~** deepest sympathy.

beiliegend ['baili:gənt] *a* (*Comm*) enclosed.

beim [baim] = **bei dem.**

beimessen ['baimɛsən] *vt irreg* attribute, ascribe (*dat* to).

Bein [bain] *nt* -(e)s, -e leg; ~**bruch** *m* fracture of the leg.

beinah(e) ['baina:(ə)] *ad* almost, nearly.

beinhalten [bə'inhaltən] *vt* contain.

beipflichten ['baipfliçtən] *vi*: **jdm/etw ~** agree with sb/sth.

Beirat ['baira:t] *m* legal adviser; (*Körperschaft*) advisory council; (*Eltern—*) parents' council.

beirren [bə'irən] *vt* confuse, muddle; **sich nicht ~ lassen** not let o.s. be confused.

beisammen [bai'zamən] *ad* together; **B~sein** *nt* -s get-together.

Beischlaf ['baiʃla:f] *m* sexual intercourse.

Beisein ['baizain] *nt* -s presence.

beiseite [bai'zaitə] *ad* to one side, aside; **stehen** on one side, aside; **etw ~ legen** (*sparen*) put sth by; **jdn/etw ~ schaffen** put sb/get sth out of the way.

beisetzen ['baizɛtsən] *vt* bury.

Beisetzung *f* funeral.

Beisitzer ['baizitsər] *m* -s, - (*bei Prüfung*) assessor.

Beispiel ['baiʃpi:l] *nt* -(e)s, -e example; **sich an jdm ein ~ nehmen** take sb as an example; **zum ~** for example; **b~haft** *a* exemplary; **b~los** *a* unprecedented, unexampled; **b~sweise** *ad* for instance *or* example.

beispringen ['baiʃpriŋən] *vi irreg*: **jdm ~** come to the aid of sb.

beißen ['baisən] *irreg vti* bite; (*stechen*:

Rauch, Säure) burn; *vr* (*Farben*) clash; **~d** a biting, caustic; (*fig auch*) sarcastic.

Beißzange ['baɪs-tsaŋə] *f* pliers *pl*.

Beistand ['baɪʃtant] *m* -(e)s, ¨e support, help; (*Jur*) adviser.

beistehen ['baɪʃteːən] *vi irreg*: **jdm ~** stand by sb.

beisteuern ['baɪʃtɔyərn] *vt* contribute.

beistimmen ['baɪʃtɪmən] *vi* (+*dat*) agree with.

Beistrich ['baɪʃtrɪç] *m* comma.

Beitrag ['baɪtraːk] *m* -(e)s, ¨e contribution; (*Zahlung*) fee, subscription; (*Versicherungs—*) premium; **b~en** ['baɪtraːgən] *vt irreg* contribute (*zu* to); (*mithelfen*) help (*zu* with); **~szahlende(r)** *mf* fee-paying member.

beitreten ['baɪtreːtən] *vi irreg* join (*einem Verein* a club).

Beitritt ['baɪtrɪt] *m* joining, membership; **~serklärung** *f* declaration of membership.

Beiwagen ['baɪvaːgən] *m* (*Motorrad—*) sidecar; (*Straßenbahn—*) extra carriage.

beiwohnen ['baɪvoːnən] *vi*: **einer Sache** (*dat*) ~ attend *or* be present at sth.

Beiwort ['baɪvɔrt] *nt* adjective.

Beize ['baɪtsə] *f* -, -n (*Holz—*) stain; (*Cook*) marinade.

beizeiten [baɪˈtsaɪtən] *ad* in time.

bejahen [bəˈjaːən] *vt Frage* say yes to, answer in the affirmative; (*gutheißen*) agree with.

bejahrt [bəˈjaːrt] a aged, elderly.

bejammern [bəˈjamərn] *vt* lament, bewail; **~swert** a lamentable.

bekämpfen [bəˈkɛmpfən] *vt Gegner* fight; *Seuche* combat; *vr* fight.

Bekämpfung *f* fight *or* struggle against.

bekannt [bəˈkant] a (well-)known; (*nicht fremd*) familiar; **mit jdm ~ sein** know sb; **jdn mit jdm ~ machen** introduce sb to sb; **sich mit etw ~ machen** familiarize o.s. with sth; **das ist mir ~** I know that; **es/sie kommt mir ~ vor** it/she seems familiar; **durch etw ~ werden** become famous because of sth; **B~e(r)** *mf* friend, acquaintance; **B~enkreis** *m* circle of friends; **B~gabe** *f* announcement; **~geben** *vt irreg* announce publicly; **~lich** *ad* as is well known, as you know; **~machen** *vt* announce; **B~machung** *f* publication; announcement; **B~schaft** *f* acquaintance.

bekehren [bəˈkeːrən] *vt* convert; *vr* become converted.

Bekehrung *f* conversion.

bekennen [bəˈkɛnən] *vt irreg* confess; *Glauben* profess; **Farbe ~** (*col*) show where one stands.

Bekenntnis [bəˈkɛntnɪs] *nt* -ses, -se admission, confession; (*Religion*) confession, denomination; **~schule** *f* denominational school.

beklagen [bəˈklaːgən] *vt* deplore, lament; *vr* complain; **~swert** a lamentable, pathetic.

beklatschen [bəˈklatʃən] *vt* applaud, clap.

bekleben [bəˈkleːbən] *vt*: **etw mit**

Bildern ~ stick pictures onto sth.

bekleiden [bəˈklaɪdən] *vt* clothe; *Amt* occupy, fill.

Bekleidung *f* clothing; **~sindustrie** *f* clothing industry, rag trade.

beklemmen [bəˈklɛmən] *vt* oppress.

beklommen [bəˈklɔmən] a anxious, uneasy; **B~heit** *f* anxiety, uneasiness.

bekommen [bəˈkɔmən] *irreg vt* get, receive; *Kind* have; *Zug* catch, get; *vi*: **jdm ~** agree with sb.

bekömmlich [bəˈkœmlɪç] a wholesome, easily digestible.

bekräftigen [bəˈkrɛftɪgən] *vt* confirm, corroborate.

Bekräftigung *f* corroboration.

bekreuzigen [bəˈkrɔytsɪgən] *vr* cross o.s.

bekritteln [bəˈkrɪtəln] *vt* criticize, pick holes in.

bekümmern [bəˈkymərn] *vt* worry, trouble.

bekunden [bəˈkʊndən] *vt* (*sagen*) state; (*zeigen*) show.

belächeln [bəˈlɛçəln] *vt* laugh at.

beladen [bəˈlaːdən] *vt irreg* load.

Belag [bəˈlaːk] *m* -(e)s, ¨e covering, coating; (*Brot—*) spread; (*Zahn—*) tartar; (*auf Zunge*) fur; (*Brems—*) lining.

belagern [bəˈlaːgərn] *vt* besiege.

Belagerung *f* siege; **~szustand** *m* state of siege.

Belang [bəˈlaŋ] *m* -(e)s importance; **~e** *pl* interests *pl*, concerns *pl*; **b~en** *vt* (*Jur*) take to court; **b~los** a trivial, unimportant; **~losigkeit** *f* triviality.

belassen [bəˈlasən] *vt irreg* (*in Zustand, Glauben*) leave; (*in Stellung*) retain; **es dabei ~** leave it at that.

belasten [bəˈlastən] *vt* (*lit*) burden; (*fig: bedrücken*) trouble, worry; (*Comm*) *Konto* debit; (*Jur*) incriminate; *vr* weigh o.s. down; (*Jur*) incriminate o.s.; **~d** a (*Jur*) incriminating.

belästigen [bəˈlɛstɪgən] *vt* annoy, pester.

Belästigung *f* annoyance, pestering.

Belastung [bəˈlastʊŋ] *f* (*lit*) load; (*fig: Sorge etc*) weight; (*Comm*) charge, debit(ing); (*Jur*) incriminatory evidence; **~sprobe** *f* capacity test; (*fig*) test; **~szeuge** *m* witness for prosecution.

belaufen [bəˈlaʊfən] *vr irreg* amount (*auf* +*acc* to).

belauschen [bəˈlaʊʃən] *vt* eavesdrop on.

belebt [bəˈleːpt] a *Straße* crowded.

Beleg [bəˈleːk] *m* -(e)s, -e (*Comm*) receipt; (*Beweis*) documentary evidence, proof; (*Beispiel*) example; **b~en** [bəˈleːgən] *vt* cover; *Kuchen, Brot* spread; *Platz* reserve, book; *Kurs, Vorlesung* register for; (*beweisen*) verify, prove; (*Mil: mit Bomben*) bomb; **~schaft** *f* personnel, staff.

belehren [bəˈleːrən] *vt* instruct, teach; **jdn eines Besseren ~** teach sb better.

Belehrung *f* instruction.

beleibt [bəˈlaɪpt] a stout, corpulent.

beleidigen [bəˈlaɪdɪgən] *vt* insult, offend.

Beleidigung *f* insult; (*Jur*) slander, libel.

belesen [bəˈleːzən] a well-read.

beleuchten [bəˈlɔʏçtən] vt light, illuminate; (fig) throw light on.
Beleuchtung f lighting, illumination.
belichten [bəˈlɪçtən] vt expose.
Belichtung f exposure; ~**smesser** m exposure meter.
Belieben [bəˈliːbən] nt: (ganz) nach ~ (just) as you wish.
beliebig [bəˈliːbɪç] a any you like, as you like; ~ **viel** as many as you like; **ein** ~**es Thema** any subject you like or want.
beliebt [bəˈliːpt] a popular; **sich bei jdm** ~ **machen** make o.s. popular with sb; **B**~**heit** f popularity.
beliefern [bəˈliːfərn] vt supply.
bellen [ˈbɛlən] vi bark.
belohnen [bəˈloːnən] vt reward.
Belohnung f reward.
belügen [bəˈlyːgən] vt irreg lie to, deceive.
belustigen [bəˈlʊstɪgən] vt amuse.
Belustigung f amusement.
bemächtigen [bəˈmɛçtɪgən] vr: **sich einer Sache** (gen) ~ take possession of sth, seize sth.
bemalen [bəˈmaːlən] vt paint.
bemängeln [bəˈmɛŋəln] vt criticize.
bemannen [bəˈmanən] vt man.
Bemannung f manning; (Naut, Aviat etc) crew.
bemänteln [bəˈmɛntəln] vt cloak, hide.
bemerk- [bəˈmɛrk] cpd: ~**bar** a perceptible, noticeable; **sich** ~**bar machen** (Person) make or get o.s. noticed; (Unruhe) become noticeable; ~**en** vt (wahrnehmen) notice, observe; (sagen) say, mention; ~**enswert** a remarkable, noteworthy; **B**~**ung** f remark; (schriftlich auch) note.
bemitleiden [bəˈmɪtlaɪdən] vt pity.
bemühen [bəˈmyːən] vr take trouble or pains.
Bemühung f trouble, pains pl, effort.
bemuttern [bəˈmʊtərn] vt mother.
benachbart [bəˈnaxbaːrt] a neighbouring.
benachrichtigen [bəˈnaːxrɪçtɪgən] vt inform.
Benachrichtigung f notification, information.
benachteiligen [bəˈnaːxtaɪlɪgən] vt (put at a) disadvantage, victimize.
benehmen [bəˈneːmən] vr irreg behave; **B**~ nt -s behaviour.
beneiden [bəˈnaɪdən] vt envy; ~**swert** a enviable.
benennen [bəˈnɛnən] vt irreg name.
Bengel [ˈbɛŋəl] m -s, - (little) rascal or rogue.
benommen [bəˈnɔmən] a dazed.
benötigen [bəˈnøːtɪgən] vt need.
benutzen [bəˈnʊtsən], **benützen** [bəˈnʏtsən] vt use.
Benutzer m -s, - user.
Benutzung f utilization, use.
Benzin [bɛntˈsiːn] nt -s, -e (Aut) petrol, gas(oline) (US); ~**kanister** m petrol can; ~**tank** m petrol tank; ~**uhr** f petrol gauge.
beobacht- [bəˈʔoːbaxt] cpd: ~**en** vt observe; **B**~**er** m -s, - observer; (eines

Unfalls) witness; (Press, TV) correspondent; **B**~**ung** f observation.
bepacken [bəˈpakən] vt load, pack.
bepflanzen [bəˈpflantsən] vt plant.
bequem [bəˈkveːm] a comfortable; Ausrede convenient; Person lazy, indolent; ~**en** vr condescend (zu to); **B**~**lichkeit** f convenience, comfort; (Faulheit) laziness, indolence.
beraten [bəˈraːtən] irreg vt advise; (besprechen) discuss, debate; vr consult; **gut/schlecht** ~ **sein** be well/ill advised; **sich** ~ **lassen** get advice.
Berater m -s, - adviser.
beratschlagen [bəˈraːtˈʃlaːgən] vti deliberate (on), confer (about).
Beratung f advice, consultation; (Besprechung) consultation; ~**sstelle** f advice centre.
berauben [bəˈraubən] vt rob.
berechenbar [bəˈrɛçənbaːr] a calculable.
berechnen [bəˈrɛçnən] vt calculate; (Comm: anrechnen) charge; ~**d** a Mensch calculating, scheming; **B**~**ung** f calculation; (Comm) charge.
berechtig- [bəˈrɛçtɪç] cpd: ~**en** vt entitle, authorize; (fig) justify; ~**t** [bəˈrɛçtɪçt] a justifiable, justified; **B**~**ung** f authorization; (fig) justification.
bereden [bəˈreːdən] vtr (besprechen) discuss; (überreden) persuade.
beredt [bəˈreːt] a eloquent.
Bereich [bəˈraɪç] m -(e)s, -e (Bezirk) area; (Phys) range; (Ressort, Gebiet) sphere.
bereichern [bəˈraɪçərn] vt enrich; vr get rich.
Bereifung [bəˈraɪfʊŋ] f (set of) tyres pl; (Vorgang) fitting with tyres.
bereinigen [bəˈraɪnɪgən] vt settle.
bereisen [bəˈraɪzən] vt travel through.
bereit [bəˈraɪt] a ready, prepared; **zu etw** ~ **sein** be ready for sth; **sich** ~ **erklären** declare o.s. willing; ~**en** vt prepare, make ready; Kummer, Freude cause; ~**halten** vt irreg keep in readiness; ~**legen** vt lay out; ~**machen** vtr prepare, get ready; ~**s** ad already; **B**~**schaft** f readiness; (Polizei) alert; **in B**~**schaft sein** be on the alert or on stand-by; **B**~**schaftsdienst** m emergency service; ~**stehen** vi irreg (Person) be prepared; (Ding) be ready; ~**stellen** vt Kisten, Pakete etc put ready; Geld etc make available; Truppen, Maschinen put at the ready; **B**~**ung** f preparation; ~**willig** a willing, ready; **B**~**willigkeit** f willingness, readiness.
bereuen [bəˈrɔʏən] vt regret.
Berg [bɛrk] m -(e)s, -e mountain, hill; **b**~**ab** ad downhill; **b**~**an**, **b**~**auf** ad uphill; ~**arbeiter** m miner; ~**bahn** f mountain railway; ~**bau** m mining; **b**~**en** [ˈbɛrgən] vt irreg (retten) rescue; Ladung salvage; (enthalten) contain; ~**führer** m mountain guide; ~**gipfel** m mountain top, peak, summit; **b**~**ig** [ˈbɛrgɪç] a mountainous, hilly; ~**kamm** m crest, ridge; ~**kette** f mountain range; ~**mann** m, pl ~**leute** miner; ~**rutsch**

m landslide; ~**schuh** *m* walking boot; ~**steigen** *nt* mountaineering; ~**steiger(in** *f*) *m* -**s**, - mountaineer, climber; ~**ung** ['bɛrgʊŋ] *f* (*von Menschen*) rescue; (*von Material*) recovery; (*Naut*) salvage; ~**wacht** *f* mountain rescue service; ~**werk** *nt* mine.

Bericht [bə'rɪçt] *m* -**(e)s**, -**e** report, account; **b**~**en** *vti* report; ~**erstatter** *m* -**s**, - reporter, (newspaper) correspondent; ~**erstattung** *f* reporting.

berichtigen [bə'rɪçtɪgən] *vt* correct.

Berichtigung *f* correction.

beritten [bə'rɪtən] *a* mounted.

Bernstein ['bɛrnʃtain] *m* amber.

bersten ['bɛrstən] *vi irreg* burst, split.

berüchtigt [bə'rʏçtɪçt] *a* notorious, infamous.

berücksichtigen [bə'rʏksɪçtɪgən] *vt* consider, bear in mind.

Berücksichtigung *f* consideration.

Beruf [bə'ru:f] *m* -**(e)s**, -**e** occupation, profession; (*Gewerbe*) trade; **b**~**en** *irreg vt* (*in Amt*) appoint (*in* +acc to; *zu* as); *vr*: **sich auf jdn/etw b**~**en** refer *or* appeal to sb/sth; **b**~**en** a competent, qualified; **b**~**lich** a professional; ~**sausbildung** *f* vocational *or* professional training; ~**sberater** *m* careers adviser; ~**sberatung** *f* vocational guidance; ~**sbezeichnung** *f* job description; ~**sgeheimnis** *nt* professional secret; ~**skrankheit** *f* occupational disease; ~**sleben** *nt* professional life; **b**~**smäßig** a professional; ~**srisiko** *nt* occupational hazard; ~**sschule** *f* vocational *or* trade school; ~**ssoldat** *m* professional soldier, regular; ~**ssportler** *m* professional (sportsman); **b**~**stätig** a employed; ~**sverkehr** *m* commuter traffic; ~**swahl** *f* choice of a job; ~**ung** *f* vocation, calling; (*Ernennung*) appointment; (*Jur*) appeal; ~**ung einlegen** appeal.

beruhen [bə'ru:ən] *vi*: **auf etw** (*dat*) ~ be based on sth; **etw auf sich** ~ **lassen** leave sth at that.

beruhigen [bə'ru:ɪgən] *vt* calm, pacify, soothe; *vr* (*Mensch*) calm (o.s.) down; (*Situation*) calm down.

Beruhigung *f* reassurance; (*der Nerven*) calming; **zu jds** ~ to reassure sb; ~**smittel** *nt* sedative; ~**spille** *f* tranquillizer.

berühmt [bə'ry:mt] *a* famous; **B**~**heit** *f* (*Ruf*) fame; (*Mensch*) celebrity.

berühren [bə'ry:rən] *vt* touch; (*gefühlsmäßig bewegen*) affect; (*flüchtig erwähnen*) mention, touch on; *vr* meet, touch.

Berührung *f* contact; ~**spunkt** *m* point of contact.

besagen [bə'za:gən] *vt* mean.

besagt *a Tag etc* in question.

besänftig- [bə'zɛnftɪg] *cpd*: ~**en** *vt* soothe, calm; ~**end** a soothing; **B**~**ung** *f* soothing, calming.

Besatz [bə'zats] *m* -**es**, -̈**e** trimming, edging; ~**ung** *f* garrison; (*Naut, Aviat*) crew; ~**ungsmacht** *f* occupying power.

besaufen [bə'zaufən] *vr irreg* (*col*) get drunk *or* stoned.

beschädig- [bə'ʃɛ:dɪg] *cpd*: ~**en** *vt* damage; **B**~**ung** *f* damage; (*Stelle*) damaged spot.

beschaffen [bə'ʃafən] *vt* get, acquire; a constituted; **B**~**heit** *f* constitution, nature.

Beschaffung *f* acquisition.

beschäftigen [bə'ʃɛftɪgən] *vt* occupy; (*beruflich*) employ; *vr* occupy *or* concern o.s.

beschäftigt a busy, occupied.

Beschäftigung *f* (*Beruf*) employment; (*Tätigkeit*) occupation; (*Befassen*) concern.

beschämen [bə'ʃɛ:mən] *vt* put to shame; ~**d** a shameful; *Hilfsbereitschaft* shaming.

beschämt a ashamed.

beschatten [bə'ʃatən] *vt* shade; *Verdächtige* shadow.

beschaulich [bə'ʃaulɪç] a contemplative.

Bescheid [bə'ʃait] *m* -**(e)s**, -**e** information; (*Weisung*) directions *pl*; ~ **wissen** be well-informed (*über* +acc about); **ich weiß** ~ I know; **jdm** ~ **geben** *or* **sagen** let sb know.

bescheiden [bə'ʃaidən] *vr irreg* content o.s.; a modest; **B**~**heit** *f* modesty.

bescheinen [bə'ʃainən] *vt irreg* shine on.

bescheinigen [bə'ʃainɪgən] *vt* certify; (*bestätigen*) acknowledge.

Bescheinigung *f* certificate; (*Quittung*) receipt.

bescheißen [bə'ʃaisən] *vt irreg* (*col*) cheat.

beschenken [bə'ʃɛŋkən] *vt* give presents to.

bescheren [bə'ʃe:rən] *vt*: **jdm etw** ~ give sb sth as a present; **jdn** ~ give presents to sb.

Bescherung *f* giving of presents; (*col*) mess.

beschildern [bə'ʃɪldərn] *vt* signpost.

beschimpfen [bə'ʃɪmpfən] *vt* abuse.

Beschimpfung *f* abuse.

Beschiß [bə'ʃɪs] *m* -**sses** (*col*) **das ist** ~ that is a swizz *or* a cheat.

Beschlag [bə'ʃla:k] *m* -**(e)s**, -̈**e** (*Metallband*) fitting; (*auf Fenster*) condensation; (*auf Metall*) tarnish; finish; (*Hufeisen*) horseshoe; **jdn/etw in** ~ **nehmen** *or* **mit** ~ **belegen** monopolize sb/sth; **b**~**en** [bə'ʃla:gən] *vti irreg* cover; *Pferd* shoe; *Fenster, Metall* cover; **b**~**en sein** be well versed (*in or auf* +dat in); *vir* (*Fenster etc*) mist over; **b**~**nahmen** *vt* seize, confiscate; requisition; ~**nahmung** *f* confiscation, sequestration.

beschleunigen [bə'ʃlɔʏnɪgən] *vt* accelerate, speed up; *vi* (*Aut*) accelerate.

Beschleunigung *f* acceleration.

beschließen [bə'ʃli:sən] *vt irreg* decide on; (*beenden*) end, close.

Beschluß [bə'ʃlus] *m* -**sses**, -**schlüsse** decision, conclusion; (*Ende*) close, end.

beschmutzen [bə'ʃmutsən] *vt* dirty, soil.

beschneiden [bə'ʃnaidən] *vt irreg* cut, prune, trim; (*Rel*) circumcise.

beschönigen [bə'ʃø:nɪgən] *vt* gloss over.

beschränken [bə'ʃrɛŋkən] *vt* limit, restrict (*auf* +acc to); *vr* restrict o.s.

beschrankt [bə'ʃraŋkt] a *Bahnübergang* with barrier.

beschränk- [bə'ʃrɛŋk] cpd: ~**t** a confined, narrow; *Mensch* limited, narrow-minded; **B~theit** f narrowness; **B~ung** f limitation.

beschreiben [bə'ʃraɪbən] vt irreg describe; *Papier* write on.

Beschreibung f description.

beschriften [bə'ʃrɪftən] vt mark, label.

Beschriftung f lettering.

beschuldigen [bə'ʃʊldɪgən] vt accuse.

Beschuldigung f accusation.

beschummeln [bə'ʃʊməln] vti (col) cheat.

beschütz- [bə'ʃʏts] cpd: ~**en** vt protect (*vor* +dat from); **B~er** m -s, - protector **B~ung** f protection.

Beschwerde [bə'ʃveːrdə] f -, -n complaint; (*Mühe*) hardship; (*pl: Leiden*) pain.

beschweren [bə'ʃveːrən] vt weight down; (*fig*) burden; vr complain.

beschwerlich a tiring, exhausting.

beschwichtigen [bə'ʃvɪçtɪgən] vt soothe, pacify.

Beschwichtigung f soothing, calming.

beschwindeln [bə'ʃvɪndəln] vt (*betrügen*) cheat; (*belügen*) fib to.

beschwingt [bə'ʃvɪŋt] a cheery, in high spirits.

beschwipst [bə'ʃvɪpst] a tipsy.

beschwören [bə'ʃvøːrən] vt irreg *Aussage* swear to; (*anflehen*) implore; *Geister* conjure up.

beseelen [bə'zeːlən] vt inspire.

besehen [bə'zeːən] vt irreg look at; **genau ~** examine closely.

beseitigen [bə'zaɪtɪgən] vt remove.

Beseitigung f removal.

Besen ['beːzən] m -s, - broom; ~**stiel** m broomstick.

besessen [bə'zɛsən] a possessed.

besetz- [bə'zɛts] cpd: ~**en** vt *Haus, Land* occupy; *Platz* take, fill; *Posten* fill; *Rolle* cast; (*mit Edelsteinen*) set; ~**t** a full; (*Tel*) engaged, busy; *Platz* taken; *WC* engaged; **B~tzeichen** nt engaged tone; **B~ung** f occupation; filling; (*von Rolle*) casting; (*die Schauspieler*) cast.

besichtigen [bə'zɪçtɪgən] vt visit, look at.

Besichtigung f visit.

Besied(e)lung [bə'ziːd(ə)lʊŋ] f population.

besiegeln [bə'ziːgəln] vt seal.

besiegen [bə'ziːgən] vt defeat, overcome.

Besiegte(r) [bə'ziːçtə(r)] m loser.

besinnen [bə'zɪnən] vr irreg (*nachdenken*) think, reflect; (*erinnern*) remember; **sich anders ~** change one's mind.

besinnlich a contemplative.

Besinnung f consciousness; **zur ~ kommen** recover consciousness; (*fig*) come to one's senses; **b~slos** a unconscious.

Besitz [bə'zɪts] m -es possession; (*Eigentum*) property; **b~anzeigend** a (*Gram*) possessive; **b~en** vt irreg possess, own; *Eigenschaft* have; ~**er(in** f) m -s, - owner, proprietor; ~**ergreifung** f, ~**nahme** f occupation, seizure.

besoffen [bə'zɔfən] a (*col*) drunk, pissed.

besohlen [bə'zoːlən] vt sole.

Besoldung [bə'zɔldʊŋ] f salary, pay.

besondere(r,s) [bə'zɔndərə(r,z)] a special; (*eigen*) particular; (*gesondert*) separate; (*eigentümlich*) peculiar.

Besonderheit [bə'zɔndərhaɪt] f peculiarity.

besonders [bə'zɔndərs] ad especially, particularly; (*getrennt*) separately.

besonnen [bə'zɔnən] a sensible, level-headed; **B~heit** f prudence.

besorg- [bə'zɔrg] cpd: ~**en** vt (*beschaffen*) acquire; (*kaufen auch*) purchase; (*erledigen*) *Geschäfte* deal with; (*sich kümmern um*) take care of; **es jdm ~en** (*col*) show sb what for; **B~nis** f -, -**se** anxiety, concern; ~**t** [bə'zɔrçt] a anxious, worried; **B~theit** f anxiety, worry; **B~ung** f acquisition; (*Kauf*) purchase.

bespielen [bə'ʃpiːlən] vt record.

bespitzeln [bə'ʃpɪtsəln] vt spy on.

besprechen [bə'ʃprɛçən] irreg vt discuss; *Tonband etc* record, speak onto; *Buch* review; vr discuss, consult.

Besprechung f meeting, discussion; (*von Buch*) review.

besser ['bɛsər] a better; **nur ein ~er ...** just a glorified ...; ~**gehen** vi irreg impers: **es geht ihm ~** he feels better; ~**n** vt make better, improve; vr improve; *Menschen* reform; **B~ung** f improvement; **gute B~ung!** get well soon; **B~wisser** m -s, - know-all.

Bestand [bə'ʃtant] m -(e)s, ̈e (*Fortbestehen*) duration, stability; (*Kassen—*) amount, balance; (*Vorrat*) stock; **eiserne(r) ~** iron rations pl; ~ **haben, von ~ sein** last long, endure.

beständig [bə'ʃtɛndɪç] a (*ausdauernd*) constant (*auch fig*); *Wetter* settled; *Stoffe* resistant; *Klagen etc* continual.

Bestand- cpd: ~**saufnahme** f stocktaking; ~**teil** m part, component; (*Zutat*) ingredient.

bestärken [bə'ʃtɛrkən] vt: **jdn in etw** (*dat*) ~ strengthen or confirm sb in sth.

bestätigen [bə'ʃtɛːtɪgən] vt confirm; (*anerkennen, Comm*) acknowledge.

Bestätigung f confirmation; acknowledgement.

bestatt- [bə'ʃtat] cpd: ~**en** vt bury; **B~er** m -s, - undertaker; **B~ung** f funeral.

bestäuben [bə'ʃtɔʏbən] vt powder, dust; *Pflanze* pollinate.

beste(r,s) ['bɛstə(r,z)] a best; **sie singt am ~n** she sings best; **so ist es am ~n** it's best that way; **am ~n gehst du gleich** you'd better go at once; **jdn zum ~n haben** pull sb's leg; **etw zum ~n geben** tell a joke/story *etc*; **aufs ~** in the best possible way; **zu jds B~n** for the benefit of sb.

bestechen [bə'ʃtɛçən] vt irreg bribe.

bestechlich a corruptible; **B~keit** f corruptibility.

Bestechung f bribery, corruption.

Besteck [bə'ʃtɛk] nt -(e)s, -e knife, fork and spoon, cutlery; (*Med*) set of instruments.

bestehen [bə'ʃteːən] *irreg vi* be; exist; *(andauern)* last; *vt Kampf, Probe, Prüfung* pass; ~ **auf** (+*dat*) insist on; ~ **aus** consist of.

bestehlen [bə'ʃteːlən] *vt irreg* rob.

besteigen [bə'ʃtaigən] *vt irreg* climb, ascend; *Pferd* mount; *Thron* ascend.

Bestell- [bə'ʃtɛl] *cpd:* ~**buch** *nt* order book; **b~en** *vt* order; *(kommen lassen)* arrange to see; *(nominieren)* name; *Acker* cultivate; *Grüße, Auftrag* pass on; ~**schein** *m* order coupon; ~**ung** *f* (*Comm*) order; *(Bestellen)* ordering.

bestenfalls ['bɛstən'fals] *ad* at best.

bestens ['bɛstəns] *ad* very well.

besteuern [bə'ʃtɔyərn] *vt* tax.

Bestie ['bɛstiə] *f* (*lit, fig*) beast.

bestimm- [bə'ʃtim] *cpd:* ~**en** *vt Regeln* lay down; *Tag, Ort* fix; *(beherrschen)* characterize; *(aussersehen)* mean; *(ernennen)* appoint; *(definieren)* define; *(veranlassen)* induce; ~**t a** *(entschlossen)* firm; *(gewiß)* certain, definite; *Artikel* definite; *ad (gewiß)* definitely, for sure; **B~theit** *f* certainty; **B~ung** *f* (*Verordnung*) regulation; *(Festsetzen)* determining; *(Verwendungszweck)* purpose; *(Schicksal)* fate; *(Definition)* definition; **B~ungsort** *m* destination.

Best- *cpd:* ~**leistung** *f* best performance; **b~möglich** *a* best possible.

bestrafen [bə'ʃtraːfən] *vt* punish.

Bestrafung *f* punishment.

bestrahlen [bə'ʃtraːlən] *vt* shine on; *(Med)* treat with X-rays.

Bestrahlung *f* (*Med*) X-ray treatment, radiotherapy.

Bestreben [bə'ʃtreːbən] *nt* **-s**, **Bestrebung** [bə'ʃtreːbuŋ] *f* endeavour, effort.

bestreichen [bə'ʃtraiçən] *vt irreg Brot* spread.

bestreiten [bə'ʃtraitən] *vt irreg (abstreiten)* dispute; *(finanzieren)* pay for, finance.

bestreuen [bə'ʃtrɔyən] *vt* sprinkle, dust; *Straße* (spread with) grit.

bestürmen [bə'ʃtyrmən] *vt (mit Fragen, Bitten etc)* overwhelm, swamp.

bestürzen [bə'ʃtyrtsən] *vt* dismay.

bestürzt *a* dismayed.

Bestürzung *f* consternation.

Besuch [bə'zuːx] *m* **-(e)s**, **-e** visit; *(Person)* visitor; **einen** ~ **machen bei jdm** pay sb a visit *or* call; ~ **haben** have visitors; **bei jdm auf** *or* **zu** ~ **sein** be visiting sb; **b~en** *vt* visit; *(Sch etc)* attend; **gut ~t** well-attended; **~er(in** *f*) *m* **-s**, - visitor, guest; ~**serlaubnis** *f* permission to visit; ~**szeit** *f* visiting hours *pl*.

betagt [bə'taːkt] *a* aged.

betasten [bə'tastən] *vt* touch, feel.

betätigen [bə'tɛːtigən] *vt (bedienen)* work, operate; *vr* involve o.s.; **sich politisch** ~ be involved in politics; **sich als etw** ~ work as sth.

Betätigung *f* activity; *(beruflich)* occupation; *(Tech)* operation.

betäuben [bə'tɔybən] *vt* stun; *(fig) Gewissen* still; *(Med)* anaesthetize.

Betäubungsmittel *nt* anaesthetic.

Bete ['beːtə] *f* ~, **-n:** **rote** ~ beetroot.

beteiligen [bə'tailigən] *vr* (**an** +*dat* **in**) take part *or* participate, share; *vt (an Geschäft: finanziell)* have a share; **jdn** ~ give sb a share *or* interest (**an** +*dat* in).

Beteiligung *f* participation; *(Anteil)* share, interest; *(Besucherzahl)* attendance.

beten ['beːtən] *vti* pray.

beteuern [bə'tɔyərn] *vt* assert; *Unschuld* protest; **jdm etw** ~ assure sb of sth.

Beteuerung *f* assertion; protest(ation), assurance.

Beton [be'tɔ̃] *m* **-s**, **-s** concrete.

betonen [be'toːnən] *vt* stress.

betonieren [betoˈniːrən] *vt* concrete.

Betonung *f* stress, emphasis.

betören [bə'tøːrən] *vt* beguile.

Betracht [bə'traxt] *m:* **in** ~ **kommen** be concerned *or* relevant; **nicht in** ~ **kommen** be out of the question; **etw in** ~ **ziehen** consider sth; **außer** ~ **bleiben** not be considered; **b~en** *vt* look at; *(fig auch)* consider; **~er(in** *f*) *m* **-s**, - onlooker.

beträchtlich [bə'trɛçtliç] *a* considerable.

Betrachtung *f* (*Ansehen*) examination; *(Erwägung)* consideration.

Betrag [bə'traːk] *m* **-(e)s**, **⁼e** amount; **b~en** [bə'traːgən] *irreg vt* amount to; *vr* behave; ~**en** *nt* **-s** behaviour.

betrauen [bə'trauən] *vt:* **jdn mit etw** ~ entrust sb with sth.

betreffen [bə'trɛfən] *vt irreg* concern, affect; **was mich betrifft** as for me; ~**d** *a* relevant, in question.

betreffs [bə'trɛfs] *prep* +*gen* concerning, regarding.

betreiben [bə'traibən] *vt irreg (ausüben)* practise; *Politik* follow; *Studien* pursue; *(vorantreiben)* push ahead; *(Tech: antreiben)* drive.

betreten [bə'treːtən] *vt irreg* enter; *Bühne etc* step onto; **B~ verboten** keep off/out; *a* embarrassed.

Betrieb [bə'triːp] *m* **-(e)s**, **-e** *(Firma)* firm, concern; *(Anlage)* plant; *(Tätigkeit)* operation; *(Treiben)* traffic; **außer** ~ **sein** be out of order; **in** ~ **sein** be in operation; ~**sausflug** *m* firm's outing; **b~sfähig** *a* in working order; ~**sferien** *pl* company holidays *pl*; ~**sklima** *nt* (working) atmosphere; ~**skosten** *pl* running costs *pl*; ~**srat** *m* workers' council; **b~ssicher** *a* safe, reliable; ~**sstoff** *m* fuel; ~**sstörung** *f* breakdown; ~**sunfall** *m* industrial accident; ~**swirtschaft** *f* economics.

betrinken [bə'triŋkən] *vr irreg* get drunk.

betroffen [bə'trɔfən] *a (bestürzt)* amazed, perplexed; **von etw** ~ **werden** *or* **sein** be affected by sth.

betrüben [bə'tryːbən] *vt* grieve.

betrübt [bə'tryːpt] *a* sorrowful, grieved.

Betrug [bə'truːk] *m* **-(e)s** deception; *(Jur)* fraud.

betrügen [bə'tryːgən] *irreg vt* cheat; *(Jur)* defraud; *Ehepartner* be unfaithful to; *vr* deceive o.s.

Betrüger m -s, - cheat, deceiver; **b~isch** a deceitful; (Jur) fraudulent.

betrunken [bə'truŋkən] a drunk.

Bett [bɛt] nt -(e)s, -en bed; **ins** or **zu ~ gehen** go to bed; **~bezug** m duvet cover; **~decke** f blanket; (Daunen~) quilt; (Überwurf) bedspread.

Bettel- ['bɛtl] cpd: **b~arm** a very poor, destitute; **~ei** [bɛtə'laɪ] f begging; **b~n** vi beg.

Bett- cpd: **b~en** vt make a bed for; **b~lägerig** a bedridden; **~laken** nt sheet.

Bettler(in f) ['bɛtlər(ɪn)] m -s, - beggar.

Bett- cpd: **b~nässer** m -s, - bedwetter; **~vorleger** m bedside rug; **~wäsche** f, **~zeug** nt bedclothes pl, bedding.

beugen ['bɔygən] vt bend; (Gram) inflect; vr (sich fügen) bow (dat to).

Beule ['bɔylə] f-, -n bump, swelling.

beunruhigen [bə'unru:igən] vt disturb, alarm; vr become worried.

Beunruhigung f worry, alarm.

beurkunden [bə'u:rkundən] vt attest, verify.

beurlauben [bə'u:rlaubən] vt give leave or holiday to.

beurteilen [bə'urtaɪlən] vt judge; Buch etc review.

Beurteilung f judgement; review; (Note) mark.

Beute ['bɔytə] f - booty, loot; **~l** m -s, - bag; (Geld~) purse; (Tabak~) pouch.

bevölkern [bə'fœlkərn] vt populate.

Bevölkerung f population.

bevollmächtigen [bə'fɔlmɛçtigən] vt authorize.

Bevollmächtigte(r) mf authorized agent.

Bevollmächtigung f authorization.

bevor [bə'fo:r] cj before; **~munden** vt insep dominate; **~stehen** vi irreg be in store (dat for); **~stehend** a imminent, approaching; **~zugen** vt insep prefer; **B~zugung** f preference.

bewachen [bə'vaxən] vt watch, guard.

Bewachung f (Bewachen) guarding; (Leute) guard, watch.

bewaffnen [bə'vafnən] vt arm.

Bewaffnung f (Vorgang) arming; (Ausrüstung) armament, arms pl.

bewahren [bə'va:rən] vt keep; **jdn vor jdm/etw ~** save sb from sb/sth.

bewähren [bə'vɛ:rən] vr prove o.s.; (Maschine) prove its worth.

bewahrheiten [bə'va:rhaɪtən] vr come true.

bewährt a reliable.

Bewährung f (Jur) probation; **~sfrist** f (period of) probation.

bewaldet [bə'valdət] a wooded.

bewältigen [bə'vɛltigən] vt overcome; Arbeit finish; Portion manage.

bewandert [bə'vandərt] a expert, knowledgeable.

bewässern [bə'vɛsərn] vt irrigate.

Bewässerung f irrigation.

Beweg- [bə've:g] cpd: **b~en** vtr move; **jdn zu etw b~en** induce sb to (do) sth;

~grund [bə've:k-] m motive; **b~lich** a movable, mobile; (flink) quick; **b~t** a Leben eventful; Meer rough; (ergriffen) touched; **~ung** f movement, motion; (innere) emotion; (körperlich) exercise; **sich** (dat) **~ung machen** take exercise; **~ungsfreiheit** f freedom of movement or action; **b~ungslos** a motionless.

Beweis [bə'vaɪs] m -es, -e proof; (Zeichen) sign; **b~bar** [bə'vaɪz-] a provable; **b~en** vt irreg prove; (zeigen) show; **~führung** f reasoning; **~kraft** f weight, conclusiveness; **b~kräftig** a convincing, conclusive; **~mittel** nt evidence.

bewenden [bə'vɛndən] vi: **etw dabei ~ lassen** leave sth at that.

Bewerb- [bə'vɛrb] cpd: **b~en** vr irreg apply (um for); **~er(in** f) m -s, - applicant; **~ung** f application.

bewerkstelligen [bə'vɛrkʃtɛligən] vt manage, accomplish.

bewerten [bə've:rtən] vt assess.

bewilligen [bə'viligən] vt grant, allow.

Bewilligung f granting.

bewirken [bə'virkən] vt cause, bring about.

bewirten [bə'virtən] vt entertain.

bewirtschaften [bə'virt-ʃaftən] vt manage.

Bewirtung f hospitality.

bewohn- [bə'vo:n] cpd: **~bar** a inhabitable; **~en** vt inhabit, live in; **B~er(in** f) m -s, - inhabitant; (von Haus) resident.

bewölkt [bə'vœlkt] a cloudy, overcast.

Bewölkung f clouds pl.

Bewunder- [bə'vundər] cpd: **~er** m -s, - admirer; **b~n** vt admire; **b~nswert** a admirable, wonderful; **~ung** f admiration.

bewußt [bə'vust] a conscious; (absichtlich) deliberate; **sich** (dat) **einer Sache ~ sein** be aware of sth; **~los** a unconscious; **B~losigkeit** f unconsciousness; **~machen** vr: **jdm/sich etw ~machen** make sb/o.s. aware of sth; **B~sein** nt consciousness; **bei B~sein** conscious.

bezahlen [bə'tsa:lən] vt pay (for); **es macht sich bezahlt** it will pay.

Bezahlung f payment.

bezaubern [bə'tsaubərn] vt enchant, charm.

bezeichnen [bə'tsaɪçnən] vt (kennzeichnen) mark; (nennen) call; (beschreiben) describe; (zeigen) show, indicate; **~d** a characteristic, typical (für of).

Bezeichnung f (Zeichen) mark, sign; (Beschreibung) description.

bezeugen [bə'tsɔygən] vt testify to.

Bezichtigung [bə'tsiçtiguŋ] f accusation.

beziehen [bə'tsi:ən] irreg vt (mit Überzug) cover; Bett make; Haus, Position move into; Standpunkt take up; (erhalten) receive; Zeitung subscribe to, take; **etw auf jdn/etw ~** relate sth to sb/sth; vr refer (auf +acc to); (Himmel) cloud over.

Beziehung f (Verbindung) connection; (Zusammenhang) relation; (Verhältnis) relationship; (Hinsicht) respect; **~en**

haben (*vorteilhaft*) have connections *or* contacts; **b~sweise** *ad or*; (*genauer gesagt auch*) that is, or rather.

Bezirk [bə'tsɪrk] *m* -(e)s, -e district.

Bezug [bə'tsu:k] *m* -(e)s, ⸚e (*Hülle*) covering; (*Comm*) ordering; (*Gehalt*) income, salary; (*Beziehung*) relationship (*zu* to); **in b~ auf** (+*acc*) with reference to; **~ nehmen auf** (+*acc*) refer to.

bezüglich [bə'tsy:klɪç] *prep* +*gen* concerning, referring to; *a* concerning; (*Gram*) relative.

Bezug- *cpd*: **~nahme** *f* reference (*auf* +*acc* to); **~spreis** *m* retail price; **~squelle** *f* source of supply.

bezwecken [bə'tsvɛkən] *vt* aim at.

bezweifeln [bə'tsvaɪfəln] *vt* doubt, query.

Bibel ['bi:bəl] *f* -, -n Bible.

Biber ['bi:bər] *m* -s, - beaver.

Biblio- *cpd*: **~graphie** [bibliogra'fi:] *f* bibliography; **~thek** [biblio'te:k] *f* -, -en library; **~thekar(in** *f*) [bibliote'ka:r(ɪn)] *m* -s, -e librarian.

biblisch ['bi:blɪʃ] *a* biblical.

bieder ['bi:dər] *a* upright, worthy; *Kleid etc* plain.

bieg- [bi:g] *cpd*: **~bar** *a* flexible; **~en** *irreg vtr* bend; *vi* turn; **~sam** ['bi:k-] *a* supple; **B~ung** *f* bend, curve.

Biene ['bi:nə] *f* -, -n bee; **~nhonig** *m* honey; **~nkorb** *m* beehive; **~nwachs** *nt* beeswax.

Bier [bi:r] *nt* -(e)s, -e beer; **~brauer** *m* brewer; **~deckel** *m*, **~filz** *m* beer mat; **~krug** *m*, **~seidel** *nt* beer mug.

bieten ['bi:tən] *irreg vt* offer; (*bei Versteigerung*) bid; *vr* (*Gelegenheit*) be open (*dat* to); **sich** (*dat*) **etw ~ lassen** put up with sth.

Bikini [bi'ki:ni] *m* -s, -s bikini.

Bilanz [bi'lants] *f* balance; (*fig*) outcome; **~ ziehen** take stock (*aus* of).

Bild [bɪlt] *nt* -(e)s, -er (*lit, fig*) picture; photo; (*Spiegel—*) reflection; **~bericht** *m* pictorial report.

bilden ['bɪldən] *vt* form; (*erziehen*) educate; (*ausmachen*) constitute; *vr* arise; (*erziehen*) educate o.s.

Bilder- ['bɪldər] *cpd*: **~buch** *nt* picture book; **~rahmen** *m* picture frame.

Bild- *cpd*: **~fläche** *f* screen; (*fig*) scene; **~hauer** *m* -s, - sculptor; **b~hübsch** *a* lovely, pretty as a picture; **b~lich** *a* figurative; pictorial; **~schirm** *m* television screen; **b~schön** *a* lovely; **~ung** ['bɪldʊŋ] *f* formation; (*Wissen, Benehmen*) education; **~ungslücke** *f* gap in one's education; **~ungspolitik** *f* educational policy; **~weite** *f* (*Phot*) distance.

Billard ['bɪljart] *nt* -s, -e billiards; **~ball** *m*, **~kugel** *f* billiard ball.

billig ['bɪlɪç] *a* cheap; (*gerecht*) fair, reasonable; **~en** ['bɪlɪgən] *vt* approve of; **B~ung** *f* approval.

Billion [bɪli'o:n] *f* billion, trillion (*US*).

bimmeln ['bɪməln] *vi* tinkle.

Binde ['bɪndə] *f* -, -n bandage; (*Arm—*) band; (*Med*) sanitary towel; **~glied** *nt* connecting link; **b~n** *vt irreg* bind, tie;

~strich *m* hyphen; **~wort** *nt* conjunction.

Bind- *cpd*: **~faden** *m* string; **~ung** *f* bond, tie; (*Ski—*) binding.

binnen ['bɪnən] *prep* +*dat or gen* within; **B~hafen** *m* inland harbour; **B~handel** *m* internal trade.

Binse ['bɪnzə] *f* -, -n rush, reed; **~nwahrheit** *f* truism.

Bio- [bio] *cpd* bio-; **~graphie** [-gra'fi:] *f* biography; **~loge** [-'lo:gə] *m* -n, -n biologist; **~logie** [-lo'gi:] *f* biology; **b~logisch** [-'lo:gɪʃ] *a* biological.

Birke ['bɪrkə] *f* -, -n birch.

Birnbaum *m* pear tree.

Birne ['bɪrnə] *f* -, -n pear; (*Elec*) (light) bulb.

bis [bɪs] *ad, prep* +*acc* (*räumlich: — zu/an* +*acc*) to, as far as; (*zeitlich*) till, until; **Sie haben ~ Dienstag Zeit** you have until *or* till Tuesday; **~ Dienstag muß es fertig sein** it must be ready by Tuesday; **~ hierher** this far; **~ in die Nacht** into the night; **~ auf weiteres** until further notice; **~bald/gleich** see you later/soon; **~ auf etw** (*acc*) (*einschließlich*) including sth; (*ausgeschlossen*) except sth; **~ zu** up to; *cj* (*mit Zahlen*) to; (*zeitlich*) until, till; **von ... ~ ...** from ... to ...

Bischof ['bɪʃɔf] *m* -s, ⸚e bishop.

bischöflich ['bɪʃø:flɪç] *a* episcopal.

bisher [bɪs'he:r] *ad*, **~ig** *a* till now, hitherto.

Biskuit [bɪs'kvi:t] *m or nt* -(e)s, -s *or* -e biscuit; **~teig** *m* sponge mixture.

bislang [bɪs'laŋ] *ad* hitherto.

Biß [bɪs] *m* -sses, -sse bite.

bißchen ['bɪsçən] *a, ad* bit.

Bissen ['bɪsən] *m* -s, - bite, morsel.

bissig ['bɪsɪç] *a Hund* snappy; *Bemerkung* cutting, biting.

Bistum ['bɪstu:m] *nt* bishopric.

bisweilen [bɪs'vaɪlən] *ad* at times, occasionally.

Bitte ['bɪtə] *f* -, -n request; **b~** *interj* please; (*wie b—?*) (I beg your) pardon; (*als Antwort auf Dank*) you're welcome; **b~ schön!** it was a pleasure; **b~n** *vti irreg* ask (*um* for); **b~nd** *a* pleading, imploring.

bitter ['bɪtər] *a* bitter; **~böse** *a* very angry; **B~keit** *f* bitterness; **~lich** *a* bitter.

blähen ['blɛːən] *vtr* swell, blow out.

Blähungen *pl* (*Med*) wind.

blam- *cpd*: **~abel** [bla'ma:bəl] *a* disgraceful; **B~age** [bla'ma:ʒə] *f* -, -n disgrace; **~ieren** [bla'mi:rən] *vr* make a fool of o.s., disgrace o.s.; *vt* let down, disgrace.

blank [blaŋk] *a* bright; (*unbedeckt*) bare; (*sauber*) clean, polished; (*col: ohne Geld*) broke; (*offensichtlich*) blatant.

blanko ['blaŋko] *ad* blank; **B~scheck** *m* blank cheque.

Bläschen ['blɛːsçən] *nt* bubble; (*Med*) spot, blister.

Blase ['bla:zə] *f* -, -n bubble; (*Med*) blister; (*Anat*) bladder; **~balg** *m* bellows *pl*; **b~n** *vti irreg* blow.

Blas- *cpd*: **~instrument** *nt* brass *or* wind instrument; **~kapelle** *f* brass band.

blaß [blas] a pale.

Blässe ['blɛsə] f- paleness, palour.

Blatt [blat] nt -(e)s, ̈er leaf; newspaper; (von Papier) sheet; (Cards) hand; **vom ~ singen/spielen** sight-read.

blättern ['blɛtərn] vi: **in etw** (dat) **~ leaf through sth.**

Blätterteig m flaky or puff pastry.

blau [blau] a blue; (col) drunk, stoned; (Cook) boiled; Auge black; **~er Fleck** bruise; **Fahrt ins B~e** mystery tour; **~äugig** a blue-eyed; **B~licht** nt flashing blue light; **~machen** vi (col) skive off work; **B~strumpf** m (fig) bluestocking.

Blech [blɛç] nt -(e)s, -e tin, sheet metal; (Back—) baking tray; **~büchse** f, **~dose** f tin, can; **b~en** vti (col) pay; **~schaden** m (Aut) damage to bodywork.

Blei [blai] nt -(e)s, -e lead; **~be** f -, -n roof over one's head; **b~ben** vi irreg stay, remain, be (alone); **b~benlassen** vt irreg leave (alone).

bleich [blaiç] a faded, pale; **~en** vt bleach.

Blei- cpd: **b~ern** a leaden; **~stift** m pencil; **~stiftspitzer** m pencil sharpener.

Blende ['blɛndə] f-, -n (Phot) aperture; **b~n** vt blind, dazzle; (fig) hoodwink; **b~nd** a (col) grand; **b~nd aussehen** look smashing.

Blick [blik] m -(e)s, -e (kurz) glance, glimpse; (Anschauen) look, gaze; (Aussicht) view; **b~en** vi look; **sich b~en lassen** put in an appearance; **~fang** m eye-catching object; **~feld** nt range of vision (auch fig).

blind [blint] a blind; Glas etc dull; **~er Passagier** stowaway; **B~darm** m appendix; **B~darmzündung** f appendicitis; **B~enschrift** ['blindən-] f braille; **B~heit** f blindness; **~lings** ad blindly; **B~schleiche** f slow worm; **~schreiben** vi irreg touch-type.

blink- [bliŋk] cpd: **~en** vi twinkle, sparkle; (Licht) flash, signal; (Aut) indicate; vt flash, signal; **B~er** m -s, -, **B~licht** nt (Aut) indicator.

blinzeln ['blintsəln] vi blink, wink.

Blitz [blits] m -es, -e (flash of) lightning; **~ableiter** m lightning conductor; **b~en** vi (aufleuchten) glint, shine; **es blitzt** (Met) there's a flash of lightning; **~licht** nt flashlight; **b~schnell** a, ad as quick as a flash.

Block [blɔk] m -(e)s, ̈e (lit, fig) block; (von Papier) pad; **~ade** [blɔ'ka:də] f-, -n blockade; **~flöte** f recorder; **b~frei** a (Pol) unaligned; **b~ieren** [blɔ'ki:rən] vt block; vi (Räder) jam; **~schrift** f block letters pl.

blöd [blø:t] a silly, stupid; **~eln** ['blø:dəln] vi (col) fool around; **B~heit** f stupidity; **B~sinn** m nonsense; **b~sinnig** a silly, idiotic.

blond [blɔnt] a blond, fair-haired.

bloß [blo:s] a (unbedeckt) bare; (nackt) naked; (nur) mere; b~ only, merely; **laß das ~!** I just don't do that!

Blöße ['blø:sə] f-, -n bareness; nakedness;

(fig) weakness; **sich** (dat) **eine ~ geben** (fig) lay o.s. open to attack.

bloß- cpd: **~legen** vt expose; **~stellen** vt show up.

blühen ['bly:ən] vi (lit) bloom, be in bloom; (fig) flourish.

Blume ['blu:mə] f-, -n flower; (von Wein) bouquet; **~nkohl** m cauliflower; **~ntopf** m flowerpot; **~nzwiebel** f bulb.

Bluse ['blu:zə] f-, -n blouse.

Blut [blu:t] nt -(e)s, -e blood; **b~arm** a anaemic; (fig) penniless; **b~befleckt** a bloodstained; **~buche** f copper beech; **~druck** m blood pressure.

Blüte ['bly:tə] f-, -n blossom; (fig) prime; **~zeit** f flowering period; (fig) prime.

Blut- cpd: **~egel** m leech; **b~en** vi bleed.

Blütenstaub m pollen.

Blut- cpd: **~er** m -s, - (Med) haemo-philiac; **~erguß** m haemorrhage; (auf Haut) bruise; **~gruppe** f blood group; **b~ig** a bloody; **b~jung** a very young; **~probe** f blood test; **~schande** f incest; **~spender** m blood donor; **~übertragung** f blood transfusion; **~ung** f bleeding, haemorrhage; **~vergiftung** f blood poisoning; **~wurst** f black pudding.

Bö(e) ['bø:(ə)] f-, -en squall.

Bock [bɔk] m -(e)s, ̈e buck, ram; (Gestell) trestle, support; (Sport) buck.

Boden ['bo:dən] m -s, ̈ ground; (Fuß—) floor; (Meeres—, Faß—) bottom; (Speicher) attic; **b~los** bottomless; (col) incredible; **~satz** m dregs pl, sediment; **~schätze** pl mineral wealth; **~turnen** nt floor exercises pl.

Bogen ['bo:gən] m -s, - (Biegung) curve; (Archit) arch; (Waffe, Mus) bow; (Papier) sheet; **~gang** m arcade; **~schütze** m archer.

Bohle ['bo:lə] f-, -n plank.

Bohne ['bo:nə] f-, -n bean; **~nkaffee** m pure coffee; **b~rn** vt wax, polish; **~rwachs** nt floor polish.

Bohr- ['bo:r] cpd: **b~en** vt bore; **~er** m -s, - drill; **~insel** f oil rig; **~maschine** f drill; **~turm** m derrick.

Boje ['bo:jə] f-, -n buoy.

Bolzen ['bɔltsən] m -s, - bolt.

Bomb- cpd: **b~ardieren** [bɔmbar'di:rən] vt bombard; (aus der Luft) bomb; **~e** ['bɔmbə] f-, -n bomb; **~enangriff** m bombing raid; **~enerfolg** m (col) huge success.

Bonbon [bõ'bõ:] m or nt -s, -s sweet.

Boot [bo:t] nt -(e)s, -e boat.

Bord [bɔrt] m -(e)s, -e (Aviat, Naut) board; **an ~** on board; nt (Brett) shelf; **~ell** [bɔr'dɛl] nt -s, -e brothel; **~funkanlage** f radio; **~stein** m kerb(stone).

borgen ['bɔrgən] vt borrow; **jdm etw ~ lend** sb sth.

borniert [bɔr'ni:rt] a narrow-minded.

Börse ['bœrzə] f-, -n stock exchange; (Geld—) purse.

Borste ['bɔrstə] f-, -n bristle.

Borte ['bɔrtə] f-, -n edging; (Band) trimming.

bös [bø:s] a bad, evil; (zornig) angry; **~artig** ['bø:z-] a malicious.

Böschung ['bœʃʊŋ] f slope; (Ufer— etc) embankment.
bos- ['boːs] cpd: ~**haft** a malicious, spiteful; B~**heit** f malice, spite.
böswillig ['bøːsvɪlɪç] a malicious.
Botanik [boˈtaːnɪk] f botany.
botanisch [boˈtaːnɪʃ] a botanical.
Bot- ['boːt] cpd: ~**e** m -**n**, -**n** messenger; ~**enjunge** m errand boy; ~**schaft** f message, news; (Pol) embassy; ~**schafter** m -**s**, - ambassador.
Bottich ['bɔtɪç] m -(e)s, -e vat, tub.
Bouillon [buˈljõː] f -, -**s** consommé.
Bowle ['boːlə] f -, -**n** punch.
Box- ['bɔks] cpd: b~**en** vi box; ~**er** m -**s**, - boxer; ~**handschuh** m boxing glove; ~**kampf** m boxing match.
boykottieren [bɔykɔˈtiːrən] vt boycott.
Branche ['brãːʃə] f -, -**n** line of business; ~**nverzeichnis** nt yellow pages pl.
Brand [brant] m -(e)s, ˑe fire; (Med) gangrene; b~**en** (branden) vi surge; (Meer) break; b~**marken** vt brand; (fig) stigmatize; ~**salbe** f ointment for burns; ~**stifter** m arsonist, fire-raiser; ~**stiftung** f arson; ~**ung** f surf; ~**wunde** f burn.
Branntwein ['brantvaɪn] m brandy.
Brat- [braːt] cpd: ~**apfel** m baked apple; b~**en** vt irreg roast, fry; ~**en** m -**s**, - roast, joint; ~**huhn** nt roast chicken; ~**kartoffeln** pl fried or roast potatoes pl; ~**pfanne** f frying pan; ~**rost** m grill.
Bratsche ['braːtʃə] f -, -**n** viola.
Brat- cpd: ~**spieß** m spit; ~**wurst** f grilled sausage.
Brauch [braʊx] m -(e)s, Bräuche custom; b~**bar** a usable, serviceable; Person capable; b~**en** vt (bedürfen) need; (müssen) have to; (verwenden) use.
Braue ['braʊə] f -, -**n** brow; b~**n** vt brew; ~'**rei** f brewery.
braun [braʊn] a brown; (von Sonne auch) tanned.
Bräune ['brɔynə] f -, -**n** brownness; (Sonnen—) tan; b~**n** vt make brown; (Sonne) tan.
braungebrannt a tanned.
Brause ['braʊzə] f -, -**n** shower bath; (von Gießkanne) rose; (Getränk) lemonade; b~**n** vi roar; (auch vr: duschen) take a shower; ~**pulver** nt lemonade powder.
Braut [braʊt] f -, Bräute bride; (Verlobte) fiancée.
Bräutigam ['brɔytɪgam] m -**s**, -e bridegroom; fiancé.
Braut- cpd: ~**jungfer** f bridesmaid; ~**paar** nt bride and bridegroom, bridal pair.
brav [braːf] a (artig) good; (ehrenhaft) worthy, honest.
Brech- ['brɛç] cpd: ~**eisen** nt crowbar; b~**en** vti irreg break; Licht refract; (fig) Mensch crush; (speien) vomit; **die Ehe** b~**en** commit adultery; ~**reiz** m nausea, retching.
Brei [braɪ] m -(e)s, -e (Masse) pulp; (Cook) slop; (Hafer—) porridge.
breit [braɪt] a wide, broad; B~**e** f -, -**n** width; breadth; (Geog) latitude; ~**en** vt:

etw über etw (acc) ~**en** spread sth over sth; B~**engrad** m degree of latitude; ~**machen** vr spread o.s. out; ~**schult(e)rig** a broad-shouldered; ~**treten** vt irreg (col) enlarge upon; B~**wandfilm** m wide-screen film.
Brems- ['brɛmz] cpd: ~**belag** m brake lining; ~**e** f -, -**n** brake; (Zool) horsefly; b~**en** vi brake, apply the brakes; vt Auto brake; (fig) slow down; ~**licht** nt brake light; ~**pedal** nt brake pedal; ~**schuh** m brake shoe; ~**spur** f tyre marks pl; ~**weg** m braking distance.
Brenn- ['brɛn] cpd: b~**bar** a inflammable; b~**en** irreg vi burn, be on fire; (Licht, Kerze etc) burn; vt Holz etc burn; Ziegel, Ton fire; Kaffee roast; **darauf** b~**en, etw zu tun** be dying to do sth; ~**material** nt fuel; ~(**n**)**essel** f nettle; ~**spiritus** m methylated spirits; ~**stoff** m liquid fuel.
brenzlig ['brɛntslɪç] a smelling of burning, burnt; (fig) precarious.
Brett [brɛt] nt -(e)s, -er board, plank; (Bord) shelf; (Spiel—) board; **Schwarze(s)** ~ notice board; ~**er** pl (Ski) skis pl; (Theat) boards pl; ~**erzaun** m wooden fence.
Brezel ['breːtsəl] f -, -**n** bretzel, pretzel.
Brief [briːf] m -(e)s, -e letter; ~**beschwerer** m -**s**, - paperweight; ~**kasten** m letterbox; b~**lich** a,ad by letter; ~**marke** f postage stamp; ~**öffner** m letter opener; ~**papier** nt notepaper; ~**tasche** f wallet; ~**träger** m postman; ~**umschlag** m envelope; ~**wechsel** m correspondence.
Brikett [briˈkɛt] nt -**s**, -**s** briquette.
brillant [brɪlˈjant] a (fig) sparkling, brilliant; B~ m -**en**, -**en** brilliant, diamond.
Brille ['brɪlə] f -, -**n** spectacles pl; (Schutz—) goggles pl; (Toiletten—) (toilet) seat.
bringen ['brɪŋən] vt irreg bring; (mitnehmen, begleiten) take; (einbringen) Profit bring in; (veröffentlichen) publish; (Theat, Cine) show; (Rad, TV) broadcast; (in einen Zustand versetzen) get; (col: tun können) manage; **jdn dazu** ~**, etw zu tun** make sb do sth; **jdn nach Hause** ~ take sb home; **jdn um etw** ~ make sb lose sth; **jdn auf eine Idee** ~ give sb an idea.
Brise ['briːzə] f -, -**n** breeze.
bröckelig ['brœkəlɪç] a crumbly.
Brocken ['brɔkən] m -**s**, - piece, bit; (Fels—) lump of rock.
brodeln ['broːdəln] vi bubble.
Brokat [broˈkaːt] m -(e)s, -e brocade.
Brombeere ['brɔmbeːrə] f blackberry, bramble.
bronchial [brɔnçiˈaːl] a bronchial.
Bronchien ['brɔnçiən] pl bronchia(l tubes) pl.
Bronze ['brõːsə] f -, -**n** bronze.
Brosame ['broːzaːmə] f -, -**n** crumb.
Brosche ['brɔʃə] f -, -**n** brooch.
Broschüre [brɔˈʃyːrə] f -, -**n** pamphlet.
Brot [broːt] nt -(e)s, -e bread; (—laib) loaf.

Brötchen ['brøːtçən] nt roll.

brotlos ['broːtloːs] a Person unemployed; Arbeit etc unprofitable.

Bruch [brux] m -(e)s, ∸e breakage; (zerbrochene Stelle) break; (fig) split, breach; (Med: Eingeweide—) rupture, hernia; (Bein— etc) fracture; (Math) fraction; ~bude f (col) shack.

brüchig ['brʏçıç] a brittle, fragile; Haus dilapidated.

Bruch- cpd: ~landung f crash landing; ~strich m (Math) line; ~stück nt fragment; ~teil m fraction.

Brücke ['brʏkə] f -, -n bridge; (Teppich) rug.

Bruder ['bruːdər] m -s, ∸ brother.

Brüder- ['bryːdər] cpd: b~lich a brotherly; ~lichkeit f fraternity; ~schaft f brotherhood, fellowship; ~schaft trinken fraternize, address each other as 'du'.

Brühe ['bryːə] f -, -n broth, stock; (pej) muck.

brüllen ['brʏlən] vi bellow, scream.

Brumm- ['brum] cpd: ~bär m grumbler; b~eln vti mumble; b~en vi (Bär, Mensch etc) growl; (Insekt, Radio) buzz; (Motoren) roar; (murren) grumble; vt growl; jdm brummt der Kopf sb's head is buzzing.

brünett [brʏˈnɛt] a brunette, dark-haired.

Brunnen ['brunən] m -s, - fountain; (tief) well; (natürlich) spring; ~kresse f watercress.

brüsk [brʏsk] a abrupt, brusque.

Brust [brust] f -, ∸e breast; (Männer—) chest.

brüsten ['brʏstən] vr boast.

Brust- cpd: ~fellentzündung f pleurisy; ~kasten m chest; ~schwimmen nt breast-stroke; ~warze f nipple.

Brüstung ['brʏstʊŋ] f parapet.

Brut [bruːt] f -, -en brood; (Brüten) hatching; b~al [bruˈtaːl] a brutal; ~alität f brutality; ~apparat m, ~kasten m incubator.

brüten ['bryːtən] vi hatch, brood (auch fig).

brutto ['bruto] ad gross; B~einkommen nt, B~gehalt nt gross salary; B~gewicht nt gross weight; B~lohn m gross wages pl.

Bub [buːp] m -en, -en boy, lad; ~e [buːbə] m -n, -n (Schurke) rogue; (Cards) jack; ~ikopf m bobbed hair, shingle.

Buch [buːx] nt -(e)s, ∸er book; (Comm) account book; ~binder m bookbinder; ~drucker m printer; ~e f -, -n beech tree; b~en vt book; Betrag enter.

Bücher- ['byːçər] cpd: ~brett nt bookshelf; ~ei [-'raı] f library; ~regal nt bookshelves pl, bookcase; ~schrank m bookcase.

Buch- cpd: ~fink m chaffinch; ~führung f book-keeping, accounting; ~halter(in f) m -s, - book-keeper; ~handel m book trade; ~händler(in f) m bookseller; ~handlung f bookshop.

Büchse ['bʏksə] f -, -n tin, can; (Holz—) box; (Gewehr) rifle; ~nfleisch nt tinned meat; ~nöffner m tin or can opener.

Buch- cpd: ~stabe m -ns, -n letter (of the alphabet); b~stabieren [buːxʃtaˈbiːrən] vt spell; b~stäblich ['buːxʃteːplıç] a literal.

Bucht ['buxt] f -, -en bay.

Buchung ['buːxʊŋ] f booking; (Comm) entry.

Buckel ['bʊkəl] m -s, - hump.

bücken ['bʏkən] vr bend.

Bückling ['bʏklıŋ] m (Fisch) kipper; (Verbeugung) bow.

Bude ['buːdə] f -, -n booth, stall; (col) digs pl.

Budget [bʏˈdʒeː] nt -s, -s budget.

Büffel ['bʏfəl] m -s, - buffalo.

Büf(f)ett [bʏˈfeː] nt -s, -s (Anrichte) sideboard; (Geschirrschrank) dresser; kaltes ~ cold buffet.

Bug [buːk] m -(e)s, -e (Naut) bow; (Aviat) nose.

Bügel ['byːgəl] m -s, - (Kleider—) hanger; (Steig—) stirrup; (Brillen—) arm; ~brett nt ironing board; ~eisen nt iron; ~falte f crease; b~n vti iron.

Bühne ['byːnə] f -, -n stage; ~nbild nt set, scenery.

Buhruf ['buːruːf] m boo.

Bulette [buˈletə] f meatball.

Bull- ['bʊl] cpd: ~dogge f bulldog; ~dozer ['buldoːzər] m -s, - bulldozer; ~e m -n, -n bull.

Bummel ['bʊməl] m -s, - stroll; (Schaufenster—) window-shopping; ~ant [-'lant] m slowcoach; ~ei [-'laı] f wandering; dawdling; skiving; b~n vi wander, stroll; (trödeln) dawdle; (faulenzen) skive, loaf around; ~streik m go-slow; ~zug m slow train.

Bummler(in f) ['bʊmlər(ın)] m -s, - (langsamer Mensch) dawdler; (Faulenzer) idler, loafer.

Bund [bunt] m -(e)s, ∸e (Freundschafts— etc) bond; (Organisation) union; (Pol) confederacy; (Hosen—, Rock—) waistband; nt -(e)s, -e bunch; (Stroh—) bundle.

Bünd- ['bʏnd] cpd: ~chen nt ribbing; (Ärmel—) cuff; ~el nt -s, -n bundle, bale; b~eln vt bundle.

Bundes- ['bundəs] in cpds Federal (esp West German); ~bahn f Federal Railways pl; ~hauptstadt f Federal capital; ~kanzler m Federal Chancellor; ~land nt Land; ~präsident m Federal President; ~rat m upper house of West German Parliament; ~republik f Federal Republic (of West Germany); ~staat m Federal state; ~straße f Federal Highway, 'A' road; ~tag m West German Parliament; ~verfassungsgericht nt Federal Constitutional Court; ~wehr f West German Armed Forces pl.

Bünd- cpd: b~ig a (kurz) concise; ~nis nt -ses, -se alliance.

Bunker ['bʊŋkər] m -s, - bunker.

bunt [bunt] a coloured; (gemischt) mixed; jdm wird es zu ~ it's getting too much for sb; B~stift m coloured pencil, crayon.

Burg [burk] f -, -en castle, fort.

Bürge ['bʏrgə] m -n, -n guarantor; b~n vi vouch; ~r(in f) m -s, - citizen; member

of the middle class; ~**krieg** m civil war;
b~**rlich** a *Rechte* civil; *Klasse* middle-
class; (*pej*) bourgeois; **gut b~rliche**
Küche good home cooking; ~**rmeister**
m mayor; ~**rrecht** nt civil rights pl;
~**rschaft** f population, citizens pl;
~**rsteig** m pavement; ~**rtum** nt citizens
pl.

Bürg- cpd: ~**in** f see **Bürge**; ~**schaft** f
surety; ~**schaft leisten** give security.

Büro [by'ro:] nt -s, -s office;
~**angestellte(r)** mf office worker;
~**klammer** f paper clip; ~**krat**
[byro'kra:t] m -en, -en bureaucrat;
~**kra'tie** f bureaucracy; b~**'kratisch** a
bureaucratic; ~**kra'tismus** m red tape;
~**schluß** m office closing time.

Bursch(e) [burʃ(ə)] m -en, -en lad,
fellow; (*Diener*) servant.

Bürste [byrstə] f -, -n brush; b~**n** vt
brush.

Bus [bus] m -ses, -se bus.

Busch [buʃ] m -(e)s, ̈e bush, shrub.

Büschel [byʃəl] nt -s, - tuft.

buschig a bushy.

Busen [bu:zən] m -s, - bosom; (*Meer*)
inlet, bay; ~**freund(in** f) m bosom friend.

Buße [bu:sə] f -, -n atonement, penance;
(*Geld*) fine.

büßen [by:sən] vti do penance (for), atone
(for).

Büste [bystə] f -, -n bust; ~**nhalter** m
bra.

Butter [butər] f - butter; ~**blume** f
buttercup; ~**brot** nt (piece of) bread and
butter; ~**brotpapier** nt greaseproof
paper; ~**dose** f butter dish; b~**weich** a
soft as butter; (*fig,col*) soft.

Butzen [butsən] m -s, - core.

C

(*see also under* K *and* Z; CH *under* SCH)

C, c [tse:] nt C, c.

Café [ka'fe:] nt -s, -s café.

Cafeteria [kafete'ri:a] f -, -s cafeteria.

Camp- [kɛmp] cpd: c~**en** vi camp;
~**er(in** f) m -s, - camper; ~**ing** nt -s
camping; ~**ingplatz** m camp(ing) site.

Caravan [kɛrəvɛn] m -s, -s caravan.

Cellist [tʃe'lɪst] m cellist.

Cello [tʃelo] nt -s, -s or **Celli** cello.

Chamäleon [ka'mɛ:leɔn] nt -s, -s
chameleon.

Champagner [ʃam'panjər] m -s, -
champagne.

Champignon [ʃampinjõ] m -s, -s button
mushroom.

Chance [ʃɑ̃:s(ə)] f -, -n chance,
opportunity.

Chaos [ka:ɔs] nt -s, - chaos.

chaotisch [ka'o:tɪʃ] a chaotic.

Charakter [ka'raktər] m -s, -e
[karak'te:rə] character; c~**fest** a of firm
character; c~**i'sieren** vt characterize;
~**istik** [karakte'rɪstɪk] f characterization;
c~**istisch** [karakte'rɪstɪʃ] a characteristic, typical (*für* of); c~**los** a unprincipled; ~**losigkeit** f lack of principle;

~**schwäche** f weakness of character;
~**stärke** f strength of character; ~**zug**
m characteristic, trait.

charmant [ʃar'mant] a charming.

Charme [ʃarm] m -s charm.

Chassis [ʃa'si:] nt -, - chassis.

Chauffeur [ʃɔ'fø:r] m chauffeur.

Chauvinismus [ʃovi'nɪsmus] m
chauvinism, jingoism.

Chauvinist [ʃovi'nɪst] m chauvinist,
jingoist.

Chef [ʃɛf] m -s, -s head; (*col*) boss; ~**arzt**
m head physician; ~**in** f (*col*) boss.

Chemie [çe'mi:] f - chemistry; ~**faser** f
man-made fibre.

Chemikalie [çemi'ka:liə] f -, -n chemical.

Chemiker(in f) [çe'mikər(ɪn)] m -s, -
(industrial) chemist.

chemisch [çe:mɪʃ] a chemical; ~**e**
Reinigung dry cleaning.

Chiffre [ʃɪfər] f -, -n (*Geheimzeichen*)
cipher; (*in Zeitung*) box number.

Chiffriermaschine [ʃɪfri:rmaʃi:nə] f
cipher machine.

Chips [tʃɪps] pl crisps pl, chips pl (*US*).

Chirurg [çi'rurk] m -en, -en surgeon;
~**ie** [-'gi:] f surgery; c~**isch** a surgical.

Chlor [klo:r] nt -s chlorine; ~**o'form** nt -s
chloroform; c~**ofor'mieren** vt
chloroform; ~**ophyll** [kloro'fyl] nt -s
chlorophyll.

Cholera [ko:lera] f - cholera.

cholerisch [ko'le:rɪʃ] a choleric.

Chor [ko:r] m -(e)s, -e or ̈e choir; (*Musik-
stück, Theat*) chorus; ~**al** [ko'ra:l] m -s,
-̈ale chorale.

Choreograph [koreo'gra:f] m -en, -en
choreographer; ~**ie** [-'fi:] f choreography.

Chor- cpd: ~**gestühl** nt choir stalls pl;
~**knabe** m choirboy.

Christ [krɪst] m -en, -en Christian;
~**baum** m Christmas tree; ~**enheit** f
Christendom; ~**entum** nt Christianity;
~**in** f Christian; ~**kind** nt ≈ Father
Christmas; (*Jesus*) baby Jesus; c~**lich** a
Christian; ~**us** m - Christ.

Chrom [kro:m] nt (*Chem*) chromium;
chrome; ~**osom** [kromo'zo:m] nt -s, -en
(*Biol*) chromosome.

Chron- [kro:n] cpd: ~**ik** f chronicle;
c~**isch** a chronic; ~**ologie** [-lo'gi:] f
chronology; c~**ologisch** [-'lo:gɪʃ] a
chronological.

Chrysantheme [kryzan'te:mə] f -, -n
chrysanthemum.

circa [tsɪrka] ad about, approximately.

Clown [klaun] m -s, -s clown.

Computer [kɔm'pju:tər] m -s, - computer.

Conférencier [kõferɑ̃si'e:] m -s, -s
compère.

Coupé [ku'pe:] nt -s, -s (*Aut*) coupé, sports
version.

Coupon [ku'põ:] m -s, -s coupon; (*Stoff*—)
length of cloth.

Cousin [ku'zɛ̃:] m -s, -s cousin; ~**e**
[ku'zi:nə] f -, -n cousin.

Creme [krɛ:m] f -, -s (*lit, fig*) cream;
(*Schuh*—) polish; (*Zahn*—) paste; (*Cook*)
mousse; c~**farben** a cream(-coloured).

Curry(pulver nt) ['kari(pʊlfər)] m or nt **-s** curry powder.

Cutter(in f) ['katər(ɪn)] m **-s**, - (Cine) editor.

D

D, d [de:] nt D, d.

da [da:] ad (dort) there; (hier) here; (dann) then; ~, **wo** where; cj as; ~**behalten** vt irreg keep.

dabei [da'baɪ] ad (räumlich) close to it; (noch dazu) besides; (zusammen mit) with them; (zeitlich) during this; (obwohl doch) but, however; **was ist schon** ~? what of it?; **es ist doch nichts** ~, **wenn . . .** it doesn't matter if . . .; **bleiben wir** ~ let's leave it at that; **es soll nicht** ~ **bleiben** this isn't the end of it; **es bleibt** ~ that's settled; **das Dumme/Schwierige** ~ the stupid/difficult part of it; **er war gerade** ~, **zu gehen** he was just leaving; ~**sein** vi irreg (anwesend) be present; (beteiligt) be involved; ~**stehen** vi irreg stand around.

Dach [dax] nt **-(e)s, ¨er** roof; ~**boden** m attic, loft; ~**decker** m **-s**, - slater, tiler; ~**fenster** nt, ~**luke** f skylight; ~**pappe** f roofing felt; ~**rinne** f gutter; ~**ziegel** m roof tile.

Dachs [daks] m **-es, -e** badger.

Dackel ['dakəl] m **-s**, - dachshund.

dadurch [da'dʊrç] ad (räumlich) through it; (durch diesen Umstand) thereby, in that way; (deshalb) because of that, for that reason; cj: ~, **daß** because.

dafür [da'fy:r] ad for it; (anstatt) instead; **er kann nichts** ~ he can't help it; **er ist bekannt** ~ he is well-known for that; **was bekomme ich** ~? what will I get for it?; **D~halten** nt **-s: nach meinem D~halten** in my opinion.

dagegen [da'ge:gən] ad against it; (im Vergleich damit) in comparison with it; (bei Tausch) to it; **ich habe nichts** ~ I don't mind; **ich war** ~ I was against it; ~**kann man nichts tun** one can't do anything about it; cj however; ~**halten** vt irreg (vergleichen) compare with it; (entgegnen) object to it.

daheim [da'haɪm] ad at home; **D~** nt **-s** home.

daher [da'he:r] ad (räumlich) from there; (Ursache) from that; ~ **kommt er auch** that's where he comes from too; cj (deshalb) that's why; ~ **die Schwierigkeiten** that's what is causing the difficulties.

dahin [da'hɪn] ad (räumlich) there; (zeitlich) then; (vergangen) gone; **das tendiert** ~ it is tending towards that; **er bringt es noch** ~, **daß ich . . .** he'll make me . . .; ~**gegen** cj on the other hand; ~**gestellt** ad: ~**gestellt bleiben** remain to be seen; ~**gestellt sein lassen** leave sth open or undecided.

dahinten [da'hɪntən] ad over there.

dahinter [da'hɪntər] ad behind it;

~**kommen** vi irreg get to the bottom of sth.

Dahlie ['da:liə] f -, **-n** dahlia.

dalassen ['da:lasən] vt irreg leave (behind).

damalig ['da:ma:lɪç] a of that time, then.

damals ['da:ma:ls] ad at that time, then.

Damast [da'mast] m **-(e)s, -e** damask.

Dame ['da:mə] f -, **-n** lady; (Schach, Cards) queen; (Spiel) draughts; **d~nhaft** a lady-like; ~**nwahl** f ladies' excuse-me; ~**spiel** nt draughts.

damit [da'mɪt] ad with it; (begründend) by that; **was meint er** ~? what does he mean by that?; **genug** ~! that's enough; ~ **basta!** and that's that; ~ **eilt es nicht** there's no hurry; cj in order that or to.

dämlich ['dɛ:mlɪç] a (col) silly, stupid.

Damm [dam] m **-(e)s, ¨e** dyke; (Stau—) dam; (Hafen—) mole; (Bahn—, Straßen—) embankment.

Dämm- ['dɛm] cpd: **d~en** vt Wasser dam up; Schmerzen keep back; **d~erig** a dim, faint; **d~ern** vi (Tag) dawn; (Abend) fall; ~**erung** f twilight; (Morgen—) dawn; (Abend—) dusk.

Dämon ['dɛ:mɔn] m **-s, -en** [dɛ'mo:nən] demon; **d~isch** [dɛ'mo:nɪʃ] a demoniacal.

Dampf [dampf] m **-(e)s, ¨e** steam; (Dunst) vapour; **d~en** vi steam.

dämpfen ['dɛmpfən] vt (Cook) steam; (bügeln auch) iron with a damp cloth; (fig) dampen, subdue.

Dampf- cpd: ~**er** m **-s**, - steamer; ~**kochtopf** m pressure cooker; ~**maschine** f steam engine; ~**schiff** nt steamship; ~**walze** f steamroller.

danach [da'na:x] ad after that; (zeitlich auch) afterwards; (gemäß) accordingly; according to which or that; **er sieht** ~ **aus** he looks it.

daneben [da'ne:bən] ad beside it; (im Vergleich) in comparison; ~**benehmen** vr irreg misbehave; ~**gehen** vi irreg miss; (Plan) fail.

Dank [daŋk] m **-(e)s** thanks pl; **vielen** or **schönen** ~ many thanks; **jdm** ~ **sagen** thank sb; **d~** prep +dat or gen thanks to; **d~bar** a grateful; Aufgabe rewarding; ~**barkeit** f gratitude; **d~e** interj thank you, thanks; **d~en** vi (+dat) thank; **d~enswert** a Arbeit worthwhile; rewarding; Bemühung kind; **d~sagen** vi express one's thanks.

dann [dan] ad then; ~ **und wann** now and then.

daran [da'ran] ad on it; (stoßen) against it; **es liegt** ~, **daß . . .** the cause of it is that . . .; **gut/schlecht** ~ **sein** be well-/badly off; **das Beste/Dümmste** ~ the best/stupidest thing about it; **ich war nahe** ~, **zu . . .** I was on the point of . . .; **er ist** ~ **. . . gestorben** he died from or of it; ~**gehen** vi irreg start; ~**setzen** vt stake; **er hat alles** ~**gesetzt, von Glasgow wegzukommen** he has done his utmost to get away from Glasgow.

darauf [da'rauf] ad (räumlich) on it; (zielgerichtet) towards it; (danach) afterwards; **es kommt ganz** ~ **an, ob . . .** it depends whether . . .; **die Tage ~** the days following *or* thereafter; **am Tag ~** the next day; **~folgend** *a* Tag, Jahr next, following; **~hin** [-'hın] *ad* (*im Hinblick darauf*) in this respect; (*aus diesem Grund*) as a result; **~legen** *vt* lay *or* put on top.

daraus [da'raus] *ad* from it; **was ist ~ geworden?** what became of it?; **~ geht hervor, daß ...** this means that ...

Darbietung ['da:rbi:toŋ] *f* performance.

darin [da'rın] *ad* in (there), in it.

Dar- ['da:r] *cpd:* **d~legen** *vt* explain, expound, set forth; **~legung** *f* explanation; **~leh(e)n** *nt* -s, - loan.

Darm [darm] *m* -(e)s, -e intestine; (*Wurst~*) skin; **~saite** *f* gut string.

Darstell- ['da:rʃtɛl] *cpd:* **d~en** *vt* (*abbilden, bedeuten*) represent; (*Theat*) act; (*beschreiben*) describe; *vr* appear to be; **~er(in** *f*) *m* -s, - actor/actress; **~ung** *f* portrayal, depiction.

darüber [da'ry:bər] *ad* (*räumlich*) over/above it; *fahren* over it; (*mehr*) more; (*währenddessen*) meanwhile; *sprechen, streiten* about it; **~ geht nichts** there's nothing like it; **seine Gedanken ~** his thoughts about *or* on it.

darum [da'rom] *ad* (*räumlich*) round it; **~ herum** round about (it); **er bittet ~** he is pleading for it; **es geht ~, daß** ... the thing is that . . .; **er würde viel ~ geben, wenn** . . . he would give a lot to . . .; *cj* that's why; **ich tue es, ~, weil** . . . I am doing it because . . .

darunter [da'runtər] *ad* (*räumlich*) under it; (*dazwischen*) among them; (*weniger*) less; **ein Stockwerk ~** one floor below (it); **was verstehen Sie ~?** what do you understand by that?; **~fallen** *vi irreg* be included; **~mischen** *vt* Mehl mix in; *vr* mingle.

das [das] *def art* the; *pron* that; **~ heißt** that is.

Dasein ['da:zaın] *nt* -s (*Leben*) life; (*Anwesenheit*) presence; (*Bestehen*) existence; **d~** *vi irreg* be there.

daß [das] *cj* that.

dasselbe [das'zɛlbə] *art, pron* the same.

dastehen ['da:ʃte:ən] *vi irreg* stand there.

Datenverarbeitung ['da:tənfɛr'arbaıtoŋ] *f* data processing.

datieren [da'ti:rən] *vt* date.

Dativ ['da:ti:f] *m* -s, -e dative.

Dattel ['datəl] *f* -, -n date.

Datum ['da:tom] *nt* -s, **Daten** date; (*pl: Angaben*) data *pl*; **das heutige ~** today's date.

Dauer ['dauər] *f* -, -n duration; (*gewisse Zeitspanne*) length; (*Bestand, Fortbestehen*) permanence; **es war nur von kurzer ~** it didn't last long; **auf die ~** in the long run; (*auf längere Zeit*) indefinitely; **~auftrag** *m* standing order; **d~haft** *a* lasting, durable; **~haftigkeit** *f* durability; **~karte** *f* season ticket; **~lauf** *m* long-distance run; **d~n** *vi* last; **es hat sehr lang gedauert, bis er** . . . it took him a long time to . . .; **d~nd** *a* constant; **~regen** *m* continuous rain; **~welle** *f* perm(anent wave); **~wurst** *f* German

salami; **~zustand** *m* permanent condition.

Daumen ['daumən] *m* -s, - thumb; **~lutscher** *m* thumb-sucker.

Daune ['daunə] *f* -, -n down; **~ndecke** *f* down duvet *or* quilt.

davon [da'fɔn] *ad* of it; (*räumlich*) away; (*weg von*) from it; (*Grund*) because of it; **das kommt ~!** that's what you get; **~ abgesehen** apart from that; **~ sprechen/wissen** talk/know of *or* about it; **was habe ich ~?** what's the point?; **~gehen** *vi irreg* leave, go away; **~kommen** *vi irreg* escape; **~laufen** *vi irreg* run away; **~tragen** *vt irreg* carry off; *Verletzung* receive.

davor [da'fo:r] *ad* (*räumlich*) in front of it; (*zeitlich*) before (that); **~ warnen** warn about it.

dazu [da'tsu:] *ad* legen, stellen by it; essen, singen with it; **und ~ noch** and in addition; **ein Beispiel/seine Gedanken ~** one example for/his thoughts on this; **wie komme ich denn ~?** why should I?; **~ fähig sein** be capable of it; **sich ~ äußern** say sth on it; **~gehören** *vi* belong to it; **~gehörig** *a* appropriate; **~kommen** *vi irreg* (*Ereignisse*) happen too; (*an einen Ort*) come along; **~mal** ['da:tsuma:l] *ad* in those days.

dazwischen [da'tsvıʃən] *ad* in between; (*räumlich auch*) between (them); (*zusammen mit*) among them; **der Unterschied ~** the difference between them; **~kommen** *vi irreg* (*hineingeraten*) get caught in it; **es ist etwas ~gekommen** something cropped up; **~reden** *vi* (*unterbrechen*) interrupt; (*sich einmischen*) interfere; **~treten** *vi irreg* intervene.

Debatte [de'batə] *f* -, -n debate.

Deck [dɛk] *nt* -(e)s, -s *or* -e deck; **an ~ gehen** go on deck; **~e** *f* -, -n cover; (*Bett~*) blanket; (*Tisch~*) tablecloth; (*Zimmer~*) ceiling; **unter einer ~ stecken** be hand in glove; **~el** *m* -s, - lid; **d~en** *vt* cover; *vr* coincide; **sie ~** lay the table; **~mantel** *m:* **unter dem ~mantel von** under the guise of; **~name** *m* assumed name; **~ung** *f* (*Schützen*) covering; (*Schutz*) cover; (*Sport*) defence; (*Übereinstimmen*) agreement; **d~ungsgleich** *a* congruent.

defekt [de'fɛkt] *m* -(e)s, -e fault, defect; **d~** *a* faulty.

defensiv [defɛn'si:f] *a* defensive.

definieren [defi'ni:rən] *vt* define.

Definition [definitsi'o:n] *f* definition.

definitiv [defini'ti:f] *a* definite.

Defizit ['de:fitsit] *nt* -s, -e deficit.

deftig ['dɛftıç] *a* Essen large; Witz coarse.

Degen ['de:gən] *m* -s, - sword.

degenerieren [degene'ri:rən] *vi* degenerate.

degradieren [degra'di:rən] *vt* degrade.

Dehn- [de:n] *cpd:* **d~bar** *a* elastic; (*fig*) Begriff loose; **~barkeit** *f* elasticity; looseness; **d~en** *vtr* stretch; **~ung** *f* stretching.

Deich [daıç] *m* -(e)s, -e dyke.

Deichsel ['daɪksəl] *f* -, -n shaft; d~n *vt* (*fig, col*) wangle.

dein [daɪn] *pron* (D~ *in Briefen*) your; ~e(r,s) yours; ~er *pron gen of* du of you; ~erseits ad on your part; ~esgleichen *pron* people like you; ~etwegen, ~etwillen ad (*für dich*) for your sake; (*wegen dir*) on your account; ~ige *pron*: der/die/das ~ige yours.

dekadent [deka'dɛnt] *a* decadent.

Dekadenz *f* decadence.

Dekan [de'ka:n] *m* -s, -e dean.

Deklination [deklinatsi'o:n] *f* declension.

deklinieren [dekli'ni:rən] *vt* decline.

Dekolleté [dekɔl'te:] *nt* -s, -s low neck-line.

Deko- [deko] *cpd*: ~rateur [-ra'tø:r] *m* window dresser; ~ration [-ratsi'o:n] *f* decoration; (*in Laden*) window dressing; d~rativ [-ra'ti:f] *a* decorative; d~rieren ['ri:rən] *vt* decorate; *Schaufenster* dress.

Delegation [delegatsi'o:n] *f* delegation.

delikat [deli'ka:t] *a* (*zart, heikel*) delicate; (*köstlich*) delicious.

Delikatesse [delika'tɛsə] *f* -, -n delicacy; (*pl: Feinkost*) delicatessen *pl*; ~n-geschäft *nt* delicatessen (shop).

Delikt [de'lɪkt] *nt* -(e)s, -e (*Jur*) offence.

Delle ['dɛlə] *f* -, -n (*col*) dent.

Delphin [dɛl'fi:n] *m* -s, -e dolphin.

Delta ['dɛltə] *nt* -s, -s delta.

dem [de(:)m] *art dat of* der.

Demagoge [dema'go:gə] *m* -n, -n demagogue.

Demarkationslinie [demarkatsi'o:nz-li:niə] *f* demarcation line.

dementieren [demɛn'ti:rən] *vt* deny.

dem- *cpd*: ~gemäß, ~nach ad accordingly; ~nächst ad shortly.

Demokrat [demo'kra:t] *m* -en, -en democrat; ~ie [-'ti:] *f* democracy; d~isch *a* democratic; d~isieren [-i'si:rən] *vt* democratize.

demolieren [demo'li:rən] *vt* demolish.

Demon- [demon] *cpd*: ~strant(in *f*) [-'strant(ɪn)] *m* demonstrator; ~stration [-stratsi'o:n] *f* demonstration; d~strativ [-stra'ti:f] *a* demonstrative; *Protest* pointed; d~strieren [-'stri:rən] *vti* demonstrate.

Demoskopie [demosko'pi:] *f* public opinion research.

Demut ['de:mu:t] *f* - humility.

demütig ['de:my:tɪç] *a* humble; ~en ['de:my:tɪgən] *vt* humiliate; D~ung *f* humiliation.

demzufolge ['de:mtsu'fɔlgə] ad accordingly.

den [de(:)n] *art acc of* der.

denen ['de:nən] *pron dat of* diese.

Denk- [dɛŋk] *cpd*: ~art *f* mentality; d~bar *a* conceivable; d~en *vti irreg* think; ~en *nt* -s thinking; ~er *m* -s, - thinker; ~fähigkeit *f* intelligence; d~faul *a* lazy; ~fehler *m* logical error; ~mal *nt* -s, 'er monument; d~würdig *a* memorable; ~zettel *m*: jdm einen ~zettel verpassen teach sb a lesson.

denn [dɛn] *cj* for; ad then; (*nach Komparativ*) than.

dennoch ['dɛn'nɔx] *cj* nevertheless.

Denunziant [denuntsi'ant] *m* informer.

deponieren [depo'ni:rən] *vt* (*Comm*) deposit.

Depot [de'po:] *nt* -s, -s warehouse; (*Bus*—, *Rail*) depot; (*Bank*—) strongroom.

Depression [deprɛsi'o:n] *f* depression.

deprimieren [depri'mi:rən] *vt* depress.

der [de(:)r] *def art* the; *rel pron* that, which; (*jemand*) who; *demon pron* this one; ~art ad so; (*solcher Art*) such; ~artig *a* such, this sort of.

derb [dɛrp] *a* sturdy; *Kost* solid; (*grob*) coarse; D~heit *f* sturdiness; solidity; coarseness.

der- *cpd*: '~'gleichen *pron* such; '~jenige *pron* he; she; it; (*rel*) the one (who); that (which); '~'maßen ad to such an extent, so; ~'selbe art, *pron* the same; '~'well(en) ad in the meantime; '~-'zeitig *a* present, current; (*damalig*) then.

des [dɛs] *art gen of* der.

Deserteur [dezɛr'tø:r] *m* deserter.

desertieren [dezɛr'ti:rən] *vi* desert.

desgleichen ['dɛs'glaɪçən] *pron* the same.

deshalb ['dɛs'halp] ad therefore, that's why.

Desinfektion [dezɪnfɛktsi'o:n] *f* disinfection; ~smittel *nt* disinfectant.

desinfizieren [dezɪnfi'tsi:rən] *vt* disinfect.

dessen ['dɛsən] *pron gen of* der, das; ~ungeachtet ad nevertheless, regardless.

Dessert [dɛ'sɛ:r] *nt* -s, -s dessert.

Destillation [dɛstɪlatsi'o:n] *f* distillation.

destillieren [dɛstɪ'li:rən] *vt* distil.

desto ['dɛsto] ad all or so much the; ~ besser all the better.

deswegen ['dɛs've:gən] *cj* therefore, hence.

Detail [de'taɪ] *nt* -s, -s detail; d~lieren [deta'ji:rən] *vt* specify, give details of.

Detektiv [detɛk'ti:f] *m* -s, -e detective.

Detektor [de'tɛktɔr] *m* (*Tech*) detector.

deut- ['dɔyt] *cpd*: ~en *vt* interpret, explain; *vi* point (auf +*acc* to or at); ~lich *a* clear; *Unterschied* distinct; D~lichkeit *f* clarity; distinctness; D~ung *f* interpretation.

Devise [de'vi:zə] *f* -, -n motto, device; (*pl: Fin*) foreign currency or exchange.

Dezember [de'tsɛmbər] *m* -(s), - December.

dezent [de'tsɛnt] *a* discreet.

dezimal [detsi'ma:l] *a* decimal; D~bruch *m* decimal (fraction); D~system *nt* decimal system.

Dia ['di:a] *nt* -s, -s *see* Diapositiv; ~betes [dia'be:tɛs] *m* -, - (*Med*) diabetes; ~gnose [dia'gno:zə] *f* -, -n diagnosis; d~gonal [diago'na:l] *a* diagonal; ~gonale *f* -, -n diagonal.

Dialekt [dia'lɛkt] *m* -(e)s, -e dialect; ~ausdruck *m* dialect expression/word; d~frei *a* pure, standard; d~isch *a* dialectal; *Logik* dialectical.

Dialog [dia'lo:k] *m* -(e)s, -e dialogue.

Diamant [dia'mant] *m* diamond.

Diapositiv [diapozi'ti:f] nt -s, -e (Phot) slide, transparency.

Diät [di'ɛ:t] f - diet; ~en pl (Pol) allowance.

dich [dıç] pron acc of du you; yourself.

dicht [dıçt] a dense; Nebel thick; Gewebe close; (undurchlässig) (water)tight; (fig) concise; ad: ~ an/bei close to; ~bevölkert a densely or heavily populated; D~e f -, -n density; thickness; closeness; (water)tightness; (fig) conciseness; ~en vt (dicht machen) make watertight; seal; (Naut) caulk; vti (Liter) compose, write; D~er(in f) m -s, - poet; (Autor) writer; ~erisch a poetical; ~halten vi irreg (col) keep mum; D~ung f (Tech) washer; (Aut) gasket; (Gedichte) poetry; (Prosa) (piece of) writing.

dick [dık] a thick; (fett) fat; durch ~ und dünn through thick and thin; D~e f -, -n thickness; fatness; ~fellig a thick-skinned; ~flüssig a viscous; D~icht nt -s, -e thicket; D~kopf m mule; D~milch f soured milk.

die [di:] def art see der.

Dieb(in f) [di:p/di:bın] m -(e)s, -e thief; d~isch a thieving; (col) immense; ~stahl m -(e)s, ⁓e theft.

Diele ['di:lə] f -, -n (Brett) board; (Flur) hall, lobby; (Eis—) ice-cream parlour; (Tanz—) dance hall.

dienen ['di:nən] vi serve (jdm sb).

Diener m -s, - servant; ~in f (maid) servant; ~schaft f servants pl.

Dienst [di:nst] m -(e)s, -e service; außer ~ retired; ~ haben be on duty; der öffentliche ~ the civil service; ~ag m Tuesday; d~ags ad on Tuesdays; ~bote m servant; d~eifrig a zealous; d~frei a off duty; ~geheimnis nt professional secret; ~gespräch nt business call; ~grad m rank; d~habend a Arzt on duty; d~lich a official; ~mädchen nt domestic servant; ~reise f business trip; ~stelle f office; d~tuend a on duty; ~vorschrift f service regulations pl; ~weg m official channels pl; ~zeit f office hours pl; (Mil) period of service.

dies- [di:s] cpd: ~bezüglich a Frage on this matter; ~e(r,s) [di:zə(r,z)] pron this (one); ~elbe [di:'zɛlbə] pron, art the same; D~elöl nt diesel oil; ~ig a drizzly; ~jährig a this year's; ~mal ad this time; ~seits prep +gen on this side; D~seits nt - this life.

Dietrich ['di:trıç] m -s, -e picklock.

differential [dıferɛntsi'a:l] a differential; D~getriebe nt differential gear; D~rechnung f differential calculus.

differenzieren [dıferɛn'tsi:rən] vt make differences in; **differenziert** complex.

Dikt- [dıkt] cpd: ~aphon [-a'fo:n] nt dictaphone; ~at [-'ta:t] nt -(e)s, -e dictation; ~ator [-'ta:tɔr] m dictator; d~atorisch [-a'to:rıʃ] a dictatorial; ~atur [-a'tu:r] f dictatorship; d~ieren [-'ti:rən] vt dictate.

Dilemma [di'lɛma] nt -s, -s or -ta dilemma.

Dilettant [dilɛ'tant] m dilettante, amateur;

d~isch a amateurish, dilettante.

Dimension [dimɛnzi'o:n] f dimension.

Ding [dıŋ] nt -(e)s, -e thing, object; d~lich a real, concrete; ~sbums ['dıŋksbums] nt - (col) thingummybob.

Diözese [diø'tse:zə] f -, -n diocese.

Diphtherie [dıfte'ri:] f diphtheria.

Diplom [di'plo:m] nt -(e)s, -e diploma, certificate; ~at [-'ma:t] m -en, -en diplomat; ~atie [-a'ti:] f diplomacy; d~atisch [-'ma:tıʃ] a diplomatic; ~ingenieur m qualified engineer.

dir [di:r] pron dat of du (to) you.

direkt [di'rɛkt] a direct; D~or m director; (Sch) principal, headmaster; D~orium [-'to:rium] nt board of directors; D~übertragung f live broadcast.

Dirigent [diri'gɛnt] m conductor.

dirigieren [diri'gi:rən] vt direct; (Mus) conduct.

Dirne ['dırnə] f -, -n prostitute.

Diskont [dıs'kɔnt] m -s, -e discount; ~satz m rate of discount.

Diskothek [dısko'te:k] f -, -en disco(theque).

Diskrepanz [dıskre'pants] f discrepancy.

diskret [dıs'kre:t] a discreet; D~ion [-tsi'o:n] f discretion.

Diskussion [dıskusi'o:n] f discussion; debate; zur ~ stehen be under discussion.

diskutabel [dısku'ta:bəl] a debatable.

diskutieren [dısku'ti:rən] vti discuss, debate.

Dissertation [dısɛrtatsi'o:n] f dissertation, doctoral thesis.

Distanz [dıs'tants] f distance.

Distel ['dıstəl] f -, -n thistle.

Disziplin [dıstsi'pli:n] f discipline.

divers [di'vɛrs] a various.

Dividende [divi'dɛndə] f -, -n dividend.

dividieren [divi'di:rən] vt divide (durch by).

doch [dɔx] ad: das ist nicht wahr! ≈ ~! that's not true! ≈ yes it is!; nicht ~! oh no!; er kam ~ noch he came after all; cj (aber) but; (trotzdem) all the same.

Docht [dɔxt] m -(e)s, -e wick.

Dock [dɔk] nt -s, -s or -e dock.

Dogge ['dɔgə] f -, -n bulldog.

Dogma ['dɔgma] nt -s, -men dogma; d~tisch [dɔ'gma:tıʃ] a dogmatic.

Doktor ['dɔktɔr] m -s, -en [-'to:rən] doctor; ~and [-'rant] m -en, -en candidate for a doctorate; ~arbeit f doctoral thesis; ~titel m doctorate.

Dokument [doku'mɛnt] nt document; ~arbericht [-'ta:rbəriçt] m documentary; ~arfilm m documentary (film); d~arisch a documentary.

Dolch [dɔlç] m -(e)s, -e dagger.

dolmetschen ['dɔlmɛtʃən] vti interpret.

Dolmetscher(in f) m -s, - interpreter.

Dom [do:m] m -(e)s, -e cathedral.

dominieren [domi'ni:rən] vt dominate; vi predominate.

Dompfaff ['do:mpfaf] m bullfinch.

Dompteur [dɔmp'tø:r] m, **Dompteuse** [dɔmp'tø:zə] f (Zirkus) trainer.

Donner ['dɔnər] m -s, - thunder; d~n vi impers thunder; ~stag m Thursday; ~wetter nt thunderstorm; (fig) dressing-down; interj good heavens!

doof [do:f] a (col) daft, stupid.

Doppel ['dɔpəl] nt -s, - duplicate; (Sport) doubles; ~bett nt double bed; ~fenster nt double glazing; ~gänger m -s, - double; ~punkt m colon; d~sinnig a ambiguous; ~stecker m two-way adaptor; d~t a double; in d~ter Ausführung in duplicate; ~verdiener pl two-income family; ~zentner m 100 kilograms; ~zimmer nt double room.

Dorf [dɔrf] nt -(e)s, ¨er village; ~bewohner m villager.

Dorn [dɔrn] m -(e)s, -en (Bot) thorn; pl -e (Schnallen—) tongue, pin; d~ig a thorny; ~röschen nt Sleeping Beauty.

dörren ['dœrən] vt dry.

Dörrobst ['dœro:pst] nt dried fruit.

Dorsch [dɔrʃ] m -(e)s, -e cod.

dort [dɔrt] ad there; ~ drüben over there; ~her from there; ~hin (to) there; ~ig a of that place; in that town.

Dose ['do:zə] f -, -n box; (Blech—) tin, can; ~nöffner m tin or can opener.

dösen ['dø:zən] vi (col) doze.

Dosis ['do:zɪs] f -, Dosen dose.

Dotter ['dɔtər] m -s, - egg yolk.

Dozent [do'tsɛnt] m university lecturer.

Drache ['draxə] m -n, -n (Tier) dragon; ~n m -, - kite.

Draht [dra:t] m -(e)s, ¨e wire; auf ~ sein be on the ball; ~gitter nt wire grating; ~seil nt cable; ~seilbahn f cable railway, funicular; ~zange f pliers pl.

drall [dral] a strapping; Frau buxom.

Drama ['dra:ma] nt -s, Dramen drama, play; ~tiker [-'ma:tikər] m -s, - dramatist; d~tisch [-'ma:tɪʃ] a dramatic.

dran [dran] ad (col) see daran.

Drang [draŋ] m -(e)s, ¨e (Trieb) impulse, urge, desire (nach for); (Druck) pressure.

drängeln ['drɛŋəln] vti push, jostle.

drängen ['drɛŋən] vt (schieben) push, press; (antreiben) urge; vi (eilig sein) be urgent; (Zeit) press; auf etw (acc) ~ press for sth.

drastisch ['drastɪʃ] a drastic.

drauf [drauf] ad (col) see darauf; D~gänger m -s, - daredevil.

draußen ['drausən] ad outside, out-of-doors.

Dreck [drɛk] m -(e)s mud, dirt; d~ig a dirty, filthy.

Dreh- ['dre:] cpd: ~achse f axis of rotation; ~arbeiten pl (Cine) shooting; ~bank f lathe; d~bar a revolving; ~buch nt (Cine) script; d~en vti turn, rotate; Zigaretten roll; Film shoot; vr turn; (handeln von) be (um about); ~orgel f barrel organ; ~tür f revolving door; ~ung f (Rotation) rotation; (Um—, Wendung) turn; ~wurm m (col) den ~ wurm haben/bekommen be/become dizzy; ~zahl f rate of revolutions; ~zahlmesser m rev(olution) counter.

drei [drai] num three; D~eck nt triangle; ~eckig a triangular; ~einhalb num three and a half; D~einigkeit [-'ainɪçkait] f, D~faltigkeit [-'faltɪçkait] f Trinity; ~erlei a inv of three kinds; ~fach a,ad triple, treble; ~hundert num three hundred; D~königsfest nt Epiphany; ~mal ad three times; thrice; ~malig a three times.

dreinreden ['drainre:dən] vi: jdm ~ (dazwischenreden) interrupt sb; (sich einmischen) interfere with sb.

dreißig ['draisɪç] num thirty.

dreist [draist] a bold, audacious; D~igkeit f boldness, audacity.

drei- cpd: ~viertel num three-quarters; D~viertelstunde f three-quarters of an hour; ~zehn num thirteen.

dreschen ['drɛʃən] vt irreg thresh.

dressieren [drɛ'si:rən] vt train.

Drill- ['dril] cpd: ~bohrer m light drill; d~en vt (bohren) drill, bore; (Mil) drill; (fig) train; ~ing m triplet.

drin [drin] ad (col) see darin.

dringen ['drɪŋən] vi irreg (Wasser, Licht, Kälte) penetrate (durch through; in +acc into); auf etw (acc) ~ insist on sth; in jdn ~ entreat sb.

dringend ['drɪŋənt], **dringlich** ['drɪŋlɪç] a urgent.

Dringlichkeit f urgency.

drinnen ['drinən] ad inside, indoors.

dritte(r,s) ['drɪtə(r,z)] a third; D~l nt -s, - third; ~ns ad thirdly.

droben ['dro:bən] ad above, up there.

Droge ['dro:gə] f -, -n drug; d~nabhängig a addicted to drugs; ~rie [-'ri:] f chemist's shop.

Drogist [dro'gɪst] m pharmacist, chemist.

drohen ['dro:ən] vi threaten (jdm sb).

dröhnen ['drø:nən] vi (Motor) roar; (Stimme, Musik) ring, resound.

Drohung ['dro:ʊŋ] f threat.

drollig ['drɔlɪç] a droll.

Droschke ['drɔʃkə] f -, -n cab; ~nkutscher m cabman.

Drossel ['drɔsəl] f -, -n thrush.

drüben ['dry:bən] ad over there, on the other side.

drüber ['dry:bər] ad (col) see darüber.

Druck [druk] m -(e)s, -e (Phys, Zwang) pressure; (Print) (Vorgang) printing; (Produkt) print; (fig: Belastung) burden, weight; ~buchstabe m block letter.

Drück- ['dryk] cpd: ~eberger m -s, - shirker, dodger; d~en vti Knopf, Hand press; (zu eng sein) pinch; (fig) Preise keep down; (fig: belasten) oppress, weigh down; jdm etw in die Hand d~en press sth into sb's hand; vr: sich vor etw (dat) d~en get out of (doing) sth; d~end a oppressive; ~er m -s, - button; (Tür—) handle; (Gewehr—) trigger.

Druck- cpd: ~er m -s, - printer; ~erei f printing works, press; ~erschwärze f printer's ink; ~fehler m misprint; ~knopf m press stud, snap fastener; ~mittel nt leverage; ~sache f printed matter; ~schrift f block or printed letters pl.

drunten ['drʊntən] ad below, down there.

Drüse ['dry:zə] f -, -n gland.

Dschungel ['dʒʊŋəl] *m* -s, - jungle.

du [duː] *pron* (D~ *in Briefen*) you.

ducken ['dukən] *vt Kopf, Person* duck; (*fig*) take down a peg or two; ~ *vr* duck.

Duckmäuser ['dukmɔʏzər] *m* -s, - yesman.

Dudelsack ['duːdəlzak] *m* bagpipes *pl*.

Duell [du'ɛl] *nt* -s, -e duel.

Duett [du'ɛt] *nt* -(e)s, -e duet.

Duft [duft] *m* -(e)s, ²e scent, odour; d~en *vi* smell, be fragrant; d~ig *a Stoff, Kleid* delicate, diaphanous; *Muster* fine.

duld- ['duld] *cpd*: ~en *vti* suffer; (*zulassen*) tolerate; ~sam *a* tolerant.

dumm [dum] *a* stupid; **das wird mir zu** ~ that's just too much; **der D~e sein** be the loser; ~**dreist** *a* impudent; ~**erweise** *ad* stupidly; **D~heit** *f* stupidity; (*Tat*) blunder, stupid mistake; **D~kopf** *m* blockhead.

dumpf [dumpf] *a Ton* hollow, dull; *Luft* close; *Erinnerung, Schmerz* vague; **D~heit** *f* hollowness, dullness; closeness, vagueness; ~**ig** *a* musty.

Düne ['dyːnə] *f* -, -n dune.

Dung [duŋ] *m* -(e)s *see* **Dünger**

düngen ['dyŋən] *vt* manure.

Dünger ['dyŋər] *m* -s, - dung, manure; (*künstlich*) fertilizer.

dunkel ['duŋkəl] *a* dark; *Stimme* deep; *Ahnung* vague; (*rätselhaft*) obscure; (*verdächtig*) dubious, shady; **im** ~**n tappen** (*fig*) grope in the dark.

Dünkel ['dyŋkəl] *m* -s self-conceit; d~**haft** *a* conceited.

Dunkel- *cpd*: ~**heit** *f* darkness; (*fig*) obscurity; ~**kammer** *f* (*Phot*) dark room; d~n *vi impers* grow dark; ~**ziffer** *f* estimated number of unnotified cases.

dünn [dyn] *a* thin; ~**flüssig** *a* watery, thin; ~**gesät** *a* scarce; **D~heit** *f* thinness.

Dunst [dunst] *m* -es, ²e vapour; (*Wetter*) haze.

dünsten ['dynstən] *vt* steam.

dunstig ['dunstɪç] *a* vaporous; *Wetter* hazy, misty.

Duplikat [dupli'kaːt] *nt* -(e)s, -e duplicate.

Dur [duːr] *nt* -, - (*Mus*) major.

durch [durç] *prep* +*acc* through; (*Mittel, Ursache*) by; (*Zeit*) during; **den Sommer** ~ during the summer; **8 Uhr** ~ **past 8 o'clock**; ~ **und** ~ completely; ~**arbeiten** *vti* work through; *vr* work one's way through; ~**'aus** *ad* completely; (*unbedingt*) definitely; ~**beißen** *irreg vt* bite through; *vr* (*fig*) battle on; ~**blättern** *vt* leaf through.

Durchblick ['durçblɪk] *m* view; (*fig*) comprehension; d~en *vi* look through; (*col: verstehen*) understand (*bei etw* sth); **etw d~en lassen** (*fig*) hint at sth.

durch'bohren *vt insep* bore through, pierce.

durchbrechen ['durçbrɛçən] *vti irreg* break; [durç'brɛçən] *vt irreg insep Schranken* break through; *Schallmauer* break; *Gewohnheit* break free from.

durch- ['durç] *cpd*: ~**brennen** *vi irreg* (*Draht, Sicherung*) burn through; (*col*) run

away; ~**bringen** *irreg vt* get through; *Geld* squander; *vr* make a living.

Durchbruch ['durçbrux] *m* (*Öffnung*) opening; (*Mil*) breach; (*von Gefühlen etc*) eruption; (*der Zähne*) cutting; (*fig*) breakthrough; **zum** ~ **kommen** break through.

durch- *cpd*: ~**dacht** [durç'daxt] *a* well thought-out; ~**'denken** *vt irreg insep* think out.

durch- ['durç] *cpd*: ~**diskutieren** *vt* talk over, discuss; ~**drängen** *vr* force one's way through; ~**drehen** *vt Fleisch* mince; *vi* (*col*) crack up.

durchdringen ['durçdrɪŋən] *vi irreg* penetrate, get through; **mit etw** ~ get one's way with sth; [durç'drɪŋən] *vt irreg insep* penetrate.

durcheinander [durç'aɪ'nandər] *ad* in a mess, in confusion; (*col: verwirrt*) confused; ~ **trinken** mix one's drinks; **D~nt** -s (*Verwirrung*) confusion; (*Unordnung*) mess; ~**bringen** *vt irreg* mess up; (*verwirren*) confuse; ~**reden** *vi* talk at the same time.

durch- ['durç] *cpd*: **D~fahrt** *f* transit; (*Verkehr*) thoroughfare; **D~fall** *m* (*Med*) diarrhoea; ~**fallen** *vi irreg* fall through; (*in Prüfung*) fail; ~**finden** *vr irreg* find one's way through.

durch'forschen *vt insep* explore.

durch- ['durç] *cpd*: ~**fressen** *vt irreg* eat through; ~**fragen** *vr* find one's way by asking.

durchführ- ['durçfyːr] *cpd*: ~**bar** *a* feasible, practicable; ~**en** *vt* carry out; **D~ung** *f* execution, performance.

Durchgang ['durçgaŋ] *m* passage(way); (*bei Produktion, Versuch*) run; (*Sport*) round; (*bei Wahl*) ballot; ~ **verboten** no thoroughfare; ~**handel** *m* transit trade; ~**slager** *nt* transit camp; ~**sstadium** *nt* transitory stage; ~**sverkehr** *m* through traffic.

durchgefroren ['durçgefroːrən] *a See* completely frozen; *Mensch* frozen stiff.

durchgehen ['durçgeːən] *irreg vt* (*behandeln*) go over; *vi* go through; (*ausreißen: Pferd*) break loose; (*Mensch*) run away; **mein Temperament ging mit mir durch** my temper got the better of me; **jdm etw** ~ **lassen** let sb get away with sth; ~**d** *a Zug* through; *Öffnungszeiten* continuous.

durch- ['durç] *cpd*: ~**greifen** *vi irreg* take strong action; ~**halten** *irreg vi* last out; *vt* keep up; ~**hecheln** *vt* (*col*) gossip about; ~**kommen** *vi irreg* get through; (*überleben*) pull through.

durch'kreuzen *vt insep* thwart, frustrate.

durch- ['durç] *cpd*: ~**lassen** *vt irreg Person* let through; *Wasser* let in; ~**lässig** *a* leaky; **D~lauf(wasser)erhitzer** *m* -s, - (hot water) geyser.

durch- *cpd*: ~**leben** *vt insep* live or go through, experience; ~**lesen** *vt irreg* read through; ~**'leuchten** *vt insep* X-ray; ~**löchern** [-'lœçərn] *vt insep* perforate; (*mit Löchern*) punch holes in; (*mit Kugeln*) riddle; ~**machen** *vt* go through; **die Nacht** ~**machen** make a night of it.

Durch- ['durç] *cpd*: ~**marsch** *m* march through; ~**messer** *m* -s, - diameter.

durch'nässen *vt insep* soak (through).

durch- ['durç] *cpd*: ~**nehmen** *vt irreg* go over; ~**numerieren** *vt* number consecutively; ~**pausen** *vt* trace; ~**peitschen** *vt* (*lit*) whip soundly; (*fig*) *Gesetzentwurf, Reform* force through.

durchqueren [durç'kve:rən] *vt insep* cross.

durch- ['durç] *cpd*: **D~reiche** *f* -, -n (serving) hatch; **D~reise** *f* transit; **auf der D~reise** passing through; *Güter* in transit; ~**ringen** *vr irreg* reach after a long struggle; ~**rosten** *vi* rust through.

durchs [durçs] = **durch das.**

Durchsage ['durçza:gə] *f* -, -n intercom or radio announcement.

durchschauen ['durçʃauən] *vi* (*lit*) look or see through; [durç'ʃauən] *vt insep* *Person, Lüge* see through.

durchscheinen ['durçʃainən] *vi irreg* shine through; ~**d** *a* translucent.

Durchschlag ['durçʃla:k] *m* (*Doppel*) carbon copy; (*Sieb*) strainer; **d~en** *irreg vt* (*entzweischlagen*) split (in two); (*sieben*) sieve; *vi* (*zum Vorschein kommen*) emerge, come out; *vr* get by; **d~end** a resounding.

durch ['durç] *cpd*: ~**schlüpfen** *vi* slip through; ~**schneiden** *vt irreg* cut through.

Durchschnitt ['durçʃnit] *m* (*Mittelwert*) average; **über/unter dem** ~ above/below average; **im** ~ on average; **d~lich** *a* average; *ad* on average; ~**sgeschwindigkeit** *f* average speed; ~**smensch** *m* average man, man in the street; ~**swert** *m* average.

durch- *cpd*: '**D~schrift** *f* copy; ~**'schwimmen** *vt irreg insep* swim across; '~**sehen** *vt irreg* look through.

durchsetzen ['durçzetsən] *vt* enforce; **seinen Kopf** ~ get one's own way; *vr* (*Erfolg haben*) succeed; (*sich behaupten*) get one's way; [durç'zetsən] *vt insep* mix.

Durchsicht ['durçzɪçt] *f* looking through, checking; **d~ig** *a* transparent; ~**igkeit** *f* transparence.

durch- *cpd*: '~**sickern** *vi* seep through; (*fig*) leak out; '~**sieben** *vt* sieve; '~**sprechen** *vt irreg* talk over; '~**stehen** *vt irreg* live through; ~**stöbern** [-'ʃtø:bərn] *vt insep* ransack, search through; '~**streichen** *vt irreg* cross out; ~**'suchen** *vt insep* search; **D~'suchung** *f* search; ~**tränken** *vt insep* soak; ~**trieben** [-'tri:bən] *a* cunning, wily; '~**wachsen** *a* (*lit*) *Speck* streaky; (*fig*: *mittelmäßig*) so-so.

durch- ['durç] *cpd*: ~**weg** *ad* throughout, completely; ~**zählen** *vt* count; *vi* count off; ~**ziehen** *irreg vt* *Faden* draw through; *vi* pass through.

durch- *cpd*: ~**'zucken** *vt insep* shoot or flash through; '**D~zug** *m* (*Luft*) draught; (*von Truppen, Vögeln*) passage; ~**'zwingen** *vtr* squeeze or force through.

dürfen ['dyrfən] *vi irreg* be allowed; **darf ich?** may I?; **es darf geraucht werden** you may smoke; **was darf es sein?** what

can I do for you?; **das darf nicht geschehen** that must not happen; **das** ~ **Sie mir glauben** you can believe me; **es dürfte Ihnen bekannt sein, daß ... as** you will probably know ...

dürftig ['dyrftɪç] *a* (*ärmlich*) needy, poor; (*unzulänglich*) inadequate.

dürr [dyr] *a* dried-up; *Land* arid; (*mager*) skinny, gaunt; **D~e** *f* -, -n aridity; (*Zeit*) drought; (*Magerkeit*) skinniness.

Durst [durst] *m* -(e)s thirst; ~ **haben** be thirsty; **d~ig** *a* thirsty.

Dusche ['duʃə] *f* -, -n shower; **d~n** *vir* have a shower.

Düse ['dy:zə] *f* -, -n nozzle; (*Flugzeug—*) jet; ~**nantrieb** *m* jet propulsion; ~**nflugzeug** *nt* jet (plane); ~**njäger** *m* jet fighter.

Dussel ['dusəl] *m* -s, - (*col*) twit.

düster ['dy:stər] *a* dark; *Gedanken, Zukunft* gloomy; **D~keit** *f* darkness, gloom; gloominess.

Dutzend ['dutsənt] *nt* -s, -e dozen; **d~(e)mal** *ad* a dozen times; ~**mensch** *m* man in the street; **d~weise** *ad* by the dozen.

duzen ['du:tsən] *vtr* use the familiar form of address or 'du' (*jdn* to or with sb).

Dynamik [dy'na:mɪk] *f* (*Phys*) dynamics; (*fig*: *Schwung*) momentum; (*von Mensch*) dynamism.

dynamisch [dy'na:mɪʃ] *a* (*lit, fig*) dynamic.

Dynamit [dyna'mi:t] *nt* -s dynamite.

Dynamo [dy'na:mo] *m* -s, -s dynamo.

D-Zug ['de:tsu:k] *m* through train.

E

E, e [e:] *nt* E, e.

Ebbe ['ebə] *f* -, -n low tide.

eben ['e:bən] *a* level; (*glatt*) smooth; *ad* just; (*bestätigend*) exactly; ~**deswegen** just because of that; ~**bürtig** *a*: **jdm** ~**bürtig sein** be sb's peer; **E~e** *f* -, -n plain; ~**erdig** *a* at ground level; ~**falls** *ad* likewise; **E~heit** *f* levelness; smoothness; ~**so** *ad* just as; ~**sogut** *ad* just as well; ~**sooft** *ad* just as often; ~**soviel** *ad* just as much; ~**soweit** *ad* just as far; ~**sowenig** *ad* just as little.

Eber ['e:bər] *m* -s, - boar; ~**esche** *f* mountain ash, rowan.

ebnen ['e:bnən] *vt* level.

Echo ['eço] *nt* -s, -s echo.

echt [eçt] *a* genuine; (*typisch*) typical; **E~heit** *f* genuineness.

Eck- ['ek] *cpd*: ~**ball** *m* corner (kick); ~**e** *f* -, -n corner; (*Math*) angle; **e~ig** *a* angular; ~**zahn** *m* eye tooth.

edel ['e:dəl] *a* noble; **E~metall** *nt* rare metal; **E~stein** *m* precious stone.

Efeu ['e:foy] *m* -s ivy.

Effekt- [e'fekt] *cpd*: ~**en** *pl* stocks *pl*; ~**enbörse** *f* Stock Exchange; ~**hasche-'rei** *f* sensationalism; **e~iv** [-'ti:f] *a* effective, actual.

egal [e'ga:l] *a* all the same.

Ego- [ego] *cpd*: ~**ismus** [-'ɪsmus] *m* selfishness, egoism; ~**ist** [-'ɪst] *m* egoist;

e~**istisch** a selfish, egoistic; e~**zentrisch** [-'tsɛntrɪʃ] a egocentric, self-centred.

Ehe ['e:ə] f -, -n marriage; e~ cj before; ~**brecher** m -s, - adulterer; ~**brecherin** f adulteress; ~**bruch** m adultery; ~**frau** f married woman; wife; ~**leute** pl married people pl; e~**lich** a matrimonial; Kind legitimate; e~**malig** a former; e~**mals** ad formerly; ~**mann** m married man; husband; ~**paar** nt married couple.

eher ['e:ər] ad (früher) sooner; (lieber) rather, sooner; (mehr) more.

Ehe- cpd: ~**ring** m wedding ring; ~**scheidung** f divorce; ~**schließung** f marriage.

eheste(r,s) ['e:əstə(r,z)] a (früheste) first, earliest; am ~**n** (liebsten) soonest; (meist) most; (wahrscheinlich) most probably.

Ehr- ['e:r] cpd: e~**bar** a honourable, respectable; e~ f -, -n honour; e~**en** vt honour; ~**engast** m guest of honour; e~**enhaft** a honourable; ~**enmann** m man of honour; ~**enmitglied** nt honorary member; ~**enplatz** m place of honour; ~**enrechte** pl civic rights pl; e~**enrührig** a defamatory; ~**enrunde** f lap of honour; ~**ensache** f point of honour; e~**envoll** a honourable; ~**enwort** nt word of honour; e~**erbietig** a respectful; ~**furcht** f awe, deep respect; ~**gefühl** nt sense of honour; ~**geiz** m ambition; e~**geizig** a ambitious; e~**lich** a honest; ~**lichkeit** f honesty; e~**los** a dishonourable; ~**ung** f honour(ing); e~**würdig** a venerable.

Ei [ai] nt -(e)s, -er egg; e~ interj well, well; (beschwichtigend) now, now.

Eich- ['aiç] cpd: ~**amt** nt Office of Weights and Measures; ~**e** f -, -n oak (tree); ~**el** f -, -n acorn; (Cards) club; e~**en** vt standardize; ~**hörnchen** nt squirrel; ~**maß** nt standard; ~**ung** f standardization.

Eid ['ait] m -(e)s, -e oath; ~**echse** ['aidɛksə] f -, -n lizard; e~**esstattliche Erklärung** affidavit; ~**genosse** m Swiss; e~**lich** a (sworn) upon oath.

Ei- cpd: ~**dotter** nt egg yolk; ~**erbecher** m eggcup; ~**erkuchen** m omelette; pancake; ~**erschale** f eggshell; ~**erstock** m ovary; ~**eruhr** f egg timer.

Eifer ['aifər] m -s zeal, enthusiasm; ~**sucht** f jealousy; e~**süchtig** a jealous (auf +acc of).

eifrig ['aifriç] a zealous, enthusiastic.

Eigelb ['aigɛlp] nt -(e)s, - egg yolk.

eigen ['aigən] a own; (-artig) peculiar; **mit der/dem ihm ~en ...** with that ... peculiar to him; **sich** (dat) **etw zu ~ machen** make sth one's own; E~**art** f peculiarity; characteristic; ~**artig** a peculiar; E~**bedarf** m one's own requirements pl; E~**gewicht** nt dead weight; ~**händig** a with one's own hand; E~**heim** nt owner-occupied house; E~**heit** f peculiarity; E~**lob** nt self-praise; ~**mächtig** a high-handed; E~**name** m proper name; ~**s** ad

expressly, on purpose; E~**schaft** f quality, property, attribute; E~**schaftswort** nt adjective; E~**sinn** m obstinacy; ~**sinnig** a obstinate; ~**tlich** a actual, real; ad actually, really; E~**tor** nt own goal; E~**tum** nt property; E~**tümer(in** f) m -s, - owner, proprietor; ~**tümlich** a peculiar; E~**tümlichkeit** f peculiarity; E~**tumswohnung** f freehold flat.

eignen ['aignən] vr be suited.

Eignung f suitability.

Eil- ['ail] cpd: ~**bote** m courier; ~**brief** m express letter; ~**e** f -, haste; **es hat keine ~e** there's no hurry; e~**en** vi (Mensch) hurry; (dringend sein) be urgent; e~**ends** ad hastily; e~**fertig** a eager, solicitous; ~**gut** nt express goods pl, fast freight (US); e~**ig** a hasty, hurried; (dringlich) urgent; **es e~ig haben** be in a hurry; ~**zug** m semi-fast train, limited stop train.

Eimer ['aimər] m -s, - bucket, pail.

ein(e) [ain(ə)] num one; indef art a, an; ad: **nicht ~ noch aus wissen** not know what to do; ~**e(r,s)** pron one; (jemand) someone.

einander [ai'nandər] pron one another, each other.

einarbeiten ['ainarbaitən] vr familiarize o.s. (in +acc with).

einarmig ['ain'armiç] a one-armed.

einatmen ['aina:tmən] vti inhale, breathe in.

einäugig ['ain'ɔygiç] a one-eyed.

Einbahnstraße ['ainba:nʃtrasə] f one-way street.

Einband ['ainbant] m binding, cover.

einbändig ['ainbɛndiç] a one-volume.

einbau- ['ainbau] cpd: ~**en** vt build in; Motor install, fit; E~**möbel** pl built-in furniture.

einbe- ['ainbə] cpd: ~**griffen** a included, inclusive; ~**rufen** vt irreg convene; (Mil) call up; E~**rufung** f convocation; call-up.

einbett- ['ainbɛt] cpd: ~**en** vt embed; E~**zimmer** nt single room.

einbeziehen ['ainbətsi:ən] vt irreg include.

einbiegen ['ainbi:gən] vi irreg turn.

einbilden ['ainbildən] vt: **sich** (dat) **etw ~** imagine sth.

Einbildung f imagination; (Dünkel) conceit; ~**skraft** f imagination.

einbinden ['ainbindən] vt irreg bind (up).

einblenden ['ainblɛndən] vt fade in.

einbleuen ['ainblɔyən] vt (col) **jdm etw ~** hammer sth into sb.

Einblick ['ainblik] m insight.

einbrechen ['ainbrɛçən] vi irreg (in Haus) break in; (in Land etc) invade; (Nacht) fall; (Winter) set in; (durchbrechen) break.

Einbrecher m -s, - burglar.

einbringen ['ainbriŋən] vt irreg bring in; Geld, Vorteil yield; (mitbringen) contribute.

Einbruch ['ainbrux] m (Haus—) break-in, burglary; (Eindringen) invasion; (des Winters) onset; (Durchbrechen) break; (Met) approach; (Mil) penetration; ~ **der Nacht** nightfall; e~**ssicher** a burglar-proof.

einbürgern ['ainbyrgərn] vt naturalize; vr

become adopted; **das hat sich so eingebürgert** that's become a custom.

Einbuße ['aɪnbuːsə] *f* loss, forfeiture.

einbüßen ['aɪnbyːsən] *vt* lose, forfeit.

eindecken ['aɪndɛkən] *vr* lay in stocks (*mit etl*).

eindeutig ['aɪndɔʏtɪç] *a* unequivocal.

eindring- ['aɪndrɪŋ] *cpd:* ~**en** *vi irreg* (*in +acc*) force one's way in(to); (*in Haus*) break in(to); (*in Land*) invade; (*Gas, Wasser*) penetrate; (*mit Bitten*) pester (*auf jdn sb*); ~**lich** *a* forcible, urgent; **E**~**ling** *m* intruder.

Eindruck ['aɪndrʊk] *m* impression; **e**~**sfähig** *a* impressionable; **e**~**svoll** *a* impressive.

eindrücken ['aɪndrʏkən] *vt* press in.

eineilig ['aɪnaɪlɪç] *a* Zwillinge identical.

eineinhalb ['aɪn'aɪn'halp] *num* one and a half.

einengen ['aɪn'ɛŋən] *vt* confine, restrict.

einer- ['aɪnər] *cpd:* **E**~**lei** *nt* -s sameness; ~**lei** *a* (*gleichartig*) the same kind of; **es ist mir** ~**lei** it is all the same to me; ~**seits** *ad* on one hand.

einfach ['aɪnfax] *a* (*Idee*) simple; (*nicht mehrfach*) single; *ad* simply; **E**~**heit** *f* simplicity.

einfädeln ['aɪnfɛːdəln] *vt* Nadel thread; (*fig*) contrive.

einfahren ['aɪnfaːrən] *irreg vt* bring in; Barriere knock down; Auto run in; *vi* drive in; (*Zug*) pull in; (*Min*) go down.

Einfahrt *f* (*Vorgang*) driving in; pulling in; (*Min*) descent; (*Ort*) entrance.

Einfall ['aɪnfal] *m* (*Idee*) idea, notion; (*Licht*—) incidence; (*Mil*) raid; **e**~**en** *vi irreg* (*Licht*) fall; (*Mil*) raid; (*einstimmen*) join in (*in +acc with*); (*einstürzen*) fall in, collapse; **etw fällt jdm ein** sth occurs to sb; **das fällt mir gar nicht ein** I wouldn't dream of it; **sich** (*dat*) **etwas e**~**en lassen** have a good idea.

einfältig ['aɪnfɛltɪç] *a* simple(-minded).

Einfamilienhaus [aɪnfa'miːliənhaʊs] *nt* detached house.

einfangen ['aɪnfaŋən] *vt irreg* catch.

einfarbig ['aɪnfarbɪç] *a* all one colour; Stoff etc self-coloured.

einfass- ['aɪnfas] *cpd:* ~**en** *vt* set; Beet enclose; Stoff edge, border; Bier barrel; **E**~**ung** *f* setting; enclosure; barrelling.

einfetten ['aɪnfɛtən] *vt* grease.

einfinden ['aɪnfɪndən] *vr irreg* come, turn up.

einfliegen ['aɪnfliːgən] *vt irreg* fly in.

einfließen ['aɪnfliːsən] *vi irreg* flow in.

einflößen ['aɪnfløːsən] *vt:* **jdm etw** ~ (*lit*) give sb sth; (*fig*) instil sth in sb.

Einfluß ['aɪnflʊs] *m* influence; ~**bereich** *m* sphere of influence; **e**~**reich** *a* influential.

einförmig ['aɪnfœrmɪç] *a* uniform; **E**~**keit** *f* uniformity.

einfrieren ['aɪnfriːrən] *irreg vi* freeze (in); *vt* freeze.

einfügen ['aɪnfyːgən] *vt* fit in; (*zusätzlich*) add.

Einfuhr ['aɪnfuːr] *f* - import; ~**artikel** *m* imported article.

einführ- ['aɪnfyːr] *cpd:* ~**en** *vt* bring in; Mensch, Sitten introduce; Ware import; **E**~**ung** *f* introduction; **E**~**ungspreis** *m* introductory price.

Eingabe ['aɪngaːbə] *f* petition; (*Daten*—) input.

Eingang ['aɪngaŋ] *m* entrance; (*Comm: Ankunft*) arrival; (*Sendung*) post; **e**~**s** *ad, prep +gen* at the outset (of); ~**sbestätigung** *f* acknowledgement of receipt; ~**shalle** *f* entrance hall.

eingeben ['aɪngeːbən] *vt irreg* Arznei give; Daten etc feed; Gedanken inspire.

eingebildet ['aɪngəbɪldət] *a* imaginary; (*eitel*) conceited.

Eingeborene(r) ['aɪngəboːrənə(r)] *mf* native.

Eingebung *f* inspiration.

einge- ['aɪngə] *cpd:* ~**denk** *prep +gen* bearing in mind; ~**fallen** *a* Gesicht gaunt; ~**fleischt** *a* inveterate; ~**fleischter Junggeselle** confirmed bachelor; ~**froren** *a* frozen.

eingehen ['aɪngeːən] *irreg vi* (*Aufnahme finden*) come in; (*verständlich sein*) be comprehensible (*jdm* to sb); (*Sendung, Geld*) be received; (*Tier, Pflanze*) die; (*Firma*) fold; (*schrumpfen*) shrink; **auf etw** (*acc*) ~ go into sth; **auf jdn** ~ respond to sb; *vt* enter into; Wette make; ~**d** *a* exhaustive, thorough.

einge- ['aɪngə] *cpd:* **E**~**machte(s)** *nt* preserves *pl;* ~**meinden** *vt* incorporate; ~**nommen** *a* (*von*) fond (of), partial (to); (*gegen*) prejudiced; ~**schrieben** *a* registered; ~**sessen** *a* old-established; ~**spielt** *a:* **aufeinander** ~**spielt sein** be in tune with each other; **E**~**ständnis** *nt* -ses, -se admission, confession; ~**stehen** *vt irreg* confess; ~**tragen** *a* (*Comm*) registered; **E**~**weide** *nt* -s, - innards *pl*, intestines *pl;* **E**~**weihte(r)** *mf* initiate; ~**wöhnen** *vt* accustom.

eingießen ['aɪngiːsən] *vt irreg* pour (out).

eingleisig ['aɪnglaɪzɪç] *a* single-track.

eingraben ['aɪngraːbən] *irreg vt* dig in; *vr* dig o.s. in.

eingreifen ['aɪngraɪfən] *vi irreg* intervene, interfere; (*Zahnrad*) mesh.

Eingriff ['aɪngrɪf] *m* intervention, interference; (*Operation*) operation.

einhaken ['aɪnhaːkən] *vt* hook in; *vr:* **sich bei jdm** ~ link arms with sb; *vi* (*sich einmischen*) intervene.

Einhalt ['aɪnhalt] *m:* ~ **gebieten** (+*dat*) put a stop to; **e**~**en** *irreg vt* Regel keep; *vi* stop.

einhändig ['aɪnhɛndɪç] *a* one-handed; ~**en** [-dɪgən] *vt* hand in.

einhängen ['aɪnhɛŋən] *vt* hang; Telefon (*auch vi*) hang up; **sich bei jdm** ~ link arms with sb.

einheim- ['aɪnhaɪm] *cpd:* ~**isch** *a* native; ~**sen** *vt* (*col*) bring home.

Einheit ['aɪnhaɪt] *f* unity; (*Maß, Mil*) unit; **e**~**lich** *a* uniform; ~**spreis** *m* uniform price.

einhellig ['aɪnhɛlɪç] *a,ad* unanimous.

einholen ['aɪnhoːlən] vt Tau haul in; Fahne, Segel lower; (Vorsprung aufholen) catch up with; Verspätung make up; Rat, Erlaubnis ask; vi (einkaufen) buy, shop.

Einhorn ['aɪnhɔrn] nt unicorn.

einhüllen ['aɪnhʏlən] vt wrap up.

einig ['aɪnɪç] a (vereint) united; **sich** (dat) ~ **sein** in agreement; ~ **werden** agree; ~**e** ['aɪnɪgə] pl some; (mehrere) several; ~**e(r,s)** a some; (mehrere) a few times; ~**en** vt unite; vr agree (auf +acc on); ~**ermaßen** ad somewhat; (leidlich) reasonably; ~**es** pron something; ~**gehen** vi irreg agree; **E~keit** f unity; (Übereinstimmung) agreement; **E~ung** f agreement; (Vereinigung) unification.

einimpfen ['aɪnɪmpfən] vt inoculate (jdm etw sb with sth); (fig) impress (jdm etw sth upon sb).

einjährig ['aɪnjɛːrɪç] a of or for one year; (Alter) one-year-old; Pflanze annual.

einkalkulieren ['aɪnkalkuliːrən] vt take into account, allow for.

Einkauf ['aɪnkaʊf] m purchase; **e~en** vt buy; vi go shopping; ~**sbummel** m shopping spree; ~**snetz** nt string bag; ~**spreis** m cost price.

einkerben ['aɪnkɛrbən] vt notch.

einklammern ['aɪnklamərn] vt put in brackets, bracket.

Einklang ['aɪnklaŋ] m harmony.

einkleiden ['aɪnklaɪdən] vt clothe; (fig) express.

einklemmen ['aɪnklɛmən] vt jam.

einknicken ['aɪnknɪkən] vt bend in; Papier fold; vi give way.

einkochen ['aɪnkɔxən] vt boil down; Obst preserve, bottle.

Einkommen ['aɪnkɔmən] nt **-s,** - income; ~**(s)steuer** f income tax.

einkreisen ['aɪnkraɪzən] vt encircle.

Einkünfte ['aɪnkʏnftə] pl income, revenue.

einlad- ['aɪnlaːd] cpd: ~**en** vt irreg Person invite; Gegenstände load; **jdn ins Kino** ~**en** take sb to the cinema; **E~ung** f invitation.

Einlage ['aɪnlaːgə] f (Programm—) interlude; (Spar—) deposit; (Schuh—) insole; (Fußstütze) support; (Zahn—) temporary filling; (Cook) noodles pl, vegetables pl etc in soup; **e~rn** vt store.

Einlaß ['aɪnlas] m **-sses, -lässe** admission.

einlassen irreg vt let in; (einsetzen) set in; vr: **sich mit jdm/auf etw** (acc) ~ get involved with sb/sth.

Einlauf ['aɪnlaʊf] m arrival; (von Pferden) finish; (Med) enema; **e~en** irreg vi arrive, come in; (in Hafen) enter; (Sport) finish; (Wasser) run in; (Stoff) shrink; vt Schuhe break in; **jdm das Haus e~en** invade sb's house; vr (Sport) warm up; (Motor, Maschine) run in.

einleben ['aɪnleːbən] vr settle down.

Einlege- ['aɪnleːgə] cpd: ~**arbeit** f inlay; **e~n** vt (einfügen) Blatt, Sohle insert; (Cook) pickle; (in Holz etc) inlay; Geld deposit; Pause have; Protest make; Veto use; Berufung lodge; **ein gutes Wort bei jdm e~n** put in a good word with sb; ~**sohle** f insole.

einleiten ['aɪnlaɪtən] vt introduce, start; Geburt induce.

Einleitung f introduction; induction.

einleuchten ['aɪnlɔyçtən] vi be clear or evident (jdm to sb); ~**d** a clear.

einliefern ['aɪnliːfərn] vt take (in +acc into).

einlösen ['aɪnløːzən] vt Scheck cash; Schuldschein, Pfand redeem; Versprechen keep.

einmachen ['aɪnmaxən] vt preserve.

einmal ['aɪnmaːl] ad once; (erstens) first; (zukünftig) sometime; **nehmen wir ~ an** just let's suppose; **noch ~** once more; **nicht ~** not even; **auf ~** all at once; **es war ~** once upon a time there was/were; **E~'eins** nt multiplication tables pl; ~**ig** a unique; (einmal geschehend) single; (prima) fantastic.

Einmann- ['aɪnman] cpd: ~**betrieb** m one-man business; ~**bus** m one-man-operated bus.

Einmarsch ['aɪnmarʃ] m entry; (Mil) invasion; **e~ieren** vi march in.

einmengen ['aɪnmɛŋən], **einmischen** ['aɪnmɪʃən] vr interfere (in +acc with).

einmünden ['aɪnmʏndən] vi run (in +acc into), join.

einmütig ['aɪnmyːtɪç] a unanimous.

Einnahme ['aɪnnaːmə] f **-, -n** (Geld) takings pl, revenue; (von Medizin) taking; (Mil) capture, taking; ~**quelle** f source of income.

einnehmen ['aɪnneːmən] vt irreg take; Stellung, Raum take up; ~ **für/gegen** persuade in favour of/against; ~**d** a charming.

einnicken ['aɪnnɪkən] vi nod off.

einnisten ['aɪnnɪstən] vr nest; (fig) settle o.s.

Einöde ['aɪnˈøːdə] f **-, -n** desert, wilderness.

einordnen ['aɪnˈɔrdnən] vt arrange, fit in; vr adapt; (Aut) get into lane.

einpacken ['aɪnpakən] vt pack (up).

einparken ['aɪnparkən] vt park.

einpendeln ['aɪnpɛndəln] vr even out.

einpferchen ['aɪnpfɛrçən] vt pen in, coop up.

einpflanzen ['aɪnpflantsən] vt plant; (Med) implant.

einplanen ['aɪnplaːnən] vt plan for.

einpräg- ['aɪnprɛːg] cpd: ~**en** vt impress, imprint; (beibringen) impress (jdm on sb); **sich** (dat) **etw ~en** memorize sth; ~**sam** a easy to remember; Melodie catchy.

einrahmen ['aɪnraːmən] vt frame.

einrasten ['aɪnrastən] vi engage.

einräumen ['aɪnrɔymən] vt (ordnend) put away; (überlassen) Platz give up; (zugestehen) admit, concede.

einrechnen ['aɪnrɛçnən] vt include; (berücksichtigen) take into account.

einreden ['aɪnreːdən] vt: **jdm/sich etw ~** talk sb/o.s. into believing sth.

einreiben ['aɪnraɪbən] vt irreg rub in.

einreichen ['aɪnraɪçən] vt hand in; Antrag submit.

Einreise ['aɪnraɪzə] f entry; ~**bestimmungen** pl entry regulations pl; ~**erlaubnis** f, ~**genehmigung** f entry permit; e~**n** vi enter (in ein Land a country).

einreißen ['aɪnraɪsən] vt irreg Papier tear; Gebäude pull down; vi tear; (Gewohnheit werden) catch on.

einrichten ['aɪnrɪçtən] vt Haus furnish; (schaffen) establish, set up; (arrangieren) arrange; (möglich machen) manage; vr (in Haus) furnish one's house; (sich vorbereiten) prepare o.s. (auf +acc for); (sich anpassen) adapt (auf +acc to).

Einrichtung f (Wohnungs—) furnishings pl; (öffentliche Anstalt) organization; (Dienste) service.

einrosten ['aɪnrɔstən] vi get rusty.

einrücken ['aɪnrykən] vi (Mil) (Soldat) join up; (in Land) move in; vt Anzeige insert; Zeile indent.

Eins [aɪns] f -, -en one; e~ num one; es ist mir alles e~ it's all one to me.

einsalzen ['aɪnzaltsən] vt salt.

einsam ['aɪnza:m] a lonely, solitary; E~**keit** f loneliness, solitude.

einsammeln ['aɪnzaməln] vt collect.

Einsatz ['aɪnzats] m (Teil) inset; (an Kleid) insertion; (Tisch) leaf; (Verwendung) use, employment; (Spiel—) stake; (Risiko) risk; (Mil) operation; (Mus) entry; im ~ in action; e~**bereit** a ready for action.

einschalten ['aɪnʃaltən] vt (einfügen) insert; Pause make; (Elec) switch on; (Aut) Gang engage; Anwalt bring in; vr (dazwischentreten) intervene.

einschärfen ['aɪnʃɛrfən] vt impress (jdm etw vth on sb).

einschätzen ['aɪnʃɛtsən] vt estimate, assess; vr rate o.s.

einschenken ['aɪnʃɛŋkən] vt pour out.

einschicken ['aɪnʃɪkən] vt send in.

einschieben ['aɪnʃi:bən] vt irreg push in; (zusätzlich) insert.

einschiffen ['aɪnʃɪfən] vt take on board; vr embark, go on board.

einschlafen ['aɪnʃla:fən] vi irreg fall asleep, go to sleep.

einschläfernd ['aɪnʃlɛ:fərnt] a (Med) soporific; (langweilig) boring; Stimme lulling.

Einschlag ['aɪnʃla:k] m impact; (Aut) lock; (fig Beimischung) touch, hint; e~**en** irreg vt knock in; Fenster smash, break; Zähne, Schädel smash in; Steuer turn; (kürzer machen) take up; Ware pack, wrap up; Weg, Richtung take; vi hit (in etw (acc) sth, auf jdn sb); (sich einigen) agree; (Anklang finden) work, succeed.

einschlägig ['aɪnʃlɛ:gɪç] a relevant.

einschleichen ['aɪnʃlaɪçən] vr irreg (in Haus, Fehler) creep in, steal in; (in Vertrauen) worm one's way in.

einschließen ['aɪnʃli:sən] irreg vt Kind lock in; Häftling lock up; Gegenstand lock away; Bergleute cut off; (umgeben) surround; (Mil) encircle; (fig) include, comprise; vr lock o.s. in.

einschließlich ad inclusive; prep +gen inclusive of, including.

einschmeicheln ['aɪnʃmaɪçəln] vr ingratiate o.s. (bei with).

einschnappen ['aɪnʃnapən] vi (Tür) click to; (fig) be touchy; **eingeschnappt sein** be in a huff.

einschneidend ['aɪnʃnaɪdənt] a incisive.

Einschnitt ['aɪnʃnɪt] m cutting; (Med) incision; (Ereignis) incident.

einschränken ['aɪnʃrɛŋkən] vt limit, restrict; Kosten cut down, reduce; vr cut down (on expenditure); ~**d** a restrictive.

Einschränkung f restriction, limitation; reduction; (von Behauptung) qualification.

Einschreib- ['aɪnʃraɪb] cpd: ~**(e)brief** m recorded delivery letter; e~**en** irreg vt write in; Post send recorded delivery; vr register; (Univ) enrol; ~**en** nt recorded delivery letter; ~**(e)sendung** f recorded delivery packet.

einschreiten ['aɪnʃraɪtən] vi irreg step in, intervene; ~ **gegen** take action against.

Einschub ['aɪnʃu:p] m -s, ²e insertion.

einschüchtern ['aɪnʃyçtərn] vt intimidate.

einsehen ['aɪnze:ən] vt irreg (hineinsehen in) realize; Akten have a look at; (verstehen) see; E~ nt -s understanding; **ein E~ haben** show understanding.

einseifen ['aɪnzaɪfən] vt soap, lather; (fig) take in, cheat.

einseitig ['aɪnzaɪtɪç] a one-sided; E~**keit** f one-sidedness.

Einsend- ['aɪnzɛnd] cpd: e~**en** vt irreg send in; ~**er** m -s, - sender, contributor; ~**ung** f sending in.

einsetzen ['aɪnzɛtsən] vt put (in); (in Amt) appoint, install; Geld stake; (verwenden) use; (Mil) employ; vi (beginnen) set in; (Mus) enter, come in; vr work hard; **sich für jdn/etw ~** support sb/sth.

Einsicht ['aɪnzɪçt] f insight; (in Akten) look, inspection; **zu der ~ kommen, daß** ... come to the conclusion that ...; e~**ig** a Mensch judicious; ~**nahme** f -, -n examination; e~**slos** a unreasonable; e~**svoll** a understanding.

Einsiedler ['aɪnzi:dlər] m hermit.

einsilbig ['aɪnzɪlbɪç] a (lit,fig) monosyllabic; E~**keit** f (fig) taciturnity.

einsinken ['aɪnzɪŋkən] vi irreg sink in.

Einsitzer ['aɪnzɪtsər] m -s, - single-seater.

einspannen ['aɪnʃpanən] vt Werkstück, Papier put (in), insert; Pferde harness; (col) Person rope in.

einsperren ['aɪnʃpɛrən] vt lock up.

einspielen ['aɪnʃpi:lən] vr (Sport) warm up; **sich aufeinander ~** become attuned to each other; vt (Film) Geld bring in; Instrument play in; **gut eingespielt** smoothly running.

einspringen ['aɪnʃprɪŋən] vi irreg (aushelfen) help out, step into the breach.

einspritzen ['aɪnʃprɪtsən] vt inject.

Einspruch ['aɪnʃprux] m protest, objection; ~**srecht** nt veto.

einspurig ['aɪnʃpu:rɪç] a single-line.

einst [aɪnst] ad once; (zukünftig) one or some day.

Einstand ['aɪnʃtant] m (Tennis) deuce;

(*Antritt*) entrance (to office).
einstechen ['aɪnʃtɛçən] *vt irreg* stick in.
einstecken ['aɪnʃtɛkən] *vt* stick in, insert; *Brief* post; (*Elec*) *Stecker* plug in; *Geld* pocket; (*mitnehmen*) take; (*überlegen sein*) put in the shade; (*hinnehmen*) swallow.
einstehen ['aɪnʃteːən] *vi irreg* guarantee (*für jdn/etw* sb/sth); (*verantworten*) answer (*für* for).
einsteigen ['aɪnʃtaɪgən] *vi irreg* get in *or* on; (*in Schiff*) go on board; (*sich beteiligen*) come in; (*hineinklettern*) climb in.
einstell- ['aɪnʃtɛl] *cpd*: ~**bar** *a* adjustable; ~**en** *vti* (*aufhören*) stop; *Geräte* adjust; *Kamera etc* focus; *Sender, Radio* tune in; (*unterstellen*) put; (*in Firma*) employ, take on; *vr* (*anfangen*) set in; (*kommen*) arrive; **sich auf jdn/etw** ~**en** adapt to sb/prepare o.s. for sth; **E~ung** *f* (*Aufhören*) suspension, cessation; adjustment; focusing; (*von Arbeiter etc*) appointment; (*Haltung*) attitude.
Einstieg ['aɪnʃtiːk] *m* -(e)s, -e entry; (*fig*) approach.
einstig ['aɪnstɪç] *a* former.
einstimm- ['aɪnʃtɪm] *cpd*: ~**en** *vi* join in; *vt* (*Mus*) tune; (*in Stimmung bringen*) put in the mood; ~**ig** *a* unanimous; (*Mus*) for one voice; **E~igkeit** *f* unanimity.
einst- ['aɪnst] *cpd*: ~**malig** *a* former; ~**mals** *ad* once, formerly.
einstöckig ['aɪnʃtœkɪç] *a* single-storeyed.
einstudieren ['aɪnʃtudiːrən] *vt* study, rehearse.
einstündig ['aɪnʃtʏndɪç] *a* one-hour.
einstürmen ['aɪnʃtʏrmən] *vi*: **auf jdn** ~ rush at sb; (*Eindrücke*) overwhelm sb.
Einsturz ['aɪnʃtʊrts] *m* collapse; ~**gefahr** *f* danger of collapse.
einstürzen ['aɪnʃtʏrtsən] *vi* fall in, collapse.
einst- ['aɪnst] *cpd*: ~**weilen** *ad* meanwhile; (*vorläufig*) temporarily, for the time being; ~**weilig** *a* temporary.
eintägig ['aɪntɛːgɪç] *a* one-day.
eintauchen ['aɪntauxən] *vt* immerse, dip in; *vi* dive.
eintauschen ['aɪntauʃən] *vt* exchange.
eintausend ['aɪntauzənt] *num* one thousand.
einteil- ['aɪntaɪl] *cpd*: ~**en** *vt* (*in Teile*) divide (up); *Menschen* assign; ~**ig** *a* one-piece.
eintönig ['aɪntøːnɪç] *a* monotonous; **E~keit** *f* monotony.
Eintopf(gericht *nt*) ['aɪntɔpf(gərɪçt)] *m* stew.
Eintracht ['aɪntraxt] *f* - concord, harmony.
einträchtig ['aɪntrɛçtɪç] *a* harmonious.
Eintrag ['aɪntraːk] *m* -(e)s, -e entry; **amtlicher** ~ entry in the register; **e~en** *irreg vt* (*in Buch*) enter; *Profit* yield; **jdm etw e~en** bring sb sth; *vr* put one's name down.
einträglich ['aɪntrɛːklɪç] *a* profitable.
eintreffen ['aɪntrɛfən] *vi irreg* happen; (*ankommen*) arrive.
eintreten ['aɪntreːtən] *irreg vi* occur; (*hineingehen*) enter (*in etw* (*acc*) sth); (*sich*

einsetzen) intercede; (*in Club, Partei*) join (*in etw* (*acc*) sth); (*in Stadium etc*) enter; *vt Tür* kick open.
Eintritt ['aɪntrɪt] *m* (*Betreten*) entrance; (*Anfang*) commencement; (*in Club etc*) joining; ~**sgeld** *nt*, ~**spreis** *m* charge for admission; ~**skarte** *f* (admission) ticket.
eintrocknen ['aɪntrɔknən] *vi* dry up.
einüben ['aɪnˈyːbən] *vt* practise, drill.
einver- ['aɪnfɛr] *cpd*: ~**leiben** *vt* incorporate; *Gebiet* annex; **sich** (*dat*) **etw** ~**leiben** (*fig*: *geistig*) acquire; **E~nehmen** *nt* -s, - agreement, understanding; ~**standen** *interj* agreed; a: ~**standen sein** agree, be agreed; **E~ständnis** *nt* understanding; (*gleiche Meinung*) agreement.
Einwand ['aɪnvant] *m* -(e)s, -e objection; ~**erer** ['aɪnvandərər] *m* immigrant; **e~ern** *vi* immigrate; ~**erung** *f* immigration; **e~frei** *a* perfect; *ad* absolutely.
einwärts ['aɪnvɛrts] *ad* inwards.
einwecken ['aɪnvɛkən] *vt* bottle, preserve.
Einwegflasche ['aɪnveːˌgflaʃə] *f* no-deposit bottle.
einweichen ['aɪnvaɪçən] *vt* soak.
einweih- ['aɪnvaɪ] *cpd*: ~**en** *vt Kirche* consecrate; *Brücke* open; *Gebäude* inaugurate; *Person* initiate (*in* +*acc* in); **E~ung** *f* consecration; opening; inauguration; initiation.
einweis- ['aɪnvaɪz] *cpd*: ~**en** *vt irreg* (*in Amt*) install; (*in Arbeit*) introduce; (*in Anstalt*) send; **E~ung** *f* installation; introduction; sending.
einwenden ['aɪnvɛndən] *vt irreg* object, oppose (*gegen* to).
einwerfen ['aɪnvɛrfən] *vt irreg* throw in; *Brief* post; *Geld* put in, insert; *Fenster* smash; (*äußern*) interpose.
einwickeln ['aɪnvɪkəln] *vt* wrap up; (*fig col*) outsmart.
einwillig- ['aɪnvɪlɪg] *cpd*: ~**en** *vi* consent, agree (*in* +*acc* to); **E~ung** *f* consent.
einwirk- ['aɪnvɪrk] *cpd*: ~**en** *vi*: **auf jdn/etw** ~**en** influence sb/sth; **E~ung** *f* influence.
Einwohner ['aɪnvoːnər] *m* -s, - inhabitant; ~'**meldeamt** *nt* registration office; ~**schaft** *f* population, inhabitants *pl*.
Einwurf ['aɪnvʊrf] *m* (*Öffnung*) slot; (*Einwand*) objection; (*Sport*) throw-in.
Einzahl ['aɪntsaːl] *f* singular; **e~en** *vt* pay in; ~**ung** *f* paying in.
einzäunen ['aɪntsɔynən] *vt* fence in.
einzeichnen ['aɪntsaɪçnən] *vt* draw in.
Einzel ['aɪntsəl] *nt* -s, - (*Tennis*) singles; *in cpds* individual; single; ~**bett** *nt* single bed; ~**fall** *m* single instance, individual case; ~**haft** *f* solitary confinement; ~**heit** *f* particular, detail; **e~n** a single; (*vereinzelt*) the odd; *ad* singly; **e~n angeben** specify; **der/die e~ne** the individual; **das e~ne** the particular; **ins e~ne gehen** go into detail(s); ~**teil** *nt* component (part); ~**zimmer** *nt* single room.
einziehen ['aɪntsiːən] *irreg vt* draw in, take in; *Kopf* duck; *Fühler, Antenne, Fahrgestell*

retract; *Steuern, Erkundigungen* collect; (*Mil*) draft, call up; (*aus dem Verkehr ziehen*) withdraw; (*konfiszieren*) confiscate; *vi* move in(to); (*Friede, Ruhe*) come; (*Flüssigkeit*) penetrate.

einzig ['aıntsıç] *a* only; (*ohnegleichen*) unique; **das ~e** the only thing; **der/die ~e** the only one; **~artig** *a* unique.

Einzug ['aıntsuːk] *m* entry, moving in.

Eis [aıs] *-es,* - ice; (*Speise—*) ice cream; **~bahn** *f* ice *or* skating rink; **~bär** *m* polar bear; **~becher** *m* sundae; **~bein** *nt* pig's trotters *pl*; **~berg** *m* iceberg; **~blumen** *pl* ice fern; **~decke** *f* sheet of ice; **~diele** *f* ice-cream parlour.

Eisen ['aızən] *nt -s,* - iron; **~bahn** *f* railway, railroad (*US*); **~bahner** *m -s,* - railwayman, railway employee, railroader (*US*); **~bahnschaffner** *m* railway guard; **~bahnübergang** *m* level crossing, grade crossing (*US*); **~bahnwagen** *m* railway carriage; **~erz** *nt* iron ore; **e~haltig** *a* containing iron.

eisern ['aızərn] *a* iron; *Gesundheit* robust; *Energie* unrelenting; *Reserve* emergency.

Eis- *cpd:* **e~frei** a clear of ice; **~hockey** *nt* ice hockey; **e~ig** ['aızıç] a icy; **e~kalt** a icy cold; **~kunstlauf** *m* figure skating; **~laufen** *nt* ice skating; **~läufer(in** *f) m* ice-skater; **~pickel** *m* ice-axe; **~schießen** *nt* ≈ curling; **~schrank** *m* fridge, ice-box (*US*); **~zapfen** *m* icicle; **~zeit** *f* ice age.

eitel ['aıtəl] *a* vain; **E~keit** *f* vanity.

Eiter ['aıtər] *m -s* pus; **e~ig** a suppurating; **e~n** *vi* suppurate.

Ei- [aı] *cpd:* **~weiß** *nt -es, -e* white of an egg; **~zelle** *f* ovum.

Ekel ['eːkəl] *m -s* nausea, disgust; *nt -s,* - (*col: Mensch*) nauseating person; **e~erregend,** **e~haft, ek(e)lig** a nauseating, disgusting; **e~n** *vt* disgust; **es ekelt jdn** *or* **jdm** *sb* is disgusted; *vr* loathe, be disgusted (*vor* +*dat* at).

Ekstase [ɛk'staːzə] *f -,* -n ecstasy.

Ekzem [ɛk'tseːm] *nt -s, -e* (*Med*) eczema.

Elan [e'laː] *m -s* elan.

elastisch [e'lastıʃ] a elastic.

Elastizität [elastitsi'tɛːt] *f* elasticity.

Elch [ɛlç] *m -(e)s, -e* elk.

Elefant [ele'fant] *m* elephant.

elegant [ele'gant] a elegant.

Eleganz [ele'gants] *f* elegance.

Elek- ['eːlek] *cpd:* **~trifizierung** [-trifi'tsiːruŋ] *f* electrification; **~triker** [-triːkər] *m -s,* - electrician; **e~trisch** [-trıʃ] a electric; **e~trisieren** [-tri'ziːrən] *vt* (*lit, fig*) electrify; *Mensch* give an electric shock to; *vr* get an electric shock; **~trizität** [-tritsi'tɛt] *f* electricity; **~trizitätswerk** *nt* electricity works, power plant.

Elektro- [e'lɛktro] *cpd:* **~de** [ɛlɛk'troːdə] *f -, -n* electrode; **~herd** *m* electric cooker; **~lyse** [-'lyːzə] *f -, -n* electrolysis; **~n** [-ɔn] *nt -s, -en* electron; **~nen(ge)hirn** [ɛlɛk'troːnən-] *nt* electronic brain; **~nenrechner** *m* computer; **e~nisch** a electronic; **~rasierer** *m -s,* - electric razor.

Element [ele'mɛnt] *nt -s, -e* element; (*Elec*) cell, battery; **e~ar** [-'taːr] a elementary; (*naturhaft*) elemental.

Elend ['eːlɛnt] *nt -(e)s* misery; **e~** a miserable; **e~iglich** ['eːlɛnd-] *ad* miserably; **~sviertel** *nt* slum.

elf [ɛlf] *num* eleven; **E~** *f -, -en* (*Sport*) eleven; **E~e** *f -, -n* elf; **E~enbein** *nt* ivory; **E~meter** *m* (*Sport*) penalty (kick).

eliminieren [elimi'niːrən] *vt* eliminate.

Elite [e'liːtə] *f -,* -n elite.

Elixier [elɪ'ksiːr] *nt -s, -e* elixir.

Ell- *cpd:* **~e** ['ɛlə] *f -, -n* ell; (*Maß*) yard; **~(en)bogen** *m* elbow; **~ipse** [ɛ'lɪpsə] *f -, -n* ellipse.

Elster ['ɛlstər] *f -, -n* magpie.

Elter- ['ɛltər] *cpd:* **e~lich** a parental; **~n** *pl* parents *pl*; **~nhaus** *nt* home; **e~nlos** a parentless.

Email [e'maːj] *nt -s, -s* enamel; **e~lieren** [emaji'rən] *vt* enamel.

Emanzipation [emantsipatsi'oːn] *f* emancipation.

emanzipieren *vt* emancipate.

Embryo ['ɛmbryo] *m -s, -nen* embryo.

Emi- [emi] *cpd:* **~grant** [-'grant] *m* emigrant; **~gration** [-gratsi'oːn] *f* emigration; **e~grieren** [-'griːrən] *vi* emigrate.

Empfang [ɛm'pfaŋ] *m -(e)s, -e* reception; (*Erhalten*) receipt; **in ~ nehmen** receive; **e~en** *irreg vt* receive; *vi* (*schwanger werden*) conceive.

Empfäng- [ɛm'pfɛŋ] *cpd:* **~er** *m -s,* - receiver; (*Comm*) addressee, consignee; **e~lich** a receptive, susceptible; **~nis** *f -, -se* conception; **~nisverhütung** *f* contraception.

Empfangs- *cpd:* **~bestätigung** *f* acknowledgement; **~dame** *f* receptionist; **~schein** *m* receipt; **~zimmer** *nt* reception room.

empfehlen [ɛm'pfeːlən] *irreg vt* recommend; *vr* take one's leave; **~swert** a recommendable.

Empfehlung *f* recommendation; **~sschreiben** *nt* letter of recommendation.

empfind- [ɛm'pfınt] *cpd:* **~en** [ɛm'pfındən] *vt irreg* feel; **~lich** a sensitive; *Stelle* sore; (*reizbar*) touchy; **E~lichkeit** *f* sensitiveness; (*Reizbarkeit*) touchiness; **~sam** a sentimental; **E~ung** *f* feeling, sentiment; **~ungslos** a unfeeling, insensitive.

empor [ɛm'poːr] *ad* up, upwards.

empören [ɛm'pøːrən] *vt* make indignant; shock; *vr* become indignant; **~d** a outrageous.

empor- *cpd:* **~kommen** *vi irreg* rise; succeed; **E~kömmling** *m* upstart, parvenu.

Empörung *f* indignation.

emsig ['ɛmzıç] a diligent, busy.

End- ['ɛnt] *in cpds* final; **~auswertung** *f* final analysis; **~bahnhof** ['ɛnt-] *m* terminus; **~e** *nt -s, -n* end; **am ~e** at the end; (*schließlich*) in the end; **am ~e sein** be at the end of one's tether; **~e Dezember** at the end of December; **zu**

~e sein be finished; e~en vi end; e~gültig a final, definite; ~ivie [ɛnˈdiːviə] f endive; e~lich a final; (Math) finite; ad finally; e~lich! at last!; e~los a endless, infinite; ~spiel nt final(s); ~spurt m (Sport) final spurt; ~station f terminus; ~ung f ending.

Energie [enɛrˈgiː] f energy; e~los a lacking in energy, weak; ~wirtschaft f energy industry.

energisch [eˈnɛrgɪʃ] a energetic.

eng [ɛŋ] a narrow; Kleidung tight; (fig) Horizont auch limited; Freundschaft, Verhältnis close; ~ an etw (dat) close to sth.

Engagement [ãgaʒəˈmãː] nt -s, -s engagement; (Verpflichtung) commitment.

engagieren [ãgaˈʒiːrən] vt engage; ein engagierter Schriftsteller a committed writer; vr commit o.s.

Enge [ˈɛŋə] f -, -n (lit,fig) narrowness; (Land—) defile; (Meer—) straits pl; jdn in die ~ treiben drive sb into a corner.

Engel [ˈɛŋəl] m -s, - angel; e~haft a angelic; ~macher m -s, - (col) backstreet abortionist.

eng- cpd: ~herzig a petty; E~paß m defile, pass; (fig, Verkehr) bottleneck.

en gros [ãˈgro] ad wholesale.

engstirnig [ˈɛŋʃtɪrnɪç] a narrow-minded.

Enkel [ˈɛŋkəl] m -s, - grandson; ~in f granddaughter; ~kind nt grandchild.

en masse [ãˈmas] ad en masse.

enorm [eˈnɔrm] a enormous.

Ensemble [ãˈsãbəl] nt -s, -s company, ensemble.

entarten [ɛntˈʔaːrtən] vi degenerate.

entbehr- [ɛntˈbeːr] cpd: ~en vt do without, dispense with; ~lich a superfluous; E~ung f privation.

entbinden [ɛntˈbɪndən] irreg vt release (gen from); (Med) deliver; vi (Med) give birth.

Entbindung f release; (Med) confinement; ~sheim nt maternity hospital.

entblößen [ɛntˈbløːsən] vt denude, uncover; (berauben) deprive (gen of).

entdeck- [ɛntˈdɛk] cpd: ~en vt discover; jdm etw ~en disclose sth to sb; E~er m -s, - discoverer; E~ung f discovery.

Ente [ˈɛntə] f -, -n duck; (fig) canard, false report.

entehren [ɛntˈʔeːrən] vt dishonour, disgrace.

enteignen [ɛntˈʔaɪgnən] vt expropriate; Besitzer dispossess.

enteisen [ɛntˈʔaɪzən] vt de-ice, defrost.

enterben [ɛntˈʔɛrbən] vt disinherit.

entfachen [ɛntˈfaxən] vt kindle.

entfallen [ɛntˈfalən] vi irreg drop, fall; (wegfallen) be dropped; jdm ~ (vergessen) slip sb's memory; auf jdn ~ be allotted to sb.

entfalten [ɛntˈfaltən] vt unfold; Talente develop; vr open; (Mensch) develop one's potential.

Entfaltung f unfolding; (von Talenten) development.

entfern- [ɛntˈfɛrn] cpd: ~en vt remove; (hinauswerfen) expel; vr go away, retire, withdraw; ~t a distant; weit davon ~t sein, etw zu tun be far from doing sth; E~ung f distance; (Wegschaffen) removal; E~ungsmesser m -s, - (Phot) rangefinder.

entfesseln [ɛntˈfɛsəln] vt (fig) arouse.

entfetten [ɛntˈfɛtən] vt take the fat from.

entfremd- [ɛntˈfrɛmd] cpd: ~en vt estrange, alienate; E~ung f alienation, estrangement.

entirost- [ɛntˈrɔst] cpd: ~en vt defrost; E~er m -s, - (Aut) defroster.

entführ- [ɛntˈfyːr] cpd: ~en vt carry off, abduct; kidnap; E~er m kidnapper; E~ung f abduction; kidnapping.

entgegen [ɛntˈgeːgən] prep +dat contrary to, against; ad towards; ~bringen vt irreg bring; (fig) show (jdm etw sb sth); ~gehen vi irreg (+dat) go to meet, go towards; ~gesetzt a opposite; (widersprechend) opposed; ~halten vt irreg (fig) object; ~kommen vi irreg approach; meet (jdm sb); (fig) accommodate (jdm sb); E~kommen nt obligingness; ~kommend a obliging; ~laufen vi irreg (+dat) run towards or to meet; (fig) run counter to; ~nehmen vt irreg receive, accept; ~sehen vi irreg (+dat) await; ~setzen vt oppose (dat to); ~treten vi irreg (+dat) (lit) step up to; (fig) oppose, counter; ~wirken vi (+dat) counteract.

entgegnen [ɛntˈgeːgnən] vt reply, retort.

Entgegnung f reply, retort.

entgehen [ɛntˈgeːən] vi irreg (fig) jdm ~ escape sb's notice; sich (dat) etw ~ lassen miss sth.

entgeistert [ɛntˈgaɪstərt] a thunderstruck.

Entgelt [ɛntˈgɛlt] nt -(e)s, -e compensation, remuneration; e~en vt irreg: jdm etw e~en repay sb for sth.

entgleisen [ɛntˈglaɪzən] vi (Rail) be derailed; (fig: Person) misbehave; ~ lassen derail.

Entgleisung f derailment; (fig) faux pas, gaffe.

entgleiten [ɛntˈglaɪtən] vi irreg slip (jdm from sb's hand).

entgräten [ɛntˈgrɛːtən] vt fillet, bone.

Enthaarungsmittel [ɛntˈhaːrʊŋsmɪtəl] nt depilatory.

enthalten [ɛntˈhaltən] irreg vt contain; vr abstain, refrain (gen from).

enthaltsam [ɛntˈhaltzaːm] a abstinent, abstemious; E~keit f abstinence.

enthemmen [ɛntˈhɛmən] vt: jdn ~ free sb from his inhibitions.

enthüllen [ɛntˈhʏlən] vt reveal, unveil.

Enthusiasmus [ɛntuziˈasmʊs] m enthusiasm.

entkernen [ɛntˈkɛrnən] vt stone; core.

entkommen [ɛntˈkɔmən] vi irreg get away, escape (dat, aus from).

entkorken [ɛntˈkɔrkən] vt uncork.

entkräften [ɛntˈkrɛftən] vt weaken, exhaust; Argument refute.

entladen [ɛntˈlaːdən] irreg vt unload; (Elec) discharge; vr (Elec, Gewehr) discharge; (Ärger etc) vent itself.

entlang [ɛntˈlaŋ] prep +acc or dat, ad along; ~ dem Fluß, den Fluß ~ along the river; ~gehen vi irreg walk along.

entlarven [ɛnt'larfən] *vt* unmask, expose.

entlassen [ɛnt'lasən] *vt irreg* discharge; *Arbeiter* dismiss.

Entlassung *f* discharge; dismissal.

entlasten [ɛnt'lastən] *vt* relieve; *Achse* relieve the load on; *Angeklagte* exonerate; *Konto* clear.

Entlastung *f* relief; (*Comm*) crediting; ~**szeuge** *m* defence witness.

entledigen [ɛnt'le:dɪgən] *vr*: **sich jds/einer Sache** ~ rid o.s. of sb/sth.

entleeren [ɛnt'le:rən] *vt* empty; evacuate.

entlegen [ɛnt'le:gən] *a* remote.

entlocken [ɛnt'lɔkən] *vt* elicit (*jdm etw sth from sb*).

entlüften [ɛnt'lʏftən] *vt* ventilate.

entmachten [ɛnt'maxtən] *vt* deprive of power.

entmenscht [ɛnt'mɛnʃt] *a* inhuman, bestial.

entmilitarisiert [ɛntmilitari'zi:rt] *a* demilitarized.

entmündigen [ɛnt'mʏndɪgən] *vt* certify.

entmutigen [ɛnt'mu:tɪgən] *vt* discourage.

Entnahme [ɛnt'na:mə] *f* -, -n removal, withdrawal.

entnehmen [ɛnt'ne:mən] *vt irreg* (+*dat*) take out (of), take (from); (*folgern*) infer (from).

entpuppen [ɛnt'pupən] *vr* (*fig*) reveal o.s., turn out (*als* to be).

entrahmen [ɛnt'ra:mən] *vt* skim.

entreißen [ɛnt'raɪsən] *vt irreg* snatch (away) (*jdm etw sth from sb*).

entrichten [ɛnt'rɪçtən] *vt* pay.

entrosten [ɛnt'rɔstən] *vt* derust.

entrüst- [ɛnt'rʏst] *cpd*: ~**en** *vt* incense, outrage; *vr* be filled with indignation; ~**et** *a* indignant, outraged; **E~ung** *f* indignation.

entsagen [ɛnt'za:gən] *vi* renounce (*dat sth*).

entschädigen [ɛnt'ʃɛ:dɪgən] *vt* compensate.

Entschädigung *f* compensation.

entschärfen [ɛnt'ʃɛrfən] *vt* defuse; *Kritik* tone down.

Entscheid [ɛnt'ʃaɪt] *m* -(e)s, -e decision; e~en *vtir irreg* decide; e~end *a* decisive; *Stimme* casting; ~**ung** *f* decision; ~**ungsspiel** *nt* play-off.

entschieden [ɛnt'ʃi:dən] *a* decided; (*entschlossen*) resolute; **E~heit** *f* firmness, determination.

entschließen [ɛnt'ʃli:sən] *vr irreg* decide.

entschlossen [ɛnt'ʃlɔsən] *a* determined, resolute; **E~heit** *f* determination.

Entschluß [ɛnt'ʃlus] *m* decision; e~freudig *a* decisive; ~**kraft** *f* determination, decisiveness.

entschuld- [ɛnt'ʃuld] *cpd*: ~**bar** *a* excusable; ~**igen** *vt* excuse; *vr* apologize; **E~igung** *f* apology; (*Grund*) excuse; **jdn um E~igung bitten** apologize to sb; **E~igung!** excuse me; (*Verzeihung*) sorry.

entschwinden [ɛnt'ʃvɪndən] *vi irreg* disappear.

entsetz- [ɛnt'zɛts] *cpd*: ~**en** *vt* horrify; (*Mil*) relieve; *vr* be horrified *or* appalled;

E~en *nt* -s horror, dismay; ~**lich** *a* dreadful, appalling; ~**t** *a* horrified.

entsichern [ɛnt'zɪçərn] *vt* release the safety catch of.

entsinnen [ɛnt'zɪnən] *vr irreg* remember (*gen* sth).

entspannen [ɛnt'ʃpanən] *vtr Körper* relax; (*Pol*) *Lage* ease.

Entspannung *f* relaxation, rest; (*Pol*) détente; ~**spolitik** *f* policy of détente; ~**sübungen** *pl* relaxation exercises *pl*.

entsprechen [ɛnt'ʃprɛçən] *vi irreg* (+*dat*) correspond to; *Anforderungen, Wünschen* meet, comply with; ~**d** *a* appropriate; *ad* accordingly.

entspringen [ɛnt'ʃprɪŋən] *vi irreg* spring (from).

entstehen [ɛnt'ʃte:ən] *vi irreg* arise, result.

Entstehung *f* genesis, origin.

entstellen [ɛnt'ʃtɛlən] *vt* disfigure; *Wahrheit* distort.

entstören [ɛnt'ʃtø:rən] *vt* (*Rad*) eliminate interference from; (*Aut*) suppress.

enttäuschen [ɛnt'tɔʏʃən] *vt* disappoint.

Enttäuschung *f* disappointment.

entwaffnen [ɛnt'vafnən] *vt* (*lit, fig*) disarm.

Entwarnung [ɛnt'varnʊŋ] *f* all clear (signal).

entwässer- [ɛnt'vɛsər] *cpd*: ~**n** *vt* drain; **E~ung** *f* drainage.

entweder ['ɛntve:dər] *cj* either.

entweichen [ɛnt'vaɪçən] *vi irreg* escape.

entweihen [ɛnt'vaɪən] *vt irreg* desecrate.

entwenden [ɛnt'vɛndən] *vt irreg* purloin, steal.

entwerfen [ɛnt'vɛrfən] *vt irreg* Zeichnung sketch; *Modell* design; *Vortrag, Gesetz etc* draft.

entwerten [ɛnt'veːrtən] *vt* devalue; (*stempeln*) cancel.

entwickeln [ɛnt'vɪkəln] *vtr* develop (*auch Phot*); *Mut, Energie* show, display.

Entwickler *m* -s, - developer.

Entwicklung [ɛnt'vɪklʊŋ] *f* development; (*Phot*) developing; ~**sabschnitt** *m* stage of development; ~**shilfe** *f* aid for developing countries; ~**sjahre** *pl* adolescence *sing*; ~**sland** *nt* developing country.

entwirren [ɛnt'vɪrən] *vt* disentangle.

entwischen [ɛnt'vɪʃən] *vi* escape.

entwöhnen [ɛnt'vø:nən] *vt* wean; *Süchtige* cure (*dat, von* of).

Entwöhnung *f* weaning; cure, curing.

entwürdigend [ɛnt'vʏrdɪgənt] *a* degrading.

Entwurf [ɛnt'vʊrf] *m* outline, design; (*Vertrags—, Konzept*) draft.

entwurzeln [ɛnt'vʊrtsəln] *vt* uproot.

entziehen [ɛnt'tsi:ən] *irreg vt* withdraw, take away (*dat* from); *Flüssigkeit* draw, extract; *vr* escape (*dat* from); (*jds Kenntnis*) be outside; (*der Pflicht*) shirk.

Entziehung *f* withdrawal; ~**sanstalt** *f* drug addiction/alcoholism treatment centre; ~**skur** *f* treatment for drug addiction/alcoholism.

entziffern [ɛnt'tsɪfərn] vt decipher; decode.

entzücken [ɛnt'tsʏkən] vt delight; E~ nt -s delight; ~d a delightful, charming.

entzünden [ɛnt'tsʏndən] vt light, set light to; (fig, Med) inflame; Streit spark off; vr (lit, fig) catch fire; (Streit) start; (Med) become inflamed.

Entzündung f (Med) inflammation.

entzwei [ɛnt'tsvaɪ] ad broken; in two; ~brechen vti irreg break in two; ~en vt set at odds; vr fall out; ~gehen vi irreg break (in two).

Enzian ['ɛntsiaːn] m -s, -e gentian.

Enzym [ɛn'tsyːm] nt -s, -e enzyme.

Epidemie [epide'miː] f epidemic.

Epilepsie [epile'psiː] f epilepsy.

episch ['eːpɪʃ] a epic.

Episode [epi'zoːdə] f -, -n episode.

Epoche [e'pɔxə] f -, -n epoch; e~machend a epoch-making.

Epos ['eːpɔs] nt -s, Epen epic (poem).

er [eːr] pron he; it.

erachten [ɛr'axtən] vt: ~ für or als consider (to be); meines E~s in my opinion.

erarbeiten [ɛr'arbaɪtən] vt (auch sich (dat) ~) work for, acquire; Theorie work out.

erbarmen [ɛr'barmən] vr have pity or mercy (gen on); E~ nt -s pity.

erbärmlich [ɛr'bɛrmlɪç] a wretched, pitiful; E~keit f wretchedness.

erbarmungs- [ɛr'barmʊŋs] cpd: ~los a pitiless, merciless; ~voll a compassionate; ~würdig a pitiable, wretched.

erbau- [ɛr'bau] cpd: ~en vt build, erect; (fig) edify; E~er m -s, - builder; ~lich a edifying; E~ung f construction; (fig) edification.

Erbe ['ɛrbə] m -n, -n heir; nt -s inheritance; (fig) heritage; e~n vt inherit.

erbeuten [ɛr'bɔytən] vt carry off; (Mil) capture.

Erb- [ɛrb] cpd: ~faktor m gene; ~fehler m hereditary defect; ~folge f (line of) succession; ~in f heiress.

erbittern [ɛr'bɪtərn] vt embitter; (erzürnen) incense.

erbittert [ɛr'bɪtərt] a Kampf fierce, bitter.

erblassen [ɛr'blasən] vi, **erbleichen** [ɛr'blaɪçən] vi irreg (turn) pale.

erblich ['ɛrplɪç] a hereditary.

Erbmasse ['ɛrbmasə] f estate; (Biol) genotype.

erbosen [ɛr'boːzən] vt anger; vr grow angry.

erbrechen [ɛr'brɛçən] vtr irreg vomit.

Erb- cpd: ~recht nt right of succession, hereditary right; law of inheritance; ~schaft f inheritance, legacy.

Erbse ['ɛrpsə] f -, -n pea.

Erb- cpd: ~stück nt heirloom; ~teil nt inherited trait; (portion of) inheritance.

Erd- ['eːrd] cpd: ~achse f earth's axis; ~atmosphäre f earth's atmosphere; ~bahn f orbit of the earth; ~beben nt earthquake; ~beere f strawberry;

~boden m ground; ~e f -, -n earth; zu ebener ~e at ground level; e~en vt (Elec) earth.

erdenkbar [ɛr'dɛŋkbaːr], **erdenklich** [-lɪç] a conceivable.

Erd- cpd: ~gas nt natural gas; ~geschoß nt ground floor; ~kunde f geography; ~nuß f peanut; ~oberfläche f surface of the earth; ~öl nt (mineral) oil.

erdreisten [ɛr'draɪstən] vr dare, have the audacity (to do sth).

erdrosseln [ɛr'drɔsəln] vt strangle, throttle.

erdrücken [ɛr'drʏkən] vt crush.

Erd- cpd: ~rutsch m landslide; ~teil m continent.

erdulden [ɛr'dʊldən] vt endure, suffer.

ereifern [ɛr'aɪfərn] vr get excited.

ereignen [ɛr'aɪgnən] vr happen.

Ereignis [ɛr'aɪgnɪs] nt -ses, -se event; e~reich a eventful.

erfahren [ɛr'faːrən] vt irreg learn, find out; (erleben) experience; a experienced.

Erfahrung f experience; e~sgemäß ad according to experience.

erfassen [ɛr'fasən] vt seize; (fig) (einbeziehen) include, register; (verstehen) grasp.

erfind- [ɛr'fɪnd] cpd: ~en vt irreg invent; E~er m -s, - inventor; ~erisch a inventive; E~ung f invention; E~ungsgabe f inventiveness.

Erfolg [ɛr'fɔlk] m -(e)s, -e success; (Folge) result; e~en vi follow; (sich ergeben) result; (stattfinden) take place; (Zahlung) be effected; e~los a unsuccessful; ~losigkeit f lack of success; e~reich a successful; e~versprechend a promising.

erforder- [ɛr'fɔrdər] cpd: ~lich a requisite, necessary; ~n vt require, demand; E~nis nt -ses,-se requirement; prerequisite.

erforsch- [ɛr'fɔrʃ] cpd: ~en vt Land explore; Problem investigate; Gewissen search; E~er m -s, - explorer; investigator; E~ung f exploration; investigation; searching.

erfragen [ɛr'fraːgən] vt inquire after, ascertain.

erfreuen [ɛr'frɔyən] vr: sich ~ an (+dat) enjoy; sich einer Sache (gen) ~ enjoy sth; vt delight.

erfreulich [ɛr'frɔylɪç] a pleasing, gratifying; ~erweise ad happily, luckily.

erfrieren [ɛr'friːrən] vi irreg freeze (to death); (Glieder) get frostbitten; (Pflanzen) be killed by frost.

erfrischen [ɛr'frɪʃən] vt refresh.

Erfrischung f refreshment; ~sraum m snack bar, cafeteria.

erfüllen [ɛr'fʏlən] vt Raum etc fill; (fig) Bitte etc fulfil; vr come true.

ergänzen [ɛr'gɛntsən] vt supplement, complete; vr complement one another.

Ergänzung f completion; (Zusatz) supplement.

ergattern [ɛr'gatərn] vt (col) get hold of, hunt up.

ergaunern [ɛr'gaunərn] vt (col) **sich** (dat) **etw ~** get hold of sth by underhand methods.

ergeben [ɛr'ge:bən] irreg vt yield, produce; vr surrender; (sich hingeben) give o.s. up, yield (dat to); (folgen) result; a devoted, humble; (dem Trunk) addicted (to); **E~heit** f devotion, humility.

Ergebnis [ɛr'ge:pnis] nt **-ses, -se** result; **e~los** a without result, fruitless.

ergehen [ɛr'ge:ən] irreg vi be issued, go out; etw **über sich ~ lassen** put up with sth; vi impers: **es ergeht ihm gut/schlecht** he's faring or getting on well/badly; vr: **sich in etw** (dat) **~** indulge in sth.

ergiebig [ɛr'gi:biç] a productive.

ergötzen [ɛr'gœtsən] vt amuse, delight.

ergreifen [ɛr'graifən] vt irreg (lit, fig) seize; Beruf take up; Maßnahmen resort to; (rühren) move; **~d** a moving, affecting.

ergriffen [ɛr'grifən] a deeply moved.

Erguß [ɛr'gus] m discharge; (fig) outpouring, effusion.

erhaben [ɛr'ha:bən] a (lit) raised, embossed; (fig) exalted, lofty; **über etw** (acc) **~ sein** be above sth.

erhalten [ɛr'haltən] vt irreg receive; (bewahren) preserve, maintain; **gut ~ in** good condition.

erhältlich [ɛr'hɛltliç] a obtainable, available.

Erhaltung f maintenance, preservation.

erhängen [ɛr'hɛŋən] vtr hang.

erhärten [ɛr'hɛrtən] vt harden; These substantiate, corroborate.

erhaschen [ɛr'haʃən] vt catch.

erheben [ɛr'he:bən] irreg vt raise; Protest, Forderungen make; Fakten ascertain, establish; vr rise (up); **sich über etw** (acc) **~** rise above sth.

erheblich [ɛr'he:pliç] a considerable.

erheitern [ɛr'haitərn] vt amuse, cheer (up).

Erheiterung f exhilaration; **zur allgemeinen ~** to everybody's amusement.

erhellen [ɛr'hɛlən] vt (lit, fig) illuminate; Geheimnis shed light on; vr brighten, light up.

erhitzen [ɛr'hitsən] vt heat; vr heat up; (fig) become heated or aroused.

erhoffen [ɛr'hɔfən] vt hope for.

erhöhen [ɛr'hø:ən] vt raise; (verstärken) increase.

erhol- [ɛr'ho:l] cpd: **~en** vr recover; (entspannen) have a rest; **~sam** a restful; **E~ung** f recovery; relaxation, rest; **~ungsbedürftig** a in need of a rest, run-down; **E~ungsheim** nt convalescent/rest home.

erhören [ɛr'hø:rən] vt Gebet etc hear; Bitte etc yield to.

Erika ['e:rika] ka] f -, **Eriken** heather.

erinnern [ɛr'inərn] vt remind (an +acc of); vr remember (an etw (acc) sth).

Erinnerung f memory; (Andenken) reminder; **~stafel** f commemorative plaque.

erkalten [ɛr'kaltən] vi go cold, cool (down).

erkält- [ɛr'kɛlt] cpd: **~en** vr catch cold; **~et a** with a cold; **~et sein** have a cold; **E~ung** f cold.

erkenn- [ɛr'kɛn] cpd: **~bar** a recognizable; **~en** vt irreg recognize; (sehen, verstehen) see; **~tlich a: sich ~tlich zeigen** show one's appreciation; **E~tlichkeit** f gratitude; (Geschenk) token of one's gratitude; **E~tnis** f -, **-se** knowledge; (das Erkennen) recognition; (Einsicht) insight; **zur E~tnis kommen** realize; **E~ung** f recognition; **E~ungsmarke** f identity disc.

Erker ['ɛrkər] m **-s, -** bay; **~fenster** nt bay window.

erklär- [ɛr'klɛ:r] cpd: **~bar** a explicable; **~en** vt explain; **~lich** a explicable; (verständlich) understandable; **E~ung** f explanation; (Aussage) declaration.

erklecklich [ɛr'klɛkliç] a considerable.

erklingen [ɛr'kliŋən] vi irreg resound, ring out.

Erkrankung [ɛr'kraŋkuŋ] f illness.

erkund- [ɛr'kund] cpd: **~en** vt find out, ascertain; (esp Mil) reconnoitre, scout; **~igen** vr inquire (nach about); **E~igung** f inquiry; **E~ung** f reconnaissance, scouting.

erlahmen [ɛr'la:mən] vi tire; (nachlassen) flag, wane.

erlangen [ɛr'laŋən] vt attain, achieve.

Erlaß [ɛr'las] m **-sses, -lässe** decree; (Aufhebung) remission.

erlassen vt irreg Verfügung issue; Gesetz enact; Strafe remit; **jdm etw ~** release sb from sth.

erlauben [ɛr'laubən] vt allow, permit (jdm etw sb to do sth); vr permit o.s., venture.

Erlaubnis [ɛr'laupnis] f -, **-se** permission.

erläutern [ɛr'lɔytərn] vt explain.

Erläuterung f explanation.

Erle ['ɛrlə] f -, **-n** alder.

erleben [ɛr'le:bən] vt experience; Zeit live through; (mit~) witness; (noch mit~) live to see.

Erlebnis [ɛr'le:pnis] nt **-ses, -se** experience.

erledigen [ɛr'le:digən] vt take care of, deal with; Antrag etc process; (col: erschöpfen) wear out; (col: ruinieren) finish; (col: umbringen) do in.

erlegen [ɛr'le:gən] vt kill.

erleichter- [ɛr'laiçtər] cpd: **~n** vt make easier; (fig) Last lighten; (lindern, beruhigen) relieve; **~t** a relieved; **E~ung** f facilitation; lightening; relief.

erleiden [ɛr'laidən] vt irreg suffer, endure.

erlernbar a learnable.

erlernen [ɛr'lɛrnən] vt learn, acquire.

erlesen [ɛr'le:zən] a select, choice.

erleuchten [ɛr'lɔyçtən] vt illuminate; (fig) inspire.

Erleuchtung f (Einfall) inspiration.

erlogen [ɛr'lo:gən] a untrue, made-up.

Erlös [ɛr'lø:s] m **-es, -e** proceeds pl.

erlöschen [ɛr'lœʃən] vi (Feuer) go out;

(*Interesse*) cease, die; (*Vertrag, Recht*) expire.

erlösen [ɛr'løːzən] *vt* redeem, save.

Erlösung *f* release; (*Rel*) redemption.

ermächtigen [ɛr'mɛçtɪgən] *vt* authorize, empower.

Ermächtigung *f* authorization; authority.

ermahnen [ɛr'maːnən] *vt* exhort, admonish.

Ermahnung *f* admonition, exhortation.

ermäßigen [ɛr'mɛsɪgən] *vt* reduce.

Ermäßigung *f* reduction.

ermessen [ɛr'mɛsən] *vt irreg* estimate, gauge; E~ *nt* -s estimation; discretion; **in jds E~ liegen** lie within sb's discretion.

ermitteln [ɛr'mɪtəln] *vt* determine; *Täter* trace; *vi*: **gegen jdn ~** investigate sb.

Ermittlung [ɛr'mɪtlʊŋ] *f* determination; (*Polizei—*) investigation.

ermöglichen [ɛr'møːklɪçən] *vt* make possible (*dat* for).

ermord- [ɛr'mɔrd] *cpd*: ~en *vt* murder; E~ung *f* murder.

ermüden [ɛr'myːdən] *vti* tire; (*Tech*) fatigue; ~d *a* tiring; (*fig*) wearisome.

Ermüdung *f* fatigue; ~serscheinung *f* sign of fatigue.

ermuntern [ɛr'mʊntərn] *vt* rouse; (*ermutigen*) encourage; (*beleben*) liven up; (*aufmuntern*) cheer up.

ermutigen [ɛr'muːtɪgən] *vt* encourage.

ernähr- [ɛr'nɛːr] *cpd*: ~en *vt* feed, nourish; *Familie* support; *vr* support o.s., earn a living; **sich ~en von** live on; E~er *m* -s, - breadwinner; E~ung *f* nourishment; nutrition; (*Unterhalt*) maintenance.

ernennen [ɛr'nɛnən] *vt irreg* appoint.

Ernennung *f* appointment.

erneu- [ɛr'nɔy] *cpd*: ~ern *vt* renew; restore; renovate; E~erung *f* renewal; restoration; renovation; ~t *a* renewed, fresh; *ad* once more.

erniedrigen [ɛr'niːdrɪgən] *vt* humiliate, degrade.

Ernst [ɛrnst] *m* -es seriousness; **das ist mein ~** I'm quite serious; **im ~** in earnest; ~ **machen mit etw** put sth into practice; e~ *a* serious; ~**fall** *m* emergency; e~**gemeint** a meant in earnest, serious; e~**haft** a serious; ~**haftigkeit** *f* seriousness; e~**lich** a serious.

Ernte ['ɛrntə] *f* -, -n harvest; ~**dankfest** *nt* harvest festival; e~**n** *vt* harvest; *Lob etc* earn.

ernüchtern [ɛr'nʏçtərn] *vt* sober up; (*fig*) bring down to earth.

Ernüchterung *f* sobering up; (*fig*) disillusionment.

Erober- [ɛr'oːbər] *cpd*: ~er *m* -s, - conqueror; e~n *vt* conquer; ~ung *f* conquest.

eröffnen [ɛr'œfnən] *vt* open; **jdm etw ~** disclose sth to sb; *vr* present itself.

Eröffnung *f* opening; ~**sansprache** *f* inaugural or opening address.

erogen [ɛro'geːn] *a* erogenous.

erörtern [ɛr'œrtərn] *vt* discuss.

Erörterung *f* discussion.

Erotik [e'roːtɪk] *f* eroticism.

erotisch *a* erotic.

erpicht [ɛr'pɪçt] *a* eager, keen (*auf +acc* on).

erpress- [ɛr'prɛs] *cpd*: ~en *vt* Geld etc extort; *Mensch* blackmail; E~er *m* -s, - blackmailer; E~ung *f* blackmail; extortion.

erproben [ɛr'proːbən] *vt* test.

erraten [ɛr'raːtən] *vt irreg* guess.

erreg- [ɛr'reːk] *cpd*: ~bar *a* excitable; (*reizbar*) irritable; E~barkeit *f* excitability; irritability; ~en *vt* excite; (*ärgern*) infuriate; (*hervorrufen*) arouse, provoke; *vr* get excited or worked up; E~er *m* -s, - causative agent; E~theit *f* excitement; (*Beunruhigung*) agitation; E~ung *f* excitement.

erreichbar *a* accessible, within reach.

erreichen [ɛr'raɪçən] *vt* reach; *Zweck* achieve; *Zug* catch.

errichten [ɛr'rɪçtən] *vt* erect, put up; (*gründen*) establish, set up.

erringen [ɛr'rɪŋən] *vt irreg* gain, win.

erröten [ɛr'røːtən] *vi* blush, flush.

Errungenschaft [ɛr'rʊŋənʃaft] *f* achievement; (*col: Anschaffung*) acquisition.

Ersatz [ɛr'zats] *m* -es substitute; replacement; (*Schaden—*) compensation; (*Mil*) reinforcements *pl*; ~**befriedigung** *f* vicarious satisfaction; ~**dienst** *m* (*Mil*) alternative service; ~**mann** *m* replacement; (*Sport*) substitute; e~**pflichtig** a liable to pay compensation; ~**reifen** *m* (*Aut*) spare tyre; ~**teil** *nt* spare (part).

ersaufen [ɛr'zaʊfən] *vi irreg* (*col*) drown.

ersäufen [ɛr'zɔyfən] *vt* drown.

erschaffen [ɛr'ʃafən] *vt irreg* create.

erscheinen [ɛr'ʃaɪnən] *vi irreg* appear.

Erscheinung *f* appearance; (*Geist*) apparition; (*Gegebenheit*) phenomenon; (*Gestalt*) figure.

erschießen [ɛr'ʃiːsən] *vt irreg* shoot (dead).

erschlaffen [ɛr'ʃlafən] *vi* go limp; (*Mensch*) become exhausted.

erschlagen [ɛr'ʃlaːgən] *vt irreg* strike dead.

erschleichen [ɛr'ʃlaɪçən] *vt irreg* obtain by stealth or dubious methods.

erschöpf- [ɛr'ʃœpf] *cpd*: ~en *vt* exhaust; ~end *a* exhaustive, thorough; ~t *a* exhausted; E~ung *f* exhaustion.

erschrecken [ɛr'ʃrɛkən] *vt* startle, frighten; *vi irreg* be frightened or startled; ~d *a* alarming, frightening.

erschrocken [ɛr'ʃrɔkən] *a* frightened, startled.

erschüttern [ɛr'ʃʏtərn] *vt* shake; (*ergreifen*) move deeply.

Erschütterung *f* shaking; shock.

erschweren [ɛr'ʃveːrən] *vt* complicate.

erschwingen [ɛr'ʃvɪŋən] *vt irreg* afford.

erschwinglich *a* within one's means.

ersehen [ɛr'zeːən] *vt irreg*: **aus etw ~, daß** gather from sth that.

ersetz- [ɛr'zɛts] *cpd*: ~bar *a* replaceable; ~en *vt* replace; **jdm Unkosten** *etc* ~en pay sb's expenses *etc*.

ersichtlich [ɛr'zɪçtlɪç] *a* evident, obvious.

erspar- [ɛr'ʃpaːr] *cpd*: ~en *vt Ärger etc* spare; *Geld* save: E~nis *f* -, -se saving.

ersprießlich [ɛr'ʃpriːslɪç] *a* profitable, useful; (*angenehm*) pleasant.

erst [eːrst] *ad* (at) first; (*nicht früher, nur*) only; (*nicht bis*) not till; ~ **einmal** first.

erstarren [ɛr'ʃtarən] *vi* stiffen; (*vor Furcht*) grow rigid; (*Materie*) solidify.

erstatten [ɛr'ʃtatən] *vt Kosten* (re)pay; **Anzeige** *etc* ~ report sb; **Bericht** ~ make a report.

Erstaufführung ['eːrstauffyːruŋ] *f* first performance.

erstaunen [ɛr'ʃtaunən] *vt* astonish; *vi* be astonished; E~ *nt* -s astonishment.

erstaunlich *a* astonishing.

erst- ['eːrst] *cpd*: E-**ausgabe** *f* first edition; ~**beste(r,s)** *a* First that comes along; ~**e(r,s)** *a* first.

erstechen [ɛr'ʃtɛçən] *vt irreg* stab (to death).

erstehen [ɛr'ʃteːən] *vt irreg* buy; *vi* (a)rise.

ersteigen [ɛr'ʃtaigən] *vt irreg* climb, ascend.

erstellen [ɛr'ʃtɛlən] *vt* erect, build.

erst- *cpd*: ~**emal** *ad* (the) first time; ~**ens** *ad* firstly, in the first place; ~**ere(r,s)** *pron* (the) former.

ersticken [ɛr'ʃtɪkən] *vt* (*lit, fig*) stifle; *Mensch* suffocate; *Flammen* smother; *vi* (*Mensch*) suffocate; (*Feuer*) be smothered; **in Arbeit** ~ be snowed under with work. **Erstickung** *f* suffocation.

erst- *cpd*: ~**klassig** *a* first-class; E~**kommunion** *f* first communion; ~**malig** *a* first; ~**mals** *ad* for the first time.

erstrebenswert [ɛr'ʃtreːbənsveːrt] *a* desirable, worthwhile.

erstrecken [ɛr'ʃtrɛkən] *vr* extend, stretch.

Ersttags- ['ɛrst-taːgz] *cpd*: ~**brief** *m* first-day cover; ~**stempel** *m* first-day (date) stamp.

ersuchen [ɛr'zuːxən] *vt* request.

ertappen [ɛr'tapən] *vt* catch, detect.

erteilen [ɛr'tailən] *vt* give.

ertönen [ɛr'töːnən] *vi* sound, ring out.

Ertrag [ɛr'traːk] *m* -(e)s, ⁻e yield; (*Gewinn*) proceeds *pl*; e~**en** *vt irreg* bear, stand.

erträglich [ɛr'treːklɪç] *a* tolerable, bearable.

ertränken [ɛr'trɛŋkən] *vt* drown.

erträumen [ɛr'trɔymən] *vt*: **sich** (*dat*) **etw** ~ dream of sth, imagine sth.

ertrinken [ɛr'trɪŋkən] *vi irreg* drown; E~ *nt* -s drowning.

erübrigen [ɛr''yːbrɪgən] *vt* spare; *vr* be unnecessary.

erwachen [ɛr'vaxən] *vi* awake.

erwachsen [ɛr'vaksən] *a* grown-up; E~**e(r)** *mf* adult; E~**enbildung** *f* adult education.

erwägen [ɛr'vɛːgən] *vt irreg* consider. **Erwägung** *f* consideration.

erwähn- [ɛr'vɛːn] *cpd*: ~**en** *vt* mention; ~**enswert** *a* worth mentioning; E~**ung** *f* mention.

erwärmen [ɛr'vɛrmən] *vt* warm, heat; *vr* get warm, warm up; **sich** ~ **für** warm to.

erwarten [ɛr'vartən] *vt* expect; (*warten auf*) wait for; **etw kaum** ~ **können** hardly be able to wait for sth.

Erwartung *f* expectation; e~**sgemäß** *ad* as expected; e~**svoll** *a* expectant.

erwecken [ɛr'vɛkən] *vt* rouse, awake; **den Anschein** ~ give the impression.

erwehren [ɛr'veːrən] *vr* fend, ward (*gen* off); (*des Lachens etc*) refrain (*gen* from).

erweichen [ɛr'vaiçən] *vti* soften.

Erweis [ɛr'vais] *m* -es, -e proof; e~**en** *irreg vt* prove; *Ehre, Dienst* do (*jdm* sb); *vr* prove (*als* to be).

Erwerb [ɛr'vɛrp] *m* -(e)s, -e acquisition; (*Beruf*) trade; e~**en** *vt irreg* acquire; e~**slos** *a* unemployed; ~**squelle** *f* source of income; e~**stätig** *a* (gainfully) employed; e~**sunfähig** *a* unemployable.

erwidern [ɛr'viːdərn] *vt* reply; (*vergelten*) return.

erwiesen [ɛr'viːzən] *a* proven.

erwischen [ɛr'vɪʃən] *vt* (*col*) catch, get.

erwünscht [ɛr'vynʃt] *a* desired.

erwürgen [ɛr'vyrgən] *vt* strangle.

Erz [eːrts] *nt* -es, -e ore.

erzähl- [ɛr'tsɛːl] *cpd*: ~**en** *vt* tell; E~**er** *m* -s, - narrator; E~**ung** *f* story, tale.

Erz- *cpd*: ~**bischof** *m* archbishop; ~**engel** *m* archangel.

erzeug- [ɛr'tsɔyg] *cpd*: ~**en** *vt* produce; *Strom* generate; E~**erpreis** *m* producer's price; E~**nis** *nt* -ses, -se product, produce; E~**ung** *f* production; generation.

erziehen [ɛr'tsiːən] *vt irreg* bring up; (*bilden*) educate, train.

Erziehung *f* bringing up; (*Bildung*) education; ~**sbeihilfe** *f* educational grant; ~**sberechtigte(r)** *mf* parent; guardian; ~**sheim** *nt* approved school.

erzielen [ɛr'tsiːlən] *vt* achieve, obtain; *Tor* score.

erzwingen [ɛr'tsvɪŋən] *vt irreg* force, obtain by force.

es [ɛs] *pron nom, acc* it.

Esche ['ɛʃə] *f* -, -n ash.

Esel ['eːzəl] *m* -s, - donkey, ass; ~**sohr** *nt* dog-ear.

Eskalation [ɛskalatsi'oːn] *f* escalation.

eßbar ['ɛsbaːr] *a* eatable, edible.

essen ['ɛsən] *vti irreg* eat; E~ *nt* -s, - meal; food; E~**szeit** *f* mealtime; dinner time.

Essig ['ɛsɪç] *m* -s, -e vinegar; ~**gurke** *f* gherkin.

Eß- ['ɛs] *cpd*: ~**kastanie** *f* sweet chestnut; ~**löffel** *m* tablespoon; ~**tisch** *m* dining table; ~**waren** *pl* victuals *pl*, food provisions *pl*; ~**zimmer** *nt* dining room.

etablieren [eta'bliːrən] *vr* become established; set up business.

Etage [e'taːʒə] *f* -, -n floor, storey; ~**nbetten** *pl* bunk beds *pl*; ~**nwohnung** *f* flat.

Etappe [e'tapə] *f* -, -n stage.

Etat [e'taː] *m* -s, -s budget; ~**jahr** *nt* financial year; ~**posten** *m* budget item.

etepetete [e:tɔpe'te:tə] a (col) fussy.
Ethik ['e:tɪk] f ethics sing.
ethisch ['e:tɪʃ] a ethical.
Etikett [eti'kɛt] nt -(e)s, -e label; tag; ~e f etiquette, manners pl; e~ieren [-'ti:rən] vt label; tag.
etliche ['ɛtlɪçə] pron pl some, quite a few; ~s a thing or two.
Etui [ɛt'vi:] nt -s, -s case.
etwa ['ɛtva] ad (ungefähr) about; (vielleicht) perhaps; (beispielsweise) for instance; **nicht** ~ by no means; ~**ig** ['ɛtva-ɪç] a possible; ~s pron something; anything; (ein wenig) a little; ad a little.
Etymologie [etymolo'gi:] f etymology.
euch [ɔʏç] pron acc of **ihr** you; yourselves; dat of **ihr** (to) you.
euer ['ɔʏər] pron gen of **ihr** of you; pron your; ~e(r,s) yours.
Eule ['ɔʏlə] f -, -n owl.
eure(r,s) ['ɔʏrə(r,z)] pron your; yours; -rseits ad on your part; ~sgleichen pron people like you; ~twegen, ~twillen ad (für euch) for your sakes; (wegen euch) on your account.
eurige pron: **der/die/das** ~ yours.
Euro- [ɔʏro] cpd: ~**krat** [-'kra:t] m -en, -en eurocrat; ~**pameister** [ɔʏ'ro:pa-] m European champion.
Euter ['ɔʏtər] nt -s, - udder.
evakuieren [evaku'i:rən] vt evacuate.
evangelisch [evaŋ'ge:lɪʃ] a Protestant.
Evangelium [evaŋ'ge:lium] nt gospel.
Eva(s)kostüm ['e:fa(s)kɔsty:m] nt: **im** ~ in one's birthday suit.
eventuell [evɛntu'ɛl] a possible; ad possibly, perhaps.
EWG [e:ve:'ge:] f - EEC, Common Market.
ewig ['e:vɪç] a eternal; **E~keit** f eternity.
exakt [ɛ'ksakt] a exact.
Examen [ɛ'ksa:mən] nt -s, - or **Examina** examination.
Exempel [ɛ'ksɛmpəl] nt -s, - example.
Exemplar [ɛksɛm'pla:r] nt -s, -e specimen; (Buch-) copy; e~isch a exemplary.
exerzieren [ɛksɛr'tsi:rən] vi drill.
Exil [ɛ'ksi:l] nt -s, -e exile.
Existenz [ɛksɪs'tɛnts] f existence; (Unterhalt) livelihood, living; (pej: Mensch) character; ~**kampf** m struggle for existence; ~**minimum** nt -s subsistence level.
existieren [ɛksɪs'ti:rən] vi exist.
exklusiv [ɛksklu'zi:f] a exclusive; ~e [-'zi:və] ad, prep +gen exclusive of, not including.
exorzieren [ɛksɔr'tsi:rən] vt exorcize.
exotisch [ɛ'kso:tɪʃ] a exotic.
Expansion [ɛkspanzi'o:n] f expansion.
Expedition [ɛkspeditsi'o:n] f expedition; (Comm) forwarding department.
Experiment [ɛksperi'mɛnt] nt experiment; e~ell [-'tɛl] a experimental; e~ieren [-'ti:rən] vi experiment.
Experte [ɛks'pɛrtə] m -n, -n expert, specialist.
explo- [ɛksplo] cpd: ~**dieren** [-'di:rən] vi explode; **E~sion** [ɛksplozi'o:n] f

explosion; ~**siv** [-'zi:f] a explosive.
Exponent [ɛkspo'nɛnt] m exponent.
Export [ɛks'pɔrt] m -(e)s, -e export; ~**eur** [-'tø:r] m exporter; ~**handel** m export trade; e~**ieren** [-'ti:rən] vt export; ~**land** nt exporting country.
Expreß- [ɛks'prɛs] cpd: ~**gut** nt express goods pl or freight; ~**zug** m express (train).
extra ['ɛkstra] a inv (col: gesondert) separate; (besondere) extra; ad (gesondert) separately; (speziell) specially; (absichtlich) on purpose; (vor Adjektiven, zusätzlich) extra; **E~** nt -s, -s extra; **E~ausgabe** f, **E~blatt** nt special edition.
Extrakt [ɛks'trakt] m -(e)s, -e extract.
extrem [ɛks'tre:m] a extreme; ~**istisch** [-'mɪstɪʃ] a (Pol) extremist; **E~itäten** [-'tɛ:tən] pl extremities pl.
Exzellenz [ɛkstsɛ'lɛnts] f excellency.
exzentrisch [ɛks'tsɛntrɪʃ] a eccentric.
Exzeß [ɛks'tsɛs] m -sses. -sse excess.

F

F, f [ɛf] nt F, f.
Fabel ['fa:bəl] f -, -n fable; f~**haft** a fabulous, marvellous.
Fabrik [fa'bri:k] f factory; ~**ant** [-'kant] m (Hersteller) manufacturer; (Besitzer) industrialist; ~**arbeiter** m factory worker; ~**at** [-'ka:t] nt -(e)s, -e manufacture, product; ~**ation** [-atsi'o:n] f manufacture, production; ~**besitzer** m factory owner; ~**gelände** nt factory premises pl.
Fach [fax] nt -(e)s, ¨er compartment; (Sachgebiet) subject; **ein Mann vom** ~ an expert; ~**arbeiter** m skilled worker; ~**arzt** m (medical) specialist; ~**ausdruck** m technical term.
Fächer ['fɛçər] m -s, - fan.
Fach- cpd: ~**kundig** a expert, specialist; f~**lich** a professional; expert; ~**mann** m, pl **-leute** specialist; ~**schule** f technical college; f~**simpeln** vi talk shop; ~**werk** nt timber frame.
Fackel ['fakəl] f -, -n torch; f~**n** vi (col) dither.
fad(e) ['fa:t, fa:də] a insipid; (langweilig) dull.
Faden ['fa:dən] m -s, ¨ thread; ~**nudeln** pl vermicelli pl; f~**scheinig** a (lit, fig) threadbare.
fähig ['fɛ:ɪç] a capable (zu, gen of); able; **F~keit** f ability.
Fähnchen ['fɛ:nçən] nt pennon, streamer.
fahnden ['fa:ndən] vi: ~ **nach** search for.
Fahndung f search; ~**sliste** f list of wanted criminals, wanted list.
Fahne ['fa:nə] f -, -n flag, standard; **eine** ~ **haben** (col) smell of drink; ~**nflucht** f desertion.
Fahrbahn f carriageway (Brit), roadway.
Fähre ['fɛ:rə] f -, -n ferry.
fahren ['fa:rən] irreg vt drive; **Rad** ride; (befördern) drive, take; **Rennen** drive in; vi (sich bewegen) go; (Schiff) sail; (abfahren) leave; **mit dem Auto/Zug** ~ go or travel by car/train; **mit der Hand** ~ **über**

(+acc) pass one's hand over.

Fahr- ['fa:r] cpd: **~er** m **-s, -** driver; **~erflucht** f hit-and-run; **~gast** m passenger; **~geld** nt fare; **~gestell** nt chassis; (Aviat) undercarriage; **~karte** f ticket; **~kartenausgabe** f, **~kartenschalter** m ticket office; f**~lässig** a negligent; f**~lässige Tötung** manslaughter; **~lässigkeit** f negligence; **~lehrer** m driving instructor; **~plan** m timetable; f**~planmäßig** a (Rail) scheduled; **~preis** m fare; **~prüfung** f driving test; **~rad** nt bicycle; **~schein** m ticket; **~schule** f driving school; **~schüler(in** f) m learner (driver); **~stuhl** m lift, elevator (US).

Fahrt [fa:rt] f **-, -en** journey; (kurz) trip; (Aut) drive; (Geschwindigkeit) speed.

Fährte ['fɛ:rtə] f**-, -n** track, trail.

Fahrt- cpd: **~kosten** pl travelling expenses pl; **~richtung** f course, direction.

Fahr- cpd: **~zeug** nt vehicle; **~zeughalter** m **-s, -** owner of a vehicle.

Fak- [fak] cpd: f**~tisch** a actual; **~tor** m factor; **~tum** nt **-s, -ten** fact; **~ul'tät** f faculty.

Falke ['falkə] m **-n, -n** falcon.

Fall [fal] m **-(e)s, ¨e** (Sturz) fall; (Sachverhalt, Jur, Gram) case; **auf jeden ~, auf alle ¨e** in any case; (bestimmt) definitely; **~e** f **-, -n** trap; f**~en** vi irreg fall; **etw** f**~en lassen** drop sth.

fällen ['fɛlən] vt Baum fell; Urteil pass.

fallenlassen vt irreg Bemerkung make; Plan abandon, drop.

fällig ['fɛlɪç] a due ; **F~keit** f (Comm) maturity.

Fall- cpd: **~obst** nt fallen fruit, windfall; f**~s** ad in case, if; **~schirm** m parachute; **~schirmjäger** pl, **~schirmtruppe** f paratroops pl; **~schirmspringer** m parachutist; **~tür** f trap door.

falsch [falʃ] a false; (unrichtig) wrong.

fälschen ['fɛlʃən] vt forge.

Fälscher m **-s, -** forger.

Falsch- cpd: **~geld** nt counterfeit money; **~heit** f falsity, falseness; (Unrichtigkeit) wrongness.

fälsch- cpd: **~lich** a false; **~licherweise** ad mistakenly; **F~ung** f forgery.

Fältchen ['fɛltçən] nt crease, wrinkle.

Falte ['faltə] f **-, -n** (Knick) fold, crease; (Haut—) wrinkle; (Rock—) pleat; f**~n** vt fold; Stirn wrinkle; f**~nlos** a without folds; without wrinkles.

familiär [famili'ɛ:r] a familiar.

Familie [fa'mi:liə] f family; **~nähnlichkeit** f family resemblance; **~nkreis** m family circle; **~nname** m surname; **~nstand** m marital status; **~nvater** m head of the family.

Fanatiker [fa'na:tikər] m **-s, -** fanatic.

fanatisch a fanatical.

Fanatismus [fana'tɪsmʊs] m fanaticism.

Fang [faŋ] m **-(e)s, ¨e** catch; (Jagen) hunting; (Kralle) talon, claw; f**~en** vt irreg catch; vr get caught; (Flugzeug) level

out; (Mensch: nicht fallen) steady o.s.; (fig) compose o.s.; (in Leistung) get back on form.

Farb- ['farb] cpd: **~abzug** m coloured print; **~aufnahme** f colour photograph; **~band** m typewriter ribbon; **~e** f **-, -n** colour; (zum Malen etc) paint; (Stoff—) dye; f**~echt** a colourfast.

färben ['fɛrbən] vt colour; Stoff, Haar dye.

farben- ['farbən] cpd: **~blind** a colourblind; **~froh, ~prächtig** a colourful, gay.

Farb- cpd: **~fernsehen** nt colour television; **~film** m colour film; f**~ig** a coloured; **~ige(r)** mf coloured; **~kasten** m paint-box; f**~los** a colourless; **~photographie** f colour photography; **~stift** m coloured pencil; **~stoff** m dye; **~ton** m hue, tone.

Färbung ['fɛrbʊŋ] f colouring; (Tendenz) bias.

Farn [farn] m **-(e)s, -e, ~kraut** nt fern; bracken.

Fasan [fa'za:n] m **-(e)s, -e(n)** pheasant.

Fasching ['faʃɪŋ] m **-s, -e** or **-s** carnival.

Faschismus [fa'ʃɪsmʊs] m fascism.

Faschist m fascist.

faseln ['fa:zəln] vi talk nonsense, drivel.

Faser ['fa:zər] f **-, -n** fibre; f**~n** vi fray.

Faß [fas] nt **-sses, Fässer** vat, barrel; (Öl) drum; **Bier vom ~** draught beer; f**~bar** a comprehensible; **~bier** nt draught beer.

fassen ['fasən] vt (ergreifen) grasp, take; (inhaltlich) hold; Entschluß etc take; (verstehen) understand; Ring etc set; (formulieren) formulate, phrase; **nicht zu ~** unbelievable; vr calm down.

faßlich ['faslɪç] a intelligible.

Fassung ['fasʊŋ] f (Umrahmung) mounting; (Lampen—) socket; (Wortlaut) version; (Beherrschung) composure; **jdn aus der ~ bringen** upset sb; f**~slos** a speechless; **~svermögen** nt capacity; (Verständnis) comprehension.

fast [fast] ad almost, nearly.

fasten ['fastən] vi fast; **F~** nt **-s** fasting; **F~zeit** f Lent.

Fastnacht f Shrove Tuesday; carnival.

fatal [fa'ta:l] a fatal; (peinlich) embarrassing.

faul [faʊl] a rotten; Person lazy; Ausreden lame; **daran ist etwas ~** there's sth fishy about it; **~en** vi rot; **~enzen** vi idle; **F~enzer** m **-s, -** idler, loafer; **F~heit** f laziness; **~ig** a putrid.

Fäulnis ['fɔʏlnɪs] f **-** decay, putrefaction.

Faust ['faʊst] f **-, Fäuste** fist; **~handschuh** m mitten.

Favorit [favo'ri:t] m **-en, -en** favourite.

Februar ['fe:brua:r] m **-(s), -e** February.

fechten ['fɛçtən] vi irreg fence.

Feder ['fe:dər] f **-, -n** feather; (Schreib—) pen nib; (Tech) spring; **~ball** m shuttlecock; **~ballspiel** nt badminton; **~bett** nt continental quilt; **~halter** m penholder, pen; f**~leicht** a light as a feather; f**~n** vi (nachgeben) be springy; (sich bewegen) bounce; vt spring; **~ung** f suspension; **~vieh** nt poultry.

Fee [fe:] *f* -, **-n** fairy; **f~nhaft** ['fe:ən-] *a* fairylike.

Fege- ['fe:gə] *cpd*: **~feuer** *nt* purgatory; **f~n** *vt* sweep.

fehl [fe:l] *a*: **~ am Platz** *or* **Ort** out of place; **~en** *vi* be wanting *or* missing; (*abwesend sein*) be absent; **etw fehlt jdm** sb lacks sth; **du fehlst mir** I miss you; **was fehlt ihm?** what's wrong with him?; **F~er** *m* **-s,** - mistake, error; (*Mangel, Schwäche*) fault; **~erfrei** *a* faultless; without any mistakes; **~erhaft** *a* incorrect; faulty; **F~geburt** *f* miscarriage; **~gehen** *vi irreg* go astray; **F~griff** *m* blunder; **F~konstruktion** *f* badly designed thing; **F~schlag** *m* failure; **~schlagen** *vi irreg* fail; **F~schluß** *m* wrong conclusion; **F~start** *m* (*Sport*) false start; **F~tritt** *m* false move; (*fig*) blunder, slip; **F~zündung** *f* (*Aut*) misfire, backfire.

Feier ['faɪər] *f* -, **-n** celebration; **~abend** *m* time to stop work; **~abend machen** stop, knock off; **was machst du am ~abend?** what are you doing after work?; **jetzt ist ~abend!** that's enough!; **f~lich** *a* solemn; **~lichkeit** *f* solemnity; *pl* festivities *pl*; **f~n** *vti* celebrate; **~tag** *m* holiday.

feig(e) ['faɪg(ə)] *a* cowardly; **F~e** *f* -, **-n** fig; **F~heit** *f* cowardice; **F~ling** *m* coward.

Feil- [faɪl] *cpd*: **~e** *f* -, **-n** file; **f~en** *vti* file; **f~schen** *vi* haggle.

fein [faɪn] *a* fine; (*vornehm*) refined; *Gehör etc* keen; **~!** great!

Feind [faɪnt] *m* **-(e)s, -e** enemy; **f~lich** *a* hostile; **~schaft** *f* enmity; **f~selig** *a* hostile; **~seligkeit** *f* hostility.

Fein- *cpd*: **f~fühlend, f~fühlig** *a* sensitive; **~gefühl** *nt* delicacy, tact; **~heit** *f* fineness; refinement; keenness; **~kostgeschäft** *nt* delicatessen (shop); **~schmecker** *m* **-s,** - gourmet.

feist [faɪst] *a* fat.

Feld [fɛlt] *nt* **-(e)s, -er** field; (*Schach*) square; (*Sport*) pitch; **~blume** *f* wild flower; **~herr** *m* commander; **~webel** *m* **-s,** - sergeant; **~weg** *m* path; **~zug** *m* (*lit, fig*) campaign.

Felge ['fɛlgə] *f* -, **-n** (wheel) rim; **~nbremse** *f* caliper brake.

Fell [fɛl] *nt* **-(e)s, -e** fur; coat; (*von Schaf*) fleece; (*von toten Tieren*) skin.

Fels [fɛls] *m* **-en, -en, Felsen** ['fɛlzən] *m* **-s,** - rock; (*von Dover etc*) cliff; **f~enfest** *a* firm; **~envorsprung** *m* ledge; **f~ig** *a* rocky; **~spalte** *f* crevice.

feminin [femi'ni:n] *a* feminine; (*pej*) effeminate.

Fenster ['fɛnstər] *nt* **-s,** - window; **~brett** *nt* windowsill; **~laden** *m* shutter; **~putzer** *m* **-s,** - window cleaner; **~scheibe** *f* windowpane; **~sims** *m* windowsill.

Ferien ['fe:rɪən] *pl* holidays *pl*, vacation (*US*); **~ haben** be on holiday; **~kurs** *m* holiday course; **~reise** *f* holiday; **~zeit** *f* holiday period.

Ferkel ['fɛrkəl] *nt* **-s,** - piglet.

fern [fɛrn] *a,ad* far-off, distant; **~ von hier** a long way (away) from here; **F~amt** *nt* (*Tel*) exchange; **F~bedienung** *f* remote control; **F~e** *f* -, **-n** distance; **~er** *a,ad* further; (*weiterhin*) in future; **F~flug** *m* long-distance flight; **F~gespräch** *nt* trunk call; **F~glas** *nt* binoculars *pl*; **~halten** *vtr irreg* keep away; **F~lenkung** *f* remote control; **~liegen** *vi irreg*: **jdm ~liegen** be far from sb's mind; **F~rohr** *nt* telescope; **F~schreiber** *m* teleprinter; **~schriftlich** *a* by telex; **F~sehapparat** *m* television set; **~sehen** *vi irreg* watch television; **F~sehen** *nt* **-s** television; **im F~sehen** on television; **F~seher** *m* television; **F~sprecher** *m* telephone; **F~sprechzelle** *f* telephone box *or* booth (*US*).

Ferse ['fɛrzə] *f* -, **-n** heel.

fertig ['fɛrtɪç] *a* (*bereit*) ready; (*beendet*) finished; (*gebrauchs~*) ready-made; **F~bau** *m* prefab(ricated house); **~bringen** *vt irreg* (*fähig sein*) manage, be capable of; (*beenden*) finish; **F~keit** *f* skill; **~machen** *vt* (*beenden*) finish; (*col*) *Person* finish; (*körperlich*) exhaust; (*moralisch*) get down; *vr* get ready; **~stellen** *vt* complete; **F~ware** *f* finished product.

Fessel ['fɛsəl] *f* -, **-n** fetter; **f~n** *vt* bind; (*mit Fesseln*) chain; (*fig*) spellbind; **f~nd** *a* fascinating, captivating.

fest [fɛst] *a* firm; *Nahrung* solid; *Gehalt* regular; *ad schlafen* soundly; **F~** *nt* **-(e)s, -e** party; festival; **~angestellt** *a* permanently employed; **F~beleuchtung** *f* illumination; **~binden** *vt irreg* tie, fasten; **~bleiben** *vi irreg* stand firm; **F~essen** *nt* banquet; **~fahren** *vr irreg* get stuck; **~halten** *irreg vt* seize, hold fast; *Ereignis* record; *vr* hold on (*an +dat* to); **~igen** *vt* strengthen; **F~igkeit** *f* strength; **~klammern** *vr* cling on (*an +dat* to); **F~land** *nt* mainland; **~legen** *vt* fix; *vr* commit o.s.; **~lich** *a* festive; **~machen** *vt* fasten; *Termin etc* fix; **F~nahme** *f* -, **-n** capture; **~nehmen** *vt irreg* capture, arrest; **F~rede** *f* address; **~schnallen** *vt* strap down; *vr* fasten one's seat belt; **~setzen** *vt* fix, settle; **F~spiel** *nt* festival; **~stehen** *vi irreg* be certain; **~stellen** *vt* establish; (*sagen*) remark; **F~ung** *f* fortress.

Fett [fɛt] *nt* **-(e)s, -e** fat, grease; **f~** *a* fat; *Essen etc* greasy; **f~arm** *a* low fat; **f~en** *vt* grease; **~fleck** *m* grease spot *or* stain; **f~gedruckt** *a* bold-type; **~gehalt** *m* fat content; **f~ig** *a* greasy, fatty; **~näpfchen** *nt*: **ins ~näpfchen treten** put one's foot in it.

Fetzen ['fɛtsən] *m* **-s,** - scrap.

feucht [fɔʏçt] *a* damp; *Luft* humid; **F~igkeit** *f* dampness; humidity.

Feuer ['fɔʏər] *nt* **-s,** - fire; (*zum Rauchen*) a light; (*fig: Schwung*) spirit; **~alarm** *nt* fire alarm; **~eifer** *m* zeal; **f~fest** *a* fireproof; **~gefahr** *f* danger of fire; **f~gefährlich** *a* inflammable; **~leiter** *f* fire escape ladder; **~löscher** *m* **-s,** - fire extinguisher; ~**melder** m -s, - fire alarm; **f**~**n** vti (lit, fig) fire; **f**~**sicher** a fire-proof; ~**stein** m flint; ~**wehr** f -, -en fire brigade; ~**werk** nt fireworks pl; ~**zeug** nt (cigarette) lighter.

Fichte ['fiçtə] f -, -n spruce, pine.

fidel [fi'de:l] a jolly.

Fieber ['fi:bər] nt -s, - fever, temperature; **f**~**haft** a feverish; ~**messer** m, ~**thermometer** nt thermometer.

fies [fi:s] a (col) nasty.

Figur [fi'gu:r] f -, -en figure; (Schach—) chessman, chess piece.

Filiale [fili'a:lə] f -, -n (Comm) branch.

Film [film] m -(e)s, -e film; ~**aufnahme** f shooting; **f**~**en** vti film; ~**kamera** f cine-camera; ~**vorführgerät** nt cine-projector.

Filter ['filtər] m -s, - filter; **f**~**n** vt filter; ~**mundstück** nt filter tip; ~**papier** nt filter paper; ~**zigarette** f tipped cigarette.

Filz [filts] m -es, -e felt; **f**~**en** vt (col) frisk; vi (Wolle) mat.

Finale [fi'na:lə] nt -s, -(s) finale; (Sport) final(s).

Finanz [fi'nants] f finance; ~**amt** nt Inland Revenue Office; ~**beamte(r)** m revenue officer; **f**~**iell** [-tsi'el] a financial; **f**~**ieren** [-'tsi:rən] vt finance; ~**minister** m Chancellor of the Exchequer (Brit), Minister of Finance.

Find- ['find] cpd: **f**~**en** irreg vt find; (meinen) think; vr be (found); (sich fassen) compose o.s.; **ich finde nichts dabei, wenn . . .** I don't see what's wrong if . . .; **das wird sich f**~**en** things will work out; ~**er** m -s, - finder; ~**erlohn** m reward; **f**~**ig** a resourceful.

Finger ['fiŋər] m -s, - finger,; ~**abdruck** m fingerprint; ~**handschuh** m glove; ~**hut** m thimble; (Bot) foxglove; ~**ring** m ring; ~**spitze** f fingertip; ~**zeig** m -(e)s, -e hint, pointer.

fingieren [fiŋ'gi:rən] vt feign.

fingiert a made-up, fictitious.

Fink ['fiŋk] m -en, -en finch.

finster ['finstər] a dark, gloomy; (verdächtig) dubious; (verdrossen) grim; Gedanke dark; **F**~**nis** f - darkness, gloom.

Finte ['fintə] f -, -n feint, trick.

firm [firm] a well-up; **F**~**a** f -, -men firm; **F**~**eninhaber** m owner of firm; **F**~**enschild** nt (shop) sign; **F**~**enzeichen** nt registered trademark.

Firnis ['firnis] m -ses, -se varnish.

Fisch [fiʃ] m -(e)s, -e fish; pl (Astrol) Pisces; **f**~**en** vti fish; ~**er** m -s, - fisherman; ~**e'rei** f fishing, fishery; ~**fang** m fishing; ~**geschäft** nt fishmonger's (shop); ~**gräte** f fishbone; ~**zug** m catch or draught of fish.

fix [fiks] a fixed; Person alert, smart; ~ **und fertig** finished; (erschöpft) done in; ~**ieren** [fi'ksi:rən] vt fix; (anstarren) stare at.

flach [flax] a flat; Gefäß shallow.

Fläche ['fleçə] f -, -n area; (Ober—) surface; ~**inhalt** m surface area.

Flach- cpd: ~**heit** f flatness; shallowness; ~**land** nt lowland.

flackern ['flakərn] vi flare, flicker.

Flagge ['flagə] f -, -n flag.

flagrant [fla'grant] a flagrant; **in** ~**i** red-handed.

Flamme ['flamə] f -, -n flame.

Flanell [fla'nɛl] m -s, -e flannel.

Flanke ['flaŋkə] f -, -n flank; (Sport: Seite) wing.

Flasche ['flaʃə] f -, -n bottle (col: Versager) wash-out; ~**nbier** nt bottled beer; ~**nöffner** m bottle opener; ~**nzug** m pulley.

flatterhaft a flighty, fickle.

flattern ['flatərn] vi flutter.

flau [flau] a weak, listless; Nachfrage slack; **jdm ist** ~ sb feels queasy.

Flaum [flaum] m -(e)s (Feder) down; (Haare) fluff.

flauschig ['flauʃiç] a fluffy.

Flausen ['flauzən] pl silly ideas pl; (Ausflüchte) weak excuses pl.

Flaute ['flautə] f -, -n calm; (Comm) recession.

Flechte ['flɛçtə] f -, -n plait; (Med) dry scab; (Bot) lichen; **f**~**n** vt irreg plait; Kranz twine.

Fleck [flɛk] m -(e)s, -e, **Flecken** m -s, - spot; (Schmutz—) stain; (Stoff—) patch; (Makel) blemish; **nicht vom** ~ **kommen** (lit, fig) not get any further; **vom** ~ **weg** straight away; **f**~**enlos** a spotless; ~**enmittel** nt, ~**enwasser** nt stain remover; **f**~**ig** a spotted; stained.

Fledermaus ['fle:dərmaus] f bat.

Flegel ['fle:gəl] m -s, - flail; (Person) lout; **f**~**haft** a loutish, unmannerly; ~**jahre** pl adolescence; **f**~**n** vr lounge about.

flehen ['fle:ən] vi implore; ~**tlich** a imploring.

Fleisch ['flaiʃ] nt -(e)s flesh; (Essen) meat; ~**brühe** f beef tea, stock; ~**er** m -s, - butcher; ~**e'rei** f butcher's (shop); **f**~**ig** a fleshy; **f**~**lich** a carnal; ~**pastete** f meat pie; ~**wolf** m mincer; ~**wunde** f flesh wound.

Fleiß ['flais] m -es diligence, industry; **f**~**ig** a diligent, industrious.

flektieren [flɛk'ti:rən] vt inflect.

flennen ['flɛnən] vi (col) cry, blubber.

fletschen ['flɛtʃən] vt Zähne show.

flexibel [flɛ'ksi:bəl] a flexible.

Flicken ['flikən] m -s, - patch; **f**~ vt mend.

Flieder ['fli:dər] m -s, - lilac.

Fliege ['fli:gə] f -, -n fly; (Kleidung) bow tie; **f**~**n** vti irreg fly; **auf jdn/etw f**~**en** (col) be mad about sb/sth; ~**npilz** m toadstool; ~**r** m -s, - flier, airman; ~**ralarm** m air-raid warning.

fliehen ['fli:ən] vi irreg flee.

Fliese ['fli:zə] f -, -n tile.

Fließ- ['fli:s] cpd: ~**arbeit** f production-line work; ~**band** nt production or assembly line; **f**~**en** vi irreg flow; **f**~**end** a flowing; Rede, Deutsch fluent; Übergänge smooth; -**heck** nt fastback; ~**papier** nt blotting paper.

flimmern ['flɪmərn] vi glimmer.

flink [flɪŋk] a nimble, lively; **F~heit** f nimbleness, liveliness.

Flinte ['flɪntə] f -, -n rifle; shotgun.

Flitter ['flɪtər] m -s, - spangle, tinsel; ~**wochen** pl honeymoon.

flitzen ['flɪtsən] vi flit.

Flocke ['flɔkə] f -, -n flake.

flockig a flaky.

Floh ['floː] m -(e)s, ¨e flea.

florieren [floˈriːrən] vi flourish.

Floskel ['flɔskəl] f -, -n empty phrase.

Floß [floːs] nt -es, ¨e raft, float.

Flosse ['flɔsə] f -, -n fin.

Flöte ['fløːtə] f -, -n flute; (Block—) recorder.

Flötist(in f) [fløˈtɪst(ɪn)] m flautist.

flott [flɔt] a lively; (elegant) smart; (Naut) afloat; **F~e** f -, -n fleet, navy.

Flöz [fløːts] nt -es, -e layer, seam.

Fluch [fluːx] m -(e)s, ¨e curse; **f~en** vi curse, swear.

Flucht [fluxt] f -, -en flight; (Fenster—) row; (Reihe—) range; (Zimmer—) suite; **f~artig** a hasty.

flücht- ['flʏçt] cpd: ~**en** vir flee, escape; ~**ig** a fugitive; (Chem) volatile; (vergänglich) transitory; (oberflächlich) superficial; (eilig) fleeting; **F~igkeit** f transitoriness; volatility; superficiality; **F~igkeitsfehler** m careless slip; **F~ling** m fugitive, refugee.

Flug [fluːk] m -(e)s, ¨e flight; **im** ~ airborne, in flight; ~**abwehr** ['fluːg-] f antiaircraft defence; ~**blatt** nt pamphlet.

Flügel ['flyːgəl] m -s, - wing; (Mus) grand piano.

Fluggast m airline passenger.

flügge ['flʏgə] a (fully-)fledged.

Flug- cpd: ~**geschwindigkeit** f flying or air speed; ~**gesellschaft** f airline (company); ~**hafen** m airport; ~**höhe** f altitude (of flight); ~**plan** m flight schedule; ~**platz** m airport; (klein) airfield; ~**post** f airmail; **f~s** [fluks] ad speedily; ~**schrift** f pamphlet; ~**strecke** f air route; ~**verkehr** m air traffic; ~**wesen** nt aviation; ~**zeug** nt (aero)plane, airplane (US); ~**zeugentführung** f hijacking of a plane; ~**zeughalle** f hangar; ~**zeugträger** m aircraft carrier.

Flunder ['flʊndər] f -, -n flounder.

flunkern ['flʊŋkərn] vi fib, tell stories.

Fluor ['fluːɔr] nt -s fluorine.

Flur [fluːr] m -(e)s, -e hall; (Treppen—) staircase.

Fluß [flʊs] m -sses, ¨sse river; (Fließen) flow; **im** ~ **sein** (fig) be in a state of flux.

flüssig ['flʏsɪç] a liquid; ~ **machen** vt Geld make available; **F~keit** f liquid; (Zustand) liquidity.

flüster- ['flʏstər] cpd: ~**n** vti whisper; **F~propaganda** f whispering campaign.

Flut [fluːt] f -, -en (lit, fig) flood; (Gezeiten) high tide; **f~en** vi flood; ~**licht** nt floodlight.

Fohlen ['foːlən] nt -s, - foal.

Föhn [føːn] m -(e)s, -e foehn, warm south wind.

Föhre ['føːrə] f -, -n Scots pine.

Folge ['fɔlgə] f -, -n series, sequence; (Fortsetzung) instalment; (Auswirkung) result; **in rascher** ~ in quick succession; **etw zur** ~ **haben** result in sth; ~ **haben** have consequences; **einer Sache** ~ **leisten** comply with sth; **f~n** vi follow (jdm sb); (gehorchen) obey (jdm sb); **jdm f~n können** (fig) follow or understand sb; **f~nd** a following; **f~ndermaßen** ad as follows, in the following way; **f~nreich**, **f~nschwer** a momentous; **f~richtig** a logical; **f~rn** vi conclude (aus +dat from); ~**rung** f conclusion; **f~widrig** a illogical.

folg- cpd: ~**lich** ad consequently; ~**sam** a obedient.

Folie ['foːliə] f -, -n foil.

Folter ['fɔltər] f -, -n torture; (Gerät) rack; **f~n** vt torture.

Fön · [føːn] m -(e)s, -e hair-dryer; **f~en** vt (blow) dry.

Fontäne [fɔnˈtɛːnə] f -, -n fountain.

foppen ['fɔpən] vt tease.

Förder- ['fœrdər] cpd: ~**band** nt conveyor belt; ~**korb** m pit cage; **f~lich** a beneficial.

fordern ['fɔrdərn] vt demand.

Förder- cpd: **f~n** vt promote; (unterstützen) help; Kohle extract; ~**ung** f promotion; help; extraction.

Forderung ['fɔrdərʊŋ] f demand.

Forelle [foˈrɛlə] f trout.

Form [fɔrm] f -, -en shape; (Gestaltung) form; (Guß—) mould; (Back—) baking tin; **in** ~ **sein** be in good form or shape; **in** ~ **von** in the shape of; **f~ali'sieren** vt formalize; ~**ali'tät** f formality; ~**at** [-ˈmaːt] nt -(e)s, -e format; (fig) distinction; ~**ati'on** f formation; **f~bar** a malleable; ~**el** f -, -n formula; [-ˈmɛl] a formal; **f~en** vt form, shape; ~**fehler** m faux-pas, gaffe; (Jur) irregularity; **f~ieren** [-ˈmiːrən] vt form; vr form up.

förmlich ['fœrmlɪç] a formal; (col) real; **F~keit** f formality.

Form- cpd: **f~los** a shapeless; Benehmen etc informal; ~**u'lar** nt -s, -e form; **f~u'lieren** vt formulate.

forsch [fɔrʃ] a energetic, vigorous; ~**en** vt search (nach for); vi (wissenschaftlich) (do) research; ~**end** a searching; **F~er** m -s, - research scientist; (Natur—) explorer.

Forschung ['fɔrʃʊŋ] f research; ~**sreise** f scientific expedition.

Forst [fɔrst] m -(e)s, -e forest; ~**arbeiter** m forestry worker; ~**wesen** nt, ~**wirtschaft** f forestry.

Förster ['fœrstər] m -s, - forester; (für Wild) gamekeeper.

fort [fɔrt] ad away; (verschwunden) gone; (vorwärts) on; **und so** ~ and so on; **in einem** ~ on and on; ~**bestehen** vi irreg survive; ~**bewegen** vtr move away; ~**bilden** vr continue one's education; ~**bleiben** vi irreg stay away; ~**bringen** vt irreg take away; **F~dauer** f continuance; ~**fahren** vi irreg depart; (fortsetzen) go on, continue; ~führen vt continue, carry on; ~gehen vi irreg go away; ~geschritten a advance; ~kommen vi irreg get on; (wegkommen) get away; ~können vi irreg be able to get away; ~müssen vi irreg have to go; ~pflanzen vr reproduce; F~pflanzung f reproduction; ~schaffen vt remove; ~schreiten vi irreg advance.

Fortschritt ['fort-frit] m advance; ~e machen make progress; f~lich ad progressive.

fort- cpd: ~setzen vt continue; F~setzung f continuation; (folgender Teil) instalment; F~setzung folgt to be continued; ~während a incessant, continual; ~ziehen irreg vt pull away; vi move on; (umziehen) move away.

Foto ['fo:to] nt -s, -s photo(graph); m -s, -s (~apparat) camera; ~graf m photographer; ~gra'phie f photography; (Bild) photograph; f~gra'phieren vt photograph; vi take photographs.

Foul nt -s, -s foul.

Fracht [fraxt] f -, -en freight; (Naut) cargo; (Preis) carriage; ~er m -s, - freighter, cargo boat; ~gut nt freight.

Frack [frak] m -(e)s, ⸚e tails pl.

Frage ['fra:gə] f -, -n question; etw in ~ stellen question sth; jdm eine ~ stellen ask sb a question, put a question to sb; nicht in ~ kommen be out of the question; ~bogen m questionnaire; f~n vti ask; ~zeichen nt question mark.

frag- cpd: ~lich a questionable, doubtful; ~los a unquestionably.

Fragment [fra'gmɛnt] nt fragment; f~arisch [-'ta:rɪʃ] a fragmentary.

fragwürdig ['fra:kvyrdɪç] a questionable, dubious.

Fraktion [fraktsi'o:n] f parliamentary party.

frank [fraŋk] a frank, candid; ~ieren [-'ki:rən] vt stamp, frank; ~o ad post-paid; carriage paid.

Franse ['franzə] f -, -n fringe; f~n vi fray.

Fratze ['fratsə] f -, -n grimace.

Frau [frau] f -, -en woman; (Ehe~) wife; (Anrede) Mrs; ~ Doktor Doctor; ~enarzt m gynaecologist; ~enbewegung f feminist movement; ~enzimmer nt female, broad (US).

Fräulein ['froylaın] nt young lady; (Anrede) Miss.

fraulich ['fraulɪç] a womanly.

frech [frɛç] a cheeky, impudent; F~dachs m cheeky monkey; F~heit f cheek, impudence.

Fregatte [fre'gatə] f frigate.

frei [fraı] a free; Stelle, Sitzplatz auch vacant; (Mitarbeiter) freelance; (Geld) available; (unbekleidet) bare; sich (dat) einen Tag ~ nehmen take a day off; von etw ~ sein be free of sth; im F~en in the open air; ~ sprechen talk without notes; F~bad nt open-air swimming pool; ~bekommen vt irreg: jdn/einen Tag ~bekommen get sb freed/get a day off; F~er m -s, - suitor; ~gebig a generous; F~gebigkeit f generosity; ~halten vt

irreg keep free; ~händig ad fahren with no hands; F~heit f freedom; ~heitlich a liberal; F~heitsstrafe f prison sentence; ~heraus ad frankly; F~karte f free ticket; ~kommen vi irreg get free; ~lassen vt irreg (set) free; F~lauf m freewheeling; ~legen vt expose; ~lich ad certainly, admittedly; ja ~lich yes of course; F~lichtbühne f open-air theatre; ~machen vt Post frank; Tage ~machen take days off; vr arrange to be free; ~sinnig a liberal; ~sprechen vt irreg acquit (von of); F~spruch m acquittal; ~stellen vt: jdm etw ~stellen leave sth (up) to sb; F~stoß m free kick; F~tag m Friday; ~tags ad on Fridays; F~übungen pl (physical) exercises pl; ~willig a voluntary; F~willige(r) mf volunteer; F~zeit f spare or free time; ~zügig a liberal, broad-minded; (mit Geld) generous.

fremd [frɛmt] a (unvertraut) strange; (ausländisch) foreign; (nicht eigen) someone else's; etw ist jdm ~ sth is foreign to sb; ~artig a strange; F~e(r) ['frɛmdə(r)] mf stranger; (Ausländer) foreigner; F~enführer m (tourist) guide; F~enlegion f foreign legion; F~enverkehr m tourism; F~enzimmer nt guest room; F~körper m foreign body; ~ländisch a foreign; F~ling m stranger; F~sprache f foreign language; ~sprachig a foreign-language; F~wort nt foreign word.

Frequenz [fre'kvɛnts] f (Rad) frequency.

fressen ['frɛsən] vti irreg eat.

Freude ['froydə] f -, -n joy, delight.

freudig a joyful, happy.

freudlos a joyless.

freuen ['froyən] vt impers make happy or pleased; vr be glad or happy; sich auf etw (acc) ~ look forward to sth; sich über etw (acc) ~ be pleased about sth.

Freund ['froynt] m -(e)s, -e friend; boyfriend; ~in [-dɪn] f friend; girlfriend; f~lich a kind, friendly; f~licherweise ad kindly; ~lichkeit f friendliness, kindness; ~schaft f friendship; f~schaftlich a friendly.

Frevel ['fre:fəl] m -s, - crime, offence (an +dat against); f~haft a wicked.

Frieden ['fri:dən] m -s, - peace; im ~ in peacetime; ~sschluß m peace agreement; ~sverhandlungen pl peace negotiations pl; ~svertrag m peace treaty; ~szeit f peacetime.

fried- ['fri:t] cpd: ~fertig a peaceable; F~hof m cemetery; ~lich a peaceful.

frieren ['fri:rən] vti irreg freeze; ich friere, es friert mich I am freezing, I'm cold.

Fries [fri:s] m -es, -e (Archit) frieze.

frigid(e) [fri'gi:t, fri'gi:də] a frigid.

Frikadelle [frika'dɛlə] f meatball.

frisch [frɪʃ] a fresh; (lebhaft) lively; ~gestrichen! wet paint!; sich ~ machen freshen (o.s.) up; F~e f- freshness; liveliness.

Friseur [fri'zø:r] m, **Friseuse** [fri'zø:zə] f hairdresser.

Frisier- [fri'zi:r] *cpd*: **f~en** *vtr* do (one's hair); *(fig)* Abrechnung fiddle, doctor; **~salon** *m* hairdressing salon; **~tisch** *m* dressing table.

Frisör [fri'zø:r] *m* **-s, e** hairdresser.

Frist [frist] *f* **-, -en** period; *(Termin)* deadline; **f~en** *vt* Dasein lead; *(kümmerlich)* eke out; **f~los** *a* Entlassung instant.

Frisur [fri'zu:r] *f* hairdo, hairstyle.

fritieren [fri'ti:rən] *vt* deep fry.

frivol [fri'vo:l] *a* frivolous.

froh [fro:] *a* happy, cheerful; **ich bin ~, daß . . .** I'm glad that . . .

fröhlich ['frø:liç] *a* merry, happy; **F~keit** *f* merriness, gaiety.

froh- *cpd*: **~'locken** *vi* exult; *(pej)* gloat; **F~sinn** *m* cheerfulness.

fromm [frɔm] *a* pious, good; *Wunsch* idle.

Frömm- ['frœm] *cpd*: **~e'lei** *f* false piety; **~igkeit** *f* piety.

frönen ['frø:nən] *vi* indulge *(etw (dat)* in sth).

Fronleichnam [fro:n'laıçna:m] *m* **-(e)s** Corpus Christi.

Front [frɔnt] *f* **-, -en** front; **f~al** [frɔn'ta:l] *a* frontal.

Frosch [frɔʃ] *m* **-(e)s, ⁻e** frog; *(Feuerwerk)* squib; **~mann** *m* frogman; **~schenkel** *m* frog's leg.

Frost [frɔst] *m* **-(e)s, ⁻e** frost; **~beule** *f* chilblain.

frösteln ['frœstəln] *vi* shiver.

Frost- *cpd*: **f~ig** *a* frosty; **~schutzmittel** *nt* anti-freeze.

Frottee [frɔ'te:] *nt or m* **-(s), -s** towelling.

frottieren [frɔ'ti:rən] *vt* rub, towel.

Frottier(hand)tuch *nt* towel.

Frucht [fruxt] *f* **-, ⁻e** *(lit, fig)* fruit; *(Getreide)* corn; **f~bar, f~bringend** *a* fruitful, fertile; **~barkeit** *f* fertility; **f~en** *vi* be of use; **f~los** *a* fruitless; **~saft** *m* fruit juice.

früh [fry:] *a,ad* early; **heute ~** this morning; **F~aufsteher** *m* **-s, -** early riser; **F~e** *f* - early morning; **~er** *a* earlier; *(ehemalig)* former; *ad* formerly; **~er war das anders** that used to be different; **~estens** *ad* at the earliest; **F~geburt** *f* premature birth/baby; **F~jahr** *nt*, **F~ling** *m* spring; **~reif** *a* precocious; **F~stück** *nt* breakfast; **~stücken** *vi* (have) breakfast; **~zeitig** *a* early; *(pej)* untimely.

frustrieren [frus'tri:rən] *vt* frustrate.

Fuchs [fuks] *m* **-es, ⁻e** fox; **f~en** *(col)* *vt* rile, annoy; *vr* be annoyed; **f~teufelswild** *a* hopping mad.

Füchsin ['fʏksın] *f* vixen.

fuchteln ['fuxtəln] *vi* gesticulate wildly.

Fuge ['fu:gə] *f* **-, -n** joint; *(Mus)* fugue.

fügen ['fy:gən] *vt* place, join; *vr* be obedient *(in +acc* to); *(anpassen)* adapt oneself (in *+acc* to); *impers* happen.

fügsam ['fy:kza:m] *a* obedient.

fühl- ['fy:l] *cpd*: **~bar** *a* perceptible, noticeable; **~en** *vtir* feel; **F~er** *m* **-s, -** feeler.

führen ['fy:rən] *vt* lead; *Geschäft* run; *Name* bear; *Buch* keep; *vi* lead; *vr* behave.

Führer ['fy:rər] *m* **-s, -** leader; *(Fremden~)* guide; **~schein** *m* driving licence.

Fuhrmann ['fu:rman] *m*, *pl* **-leute** carter.

Führung ['fy:rʊŋ] *f* leadership; *(eines Unternehmens)* management; *(Mil)* command; *(Benehmen)* conduct; *(Museums~)* conducted tour; **~szeugnis** *nt* certificate of good conduct.

Fuhrwerk ['fu:rvɛrk] *nt* cart.

Fülle ['fʏlə] *f* - wealth, abundance; **f~n** *vtr* fill; *(Cook)* stuff; **~n** *nt* **-s, -** foal; **~r** *m* **-s, -**, **Füllfederhalter** *m* fountain pen.

Füllung *f* filling; *(Holz~)* panel.

fummeln ['fuməln] *vi (col)* fumble.

Fund [fʊnt] *m* **-(e)s, -e** find; **~ament** [-da'mɛnt] *nt* foundation; **f~amen'tal** *a* fundamental; **~büro** *nt* lost property office, lost and found; **~grube** *f (fig)* treasure trove; **f~ieren** [-'di:rən] *vt* back up; **f~iert** *a* sound.

fünf [fʏnf] *num* five; **~hundert** *num* five hundred; **~te** *num* fifth; **F~tel** *nt* **-s, -** fifth; **~zehn** *num* fifteen; **~zig** *num* fifty.

fungieren [fʊŋ'gi:rən] *vi* function; *(Person)* act.

Funk [fʊŋk] *m* **-s** radio, wireless; **~e(n)** *m* **-ns, -n** *(lit, fig)* spark; **~eln** *vi* sparkle; **f~en** *vt* radio; **~er** *m* **-s, -** radio operator; **~gerät** *nt* radio set; **~haus** *nt* broadcasting centre; **~spruch** *m* radio signal; **~station** *f* radio station.

Funktion [fʊŋktsi'o:n] *f* function; **f~ieren** [-'ni:rən] *vi* work, function.

für [fy:r] *prep +acc* for; **was ~** what kind or sort of; **das F~ und Wider** the pros and cons *pl*; **Schritt ~ Schritt** step by step; **F~bitte** *f* intercession.

Furche ['fʊrçə] *f* **-, -n** furrow; **f~n** *vt* furrow.

Furcht [fʊrçt] *f* - fear; **f~bar** *a* terrible, frightful.

fürcht- ['fʏrçt] *cpd*: **~en** *vt* be afraid of, fear; *vr* be afraid *(vor +dat* of); **~erlich** *a* awful.

furcht- *cpd*: **~los** *a* fearless; **~sam** *a* timid.

füreinander [fy:r'aı'nandər] *ad* for each other.

Furnier [fʊr'ni:r] *nt* **-s, -e** veneer.

fürs [fy:rs] **= für das.**

Fürsorge ['fy:rzɔrgə] *f* care; *(Sozial~)* welfare; **~amt** *nt* welfare office; **~r(in** *f)* *m* **-s, -** welfare worker; **~unterstützung** *f* social security, welfare benefit *(US)*.

Für- *cpd*: **~sprache** *f* recommendation; *(um Gnade)* intercession; **~sprecher** *m* advocate.

Fürst [fʏrst] *m* **-en, -en** prince; **~in** *f* princess; **~entum** *nt* principality; **f~lich** *a* princely.

Furt [fʊrt] *f* **-, -en** ford.

Fürwort ['fy:rvɔrt] *nt* pronoun.

Fuß [fu:s] *m* **-es, ⁻e** foot; *(von Glas, Säule etc)* base; *(von Möbel)* leg; **zu ~** on foot; **~ball** *m* football; **~ballspiel** *nt* football match; **~ballspieler** *m* footballer; **~boden** *m* floor; **~bremse** *f (Aut)* foot-brake; **f~en** *vi* rest, be based *(auf +dat* on); **~ende** *nt* foot; **~gänger(in** *f)* *m* **-s, -**

pedestrian; ~**gängerzone** f pedestrian precinct; ~**note** f footnote; ~**pfleger(in** f) m chiropodist; ~**spur** f footprint; ~**tritt** m kick; (Spur) footstep; ~**weg** m footpath.

Futter ['futər] nt -s, - fodder, feed; (Stoff) lining; ~**al** [-'ra:l] nt -s, -e case.

füttern ['fytərn] vt feed; Kleidung line.

Futur [fu'tu:r] nt -s, -e future.

G

G, g [ge:] nt G, g.

Gabe ['ga:bə] f -, -n gift.

Gabel ['ga:bəl] f -, -n fork; ~**frühstück** nt mid-morning snack; ~**ung** f fork.

gackern ['gakərn] vi cackle.

gaffen ['gafən] vi gape.

Gage ['ga:ʒə] f -, -n fee; salary.

gähnen ['gɛ:nən] vi yawn.

Gala ['gala] f - formal dress; ~**vorstellung** f (Theat) gala performance.

galant [ga'lant] a gallant, courteous.

Galerie [galə'ri:] f gallery.

Galgen ['galgən] m -s, - gallows pl; ~**frist** f respite; ~**humor** m macabre humour.

Galle ['galə] f -, -n gall; (Organ) gallbladder.

Galopp [ga'lɔp] m -s, -s or -e gallop; g~**ieren** [-'pi:rən] vi gallop.

galvanisieren [galvani'zi:rən] vt galvanize.

Gamasche [ga'maʃə] f -, -n gaiter; (kurz) spat.

Gammler ['gamlər] m -s, - loafer, layabout.

Gang [gaŋ] m -(e)s, ⁓e walk; (Boten—) errand; (—art) gait; (Abschnitt eines Vorgangs) operation; (Essens—, Ablauf) course; (Flur etc) corridor; (Durch—) passage; (Tech) gear; **in ~ bringen** start up; (fig) get off the ground; **in ~ sein** be in operation; (fig) be underway; [gɛŋ] f -, -s gang; g~ a: g~ **und gäbe** usual, normal; g~**bar** a passable; Methode practicable.

Gängel- ['gɛŋəl] cpd: ~**band** nt: jdn am ~**band halten** (fig) spoonfeed sb; g~**n** vt spoonfeed.

gängig ['gɛŋɪç] a common, current; Ware in demand, selling well.

Ganove [ga'no:və] m -n, -n (col) crook.

Gans [gans] f -, ⁓e goose.

Gänse- ['gɛnzə] cpd: ~**blümchen** nt daisy; ~**braten** m roast goose; ~**füßchen** pl (col) inverted commas pl (Brit), quotes pl; ~**haut** f goose pimples pl; ~**marsch** m: **im** ~**marsch** in single file; ~**rich** m -s, -e gander.

ganz [gants] a whole; (vollständig) complete; ~ **Europa** all Europe; **sein** ~**es Geld** all his money; ad quite; (völlig) completely; ~ **und gar nicht** not at all; **es sieht** ~ **so aus** it really looks like it; **aufs G**~**e gehen** go for the lot.

gänzlich ['gɛntslɪç] a,ad complete(ly), entire(ly).

gar [ga:r] a cooked, done; ad quite; ~ **nicht/nichts/keiner** not/nothing/nobody at all; ~ **nicht schlecht** not bad at all.

Garage [ga'ra:ʒə] f -, -n garage.

Garantie [garan'ti:] f guarantee; g~**ren** vt guarantee.

Garbe ['garbə] f -, -n sheaf; (Mil) burst of fire.

Garde ['gardə] f -, -n guard(s); **die alte** ~ the old guard; ~'**robe** f -, -n wardrobe; (Abgabe) cloakroom; ~'**robenfrau** f cloakroom attendant; ~'**robenständer** m hallstand.

Gardine [gar'di:nə] f curtain.

gären ['gɛ:rən] vi irreg ferment.

Garn [garn] nt -(e)s, -e thread; yarn (auch fig).

Garnele [gar'ne:lə] f -, -n shrimp, prawn.

garnieren [gar'ni:rən] vt decorate; Speisen garnish.

Garnison [garni'zo:n] f -, -en garrison.

Garnitur [garni'tu:r] f (Satz) set; (Unterwäsche) set of (matching) underwear; (fig) **erste** ~ top rank; **zweite** ~ second rate.

garstig ['garstɪç] a nasty, horrid.

Garten ['gartən] m -s, ⁓ garden; ~**arbeit** f gardening; ~**bau** m horticulture; ~**fest** nt garden party; ~**gerät** nt gardening tool; ~**haus** nt summerhouse; ~**kresse** f cress; ~**lokal** nt beer garden; ~**schere** f pruning shears pl; ~**tür** f garden gate.

Gärtner(in f) ['gɛrtnər(ɪn)] m -s, - gardener; ~**ei** [-'raɪ] f nursery; (Gemüse-) market garden (Brit), truck farm (US); g~**n** vi garden.

Gärung ['gɛ:ruŋ] f fermentation.

Gas [ga:s] nt -es, -e gas; ~ **geben** (Aut) accelerate, step on the gas; g~**förmig** a gaseous; ~**herd** m, ~**kocher** m gas cooker; ~**leitung** f gas pipeline; ~**maske** f gasmask; ~**pedal** nt accelerator, gas pedal.

Gasse ['gasə] f -, -n lane, alley; ~**njunge** m street urchin.

Gast [gast] m -es, ⁓e guest; ~**arbeiter(in** f) m foreign worker.

Gästebuch ['gɛstəbu:x] nt visitors' book, guest book.

Gast- cpd: g~**freundlich** a hospitable; ~**geber** m -s, - host; ~**geberin** f hostess; ~**haus** nt, ~**hof** m hotel, inn; g~**ieren** [-'ti:rən] vi (Theat) (appear as a) guest; g~**lich** a hospitable; ~**lichkeit** f hospitality; ~**rolle** f guest role.

gastronomisch [gastro'no:mɪʃ] a gastronomic(al).

Gast- cpd: ~**spiel** nt (Sport) away game; ~**stätte** f restaurant; pub; ~**wirt** m innkeeper; ~**wirtschaft** f hotel, inn; ~**zimmer** nt (guest) room.

Gas- cpd: ~**vergiftung** f gas poisoning; ~**werk** nt gasworks sing or pl; ~**zähler** m gas meter.

Gatte ['gatə] m -n, -n husband, spouse; **die** ~**n** husband and wife.

Gatter ['gatər] nt -s, - railing, grating; (Eingang) gate.

Gattin f wife, spouse.

Gattung ['gatʊŋ] f genus; kind.
Gaukler ['gaʊklər] m -s, - juggler, conjurer.
Gaul [gaʊl] m -(e)s, **Gäule** horse; nag.
Gaumen ['gaʊmən] m -s, - palate.
Gauner ['gaʊnər] m -s, - rogue; ~ei [-'raɪ] f swindle.
Gaze ['ga:zə] f -, -n gauze.
Gebäck [gə'bɛk] nt -(e)s, -e pastry.
Gebälk [gə'bɛlk] nt -(e)s timberwork.
Gebärde [gə'bɛːrdə] f -, -n gesture; g~n vr behave.
gebären [gə'bɛːrən] vt irreg give birth to, bear.
Gebärmutter f uterus, womb.
Gebäude [gə'bɔʏdə] nt -s, - building; ~komplex m (building) complex.
Gebein [gə'baɪn] nt -(e)s, -e bones pl.
Gebell [gə'bɛl] nt -(e)s barking.
geben ['ge:bən] irreg vti (jdm etw) give (sb sth or sth to sb); Karten deal; **ein Wort gab das andere** one angry word led to another; v impers **es gibt** there is/are; there will be; **gegeben** given; **zu gegebener Zeit** in good time; vr (sich verhalten) behave, act; (aufhören) abate; **sich geschlagen** ~ admit defeat; **das wird sich schon** ~ that'll soon sort itself out.
Gebet [gə'be:t] nt -(e)s, -e prayer.
Gebiet [gə'bi:t] nt -(e)s, -e area; (Hoheits—) territory; (fig) field; g~en vt irreg command, demand; ~er m -s, - master; (Herrscher) ruler; g~erisch a imperious.
Gebilde [gə'bɪldə] nt -s, - object, structure; g~t a cultured, educated.
Gebimmel [gə'bɪml] nt -s (continual) ringing.
Gebirge [gə'bɪrgə] nt -s, - mountain chain.
gebirgig a mountainous.
Gebirgszug [gə'bɪrksts:k] m mountain range.
Gebiß [gə'bɪs] nt -sses, -sse teeth pl; (künstlich) dentures pl.
geblümt [gə'bly:mt] a flowery.
Geblüt [gə'bly:t] nt -(e)s blood, race.
geboren [gə'bo:rən] a born; Frau née.
geborgen [gə'bɔrgən] a secure, safe.
Gebot [gə'bo:t] nt -(e)s, -e command(ment Bibl); (bei Auktion) bid.
Gebräu [gə'brɔʏ] nt -(e)s, -e brew, concoction.
Gebrauch [gə'braʊx] m -(e)s, **Gebräuche** use; (Sitte) custom; g~en vt use.
gebräuchlich [gə'brɔʏçlɪç] a usual, customary.
Gebrauchs- cpd: ~**anweisung** f directions pl for use; ~**artikel** m article of everyday use; g~**fertig** a ready for use; ~**gegenstand** m commodity.
gebraucht [gə'braʊxt] a used; G~**wagen** m secondhand or used car.
gebrechlich [gə'brɛçlɪç] a frail; G~**keit** f frailty.
Gebrüder [gə'bry:dər] pl brothers pl.
Gebrüll [gə'brʏl] nt -(e)s roaring.
Gebühr [gə'by:r] f -, -en charge, fee; **nach** ~ fittingly; **über** ~ unduly; g~en vi:

jdm g~en be sb's due or due to sb; vr be fitting; g~**end** a,ad fitting(ly), appropriate(ly); ~**enerlaß** m remission of fees; ~**enermäßigung** f reduction of fees; g~**enfrei** a free of charge; g~**enpflichtig** a subject to charges.
Geburt [gə'bu:rt] f -, -en birth; ~**enbeschränkung** f, ~**enkontrolle** f, ~**enregelung** f birth control; ~**enziffer** f birth-rate.
gebürtig [gə'bʏrtɪç] a born in, native of; ~e **Schweizerin** native of Switzerland, Swiss-born.
Geburts- cpd: ~**anzeige** f birth notice; ~**datum** nt date of birth; ~**jahr** nt year of birth; ~**ort** m birthplace; ~**tag** m birthday; ~**urkunde** f birth certificate.
Gebüsch [gə'bʏʃ] nt -(e)s, -e bushes pl.
Gedächtnis [gə'dɛçtnɪs] nt -ses, -se memory; ~**feier** f commemoration; ~**schwund** m loss of memory, failing memory; ~**verlust** m amnesia.
Gedanke [gə'daŋkə] m -ns, -n thought; **sich über etw** (acc) ~**n machen** think about sth; ~**naustausch** m exchange of ideas; g~**nlos** a thoughtless; ~**nlosigkeit** f thoughtlessness; ~**nstrich** m dash; ~**nübertragung** f thought transference, telepathy; g~**nverloren** a lost in thought; g~**nvoll** a thoughtful.
Gedärm [gə'dɛrm] nt -(e)s, -e intestines pl, bowels pl.
Gedeck [gə'dɛk] nt -(e)s, -e cover(ing); (Speisenfolge) menu; **ein** ~ **auflegen** lay a place.
gedeihen [gə'daɪən] vi irreg thrive, prosper.
gedenken [gə'dɛŋkən] vi irreg (sich erinnern) (+gen) remember; (beabsichtigen) intend.
Gedenk- cpd: ~**feier** f commemoration; ~**minute** f minute's silence; ~**tag** m remembrance day.
Gedicht [gə'dɪçt] nt -(e)s, -e poem.
gediegen [gə'di:gən] a (good) quality; Mensch reliable, honest; G~**heit** f quality; reliability, honesty.
Gedränge [gə'drɛŋə] nt -s crush, crowd; **ins** ~ **kommen** (fig) get into difficulties.
gedrängt a compressed; ~ **voll** packed.
gedrungen [gə'drʊŋən] a thickset, stocky.
Geduld [gə'dʊlt] f - patience; g~**en** [gə'dʊldən] vr be patient; g~**ig** a patient, forbearing; ~**sprobe** f trial of (one's) patience.
gedunsen [gə'dʊnzən] a bloated.
geeignet [gə'aɪgnət] a suitable.
Gefahr [gə'fa:r] f -, -en danger; ~ **laufen, etw zu tun** run the risk of doing sth; **auf eigene** ~ at one's own risk.
gefährden [gə'fɛːrdən] vt endanger.
Gefahren- cpd: ~**quelle** f source of danger; ~**zulage** f danger money.
gefährlich [gə'fɛːrlɪç] a dangerous.
Gefährte [gə'fɛːrtə] m -n, -n, **Gefährtin** f companion.
Gefälle [gə'fɛlə] nt -s, - gradient, incline.
Gefallen [gə'falən] m -s, - favour; nt -s pleasure; **an etw** (dat) ~ **finden** derive

pleasure from sth; **jdm etw zu ~ tun** do sth to please sb; **g~** *vi irreg*: **jdm g~** please sb; **er/es gef*ä*llt mir** I like him/it; **das gefällt mir an ihm** that's one thing I like about him; **sich** (*dat*) **etw g~ lassen** put up with sth; *ptp of* **fallen**.

gefällig [gə'fɛlıç] a (*hilfsbereit*) obliging; (*erfreulich*) pleasant; **G~keit** f favour; helpfulness; **etw aus G~keit tun** do sth as a favour.

gefälligst ad kindly.

gefallsüchtig a eager to please.

gefangen [gə'faŋən] a captured; (*fig*) captivated; **G~e(r)** m prisoner, captive; **G~enlager** nt prisoner-of-war camp; **~halten** vt irreg keep prisoner; **G~nahme** f -, -n capture; **G~schaft** f captivity.

Gefängnis [gə'fɛŋnıs] nt -ses, -se prison; **~strafe** f prison sentence; **~wärter** m prison warder.

Gefasel [gə'fa:zəl] nt -s twaddle, drivel.

Gefäß [gə'fɛ:s] nt -es, -e vessel (*auch* Anat), container.

gefaßt [gə'fast] a composed, calm; **auf etw** (*acc*) **~ sein** be prepared or ready for sth.

Gefecht [gə'fɛçt] nt -(e)s, -e fight; (*Mil*) engagement.

gefeit [gə'faıt] a: **gegen etw ~ sein** be immune to sth.

Gefieder [gə'fi:dər] nt -s, - plumage, feathers pl; **g~t** a feathered.

gefleckt [gə'flɛkt] a spotted, mottled.

geflissentlich [gə'flısəntlıç] a,ad intentional(ly).

Geflügel [gə'fly:gəl] nt -s poultry.

Gefolge [gə'fɔlgə] nt -s, - retinue.

Gefolg- cpd: **~schaft** f following; (*Arbeiter*) personnel; **~smann** m follower.

gefragt [ge'fra:kt] a in demand.

gefräßig [gə'frɛ:sıç] a voracious.

Gefreite(r) [gə'fraıtə(r)] m -n, -n lance corporal; (*Naut*) able seaman; (*Aviat*) aircraftman.

gefrieren [gə'fri:rən] vi irreg freeze.

Gefrier- cpd: **~fach** nt icebox; **~fleisch** nt frozen meat; **g~getrocknet** a freeze-dried; **~punkt** m freezing point; **~schutzmittel** nt antifreeze; **~truhe** f deep-freeze.

Gefüge [gə'fy:gə] nt -s, - structure.

gefügig a pliant; *Mensch* obedient.

Gefühl [gə'fy:l] nt -(e)s, -e feeling; **etw im ~ haben** have a feel for sth; **g~los** a unfeeling; **g~sbetont** a emotional; **~sduselei** [-zdu:zə'laı] f emotionalism; **g~smäßig** a instinctive.

gegebenenfalls [gə'ge:bənənfals] ad if need be.

gegen ['ge:gən] prep +acc against; (*in Richtung auf, jdn betreffend, kurz vor*) towards; (*im Austausch für*) (in return) for; (*ungefähr*) round about; **G~angriff** m counter-attack; **G~beweis** m counter-evidence.

Gegend ['ge:gənt] f -, -en area, district.

Gegen- cpd: **g~el'nander** ad against one another; **~fahrbahn** f oncoming

carriageway; **~frage** f counter-question; **~gewicht** nt counterbalance; **~gift** nt antidote; **~leistung** f service in return; **~lichtaufnahme** f contre-jour photograph; **~maßnahme** f counter-measure; **~probe** f cross-check; **~satz** m contrast; **~sätze überbrücken** overcome differences; **g~sätzlich** a contrary, opposite; (*widersprüchlich*) contradictory; **~schlag** m counter attack; **~seite** f opposite side; (*Rückseite*) reverse; **g~seitig** a mutual, reciprocal; **sich g~seitig helfen** help each other; **~seitigkeit** f reciprocity; **~spieler** m opponent; **~stand** m object; **g~ständlich** a objective, concrete; **~stimme** f vote against; **~stoß** m counterblow; **~stück** nt counterpart; **~teil** nt opposite; **im ~teil** on the contrary; **ins ~teil umschlagen** swing to the other extreme; **g~teilig** a opposite, contrary.

gegenüber [ge:gən''y:bər] prep +dat opposite; (*zu* to(wards); (*angesichts*) in the face of; ad opposite; **G~** nt -s, - person opposite; **~liegen** vr irreg face each other; **~stehen** vr irreg be opposed (to each other); **~stellen** vt confront; (*fig*) contrast; **G~stellung** f confrontation; (*fig*) contrast; **~treten** vi irreg (+dat) face.

Gegen- cpd: **~verkehr** m oncoming traffic; **~vorschlag** m counterproposal; **~wart** f present; **g~wärtig** a present; **das ist mir nicht mehr g~wärtig** that has slipped my mind; ad at present; **~wert** m equivalent; **~wind** m headwind; **~wirkung** f reaction; **g~zeichnen** vti countersign; **~zug** m counter-move; (*Rail*) corresponding train in the other direction.

Gegner ['ge:gnər] m -s, - opponent; **g~isch** a opposing; **~schaft** f opposition.

Gehackte(s) [ge'hakt(z)] nt mince(d meat).

Gehalt [gə'halt] m -(e)s, -e content; nt -(e)s, -er salary; **~sempfänger** m salary earner; **~serhöhung** f salary increase; **~szulage** f salary increment.

geharnischt [gə'harnıʃt] a (*fig*) forceful, angry.

gehässig [gə'hɛsıç] a spiteful, nasty; **G~keit** f spite(fulness).

Gehäuse [gə'hɔyzə] nt -s, - case; casing; (*von Apfel etc*) core.

Gehege [gə'he:gə] nt -s, - enclosure, preserve; **jdm ins ~ kommen** (*fig*) poach on sb's preserve.

geheim [gə'haım] a secret; **G~dienst** m secret service, intelligence service; **~halten** vt irreg keep secret; **G~nis** nt -ses, -se secret; mystery; **~niskrämer** m secretive type; **~nisvoll** a mysterious; **G~polizei** f secret police; **G~schrift** f code, secret writing.

Geheiß [gə'haıs] nt -es command; **auf jds ~** at sb's behest.

gehen ['ge:ən] irreg vti go; (*zu Fuß —*) walk; **~ nach** (*Fenster*) face; v impers: **wie**

geht es (dir)? how are you or things?; mir/ihm geht es gut I'm/he's (doing) fine; geht das? is that possible?; geht's noch? can you manage?; es geht not too bad, O.K.; das geht nicht that's not on; es geht um etw sth is concerned, it's about sth.

geheuer [gə'hɔyər] a: nicht ~ eery; (fragwürdig) dubious.

Geheul [gə'hɔyl] nt -(e)s howling.

Gehilfe [gə'hilfə] m -n, -n, Gehilfin f assistant.

Gehirn [gə'hirn] nt -(e)s, -e brain; ~erschütterung f concussion; ~wäsche f brainwashing.

Gehör [gə'hø:r] nt -(e)s hearing; musikalisches ~ ear; ~ finden gain a hearing; jdm ~ schenken give sb a hearing.

gehorchen [gə'hɔrçən] vi obey (jdm sb).

gehören [gə'hø:rən] vi belong; vr impers be right or proper.

gehörig a proper; ~ zu or +dat belonging to; part of.

gehorsam [gə'ho:rza:m] a obedient; G~ m -s obedience.

Gehsteig m, Gehweg m ['ge:-] pavement, sidewalk (US).

Geier ['gaiər] m -s, - vulture.

geifern ['gaifərn] vi salivate; (fig) bitch.

Geige ['gaigə] f -, -n violin; ~r m -s, - violinist; ~rzähler m geiger counter.

geil [gail] a randy, horny (US).

Geisel ['gaizəl] f -, -n hostage.

Geißel ['gaisəl] f -, -n scourge, whip; g~n vt scourge.

Geist [gaist] m -(e)s, -er spirit; (Gespenst) ghost; (Verstand) mind; g~erhaft a ghostly; g~esabwesend a absentminded; ~esblitz m brainwave; ~esgegenwart f presence of mind; ~eshaltung f mental attitude; g~eskrank a mentally ill; ~eskranke(r) mf mentally ill person; ~eskrankheit f mental illness; ~esstörung f mental disturbance; ~eswissenschaften pl arts (subjects) pl; ~eszustand m state of mind; g~ig a intellectual; mental; Getränke alcoholic; g~ig behindert mentally handicapped; g~lich a spiritual, religious; clerical; ~liche(r) m clergyman; ~lichkeit f clergy; g~los a uninspired, dull; g~reich a clever; witty; g~tötend a soul-destroying; g~voll a intellectual; (weise) wise.

Geiz [gaits] m -es miserliness, meanness; g~en vi be miserly; ~hals m, ~kragen m miser; g~ig a miserly, mean.

Geklapper [gə'klapər] nt -s rattling.

geknickt [gə'knikt] a (fig) dejected.

gekonnt [gə'kɔnt] a skilful.

Gekritzel [gə'kritsəl] nt -s scrawl, scribble.

gekünstelt [ge'kynstəlt] a artificial, affected.

Gelächter [gə'lɛçtər] nt -s, - laughter.

geladen [ge'la:dən] a loaded; (Elec) live; (fig) furious.

Gelage [gə'la:gə] nt -s, - feast, banquet.

gelähmt [gə'lɛ:mt] a paralysed.

Gelände [gə'lɛndə] nt -s, - land, terrain; (von Fabrik, Sport—) grounds pl; (Bau—) site; g~gängig a able to go crosscountry; ~lauf m cross-country race.

Geländer [gə'lɛndər] nt -s, - railing; (Treppen—) banister(s).

gelangen [gə'laŋən] vi (an +acc or zu) reach; (erwerben) attain; in jds Besitz ~ to come into sb's possession.

gelassen [gə'lasən] a calm, composed; G~heit f calmness, composure.

Gelatine [ʒela'ti:nə] f gelatine.

geläufig [gə'lɔyfiç] a (üblich) common; das ist mir nicht ~ I'm not familiar with that; G~keit f commonness; familiarity.

gelaunt [gə'launt] a: schlecht/gut ~ in a bad/good mood; wie ist er ~? what sort of mood is he in?

Geläut(e) [gə'lɔyt(ə)] nt -(e)s, -(e) ringing; (Läutwerk) chime.

gelb [gɛlp] a yellow; (Ampellicht) amber; ~lich a yellowish; G~sucht f jaundice.

Geld [gɛlt] nt -(e)s, -er money; etw zu ~ machen sell sth off; ~anlage f investment; ~beutel m, ~börse f purse; ~einwurf m slot; ~geber m -s, - financial backer; g~gierig a avaricious; ~mittel pl capital, means pl; ~schein m banknote; ~schrank m safe, strongbox; ~strafe f fine; ~stück nt coin; ~verlegenheit f: in ~verlegenheit sein/kommen to be/run short of money; ~verleiher m -s, - moneylender; ~wechsel m exchange (of money).

Gelee [ʒe'le:] nt or m -s, -s jelly.

gelegen [gə'le:gən] a situated; (passend) convenient, opportune; etw kommt jdm ~ sth is convenient for sb.

Gelegenheit [gə'le:gənhait] f opportunity; (Anlaß) occasion; bei jeder ~ at every opportunity; ~arbeit f casual work; ~arbeiter m casual worker; ~skauf m bargain.

gelegentlich [gə'le:gəntliç] a occasional; ad occasionally; (bei Gelegenheit) some time (or other); prep +gen on the occasion of.

gelehrig [gə'le:riç] a quick to learn, intelligent.

gelehrt a learned; G~e(r) mf scholar; G~heit f scholarliness.

Geleise [gə'laizə] nt -s, - track; see Gleis.

Geleit [gə'lait] nt -(e)s, -e escort; g~en vt escort; ~schutz m escort.

Gelenk [gə'lɛŋk] nt -(e)s, -e joint; g~ig a supple.

gelernt [gə'lɛrnt] a skilled.

Geliebte(r) [gə'li:ptə(r)] mf sweetheart, beloved.

gelind(e) [gə'lint, gə'lində] a mild, light; (fig) Wut fierce; ~e gesagt to put it mildly.

gelingen [gə'liŋən] vi irreg succeed; die Arbeit gelingt mir nicht I'm not being very successful with this piece of work; es ist mir gelungen, etw zu tun I succeeded in doing sth.

gellen ['gɛlən] vi shrill.

geloben [gə'lo:bən] *vti* vow, swear.

gelten ['gɛltən] *irreg vt* (*wert sein*) be worth; **etw gilt bei jdm viel/wenig** sb values sth highly/sb doesn't value sth very highly; **jdm viel/wenig ~** mean a lot/not mean much to sb; **was gilt die Wette?** do you want to bet?; *vi* (*gültig sein*) be valid; (*erlaubt sein*) be allowed; **jdm ~** (*gemünzt sein auf*) be meant for *or* aimed at sb; **etw ~ lassen** accept sth; **als** *or* **für etw ~** be considered to be sth; **jdm** *or* **für jdn ~** (*betreffen*) apply to *or* for sb; *v impers* **es gilt, etw zu tun** it is necessary to do sth; **~d** *a* prevailing; **etw ~d machen** to assert sth; **sich ~d machen** make itself/o.s. felt.

Geltung ['gɛltuŋ] *f:* **~ haben** have validity; **sich/etw** (*dat*) **verschaffen** establish oneself/sth; **etw zur ~ bringen** show sth to its best advantage; **zur ~ kommen** be seen/heard *etc* to its best advantage; **~sbedürfnis** *nt* desire for admiration.

Gelübde [gə'lypdə] *nt* -s, - vow.

gelungen [gə'luŋən] a successful.

gemächlich [gə'mɛ:çlɪç] a leisurely.

Gemahl [gə'ma:l] *m* -(e)s, -e husband; **~in** *f* wife.

Gemälde [gə'mɛ:ldə] *nt* -s, - picture, painting.

gemäß [gə'mɛ:s] *prep* +*dat* in accordance with; *a* appropriate (*dat* to); **~igt** *a* moderate; *Klima* temperate.

gemein [gə'main] *a* common; (*niederträchtig*) mean; **etw ~ haben** (**mit**) have sth in common (with).

Gemeinde [gə'maində] *f* -, -n district, community; (*Pfarr—*) parish; (*Kirchen—*) congregation; **~steuer** *f* local rates *pl*; **~verwaltung** *f* local administration; **~vorstand** *m* local council; **~wahl** *f* local election.

Gemein- *cpd:* **g~gefährlich** a dangerous to the public; **~gut** *nt* public property; **~heit** *f* commonness; mean thing to do/to say; **g~hin** *ad* generally; **~nutz** *m* public good; **~platz** *m* commonplace, platitude; **g~sam** a joint, common (*auch Math*); **g~same Sache mit jdm machen** be in cahoots with sb; *ad* together, jointly; **etw g~sam haben** have sth in common; **~samkeit** *f* community, having in common; **~schaft** *f* community; **in ~schaft mit** jointly *or* together with; **g~schaftlich** a see **g~sam**; **~schaftsarbeit** *f* teamwork; team effort; **~schaftserziehung** *f* coeducation; **~sinn** *m* public spirit; **g~verständlich** a generally comprehensible; **~wohl** *nt* common good.

Gemenge [gə'mɛŋə] *nt* -s, - mixture; (*Hand—*) scuffle.

gemessen [gə'mɛsən] a measured.

Gemetzel [gə'mɛtsəl] *nt* -s, - slaughter, carnage, butchery.

Gemisch [gə'mɪʃ] *nt* -es, -e mixture; **g~t** a mixed.

Gemse ['gɛmzə] *f* -, -n chamois.

Gemunkel [gə'muŋkəl] *nt* -s gossip.

Gemurmel [gə'murməl] *nt* -s murmur(ing).

Gemüse [gə'my:zə] *nt* -s, - vegetables *pl*; **~garten** *m* vegetable garden; **~händler** *m* greengrocer.

Gemüt [gə'my:t] *nt* -(e)s, -er disposition, nature; person; **sich** (*dat*) **etw zu ~e führen** (*col*) indulge in sth; **die ~er erregen** arouse strong feelings; **g~lich** a comfortable, cosy; *Person* good-natured; **~lichkeit** *f* comfortableness, cosiness; amiability; **~sbewegung** *f* emotion; **~smensch** *m* sentimental person; **~sruhe** *f* composure; **~szustand** *m* state of mind; **g~voll** a warm, tender.

genau [gə'nau] *a,ad* exact(ly), precise(ly); **etw ~ nehmen** take sth seriously; **~genommen** *ad* strictly speaking; **G~igkeit** *f* exactness, accuracy.

genehm [gə'ne:m] a agreeable, acceptable; **~igen** *vt* approve, authorize; **sich** (*dat*) **etw ~igen** indulge in sth; **G~igung** *f* approval, authorization.

geneigt [gə'naikt] a well-disposed, willing; **~ sein, etw zu tun** be inclined to do sth.

General [gene'ra:l] *m* -s, -e *or* -e general; **~direktor** *m* director general; **~konsulat** *nt* consulate general; **~probe** *f* dress rehearsal; **~stabskarte** *f* ordnance survey map; **~streik** *m* general strike; **g~überholen** *vt* thoroughly overhaul.

Generation [generatsi'o:n] *f* generation; **~skonflikt** *m* generation gap.

Generator [gene'ra:tɔr] *m* generator, dynamo.

genesen [ge'ne:zən] *vi irreg* convalesce, recover, get well; **G~de(r)** *mf* convalescent.

Genesung *f* recovery, convalescence.

genetisch [ge'ne:tɪʃ] a genetic.

genial [geni'a:l] a brilliant; **G~i'tät** *f* brilliance, genius.

Genick [gə'nɪk] *nt* -(e)s, -e (back of the) neck; **~starre** *f* stiff neck.

Genie [ʒe'ni:] *nt* -s, -s genius.

genieren [ʒe'ni:rən] *vt* bother; **geniert es Sie, wenn . . .?** do you mind if . . .?; *vr* feel awkward *or* self-conscious.

genießbar a edible; drinkable.

genießen [gə'ni:sən] *vt irreg* enjoy; eat; drink.

Genießer *m* -s, - epicure; pleasure lover; **g~isch** a appreciative; *ad* with relish.

Genosse [gə'nɔsə] *m* -n, -n, **Genossin** *f* comrade (*esp Pol*), companion; **~nschaft** *f* cooperative (association).

genug [gə'nu:k] *ad* enough.

Genüge [gə'ny:gə] *f* -: **jdm/etw ~ tun** *or* **leisten** satisfy sb/sth; **g~n** *vi* be enough, suffice; (+*dat*) satisfied; **g~nd** a sufficient.

genügsam [gə'ny:kza:m] a modest, easily satisfied; **G~keit** *f* moderation.

Genugtuung [gə'nu:ktu:uŋ] *f* satisfaction.

Genuß [gə'nus] *m* -sses, -sse pleasure; (*Zusichnehmen*) consumption; **in den ~ von etw kommen** receive the benefit of sth; **~mittel** *pl* (semi-)luxury items *pl*.

genüßlich [gə'nʏslɪç] *ad* with relish.

Geograph [geo'gra:f] m -en, -en geographer; ~ie [-'fi:] f geography; g~isch a geographical.

Geologe [geo'lo:gə] m -n, -n geologist; ~gie ['gi:] f geology.

Geometrie [geome'tri:] f geometry.

Gepäck [gə'pɛk] nt -(e)s luggage, baggage; ~abfertigung f, ~annahme f, ~ausgabe f luggage desk/office; ~aufbewahrung f left-luggage office, check-room (US); ~netz nt luggage-rack; ~träger m porter; (Fahrrad) carrier; ~wagen m luggage van, baggage car (US).

gepflegt [gə'pfle:kt] a well-groomed; Park etc well looked after.

Gepflogenheit [gə'pflo:gənhait] f custom.

Geplapper [gə'plapər] nt -s chatter.

Geplauder [gə'plaudər] nt -s chat(ting).

Gepolter [gə'poltər] nt -s din.

gerade [gə'ra:də] a straight; Zahl even; ad (genau) exactly; (örtlich) straight; (eben) just; warum ~ ich? why me?; ~ weil just or precisely because; nicht ~ schön not exactly nice; das ist es ja ~ that's just it; jetzt ~ nicht! not now!; ~ noch just; ~ neben right next to; G~ f -n, -n straight line; ~aus straight ahead; ~heraus a straight out, bluntly; ~so ad just so; ~so dumm etc just as stupid etc; ~so wie just as; ~zu ad (beinahe) virtually, almost.

geradlinig a rectilinear.

Gerät [gə'rɛ:t] nt -(e)s, -e device; (Werkzeug) tool; (Sport) apparatus; (Zubehör) equipment no pl.

geraten [gə'ra:tən] vi irreg (gelingen) turn out well (jdm for sb); (gedeihen) thrive; gut/schlecht ~ turn out well/badly; an jdn ~ come across sb; in etw (acc) ~ get into sth; in Angst ~ get frightened; nach jdm ~ take after sb.

Geratewohl [gəra:tə'vo:l] nt: aufs ~ on the off chance; (bei Wahl) at random.

geraum [gə'raum] a: seit ~er Zeit for some considerable time.

geräumig [gə'rɔymiç] a roomy.

Geräusch [gə'rɔyʃ] nt -(e)s, -e sound, noise; g~los a silent; g~voll a noisy.

gerben ['gɛrbən] vt tan.

Gerber m -s, - tanner; ~ei ['rai] f tannery.

gerecht [gə'rɛçt] a just, fair; jdm/etw ~ werden do justice to sb/sth; G~igkeit f justice, fairness.

Gerede [gə're:də] nt -s talk, gossip.

gereizt [gə'raitst] a irritable; G~heit f irritation.

Gericht [gə'riçt] nt -(e)s, -e court; (Essen) dish; mit jdm ins ~ gehen (fig) judge sb harshly; über jdn zu ~ sitzen sit in judgement on sb; das Letzte ~ the Last Judgement; g~lich a,ad judicial(ly), legal(ly); ~sbarkeit f jurisdiction; ~shof m court (of law); ~skosten pl (legal) costs pl; ~ssaal m courtroom; ~sverfahren nt legal proceedings pl; ~sverhandlung f court proceedings pl; ~svollzieher m bailiff.

gerieben [gə'ri:bən] a grated; (col: schlau) smart, wily.

gering [gə'riŋ] a slight, small; (niedrig) low; Zeit short; ~achten vt think little of; ~fügig a slight, trivial; ~schätzig a disparaging; G~schätzung f disdain; ~ste(r,s) a slightest, least; ~stenfalls ad at the very least.

gerinnen [gə'rinən] vi irreg congeal; (Blut) clot; (Milch) curdle.

Gerinnsel [gə'rinzəl] nt -s, - clot.

Gerippe [gə'ripə] nt -s, - skeleton.

gerissen [gə'risən] a wily, smart.

gern(e) ['gɛrn(ə)] ad willingly, gladly; ~ haben, ~ mögen like; etwas ~ tun like doing something; G~egroß m -, -e show-off.

Geröll [gə'rœl] nt -(e)s, -e scree.

Gerste ['gɛrstə] f -, -n barley; ~nkorn nt (im Auge) stye.

Gerte ['gɛrtə] f -, -n switch, rod; g~nschlank a willowy.

Geruch [gə'rux] m -(e)s, -e smell, odour; g~los a odourless; g~tilgend a deodorant.

Gerücht [gə'rçt] nt -(e)s, -e rumour.

geruhen [gə'ru:ən] vi deign.

Gerümpel [gə'rympəl] nt -s junk.

Gerüst [gə'ryst] nt -(e)s, -e (Bau—) scaffold(ing); frame.

gesamt [gə'zamt] a whole, entire; Kosten total; Werke complete; im ~en all in all; G~ausgabe f complete edition; ~deutsch a all-German; G~eindruck m general impression; G~heit f totality, whole.

Gesandte(r) [gə'zantə(r)] m envoy.

Gesandtschaft [gə'zant-ʃaft] f legation.

Gesang [gə'zaŋ] m -(e)s, -e song; (Singen) singing; ~buch nt (Rel) hymn book; ~verein m choral society.

Gesäß [gə'zɛ:s] nt -es, -e seat, bottom.

Geschäft [gə'ʃɛft] nt -(e)s, -e business; (Laden) shop; (—sabschluß) deal; ~emacher m -s, - profiteer; g~ig a active, busy; (pej) officious; g~lich a commercial; ad on business; ~sbericht m financial report; ~sführer m manager; (Klub) secretary; ~sjahr nt financial year; ~slage f business conditions pl; ~smann m businessman; g~smäßig a businesslike; ~sreise f business trip; ~sschluß m closing time; ~ssinn m business sense; ~sstelle f office, place of business; g~stüchtig a efficient; ~sviertel nt business quarter; shopping centre; ~swagen m company car; ~szweig m branch (of a business).

geschehen [gə'ʃe:ən] vi irreg happen; es war um ihn ~ that was the end of him.

gescheit [gə'ʃait] a clever.

Geschenk [gə'ʃɛŋk] nt -(e)s, -e present, gift; ~packung f gift pack.

Geschicht- [gə'ʃiçt] cpd: ~e f -, -n story; (Sache) affair; (Historie) history; ~enerzähler m storyteller; g~lich a historical; ~sschreiber m historian.

Geschick [gə'ʃik] nt -(e)s, -e aptitude; (Schicksal) fate; ~lichkeit f skill, dexterity; g~t a skilful.

geschieden [gə'ʃiːdən] a divorced.
Geschirr [gə'ʃir] nt -(e)s, -e crockery; pots and pans pl; (Pferd) harness; ~spülmaschine f dishwashing machine; ~tuch nt dish cloth.
Geschlecht [gə'ʃleçt] nt -(e)s, -er sex; (Gram) gender; (Art) species; family; g~lich a sexual; ~skrankheit f venereal disease; ~steil nt or m genitals pl; ~sverkehr m sexual intercourse; ~swort nt (Gram) article.
Geschmack [gə'ʃmak] m -(e)s, -e taste; nach jds ~ to sb's taste; ~ finden an etw (dat) (come to) like sth; g~los a tasteless; (fig) in bad taste; ~(s)sache f matter of taste; ~sinn m sense of taste; g~voll a tasteful.
Geschmeide [gə'ʃmaidə] nt -s, - jewellery.
geschmeidig a supple; (formbar) malleable.
Geschmeiß [gə'ʃmais] nt vermin pl.
Geschmiere [gə'ʃmiːrə] nt -s scrawl; (Bild) daub.
Geschöpf [gə'ʃœpf] nt -(e)s, -e creature.
Geschoß [gə'ʃɔs] nt -sses, -sse (Mil) projectile, missile; (Stockwerk) floor.
geschraubt [gə'ʃraupt] a stilted, artificial.
Geschrei [gə'ʃrai] nt -s cries pl, shouting; (fig: Aufhebens) noise, fuss.
Geschütz [gə'ʃyts] nt -es, -e gun, cannon; ein schweres ~ auffahren (fig) bring out the big guns; ~feuer nt artillery fire, gunfire; g~t a protected.
Geschwader [gə'ʃvaːdər] nt -s, - (Naut) squadron; (Aviat) group.
Geschwafel [gə'ʃvaːfəl] nt -s silly talk.
Geschwätz [gə'ʃvɛts] nt -es chatter, gossip; g~ig a talkative; ~igkeit f talkativeness.
geschweige [gə'ʃvaigə] ad: ~ (denn) let alone, not to mention.
geschwind [gə'ʃvint] a quick, swift; G~igkeit [-diçkait] f speed, velocity; G~igkeitsbegrenzung f speed limit; G~igkeitsmesser m (Aut) speedometer; G~igkeitsüberschreitung f exceeding the speed limit.
Geschwister [gə'ʃvistər] pl brothers and sisters pl.
geschwollen [gə'ʃvɔlən] a pompous.
Geschworene(r) [gə'ʃvoːrənə(r)] mf juror; pl jury.
Geschwulst [gə'ʃvulst] f -, -e swelling; growth, tumour.
Geschwür [gə'ʃvyːr] nt -(e)s, -e ulcer.
Gesell- [gə'zɛl] cpd: ~e m -n, -n fellow; (Handwerk~) journeyman; g~ig a sociable; ~igkeit f sociability; ~schaft f society; (Begleitung, Comm) company; (Abend~schaft etc) party; g~schaftlich a social; ~schaftsanzug m evening dress; g~schaftsfähig a socially acceptable; ~schaftsordnung f social structure; ~schaftsreise f group tour; ~schaftsschicht f social stratum.
Gesetz [gə'zɛts] nt -es, -e law; ~buch nt statute book; ~entwurf m, ~esvorlage f bill; g~gebend a legislative; ~geber m -s, - legislator; ~gebung f legislation;

g~lich a legal, lawful; ~lichkeit f legality, lawfulness; g~los a lawless; g~mäßig a lawful; g~t a Mensch sedate; g~tenfalls ad supposing (that); g~widrig a illegal, unlawful.
Gesicht [gə'zıçt] nt -(e)s, -er face; das zweite ~ second sight; das ist mir nie zu ~ gekommen I've never laid eyes on that; ~sausdruck m (facial) expression; ~sfarbe f complexion; ~spunkt m point of view; ~szüge pl features pl.
Gesindel [gə'zındəl] nt -s rabble.
gesinnt [gə'zınt] a disposed, minded.
Gesinnung [gə'zınʊŋ] f disposition; (Ansicht) views pl; ~sgenosse m likeminded person; ~slosigkeit f lack of conviction; ~swandel m change of opinion, volte-face.
gesittet [gə'zıtət] a well-mannered.
Gespann [gə'ʃpan] nt -(e)s, -e team; (col) couple; g~t a tense, strained; (begierig) eager; ich bin g~t, ob I wonder if or whether; auf etw/jdn g~t sein look forward to sth/meeting sb.
Gespenst [gə'ʃpɛnst] nt -(e)s, -er ghost, spectre; g~erhaft a ghostly.
Gespiele [gə'ʃpiːlə] m-n, -n, Gespielin f playmate.
Gespött [gə'ʃpœt] nt -(e)s mockery; zum ~ werden become a laughing stock.
Gespräch [gə'ʃprɛːç] nt -(e)s, -e conversation; discussion(s); (Anruf) call; zum ~ werden become a topic of conversation; g~ig a talkative; ~igkeit f talkativeness; ~sthema nt subject or topic (of conversation).
Gespür [gə'ʃpyːr] nt -s feeling.
Gestalt [gə'ʃtalt] f -, -en form, shape; (Person) figure; in ~ von in the form of; ~ annehmen take shape; g~en vt (formen) shape, form; (organisieren) arrange, organize; vr turn out (zu to be); ~ung f formation; organization.
geständig [gə'ʃtɛndıç] a: ~ sein have confessed.
Geständnis [gə'ʃtɛntnıs] nt -ses, -se confession.
Gestank [gə'ʃtaŋk] m -(e)s stench.
gestatten [gə'ʃtatən] vt permit, allow; ~ Sie? may I?; sich (dat) ~, etw zu tun take the liberty of doing sth.
Geste ['gɛstə] f -, -n gesture.
gestehen [gə'ʃteːən] vt irreg confess.
Gestein [gə'ʃtain] nt -(e)s, -e rock.
Gestell [gə'ʃtɛl] nt -(e)s, -e frame; (Regal) rack, stand.
gestern ['gɛstərn] ad yesterday; ~ abend/morgen yesterday evening/morning.
gestikulieren [gɛstikuˈliːrən] vi gesticulate.
Gestirn [gə'ʃtırn] nt -(e)s, -e star; (Sternbild) constellation.
Gestöber [gə'ʃtøːbər] nt -s, - flurry, blizzard.
Gesträuch [gə'ʃtrɔyç] nt -(e)s, -e shrubbery, bushes pl.
gestreift [gə'ʃtraift] a striped.
gestrig ['gɛstrıç] a yesterday's.

Gestrüpp [gəˈʃtryp] nt -(e)s, -e under-growth.

Gestüt [gəˈʃty:t] nt -(e)s, -e stud farm.

Gesuch [gəˈzu:x] nt -(e)s, -e petition; (Antrag) application; g~t a (Comm) in demand; wanted; (fig) contrived.

gesund [gəˈzʊnt] a healthy; wieder ~ werden get better; G~heit f health(iness); G~heit! bless you!; ~heitlich a,ad health attr, physical; wie geht es Ihnen ~heitlich? how's your health?; ~heitsschädlich a unhealthy; G~heitswesen nt health service; G~heitszustand m state of health.

Getöse [gəˈtø:zə] nt -s din, racket.

Getränk [gəˈtrɛŋk] nt -(e)s, -e drink.

getrauen [gəˈtraʊən] vr dare, venture.

Getreide [gəˈtraɪdə] nt -s, - cereals pl, grain; ~speicher m granary.

getrennt [gəˈtrɛnt] a separate.

getreu [gəˈtrɔy] a faithful.

Getriebe [gəˈtri:bə] nt -s, - (Leute) bustle; (Aut) gearbox; ~öl nt transmission oil.

getrost [gəˈtro:st] ad without any bother; ~ sterben die in peace.

Getue [gəˈtu:ə] nt -s fuss.

geübt [gəˈy:pt] a experienced.

Gewächs [gəˈvɛks] nt -es, -e growth; (Pflanze) plant.

gewachsen [gəˈvaksən] a: jdm/etw ~ sein be sb's equal/equal to sth.

Gewächshaus nt greenhouse.

gewagt [gəˈva:kt] a daring, risky.

gewählt [gəˈvɛ:lt] a Sprache refined, elegant.

Gewähr [gəˈvɛ:r] f - guarantee; keine ~ übernehmen für accept no responsibility for; g~en vt grant; (geben) provide; g~leisten vt guarantee.

Gewahrsam [gəˈva:rza:m] m -s, -e safe-keeping; (Polizei~) custody.

Gewähr- cpd: ~smann m informant, source; ~ung f granting.

Gewalt [gəˈvalt] f -, -en power; (große Kraft) force; (~taten) violence; mit aller ~ with all one's might; ~anwendung f use of force; ~herrschaft f tyranny; g~ig a tremendous, Irrtum huge; ~marsch m forced march; g~sam a forcible; g~tätig a violent.

Gewand [gəˈvant] nt -(e)s, -er garment.

gewandt [gəˈvant] a deft, skilful; (erfahren) experienced; G~heit f dexterity, skill.

Gewässer [gəˈvɛsər] nt -s, - waters pl.

Gewebe [gəˈve:bə] nt -s, - (Stoff) fabric; (Biol) tissue.

Gewehr [gəˈve:r] nt -(e)s, -e gun; rifle; ~lauf m rifle barrel.

Geweih [gəˈvaɪ] nt -(e)s, -e antlers pl.

Gewerb- [gəˈvɛrb] cpd: ~e nt -s, - trade, occupation; Handel und ~e trade and industry; ~eschule f technical school; g~etreibend a carrying on a trade; industrial; g~lich a industrial; trade attr; g~smäßig a professional; ~szweig m line of trade.

Gewerkschaft [gəˈvɛrkʃaft] f trade union;

~ler m -s, - trade unionist; ~sbund m trade unions federation.

Gewicht [gəˈvɪçt] nt -(e)s, -e weight; (fig) importance; g~ig a weighty.

gewieft [gəˈvi:ft] a, gewiegt [gəˈvi:kt] a shrewd, cunning.

gewillt [gəˈvɪlt] a willing, prepared.

Gewimmel [gəˈvɪməl] nt -s swarm.

Gewinde [gəˈvɪndə] nt -s, - (Kranz) wreath; (von Schraube) thread.

Gewinn [gəˈvɪn] m -(e)s, -e profit; (bei Spiel) winnings pl; etw mit ~ verkaufen sell sth at a profit; ~beteiligung f profit-sharing; g~bringend a profitable; g~en vt irreg win; (erwerben) gain; Kohle, Öl extract; vi win; (profitieren) gain; an etw (dat) g~en gain in sth; g~end a winning, attractive; ~er(in f) m -s, - winner; ~spanne f profit margin; ~sucht f love of gain; ~(n)ummer f winning number; ~ung f winning; gaining; (von Kohle etc) extraction.

Gewirr [gəˈvɪr] nt -(e)s, -e tangle; (von Straßen) maze.

gewiß [gəˈvɪs] a,ad certain(ly).

Gewissen [gəˈvɪsən] nt -s, - conscience; g~haft a conscientious; ~haftigkeit f conscientiousness; g~los a unscrupulous; ~sbisse pl. pangs of conscience pl, qualms pl; ~sfrage f matter of conscience; ~sfreiheit f freedom of conscience; ~skonflikt m moral conflict.

gewissermaßen [gəvɪsərˈma:sən] ad more or less, in a way.

Gewiß- cpd: ~heit f certainty; g~lich ad surely.

Gewitter [gəˈvɪtər] nt -s, - thunderstorm; g~n vi impers: es gewittert there's a thunderstorm; g~schwül a sultry and thundery.

gewitzigt [gəˈvɪtsɪçt] a: ~ sein have learned by experience.

gewitzt [gəˈvɪtst] a shrewd, cunning.

gewogen [gəˈvo:gən] a well-disposed (+dat towards).

gewöhnen [gəˈvø:nən] vt: jdn an etw (acc) ~ accustom sb to sth; (erziehen zu) teach sb sth; vr: sich an etw (acc) ~ get used or accustomed to sth.

Gewohnheit [gəˈvo:nhaɪt] f habit; (Brauch) custom; aus ~ from habit; zur ~ werden become a habit; ~s- in cpds habitual; ~smensch m creature of habit; ~srecht nt common law; ~stier nt (col) creature of habit.

gewöhnlich [gəˈvø:nlɪç] a usual; ordinary; (pej) common; wie ~ as usual.

gewohnt [gəˈvo:nt] a usual; etw ~ sein be used to sth.

Gewöhnung f getting accustomed (an +acc to).

Gewölbe [gəˈvœlbə] nt -s, - vault.

Gewühl [gəˈvy:l] nt -(e)s throng.

Gewürz [gəˈvʏrts] nt -es, -e spice, seasoning; ~nelke f clove.

gezähnt [gəˈtsɛ:nt] a serrated, toothed.

Gezeiten [gəˈtsaɪtən] pl tides pl.

Gezeter [gəˈtse:tər] nt -s clamour, yelling.

gezielt [gəˈtsi:lt] a with a particular aim in mind, purposeful; Kritik pointed.

geziemen [gə'tsi:mən] *vr impers* be fitting; ~**d** a proper.

geziert [gə'tsi:rt] *a* affected; **G**~**heit** *f* affectation.

Gezwitscher [gə'tsvɪtʃər] *nt* -s twitter(ing), chirping.

gezwungen [gə'tsvʊŋən] *a* forced; ~**ermaßen** *ad* of necessity.

Gicht ['gɪçt] *f* - gout; **g**~**isch** *a* gouty.

Giebel ['gi:bəl] *m* -s, - gable; ~**dach** *nt* gable(d) roof; ~**fenster** *nt* gable window.

Gier [gi:r] *f* - greed; **g**~**ig** *a* greedy.

Gieß- ['gi:s] *cpd:* ~**bach** *m* torrent; **g**~**en** *vt irreg* pour; *Blumen* water; *Metall* cast; *Wachs* mould; ~**e'rei** *f* foundry; ~**kanne** *f* watering can.

Gift [gɪft] *nt* -(e)s, -e poison; **g**~**ig** *a* poisonous; *(fig: boshaft)* venomous; ~**zahn** *m* fang.

Gilde ['gɪldə] *f* -, -n guild.

Ginster ['gɪnstər] *m* -s, - broom.

Gipfel ['gɪpfəl] *m* -s, - summit, peak; *(fig)* height; **g**~**n** *vi* culminate; ~**treffen** *nt* summit (meeting).

Gips [gɪps] *m* -es, -e plaster; *(Med)* plaster (of Paris); ~**abdruck** *m* plaster cast; **g**~**en** *vt* plaster; ~**figur** *f* plaster figure; ~**verband** *m* plaster (cast).

Giraffe [gi'rafə] *f* -, -n giraffe.

Girlande [gɪr'landə] *f* -, -n garland.

Giro ['ʒi:ro] *nt* -s, -s giro; ~**konto** *nt* current account.

girren ['gɪrən] *vi* coo.

Gischt [gɪʃt] *m* -(e)s, -e spray, foam.

Gitarre [gi'tarə] *f* -, -n guitar.

Gitter ['gɪtər] *nt* -s, - grating, bars *pl*; *(für Pflanzen)* trellis; *(Zaun)* rai'ling(s); ~**bett** *nt* cot; ~**fenster** *nt* barred window; ~**zaun** *m* railing(s).

Glacéhandschuh [gla'se:hant-ʃu:] *m* kid glove.

Gladiole [gladi'o:lə] *f* -, -n gladiolus.

Glanz [glants] *m* -es shine, lustre; *(fig)* splendour.

glänzen ['glɛntsən] *vi* shine *(also fig)*, gleam; *vt* polish; ~**d** *a* shining; *(fig)* brilliant.

Glanz- *cpd:* ~**leistung** *f* brilliant achievement; **g**~**los** *a* dull; ~**zeit** *f* heyday.

Glas [gla:s] *nt* -es, ¨er glass; ~**bläser** *m* -s, - glass blower; ~**er** *m* -s, - glazier; **g**~**ieren** [gla'zi:rən] *vt* glaze; **g**~**ig** *a* glassy; ~**scheibe** *f* pane; ~**ur** [gla'zu:r] *f* glaze; *(Cook)* icing.

glatt [glat] *a* smooth; *(rutschig)* slippery; *Absage* flat; *Lüge* downright; **G**~**eis** *nt* (black) ice; **jdn aufs G**~**eis führen** *(fig)* take sb for a ride.

Glätte ['glɛtə] *f* -, -n smoothness; slipperiness; **g**~**n** *vt* smooth out.

Glatze ['glatsə] *f* -, -n bald head; **eine** ~ **bekommen** go bald.

glatzköpfig *a* bald.

Glaube ['glaubə] *m* -ns, -n faith *(an +acc* in); belief *(an +acc* in); **g**~**n** *vti* believe *(an +acc* in, **jdm** sb); think; ~**nsbekenntnis** *nt* creed.

glaubhaft ['glaubhaft] *a* credible; **G**~**igkeit** *f* credibility.

gläubig ['glɔybɪç] *a* (Rel) devout; *(vertrauensvoll)* trustful; **G**~**e(r)** *mf* believer; **die G**~**en** the faithful; **G**~**er** *m* -s, - creditor.

glaubwürdig ['glaubvyrdɪç] *a* credible; *Mensch* trustworthy; **G**~**keit** *f* credibility; trustworthiness.

gleich [glaɪç] *a* equal; *(identisch)* (the) same, identical; **es ist mir** ~ it's all the same to me; **2 mal 2** ~ 4 2 times 2 is *or* equals 4; *ad* equally; *(sofort)* straight away; *(bald)* in a minute; ~ **groß** the same size; ~ **nach/an** right after/at; ~**altrig** *a* of the same age; ~**artig** *a* similar; ~**bedeutend** *a* synonymous; ~**berechtigt** *a* having equal rights; **G**~**berechtigung** *f* equal rights *pl*; ~**bleibend** *a* constant; ~**en** *vi irreg*: **jdm/etw** ~**en** be like sb/sth; *vr* be alike; ~**ermaßen** *ad* equally; ~**falls** *ad* likewise; **danke** ~**falls!** the same to you; **G**~**förmigkeit** *f* uniformity; ~**gesinnt** *a* like-minded; **G**~**gewicht** *nt* equilibrium, balance; ~**gültig** *a* indifferent; *(unbedeutend)* unimportant; **G**~**gültigkeit** *f* indifference; **G**~**heit** *f* equality; ~**kommen** *vi irreg +dat* be equal to; **G**~**mache'rei** *f* egalitarianism; ~**mäßig** *a* even, equal; **G**~**mut** *m* equanimity; **G**~**nis** *nt* -ses, -se parable; ~**sam** *ad* as it were; ~**sehen** *vi irreg (jdm)* be *or* look like (sb); **G**~**strom** *m* *(Elec)* direct current; ~**tun** *vi irreg*: **es jdm** ~**tun** match sb; **G**~**ung** *f* equation; ~**viel** *ad* no matter; ~**wohl** *ad* nevertheless; ~**zeitig** *a* simultaneous.

Gleis [glaɪs] *nt* -es, -e track, rails *pl*; *(Bahnsteig)* platform.

Gleit- ['glaɪt] *cpd:* gliding; sliding; **g**~**en** *vi irreg* glide; *(rutschen)* slide; ~**flug** *m* glide; gliding.

Gletscher ['glɛtʃər] *m* -s, - glacier; ~**spalte** *f* crevasse.

Glied [gli:t] *nt* -(e)s, -er member; *(Arm, Bein)* limb; *(von Kette)* link; *(Mil)* rank(s); **g**~**ern** *vt* organize, structure; ~**erung** *f* structure, organization; ~**maßen** *pl* limbs *pl*.

Glimm- ['glɪm] *cpd:* **g**~**en** *vi irreg* glow, gleam; ~**er** *m* -s, - glow, gleam; *(Mineral)* mica; ~**stengel** *m (col)* fag.

glimpflich ['glɪmpflɪç] *a* mild, lenient; ~ **davonkommen** get off lightly.

glitzern ['glɪtsərn] *vi* glitter, twinkle.

Globus ['glo:bus] *m* - *or* -ses, **Globen** *or* -se globe.

Glöckchen ['glœkçən] *nt* (little) bell.

Glocke ['glɔkə] *f* -, -n bell; **etw an die große** ~ **hängen** *(fig)* shout sth from the rooftops; ~**ngeläut** *nt* peal of bells; ~**nspiel** *nt* chime(s); *(Mus)* glockenspiel.

Glorie ['glo:riə] *f* -, -n glory; *(von Heiligen)* halo.

Glosse ['glɔsə] *f* -, -n comment.

glotzen ['glɔtsən] *vi (col)* stare.

Glück [glʏk] *nt* -(e)s luck, fortune; *(Freude)* happiness; ~ **haben** be lucky; **viel** ~ good luck; **zum** ~ fortunately;

g~en vi succeed; **es glückte ihm, es zu bekommen** he succeeded in getting it.
gluckern ['glukərn] vi glug.
Glück- cpd: g~**lich** a fortunate; (froh) happy; g~**licherweise** ad fortunately; ~**sbringer** m -s, - lucky charm; g~-'**selig** a blissful; ~**sfall** m stroke of luck; ~**skind** nt lucky person; ~**ssache** f matter of luck; ~**sspiel** nt game of chance; ~**sstern** m lucky star; g~**strahlend** a radiant (with happiness); ~**wunsch** m congratulations pl, best wishes pl.
Glüh- ['gly:] cpd: ~**birne** f light bulb; g~**en** vi glow; ~**wein** m mulled wine; ~**würmchen** nt glow-worm.
Glut [glu:t] f -, -en (Röte) glow; (Feuers—) fire; (Hitze) heat; (fig) ardour.
Gnade ['gna:də] f -, -n (Gunst) favour; (Erbarmen) mercy; (Milde) clemency; ~**nfrist** f reprieve, respite; ~**ngesuch** nt petition for clemency; ~**nstoß** m coup de grâce.
gnädig ['gnɛ:dɪç] a gracious; (voll Erbarmen) merciful.
Gold [gɔlt] nt -(e)s gold; g~**en** a golden; ~**fisch** m goldfish; ~**grube** f goldmine; ~**regen** m laburnum; ~**schnitt** m gilt edging; ~**währung** f gold standard.
Golf [gɔlf] m -(e)s, -e gulf; nt -s golf; ~**platz** m golf course; ~**schläger** m golf club; ~**spieler** m golfer; ~**strom** m Gulf Stream.
Gondel ['gɔndəl] f -, -n gondola; (Seilbahn) cable-car.
gönnen ['gœnən] vt: **jdm etw** ~ not begrudge sb sth; **sich** (dat) **etw** ~ allow oneself sth.
Gönner m -s, - patron; g~**haft** a patronizing; ~**miene** f patronizing air.
Gosse ['gɔsə] f -, -n gutter.
Gott [gɔt] m -es, "er god; **um** ~**es Willen!** for heaven's sake!; ~ **sei Dank!** thank God!; ~**esdienst** m service; ~**eshaus** nt place of worship; ~**heit** f deity.
Gött- [gœt] cpd: ~**in** f goddess; g~**lich** a divine.
Gott- cpd: g~**los** a godless; ~**vertrauen** nt trust in God.
Götze ['gœtsə] m -n, -n idol.
Grab [gra:p] nt -(e)s, "er grave; g~**en** ['gra:bən] vt irreg dig; ~**en** m -s, " ditch; (Mil) trench; ~**rede** f funeral oration; ~**stein** m gravestone.
Grad [gra:t] m -(e)s, -e degree; ~**einteilung** f graduation; g~**weise** ad gradually.
Graf [gra:f] m -en, -en count, earl; ~**schaft** f county.
Gräfin ['grɛ:fin] f countess.
Gram [gra:m] m -(e)s grief, sorrow.
grämen ['grɛ:mən] vr grieve.
Gramm [gram] nt -s, -e gram(me); ~**atik** [-'matik] f grammar; g~**atisch** a grammatical; g~**o'phon** nt -s, -e gramophone.
Granat [gra'na:t] m -(e)s, -e (Stein) garnet; ~**apfel** m pomegranate; ~**e** f -, -n (Mil) shell; (Hand—) grenade.

Granit [gra'ni:t] m -s, -e granite.
graphisch ['gra:fiʃ] a graphic; ~**e Darstellung** graph.
Gras [gra:s] nt -es, "er grass; g~**en** vi graze; ~**halm** m blade of grass; g~**ig** a grassy; ~**narbe** f turf.
grassieren [gra'si:rən] vi be rampant, rage.
gräßlich ['grɛsliç] a horrible.
Grat [gra:t] m -(e)s, -e ridge.
Gräte ['grɛ:tə] f -, -n fishbone.
gratis ['gra:tis] a,ad free (of charge); G~**probe** f free sample.
Gratulation [gratulatsi'o:n] f congratulation(s).
gratulieren [gratu'li:rən] vi: **jdm** ~ (**zu etw**) congratulate sb (on sth); (**ich**) **gratuliere!** congratulations!
grau [grau] a grey; ~**en** vi (Tag) dawn; vi impers: **es graut jdm vor etw** sb dreads sth, sb is afraid of sth; vr: **sich** ~**en vor** dread, have a horror of; G~**en** nt -s horror; ~**enhaft** a horrible; ~**haarig** a grey-haired; ~**meliert** a grey-flecked.
grausam ['grauza:m] a cruel; G~**keit** f cruelty.
Grausen ['grauzən] nt -s horror; g~ vi impers, vr see **grauen**.
gravieren [gra'vi:rən] vt engrave; ~**d** a grave.
Grazie ['gra:tsiə] f -, -n grace.
graziös [gratsi'ø:s] a graceful.
greif- [graif] cpd: ~**bar** a tangible, concrete; **in** ~**barer Nähe** within reach; ~**en** vt irreg seize; grip; **nach etw** ~**en** reach for sth; **um sich** ~**en** (fig) spread; **zu etw** ~**en** (fig) turn to sth.
Greis [grais] m -es, -e old man; ~**enalter** nt old age; g~**enhaft** a senile.
grell [grɛl] a harsh.
Grenz- ['grɛnts] cpd: ~**beamte(r)** m frontier official; ~**e** f -, -n boundary; (Staats—) frontier; (Schranke) limit; g~**en** vi border (**an** +acc on); g~**enlos** a boundless; ~**fall** m borderline case; ~**linie** f boundary; ~**übergang** m frontier crossing.
Greuel ['grɔyəl] m -s, - horror, revulsion; **etw ist jdm ein** ~ sb loathes sth; ~**tat** f atrocity.
greulich ['grɔyliç] a horrible.
griesgrämig ['gri:sgrɛ:miç] a grumpy.
Grieß [gri:s] m -es, -e (Cook) semolina.
Griff [grif] m -(e)s, -e grip; (Vorrichtung) handle; g~**bereit** a handy.
Griffel ['grifəl] m -s, - slate pencil; (Bot) style.
Grille ['grilə] f -, -n cricket; (fig) whim; g~**n** vt grill.
Grimasse [gri'masə] f -, -n grimace.
Grimm [grim] m -(e)s fury; g~**ig** a furious; (heftig) fierce, severe.
grinsen ['grinzən] vi grin.
Grippe ['gripə] f -, -n influenza, flu.
grob [gro:p] a coarse, gross; Fehler, Verstoß gross; G~**heit** f coarseness; coarse expression; g~**ian** ['gro:bia:n] m -s, -e ruffian; ~**knochig** a large-boned.
Groll [grɔl] m -(e)s resentment; g~**en** vi

bear ill will (+*dat* or *mit* towards); (*Donner*) rumble.

groß [gro:s] *a* big, large; (*hoch*) tall; (*fig*) great; **im ~en und ganzen** on the whole; *ad* greatly; **~artig** *a* great, splendid; **G~aufnahme** *f* (*Cine*) close-up.

Größe ['grø:sə] *f* -, -n size; (*fig*) greatness; (*Länge*) height.

Groß- *cpd*: **~einkauf** *m* bulk purchase; **~eltern** *pl* grandparents *pl*; **g~enteils** *ad* mostly.

Größen- *cpd*: **~unterschied** *m* difference in size; **~wahn** *m* megalomania.

Groß- *cpd*: **~format** *nt* large size; **~handel** *m* wholesale trade; **~händler** *m* wholesaler; **g~herzig** *a* generous; **~macht** *f* great power; **~maul** *m* braggart; **~mut** *f* - magnanimity; **g~mütig** *a* magnanimous; **~mutter** *f* grandmother; **g~spurig** *a* pompous; **~stadt** *f* city, large town.

größte(r,s) [grø:stə(r,z)] *a superl* of **groß**; **~nteils** *ad* for the most part.

Groß- *cpd*: **~tuer** *m* -s, - boaster; **g~tun** *vi irreg* boast; **~vater** *m* grandfather; **g~ziehen** *vt irreg* raise; **g~zügig** *a* generous; *Planung* on a large scale.

grotesk [gro'tɛsk] *a* grotesque.

Grotte ['grɔtə] *f* -, -n grotto.

Grübchen ['gry:pçən] *nt* dimple.

Grube ['gru:bə] *f* -, -n pit; mine; **~narbeiter** *m* miner; **~ngas** *nt* firedamp.

grübeln ['gry:bəln] *vi* brood.

Grübler ['gry:blər] *m* -s, - brooder; **g~isch** *a* brooding, pensive.

Gruft [gruft] *f* -, -e tomb, vault.

grün [gry:n] *a* green; **G~anlage** *f* park.

Grund [grunt] *m* ground; (*von See, Gefäß*) bottom; (*fig*) reason; **im ~e genommen** basically; **~ausbildung** *f* basic training; **~bedeutung** *f* basic meaning; **~bedingung** *f* fundamental condition; **~besitz** *m* land(ed property), real estate; **~buch** *nt* land register; **g~ehrlich** *a* thoroughly honest.

gründ- [grynd] *cpd*: **~en** *vt* found; **~en auf** (+*acc*) base on; *vr* be based (*auf* +*dat* on); **G~er** *m* -s, - founder; **~lich** *a* thorough; **G~ung** *f* foundation.

Grund- *cpd*: **g~falsch** *a* utterly wrong; **~gebühr** *f* basic charge; **~gedanke** *m* basic idea; **~gesetz** *nt* constitution; **~lage** *f* foundation; **g~legend** *a* fundamental; **g~los** *a* groundless; **~mauer** *f* foundation wall; **~regel** *f* basic rule; **~riß** *m* plan; (*fig*) outline; **~satz** *m* principle; **g~sätzlich** *a,ad* fundamental(ly); *Frage* of principle; (*prinzipiell*) on principle; **~schule** *f* elementary school; **~stein** *m* foundation stone; **~steuer** *f* rates *pl*; **~stück** *nt* estate; plot; **g~verschieden** *a* utterly different; **~zug** *m* characteristic.

Grün- *cpd*: **~e** *nt* -nt *lm* **~en** in the open air; **~kohl** *m* kale; **~schnabel** *m* greenhorn; **~span** *m* verdigris; **~streifen** *m* central reservation.

grunzen ['gruntsən] *vi* grunt.

Gruppe ['grupə] *f* -, -n group; **g~nweise** *ad* in groups.

gruppieren [gru'pi:rən] *vtr* group.

gruselig *a* creepy.

gruseln ['gru:zəln] *vi impers*: **es gruselt jdm vor etw** sth gives sb the creeps; *vr* have the creeps.

Gruß [gru:s] *m* -es, -e greeting; (*Mil*) salute; **viele e best wishes**; **e an** (+*acc*) regards to.

grüßen ['gry:sən] *vt* greet; (*Mil*) salute; **jdn von jdm ~** give sb sb's regards; **jdn ~ lassen** send sb one's regards.

gucken ['gukən] *vi* look.

Gulasch ['gu:laʃ] *nt* -(e)s, -e goulash.

gültig ['gyltiç] *a* valid; **G~keit** *f* validity; **G~keitsdauer** *f* period of validity.

Gummi ['gumi] *nt* or *m* -s, -s rubber; (*~harze*) gum; (*~band* *nt*) rubber or elastic band; (*Hosen~*) elastic; **g~eren** [gu'mi:rən] *vt* gum; **~knüppel** *m* rubber truncheon; **~strumpf** *m* elastic stocking.

Gunst [gunst] *f* - favour.

günstig ['gynstiç] *a* favourable.

Gurgel ['gurgəl] *f* -, -n throat; **g~n** *vi* gurgle; (*im Mund*) gargle.

Gurke ['gurkə] *f* -, -n cucumber; **saure ~** pickled cucumber, gherkin.

Gurt [gurt] *m* -(e)s, -e belt.

Gürtel ['gyrtəl] *m* -s, - belt; (*Geog*) zone; **~reifen** *m* radial tyre.

Guß [gus] *m* -sses, Güsse casting; (*Regen~*) downpour; (*Cook*) glazing; **~eisen** *nt* cast iron.

Gut [gu:t] *nt* -(e)s, -er (*Besitz*) possession; (*pl*: *Waren*) goods *pl*; **g~** *a* good; *ad* well; **laß es g~ sein** that'll do; **~achten** *nt* -s, - (*expert*) opinion; **~achter** *m* -s, - expert; **g~artig** *a* good-natured; (*Med*) benign; **~bürgerlich** *a* *Küche* (good) plain; **~dünken** *nt*: **nach ~dünken** at one's discretion.

Güte ['gy:tə] *f* - goodness, kindness; (*Qualität*) quality.

Güter- *cpd*: **~abfertigung** *f* (*Rail*) goods office; **~bahnhof** *m* goods station; **~wagen** *m* goods waggon, freight car (*US*); **~zug** *m* goods train, freight train (*US*).

Gut- *cpd*: **g~gehen** *v impers irreg* work, come off; **es geht jdm g~** sb's doing fine; **g~gelaunt** *a* good-humoured, in a good mood; **g~gemeint** *a* well meant; **g~gläubig** *a* trusting; **~haben** *nt* -s credit; **g~heißen** *vt irreg* approve (of); **g~herzig** *a* kind(-hearted).

gütig ['gy:tiç] *a* kind.

gütlich ['gy:tliç] *a* amicable.

Gut- *cpd*: **g~mütig** *a* good-natured; **~mütigkeit** *f* good nature; **~sbesitzer** *m* landowner; **~schein** *m* voucher; **g~schreiben** *vt irreg* credit; **~schrift** *f* credit; **~sherr** *m* squire; **g~tun** *vi irreg*: **jdm g~tun** do sb good; **g~willig** *a* willing.

Gymnasium [gym'na:zium] *nt* grammar school (*Brit*), high school (*US*).

Gymnastik [gym'nastik] *f* exercises *pl*, keep fit.

H

H, h [ha:] *nt* H, h.

Haar [ha:r] *nt* -(e)s, -e hair; **um ein ~** nearly; **~bürste** *f* hairbrush; **h~en** *vir* lose hair; **~esbreite** *f*: **um ~esbreite** by a hair's-breadth; **h~genau** *ad* precisely; **h~ig** *a* hairy; (*fig*) nasty; **~klemme** *f* hair grip; **h~los** *a* hairless; **~nadel** *f* hairpin; **h~scharf** *ad* beobachten very sharply; *daneben* by a hair's breadth; **~schnitt** *m* haircut; **~schopf** *m* head of hair; **~spalte'rei** *f* hairsplitting; **~spange** *f* hair slide; **h~sträubend** *a* hair-raising; **~teil** *nt* hairpiece; **~waschmittel** *nt* shampoo.

Habe ['ha:bə] *f* - property.

haben ['ha:bən] *vt, v aux irreg* have; **Hunger/Angst ~** be hungry/afraid; **woher hast du das?** where did you get that from?; **was hast du denn?** what's the matter (with you)?; **H~** *nt* -s, - credit.

Habgier *f* avarice; **h~ig** *a* avaricious.

Habicht ['ha:bɪçt] *m* -(e)s, -e hawk.

Habseligkeiten *pl* belongings *pl*.

Hachse ['haksə] *f* -, -n (*Cook*) knuckle.

Hacke ['hakə] *f* -, -n hoe; (*Ferse*) heel; **h~n** *vt* hack, chop; *Erde* hoe.

Hackfleisch *nt* mince, minced meat.

Häcksel ['hɛksəl] *m or nt* -s chopped straw, chaff.

hadern ['ha:dərn] *vi* quarrel.

Hafen ['ha:fən] *m* -s, ̈ harbour, port; **~arbeiter** *m* docker; **~damm** *m* jetty, mole; **~stadt** *f* port.

Hafer ['ha:fər] *m* -s, - oats *pl*; **~brei** *m* porridge; **~flocken** *pl* porridge oats *pl*; **~schleim** *m* gruel.

Haft [haft] *f* - custody; **h~bar** *a* liable, responsible; **~befehl** *m* warrant (of arrest); **h~en** *vi* stick, cling; **h~en für** be liable *or* responsible for; **h~enbleiben** *vi irreg* stick (*an* +*dat* to); **~pflicht** *f* liability; **~pflichtversicherung** *f* third party insurance; **~schalen** *pl* contact lenses *pl*; **~ung** *f* liability.

Hage- ['ha:gə] *cpd*: **~butte** *f* -, -n rose hip; **~dorn** *m* hawthorn.

Hagel ['ha:gəl] *m* -s hail; **h~n** *vi impers* hail.

hager ['ha:gər] *a* gaunt.

Häher ['hɛ:ər] *m* -s, - jay.

Hahn [ha:n] *m* -(e)s, ̈e cock; (*Wasser~*) tap, faucet (*US*).

Hähnchen ['hɛ:nçən] *nt* cockerel; (*Cook*) chicken.

Hai(fisch) ['hai(fɪʃ)] *m* -(e)s, -e shark.

Häkchen ['hɛ:kçən] *nt* small hook.

Häkel- ['hɛ:kəl] *cpd*: **~arbeit** *f* crochet work; **h~n** *vt* crochet; **~nadel** *f* crochet hook.

Haken ['ha:kən] *m* -s, - hook; (*fig*) catch; **~kreuz** *nt* swastika; **~nase** *f* hooked nose.

halb [halp] *a* half; **~ eins** half past twelve; **ein ~es Dutzend** half a dozen; **H~dunkel** *nt* semi-darkness.

halber ['halbər] *prep* +*gen* (*wegen*) on account of; (*für*) for the sake of.

Halb- *cpd*: **~heit** *f* half-measure; **h~ieren** *vt* halve; **~insel** *f* peninsula; **h~jährlich** *a* half-yearly; **~kreis** *m* semicircle; **~kugel** *f* hemisphere; **h~laut** *a* in an undertone; **~links** *m* -, - (*Sport*) inside-left; **~mond** *m* half-moon; (*fig*) crescent; **h~offen** *a* half-open; **~rechts** *m* -, - (*Sport*) inside-right; **~schuh** *m* shoe; **~tagsarbeit** *f* part-time work; **h~wegs** *ad* half-way; **h~wegs besser** more or less better; **~wüchsige(r)** *mf* adolescent; **~zeit** *f* (*Sport*) half; (*Pause*) half-time.

Halde ['haldə] *f* -, -n tip; (*Schlacken~*) slag heap.

Hälfte ['hɛlftə] *f* -, -n *f* half.

Halfter ['halftər] *f* -, -n, *or nt* -s, - halter; (*Pistolen~*) holster.

Hall [hal] *m* -(e)s, -e sound.

Halle ['halə] *f* -, -n hall; (*Aviat*) hangar; **h~n** *vi* echo, resound; **~nbad** *nt* indoor swimming pool.

hallo [ha'lo:] *interj* hallo.

Halluzination [halutsinatsi'o:n] *f* hallucination.

Halm ['halm] *m* -(e)s, -e blade, stalk.

Hals [hals] *m* -es, ̈e neck; (*Kehle*) throat; **~ über Kopf** in a rush; **~kette** *f* necklace; **~krause** *f* ruff; **~-Nasen-Ohren-Arzt** *m* ear nose and throat specialist; **~schlagader** *f* carotid artery; **~schmerzen** *pl* sore throat; **h~starrig** *a* stubborn, obstinate; **~tuch** *nt* scarf; **~weh** *nt* sore throat; **~wirbel** *m* cervical vertebra.

Halt [halt] *m* -(e)s, -e stop; (*fester ~*) hold; (*innerer ~*) stability; **h~!** stop!, halt!; **h~bar** *a* durable; *Lebensmittel* non-perishable; (*Mil, fig*) tenable; **~barkeit** *f* durability; (non-)perishability; tenability.

halten ['haltən] *irreg vt* keep; (*fest~*) hold; **~ für** regard as; **~ von** think of; *vi* hold; (*frisch bleiben*) keep; (*stoppen*) stop; **an sich ~** restrain oneself; *vr* (*frisch bleiben*) keep; (*sich behaupten*) hold out; **sich rechts/links ~** keep to the right/left.

Halt- *cpd*: **~estelle** *f* stop; **h~los** *a* unstable; **~losigkeit** *f* instability; **h~machen** *vi* stop; **~ung** *f* posture; (*fig*) attitude; (*Selbstbeherrschung*) composure; **~verbot** *nt* ban on stopping.

Halunke [ha'luŋkə] *m* -n, -n rascal.

hämisch ['hɛ:mɪʃ] *a* malicious.

Hammel ['haməl] *m* -s, ̈ *or* - wether; **~fleisch** *nt* mutton; **~keule** *f* leg of mutton.

Hammer ['hamər] *m* -s, ̈ hammer.

hämmern ['hɛmərn] *vti* hammer.

Hampelmann ['hampəlman] *m* (*lit, fig*) puppet.

Hamster ['hamstər] *m* -s, - hamster; **~ei** [-'rai] *f* hoarding; **~er** *m* -s, - hoarder; **h~n** *vi* hoard.

Hand [hant] *f* -, ̈e hand; **~arbeit** *f* manual work; (*Nadelarbeit*) needlework; **~arbeiter** *m* manual worker; **~besen** *m* brush; **~bremse** *f* handbrake; **~buch** *nt* handbook, manual.

Hände- ['hɛndə] *cpd*: **~druck** *m* handshake; **~klatschen** *nt* clapping, applause.

Handel ['handəl] *m* -s trade; (*Geschäft*) transaction; **haben** quarrel.

handeln ['handəln] *vi* trade; act; ~ **von** be about; *vr impers*: **sich** ~ **um** be a question of, be about; H~ *nt* -s action.

Handels- *cpd*: ~**bilanz** *f* balance of trade; **h~einig** a: **mit jdm h~einig werden** conclude a deal with sb; ~**kammer** *f* chamber of commerce; ~**marine** *f* merchant navy; ~**recht** *nt* commercial law; ~**reisende(r)** *m* commercial traveller; ~**schule** *f* business school; ~**vertreter** *m* sales representative.

Hand- *cpd*: ~**feger** *m* -s, - brush; **h~fest** a hefty; **h~gearbeitet** a handmade; ~**gelenk** *nt* wrist; ~**gemenge** *nt* scuffle; ~**gepäck** *nt* hand-luggage; **h~geschrieben** a handwritten; **h~greiflich** a palpable; **h~greiflich werden** become violent; ~**griff** *m* flick of the wrist; **h~haben** *vt irreg insep* handle; ~**karren** *m* handcart; ~**kuß** *m* kiss on the hand.

Händler ['hɛndlər] *m* -s, - trader, dealer.

handlich ['hantlıç] a handy.

Handlung ['handluŋ] *f* -, -en act(ion); (*in Buch*) plot; (*Geschäft*) shop; ~**sbevollmächtige(r)** *mf* authorized agent; ~**sweise** *f* manner of dealing.

Hand- *cpd*: ~**pflege** *f* manicure; ~**schelle** *f* handcuff; ~**schlag** *m* handshake; ~**schrift** *f* handwriting; (*Text*) manuscript; ~**schuh** *m* glove; ~**tasche** *f* handbag; ~**tuch** *nt* towel; ~**werk** *nt* trade, craft; ~**werker** *m* -s - craftsman, artisan; ~**werkzeug** *nt* tools *pl*.

Hanf [hanf] *m* -(e)s hemp.

Hang [haŋ] *m* -(e)s, -e inclination; (*Ab*—) slope.

Hänge- ['hɛŋə] *in cpds* hanging; ~**brücke** *f* suspension bridge; ~**matte** *f* hammock.

hängen ['hɛŋən] *irreg vi* hang; ~ **an** (*fig*) be attached to; *vt* hang (*an* +*acc* on(to)); **sich** ~ **an** (+*acc*) hang on to, cling to; ~**bleiben** *vi irreg* be caught (*an* +*dat* on); (*fig*) remain, stick.

Hängeschloß *nt* padlock.

hänseln ['hɛnzəln] *vt* tease.

hantieren [han'ti:rən] *vi* work, be busy; **mit etw** ~ handle sth.

hapern ['ha:pərn] *vi impers*: **es hapert an etw** (*dat*) sth leaves something to be desired.

Happen ['hapən] *m* -s, - mouthful.

Harfe ['harfə] *f* -, -n harp.

Harke ['harkə] *f* -, -n rake; **h~n** *vti* rake.

harmlos ['harmlo:s] a harmless; **H~igkeit** *f* harmlessness.

Harmonie [harmo'ni:] *f* harmony; **h~ren** *vi* harmonize.

Harmonika [har'mo:nika] *f* -, -s (*Zieh*—) concertina.

harmonisch [har'mo:nıʃ] a harmonious.

Harmonium [har'mo:nium] *nt* -s, -nien or -s harmonium.

Harn [harn] *m* -(e)s, -e urine; ~**blase** *f* bladder.

Harnisch ['harnıʃ] *m* -(e)s, -e armour; **jdn in** ~ **bringen** infuriate sb; **in** ~ **geraten** become angry.

Harpune [har'pu:nə] *f* -, -n harpoon.

harren ['harən] *vi* wait (*auf* +*acc* for).

hart [hart] a hard; (*fig*) harsh.

Härte ['hɛrtə] *f* -, -n hardness; (*fig*) harshness; **h**~n *vtr* harden.

hart- *cpd*: ~**gekocht** a hard-boiled; ~**gesotten** a tough, hard-boiled; ~**herzig** a hard-hearted; ~**näckig** a stubborn; **H~näckigkeit** *f* stubbornness.

Harz [ha:rts] *nt* -es, -e resin.

Haschee [ha'ʃe:] *nt* -s, -s hash.

haschen ['haʃən] *vt* catch, snatch; *vi* (*col*) smoke hash.

Haschisch ['haʃıʃ] *nt* - hashish.

Hase ['ha:zə] *m* -n, -n hare.

Haselnuß ['ha:zəlnus] *f* hazelnut.

Hasen- *cpd*: ~**fuß** *m* coward; ~**scharte** *f* harelip.

Haspe ['haspə] *f* -, -n hinge; ~**l** *f* -, -n reel, bobbin; (*Winde*) winch.

Haß [has] *m* -sses hate, hatred.

hassen ['hasən] *vt* hate; ~**enswert** a hateful.

häßlich ['hɛslıç] a ugly; (*gemein*) nasty; **H~keit** *f* ugliness; nastiness.

Hast [hast] *f* - haste; **h~en** *vir* rush; **h~ig** a hasty.

hätscheln ['hɛtʃəln] *vt* pamper; (*zärtlich*) cuddle.

Haube ['haubə] *f* -, -n hood; (*Mütze*) cap; (*Aut*) bonnet, hood (*US*).

Hauch [haux] *m* -(e)s, -e breath; (*Luft*—) breeze; (*fig*) trace; **h**~en *vi* breathe; **h~fein** a very fine.

Haue ['hauə] *f* -, -n hoe, pick; (*col*) hiding; **h**~n *vt irreg* hew, cut; (*col*) thrash.

Haufen ['haufən] *m* -s, - heap; (*Leute*) crowd; **ein** ~ (**x**) (*col*) loads or a lot (of x); **auf einem** ~ in one heap; **h~weise** ad in heaps; in droves; **etw h~weise haben** have piles of sth.

häufen ['hɔyfən] *vt* pile up; *vr* accumulate.

häufig ['hɔyfıç] a,ad frequent(ly); **H~keit** *f* frequency.

Haupt [haupt] *nt* -(e)s, **Häupter** head; (*Ober*—) chief; *in cpds* main; ~**bahnhof** *m* central station; **h~beruflich** ad as one's main occupation; ~**buch** *nt* (*Comm*) ledger; ~**darsteller(in** *f*) *m* leading actor/actress; ~**eingang** *m* main entrance; ~**fach** *nt* main subject; ~**film** *m* main film.

Häuptling ['hɔyptlıŋ] *m* chief(tain).

Haupt- *cpd*: ~**mann** *m, pl* -**leute** (*Mil*) captain; ~**postamt** *nt* main post office; ~**quartier** *nt* headquarters *pl*; ~**rolle** *f* leading part; ~**sache** *f* main thing; **h~sächlich** a,ad chief(ly); ~**satz** *m* main clause; ~**schlagader** *f* aorta; ~**stadt** *f* capital; ~**straße** *f* main street; ~**wort** *nt* noun.

Haus [haus] *nt* -es, **Häuser** house; **nach** ~**e** home; **zu** ~ at home; ~**angestellte** *f* domestic servant; ~**arbeit** *f* housework; (*Sch*) homework; ~**arzt** *m* family doctor; ~**aufgabe** *f* (*Sch*) homework; ~**besitzer(in** *f*) *m*, ~**eigentümer(in** *f*) *m* house-owner.

hausen ['hauzən] *vi* live (in poverty); (*pej*) wreak havoc.

Häuser- ['hɔyzər] cpd: ~**block** m block (of houses); ~**makler** m estate agent.

Haus- cpd: ~**frau** f housewife; ~**freund** m family friend; (col) lover; h~**gemacht** a home-made; ~**halt** m household; (Pol) budget; h~**halten** vi irreg keep house; (sparen) economize; ~**hälterin** f housekeeper; ~**haltsgeld** nt housekeeping (money); ~**haltsgerät** nt domestic appliance; ~**haltsplan** m budget; ~**haltung** f housekeeping; ~**herr** m host; (Vermieter) landlord; h~**hoch** ad: h~**hoch verlieren** lose by a mile.

hausieren [hau'zi:rən] vi hawk, peddle.

Hausierer m -s, - hawker, peddlar.

häuslich ['hɔyslɪç] a domestic; **H~keit** f domesticity.

Haus- cpd: ~**meister** m caretaker, janitor; ~**ordnung** f house rules pl; ~**putz** m house cleaning; ~**schlüssel** m front-door key; ~**schuh** m slipper; ~**suchung** f police raid; ~**tier** nt domestic animal; ~**verwalter** m caretaker; ~**wirt** m landlord; ~**wirtschaft** f domestic science.

Haut [haut] f -, **Häute** skin; (Tier—) hide.

häuten ['hɔytən] vt skin; vr slough one's skin.

Haut- cpd: h~**eng** a skin-tight; ~**farbe** f complexion.

Haxe ['haksə] f -, -n see **Hachse**.

Hebamme ['he:p'amə] f -, -n midwife.

Hebel ['he:bəl] m -s, - lever.

heben ['he:bən] vt irreg raise, lift.

hecheln ['hɛçəln] vi (Hund) pant.

Hecht [hɛçt] m -(e)s, -e pike.

Heck [hɛk] nt -(e)s, -e stern; (von Auto) rear.

Hecke ['hɛkə] f -, -n hedge; ~**nrose** f dog rose; ~**schütze** m sniper.

Heer [he:r] nt -(e)s, -e army.

Hefe ['he:fə] f -, -n yeast.

Heft [hɛft] nt -(e)s, -e exercise book; (Zeitschrift) number; (von Messer) haft; h~**en** vt fasten (an +acc to); (nähen) tack; ~**er** m -s, - folder.

heftig a fierce, violent; **H~keit** f fierceness, violence.

Heft- cpd: ~**klammer** f paper clip; ~**maschine** f stapling machine; ~**pflaster** nt sticking plaster; ~**zwecke** f drawing pin.

hegen ['he:gən] vt nurse; (fig) harbour, foster.

Hehl [he:l] m or nt: **kein(en)** ~ **aus etw** (dat) **machen** make no secret of sth; ~**er** m -s, - receiver (of stolen goods), fence.

Heide ['haɪdə] f -, -n heath, moor; (—kraut) heather; m -n, -n, **Heidin** f heathen, pagan; ~**kraut** nt heather; ~**lbeere** f bilberry; h~**nmäßig** a (col) terrific; ~**ntum** nt paganism.

heidnisch ['haɪdnɪʃ] a heathen, pagan.

heikel ['haɪkəl] a awkward, thorny; (wählerisch) fussy.

Heil [haɪl] nt -(e)s well-being; (Seelen—) salvation; h~ a in one piece, intact; h~ interj hail; ~**and** m -(e)s, -e saviour; h~**bar** a curable; h~**en** vt cure; vi heal;

h~**froh** a very relieved; ~**gymnastin** f physiotherapist.

heilig ['haɪlɪç] a holy; **H~abend** m Christmas Eve; **H~e(r)** mf saint; ~**en** vt sanctify, hallow; **H~enschein** m halo; **H~keit** f holiness; ~**sprechen** vt irreg canonize; **H~tum** nt shrine; (Gegenstand) relic.

Heil- cpd: h~**los** a unholy; ~**mittel** nt remedy; h~**sam** a (fig) salutary; ~**sarmee** f Salvation Army; ~**ung** f cure.

Heim [haɪm] nt -(e), -e home; h~ ad home.

Heimat ['haɪma:t] f -, -en home (town/country etc); ~**land** nt homeland; h~**lich** a native, home attr; (Gefühle nostalgic; h~**los** a homeless; ~**ort** m home town/area; ~**vertriebene(r)** mf displaced person.

Heim- cpd: h~**begleiten** vt accompany home; h~**elig** a homely; h~**fahren** vi irreg drive/go home; ~**fahrt** f journey home; ~**gang** m return home; (Tod) decease; h~**gehen** vi irreg go home; (sterben) pass away; h~**isch** a (gebürtig) native; **sich** h~**isch fühlen** feel at home; ~**kehr** f -, -en homecoming; h~**kehren** vi return home; h~**lich** a secret; ~**lichkeit** f secrecy; ~**reise** f journey home; h~**suchen** vt afflict; (Geist) haunt; h~**tückisch** a malicious; h~**wärts** ad homewards; ~**weg** m way home; ~**weh** nt homesickness; ~**weh haben be** homesick; h~**zahlen** vt: **jdm etw** h~**zahlen** pay back sb for sth.

Heirat ['haɪra:t] f -, -en marriage; h~**en** vti marry; ~**santrag** m proposal.

heiser ['haɪzər] a hoarse; **H~keit** f hoarseness.

heiß [haɪs] a hot; ~**e(r) Draht** hot line; ~**blütig** a hot-blooded.

heißen ['haɪsən] irreg vi be called; (bedeuten) mean; vt command; (nennen) name; v impers it says; **it is said.**

Heiß- cpd: h~**ersehnt** a longed for; ~**hunger** m ravenous hunger; h~**laufen** vir irreg overheat.

heiter ['haɪtər] a cheerful; (Wetter) bright; **H~keit** f cheerfulness; (Belustigung) amusement.

Heiz- ['haɪts] cpd: h~**bar** a heated; (Raum with heating); **leicht** h~**bar** easily heated; ~**decke** f electric blanket; h~**en** vt heat; ~**er** m -s, - stoker; ~**körper** m radiator; ~**öl** nt fuel oil; ~**sonne** f electric fire; ~**ung** f heating; ~**ungsanlage** f heating system.

hektisch ['hɛktɪʃ] a hectic.

Held [hɛlt] m -en, -en hero; ~**in** f heroine.

helfen ['hɛlfən] irreg vi help (jdm sb, bei with); (nützen) be of use; **sich** (dat) **zu** ~ **wissen** be resourceful; v impers: **es hilft nichts, du mußt** . . . it's no use, you have to . . .

Helfer m -s, - helper, assistant; ~**shelfer** m accomplice.

hell [hɛl] a clear, bright; (Farbe) light; ~**blau** a light blue; ~**blond** a ash-blond;

H~e f - clearness, brightness; H~er m
-s, - farthing; ~hörig a keen of hearing;
Wand poorly soundproofed; H~igkeit f
clearness, brightness; lightness;
H~seher m clairvoyant; ~wach a wide-
awake.

Helm ['hɛlm] m ~(e)s, -e (auf Kopf)
helmet.

Hemd [hɛmt] nt ~(e)s, -en shirt; (Unter—)
vest; ~bluse f blouse; ~enknopf m shirt
button.

hemmen ['hɛmən] vt check, hold up;
gehemmt sein be inhibited.

Hemmung f check; (Psych) inhibition;
h~slos a unrestrained, without restraint.

Hengst [hɛŋst] m -es, -e stallion.

Henkel ['hɛŋkəl] m -s, - handle; ~krug m
jug.

henken ['hɛŋkən] vt hang.

Henker m -s, - hangman.

Henne ['hɛnə] f -, -n hen.

her [heːr] ad here; (Zeit) ago; ~ damit!
hand it over!

herab [hɛˈrap] ad down(ward(s));
~hängen vi irreg hang down; ~lassen
irreg vt let down; vr condescend;
H~lassung f condescension; ~sehen vi
irreg look down (auf +acc on); ~setzen vt
lower, reduce; (fig) belittle, disparage;
H~setzung f reduction; disparagement;
~würdigen vt belittle, disparage.

heran [hɛˈran] ad: näher ~! come up
closer!; ~ zu mir! come up to me!;
~bilden vt train; ~bringen vt irreg
bring up (an +acc to); ~fahren vi irreg
drive up (an +acc to); ~kommen vi irreg
(an +acc) approach, come near;
~machen vr: sich an jdn ~machen
make up to sb; ~wachsen vi irreg grow
up; ~ziehen vt irreg pull nearer;
(aufziehen) raise; (ausbilden) train; jdn zu
etw ~ziehen call upon sb to help in sth.

herauf [hɛˈrauf] ad up(ward(s)), up here;
~beschwören vt irreg conjure up, evoke;
~bringen vt irreg bring up; ~ziehen
irreg vt draw or pull up; vi approach;
(Sturm) gather.

heraus [hɛˈraus] ad out; outside; from;
~arbeiten vt work out; ~bekommen vt
irreg get out; (fig) find or figure out;
~bringen vt irreg bring out; Geheimnis
elicit; ~finden vt irreg find out;
~fordern vt challenge; H~forderung f
challenge; provocation; ~geben vt irreg
give up, surrender; Geld give back; Buch
edit; (veröffentlichen) publish; ~geber m
-s, - editor; (Verleger) publisher; ~gehen
vi irreg: aus sich (dat) ~gehen come out
of one's shell; ~halten vr irreg: sich aus
etw ~halten keep out of sth; ~hängen
vti irreg hang out; ~holen vt get out (aus
of); ~kommen vi irreg come out; dabei
kommt nichts ~ nothing will come of it;
~nehmen vt irreg take out; sich (dat)
Freiheiten ~nehmen take liberties;
~reißen vt irreg tear out; pull out;
~rücken vt Geld fork out, hand over; mit
etw ~rücken (fig) come out with sth;
~rutschen vi irreg slip out; ~schlagen vt
irreg knock out; (fig) obtain; ~stellen vr

turn out (als to be); ~wachsen vi irreg
grow out (aus of); ~ziehen vt irreg pull
out, extract.

herb [hɛrp] a (slightly) bitter, acid; Wein
dry; (fig) (schmerzlich) bitter; (streng)
stern, austere.

herbei [hɛrˈbai] ad (over) here; ~führen
vt bring about; ~lassen vr irreg: sich
~lassen zu condescend or deign to;
~schaffen vt procure.

herbemühen ['hɛrbəmyːən] vr take the
trouble to come.

Herberge ['hɛrbɛrgə] f -, -n shelter;
hostel, inn.

Herbergsmutter f, **Herbergsvater** m
warden.

her- ['hɛr] cpd: ~bitten vt irreg ask to
come (here); ~bringen vt irreg bring
here.

Herbst [hɛrpst] m ~(e)s, -e autumn, fall
(US); h~lich a autumnal.

Herd [heːrt] m ~(e)s, -e cooker; (fig, Med)
focus, centre.

Herde ['heːrdə] f -, -n herd; (Schaf—)
flock.

herein [hɛˈrain] ad in (here), here; ~!
come in!; ~bitten vt irreg ask in;
~brechen vi irreg set in; ~bringen vt
irreg bring in; ~dürfen vi irreg have permission to enter; H~fall m letdown;
~fallen vi irreg be caught, taken in;
~fallen auf (+acc) fall for; ~kommen
vi irreg come in; ~lassen vt irreg admit;
~legen vt: jdn ~legen take sb in;
~platzen vi burst in.

Her- ['hɛr] cpd: ~fahrt f journey here;
h~fallen vi irreg: h~fallen über fall
upon; ~gang m course of events, circumstances pl; h~geben vt irreg give, hand
(over); sich zu etw h~geben lend one's
name to sth; h~gehen vt irreg: hinter
jdm h~gehen follow sb; es geht hoch
h~ there are a lot of goings-on;
h~halten vt irreg hold out; h~halten
müssen (col) have to suffer; h~hören vi
listen; hör mal h~! listen here!

Hering ['heːrɪŋ] m -s, -e herring.

her- ['hɛr] cpd: ~kommen vi irreg come;
komm mal ~! come here!; ~kömmlich
a traditional; H~kunft f -, -künfte origin;
~laufen vi irreg; ~laufen hinter
(+dat) run after; ~leiten vr derive;
~machen vr: sich ~machen über
(+acc) set about or upon.

Hermelin [hɛrməˈliːn] m or nt -s, -e
ermine.

hermetisch [hɛrˈmeːtɪʃ] a,ad her-
metic(ally).

her- cpd: ~'nach ad afterwards; ~-
'nieder ad down.

heroisch [heˈroːɪʃ] a heroic.

Herold ['heːrɔlt] m ~(e)s, -e herald.

Herr [hɛr] m ~(e)n, -en master; (Mann)
gentleman; (adliger, Rel) Lord; (vor
Namen) Mr.; mein ~! sir!; meine ~en!
gentlemen!; ~enbekanntschaft f gentleman friend; ~endoppel nt men's doubles;
~eneinzel nt men's singles; ~enhaus nt
mansion; h~enlos a ownerless.

herrichten ['hɛrrɪçtən] vt prepare.

Herr- *cpd:* ~**in** *f* mistress; **h~isch** *a* domineering; **h~lich** *a* marvellous, splendid; ~**lichkeit** *f* splendour, magnificence; ~**schaft** *f* power, rule; (*Herr und Herrin*) master and mistress; **meine ~schaften!** ladies and gentlemen!

herrschen ['hɛrʃən] *vt* rule; (*bestehen*) prevail, be.

Herrscher(in *f*) *m* -**s,** - ruler.

Herrschsucht *f* domineering behaviour.

her- ['hɛr] *cpd:* ~**rühren** *vi* arise, originate; ~**sagen** *vt* recite; ~**stammen** *vi* descend, come from; ~**stellen** *vt* make, manufacture; **H~steller** *m* -**s,** - manufacturer; **H~stellung** *f* manufacture; **H~stellungskosten** *pl* manufacturing costs *pl*.

herüber [hɛ'ry:bər] *ad* over (here), across.

herum [hɛ'rʊm] *ad* about, (a)round; **um etw ~** around sth; ~**ärgern** *vr* get annoyed (*mit* with); ~**führen** *vt* show around; ~**gehen** *vi irreg* walk *or* go round (*um etw* sth); walk about; ~**irren** *vi* wander about; ~**kriegen** *vt* bring *or* talk around; ~**lungern** *vi* lounge about; ~**sprechen** *vr irreg* get around, be spread; ~**treiben** *vr irreg* drift about; ~**ziehen** *vir irreg* wander about.

herunter [hɛ'rʊntər] *ad* downward(s), down (there); ~**gekommen** *a* run-down; ~**hängen** *vi irreg* hang down; ~**holen** *vt* bring down; ~**kommen** *vi irreg* come down; (*fig*) come down in the world; ~**machen** *vt* take down; (*schimpfen*) abuse, criticise severely.

hervor [hɛr'fo:r] *ad* out, forth; ~**brechen** *vi irreg* burst forth, break out; ~**bringen** *vt irreg* produce; *Wort* utter; ~**gehen** *vi irreg* emerge, result; ~**heben** *vt irreg* stress; (*als Kontrast*) set off; ~**ragend** *a* excellent; (*lit*) projecting; ~**rufen** *vt irreg* cause, give rise to; ~**treten** *vi irreg* come out.

Herz [hɛrts] *nt* -**ens, -en** heart; ~**anfall** *m* heart attack; **h~en** *vt* caress, embrace; ~**enslust** *f:* **nach ~enslust** to one's heart's content; ~**fehler** *m* heart defect; **h~haft** *a* hearty; ~**infarkt** *m* heart attack; ~**klopfen** *nt* palpitation; **h~lich** *a* cordial; **h~lichen Glückwunsch** congratulations *pl;* **h~liche Grüße** best wishes; ~**lichkeit** *f* cordiality; **h~los** *a* heartless; ~**losigkeit** *f* heartlessness.

Herzog ['hɛrtso:k] *m* -**(e)s,** ⁻**e** duke; ~**in** *f* duchess; **h~lich** *a* ducal; ~**tum** *nt* duchy.

Herz- *cpd:* ~**schlag** *m* heartbeat; (*Med*) heart attack; **h~zerreißend** *a* heart-rending.

heterogen [hetero'ge:n] *a* heterogeneous.

Hetze ['hɛtsə] *f* -, -**n** (*Eile*) rush; **h~n** *vt* hunt; (*verfolgen*) chase; **jdn/etw auf jdn/etw ~** set sb/sth on sb/sth; *vi* (*eilen*) rush; **h~n gegen** stir up feeling against; **h~n zu** agitate for; ~'**rei** *f* agitation; (*Eile*) rush.

Heu [hɔy] *nt* -**(e)s** hay; ~**boden** *m* hayloft.

Heuchelei [hɔyçə'laɪ] *f* hypocrisy.

heucheln ['hɔyçəln] *vt* pretend, feign; *vi* be hypocritical.

Heuchler(in *f*) ['hɔyçlər(ɪn)] *m* -**s,** - hypocrite; **h~isch** *a* hypocritical.

Heuer ['hɔyər] *f* -, -**n** (*Naut*) pay; **h~** *ad* this year.

Heugabel *f* pitchfork.

heulen ['hɔylən] *vi* howl; cry; **das ~de Elend bekommen** get the blues.

heurig ['hɔyrɪç] *a* this year's.

Heu- *cpd:* ~**schnupfen** *m* hay fever; ~**schrecke** *f* grasshopper, locust.

heute ['hɔytə] *ad* today; ~ **abend/früh** this evening/morning; **das H~** today.

heutig ['hɔytɪç] *a* today's.

heutzutage ['hɔyttsuta:gə] *ad* nowadays.

Hexe ['hɛksə] *f* -, -**n** witch; **h~n** *vi* practise witchcraft; **ich kann doch nicht h~n** I can't work miracles; ~**nkessel** *m* (*lit, fig*) cauldron; ~**nmeister** *m* wizard; ~**nschuß** *m* lumbago; ~'**rei** *f* witchcraft.

Hieb [hi:p] *m* -**(e)s, -e** blow; (*Wunde*) cut, gash; (*Stichelei*) cutting remark; ~**e bekommen** get a thrashing.

hier [hi:r] *ad* here; ~**auf** *ad* thereupon; (*danach*) after that; ~**behalten** *vt irreg* keep here; ~**bei** *ad* herewith, enclosed; ~**bleiben** *vi irreg* stay here; ~**durch** *ad* by this means; (*örtlich*) through here; ~**her** *ad* this way, here; ~**lassen** *vt irreg* leave here; ~**mit** *ad* hereby; ~**nach** *ad* hereafter; ~**von** *ad* about this, hereof; ~**zulande** *ad* in this country.

hiesig ['hi:zɪç] *a* of this place, local.

Hilfe ['hɪlfə] *f* -, -**n** help; aid; **Erste ~** first aid; ~**!** help!

Hilf- *cpd:* **h~los** *a* helpless; ~**losigkeit** *f* helplessness; **h~reich** *a* helpful; ~**saktion** *f* relief measures *pl;* ~**sarbeiter** *m* labourer; **h~sbedürftig** *a* needy; **h~sbereit** *a* ready to help; ~**skraft** *f* assistant, helper; ~**sschule** *f* school for backward children; ~**szeitwort** *nt* auxiliary verb.

Himbeere ['hɪmbe:rə] *f* -, -**n** raspberry.

Himmel ['hɪməl] *m* -**s,** - sky; (*Rel, liter*) heaven; **h~angst** *a:* **es ist mir h~angst** I'm scared to death; **h~blau** *a* sky-blue; ~**fahrt** *f* Ascension; **h~schreiend** *a* outrageous; ~**srichtung** *f* direction.

himmlisch ['hɪmlɪʃ] *a* heavenly.

hin [hɪn] *ad* there; ~ **und her** to and fro; **bis zur Mauer ~** up to the wall; **Geld ~, Geld her** money or no money; **mein Glück ist ~** my happiness has gone.

hinab [hɪ'nap] *ad* down; ~**gehen** *vi irreg* go down; ~**sehen** *vi irreg* look down.

hinauf [hɪ'nauf] *ad* up; ~**arbeiten** *vr* work one's way up; ~**steigen** *vi irreg* climb.

hinaus [hɪ'naus] *ad* out; ~**befördern** *vt* kick/throw out; ~**gehen** *vi irreg* go out; ~**gehen über** (+*acc*) exceed; ~**laufen** *vi irreg* run out; ~**laufen auf** (+*acc*) come to, amount to; ~**schieben** *vt irreg* put off, postpone; ~**werfen** *vt irreg* throw out; ~**wollen** *vi* want to go out; ~**wollen auf** (+*acc*) drive at, get at; ~**ziehen** *irreg vt* draw out; *vr* be protracted.

Hinblick ['hɪnblɪk] *m:* **in** *or* **im ~ auf** (+*acc*) in view of.

hinder- ['hɪndər] *cpd:* ~**lich** *a* awkward;

~n vt hinder, hamper; **jdn an etw** (dat) **~n** prevent sb from doing sth; **H~nis** nt **-ses, -se** obstacle.

hindeuten ['hɪndɔʏtən] vi point (auf +acc to).

hindurch [hɪn'dʊrç] ad through; across; (zeitlich) over.

hinein [hɪ'naɪn] ad in; **~fallen** vi irreg fall in; **~fallen in** (+acc) fall into; **~gehen** vi irreg go in; **~gehen in** (+acc) go into, enter; **~geraten** vi irreg: **~geraten in** (+acc) get into; **~passen** vi fit in; **~passen in** (+acc) fit into; **~reden** vi: **jdm ~reden** interfere in sb's affairs; **~steigern** vr get worked up; **~versetzen** vr: **sich ~versetzen in** (+acc) put oneself in the position of.

hin- ['hɪn] cpd: **~fahren** irreg vi go; drive; vt take; drive; **H~fahrt** f journey there; **~fallen** vi irreg fall down; **~fällig** a frail, decrepit; Regel etc unnecessary, otiose; **H~gabe** f devotion; **~geben** vr irreg +dat give oneself up to, devote oneself to; **~gehen** vi irreg go; (Zeit) pass; **~halten** vt irreg hold out; (warten lassen) put off, stall.

hinken ['hɪŋkən] vi limp; (Vergleich) be unconvincing.

hin- ['hɪn] cpd: **~legen** vt put down; vr lie down; **~nehmen** vt irreg (fig) put up with, take; **~reichen** vi be adequate; vt: **jdm etw ~reichen** hand sb sth; **H~reise** f journey out; **~reißen** vt irreg carry away, enrapture; **sich ~reißen lassen, etw zu tun get** carried away and do sth; **~richten** vt execute; **H~richtung** f execution; **~sichtlich** prep +gen with regard to; **~spiel** nt (Sport) first leg; **~stellen** vt put (down); vr place o.s.

hintanstellen [hɪnt'anʃtɛlən] vt (fig) ignore.

hinten ['hɪntən] ad at the back; behind; **~herum** ad round the back; (fig) secretly.

hinter ['hɪntər] prep +dat or acc behind; (nach) after; **~ jdm hersein** be after sb; **H~achse** f rear axle; **H~bein** nt hind leg; **sich auf die H~beine stellen** get tough; **H~bliebene(r)** mf surviving relative; **~drein** ad afterwards; **~e(r,s)** a rear, back; **~einander** ad one after the other; **H~gedanke** m ulterior motive; **~gehen** vt irreg deceive; **H~grund** m background; **H~halt** m ambush; **~hältig** a underhand, sneaky; **~her** ad afterwards, after; **H~hof** m backyard; **H~kopf** m back of one's head; **~'lassen** vt irreg leave; **H~'lassenschaft** f (testator's) estate; **~'legen** vt deposit; **H~list** f cunning, trickery; (Handlung) trick, dodge; **~listig** a cunning, crafty; **H~mann** m, pl **~männer** person behind; **H~rad** nt back wheel; **H~radantrieb** m (Aut) rear wheel drive; **~rücks** ad from behind; **H~teil** nt behind; **H~treffen** nt: **ins H~treffen kommen** lose ground; **~'treiben** vt irreg prevent, frustrate; **H~tür** f back door; (fig: Ausweg) escape, loophole; **~'ziehen**

vt irreg Steuern evade (paying).

hinüber [hɪ'ny:bər] ad across, over; **~gehen** vi irreg go over or across.

hinunter [hɪ'nʊntər] ad down; **~bringen** vt irreg take down; **~schlucken** vt (lit, fig) swallow; **~steigen** vi irreg descend.

hin- ['hɪn] cpd: **H~weg** m journey out; **~'weghelfen** vi irreg: **jdm über etw** (acc) **~weghelfen** help sb to get over sth; **~'wegsetzen** vr: **sich ~wegsetzen über** (+acc) disregard; **H~weis** m **-es, -e** (Andeutung) hint; (Anweisung) instruction; (Verweis) reference; **~weisen** vi irreg (auf +acc) (anzeigen) point to; (sagen) point out, refer to; **~werfen** vt irreg throw down; **~ziehen** vr irreg (fig) drag on; **~zielen** vi aim (auf +acc at).

hinzu [hɪn'tsu:] ad in addition; **~fügen** vt add.

Hirn [hɪrn] nt **-(e)s, -e** brain(s); **~gespinst** nt **-(e)s, -e** fantasy; **h~verbrannt** a half-baked, crazy.

Hirsch [hɪrʃ] m **-(e)s, -e** stag.

Hirse ['hɪrzə] f **-, -n** millet.

Hirt ['hɪrt] m **-en, -en** herdsman; (Schaf~, fig) shepherd.

hissen ['hɪsən] vt hoist.

Historiker [hɪs'to:rikər] m **-s, -** historian.

historisch [hɪs'to:rɪʃ] a historical.

Hitze ['hɪtsə] f **-** heat; **h~beständig** a heat-resistant; **~welle** f heatwave.

hitzig a hot-tempered; Debatte heated.

Hitz- cpd: **~kopf** m hothead; **h~köpfig** a fiery, hotheaded; **~schlag** m heatstroke.

Hobel ['ho:bəl] m **-s, -** plane; **~bank** f carpenter's bench; **h~n** vti plane; **~späne** pl wood shavings pl.

hoch [ho:x] a high; **H~** nt **-s, -s** (Ruf) cheer; (Met) anticyclone; **~achten** vt respect; **H~achtung** f respect, esteem; **~achtungsvoll** ad yours faithfully; **H~amt** nt high mass; **~arbeiten** vr work one's way up; **~begabt** a extremely gifted; **~betagt** a very old, aged; **H~betrieb** m intense activity; (Comm) peak time; **~bringen** vt irreg bring up; **H~burg** f stronghold; **H~deutsch** nt High German; **~dotiert** a highly paid; **H~druck** m high pressure; **H~ebene** f plateau; **~erfreut** a highly delighted; **~fliegend** a (fig) high-flown; **H~form** f top form; **~gradig** a intense, extreme; **~halten** vt irreg hold up; (fig) uphold, cherish; **H~haus** nt multi-storey building; **~heben** vt irreg lift up; **H~konjunktur** f boom; **H~land** nt highlands pl; **~leben** vi: **jdn ~leben lassen** give sb three cheers; **H~mut** m pride; **~mütig** a proud, haughty; **~näsig** a stuck-up, snooty; **H~ofen** m blast furnace; **~prozentig** a Alkohol strong; **H~rechnung** f projected result; **H~schätzung** f high esteem; **H~schule** f college; university; **H~sommer** m middle of summer; **H~spannung** f high tension; **H~sprache** f standard language; **~springen** vi irreg jump up, **H~sprung** m high jump.

höchst [høːçst] *ad* highly, extremely; ~**e(r,s)** *a* highest; (*äußerste*) extreme.

Hochstapler ['hoːxstaːplər] *m* -s, - swindler.

Höchst- *cpd*: **h**~**ens** *ad* at the most; ~**geschwindigkeit** *f* maximum speed; **h**~**persönlich** *ad* in person; ~**preis** *m* maximum price; **h**~**wahrscheinlich** *ad* most probably.

Hoch- *cpd* **h**~**trabend** *a* pompous; ~**verrat** *m* high treason; ~**wasser** *nt* high water; (*Überschwemmung*) floods *pl*; **h**~**wertig** *a* high-class, first-rate; ~**würden** *m* Reverend; ~**zahl** *f* (*Math*) exponent.

Hochzeit ['hoːxtsait] *f* -, -en wedding; ~**sreise** *f* honeymoon.

hocken ['hɔkən] *vir* squat, crouch.

Hocker *m* -s, - stool.

Höcker ['hœkər] *m* -s, - hump.

Hode ['hoːdə] *m* -n, -n testicle.

Hof [hoːf] *m* -(e)s, ̈e (*Hinter*—) yard; (*Bauern*—) farm; (*Königs*—) court.

hoffen ['hɔfən] *vi* hope (*auf* +acc for); ~**tlich** *ad* I hope, hopefully.

Hoffnung ['hɔfnuŋ] *f* hope; **h**~**slos** *a* hopeless; ~**slosigkeit** *f* hopelessness; ~**sschimmer** *m* glimmer of hope; **h**~**svoll** *a* hopeful.

höflich ['høːflɪç] *a* polite, courteous; **H**~**keit** *f* courtesy, politeness.

hohe(r,s) ['hoːə(r,z)] *a see* hoch.

Höhe ['høːə] *f* -, -n height; (*An*—) hill.

Hoheit ['hoːhait] *f* -(*Pol*) sovereignty; (*Titel*) Highness; ~**sgebiet** *nt* sovereign territory; ~**sgewässer** *nt* territorial waters *pl*; ~**szeichen** *nt* national emblem.

Höhen- ['høːən] *cpd*: ~**angabe** *f* altitude reading; (*auf Karte*) height marking; ~**messer** *m* -s, - altimeter; ~**sonne** *f* sun lamp; ~**unterschied** *m* difference in altitude; ~**zug** *m* mountain chain.

Höhepunkt *m* climax.

höher *a,ad* higher.

hohl [hoːl] *a* hollow.

Höhle ['høːlə] *f* -, -n cave, hole; (*Mund*—) cavity; (*fig, Zool*) den.

Hohl- *cpd*: ~**heit** *f* hollowness; ~**maß** *nt* measure of volume; ~**saum** *m* hemstitch.

Hohn [hoːn] *m* -(e)s scorn.

höhnen ['høːnən] *vt* taunt, scoff at.

höhnisch ['høːnɪʃ] *a* scornful, taunting.

hold [hɔlt] *a* charming, sweet.

holen ['hoːlən] *vt* get, fetch; *Atem* take; **jdn/etw** ~ **lassen** send for sb/sth.

Hölle ['hœlə] *f* -, -n hell; ~**nangst** *f*: **eine** ~**nangst haben** be scared to death.

höllisch ['hœlɪʃ] *a* hellish, infernal.

holperig ['hɔlpərɪç] *a* rough, bumpy.

holpern ['hɔlpərn] *vi* jolt.

Holunder [hoˈlundər] *m* -s, - elder.

Holz [hɔlts] *nt* -es, ̈er wood.

hölzern ['hœltsərn] *a* (*lit, fig*) wooden.

Holz- *cpd*: ~**fäller** *m* -s, - lumberjack, woodcutter; **h**~**ig** *a* woody, ~**klotz** *m* wooden block; ~**kohle** *f* charcoal; ~**scheit** *nt* log; ~**schuh** *m* clog; ~**weg** *m* (*fig*) wrong track; ~**wolle** *f* fine wood

shavings *pl*; ~**wurm** *m* woodworm.

homosexuell [homozɛksuˈɛl] *a* homosexual.

Honig ['hoːnɪç] *m* -s, -e honey; ~**wabe** *f* honeycomb.

Honorar [honoˈraːr] *nt* -s, -e fee.

honorieren [honoˈriːrən] *vt* remunerate; *Scheck* honour.

Hopfen ['hɔpfən] *m* -s, - hops *pl*.

hopsen ['hɔpsən] *vi* hop.

Hör- *cpd*: ~**apparat** *m* hearing aid; **h**~**bar** *a* audible.

horch [hɔrç] *interj* listen; ~**en** *vi* listen; (*pej*) eavesdrop; **H**~**er** *m* -s, - listener; eavesdropper.

Horde ['hɔrdə] *f* -, -n horde.

hören ['høːrən] *vti* hear; **H**~**sagen** *nt*: **vom H**~**sagen** from hearsay.

Hörer *m* -s, - hearer; (*Rad*) listener; (*Univ*) student; (*Telefon*—) receiver.

Horizont [horiˈtsɔnt] *m* -(e)s, -e horizon; **h**~**al** [-ˈtaːl] *a* horizontal.

Hormon [hɔrˈmoːn] *nt* -s, -e hormone.

Hörmuschel *f* (*Tel*) earpiece.

Horn [hɔrn] *nt* -(e)s, ̈er horn; ~**haut** *f* horny skin.

Hornisse [hɔrˈnɪsə] *f* -, -n hornet.

Horoskop [horoˈskoːp] *nt* -s, -e horoscope.

Hör- *cpd* ~**rohr** *nt* ear trumpet; (*Med*) stethoscope; ~**saal** *m* lecture room; ~**spiel** *nt* radio play.

Hort [hɔrt] *m* -(e)s, -e hoard; (*Sch*) nursery school; **h**~**en** *vt* hoard.

Hose ['hoːzə] *f* -, -n trousers *pl*, pants (*US*) *pl*; ~**nanzug** *m* trouser suit; ~**nrock** *m* culottes *pl*; ~**ntasche** *f* (trouser) pocket; ~**nträger** *m* braces *pl*, suspenders (*US*) *pl*.

Hostie ['hɔstiə] *f* (*Rel*) host.

Hotel [hoˈtɛl] *nt* -s, -s hotel; ~**ier** [hotɛliˈeː] *m* -s, -s hotelkeeper, hotelier.

Hub [huːp] *m* -(e)s, ̈e lift; (*Tech*) stroke.

hüben ['hyːbən] *ad* on this side, over here.

Hubraum *m* (*Aut*) cubic capacity.

hübsch [hypʃ] *a* pretty, nice.

Hubschrauber *m* -s, - helicopter.

hudeln ['huːdəln] *vi* be sloppy.

Huf [huːf] *m* -(e)s, -e hoof; ~**eisen** *nt* horseshoe; ~**nagel** *m* horseshoe nail.

Hüft- [hyft] *cpd*: ~**e** *f* -, -n hip; ~**gürtel** *m*, ~**halter** *m* -s, - girdle.

Hügel ['hyːgəl] *m* -s, - hill; **h**~**ig** *a* hilly.

Huhn [huːn] *nt* -(e)s, ̈er hen; (*Cook*) chicken.

Hühner- ['hyːnər] *cpd*: ~**auge** *nt* corn; ~**brühe** *f* chicken broth.

Huld [hult] *f* -, favour; **h**~**igen** ['huldɪgən] *vi* pay homage (*jdm* to sb); ~**igung** *f* homage.

Hülle ['hylə] *f* -, -n cover(ing); wrapping; **in** ~ **und Fülle** galore; **h**~**n** *vt* cover, wrap (*in* +acc with).

Hülse ['hylzə] *f* -, -n husk, shell; ~**nfrucht** *f* legume.

human [huˈmaːn] *a* humane; ~**itär** *a* humanitarian; **H**~**ität** *f* humanity.

Hummel ['huməl] *f* -, -n bumblebee.

Hummer ['humər] *m* -s, - lobster.

Humor [huˈmoːr] *m* -s, -e humour; ~

haben have a sense of humour; ~**ist** [-'rɪst] *m* humorist; **h**~**istisch** *a*, **h**~**voll** *a* humorous.

humpeln ['hʊmpəln] *vi* hobble.

Humpen ['hʊmpən] *m* -s, - tankard.

Hund [hʊnt] *m* -(e)s, -e dog; ~**ehütte** *f* (dog) kennel; ~**ekuchen** *m* dog biscuit; **h**~**emüde** *a* (col) dog-tired.

hundert ['hʊndərt] *num* hundred; **H**~-'**jahrfeier** *f* centenary; ~**prozentig** *a,ad* one hundred per cent.

Hündin ['hʏndɪn] *f* bitch.

Hunger ['hʊŋər] *m* -s hunger; ~ **haben** be hungry; ~**lohn** *m* starvation wages *pl*; **h**~**n** *vi* starve; ~**snot** *f* famine; ~**streik** *m* hunger strike.

hungrig ['hʊŋrɪç] *a* hungry.

Hupe ['hu:pə] *f* -, -n horn, hooter; **h**~**n** *vi* hoot, sound one's horn.

hüpfen ['hʏpfən] *vi* hop, jump.

Hürde ['hʏrdə] *f* -, -n hurdle; (*für Schafe*) pen; ~**nlauf** *m* hurdling.

Hure ['hu:rə] *f* -, -n whore.

hurtig ['hʊrtɪç] *a,ad* brisk(ly), quick(ly).

huschen ['hʊʃən] *vi* flit, scurry.

Husten ['hu:stən] *m* -s cough; **h**~ *vi* cough; ~**anfall** *m* coughing fit; ~**bonbon** *m* or *nt* cough drop; ~**saft** *m* cough mixture.

Hut [hu:t] *m* -(e)s, -e hat; *f* -care; **auf der** ~ **sein** be on one's guard.

hüten ['hy:tən] *vt* guard; *vr* watch out; **sich** ~, **zu** take care not to; **sich** ~ **vor** beware of.

Hütte ['hʏtə] *f* -, -n hut, cottage; (*Eisen*—) forge; ~**nwerk** *nt* foundry.

hutzelig ['hʊtsəlɪç] *a* shrivelled.

Hyäne [hy'ɛ:nə] *f* -, -n hyena.

Hyazinthe [hya'tsɪntə] *f* -, -n hyacinth.

Hydr- *cpd*: ~**ant** [hy'drant] *m* hydrant; **h**~**aulisch** [hy'draʊlɪʃ] *a* hydraulic; ~**ierung** [hy'dri:rʊŋ] *f* hydrogenation.

Hygiene [hygi'e:nə] *f* - hygiene.

hygienisch [hygi'e:nɪʃ] *a* hygienic.

Hymne ['hʏmnə] *f* -, -n hymn, anthem.

hyper- ['hypər] *pref* hyper-.

Hypno- [hyp'no] *cpd*: ~**se** *f* -, -n hypnosis; **h**~**tisch** *a* hypnotic; ~**tiseur** [-ti'zø:r] *m* hypnotist; **h**~**ti'sieren** *vt* hypnotize.

Hypothek [hypo'te:k] *f* -, -en mortgage.

Hypothese [hypo'te:zə] *f* -, -n hypothesis.

hypothetisch [hypo'te:tɪʃ] *a* hypothetical.

Hysterie [hyste'ri:] *f* hysteria.

hysterisch [hys'te:rɪʃ] *a* hysterical.

I

I, i [i:] *nt* I, i.

ich [ɪç] *pron* I; ~ **bin's!** it's me!; **I**~ *nt* -(s), -(s) self; (*Psych*) ego.

Ideal [ide'a:l] *nt* -s, -e ideal; **i**~ *a* ideal; ~**ist** [-'lɪst] *m* idealist; **i**~**istisch** [-'lɪstɪʃ] *a* idealistic.

Idee [i'de:] *f* -, -n [i'de:ən] idea; **i**~**ll** [ide'ɛl] *a* ideal.

identi- [i'dɛnti] *cpd*: ~**fizieren** [-fi'tsi:rən] *vt* identify; ~**sch** *a* identical; **I**~**tät** [-'tɛ:t] *f* identity.

Ideo- [ideo] *cpd*: ~**loge** [-'lo:gə] *m* -n, -n

ideologist; ~**logie** [-lo'gi:] *f* ideology; **i**~**logisch** [-'lo:gɪʃ] *a* ideological.

idiomatisch [idio'ma:tɪʃ] *a* idiomatic.

Idiot [idi'o:t] *m* -en, -en idiot; **i**~**isch** *a* idiotic.

idyllisch [i'dʏlɪʃ] *a* idyllic.

Igel ['i:gəl] *m* -s, - hedgehog.

ignorieren [ɪgno'ri:rən] *vt* ignore.

ihm [i:m] *pron dat of* **er, es** (to) him, (to) it.

ihn [i:n] *pron acc of* **er** him, it; ~**en** *pron dat of* **sie** *pl* (to) them; **I**~**en** *pron dat of* **Sie** (to) you.

ihr [i:r] *pron nom pl* you; *dat of* **sie** *sing* (to) her; ~**(e)** *poss pron sing* her; its; *pl* their; **I**~**(e)** *poss pron* your; ~**e(r,s)** *poss pron sing* hers; its; *pl* theirs; **I**~**e(r,s)** *poss pron* yours; ~**er** *pron gen of* **sie** *sing/pl of* her/them; **I**~**er** *pron gen of* **Sie** of you; ~**erseits** *ad* for her/their part; ~**esgleichen** *pron* people like her/them; (*von Dingen*) others like it; ~**etwegen**, ~**etwillen** *ad* (*für sie*) for her/its/their sake; (*wegen ihr*) on her/its/their account; ~**ige** *pron*: **der/die/das** ~**ige** hers; its; theirs.

Ikone [i'ko:nə] *f* -, -n icon.

illegal ['ɪlega:l] *a* illegal.

Illusion [ɪluzi'o:n] *f* illusion.

illusorisch [ɪlu'zo:rɪʃ] *a* illusory.

illustrieren [ɪlus'tri:rən] *vt* illustrate.

Illustrierte *f* -n, -n picture magazine.

Iltis ['ɪltɪs] *m* -ses, -se polecat.

im [ɪm] = **in dem**.

imaginär [imagi'nɛ:r] *a* imaginary.

Imbiß ['ɪmbɪs] *m* -sses, -sse snack; ~**halle** *f*, ~**stube** *f* snack bar.

imitieren [imi'ti:rən] *vt* imitate.

Imker ['ɪmkər] *m* -s, - beekeeper.

Immatrikulation [ɪmatrikulatsi'o:n] *f* (*Univ*) registration.

immatrikulieren [ɪmatriku'li:rən] *vir* register.

immer ['ɪmər] *ad* always; ~ **wieder** again and again; ~ **noch** still; ~ **noch nicht** still not; **für** ~ forever; ~ **wenn ich ...** everytime I . . . ; ~ **schöner/trauriger** more and more beautiful/sadder and sadder; **was/wer (auch)** ~ whatever/whoever; ~**hin** *ad* all the same; ~**zu** *ad* all the time.

Immobilien [ɪmo'bi:liən] *pl* real estate.

immun [ɪ'mu:n] *a* immune; **I**~**ität** [-i'tɛ:t] *f* immunity.

Imperativ ['ɪmperati:f] *m* -s, -e imperative.

Imperfekt ['ɪmpɛrfɛkt] *nt* -s, -e imperfect (tense).

Imperialist [ɪmperia'lɪst] *m* imperialist; **i**~**isch** *a* imperialistic.

Impf- [ɪmpf] *cpd*: **i**~**en** *vt* vaccinate; ~**stoff** *m* vaccine; ~**ung** *f* vaccination; ~**zwang** *m* compulsory vaccination.

implizieren [ɪmpli'tsi:rən] *vt* imply (*mit* by).

imponieren [ɪmpo'ni:rən] *vi* impress (*jdm* sb).

Import [ɪm'pɔrt] *m* -(e)s, -e import; **i**~**ieren** [-'ti:rən] *vt* import.

imposant [ɪmpo'zant] *a* imposing.

impotent ['ɪmpotɛnt] a impotent.
imprägnieren [ɪmprɛ'gniːrən] vt (water)proof.
Improvisation [ɪmprovizatsi'oːn] f improvization.
improvisieren [ɪmprovi'ziːrən] vti improvize.
Impuls [ɪm'puls] m -es, -e impulse; **i~iv** [-'ziːf] a impulsive.
imstande [ɪm'ʃtandə] a: ~ **sein** be in a position; (fähig) be able.
in [ɪn] prep +acc in(to); to; +dat in; ~ **der/die Stadt** in/into town; ~ **der/die Schule** at/to school.
Inanspruchnahme [ɪn'ʔanʃpruxnaːmə] f -, -n demands pl (gen on).
Inbegriff ['ɪnbəɡrɪf] m embodiment, personification; **i~en** ad included.
inbrünstig ['ɪnbrʏnstɪç] a ardent.
indem [ɪn'deːm] cj while; ~ **man etw macht** (dadurch) by doing sth.
indes(sen) [ɪn'dɛs(ən)] ad meanwhile; cj while.
Indianer(in f) [ɪndi'aːnər(ɪn)] m -s, - Red Indian.
indianisch a Red Indian.
indigniert [ɪndɪ'gniːrt] a indignant.
Indikativ ['ɪndikatiːf] m -s, -e indicative.
indirekt ['ɪndirɛkt] a indirect.
indiskret ['ɪndiskreːt] a indiscreet; **I~ion** [ɪndɪskretsi'oːn] f indiscretion.
indiskutabel ['ɪndɪskutaːbəl] a out of the question.
Individu- [ɪndividu] cpd: ~**alist** [-a'lɪst] m individualist; ~**alität** [-ali'tɛt] f individuality; **i~ell** [-'ɛl] a individual; ~**um** [ɪndi'viːduum] nt -s, -en individual.
Indiz [ɪn'diːts] nt -es, -ien sign (für of); (Jur) clue; ~**ienbeweis** m circumstantial evidence.
indoktrinieren [ɪndɔktri'niːrən] vt indoctrinate.
industrialisieren [ɪndustriali'ziːrən] vt industrialize.
Industrie [ɪndus'triː] f industry; in cpds industrial; ~**gebiet** nt industrial area; **i~ll** [ɪndustri'ɛl] a industrial; ~**zweig** m branch of industry.
ineinander [ɪn'aɪnandər] ad in(to) one another or each other.
Infanterie [ɪnfantə'riː] f infantry.
Infarkt [ɪn'farkt] m -(e)s, -e coronary (thrombosis).
Infektion [ɪnfɛktsi'oːn] f infection; ~**skrankheit** f infectious disease.
Infinitiv ['ɪnfinitiːf] m -s, -e infinitive.
infizieren [ɪnfi'tsiːrən] vt infect; vr be infected (bei by).
Inflation [ɪnflatsi'oːn] f inflation.
inflatorisch [ɪnfla'toːrɪʃ] a inflationary.
infolge [ɪn'fɔlɡə] prep +gen as a result of, owing to; ~**dessen** [-'dɛsən] ad consequently.
Informatik [ɪnfɔr'maːtɪk] f information studies pl.
Information [ɪnfɔrmatsi'oːn] f information no pl.
informieren [ɪnfɔr'miːrən] vt inform; vr find out (über +acc about).

Infusion [ɪnfuzi'oːn] f infusion.
Ingenieur [ɪnʒeni'øːr] m engineer; ~**schule** f school of engineering.
Ingwer ['ɪŋvər] m -s ginger.
Inhaber(in f) [ɪn'haːbər(ɪn)] m -s, - owner; (Haus—) occupier; (Lizenz—) licensee, holder; (Fin) bearer.
inhaftieren [ɪnhaf'tiːrən] vt take into custody.
inhalieren [ɪnha'liːrən] vti inhale.
Inhalt ['ɪnhalt] m -(e)s, -e contents pl; (eines Buchs etc) content; (Math) area; volume; ~**lich** a as regards content; ~**sangabe** f summary; **i~slos** a empty; **i~(s)reich** a full; ~**sverzeichnis** nt table of contents.
inhuman ['ɪnhumaːn] a inhuman.
Initiative [initsia'tiːvə] f initiative.
Injektion [ɪnjɛktsi'oːn] f injection.
inklusive [ɪnklu'ziːvə] prep, ad inclusive (gen of).
inkognito [ɪn'kɔɡnito] ad incognito.
inkonsequent ['ɪnkɔnzekvɛnt] a inconsistent.
inkorrekt ['ɪnkɔrɛkt] a incorrect.
Inkrafttreten [ɪn'krafttreːtən] nt -s coming into force.
Inland ['ɪnlant] nt -(e)s (Geog) inland; (Pol, Comm) home (country); ~**sporto** nt inland postage.
inmitten [ɪn'mɪtən] prep +gen in the middle of; ~ **von** amongst.
innehaben ['ɪnəhaːbən] vt irreg hold.
innen ['ɪnən] ad inside; **I~aufnahme** f indoor photograph; **I~einrichtung** f (interior) furnishings pl; **I~minister** m minister of the interior, Home Secretary (Brit); **I~politik** f domestic policy; **I~stadt** f town/city centre.
inner- ['ɪnər] cpd: ~**e(r,s)** a inner; (im Körper, inländisch) internal; **I~e(s)** nt inside; (Mitte) centre; (fig) heart; **I~eien** [-'raɪən] pl innards pl; ~**halb** ad, prep +gen within; (räumlich) inside; ~**lich** a internal; (geistig) inward; **I~ste(s)** nt heart; ~**ste(r,s)** a innermost.
innig ['ɪnɪç] a profound; Freundschaft intimate.
inoffiziell ['ɪnʔofitsiɛl] a unofficial.
ins [ɪns] = **in das**.
Insasse ['ɪnzasə] m -n, -n (Anstalt) inmate; (Aut) passenger.
insbesondere [ɪnsbə'zɔndərə] ad (e)specially.
Inschrift ['ɪnʃrɪft] f inscription.
Insekt [ɪn'zɛkt] nt -s, -en insect.
Insel ['ɪnzəl] f -, -n island.
Inser- cpd: ~**at** [ɪnze'raːt] nt -(e)s, -e advertisement; ~**ent** [ɪnze'rɛnt] m advertiser; **i~ieren** [ɪnze'riːrən] vti advertise.
insgeheim [ɪnsɡə'haɪm] ad secretly.
insgesamt [ɪnsɡə'zamt] ad altogether, all in all.
insofern ['ɪnzoˈfɛrn], **insoweit** ['ɪnzo'vaɪt] ad in this respect; ~ **als** in so far as; cj if; (deshalb) (and) so.
Installateur [ɪnstala'tøːr] m electrician; plumber.
Instand- [ɪn'ʃtant] cpd: ~**haltung** f main-

tenance; **~setzung** f overhaul; (eines Gebäudes) restoration.
Instanz [in'stants] f authority; (Jur) court; **~enweg** m official channels pl.
Instinkt [in'stiŋkt] m **-(e)s, -e** instinct; **i~iv** [-'ti:f] a instinctive.
Institut [insti'tu:t] nt **-(e)s, -e** institute.
Instrument [instru'mɛnt] nt instrument.
inszenieren [instse'ni:rən] vt direct; (fig) stage-manage.
Intell- [intɛl] cpd: **i~ektuell** [-ɛktu'ɛl] a intellectual; **i~igent** [-i'gɛnt] a intelligent; **~igenz** [-i'gɛnts] f intelligence; (Leute) intelligentsia pl.
Intendant [intɛn'dant] m director.
intensiv [intɛn'zi:f] a intensive.
Interess- cpd: **i~ant** [intɛrɛ'sant] a interesting; **i~anterweise** ad interestingly enough; **~e** [inte'rɛsə] nt **-s, -n** interest; **~e haben** be interested (an +dat in); **~ent** [intɛrɛ'sɛnt] m interested party; **i~ieren** [intɛrɛ'si:rən] vt interest; vr be interested (für in).
Inter- [intɛr] cpd: **~nat** [-'na:t] nt **-(e)s, -e** boarding school; **i~national** [-natsio'na:l] a international; **i~nieren** [-'ni:rən] vt intern; **i~pretieren** [-pre'ti:rən] vt interpret; **~punktion** [-puŋktsi'o:n] f punctuation; **~vall** [-'val] nt **-s, -e** interval; **~view** [-'vju:] nt **-s, -s** interview; **i~viewen** [-'vju:ən] vt interview.
intim [in'ti:m] a intimate; **I~ität** [intimi'tɛ:t] f intimacy.
intolerant ['intolerant] a intolerant.
intransitiv ['intranziti:f] a (Gram) intransitive.
Intrige [in'tri:gə] f **-, -n** intrigue, plot.
Invasion [invazi'o:n] f invasion.
Inventar [invɛn'ta:r] nt **-s, -e** inventory.
Inventur [invɛn'tu:r] f stocktaking; **~ machen** stocktake.
investieren [invɛs'ti:rən] vt invest.
inwiefern [invi'fɛrn], **inwieweit** [invi'vait] ad how far, to what extent.
inzwischen [in'tsviʃən] ad meanwhile.
irdisch ['irdiʃ] a earthly.
irgend ['irgənt] ad at all; **wann/was/wer ~** whenever/whatever/whoever; **~ jemand/etwas** somebody/something; anybody/anything; **~ein(e,s)** a some, any; **~einmal** ad sometime or other; (fragend) ever; **~wann** ad sometime; **~wie** ad somehow; **~wo** ad somewhere, anywhere.
Ironie [iro'ni:] f irony.
ironisch [i'ro:niʃ] a ironic(al).
irre ['irə] a crazy, mad; **I~(r)** mf lunatic; **~führen** vt mislead; **~machen** vt confuse; **~n** vir be mistaken; (umher—) wander, stray; **I~nanstalt** f lunatic asylum.
irrig ['iriç] a incorrect, wrong.
Irr- cpd: **i~sinnig** a mad, crazy; (col) terrific; **~tum** m **-s, -tümer** mistake, error; **i~tümlich** a mistaken.
Isolation [izolatsi'o:n] f isolation; (Elec) insulation.
Isolator [izo'la:tor] m insulator.
Isolier- [izo'li:r] cpd: **~band** nt insulating tape; **i~en** vt isolate; (Elec) insulate;

~station f (Med) isolation ward; **~ung** f isolation; (Elec) insulation.

J

J, j [jɔt] nt J, j.
ja [ja:] ad yes; **tu das ~ nicht!** don't do that!
Jacht [jaxt] f **-, -en** yacht.
Jacke ['jakə] f **-, -n** jacket; (Woll—) cardigan.
Jackett [ʒa'kɛt] nt **-s, -s** or **-e** jacket.
Jagd [ja:kt] f **-, -en** hunt; (Jagen) hunting; **~beute** f kill; **~flugzeug** nt fighter; **~gewehr** nt sporting gun.
jagen ['ja:gən] vi hunt; (eilen) race; vt hunt; (weg—) drive (off); (verfolgen) chase.
Jäger ['jɛ:gər] m **-s, -** hunter.
jäh [jɛ:] a sudden, abrupt; (steil) steep, precipitous; **~lings** ad abruptly.
Jahr [ja:r] nt **-(e)s, -e** year; **j~elang** ad for years; **~esabonnement** nt annual subscription; **~esabschluß** m end of the year; (Comm) annual statement of account; **~esbericht** m annual report; **~eswechsel** m turn of the year; **~eszahl** f date, year; **~eszeit** f season; **~gang** m age group; (von Wein) vintage; **~hundert** nt **-s, -e** century; **~'hundertfeier** f centenary.
jährlich ['jɛ:rliç] a,ad yearly.
Jahr- cpd: **~markt** m fair; **~'zehnt** nt decade.
Jähzorn ['jɛ:tsɔrn] m sudden anger; hot temper; **j~ig** a hot-tempered.
Jalousie [ʒalu'zi:] f venetian blind.
Jammer ['jamər] m **-s** misery; **es ist ein ~, daß . . .** it is a crying shame that . . .
jämmerlich ['jɛmərliç] a wretched, pathetic; **J~keit** f wretchedness.
jammer- cpd: **~n** vi wail; vt impers: **es jammert jdn** it makes sb feel sorry; **~schade** a: **es ist ~schade** it is a crying shame.
Januar ['janua:r] m **-s, -e** January.
Jargon [ʒar'gõ:] m **-s, -s** jargon.
jäten ['jɛ:tən] vt: **Unkraut ~** weed.
jauchzen ['jauxtsən] vi rejoice, shout (with joy).
Jauchzer m **-s, -** shout of joy.
jaulen ['jaulən] vi howl.
ja- cpd: **~'wohl** ad yes (of course); **J~wort** nt consent.
Jazz [dʒɛs] m **-** Jazz.
je [je:] ad ever; (jeweils) each; **~ nach** depending on; **~ nachdem** it depends; **~ . . . desto** or **~ . . . the . . . the.**
jede(r,s) ['je:də(r,z)] a every, each; pron everybody; (— einzelne) each; **ohne ~ x** without any x; **~nfalls** ad in any case; **~rmann** pron everone; **~rzeit** ad at any time; **~smal** ad every time, each time.
jedoch [je'dɔx] ad however.
jeher ['je:he:r] ad: **von ~** all along.
jemals ['je:ma:ls] ad ever.
jemand ['je:mant] pron somebody; anybody.
jene(r,s) ['je:nə(r,z)] a that; pron that one.
jenseits ['je:nzaits] ad on the other side;

prep +*gen* on the other side of, beyond; **das J~** the hereafter, the beyond.

jetzig ['jɛtsɪç] *a* present.

jetzt [jɛtst] *ad* now.

je~ *cpd*: **~weilig** *a* respective; **~weils** *ad* **~weils zwei zusammen** two at a time; **zu ~weils 5 DM** at 5 marks each; **~weils das erste** the first each time.

Joch [jɔx] *nt* -(e)s, -e yoke.

Jockei ['dʒɔke] *m* -s, -s jockey.

Jod [joːt] *nt* -(e)s iodine.

jodeln ['joːdəln] *vi* yodel.

Joghurt ['joːgurt] *m or nt* -s, -s yogurt.

Johannisbeere [jo'hanɪsbeːrə] *f* redcurrant; **schwarze ~** blackcurrant.

johlen ['joːlən] *vi* yell.

Jolle ['jɔlə] *f* -, -n dinghy.

jonglieren [ʒõ'gliːrən] *vi* juggle.

Joppe ['jɔpə] *f* -, -n jacket.

Journal- [ʒur'naːl] *cpd*: **~ismus** [-'lɪsmus] *m* journalism; **~ist(in** *f)* [-'lɪst] *m* journalist; **j~istisch** *a* journalistic.

Jubel ['juːbəl] *m* -s rejoicing; **j~n** *vi* rejoice.

Jubiläum [jubi'lɛːum] *nt* -s, **Jubiläen** anniversary, jubilee.

jucken ['jukən] *vi* itch; *vt* **es juckt mich am Arm** my arm is itching; **das juckt mich** that's itchy.

Juckreiz ['jukraits] *m* itch.

Jude ['juːdə] *m* -n, -n Jew; **~ntum** *nt* - Judaism; Jewry; **~nverfolgung** *f* persecution of the Jews.

Jüd- ['jyːd] *cpd*: **~in** *f* Jewess; **j~isch** *a* Jewish.

Judo ['juːdo] *nt* -(s) judo.

Jugend ['juːgənt] *f* - youth; **~herberge** *f* youth hostel; **~kriminalität** *f* juvenile crime; **j~lich** *a* youthful; **~liche(r)** *mf* teenager, young person; **~richter** *m* juvenile court judge.

Juli ['juːli] *m* -(s), -s July.

jung [juŋ] *a* young; **J~e** *m* -n, -n boy, lad; **J~e(s)** *nt* young animal; (*pl*) young *pl*.

Jünger ['jyŋər] *m* -s, - disciple; **j~** *a* younger.

Jung- *cpd*: **~fer** *f* -, -n: **alte ~fer** old maid; **~fernfahrt** *f* maiden voyage; **~frau** *f* virgin; (*Astrol*) Virgo; **~geselle** *m* bachelor.

Jüngling ['jyŋlɪŋ] *m* youth.

jüngst ['jyŋst] *ad* lately, recently; **~e(r,s)** *a* youngest; (*neueste*) latest.

Juni ['juːni] *m* -(s), -s June.

Junior ['juːnior] *m* -s, -en [-'oːrən] junior.

Jurist [ju'rɪst] *m* jurist, lawyer; **j~isch** *a* legal.

Justiz [jus'tiːts] *f* - justice; **~beamte(r)** *m* judicial officer; **~irrtum** *m* miscarriage of justice.

Juwel [ju've:l] *nt or m* -s, -en jewel; **~ier** *m* [-'liːr] *m* -s, -e jeweller; **~iergeschäft** *nt* jeweller's (shop).

Jux [juks] *m* -es, -e joke, lark.

K

K, k [kaː] *nt* K, k.

Kabarett [kaba'rɛt] *nt* -s, -e or -s cabaret; **~ist** [-'tɪst] *m* cabaret artiste.

Kabel ['kaːbəl] *nt* -s, - (*Elec*) wire; (*stark*) cable; **~jau** [-jau] *m* -s, -e or -s cod; **k~n** *vti* cable.

Kabine [ka'biːnə] *f* cabin; (*Zelle*) cubicle.

Kabinett [kabi'nɛt] *nt* -s, -e (*Pol*) cabinet; small room.

Kachel ['kaxəl] *f* -, -n tile; **k~n** *vt* tile; **~ofen** *m* tiled stove.

Kadaver [ka'daːvər] *m* -s, - carcass.

Kadett [ka'dɛt] *m* -en, -en cadet.

Käfer ['kɛːfər] *m* -s, - beetle.

Kaffee ['kafe] *m* -s, -s coffee; **~kanne** *f* coffeepot; **~klatsch** *m*, **~kränzchen** *nt* hen party; coffee morning; **~löffel** *m* coffee spoon; **~mühle** *f* coffee grinder; **~satz** *m* coffee grounds *pl*.

Käfig ['kɛːfiç] *m* -s, -e cage.

kahl [kaːl] *a* bald; **~fressen** *vt irreg* strip bare; **~geschoren** *a* shaven, shorn; **K~heit** *f* baldness; **~köpfig** *a* baldheaded.

Kahn [kaːn] *m* -(e)s, -e boat, barge.

Kai [kai] *m* -s, -e or -s quay.

Kaiser ['kaizər] *m* -s, - emperor; **~in** *f* empress; **k~lich** *a* imperial; **~reich** *nt* empire; **~schnitt** *m* (*Med*) Caesarian (section).

Kajüte [ka'jyːtə] *f* -, -n cabin.

Kakao [ka'kaːo] *m* -s, -s cocoa.

Kaktee [kak'teː(ə)] *f* -, -n, **Kaktus** ['kaktus] *m* -, -se cactus.

Kalb [kalp] *nt* -(e)s, -er calf; **k~en** ['kalbən] *vi* calve; **~fleisch** *nt* veal; **~sleder** *nt* calf(skin).

Kalender [ka'lɛndər] *m* -s, - calendar; (*Taschen~*) diary.

Kali ['kaːli] *nt* -s, -s potash.

Kaliber [ka'liːbər] *nt* -s, - (*lit, fig*) calibre.

Kalk [kalk] *m* -(e)s, -e lime; (*Biol*) calcium; **~stein** *m* limestone.

Kalkulation [kalkulatsi'oːn] *f* calculation.

kalkulieren [kalku'liːrən] *vt* calculate.

Kalorie [kalo'riː] *f* calorie.

kalt [kalt] *a* cold; **mir ist (es) ~** I am cold; **~bleiben** *vi irreg* be unmoved; **~blütig** *a* cold-blooded; (*ruhig*) cool; **K~blütigkeit** *f* cold-bloodedness; coolness.

Kälte ['kɛltə] *f* - cold; coldness; **~grad** *m* degree of frost or below zero; **~welle** *f* cold spell.

kalt- *cpd*: **~herzig** *a* cold-hearted; **~schnäuzig** *a* cold, unfeeling; **~stellen** *vt* chill; (*fig*) leave out in the cold.

Kamel [ka'meːl] *nt or m* -(e)s, -e camel.

Kamera ['kamera] *f* -, -s camera.

Kamerad [kamə'raːt] *m* -en, -en comrade, friend; **~schaft** *f* comradeship; **k~schaftlich** *a* comradely.

Kamera- *cpd*: **~führung** *f* camera work; **~mann** *m* cameraman.

Kamille [ka'mɪlə] *f* -, -n camomile; **~ntee** *m* camomile tea.

Kamin [ka'mi:n] *m* -s, -e (*außen*) chimney; (*innen*) fireside, fireplace; ~**feger**, ~**kehrer** *m* -s, - chimney sweep.

Kamm [kam] *m* -(e)s, ¨e comb; (*Berg*—) ridge; (*Hahnen*—) crest.

kämmen ['kɛmən] *vt* comb.

Kammer ['kamər] *f* -, -n chamber; small bedroom; ~**diener** *m* valet.

Kampf [kampf] *m* -(e)s, ¨e fight, battle; (*Wettbewerb*) contest; (*fig: Anstrengung*) struggle; **k**~**bereit** *a* ready for action.

kämpfen ['kɛmpfən] *vi* fight.

Kämpfer *m* -s, - fighter, combatant.

Kampfer ['kampfər] *m* -s camphor.

Kampf- *cpd:* ~**handlung** *f* action; **k**~**los** *a* without a fight; **k**~**lustig** *a* pugnacious; ~**richter** *m* (*Sport*) referee; (*Tennis*) umpire.

Kanal [ka'na:l] *m* -s, **Kanäle** (*Fluß*) canal; (*Rinne, Ärmel*—) channel; (*für Abfluß*) drain; ~**isation** [-izatsi'o:n] *f* sewage system; **k**~**isieren** [-i'zi:rən] *vt* provide with a sewage system.

Kanarienvogel [ka'na:riənfo:gəl] *m* canary.

Kandi- [kandi] *cpd:* ~**dat** [-'da:t] *m* -en, -en candidate; ~**datur** [-da'tu:r] *f* candidature, candidacy; **k**~**dieren** [-'di:rən] *vi* stand, run.

Kandis(zucker) ['kandis] *m* - candy.

Känguruh ['kɛŋguru] *nt* -s, -s kangaroo.

Kaninchen [ka'ni:nçən] *nt* rabbit.

Kanister [ka'nistər] *m* -s, - can, canister.

Kanne ['kanə] *f* -, -n (*Krug*) jug; (*Kaffee*—) pot; (*Milch*—) churn; (*Gieß*—) can.

Kanon ['ka:nɔn] *m* -s, -s canon.

Kanone [ka'no:nə] *f* -, -n gun; (*Hist*) cannon; (*fig: Mensch*) ace.

Kantate [kan'ta:tə] *f* -, -n cantata.

Kante ['kantə] *f* -, -n edge.

Kantine [kan'ti:nə] *f* canteen.

Kantor ['kantɔr] *m* choirmaster.

Kanu [ˈka:nu] *nt* -s, -s canoe.

Kanzel ['kantsəl] *f* -, -n pulpit.

Kanzlei [kants'lai] *f* chancery; (*Büro*) chambers *pl.*

Kanzler ['kantslər] *m* -s, - chancellor.

Kap [kap] *nt* -s, -s cape.

Kapazität [kapasi'tɛ:t] *f* capacity; (*Fachmann*) authority.

Kapelle [ka'pɛlə] *f* (*Gebäude*) chapel; (*Mus*) band.

Kaper ['ka:pər] *f* -, -n caper; **k**~**n** *vt* capture.

kapieren [ka'pi:rən] *vti* (*col*) understand.

Kapital [kapi'ta:l] *nt* -s, -e or -**ien** capital; ~**anlage** *f* investment; ~**ismus** [-'lismʊs] *m* capitalism; ~**ist** [-'list] *m* capitalist; **k**~**kräftig** *a* wealthy; ~**markt** *m* money market.

Kapitän [kapi'tɛ:n] *m* -s, -e captain.

Kapitel [ka'pitəl] *nt* -s, - chapter.

Kapitulation [kapitulatsi'o:n] *f* capitulation.

kapitulieren [kapitu'li:rən] *vi* capitulate.

Kaplan [ka'pla:n] *m* -s, **Kapläne** chaplain.

Kappe ['kapə] *f* -, -n cap; (*Kapuze*) hood; **k**~**n** *vt* cut.

Kapsel ['kapsəl] *f* -, -n capsule.

kaputt [ka'pʊt] *a* (*col*) smashed, broken; *Person* exhausted, finished; ~**gehen** *vi irreg* break; (*Schuhe*) fall apart; (*Firma*) go bust; (*Stoff*) wear out; (*sterben*) cop it; ~**lachen** *vr* laugh o.s. silly; ~**machen** *vt* break; *Mensch* exhaust, wear out.

Kapuze [ka'pu:tsə] *f* -, -n hood.

Karaffe [ka'rafə] *f* -, -n caraffe; (*geschliffen*) decanter.

Karambolage [karambo'la:ʒə] *f* -, -n (*Zusammenstoß*) crash.

Karamel [kara'mɛl] *m* -s caramel; ~**bonbon** *m* or *nt* toffee.

Karat [ka'ra:t] *nt* -(e)s, -e carat; ~**e** *nt* -s karate.

Karawane [kara'va:nə] *f* -, -n caravan.

Kardinal [kardi'na:l] *m* -s, **Kardinäle** cardinal; ~**zahl** *f* cardinal number.

Karfreitag [ka:r'fraita:k] *m* Good Friday.

karg [kark] *a* scanty, poor; *Mahlzeit auch* meagre; ~ **mit Worten sein** use few words; **K**~**heit** *f* poverty, scantiness; meagreness.

kärglich ['kɛrkliç] *a* poor, scanty.

kariert [ka'ri:rt] *a* *Stoff* checked; *Papier* squared.

Karies ['ka:riɛs] *f* - caries.

Karikatur [karika'tu:r] *f* caricature; ~**ist** [-'rist] *m* cartoonist.

karikieren [kari'ki:rən] *vt* caricature.

Karneval ['karnəval] *m* -s, -e or -s carnival.

Karo ['ka:ro] *nt* -s, -s square; (*Cards*) diamonds; ~**-As** *nt* ace of diamonds.

Karosse [ka'rɔsə] *f* -, -n coach, carriage; ~**rie** [-'ri:] *f* (*Aut*) body(work).

Karotte [ka'rɔtə] *f* -, -n carrot.

Karpfen ['karpfən] *m* -s, - carp.

Karre ['karə] *f* -, -n, ~**n** *m* -s, - cart, barrow; **k**~**n** *vt* cart, transport.

Karriere [kari'ɛ:rə] *f* -, -n career; ~ **machen** get on, get to the top; ~**macher** *m* -s, - careerist.

Karte ['kartə] *f* -, -n card; (*Land*—) map; (*Speise*—) menu; (*Eintritts*—, *Fahr*—) ticket; **alles auf eine** ~ **setzen** put all one's eggs in one basket.

Kartei [kar'tai] *f* card index; ~**karte** *f* index card.

Kartell [kar'tɛl] *nt* -s, -e cartel.

Karten- *cpd:* ~**haus** *nt* (*lit, fig*) house of cards; ~**spiel** *nt* card game; pack of cards.

Kartoffel [kar'tɔfəl] *f* -, -n potato; ~**brei** *m*, ~**püree** *nt* mashed potatoes *pl*; ~**salat** *m* potato salad.

Karton [kar'tõ:] *m* -s, -s cardboard; (*Schachtel*) cardboard box; **k**~**iert** [karto'ni:rt] *a* hardback.

Karussell [karu'sɛl] *nt* -s, -s roundabout (*Brit*), merry-go-round.

Karwoche ['ka:rvɔxə] *f* Holy Week.

Kaschemme [ka'ʃɛmə] *f* -, -n dive.

Käse ['kɛ:zə] *m* -s, - cheese; ~**blatt** *nt* (*col*) (local) rag; ~**kuchen** *m* cheesecake.

Kaserne [ka'zɛrnə] *f* -, **-n** barracks *pl*; ~**nhof** *m* parade ground.

Kasino [ka'zi:no] *nt* **-s**, **-s** club; (*Mil*) officers' mess; (*Spiel*—) casino.

Kasper ['kaspər] *m* **-s**, - Punch; (*fig*) clown.

Kasse ['kasə] *f* -, **-n** (*Geldkasten*) cashbox; (*in Geschäft*) till, cash register; (*Kino*—, *Theater*— *etc*) box office; ticket office; (*Kranken*—) health insurance; (*Spar*—) savings bank; ~ **machen** count the money; **getrennte** ~ **führen** pay separately; **an der** ~ (*in Geschäft*) at the desk; **gut bei** ~ **sein** be in the money; ~**narzt** *m* panel doctor (*Brit*); ~**nbestand** *m* cash balance; ~**npatient** *m* panel patient (*Brit*); ~**nprüfung** *f* audit; ~**nsturz** *m*: ~**nsturz machen** check one's money; ~**nzettel** *m* receipt.

Kasserolle [kasə'rɔlə] *f* -, **-n** casserole.

Kassette [ka'sɛtə] *f* small box; (*Tonband*, *Phot*) cassette; (*Bücher*—) case; ~**nrecorder** *m* **-s**, - cassette recorder.

kassieren [ka'si:rən] *vt* take; *vi*: **darf ich** ~? would you like to pay now?

Kassierer [ka'si:rər] *m* **-s**, - cashier; (*von Klub*) treasurer.

Kastanie [kas'ta:niə] *f* chestnut; ~**nbaum** *m* chestnut tree.

Kästchen ['kɛstçən] *nt* small box, casket.

Kaste ['kastə] *f* -, **-n** caste.

Kasten ['kastən] *m* **-s**, ⁺ box (*Sport auch*), case; (*Truhe*) chest; ~**wagen** *m* van.

kastrieren [kas'tri:rən] *vt* castrate.

Katalog [kata'lo:k] *m* **-(e)s**, **-e** catalogue; **k**~**isieren** [katalogi'zi:rən] *vt* catalogue.

Katapult [kata'pʊlt] *m or nt* **-(e)s**, **-e** catapult.

Katarrh [ka'tar] *m* **-s**, **-e** catarrh.

katastrophal [katastro'fa:l] *a* catastrophic.

Katastrophe [kata'stro:fə] *f* -, **-n** catastrophe, disaster.

Kategorie [katego'ri:] *f* category.

kategorisch [kate'go:rɪʃ] *a* categorical.

kategorisieren [kategori'zi:rən] *vt* categorize.

Kater ['ka:tər] *m* **-s**, - tomcat; (*col*) hangover.

Katheder [ka'te:dər] *nt* **-s**, - lecture desk.

Kathedrale [kate'dra:lə] *f* -, **-n** cathedral.

Kathode [ka'to:də] *f* -, **-n** cathode.

Katholik [kato'li:k] *m* **-en**, **-en** Catholic.

katholisch [ka'to:lɪʃ] *a* Catholic.

Katholizismus [katoli'tsɪsmʊs] *m* Catholicism.

Kätzchen ['kɛtsçən] *nt* kitten.

Katze ['katsə] *f* -, **-n** cat; **für die Katz** (*col*) in vain, for nothing; ~**nauge** *nt* cat's eye; (*Fahrrad*) rear light; ~**njammer** *m* (*col*) hangover; ~**nsprung** *m* (*col*) stone's throw; short journey; ~**nwäsche** *f* lick and a promise.

Kauderwelsch ['kaʊdərvɛlʃ] *nt* **-(s)** jargon; (*col*) double Dutch.

kauen ['kaʊən] *vti* chew.

kauern ['kaʊərn] *vi* crouch.

Kauf [kaʊf] *m* **-(e)s**, **Käufe** purchase, buy; (*Kaufen*) buying; **ein guter** ~ a bargain; **etw in** ~ **nehmen** put up with sth; **k**~**en** *vt* buy.

Käufer(in *f*) ['kɔʏfər(ɪn)] *m* **-s**, - buyer.

Kauf- *cpd*: ~**haus** *nt* department store; ~**kraft** *f* purchasing power; ~**laden** *m* shop, store.

käuflich ['kɔʏflɪç] *a,ad* purchasable, for sale; (*pej*) venal; ~ **erwerben** purchase.

Kauf- *cpd*: **k**~**lustig** *a* interested in buying; ~**mann** *m, pl* -**leute** businessman; shopkeeper; **k**~**männisch** *a* commercial; ~**männischer Angestellter** clerk.

Kaugummi ['kaʊgʊmi] *m* chewing gum.

Kaulquappe ['kaʊlkvapə] *f* -, **-n** tadpole.

kaum [kaʊm] *ad* hardly, scarcely.

Kaution [kaʊtsi'o:n] *f* deposit; (*Jur*) bail.

Kautschuk ['kaʊtʃʊk] *m* **-s**, **-e** india-rubber.

Kauz [kaʊts] *m* **-es**, **Käuze** owl; (*fig*) queer fellow.

Kavalier [kava'li:r] *m* **-s**, **-e** gentleman, cavalier; ~**sdelikt** *nt* peccadillo.

Kavallerie [kavalə'ri:] *f* cavalry.

Kavallerist [kavalə'rɪst] *m* trooper, cavalryman.

Kaviar ['ka:viar] *m* caviar.

keck [kɛk] *a* daring, bold; **K**~**heit** *f* daring, boldness.

Kegel ['ke:gəl] *m* **-s**, - skittle; (*Math*) cone; ~**bahn** *f* skittle alley; bowling alley; **k**~**förmig** *a* conical; **k**~**n** *vi* play skittles.

Kehle ['ke:lə] *f* -, **-n** throat.

Kehl- *cpd*: ~**kopf** *m* larynx; ~**laut** *m* guttural.

Kehre ['ke:rə] *f* -, **-n** turn(ing); bend; **k**~**n** *vti* (*wenden*) turn; (*mit Besen*) sweep; **sich an etw** (*dat*) **nicht k**~**n** not heed sth.

Kehr- *cpd*: ~**icht** *m* **-s** sweepings *pl*; ~**maschine** *f* sweeper; ~**reim** *m* refrain; ~**seite** *f* reverse, other side; wrong side; bad side; **k**~**tmachen** *vi* turn about, about-turn.

keifen ['kaɪfən] *vi* scold, nag.

Keil [kaɪl] *m* **-(e)s**, **-e** wedge; (*Mil*) arrowhead; **k**~**en** *vt* wedge; *vr* fight; ~**e'rei** *f* (*col*) punch-up; ~**riemen** *m* (*Aut*) fan belt.

Keim [kaɪm] *m* **-(e)s**, **-e** bud; (*Med*, *fig*) germ; **etw im** ~ **ersticken** nip sth in the bud; **k**~**en** *vi* germinate; **k**~**frei** *a* sterile; **k**~**tötend** *a* antiseptic, germicidal; ~**zelle** *f* (*fig*) nucleus.

kein [kaɪn] *a* no, not any; ~**e(r,s)** *pron* no one, nobody; none; ~**esfalls** *ad* on no account; ~**eswegs** *ad* by no means; ~**mal** *ad* not once.

Keks [ke:ks] *m or nt* **-es**, **-e** biscuit.

Kelch [kɛlç] *m* **-(e)s**, **-e** cup, goblet, chalice.

Kelle ['kɛlə] *f* -, **-n** ladle; (*Maurer*—) trowel.

Keller ['kɛlər] *m* **-s**, - cellar; ~**assel** *f* -, **-n** woodlouse; ~**wohnung** *f* basement flat.

Kellner ['kɛlnər] *m* **-s**, - waiter; ~**in** *f* waitress.

keltern ['kɛltərn] *vt* press.

kennen ['kɛnən] vt irreg know; ~**lernen** vt get to know; **sich** ~**lernen** get to know each other; (zum erstenmal) meet.

Kenn- cpd: ~**er** m -s, - connoisseur; ~**karte** f identity card; k~**tlich** a distinguishable, discernible; **etw** k~**tlich machen** mark sth; ~**tnis** f -, -**se** knowledge no pl; **etw zur** ~**tnis nehmen** note sth; **von etw** ~**tnis nehmen** take notice of sth; **jdn in** ~**tnis setzen** inform sb; ~**zeichen** nt mark, characteristic; k~**zeichnen** vt insep characterize; k~**zeichnenderweise** ad characteristically; ~**ziffer** f reference number.

kentern ['kɛntərn] vi capsize.

Keramik [ke'raːmɪk] f -, -**en** ceramics pl, pottery.

Kerb- [kɛrb] cpd: ~**e** f -, -**n** notch, groove; ~**el** m -s, - chervil; k~**en** vt notch; ~**holz** nt: **etw auf dem** ~**holz haben** have done sth wrong.

Kerker ['kɛrkər] m -s, - prison.

Kerl [kɛrl] m -s, -**e** chap, bloke (Brit), guy.

Kern [kɛrn] m -(**e**)**s**, -**e** (Obst—) pip, stone; (Nuß—) kernel; (Atom—) nucleus; (fig) heart, core; ~**energie** f nuclear energy; ~**forschung** f nuclear research; ~**frage** f central issue; ~**gehäuse** nt core; k~**gesund** a thoroughly healthy, fit as a fiddle; k~**ig** a robust; Ausspruch pithy; ~**kraftwerk** nt nuclear power station; k~**los** a seedless, pipless; ~**physik** f nuclear physics; ~**reaktion** f nuclear reaction; ~**spaltung** f nuclear fission; ~**waffen** pl nuclear weapons pl.

Kerze ['kɛrtsə] f -, -**n** candle; (Zünd—) plug; k~**ngerade** a straight as a die; ~**nständer** m candle holder.

keß [kɛs] a saucy.

Kessel ['kɛsəl] m -s, - kettle; (von Lokomotive etc) boiler; (Geog) depression; (Mil) encirclement; ~**treiben** nt -s, - (fig) witch hunt.

Kette ['kɛtə] f -, -**n** chain; k~**n** vt chain; ~**nhund** m watchdog; ~**nladen** m chain store; ~**nrauchen** nt chain smoking; ~**nreaktion** f chain reaction.

Ketzer ['kɛtsər] m -s, - heretic; k~**isch** a heretical.

keuchen ['kɔʏçən] vi pant, gasp.

Keuchhusten m whooping cough.

Keule ['kɔʏlə] f -, -**n** club; (Cook) leg.

keusch [kɔʏʃ] a chaste; ~**heit** f chastity.

Kfz [kaːɛftseː] abbr of **Kraftfahrzeug**.

kichern ['kɪçərn] vi giggle.

kidnappen ['kɪdnæpən] vt kidnap.

Kiebitz ['kiːbɪts] m -es, -**e** peewit.

Kiefer ['kiːfər] m -s, - jaw; f -, -**n** pine; ~**nzapfen** m pine cone.

Kiel [kiːl] m -(**e**)**s**, -**e** (Feder—) quill; (Naut) keel; k~**holen** vt Person keelhaul; Schiff career; ~**wasser** nt wake.

Kieme ['kiːmə] f -, -**n** gill.

Kies [kiːs] m -es, -**e** gravel; ~**el** [kiːzəl] m -s, - pebble; ~**elstein** m pebble; ~**grube** f gravel pit; ~**weg** m gravel path.

Kilo ['kiːlo] kilo; ~**gramm** [kilo'gram] nt -s, -**e** kilogram; ~**meter** [kilo'meːtər] m kilometre; ~**meterzähler** m ≈ milometer.

Kimme ['kɪmə] f -, -**n** notch; (Gewehr) backsight.

Kind [kɪnt] nt -(**e**)**s**, -**er** child; **von** ~ **auf** from childhood; **sich bei jdm lieb** ~ **machen** ingratiate o.s. with sb; ~**erbett** ['kɪndərbɛt] nt cot; ~**erei** [kɪndə'raɪ] f childishness; ~**ergarten** m nursery school, playgroup; ~**ergeld** nt family allowance; ~**erlähmung** f poliomyelitis; k~**erleicht** a childishly easy; k~**erlos** a childless; ~**ermädchen** nt nursemaid; k~**erreich** a with a lot of children; ~**erspiel** nt child's play; ~**erstube** f: **eine gute** ~**erstube haben be** well-mannered; ~**erwagen** m pram, baby carriage (US); ~**esalter** nt infancy; ~**esbeine** pl: **von** ~**esbeinen an** from early childhood; ~**heit** f childhood; k~**isch** a childish; k~**lich** a childlike; k~**sköpfig** a childish.

Kinn [kɪn] nt -(**e**)**s**, -**e** chin; ~**haken** m (Boxen) uppercut; ~**lade** f jaw.

Kino ['kiːno] nt -s, -**s** cinema; ~**besucher** m cinema-goer; ~**programm** nt film programme.

Kiosk [ki'ɔsk] m -(**e**)**s**, -**e** kiosk.

Kipp- ['kɪp] cpd: ~**e** f -, -**n** cigarette end; (col) fag; **auf der** ~**e stehen** (fig) be touch and go; k~**en** vi topple over, overturn; vt tilt.

Kirch- ['kɪrç] cpd: ~**e** f -, -**n** church; ~**endiener** m churchwarden; ~**enfest** nt church festival; ~**enlied** nt hymn; ~**gänger** m -s, - churchgoer; ~**hof** m churchyard; k~**lich** a ecclesiastical; ~**turm** m church tower, steeple.

Kirsche ['kɪrʃə] f -, -**n** cherry.

Kissen ['kɪsən] nt -s, - cushion; (Kopf—) pillow; ~**bezug** m pillowslip.

Kiste ['kɪstə] f -, -**n** box; chest.

Kitsch [kɪtʃ] m -(**e**)**s** trash; k~**ig** a trashy.

Kitt [kɪt] m -(**e**)**s**, -**e** putty; ~**chen** nt (col) clink; ~**el** m -s, - overall, smock; k~**en** vt putty; (fig) Ehe etc cement.

Kitz [kɪts] nt -es, -**e** kid; (Reh—) fawn.

kitzel- ['kɪtsəl] cpd: ~**ig** a (lit, fig) ticklish; ~**n** vi tickle.

klaffen ['klafən] vi gape.

kläffen ['klɛfən] vi yelp.

Klage ['klaːgə] f -, -**n** complaint; (Jur) action; k~**n** vi (weh—) lament, wail; (sich beschweren) complain; (Jur) take legal action.

Kläger(in f**)** ['klɛːgər(ɪn)] m -s, - plaintiff.

kläglich ['klɛːklɪç] a wretched.

Klamm [klam] f -, -**en** ravine; k~ a Finger numb; (feucht) damp.

Klammer ['klamər] f -, -**n** clamp; (in Text) bracket; (Büro—) clip; (Wäsche—) peg; (Zahn—) brace; k~**n** vr cling (an +acc to).

Klang [klaŋ] m -(**e**)**s**, ⁻**e** sound; k~**voll** a sonorous.

Klappe ['klapə] f -, -**n** valve; (Ofen—) damper; (col: Mund) trap; k~**n** vi (Geräusch) click; vti Sitz etc tip; v impers work.

Klapper ['klapər] f -, -**n** rattle; k~**ig** a run-down, worn-out; k~**n** vi clatter, rattle;

~schlange *f* rattlesnake; **~storch** *m* stork.

Klapp- *cpd:* **~messer** *nt* jack-knife; **~rad** *nt* collapsible bicycle; **~stuhl** *m* folding chair.

Klaps [klaps] *m* **-es, -e** slap; **k~en** *vt* slap.

klar [klaːr] *a* clear; (*Naut*) ready for sea; (*Mil*) ready for action; **sich** (*dat*) **im K~en sein über** (+*acc*) be clear about; **ins K~e kommen** get clear.

Klär- [klɛːr] *cpd:* **~anlage** *f* purification plant; **k~en** *vt* Flüßigkeit purify; Probleme clarify; *vr* clear (itself) up.

Klar- *cpd:* **~heit** *f* clarity; **~inette** [klariˈnɛtə] *f* clarinet; **k~legen** *vt* clear up, explain; **k~machen** *vt* Schiff get ready for sea; **jdm etw k~machen** make sth clear to sb; **k~sehen** *vi irreg* see clearly; **~sichtfolie** *f* transparent film; **k~stellen** *vt* clarify.

Klärung [klɛːrʊŋ] *f* purification; clarification.

Klasse [klasə] *f* -, **-n** class; (*Sch auch*) form; **k~ a** (*col*) smashing; **~narbeit** *f* test; **~nbewußtsein** *nt* class consciousness; **~ngesellschaft** *f* class society; **~nkampf** *m* class conflict; **~nlehrer** *m* form master; **k~nlos** *a* classless; **~nsprecher(in** *f*) *m* form prefect; **~nzimmer** *nt* classroom.

klassifizieren [klasifiˈtsiːrən] *vt* classify.

Klassifizierung *f* classification.

Klassik [klasɪk] *f* (*Zeit*) classical period; (*Stil*) classicism; **~er** *m* -s, - classic.

klassisch *a* (*lit, fig*) classical.

Klatsch [klatʃ] *m* **-(e)s, -e** smack, crack; (*Gerede*) gossip; **~base** *f* gossip, scandalmonger; **~e** *f* -, *a* (*col*) crib; **k~en** *vi* (*Geräusch*) clash; (*reden*) gossip; (*Beifall*) applaud, clap; **~mohn** *m* (corn) poppy; **k~naß** a soaking wet; **~spalte** *f* gossip column.

klauben [klaʊbən] *vt* pick.

Klaue [klaʊə] *f* -, **-n** claw; (*col: Schrift*) scrawl; **k~n** *vt* claw; (*col*) pinch.

Klause [klaʊzə] *f* -, **-n** cell; hermitage.

Klausel [klaʊzəl] *f* -, **-n** clause.

Klausur [klaʊˈzuːr] *f* seclusion; **~arbeit** *f* examination paper.

Klaviatur [klaviaˈtuːr] *f* keyboard.

Klavier [klaˈviːr] *nt* **-s, -e** piano.

Kleb- [kleːb] *cpd:* **~emittel** *nt* glue; **k~en** *vt stick* (*an* +*acc* to); **k~rig** *a* sticky; **~stoff** *m* glue; **~streifen** *m* adhesive tape.

kleckern [klɛkərn] *vi* slobber.

Klecks [klɛks] *m* **-es, -e** blot, stain; **k~en** *vi* blot; (*pej*) daub.

Klee [kleː] *m* -s clover; **~blatt** *nt* cloverleaf; (*fig*) trio.

Kleid [klaɪt] *nt* **-(e)s, -er** garment; (*Frauen*—) dress; *pl* clothes *pl*; **k~en** [klaɪdən] *vt* clothe, dress; (*auch +i*) suit; *vr* dress; **~erbügel** *m* coat hanger; **~erbürste** *f* clothes brush; **~erschrank** *m* wardrobe; **k~sam** *a* becoming; **~ung** *f* clothing; **~ungsstück** *nt* garment.

Kleie [klaɪə] *f* -, **-n** bran.

klein [klaɪn] *a* little, small;

K~bürgertum *nt* petite bourgeoisie; **K~e(r,s)** little one; **K~format** *nt* small size; **im K~format** small-scale; **K~geld** *nt* small change; **~gläubig** *a* of little faith; **~hacken** *vt* chop up, mince; **K~holz** *nt* firewood; **K~holz aus jdm machen** make mincemeat of sb; **K~igkeit** *f* trifle; **K~kind** *nt* infant; **K~kram** *m* details *pl*; **~laut** *a* dejected, quiet; **~lich** *a* petty, paltry; **K~lichkeit** *f* pettiness, paltriness; **~mütig** *a* fainthearted; **K~od** [klaɪnoːt] *nt* **-s, -odien** gem, jewel; treasure; **~schneiden** *vt irreg* chop up; **~städtisch** *a* provincial; **~stmöglich** *a* smallest possible.

Kleister [klaɪstər] *m* **-s, -** paste; **k~n** *vt* paste.

Klemme [klɛmə] *f* -, **-n** clip; (*Med*) clamp; (*fig*) jam; **k~n** *vt* (*festhalten*) jam; (*quetschen*) pinch, nip; *vr* catch o.s.; (*sich hineinzwängen*) squeeze o.s.; **sich hinter jdn/etw k~n** get on to sb/get down to sth; *vi* (*Tür*) stick, jam.

Klempner [klɛmpnər] *m* **-s, -** plumber.

Kleptomanie [klɛptomaˈniː] *f* kleptomania.

Kleriker [kleːrikər] *m* **-s, -** cleric.

Klerus [kleːrʊs] *m* - clergy.

Klette [klɛtə] *f* -, **-n** burr.

Kletter- [klɛtər] *cpd:* **~er** *m* **-s, -** climber; **k~n** *vi* climb; **~pflanze** *f* creeper; **~seil** *nt* climbing rope.

klicken [klɪkən] *vi* click.

Klient(in *f*) [kliˈɛnt(ɪn)] *m* client.

Klima [kliːma] *nt* **-s, -s** *or* **-te** [kliˈmaːtə] climate; **~anlage** *f* air conditioning; **k~tisieren** [-iˈtsiːrən] *vt* air-condition; **~wechsel** *m* change of air.

klimpern [klɪmpərn] *vi* tinkle; (*mit Gitarre*) strum.

Klinge [klɪŋə] *f* -, **-n** blade, sword.

Klingel [klɪŋəl] *f* -, **-n** bell; **~beutel** *m* collection bag; **k~n** *vi* ring.

klingen [klɪŋən] *vi irreg* sound; (*Gläser*) clink.

Klinik [kliːnɪk] *f* -, hospital, clinic.

klinisch [kliːnɪʃ] *a* clinical.

Klinke [klɪŋkə] *f* -, **-n** handle.

Klinker [klɪŋkər] *m* **-s, -** clinker.

Klippe [klɪpə] *f* -, **-n** cliff; (*im Meer*) reef; (*fig*) hurdle; **k~nreich** *a* rocky.

klipp und klar [klɪpˈʊntklaːr] *a* clear and concise.

Klips [klɪps] *m* **-es, -e** clip; (*Ohr—*) earring.

klirren [klɪrən] *vi* clank, jangle; (*Gläser*) clink; **~de Kälte** biting cold.

Klischee [kliˈʃeː] *nt* **-s, -s** (*Druckplatte*) plate, block; (*fig*) cliché; **~vorstellung** *f* stereotyped idea.

Klo [kloː] *nt* **-s, -s** (*col*) loo.

Kloake [kloˈaːkə] *f* -, **-n** sewer.

klobig [kloːbɪç] *a* clumsy.

klopfen [klɔpfən] *vti* knock; (*Herz*) thump; **es klopft** sb's knocking; **jdm auf die Schulter** ~ tap sb on the shoulder; *vt* beat.

Klopfer *m* **-s, -** (*Teppich-*) beater; (*Tür—*) knocker.

Klöppel ['klœpəl] m -s, - (von Glocke) clapper; **k~n** vi make lace.

Klops [klɔps] m -es, -e meatball.

Klosett [klo'zɛt] nt -s, -e or -s lavatory, toilet; **~papier** nt toilet paper.

Kloß [klo:s] m -es, ⁻e (Erd—) clod; (im Hals) lump; (Cook) dumpling.

Kloster ['klo:stər] nt -s, ⁻ (Männer—) monastery; (Frauen—) convent.

klösterlich ['klø:stərlıç] a monastic; convent.

Klotz [klɔts] m -es, ⁻e log; (Hack—) block; **ein ~ am Bein** (fig) drag, millstone round (sb's) neck.

Klub [klʊp] m -s, -s club; **~sessel** m easy chair.

Kluft [klʊft] f -, ⁻e cleft, gap; (Geol) gorge, chasm.

klug [klu:k] a clever, intelligent; **K~heit** f cleverness, intelligence.

Klümpchen ['klʏmpçən] nt clot, blob.

Klumpen ['klʊmpən] m -s, - (Erd—) clod; (Blut—) lump, clot; (Gold—) nugget; (Cook) lump; **k~** vi go lumpy, clot.

Klumpfuß ['klʊmpfu:s] m club-foot.

knabbern ['knabərn] vti nibble.

Knabe ['kna:bə] m -n, -n boy; **k~nhaft** a boyish.

Knäckebrot ['knɛkəbro:t] nt crispbread.

knacken ['knakən] vti (lit, fig) crack.

Knall [knal] m -(e)s, -e bang; (Peitschen—) crack; **~ und Fall** (col) unexpectedly; **~bonbon** m cracker; **~effekt** m surprise effect, spectacular effect; **k~en** vi bang; crack; **k~rot** a bright red.

knapp [knap] a tight; Geld scarce; Sprache concise; **K~e** m -n, -n (Edelmann) young knight; **~halten** vt irreg stint; **K~heit** f tightness; scarcity; conciseness.

knarren ['knarən] vi creak.

knattern ['knatərn] vi rattle; (MG) chatter.

Knäuel ['knɔʏəl] m or nt -s, - (Woll—) ball; (Menschen—) knot.

Knauf [knauf] m -(e)s, **Knäufe** knob; (Schwert—) pommel.

Knauser ['knauzər] m -s, - miser; **k~ig** a miserly; **k~n** vi be mean.

knautschen ['knautʃən] vti crumple.

Knebel ['kne:bəl] m -s, - gag; **k~n** vt gag; (Naut) fasten.

Knecht [knɛçt] m -(e)s, -e farm labourer; servant; **k~en** vt enslave; **~schaft** f servitude.

kneifen ['knaɪfən] vti irreg pinch; (sich drücken) back out; **vor etw ~** dodge sth.

Kneipe ['knaɪpə] f -, -n (col) pub.

Knet- [kne:t] cpd: **k~en** vt knead; Wachs mould; **~masse** f Plasticine ®.

Knick [knɪk] m -(e)s, -e (Sprung) crack; (Kurve) bend; (Falte) fold; **k~en** vti (springen) crack; (brechen) break; Papier fold; **geknickt sein** be downcast.

Knicks [knɪks] m -es, -e curtsey; **k~en** vi curtsey.

Knie [kni:] nt -s, - knee; **~beuge** f -, -n knee bend; **k~n** vi kneel; **~fall** m genuflection; **~gelenk** nt knee joint; **~kehle** f

back of the knee; **~scheibe** f kneecap; **~strumpf** m knee-length sock.

Kniff [knɪf] m -(e)s, -e (Zwicken) pinch; (Falte) fold; (fig) trick, knack; **k~elig** a tricky.

knipsen ['knɪpsən] vti Fahrkarte punch; (Phot) take a snap (of), snap.

Knirps [knɪrps] m -es, -e little chap; ® (Schirm) telescopic umbrella.

knirschen ['knɪrʃən] vi crunch; **mit den Zähnen ~** grind one's teeth.

knistern ['knɪstərn] vi crackle.

Knitter- ['knɪtər] cpd: **~falte** f crease; **k~frei** a non-crease; **k~n** vi crease.

Knoblauch ['kno:plaux] m -(e)s garlic.

Knöchel ['knœçəl] m -s, - knuckle; (Fuß—) ankle.

Knochen ['knɔxən] m -s, - bone; **~bau** m bone structure; **~bruch** m fracture; **~gerüst** nt skeleton.

knöchern ['knœçərn] a bone.

knochig ['knɔxıç] a bony.

Knödel ['knø:dəl] m -s, - dumpling.

Knolle ['knɔlə] f -, -n bulb.

Knopf [knɔpf] m -(e)s, ⁻e button; (Kragen—) stud; **~loch** nt buttonhole.

knöpfen ['knœpfən] vt button.

Knorpel ['knɔrpəl] m -s, - cartilage, gristle; **k~ig** a gristly.

knorrig ['knɔrıç] a gnarled, knotted.

Knospe ['knɔspə] f -, -n bud; **k~n** vi bud.

Knoten ['kno:tən] m -s, - knot; (Bot) node; (Med) lump; **k~** vt knot; **~punkt** m junction.

knuffen ['knʊfən] vt (col) cuff.

Knüller ['knʏlər] m -s, - (col) hit; (Reportage) scoop.

knüpfen ['knʏpfən] vt tie; Teppich knot; Freundschaft form.

Knüppel ['knʏpəl] m -s, - cudgel; (Polizei—) baton, truncheon; (Aviat) (joy)stick; **~schaltung** f (Aut) floor-mounted gear change.

knurren ['knʊrən] vi (Hund) snarl, growl; (Magen) rumble; (Mensch) mutter.

knusperig ['knʊspərıç] a crisp; Keks crunchy.

Koalition [koalitsi'o:n] f coalition.

Kobalt ['ko:balt] nt -s cobalt.

Kobold ['ko:bɔlt] m -(e)s, -e goblin, imp.

Kobra ['ko:bra] f -, -s cobra.

Koch [kɔx] m -(e)s, ⁻e cook; **~buch** nt cookery book; **k~en** vti cook; Wasser boil; **~er** m -s, - stove, cooker.

Köcher ['kœçər] m -s, - quiver.

Kochgelegenheit ['kɔxgəle:gənhaɪt] f cooking facilities pl.

Köchin ['kœçın] f cook.

Koch- cpd: **~löffel** m kitchen spoon; **~nische** f kitchenette; **~platte** f boiling ring, hotplate; **~salz** nt cooking salt; **~topf** m saucepan, pot.

Köder ['kø:dər] m -s, - bait, lure; **k~n** vt lure, entice.

Koexistenz [koeksıs'tɛnts] f coexistence.

Koffein [kɔfe'i:n] nt -s caffeine; **k~frei** a decaffeinated.

Koffer ['kɔfər] m -s, - suitcase; (Schrank—) trunk; **~radio** nt portable radio; ~**raum** m (Aut) boot, trunk (US).

Kognak ['konjak] m **-s, -s** brandy, cognac.

Kohl [ko:l] m **-(e)s, -e** cabbage.

Kohle ['ko:lə] f **-, -n** coal; (Holz—) charcoal; (Chem) carbon; ~**hydrat** nt **-(e)s, -e** carbohydrate; ~**ndioxyd** nt **-(e)s, -e** carbon dioxide; ~**ngrube** f coal pit, mine; ~**nhändler** m coal merchant, coalman; ~**nsäure** f carbon dioxide; ~**nstoff** m carbon; ~**papier** nt carbon paper; ~**stift** m charcoal pencil.

Köhler ['kø:lər] m **-s, -** charcoal burner.

Kohl- cpd: ~**rübe** f turnip; **k**~**schwarz** a coal-black.

Koje ['ko:jə] f **-, -n** cabin; (Bett) bunk.

Kokain [koka'i:n] nt **-s** cocaine.

kokett [ko'ket] a coquettish, flirtatious; ~**ieren** [-'ti:rən] vi flirt.

Kokosnuß ['ko:kosnus] f coconut.

Koks [ko:ks] m **-es, -e** coke.

Kolben ['kolbən] m **-s, -** (Gewehr—) rifle butt; (Keule) club; (Chem) flask; (Tech) piston; (Mais—) cob.

Kolchose [kol'ço:zə] f **-, -n** collective farm.

Kolik ['ko:lik] f colic, gripe.

Kollaps [ko'laps] m **-es, -e** collapse.

Kolleg [ko'le:k] nt **-s, -s** or **-ien** lecture course; ~**e** [ko'le:gə] m **-n, -n, ~in** f colleague; ~**ium** nt board; (Sch) staff.

Kollekte [ko'lektə] f **-, -n** (Rel) collection.

kollektiv [kolɛk'ti:f] a collective.

kollidieren [koli'di:rən] vi collide; (zeitlich) clash.

Kollision [kolizi'o:n] f collision; (zeitlich) clash.

kolonial [koloni'a:l] a colonial; **K**~**warenhändler** m grocer.

Kolonie [kolo'ni:] f colony.

kolonisieren [koloni'zi:rən] vt colonize.

Kolonist [kolo'nist] m colonist.

Kolonne [ko'lonə] f **-, -n** column; (von Fahrzeugen) convoy.

Koloß [ko'los] m **-sses, -sse** colossus.

kolossal [kolo'sa:l] a colossal.

Kombi- ['kombi] cpd: ~**nation** [-natsi'o:n] f combination; (Vermutung) conjecture; (Hemdhose) combinations pl; (Aviat) flying suit; **k**~**nieren** [-'ni:rən] vt combine; vi deduce, work out; (vermuten) guess; ~**wagen** m station wagon; ~**zange** f (pair of) pliers.

Komet [ko'me:t] m **-en, -en** comet.

Komfort [kom'fo:r] m **-s** luxury.

Komik ['ko:mik] f humour, comedy; ~**er** m **-s, -** comedian.

komisch ['ko:miʃ] a funny.

Komitee [komi'te:] nt **-s, -s** committee.

Komma ['koma] nt **-s, -s** or **-ta** comma.

Kommand- [ko'mand] cpd: ~**ant** [-'dant] m commander, commanding officer; ~**eur** [-'dø:r] m commanding officer; **k**~**ieren** [-'di:rən] vti command; ~**o** nt **-s, -s** command, order; (Truppe) detachment, squad; **auf** ~**o** to order.

kommen ['komən] vi irreg come; (näher —) approach; (passieren) happen; (gelangen, geraten) get; (Blumen, Zähne, Tränen etc) appear; (in die Schule, das

Zuchthaus etc) go; ~ **lassen** send for; **das kommt in den Schrank** that goes in the cupboard; **zu sich** ~ come round or to; **zu etw** ~ acquire sth; **um etw** ~ lose sth; **nichts auf jdn/etw** ~ **lassen** have nothing said against sb/sth; **jdm frech** ~ get cheeky with sb; **auf jeden vierten kommt ein Platz** there's one place to every fourth person; **wer kommt zuerst?** who's first?; **unter ein Auto** ~ be run over by a car; **wie hoch kommt das?** what does that cost?; **K**~ nt **-s** coming.

Kommentar [komen'ta:r] m commentary; **kein** ~ no comment; **k**~**los** a without comment.

Kommentator [komen'ta:tor] m (TV) commentator.

kommentieren [komen'ti:rən] vt comment on.

kommerziell [komɛrtsi'ɛl] a commercial.

Kommilitone [komili'to:nə] m **-n, -n** fellow student.

Kommiß [ko'mis] m **-sses** (life in the) army; ~**brot** nt army bread.

Kommissar [komi'sa:r] m police inspector.

Kommission [komisi'o:n] f (Comm) commission; (Ausschuß) committee.

Kommode [ko'mo:də] f **-, -n** (chest of) drawers.

Kommune [ko'mu:nə] f **-, -n** commune.

Kommunikation [komunikatsi'o:n] f communication.

Kommunion [komuni'o:n] f communion.

Kommuniqué [komyni'ke:] nt **-s, -s** communiqué.

Kommunismus [komu'nismus] m communism.

Kommunist [komu'nist] m communist; **k**~**isch** a communist.

kommunizieren [komuni'tsi:rən] vi communicate; (Eccl) receive communion.

Komödiant [komødi'ant] m comedian; ~**in** f comedienne.

Komödie [ko'mø:diə] f comedy.

Kompagnon [kompan'jõ:] m **-s, -s** (Comm) partner.

kompakt [kom'pakt] a compact.

Kompanie [kompa'ni:] f company.

Komparativ ['komparati:f] m **-s, -e** comparative.

Kompaß ['kompas] m **-sses, -sse** compass.

kompetent [kompe'tɛnt] a competent.

Kompetenz f competence, authority.

komplett [kom'plet] a complete.

Komplikation [komplikatsi'o:n] f complication.

Kompliment [kompli'mɛnt] nt compliment.

Komplize [kom'pli:tsə] m **-n, -n** accomplice.

komplizieren [kompli'tsi:rən] vt complicate.

Komplott [kom'plot] nt **-(e)s, -e** plot.

komponieren [kompo'ni:rən] vt compose.

Komponist [kompo'nist] m composer.

Komposition [kompozitsi'o:n] f composition.

Kompost [kɔm'pɔst] *m* -(e)s, -e compost; ~**haufen** *m* compost heap.

Kompott [kɔm'pɔt] *nt* -(e)s, -e stewed fruit.

Kompresse [kɔm'prɛsə] *f* -, -n compress.

Kompressor [kɔm'prɛsɔr] *m* coɪnpressor.

Kompromiß [kɔmpro'mɪs] *m* -sses, -sse compromise; k~**bereit** *a* willing to compromise; ~**lösung** *f* compromise solution.

kompromittieren [kɔmprɔmɪ'tiːrən] *vt* compromise.

Kondens- [kɔn'dɛns] *cpd:* ~**ation** [kɔndɛnzatsi'oːn] *f* condensation; ~**ator** [kɔndɛn'zaːtɔr] *m* condenser; k~**ieren** [kɔndɛn'ziːrən] *vt* condense; ~**milch** *f* condensed milk; ~**streifen** *m* vapour trail.

Kondition- [kɔnditsi'oːn] *cpd:* ~**alsatz** [kɔnditsio'naːlzats] *m* conditional clause; ~**straining** *nt* fitness training.

Konditor [kɔn'diːtɔr] *m* pastrycook; ~**ei** [kɔndito'raɪ] *f* café; cake shop.

kondolieren [kɔndo'liːrən] *vi* condole (*jdm* with sb).

Kondom [kɔn'doːm] *nt* -s, -e condom.

Konfektion [kɔnfɛktsi'oːn] *f* production of ready-made clothing; ~**skleidung** *f* ready-made clothing.

Konferenz [kɔnfe'rɛnts] *f* conference, meeting.

konferieren [kɔnfe'riːrən] *vi* confer, have a meeting.

Konfession [kɔnfɛsi'oːn] *f* religion; (*christlich*) denomination; k~**ell** [-'nɛl] *a* denominational; k~**slos** *a* non-denominational; ~**sschule** *f* denominational school.

Konfetti [kɔn'fɛti] *nt* -(s) confetti.

Konfirmand [kɔnfɪr'mant] *m* candidate for confirmation.

Konfirmation [kɔnfɪrmatsi'oːn] *f* (*Eccl*) confirmation.

konfirmieren [kɔnfɪr'miːrən] *vt* confirm.

konfiszieren [kɔnfɪs'tsiːrən] *vt* confiscate.

Konfitüre [kɔnfi'tyːrə] *f* -, -n jam.

Konflikt [kɔn'flɪkt] *m* -(e)s, -e conflict.

konform [kɔn'fɔrm] *a* concurring; ~ **gehen** be in agreement.

konfrontieren [kɔnfrɔn'tiːrən] *vt* confront.

konfus [kɔn'fuːs] *a* confused.

Kongreß [kɔn'grɛs] *m* -sses, -sse congress.

Kongruenz [kɔngru'ɛnts] *f* agreement, congruence.

König [kø'nɪç] *m* -(e)s, -e king; ~**in** ['kø'nɪgɪn] *f* queen; k~**lich** *a* royal; ~**reich** *nt* kingdom; ~**tum** *nt* -(e)s, -tümer kingship.

konisch ['koːnɪʃ] *a* conical.

Konjugation [kɔnjugatsi'oːn] *f* conjugation.

konjugieren [kɔnju'giːrən] *vt* conjugate.

Konjunktion [kɔnjʊŋktsi'oːn] *f* conjunction.

Konjunktiv ['kɔnjʊŋktiːf] *m* -s, -e subjunctive.

Konjunktur [kɔnjʊŋk'tuːr] *f* economic situation; (*Hoch*—) boom.

konkav [kɔn'kaːf] *a* concave.

konkret [kɔn'kreːt] *a* concrete.

Konkurrent(in *f*) [kɔnkʊ'rɛnt(ɪn)] *m* competitor.

Konkurrenz [kɔnkʊ'rɛnts] *f* competition; k~**fähig** *a* competitive; ~**kampf** *m* competition; (*col*) rat race.

konkurrieren [kɔnkʊ'riːrən] *vi* compete.

Konkurs [kɔn'kʊrs] *m* -es, -e bankruptcy.

können ['kœnən] *vti irreg* be able to, can; (*wissen*) know; ~ **Sie Deutsch?** can you speak German?; **ich kann nicht . . .** I can't *or* cannot . . .; **kann ich gehen?** can I go?; **das kann sein** that's possible; **ich kann nicht mehr** I can't go on; **K~** *nt* -s ability.

konsequent [kɔnze'kvɛnt] *a* consistent.

Konsequenz [kɔnze'kvɛnts] *f* consistency; (*Folgerung*) conclusion.

Konserv- [kɔn'zɛrv] *cpd:* k~**ativ** [-a'tiːf] *a* conservative; ~**atorium** [-a'toːriʊm] *nt* academy of music, conservatory; ~**e** *f* -, -n tinned food; ~**enbüchse** *f* tin, can; k~**ieren** [-'viːrən] *vt* preserve; ~**ierung** *f* preservation; ~**ierungsmittel** *nt* preservative.

Konsonant [kɔnzo'nant] *m* consonant.

konstant [kɔn'stant] *a* constant.

Konstitution [kɔnstitutsi'oːn] *f* constitution; k~**ell** [-'nɛl] *a* constitutional.

konstruieren [kɔnstru'iːrən] *vt* construct.

Konstrukteur [kɔnstrʊk'tøːr] *m* engineer, designer.

Konstruktion [kɔnstrʊktsi'oːn] *f* construction.

konstruktiv [kɔnstrʊk'tiːf] *a* constructive.

Konsul ['kɔnzul] *m* -s, -n consul; ~**at** [-'laːt] *nt* consulate.

konsultieren [kɔnzul'tiːrən] *vt* consult.

Konsum [kɔn'zuːm] *m* -s consumption; ~**artikel** *m* consumer article; ~**ent** [-'mɛnt] *m* consumer; k~**ieren** [-'miːrən] *vt* consume.

Kontakt [kɔn'takt] *m* -(e)s, -e contact; k~**arm** *a* unsociable; k~**freudig** *a* sociable; ~**linsen** *pl* contact lenses *pl*.

Konterfei ['kɔntərfaɪ] *nt* -s, -s picture.

kontern ['kɔntərn] *vti* counter.

Konterrevolution [kɔntərrevolutsio'oːn] *f* counter-revolution.

Kontinent ['kɔntinɛnt] *m* continent.

Kontingent [kɔntɪŋ'gɛnt] *nt* -(e)s, -e quota; (*Truppen*—) contingent.

kontinuierlich [kɔntinu'iːrlɪç] *a* continuous.

Kontinuität [kɔntinui'tɛːt] *f* continuity.

Konto ['kɔnto] *nt* -s, **Konten** account; ~**auszug** *m* statement (of account); ~**inhaber(in** *f*) *m* account holder; ~**r** [kɔn'toːr] *nt* -s, -e office; ~**rist** [-'rɪst] *m* clerk, office worker; ~**stand** *m* state of account.

Kontra ['kɔntra] *nt* -s, -s (*Cards*) double; **jdm** ~ **geben** (*fig*) contradict sb; ~**baß** *m* double bass; ~**hent** [-'hɛnt] *m* contracting party; ~**punkt** *m* counterpoint.

Kontrast [kɔn'trast] *m* -(e)s, -e contrast.

Kontroll- [kɔn'trɔl] *cpd:* ~**e** *f* -, -n control, supervision; (*Paß*—) passport control; ~**eur** [-'løːr] *m* inspector; k~**ieren**

[-'li:rən] vt control, supervise; (nachprüfen) check.

Kontur [kɔn'tu:r] f contour.

Konvention [kɔnvɛntsi'o:n] f convention; **k~ell** [-'nɛl] a conventional.

Konversation [kɔnvɛrzatsi'o:n] f conversation; **~slexikon** nt encyclopaedia.

konvex [kɔn'vɛks] a convex.

Konvoi ['kɔnvɔy] m -s, -s convoy.

Konzentration [kɔntsɛntratsi'o:n] f concentration; **~slager** nt concentration camp.

konzentrieren [kɔntsɛn'tri:rən] vtr concentrate.

konzentriert a concentrated; ad zuhören, arbeiten intently.

Konzept [kɔn'tsɛpt] nt -(e)s, -e rough draft; **jdn aus dem ~ bringen** confuse sb.

Konzern [kɔn'tsɛrn] m -s, -e combine.

Konzert [kɔn'tsɛrt] nt -(e)s, -e concert; (Stück) concerto; **~saal** m concert hall.

Konzession [kɔntsɛsi'o:n] f licence; (Zugeständnis) concession; **k~ieren** [-'ni:rən] vt license.

Konzil [kɔn'tsi:l] nt -s, -e or -ien council.

konzipieren [kɔntsi'pi:rən] vt conceive.

Kopf [kɔpf] m -(e)s, -̈e head; **~bedeckung** f headgear.

köpfen ['kœpfən] vt behead; Baum lop; Ei take the top off; Ball head.

Kopf- cpd: **~haut** f scalp; **~hörer** m headphone; **~kissen** nt pillow; **k~los** a panic-stricken; **~losigkeit** f panic; **k~rechnen** vi do mental arithmetic; **~salat** m lettuce; **~schmerzen** pl headache; **~sprung** m header, dive; **~stand** m headstand; **~tuch** nt headscarf; **k~über** ad head over heels; **~weh** nt headache; **~zerbrechen** nt: **jdm ~zerbrechen machen** give sb a lot of headaches.

Kopie [ko'pi:] f copy; **k~ren** vt copy.

Koppel ['kɔpəl] f -, -n (Weide) enclosure; nt -s, - (Gürtel) belt; **k~n** vt couple; **~ung** f coupling; **~ungsmanöver** nt docking manoeuvre.

Koralle [ko'ralə] f -, -n coral; **~nkette** f coral necklace; **~nriff** nt coral reef.

Korb [kɔrp] m -(e)s, -̈e basket; **jdm einen ~ geben** (fig) turn sb down; **~ball** m basketball; **~stuhl** m wicker chair.

Kord [kɔrt] m -(e)s, -e corduroy.

Kordel ['kɔrdəl] f -, -n cord, string.

Kork [kɔrk] m -(e)s, -e cork; **~en** m -s, - stopper, cork; **~enzieher** m -s, - corkscrew.

Korn [kɔrn] nt -(e)s, -̈er corn, grain; (Gewehr) sight; **~blume** f cornflower; **~kammer** f granary.

Körnchen ['kœrnçən] nt grain, granule.

Körper ['kœrpər] m -s, - body; **~bau** m build; **k~behindert** a disabled; **~gewicht** nt weight; **~größe** f height; **~haltung** f carriage, deportment; **k~lich** a physical; **~pflege** f personal hygiene; **~schaft** f corporation; **~teil** m part of the body.

Korps [ko:r] nt -, - (Mil) corps; students' club.

korpulent [kɔrpu'lɛnt] a corpulent.

korrekt [kɔ'rɛkt] a correct; **K~heit** f correctness; **K~or** m proofreader; **K~ur** [-'tu:r] f (eines Textes) proofreading; (Text) proof; (Sch) marking, correction.

Korrespond- [kɔrɛspɔnd] cpd: **~ent(in f)** [-'dɛnt(ɪn)] m correspondent; **~enz** [-'dɛnts] f correspondence; **k~ieren** [-'di:rən] vi correspond.

Korridor ['kɔrido:r] m -s, -e corridor.

korrigieren [kɔri'gi:rən] vt correct.

korrumpieren [kɔrum'pi:rən] vt corrupt.

Korruption [kɔruptsi'o:n] f corruption.

Korsett [kɔr'zɛt] nt -(e)s, -e corset.

Kose- ['ko:zə] cpd: **~form** f pet form; **k~n** vi caress; vi bill and coo; **~name** m pet name; **~wort** nt term of endearment.

Kosmetik [kɔs'me:tɪk] f cosmetics pl; **~erin** f beautician.

kosmetisch a cosmetic; Chirurgie plastic.

kosmisch ['kɔsmɪʃ] a cosmic.

Kosmo- [kɔsmo] cpd: **~naut** [-'naut] m -en, -en cosmonaut; **~polit** [-po'li:t] m -en, -en cosmopolitan; **k~politisch** [-po'li:tɪʃ] a cosmopolitan; **~s** m - cosmos.

Kost [kɔst] f - (Nahrung) food; (Verpflegung) board; **k~bar** a precious; (teuer) costly, expensive; **~barkeit** f preciousness; costliness, expensiveness; (Wertstück) valuable; **~en** pl cost(s); (Ausgaben) expenses pl; **auf ~ von** at the expense of; **k~en** vt vi cost; vti (versuchen) taste; **~enanschlag** m estimate; **k~enlos** a free (of charge); **~geld** nt board.

köstlich ['kœstlɪç] a precious; Einfall delightful; Essen delicious; **sich ~ amüsieren** have a marvellous time.

Kost- cpd: **~probe** f taste; (fig) sample; **k~spielig** a expensive.

Kostüm [kɔs'ty:m] nt -s, -e costume; (Damen—) suit; **~fest** nt fancy-dress party; **k~ieren** [kɔsty'mi:rən] vtr dress up; **~verleih** m costume agency.

Kot [ko:t] m -(e)s excrement.

Kotelett [kɔtə'lɛt] nt -(e)s, -e or -s cutlet, chop; **~en** pl sideboards pl.

Köter ['kø:tər] m -s, - cur.

Kotflügel m (Aut) wing.

Krabbe ['krabə] f -, -n shrimp; **k~ln** vi crawl.

Krach [krax] m -(e)s, -s or -e crash; (andauernd) noise; (col: Streit) quarrel, row; **k~en** vi crash; (beim Brechen) crack; vr (col) row, quarrel.

krächzen ['krɛçtsən] vi croak.

Kraft [kraft] f -, -̈e strength, power, force; (Arbeits—) worker; **in ~ treten** come into effect; **k~ prep +gen** by virtue of; **~ausdruck** m swearword; **~fahrer** m motor driver; **~fahrzeug** nt motor vehicle; **~fahrzeugbrief** m logbook; **~fahrzeugsteuer** f ≈ road tax.

kräftig ['krɛftɪç] a strong; **~en** [krɛftɪgən] vt strengthen.

Kraft- cpd: **k~los** a weak; powerless; (Jur) invalid; **~probe** f trial of strength; **~rad** nt motorcycle; **k~voll** a vigorous;

~**wagen** m motor vehicle; ~**werk** nt power station.

Kragen ['kra:gən] m -s, - collar; ~**weite** f collar size.

Krähe ['krɛ:ə] f -, -n crow; **k**~**n** vi crow.

krakeelen [kra'ke:lən] vi (col) make a din.

Kralle ['kralə] f -, -n claw; (Vogel—) talon; **k**~**n** vt clutch; (krampfhaft) claw.

Kram [kra:m] m -(e)s stuff, rubbish; **k**~**en** vi rummage; ~**laden** m (pej) small shop.

Krampf [krampf] m -(e)s, ⁻e cramp; (zuckend) spasm; ~**ader** f varicose vein; **k**~**haft** a convulsive; (fig) Versuche desperate.

Kran [kra:n] m -(e)s, ⁻e crane; (Wasser—) tap.

Kranich ['kra:nɪç] m -s, -e (Zool) crane.

krank [krank] a ill, sick; **K**~**e(r)** mf sick person; invalid, patient.

kränkeln ['krɛŋkəln] vi be in bad health.

kranken ['krankən] vi: **an etw** (dat) ~ (fig) suffer from sth.

kränken ['krɛŋkən] vt hurt.

Kranken- cpd: ~**bericht** m medical report; ~**geld** nt sick pay; ~**haus** nt hospital; ~**kasse** f health insurance; ~**pfleger** m nursing orderly; ~**schwester** f nurse; ~**versicherung** f health insurance; ~**wagen** m ambulance.

Krank- cpd: **k**~**haft** a diseased; Angst etc morbid; ~**heit** f illness, disease; ~**heitserreger** m disease-carrying agent.

kränk- ['krɛŋk] cpd: ~**lich** a sickly; **K**~**ung** f insult, offence.

Kranz [krants] m -es, ⁻e wreath, garland.

Kränzchen ['krɛntsçən] nt small wreath; ladies' party.

Krapfen ['krapfən] m -s, - fritter; (Berliner) doughnut.

kraß [kras] a crass.

Krater ['kra:tər] m -s, - crater.

Kratz- ['krats] cpd: ~**bürste** f (fig) crosspatch; **k**~**en** vti scratch; ~**er** m -s, - scratch; (Werkzeug) scraper.

Kraul(schwimmen) ['kraul(ʃvɪmən)] nt -s crawl; **k**~**en** vi (schwimmen) do the crawl; vt (streicheln) tickle.

kraus [kraus] a crinkly; Haar frizzy; Stirn wrinkled; **K**~**e** ['krauzə] f -, -n frill, ruffle.

kräuseln ['krɔyzəln] vt Haar make frizzy; Stoff gather; Stirn wrinkle; vr (Haar) go frizzy; (Stirn) wrinkle; (Wasser) ripple.

Kraut [kraut] nt -(e)s, Kräuter plant; (Gewürz) herb; (Gemüse) cabbage.

Krawall [kra'val] m -s, -e row, uproar.

Krawatte [kra'vatə] f -, -n tie.

kreativ [krea'ti:f] a creative.

Kreatur [krea'tu:r] f creature.

Krebs [kre:ps] m -es, -e crab; (Med, Astrol) cancer.

Kredit [kre'di:t] m -(e)s, -e credit.

Kreide ['kraɪdə] f -, -n chalk; **k**~**bleich** a as white as a sheet.

Kreis [kraɪs] m -es, -e circle; (Stadt— etc) district; **im** ~ **gehen** (lit, fig) go round in circles.

kreischen ['kraɪʃən] vi shriek, screech.

Kreis- cpd: ~**el** ['kraɪzəl] m -s, - top; (Verkehrs—) roundabout; **k**~**en** ['kraɪzən] vi spin; **k**~**förmig** a circular; ~**lauf** m (Physiol) circulation; (fig: der Natur etc) cycle; ~**säge** f circular saw; ~**stadt** f county town; ~**verkehr** m roundabout traffic.

Kreißsaal ['kraɪs-za:l] m delivery room.

Krem [kre:m] f -, -s cream, mousse.

Krematorium [krema'to:rium] nt crematorium.

Krempe ['krɛmpə] f -, -n brim; ~**l** m -s (col) rubbish.

krepieren [kre'pi:rən] vi (col: sterben) die, kick the bucket.

Krepp [krɛp] m -s, -s or -e crepe; ~**papier** nt crepe paper; ~**sohle** f crepe sole.

Kresse ['krɛsə] f -, -n cress.

Kreuz [krɔyts] nt -es, -e cross; (Anat) small of the back; (Cards) clubs; **k**~**en** vtr cross; vi (Naut) cruise; ~**er** m -s, - (Schiff) cruiser; ~**fahrt** f cruise; ~**feuer** nt (fig) **im** ~**feuer stehen** be caught in the crossfire; ~**gang** m cloisters pl; **k**~**igen** vt crucify; ~**igung** f crucifixion; ~**otter** f adder; ~**ung** f (Verkehrs—) crossing, junction; (Züchten) cross; ~**verhör** nt cross-examination; ~**weg** m crossroads; (Rel) Way of the Cross; ~**worträtsel** nt crossword puzzle; ~**zeichen** nt sign of the cross; ~**zug** m crusade.

Kriech- ['kri:ç] cpd: **k**~**en** vi irreg crawl, creep; (pej) grovel, crawl; ~**er** m -s, - crawler; ~**spur** f crawler lane; ~**tier** nt reptile.

Krieg [kri:k] m -(e)s, -e war; **k**~**en** ['kri:gən] vt (col) get; ~**er** m -s, - warrior; **k**~**erisch** a warlike; ~**führung** f warfare; ~**bemalung** f war paint; ~**serklärung** f declaration of war; ~**sfuß** m: **mit jdm/etw auf** ~**sfuß stehen** be at loggerheads with sb/not get on with sth; ~**sgefangene(r)** m prisoner of war; ~**sgefangenschaft** f captivity; ~**sgericht** nt court-martial; ~**sschiff** nt warship; ~**sschuld** f war guilt; ~**sverbrecher** m war criminal; ~**sversehrte(r)** m person disabled in the war; ~**szustand** m state of war.

Krimi ['kri:mi] m -s, -s (col) thriller; **k**~**nal** [-'na:l] a criminal; ~**'nalbeamte(r)** m detective; ~**nalität** f criminality; ~**'nalpolizei** f detective force, CID (Brit); ~**'nalroman** m detective story; **k**~**nell** [-'nɛl] a criminal; ~**'nelle(r)** m criminal.

Krippe ['krɪpə] f -, -n manger, crib; (Kinder—) crèche.

Krise ['kri:zə] f -, -n crisis; **k**~**n** vi: **es kriselt** there's a crisis; ~**nherd** m trouble spot.

Kristall [krɪs'tal] m -s, -e crystal; nt -s (Glas) crystal.

Kriterium [kri'te:rium] nt criterion.

Kritik [kri'ti:k] f criticism; (Zeitungs—) review, write-up; ~**er** ['kri'ti:kər] m -s, - critic; **k**~**los** a uncritical.

kritisch ['kri:tɪʃ] a critical.

kritisieren [kriti'zi:rən] vti criticize.

kritteln ['krıtəln] vi find fault, carp.

kritzeln ['krıtsəln] vti scribble, scrawl.

Krokodil [kroko'di:l] nt -s, -e crocodile.

Krokus ['kro:kus] m -, - or -se crocus.

Krone ['kro:nə] f -, -n crown; (Baum—) top.

krönen ['krø:nən] vt crown.

Kron- cpd: ~**korken** m bottle top; ~**leuchter** m chandelier; ~**prinz** m crown prince.

Krönung ['krø:nuŋ] f coronation.

Kropf [krɔpf] m -(e)s, ˝e (Med) goitre; (im Vogel) crop.

Kröte ['krø:tə] f -, -n toad.

Krücke ['krʏkə] f -, -n crutch.

Krug [kru:k] m -(e)s, ˝e jug; (Bier—) mug.

Krümel ['kry:məl] m -s, - crumb; k~**n** vti crumble.

krumm [krum] a (lit, fig) crooked; (kurvig) curved; ~**beinig** a bandy-legged.

krümm- ['krʏm] cpd: ~**en** vtr curve, bend; K~**ung** f bend, curve.

krumm- cpd: ~**lachen** vr (col) laugh o.s. silly; ~**nehmen** vt irreg (col) jdm etw ~ **nehmen** take sth amiss.

Krüppel ['krʏpəl] m -s, - cripple.

Kruste ['krustə] f -, -n crust.

Kruzifix [krutsi'fıks] nt -es, -e crucifix.

Kübel ['ky:bəl] m -s, - tub; (Eimer) pail.

Küche ['kʏçə] f -n kitchen; (Kochen) cooking, cuisine.

Kuchen ['ku:xən] m -s, - cake; ~**blech** nt baking tray; ~**form** f baking tin; ~**gabel** f pastry fork; ~**teig** m cake mixture.

Küchen- cpd: ~**herd** m range; (Gas, Elec) cooker, stove; ~**schabe** f cockroach; ~**nschrank** m kitchen cabinet.

Kuckuck ['kukuk] m -s, -e cuckoo.

Kufe ['ku:fə] f -, -n (Faß) vat; (Schlitten—) runner; (Aviat) skid.

Kugel ['ku:gəl] f -, -n ball; (Math) sphere; (Mil) bullet; (Erd—) globe; (Sport) shot; k~**förmig** a spherical; ~**lager** nt ball bearing; k~**n** vt roll; (Sport) bowl; vr (vor Lachen) double up; k~**rund** a Gegenstand round; (col) Person tubby; ~**schreiber** m ball-point (pen), biro ˚; k~**sicher** a bulletproof; ~**stoßen** nt -s shot-put.

Kuh [ku:] f -, ˝e cow.

kühl [ky:l] a (lit, fig) cool; K~**anlage** f refrigerating plant; K~**e** f - coolness; ~**en** vt cool; K~**er** m -s, - (Aut) radiator; K~**erhaube** (Aut) bonnet, hood (US); K~**raum** m cold-storage chamber; K~**schrank** m refrigerator; K~**truhe** f freezer; K~**ung** f cooling; K~**wagen** m (Rail) refrigerator van; K~**wasser** nt cooling water.

kühn [ky:n] a bold, daring; K~**heit** f boldness.

Küken ['ky:kən] nt -s, - chicken.

kulant [ku'lant] a obliging.

Kuli ['ku:li] m -s, -s coolie; (col: Kugelschreiber) biro ˚.

Kulisse [ku'lısə] f -, -n scene.

kullern ['kulərn] vi roll.

Kult [kult] m -(e)s, -e worship, cult; mit etw ~ **treiben** make a cult out of sth; k~**ivieren** [-i'vi:rən] vt cultivate;

k~iviert a cultivated, refined; ~**ur** [kul'tu:r] f culture; (Zivilization; (das Boden) cultivation; k~**urell** [-u'rɛl] a cultural; ~**urfilm** m documentary film.

Kümmel ['kʏməl] m -s, - caraway seed; (Branntwein) kümmel.

Kummer ['kumər] m -s grief, sorrow.

kümmer- ['kʏmər] cpd: ~**lich** a miserable, wretched; ~**n** vr: sich um jdn ~ **n** look after sb; sich um etw ~ **n** see to sth; vt concern; das kümmert mich nicht that doesn't worry me.

Kumpan [kum'pa:n] m -s, -e mate; (pej) accomplice.

Kumpel ['kumpəl] m -s, - (col) mate.

kündbar ['kʏntba:r] a redeemable, recallable; Vertrag terminable.

Kunde ['kundə] m -n, -n, **Kundin** f customer; f -, -n (Botschaft) news; ~**ndienst** m after-sales service.

Kund- cpd: ~**gabe** f announcement; k~**geben** vt irreg announce; ~**gebung** f announcement; (Versammlung) rally; k~**ig** a expert, experienced.

Künd- ['kʏnd] cpd: k~**igen** vi give in one's notice; jdm k~**igen** give sb his notice; vt cancel; (jdm) die Stellung/Wohnung ~ give (sb) notice; ~**igung** f notice; ~**igungsfrist** f period of notice.

Kundschaft f customers pl, clientele.

künftig ['kʏnftıç] a future; ad in future.

Kunst [kunst] f -, ˝e art; (Können) skill; das ist doch keine ~ it's easy; ~**akademie** f academy of art; ~**dünger** m artificial manure; ~**faser** f synthetic fibre; ~**fertigkeit** f skilfulness; ~**geschichte** f history of art; ~**gewerbe** nt arts and crafts pl; ~**griff** m trick, knack; ~**händler** m art dealer; ~**harz** nt artificial resin.

Künstler(in f) ['kʏnstlər(ın)] m -s, - artist; k~**isch** a artistic; ~**name** m stagename; pseudonym.

künstlich ['kʏnstlıç] a artificial.

Kunst- cpd: ~**sammler** m -s, - art collector; ~**seide** f artificial silk; ~**stoff** m synthetic material; ~**stopfen** nt -s invisible mending; ~**stück** nt trick; ~**turnen** nt gymnastics; k~**voll** a ingenious, artistic; ~**werk** nt work of art.

kunterbunt ['kuntərbunt] a higgledy-piggledy.

Kupfer ['kupfər] nt -s, - copper; ~**geld** nt coppers pl; k~**n** a copper; ~**stich** m copperplate engraving.

Kuppe ['kupə] f -, -n (Berg—) top; (Finger—) tip; ~**l** f -, -n cupola, dome; ~**lei** f (Jur) procuring; k~**ln** vi (Jur) procure; (Aut) declutch; vt join.

Kupp- ['kup] cpd: ~**ler** m -s, - pimp; ~**lerin** f matchmaker; ~**lung** f coupling; (Aut) clutch.

Kur [ku:r] f -, -en cure, treatment.

Kür [ky:r] f -, -en (Sport) free skating/exercises pl.

Kurbel ['kurbəl] f -, -n crank, winch; (Aut) starting handle; ~**welle** f crankshaft.

Kürbis ['kʏrbıs] m -ses, -se pumpkin; (exotisch) gourd.

Kur- ['ku:r] cpd: ~**gast** m visitor (to a

health resort); **k~ieren** [ku'ri:rən] vt cure; **k~ios** [kuri'o:s] a curious, odd; **~losität** f curiosity; **~ort** m health resort; **~pfuscher** m quack.

Kurs [kurs] m **-es, -e** course; (Fin) rate; **hoch im ~ stehen** (fig) be highly thought of; **~buch** nt timetable; **k~ieren** [kur'zi:rən] vi circulate; **k~iv** ad in italics; **~ive** [kur'zi:və] f -, -n italics pl; **~us** ['kurzus] m -, **Kurse** course; **~wagen** m (Rail) through carriage.

Kurve ['kurvə] f -, -n curve; (Straßen-auch) bend; **k~nreich, kurvig** a Straße bendy.

kurz [kurts] a short; **zu ~ kommen** come off badly; **den eren ziehen** get the worst of it; **K~arbeit** f short-time work; **~ärm(e)lig** a short-sleeved.

Kürze ['kyrtsə] f -, -n shortness, brevity; **k~n** vt cut short; (in der Länge) shorten; Gehalt reduce.

kurz- cpd: **~erhand** ad on the spot; **K~fassung** f shortened version; **~fristig** a short-term; **~gefaßt** a concise; **K~geschichte** f short story; **~halten** vt irreg keep short; **~lebig** a shortlived.

kürzlich ['kyrtslıç] ad lately, recently.

Kurz- cpd: **~schluß** m (Elec) short circuit; **~schrift** f shorthand; **k~sichtig** a short-sighted; **~welle** f shortwave.

kuscheln ['kuʃəln] vr snuggle up.

Kusine [ku'zi:nə] f cousin.

Kuß [kus] m **-sses, ̈sse** kiss.

küssen ['kysən] vtr kiss.

Küste ['kystə] f -, -n coast, shore; **~nwache** f coastguard (station).

Küster ['kystər] m **-s,** - sexton, verger.

Kutsche ['kutʃə] f -, -n coach, carriage; **~r** m **-s,** - coachman.

Kutte ['kutə] f -, -n cowl.

Kuvert [ku'vert] nt **-s, -e** or **-s** envelope, cover.

Kybernetik [kyber'ne:tık] f cybernetics.

kybernetisch [kyber'ne:tıʃ] a cybernetic.

L

L, l [ɛl] nt L, l.

laben ['la:bən] vtr refresh (o.s.); (fig) relish (an etw (dat) sth).

Labor [la'bo:r] nt **-s, -e** or **-s** lab; **~ant(in** f) [labo'rant(ın)] m lab(oratory) assistant; **~atorium** [labora'to:rium] nt laboratory.

Labyrinth [laby'rınt] nt **-s, -e** labyrinth.

Lache ['laxə] f -, -n (Wasser) pool, puddle; (col: Gelächter) laugh.

lächeln ['lɛçəln] vi smile; **L~** nt **-s** smile.

lachen ['laxən] vi laugh.

lächerlich ['lɛçərlıç] a ridiculous; **L~keit** f absurdity.

Lach- cpd: **~gas** nt laughing gas; **l~haft** a laughable.

Lachs [laks] m **-es, -e** salmon.

Lack [lak] m **-(e)s, -e** lacquer, varnish; (von Auto) paint; **l~ieren** [la'ki:rən] vt varnish; Auto spray; **l~ierer** [la'ki:rər] m **-s,** - varnisher; **~leder** nt patent leather.

Lackmus ['lakmus] m or nt - litmus.

Lade ['la:də] f -, -n box, chest; **~baum** m derrick; **~fähigkeit** f load capacity.

laden ['la:dən] vt irreg Lasten load; (Jur) summon; (einladen) invite.

Laden ['la:dən] m **-s,** ̈ shop; (Fenster-) shutter; **~besitzer** m shopkeeper; **~dieb** m shoplifter; **~diebstahl** m shoplifting; **~hüter** m **-s,** - unsaleable item; **~preis** m retail price; **~schluß** m closing time; **~tisch** m counter.

Laderaum m (Naut) hold.

Ladung ['la:duŋ] f (Last) cargo, load; (Beladen) loading; (Jur) summons; (Einladung) invitation; (Spreng-) charge.

Lage ['la:gə] f -, -n position, situation; (Schicht) layer; **in der ~ sein** be in a position; **l~nweise** ad in layers.

Lager ['la:gər] nt **-s,** - camp; (Comm) warehouse; (Schlaf-) bed; (von Tier) lair; (Tech) bearing; **~arbeiter(in** f) m storehand; **~bestand** m stocks pl; **~geld** nt storage (charges pl); **~haus** nt warehouse, store.

lagern ['la:gərn] vi (Dinge) be stored; (Menschen) camp; (auch vr: rasten) lie down; vt store; (betten) lay down; Maschine bed.

Lager- cpd: **~schuppen** m store shed; **~stätte** f resting place; **~ung** f storage.

Lagune [la'gu:nə] f -, -n lagoon.

lahm [la:m] a lame; **~en** vi be lame, liınp.

lähmen ['lɛ:mən] vt paralyse.

lahmlegen vt paralyse.

Lähmung f paralysis.

Laib [laıp] m **-s, -e** loaf.

Laich [laıç] m **-(e)s, -e** spawn; **l~en** vi spawn.

Laie ['laıə] m **-n, -n** layman; **l~nhaft** a amateurish.

Lakai [la'kaı] m **-en, -en** lackey.

Laken ['la:kən] nt **-s,** - sheet.

Lakritze [la'krıtsə] f -, -n liquorice.

lallen ['lalən] vti slur; (Baby) babble.

Lamelle [la'mɛlə] f lamella; (Elec) lamina; (Tech) plate.

lamentieren [lamen'ti:rən] vi lament.

Lametta [la'mɛta] nt **-s** tinsel.

Lamm [lam] nt **-(e)s, ̈er** lamb; **~fell** nt lambskin; **l~fromm** a like a lamb; **~wolle** f lambswool.

Lampe ['lampə] f -, -n lamp; **~nfieber** nt stage fright; **~nschirm** m lampshade.

Lampion [lãpi'õ:] m **-s, -s** Chinese lantern.

Land [lant] nt **-(e)s, ̈er** land; (Nation, nicht Stadt) country; (Bundes-) state; **auf dem ~(e)** in the country; **~arbeiter** m farm or agricultural worker; **~besitz** m landed property; **~besitzer** m landowner; **~ebahn** f runway; **l~einwärts** ad inland; **l~en** ['landən] vti land.

Ländereien [lɛndə'raıən] pl estates pl.

Landes- ['landəs] cpd: **~farben** pl national colours pl; **~innere(s)** nt inland region; **~tracht** f national costume; **l~üblich** a customary; **~verrat** m high treason; **~verweisung** f banishment; **~währung** f national currency.

Land- cpd: **~gut** nt estate; **~haus** nt

country house; ~karte f map; ~kreis m administrative region; l~läufig a customary.

ländlich ['lɛntlɪç] a rural.

Land- cpd: ~schaft f countryside; (Art) landscape; l~schaftlich a scenic; regional; ~smann m, ~smännin f, pl -sleute compatriot, fellow countryman or countrywoman; ~straße f country road; ~streicher m -s, - tramp; ~strich m region; ~tag m (Pol) regional parliament.

Landung ['landʊŋ] f landing; ~sboot nt landing craft; ~sbrücke f jetty, pier; ~sstelle f landing place.

Land- cpd: ~vermesser m surveyor; ~wirt m farmer; ~wirtschaft f agriculture; ~zunge f spit.

lang [laŋ] a long; Mensch tall; ~atmig a long-winded; ~e ad for a long time; dauern, brauchen a long time.

Länge ['lɛŋə] f -, -n length; (Geog) longitude; ~ngrad m longitude; ~nmaß nt linear measure.

langen ['laŋən] vi (ausreichen) do, suffice; (fassen) reach (nach for); es langt mir I've had enough.

lang- cpd: L~eweile f boredom; ~lebig a long-lived.

länglich a longish.

lang- cpd: L~mut f forbearance, patience; ~mütig a forbearing.

längs [lɛŋs] prep +gen or dat along; ad lengthwise.

lang- cpd: ~sam a slow; L~samkeit f slowness; L~schläfer(in f) m late riser; L~spielplatte f long-playing record.

längst ['lɛŋst] ad das ist ~ fertig that was finished a long time ago, that has been finished for a long time; ~e(r,s) a longest.

lang- cpd: ~weilig a boring, tedious; L~welle f long wave; ~wierig a lengthy, long-drawn-out.

Lanze ['lantsə] f -, -n lance.

Lanzette [lan'tsɛtə] f lancet.

lapidar [lapi'da:r] a terse, pithy.

Lappalie [la'pa:liə] f trifle.

Lappen ['lapən] m -s, - cloth, rag; (Anat) lobe.

läppisch ['lɛpɪʃ] a foolish.

Lapsus ['lapsʊs] m -, - slip.

Lärche ['lɛrçə] f -, -n larch.

Lärm [lɛrm] m -(e)s noise; l~en vi be noisy, make a noise.

Larve ['larfə] f -, -n mask; (Biol) larva.

lasch [laʃ] a slack; Geschmack tasteless.

Lasche ['laʃə] f -, -n (Schuh-) tongue; (Rail) fishplate.

Laser ['leːzə] m -s, - laser.

lassen ['lasən] vti irreg leave; (erlauben) let; (aufhören mit) stop; (veranlassen) make; etw machen ~ to have sth done; es läßt sich machen it can be done; es läßt sich öffnen it can be opened, it opens.

lässig ['lɛsɪç] a casual; L~keit f casualness.

läßlich ['lɛslɪç] a pardonable, venial.

Last [last] f -, -en load, burden; (Naut, Aviat) cargo; (usu pl: Gebühr) charge; jdm zur ~ fallen be a burden to sb; ~auto nt lorry, truck; l~en vi (auf +dat) weigh on.

Laster ['lastə] nt -s, - vice.

Lästerer ['lɛstərər] m -s, - mocker; (Gottes-) blasphemer.

lasterhaft a immoral.

lästerlich a scandalous.

lästern ['lɛstərn] vti Gott blaspheme; (schlecht sprechen) mock.

Lästerung f jibe; (Gottes-) blasphemy.

lästig ['lɛstɪç] a troublesome, tiresome.

Last- cpd: ~kahn m barge; ~kraftwagen m heavy goods vehicle; ~schrift f debiting; debit item; ~tier nt beast of burden; ~träger m porter; ~wagen m lorry, truck.

latent [la'tɛnt] a latent.

Laterne [la'tɛrnə] f -, -n lantern; (Straßen-) lamp, light; ~npfahl m lamppost.

Latrine [la'tri:nə] f latrine.

Latsche ['latʃə] f -, -n dwarf pine; l~n ['la:tʃən] vi (col) (gehen) wander, go; (lässig) slouch.

Latte ['latə] f -, -n lath; (Sport) goalpost; (quer) crossbar; ~nzaun m lattice fence.

Latz [lats] m -es, ⁻e bib; (Hosen-) flies pl.

Lätzchen ['lɛtsçən] nt bib.

Latzhose f dungarees pl.

lau [lau] a Nacht balmy; Wasser lukewarm.

Laub [laup] nt -(e)s foliage; ~baum m deciduous tree; ~e ['laubə] f -, -n arbour; ~frosch m tree frog; ~säge f fretsaw.

Lauch [laux] m -(e)s, -e leek.

Lauer ['lauər] f: auf der ~ sein or liegen, l~n vi lie in wait; (Gefahr) lurk.

Lauf [lauf] m -(e)s, Läufe run; (Wett-) race; (Entwicklung, Astron) course; (Gewehr-) barrel; einer Sache ihren ~ lassen let sth take its course; ~bahn f career; ~bursche m errand boy.

laufen ['laufən] vti irreg run; (col: gehen) walk; ~d a running; Monat, Ausgaben current; auf dem ~den sein/halten be/keep up to date; am ~den Band (fig) continuously; ~ lassen vt irreg leave running; ~ lassen vt irreg Person let go.

Läufer ['lɔyfər] m -s, - (Teppich, Sport) runner; (Fußball) half-back; (Schach) bishop.

Lauf- cpd: ~kundschaft f passing trade; ~masche f run, ladder (Brit); im ~schritt at a run; ~stall m playpen; ~steg m dais; ~zettel m circular.

Lauge ['laugə] f -, -n soapy water; (Chem) alkaline solution.

Laune ['launə] f -, -n mood, humour; (Einfall) caprice; (schlechte) temper; l~nhaft a capricious, changeable.

launisch a moody; bad-tempered.

Laus [laus] f -, Läuse louse; ~bub m rascal, imp.

lauschen ['lauʃən] vi eavesdrop, listen in.

lauschig ['lauʃɪç] a snug.

lausen ['lauzən] vt delouse.

laut [laut] a loud; ad loudly; lesen aloud;

prep +gen or dat according to; **L**~ m -(e)s, -e sound.

Laute ['lautə] f-, -n lute.

lauten ['lautən] vi say; (Urteil) be.

läuten ['lɔytən] vti ring, sound.

lauter ['lautər] a Wasser clear, pure; Wahrheit, Charakter honest; inv Freude, Dummheit etc sheer; (mit pl) nothing but, only; **L**~keit f purity; honesty, integrity.

läutern ['lɔytərn] vt purify.

Läuterung f purification.

laut- cpd: ~hals ad at the top of one's voice; ~los a noiseless, silent; ~malend a onomatopoeic; **L**~schrift f phonetics pl; **L**~sprecher m loudspeaker; **L**~sprecherwagen m loudspeaker van; ~stark a vociferous; **L**~stärke f (Rad) volume.

lauwarm ['lauvarm] a (lit, fig) lukewarm.

Lava ['la:va] f-, **Laven** lava.

Lavendel [la'vɛndəl] m -s, - lavender.

Lawine [la'vi:nə] f avalanche; ~ngefahr f danger of avalanches.

lax [laks] a lax.

Lazarett [latsa'rɛt] nt -(e)s, -e (Mil) hospital, infirmary.

Lebe- cpd: ~hoch nt three cheers pl; ~mann m, pl ~männer man about town.

leben ['le:bən] vti live; **L**~ nt -s, - life; ~d a living; ~dig [le'bɛndɪç] a living, alive; (lebhaft) lively; **L**~digkeit f liveliness.

Lebens- cpd: ~alter nt age; ~art f way of life; ~erwartung f life expectancy; l~fähig a able to live; l~froh a full of the joys of life; ~gefahr f: ~gefahr! danger!; in ~gefahr dangerously ill; l~gefährlich a dangerous; Verletzung critical; ~haltungskosten pl cost of living sing; ~jahr nt year of life; ~lage f situation in life; ~lauf m curriculum vitae; l~lustig a cheerful, lively; ~mittel pl food sing; ~mittelgeschäft nt grocer's; l~müde a tired of life; ~retter m lifesaver; ~standard m standard of living; **L**~stellung f permanent post; ~unterhalt m livelihood; ~versicherung f life insurance; ~wandel m way of life; ~weise f way of life, habits pl; ~zeichen nt sign of life; ~zeit f lifetime.

Leber ['le:bər] f-, -n liver; ~fleck m mole; ~tran m cod-liver oil; ~wurst f liver sausage.

Lebe- cpd: ~wesen nt creature; ~wohl nt farewell, goodbye.

leb- ['le:p] cpd: ~haft a lively, vivacious; **L**~haftigkeit f liveliness, vivacity; **L**~kuchen m gingerbread; ~los a lifeless.

lechzen ['lɛçtsən] vi: nach etw ~ long for sth.

leck [lɛk] a leaky, leaking; **L**~ nt -(e)s, -e leak; ~en vi (Loch haben) leak; vti (schlecken) lick.

lecker ['lɛkər] a delicious, tasty; **L**~bissen m dainty morsel; **L**~maul nt: ein **L**~maul sein enjoy one's food.

Leder ['le:dər] nt -s, - leather; l~n a leather; ~waren pl leather goods pl.

ledig ['le:dɪç] a single; einer Sache ~ sein be free of sth; ~lich ad merely, solely.

leer [le:r] a empty; vacant; **L**~e f - emptiness; ~en vt empty; vr become empty; **L**~gewicht nt weight when empty; **L**~lauf m neutral; ~stehend a empty; **L**~ung f emptying; (Post) collection.

legal [le'ga:l] a legal, lawful; ~i'sieren vt legalize; **L**~i'tät f legality.

legen ['le:gən] vt lay, put, place; Ei lay; vr lie down; (fig) subside.

Legende [le'gɛndə] f-, -n legend.

leger [le'ʒɛːr] a casual.

legieren [le'gi:rən] vt alloy.

Legierung f alloy.

Legislative [legisla'ti:və] f legislature.

legitim [legi'ti:m] a legitimate; **L**~ation [-atsi'o:n] f legitimation; ~ieren [-'mi:rən] vt legitimate; vr prove one's identity; **L**~i'tät f legitimacy.

Lehm [le:m] m -(e)s, -e loam; l~ig a loamy.

Lehne ['le:nə] f -, -n arm; back; l~n vtr lean.

Lehnstuhl m armchair.

Lehr- cpd: ~amt nt teaching profession; ~brief m indentures pl; ~buch nt textbook.

Lehre ['le:rə] f -, -n teaching, doctrine; (beruflich) apprenticeship; (moralisch) lesson; (Tech) gauge; l~n vt teach; ~r(in f) m -s, - teacher.

Lehr- cpd: ~gang m course; ~jahre pl apprenticeship; ~kraft f teacher; ~ling m apprentice; ~plan m syllabus; l~reich a instructive; ~satz m proposition; ~stelle f apprenticeship; ~stuhl m chair; ~zeit f apprenticeship.

Leib [laip] m -(e)s, -er body; halt ihn mir vom ~! keep him away from me; ~eserziehung ['laibəs-] f physical education; ~esübung f physical exercise; l~haftig a personified; Teufel incarnate; l~lich a bodily; Vater etc own; ~wache f bodyguard.

Leiche ['laiçə] f -, -n corpse; ~nbeschauer m -s, - doctor who makes out death certificate; l~nhemd nt shroud; ~nträger m bearer; ~nwagen m hearse.

Leichnam ['laiçna:m] m -(e)s, -e corpse.

leicht [laiçt] a light; (einfach) easy; **L**~athletik f athletics sing; ~fallen vi irreg: jdm ~fallen be easy for sb; ~fertig a frivolous; ~gläubig a gullible, credulous; **L**~gläubigkeit f gullibility, credulity; ~hin ad lightly; **L**~igkeit f easiness; mit **L**~igkeit with ease; ~lebig a easy-going; ~machen vt: es sich (dat) ~machen make things easy for oneself; ~nehmen vt irreg take lightly; **L**~sinn m carelessness; ~sinnig a careless.

Leid [lait] nt -(e)s grief, sorrow; l~ a: etw l~ haben or sein be tired of sth; es tut mir/ihm l~ I am/he is sorry; er/das tut mir l~ I am sorry for him/it; l~en ['laidən] irreg vt suffer; (erlauben) permit; jdn/etw nicht l~en können not be able to stand sb/sth; *vi* suffer; ~**en** *nt* -**s**, - suffering; (*Krankheit*) complaint; ~**enschaft** *f* passion; l~**enschaftlich** *a* passionate.

leider ['laɪdər] *ad* unfortunately; **ja**, ~ yes, I'm afraid so; ~ **nicht** I'm afraid not.

leidig ['laɪdɪç] *a* miserable, tiresome.

leidlich *a* tolerable; *ad* tolerably.

Leid- *cpd:* ~**tragende(r)** *mf* bereaved; (*Benachteiligter*) one who suffers; ~**wesen** *nt:* **zu jds** ~**wesen** to sb's dismay.

Leier ['laɪər] *f* -, -**n** lyre; (*fig*) old story; ~**kasten** *m* barrel organ; **l~n** *vti* Kurbel turn; (*col*) Gedicht rattle off.

Leihbibliothek *f* lending library.

leihen ['laɪən] *vt irreg* lend; **sich** (*dat*) **etw** ~ borrow sth.

Leih- *cpd:* ~**gebühr** *f* hire charge; ~**haus** *nt* pawnshop; ~**schein** *m* pawn ticket; (*Buch-* etc) borrowing slip; ~**wagen** *m* hired car.

Leim [laɪm] *m* -**(e)s**, -**e** glue; **l~en** *vt* glue.

Leine ['laɪnə] *f* -, -**n** line, cord; (*Hunde—*) leash, lead; ~**n** *nt* -**s**, - linen; **l~n** *a* linen.

Lein- *cpd:* ~**tuch** *nt* (*Bett—*) sheet; linen cloth; ~**wand** *f* (*Art*) canvas; (*Cine*) screen.

leise ['laɪzə] *a* quiet; (*sanft*) soft, gentle.

Leiste ['laɪstə] *f* -, -**n** ledge; (*Zier—*) strip; (*Anat*) groin.

leisten ['laɪstən] *vt* Arbeit do; Gesellschaft keep; Ersatz supply; (*vollbringen*) achieve; **sich** (*dat*) **etw** ~ **können** be able to afford sth.

Leistung *f* performance; (*gute*) achievement; ~**sdruck** *m* pressure; **l~sfähig** *a* efficient; ~**sfähigkeit** *f* efficiency; ~**szulage** *f* productivity bonus.

Leit- *cpd:* ~**artikel** *m* leading article; ~**bild** *nt* model.

leiten ['laɪtən] *vt* lead; Firma manage; (*in eine Richtung*) direct; (*Elec*) conduct.

Leiter ['laɪtər] *m* -**s**, - leader, head; (*Elec*) conductor; *f* -, -**n** ladder.

Leit- *cpd:* ~**faden** *m* guide; ~**fähigkeit** *f* conductivity; ~**motiv** *nt* leitmotiv; ~**planke** *f* -, -**n** crash barrier.

Leitung *f* (*Führung*) direction; (*Cine, Theat* etc) production; (*von Firma*) management; directors *pl*; (*Wasser—*) pipe; (*Kabel*) cable; **eine lange** ~ **haben** be slow on the uptake; ~**sdraht** *m* wire; ~**smast** *m* telegraph pole; ~**srohr** *nt* pipe; ~**swasser** *nt* tap water.

Lektion [lɛktsi'oːn] *f* lesson.

Lektor(in *f*) *m* ['lɛktɔr(ɪn)] (*Univ*) lector; (*Verlag*) editor.

Lektüre [lɛk'tyːrə] *f* -, -**n** (*Lesen*) reading; (*Lesestoff*) reading matter.

Lende ['lɛndə] *f* -, -**n** loin; ~**nbraten** *m* roast sirloin; ~**nstück** *nt* fillet.

lenk- ['lɛŋk] *cpd:* ~**bar** *a* Fahrzeug steerable; Kind manageable; ~**en** *vt* steer; Kind guide; Blick, Aufmerksamkeit direct (*auf* +*acc* at); **L~rad** *nt* steering wheel; **L~stange** *f* handlebars *pl*.

Lenz [lɛnts] *m* -**es**, -**e** (*liter*) spring.

Leopard [leo'part] *m* -**en**, -**en** leopard.

Lepra ['leːpra] *f* - leprosy.

Lerche ['lɛrçə] *f* -, -**n** lark.

lern- [lɛrn] *cpd:* ~**begierig** *a* eager to learn; ~**en** *vt* learn.

lesbar ['leːsbaːr] *a* legible.

Lesbierin ['lɛsbiərɪn] *f* lesbian.

lesbisch ['lɛsbɪʃ] *a* lesbian.

Lese ['leːzə] *f* -, -**n** gleaning; (*Wein*) harvest; ~**buch** *nt* reading book, reader; **l~n** *vti irreg* read; (*ernten*) gather, pick; ~**r(in** *f*) *m* -**s**, - reader; ~**rbrief** *m* reader's letter; **l~rlich** *a* legible; ~**saal** *m* reading room; ~**zeichen** *nt* bookmark.

Lesung ['leːzʊŋ] *f* (*Parl*) reading; (*Eccl*) lesson.

letzte(r, s) ['lɛtstə(r,z)] *a* last; (*neueste*) latest; **zum** ~**nmal** *ad* for the last time; ~**ns** *ad* lately; ~**re(r,s)** *a* latter.

Leuchte ['lɔʏçtə] *f* -, -**n** lamp, light; **l~n** *vi* shine, gleam; ~**r** *m* -**s**, - candlestick.

Leucht- *cpd:* ~**farbe** *f* fluorescent colour; ~**feuer** *nt* beacon; ~**käfer** *m* glowworm; ~**kugel** *f*, ~**rakete** *f* flare; ~**reklame** *f* neon sign; ~**röhre** *f* strip light; ~**turm** *m* lighthouse; ~**zifferblatt** *nt* luminous dial.

leugnen ['lɔʏgnən] *vti* deny.

Leugnung *f* denial.

Leukämie [lɔʏkɛ'miː] *f* leukaemia.

Leukoplast® [lɔʏko'plast] *nt* -**(e)s**, -**e** elastoplast®.

Leumund ['lɔʏmʊnt] *m* -**(e)s**, -**e** reputation; ~**szeugnis** *nt* character reference.

Leute ['lɔʏtə] *pl* people *pl*.

Leutnant ['lɔʏtnant] *m* -**s**, -**s** or -**e** lieutenant.

leutselig ['lɔʏtzɛːlɪç] *a* affable; **L~keit** *f* affability.

Lexikon ['lɛksikɔn] *nt* -**s**, **Lexiken** or **Lexika** dictionary.

Libelle [li'bɛlə] *f* -, -**n** dragonfly; (*Tech*) spirit level.

liberal [libe'raːl] *a* liberal; **L~ismus** [libera'lɪsmʊs] *m* liberalism.

Libero ['liːbero] *m* -**s**, -**s** (*Fußball*) sweeper.

Licht [lɪçt] *nt* -**(e)s**, -**er** light; **l~** *a* light, bright; ~**bild** *nt* photograph; (*Dia*) slide; ~**blick** *m* cheering prospect; **l~empfindlich** *a* sensitive to light; **l~en** *vt* clear; Anker weigh; *vr* clear up; (*Haar*) thin; **l~erloh** *ad:* **l~erloh brennen** blaze; ~**hupe** *f* flashing of headlights; ~**jahr** *nt* light year; ~**maschine** *f* dynamo; ~**meß** *f* - Candlemas; ~**schalter** *m* light switch.

Lichtung *f* clearing, glade.

Lid [liːt] *nt* -**(e)s**, -**er** eyelid; ~**schatten** *m* eyeshadow.

lieb [liːp] *a* dear; ~**äugeln** *vi insep* ogle (*mit jdm/etw* sb/sth).

Liebe ['liːbə] *f* -, -**n** love; **l~bedürftig** *a:* **l~bedürftig sein** need love; ~**lei** *f* flirtation; **l~n** *vt* love; like; **l~nswert** *a* loveable; **l~nswürdig** *a* kind; **l~nswürdigerweise** *ad* kindly; ~**nswürdigkeit** *f* kindness.

lieber ['liːbər] *ad* rather, preferably; **ich**

gehe ~ **nicht** I'd rather not go; *see* **gern**, **lieb**.

Liebes- *cpd*: ~**brief** *m* love letter; ~**dienst** *m* good turn; ~**kummer** *m*: ~**kummer haben** be lovesick; ~**paar** *nt* courting couple, lovers *pl*.

liebevoll *a* loving.

lieb- ['li:p] *cpd*: ~**gewinnen** *vt irreg* get fond of; ~**haben** *vt irreg* be fond of; **L~haber** *m* -**s**, - lover; **L~habe'rei** *f* hobby; ~**kosen** ['li:p'ko:zən] *vt insep* caress; ~**lich** a lovely, charming; **L~ling** *m* darling; **L~lings-** *in cpds* favourite; ~**los** a unloving; **L~schaft** *f* love affair.

Lied [li:t] *nt* -(e)s, -er song; (*Eccl*) hymn; ~**erbuch** *nt* songbook; hymn book.

liederlich ['li:dərlıç] a slovenly; *Lebenswandel* loose, immoral; **L~keit** *f* slovenliness; immorality.

Lieferant [li:fə'rant] *m* supplier.

liefern ['li:fərn] *vt* deliver; (*versorgen mit*) supply; *Beweis* produce.

Liefer- *cpd*: ~**schein** *m* delivery note; ~**termin** *m* delivery date; ~**ung** *f* delivery; supply; ~**wagen** *m* van.

Liege ['li:gə] *f* -, -n bed.

liegen ['li:gən] *vi irreg* lie; (*sich befinden*) be; **mir liegt nichts/viel daran** it doesn't matter to me/it matters a lot to me; **es liegt bei Ihnen, ob . . .** it rests with you whether . . .; **Sprachen** ~ **mir nicht** languages are not my line; **woran liegt es?** what's the cause?; ~**bleiben** *vi irreg* (*Person*) stay in bed; stay lying down; (*Ding*) be left (behind); ~**lassen** *vt irreg* (*vergessen*) leave behind; **L~schaft** *f* real estate.

Liege- *cpd*: ~**sitz** *m* (*Aut*) reclining seat; ~**stuhl** *m* deck chair; ~**wagen** *m* (*Rail*) couchette.

Lift [lıft] *m* -(e)s, -e *or* -s lift.

Likör [li'kø:r] *m* -s, -e liqueur.

lila ['li:la] a purple, lilac; **L~** *nt* -s, -s (*Farbe*) purple, lilac.

Lilie ['li:liə] *f* lily.

Limonade [limo'na:də] *f* lemonade.

lind [lınt] a gentle, mild; **L~e** ['lındə] *f* -, -n lime tree, linden; ~**ern** *vt* alleviate, soothe; **L~erung** *f* alleviation; ~**grün** a lime green.

Lineal [line'a:l] *nt* -s, -e ruler.

Linie ['li:niə] *f* line; ~**nblatt** *nt* ruled sheet; ~**nflug** *m* scheduled flight; ~**nrichter** *m* linesman.

liniieren [lini'i:rən] *vt* line.

Linke ['lıŋkə] *f* -, -n left side; left hand; (*Pol*) left; **l~(r,s)** a left; **l~ Masche** purl.

linkisch a awkward, gauche.

links [lıŋks] *ad* left; to *or* on the left; ~ **von mir** on *or* to my left; **L~außen** [lıŋks'aʊsən] *m* -s, - (*Sport*) outside left; **L~händer(in** *f*) *m* -s, - left-handed person; **L~kurve** *f* left-hand bend; **L~verkehr** *m* traffic on the left.

Linoleum [li'no:leʊm] *nt* -s lino(leum).

Linse ['lınzə] *f* -, -n lentil; (*optisch*) lens.

Lippe ['lıpə] *f* -, -n lip; ~**nstift** *m* lipstick.

liquidieren [likvi'di:rən] *vt* liquidate.

lispeln ['lıspəln] *vi* lisp.

List [lıst] *f* -, -en cunning; trick, ruse.

Liste ['lıstə] *f* -, -n list.

listig ['lıstıç] a cunning, sly.

Litanei [lita'naı] *f* litany.

Liter ['li:tər] *nt or m* -s, - litre.

literarisch [lite'ra:rıʃ] a literary.

Literatur [litera'tu:r] *f* literature; ~**preis** *m* award for literature.

Litfaßsäule ['lıtfaszɔylə] *f* advertising pillar.

Lithographie [litogra'fi:] *f* lithography.

Liturgie [litur'gi:] *f* liturgy.

liturgisch [li'turgıʃ] a liturgical.

Litze ['lıtsə] *f* -, -n braid; (*Elec*) flex.

live [laıf] ad (*Rad, TV*) live.

Livree [li'vre:] *f* -, -n livery.

Lizenz [li'tsɛnts] *f* licence.

Lkw [ɛlka:'ve:] *m* **Lastkraftwagen**.

Lob [lo:p] *nt* -(e)s praise; **l~en** ['lo:bən] *vt* praise; **l~enswert** a praiseworthy.

löblich ['lø:plıç] a praiseworthy, laudable.

Lobrede *f* eulogy.

Loch [lɔx] *nt* -(e)s, "er hole; **l~en** *vt* punch holes in; ~**er** *m* -s, - punch.

löcherig ['lœçərıç] a full of holes.

Loch- *cpd*: ~**karte** *f* punch card; ~**streifen** *m* punch tape.

Locke ['lɔkə] *f* -, -n lock, curl; **l~n** *vt* entice; *Haare* curl; ~**nwickler** *m* -s, - curler.

locker ['lɔkər] a loose; ~**lassen** *vi irreg*: **nicht ~lassen** not let up; ~**n** *vt* loosen.

lockig ['lɔkıç] a curly.

Lock- *cpd*: ~**ruf** *m* call; ~**ung** *f* enticement; ~**vogel** *m* decoy, bait.

Lodenmantel ['lo:dənmantəl] *m* thick woollen coat.

lodern ['lo:dərn] *vi* blaze.

Löffel ['lœfəl] *m* -s, - spoon; **l~n** *vt* (eat with a) spoon; **l~weise** ad by spoonfuls.

Logarithmentafel [loga'rıtmənta:fəl] *f* log(arithm) tables *pl*.

Logarithmus [loga'rıtmʊs] *m* logarithm.

Loge ['lo:ʒə] *f* -, -n (*Theat*) box; (*Freimaurer*) (masonic) lodge; (*Pförtner*—) office.

logieren [lo'ʒi:rən] *vi* lodge, stay.

Logik ['lo:gık] *f* logic.

logisch ['lo:gıʃ] a logical.

Lohn [lo:n] *m* -(e)s, "e reward; (*Arbeits*—) pay, wages *pl*; ~**büro** *nt* wages office; ~**empfänger** *m* wage earner.

lohnen ['lo:nən] *vt* (*liter*) reward (*jdm etw* sb for sth); *vr impers* be worth it; ~**d** a worthwhile.

Lohn- *cpd*: ~**steuer** *f* income tax; ~**streifen** *m* pay slip; ~**tüte** *f* pay packet.

lokal [lo'ka:l] a local; **L~** *nt* -(e)s, -e pub(lic house); ~**i'sieren** *vt* localize; **L~i'sierung** *f* localization.

Lokomotive [lokomo'ti:və] *f* -, -n locomotive.

Lokomotivführer *m* engine driver.

Lorbeer ['lɔrbe:r] *m* -s, -en (*lit, fig*) laurel; ~**blatt** *nt* (*Cook*) bay leaf.

Lore ['lo:rə] *f* -, -n (*Min*) truck.

Los [lo:s] *nt* -es, -e (*Schicksal*) lot, fate; lottery ticket.

los [lo:s] *a* loose; **~! go on!**; *etw ~* **sein** be rid of sth; **was ist ~?** what's the matter?; **dort ist nichts/viel ~** there's nothing/a lot going on there; *etw ~* **haben** (*col*) be clever; **~ binden** *vt irreg* untie.

löschen ['lœʃən] *vt Feuer, Licht* put out, extinguish; *Durst* quench; (*Comm*) cancel; *Tonband* erase; *Fracht* unload; *vi* (*Feuerwehr*) put out a fire; (*Papier*) blot.

Lösch- *cpd:* **~fahrzeug** *nt* fire engine; fire boat; **~gerät** *nt* fire extinguisher; **~papier** *nt* blotting paper; **~ung** *f* extinguishing; (*Comm*) cancellation; (*Fracht*) unloading.

lose ['lo:zə] *a* loose.

Lösegeld *nt* ransom.

losen ['lo:zən] *vi* draw lots.

lösen ['lø:zən] *vt* loosen; *Rätsel etc* solve; *Verlobung* call off; (*Chem*) dissolve; *Partnerschaft* break up; *Fahrkarte* buy; *vr* (*aufgehen*) come loose; (*Zucker etc*) dissolve; (*Problem, Schwierigkeit*) (re)solve itself.

los- *cpd:* **~fahren** *vi irreg* leave; **~gehen** *vi irreg* set out; (*anfangen*) start; (*Bombe*) go off; **auf jdn ~gehen** go for sb; **~kaufen** *vt Gefangene, Geißeln* pay ransom for; **~kommen** *vi irreg:* **von etw ~kommen** get away from sth; **~lassen** *vt irreg Seil* let go of; *Schimpfe* let loose; **~laufen** *vi irreg* run off.

löslich ['lø:slɪç] *a* soluble; **L~keit** *f* solubility.

los- *cpd:* **~lösen** *vtr* free; **~machen** *vt* loosen; *Boot* unmoor; *vr* get free; **~sagen** *vr* renounce (*von jdm/etw* sb/sth); **~schrauben** *vt* unscrew; **~sprechen** *vt irreg* absolve.

Losung ['lo:zʊŋ] *f* watchword, slogan.

Lösung ['lø:zʊŋ] *f* (*Lockermachen*) loosening; (*eines Rätsels, Chem*) solution; **~smittel** *nt* solvent.

los- *cpd:* **~werden** *vt irreg* get rid of; **~ziehen** *vi irreg* (*sich aufmachen*) set out; **gegen jdn ~ziehen** run sb down.

Lot [lo:t] *nt* **-(e)s, -e** plummet; **im ~** vertical; (*fig*) on an even keel; **l~en** *vti* plumb, sound.

löten ['lø:tən] *vt* solder.

Lötkolben *m* soldering iron.

Lotse ['lo:tsə] *m* **-n, -n** pilot; (*Aviat*) air traffic controller; *see* **Schüler ~**; **l~n** *vt* pilot; (*col*) lure.

Lotterie [lɔtə'ri:] *f* lottery.

Löwe ['lø:və] *m* **-n, -n** lion; (*Astrol*) Leo; **~nanteil** *m* lion's share; **~nmaul** *nt* snapdragon; **~nzahn** *m* dandelion.

Löwin ['lø:vɪn] *f* lioness.

loyal [loa'ja:l] *a* loyal; **L~ität** *f* loyalty.

Luchs [luks] *m* **-es, -e** lynx.

Lücke ['lʏkə] *f* **-, -n** gap; **~nbüßer** *m* **-s, -** stopgap; **l~nhaft** *a* defective, full of gaps; **l~nlos** *a* complete.

Luder ['lu:dər] *nt* **-s, -** (*pej: Frau*) hussy; (*bedauernswert*) poor wretch.

Luft [luft] *f* **-, ¨e** air; (*Atem*) breath; **in der ~ liegen** be in the air; **jdn wie ~ behandeln** ignore sb; **~angriff** *m* air raid; **~ballon** *m* balloon; **~blase** *f* air

bubble; **l~dicht** *a* airtight; **~druck** *m* atmospheric pressure.

lüften ['lʏftən] *vti* air; *Hut* lift, raise.

Luft- *cpd:* **~fahrt** *f* aviation; **l~gekühlt** *a* air-cooled; **l~ig** *a Ort* breezy; *Raum* airy; *Kleider* summery; **~kissenfahrzeug** *nt* hovercraft; **~krieg** *m* war in the air; aerial warfare; **~kurort** *m* health resort; **l~leer** *a:* **~leerer Raum** vacuum; **~linie** *f:* **in der ~linie** as the crow flies; **~loch** *nt* air-hole; (*Aviat*) air-pocket; **~matratze** *f* lilo [R], air mattress; **~pirat** *m* hijacker; **~post** *f* airmail; **~röhre** *f* (*Anat*) wind pipe; **~schlange** *f* streamer; **~schutz** *m* anti-aircraft defence; **~schutzkeller** *m* air-raid shelter; **~sprung** *m:* (*fig*) **einen ~sprung machen** jump for joy.

Lüftung ['lʏftʊŋ] *f* ventilation.

Luft- *cpd:* **~verkehr** *m* air traffic; **~waffe** *f* air force; **~zug** *m* draught.

Lüge ['ly:gə] *f* **-, -n** lie; **jdn/etw ~n strafen** give the lie to sb/sth; **l~n** *vi irreg* lie.

Lügner(in *f*) *m* **-s, -** liar.

Luke ['lu:kə] *f* **-, -n** dormer window, hatch.

Lümmel ['lʏməl] *m* **-s, -** lout; **l~n** *vr* lounge (about).

Lump [lump] *m* **-en, -en** scamp, rascal.

Lumpen ['lumpən] *m* **-s, -** rag; **sich nicht l~ lassen** not be mean.

lumpig ['lumpɪç] *a* shabby.

Lunge ['luŋə] *f* **-, -n** lung; **~nentzündung** *f* pneumonia; **l~nkrank** *a* consumptive.

lungern ['luŋərn] *vi* hang about.

Lunte ['luntə] *f* **-, -n** fuse; **~ riechen** smell a rat.

Lupe ['lu:pə] *f* **-, -n** magnifying glass; **unter die ~ nehmen** (*fig*) scrutinize.

Lupine [lu'pi:nə] *f* lupin.

Lust [lust] *f* **-, ¨e** joy, delight; (*Neigung*) desire; **~ haben zu** *or* **auf etw** (*acc*)**/etw zu tun** feel like sth/doing sth.

lüstern ['lystərn] *a* lustful, lecherous.

Lustgefühl *nt* pleasurable feeling.

lustig ['lustɪç] *a* (*komisch*) amusing, funny; (*fröhlich*) cheerful.

Lüstling *m* lecher.

Lust- *cpd:* **l~los** *a* unenthusiastic; **~mord** *m* sex(ual) murder; **~spiel** *nt* comedy; **l~wandeln** *vi* stroll about.

lutschen ['lutʃən] *vti* suck; **am Daumen ~** suck one's thumb.

Lutscher *m* **-s, -** lollipop.

luxuriös [luksuri'ø:s] *a* luxurious.

Luxus ['luksus] *m* **-** luxury; **~artikel** *pl* luxury goods *pl*; **~hotel** *nt* luxury hotel; **~steuer** *f* tax on luxuries.

Lymphe ['lʏmfə] *f* **-, -n** lymph.

lynchen ['lʏnçən] *vt* lynch.

Lyrik ['ly:rɪk] *f* lyric poetry; **~er** *m* **-s, -** lyric poet.

lyrisch ['ly:rɪʃ] *a* lyrical.

M

M, m [ɛm] *nt* M, m.

Mach- [max] *cpd:* **~art** *f* make; **m~bar** *a* feasible; **~e** *f* - (*col*) show, sham;

m ~en vt make; (tun) do; (col: reparieren) fix; (betragen) be; **das macht nichts** that doesn't matter; **mach's gut!** good luck!; vr come along (nicely); **sich an etw** (acc) **m ~en** set about sth; vi: **in etw** (dat) **m ~en** (Comm) be or deal in sth.

Macht [maxt] f **-s, ¨e** power; **~haber** m **-s, -** ruler.

mächtig ['mɛçtɪç] a powerful, mighty; (col: ungeheuer) enormous.

Macht- cpd: **m ~los** a powerless; **~probe** f trial of strength; **~stellung** f position of power; **~wort** nt: **ein ~wort sprechen** lay down the law.

Machwerk nt work; (schlechte Arbeit) botched-up job.

Mädchen ['mɛːtçən] nt girl; **m ~haft** a girlish; **~name** m maiden name.

Made ['maːdə] f **-, -n** maggot.

madig ['maːdɪç] a maggoty; **jdm etw ~ machen** spoil sth for sb.

Magazin [maga'tsiːn] nt **-s, -e** magazine.

Magd [maːkt] f **-, ¨e** maid(servant).

Magen ['maːgən] m **-s, -** or **¨** stomach; **~schmerzen** pl stomachache.

mager ['maːgər] a lean; (dünn) thin; **M ~keit** f leanness; thinness.

Magie [ma'giː] f magic; **~r** ['maːgiər] m **-s, -** magician.

magisch ['maːgɪʃ] a magical.

Magnet [ma'gneːt] m **-s** or **-en, -en** magnet; **m ~isch** a magnetic; **m ~i-'sieren** vt magnetize; **~nadel** f magnetic needle.

Mahagoni [maha'goːni] nt **-s** mahogany.

mähen ['mɛːən] vti mow.

Mahl [maːl] nt **-(e)s, -e** meal; **m ~en** vt irreg. grind; **~stein** m grindstone; **~zeit** f meal; interj enjoy your meal.

Mahnbrief m reminder.

Mähne ['mɛːnə] f **-, -n** mane.

Mahn- [maːn] cpd: **m ~en** vt remind; (warnend) warn; (wegen Schuld) demand payment from; **~ung** f reminder; admonition, warning.

Mähre ['mɛːrə] f **-, -n** mare.

Mai [maɪ] m **-(e)s, -e** May; **~glöckchen** nt lily of the valley; **~käfer** m cockchafer.

Mais [maɪs] m **-es, -e** maize, corn (US); **~kolben** m corncob.

Majestät [majɛs'tɛːt] f majesty; **m ~isch** a majestic.

Major [ma'joːr] m **-s, -e** (Mil) major; (Aviat) squadron leader.

Majoran [majo'raːn] m **-s, -e** marjoram.

makaber [ma'kaːbər] a macabre.

Makel ['maːkəl] m **-s, -** blemish; (moralisch) stain; **m ~los** a immaculate, spotless.

mäkeln ['mɛːkəln] vi find fault.

Makkaroni [maka'roːni] pl macaroni sing.

Makler ['maːklər] m **-s, -** broker.

Makrele [ma'kreːlə] f **-, -n** mackerel.

Makrone [ma'kroːnə] f **-, -n** macaroon.

Mal [maːl] nt **-(e)s, -e** mark, sign; (Zeitpunkt) time; **m ~** ad times; (col) see **einmal**; **-m ~** suff -times; **m ~en** vti paint; **~er** m **-s, -** painter; **~e'rei** f

painting; **m ~erisch** a picturesque; **~kasten** m paintbox; **m ~nehmen** vti irreg multiply.

Malz [malts] nt **-es** malt; **~bonbon** nt cough drop; **~kaffee** m malt coffee.

Mama ['mamaː] f **-, -s, Mami** ['mami] f **-, -s** (col) mum(my).

Mammut ['mamʊt] nt **-s, -e** or **-s** mammoth.

man [man] pron one, people pl, you.

manche(r,s) ['mançə(r,z)] a many a; (pl) a number of; pron some; **~rlei** a inv various; pron a variety of things.

manchmal ad sometimes.

Mandant(in f) [man'dant(ɪn)] m (Jur) client.

Mandarine [manda'riːnə] f mandarin, tangerine.

Mandat [man'daːt] nt **-(e)s, -e** mandate.

Mandel ['mandəl] f **-, -n** almond; (Anat) tonsil.

Manege [ma'neːʒə] f **-, -n** ring, arena.

Mangel ['maŋəl] f **-, -** mangle; **m ~s, -** lack; (Knappheit) shortage (an + dat of); (Fehler) defect, fault; **~erscheinung** f deficiency symptom; **m ~haft** a poor; (fehlerhaft) defective, faulty; **m ~n** vi impers: **es mangelt jdm an etw** (dat) sb lacks sth; vt Wäsche mangle; **m ~s** prep +gen for lack of.

Manie [ma'niː] f mania.

Manier [ma'niːr] f **-** manner; style; (pej) mannerism; **~en** pl manners pl; **m ~iert** [mani'riːrt] a mannered, affected; **m ~lich** a well-mannered.

Manifest [mani'fɛst] nt **-es, -e** manifesto.

Maniküre [mani'kyːrə] f **-, -n** manicure; **m ~n** vt manicure.

manipulieren [manipu'liːrən] vt manipulate.

Manko ['maŋko] nt **-s, -s** deficiency; (Comm) deficit.

Mann [man] m **-(e)s, ¨er** man; (Ehe—) husband; (Naut) hand; **seinen ~ stehen** hold one's own.

Männchen ['mɛnçən] nt little man; (Tier) male.

Mannequin [manə'kɛ̃] nt **-s, -s** fashion model.

mannigfaltig ['manɪçfaltɪç] a various, varied; **M ~keit** f variety.

männlich ['mɛnlɪç] a (Biol) male; (fig, Gram) masculine.

Mann- cpd: **~schaft** f (Sport, fig) team; (Naut, Aviat) crew; (Mil) other ranks pl; **~sleute** pl (col) menfolk pl; **~weib** nt (pej) mannish woman.

Manöver [ma'nøːvər] nt **-s, -** manoeuvre.

manövrieren [manø'vriːrən] vti manoeuvre.

Mansarde [man'zardə] f **-, -n** attic.

Manschette [man'ʃɛtə] f cuff; (Papier—) paper frill; (Tech) collar; sleeve; **~knopf** m cufflink.

Mantel ['mantəl] m **-s, ¨** coat; (Tech) casing, jacket.

Manuskript [manu'skrɪpt] nt **-(e)s, -e** manuscript.

Mappe ['mapə] f -, -n briefcase; (Akten—) folder.

Märchen ['mɛːrçən] nt fairy tale; m~**haft** a fabulous; ~**prinz** m prince charming.

Marder ['mardər] m -s, - marten.

Margarine [marga'riːnə] f margarine.

Marienkäfer [ma'riːənkeːfər] m ladybird.

Marine [ma'riːnə] f navy; m~**blau** a navy-blue.

marinieren [mari'niːrən] vt marinate.

Marionette [mario'nɛtə] f puppet.

Mark [mark] f -, - (Münze) mark; nt -(e)s (Knochen—) marrow; **durch** ~ **und Bein gehen** go right through sb; m~**ant** [mar'kant] a striking.

Marke ['markə] f -, -n mark; (Warensorte) brand; (Fabrikat) make; (Rabatt—, Brief—) stamp; (Essens—) ticket; (aus Metall etc) token, disc.

Mark- cpd: m~**ieren** [mar'kiːrən] vt mark; vti (col) act; ~**ierung** f marking; m~**ig** ['makɪç] a (fig) pithy; ~**ise** [mar'kiːzə] f -, -n awning; ~**stück** nt one-mark piece.

Markt [markt] m -(e)s, ⁻e market; ~**forschung** f market research; ~**platz** m market place; ~**wirtschaft** f market economy.

Marmelade [marmə'laːdə] f -, -n jam.

Marmor ['marmər] m -s, -e marble; m~**ieren** [-'riːrən] vt marble; m~**n** a marble.

Marone [ma'roːnə] f -, -n or **Maroni** chestnut.

Marotte [ma'rɔtə] f -, -n fad, quirk.

Marsch [marʃ] m -(e)s, ⁻e march; m~ interj march; f -, -en marsh; ~**befehl** m marching orders pl; m~**bereit** a ready to move; m~**ieren** [mar'ʃiːrən] vi march.

Marter ['martər] f -, -n torment; m~**n** vt torture.

Märtyrer(in f) ['mɛrtyrər(ɪn)] m -s, - martyr.

März [mɛrts] m -(es), -e March.

Marzipan [martsi'paːn] nt -s, -e marzipan.

Masche ['maʃə] f -, -n mesh; (Strick—) stitch; **das ist die neueste** ~ that's the latest dodge; ~**ndraht** m wire mesh; m~**nfest** a runproof.

Maschine [ma'ʃiːnə] f machine; (Motor) engine; m~**ll** [maʃi'nɛl] a machine(-); mechanical; ~**nbauer** m mechanical engineer; ~**ngewehr** nt machine gun; ~**npistole** f submachine gun; ~**nschaden** m mechanical fault; ~**nschlosser** m fitter; ~**nschrift** f type-script; m~**schreiben** vi irreg type.

Maschinist [maʃi'nɪst] m engineer.

Maser ['maːzər] f -, -n grain; speckle; ~**n** pl (Med) measles sing; ~**ung** f grain(ing).

Maske ['maskə] f -, -n mask; ~**nball** m fancy-dress ball; ~**rade** [-'raːdə] f masquerade.

maskieren [mas'kiːrən] vt mask; (verkleiden) dress up; vr disguise o.s., dress up.

Maß [maːs] nt -es, -e measure; (Mäßigung) moderation; (Grad) degree, extent; f -, -(e) litre of beer.

Massage [ma'saːʒə] f -, -n massage.

Maß- cpd: ~**anzug** m made-to-measure suit; ~**arbeit** f (fig) neat piece of work.

Masse ['masə] f -, -n mass; ~**nartikel** m mass-produced article; ~**ngrab** nt mass grave; m~**nhaft** a loads of; ~**nmedien** pl mass media pl.

Mass- cpd: ~**eur** [ma'søːr] m masseur; ~**euse** [ma'søːzə] f masseuse.

maß- cpd: ~**gebend** a authoritative; ~**halten** vi irreg exercise moderation.

massieren [ma'siːrən] vt massage; (Mil) mass.

massig ['masɪç] a massive; (col) massive amount of.

mäßig ['mɛːsɪç] a moderate; ~**en** ['mɛːsɪgən] vt restrain, moderate; M~**keit** f moderation.

massiv [ma'siːf] a solid; (fig) heavy, rough; M~ nt -s, -e massif.

Maß- cpd: ~**krug** m tankard; m~**los** a extreme; ~**nahme** f -, -n measure, step; m~**regeln** vt insep reprimand; ~**stab** m rule, measure; (fig) standard; (Geog) scale; m~**voll** a moderate.

Mast ['mast] m -(e)s, -e(n) mast; (Elec) pylon.

mästen ['mɛstən] vt fatten.

Material [materi'aːl] nt -s, -ien material(s); ~**fehler** m material defect; ~**ismus** [-'lɪsmus] m materialism; ~**ist** [-'lɪst] m materialist; m~**istisch** [-'lɪstɪʃ] a materialistic.

Materie [ma'teːriə] f matter, substance; m~**ll** [materi'ɛl] a material.

Mathematik [matema'tiːk] f mathematics sing; ~**er(in** f) [mate'maːtikər(ɪn)] m -s, - mathematician.

mathematisch [mate'maːtɪʃ] a mathematical.

Matratze [ma'tratsə] f -, -n mattress.

Matrize [ma'triːtsə] f -, -n matrix; (zum Abziehen) stencil.

Matrose [ma'troːzə] m -n, -n sailor.

Matsch [matʃ] m -(e)s mud; (Schnee—) slush; m~**ig** a muddy; slushy.

matt [mat] a weak; (glanzlos) dull; (Phot) matt; (Schach) mate.

Matte ['matə] f -, -n mat.

Matt- cpd: ~**igkeit** f weakness; dullness; ~**scheibe** f (TV) screen; ~**scheibe haben** (col) be not quite with it.

Mauer ['mauər] f -, -n wall; m~**n** vti build; lay bricks; ~**werk** nt brickwork; (Stein) masonry.

Maul [maul] nt -(e)s, **Mäuler** mouth; m~**en** vi (col) grumble; ~**esel** m mule; ~**korb** m muzzle; ~**sperre** f lockjaw; ~**tier** nt mule; ~**wurf** m mole; ~**wurfshaufen** m molehill.

Maurer ['maurər] m -s, - bricklayer.

Maus [maus] f -, **Mäuse** mouse.

mäuschenstill ['mɔysçən'ʃtɪl] a very quiet.

Maus- cpd: ~**efalle** f mousetrap; m~**en** vt (col) flinch; vi catch mice; m~**ern** vr moult; m~**(e)tot** a stone dead.

maximal [maksi'maːl] a maximum.

Maxime [ma'ksi:mə] *f* -, -n maxim.
Mayonnaise [majɔ'nɛ:zə] *f* -, -n mayonnaise.
Mechan- [me'ça:n] *cpd:* ~**ik** *f* mechanics *sing;* (*Getriebe*) mechanics *pl;* ~**iker** *m* -s, - mechanic, engineer; **m**~**isch** *a* mechanical; **m**~**i'sieren** *vt* mechanize; ~**i'sierung** *f* mechanization; ~**ismus** [meça'nısmus] *m* mechanism.
meckern ['mɛkərn] *vi* bleat; (*col*) moan.
Medaille [me'daljə] *f* -, -n medal.
Medaillon [medal'jõ:] *nt* -s, -s (*Schmuck*) locket.
Medikament [medika'mɛnt] *nt* medicine.
meditieren [medi'ti:rən] *vi* meditate.
Medizin [medi'tsi:n] *f* -, en medicine; **m**~**isch** *a* medical.
Meer [me:r] *nt* -(e)s, -e sea; ~**busen** *m* bay, gulf; ~**enge** *f* straits *pl;* ~**esspiegel** *m* sea level; ~**rettich** *m* horseradish; ~**schweinchen** *nt* guinea-pig.
Megaphon [mega'fo:n] *nt* -s, -e megaphone.
Mehl ['me:l] *nt* -(e)s, -e flour; **m**~**ig** *a* floury.
mehr [me:r] *a,ad* more; **M**~**aufwand** *m* additional expenditure; ~**deutig** *a* ambiguous; ~**ere** *a* several; ~**eres** *pron* several things; ~**fach** *a* multiple; (*wiederholt*) repeated; **M**~**heit** *f* majority; ~**malig** *a* repeated; ~**mals** *ad* repeatedly; ~**stimmig** *a* for several voices; ~**stimmig singen** harmonize; **M**~**wertsteuer** *f* value added tax, VAT; **M**~**zahl** *f* majority; (*Gram*) plural.
meiden ['maidən] *vt irreg* avoid.
Meile ['mailə] *f* -, -n mile; ~**nstein** *m* milestone; **m**~**nweit** *a* for miles.
mein [main] *pron* my; ~**e(r,s)** mine.
Meineid ['main'ait] *m* perjury.
meinen ['mainən] *vti* think; (*sagen*) say; (*sagen wollen*) mean; **das will ich** ~ I should think so.
mein- *cpd:* ~**er** *pron gen of* ich of me; ~**erseits** *ad* for my part; ~**esgleichen** *pron* people like me; ~**etwegen**, ~**etwillen** *ad* (*für mich*) for my sake; (*wegen mir*) on my account; (*von mir aus*) as far as I'm concerned; I don't care *or* mind; ~**ige** *pron:* **der/die/das** ~**ige** mine.
Meinung ['mainuŋ] *f* opinion; **jdm die** ~ **sagen** give sb a piece of one's mind; ~**saustausch** *m* exchange of views; ~**sumfrage** *f* opinion poll; ~**sverschiedenheit** *f* difference of opinion.
Meise ['maizə] *f* -, -n tit(mouse).
Meißel ['maisəl] *m* -s, - chisel; **m**~**n** *vt* chisel.
meist ['maist] *a,ad* most(ly); ~**ens** *ad* generally, usually.
Meister ['maistər] *m* -s, - master; (*Sport*) champion; ~**haft** *a* masterly; **m**~**n** *vt* master; ~**schaft** *f* mastery; (*Sport*) championship; ~**stück** *nt*, ~**werk** *nt* masterpiece.
Melancholie [melaŋko'li:] *f* melancholy.
melancholisch [melaŋ'ko:lɪʃ] *a* melancholy.

Melde- ['mɛldə] *cpd:* ~**frist** *f* registration period; **m**~**n** *vt* report; (*freiwillig*) volunteer; (*auf etw, am Telefon*) answer; **sich zu Wort m**~**n** ask to speak; ~**pflicht** *f* obligation to register with the police; ~**stelle** *f* registration office.
Meldung ['mɛldoŋ] *f* announcement; (*Bericht*) report.
meliert [me'li:rt] *a* mottled, speckled.
melken ['mɛlkən] *vt irreg* milk.
Melodie [melo'di:] *f* melody, tune.
melodisch [me'lo:dɪʃ] *a* melodious, tuneful.
Melone [me'lo:nə] *f* -, -n melon; (*Hut*) bowler (hat).
Membran(e) [mɛm'bra:n(ə)] *f* -, -en (*Tech*) diaphragm.
Memoiren [memo'a:rən] *pl* memoirs *pl.*
Menge ['mɛŋə] *f* -, -n quantity; (*Menschen*—) crowd; (*große Anzahl*) lot (of); **m**~**n** *vt* mix; *vr:* **sich m**~**n in** (+*acc*) meddle with; ~**nlehre** *f* (*Math*) set theory; ~**nrabatt** *m* bulk discount.
Mensch [mɛnʃ] *m* -en, -en human being, man; person; **kein** ~ nobody; *nt* -(e)s, -er hussy; ~**enalter** *nt* generation; ~**enfeind** *m* misanthrope; **m**~**enfreundlich** *a* philanthropical; ~**enkenner** *m* -s, - judge of human nature; ~**enliebe** *f* philanthropy; **m**~**enmöglich** *a* humanly possible; ~**enrecht** *nt* human rights *pl;* **m**~**enscheu** *a* shy; **m**~**enunwürdig** *a* degrading; ~**enverstand** *m:* **gesunder** ~**enverstand** common sense; ~**heit** *f* humanity, mankind; **m**~**lich** *a* human; (*human*) humane; ~**lichkeit** *f* humanity.
Menstruation [mɛnstruatsi'o:n] *f* menstruation.
Mentalität [mɛntali'tɛ:t] *f* mentality.
Menü [me'ny:] *nt* -s, -s menu.
Merk- [mɛrk] *cpd:* ~**blatt** *nt* instruction sheet *or* leaflet; **m**~**en** *vt* notice; **sich** (*dat*) **etw m**~**en** remember sth; **m**~**lich** *a* noticeable; ~**mal** *nt* sign, characteristic; **m**~**würdig** *a* odd.
Meß- [mɛs] *cpd:* **m**~**bar** *a* measurable; ~**becher** *m* measuring cup; ~**buch** *nt* missal.
Messe ['mɛsə] *f* -, -n fair; (*Eccl*) mass; (*Mil*) mess; **m**~**n** *irreg vt* measure; *vr:* compete; ~**r** *nt* -s, - knife; ~**rspitze** *f* knife point; (*in Rezept*) pinch; ~**stand** *m* exhibition stand.
Meß- *cpd:* ~**gerät** *nt* measuring device, gauge; ~**gewand** *nt* chasuble.
Messing ['mɛsɪŋ] *nt* -s brass.
Metall [me'tal] *nt* -s, -e metal; **m**~**en**, **m**~**isch** *a* metallic.
Metaphysik [metafy'zi:k] *f* metaphysics *sing.*
Metastase [meta'sta:zə] *f* -, -n (*Med*) secondary growth.
Meteor [mete'o:r] *nt* -s, -e meteor.
Meter ['me:tər] *nt or m* -s, - metre; ~**maß** *nt* tape measure.
Methode [me'to:də] *f* -, -n method.
methodisch [me'to:dɪʃ] *a* methodical.

Metropole [metro'po:lə] f -, -n metropolis.

Metzger ['mɛtsgər] m -s, - butcher; ~ei [-'rai] f butcher's (shop).

Meuchelmord ['mɔyçəlmɔrt] m assassination.

Meute ['mɔytə] f -, -n pack; ~'rei f mutiny; ~rer m -s, - mutineer; m~rn vi mutiny.

miauen [mi'auən] vi miaow.

mich [miç] pron acc of **ich** me; myself.

Miene ['mi:nə] f -, -n look, expression.

mies [mi:s] a (col) lousy.

Miet- ['mi:t] cpd: ~**auto** nt hired car; ~**e** f -, -n rent; **zur** ~**e wohnen** live in rented accommodation; m~**en** vt rent; Auto hire; ~**er(in** f) m -s, - tenant; ~**shaus** nt tenement, block of flats; ~**vertrag** m tenancy agreement.

Migräne [mi'grɛ:nə] f -, -n migraine.

Mikro- cpd: ~**be** [mi'kro:bə] f -, -n microbe; ~**fon**, ~**phon** [mikro'fo:n] nt -s, -e microphone; ~**skop** [mikro'sko:p] nt -s, -e microscope; m~**skopisch** a microscopic.

Milch [milç] f - milk; (Fisch—) milt, roe; ~**glas** nt frosted glass; m~**ig** a milky; ~**kaffee** m white coffee; ~**pulver** nt powdered milk; ~**straße** f Milky Way; ~**zahn** m milk tooth.

mild [milt] a mild; Richter lenient; (freundlich) kind, charitable; M~**e** ['mildə] f-, -n mildness; leniency; ~**ern** vt mitigate, soften; Schmerz alleviate; ~**ernde Umstände** extenuating circumstances.

Milieu [mili'ø] nt -s, -s background, environment; m~**geschädigt** a maladjusted.

Mili- [mili] cpd: m~**tant** [-'tant] a militant; ~**tär** [-'tɛ:r] nt -s military, army; ~**'tärgericht** nt military court; m~**'tärisch** a military; ~**tarismus** [-ta'rismus] m militarism; m~**ta'ristisch** a militaristic; ~**'tärpflicht** f (compulsory) military service.

Milli- ['mili] cpd: ~**ardär** [-ar'dɛ:r] m multimillionaire; ~**arde** [-'ardə] f -, -n milliard; billion (esp US); ~**meter** m millimetre; ~**on** [-'o:n] f-, -en million; ~**onär** [-o'nɛ:r] m millionaire.

Milz [milts] f -, -en spleen.

Mimik ['mi:mik] f mime.

Mimose [mi'mo:zə] f -, -n mimosa; (fig) sensitive person.

minder ['mindər] a inferior; ad less; M~**heit** f minority; ~**jährig** a minor; M~**jährigkeit** f minority; ~**n** vtr decrease, diminish; M~**ung** f decrease; ~**wertig** a inferior; M~**wertigkeitsgefühl** nt, M~**wertigkeitskomplex** m inferiority complex.

Mindest- ['mindəst] cpd: ~**alter** nt minimum age; ~**betrag** m minimum amount; m~**e** a least; m~**ens, zum** m~**en** ad at least; ~**lohn** m minimum wage; ~**maß** nt minimum.

Mine ['mi:nə] f -, -n mine; (Bleistift—) lead; (Kugelschreiber—) refill; ~**nfeld** nt minefield.

Mineral [mine'ra:l] nt -s, -e or -ien mineral; m~**isch** a mineral; ~**wasser** nt mineral water.

Miniatur [minia'tu:r] f miniature.

minimal [mini'ma:l] a minimal.

Minister [mi'nistər] m -s, - minister; m~**iell** [ministeri'ɛl] a ministerial; ~**ium** [minis'te:rium] nt ministry; ~**präsident** m prime minister.

minus ['mi:nus] ad minus; M~ nt -, - deficit; M~**pol** m negative pole; M~**zeichen** nt minus sign.

Minute [mi'nu:tə] f -, -n minute; ~**nzeiger** m minute hand.

mir [mi:r] pron dat of **ich** (to) me; ~ **nichts, dir nichts** just like that.

Misch- ['miʃ] cpd: ~**ehe** f mixed marriage; m~**en** vt mix; ~**ling** m half-caste; ~**ung** f mixture.

Miß- ['mis] cpd: m~**'achten** vt insep disregard; ~**'achtung** f disregard; ~**behagen** nt discomfort, uneasiness; ~**bildung** f deformity; m~**'billigen** vt insep disapprove of; ~**billigung** f disapproval; ~**brauch** m abuse; (falscher Gebrauch) misuse; m~**'brauchen** vt insep abuse; misuse (zu for); m~**'deuten** vt insep misinterpret; ~**erfolg** m failure.

Misse- ['misə] cpd: ~**tat** f misdeed; ~**täter(in** f) m criminal; (col) scoundrel.

Miß- cpd: m~**'fallen** vi irreg insep displease (jdm sb); ~**fallen** nt -s displeasure; ~**geburt** f freak; (fig) abortion; ~**geschick** nt misfortune; m~**glücken** [mis'glykən] vi insep fail; jdm m~**glückt etw** sb does not succeed with sth; ~**griff** m mistake; ~**gunst** f envy; m~**günstig** a envious; m~**'handeln** vt insep ill-treat; ~**'handlung** f ill-treatment; ~**helligkeit** f: ~**helligkeiten haben** be at variance.

Mission [misi'o:n] f mission; ~**ar** [misio'na:r] m missionary.

Miß- cpd: ~**klang** m discord; ~**kredit** m discredit; ~**lingen** [mis'liŋən] vi irreg insep fail; ~**'lingen** nt -s failure; ~**mut** nt bad temper; m~**mutig** a cross; m~**'raten** vi irreg insep turn out badly; a ill-bred; ~**stand** m state of affairs; abuse; ~**stimmung** f ill-humour, discord; m~**'trauen** vi insep mistrust; ~**trauen** nt -s distrust, suspicion (of); ~**trauensantrag** m (Pol) motion of no confidence; ~**trauensvotum** nt -s, -voten (Pol) vote of no confidence; m~**trauisch** a distrustful, suspicious; ~**verhältnis** nt disproportion; ~**verständnis** nt misunderstanding; m~**verstehen** vt irreg insep misunderstand.

Mist [mist] m -(e)s dung; dirt; (col) rubbish; ~**el** f -, -n mistletoe; ~**haufen** m dungheap.

mit [mit] prep +dat with; (mittels) by; ~ **der Bahn** by train; ~ **10 Jahren** at the age of 10; ad along, too; **wollen Sie** ~? do you want to come along?

Mitarbeit ['mit'arbait] f cooperation; m~**en** vi cooperate, collaborate; ~**er(in** f) m collaborator; co-worker; pl staff.

Mit- cpd: ~**bestimmung** f participation in decision-making; (Pol) determination

m~**bringen** vt irreg bring along;
~**bürger(in** f) m fellow citizen;
m~**denken** vi irreg follow; **du hast ja**
m~**gedacht!** good thinking!

miteinander [mɪt'aɪ'nandər] ad together,
with one another.

Mit- cpd: m~**erleben** vt see, witness;
~**esser** ['mɪt'ɛsər] m -s, - blackhead;
m~**geben** vt irreg give; ~**gefühl** nt
sympathy; m~**gehen** vi irreg go/come
along; m~**genommen** a done in, in a bad
way; ~**gift** f dowry.

Mitglied ['mɪtgliːt] nt member;
~**sbeitrag** m membership fee; ~**schaft**
f membership.

Mit- cpd: m~**halten** vi irreg keep up;
~**hilfe** f help, assistance; m~**hören** vt
listen in to; m~**kommen** vi irreg come
along; (verstehen) keep up, follow;
~**läufer** m hanger-on; (Pol) fellow-
traveller.

Mitleid nt sympathy; (Erbarmen)
compassion; ~**enschaft** f: in ~**enschaft**
ziehen affect; m~**ig** a sympathetic;
m~**slos** a pitiless, merciless.

Mit- cpd: m~**machen** vt join in, take part
in; ~**mensch** m fellow man;
m~**nehmen** vt irreg take along/away;
(anstrengen) wear out, exhaust.

mitsamt [mɪt'zamt] prep +dat together
with.

Mitschuld f complicity; m~**ig** a also
guilty (an +dat of); ~**ige(r)** mf
accomplice.

Mit- cpd: ~**schüler(in** f) m schoolmate;
m~**spielen** vi join in, take part;
~**spieler(in** f) m partner;
~**spracherecht** ['mɪtʃpraːxərɛçt] nt
voice, say.

Mittag ['mɪtaːk] m -(e)s, -e midday,
lunchtime; (zu) ~ **essen** have lunch;
m~ ad at lunchtime or noon; ~**essen** nt
lunch, dinner; m~**s** ad at lunchtime or
noon; ~**spause** f lunch break; ~**sschlaf**
m early afternoon nap, siesta.

Mittäter(in f) [mɪttɛːtər(ɪn)] m
accomplice.

Mitte ['mɪtə] f -, -n middle; **aus unserer**
~ from our midst.

mitteil- ['mɪttaɪl] cpd: ~**en** vt: **jdm etw**
~**en** inform sb of sth, communicate sth to
sb; ~**sam** a communicative; M~**ung** f
communication.

Mittel ['mɪtəl] nt -s - means; method;
(Math) average; (Med) medicine; **ein** ~
zum Zweck a means to an end; ~**alter**
nt Middle Ages pl; m~**alterlich** a
mediaeval; m~**bar** a indirect; ~**ding** nt
cross; m~**los** a without means;
m~**mäßig** a mediocre, middling;
~**mäßigkeit** f mediocrity; ~**punkt** m
centre; m~**s** prep +gen by means of;
~**stand** m middle class; ~**streifen** m
central reservation; m~**stürmer** m centre-
forward; ~**weg** m middle course;
~**welle** f (Rad) medium wave; ~**wert** m
average value, mean.

mitten ['mɪtən] ad in the middle; ~ **auf**
der Straße/in der Nacht in the middle
of the street/night; ~**hindurch** ad

[-hɪn'dʊrç] through the middle.

Mitternacht ['mɪtərnaxt] f midnight;
m~**s** ad at midnight.

mittlere(r,s) ['mɪtlərə(r,z)] a middle;
(durchschnittlich) medium, average.

mittlerweile ['mɪtlərvaɪlə] ad meanwhile.

Mittwoch [mɪtvɔx] m -(e)s, -e
Wednesday; m~**s** ad on Wednesdays.

mitunter [mɪt'ʊntər] ad occasionally,
sometimes.

Mit- cpd: m~**verantwortlich** a also
responsible; ~**verschulden** ['mɪtfɛr-
ʃʊldən] nt contributory negligence; m~-
wirken vi contribute (bei to); (Theat) take
part (bei in); ~**wirkung** f contribution;
participation; ~**wisser** ['mɪtvɪsər] m -s, -
sb in the know.

Möbel ['møːbəl] nt -s, - (piece of)
furniture; ~**wagen** m furniture or
removal van.

mobil [mo'biːl] a mobile; (Mil) mobilized;
M~iar [mobiliˈaːr] nt -s, -e movable
assets pl; **M~machung** f mobilization.

möblieren [mø'bliːrən] vt furnish;
möbliert wohnen live in furnished
accommodation.

Mode ['moːdə] f -, -n fashion.

Modell [mo'dɛl] nt -s, -e model;
m~**ieren** [-'liːrən] vt model.

Mode- cpd: ~**(n)schau** f fashion show;
m~**rn** [mo'dɛrn] a modern; (modisch)
fashionable; m~**rnisieren** vt modernize;
~**schmuck** m fashion jewellery; ~**wort**
nt fashionable word.

modisch ['moːdɪʃ] a fashionable.

mogeln [mo'gəln] vi (col) cheat.

mögen ['møːgən] vti irreg like; **ich möchte**
. . . I would like . . .; das mag wohl sein
that may well be so.

möglich ['møːklɪç] a possible; ~**erweise**
ad possibly; **M~keit** f possibility; **nach**
M~keit if possible; ~**st** ad as . . . as
possible.

Mohn [moːn] m -(e)s, -e (—blume) poppy;
(—samen) poppy seed.

Möhre ['møːrə] f -, -n, **Mohrrübe** f
carrot.

mokieren [mo'kiːrən] vr make fun (über
+acc of).

Mole ['moːlə] f -, -n (harbour) mole; ~**kül**
[mole'kyːl] nt -s, -e molecule.

Molkerei [mɔlkə'raɪ] f dairy.

Moll [mɔl] nt -, - (Mus) minor (key);
m~**ig** a cosy; (dicklich) plump.

Moment [mo'mɛnt] m -(e)s, -e moment;
im ~ at the moment; nt factor, element;
m~**an** [-'taːn] a momentary; ad at the
moment.

Monarch [mo'narç] m -en, -en monarch;
~**ie** [monar'çiː] f monarchy.

Monat ['moːnat] m -(e)s, -e month;
m~**elang** ad for months; m~**lich** a
monthly; ~**skarte** f monthly ticket.

Mönch ['mœnç] m -(e)s, -e monk.

Mond [moːnt] m -(e)s, -e moon; (—bahn) f
lunar (excursion) module; ~**finsternis** f
eclipse of the moon; m~**hell** a moonlit;
~**landung** f moon landing; ~**schein** m
moonlight; ~**sonde** f moon probe.

Mono- [mono] in cpds mono; **~log** [-'lo:k] m -s, -e monologue; **~pol** [-'po:l] nt -s, -e monopoly; **m~polisieren** [-poli'zi:rən] vt monopolize; **m~ton** [-'to:n] a monotonous; **~tonie** [-to'ni:] f monotopy.

Monsun [mɔn'zu:n] m -s, -e monsoon.

Montag ['mo:nta:k] m -(e)s, -e Monday; **m~s** ad on Mondays.

Montage ['mɔn'ta:ʒə] f -, -n (Phot etc) montage; (Tech) assembly; (Einbauen) fitting.

Monteur [mɔn'tø:r] m fitter, assembly man.

montieren [mɔn'ti:rən] vt assemble, set up.

Monument [monu'mɛnt] nt monument; **m~al** [-'ta:l] a monumental.

Moor [mo:r] nt -(e)s, -e moor.

Moos [mo:s] nt -es, -e moss.

Moped ['mo:pet] nt -s, -s moped.

Mops [mɔps] m -es, -̈e pug.

Moral [mo'ra:l] f -, -en morality; (einer Geschichte) moral; **m~isch** a moral.

Moräne [mo'rɛ:nə] f -, -n moraine.

Morast [mo'rast] m -(e)s, -e morass, mire; **m~ig** a boggy.

Mord [mɔrt] m -(e)s, -e murder; **~anschlag** m murder attempt.

Mörder ['mœrdər] m -s, - murderer; **~in** f murderess.

Mord- cpd: **~kommission** f murder squad; **~sglück** nt (col) amazing luck; **m~smäßig** a (col) terrific, enormous; **~sschreck** m (col) terrible fright; **~verdacht** m suspicion of murder; **~waffe** f murder weapon.

morgen ['mɔrgən] ad, **M~** nt tomorrow; **~ früh** tomorrow morning; **M~** m -s, - morning; **M~mantel** m, **M~rock** m dressing gown; **M~röte** f dawn; **~s** ad in the morning.

morgig ['mɔrgiç] a tomorrow's; **der ~e Tag** tomorrow.

Morphium ['mɔrfiʊm] nt morphine.

morsch [mɔrʃ] a rotten.

Morse- ['mɔrzə] cpd: **~alphabet** nt Morse code; **m~n** vi send a message by morse code.

Mörtel ['mœrtəl] m -s, - mortar.

Mosaik [moza'i:k] nt -s, -en or -e mosaic.

Moschee [mɔ'ʃe:] f -, -n [mɔ'ʃe:ən] mosque.

Moskito [mɔs'ki:to] m -s, -s mosquito.

Most [mɔst] m -(e)s, -e (unfermented) fruit juice; (Apfelwein) cider.

Motel [mo'tel] nt -s, -s motel.

Motiv [mo'ti:f] nt -s, -e motive; (Mus) theme; **m~ieren** [moti'vi:rən] vt motivate; **~ierung** f motivation.

Motor ['mo:tɔr] m -s, -en [mo'to:rən] engine; (esp Elec) motor; **~boot** nt motorboat; **~enöl** nt motor oil; **m~isieren** [motori'zi:rən] vt motorize; **~rad** nt motorcycle; **~roller** m motor scooter; **~schaden** m engine trouble or failure.

Motte ['mɔtə] f -, -n moth; **~nkugel** f, **~npulver** nt mothball(s).

Motto ['mɔto] nt -s, -s motto.

Möwe ['mø:və] f -, -n seagull.

Mucke ['mʊkə] f -, -n (usu pl) caprice; (von

Ding) snag, bug; **seine ~n haben** be temperamental.

Mücke ['mʏkə] f -, -n midge, gnat; **~nstich** m midge or gnat bite.

mucksen ['mʊksən] vr (col) budge; (Laut geben) open one's mouth.

müde ['my:də] a tired.

Müdigkeit ['my:dɪçkait] f tiredness.

Muff [mʊf] m -(e)s, -e (Handwärmer) muff; **~el** m -s, - (col) killjoy, sourpuss; **m~ig** a Luft musty.

Mühe ['my:ə] f -, -n trouble, pains pl; **mit Müh und Not** with great difficulty; **sich** (dat) **~ geben** go to a lot of trouble; **m~los** a without trouble, easy.

muhen ['mu:ən] vi low, moo.

mühevoll a laborious, arduous.

Mühle ['my:lə] f -, -n mill; (Kaffee~) grinder.

Müh- cpd: **~sal** f -, -e hardship, tribulation; **m~sam** a arduous, troublesome; **m~selig** a arduous, laborious.

Mulatte [mu'latə] m -, -n, **Mulattin** f mulatto.

Mulde ['mʊldə] f -, -n hollow, depression.

Mull [mʊl] m -(e)s, -e thin muslin; **~binde** f gauze bandage.

Müll [mʏl] m -(e)s refuse; **~abfuhr** f rubbish disposal; (Leute) dustmen pl; **~abladeplatz** m rubbish dump; **~eimer** m dustbin, garbage can (US); **~er** m -s, - miller; **~haufen** m rubbish heap; **~schlucker** m -s, - garbage disposal unit; **~wagen** m dustcart, garbage truck (US).

mulmig ['mʊlmɪç] a rotten; (col) dodgy; **jdm ist ~** sb feels funny.

multiplizieren [multipli'tsi:rən] vt multiply.

Mumie ['mu:miə] f mummy.

Mumm [mʊm] m -s (col) gumption, nerve.

Mund [mʊnt] m -(e)s, -̈er ['mʏndər] mouth; **~art** f dialect.

Mündel ['mʏndəl] nt -s, - ward.

münden ['mʏndən] vi flow (in +acc into).

Mund- cpd: **m~faul** a taciturn; **~fäule** f - (Med) ulcerative stomatitis; **~geruch** m bad breath; **~harmonika** f mouth organ.

mündig ['mʏndɪç] a of age; **M~keit** f majority.

mündlich ['mʏntlɪç] a oral.

Mund- cpd: **~stück** nt mouthpiece; (Zigaretten~) tip; **m~tot** a: **jdn m~tot machen** muzzle sb.

Mündung ['mʏndʊŋ] f mouth; (Gewehr) muzzle.

Mund- cpd: **~wasser** nt mouthwash; **~werk** nt: **ein großes ~werk haben** have a big mouth; **~winkel** m corner of the mouth.

Munition [munitsi'o:n] f ammunition; **~slager** nt ammunition dump.

munkeln ['mʊŋkəln] vi whisper, mutter.

Münster ['mʏnstər] nt -s, - minster.

munter ['mʊntər] a lively; **M~keit** f liveliness.

Münze ['mʏntsə] f -, -n coin; **m~n** vt coin, mint; **auf jdn gemünzt sein** be aimed at sb.

Münzfernsprecher ['mʏntsfɛrnʃprɛçər] *m* callbox, pay phone (*US*).

mürb(e) ['mʏrb(ə)] *a Gestein* crumbly; *Holz* rotten; *Gebäck* crisp; **jdn ~ machen** wear sb down; **M~(e)teig** *m* shortcrust pastry.

murmeln ['murməln] *vti* murmur, mutter.

Murmeltier ['murməlti:r] *nt* marmot.

murren ['murən] *vi* grumble, grouse.

mürrisch ['mʏrɪʃ] *a* sullen.

Mus [mu:s] *nt* **-es, -e** puree.

Muschel ['muʃəl] *f* **-, -n** mussel; (*—schale*) shell; (*Telefon—*) receiver.

Muse ['mu:zə] *f* **-, -n** muse.

Museum [mu'ze:um] *nt* **-s, Museen** museum.

Musik [mu'zi:k] *f* music; (*Kapelle*) band; **m~alisch** [-'ka:lɪʃ] *a* musical; **~box** *f* jukebox; **~er** ['mu:zikər] *m* **-s, -** musician; **~hochschule** *f* music school; **~instrument** *nt* musical instrument; **~truhe** *f* radiogram.

musizieren [muzi'tsi:rən] *vi* make music.

Muskat [mus'ka:t] *m* **-(e)s, -e** nutmeg.

Muskel ['muskəl] *m* **-s, -n** muscle; **~kater** *m*: **einen ~kater haben** be stiff.

Muskulatur [muskula'tu:r] *f* muscular system.

muskulös [musku'lø:s] *a* muscular.

Muß [mus] *nt* **-** necessity, must.

Muße ['mu:sə] *f* **-** leisure.

müssen ['mʏsən] *vi irreg* must, have to; **er hat gehen ~** he (has) had to go.

müßig ['my:sɪç] *a* idle; **M~gang** *m* idleness.

Muster ['mustər] *nt* **-s, -** model; (*Dessin*) pattern; (*Probe*) sample; **~ ohne Wert** free sample; **m~gültig** *a* exemplary; **m~n** *vt Tapete* pattern; (*fig, Mil*) examine; *Truppen* inspect; **~schüler** *m* model pupil; **~ung** *f* (*von Stoff*) pattern; (*Mil*) inspection.

Mut [mu:t] *m* courage; **nur ~!** cheer up!; **jdm ~ machen** encourage sb; **m~ig** *a* courageous; **m~los** *a* discouraged, despondent.

mutmaßlich ['mu:tma:slɪç] *a* presumed; *ad* probably.

Mutter ['mutər] *f* **-, ˮ** mother; *pl* **~n** (*Schrauben—*) nut; **~land** *nt* mother country.

mütterlich ['mʏtərlɪç] *a* motherly; **~erseits** *ad* on the mother's side.

Mutter- *cpd*: **~liebe** *f* motherly love; **~mal** *nt* birthmark, mole; **~schaft** *f* motherhood, maternity; **~schutz** *m* maternity regulations; **'m~seelen-a'llein** *a* all alone; **~sprache** *f* native language; **~tag** *m* Mother's Day.

mutwillig ['mu:tvɪlɪç] *a* malicious, deliberate.

Mütze ['mʏtsə] *f* **-, -n** cap.

mysteriös [mʏsteri'ø:s] *a* mysterious.

Mystik ['mʏstɪk] *f* mysticism; **~er** *m* **-s, -** mystic.

Mythos ['my:tɔs] *m* **-, Mythen** myth.

N

N, n [ɛn] *nt* N, n.

na [na] *interj* well.

Nabel ['na:bəl] *m* **-s, -** navel; **~schnur** *f* umbilical cord.

nach [na:x] *prep +dat* after; (*in Richtung*) to; (*gemäß*) according to; **~ oben/hinten** up/back; **ihm ~!** after him!; **~ wie vor** still; **~ und ~** gradually; **dem Namen ~ judging by his name; **~äffen** *vt* ape; **~ahmen** *vt* imitate; **N~ahmung** *f* imitation.

Nachbar(in *f*) ['naxba:r(ɪn)] *m* **-s, -n** neighbour; **~haus** *nt*: **im ~haus** next door; **n~lich** *a* neighbourly; **~schaft** *f* neighbourhood; **~staat** *m* neighbouring state.

nach- *cpd*: **~bestellen** *vt* order again; **N~bestellung** *f* (*Comm*) repeat order; **~bilden** *vt* copy; **N~bildung** imitation, copy; **~blicken** *vi* look or gaze after; **~datieren** *vt* postdate.

nachdem [na:x'de:m] *cj* after; (*weil*) since; **je ~ (ob)** it depends (whether).

nach- *cpd*: **~denken** *vi irreg* think (*über +acc* about); **N~denken** *nt* **-s** reflection, meditation; **~denklich** *a* thoughtful, pensive.

Nachdruck ['na:xdruk] *m* emphasis; (*Print*) reprint, reproduction.

nachdrücklich ['na:xdrʏklɪç] *a* emphatic.

nacheifern ['na:xaɪfərn] *vi* emulate (*jdm* sb).

nacheinander [na:x'aɪ'nandər] *ad* one after the other.

nachempfinden ['na:xɛmpfɪndən] *vt irreg*: **jdm etw ~** feel sth with sb.

Nacherzählung ['na:xɛrtsɛ:luŋ] *f* reproduction (of a story).

Nachfahr ['na:xfa:r] *m* **-s, -en** descendant.

Nachfolge ['na:xfɔlgə] *f* succession; **n~n** *vi* (*lit*) follow (*jdm/etw* sb/sth); **~r(in** *f*) *m* **-s, -** successor.

nach- *cpd*: **~forschen** *vti* investigate; **N~forschung** *f* investigation.

Nachfrage ['na:xfra:gə] *f* inquiry; (*Comm*) demand; **n~n** *vi* inquire.

nach- *cpd*: **~fühlen** *vt* see **~empfinden**; **~füllen** *vt* refill; **~geben** *vi irreg* give way, yield.

Nach- *cpd*: **~gebühr** *f* surcharge; (*Post*) excess postage; **~geburt** *f* afterbirth.

nachgehen ['na:xge:ən] *vi irreg* follow (*jdm* sb); (*erforschen*) inquire (*einer Sache* into sth); (*Uhr*) be slow.

Nachgeschmack ['na:xgəʃmak] *m* aftertaste.

nachgiebig ['na:xgi:bɪç] *a* soft, accommodating; **N~keit** *f* softness.

Nachhall ['na:xhal] *m* resonance; **n~en** *vi* resound.

nachhaltig ['na:xhaltɪç] *a* lasting; *Widerstand* persistent.

nachhelfen ['na:xhɛlfən] *vi irreg* assist, help (*jdm* sb).

nachher [na:x'he:r] *ad* afterwards.

Nachhilfeunterricht ['naːxhɪlfə‐ʊntərrɪçt] *m* extra tuition.

nachholen ['naːxhoːlən] *vt* catch up with; *Versäumtes* make up for.

Nachkomme ['naːxkɔmə] *m* -, -n descendant; n~n *vi irreg* follow; *einer Verpflichtung* fulfil; ~nschaft *f* descendants *pl*.

Nachkriegs- ['naːxkriːks] *in cpds* postwar; ~zeit *f* postwar period.

Nach- *cpd*: ~laß *m* -lasses, -lässe (*Comm*) discount, rebate; (*Erbe*) estate; n~lassen *irreg vt Strafe* remit; *Summe* take off; *Schulden* cancel; *vi* decrease, ease off; (*Sturm auch*) die down; (*schlechter werden*) deteriorate; **er hat n~gelassen** he has got worse; n~lässig *a* negligent, careless; n~lässigkeit *f* negligence, carelessness.

nachlaufen ['naːxlaʊfən] *vi irreg* run after, chase (*jdm* sb).

nachmachen ['naːxmaxən] *vt* imitate, copy (*jdm etw* sth from sb); (*fälschen*) counterfeit.

Nachmittag ['naːxmɪtaːk] *m* afternoon; **am ~, n~s** *ad* in the afternoon.

Nach- *cpd*: ~nahme *f* -, -n cash on delivery; **per ~nahme** C.O.D.; ~name *m* surname; ~porto *nt* excess postage.

nachprüfen ['naːxpryːfən] *vt* check, verify.

nachrechnen ['naːxrɛçnən] *vt* check.

Nachrede ['naːxreːdə] *f*: **üble** ~ libel; slander.

Nachricht ['naːxrɪçt] *f* -, -en (piece of) news; (*Mitteilung*) message; ~en *pl* news; ~enagentur *f* news agency; ~endienst *m* (*Mil*) intelligence service; ~ensprecher(in *f*) *m* newsreader; ~entechnik *f* telecommunications *sing*.

nachrücken ['naːxrʏkən] *vi* move up.

Nachruf ['naːxruːf] *m* obituary (notice).

nachsagen ['naːxzaːgən] *vt* repeat; **jdm etw ~** say sth of sb.

nachschicken ['naːxʃɪkən] *vt* forward.

Nachschlag- ['naːxʃlaːg] *cpd*: n~en *vt irreg* look up; *vi*: **jdm n~en** take after sb; ~ewerk *nt* reference boook.

Nach- *cpd*: ~schlüssel *m* master key; ~schub *m* supplies *pl*; (*Truppen*) reinforcements *pl*.

nachsehen ['naːxzeːən] *irreg vt* (*prüfen*) check; **jdm etw ~** forgive sb sth; *vi* look after (*jdm* sb); (*erforschen*) look and see; **das N~ haben** come off worst.

nachsenden ['naːxzɛndən] *vt irreg* send on, forward.

Nachsicht ['naːxzɪçt] *f* - indulgence, leniency; n~ig *a* indulgent, lenient.

nachsitzen ['naːxzɪtsən] *vi irreg* (*Sch*) be kept in.

Nachspeise ['naːxʃpaɪzə] *f* dessert, sweet, pudding.

Nachspiel ['naːxʃpiːl] *nt* epilogue; (*fig*) sequel.

nachsprechen ['naːxʃprɛçən] *vt irreg* repeat (*jdm* after sb).

nächst [nɛːçst] *prep* +*dat* (*räumlich*) next to; (*außer*) apart from; ~beste(r,s) *a* first that comes along; (*zweitbeste*) next best;

N~e(r) *mf* neighbour; ~e(r,s) next; (*nächstgelegen*) nearest; **N~enliebe** *f* love for one's fellow men; ~ens *ad* shortly, soon; ~liegend *a* (*lit*) nearest; (*fig*) obvious; ~möglich *a* next possible.

nachsuchen ['naːxzuːxən] *vi*: **um etw ~** ask *or* apply for sth.

Nacht [naxt] *f* -, "e night.

Nachteil ['naːxtaɪl] *m* disadvantage; n~ig *a* disadvantageous.

Nachthemd *nt* nightshirt; nightdress.

Nachtigall ['naxtɪgal] *f* -, -en nightingale.

Nachtisch ['naːxtɪʃ] *m* see **Nachspeise**.

nächtlich ['nɛçtlɪç] *a* nightly.

Nach- *cpd*: ~trag *m* -(e)s, -träge supplement; n~tragen *vt irreg* carry (*jdm* after sb); (*zufügen*) add; **jdm etw n~tragen** hold sth against sb; n~tragend *a* resentful; n~träglich *a,ad* later, subsequent(ly); additional(ly); n~trauern *vi*: **jdm/etw n~trauern** mourn the loss of sb/sth.

Nacht- *cpd*: ~ruhe *f* sleep; n~s *ad* by night; ~schicht *f* nightshift; n~süber *ad* during the night; ~tarif *m* off-peak tariff; ~tisch *m* bedside table; ~topf *m* chamberpot; ~wächter *m* night watchman.

Nach- *cpd*: ~untersuchung *f* checkup; n~wachsen *vi irreg* grow again; ~wehen *pl* afterpains *pl*; (*fig*) aftereffects *pl*.

Nachweis ['naːxvaɪs] *m* -es, -e proof; n~bar *a* provable, demonstrable; n~en ['naːxvaɪzən] *vt irreg* prove; **jdm etw n~en** point sth out to sb; n~lich *a* evident, demonstrable.

nach- *cpd*: ~winken *vi* wave (*jdm* after sb); ~wirken *vi* have after-effects; **N~wirkung** *f* after-effect; **N~wort** *nt* appendix; **N~wuchs** *m* offspring; (*beruflich etc*) new recruits *pl*; ~zahlen *vti* pay extra; **N~zahlung** *f* additional payment; (*zurückdatiert*) back pay; ~zählen *vt* count again; **N~zügler** *m* -s, - straggler.

Nacken ['nakən] *m* -s, - nape of the neck.

nackt [nakt] *a* naked; *Tatsachen* plain, bare; **N~heit** *f* nakedness; **N~kultur** *f* nudism.

Nadel ['naːdəl] *f* -, -n needle; (*Steck—*) pin; ~kissen *nt* pincushion; ~öhr *nt* eye of a needle; ~wald *m* coniferous forest.

Nagel ['naːgəl] *m* -s, " nail; ~feile *f* nailfile; ~haut *f* cuticle; ~lack *m* nail varnish; n~n *vti* nail; n~neu *a* brandnew; ~schere *f* nail scissors *pl*.

nagen ['naːgən] *vti* gnaw.

Nagetier ['naːgətiːr] *nt* rodent.

nah(e) ['naː(ə)] *a,ad* (*räumlich*) near(by); *Verwandte* near; *Freunde* close; (*zeitlich*) near, close; *prep* +*dat* near (to), close to; **N~aufnahme** *f* close-up.

Nähe ['nɛːə] *f* - nearness, proximity; (*Umgebung*) vicinity; **in der ~** close by; at hand; **aus der ~** from close to.

nahe- *cpd*: ~bei *ad* nearby; ~gehen *vi irreg* grieve (*jdm* sb); ~kommen *vi irreg* get close (*jdm* to sb); ~legen *vt*: **jdm etw ~legen** suggest sth to sb; ~liegen *vi* irreg be obvious; **~liegend** a obvious; **~n** vir approach, draw near.

Näh- ['nɛ:] cpd: **~en** vti sew; **n~er** a,ad nearer; Erklärung, Erkundigung more detailed; **~ere(s)** nt details pl, particulars pl; **~erei** f sewing, needlework; **~erin** f seamstress; **n~erkommen** vir irreg get closer; **n~ern** vr approach; **~erungswert** m approximate value.

nahe- cpd: **~stehen** vi irreg be close (jdm to sb); **einer Sache ~stehen** sympathize with sth; **~stehend** a close; **~treten** vi irreg: **jdm (zu) ~treten** offend sb; **~zu** ad nearly.

Näh- cpd: **~garn** nt thread; **~kasten** m workbox; **~maschine** f sewing machine; **~nadel** f needle.

nähren ['nɛ:rən] vtr feed.

nahrhaft ['na:rhaft] a nourishing, nutritious.

Nähr- ['nɛ:r] cpd: **~gehalt** m nutritional value; **~stoffe** pl nutrients pl.

Nahrung [na:ruŋ] f food; (fig auch) sustenance; **~smittel** nt foodstuffs pl; **~smittelindustrie** f food industry; **~ssuche** f search for food.

Nährwert m nutritional value.

Naht [na:t] f -, -̈e seam; (Med) suture; (Tech) join; **n~los** a seamless; **n~los ineinander übergehen** follow without a gap.

Nah- cpd: **~verkehr** m local traffic; **~verkehrszug** m local train; **~ziel** nt immediate objective.

naiv [na'i:f] a naive; **N~ität** [naivi'tɛ:t] f naivety.

Name ['na:mə] m -ns, -n name; **im ~n von** on behalf of; **n~ns** ad by the name of; **n~ntlich** a by name; ad particularly, especially.

namhaft ['na:mhaft] a (berühmt) famed, renowned; (beträchtlich) considerable; **~machen** name.

nämlich ['nɛ:mlıç] ad that is to say, namely; (denn) since; **der/die/das ~e** the same.

Napf [napf] m -(e)s, -̈e bowl, dish.

Narbe ['narbə] f -, -n scar.

narbig ['narbıç] a scarred.

Narkose [nar'ko:zə] f -, -n anaesthetic.

Narr [nar] m -en, -en fool; **n~en** vt fool; **~heit** f foolishness.

Närr- ['nɛr] cpd: **~in** f fool; **n~isch** a foolish, crazy.

Narzisse [nar'tsısə] f -, -n narcissus; daffodil.

nasch- ['naʃ] cpd: **~en** vti nibble; eat secretly; **~haft** a sweet-toothed.

Nase ['na:zə] f -, -n nose; **~nbluten** nt -s nosebleed; **~nloch** nt nostril; **~nrücken** m bridge of the nose; **~ntropfen** pl nose drops pl; **n~weis** a pert, cheeky; (neugierig) nosey.

Nashorn ['na:shɔrn] nt rhinoceros.

naß [nas] a wet.

Nässe ['nɛsə] f - wetness; **n~n** vt wet.

Naß- cpd: **n~kalt** a wet and cold; **~rasur** f wet shave.

Nation [natsi'o:n] f nation.

national [natsio'na:l] a national;

N~hymne f national anthem; **~isieren** [-i'zi:rən] vt nationalize; **N~i'sierung** f nationalization; **N~ismus** [-'lısmʊs] m nationalism; **~istisch** [-'lıstıʃ] a nationalistic; **N~i'tät** f nationality; **N~mannschaft** f national team; **N~sozialismus** m national socialism.

Natron ['na:trɔn] nt -s soda.

Natter ['natər] f -, -n adder.

Natur [na'tu:r] f nature; (körperlich) constitution; **~alien** [natu'ra:liən] pl natural produce; **in ~alien** in kind; **~a'lismus** m naturalism; **~erscheinung** f natural phenomenon or event; **n~farben** a natural coloured; **n~gemäß** a natural; **~geschichte** f natural history; **~gesetz** nt law of nature; **~katastrophe** f natural disaster.

natürlich [na'ty:rlıç] a natural; ad naturally; **~erweise** ad naturally, of course; **N~keit** f naturalness.

Natur- cpd: **~produkt** nt natural product; **n~rein** a natural, pure; **~schutzgebiet** nt nature reserve; **~wissenschaft** f natural science; **~wissenschaftler(in f)** m scientist; **~zustand** m natural state.

nautisch ['nautıʃ] a nautical.

Navelorange ['na:vəlorã:ʒə] f navel orange.

Navigation [navigatsi'o:n] f navigation; **~sfehler** m navigational error; **~sinstrumente** m pl navigation instruments pl.

Nazi ['na:tsi] m -s, -s Nazi.

Nebel ['ne:bəl] m -s, - fog, mist; **n~ig** a foggy, misty; **~scheinwerfer** m foglamp.

neben ['ne:bən] prep +acc or dat next to; (außer) apart from, besides; **~an** [ne:bən'an] ad next door; **N~anschluß** m (Tel) extension; **~bei** [ne:bən'bai] ad at the same time; (außerdem) additionally; (beiläufig) incidentally; **N~beschäftigung** f sideline; **N~buhler(in f)** m -s, - rival; **~einander** [ne:bən'ai'nandər] ad side by side; **~einanderlegen** vt put next to each other; **N~eingang** m side entrance; **N~erscheinung** f side effect; **N~fach** nt subsidiary subject; **N~fluß** m tributary; **N~geräusch** nt (Rad) atmospherics pl, interference; **~her** [ne:bən'he:r] ad (zusätzlich) besides; (gleichzeitig) at the same time; (daneben) alongside; **~herfahren** vi irreg drive alongside; **N~kosten** pl extra charges pl, extras pl; **N~produkt** nt by-product; **N~rolle** f minor part; **N~sache** f trifle, side issue; **n~sächlich** a minor, peripheral; **N~straße** f side street; **N~zimmer** nt adjoining room.

Necessaire [nesɛ'sɛ:r] nt -s, -s (Näh—) needlework box; (Nagel—) manicure case.

neck- ['nɛk] cpd: **~en** vt tease; **N~e'rei** f teasing; **~isch** a coy; Einfall, Lied amusing.

Neffe ['nɛfə] m -n, -n nephew.

negativ [nega'ti:f] a negative; **N~** nt -s, -e (Phot) negative.

Neger ['ne:gər] m -s, - negro; **~in** f negress.

negieren [ne'gi:rən] *vt* (*bestreiten*) deny; (*verneinen*) negate.

nehmen ['ne:mən] *vt irreg* take; **jdn zu sich ~** take sb in; **sich ernst ~** take o.s. seriously; **nimm dir noch einmal** help yourself.

Neid [naɪt] *m* -(e)s envy; **~er** *m* -s, - envier; **n~isch** *a* envious, jealous.

neigen ['naɪgən] *vt* incline, lean; *Kopf* bow; *vi*: **zu etw ~** tend to sth.

Neigung *f* (*des Geländes*) slope; (*Tendenz*) tendency, inclination; (*Vorliebe*) liking; (*Zuneigung*) affection; **~swinkel** *m* angle of inclination.

nein [naɪn] *ad* no.

Nelke ['nɛlkə] *f* -, -n carnation, pink; (*Gewürz*) clove.

Nenn- ['nɛn] *cpd*: **n~en** *vt irreg* name; (*mit Namen*) call; **n~enswert** *a* worth mentioning; **~er** *m* -s, - denominator; **~ung** *f* naming; **~wert** *m* nominal value; (*Comm*) par.

Neon ['ne:ɔn] *nt* -s neon; **~licht** *nt* neon light; **~röhre** *f* neon tube.

Nerv [nɛrf] *m* -s, -en nerve; **jdm auf die ~en gehen** get on sb's nerves; **n~enaufreibend** *a* nerve-racking; **~enbündel** *nt* bundle of nerves; **~enheilanstalt** *f* mental home; **n~enkrank** *a* mentally ill; **~enschwäche** *f* neurasthenia; **~ensystem** *nt* nervous system; **~enzusammenbruch** *m* nervous breakdown; **n~ös** [nɛr'vø:s] *a* nervous; **~osität** *f* nervousness; **n~tötend** *a* nerve-racking; *Arbeit* soul-destroying.

Nerz [nɛrts] *m* -es, -e mink.

Nessel ['nɛsəl] *f* -, -n nettle.

Nest [nɛst] *nt* -(e)s, -er nest; (*col: Ort*) dump; **n~eln** *vi* fumble *or* fiddle about (*an* +*dat* with).

nett [nɛt] *a* nice; (*freundlich auch*) kind; **~erweise** *ad* kindly; **~o** *ad* net.

Netz [nɛts] *nt* -es, -e net; (*Gepäck~*) rack; (*Einkaufs~*) string bag; (*Spinnen~*) web; (*System*) network; **jdm ins ~ gehen** (*fig*) fall into sb's trap; **~anschluß** *m* mains connection; **~haut** *f* retina.

neu [nɔy] *a* new; *Sprache, Geschichte* modern; **seit ~estem** (since) recently; **~ schreiben** rewrite, write again; **N~anschaffung** *f* new purchase *or* acquisition; **~artig** *a* a new kind of; **N~auflage** *f*, **N~ausgabe** *f* new edition; **N~bau** *m* -s, -ten new building; **~erdings** *ad* (*kürzlich*) (since) recently; (*von neuem*) again; **N~erung** *f* innovation, new departure; **N~gier** *f* curiosity; **~gierig** *a* curious; **N~heit** *f* newness; novelty; **N~igkeit** *f* news; **N~jahr** *nt* New Year; **~lich** *ad* recently, the other day; **N~ling** *m* novice; **N~mond** *m* new moon.

neun [nɔyn] *num* nine; **~zehn** *num* nineteen; **~zig** *num* ninety.

neureich *a* nouveau riche; **N~e(r)** *m/f* nouveau riche.

Neur- *cpd*: **~ose** [nɔy'ro:zə] *f* -, -n neurosis; **~otiker** [nɔy'ro:tikər] *m* -s, - neurotic; **n~otisch** *a* neurotic.

Neutr- *cpd*: **n~al** [nɔy'tra:l] *a* neutral; **~alität** *f* neutrality; **n~alisieren** *vt* neutralize; **~on** ['nɔytrɔn] *nt* -s, -en neutron; **~um** ['nɔytrum] *nt* -s, -a *or* -en neuter.

Neu- *cpd*: **~wert** *m* purchase price; **~zeit** *f* modern age; **n~zeitlich** *a* modern, recent.

nicht [nɪçt] *ad* not; *pref* non-; **~ wahr?** isn't it/he?, don't you *etc*; **~ doch!** don't!; **~ berühren!** do not touch! **was du ~ sagst!** the things you say!; **N~achtung** *f* disregard; **N~angriffspakt** *m* non-aggression pact.

Nichte ['nɪçtə] *f* -, -n niece.

nichtig ['nɪçtɪç] *a* (*ungültig*) null, void; (*wertlos*) futile; **N~keit** *f* nullity, invalidity; (*Sinnlosigkeit*) futility.

Nicht- *cpd*: **~raucher(in** *f*) *m* nonsmoker; **n~rostend** *a* stainless.

nichts [nɪçts] *pron* nothing; **für ~ und wieder ~** for nothing at all; **N~** *nt* -es nothingness; (*pej: Person*) nonentity; **~destoweniger** *ad* nevertheless; **N~nutz** *m* -es, -e good-for-nothing; **~nutzig** *a* worthless, useless; **~sagend** *a* meaningless; **N~tun** *nt* -s idleness.

Nickel ['nɪkəl] *nt* -s nickel.

nicken ['nɪkən] *vi* nod.

Nickerchen ['nɪkərçən] *nt* nap.

nie [ni:] *ad* never; **~ wieder** *or* **mehr** never again; **~ und nimmer** never ever.

nieder ['ni:dər] *a* low; (*gering*) inferior; *ad* down; **N~gang** *m* decline; **~gehen** *vi irreg* descend; (*Aviat*) come down; (*Regen*) fall; (*Boxer*) go down; **~geschlagen** *a* depressed, dejected; **N~geschlagenheit** *f* depression, dejection; **N~lage** *f* defeat; (*Lager*) depot; (*Filiale*) branch; **~lassen** *vr irreg* (*sich setzen*) sit down; (*an Ort*) settle (down); (*Arzt, Rechtsanwalt*) set up a practice; **N~lassung** *f* settlement; (*Comm*) branch; **~legen** *vt* lay down; *Arbeit* stop; *Amt* resign; **~machen** *vt* mow down; **N~schlag** *m* (*Chem*) precipitate, sediment; (*Met*) precipitation; rainfall; (*Boxen*) knockdown; **~schlagen** *irreg vt Gegner* beat down; *Augen* lower; (*Jur*) *Prozeß* dismiss; *Aufstand* put down; *vr* (*Chem*) precipitate; **N~schrift** *f* transcription; **~trächtig** *a* base, mean; **N~trächtigkeit** *f* meanness, baseness; outrage; **N~ung** *f* (*Geog*) depression; flats *pl*.

niedlich ['ni:tlɪç] *a* sweet, nice, cute.

niedrig ['ni:drɪç] *a* low; *Stand* lowly, humble; *Gesinnung* mean.

niemals ['ni:ma:ls] *ad* never.

niemand ['ni:mant] *pron* nobody, no one; **N~sland** *nt* no-man's land.

Niere ['ni:rə] *f* -, -n kidney; **~nentzündung** *f* kidney infection.

nieseln ['ni:zəln] *vi* drizzle.

niesen ['ni:zən] *vi* sneeze.

Niet ['ni:t] *m* -(e)s, -e, -e *f* -, -n (*Tech*) rivet; (*Los*) blank; (*Reinfall*) flop; (*Mensch*) failure; **n~en** *vt* rivet.

Nihil- *cpd*: **~ismus** [nihi'lɪsmus] *m*

nihilism; ~ist [nihi'list] m nihilist; n~istisch a nihilistic.

Nikotin [niko'ti:n] nt -s nicotine.

Nilpferd ['ni:lpfe:rt] nt hippopotamus.

nimmersatt ['nɪmərzat] a insatiable; N~ m -(e)s, -e glutton.

nippen ['nɪpən] vti sip.

Nippsachen ['nɪpzaxən] pl knick-knacks pl.

nirgends ['nɪrgənts], nirgendwo ['nɪrgəntvo:] ad nowhere.

Nische ['ni:ʃə] f -, -n niche.

nisten ['nɪstən] vi nest.

Nitrat [ni'tra:t] nt -(e)s, -e nitrate.

Niveau [ni'vo:] nt -s, -s level.

Nixe ['nɪksə] f -, -n water nymph.

noch [nɔx] ad still; (in Zukunft) still, yet; one day; (außerdem) else; cj nor; ~ nie never (yet); ~ nicht not yet; immer ~ still; ~ heute today; ~ vor einer Woche only a week ago; und wenn es ~ so schwer ist however hard it is; ~ einmal again; ~ dreimal three more times; ~ und ~ heaps of; (mit Verb) again and again; ~mal(s) ad again, once more; ~malig a repeated.

Nockenwelle ['nɔkənvɛlə] f camshaft.

Nominativ ['no:minati:f] m -s, -e nominative.

nominell [nomi'nɛl] a nominal.

Nonne ['nɔnə] f -, -n nun; ~nkloster nt convent.

Nord(en) ['nɔrd(ən)] m -s north; n~isch a northern; n~ische Kombination (Ski) nordic combination.

nördlich ['nœrtlɪç] a northerly, northern; ~ von, ~ prep +gen (to the) north of.

Nord- cpd: ~pol m North Pole; n~wärts ad northwards.

Nörg- ['nœrg] cpd: ~e'lei f grumbling; n~eln vi grumble; ~ler m -s, - grumbler.

Norm [nɔrm] f -, -en norm; (Größenvorschrift) standard; n~al [nɔr'ma:l] a normal; n~alerweise ad normally; n~ali'sieren vt normalize; vr return to normal; n~en vt standardize.

Not [no:t] f -, ¨e need; (Mangel) want; (Mühe) trouble; (Zwang) necessity; zur ~ if necessary; (gerade noch) just about; ~ar [no'ta:r] m -s, -e notary; n~ari'ell a notarial; ~ausgang m emergency exit; ~behelf m -s, -e makeshift; ~bremse f emergency brake; n~dürftig a scanty; (behelfsmäßig) makeshift; sich n~dürftig verständigen just about understand each other.

Note ['no:tə] f -, -n note; (Sch) mark; ~nblatt nt sheet of music; ~nschlüssel m clef; ~nständer m music stand.

Not- cpd: ~fall m (case of) emergency; n~falls ad if need be; n~gedrungen a necessary, unavoidable; etw n~gedrungen machen be forced to do sth.

notieren [no'ti:rən] vt note; (Comm) quote.

Notierung f (Comm) quotation.

nötig ['nø:tɪç] a necessary; etw ~ haben need sth; ~en vt compel, force; ~enfalls ad if necessary.

Notiz [no'ti:ts] f -, -en note; (Zeitungs—)

item; ~ nehmen take notice; ~buch nt notebook; ~zettel m piece of paper.

Not- cpd: ~lage f crisis, emergency; n~landen vi make a forced or emergency landing; n~leidend a needy; ~lösung f temporary solution; ~lüge f white lie.

notorisch [no'to:rɪʃ] a notorious.

Not- cpd: ~ruf m emergency call; ~stand m state of emergency; ~standsgesetz nt emergency law; ~unterkunft f emergency accommodation; ~verband m emergency dressing; ~wehr f - self-defence; n~wendig a necessary; ~wendigkeit f necessity; ~zucht f rape.

Novelle [no'vɛlə] f -, -n short story; (Jur) amendment.

November [no'vɛmbər] m -(s), - November.

Nu [nu:] m: im ~ in an instant.

Nuance [ny'ã:sə] f -, -n nuance.

nüchtern ['nʏçtərn] a sober; Magen empty; Urteil prudent; N~heit f sobriety.

Nudel ['nu:dəl] f -, -n noodle.

Null [nʊl] f -, -en nought, zero; (pej: Mensch) washout; n~ num zero; Fehler no; n~ Uhr midnight; n~ und nichtig null and void; ~punkt m zero; auf dem ~punkt at zero.

numerieren [nume'ri:rən] vt number.

numerisch [nu'me:rɪʃ] a numerical.

Nummer ['nʊmər] f -, -n number; ~nscheibe f telephone dial; ~nschild nt (Aut) number or license (US) plate.

nun [nu:n] ad now; interj well.

nur [nu:r] ad just, only.

Nuß [nʊs] f -, Nüsse nut; ~baum m walnut tree; hazelnut tree; ~knacker m -s, - nutcracker.

Nüster ['nʏstər] f -, -n nostril.

Nutte ['nʊtə] f -, -n tart.

nutz [nʊts], nütze ['nʏtsə] a: zu nichts ~ sein be useless; ~bar a: ~bar machen utilize; N~barmachung v utilization; ~bringend a profitable; ~en, nützen vt use (zu etw for sth); vi be of use; was nützt es? what's the use?, what use is it?; N~en m -s usefulness; profit; von N~en useful.

nützlich ['nʏtslɪç] a useful; N~keit f usefulness.

Nutz- cpd: n~los a useless; ~losigkeit f uselessness; ~nießer m -s, - beneficiary.

Nymphe ['nʏmfə] f -, -n nymph.

O

O, o [o:] nt O, o.

Oase [o'a:zə] f -, -n oasis.

ob [ɔp] cj if, whether; ~ das wohl wahr ist? can that be true?; und ~! you bet!

Obacht ['o:baxt] f: ~ geben pay attention.

Obdach ['ɔpdax] nt -(e)s shelter, lodging; o~los a homeless; ~lose(r) mf homeless person.

Obduktion [ɔpdʊktsi'o:n] f post-mortem.

obduzieren [ɔpduˈtsiːrən] vt do a post mortem on.

O-Beine [ˈoːbainə] pl bow or bandy legs pl.

oben [ˈoːbən] ad above; (in Haus) upstairs; **nach ~** up; **von ~** down; **~ ohne** topless; **jdn von ~ bis unten ansehen** look sb up and down; **Befehl von ~** orders from above; **~an** ad at the top; **~auf** ad up above, on the top; a (munter) in form; **~drein** ad into the bargain; **~erwähnt**, **~genannt** a above-mentioned; **~hin** ad cursorily, superficially.

Ober [ˈoːbər] m -s, - waiter; **~arm** m upper arm; **~arzt** m senior physician; **~aufsicht** f supervision; **~befehl** m supreme command; **~befehlshaber** m commander-in-chief; **~begriff** m generic term; **~bekleidung** f outer clothing; **~'bürgermeister** m lord mayor; **~deck** nt upper or top deck; **o~e(r,s)** a upper; **die ~en** the bosses; (Eccl) the superiors; **~fläche** f surface; **o~flächlich** a superficial; **~geschoß** nt upper storey; **o~halb** ad, prep +gen above; **~haupt** nt head, chief; **~haus** nt upper house; House of Lords; **~hemd** nt shirt; **~herrschaft** f supremacy, sovereignty; **~in** f matron; (Eccl) Mother Superior; **o~irdisch** a above ground; Leitung overhead; **~kellner** m head waiter; **~kiefer** m upper jaw; **~kommando** nt supreme command; **~körper** m trunk, upper part of body; **~leitung** f direction; (Elec) overhead cable; **~licht** nt skylight; **~lippe** f upper lip; **~prima** f-, **~primen** final year of secondary school; **~schenkel** m thigh; **~schicht** f upper classes pl; **~schule** f grammar school (Brit), high school (US); **~schwester** f (Med) matron; **~sekunda** f -, **-sekunden** seventh year of secondary school.

Oberst [ˈoːbərst] m -en or -s, -en or -e colonel; **o~e(r,s)** a very top, topmost.

Ober- cpd: **~stufe** f upper school; **~teil** nt upper part; **~tertia** f -tertsia] f -, **-tertien** fifth year of secondary school; **~wasser** nt: **~wasser haben/ bekommen** be/get on top (of things); **~weite** f bust/chest measurement.

obgleich [ɔpˈɡlaiç] cj although.

Obhut [ˈɔphuːt] f - care, protection; **in jds ~ sein** in sb's care.

obig [ˈoːbiç] a above.

Objekt [ɔpˈjɛkt] nt -(e)s, -e object; **~iv** [-ˈtiːf] nt -s, -e lens; **o~iv** a objective; **~ivi'tät** f objectivity.

Oblate [oˈblaːtə] f -, -n (Gebäck) wafer; (Eccl) host.

obligatorisch [obligaˈtoːriʃ] a compulsory, obligatory.

Oboe [oˈboːə] f -, -n oboe.

Obrigkeit [ˈoːbriçkait] f (Behörden) authorities pl, administration; (Regierung) government.

obschon [ɔpˈʃoːn] cj although.

Observatorium [ɔpzɛrvaˈtoːriʊm] nt observatory.

obskur [ɔpsˈkuːr] a obscure; (verdächtig) dubious.

Obst [oːpst] nt -(e)s fruit; **~bau** m fruit-

growing; **~baum** m fruit tree; **~garten** m orchard; **~händler** m fruiterer, fruit merchant; **~kuchen** m fruit tart.

obszön [ɔpsˈtsøːn] a obscene; **O~i'tät** f obscenity.

obwohl [ɔpˈvoːl] cj although.

Ochse [ˈɔksə] m -n, -n ox; **o~n** vti (col) cram, swot; **~nschwanzsuppe** f oxtail soup; **~nzunge** f oxtongue.

öd(e) [ˈøːd(ə)] a Land waste, barren; (fig) dull; **Ö~e** f -, -n desert, waste(land); (fig) tedium.

oder [ˈoːdər] cj or.

Ofen [ˈoːfən] m -s, ̈ oven; (Heiz~) fire, heater; (Kohle~) stove; (Hoch~) furnace; (Herd) cooker, stove; **~rohr** nt stovepipe.

offen [ˈɔfən] a open; (aufrichtig) frank; Stelle vacant; **~ gesagt** to be honest; **~bar** a obvious; **~baren** [ɔfənˈbaːrən] vt reveal, manifest; **O~'barung** f (Rel) revelation; **~bleiben** vi irreg (Fenster) stay open; (Frage, Entscheidung) remain open; **~halten** vi irreg keep open; **O~heit** f candour, frankness; **~herzig** a candid, frank; Kleid revealing; **O~herzigkeit** f frankness; **~kundig** a well-known; (klar) evident; **~lassen** vt irreg leave open; **~sichtlich** a evident, obvious; **~siv** [ɔfɛnˈziːf] a offensive; **O~'sive** f -, -n offensive; **~stehen** vi irreg be open; (Rechnung) be unpaid; **es steht Ihnen ~**, **es zu tun** you are at liberty to do it.

öffentlich [ˈœfəntliç] a public; **Ö~keit** f (Leute) public; (einer Versammlung etc) public nature; **in aller Ö~keit** in public; **an die Ö~keit dringen** reach the public ear.

offerieren [ɔfeˈriːrən] vt offer.

Offerte [ɔˈfɛrtə] f -, -n offer.

offiziell [ɔfitsiˈɛl] a official.

Offizier [ɔfiˈtsiːr] m -s, -e officer; **~skasino** nt officers' mess.

öffnen [ˈœfnən] vtr open; **jdm die Tür ~** open the door for sb.

Öffner [ˈœfnər] m -s, - opener.

Öffnung [ˈœfnʊŋ] f opening; **~szeiten** pl opening times pl.

oft [ɔft] ad often.

öfter [ˈœftər] ad more often or frequently; **~s** ad often, frequently.

oftmals ad often, frequently.

ohne [ˈoːnə] prep +acc, cj without; **das ist nicht ~** (col) it's not bad; **~ weiteres** without a second thought; (sofort) immediately; **~dies** [oːnəˈdiːs] ad anyway; **~einander** [oːnəˈnandər] ad without each other; **~gleichen** [oːnəˈɡlaiçən] a unsurpassed, without equal; **~hin** [oːnəˈhin] ad anyway, in any case.

Ohnmacht [ˈoːnmaxt] f faint; (fig) impotence; **in ~ fallen** faint.

ohnmächtig [ˈoːnmɛçtiç] a in a faint, unconscious; (fig) weak, impotent; **sie ist ~** she has fainted.

Ohr [oːr] nt -(e)s, -en ear; (Gehör) hearing.

Öhr [øːr] nt -(e)s, -e eye.

Ohr- cpd: **~enarzt** m ear specialist; **o~enbetäubend** a deafening; **~en-**

schmalz *nt* earwax; ~enschmerzen *pl* earache; ~enschützer *m* -s, - earmuff; ~feige *f* slap on the face; box on the ears; o~feigen *vt* slap sb's face; box sb's ears; ~läppchen *nt* ear lobe; ~ringe *pl* earrings *pl*; ~wurm *m* earwig; (*Mus*) catchy tune.

okkupieren [ɔku'pi:rən] *vt* occupy.

ökonomisch [öko'no:mɪʃ] *a* economical.

Oktanzahl [ɔk'ta:ntsa:l] *f* (*bei Benzin*) octane.

Oktave [ɔk'ta:fə] *f* -, -n octave.

Oktober [ɔk'to:bər] *m* -(s), - October.

ökumenisch [öku'me:nɪʃ] *a* ecumenical.

Öl [ö:l] *nt* -(e)s, -e oil; ~baum *m* olive tree; ö~en *vt* oil; (*Tech*) lubricate; ~farbe *f* oil paint; ~feld *nt* oilfield; ~film *m* film of oil; ~heizung *f* oil-fired central heating; ö~ig *a* oily.

oliv [o'li:f] *a* olive-green; **O~e** [o'li:və] *f* -, -n olive.

Öl- *cpd*: ~meßstab *m* dipstick; ~pest *f* oil pollution; ~sardine *f* sardine; ~scheich *m* oil sheik; ~standanzeiger *m* (*Aut*) oil gauge; ~ung *f* lubrication; oiling; (*Eccl*) anointment; **die Letzte** ~ung Extreme Unction; ~wechsel *m* oil change; ~zeug *nt* oilskins *pl*.

Olymp- [o'lʏmp] *cpd*: ~iade [-i'a:də] *f* Olympic Games *pl*; ~iasieger(in *f*) [-iazi:gər(ɪn)] *m* Olympic champion; ~iateilnehmer(in *f*) *m*, ~ionike [-io'ni:kə] *m*, ~io'nikin *f* Olympic competitor; o~isch *a* Olympic.

Oma ['o:ma] *f* -, -s (*col*) granny.

Omelett [ɔm(ə)'lɛt] *nt* -(e)s, -s, **Omelette** *f* omlet(te).

Omen ['o:mɛn] *nt* -s, - *or* **Omina** omen.

Omnibus ['ɔmnibus] *m* (omni)bus.

Onanie [ona'ni:] *f* masturbation; o~ren *vi* masturbate.

Onkel ['ɔŋkəl] *m* -s, - uncle.

Opa ['o:pa] *m* -s, -s (*col*) grandpa.

Opal [o'pa:l] *m* -s, -e opal.

Oper ['o:pər] *f* -, -n opera; opera house; ~ation [operatsi'o:n] *f* operation; ~ationssaal *m* operating theatre; ~ette [ope'rɛtə] *f* operetta; o~ieren [ope'ri:rən] *vti* operate; ~nglas *nt* opera glasses *pl*; ~nhaus *nt* opera house; ~nsänger(in *f*) *m* operatic singer.

Opfer ['ɔpfər] *nt* -s, - sacrifice; (*Mensch*) victim; o~n *vt* sacrifice; ~stock *m* (*Eccl*) offertory box; ~ung *f* sacrifice.

Opium ['o:pium] *nt* -s opium.

opponieren [ɔpo'ni:rən] *vi* oppose (*gegen jdn/etw* sb/sth).

opportun [ɔpɔr'tu:n] *a* opportune; **O~ismus** [-'nɪsmus] *m* opportunism; **O~ist** [-'nɪst] *m* opportunist.

Opposition [ɔpozitsi'o:n] *f* opposition; o~ell [-'nɛl] *a* opposing.

Optik ['ɔptɪk] *f* optics *sing*; ~er *m* -s, - optician.

optimal [ɔpti'ma:l] *a* optimal, optimum.

Optimismus [ɔpti'mɪsmus] *m* optimism.

Optimist [ɔpti'mɪst] *m* optimist; o~isch *a* optimistic.

optisch ['ɔptɪʃ] *a* optical.

Orakel [o'ra:kəl] *nt* -s, - oracle.

Orange [o'rã:ʒə] *f* -, -n orange; o~ *a* orange; ~ade [orã'ʒa:də] *f* orangeade; ~at [orã'ʒa:t] *nt* -s, -e candied peel; ~nmarmelade *f* marmelade; ~nschale *f* orange peel.

Orchester [ɔr'kɛstər] *nt* -s, - orchestra.

Orchidee [ɔrçi'de:ə] *f* -, -n orchid.

Orden ['ɔrdən] *m* -s, - (*Eccl*) order; (*Mil*) decoration; ~sschwester *f* nun.

ordentlich ['ɔrdəntlɪç] *a* (*anständig*) decent, respectable; (*geordnet*) tidy, neat; (*col*: annehmbar) not bad; (*col*: tüchtig) real, proper; ~er Professor (full) professor; *ad* properly; **O~keit** *f* respectability; tidiness, neatness.

Ordinalzahl [ɔrdi'na:ltsa:l] *f* ordinal number.

ordinär [ɔrdi'nɛ:r] *a* common, vulgar.

ordnen ['ɔrdnən] *vt* order, put in order.

Ordner *m* -s, - steward; (*Comm*) file.

Ordnung *f* order; (*Ordnen*) ordering; (*Geordnetsein*) tidiness; o~sgemäß *a* proper, according to the rules; o~shalber *ad* as a matter of form; ~sliebe *f* tidiness, orderliness; ~sstrafe *f* fine; o~swidrig *a* contrary to the rules, irregular; ~szahl *f* ordinal number.

Organ [ɔr'ga:n] *nt* -s, -e organ; (*Stimme*) voice; ~isation [-izatsi'o:n] *f* organisation; ~isationstalent *nt* organizing ability; (*Person*) good organizer; ~isator [-i'za:tor] *m* organizer; o~isch *a* organic; o~isieren [-i'zi:rən] *vt* organize, arrange; (*col*: beschaffen) acquire; *vr* organize; ~ismus ['nɪsmus] *m* organism; ~ist [-'nɪst] *m* organist; ~verpflanzung *f* transplantation (of organs).

Orgasmus [ɔr'gasmus] *m* orgasm.

Orgel ['ɔrgəl] *f* -, -n organ; ~pfeife *f* organ pipe; **wie die ~pfeifen stehen** stand in order of height.

Orgie ['ɔrgiə] *f* orgy.

Orient [o'riɛnt] *m* -s Orient, east; ~ale [-'ta:lə] *m* -n, -n Oriental; o~alisch [-'ta:lɪʃ] *a* oriental; o~ieren [-'ti:rən] *vt* (*örtlich*) locate; (*fig*) inform; *vr* find one's way *or* bearings; inform oneself; ~ierung [-'ti:rʊŋ] *f* orientation; (*fig*) information; ~ierungssinn *m* sense of direction.

original [origi'na:l] *a* original; **O~** *nt* -s, -e original; **O~fassung** *f* original version; **O~i'tät** *f* originality.

originell [origi'nɛl] *a* original.

Orkan [ɔr'ka:n] *m* -(e)s, -e hurricane.

Ornament [ɔrna'mɛnt] *nt* decoration, ornament; o~al [-'ta:l] *a* decorative, ornamental.

Ort [ɔrt] *m* -(e)s, -e *or* ¨er place; **an ~ und Stelle** on the spot; o~en *vt* locate.

ortho- [ɔrto] *cpd*: ~dox [-'dɔks] *a* orthodox; **O~graphie** [-gra'fi:] *f* spelling, orthography; ~'graphisch *a* orthographic; **O~päde** [-'pɛ:də] *m* -n, -n orthopaedic specialist, orthopaedist; **O~pädie** [-pɛ'di:] *f* orthopaedics *sing*; ~'pädisch *a* orthopaedic.

örtlich ['œrtlɪç] *a* local; **Ö~keit** *f* locality.

Ort- *cpd*: ~sangabe *f* (name of the) town; o~sansässig *a* local; ~schaft *f* village, small town; o~sfremd *a* non-local;

~sfremde(r) mf stranger; ~sgespräch nt local (phone)call; ~sname m placename; ~snetz nt (Tel) local telephone exchange area; ~ssinn m sense of direction; ~szeit f local time; ~ung f locating.

Öse ['ø:zə] f -, -n loop, eye.

Ost- [ɔst] cpd: ~block m (Pol) Eastern bloc; ~en m -s east; o~entativ [ɔstɛntaˈtiːf] a pointed, ostentatious.

Oster- ['oːstər] cpd: ~ei nt Easter egg; ~fest nt Easter; ~glocke f daffodil; ~hase m Easter bunny; ~montag m Easter Monday; ~n nt -s, - Easter; ~sonntag m Easter Day or Sunday.

östlich ['œstlɪç] a eastern, easterly.

Ost- cpd: ~see f Baltic Sea; o~wärts ad eastwards; ~wind m east wind.

oszillieren [ɔstsɪˈliːrən] vi oscillate.

Otter ['ɔtər] m -s, - otter; f -, -n (Schlange) adder.

Ouvertüre [uvɛrˈtyːrə] f -, -n overture.

oval [oˈvaːl] a oval.

Ovation [ovatsiˈoːn] f ovation.

Ovulation [ovulatsiˈoːn] f ovulation.

Oxyd [ɔˈksyːt] nt -(e)s, -e oxide; o~leren [ɔksyˈdiːrən] vti oxidize; ~lerung f oxidization.

Ozean ['oːtseaːn] m -s, -e ocean; ~dampfer m (ocean-going) liner; o~isch [otseˈaːnɪʃ] a oceanic.

Ozon [oˈtsoːn] nt -s ozone.

P

P, p [peː] nt P, p.

Paar [paːr] nt -(e)s, -e pair; (Ehe—) couple; ein p~ a few; p~en vtr couple; Tiere mate; ~lauf m pair skating; p~mal ad: ein p~mal a few times; ~ung f combination; mating; p~weise ad in pairs; in couples.

Pacht [paxt] f -, -en lease; p~en vt lease.

Pächter ['pɛçtər] m -s, - leaseholder, tenant.

Pack [pak] m -(e)s, -e or -e bundle, pack; nt -(e)s (pej) mob, rabble.

Päckchen ['pɛkçən] nt small package; (Zigaretten) packet; (Post—) small parcel.

Pack- cpd: p~en vt pack; (fassen) grasp, seize; (col: schaffen) manage; (fig: fesseln) grip; ~en m -s, - bundle; (fig: Menge) heaps of; ~esel m (lit, fig) packhorse; ~papier nt brown paper, wrapping paper; ~ung f packet; (Pralinen—) box; (Med) compress.

Pädagog- [pɛdaˈgoːg] cpd: ~e m -n, -n teacher; ~ik f education; p~isch a educational, pedagogical.

Paddel ['padəl] nt -s, - paddle; ~boot nt canoe; p~n vi paddle.

paffen ['pafən] vti puff.

Page ['paːʒə] m -n, -n page; ~nkopf m pageboy.

Paillette [paiˈjɛtə] f sequin.

Paket [paˈkeːt] nt -(e)s, -e packet; (Post—) parcel; ~karte f dispatch note; ~post f parcel post; ~schalter m parcels counter.

Pakt [pakt] m -(e)s, -e pact.

Palast [paˈlast] m -es, Paläste palace.

Palette [paˈlɛtə] f palette; (Lade—) pallet.

Palme ['palmə] f -, -n palm (tree).

Palmsonntag m Palm Sunday.

Pampelmuse ['pampəlmuːzə] f -, -n grapefruit.

pampig ['pampɪç] a (col: frech) fresh.

panieren [paˈniːrən] vt (Cook) coat with egg and breadcrumbs.

Paniermehl [paˈniːrmeːl] nt breadcrumbs pl.

Panik ['paːnɪk] f panic.

panisch ['paːnɪʃ] a panic-stricken.

Panne ['panə] f -, -n (Aut etc) breakdown; (Mißgeschick) slip.

panschen ['panʃən] vi splash about; vt water down.

Panther ['pantər] m -s, - panther.

Pantoffel [panˈtɔfəl] m -s, -n slipper; ~held m (col) henpecked husband.

Pantomime [pantoˈmiːmə] f -, -n mime.

Panzer ['pantsər] m -s, - armour; (Platte) armour plate; (Fahrzeug) tank; ~glas nt bulletproof glass; p~n vtr armour; (fig) arm o.s.; ~schrank m strongbox.

Papa [paˈpaː] m -s, -s (col) dad, daddy; ~gei [-ˈgai] m -s, -en parrot.

Papier [paˈpiːr] nt -s, -e paper; (Wert—) share; ~fabrik f paper mill; ~geld nt paper money; ~korb m wastepaper basket; ~krieg m red tape; angry correspondence; ~tüte f paper bag.

Papp- [pap] cpd: ~deckel m, ~e f -, -n cardboard; ~einband m pasteboard; ~el f -, -n poplar; p~en vti (col) stick; ~enstiel m (col): keinen ~enstiel wert sein not be worth a thing; für einen ~enstiel bekommen get for a song; p~erlapapp interj rubbish; p~ig a sticky; ~maché [-maˈʃeː] nt -s, -s papiermâché.

Paprika ['paprika] m -s, -s (Gewürz) paprika; (—schote) pepper.

Papst [paːpst] m -(e)s, -e pope.

päpstlich ['pɛːpstlɪç] a papal.

Parabel [paˈraːbəl] f -, -n parable; (Math) parabola.

Parade [paˈraːdə] f (Mil) parade, review; (Sport) parry; ~marsch m march-past; ~schritt m goose-step.

Paradies [paraˈdiːs] nt -es, -e paradise; p~isch a heavenly.

paradox [paraˈdɔks] a paradoxical; P~ nt -es, -e paradox.

Paragraph [paraˈgraːf] m -en, -en paragraph; (Jur) section.

parallel [paraˈleːl] a parallel; P~e f parallel.

paramilitärisch [paramiliˈtɛːrɪʃ] a paramilitary.

Paranuß ['paːranus] f Brazil nut.

paraphieren [paraˈfiːrən] vt Vertrag initial.

Parasit [paraˈziːt] m -en, -en (lit, fig) parasite.

parat [paˈraːt] a ready.

Pärchen ['pɛːrçən] nt couple.

Parfüm [parˈfyːm] nt -s, -s or -e perfume;

~erie [-ɔ'ri:] f perfumery; ~flasche f scent bottle; p~leren [-'mi:rən] vt scent, perfume.

parieren [pa'ri:rən] vt parry; vi (col) obey.

Parität [pari'tɛ:t] f parity.

Park [park] m -s, -s park; ~anlage f park; (um Gebäude) grounds pl; p~en vti park; ~ett [par'kɛt] nt -(e)s, -e parquet (floor); (Theat) stalls pl; ~haus nt multi-storey car park; ~lücke f parking space; ~platz m parking place; car park, parking lot (US); ~scheibe f parking disc; ~uhr f parking meter; ~verbot nt no parking.

Parlament [parla'mɛnt] nt parliament; ~arier [-'ta:riər] m -s, - parliamentarian; p~arisch [-'ta:rɪʃ] a parliamentary; ~sbeschluß m vote of parliament; ~smitglied nt member of parliament; ~ssitzung f sitting (of parliament).

Parodie [paro'di:] f parody; p~ren vt parody.

Parole [pa'ro:lə] f -, -n password; (Wahlspruch) motto.

Partei [par'tai] f party; ~ ergreifen für jdn take sb's side; ~führung f party leadership; ~genosse m party member; p~isch a partial, biased; p~los a neutral; ~nahme f -, -n support, taking the part of; ~tag m party conference.

Parterre [par'tɛr] nt -s, -s ground floor; (Theat) stalls pl.

Partie [par'ti:] f part; (Spiel) game; (Ausflug) outing; (Mann, Frau) catch; (Comm) lot; mit von der ~ sein join in.

Partikel [par'ti:kəl] f -, -n particle.

Partisan [parti'za:n] m -s or -en, -en partisan.

Partitur [parti'tu:r] f (Mus) score.

Partizip [parti'tsi:p] nt -s, -ien participle.

Partner(in f) ['partnər] m -s, - partner; p~schaftlich a as partners.

Party ['pa:rti] f -, -s or Parties party.

Parzelle [par'tsɛlə] f plot, allotment.

Paß [pas] m -sses, -̈sse pass; (Ausweis) passport.

Pass- cpd: p~abel [pa'sa:bəl] a passable, reasonable; ~age [pa'sa:ʒə] f -, -n passage; ~agier [pasa'ʒi:r] m -s, -e passenger; ~agierdampfer m passenger steamer; ~agierflugzeug nt airliner; ~ant [pa'sant] m passer-by.

Paß- cpd: ~amt nt passport office; ~bild nt passport photograph.

passen ['pasən] vi fit; (Farbe) go (zu with); (auf Frage, Cards, Sport) pass; das paßt mir nicht that doesn't suit me; er paßt nicht zu dir he's not right for you; ~d a suitable; (zusammen-) matching; (ange-bracht) fitting; Zeit convenient.

passier- [pa'si:r] cpd: ~bar a passable; ~en vt pass; (durch Sieb) strain; vi happen; P~schein m pass, permit.

Passion [pasi'o:n] f passion; p~iert [-'ni:rt] a enthusiastic, passionate; ~sspiel nt Passion Play.

passiv ['pasi:f] a passive; P~ nt -s, -e passive; P~a pl (Comm) liabilities pl; P~i'tät f passiveness.

Paß- cpd: ~kontrolle f passport control;

~stelle f passport office; ~straße f (mountain) pass; ~zwang m require-ment to carry a passport.

Paste ['pastə] f -, -n paste.

Pastell [pas'tɛl] nt -(e)s, -e pastel.

Pastete [pas'te:tə] f -, -n pie.

pasteurisieren [pastöri'zi:rən] vt pasteurize.

Pastor ['pastɔr] m vicar; pastor, minister.

Pate ['pa:tə] m -n, -n godfather; ~nkind nt godchild.

Patent [pa'tɛnt] nt -(e)s, -e patent; (Mil) commission; p~ a clever; ~amt nt patent office; p~leren [-'ti:rən] vt patent; ~inhaber m patentee; ~schutz m patent right.

Pater ['pa:tər] m -s, - or Patres (Eccl) Father.

pathetisch [pa'te:tɪʃ] a emotional; bom-bastic.

Pathologe [pato'lo:gə] m -n, -n pathologist.

pathologisch a pathological.

Pathos ['pa:tɔs] nt - emotiveness, emotionalism.

Patient(in f) [patsi'ɛnt(ɪn)] m patient.

Patin ['pa:tɪn] f godmother; ~a ['pa:tina] f - patina.

Patriarch [patri'arç] m -en, -en patriarch; p~alisch [-'ça:lɪʃ] a patriarchal.

Patriot [patri'o:t] m -en, -en patriot; p~isch a patriotic; ~ismus [-'tɪsmʊs] m patriotism.

Patron [pa'tro:n] m -s, -e patron; (pej) beggar; ~e f -, -n cartridge; ~enhülse f cartridge case; ~in f patroness.

Patrouille [pa'truljə] f -, -n patrol.

patrouillieren [patrul'ji:rən] vi patrol.

patsch [patʃ] interj splash; P~e f -, -n (col: Händchen) paw; (Fliegen—) swat; (Feuer—) beater; (Bedrängnis) mess, jam; ~en vti smack, slap; (im Wasser) splash; ~naß a soaking wet.

patzig ['patsɪç] a (col) cheeky, saucy.

Pauke ['paukə] f -, -n kettledrum; auf die ~ hauen live it up; p~n vti (Sch) swot, cram; ~r m -s, - (col) teacher.

pausbäckig ['pausbɛkɪç] a a chubby-cheeked.

pauschal [pau'ʃa:l] a Kosten inclusive; Urteil sweeping; P~e f -, -n, P~gebühr f flat rate; P~preis m all-in price; P~reise f package tour; P~summe f lump sum.

Pause ['pauzə] f -, -n break; (Theat) interval; (Innehalten) pause; (Kopie) tracing; p~n vt trace; p~nlos a non-stop; ~nzeichen nt call sign; (Mus) rest.

pausieren [pau'zi:rən] vi make a break.

Pauspapier ['pauzpapi:r] nt tracing paper.

Pavian ['pa:via:n] m -s, -e baboon.

Pazifist [patsi'fɪst] m pacifist; p~isch a pacifist.

Pech [pɛç] nt -s, -e pitch; (fig) bad luck; ~ haben be unlucky; p~schwarz a pitch-black; ~strähne m (col) unlucky patch; ~vogel m (col) unlucky person.

Pedal [pe'daːl] nt -s, -e pedal.

Pedant [pe'dant] m pedant; ~e'rie f pedantry; p~isch a pedantic.

Peddigrohr ['pɛdɪçroːr] nt cane.

Pegel ['peːgəl] m -s, - water gauge; ~stand m water level.

peilen ['paɪlən] vt get a fix on.

Pein [paɪn] f - agony, pain; p~igen vt torture; (plagen) torment; p~lich a (unangenehm) embarrassing, awkward, painful; (genau) painstaking; P~lichkeit f painfulness, awkwardness; scrupulousness.

Peitsche ['paɪtʃə] f -, -n whip; p~n vt whip; (Regen) lash.

Pelikan ['peːlikaːn] m -s, -e pelican.

Pelle ['pɛlə] f -, -n skin; p~n vt skin, peel.

Pellkartoffeln pl jacket potatoes pl.

Pelz [pɛlts] m -es, -e fur.

Pendel ['pɛndəl] nt -s, - pendulum; ~verkehr m shuttle traffic; (für Pendler) commuter traffic.

Pendler ['pɛndlər] m -s, - commuter.

penetrant [pene'trant] a sharp; Person pushing.

Penis ['peːnɪs] m -, -se penis.

Pension [penzi'oːn] f (Geld) pension; (Ruhestand) retirement; (für Gäste) boarding or guest-house; **halbe/volle** ~ half/full board; ~är(in f) [-'nɛːr(ɪn)] m -s, -e pensioner; ~at [-'naːt] nt -(e)s, -e boarding school; p~ieren [-'niːrən] vt pension (off); p~iert a retired; ~ierung f retirement; ~sgast m boarder, paying guest.

Pensum ['pɛnzʊm] nt -s, **Pensen** quota; (Sch) curriculum.

per [pɛr] prep +acc by, per; (pro) per; (bis) by.

Perfekt ['pɛrfɛkt] nt -(e)s, -e perfect; p~ [pɛr'fɛkt] a perfect; ~ionismus [pɛrfɛktsio'nɪsmʊs] m perfectionism.

perforieren [pɛrfo'riːrən] vt perforate.

Pergament [pɛrga'mɛnt] nt parchment; ~papier nt greaseproof paper.

Periode [peri'oːdə] f -, -n period.

periodisch [peri'oːdɪʃ] a periodic; (dezimal) recurring.

Peripherie [perife'riː] f periphery; (um Stadt) outskirts pl; (Math) circumference.

Perle ['pɛrlə] f -, -n (lit, fig) pearl; p~n vi sparkle; (Tropfen) trickle.

Perlmutt ['pɛrlmʊt] nt -s mother-of-pearl.

perplex [pɛr'plɛks] a dumbfounded.

Persianer [pɛrzi'aːnər] m -s, - Persian lamb.

Person [pɛr'zoːn] f -, -en person; **ich für meine** ~ personally I; **klein von** ~ of small build; ~al [-'naːl] nt -s personnel; (Bedienung) servants pl; ~alausweis m identity card; ~alien [-'naːliən] pl particulars pl; ~ali'tät f personality; ~alpronomen nt personal pronoun; ~enaufzug m lift, elevator (US); ~enkraftwagen m private motorcar; ~enkreis m group of people; ~enschaden m injury to persons; ~enwaage f scales pl; ~enzug m stopping train; passenger train; p~ifizieren [-ifi'tsiːrən] vt personify.

persönlich [pɛr'zøːnlɪç] a personal; ad in person; personally; P~keit f personality.

Perspektive [pɛrspɛk'tiːvə] f perspective.

Perücke [pe'rʏkə] f -, -n wig.

pervers [pɛr'vɛrs] a perverse; P~i'tät f perversity.

Pessimismus [pɛsi'mɪsmʊs] m pessimism.

Pessimist [pɛsi'mɪst] m pessimist; p~isch a pessimistic.

Pest [pɛst] f - plague.

Petersilie [petər'ziːliə] f parsley.

Petroleum [pe'troːleum] nt -s paraffin, kerosene (US).

petzen ['pɛtsən] vi (col) tell tales.

Pfad [pfaːt] m -(e)s, -e path; ~finder m -s, - boy scout; ~finderin f girl guide.

Pfahl [pfaːl] m -(e)s, ˝e post, stake; ~bau m pile dwelling.

Pfand [pfant] nt -(e)s, ˝er pledge, security; (Flaschen—) deposit; (im Spiel) forfeit; (fig: der Liebe etc) pledge; ~brief m bond.

pfänden ['pfɛndən] vt seize, distrain.

Pfänderspiel nt game of forfeits.

Pfand- cpd: ~haus nt pawnshop; ~leiher m -s, - pawnbroker; ~schein m pawn ticket.

Pfändung ['pfɛndʊŋ] f seizure, distraint.

Pfanne ['pfanə] f -, -n (frying) pan.

Pfannkuchen m pancake; (Berliner) doughnut.

Pfarr- ['pfar] cpd: ~ei [-'raɪ] f parish; ~er m -s, - priest; (evangelisch) vicar; minister; ~haus nt vicarage; manse.

Pfau [pfau] m -(e)s, -en peacock; ~enauge nt peacock butterfly.

Pfeffer ['pfɛfər] m -s, - pepper; ~korn nt peppercorn; ~kuchen m gingerbread; ~minz nt -es, -e peppermint; ~mühle f pepper-mill; p~n vt pepper; (col: werfen) fling; **gepfefferte Preise/Witze** steep prices/spicy jokes.

Pfeife ['pfaɪfə] f -, -n whistle; (Tabak—, Orgel—) pipe; p~n vti irreg whistle; ~r m -s, - piper.

Pfeil [pfaɪl] m -(e)s, -e arrow.

Pfeiler ['pfaɪlər] m -s, - pillar, prop; (Brücken—) pier.

Pfennig ['pfɛnɪç] m -(e)s, -e pfennig (hundredth part of a mark).

Pferd [pfeːrt] nt -(e)s, -e horse; ~erennen nt horse-race; horse-racing; ~eschwanz m (Frisur) ponytail; ~estall m stable.

Pfiff [pfɪf] m -(e)s, -e whistle; (Kniff) trick; ~erling ['pfɪfərlɪŋ] m yellow chanterelle; **keinen** ~erling **wert** not worth a thing; p~ig a sly, sharp.

Pfingsten ['pfɪŋstən] nt -, -Whitsun.

Pfingstrose ['pfɪŋstroːzə] f peony.

Pfirsich ['pfɪrzɪç] m -e peach.

Pflanz- ['pflants] cpd: ~e f -, -n plant; p~en vt plant; ~enfett nt vegetable fat; ~er m -s, - planter; ~ung f plantation.

Pflaster ['pflastər] nt -s, - plaster; (Straße) pavement; p~müde a dead on one's feet; p~n vt pave; ~stein m paving stone.

Pflaume ['pflaumə] f -, -n plum.
Pflege ['pfleːgə] f -, -n care; (von Idee) cultivation; (Kranken—) nursing; **in ~ sein** (Kind) be fostered out; **p~bedürftig** a needing care; **~eltern** pl foster parents pl; **~kind** nt foster child; **p~leicht** a easy-care; **~mutter** f foster mother; **p~n** vt look after; Kranke nurse; Beziehungen foster; **~r** m -s, - orderly; male nurse; **~rin** f nurse, attendant; **~vater** m foster father.
Pflicht [pflɪçt] f -, -en duty; (Sport) compulsory section; **p~bewußt** a conscientious; **~fach** nt (Sch) compulsory subject; **~gefühl** nt sense of duty; **p~gemäß** a dutiful; ad as in duty bound; **p~vergessen** a irresponsible; **~versicherung** f compulsory insurance.
Pflock [pflɔk] m -(e)s, ¨e peg; (für Tiere) stake.
pflücken ['pflʏkən] vt pick; Blumen auch pluck.
Pflug [pfluːk] m -(e)s, ¨e plough.
pflügen ['pflyːgən] vt plough.
Pforte ['pfɔrtə] f -, -n gate; door.
Pförtner ['pfœrtnər] m -s, - porter, door-keeper, doorman.
Pfosten ['pfɔstən] m -s, - post.
Pfote ['pfoːtə] f -, -n paw; (col: Schrift) scrawl.
Pfropf [pfrɔpf] m -(e)s, -e (Flaschen—) stopper; (Blut—) clot; **p~en** vt (stopfen) cram; Baum graft; **P~en** m -s, -e see Pfropf.
pfui [pfʊi] interj ugh; (na na) tut tut.
Pfund [pfʊnt] nt -(e)s, -e pound; **p~ig** a (col) great; **p~weise** ad by the pound.
pfuschen ['pfʊʃən] vi (col) be sloppy; **jdm in etw** (acc) **~** interfere in sth.
Pfuscher ['pfʊʃər] m -s, - (col) sloppy worker; (Kur—) quack; **~ei** [-'rai] f (col) sloppy work; (Kur—) quackery.
Pfütze ['pfʏtsə] f -, -n puddle.
Phänomen [fɛnoˈmeːn] nt -s, -e phenomenon; **p~al** [-'naːl] a phenomenal.
Phantasie [fantaˈziː] f imagination; **p~los** a unimaginative; **p~ren** vi fantasize; **p~voll** a imaginative.
phantastisch [fanˈtastɪʃ] a fantastic.
Pharisäer [fariˈzɛːər] m -s, - (lit, fig) pharisee.
Pharmazeut(in f) [farmaˈtsɔʏt(ɪn)] m -en, -en pharmacist.
Phase ['faːzə] f -, -n phase.
Philanthrop [filanˈtroːp] m -en, -en philanthropist; **p~isch** a philanthropic.
Philologe [filoˈloːgə] m -n, -n philologist.
Philologie [filoloˈgiː] f philology.
Philosoph [filoˈzoːf] m -en, -en philosopher; **~ie** [-'fiː] f philosophy; **p~isch** a philosophical.
Phlegma ['flɛgma] nt -s lethargy; **p~tisch** [flɛˈgmaːtɪʃ] a lethargic.
Phonet- [foˈneːt] cpd: **~ik** f phonetics sing; **p~isch** a phonetic.
Phosphor ['fɔsfɔr] m -s phosphorus; **p~eszieren** [fɔsforɛsˈtsiːrən] vi phosphoresce.
Photo ['foːto] nt -s, -s etc see Foto.

Phrase ['fraːzə] f -, -n phrase; (pej) hollow phrase.
Physik [fyˈziːk] f physics sing; **p~alisch** [-'kaːlɪʃ] a of physics; **~er(in** f) ['fyːzikər(ɪn)] m -s, - physicist.
Physiologe [fyzioˈloːgə] m -n, -n physiologist.
Physiologie [fyzioloˈgiː] f physiology.
physisch ['fyːzɪʃ] a physical.
Pianist(in f) [piaˈnɪst(ɪn)] m pianist.
picheln ['pɪçəln] vi (col) booze.
Pickel ['pɪkəl] m -s, - pimple; (Werkzeug) pickaxe; (Berg—) ice-axe; **p~ig** a pimply.
picken ['pɪkən] vi pick, peck.
Picknick ['pɪknɪk] nt -s, -e or -s picnic; **~ machen** have a picnic.
piepen ['piːpən], **piepsen** ['piːpsən] vi chirp.
piesacken ['piːzakən] vt (col) torment.
Pietät [pieˈtɛːt] f piety, reverence; **p~los** a impious, irreverent.
Pigment [pɪgˈmɛnt] nt pigment.
Pik [piːk] nt -s, -s (Cards) spades; **einen ~ auf jdn haben** (col) have it in for sb; **p~ant** [piˈkant] a spicy, piquant; (anzüglich) suggestive; **p~iert** [piˈkiːrt] a offended.
Pilger ['pɪlgər] m -s, - pilgrim; **~fahrt** f pilgrimage.
Pille ['pɪlə] f -, -n pill.
Pilot [piˈloːt] m -en, -en pilot.
Pilz [pɪlts] m -es, -e fungus; (eßbar) mushroom; (giftig) toadstool; **~krankheit** f fungal disease.
pingelig ['pɪŋəlɪç] a (col) fussy.
Pinguin ['pɪŋguiːn] m -s, -e penguin.
Pinie ['piːniə] f pine.
pinkeln ['pɪŋkəln] vi (col) pee.
Pinsel ['pɪnzəl] m -s, - paintbrush.
Pinzette [pɪnˈtsɛtə] f tweezers pl.
Pionier [pioˈniːr] m -s, -e pioneer; (Mil) sapper, engineer.
Pirat [piˈraːt] m -en, -en pirate; **~ensender** m pirate radio station.
Pirsch [pɪrʃ] f - stalking.
Piste ['pɪstə] f -, -n (Ski) run, piste; (Aviat) runway.
Pistole [pɪsˈtoːlə] f -, -n pistol.
Pizza ['pɪtsa] f -, -s pizza.
Pkw [peːkaːˈveː] m -(s), -(s) see Personenkraftwagen.
Plackerei [plakəˈrai] f drudgery.
plädieren [plɛˈdiːrən] vi plead.
Plädoyer [plɛdoaˈjeː] nt -s, -s speech for the defence; (fig) plea.
Plage ['plaːgə] f -, -n plague; (Mühe) nuisance; **~geist** m pest, nuisance; **p~n** vt torment; vr toil, slave.
Plakat [plaˈkaːt] nt -(e)s, -e placard; poster.
Plan [plaːn] m -(e)s, ¨e plan; (Karte) map; **~e** f -, -n tarpaulin; **p~en** vt plan; Mord etc plot; **~er** m -s, - planner; **~et** [plaˈneːt] m -en -en planet; **~etenbahn** f orbit (of a planet); **p~gemäß** a according to schedule or plan; (Rail) on time; **p~ieren** [plaˈniːrən] vt plane, level; **~ierraupe** f bulldozer.
Planke ['plaŋkə] f -, -n plank.

Plänkelei [plɛŋkə'laɪ] f skirmish(ing).
plänkeln ['plɛŋkəln] vi skirmish.
Plankton ['plaŋktɔn] nt -s plankton.
Plan- cpd: p~los a Vorgehen unsystematic; Umherlaufen aimless; p~mäßig a according to plan; systematic; (Rail) scheduled.
Plansch- ['planʃ] cpd: ~becken nt paddling pool; p~en vi splash.
Plan- cpd: ~soll nt -s output target; ~stelle f post.
Plantage [plan'ta:ʒə] f -, -n plantation.
Plan- cpd: ~ung f planning; ~wagen m covered wagon; ~wirtschaft f planned economy.
plappern ['plapərn] vi chatter.
plärren ['plɛrən] vi (Mensch) cry, whine; (Radio) blare.
Plasma ['plasma] nt -s, **Plasmen** plasma.
Plastik ['plastɪk] f sculpture; nt -s (Kunststoff) plastic; ~folie f plastic film.
Plastilin [plasti'li:n] nt -s plasticine.
plastisch ['plastɪʃ] a plastic; stell dir das ~ vor! just picture it!
Platane [pla'ta:nə] f -, -n plane (tree).
Platin [pla'ti:n] nt -s platinum.
Platitüde [plati'ty:də] f -, -n platitude.
platonisch [pla'to:nɪʃ] a platonic.
platsch [platʃ] interj splash; ~en vi splash; ~naß a drenched.
plätschern ['plɛtʃərn] vi babble.
platt [plat] a flat; (col: überrascht) flabbergasted; (fig: geistlos) flat, boring; ~deutsch a low German; P~e f -, -n (Speisen-, Phot, Tech) plate; (Stein-) flag; (Kachel) tile; (Schall-) record.
Plätt- ['plɛt] cpd: ~eisen nt iron; p~en vti iron.
Platt- cpd: ~enspieler m record player; ~enteller m turntable; ~fuß m flat foot; (Reifen) flat tyre.
Platz [plats] m -es, ¨e place; (Sitz-) seat; (Raum) space, room; (in Stadt) square; (Sport-) playing field; jdm ~ machen make room for sb; ~angst f (Med) agoraphobia; (col) claustrophobia; ~anweiser(in f) m -s, - usher(ette).
Plätzchen ['plɛtsçən] nt spot; (Gebäck) biscuit.
Platz- cpd: p~en vi burst; (Bombe) explode; vor Wut p~en (col) be bursting with anger; ~karte f seat reservation; ~mangel m lack of space; ~patrone f blank cartridge; ~regen m downpour; ~wunde f cut.
Plauderei [plaudə'raɪ] f chat, conversation; (Rad) talk.
plaudern ['plaudərn] vi chat, talk.
plausibel [plau'zi:bəl] a plausible.
plazieren [pla'tsi:rən] vt place; vr (Sport) be placed; (Tennis) be seeded.
Plebejer [ple'be:jər] m -s, - plebeian.
plebejisch [ple'be:jɪʃ] a plebeian.
pleite ['plaɪtə] a (col) broke; P~ f -, -n bankruptcy; (col: Reinfall) flop; P~ machen go bust.
Plenum ['ple:num] nt -s plenum.

Pleuelstange ['plɔyəlʃtaŋə] f connecting rod.
Plissee [plɪ'se:] nt -s, -s pleat.
Plombe ['plɔmbə] f -, -n lead seal; (Zahn-) filling.
plombieren [plɔm'bi:rən] vt seal; Zahn fill.
plötzlich ['plœtslɪç] a sudden; ad suddenly.
plump [plump] a clumsy; Hände coarse; Körper shapeless; ~sen vi (col) plump down, fall.
Plunder ['plundər] m -s rubbish.
plündern ['plʏndərn] vti plunder; Stadt sack.
Plünderung ['plʏndəruŋ] f plundering, sack, pillage.
Plural ['plu:ra:l] m -s, -e plural; p~istisch [plura'lɪstɪʃ] a pluralistic.
Plus [plus] nt -, - plus; (Fin) profit; (Vorteil) advantage; p~ ad plus.
Plüsch [ply:ʃ] m -(e)s, -e plush.
Plus- cpd: ~pol m (Elec) positive pole; ~punkt m point; (fig) point in sb's favour; ~quamperfekt nt -s, -e pluperfect.
Po [po:] m -s, -s (col) bottom, bum.
Pöbel ['pø:bəl] m -s mob, rabble; ~ei [-'laɪ] f vulgarity; p~haft a low, vulgar.
pochen ['pɔxən] vi knock; (Herz) pound; auf etw (acc) ~ (fig) insist on sth.
Pocken ['pɔkən] pl smallpox.
Podium ['po:dium] nt podium; ~sdiskussion f panel discussion.
Poesie [poe'zi:] f poetry.
Poet [po'e:t] m -en, -en poet; p~isch a poetic.
Pointe [po'ɛ:tə] f -, -n point.
Pokal [po'ka:l] m -s, -e goblet; (Sport) cup; ~spiel nt cup-tie.
Pökel- ['pø:kəl] cpd: ~fleisch nt salt meat; p~n vt pickle, salt.
Pol [po:l] m -s, -e pole; p~ar [po'la:r] a polar; ~arkreis m arctic circle.
Polemik [po'le:mɪk] f polemics.
polemisch a polemical.
polemisieren [polemi'zi:rən] vi polemicize.
Police [po'li:s(ə)] f -, -n insurance policy.
Polier [po'li:r] m -s, -e foreman; p~en vt polish.
Poliklinik [poli'kli:nɪk] f outpatients.
Politik [poli'ti:k] f politics sing; (eine bestimmte) policy; ~er(in f) [po'li:tikər(ɪn)] m -s, - politician.
politisch [po'li:tɪʃ] a political.
politisieren [politi'zi:rən] vi talk politics; vt politicize.
Politur [poli'tu:r] f polish.
Polizei [poli'tsaɪ] f police; ~beamte(r) m police officer; p~lich a police; sich p~lich melden register with the police; ~revier nt police station; ~spitzel m police spy, informer; ~staat m police state; ~streife f police patrol; ~stunde f closing time; p~widrig a illegal.
Polizist [poli'tsɪst] m -en, -en policeman; ~in f policewoman.
Pollen ['pɔlən] m -s, - pollen.
Polster ['pɔlstər] nt -s, - cushion; (Polsterung) upholstery; (in Kleidung) padding; (fig: Geld) reserves pl; ~er m -s,

- upholsterer; ~**möbel** pl upholstered furniture; **p~n** vt upholster; pad; ~**ung** f upholstery.

Polter- ['pɔltər] cpd: ~**abend** m party on eve of wedding; **p~n** vi (Krach machen) crash; (schimpfen) rant.

Polygamie [polyga'miː] f polygamy.

Polyp [po'lyːp] m **-en -en** polyp; (pl: Med) adenoids pl; (col) cop.

Pomade [po'maːdə] f pomade.

Pommes frites [pɔm'friːt] pl chips pl, French fried potatoes pl.

Pomp [pɔmp] m **-(e)s** pomp.

Pony ['pɔni] m **-s, -s** (Frisur) fringe; nt **-s, -s** (Pferd) pony.

Popo [po'poː] m **-s, -s** bottom, bum.

populär [popu'lɛːr] a popular.

Popularität [populari'tɛːt] f popularity.

Pore ['poːrə] f **-, -n** pore.

Pornographie [pɔrnogra'fiː] f pornography.

porös [po'røːs] a porous.

Porree ['pɔre] m **-s, -s** leek.

Portal [pɔr'taːl] nt **-s, -e** portal.

Portemonnaie [pɔrtmɔ'neː] nt **-s, -s** purse.

Portier [pɔrti'eː] m **-s, -s** porter; see **Pförtner**.

Portion [pɔrtsi'oːn] f portion, helping; (col: Anteil) amount.

Porto ['pɔrto] nt **-s, -s** postage; **p~frei** a post-free, (postage) prepaid.

Porträt [pɔr'trɛː] nt **-s, -s** portrait; **p~ieren** [pɔrtrɛ'tiːrən] vt paint, portray.

Porzellan [pɔrtse'laːn] nt **-s, -e** china, porcelain; (Geschirr) china.

Posaune [po'zaunə] f **-, -n** trombone.

Pose ['poːzə] f **-, -n** pose.

posieren [po'ziːrən] vi pose.

Position [pozitsi'oːn] f position; ~**slichter** pl (Aviat) position lights pl.

positiv ['poːzitiːf] a positive; **P~** nt **-s, -e** (Phot) positive.

Positur [pozi'tuːr] f posture, attitude.

possessiv ['pɔsesiːf] a possessive; **P~(pronomen)** nt **-s, -e** possessive pronoun.

possierlich [po'siːrlıç] a funny.

Post [pɔst] f **-, -en** post (office); (Briefe) mail; ~**amt** nt post office; ~**anweisung** f postal order, money order; ~**bote** m postman; ~**en** m **-s, -** post, position; (Comm) item; (auf Liste) entry; (Mil) sentry; (Streik~) picket; ~**fach** nt post-office box; ~**karte** f postcard; **p~lagernd** ad poste restante; ~**leitzahl** f postal code; ~**scheckkonto** nt postal giro account; ~**sparkasse** f post office savings bank; ~**stempel** m postmark; **p~wendend** ad by return (of post).

potent [po'tɛnt] a potent; (fig) high-powered.

Potential [potɛntsi'aːl] nt **-s, -e** potential.

potentiell [potɛntsi'ɛl] a potential.

Potenz [po'tɛnts] f power; (eines Mannes) potency.

Pracht [praxt] f **-** splendour, magnificence.

prächtig ['prɛçtıç] a splendid.

Pracht- cpd: ~**stück** nt showpiece; **p~voll** a splendid, magnificent.

Prädikat [prɛdi'kaːt] nt **-(e)s, -e** title; (Gram) predicate; (Zensur) distinction.

prägen ['prɛːgən] vt stamp; Münze mint; Ausdruck coin; Charakter form.

prägnant [prɛ'gnant] a precise, terse.

Prägnanz [prɛ'gnants] f conciseness, terseness.

Prägung ['prɛːgʊŋ] f minting; forming; (Eigenart) character, stamp.

prahlen ['praːlən] vi boast, brag.

Prahlerei [praːlə'rai] f boasting.

prahlerisch a boastful.

Praktik ['praktık] f practice; **p~abel** [-'kaːbəl] a practicable; ~**ant(in** f) [-'kant(ın)] m trainee; ~**um** nt **-s, Praktika** or **Praktiken** practical training.

praktisch ['praktıʃ] a practical, handy; ~**er Arzt** general practitioner.

praktizieren [prakti'tsiːrən] vti practise.

Praline [pra'liːnə] f chocolate.

prall [pral] a firmly rounded; Segel taut; Arme plump; Sonne blazing; ~**en** vi bounce, rebound; (Sonne) blaze.

Prämie ['prɛːmiə] f premium; (Belohnung) award, prize; **p~ren** [prɛ'miːrən] vt give an award to.

Pranger ['praŋər] m **-s, -** (Hist) pillory; **jdn an den ~ stellen** (fig) pillory sb.

Präparat [prɛpa'raːt] nt **-(e)s, -e** (B...) preparation; (Med) medicine.

Präposition [prɛpozitsi'oːn] f preposition.

Prärie [prɛ'riː] f prairie.

Präsens ['prɛːzɛns] nt **-** present tense.

präsentieren [prɛzɛn'tiːrən] vt present.

Präservativ [prɛzɛrva'tiːf] nt **-s, -e** contraceptive.

Präsident(in f) [prɛzi'dɛnt(ın)] m president; ~**schaft** f presidency; ~**schaftskandidat** m presidential candidate.

Präsidium [prɛ'ziːdiʊm] nt presidency, chair(manship); (Polizei~) police headquarters pl.

prasseln ['prasəln] vi (Feuer) crackle; (Hagel) drum; (Wörter) rain down.

prassen ['prasən] vi live it up.

Präteritum [prɛ'teːritʊm] nt **-s, Präterita** preterite.

Pratze ['pratsə] f **-, -n** paw.

Präventiv- [prɛvɛn'tiːf] in cpds preventive.

Praxis ['praksıs] f **-, Praxen** practice; (Behandlungsraum) surgery; (von Anwalt) office.

Präzedenzfall [prɛtse'dɛntsfal] m precedent.

präzis [prɛ'tsiːs] a precise; **P~ion** [prɛtsizi'oːn] f precision.

predigen ['preːdıgən] vti preach.

Prediger m **-s, -** preacher.

Predigt ['preːdıçt] f **-, -en** sermon.

Preis [prais] m **-es, -e** price; (Sieges~) prize; **um keinen ~** not at any price; ~**elbeere** f cranberry; **p~en** [praizən] vi irreg praise; **p~geben** vt irreg abandon; (opfern) sacrifice; (zeigen) expose;

p~gekrönt a prize-winning; ~gericht nt jury; p~günstig a inexpensive; ~lage f price range; p~lich a price, in price; ~sturz m slump; ~träger(in f) m prizewinner; p~wert a inexpensive.

prekär [pre'kɛːr] a precarious.

Prell- [prɛl] cpd: ~bock m buffers pl; p~en vt bump; (fig) cheat, swindle; ~ung f bruise.

Premiere [prəmi'ɛːrə] f -, -n premiere.

Premierminister [prəmi'eːmɪnɪstər] m prime minister, premier.

Presse ['prɛsə] f -, -n press; ~freiheit f freedom of the press; ~meldung f press report; p~n vt press.

pressieren [prɛ'siːrən] vi (be in a) hurry.

Preß- ['prɛs] cpd: ~luft f compressed air; ~luftbohrer m pneumatic drill.

Prestige [prɛs'tiːʒə] nt -s prestige.

prickeln ['prɪkəln] vti tingle, tickle.

Priester ['priːstər] m -s, - priest.

prima ['priːma] a first-class, excellent; P~ f-, Primen sixth form, top class.

primär [pri'mɛːr] a primary.

Primel ['priːməl] f -, -n primrose.

primitiv [primi'tiːf] a primitive.

Prinz [prɪnts] m -en, -en prince; ~essin [prɪn'tsɛsɪn] f princess.

Prinzip [prɪn'tsiːp] nt -s, -ien principle; p~iell [-i'ɛl] a,ad on principle; p~ienlos a unprincipled.

Priorität [priori'tɛːt] f priority.

Prise ['priːzə] f -, -n pinch.

Prisma ['prɪsma] nt -s, Prismen prism.

privat [pri'vaːt] a privat; P~ in cpds private.

pro [proː] prep +acc per; P~ nt - pro.

Probe ['proːbə] f -, -n test; (Teststück) sample; (Theat) rehearsal; jdn auf die ~ stellen put sb to the test; ~exemplar nt specimen copy; ~fahrt f test drive; p~n vt try; (Theat) rehearse; p~weise ad on approval; ~zeit f probation period.

probieren [pro'biːrən] vti try; Wein, Speise taste, sample.

Problem [pro'bleːm] nt -s, -e problem; ~atik [-'maːtɪk] f problem; p~atisch [-'maːtɪʃ] a problematic; p~los a problemfree.

Produkt [pro'dukt] nt -(e)s, -e product; (Agr) produce no pl; ~ion [produktsi'oːn] f production; output; p~iv [-'tiːf] a productive; ~ivität productivity.

Produzent [produ'tsɛnt] m manufacturer; (Film) producer.

produzieren [produ'tsiːrən] vt produce.

Professor [pro'fɛsɔr] m professor.

Professur [profɛ'suːr] f chair.

Profil [pro'fiːl] nt -s, -e profile; (fig) image; p~ieren [profi'liːrən] vr create an image for o.s.

Profit [pro'fiːt] m -(e)s, -e profit; p~ieren [profi'tiːrən] vi profit (von from).

Prognose [pro'gnoːzə] f -, -n prediction, prognosis.

Programm [pro'gram] nt -s, -e programme; p~(m)äßig a according to plan; p~ieren [-'miːrən] vt programme; ~ierer(in f) m -s, - programmer.

progressiv [progrɛ'siːf] a progressive.

Projekt [pro'jɛkt] nt -(e)s, -e project; ~or [pro'jɛktɔr] m projector.

projizieren [proji'tsiːrən] vt project.

proklamieren [prokla'miːrən] vt proclaim.

Prolet [pro'leːt] m -en, -en prole, pleb; ~ariat [-ari'aːt] nt -(e)s, -e proletariat; ~arier [-'taːriər] m -s, - proletarian.

Prolog [pro'loːk] m -(e)s, -e prologue.

Promenade [promə'naːdə] f promenade.

Promille [pro'mɪlə] nt -(s), - alcohol level.

prominent [promi'nɛnt] a prominent.

Prominenz [promi'nɛnts] f VIPs pl.

Promotion [promotsi'oːn] f doctorate, Ph.D.

promovieren [promo'viːrən] vi do a doctorate or Ph.D.

prompt [prɔmpt] a prompt.

Pronomen [pro'noːmen] nt -s, - pronoun.

Propaganda [propa'ganda] f - propaganda.

Propeller [pro'pɛlər] m -s, - propeller.

Prophet [pro'feːt] m -en, -en prophet; ~in f prophetess.

prophezeien [profe'tsaɪən] vt prophesy.

Prophezeiung f prophecy.

Proportion [proportsi'oːn] f proportion; p~al [-'naːl] a proportional.

Prosa ['proːza] f - prose; p~isch [pro'zaːɪʃ] a prosaic.

prosit ['proːzɪt] interj cheers.

Prospekt [pro'spɛkt] m -(e)s, -e leaflet, brochure.

prost [proːst] interj cheers.

Prostituierte [prostitu'iːrtə] f -n, -n prostitute.

Prostitution [prostitutsi'oːn] f prostitution.

Protest [pro'tɛst] m -(e)s, -e protest; ~ant(in f) [protɛs'tant] m Protestant; p~antisch [protɛs'tantɪʃ] a Protestant; p~ieren [protɛs'tiːrən] vi protest; ~kundgebung f (protest) rally.

Prothese [pro'teːzə] f -, -n artificial limb; (Zahn-) dentures pl.

Protokoll [proto'kɔl] nt -s, -e register; (von Sitzung) minutes pl; (diplomatisch) protocol; (Polizei-) statement; p~ieren [-'liːrən] vt take down in the minutes.

Proton [pro'toːn] nt -s, -en proton.

Protz [prɔts] m -en, -e(n) swank; p~en vi show off; p~ig a ostentatious.

Proviant [provi'ant] m -s, -e provisions pl, supplies pl.

Provinz [pro'vɪnts] f -, -en province; p~iell [provin'tsiɛl] a provincial.

Provision [provizi'oːn] f (Comm) commission.

provisorisch [provi'zoːrɪʃ] a provisional.

Provokation [provokatsi'oːn] f provocation.

provozieren [provo'tsiːrən] vt provoke.

Prozedur [protse'duːr] f procedure; (pej) carry-on.

Prozent [pro'tsɛnt] nt -(e)s, -e per cent, percentage; ~rechnung f percentage calculation; ~satz m percentage; p~ual

[-u'a:l] a percentage; as a percentage.

Prozeß [pro'tsɛs] m **-sses, -sse** trial, case; ~**kosten** pl (legal) costs pl.

prozessieren [protsɛ'si:rən] vi bring an action, go to law (mit against).

Prozession [protsɛsi'o:n] f procession.

prüde ['pry:də] a prudish; **P~rie** [-'ri:] f prudery.

Prüf- ['pry:f] cpd: p~**en** vt examine, test; (nach—) check; ~**er** m **-s,** - examiner; ~**ling** m examinee; ~**stein** m touchstone; ~**ung** f examination; checking; ~**ungsausschuß** m, ~**ungskommission** f examining board.

Prügel ['pry:gəl] m **-s,** - cudgel; pl beating; ~**ei** [-'lai] f fight; ~**knabe** m scapegoat; p~**n** vt beat; vr fight; ~**strafe** f corporal punishment.

Prunk [pruŋk] m **-(e)s** pomp, show; p~**voll** a splendid, magnificent.

Psalm [psalm] m **-s, -en** psalm.

pseudo- [psɔydo] in cpds pseudo.

Psych- ['psyç] cpd: ~**iater** [-i'a:tər] m **-s,** - psychiatrist; p~**isch** a psychological; ~**oanalyse** [-o'analy:zə] f psychoanalysis; ~**ologe** [-o'lo:gə] m **-n,** -n psychologist; ~**olo'gie** f psychology; p~**ologisch** a psychological.

Pubertät [pubɛr'tɛ:t] f puberty.

Publikum ['pu:blikum] nt **-s** audience; (Sport) crowd.

publizieren [publi'tsi:rən] vt publish, publicize.

Pudding ['pudɪŋ] m **-s, -e** or **-s** blancmange.

Pudel ['pu:dəl] m **-s** poodle.

Puder ['pu:dər] m **-s,** - powder; ~**dose** f powder compact; p~**n** vt powder; ~**zucker** m icing sugar.

Puff [puf] m **-e** (Wäsche—) linen basket; (Sitz—) pouf; pl **-e** (col: Stoß) push; pl **-s** (col: Bordell) brothel; ~**er** m **-s,** - buffer; ~**erstaat** m buffer state.

Pulli ['puli] m **-s, -s** (col), **Pullover** [pu'lo:vər] m **-s,** - pullover, jumper.

Puls [puls] m **-es, -e** pulse; ~**ader** f artery; p~**ieren** [pul'zi:rən] vi throb, pulsate.

Pult [pult] nt **-(e)s, -e** desk.

Pulver ['pulfər] nt **-s,** - powder; p~**ig** a powdery; p~**isieren** [pulveri'zi:rən] vt pulverize; ~**schnee** m powdery snow.

pummelig ['puməlɪç] a chubby.

Pumpe ['pumpə] f **-, -n** pump; p~**n** vt pump; (col) lend; borrow.

Punkt [puŋkt] m **-(e)s, -e** point; (bei Muster) dot; (Satzzeichen) full stop; p~**ieren** [-'ti:rən] vt dot; (Med) aspirate.

pünktlich ['pyŋktlɪç] a punctual; **P~keit** f punctuality.

Punkt- cpd: ~**sieg** m victory on points; ~**zahl** f score.

Punsch [punʃ] m **-(e)s, -e** punch.

Pupille [pu'pɪlə] f **-, -n** pupil.

Puppe ['pupə] f **-, -n** doll; (Marionette) puppet; (Insekten—) pupa, chrysalis; ~**nspieler** m puppeteer; ~**nstube** f doll's house.

pur [pu:r] a pure; (völlig) sheer; Whisky neat.

Püree [py're:] nt **-s, -s** mashed potatoes pl.

Purzel- ['purtsəl] cpd: ~**baum** m somersault; p~**n** vi tumble.

Puste ['pu:stə] f - (col) puff; (fig) steam; ~**l** ['pustəl] f **-, -n** pustule; p~**n** vi puff, blow.

Pute ['pu:tə] f **-, -n** turkey-hen; ~**r** m **-s,** - turkey-cock.

Putsch [putʃ] m **-(e)s, -e** revolt, putsch; p~**en** vi revolt; ~**ist** [pu'tʃɪst] m rebel.

Putz [puts] m **-es** (Mörtel) plaster, roughcast; p~**en** vt clean; Nase wipe, blow; vr clean oneself; dress oneself up; ~**frau** f charwoman; p~**ig** a quaint, funny; ~**lappen** m cloth; ~**tag** m cleaning day; ~**zeug** nt cleaning things pl.

Puzzle ['pasəl] nt **-s, -s** jigsaw.

Pyjama [pi'dʒa:ma] m **-s, -s** pyjamas pl.

Pyramide [pyra'mi:də] f **-, -n** pyramid.

Q

Q, q [ku:] nt Q, q.

quabb(e)lig ['kvab(ə)lɪç] a wobbly; Frosch slimy.

Quacksalber ['kvakzalbər] m **-s,** - quack (doctor).

Quader ['kva:dər] m **-s,** - square stone; (Math) cuboid.

Quadrat [kva'dra:t] nt **-(e)s, -e** square; q~**isch** a square; ~**meter** m square metre.

quadrieren [kva'dri:rən] vt square.

quaken ['kva:kən] vi croak; (Ente) quack.

quäken ['kvɛ:kən] vi screech; ~**d** a screeching.

Qual [kva:l] f **-, -en** pain, agony; (seelisch) anguish.

Quäl- [kvɛ:l] cpd: q~**en** vt torment; vr struggle; (geistig) torment oneself; ~**erei** [-ə'rai] f torture, torment; ~**geist** m pest.

qualifizieren [kvalifi'tsi:rən] vtr qualify; (einstufen) label.

Qualität [kvali'tɛ:t] f quality; ~**sware** f article of high quality.

Qualle ['kvalə] f **-, -n** jellyfish.

Qualm [kvalm] m **-(e)s** thick smoke; q~**en** vti smoke.

qualvoll ['kva:lfɔl] a excruciating, painful, agonizing.

Quant- ['kvant] cpd: ~**entheorie** f quantum theory; ~**ität** [-i'tɛ:t] f quantity; q~**itativ** [-ita'ti:f] a quantitative; ~**um** nt **-s, Quanten** quantity, amount.

Quarantäne [karan'tɛ:nə] f **-, -n** quarantine.

Quark [kvark] m **-s** curd cheese; (col) rubbish.

Quarta ['kvarta] f **-, Quarten** third year of secondary school; ~**l** [kvar'ta:l] nt **-s, -e** quarter (year).

Quartier [kvar'ti:r] nt **-s, -e** accommodation; (Mil) quarters pl; (Stadt—) district.

Quarz [kva:rts] m **-es, -e** quartz.

quasseln ['kvasəln] vi (col) natter.

Quatsch [kvatʃ] m **-es** rubbish; q~**en** vi chat, natter.

Quecksilber ['kvɛkzɪlbər] nt mercury.

Quelle ['kvɛlə] f **-, -n** spring; (eines Flusses)

source; q~n vi (hervor—) pour or gush forth; (schwellen) swell.

quengel- ['kvɛŋəl] cpd: Q~ei [-'laɪ] f (col) whining; ~ig a (col) whining; ~n vi (col) whine.

quer [kveːr] ad crossways, diagonally; (rechtwinklig) at right angles; ~ auf dem Bett across the bed; Q~balken m crossbeam; ~feldein ad across country; Q~flöte f flute; Q~kopf m awkward customer; Q~schiff nt transept; Q~schnitt m cross-section; ~schnittsgelähmt a paralysed below the waist; Q~straße f intersecting road; Q~treiber m -s, - obstructionist; Q~verbindung f connection, link.

quetschen ['kvɛtʃən] vt squash, crush; (Med) bruise.

Quetschung f bruise, contusion.

quieken ['kviːkən] vi squeak.

quietschen ['kviːtʃən] vi squeak.

Quint- ['kvɪnt] cpd: ~a f -, -en second form in secondary school; ~essenz [-'ɛsɛnts] f quintessence; ~ett [-'tɛt] nt -(e)s, -e quintet.

Quirl [kvɪrl] m -(e)s, -e whisk.

quitt [kvɪt] a quits, even; Q~e f -, -n quince; ~engelb a sickly yellow; ~ieren [-'tiːrən] vt give a receipt for; Dienst leave; Q~ung f receipt.

Quiz [kvɪs] nt -, - quiz.

Quote ['kvoːtə] f -, -n number, rate.

R

R, r [ɛr] nt R, r.

Rabatt [ra'bat] m -(e)s, -e discount; ~e f -, -n flowerbed, border; ~marke f trading stamp.

Rabe ['raːbə] m -n, -n raven; ~nmutter f bad mother.

rabiat [rabi'aːt] a furious.

Rache ['raxə] f revenge, vengeance; ~n m -s, - throat.

rächen ['rɛçən] vt avenge, revenge; vr take (one's) revenge; das wird sich ~ you'll pay for that.

Rach- ['rax] cpd: ~'tis [ra'xiːtɪs] f rickets sing; ~sucht f vindictiveness; r~süchtig a vindictive.

Racker ['rakər] m -s, - rascal, scamp.

Rad [raːt] nt -(e)s, ̈er wheel; (Fahr—) bike; ~ar ['raːdaːr] m or nt -s radar; ~arkontrolle f radar-controlled speed trap; ~au [ra'dau] m -s (col) row; ~dampfer m paddle steamer; r~ebrechen vi insep: deutsch etc r~ebrechen speak broken German etc; r~eln vi, r~fahren vi irreg cycle; ~fahrer(in f) m cyclist; ~fahrweg m cycle track or path.

Radier- [ra'diːr] cpd: r~en vt rub out, erase; (Art) etch; ~gummi m rubber, eraser; ~ung f etching.

Radieschen [ra'diːsçən] nt radish.

radikal [radi'kaːl] a, R~e(r) mf radical.

Radio ['raːdio] nt -s, -s radio, wireless; r~ak'tiv a radioactive; ~aktivi'tät f radioactivity; ~apparat m radio, wireless set.

Radium ['raːdiʊm] nt -s radium.

Radius ['raːdiʊs] m -, Radien radius.

Rad- cpd: ~kappe f (Aut) hub cap; ~ler(in f) m -s, - cyclist; ~rennbahn f cycling (race)track; ~rennen nt cycle race; cycle racing; ~sport m cycling.

raff- [raf] cpd: ~en vt snatch, pick up; Stoff gather (up); Geld pile up, rake in; R~inade [-i'naːdə] f refined sugar; ~inieren [-i'niːrən] vt refine; ~i'niert a crafty, cunning; Zucker refined.

ragen ['raːgən] vi tower, rise.

Rahm [raːm] m -s cream; ~en m -s, - frame(work); im ~en des Möglichen within the bounds of possibility; r~en vt frame; r~ig a creamy.

Rakete [ra'keːtə] f -, -n rocket; ferngelenkte ~ guided missile.

rammen ['ramən] vt ram.

Rampe ['rampə] f -, -n ramp; ~nlicht vt (Theat) footlights pl.

ramponieren [rampo'niːrən] vt (col) damage.

Ramsch [ramʃ] m -(e)s, -e junk.

ran [ran] ad (col) = heran.

Rand [rant] m -(e)s, ̈er edge; (von Brille, Tasse etc) rim; (Hut—) brim; (auf Papier) margin; (Schmutz—, unter Augen) ring; (fig) verge, brink; außer ~ und Band wild; am ~e bemerkt mentioned in passing; r~alieren [randa'liːrən] vi (go on the) rampage; ~bemerkung f marginal note; (fig) odd comment; ~erscheinung f unimportant side effect, marginal phenomenon.

Rang [raŋ] m -(e)s, ̈e rank; (Stand) standing; (Wert) quality; (Theat) circle; ~abzeichen nt badge of rank; ~älteste(r) m senior officer.

Rangier- [rãʒiːr] cpd: ~bahnhof m marshalling yard; r~en vt (Rail) shunt, switch (US); vi rank, be classed; ~gleis nt siding.

Rang- cpd: ~ordnung f hierarchy; (Mil) rank; ~unterschied m social distinction; (Mil) difference in rank.

Ranke ['raŋkə] f -, -n tendril, shoot.

Ränke ['rɛŋkə] pl intrigues pl; ~schmied m intriguer; r~voll a scheming.

Ranzen ['rantsən] m -s, - satchel; (col: Bauch) gut, belly.

ranzig ['rantsɪç] a rancid.

Rappe ['rapə] m -n, -n black horse.

Raps [raps] m -es, -e (Bot) rape.

rar [raːr] a rare; sich ~ machen (col) keep oneself to oneself; R~i'tät f rarity; (Sammelobjekt) curio.

rasant [ra'zant] a quick, rapid.

rasch [raʃ] a quick; ~eln vi rustle.

Rasen ['raːzən] m -s, - lawn; grass; r~ vi rave; (schnell) race; r~d a furious; r~de Kopfschmerzen a splitting head-ache; ~mäher m -s, -, ~mähmaschine f lawnmower; ~platz m lawn.

Raserei [raːzə'raɪ] f raving, ranting; (Schnelle) reckless speeding.

Rasier- [ra'ziːr] cpd: ~apparat m shaver; ~creme f shaving cream; r~en vtr shave; ~klinge f razor blade; ~messer nt razor; ~pinsel m shaving brush;

~seife *f* shaving soap *or* stick; ~wasser *nt* shaving lotion.

Rasse ['rasə] *f* -, -n race; *(Tier—)* breed; ~hund *m* thoroughbred dog; ~l *f* -, -n rattle; r~ln *vi* rattle, clatter; ~nhaß *m* race *or* racial hatred; ~ntrennung *f* racial segregation.

Rast [rast] *f* -, -en rest; r~en *vi* rest; ~haus *nt (Aut)* service station; r~los *a* tireless; *(unruhig)* restless; ~platz *m (Aut)* layby.

Rasur [ra'zu:r] *f* shaving; *(Radieren)* erasure.

Rat [ra:t] *m* -(e)s, ~schläge (piece of) advice; **jdn zu ~e ziehen** consult sb; **keinen ~ wissen** not know what to do; ~e *f* -, -n instalment; r~en *vti irreg* guess; *(empfehlen)* advise *(jdm sb)*; r~enweise *ad* by instalments; ~enzahlung *f* hire purchase; ~geber *m* -s, - adviser; ~haus *nt* town hall.

ratifizier- [ratifi'tsi:r] *cpd*: ~en *vt* ratify; R~ung *f* ratification.

Ration [ratsi'o:n] *f* ration; r~al [-'na:l] *a* rational; r~alisieren *vt* rationalize; r~ell [-'nɛl] *a* efficient; r~ieren [-'ni:rən] *vt* ration.

Rat- *cpd*: r~los *a* at a loss, helpless; ~losigkeit *f* helplessness; r~sam *a* advisable; ~schlag *m* -(s)piece of advice.

Rätsel ['rɛ:tsəl] *nt* -s, - puzzle; *(Wort—)* riddle; r~haft *a* mysterious; **es ist mir r~haft** it's a mystery to me.

Rats- *cpd*: r~herr *m* councillor; ~keller *m* town-hall restaurant.

Ratte ['ratə] *f* -, -n rat; ~nfänger *m* -s, - ratcatcher.

rattern ['ratərn] *vi* rattle, clatter.

Raub [raup] *m* -(e)s robbery; *(Beute)* loot, booty; ~bau *m* ruthless exploitation; r~en [rauben] *vt* rob; *Mensch* kidnap, abduct.

Räuber ['rɔybər] *m* -s, - robber; r~isch *a* thieving.

Raub- *cpd*: r~gierig *a* rapacious; ~mord *m* robbery with murder; ~tier *nt* predator; ~überfall *m* robbery with violence; ~vogel *m* bird of prey.

Rauch ['raux] *m* -(e)s smoke; r~en *vti* smoke; ~er *m* -s, - smoker; ~erabteil *nt (Rail)* smoker.

räuchern [rɔyçərn] *vt* smoke, cure.

Rauch- *cpd*: ~fahne *f* smoke trail; ~fleisch *nt* smoked meat; r~ig *a* smoky.

räudig ['rɔydiç] *a* mangy.

rauf [rauf] *ad (col)* = **herauf**; R~bold *m* -(e)s, -e rowdy, hooligan; ~en *vt Haare* pull out; *vir* fight; R~e'rei *f* brawl, fight; ~lustig *a* spoiling for a fight, rowdy.

rauh [rau] *a* rough, coarse; *Wetter* harsh; ~haarig *a* wire-haired; R~reif *m* hoarfrost.

Raum [raum] *m* -(e)s, Räume space; *(Zimmer, Platz)* room; *(Gebiet)* area; ~bild *nt* 3D picture.

räumen ['rɔymən] *vt* clear; *Wohnung, Platz* vacate; *(wegbringen)* shift, move; *(in Schrank etc)* put away.

Raum- *cpd*: ~fahrt *f* space travel;

~inhalt *m* cubic capacity, volume.

räumlich ['rɔymliç] *a* spatial; R~keiten *pl* premises *pl*.

Raum- *cpd*: ~mangel *m* lack of space; ~meter *m* cubic metre; ~pflegerin *f* cleaner; ~schiff *nt* spaceship; ~schiffahrt *f* space travel; r~sparend *a* space-saving.

Räumung ['rɔymuŋ] *f* vacating, evacuation; clearing (away); ~sverkauf *m* clearance sale.

raunen ['raunən] *vti* whisper mysteriously.

Raupe ['raupə] *f* -, -n caterpillar; *(—nkette)* (caterpillar) track; ~n-schlepper *m* caterpillar tractor.

raus [raus] *ad (col)* = **heraus, hinaus.**

Rausch [rauʃ] *m* -(e)s, Räusche intoxication; r~en *vi (Wasser)* rush; *(Baum)* rustle; *(Radio etc)* hiss; *(Mensch)* sweep, sail; r~end *a Beifall* thunderous; *Fest* sumptuous; ~gift *nt* drug; ~giftsüchtige(r) *mf* drug addict.

räuspern ['rɔyspərn] *vr* clear one's throat.

Raute ['rautə] *f* -, -n diamond; *(Math)* rhombus; r~nförmig *a* rhombic.

Razzia ['ratsia] *f* -, Razzien raid.

Reagenzglas [rea'gɛntsgla:s] *nt* test tube.

reagieren [rea'gi:rən] *vi* react *(auf +acc* to).

Reakt- *cpd*: ~ion [reaktsi'o:n] *f* reaction; r~io'när *a* reactionary; ~ionsge-schwindigkeit *f* speed of reaction; ~or [re'aktor] *m* reactor.

real [re'a:l] *a* real, material; R~ismus [-'lismus] *m* realism; R~ist [-'list] *m* realist; ~istisch *a* realistic.

Rebe ['re:bə] *f* -, -n vine.

Rebell [re'bɛl] *m* -en, -en rebel; ~i'on *f* rebellion; r~isch *a* rebellious.

Reb- *cpd*: ~ensaft *m* grape juice; ~huhn ['rɛphu:n] *nt* partridge; ~stock *m* vine.

Rechen ['rɛçən] *m* -s, - rake; r~ *vti* rake; ~aufgabe *f* sum, mathematical problem; ~fehler *m* miscalculation; ~maschine *f* calculating machine; ~schaft *f* account; ~schaftsbericht *m* report; ~schieber *m* slide rule.

Rech- ['rɛç] *cpd*: r~nen *vti* calculate; **jdn/etw r~nen zu *or* unter** *(+acc)* count sb/sth among; r~nen **mit** reckon with; r~nen **auf** *(+acc)* count on; ~ner *m* -s, calculator; ~nung *f* calculation(s); *(Comm)* bill, check *(US)*; **jdm/etw ~nung tragen** take sb/sth into account; ~nungsbuch *nt* account book; ~nungsjahr *nt* financial year; ~nungsprüfer *m* auditor; ~nungsprüfung *f* audit(ing).

recht [rɛçt] *a, ad* right; *(vor Adjektiv)* really, quite; **das ist mir ~** that suits me; **jetzt erst ~** now more than ever; ~ **haben be right; jdm ~ geben** agree with sb; R~ *nt* -(e)s, -e right; *(Jur)* law; R~ **sprechen** administer justice; **mit R~** rightly, justly; **von R~s wegen** by rights; R~e *f* -n, -n right (hand); *(Pol)* Right; ~e(r,s) *adj m*; *(Pol)* right-wing; R~e(r) *mf* right person; R~e(s) *nt* right thing; **etwas/nichts R~es** something/nothing proper; **R~eck** *nt* **-s, -e** rectangle; **~eckig** a rectangular; **~fertigen** *vtr insep* justify (o.s.); **R~fertigung** *f* justification; **~haberisch** a dogmatic; **~lich** a, **~mäßig** a legal, lawful.

rechts [reçts] *ad* on/to the right; **R~anwalt** *m*, **R~anwältin** *f* lawyer, barrister; **R~'außen** *m* **-, -** (*Sport*) outside right; **R~beistand** *m* legal adviser.

Recht- *cpd*: **r~schaffen** a upright; **~schreibung** *f* spelling.

Rechts- *cpd*: **~drehung** *f* clockwise rotation; **~fall** *m* (law) case; **~frage** *f* legal question; **~händer** *m* **-s, -** right-handed person; **r~kräftig** a valid, legal; **~kurve** *f* right-hand bend; **~pflege** *f* administration of justice; **r~radikal** a (*Pol*) extreme right-wing; **~spruch** *m* verdict; **~verkehr** *m* driving on the right; **r~widrig** a illegal; **~wissenschaft** *f* jurisprudence.

recht- *cpd*: **~winklig** a right-angled; **~zeitig** a timely; *ad* in time.

Reck [rɛk] *nt* **-(e)s, -e** horizontal bar; **r~en** *vtr* stretch.

Redak- *cpd*: **~teur** [redak'tøːr] *m* editor; **~tion** [redaktsi'oːn] *f* editing; (*Leute*) editorial staff; (*Büro*) editorial office(s).

Rede ['reːdə] *f* **-, -n** speech; (*Gespräch*) talk; **jdn zur ~ stellen** take sb to task; **~freiheit** *f* freedom of speech; **r~gewandt** a eloquent; **r~n** *vi* talk, speak; *vt* say; *Unsinn etc* talk; **~n** *nt* **-s** talking, speech; **~nsart** *f* set phrase; **~wendung** *f* expression, idiom.

red- *cpd*: **~lich** ['reːtlɪç] a honest; **R~lichkeit** *f* honesty; **R~ner** *m* **-s, -** speaker, orator; **~selig** ['reːtzeːlɪç] a talkative, loquacious; **R~seligkeit** *f* talkativeness.

reduzieren [redu'tsiːrən] *vt* reduce.

Reede ['reːdə] *f* **-, -n** protected anchorage; **~r** *m* **-s, -** shipowner; **~'rei** *f* shipping line or firm.

reell [re'ɛl] a fair, honest; (*Math*) real.

Refer- *cpd*: **~at** [refe'raːt] *nt* **-(e)s, -e** report; (*Vortrag*) paper; (*Gebiet*) section; **~ent** [refe'rɛnt] *m* speaker; (*Berichterstatter*) reporter; (*Sachbearbeiter*) expert; **~enz** [refe'rɛnts] *f* reference; **r~ieren** [refe'riːrən] *vi*: **r~ieren über** (*+acc*) speak or talk on.

reflektieren [reflɛk'tiːrən] *vti* reflect; **~ auf** (*+acc*) be interested in.

Reflex [re'flɛks] *m* **-es, -e** reflex; **~bewegung** *f* reflex action; **r~iv** [-'ksiːf] a (*Gram*) reflexive.

Reform [re'fɔrm] *f* **-, -en** reform; **~a-tion** *f* reformation; **~ator** [-'maːtɔr] *m* reformer; **r~atorisch** a reformatory, reforming; **~haus** *nt* health food shop; **r~ieren** [-'miːrən] *vt* reform.

Refrain [rə'frɛː] *m* **-s, -s** refrain, chorus.

Regal [re'gaːl] *nt* **-s, -e** (book)shelves *pl*, bookcase; stand, rack.

rege ['reːgə] a lively, active; *Geschäft* brisk.

Regel ['reːgəl] *f* **-, -n** rule; (*Med*) period; **r~los** a irregular, unsystematic; **r~mäßig** a regular; **~mäßigkeit** *f*

regularity; **r~n** *vt* regulate, control; *Angelegenheit* settle; *vr*: **sich von selbst r~n** take care of itself; **r~recht** a regular, proper, thorough; **~ung** *f* regulation; settlement; **r~widrig** a irregular, against the rules.

regen ['reːgən] *vtr* move, stir; **R~** *m* **-s, -** rain; **R~bogen** *m* rainbow; **R~bogenhaut** *f* (*Anat*) iris; **R~guß** *m* downpour; **R~mantel** *m* raincoat, mac(kintosh); **R~menge** *f* rainfall; **R~schauer** *m* shower (of rain); **R~schirm** *m* umbrella.

Regent [re'gɛnt] *m* regent; **~schaft** *f* regency.

Regen- *cpd*: **~tag** *m* rainy day; **~wurm** *m* earthworm; **~zeit** *f* rainy season, rains *pl*.

Regie [re'ʒiː] *f* (*Film etc*) direction; (*Theat*) production; **r~ren** [re'giːrən] *vti* govern, rule; **~rung** *f* government; (*Monarchie*) reign; **~rungswechsel** *m* change of government; **~rungszeit** *f* period in government; (*von König*) reign.

Regiment [regi'mɛnt] *nt* **-s, -er** regiment.

Region [regi'oːn] *f* region.

Regisseur [reʒɪ'søːr] *m* director; (*Theat*) (stage) producer.

Register [re'gɪstər] *nt* **-s, -** register; (*in Buch*) table of contents, index.

Registratur [regɪstra'tuːr] *f* registry, record office.

registrieren [regɪs'triːrən] *vt* register.

reg- ['reːg] *cpd*: **R~ler** *m* **-s, -** regulator, governor; **~los** ['reːkloːs] a motionless; **~nen** *vi impers* rain; **~nerisch** a rainy; **~sam** ['reːkzaːm] a active.

regulär [regu'lɛːr] a regular.

regulieren [regu'liːrən] *vt* regulate; (*Comm*) settle.

Regung ['reːguŋ] *f* motion; (*Gefühl*) feeling, impulse; **r~slos** a motionless.

Reh [reː] *nt* **-(e)s, -e** deer, roe; **~bock** *m* roebuck; **~kalb** *nt*, **~kitz** *nt* fawn.

Reib- ['raɪb] *cpd*: **~e** *f* **-, -n,** **~eisen** *nt* grater; **r~en** *vt irreg* rub; (*Cook*) grate; **~e'rei** *f* friction *no pl*; **~fläche** *f* rough surface; **~ung** *f* friction; **r~ungslos** a smooth.

reich [raɪç] a rich; **R~** *nt* **-(e)s, -e** empire, kingdom; (*fig*) realm; **das Dritte R~** the Third Reich; **~en** *vi* reach; (*genügen*) be enough or sufficient (*jdm for* sb); *vt* hold out; (*geben*) pass, hand; (*anbieten*) offer; **~haltig** a ample, rich; **~lich** a ample, plenty of; **R~tum** *m* **-s, -tümer** wealth; **R~weite** *f* range.

reif [raɪf] a ripe; *Mensch, Urteil* mature; **R~** *m* **-(e)s** hoarfrost; **-(e)s, -e** (*Ring*) ring, hoop; **R~e** *f* **-** ripeness; maturity; **~en** *vi* mature; ripen; **R~en** *m* **-s, -** ring, hoop; (*Fahrzeug~*) tyre; **R~enschaden** *m* puncture; **R~eprüfung** *f* school leaving exam; **R~ezeugnis** *nt* school leaving certificate.

Reihe ['raɪə] *f* **-, -n** row; (*von Tagen etc, col*: *Anzahl*) series *sing*; **der ~ nach** in turn; **er ist an der ~** it's his turn; **an die ~ kommen** have one's turn; **r~n** *vt* set in a row; arrange in series; *Perlen* string;

~**nfolge** f sequence; **alphabetische**
~**nfolge** alphabetical order; ~**nhaus** nt
terraced house; ~ r m -s, - heron.
Reim [raɪm] m -(e)s, -e rhyme; r~**en** vt
rhyme.
rein [raɪn] ad (col) = **herein, hinein**; a,
ad pure(ly); (sauber) clean; **etw ins** ~ e
schreiben make a fair copy of sth; **etw
ins** ~ e **bringen** clear up sth; **R~** in cpds
(Comm) net(t); **R~(e)machefrau** f
charwoman; **R~fall** m (col) let-down;
R~gewinn m net profit; **R~heit** f
purity; cleanliness; ~**igen** vt clean;
Wasser purify; **R~igung** f cleaning;
purification; (Geschäft) cleaners;
chemische R~igung dry cleaning; dry
cleaners; ~**lich** a clean; **R~lichkeit** f
cleanliness; ~**rassig** a pedigree;
R~schrift f fair copy; ~**waschen** vr
irreg clear oneself.
Reis [raɪs] m -es, -e rice; nt -es, -er twig,
sprig.
Reise ['raɪzə] f -, -n journey; (Schiff—)
voyage; ~**n** pl travels pl; ~**andenken** nt
souvenir; ~**büro** nt travel agency;
r~**fertig** a ready to start; ~**führer** m
guide(book); (Mensch) travel guide;
~**gepäck** nt luggage; ~**gesellschaft** f
party of travellers; ~**kosten** pl travelling
expenses pl; ~**leiter** m courier;
~**lektüre** f reading matter for the
journey; r~**n** vi travel; go (nach to);
~**nde(r)** mf traveller; ~**paß** m passport;
~**pläne** pl plans pl for a journey;
~**proviant** m provisions pl for the
journey; ~**scheck** m traveller's cheque;
~**tasche** f travelling bag or case;
~**verkehr** m tourist/holiday traffic;
~**wetter** nt holiday weather; ~**ziel** nt
destination.
Reisig ['raɪzɪç] nt -s brushwood.
Reiß- [raɪs] cpd: ~**aus nehmen** run
away, flee; ~**brett** nt drawing board;
r~**en** vti irreg tear; (ziehen) pull, drag;
Witz crack; **etw an sich r~en** snatch sth
up; (fig) take over sth; **sich um etw
r~en** scramble for sth; r~**end** a Fluß
torrential; (Comm) rapid; ~**er** m -s, - (col)
thriller; r~**erisch** a sensationalistic;
~**leine** f (Aviat) ripcord; ~**nagel** m
drawing pin, thumbtack (US); ~**schiene** f
drawing rule, square; ~**verschluß** m
zip(per), zip fastener; ~**zeug** nt geometry
set; ~**zwecke** f = ~ **nagel**.
Reit- ['raɪt] cpd: r~**en** vti irreg ride;
~**er(in** f) m -s, - rider; (Mil) cavalryman,
trooper; ~**e'rei** f cavalry; ~**hose** f riding
breeches pl; ~**pferd** nt saddle horse;
~**stiefel** m riding boot; ~**zeug** nt riding
outfit.
Reiz [raɪts] m -es, -e stimulus; (angenehm)
charm; (Verlockung) attraction; r~**bar** a
irritable; ~**barkeit** f irritability; r~**en** vt
stimulate; (unangenehm) irritate;
(verlocken) appeal to, attract; r~**end** a
charming; r~**los** a unattractive; r~**voll**
a attractive; ~**wäsche** f sexy underwear.
rekeln ['re:kəln] vr stretch out; (lümmeln)
lounge or loll about.
Reklam- ['re:klam] cpd: ~**ation** [reklamatsi'o:n] f

complaint; ~**e** [re'kla:mə] f -, -n advertising; advertisement; ~**e machen für etw**
advertise sth; r~**ieren** [rekla'mi:rən] vti
complain (about); (zurückfordern) reclaim.
rekon- [rekon] cpd: ~**struieren**
[stru'i:rən] vt reconstruct; **R~valeszenz**
[-vales'tsɛnts] f convalescence.
Rekord [re'kɔrt] m -(e)s, -e record;
~**leistung** f record performance.
Rekrut [re'kru:t] m -en, -en recruit;
r~**ieren** ['-ti:rən] vt recruit; vr be
recruited.
Rektor ['rɛktɔr] m (Univ) rector, vice-
chancellor; (Sch) headmaster; ~**at** [-'ra:t]
nt -(e)s, -e rectorate, vice-chancellorship;
headship; (Zimmer) rector's etc office.
Relais [rə'lɛ:] nt -, - relay.
relativ [rela'ti:f] a relative; **R~ität**
[relativi'tɛ:t] f relativity.
relevant [rele'vant] a relevant.
Relief [reli'ɛf] nt -s, -s relief.
Religion [religi'o:n] f religion; ~**slehre** f,
~**sunterricht** m religious instruction.
religiös [religi'ø:s] a religious.
Relikt [re'likt] nt -(e)s, -e relic.
Reling ['re:lɪŋ] f -, -s (Naut) rail.
Reliquie [re'li:kviə] f relic.
Reminiszenz [reminis'tsɛnts] f
reminiscence, recollection.
Remoulade [remu'la:də] f remoulade.
Ren [rɛn] nt -s, -s or -e reindeer.
Rendezvous [rãde'vu:] nt -, - rendezvous.
Renn- ['rɛn] cpd: ~**bahn** f racecourse;
(Aut) circuit, race track; r~**en** vti irreg
run, race; **R~en** nt -s, - running;
(Wettbewerb) race; ~**fahrer** m racing
driver; ~**pferd** nt racehorse; ~**platz** m
racecourse; ~**wagen** m racing car.
renovier- [reno'vi:r] cpd: ~**en** vt renovate; **R~ung** f renovation.
rentabel [rɛn'ta:bəl] a profitable,
lucrative.
Rentabilität [rɛntabili'tɛ:t] f profitability.
Rente ['rɛntə] f -, -n pension;
~**nempfänger** m pensioner.
Rentier ['rɛnti:r] nt reindeer.
rentieren [rɛn'ti:rən] vr pay, be profitable.
Rentner(in f) ['rɛntnər(ın)] m -s, -
pensioner.
Repar- [repa] cpd: ~**ation** [-atsi'o:n] f
reparation; ~**atur** [-ra'tu:r] f repairing;
repair; r~**a'turbedürftig** a in need of
repair; ~**a'turwerkstatt** f repair shop;
(Aut) garage; r~**ieren** [-'ri:rən] vt repair.
Repertoire [reportʊ'a:r] nt -s, -s
repertoire.
Report- cpd: ~**age** [repɔr'ta:ʒə] f -, -n
(on-the-spot) report; (TV, Rad) live
commentary or coverage; ~**er** [re'pɔrtər]
m -s, - reporter, commentator.
Repräsent- cpd: ~**ant** [reprɛzɛn'tant] m
representative; r~**a'tiv** a representative;
Geschenk etc prestigious; r~**ieren**
[reprɛzɛn'ti:rən] vti represent.
Repressalien [reprɛ'sa:liən] pl reprisals
pl.
Reproduktion [reprodʊktsi'o:n] f
reproduction.

reproduzieren [reprodu'tsi:rən] *vt* reproduce.

Reptil [rɛp'ti:l] *nt* **-s, -ien** reptile.

Republik [repu'bli:k] *f* republic; **~aner** ['-ka:nər] *m* **-s, -** republican; **r~anisch** ['-ka:nıʃ] *a* republican.

Reserv- *cpd*: **~at** [rezɛr'va:t] *nt* **-(e)s, -e** reservation; **~e** [re'zɛrvə] *f* **-, -n** reserve; **~erad** *nt* (Aut) spare wheel; **~espieler** *m* reserve; **~etank** *m* reserve tank; **r~ieren** [rezɛr'vi:rən] *vt* reserve; **~ist** [rezɛr'vıst] *m* reservist; **~oir** [rezɛrvo'a:r] *nt* **-s, -e** reservoir.

Residenz [rezi'dɛnts] *f* residence, seat.

Resignation [rezıgnatsi'o:n] *f* resignation.

resignieren [rezı'gni:rən] *vi* resign.

resolut [rezo'lu:t] *a* resolute; **R~ion** [rezolutsi'o:n] *f* resolution.

Resonanz [rezo'nants] *f* (lit, fig) resonance; **~boden** *m* sounding board; **~kasten** *m* resonance box.

Resopal ® [rezo'pa:l] *nt* **-s** formica ®.

Resozialisierung [rezotsiali'zi:ruŋ] *f* rehabilitation.

Respekt [re'spɛkt] *m* **-(e)s** respect; **r~abel** ['-ta:bəl] *a* respectable; **r~ieren** [-'ti:rən] *vt* respect; **r~los** *a* disrespectful; **~sperson** *f* person commanding respect; **r~voll** *a* respectful.

Ressort [rɛ'so:r] *nt* **-s, -s** department.

Rest [rɛst] *m* **-(e)s, -e** remainder, rest; (Über-) remains *pl*; **~er** *pl* (Comm) remnants *pl*.

Restaur- *cpd*: **~ant** [rɛsto'rã:] *nt* **-s, -s** restaurant; **~ation** [rɛstauratsi'o:n] *f* restoration; **r~ieren** [rɛstau'ri:rən] *vt* restore.

Rest- *cpd*: **~betrag** *m* remainder, outstanding sum; **r~lich** *a* remaining; **r~los** *a* complete.

Resultat [rezul'ta:t] *nt* **-(e)s, -e** result.

Retorte [re'tɔrtə] *f* **-, -n** retort.

retten ['rɛtən] *vt* save, rescue.

Retter *m* **-s, -** rescuer, saviour.

Rettich ['rɛtıç] *m* **-s, -e** radish.

Rettung *f* rescue; (Hilfe) help; **seine letzte ~** his last hope; **~sboot** *nt* lifeboat; **~sgürtel** *m*, **~sring** *m* lifebelt, life preserver (US); **r~slos** *a* hopeless.

retuschieren [retu'ʃi:rən] *vt* (Phot) retouch.

Reue ['rɔyə] *f* **-** remorse; (Bedauern) regret; **r~n** *vt*: **es reut ihn** he regrets (it) or is sorry (about it).

reuig ['rɔyıç] *a* penitent.

Revanche [re'vã:ʃə] *f* **-, -n** revenge; (Sport) return match.

revanchieren [revã'ʃi:rən] *vr* (sich rächen) get one's own back, have one's revenge; (erwidern) reciprocate, return the compliment.

Revers [re've:r] *m* or *nt* **-, -** lapel.

revidieren [revi'di:rən] *vt* revise.

Revier [re'vi:r] *nt* **-s, -e** district; (Jagd-) preserve; police station/beat; (Mil) sickbay.

Revision [revizi'o:n] *f* revision; (Comm) auditing; (Jur) appeal.

Revolte [re'vɔltə] *f* **-, -n** revolt.

Revolution [revolutsi'o:n] *f* revolution; **~är** ['-'nɛ:r] *m* **-s, -e** revolutionary; **r~ieren** [-'ni:rən] *vt* revolutionize.

Revolver [re'vɔlvər] *m* **-s, -** revolver.

Rezen- [retsɛn] *cpd*: **~sent** [-'zɛnt] *m* reviewer, critic; **r~sieren** [-'zi:rən] *vt* review; **~sion** [-zi'o:n] *f* review, criticism.

Rezept [re'tsɛpt] *nt* **-(e)s, -e** recipe; (Med) prescription; **r~pflichtig** *a* available only on prescription.

rezitieren [retsi'ti:rən] *vt* recite.

Rhabarber [ra'barbər] *m* **-s** rhubarb.

Rhesusfaktor ['re:zusfaktor] *m* rhesus factor.

Rhetorik [re'to:rık] *f* rhetoric.

rhetorisch [re'to:rıʃ] *a* rhetorical.

Rheuma ['rɔyma] *nt* **-s, Rheumatismus** [rɔyma'tısmus] *m* rheumatism.

Rhinozeros [ri'no:tserɔs] *nt* **-** or **-ses, -se** rhinoceros.

rhyth- ['rʏt] *cpd*: **~misch** *a* rythmical; **R~mus** *m* rhythm.

Richt- ['rıçt] *cpd*: **r~en** *vt* direct (an +acc at; (fig) to); Waffe aim (auf +acc at); (einstellen) adjust; (instand setzen) repair; (zurechtmachen) prepare; (bestrafen) pass judgement on; *vr*: **sich r~en nach** go by; **~en(in** *f*) *m* **-s, -** judge; **r~erlich** *a* judicial; **r~ig** *a* right, correct; (echt) proper; *ad* (col: sehr) really; **der/die ~ige** the right one/person; **das ~ige** the right thing; **~igkeit** *f* correctness; **~igstellung** *f* correction, rectification; **~preis** *m* recommended price; **~ung** *f* direction; tendency, orientation.

riechen ['ri:çən] *vti irreg* smell (an etw (dat) sth; nach of); **ich kann das/ihn nicht ~** (col) I can't stand it/him.

Ried [ri:t] *nt* **-(e)s, -e** reed; marsh.

Riege ['ri:gə] *f* **-, -n** team, squad.

Riegel ['ri:gəl] *m* **-s, -** bolt, bar.

Riemen ['ri:mən] *m* **-s, -** strap; (Gürtel, Tech) belt; (Naut) oar.

Riese ['ri:zə] *m* **-n, -n** giant; **r~ln** *vi* trickle; (Schnee) fall gently; **~nerfolg** *m* enormous success; **r~ngroß** *a*, **r~nhaft** *a* colossal, gigantic, huge.

ries- ['ri:z] *cpd*: **~ig** *a* enormous, huge, vast; **R~in** *f* giantess.

Riff [rıf] *nt* **-(e)s, -e** reef.

Rille ['rılə] *f* **-, -n** groove.

Rind [rınt] *nt* **-(e)s, -er** ox; cow; cattle *pl*; (Cook) beef; **~e** *f* ['rındə] **-, -n** rind; (Baum—) bark; (Brot—) crust; **~fleisch** *nt* beef; **~sbraten** *m* roast beef; **~vieh** *nt* cattle *pl*; (col) blockhead, stupid oaf.

Ring [rıŋ] *m* **-(e)s, -e** ring; **~buch** *nt* loose-leaf book; **~elnatter** *f* grass snake; **r~en** *vi irreg* wrestle; **~en** *nt* **-s** wrestling; **~finger** *m* ring finger; **r~förmig** *a* ring-shaped; **~kampf** *m* wrestling bout; **~richter** *m* referee; **r~s um** *ad* round; **r~sherum** *ad* round about; **~straße** *f* ring road; **r~sum(her)** *ad* (rundherum) round about; (überall) all round.

Rinn- ['rın] *cpd*: **~e** *f* **-, -n** gutter, drain; **r~en** *vi irreg* run, trickle; **~sal** *nt* **-s, -e** trickle of water; **~stein** *m* gutter.

Rippchen ['rıpçən] *nt* small rib; cutlet.

Rippe ['rɪpə] f -, -n rib; ~nfellentzündung f pleurisy.

Risiko ['ri:ziko] nt -s, -s or **Risiken** risk.

riskant [rɪs'kant] a risky, hazardous.

riskieren [rɪs'ki:rən] vt risk.

Riß [rɪs] m -sses, -sse tear; (in Mauer, Tasse etc) crack; (in Haut) scratch; (Tech) design.

rissig ['rɪsɪç] a torn; cracked; scratched.

Ritt [rɪt] m -(e)s, -e ride; ~er m -s, knight; r~erlich a chivalrous; ~erschlag m knighting; ~ertum nt -s chivalry; ~erzeit f age of chivalry; r~lings ad astride.

Ritus ['ri:tʊs] m -, **Riten** rite.

Ritze ['rɪtsə] f -, -n crack, chink; r~n vt scratch.

Rivale [ri'va:lə] m -n, -n rival.

Rivalität [rivali'tɛ:t] f rivalry.

Rizinusöl ['ri:tsinusø:l] nt castor oil.

Robbe ['rɔbə] f -, -n seal.

Robe ['ro:bə] f -, -n robe.

Roboter ['rɔbɔtər] m -s, - robot.

röcheln ['rœçəln] vi wheeze.

Rock [rɔk] m -(e)s, ⁼e skirt; (Jackett) jacket; (Uniform~) tunic.

Rodel ['ro:dəl] m -s, - toboggan; ~bahn f toboggan run; r~n vi toboggan.

roden ['ro:dən] vti clear.

Rogen ['ro:gən] m -s, - roe, spawn.

Roggen ['rɔgən] m -s, - rye; ~brot nt rye bread, black bread.

roh [ro:] a raw; Mensch coarse, crude; R~bau m shell of a building; R~eisen nt pig iron; R~ling m ruffian; R~material nt raw material; R~öl nt crude oil.

Rohr ['ro:r] nt -(e)s, -e pipe, tube; (Bot) cane; (Schilf) reed; (Gewehr~) barrel; ~bruch m burst pipe.

Röhre ['rø:rə] f -, -n tube, pipe; (Rad etc) valve; (Back~) oven.

Rohr- cpd: ~geflecht nt wickerwork; ~leger m -s, - plumber; ~leitung f pipeline; ~post f pneumatic post; ~stock m cane; ~stuhl m basket chair; ~zucker m cane sugar.

Roh- cpd: ~seide f raw silk; ~stoff m raw material.

Rokoko ['rɔkoko] nt -s rococo.

Roll- ['rɔl] cpd: ~(l)aden m shutter; ~bahn f, ~feld nt (Aviat) runway.

Rolle ['rɔlə] f -, -n roll; (Theat, soziologisch) role; (Garn~ etc) reel, spool; (Walze) roller; (Wäsche~) mangle; keine ~ spielen not matter; r~n vti roll; (Aviat) taxi; Wäsche mangle; ~nbesetzung f (Theat) cast; ~r m -s, - scooter; (Welle) roller.

Roll- cpd: ~mops m pickled herring; ~schuh m roller skate; ~stuhl m wheelchair; ~treppe f escalator.

Roman [ro'ma:n] m -s, -e novel; ~schreiber m, ~schriftsteller m novelist; ~tik [ro'mantɪk] f romanticism; ~tiker [ro'mantɪkər] m -s, - romanticist; r~tisch [ro'mantɪʃ] a romantic; ~ze [ro'mantsə] f -, -n romance.

Römer ['rø:mər] m -s, - wineglass; (Mensch) Roman.

röntgen ['rœntgən] vt X-ray; R~aufnahme f, R~bild nt X-ray; R~strahlen pl X-rays pl.

rosa ['ro:za] a pink, rose(-coloured).

Rose ['ro:zə] f -, -n rose; ~nkohl m Brussels sprouts pl; ~nkranz m rosary; ~nmontag m Shrove Monday.

Rosette [ro'zɛtə] f rosette; rose window.

rosig ['ro:zɪç] a rosy.

Rosine [ro'zi:nə] f raisin, currant.

Roß [rɔs] nt -sses, -sse horse, steed; ~kastanie f horse chestnut.

Rost [rɔst] m -(e)s, -e rust; (Gitter) grill, gridiron; (Bett~) springs pl; ~braten m roast(ed) meat, joint; r~en vi rust.

rösten ['rø:stən] vt roast; toast; grill.

Rost- cpd: r~frei a rust-free; rustproof; stainless; r~ig a rusty; ~schutz m rustproofing.

rot [ro:t] a red; R~ation [rotatsi'o:n] f rotation; ~bäckig a red-cheeked; ~blond a strawberry blond.

Röte ['rø:tə] f - redness; ~ln pl German measles sing; r~n vtr redden.

rot- cpd: ~haarig a red-haired; ~ieren [ro'ti:rən] vi rotate; R~käppchen nt Little Red Riding Hood; ~kehlchen nt robin; R~stift m red pencil; R~wein m red wine.

Rotz [rɔts] m -es, -e (col) snot.

Roulade [ru'la:də] f (Cook) beef olive.

Route ['ru:tə] f -, -n route.

Routine [ru'ti:nə] f experience; routine.

Rübe ['ry:bə] f -, -n turnip; gelbe ~ carrot; rote ~ beetroot; ~nzucker m beet sugar.

Rubin [ru'bi:n] m -s, -e ruby.

Rubrik [ru'bri:k] f heading; (Spalte) column.

Ruck [rʊk] m -(e)s, -e jerk, jolt.

Rück- ['rʏk] cpd: ~antwort f reply, answer; r~bezüglich a reflexive; r~blenden vi flash back; r~blickend a retrospective; r~en vti move; ~en m -s, - back; (Berg~) ridge; ~endeckung f backing; ~enlehne f back (of chair); ~enmark nt spinal cord; ~enschwimmen nt backstroke; ~enwind m following wind; ~erstattung f return, restitution; ~fahrt f return journey; ~fall m relapse; r~fällig a relapsing; r~fällig werden relapse; ~flug m return flight; ~frage f question; ~gabe f return; ~gang m decline, fall; r~gängig a: etw r~gängig machen cancel sth; ~grat nt -(e)s, -e spine, backbone; ~griff m recourse; ~halt m backing; reserve; r~haltlos a unreserved; ~kehr f -, -en return; ~koppelung f feedback; ~lage f reserve, savings pl; r~läufig a declining, falling; ~licht nt back light; r~lings ad from behind; backwards; ~nahme f -, -n taking back; ~porto nt return postage; ~reise f return journey; (Naut) home voyage; ~ruf m recall.

Rucksack ['rʊkzak] m rucksack.

Rück- cpd: ~schau f reflection;

r~schauend a, ad retrospective, in retrospect; ~schluß m conclusion; ~schritt m retrogression; r~schrittlich a reactionary; retrograde; ~seite f back; (von Münze etc) reverse; ~sicht f consideration; ~sicht nehmen auf (+acc) show consideration for; r~sichtslos a inconsiderate; Fahren reckless; (unbarmherzig) ruthless; r~sichtsvoll a considerate; ~sitz m back seat; ~spiegel m (Aut) rear-view mirror; ~spiel nt return match; ~sprache f further discussion or talk; ~stand m arrears pl; r~ständig a backward, out-of-date; Zahlungen in arrears; ~stoß m recoil; ~strahler m -s, - rear reflector; ~tritt m resignation; ~trittbremse f pedal brake; ~vergütung f repayment; (Comm) refund; ~versicherung f reinsurance; r~wärtig a rear; r~wärts ad backward(s), back; ~wärtsgang m (Aut) reverse gear; ~weg m return journey, way back; r~wirkend a retroactive; ~wirkung f reaction; retrospective effect; ~zahlung f repayment; ~zug m retreat.

Rüde [ˈryːdə] m -n, -n male dog/fox/wolf; r~ a blunt, gruff.

Rudel [ˈruːdəl] nt -s, - pack; herd.

Ruder [ˈruːdər] nt -s, - oar; (Steuer) rudder; ~boot nt rowing boat; ~er m -s, - rower; r~n vti row.

Ruf [ruːf] m -(e)s, -e call, cry; (Ansehen) reputation; r~en vti irreg call; cry; ~name m usual (first) name; ~nummer f (tele)phone number; ~zeichen nt (Rad) call sign; (Tel) ringing tone.

Rüge [ˈryːgə] f -, -n reprimand, rebuke; r~n vt reprimand.

Ruhe [ˈruːə] f - rest; (Ungestörtheit) peace, quiet; (Gelassenheit, Stille) calm; (Schweigen) silence; sich zur ~ setzen retire; ~! be quiet!, silence!; r~los a restless; r~n vi rest; ~pause f break; ~platz m resting place; ~stand m retirement; letzte ~stätte f final resting place; ~störung f breach of the peace; ~tag m closing day.

ruhig [ˈruːɪç] a quiet; (bewegungslos) still; Hand steady; (gelassen, friedlich) calm; Gewissen clear; tu das ~ feel free to do that.

Ruhm [ruːm] m -(e)s fame, glory.

rühm- [ˈryːm] cpd: ~en vt praise; vr boast; ~lich a laudable.

ruhm- cpd: ~los a inglorious; ~reich a glorious.

Ruhr [ruːr] f - dysentery.

Rühr- [ˈryːr] cpd: ~ei nt scrambled egg; r~en vtr (lit, fig) move, stir (auch Cook); vi: r~en von come or stem from; r~en an (+acc) touch; (fig) touch on; r~end a touching, moving; r~ig a active, lively; r~selig a sentimental, emotional; ~ung f emotion.

Ruin [ruˈiːn] m -s, ~e, f -, -n ruin; r~ieren [ruiˈniːrən] vt ruin.

rülpsen [ˈrylpsən] vi burp, belch.

Rum [rum] m -s, -s rum.

Rummel [ˈruməl] m -s (col) hubbub; (Jahrmarkt) fair; ~platz m fairground, fair.

rumoren [ruˈmoːrən] vi be noisy, make a noise.

Rumpel- [ˈrumpəl] cpd: ~kammer f junk room; r~n vi rumble; (holpern) jolt.

Rumpf [rumpf] m -(e)s, ̈e trunk, torso; (Aviat) fuselage; (Naut) hull.

rümpfen [ˈrympfən] vt Nase turn up.

rund [runt] a round; ad (etwa) around; ~ um etw round sth; R~bogen m Norman or Romanesque arch; R~brief m circular; R~e f [ˈrundə] f -, -n round; (in Rennen) lap; (Gesellschaft) circle; ~en vt make round; vr (fig) take shape; ~erneuert a Reifen remoulded; R~fahrt f (round) trip.

Rundfunk [ˈruntfuŋk] m -(e)s broadcasting; (~anstalt) broadcasting service; im ~ on the radio; ~empfang m reception; ~gebühr f licence; ~gerät nt wireless set; ~sendung f broadcast, radio programme.

Rund- cpd: r~heraus ad straight out, bluntly; r~herum ad round about; all round; r~lich a plump, rounded; ~reise f round trip; ~schreiben nt (Comm) circular; ~ung f curve, roundness.

runter [ˈruntər] ad (col) = herunter, hinunter.

Runzel [ˈruntsəl] f -, -n wrinkle; r~ig a wrinkled; r~n vt wrinkle; die Stirn r~n frown.

Rüpel [ˈryːpəl] m -s, - lout; r~haft a loutish.

rupfen [ˈrupfən] vt pluck; R~ m -s, - sackcloth.

ruppig [ˈrupɪç] a rough, gruff.

Rüsche [ˈryːʃə] f -, -n frill.

Ruß [ruːs] m -es soot; r~en vi smoke; (Ofen) be sooty; r~ig a sooty.

Rüssel [ˈrysəl] m -s, - snout; (Elefanten—) trunk.

rüsten [ˈrystən] vtri prepare; (Mil) arm.

rüstig [ˈrystɪç] a sprightly, vigorous; R~keit f sprightliness, vigour.

Rüstung [ˈrystuŋ] f preparation; arming; (Ritter—) armour; (Waffen etc) armaments pl; ~skontrolle f armaments control.

Rüstzeug nt tools pl; (fig) capacity.

Rute [ˈruːtə] f -, -n rod, switch.

Rutsch [rutʃ] m -(e)s, -e slide; (Erd—) landslide; ~bahn f slide; r~en vi slide; (ausr—en) slip; r~ig a slippery.

rütteln [ˈrytəln] vti shake, jolt.

S

S,s [ɛs] nt S,s.

Saal [zaːl] m -(e)s, Säle hall; room.

Saat [zaːt] f -, -en seed; (Pflanzen) crop; (Säen) sowing.

sabbern [ˈzabərn] vi (col) dribble.

Säbel [ˈzɛːbəl] m -s, - sabre, sword.

Sabotage [zaboˈtaːʒə] f -, -n sabotage.

sabotieren [zaboˈtiːrən] vt sabotage.

Sach- [zax] cpd: ~**bearbeiter** m specialist; s~**dienlich** a relevant, helpful; ~**e** f -, -n thing; (Angelegenheit) affair, business; (Frage) matter; (Pflicht) task; **zur** ~**e** to the point; s~**gemäß** a appropriate, suitable; s~**kundig** a expert; ~**lage** f situation, state of affairs; s~**lich** a matter-of-fact, objective; Irrtum, Angabe factual.

sächlich ['zɛxlɪç] a neuter.

Sach- cpd: ~**schaden** m material damage; s~**t(e)** ad softly, gently; ~**verständige(r)** mf expert.

Sack [zak] m -(e)s, ¨e sack; s~**en** vi sag, sink; ~**gasse** f cul-de-sac, dead-end street (US).

Sadismus [za'dɪsmus] m sadism.

Sadist [za'dɪst] m sadist; s~**isch** a sadistic.

säen ['zɛ:ən] vti sow.

Saft [zaft] m -(e)s, ¨e juice; (Bot) sap; s~**ig** a juicy; s~**los** a dry.

Sage ['za:gə] f -, -n saga.

Säge ['zɛ:gə] f -, -n saw; ~**mehl** nt sawdust; s~**n** vti saw.

sagen ['za:gən] vti say (jdm to sb), tell (jdm sb); ~**haft** a legendary; (col) great, smashing.

Sägewerk nt sawmill.

Sahne ['za:nə] f -, cream.

Saison [zɛ'zõ] f -, -s season; ~**arbeiter** m seasonal worker.

Saite ['zaitə] f -, -n string; ~**ninstrument** nt string instrument.

Sakko ['zako] m or nt -s, -s jacket.

Sakrament [zakra'ment] nt sacrament.

Sakristei [zakrıs'tai] f sacristy.

Salat [za'la:t] m -(e)s, -e salad; (Kopfsalat) lettuce; ~**soße** f salad dressing.

Salb- ['zalp] cpd: ~**e** f -, -n ointment; ~**ei** [zal'bai] m or f -s or - sage; s~**en** vt anoint; ~**ung** f anointing; s~**ungsvoll** a unctuous.

Saldo ['zaldo] m -s, **Salden** balance.

Salmiak [zalmi'ak] m -s sal ammoniac; ~**geist** m liquid ammonia.

Salon [za'lõ:] m -s, -s salon.

salopp [za'lɔp] a casual.

Salpeter [zal'pe:tər] m -s saltpetre; ~**säure** f nitric acid.

Salut [za'lu:t] m -(e)s, -e salute; s~**ieren** [-'ti:rən] vi salute.

Salve ['zalvə] f -, -n salvo.

Salz [zalts] nt -es, -e salt; s~**en** vt irreg salt; s~**ig** a salty; ~**kartoffeln** pl boiled potatoes pl; ~**säure** f hydrochloric acid.

Samen ['za:mən] m -s, - seed; (Anat) sperm.

Sammel- ['zaməl] cpd: ~**band** m anthology; ~**becken** nt reservoir; ~**bestellung** f collective order; s~**n** vt collect; vr assemble, gather; (konzentrieren) concentrate; ~**name** m collective term; ~**surium** [-'zu:rɪum] nt hotchpotch.

Sammlung ['zamluŋ] f collection; assembly, gathering; concentration.

Samstag ['zamsta:k] m Saturday; s~**s** ad (on) Saturdays.

Samt [zamt] m -(e)s, -e velvet; s~ prep +dat (along) with, together with; s~ **und sonders** each and every one (of them).

sämtlich ['zɛmtlıç] a all (the), entire.

Sand [zant] m -(e)s, -e sand; ~**ale** [zan'da:lə] f -, -n sandal; ~**bank** f sand-bank; s~**ig** ['zandıç] a sandy; ~**kasten** m sandpit; ~**kuchen** m Madeira cake; ~**papier** nt sandpaper; ~**stein** m sand-stone; ~**uhr** f hourglass.

sanft [zanft] a soft, gentle; ~**mütig** a gentle, meek.

Sänger(in f) ['zɛŋər(ın)] m -s, - singer.

Sani- cpd: s~**eren** [za'ni:rən] vt re-develop; Betrieb make financially sound; vr line one's pocket; become financially sound; ~**erung** f redevelopment; making viable; s~**tär** [zani'tɛ:r] a sanitary; s~**täre Anlagen** sanitation; ~**täter** [zani'tɛ:tər] m -s, - first-aid attendant; (Mil) (medical) orderly.

sanktionieren [zaŋktsio'ni:rən] vt sanction.

Saphir ['za:fi:r] m -s, -e sapphire.

Sardelle [zar'dɛlə] f anchovy.

Sardine [zar'di:nə] f sardine.

Sarg [zark] m -(e)s, ¨e coffin.

Sarkasmus [zar'kasmus] m sarcasm.

sarkastisch [zar'kastıʃ] a sarcastic.

Satan ['za:tan] m -s, -e Satan; devil.

Satellit [zatɛ'li:t] m -en, -en satellite.

Satire [za'ti:rə] f -, -n satire.

satirisch [za'ti:rıʃ] a satirical.

satt [zat] a full; Farbe rich, deep; jdn/etw ~ **sein** or **haben** be fed up with sb/sth; **sich** ~ **hören/sehen an** (+dat) see/hear enough of; **sich** ~ **essen** eat one's fill; ~ **machen** be filling.

Sattel ['zatəl] m -s, ¨ saddle; (Berg) ridge; s~**fest** a (fig) proficient; s~**n** vt saddle.

sättigen ['zɛtıgən] vt satisfy; (Chem) saturate.

Satz [zats] m -es, ¨e (Gram) sentence; (Neben-, Adverbial-) clause; (Theorem) theorem; (Mus) movement; (Tennis, Briefmarken etc) set; (Kaffee) grounds pl; (Comm) rate; (Sprung) jump; ~**gegenstand** m (Gram) subject; ~**lehre** f syntax; ~**teil** m constituent (of a sentence); ~**ung** f statute, rule; s~**ungsgemäß** a statutory; ~**zeichen** nt punctuation mark.

Sau [zau] f -, **Säue** sow; (col) dirty dog.

sauber ['zaubər] a clean; (ironisch) fine; ~**halten** vt irreg keep clean; S~**keit** f cleanness; (einer Person) cleanliness.

säuber- ['zɔybər] cpd: ~**lich** ad neatly; ~**n** vt clean; (Pol etc) purge; S~**ung** f cleaning; purge.

Sauce ['zo:sə] f -, -n sauce, gravy.

sauer ['zauər] a sour; (Chem) acid; (col) cross.

Sauerei [zauə'rai] f (col) rotten state of affairs; scandal; (Schmutz etc) mess; (Unanständigkeit) obscenity.

säuerlich ['zɔyərlıç] a sourish, tart.

Sauer- cpd: ~**milch** f sour milk; ~**stoff** m oxygen; ~**stoffgerät** nt breathing apparatus; ~**teig** m leaven.

saufen ['zaufən] vti irreg (col) drink, booze.

Säufer ['zɔyfər] m -s, - (col) boozer.

Sauferei [zaufə'rai] f drinking, boozing; booze-up.

saugen ['zaugən] vti irreg suck.

säugen ['zɔygən] vt suckle.

Sauger ['zaugər] m -s, - dummy, comforter (US); (auf Flasche) teat; (Staub—) vacuum cleaner, hoover ®.

Säug- ['zɔyg] cpd: ~etier nt mammal; ~ling m infant, baby.

Säule ['zɔylə] f -, -n column, pillar; ~ngang m arcade.

Saum [zaum] m -(e)s, Säume hem; (Naht) seam.

säumen ['zɔymən] vt hem; seam; vi delay, hesitate.

Sauna ['zauna] f -, -s sauna.

Säure ['zɔyrə] f -, -n acid; (Geschmack) sourness, acidity; s~beständig a acid-proof; s~haltig a acidic.

säuseln ['zɔyzəln] vi murmur, rustle.

sausen ['zauzən] vi blow; (col: eilen) rush; (Ohren) buzz; etw ~ lassen (col) give sth a miss.

Saustall ['zauʃtal] m (col) pigsty.

Saxophon [zakso'foːn] nt -s, -e saxophone.

Schabe ['ʃaːbə] f -, -n cockroach; s~n vt scrape; ~rnack ['ʃaːbərnak] m -(e)s, -e trick, prank.

schäbig ['ʃɛːbɪç] a shabby; S~keit f shabbiness.

Schablone [ʃa'bloːnə] f -, -n stencil; (Muster) pattern; (fig) convention; s~nhaft a stereotyped, conventional.

Schach [ʃax] nt -s, -s chess; (Stellung) check; ~brett nt chessboard; ~figur f chessman; 's~'matt a checkmate; ~partie f, ~spiel nt game of chess.

Schacht [ʃaxt] m -(e)s, -e shaft; ~el f -, -n box; (pej: Frau) bag, cow.

schade ['ʃaːdə] a a pity or shame; sich (dat) zu ~ sein für etw consider oneself too good for sth; interj (what a) pity or shame.

Schädel ['ʃɛːdəl] m -s, - skull; ~bruch m fractured skull.

Schaden ['ʃaːdən] m -s, ·· damage; (Verletzung) injury; (Nachteil) disadvantage; s~ vi (+dat) hurt; einer Sache s~ damage sth; ~ersatz m compensation, damages pl; s~ersatzpflichtig a liable for damages; ~freude f malicious delight; s~froh a gloating, with malicious delight.

schadhaft ['ʃaːthaft] a faulty, damaged.

schäd- ['ʃɛːt] cpd: ~igen ['ʃɛːdɪgən] vt damage; Person do harm to, harm; S~igung f damage; harm; ~lich a harmful (für to); S~lichkeit f harmfulness; S~ling m pest; S~lingsbekämpfungsmittel nt pesticide.

schadlos ['ʃaːtloːs] a: sich ~ halten an (+dat) take advantage of.

Schaf [ʃaːf] nt -(e)s, -e sheep; ~bock m ram.

Schäfchen ['ʃɛːfçən] nt lamb; ~wolken pl cirrus clouds pl.

Schäfer ['ʃɛːfər] m -s, -e shepherd; ~hund m Alsatian; ~in f shepherdess.

schaffen ['ʃafən] vt irreg create; Platz make; sich (dat) etw ~ get o.s. sth; vt (erreichen) manage, do; (erledigen) finish;

Prüfung pass; (transportieren) take; vi (col: arbeiten) work; sich an etw (dat) zu ~ machen busy oneself with sth; S~ nt -s (creative) activity; S~sdrang m creative urge; energy; S~skraft f creativity.

Schaffner(in f) ['ʃafnər(ɪn)] m -s, - (Bus) conductor/conductress; (Rail) guard.

Schaft [ʃaft] m -(e)s, -e shaft; (von Gewehr) stock; (von Stiefel) leg; (Bot) stalk; tree trunk; ~stiefel m high boot.

Schakal [ʃa'kaːl] m -s, -e jackal.

Schäker ['ʃɛːkər] m -s, - flirt; joker; s~n vi flirt; joke.

schal [ʃaːl] a flat; (fig) insipid; S~ m -s, -e or -s scarf.

Schälchen ['ʃɛːlçən] nt cup, bowl.

Schale ['ʃaːlə] f -, -n skin; (abgeschält) peel; (Nuß—, Muschel—, Ei—) shell; (Geschirr) dish, bowl.

schälen ['ʃɛːlən] vt peel; shell; vr peel.

Schall [ʃal] m -(e)s, -e sound; ~dämpfer m -s, - (Aut) silencer; s~dicht a soundproof; s~en vi (re)sound; s~end a resounding, loud; ~mauer f sound barrier; ~platte f (gramophone) record.

Schalt- ['ʃalt] cpd: ~bild nt circuit diagram; ~brett nt switchboard; s~en vt switch, turn; vi (Aut) change (gear); (col: begreifen) catch on; s~en und walten do as one pleases; ~er m -s, - counter; (an Gerät) switch; ~erbeamte(r) m counter clerk; ~hebel m switch; (Aut) gear-lever; ~jahr nt leap year; ~ung f switching; (Elec) circuit; (Aut) gear change.

Scham [ʃaːm] f - shame; (—gefühl) modesty; (Organe) private parts pl.

schämen ['ʃɛːmən] vr be ashamed.

Scham- cpd: ~haare pl pubic hair; s~haft a modest, bashful; s~los a shameless.

Schande ['ʃandə] f - disgrace.

schändlich ['ʃɛntlɪç] a disgraceful, shameful; S~keit f disgracefulness.

Schandtat ['ʃanttaːt] f (col) escapade, shenanigan.

Schändung ['ʃɛnduŋ] f violation, defilement.

Schank- ['ʃaŋk] cpd: ~erlaubnis f, ~konzession f (publican's) licence; ~tisch m bar.

Schanze ['ʃantsə] f -, -n (Mil) fieldwork, earthworks pl; (Sprung—) skijump.

Schar [ʃaːr] f -, -en band, company; (Vögel) flock; (Menge) crowd; in ~en in droves; ~ade [ʃa'raːdə] f charade; s~en vr assemble, rally; s~enweise ad in droves.

scharf [ʃarf] a sharp; Essen hot; Munition live; ~ nachdenken think hard; auf etw (acc) ~ sein (col) be keen on sth; S~blick m (fig) penetration.

Schärf- ['ʃɛrf] cpd: ~e f -, -n sharpness; (Strenge) rigour; s~en vt sharpen.

Scharf- cpd: ~machen vt (col) stir up; ~richter m executioner; ~schießen nt firing live ammunition; ~schütze m marksman, sharpshooter; ~sinn m penetration, astuteness; s~sinnig a astute, shrewd.

Scharmützel [ʃar'mʏtsəl] nt -s, - skirmish.

Scharnier [ʃar'niːr] nt -s, -e hinge.

Schärpe ['ʃɛrpə] f -, -n sash.

scharren ['ʃarən] vti scrape, scratch.

Scharte ['ʃartə] f -, -n notch, nick; (Berg) wind gap.

schartig ['ʃartıç] a jagged.

Schaschlik ['ʃaʃlık] m or nt -s, -s (shish) kebab.

Schatten ['ʃatən] m -s, - shadow; ~**bild** nt, ~**riß** m silhouette; ~**seite** f shady side, dark side.

schattieren [ʃa'tiːrən] vti shade.

Schattierung f shading.

schattig ['ʃatıç] a shady.

Schatulle [ʃa'tulə] f -, -n casket; (Geld—) coffer.

Schatz [ʃats] m -es, ⁻e treasure; (Person) darling; ~**amt** nt treasury.

schätz- ['ʃɛts] cpd: ~**bar** a assessable; **S~chen** nt darling, love; ~**en** vt (abschätzen) estimate; Gegenstand value; (würdigen) value, esteem; (vermuten) reckon; ~**enlernen** vt learn to appreciate; **S~ung** f estimate; estimation; valuation; **nach meiner S~ung ...** I reckon that ...; ~**ungsweise** ad approximately; it is thought; **S~wert** m estimated value.

Schau [ʃau] f - show; (Ausstellung) display, exhibition; **etw zur ~ stellen** make a show of sth, show sth off; ~**bild** nt diagram.

Schauder ['ʃaudər] m -s, -s shudder; (wegen Kälte) shiver; **s~haft** a horrible; **s~n** vi shudder; shiver.

schauen ['ʃauən] vi look.

Schauer ['ʃauər] m -s, - (Regen—) shower; (Schreck) shudder; ~**geschichte** f horror story; **s~lich** a horrific, spine-chilling.

Schaufel ['ʃaufəl] f -, -n shovel; (Naut) paddle; (Tech) scoop; **s~n** vt shovel, scoop.

Schau- cpd: ~**fenster** nt shop window; ~**fensterauslage** f window display; ~**fensterbummel** m window shopping (expedition); ~**fensterdekorateur** m window dresser; ~**geschäft** nt show business; ~**kasten** m showcase.

Schaukel ['ʃaukəl] f -, -n swing; **s~n** vi swing, rock; ~**pferd** nt rocking horse; ~**stuhl** m rocking chair.

Schaulustige(r) ['ʃaulustıgə(r)] mf onlooker.

Schaum [ʃaum] m -(e)s, **Schäume** foam; (Seifen—) lather.

schäumen ['ʃɔʏmən] vi foam.

Schaum- cpd: ~**gummi** m foam (rubber); **s~ig** a frothy, foamy; ~**krone** f white crest; ~**schläger** m (fig) windbag; ~**wein** m sparkling wine.

Schau- cpd: ~**platz** m scene; **s~rig** a horrific, dreadful; ~**spiel** nt spectacle; (Theat) play; ~**spieler** m actor; ~**spielerin** f actress; **s~spielern** vi insep act.

Scheck [ʃɛk] m -s, -s cheque; ~**buch** nt cheque book; **s~ig** a dappled, piebald.

scheel [ʃeːl] a (col) dirty; **jdn ~ ansehen** give sb a dirty look.

scheffeln ['ʃɛfəln] vt amass.

Scheibe ['ʃaibə] f -, -n disc; (Brot etc) slice; (Glas—) pane (Mil) target; ~**nbremse** f (Aut) disc brake; ~**nwaschanlage** f (Aut) windscreen washers pl; ~**nwischer** m (Aut) windscreen wiper.

Scheich [ʃaiç] m -s, -e or -s sheik(h).

Scheide ['ʃaidə] f -, -n sheath; (Grenze) boundary; (Anat) vagina; **s~n** irreg vt separate; Ehe dissolve; **sich s~n lassen** get a divorce; vi (de)part.

Scheidung f (Ehe—) divorce; ~**sgrund** m grounds pl for divorce; ~**sklage** f divorce suit.

Schein [ʃain] m -(e)s, -e light; (An—) appearance; (Geld) (bank)note; (Bescheinigung) certificate; **zum ~ in** pretence; **s~bar** a apparent; **s~en** vi irreg shine; (Anschein haben) seem; **s~heilig** a hypocritical; ~**tod** m apparent death; ~**werfer** m -s, - floodlight; spotlight; (Such—) searchlight; (Aut) headlamp.

Scheiß- ['ʃais] in cpds (col) bloody; ~**e** f - (col) shit.

Scheit [ʃait] nt -(e)s, -e or -er log, billet.

Scheitel ['ʃaitəl] m -s, - top; (Haar) parting; **s~n** vt part; ~**punkt** m zenith, apex.

scheitern ['ʃaitərn] vi fail.

Schelle ['ʃɛlə] f -, -n small bell; **s~n** vi ring.

Schellfisch ['ʃɛlfıʃ] m haddock.

Schelm [ʃɛlm] m -(e)s, -e rogue; **s~isch** a mischievous, roguish.

Schelte ['ʃɛltə] f -, -n scolding; **s~n** vt irreg scold.

Schema ['ʃema] nt -s, -s or -ta scheme, plan; (Darstellung) schema; **nach ~ quite** mechanically; **s~tisch** [ʃe'maːtıʃ] a schematic; (pej) mechanical.

Schemel ['ʃeːməl] m -s, - (foot)stool.

Schenkel ['ʃɛŋkəl] m -s, - thigh.

schenken ['ʃɛŋkən] vt (lit, fig) give; Getränk pour; **sich** (dat) **etw ~** (col) skip sth; **das ist geschenkt!** (billig) that's a giveaway!; (nichts wert) that's worthless!

Schenkung ['ʃɛŋkuŋ] f gift; ~**surkunde** f deed of gift.

Scherbe ['ʃɛrbə] f -, -n broken piece, fragment; (archäologisch) potsherd.

Schere ['ʃeːrə] f -, -n scissors pl; (groß) shears pl; **s~n** vt irreg cut; Schaf shear; (sich kümmern) bother; vr care; **scher dich** (zum Teufel)! get lost!; ~**n-schleifer** m -s, - knife-grinder; ~**'rei** f (col) bother, trouble.

Scherflein ['ʃɛrflain] nt mite, bit.

Scherz [ʃɛrts] m -es, -e joke; fun; ~**frage** f conundrum; **s~haft** a joking, jocular.

scheu [ʃɔʏ] a shy; **S~** f - shyness; (Angst) fear (vor +dat of); (Ehrfurcht) awe; **S~che** f -, -n scarecrow; ~**chen** vt scare (off); ~**en** vr: **sich ~en vor** (+dat) be afraid of, shrink from; vt shun; vi (Pferd) shy.

Scheuer- ['ʃɔʏər] cpd: ~**bürste** f scrubbing brush; ~**lappen** m floorcloth;

~leiste f skirting board; **s~n** vt scour, scrub.

Scheuklappe f blinker.

Scheune ['ʃɔynə] f -, -n barn.

Scheusal ['ʃɔyza:l] nt -s, -e monster.

scheußlich ['ʃɔyslɪç] a dreadful, frightful; **S~keit** f dreadfulness.

Schi [ʃi:] m see **Ski**.

Schicht [ʃɪçt] f -, -en layer; (Klasse) class, level; (in Fabrik etc) shift; **~arbeit** f shift work; **s~en** vt layer, stack.

schick [ʃɪk] a stylish, chic; **~en** vt send; vr resign oneself (in +acc to); v impers (anständig sein) be fitting; **~lich** a proper, fitting; **S~sal** nt -s, -e fate; **~salsschlag** m great misfortune, blow.

Schieb- ['ʃi:b] cpd: **~edach** nt (Aut) sunshine roof; **~en** vti irreg push; Schuld put (auf jdn on sb); **~er** m -s, - slide; (Besteckteil) pusher; (Person) profiteer; **~etür** f sliding door; **~lehre** f (Math) calliper rule; **~ung** f fiddle.

Schieds- ['ʃi:ts] cpd: **~gericht** nt court of arbitration; **~richter** m referee, umpire; (Schlichter) arbitrator; **s~richtern** vti insep referee, umpire; arbitrate; **~spruch** m (arbitration) award.

schief [ʃi:f] a crooked; Ebene sloping; Turm leaning; Winkel oblique; Blick funny; Vergleich distorted; ad crooked(ly); ansehen askance; etw **~ stellen** slope sth.

Schiefer ['ʃi:fər] m -s, - slate; **~dach** nt slate roof; **~tafel** f (child's) slate.

schief- cpd: **~gehen** vi irreg (col) go wrong; **~lachen** vr (col) double up with laughter; **~liegen** vi irreg (col) be wrong.

schielen ['ʃi:lən] vi squint; **nach etw ~** (fig) eye sth.

Schienbein nt shinbone.

Schiene ['ʃi:nə] f -, -n rail; (Med) splint; **s~n** vt put in splints; **~nstrang** m (Rail etc) (section of) track.

schier [ʃi:r] a pure; Fleisch lean and boneless; (fig) sheer; ad nearly, almost.

Schieß- ['ʃi:s] cpd: **~bude** f shooting gallery; **~budenfigur** f (col) clown, ludicrous figure; **s~en** vti irreg shoot (auf +acc at); (Salat etc) run to seed; Ball kick; Geschoß fire; **~e'rei** f shooting incident, shoot-up; **~platz** m firing range; **~pulver** nt gunpowder; **~scharte** f embrasure; **~stand** m rifle or shooting range.

Schiff [ʃɪf] nt -(e)s, -e ship, vessel; (Kirchen—) nave; **s~bar** a navigable; **~bau** m shipbuilding; **~bruch** m shipwreck; **s~brüchig** a shipwrecked; **~chen** nt small boat; (Weben) shuttle; (Mütze) forage cap; **~er** m -s, - bargeman, boatman; **~(f)ahrt** f shipping; (Reise) voyage; **~(f)ahrtslinie** f shipping route; **~sjunge** m cabin boy; **~sladung** f cargo, shipload; **~splanke** f gangplank.

Schikane [ʃi'ka:nə] f -, -n harassment; dirty trick; **mit allen ~n** with all the trimmings.

schikanieren [ʃika'ni:rən] vt harass, torment.

Schild [ʃɪlt] m -(e)s, -e shield; (Mützen—)

peak, visor; etw im **~ führen** be up to sth; nt -(e)s, -er sign; nameplate; (Etikett) label; **~bürger** m duffer, blockhead; **~drüse** f thyroid gland; **s~ern** ['ʃɪldərn] vt depict, portray; **~erung** f description, portrayal; **~kröte** f tortoise; (Wasser—) turtle.

Schilf [ʃɪlf] nt -(e)s, -e, **~rohr** nt (Pflanze) reed; (Material) reeds pl, rushes pl.

schillern ['ʃɪlərn] vi shimmer; **~d** a iridescent.

Schimmel ['ʃɪməl] m -s, - mould; (Pferd) white horse; **s~ig** a mouldy; **s~n** vi get mouldy.

Schimmer ['ʃɪmər] m -s glimmer; **s~n** vi glimmer, shimmer.

Schimpanse [ʃɪm'panzə] m -n, -n chimpanzee.

Schimpf [ʃɪmpf] m -(e)s, -e disgrace; **s~en** vti scold; vi curse, complain; **~wort** nt term of abuse.

Schind- ['ʃɪnd] cpd: **~el** f -, -n shingle; **s~en** irreg vt maltreat, drive too hard; (col) Eindruck **s~en** create an impression; vr sweat and strain, toil away (mit at); **~er** m -s, - knacker; (fig) slave driver; **~e'rei** f grind, drudgery; **~luder** nt: **~luder treiben mit** muck or mess about; Vorrecht abuse.

Schinken ['ʃɪŋkən] m -s, - ham.

Schippe ['ʃɪpə] f -, -n shovel; **s~n** vt shovel.

Schirm [ʃɪrm] m -(e)s, -e (Regen—) umbrella; (Sonnen—) parasol, sunshade; (Wand—, Bild—) screen; (Lampen—) (lamp)shade; (Mützen—) peak; (Pilz—) cap; **~bildaufnahme** f X-ray; **~herr** m patron, protector; **~mütze** f peaked cap; **~ständer** m umbrella stand.

schizophren [ʃitso'fre:n] a schizophrenic.

Schlacht [ʃlaxt] f -, -en battle; **s~en** vt slaughter, kill; **~enbummler** m football supporter; **~er** m -s, - butcher; **~feld** nt battlefield; **~haus** nt, **~hof** m slaughterhouse, abattoir; **~plan** m (lit, fig) battle plan; **~ruf** m battle cry, war cry; **~schiff** nt battle ship; **~vieh** nt animals kept for meat; beef cattle.

Schlacke ['ʃlakə] f -, -n slag.

Schlaf [ʃla:f] m -(e)s sleep; **~anzug** m pyjamas pl.

Schläf- ['ʃlɛ:f] cpd: **~chen** nt nap; **~e** f -, -n temple.

schlafen ['ʃla:fən] vi irreg sleep; **S~gehen** nt -s going to bed; **S~szeit** f bedtime.

Schläfer(in f) ['ʃlɛ:fər(ɪn)] m -s, - sleeper.

schlaff [ʃlaf] a slack; (energielos) limp; (erschöpft) exhausted; **S~heit** f slackness; limpness; exhaustion.

Schlaf- cpd: **~gelegenheit** f sleeping accommodation; **~lied** nt lullaby; **s~los** a sleepless; **~losigkeit** f sleeplessness, insomnia; **~mittel** nt soporific, sleeping pill.

schläfrig ['ʃlɛ:frɪç] a sleepy.

Schlaf- cpd: **~saal** m dormitory; **~sack** m sleeping bag; **~tablette** f sleeping pill; **s~trunken** a drowsy, half-asleep; **~wagen** m sleeping car, sleeper;

s~wandeln *vi insep* sleepwalk; ~zimmer *nt* bedroom.

Schlag [ʃlaːk] *m* -(e)s, ⁼e (*lit, fig*) blow; stroke (*auch Med*); (*Puls-, Herz—*) beat; *pl: Tracht Prügel*) beating; (*Elec*) shock; (*Blitz—*) bolt, stroke; (*Autotür*) car door; (*col: Portion*) helping; (*Art*) kind, type; **mit einem ~** all at once; **~ auf ~** in rapid succession; **~ader** *f* artery; **~anfall** *m* stroke; **s~artig** a sudden, without warning; **~baum** *m* barrier; **s~en** ['ʃlaːgən] *irreg vti* strike, hit; (*wiederholt ~, besiegen*) beat; (*Glocke*) ring; *Stunde* strike; *Sahne* whip; *Schlacht* fight; (*einwickeln*) wrap; **nach jdm s~en** (*fig*) take after sb; *vr* fight; **sich gut s~en** (*fig*) do well; **s~end a** *Beweis* convincing; **s~ende Wetter** (*Min*) firedamp; **~er** ['ʃlaːgər] *m* -s, - (*lit, fig*) hit; **~ersänger(in** *f*) *m* pop singer.

Schläg- ['ʃlɛːg] *cpd:* **~er** *m* -s, - brawler; (*Sport*) bat; (*Tennis etc*) racket; (*golf*) club; hockey stick; (*Waffe*) rapier; **~e'rei** *f* fight, punch-up.

Schlag- *cpd:* **s~fertig** a quick-witted; **~fertigkeit** *f* ready wit, quickness of repartee; **~instrument** *nt* percussion instrument; **~loch** *nt* pothole; **~rahm** *m*, **~sahne** *f* (whipped) cream; **~seite** *f* (*Naut*) list; **~wort** *nt* slogan, catch phrase; **~zeile** *f* headline; **~zeug** *nt* percussion; drums *pl*; **~zeuger** *m* -s, - drummer.

Schlamassel [ʃla'masəl] *m* -s, - (*col*) mess.

Schlamm [ʃlam] *m* -(e)s, -e mud; **s~ig** a muddy.

Schlamp- ['ʃlamp] *cpd:* **~e** *f* -, -n (*col*) slattern, slut; **s~en** *vi* (*col*) be sloppy; **~e'rei** *f* (*col*) disorder, untidiness; sloppy work; **s~ig** a (*col*) slovenly, sloppy.

Schlange ['ʃlaŋə] *f* -, -n snake; (*Menschen—*) queue (*Brit*), line-up (*US*); **~ stehen** (form a) queue, line up.

schlängeln ['ʃlɛŋəln] *vr* twist, wind; (*Fluß*) meander.

Schlangen- *cpd:* **~biß** *m* snake bite; **~ngift** *nt* snake venom; **~linie** *f* wavy line.

schlank [ʃlaŋk] a slim, slender; **S~heit** *f* slimness, slenderness; **S~heitskur** *f* diet.

schlapp [ʃlap] a limp; (*locker*) slack; **S~e** *f* -, -n (*col*) setback; **S~heit** *f* limpness; slackness; **S~hut** *m* slouch hat; **~machen** *vi* (*col*) wilt, droop.

Schlaraffenland [ʃla'rafənlant] *nt* land of milk and honey.

schlau [ʃlau] a crafty, cunning.

Schlauch [ʃlaux] *m* -(e)s, Schläuche hose; (*in Reifen*) inner tube; (*col: Anstrengung*) grind; **~boot** *nt* rubber dinghy; **s~en** *vt* (*col*) tell on, exhaust; **s~los a** *Reifen* tubeless.

Schlau- *cpd:* **~heit** *f*, **Schläue** ['ʃlɔyə] *f* - cunning; **~kopf** *m* clever dick.

schlecht [ʃlɛçt] a bad; **~ und recht** after a fashion; **jdm ist ~** sb feels sick or bad; **~erdings** *ad* simply; **~gehen** *vi impers irreg*: **jdm geht es ~** sb is in a bad way; **S~heit** *f* badness; **'~'hin** *ad* simply; **der Dramatiker ~hin** THE playwright;

S~igkeit *f* badness; bad deed; **~machen** *vt* run down; **etw ~ machen** do sth badly; **~weg** *ad* simply.

schlecken ['ʃlɛkən] *vti* lick.

Schlegel ['ʃleːgəl] *m* -s, - (*drum*)stick; (*Hammer*) mallet, hammer; (*Cook*) leg.

Schleie ['ʃlaiə] *f* -, -n tench.

schleichen ['ʃlaiçən] *vi irreg* creep, crawl; **~d** a gradual; creeping.

Schleier ['ʃlaiər] *m* -s, - veil; **s~haft** a (*col*) **jdm s~haft sein** be a mystery to sb.

Schleif- ['ʃlaif] *cpd:* **~e** *f* -, -n loop; (*Band*) bow; **s~en** *vt* drag; (*Mil*) *Festung* raze; *vi* drag; *vt irreg* grind; *Edelstein* cut; (*Mil*) *Soldaten* drill; **~stein** *m* grindstone.

Schleim [ʃlaim] *m* -(e)s, -e slime; (*Med*) mucus; (*Cook*) gruel; **s~ig** a slimy.

Schlemm- ['ʃlɛm] *cpd:* **s~en** *vi* feast; **~er** *m* -s, - gourmet; **~e'rei** *f* gluttony, feasting.

schlendern ['ʃlɛndərn] *vi* stroll.

Schlendrian ['ʃlɛndriaːn] *m* -(e)s sloppy way of working.

schlenkern ['ʃlɛŋkərn] *vti* swing, dangle.

Schlepp- ['ʃlɛp] *cpd:* **~e** *f* -, -n train; **s~en** *vt* drag; *Auto, Schiff* tow; (*tragen*) lug; **s~end** a dragging, slow; **~er** *m* -s, - tractor; (*Schiff*) tug; **~tau** *nt* towrope; **jdn ins ~tau nehmen** (*fig*) take sb in tow.

Schleuder ['ʃlɔydər] *f* -, -n catapult; (*Wäsche—*) spin-drier; (*Butter— etc*) centrifuge; **s~n** *vt* hurl; *Wäsche* spin-dry; *vi* (*Aut*) skid; (*Preise*) give-away price; **~sitz** *m* (*Aviat*) ejector seat; (*fig*) hot seat; **~ware** *f* cheap or cut-price goods *pl*.

schleunig [ʃlɔyniç] a quick, prompt; **~st** *ad* straight away.

Schleuse ['ʃlɔyzə] *f* -, -n lock; (*—ntor*) sluice.

Schlich [ʃliç] *m* -(e)s, -e dodge, trick.

schlicht [ʃliçt] a simple, plain; **~en** *vt* smooth, dress; *Streit* settle; **S~er** *m* -s, - mediator, arbitrator; **S~ung** *f* settlement; arbitration.

Schlick [ʃlik] *m* -(e)s, -e mud; (*Öl—*) slick.

Schließ- ['ʃliːs] *cpd:* **~e** *f* -, -n fastener; **s~en** *irreg vtir* close, shut; (*beenden*) close; *Freundschaft, Bündnis, Ehe* enter into; (*folgern*) infer (*aus +dat* from); **etw in sich s~en** include sth; **~fach** *nt* locker; **s~lich** *ad* finally; (*— doch*) after all.

Schliff [ʃlif] *m* -(e)s, -e cut(ting); (*fig*) polish.

schlimm [ʃlim] a bad; **~er** a worse; **~ste(r,s)** a worst; **~stenfalls** *ad* at (the) worst.

Schling- ['ʃliŋ] *cpd:* **~e** *f* -, -n loop; (*esp Henkers—*) noose; (*Falle*) snare; (*Med*) sling; **~el** *m* -s, - rascal; **s~en** *irreg vt* wind; *vti* (*essen*) bolt (one's food), gobble; **s~ern** *vi* roll.

Schlips [ʃlips] *m* -es, -e tie.

Schlitten ['ʃlitən] *m* -s, - sledge, sleigh; **~bahn** *f* toboggan run; **~fahren** *nt* -s tobogganing.

schlittern ['ʃlitərn] *vi* slide.

Schlittschuh ['ʃlit-ʃuː] *m* skate; **~ laufen** skate; **~bahn** *f* skating rink; **~läufer(in** *f*) *m* skater.

Schlitz [ʃlits] *m* -es, -e slit; (*für Münze*)

slot; (Hosen—) flies pl; s~äugig a slant-eyed; s~en vt slit.

schlohweiß [ʃloːˈvaɪs] a snow-white.

Schloß [ʃlɔs] nt -sses, ¨sser lock; (an Schmuck etc) clasp; (Bau) castle; chateau.

Schlosser [ˈʃlɔsər] m -s, - (Auto—) fitter; (für Schlüssel etc) locksmith; ~ei [-ˈraɪ] f metal (working) shop.

Schlot [ʃloːt] m -(e)s, -e chimney; (Naut) funnel.

schlottern [ˈʃlɔtərn] vi shake, tremble; (Kleidung) be baggy.

Schlucht [ʃluxt] f-, -en gorge, ravine.

schluchzen [ˈʃluxtsən] vi sob.

Schluck [ʃluk] m -(e)s, -e swallow; (Menge) drop; ~auf m -s, ~en m -s, -hiccups pl; s~en vti swallow.

schludern [ˈʃluːdərn] vi skimp, do sloppy work.

Schlummer [ˈʃlumər] m -s slumber; s~n vi slumber.

Schlund [ʃlunt] m -(e)s, ¨e gullet; (fig) jaw.

schlüpfen [ˈʃlʏpfən] vi slip; (Vogel etc) hatch (out).

Schlüpfer [ˈʃlʏpfər] m -s, - panties pl, knickers pl.

Schlupfloch [ˈʃlupflɔx] nt hole; hide-out; (fig) loophole.

schlüpfrig [ˈʃlʏpfrɪç] a slippery; (fig) lewd; S~keit f slipperiness; (fig) lewdness.

schlurfen [ˈʃlurfən] vi shuffle.

schlürfen [ˈʃlʏrfən] vti slurp.

Schluß [ʃlus] m -sses, ¨sse end; (—folgerung) conclusion; am ~ at the end; ~ machen mit finish with.

Schlüssel [ˈʃlʏsəl] m -s, - (lit, fig) key; (Schraub—) spanner, wrench; (Mus) clef; ~bein nt collarbone; ~blume f cowslip, primrose; ~bund m bunch of keys; ~kind nt latchkey child; ~loch nt keyhole; ~position f key position; ~wort f combination.

schlüssig [ˈʃlʏsɪç] a conclusive.

Schluß- cpd: ~licht nt taillight; (fig) tailender; ~strich m (fig) final stroke; ~verkauf m clearance sale; ~wort nt concluding words pl.

Schmach [ʃmaːx] f- disgrace, ignominy.

schmachten [ˈʃmaːxtən] vi languish; long (nach for).

schmächtig [ˈʃmɛçtɪç] a slight.

schmachvoll a ignominious, humiliating.

schmackhaft [ˈʃmakhaft] a tasty.

schmäh- [ʃmɛː] cpd: ~en vt abuse, revile; ~lich a ignominious, shameful; S~ung f abuse.

schmal [ʃmaːl] a narrow; Person, Buch etc slender, slim; (karg) meagre.

schmälern [ˈʃmɛːlərn] vt diminish; (fig) belittle.

Schmal- cpd: ~film m cine film; ~spur f narrow gauge.

Schmalz [ʃmalts] nt -es, -e dripping, lard; (fig) sentiment, schmaltz; s~ig a (fig) schmaltzy, slushy.

schmarotzen [ʃmaˈrɔtsən] vi sponge; (Bot) be parasitic.

Schmarotzer m -s, - parasite; sponger.

Schmarren [ˈʃmarən] m -s, - (Aus) small

piece of pancake; (fig) rubbish, tripe.

schmatzen [ˈʃmatsən] vi smack one's lips; eat noisily.

Schmaus [ʃmaus] m -es, **Schmäuse** feast; s~en vi feast.

schmecken [ˈʃmɛkən] vti taste; es schmeckt ihm he likes it.

Schmeichel- [ˈʃmaɪçəl] cpd: ~ei [-ˈlaɪ] f flattery; s~haft a flattering; s~n vi flatter.

schmeißen [ˈʃmaɪsən] vt irreg (col) throw, chuck.

Schmeißfliege f bluebottle.

Schmelz [ʃmɛlts] m -es, -e enamel; (Glasur) glaze; (von Stimme) melodiousness; s~bar a fusible; s~en vti irreg melt; Erz smelt; ~hütte f smelting works pl; ~punkt m melting point; ~wasser nt melted snow.

Schmerz [ʃmɛrts] m -es, -en pain; (Trauer) grief; s~empfindlich a sensitive to pain; s~en vti hurt; ~ensgeld nt compensation; s~haft, s~lich a painful; s~los a painless; s~stillend a soothing.

Schmetterling [ˈʃmɛtərlɪŋ] m butterfly.

schmettern [ˈʃmɛtərn] vti smash; Melodie sing loudly, bellow out; (Trompete) blare.

Schmied [ʃmiːt] m -(e)s, -e blacksmith; ~e [ˈʃmiːdə] f -, -n smithy, forge; ~eisen nt wrought iron; s~en vt forge; Pläne devise, concoct.

schmiegen [ˈʃmiːgən] vt press, nestle; vr cling, nestle (up) (an +acc to).

schmiegsam [ˈʃmiːkzaːm] a flexible, pliable.

Schmier- [ˈʃmiːr] cpd: ~e f -, -n grease; (Theat) greasepaint, make-up; s~en vt smear; (ölen) lubricate, grease; (bestechen) bribe; vti (schreiben) scrawl; ~fett nt grease; ~fink m messy person; ~geld nt bribe; s~ig a greasy; ~mittel nt lubricant; ~seife f soft soap.

Schminke [ˈʃmɪŋkə] f -, -n make-up; s~n vtr make up.

schmirgel- [ˈʃmɪrgəl] cpd: ~n vt sand (down); S~papier nt emery paper.

Schmöker [ˈʃmøːkər] m -s, - (col) (trashy) old book; s~n vi (col) browse.

schmollen [ˈʃmɔlən] vi sulk, pout; ~d a sulky.

Schmor- [ʃmoːr] cpd: ~braten m stewed or braised meat; s~en vt stew, braise.

Schmuck [ʃmuk] m -(e)s, -e jewellery; (Verzierung) decoration.

schmücken [ˈʃmʏkən] vt decorate.

Schmuck- cpd: s~los a unadorned, plain; ~losigkeit f simplicity; ~sachen pl jewels pl, jewellery.

Schmuggel [ˈʃmugəl] m -s smuggling; s~n vti smuggle.

Schmuggler m -s, - smuggler.

schmunzeln [ˈʃmuntsəln] vi smile benignly.

Schmutz [ʃmuts] m -es dirt, filth; s~en vi get dirty; ~fink m filthy creature; ~fleck m stain; s~ig a dirty.

Schnabel [ˈʃnaːbəl] m -s, ¨ beak, bill; (Ausguß) spout.

Schnake [ˈʃnaːkə] f -, -n cranefly; (Stechmücke) gnat.

Schnalle ['ʃnalə] f -, -n buckle, clasp; s~n vt buckle.

schnalzen ['ʃnaltsən] vi snap; (mit Zunge) click.

Schnapp- ['ʃnap] cpd: s~en vt grab, catch; vi snap; ~schloß nt spring lock; ~schuß m (Phot) snapshot.

Schnaps [ʃnaps] m -es, ⁻e spirits pl; schnapps.

schnarchen ['ʃnarçən] vi snore.

schnattern ['ʃnatərn] vi chatter; (zittern) shiver.

schnauben ['ʃnaubən] vi snort; vr blow one's nose.

schnaufen ['ʃnaufən] vi puff, pant.

Schnauz- ['ʃnauts] cpd: ~bart m moustache; ~e f -, -n snout, muzzle; (Ausguß) spout; (col) gob.

Schnecke ['ʃnɛkə] f -, -n snail; ~nhaus nt snail's shell.

Schnee ['ʃneː] m -s snow; (Ei—) beaten egg white; ~ball m snowball; ~flocke f snowflake; ~gestöber nt snowstorm; ~glöckchen nt snowdrop; ~kette f (Aut) (snow) chain; ~pflug m snowplough; ~schmelze f -, -n thaw; ~wehe f snowdrift; ~wittchen nt Snow White.

Schneid [ʃnait] m -(e)s (col) pluck; ~e ['ʃnaidə] f -, -n edge; (Klinge) blade; s~en vtr irreg cut (o.s.); (kreuzen) cross, intersect; s~end a cutting; ~er m -s, - tailor; ~erin f dressmaker; s~ern vt make; vi be a tailor; ~ezahn m incisor; s~ig a dashing; (mutig) plucky.

schneien ['ʃnaiən] vi snow.

Schneise ['ʃnaizə] f -, -n clearing.

schnell [ʃnɛl] a,ad quick(ly), fast; ~en vi shoot, fly; S~hefter m -s, - loose-leaf binder; S~igkeit f speed; ~stens ad as quickly as possible; S~straße f expressway; S~zug m fast or express train.

schneuzen ['ʃnɔytsən] vr blow one's nose.

schnippisch ['ʃnɪpɪʃ] a sharp-tongued.

Schnitt [ʃnɪt] m -(e)s, -e cut(ting); (—punkt) intersection; (Quer—) (cross) section; (Durch—) average; (—muster) pattern; (Ernte) crop; (an Buch) edge; (col: Gewinn) profit; ~blumen pl cut flowers pl; ~e f -, -n slice; (belegt) sandwich; ~fläche f section; ~lauch m chive; ~muster nt pattern; ~punkt m (point of) intersection; ~wunde f cut.

Schnitz- ['ʃnɪts] cpd: ~arbeit f wood carving; ~el nt -s, - chip; (Cook) escalope; s~en vt carve; ~er m -s, - carver; (col) blunder; ~erei f carving, carved woodwork.

schnodderig ['ʃnɔdəriç] a (col) snotty.

schnöde ['ʃnøːdə] a base, mean.

Schnorchel ['ʃnɔrçəl] m -s, - snorkel.

Schnörkel ['ʃnœrkəl] m -s, - flourish; (Archit) scroll.

schnorren ['ʃnɔrən] vti cadge.

schnüffeln ['ʃnyfəln] vi sniff.

Schnüffler m -s, - snooper.

Schnuller ['ʃnʊlər] m -s, - dummy, comforter (US).

Schnupfen ['ʃnʊpfən] m -s, - cold.

schnuppern ['ʃnʊpərn] vi sniff.

Schnur [ʃnuːr] f -, ⁻e string, cord; (Elec)

flex; s~gerade a straight (as a die or arrow).

schnüren ['ʃnyːrən] vt tie.

Schnurr- ['ʃnʊr] cpd: ~bart m moustache; s~en vi purr; (Kreisel) hum.

Schnür- ['ʃnyːr] cpd: ~schuh m lace-up (shoe); ~senkel m shoelace.

schnurstracks ad straight (away).

Schock [ʃɔk] m -(e)s, -e shock; s~ieren [ʃɔˈkiːrən] vt shock, outrage.

Schöffe ['ʃœfə] m -n, -n lay magistrate; ~ngericht nt magistrates' court.

Schöffin f lay magistrate.

Schokolade [ʃokoˈlaːdə] f -, -n chocolate.

Scholle ['ʃɔlə] f -, -n clod; (Eis—) ice floe; (Fisch) plaice.

schon [ʃoːn] ad already; (zwar) certainly; warst du ~ einmal da? have you ever been there?; ich war ~ einmal da I've been there before; das ist ~ immer so that has always been the case; das wird ~ (noch) gut that'll be OK; wenn ich das ~ höre . . . I only have to hear that . . .; ~ der Gedanke the very thought.

schön [ʃøːn] a beautiful; (nett) nice; ~e Grüße best wishes; ~en Dank (many) thanks.

schonen ['ʃoːnən] vt look after; vr take it easy; ~d a careful, gentle.

Schön- cpd: ~geist m cultured person, aesthete; ~heit f beauty; ~heitsfehler m blemish, flaw; ~heitsoperation f cosmetic plastic surgery; s~machen vr make oneself look nice.

Schon- cpd: ~ung f good care; (Nachsicht) consideration; (Forst) plantation of young trees; s~ungslos a unsparing, harsh; ~zeit f close season.

Schöpf- ['ʃœpf] cpd: s~en vt scoop, ladle; (Mut) summon up; (Luft) breath in; ~er m -s, - creator; s~erisch a creative; ~kelle f ladle; ~löffel m skimmer, scoop; ~ung f creation.

Schorf ['ʃɔrf] m -(e)s, -e scab.

Schornstein ['ʃɔrnʃtain] m chimney; (Naut) funnel; ~feger m -s, - chimney sweep.

Schoß [ʃoːs] m -es, ⁻e lap; (Rock—) coat tail; ~hund m pet dog, lapdog.

Schote ['ʃoːtə] f -, -n pod.

Schotter ['ʃɔtər] m -s broken stone, road metal; (Rail) ballast.

schraffieren [ʃraˈfiːrən] vt hatch.

schräg [ʃrɛːk] a slanting, not straight; etw ~ stellen put sth at an angle; ~gegenüber diagonally opposite; S~e f -, -n slant; S~schrift f italics pl; S~streifen m bias binding; S~strich m oblique stroke.

Schramme ['ʃramə] f -, -n scratch; s~n vt scratch.

Schrank [ʃraŋk] m -(e)s, ⁻e cupboard; (Kleider—) wardrobe; ~e f -, -n barrier; s~enlos a boundless; (zügellos) unrestrained; ~enwärter m (Rail) level crossing attendant; ~koffer m trunk.

Schraube ['ʃraubə] f -, -n screw; s~n vt screw; ~nschlüssel m spanner; ~nzieher m -s, - screwdriver.

Schraubstock ['ʃraubʃtɔk] m (Tech) vice.
Schrebergarten ['ʃre:bərgartən] m allotment.
Schreck [ʃrɛk] m -(e)s, -e, ~en m -s, - terror; fright; **s~en** vt frighten, scare; ~gespenst nt spectre, nightmare; **s~haft** a jumpy, easily frightened; **s~lich** a terrible, dreadful; ~schuß m shot fired in the air.
Schrei [ʃraɪ] m -(e)s, -e scream; (Ruf) shout.
Schreib- ['ʃraɪb] cpd: ~block m writing pad; **s~en** vti irreg write; (buchstabieren) spell; ~en nt -s, - letter, communication; ~er m -s, - writer; (Büro~) clerk; **s~faul** a bad about writing letters; ~fehler m spelling mistake; ~maschine f typewriter; ~papier nt notepaper; ~tisch m desk; ~ung f spelling; ~waren pl stationery; ~weise f spelling; way of writing; ~zeug nt writing materials pl.
schreien ['ʃraɪən] vti irreg scream; (rufen) shout; ~d a (fig) glaring; Farbe loud.
Schreiner ['ʃraɪnər] m -s, - joiner; (Zimmermann) carpenter; (Möbel~) cabinetmaker; ~ei [-'raɪ] f joiner's workshop.
schreiten ['ʃraɪtən] vi irreg stride.
Schrift [ʃrɪft] f -, -en writing; handwriting; (~art) script; (Gedrucktes) pamphlet, work; ~deutsch nt written German; ~führer m secretary; **s~lich** a written; ad in writing; ~setzer m compositor; ~sprache f written language; ~steller(in f) m -s, - writer; ~stück nt document.
schrill [ʃrɪl] a shrill; ~en vi sound or ring shrilly.
Schritt [ʃrɪt] m -(e)s, -e step; (Gangart) walk; (Tempo) pace; (von Hose) crutch; ~macher m -s, pacemaker; ~(t)empo nt: im ~(t)empo at a walking pace.
schroff [ʃrɔf] a steep; (zackig) jagged; (fig) brusque; (ungeduldig) abrupt.
schröpfen ['ʃrœpfən] vt (fig) fleece.
Schrot [ʃro:t] m or nt -(e)s, -e (Blei) (small) shot; (Getreide) coarsely ground grain, groats pl; ~flinte f shotgun.
Schrott [ʃrɔt] m -(e)s, -e scrap metal; ~haufen m scrap heap; **s~reif** a ready for the scrap heap.
schrubben ['ʃrubən] vt scrub.
Schrubber m -s, - scrubbing brush.
Schrulle ['ʃrulə] f -, -n eccentricity, queer idea/habit.
schrumpfen ['ʃrumpfən] vi shrink; (Apfel) shrivel.
Schub- ['ʃu:b] cpd: ~fach nt drawer; ~karren m wheelbarrow; ~lade f drawer.
schüchtern ['ʃʏçtərn] a shy; **S~heit** f shyness.
Schuft [ʃuft] m -(e)s, -e scoundrel; **s~en** vi (col) graft, slave away.
Schuh [ʃu:] m -(e)s, -e shoe; ~band nt shoelace; ~creme f shoe polish; ~löffel m shoehorn; ~macher m -s, - shoemaker.
Schul- ['ʃu:l] cpd: ~aufgaben pl

homework; ~besuch m school attendance.
Schuld [ʃult] f -, -en guilt; (Fin) debt; (Verschulden) fault; **s~** a: **s~ sein** or **haben** be to blame (an +dat for); **er ist** or **hat s~** it's his fault; **jdm s~ geben** blame sb; **s~en** ['ʃuldən] vt owe; **s~enfrei** a free from debt; ~gefühl nt feeling of guilt; **s~ig** a guilty (an +dat of); (gebührend) due; **jdm etw s~ig sein** owe sb sth; **jdm etw s~ig bleiben** not provide sb with sth; **s~los** a innocent, without guilt; ~ner m -s, - debtor; ~schein m promissory note, IOU; ~spruch m verdict of guilty.
Schule ['ʃu:lə] f -, -n school; **s~n** vt train, school.
Schüler(in f) ['ʃy:lər(ɪn)] m -s, - pupil.
Schul- ['ʃu:l] cpd: ~ferien pl school holidays pl; **s~frei** a: **s~freier Tag** holiday; **s~frei sein** be a holiday; ~funk m schools' broadcasts pl; ~geld nt school fees pl; ~hof m playground; ~jahr nt school year; ~junge m schoolboy; ~mädchen nt schoolgirl; **s~pflichtig** a of school age; ~schiff nt (Naut) training ship; ~stunde f period, lesson; ~tasche f satchel.
Schulter ['ʃultər] f -, -n shoulder; ~blatt nt shoulder blade; **s~n** vt shoulder.
Schul- cpd: ~ung f education, schooling; ~wesen nt educational system; ~zeugnis nt school report.
Schund [ʃunt] m -(e)s trash, garbage; ~roman m trashy novel.
Schuppe ['ʃupə] f -, -n scale; pl (Haar~) dandruff; **s~n** vt scale; vr peel; ~n m -s, - shed.
schuppig ['ʃupɪç] a scaly.
Schur [ʃu:r] f -, -en shearing.
Schür- ['ʃy:r] cpd: ~eisen nt poker; **s~en** vt rake; (fig) stir up; **s~fen** ['ʃʏrfən] vti scrape, scratch; (Min) prospect, dig; ~fung f abrasion; (Min) prospecting; ~haken m poker.
Schurke ['ʃurkə] m -n, -n rogue.
Schurz [ʃurts] m -es, -e, **Schürze** ['ʃʏrtsə] f -, -n apron.
Schuß [ʃus] m -sses, -̈sse shot; (Weben) woof; ~bereich m effective range.
Schüssel ['ʃʏsəl] f -, -n bowl.
Schuß- cpd: ~linie f line of fire; ~verletzung f bullet wound; ~waffe f firearm; ~weite f range (of fire).
Schuster ['ʃu:stər] m -s, - cobbler, shoemaker.
Schutt [ʃut] m -(e)s rubbish; (Bau~) rubble; ~abladeplatz m refuse dump.
Schütt- ['ʃʏt] cpd: ~elfrost m shivering; **s~eln** vtr shake; **s~en** vt pour; (Zucker, Kies etc) tip; (ver~) spill; vi impers pour (down); **s~er** a Haare sparse, thin.
Schutt- cpd: ~halde f dump; ~haufen m heap of rubble.
Schutz [ʃuts] m -es protection; (Unterschlupf) shelter; **jdn in ~ nehmen** stand up for sb; ~anzug m overalls pl; ~befohlene(r) mf charge; ~blech nt mudguard; ~brille f goggles pl.
Schütze ['ʃʏtsə] m -n, -n gunman;

(Gewehr—) rifleman; (Scharf—, Sport—) marksman; (Astrol) Sagittarius.

Schutz- cpd: **~engel** m guardian angel; **~gebiet** nt protectorate; (Natur—) reserve; **~haft** f protective custody; **~impfung** f immunisation; **s~los** a defenceless; **~mann** m, pl -leute or -männer policeman; **~maßnahme** f precaution; **~patron** m patron saint; **~umschlag** m (book) jacket; **~vorrichtung** f safety device.

schwach [ʃvax] a weak, feeble.

Schwäche [ʃvɛçə] f -, -n weakness; **s~n** vt weaken.

Schwach- cpd: **~heit** f weakness; **s~köpfig** a silly, lame-brained.

Schwäch- cpd: **s~lich** a weakly, delicate; **~ling** m weakling.

Schwach- cpd: **~sinn** m imbecility; **s~sinnig** a mentally deficient; Idee idiotic; **~strom** m weak current.

Schwächung [ʃvɛçʊŋ] f weakening.

Schwaden [ʃvaːdən] m -s, - cloud.

schwafeln [ʃvaːfəln] vti blather, drivel.

Schwager [ʃvaːgər] m -s, ˝ brother-in-law.

Schwägerin [ʃvɛːgərin] f sister-in-law.

Schwalbe [ʃvalbə] f -, -n swallow.

Schwall [ʃval] m -(e)s, -e surge; (Worte) flood, torrent.

Schwamm [ʃvam] m -(e)s, ˝e sponge; (Pilz) fungus; **s~ig** a spongy; Gesicht puffy.

Schwan [ʃvaːn] m -(e)s, ˝e swan; **s~en** vi impers: **jdm schwant etw** sb has a foreboding of sth.

schwanger [ʃvaŋər] a pregnant.

schwängern [ʃvɛŋərn] vt make pregnant.

Schwangerschaft f pregnancy.

Schwank [ʃvaŋk] m -(e)s, ˝e funny story; **s~en** vi sway; (taumeln) stagger, reel; (Preise, Zahlen) fluctuate; (zögern) hesitate, vacillate; **~ung** f fluctuation.

Schwanz [ʃvants] m -es, ˝e tail.

schwänzen [ʃvɛntsən] (col) vt skip, cut; vi play truant.

Schwänzer [ʃvɛntsər] m -s, - (col) truant.

Schwarm [ʃvarm] m -(e)s, ˝e swarm; (col) heart-throb, idol.

schwärm- [ʃvɛrm] cpd: **~en** vi swarm; **~en für** be mad or wild about; **S~erei** f [-əˈraɪ] f enthusiasm; **~erisch** a impassioned, effusive.

Schwarte [ʃvaːrtə] f -, -n hard skin; (Speck—) rind.

schwarz [ʃvarts] a black; **ins S~e treffen** (lit, fig) hit the bull's eye; **S~arbeit** f illicit work, moonlighting; **S~brot** nt black bread.

Schwärze [ʃvɛrtsə] f -, -n blackness; (Farbe) blacking; (Drucker—) printer's ink; **s~n** vt blacken.

Schwarz- cpd: **s~fahren** vi irreg travel without paying; drive without a licence; **~handel** m black-market (trade); **s~hören** vi listen to the radio without a licence.

schwärzlich [ʃvɛrtslɪç] a blackish, darkish.

Schwarz- cpd: **~markt** m black market; **s~sehen** vi irreg (col) see the gloomy side

of things; (TV) watch TV without a licence; **~seher** m pessimist; (TV) viewer without a licence; **s~weiß** a black and white.

schwatzen [ʃvatsən], **schwätzen** [ʃvɛtsən] vi chatter.

Schwätzer [ʃvɛtsər] m -s, - gasbag; **~in** f chatterbox, gossip.

schwatzhaft a talkative, gossipy.

Schwebe [ʃveːbə] f: **in der ~** (fig) in abeyance; **~bahn** f overhead railway; **~balken** m (Sport) beam; **s~n** vi drift, float; (hoch) soar; (unentschieden sein) be in the balance.

Schwefel [ʃveːfəl] m -s sulphur; **s~ig** a sulphurous; **~säure** f sulphuric acid.

Schweif [ʃvaɪf] m -(e)s, -e tail; **s~en** vi wander, roam.

Schweig- [ʃvaɪg] cpd: **~egeld** nt hush money; **s~en** vi irreg be silent; stop talking; **~en** nt -s silence; **s~sam** [ʃvaɪkzaːm] a silent, taciturn; **~samkeit** f taciturnity, quietness.

Schwein [ʃvaɪn] nt -(e)s, -e pig; (fig) (good) luck; **~efleisch** nt pork; **~ehund** m (col) stinker, swine; **~erei** [-əˈraɪ] f mess; (Gemeinheit) dirty trick; **~estall** m pigsty; **s~isch** a filthy; **~sleder** nt pigskin.

Schweiß [ʃvaɪs] m -es sweat, perspiration; **s~en** vti weld; **~er** m -s, - welder; **~füße** pl sweaty feet pl; **~naht** f weld.

schwelen [ʃveːlən] vi smoulder.

schwelgen [ʃvɛlgən] vi indulge.

Schwelle [ʃvɛlə] f -, -n threshold (auch fig); doorstep; (Rail) sleeper; **s~n** vi irreg swell.

Schwellung f swelling.

Schwengel [ʃvɛŋəl] m -s, - pump handle; (Glocken-) clapper.

Schwenk- [ʃvɛŋk] cpd: **s~bar** a swivel-mounted; **s~en** vt swing; Fahne wave; (abspülen) rinse; vi turn, swivel; (Mil) wheel; **~ung** f turn; wheel.

schwer [ʃveːr] a heavy; (schwierig) difficult, hard; (schlimm) serious, bad; ad (sehr) very (much); verletzt etc seriously, badly; **S~arbeiter** m manual worker, labourer; **S~e** f -, -n weight, heaviness; (Phys) gravity; **~elos** a weightless; Kammer zero-G; **S~enöter** m -s, - casanova, ladies' man; **~erziehbar** a difficult (to bring up); **~fallen** vi irreg: **jdm ~fallen** be difficult for sb; **~fällig** a ponderous; **S~gewicht** nt heavyweight; (fig) emphasis; **~hörig** a hard of hearing; **S~industrie** f heavy industry; **S~kraft** f gravity; **S~kranke(r)** mf person who is seriously ill; **~lich** ad hardly; **~machen** vt: **jdm/sich etw ~machen** make sth difficult for sb/o.s.; **S~metall** nt heavy metal; **~mütig** a melancholy; **~nehmen** vt irreg take to heart; **S~punkt** m centre of gravity; (fig) emphasis, crucial point.

Schwert [ʃveːrt] nt -(e)s, -er sword; **~lilie** f iris.

schwer- cpd: **~tun** vi irreg: **sich** (dat or acc) **~tun** have difficulties; **S~verbrecher(in** f) m criminal, serious offender; **~verdaulich** a indigestible, heavy; ~**verletzt** a badly injured; ~**verwundet** a seriously wounded; ~**wiegend** a weighty, important.

Schwester ['ʃvɛstər] f -, -n sister; (Med) nurse; s~**lich** a sisterly.

Schwieger- ['ʃviːgər] cpd: ~**eltern** pl parents-in-law pl; ~**mutter** f mother-in-law; ~**sohn** m son-in-law; ~**tochter** f daughter-in-law; ~**vater** m father-in-law.

Schwiele ['ʃviːlə] f -, -n callus.

schwierig ['ʃviːrɪç] a difficult, hard; S~**keit** f difficulty.

Schwimm- ['ʃvɪm] cpd: ~**bad** nt swimming baths pl; ~**becken** nt swimming pool; s~**en** vi irreg swim; (treiben, nicht sinken) float; (fig: unsicher sein) be all at sea; ~**er** m -s, - swimmer; (Angeln) float; ~**lehrer** m swimming instructor; ~**sport** m swimming; ~**weste** f life jacket.

Schwindel ['ʃvɪndəl] m -s giddiness; dizzy spell; (Betrug) swindle, fraud; (Zeug) stuff; s~**frei** a free from giddiness; s~**n** vi (col: lügen) fib; **jdm schwindelt es** sb feels giddy.

schwinden ['ʃvɪndən] vi irreg disappear; (sich verringern) decrease; (Kräfte) decline.

Schwind- [ʃvɪnd] cpd: ~**ler** m -s, - swindler; (Lügner) liar; s~**lig** a giddy; **mir ist** s~**lig** I feel giddy.

Schwing- ['ʃvɪŋ] cpd: s~**en** vti irreg swing; Waffe etc brandish; (vibrieren) vibrate; (klingen) sound; ~**er** m -s, - (Boxen) swing; ~**tür** f swing door(s); ~**ung** f vibration; (Phys) oscillation.

Schwips [ʃvɪps] m -es, -e **einen** ~ **haben** be tipsy.

schwirren ['ʃvɪrən] vi buzz.

schwitzen ['ʃvɪtsən] vi sweat, perspire.

schwören ['ʃvøːrən] vti irreg swear.

schwul [ʃvuːl] a (col) gay, queer.

schwül [ʃvyːl] a sultry, close; S~**e** f - - sultriness, closeness.

Schwulst [ʃvʊlst] f -(e)s, -̈e bombast.

schwülstig ['ʃvʏlstɪç] a pompous.

Schwund [ʃvʊnt] m -(e)s loss; (Schrumpfen) shrinkage.

Schwung [ʃvʊŋ] m -(e)s, -̈e swing; (Triebkraft) momentum; (fig: Energie) verve, energy; (col: Menge) batch; s~**haft** a brisk, lively; ~**rad** nt flywheel; s~**voll** a vigorous.

Schwur [ʃvuːr] m -(e)s, -̈e oath; ~**gericht** nt court with a jury.

sechs [zɛks] num six; ~**hundert** num six hundred; ~**te(r,s)** a sixth; S~**tel** nt -s - sixth.

sechzehn ['zɛçtseːn] num sixteen.

sechzig ['zɛçtsɪç] num sixty.

See [zeː] f -, -n sea; m -s, -n lake; ~**bad** nt seaside resort; ~**fahrt** f seefaring; (Reise) voyage; ~**gang** m (motion of the) sea; ~**gras** nt seaweed; ~**hund** m seal; ~**igel** ['zeːˈiːgəl] m sea urchin; s~**krank** a seasick; ~**krankheit** f seasickness; ~**lachs** m rock salmon.

Seel- ['zeːl] cpd: ~**e** f -, -n soul; ~**enfriede(n)** m peace of mind; s~**enruhig** ad calmly.

Seeleute ['zeːlɔɪtə] pl seamen pl.

Seel- cpd: s~**isch** a mental; ~**sorge** f pastoral duties pl; ~**sorger** m -s, - clergyman.

See- cpd: ~**macht** f naval power; ~**mann** m, pl -**leute** seaman, sailor; ~**meile** f nautical mile; ~**not** f distress; ~**pferd(chen)** nt sea horse; ~**räuber** m pirate; ~**rose** f water lily; ~**stern** m starfish; s~**tüchtig** a seaworthy; ~**weg** m sea route; **auf dem** ~**weg by sea**; ~**zunge** f sole.

Segel ['zeːgəl] nt -s, - sail; ~**boot** nt yacht; ~**fliegen** nt -s gliding; ~**flieger** m glider pilot; ~**flugzeug** nt glider; s~**n** vti sail; ~**schiff** nt sailing vessel; ~**sport** m sailing; ~**tuch** nt canvas.

Segen ['zeːgən] m -s, - blessing; s~**sreich** a beneficial.

Segler ['zeːglər] m -s, - sailor, yachtsman; (Boot) sailing boat.

segnen ['zeːgnən] vt bless.

Seh- [zeː] cpd: s~**en** vti irreg see; (in bestimmter Richtung) look; s~**enswert** a worth seeing; ~**enswürdigkeiten** pl sights pl (of a town); ~**er** m -s, - seer; ~**fehler** m sight defect.

Sehn- ['zeːn] cpd: ~**e** f -, -n sinew; (an Bogen) string; s~**en** vr long, yearn (nach for); s~**ig** a sinewy; s~**lich** a ardent; ~**sucht** f longing; s~**süchtig** a longing.

sehr [zeːr] ad (vor a,ad) very; (mit Verben) a lot, (very) much; **zu** ~ too much.

seicht [zaɪçt] a (lit, fig) shallow.

Seide ['zaɪdə] f -, -n silk; ~**l** nt -s, - tankard, beer mug; s~**n** a silk; ~**npapier** nt tissue paper.

seidig ['zaɪdɪç] a silky.

Seife ['zaɪfə] f -, -n soap; ~**nlauge** f soapsuds pl; ~**nschale** f soap dish; ~**nschaum** m lather.

seifig ['zaɪfɪç] a soapy.

seihen ['zaɪən] vt strain, filter.

Seil [zaɪl] nt -(e)s, -e rope; cable; ~**bahn** f cable railway; ~**hüpfen** nt -s, ~**springen** nt -s skipping; ~**tänzer(in** f) m tightrope walker; ~**zug** m tackle.

sein [zaɪn] vi irreg be; **laß das** ~! leave that!; stop that!; **es ist an dir, zu . . .** it's up to you to . . .

sein [zaɪn] pron his; its; ~**e(r,s)** his; its; ~**er** pron gen of er of him; ~**erseits** ad for his part; ~**erzeit** ad in those days, formerly; ~**esgleichen** pron people like him; ~**etwegen**, ~**etwillen** ad (für ihn) for his sake; (wegen ihm) on his account; (von ihm aus) as far as he is concerned; ~**ige** pron: **der/die/das** ~ his.

Seismograph [zaɪsmoˈgraːf] m -en, -en seismograph.

seit [zaɪt] prep, cj since; **er ist** ~ **einer Woche hier** he has been here for a week; ~ **langem** for a long time; ~**dem** [zaɪtˈdeːm] ad,cj since.

Seite ['zaɪtə] f -, -n side; (Buch-) page; (Mil) flank; ~**nansicht** f side view; ~**nhieb** m (fig) passing shot, dig; ~**nruder** nt (Aviat) rudder; s~**ns** prep +gen on the part of; ~**nschiff** nt aisle; ~**nsprung** m extra-marital escapade; ~**nstechen** nt (a) stitch; ~**nstraße** f side road; ~**nwagen** m sidecar; ~**nzahl** f page number; number of pages.

seit- cpd: ~**her** [zaɪt'he:r] ad,cj since (then); ~**lich** a on one or the side; side; ~**wärts** ad sidewards.

Sekretär [zekre'tɛ:r] m secretary; (Möbel) bureau; ~**in** f secretary.

Sekretariat [zekretari'a:t] nt -(e)s, -e secretary's office, secretariat.

Sekt [zɛkt] m -(e)s, -e champagne; ~**e** f -, -n sect.

sekundär [zekun'dɛ:r] a secondary.

Sekunde [ze'kundə] f -, -n second.

selber ['zɛlbər] = **selbst**.

selbst [zɛlpst] pron myself; itself; themselves etc; von ~ by itself etc; ad even; S~ nt - self; S~**achtung** f self-respect; ~**ändig** ['zɛlpʃtɛndɪç] a independent; S~**ändigkeit** f independence; S~**auslöser** m (Phot) delayed-action shutter release; S~**bedienung** f self-service; S~**befriedigung** f masturbation; S~**beherrschung** f self-control; ~**bewußt** a (self-)confident; S~**bewußtsein** nt self-confidence; S~**erhaltung** f self-preservation; S~**erkenntnis** f self-knowledge; ~**gefällig** a smug, self-satisfied; ~**gemacht** a home-made; S~**gespräch** nt conversation with oneself; S~**kostenpreis** m cost price; ~**los** a unselfish, selfless; S~**mord** m suicide; S~**mörder(in** f) m suicide; ~**mörderisch** a suicidal; ~**sicher** a self-assured; ~**süchtig** a selfish; ~**tätig** a auto-matic; ~**verständlich** a obvious; ad naturally; **ich halte das für** ~**verständlich** I take that for granted; S~**vertrauen** nt self-confidence; S~**verwaltung** f autonomy, self-government; S~**zweck** m end in itself.

selig ['ze:lɪç] a happy, blissful; (Rel) blessed; (tot) late; S~**keit** f bliss.

Sellerie ['zɛləri] m -s, -(s) or f -, -n celery.

selten ['zɛltən] a rare; ad seldom, rarely; S~**heit** f rarity.

Selterswasser ['zɛltərsvasər] nt soda water.

seltsam ['zɛltza:m] a strange, curious; ~**erweise** ad curiously, strangely; S~**keit** f strangeness.

Semester [ze'mɛstər] nt -s, - semester.

Semi- [zemi] in cpds semi-; ~**kolon** [-'ko:lɔn] nt -s, -s semicolon; ~**nar** [-'na:r] nt -s, -e seminary; (Kurs) seminar; (Univ: Ort) department building.

Semmel ['zɛməl] f -, -n roll.

Senat [ze'na:t] m -(e)s, -e senate, council.

Sende- ['zɛndə] cpd: ~**bereich** m range of transmission; ~**folge** f (Serie) series; s~**n** vt irreg send; vti (Rad, TV) transmit, broadcast; ~**r** m -s, - station; (Anlage) transmitter; ~**reihe** f series (of broadcasts); ~**station** f, ~**stelle** f transmitting station.

Sendung ['zɛnduŋ] f -, -en consignment; (Aufgabe) mission; (Rad, TV) transmission; (Programm) programme.

Senf [zɛnf] m -(e)s, -e mustard.

sengen ['zɛŋən] vt singe; vi scorch.

Senk- ['zɛŋk] cpd: ~**blei** nt plumb; ~**e** f -, -n depression; ~**el** m -s, - (shoe)lace; s~**en** vt lower; vr sink, drop gradually; ~**fuß** m flat foot; s~**recht** a vertical, perpendicular; ~**rechte** f -n, -n perpendicular; ~**rechtstarter** m (Aviat) vertical take-off plane; (fig) high-flier.

Sensation [zenzatsi'o:n] f sensation; s~**ell** [-'nɛl] a sensational; ~**ssucht** f sensationalism.

Sense ['zɛnzə] f -, -n scythe.

sensibel [zɛn'zi:bəl] a sensitive.

Sensibilität [zɛnzibili'tɛ:t] f sensitivity.

sentimental [zentimɛn'ta:l] a sentimental; S~**ität** f sentimentality.

separat [zepa'ra:t] a separate.

September [zɛp'tɛmbər] m -(s), - September.

septisch ['zɛptɪʃ] a septic.

Serie ['ze:riə] f series; ~**nherstellung** f mass production; ~**nweise** ad in series.

seriös [zeri'ø:s] a serious, bona fide.

Serpentine [zɛrpɛn'ti:n(ə)] f hairpin (bend).

Serum ['ze:rum] nt -s, **Seren** serum.

Service [zɛr'vi:s] nt -(s), - set, service; ['zø:rvɪs] m -, -s service.

servieren [zɛr'vi:rən] vti serve.

Serviette [zɛrvi'ɛtə] f napkin, serviette.

Sessel ['zɛsəl] m -s, - armchair; ~**lift** m chairlift.

seßhaft ['zɛshaft] a settled; (ansässig) resident.

Sets [zɛts] pl tablemats pl.

setzen ['zɛtsən] vt put, set; Baum etc plant; Segel, (Print) set; vr settle; (person) sit down; vi leap.

Setz- [zɛts] cpd: ~**er** m -s, - (Print) compositor; ~**e'rei** f caseroom; ~**ling** m young plant; ~**maschine** f (Print) typesetting machine.

Seuche ['zɔyçə] f -, -n epidemic; ~**ngebiet** nt infected area.

seufzen ['zɔyftsən] vti sigh.

Seufzer ['zɔyftsər] m -s, - sigh.

Sex [zɛks] m -(es) sex; ~**ualität** [-uali'tɛt] f sex, sexuality; s~**uell** [-u'ɛl] a sexual.

Sexta ['zɛksta] f -, **Sexten** first year of secondary school.

sezieren [ze'tsi:rən] vt dissect.

sich [zɪç] pron himself; herself; itself; oneself; yourself; yourselves; themselves; each other.

Sichel ['zɪçəl] f -, -n sickle; (Mond—) crescent.

sicher ['zɪçər] a safe (vor +dat from); (gewiß) certain (+gen of); (zuverlässig) secure, reliable, (selbst—) confident; ~**gehen** vi irreg make sure.

Sicherheit ['zɪçərhaɪt] f safety; security (auch Fin); (Gewißheit) certainty; (Selbst—) confidence; ~**sabstand** m safe distance; ~**sglas** nt safety glass; s~**shalber** ad for safety; to be on the safe side; ~**snadel** f safety pin; ~**sschloß** nt safety lock; ~**sverschluß** m safety clasp; ~**svorkehrung** f safety precaution.

sicher- cpd: **~lich** ad certainly, surely; **~n** vt secure; (schützen) protect; Waffe put the safety catch on; jdm/sich etw **~n** secure sth for sb/(for o.s.); **~stellen** vt impound; **S~ung** f (Sichern) securing; (Vorrichtung) safety device; (an Waffen) safety catch; (Elec) fuse.

Sicht [zɪçt] f - sight; (Aus—) view; auf or nach **~** (Fin) at sight; auf lange **~** on a long-term basis; s**~bar** a visible; **~barkeit** f visibility; s**~en** vt sight; (auswählen) sort out; s**~lich** a evident, obvious; **~verhältnisse** pl visibility; **~vermerk** m visa; **~weite** f visibility.

sickern ['zɪkərn] vi trickle, seep.

Sie [zi:] pron sing, pl, nom, acc you.

sie [zi:] pron sing nom she; acc her; pl nom they; acc them.

Sieb [zi:p] nt **-(e)s, -e** sieve; (Cook) strainer; s**~en** ['zi:bən] vt sift; Flüssigkeit strain.

sieben ['zi:bən] num seven; **~hundert** num seven hundred; **S~sachen** pl belongings pl.

siebte(r,s) ['zi:ptə(r,z)] a seventh; **S~l** nt **-s, -** seventh.

siebzehn ['zi:ptse:n] num seventeen.

siebzig ['zi:ptsɪç] num seventy.

sied- [zi:d] cpd: **~eln** vi settle; **~en** vti boil, simmer; **S~epunkt** m boiling point; **S~ler** m **-s, -** settler; **S~lung** f settlement; (Häuser—) housing estate.

Sieg [zi:k] m **-(e)s, -e** victory; **~el** ['zi:gəl] nt **-s** - seal; **~ellack** m sealing wax; **~elring** m signet ring; s**~en** vi be victorious; (Sport) win; **~er** m **-s, -** victor; (Sport etc) winner; s**~essicher** a sure of victory; **~eszug** m triumphal procession; s**~reich** a victorious.

siehe [zi:ə] (Imperativ) see; (— da) behold.

siezen ['zi:tsən] vt address as 'Sie'.

Signal [zɪ'gna:l] nt **-s, -e** signal.

Signatur [zɪgna'tu:r] f signature.

Silbe ['zɪlbə] f **-, -n** syllable.

Silber ['zɪlbər] nt **-s** silver; **~bergwerk** nt silver mine; **~blick** m: einen **~blick** haben have a slight squint; s**~n** a silver; **~papier** nt silver paper.

Silhouette [zɪlu'ɛtə] f silhouette.

Silo ['zi:lo] nt or m **-s, -s** silo.

Silvester(abend m) [zɪl'vɛstər(a:bənt)] nt **-s, -** New Year's Eve, Hogmanay (Scot).

simpel ['zɪmpəl] a simple; **S~** m **-s, -** (col) simpleton.

Sims [zɪms] nt or m **-es, -e** (Kamin—) mantlepiece; (Fenster—) (window)sill.

simulieren [zimu'li:rən] vti simulate; (vortäuschen) feign.

simultan [zimul'ta:n] a simultaneous.

Sinfonie [zɪnfo'ni:] f symphony.

singen ['zɪŋən] vti irreg sing.

Singular ['zɪŋgula:r] m singular.

Singvogel ['zɪŋfo:gəl] m songbird.

sinken ['zɪŋkən] vi irreg sink; (Preise etc) fall, go down.

Sinn [zɪn] m **-(e)s, -e** mind; (Wahrnehmungs—) sense; (Bedeutung) sense, meaning; **für etw** sense of sth; **von ~en sein** be out of one's mind;

~bild nt symbol; s**~bildlich** a symbolic; s**~en** vi irreg ponder; **auf etw** (acc) s**~en** contemplate sth; **~enmensch** m sensualist; **~estäuschung** f illusion; s**~gemäß** a faithful; Wiedergabe in one's own words; s**~ig** a clever; s**~lich** a sensual, sensuous; Wahrnehmung sensory; **~lichkeit** f sensuality; s**~los** a senseless; meaningless; **~losigkeit** f senselessness; meaninglessness; s**~voll** a meaningful; (vernünftig) sensible.

Sintflut ['zɪntflu:t] f Flood.

Sinus ['zi:nus] m **-, -** or **-se** (Anat) sinus; (Math) sine.

Siphon [zi'fɔ:] m **-s, -s** siphon.

Sippe ['zɪpə] f **-, -n** clan, kin.

Sippschaft ['zɪpʃaft] f (pej) relations pl, tribe; (Bande) gang.

Sirene [zi're:nə] f **-, -n** siren.

Sirup ['zi:rup] m **-s, -e** syrup.

Sitt- [zɪt] cpd: **~e** f **-, -n** custom; pl morals pl; **~enpolizei** f vice squad; s**~lich** a moral; **~lichkeit** f morality; **~lichkeitsverbrechen** nt sex offence; s**~sam** a modest, demure.

Situation [zituatsi'o:n] f situation.

Sitz [zɪts] m **-es, -e** seat; der Anzug hat einen guten **~** the suit is a good fit; s**~en** vi irreg sit; (Bemerkung, Schlag) strike home, tell; (Gelerntes) have sunk in; s**~en bleiben** remain seated; s**~enbleiben** vi irreg (Sch) have to repeat a year; auf etw (dat) s**~enbleiben** be lumbered with sth; s**~end** a Tätigkeit sedentary; s**~enlassen** vt irreg (Sch) make (sb) repeat a year; Mädchen jilt; Wartenden stand up; etw auf sich (dat) s**~enlassen** take sth lying down; **~gelegenheit** f place to sit down; **~platz** m seat; **~streik** m sit-down strike; **~ung** f meeting.

Skala ['ska:la] f **-, Skalen** scale.

Skalpell [skal'pɛl] nt **-s, -e** scalpel.

Skandal [skan'da:l] m **-s, -e** scandal; s**~ös** [skanda'lø:s] a scandalous.

Skelett [ske'lɛt] nt **-(e)s, -e** skeleton.

Skepsis ['skɛpsɪs] f - scepticism.

skeptisch ['skɛptɪʃ] a sceptical.

Ski, Schi [ʃi:] m **-s, -er** ski; **~** laufen or fahren ski; **~fahrer** m, **~läufer** m skier; **~lehrer** m ski instructor; **~lift** m ski-lift; **~springen** nt ski-jumping.

Skizze ['skɪtsə] f **-, -n** sketch.

skizzieren [skɪ'tsi:rən] vti sketch.

Sklave ['skla:və] m **-n, -n, Sklavin** f slave; **~rei** f slavery.

Skonto ['skɔnto] m or nt **-s, -s** discount.

Skorpion [skɔrpi'o:n] m **-s, -e** scorpion; (Astrol) Scorpio.

Skrupel ['skru:pəl] m **-s, -** scruple; s**~los** a unscrupulous.

Slalom ['sla:lɔm] m **-s, -s** slalom.

Smaragd [sma'rakt] m **-(e)s, -e** emerald.

Smoking ['smo:kɪŋ] m **-s, -s** dinner jacket.

so [zo:] ad so; (auf diese Weise) like this; (etwa) roughly; **~** ein such a; **~, das ist fertig** well, that's finished; **~** etwas! well, well!; **~ ... wie ... as ... as ... ;** **~** daß so that, with the result that; cj so; (vor a) as.

Socke ['zɔkə] *f* -, -n sock.
Sockel ['zɔkəl] *m* -s, - pedestal, base.
Sodawasser ['zo:davasər] *nt* soda water.
Sodbrennen ['zo:tbrenən] *nt* -s, - heartburn.
soeben [zo'e:bən] *ad* just (now).
Sofa ['zo:fa] *nt* -s, -s sofa.
sofern [zo'fern] *cj* if, provided (that).
sofort [zo'fɔrt] *ad* immediately, at once; ~ ig a immediate.
Sog [zo:k] *m* -(e)s, -e suction.
so- *cpd*: ~**gar** [zo'ga:r] *ad* even; ~**genannt** ['zo:gənant] *a* so-called; ~**gleich** [zo'glaiç] *ad* straight away, at once.
Sohle ['zo:lə] *f* -, -n sole; *(Tal— etc)* bottom; *(Min)* level.
Sohn [zo:n] *m* -(e)s, -̈e son.
solang(e) [zo'laŋ(ə)] *cj* as or so long as.
Solbad ['zo:lba:t] *nt* saltwater bath.
solch [zɔlç] *pron* such; **ein** ~ **e(r,s)** . . . such a . . .
Sold [zɔlt] *m* -(e)s, -e pay; ~**at** [zɔl'da:t] *m* -en, -en soldier; **s**~**atisch** a soldierly.
Söldner ['zœldnər] *m* -s, - mercenary.
solid(e) [zo'li:d(ə)] *a* staid, respectable; ~**arisch** [zoli'da:rɪʃ] *a* in/with solidarity; **sich** ~**arisch erklären** declare one's solidarity.
Solist(in *f)* [zo'lɪst(ɪn)] *m* soloist.
Soll [zɔl] *nt* -(s), -(s) *(Fin)* debit (side); *(Arbeitsmenge)* quota, target.
sollen ['zɔlən] *vi* be supposed to; *(Verpflichtung)* shall, ought to; **du hättest nicht gehen** ~ you shouldn't have gone; **soll ich?** shall I?; **was soll das?** what's that supposed to mean?
Solo ['zo:lo] *nt* -s, -s or **Soli** solo.
somit [zo'mɪt] *cj* and so, therefore.
Sommer ['zɔmər] *m* -s, - summer; **s**~**lich** *a* summery; summer; ~**sprossen** *pl* freckles *pl.*
Sonate [zo'na:tə] *f* -, -n sonata.
Sonde ['zɔndə] *f* -, -n probe.
Sonder- ['zɔndər] *in cpds* special; ~**angebot** *nt* special offer; **s**~**bar** a strange, odd; ~**fahrt** *f* special trip; ~**fall** *m* special case; **s**~**gleichen** a inv without parallel, unparalleled; **s**~**lich** a particular; *(außergewöhnlich)* remarkable; *(eigenartig)* peculiar; ~**ling** *m* eccentric; **s**~**n** *cj* but; **nicht nur . . ., s**~**n** a but also; **vt** separate; ~**zug** *m* special train.
sondieren [zɔn'di:rən] *vt* suss out; *Gelände* scout out.
Sonett [zo'nɛt] *nt* -(e)s, -e sonnet.
Sonnabend ['zɔn'a:bənt] *m* Saturday.
Sonne ['zɔnə] *f* -, -n sun; **s**~**n** *vt* put out in the sun; *vr* sun oneself; ~**naufgang** *m* sunrise; **s**~**nbaden** *vi* sunbathe; ~**nbrand** *m* sunburn; ~**nbrille** *f* sunglasses *pl*; ~**nfinsternis** *f* solar eclipse; ~**nschein** *m* sunshine; ~**nschirm** *m* parasol, sunshade; ~**nstich** *m* sunstroke; ~**nuhr** *f* sundial; ~**nuntergang** *m* sunset; ~**nwende** *f* solstice.
sonnig ['zɔnɪç] a sunny.

Sonntag ['zɔnta:k] *m* Sunday; **s**~**s** *ad* (on) Sundays.
sonst [zɔnst] *ad* otherwise *(auch cj)*; *(mit pron, in Fragen)* else; *(zu anderer Zeit)* at other times, normally; ~ **noch etwas?** anything else?; ~ **nichts** nothing else; ~**ig** *a* other; ~**jemand** *pron* anybody (at all); ~**wo(hin)** *ad* somewhere else; ~**woher** *ad* from somewhere else.
sooft [zo'ɔft] *cj* whenever.
Sopran [zo'pra:n] *m* -s, -e soprano; ~**istin** [zopra'nɪstɪn] *f* soprano.
Sorge ['zɔrgə] *f* -, -n care, worry; **s**~**n** *vi*: **für jdn s**~**n** look after sb; **für etw s**~**n** take care of or see to sth; *vr* worry *(um* about); **s**~**nfrei** a carefree; ~**nkind** *nt* problem child; **s**~**nvoll** a troubled, worried; ~**recht** *nt* custody (of a child).
Sorg- [zɔrk] *cpd*: ~**falt** *f* - care(fulness); **s**~**fältig** a careful; **s**~**los** a careless; *(ohne Sorgen)* carefree; **s**~**sam** a careful.
Sorte ['zɔrtə] *f* -, -n sort; *(Waren—)* brand; ~**n** *pl (Fin)* foreign currency.
sortieren [zɔr'ti:rən] *vt* sort (out).
Sortiment [zɔrti'mɛnt] *nt* assortment.
sosehr [zo'ze:r] *cj* as much as.
Soße ['zo:sə] *f* -, -n sauce; *(Braten—)* gravy.
Souffleur [zu'flø:r] *m*, **Souffleuse** [zu'flø:zə] *f* prompter.
souffiieren [zu'fli:rən] *vti* prompt.
souverän [zuvə're:n] *a* sovereign; *(überlegen)* superior.
so- *cpd*: ~**viel** [zo'fi:l] *cj* as far as; *pron* as much *(wie* as); **rede nicht** ~**viel** don't talk so much; ~**weit** [zo'vait] *cj* as far as; *a*: ~**weit sein** be ready; *vr* worry *(um* about); ~**weit wie** or **als möglich** as far as possible; **ich bin** ~**weit zufrieden** by and large I'm quite satisfied; ~**wenig** [zo've:nɪç] *cj* little as; *pron* as little *(wie* as); ~**wie** [zo'vi:] *cj (sobald)* as soon as; *(ebenso)* as well as; ~**wieso** [zovi'zo:] *ad* anyway; ~**wohl** [zo'vo:l] *cj*: ~**wohl . . . als** or **wie auch** both . . . and.
sozial [zotsi'a:l] a social; **S**~**abgaben** *pl* national insurance contributions *pl*; **S**~**demokrat** *m* social democrat; ~**i-'sieren** *vt* socialize; **S**~**ismus** [-'lɪsmʊs] *m* socialism; **S**~**ist** [-'lɪst] *m* socialist; ~**istisch** a socialist; **S**~**politik** *f* social welfare policy; **S**~**produkt** *nt* (gross/net) national product; **S**~**staat** *m* welfare state.
Sozio- [zotsio] *cpd*: ~**loge** [-'lo:gə] *m* -n, -n sociologist; ~**logie** [-'lo:gi:] *f* sociology; **s**~**logisch** [-'lo:gɪʃ] a sociological.
Sozius ['zo:tsius] *m* -, -se *(Comm)* partner; *(Motorrad)* pillion rider; ~**sitz** *m* pillion (seat).
sozusagen [zotsu'za:gən] *ad* so to speak.
Spachtel ['ʃpaxtəl] *m* -s, - spatula.
spähen ['ʃpe:ən] *vi* peep, peek.
Spalier [ʃpa'li:r] *nt* -s, -e *(Gerüst)* trellis; *(Leute)* guard of honour.
Spalt [ʃpalt] *m* -(e)s, -e crack; *(Tür—)* chink; *(fig: Kluft)* split; ~**e** *f* -, -n crack, fissure; *(Gletscher—)* crevasse; *(in Text)* column; **s**~**en** *vtr (lit, fig)* split; ~**ung** *f* splitting.

Span [ʃpaːn] -(e)s, ⁻e shaving; ~ferkel nt sucking-pig.

Spange [ˈʃpaŋə] f -, -n clasp; (Haar—) hair slide; (Schnalle) buckle; (Armreif) bangle.

Spann [ˈʃpan] cpd: ~beton m pre-stressed concrete; ~e f -, -n (Zeit—) space; (Differenz) gap; s~en vt (straffen) tighten, tauten; (befestigen) brace; vi be tight; s~end a exciting, gripping; ~kraft f elasticity; (fig) energy; ~ung f tension; (Elec) voltage; (fig) suspense; (unangenehm) tension.

Spar- [ˈʃpaːr] cpd: ~buch nt savings book; ~büchse f moneybox; s~en vti save; sich (dat) etw s~en save oneself sth; Bemerkung keep sth to oneself; mit etw (dat) s~en be sparing with sth; an etw (dat) s~en economize on sth; ~er m -s, - saver.

Spargel [ˈʃpargəl] m -s, - asparagus.

Spar- cpd: ~kasse f savings bank; ~konto nt savings account.

spärlich [ˈʃpɛːrlɪç] a meagre; Bekleidung scanty.

Spar- cpd: ~maßnahme f economy measure, cut; s~sam a economical, thrifty; ~samkeit f thrift, economizing; ~schwein nt piggy bank.

Sparte [ˈʃpartə] f -, -n field; line of business; (Press) column.

Spaß [ʃpaːs] m -es, ⁻e joke; (Freude) fun; jdm ~ machen be fun (for sb); s~en vi joke; mit ihm ist nicht zu s~en you can't take liberties with him; s~eshalber ad for the fun of it; s~haft, s~ig a funny, droll; ~macher m -s, - joker, funny man; ~verderber m -s, - spoilsport.

spät [ʃpɛːt] a, ad late; ~er a, ad later; ~estens ad at the latest.

Spaten [ˈʃpaːtən] m -s, - spade.

Spatz [ʃpats] m -en, -en sparrow.

spazier- [ʃpaˈtsiːr] cpd: ~en vi stroll, walk; ~enfahren vi irreg go for a drive; ~engehen vi irreg go for a walk; S~gang m walk; S~stock m walking stick; S~weg m path, walk.

Specht [ʃpɛçt] m -(e)s, -e woodpecker.

Speck [ʃpɛk] m -(e)s, -e bacon.

Spediteur [ʃpediˈtøːr] m carrier; (Möbel—) furniture remover.

Spedition [ʃpediˈtsiˈoːn] f carriage; (—sfirma) road haulage contractor; removal firm.

Speer [ʃpeːr] m -(e)s, -e spear; (Sport) javelin.

Speiche [ˈʃpaɪçə] f -, -n spoke.

Speichel [ˈʃpaɪçəl] m -s saliva, spit(tle).

Speicher [ˈʃpaɪçər] m -s, - storehouse; (Dach—) attic, loft; (Korn—) granary; (Wasser—) tank; (Tech) store; s~n vt store.

speien [ˈʃpaɪən] vti irreg spit; (erbrechen) vomit; (Vulkan) spew.

Speise [ˈʃpaɪzə] f -, -n food; ~eis [ˈ-ʔaɪs] nt ice-cream; ~kammer f larder, pantry; ~karte f menu; s~n vt feed; eat; vi dine; ~röhre f gullet, oesophagus; ~saal m dining room; ~wagen m dining car; ~zettel m menu.

Spektakel [ʃpɛkˈtaːkəl] m -s, - (col) row; nt -s, - spectacle.

Speku- [ʃpeku] cpd: ~lant [-ˈlant] m speculator; ~lation [-latsiˈoːn] f speculation; s~lieren [-ˈliːrən] vi (fig) speculate; auf etw (acc) s~lieren have hopes of sth.

Spelunke [ʃpeˈluŋkə] f -, -n dive.

Spende [ˈʃpɛndə] f -, -n donation; s~n vt donate, give; ~r m -s, - donor, donator.

spendieren [ʃpɛnˈdiːrən] vt pay for, buy; jdm etw ~ treat sb to sth, stand sb sth.

Sperling [ˈʃpɛrlɪŋ] m sparrow.

Sperma [ˈʃpɛrma] nt -s, Spermen sperm.

Sperr- [ˈʃpɛr] cpd: s~angelweit [ˈ-ʔaŋəlˈvaɪt] a wide open; ~e f -, -n barrier; (Verbot) ban; s~en vt block; (Sport) suspend; (vom Ball) obstruct; (einschließen) lock; (verbieten) ban; vr baulk, jib(e); ~gebiet nt prohibited area; ~holz nt plywood; s~ig a bulky; ~müll m bulky refuse; ~sitz m (Theat) stalls pl; ~stunde f, ~zeit f closing time.

Spesen [ˈʃpeːzən] pl expenses pl.

Spezial- [ʃpetsiˈaːl] in cpds special; s~i-ˈsieren vr specialize; ~iˈsierung f specialization; ~ist [-ˈlɪst] m specialist; ~iˈtät f speciality.

speziell [ʃpetsiˈɛl] a special.

spezifisch [ʃpeˈtsiːfɪʃ] a specific.

Sphäre [ˈsfɛːrə] f -, -n sphere.

spicken [ˈʃpɪkən] vt lard; vi (Sch) copy, crib.

Spiegel [ˈʃpiːgəl] m -s, - mirror; (Wasser—) level; (Mil) tab; ~bild nt reflection; s~bildlich a reversed; ~ei [-ˈʔaɪ] nt fried egg; ~fechterei [-fɛçtəˈraɪ] f shadow-boxing, bluff; s~n vt mirror, reflect; vr be reflected; vi gleam; (wider—) be reflective; ~schrift f mirror-writing; ~ung f reflection.

Spiel [ʃpiːl] nt -(e)s, -e game; (Schau—) play; (Tätigkeit) play(ing); (Cards) deck; (Tech) (free) play; s~en vti play; (um Geld) gamble; (Theat) perform, act; s~end ad easily; ~er m -s, - player; (um Geld) gambler; ~erei f trifling pastime; s~erisch a playful; Leichtigkeit effortless; s~erisches Können skill as a player; acting ability; ~feld nt pitch, field; ~film m feature film; ~plan m (Theat) programme; ~platz m playground; ~raum m room to manoeuvre, scope; ~sachen pl toys pl; ~verderber m -s, - spoilsport; ~waren pl, ~zeug nt toys pl.

Spieß [ʃpiːs] m -es, -e spear; (Brat—) spit; ~bürger m, ~er m -s, - bourgeois; ~rutenlaufen nt running the gauntlet.

Spikes [spaɪks] pl spikes pl; (Aut) studs pl.

Spinat [ʃpiˈnaːt] m -(e)s, -e spinach.

Spind [ʃpɪnt] m or nt -(e)s, -e locker.

Spinn- [ˈʃpɪn] cpd: ~e f -, -n spider; s~en vti irreg spin; (col) talk rubbish; (verrückt) be crazy or mad; ~erei f spinning mill; ~(en)gewebe nt cobweb; ~rad nt spinning-wheel; ~webe f cobweb.

Spion [ʃpiˈoːn] m -s, -e spy; (in Tür) spyhole; ~age [ʃpioˈnaːʒə] f -, -n espionage; s~ieren [ʃpioˈniːrən] vi spy.

Spirale [ʃpiˈraːlə] f -, -n spiral.

Spirituosen [ʃpiritu'o:zən] *pl* spirits *pl.*

Spiritus ['spi:ritus] *m* -, -se (methylated) spirit.

Spital [ʃpi'ta:l] *nt* -s, ̈er hospital.

spitz [ʃpits] a pointed; *Winkel* acute; *(fig) Zunge* sharp; *Bemerkung* caustic; S~ *m* -es, -e spitz; S~**bogen** *m* pointed arch; S~**bube** *m* rogue; S~e *f* -, -n point, tip; *(Berg—)* peak; *(Bemerkung)* taunt, dig; *(erster Platz)* lead, top; *(usu pl: Gewebe)* lace; S~**el** *m* -s, - police informer; ~**en** *vt* sharpen; S~**en-** *in cpds* top; S~**en-leistung** *f* top performance; S~**enlohn** *m* top wages *pl*; S~**ensportler** *m* top-class sportsman; S~**findig** a (over)subtle; ~**ig** a see **spitz**; S~**name** *m* nickname.

Splitter ['ʃplitər] *m* -s, - splinter; s~**nackt** a stark naked.

spontan [ʃpɔn'ta:n] a spontaneous.

Sport ['ʃpɔrt] *m* -(e)s, -e sport; *(fig)* hobby; ~**lehrer(in** *f*) *m* games or P.E. teacher; ~**ler(in** *f*) *m* -s, - sportsman/woman; s~**lich** a sporting; *Mensch* sporty; ~**platz** *m* playing or sports field; ~**verein** *m* sports club; ~**wagen** *m* sports car; ~**zeug** *nt* sports gear.

Spott [ʃpɔt] *m* -(e)s mockery, ridicule; s~**billig** a dirt-cheap; s~**en** *vi* mock *(über +acc* at), ridicule.

spöttisch ['ʃpœtiʃ] a mocking.

Sprach- ['ʃpra:x] *cpd*: s~**begabt** a good at languages; ~**e** *f* -, -n language; ~**fehler** *m* speech defect; ~**fertigkeit** *f* fluency; ~**führer** *m* phrasebook; ~**gebrauch** *m* (linguistic) usage; ~**gefühl** *nt* feeling for language; s~**lich** a linguistic; s~**los** a speechless; ~**rohr** *nt* megaphone; *(fig)* mouthpiece.

Spray [spre:] *m* or *nt* -s, -s spray.

Sprech- ['ʃprɛç] *cpd*: ~**anlage** *f* intercom; s~**en** *irreg* *vi* speak, talk *(mit* to); *das spricht für ihn* that's a point in his favour; *vt* say; *Sprache* speak; *Person* speak to; ~**er(in** *f*) *m* -s, - speaker; *(für Gruppe)* spokesman; *(Rad, TV)* announcer; ~**stunde** *f* consultation hour; *(doctor's)* surgery; ~**stundenhilfe** *f* *(doctor's)* receptionist; ~**zimmer** *nt* consulting room, surgery.

spreizen ['ʃpraitsən] *vt* spread; *vr* put on airs.

Spreng- ['ʃprɛŋ] *cpd*: ~**arbeiten** *pl* blasting operations *pl*; s~**en** *vt* sprinkle; *(mit Sprengstoff)* blow up; *Gestein* blast; *Versammlung* break up; ~**ladung** *f* explosive charge; ~**stoff** *m* explosive(s).

Spreu [ʃprɔy] *f* - chaff.

Sprich- ['ʃpriç] *cpd*: ~**wort** *nt* proverb; s~**wörtlich** a proverbial.

Spring- ['ʃpriŋ] *cpd*: ~**brunnen** *m* fountain; s~**en** *vi* *irreg* jump; *(Glas)* crack; *(mit Kopfsprung)* dive; ~**er** *m* -s, - jumper; *(Schach)* knight.

Sprit [ʃprit] *m* -(e)s, -e *(col)* petrol, fuel.

Spritz- ['ʃprits] *cpd*: ~**e** *f* -, -n syringe; injection; *(an Schlauch)* nozzle; s~**en** *vt* spray; *(Med)* inject; *vi* splash; *(heraus—)* spurt; *(Med)* give injections; ~**pistole** *f* spray gun.

spröde ['ʃprø:də] a brittle; *Person* reserved, coy.

Sproß [ʃprɔs] *m* -sses, -sse shoot; *(Kind)* scion.

Sprosse ['ʃprɔsə] *f* -, -n rung.

Sprößling ['ʃprœsliŋ] *m* offspring *no pl.*

Spruch [ʃprux] *m* -(e)s, ̈e saying, maxim; *(Jur)* judgement.

Sprudel ['ʃpru:dəl] *m* -s, - mineral water; lemonade; s~**n** *vi* bubble.

Sprüh- ['ʃpry:] *cpd*: ~**dose** *f* aerosol (can); s~**en** *vti* spray; *(fig)* sparkle; ~**regen** *m* drizzle.

Sprung [ʃpruŋ] *m* -(e)s, ̈e jump; *(Riß)* crack; ~**brett** *nt* springboard; s~**haft** a erratic; *Aufstieg* rapid; ~**schanze** *f* ski-jump.

Spucke ['ʃpukə] *f* - spit; s~**en** *vti* spit.

Spuk [ʃpu:k] *m* -(e)s, -e haunting; *(fig)* nightmare; s~**en** *vi* *(Geist)* walk; *hier spukt es* this place is haunted.

Spule ['ʃpu:lə] *f* -, -n spool; *(Elec)* coil.

Spül- ['ʃpy:l] *cpd*: ~**e** *f* -, -n (kitchen) sink; s~**en** *vti* rinse; *Geschirr* wash up; *Toilette* flush; ~**maschine** *f* dishwasher; ~**stein** *m* sink; ~**ung** *f* rinsing; flush; *(Med)* irrigation.

Spur [ʃpu:r] *f* -, -en trace; *(Fuß—, Rad—, Tonband—)* track; *(Fährte)* trail; *(Fahr—)* lane; s~**los** *ad* without (a) trace.

spür- ['ʃpy:r] *cpd*: ~**bar** a noticeable, perceptible; ~**en** *vt* feel; S~**hund** *m* tracker dog; *(fig)* sleuth.

Spurt [ʃpurt] *m* -(e)s, -s or -e spurt.

sputen ['ʃpu:tən] *vr* make haste.

Staat [ʃta:t] *m* -(e)s, -en state; *(Prunk)* show; *(Kleidung)* finery; *mit etw ~ machen* show off or parade sth; s~**enlos** a stateless; s~**lich** a state(-); state-run; ~**sangehörigkeit** *f* nationality; ~**sanwalt** *m* public prosecutor; ~**sbürger** *m* citizen; ~**sdienst** *m* civil service; s~**seigen** a state-owned; ~**sexamen** *nt* *(Univ)* degree; s~**sfeindlich** a subversive; ~**smann** *m, pl* -**männer** statesman; ~**ssekretär** *m* secretary of state.

Stab [ʃta:p] *m* -(e)s, ̈e rod; *(Gitter—)* bar; *(Menschen)* staff; ~**hochsprung** *m* pole vault; s~**il** [ʃta'bi:l] a stable; *Möbel* sturdy; s~**ilisieren** *vt* stabilize; ~**reim** *m* alliteration.

Stachel ['ʃtaxəl] *m* -s, -n spike; *(von Tier)* spine; *(von Insekten)* sting; ~**beere** *f* gooseberry; ~**draht** *m* barbed wire; s~**ig** a prickly; ~**schwein** *nt* porcupine.

Stadion ['ʃta:diɔn] *nt* -s, **Stadien** stadium.

Stadium ['ʃta:diʊm] *nt* stage, phase.

Stadt [ʃtat] *f* -, ̈e town.

Städt- ['ʃtɛ:t] *cpd*: ~**chen** *nt* small town; ~**ebau** *m* town planning; ~**er(in** *f*) *m* -s, - town dweller; s~**isch** a municipal; *(nicht ländlich)* urban.

Stadt- *cpd*: ~**mauer** *f* city wall(s); ~**plan** *m* street map; ~**rand** *m* outskirts *pl*; ~**teil** *m* district, part of town.

Staffel ['ʃtafəl] *f* -, -n rung; *(Sport)* relay (team); *(Aviat)* squadron; ~**ei** ['lai] *f* easel; s~**n** *vt* graduate; ~**ung** *f* graduation.

Stahl [ʃtaːl] m -(e)s, ᵉe steel; ~helm m steel helmet.

Stall [ʃtal] m -(e)s, ᵉe stable; (Kaninchen—) hutch; (Schweine—) sty; (Hühner—) henhouse.

Stamm [ʃtam] m -(e)s, ᵉe (Baum—) trunk; (Menschen—) tribe; (Gram) stem; ~baum m family tree; (von Tier) pedigree; s~eln vti stammer; s~en vi: s~en von or aus come from; ~gast m regular (customer); ~halter m -s, - son and heir.

stämmig ['ʃtɛmiç] a sturdy; Mensch stocky; S~keit f sturdiness; stockiness.

stampfen ['ʃtampfən] vti stamp; (stapfen) tramp; (mit Werkzeug) pound.

Stand [ʃtant] m -(e)s, ᵉe position; (Wasser—, Benzin— etc) level; (Stehen) standing position; (Zustand) state; (Spiel—) score; (Messe— etc) stand; (Klasse) class; (Beruf) profession.

Standard ['ʃtandart] m -s, -s standard.

Ständ- ['ʃtɛnd] cpd: ~chen nt serenade; ~er m -s, - stand.

Stand- ['ʃtand] cpd: ~esamt nt registry office; ~esbeamte(r) m registrar; ~esbewußtsein nt status consciousness; s~esgemäß a,ad according to one's social position; ~esunterschied m social difference; s~haft a steadfast; ~haftigkeit f steadfastness; s~halten vi irreg stand firm (jdm/ etw against sb/sth), resist (jdm/ etw sb/sth).

ständig ['ʃtɛndiç] a permanent; (ununterbrochen) constant, continual.

Stand- cpd: ~licht nt sidelights pl, parking lights pl (US); ~ort m location; (Mil) garrison; ~punkt m standpoint.

Stange ['ʃtaŋə] f -, -n stick; (Stab) pole, bar; rod; (Zigaretten) carton; **von der** ~ (Comm) off the peg; **eine** ~ **Geld** quite a packet.

Stanniol [ʃtaniˈoːl] nt -s, -e tinfoil.

Stanze ['ʃtantsə] f -, -n stanza; (Tech) stamp; s~n vt stamp.

Stapel ['ʃtaːpəl] m -s, - pile; (Naut) stocks pl; ~lauf m launch; s~n vt pile (up).

Star [ʃtaːr] m -(e)s, -e starling; (Med) cataract; m -s, -s (Film etc) star.

stark [ʃtark] a strong; (heftig, groß) heavy; (Maßangabe) thick.

Stärke ['ʃtɛrkə] f -, -n strength; heaviness; thickness; (Cook, Wäsche—) starch; s~n vt strengthen; Wäsche starch.

Starkstrom m heavy current.

Stärkung ['ʃtɛrkʊŋ] f strengthening; (Essen) refreshment.

starr [ʃtar] a stiff; (unnachgiebig) rigid; Blick staring; ~en vi stare; ~en vor or von be covered in; Waffen be bristling with; S~heit f rigidity; ~köpfig a stubborn; S~sinn m obstinacy.

Start [ʃtart] m -(e)s, -e start; (Aviat) takeoff; ~automatik f (Aut) automatic choke; ~bahn f runway; s~en vti start; take off; ~er m -s, - starter; ~erlaubnis f takeoff clearance; ~zeichen nt start signal.

Station [ʃtatsi̯oːn] f station; hospital ward; s~ieren ['-niːrən] vt station.

Statist [ʃtaˈtɪst] m extra, supernumerary;

~ik f statistics; ~iker m -s, - statistician; s~isch a statistical.

Stativ [ʃtaˈtiːf] nt -s, -e tripod.

statt [ʃtat] cj, prep +gen or dat instead of; S~ f - place.

Stätte ['ʃtɛtə] f -, -n place.

statt- cpd: ~finden vi irreg take place; ~haft a admissible; ~lich a imposing, handsome.

Statue ['ʃtaːtuə] f -, n statue.

Statur [ʃtaˈtuːr] f stature.

Status ['ʃtaːtus] m -, - status.

Stau [ʃtaʊ] m -(e)s, -e blockage; (Verkehrs—) (traffic) jam.

Staub [ʃtaʊp] m -(e)s dust; s~en ['ʃtaʊbən] vi be dusty; ~faden m stamen; s~ig a dusty; ~sauger m vacuum cleaner; ~tuch nt duster.

Staudamm m dam.

Staude ['ʃtaʊdə] f -, -n shrub.

stauen ['ʃtaʊən] vt Wasser dam up; Blut stop the flow of; vr (Wasser) become dammed up; (Med, Verkehr) become congested; (Menschen) collect together; (Gefühle) build up.

staunen ['ʃtaʊnən] vi be astonished; S~ nt -s amazement.

Stauung ['ʃtaʊʊŋ] f (von Wasser) dammingup; (von Blut, Verkehr) congestion.

Stech- ['ʃtɛç] cpd: ~becken nt bedpan; s~en vt irreg (mit Nadel etc) prick; (mit Messer) stab; (mit Finger) poke; (Biene etc) sting; (Mücke) bite; (Sonne) burn; (Cards) take; (Art) engrave; Torf, Spargel cut; **in See** s~en put to sea; ~en nt -s, - (Sport) play-off; jump-off; s~end a piercing, stabbing; Geruch pungent; ~ginster m gorse; ~palme f holly; ~uhr f time clock.

Steck- ['ʃtɛk] cpd: ~brief m 'wanted' poster; ~dose f (wall) socket; s~en vt put, insert; Nadel stick; Pflanzen plant; (beim Nähen) pin; vi irreg be; (festsitzen) be stuck; (Nadeln) stick; s~enbleiben vi irreg get stuck; s~enlassen vt irreg leave in; ~enpferd nt hobby-horse; ~er m -s, - plug; ~nadel f pin; ~rübe f swede, turnip; ~zwiebel f bulb.

Steg [ʃteːk] m -(e)s, -e small bridge; (Anlege—) landing stage; ~reif m: **aus dem** ~reif just like that.

stehen ['ʃteːən] irreg vi stand (zu by); (sich befinden) be; (in Zeitung) say; (still—) have stopped; jdm ~ suit sb; vi impers: **es steht schlecht um things are bad for; wie steht's?** how are things?; (Sport) what's the score?; ~ **bleiben** remain standing; ~bleiben vi irreg (Uhr) stop; (Fehler) stay as it is; ~lassen vt irreg leave; Bart grow.

stehlen ['ʃteːlən] vt irreg steal.

steif [ʃtaɪf] a stiff; S~heit f stiffness.

Steig- ['ʃtaɪk] cpd: ~bügel m stirrup; ~e ['ʃtaɪgə] f -, -n (Straße) steep road; (Kiste) crate; ~eisen nt crampon; s~en vi irreg rise; (klettern) climb; s~en in (+acc)/auf (+acc) get in/on; s~ern vt raise; (Gram) compare; vi (Auktion) bid; vr increase; ~erung f raising; (Gram) comparison; ~ung f incline, gradient, rise.

steil [ʃtail] a steep.

Stein [ʃtain] m -(e)s, -e stone; (in Uhr) jewel; s~alt a ancient; ~bock m (Astrol) Capricorn; ~bruch m quarry; ~butt m -s, -e turbot; s~ern a (made of) stone; (fig) stony; ~gut nt stoneware; s~hart a hard as stone; s~ig a stony; s~igen vt stone; ~kohle f mineral coal; ~metz m -es, -e stonemason.

Steiß [ʃtais] m -es, -e rump.

Stell- ['ʃtɛl] cpd: ~dichein nt -(s), -(s) rendezvous; ~e f -, -n place; (Arbeit) post, job; (Amt) office; s~en vt put; Uhr etc set; (zur Verfügung —) supply; (fassen) Dieb apprehend; vr (sich aufstellen) stand; (sich einfinden) present oneself; (bei Polizei) give oneself up; (vorgeben) pretend (to be); sich zu etw s~en have an opinion of sth; ~enangebot nt offer of a post; (Zeitung) vacancies; ~ennachweis m, ~envermittlung f employment agency; ~ung f position; (Mil) line; ~ung nehmen zu comment on; ~ungnahme f -, -n comment; s~vertretend a deputy, acting; ~vertreter m deputy; ~werk nt (Rail) signal box.

Stelze ['ʃtɛltsə] f -, -n stilt.

Stemm- ['ʃtɛm] cpd: ~bogen m (Ski) stem turn; s~en vt lift (up); (drücken) press; sich s~en gegen (fig) resist, oppose.

Stempel ['ʃtɛmpəl] m -s, - stamp; (Bot) pistil; ~kissen nt inkpad; s~n vt stamp; Briefmarke cancel; s~n gehen (col) be/go on the dole.

Stengel ['ʃtɛŋəl] m -s, - stalk.

Steno- [ʃteno] cpd: ~gramm [-'gram] nt shorthand report; ~graphie [-gra'fi:] f shorthand; s~graphieren [-gra'fi:rən] vti write (in) shorthand; ~typist(in f) [-ty'pɪst(ɪn)] m shorthand typist.

Stepp- ['ʃtɛp] cpd: ~decke f quilt; ~e f -, -n prairie; steppe; s~en vt stitch; vi tapdance.

Sterb- ['ʃtɛrb] cpd: ~ebett nt deathbed; ~efall m death; s~en vi irreg die; ~eurkunde f death certificate; s~lich ['ʃtɛrplɪç] a mortal; ~lichkeit f mortality; ~lichkeitsziffer f death rate.

stereo- [ʃte:reo] in cpds stereo(-); ~typ [stereo'ty:p] a stereotype.

steril [ʃte'ri:l] a sterile; ~i'sieren vt sterilize; S~i'sierung f sterilization.

Stern [ʃtɛrn] m -(e)s, -e star; ~bild nt constellation; ~chen nt asterisk; ~schnuppe f -, -n meteor, falling star; ~stunde f historic moment.

stet [ʃte:t] a steady; ~ig a constant, continual; ~s ad continually, always.

Steuer ['ʃtɔyər] nt -s, - (Naut) helm; (—ruder) rudder; (Aut) steering wheel; f -, -n tax; ~bord nt starboard; ~erklärung f tax return; ~klasse f tax group; ~knüppel m control column; (Aviat) joystick; ~mann m, pl -männer or -leute helmsman; s~n vti steer; Flugzeug pilot; Entwicklung, Tonstärke control; s~pflichtig a taxable; Person liable to pay tax; ~rad nt steering wheel; ~ung f steering (auch Aut); piloting; control;

(Vorrichtung) controls pl; ~zahler m -s, - taxpayer; ~zuschlag m additional tax.

Steward ['stju:ərt] m -s, -s steward; ~eß ['stju:ɔrdɛs] f -, -essen stewardess; air hostess.

stibitzen [ʃti'bɪtsən] vt (col) pilfer, steal.

Stich [ʃtɪç] m -(e)s, -e (Insekten—) sting; (Messer—) stab; (beim Nähen) stitch; (Färbung) tinge; (Cards) trick; (Art) engraving; jdn im ~ lassen leave sb in the lurch; ~el m -s, - engraving tool, style; ~e'lei f jibe, taunt; s~eln vi (fig) jibe; s~haltig a sound, tenable; ~probe f spot check; ~wahl f final ballot; ~wort nt cue; (in Wörterbuch) headword; (für Vortrag) note; ~wortverzeichnis nt index.

Stick- [ʃtɪk] cpd: s~en vti embroider; ~e'rei f embroidery; s~ig a stuffy, close; ~stoff m nitrogen.

Stiefel ['ʃti:fəl] m -s, - boot.

Stief- ['ʃti:f] in cpds step; ~kind nt stepchild; (fig) Cinderella; ~mutter f stepmother; ~mütterchen nt pansy.

Stiege ['ʃti:gə] f -, -n staircase.

Stiel [ʃti:l] m -(e)s, -e handle; (Bot) stalk.

stier [ʃti:r] a staring, fixed; S~ m -(e)s, -e bull; (Astrol) Taurus; ~en vi stare.

Stift [ʃtɪft] m -(e)s, -e peg; (Nagel) tack; (Farb—) crayon; (Blei—) pencil; nt -(e)s, -e (charitable) foundation; (Eccl) religious institution; s~en vt found; Unruhe cause; (spenden) contribute; ~er(in f) m -s, - founder; ~ung f donation; (Organisation) foundation; ~zahn m crown tooth.

Stil [ʃti:l] m -(e)s, -e style; ~blüte f howler.

still [ʃtɪl] a quiet; (unbewegt) still; (heimlich) secret; S~e f -, -n stillness, quietness; in aller S~e quietly; ~en vt stop; (befriedigen) satisfy; Säugling breast-feed; ~gestanden interj attention; ~halten vi irreg keep still; s~(l)egen vt close down; ~schweigen vi irreg silent; S~schweigen nt silence; ~schweigend a,ad silent(ly); Einverständnis tacit(ly); S~stand m standstill; ~stehen vi irreg stand still.

Stimm- ['ʃtɪm] cpd: ~abgabe f voting; ~bänder pl vocal chords pl; s~berechtigt a entitled to vote; ~e f -, -n voice; (Wahl—) vote; s~en vt (Mus) tune; das stimmte ihn traurig that made him feel sad; vi be right; s~en für/gegen vote for/against; ~enmehrheit f majority (of votes); ~enthaltung f abstention; ~gabel f tuning fork; s~haft a voiced; ~lage f register; s~los a voiceless; ~recht nt right to vote; ~ung f mood; atmosphere; s~ungsvoll a enjoyable; full of atmosphere; ~zettel m ballot paper.

stinken ['ʃtɪŋkən] vi irreg stink.

Stipendium [ʃti'pɛndium] nt grant.

Stirn [ʃtɪrn] f -, -en forehead, brow; (Frechheit) impudence; ~höhle f sinus; ~runzeln nt -s frown(ing).

stöbern ['ʃtøːbərn] vi rummage.

stochern ['ʃtɔxərn] vi poke (about).

Stock [ʃtɔk] m -(e)s, -e stick; (Bot) stock; pl

-werke storey; s~-in cpds vor a (col)
completely; s~en vi stop, pause; s~end
a halting; s~finster a (col) pitch-dark;
s~taub a stone-deaf; ~ung f stoppage;
~werk nt storey, floor.

Stoff [ʃtɔf] m -(e)s, -e (Gewebe) material,
cloth; (Materie) matter; (von Buch etc)
subject (matter); s~lich a material; with
regard to subject matter; ~wechsel m
metabolism.

stöhnen ['ʃtøːnən] vi groan.

stoisch ['ʃtoːɪʃ] a stoical.

Stollen ['ʃtɔlən] m -s, - (Min) gallery;
(Cook) cake eaten at Christmas; (von
Schuhen) stud.

stolpern ['ʃtɔlpərn] vi stumble, trip.

Stolz [ʃtɔlts] m -es pride; s~ a proud;
s~ieren [ʃtɔlˈtsiːrən] vi strut.

Stopf- ['ʃtɔpf] cpd: s~en vt (hinein-) stuff;
(voll-) fill (up); (nähen) darn; vi (Med)
cause constipation; ~garn nt darning
thread.

Stoppel ['ʃtɔpəl] f -, -n stubble.

Stopp- ['ʃtɔp] cpd: s~en vti stop; (mit Uhr)
time; ~schild nt stop sign; ~uhr f stop-
watch.

Stöpsel ['ʃtœpsəl] m -s, - plug; (für
Flaschen) stopper.

Stör [ʃtøːr] m -(e)s, -e sturgeon.

Storch m -(e)s, -e stork.

Stör- [ʃtøːr] cpd: s~en vt disturb;
(behindern, Rad) interfere with; vr sich an
etw (dat) s~en let sth bother one;
s~end a disturbing, annoying; ~enfried
m -(e)s, -e troublemaker.

störrig ['ʃtœrɪç], **störrisch** ['ʃtœrɪʃ] a
stubborn, perverse.

Stör- cpd: ~sender m jammer; ~ung f
disturbance; interference.

Stoß [ʃtoːs] m -es, -e (Schub) push; (Schlag)
blow; knock; (mit Schwert) thrust; (mit Fuß)
kick; (Erd-) shock; (Haufen) pile;
~dämpfer m -s, - shock absorber; s~en
irreg vt (mit Druck) shove, push; (mit
Schlag) knock, bump; (mit Fuß) kick;
Schwert etc thrust; (an-) Kopf etc bump;
(zerkleinern) pulverize; vr get a knock;
sich s~en an (+dat) (fig) take exception
to; vi: s~en an or auf (+acc) bump into;
(finden) come across; (angrenzen) be next
to; ~stange f (Aut) bumper.

Stotterer ['ʃtɔtərər] m -s, - stutterer.

stottern ['ʃtɔtərn] vti stutter.

stracks [ʃtraks] ad straight.

Straf- ['ʃtraː] cpd: ~anstalt f penal
institution; ~arbeit f (Sch) punishment;
lines pl; s~bar a punishable; ~barkeit f
criminal nature; ~e f -, -n punishment;
(Jur) penalty; (Gefängnis-) sentence;
(Geld-) fine; s~en vt punish.

straff [ʃtraf] a tight; (streng) strict; Stil etc
concise; Haltung erect; ~en vt tighten,
tauten.

Straf- cpd: ~gefangene(r) mf prisoner,
convict; ~gesetzbuch nt penal code;
~kolonie f penal colony.

Sträf- ['ʃtrɛː] cpd: s~lich a criminal;
~ling m convict.

Straf- cpd: ~porto nt excess postage
(charge); ~predigt f severe lecture;

~raum m (Sport) penalty area; ~recht
nt criminal law; ~stoß m (Sport) penalty
(kick); ~tat f punishable act; ~zettel m
ticket.

Strahl [ʃtraːl] m -s, -en ray, beam;
(Wasser-) jet; s~en vi radiate; (fig)
beam; ~enbehandlung, ~entherapie f
radiotherapy; ~ung f radiation.

Strähne ['ʃtrɛːnə] f-, -n strand.

stramm [ʃtram] a tight; Haltung erect;
Mensch robust; ~stehen vi irreg (Mil)
stand to attention.

strampeln ['ʃtrampəln] vi kick (about),
fidget.

Strand [ʃtrant] m -(e)s, -e shore; (mit
Sand) beach; ~bad nt open-air swimming
pool, lido; s~en ['ʃtrandən] vi run
aground; (fig: Mensch) fail; ~gut nt
flotsam; ~korb m beach chair.

Strang [ʃtraŋ] m -(e)s, -e cord, rope;
(Bündel) skein; (Schienen-) track; über
die e schlagen (col) kick over the traces.

Strapaz- cpd: ~e [ʃtraˈpaːtsə] f- -n strain,
exertion; s~ieren [ʃtrapaˈtsiːrən] vt
Material treat roughly, punish; Mensch,
Kräfte wear out, exhaust; s~ierfähig a
hard-wearing; s~iös [ʃtrapatsiˈøːs] a
exhausting, tough.

Straße ['ʃtraːsə] f -, -n street, road;
~nbahn f tram, streetcar (US);
~nbeleuchtung f street lighting;
~nfeger, ~nkehrer m -s, -
roadsweeper; ~nsperre f roadblock;
~nverkehrsordnung f highway code.

Strateg- [ʃtraˈteːg] cpd: ~e m -n, -n
strategist; ~ie [ʃtrateˈgiː] f strategy;
s~isch a strategic.

Stratosphäre [ʃtratoˈsfɛːrə] f -
stratosphere.

sträuben ['ʃtrɔybən] vt ruffle; vr bristle;
(Mensch) resist (gegen etw sth).

Strauch [ʃtraʊx] m -(e)s, Sträucher
bush, shrub; s~eln vi stumble, stagger.

Strauß [ʃtraʊs] m -es, Sträuße bunch;
bouquet; pl -e ostrich.

Streb- [ʃtreːb] cpd: ~e f -, -n strut;
~ebalken m buttress; s~en vi strive
(nach for); endeavour; s~en zu or nach
(sich bewegen) make for; ~er m -s, - (pej)
pusher, climber; (Sch) swot; s~sam a
industrious; ~samkeit f industry.

Strecke ['ʃtrɛkə] f -, -n stretch;
(Entfernung) distance; (Rail) line; (Math)
line; s~n vt stretch; Waffen lay down;
(Cook) eke out; vr stretch (oneself); vi (Sch)
put one's hand up.

Streich [ʃtraɪç] m -(e)s, -e trick, prank;
(Hieb) blow; s~eln vt stroke; s~en irreg
vt (berühren) stroke; (auftragen) spread;
(anmalen) paint; (durch-) delete; (nicht
genehmigen) cancel; vi (berühren) brush;
(schleichen) prowl; ~holz nt match;
~instrument nt string instrument.

Streif- ['ʃtraɪf] cpd: ~band nt wrapper;
~e f -, -n patrol; s~en vt (leicht
berühren) brush against, graze; (Blick)
skim over; Thema, Problem touch on; (ab-)
take off; vi (gehen) roam; ~en m -s, -
(Linie) stripe; (Stück) strip; (Film) film;
~endienst m patrol duty; ~enwagen m

patrol car; ~schuß m graze, grazing shot; ~zug m scouting trip.
Streik [ʃtraɪk] m -(e)s, -s strike; ~brecher m -s, - blackleg, strikebreaker; s~en vi strike; ~kasse f strike fund; ~posten m (strike) picket.
Streit [ʃtraɪt] m -(e)s, -e argument; dispute; s~en vir irreg argue; dispute; ~frage f point at issue; s~ig a: jdm etw s~ig machen dispute sb's right to sth; ~igkeiten pl quarrel, dispute; ~kräfte pl (Mil) armed forces pl; s~lustig a quarrelsome; ~sucht f quarrelsomeness.
streng [ʃtrɛŋ] a severe; Lehrer, Maßnahme strict; Geruch etc sharp; S~e f - severity; strictness; sharpness; ~genommen ad strictly speaking; ~gläubig a orthodox, strict.
Streu [ʃtrɔy] f -, -en litter, bed of straw; s~en vt strew, scatter, spread; ~ung f dispersion.
Strich [ʃtrɪç] m -(e)s, -e (Linie) line; (Feder-, Pinsel—) stroke; (von Geweben) nap; (von Fell) pile; auf den ~ gehen (col) walk the streets; jdm gegen den ~ gehen rub sb up the wrong way; einen ~ machen durch (lit) cross out; (fig) foil; ~einteilung f calibration; ~mädchen nt streetwalker; ~punkt m semicolon; s~weise ad here and there.
Strick [ʃtrɪk] m -(e)s, -e rope; (col: Kind) rascal; s~en vti knit; ~jacke f cardigan; ~leiter f rope ladder; ~nadel f knitting needle; ~waren pl knitwear.
Strieme [ˈʃtriːmə] f -, -n, Striemen [ˈʃtriːmən] m -s, - weal.
strikt [ˈʃtrɪkt] a strict.
strittig [ˈʃtrɪtɪç] a disputed, in dispute.
Stroh [ʃtroː] nt -(e)s straw; ~blume f everlasting flower; ~dach nt thatched roof; ~halm m (drinking) straw; ~mann m, pl -männer dummy, straw man; ~witwe f grass widow.
Strolch [ʃtrɔlç] m -(e)s, -e layabout, bum.
Strom [ʃtroːm] m -(e)s, ꞉e river; (fig) stream; (Elec) current; s~abwärts [-ˈapvɛrts] ad downstream; s~aufwärts [-ˈaufvɛrts] ad upstream.
strömen [ˈʃtrøːmən] vi stream, pour.
Strom- cpd: ~kreis m ꞉ circuit; s~linienförmig a streamlined; ~rechnung f electricity bill; ~sperre f power cut; ~stärke f amperage.
Strömung [ˈʃtrøːmʊŋ] f current.
Strophe [ˈʃtroːfə] f -, -n verse.
strotzen [ˈʃtrɔtsən] vi: ~vor or von abound in, be full of.
Strudel [ˈʃtruːdəl] m -s, - whirlpool, vortex; (Cook) strudel; s~n vi swirl, eddy.
Struktur [ʃtrʊkˈtuːr] f structure; s~ell [-ˈrɛl] a structural.
Strumpf [ʃtrʊmpf] m -(e)s, ꞉e stocking; ~band nt garter; ~hose f (pair of) tights.
Strunk [ʃtrʊŋk] m -(e)s, ꞉e stump.
struppig [ˈʃtrʊpɪç] a shaggy, unkempt.
Stube [ˈʃtuːbə] f -, -n room; ~narrest m confinement to one's room; (Mil) confinement to quarters; ~nhocker m

(col) stay-at-home; s~nrein a house-trained.
Stuck [ʃtʊk] m -(e)s stucco.
Stück [ʃtʏk] nt -(e)s, -e piece; (etwas) bit; (Theat) play; ~arbeit f piecework; ~chen nt little piece; ~lohn m piecework wages pl; s~weise ad bit by bit, piecemeal; (Comm) individually; ~werk nt bits and pieces pl.
Student(in f) [ʃtuˈdɛnt(ɪn)] m student; s~isch a student, academic.
Studie [ˈʃtuːdiə] f study.
studieren [ʃtuˈdiːrən] vti study.
Studio [ˈʃtuːdio] nt -s, -s studio.
Studium [ˈʃtuːdiʊm] nt studies pl.
Stufe [ˈʃtuːfə] f -, -n step; (Entwicklungs—) stage; ~nleiter f (fig) ladder; s~nweise ad gradually.
Stuhl [ʃtuːl] m -(e)s, ꞉e chair; ~gang m bowel movement.
stülpen [ˈʃtʏlpən] vt (umdrehen) turn upside down; (bedecken) put.
stumm [ʃtʊm] a silent; (Med) dumb; S~el m -s, - stump; (Zigaretten-) stub; S~film m silent film; S~heit f silence; dumbness.
Stümper [ˈʃtʏmpər] m -s, - incompetent, duffer; s~haft a bungling, incompetent; s~n vi (col) bungle.
stumpf [ʃtʊmpf] a blunt; (teilnahmslos, glanzlos) dull; Winkel obtuse; S~ m -(e)s, ꞉e stump; S~heit f bluntness; dullness; S~sinn m tediousness; ~sinnig a dull.
Stunde [ˈʃtʊndə] f -, -n hour; s~n vt: jdm etw s~en give sb time to pay sth; ~ngeschwindigkeit f average speed per hour; ~nkilometer pl kilometres per hour; s~nlang a for hours; ~nlohn m hourly wage; ~nplan m timetable; s~nweise a by the hour; every hour.
stündlich [ˈʃtʏntlɪç] a hourly.
Stups [ʃtʊps] m -es, -e (col) push; ~nase f snub nose.
stur [ʃtuːr] a obstinate, pigheaded.
Sturm [ʃtʊrm] m -(e)s, ꞉e storm, gale; (Mil etc) attack, assault.
stürm- [ˈʃtʏrm] cpd: ~en vi (Wind) blow hard, rage; (rennen) storm; vt (Mil, fig) storm; v impers es ~t there's a gale blowing; S~er m -s, - (Sport) forward, striker; ~isch a stormy.
Sturm- cpd: ~warnung f gale warning; ~wind m storm, gale.
Sturz [ʃtʊrts] m -es, ꞉e fall; (Pol) overthrow.
stürzen [ˈʃtʏrtsən] vt (werfen) hurl; (Pol) overthrow; (umkehren) overturn; vr rush; (hinein—) plunge; vi fall; (Aviat) dive; (rennen) dash.
Sturz- cpd: ~flug m nose-dive; ~helm m crash helmet.
Stute [ˈʃtuːtə] f -, -n mare.
Stütz- [ʃtʏts] cpd: ~balken m brace, joist; ~e f -, -n support; help; s~en vt (lit, fig) support; Ellbogen etc prop up.
stutz- [ʃtʊts] cpd: ~en vt trim; Ohr, Schwanz dock; Flügel clip; vi hesitate; become suspicious; ~ig a perplexed, puzzled; (mißtrauisch) suspicious.
Stütz- cpd: ~mauer f supporting wall;

~punkt *m* point of support; *(von Hebel)* fulcrum; *(Mil, fig)* base.

Styropor ³ [ʃtyro'po:r] *nt* **-s** polystyrene.

Subjekt [zʊp'jɛkt] *nt* **-(e)s, -e** subject; **s~iv** [-'ti:f] *a* subjective; **~ivi'tät** *f* subjectivity.

Substantiv [zʊpstan'ti:f] *nt* **-s, -e** noun.

Substanz [zʊp'stants] *f* substance.

subtil [zʊp'ti:l] *a* subtle.

subtrahieren [zʊptra'hi:rən] *vt* subtract.

Subvention [zʊpvɛntsi'o:n] *f* subsidy; **s~ieren** [-'ni:rən] *vt* subsidize.

subversiv [zʊpvɛr'zi:f] *a* subversive.

Such- ['zu:x] *cpd*: **~aktion** *f* search; **~e** *f* **-, -n** search; **s~en** *vti* look (for), seek; *(ver~)* try; **~er** *m* **-s, -** seeker, searcher; *(Phot)* viewfinder.

Sucht [zʊxt] *f* **-, ⁻e** mania; *(Med)* addiction, craving.

süchtig ['zʏçtɪç] *a* addicted; **S~e(r)** *mf* addict.

Süd- [zy:t] *cpd*: **~en** ['zy:dən] *m* **-s** south; **~früchte** *pl* Mediterranean fruit; **s~lich** *a* southern; **s~lich von** (to the) south of; **s~wärts** *ad* southwards.

süff- *cpd*: **~ig** ['zʏfɪç] *a* Wein pleasant to the taste; **~isant** [zyfi'zant] *a* smug.

suggerieren [zʊge'ri:rən] *vt* suggest *(jdm etw* sth to sb).

Sühne ['zy:nə] *f* **-, -n** atonement, expiation; **s~n** *vt* atone for, expiate.

Sulfonamid [zulfona'mi:t] *nt* **-(e)s, -e** *(Med)* sulphonamide.

Sultan ['zʊltan] *m* **-s, -e** sultan; **~ine** [zulta'ni:nə] *f* sultana.

Sülze ['zʏltsə] *f* **-, -n** brawn.

Summ- [zʊm] *cpd*: **s~arisch** [zʊ'ma:rɪʃ] *a* summary; **~e** *f* **-, -n** sum, total; **s~en** *vti* buzz; *Lied* hum; **s~ieren** [zʊ'mi:rən] *vtr* add up (to).

Sumpf [zʊmpf] *m* **-(e)s, ⁻e** swamp, marsh; **s~ig** *a* marshy.

Sünde ['zʏndə] *f* **-, -n** sin; **~nbock** *m (col)* scapegoat; **~nfall** *m* Fall (of man); **~r(in** *f) m* **-s, -** sinner.

Super ['zu:pər] *nt* **-s** *(Benzin)* four star (petrol); **~lativ** [-lati:f] *m* **-s, -e** superlative; **~markt** *m* supermarket.

Suppe ['zʊpə] *f* **-, -n** soup.

surren ['zʊrən] *vi* buzz, hum.

Surrogat [zʊro'ga:t] *nt* **-(e)s, -e** substitute, surrogate.

suspekt [zʊs'pɛkt] *a* suspect.

süß [zy:s] *a* sweet; **S~e** *f* **-** sweetness; **~en** *vt* sweeten; **S~igkeit** *f* sweetness; *(Bonbon etc)* sweet, candy *(US)*; **~lich** *a* sweetish; *(fig)* sugary; **S~speise** *f* pudding, sweet; **S~stoff** *m* sweetening agent; **S~wasser** *nt* fresh water.

Sylvester [zʏl'vɛstər] *nt* **-s, -** *see* **Silvester.**

Symbol [zʏm'bo:l] *nt* **-s, -e** symbol; **s~isch** *a* symbolic(al).

Symmetrie [zʏme'tri:] *f* symmetry; **~achse** *f* symmetric axis.

symmetrisch [zʏ'me:trɪʃ] *a* symmetrical.

Sympath- *cpd*: **~ie** [zʏmpa'ti:] *f* liking, sympathy; **s~isch** [zʏm'pa:tɪʃ] *a* likeable,

congenial; **er ist mir s~isch** I like him; **s~i'sieren** *vi* sympathize.

Symptom [zʏmp'to:m] *nt* **-s, -e** symptom; **s~atisch** [zʏmpto'ma:tɪʃ] *a* symptomatic.

Synagoge [zyna'go:gə] *f* **-, -n** synagogue.

synchron [zʏn'kro:n] *a* synchronous; **S~getriebe** *nt* synchromesh (gears *pl*); **~i'sieren** *vt* synchronize; *Film* dub.

Syndikat [zʏndi'ka:t] *nt* **-(e)s, -e** combine, syndicate.

Synonym [zyno'ny:m] *nt* **-s, -e** synonym; **s~** *a* synonymous.

Syntax ['zʏntaks] *f* **-, -en** syntax.

Synthese [zʏn'te:zə] *f* **-, -n** synthesis.

synthetisch [zʏn'te:tɪʃ] *a* synthetic.

Syphilis ['zyfilɪs] *f* **-** syphilis.

System [zʏs'te:m] *nt* **-s, -e** system; **s~atisch** [zʏste'ma:tɪʃ] *a* systematic; **s~ati'sieren** *vt* systematize.

Szene ['stse:nə] *f* **-, -n** scene; **~rie** [stsenə'ri:] *f* scenery.

Szepter ['stsɛptər] *nt* **-s, -** sceptre.

T

T, t [te:] T, t.

Tabak ['ta:bak] *m* **-s, -e** tobacco.

Tabell- [ta'bɛl] *cpd*: **t~arisch** [tabɛ'la:rɪʃ] *a* tabular; **~e** *f* table; **~enführer** *m* top of the table, league leader.

Tabernakel [tabɛr'na:kəl] *m* **-s, -** tabernacle.

Tablette [ta'blɛtə] *f* tablet, pill.

Tachometer [taxo'me:tər] *m* **-s, -** *(Aut)* speedometer.

Tadel ['ta:dəl] *m* **-s, -** censure, scolding; *(Fehler)* fault, blemish; **t~los** *a* faultless, irreproachable; **t~n** *vt* scold; **t~nswert** *a* blameworthy.

Tafel ['ta:fəl] *f* **-, -n** table *(auch Math)*; *(Anschlag—)* board; *(Wand—)* blackboard; *(Schiefer—)* slate; *(Gedenk—)* plaque; *(Illustration)* plate; *(Schalt—)* panel; *(Schokolade etc)* bar.

Täfel- ['tɛ:fəl] *cpd*: **t~n** *vt* panel; **~ung** *f* panelling.

Taft [taft] *m* **-(e)s, -e** tafetta.

Tag [ta:k] *m* **-(e)s, -e** day; daylight; **unter/über ~** *(Min)* underground/on the surface; **an den ~ kommen** come to light; **guten ~!** good morning/afternoon!; **t~aus, t~ein** day in, day out; **~dienst** *m* day duty; **~ebuch** ['ta:gəbu:x] *nt* diary, journal; **~edieb** *m* idler; **~egeld** *nt* daily allowance; **t~elang** *ad* for days; **t~en** *vi* sit, meet; *v impers*: **es tagt** dawn is breaking; **~esablauf** *m* course of the day; **~esanbruch** *m* dawn; **~eslicht** *nt* daylight; **~esordnung** *f* agenda; **~essatz** *m* daily rate; **~eszeit** *f* time of day; **~eszeitung** *f* daily (paper).

täglich ['tɛ:klɪç] *a,ad* daily.

Tag- *cpd*: **t~süber** *ad* during the day; **~ung** *f* conference.

Taille ['taljə] *f* **-, -n** waist.

Takel ['ta:kəl] *nt* **-s, -** tackle; **t~n** *vt* rig.

Takt [takt] *m* **-(e)s, -e** tact; *(Mus)* time; **~gefühl** *nt* tact; **~ik** *f* tactics *pl*; **t~isch** *a* tactical; **t~los** *a* tactless; **~losigkeit** *f*

tactlessness; ~**stock** m (conductor's) baton; t~**voll** a tactful.
Tal [ta:l] nt -(e)s, ¨er valley.
Talar [ta'la:r] m -s, -e (Jur) robe; (Univ) gown.
Talent [ta'lɛnt] nt -(e)s, -e talent; t~**iert** [talɛn'ti:rt], t~**voll** a talented, gifted.
Taler ['ta:lər] m -s, - taler, florin.
Talg [talk] m -(e)s, -e tallow; ~**drüse** f sebaceous gland.
Talisman ['ta:lisman] m -s, -e talisman.
Tal- cpd: ~**sohle** f bottom of a valley; ~**sperre** f dam.
Tamburin [tambu'ri:n] nt -s, -e tambourine.
Tampon ['tampon] m -s, -s tampon.
Tang [taŋ] m -(e)s, -e seaweed; ~**ente** [taŋ'gɛntə] f -, -n tangent; t~**ieren** [taŋgi'rən] vt (lit) be tangent to; (fig) affect.
Tank [taŋk] m -s, -s tank; t~**en** vi fill up with petrol or gas (US); (Aviat) (re)fuel; ~**er** m -s, -, ~**schiff** nt tanker; ~**stelle** f petrol or gas (US) station; ~**wart** m petrol pump or gas station (US) attendant.
Tanne ['tanə] f -, -n fir; ~**nbaum** m fir tree; ~ **nzapfen** m fir cone.
Tante ['tantə] f -, -n aunt.
Tanz [tants] m -es, ¨e dance.
Tänz- ['tɛnts] cpd: t~**eln** vi dance along; ~**er(in** f) m -s, - dancer.
Tanz- cpd: t~**en** vti dance; ~**fläche** f (dance) floor; ~**schule** f dancing school.
Tape- cpd: ~**te** [ta'pe:tə] f -, -n wallpaper; ~**tenwechsel** m (fig) change of scenery; t~**zieren** [tape'tsi:rən] vt (wall)paper; ~**zierer** [tape'tsi:rər] m -s, - (interior) decorator.
tapfer ['tapfər] a brave; T~**keit** f courage, bravery.
tappen ['tapən] vi walk uncertainly or clumsily.
täppisch ['tɛpɪʃ] a clumsy.
Tarif [ta'ri:f] m -s, -e tariff, (scale of) fares/charges; ~**lohn** m standard wage rate.
Tarn ['tarn] cpd: t~**en** vt camouflage; Person, Absicht disguise; ~**farbe** f camouflage paint; ~**ung** f camouflaging, disguising.
Tasche ['taʃə] f -, -n pocket; handbag; ~**n** in cpds pocket; ~**nbuch** nt paperback; ~**ndieb** m pickpocket; ~**ngeld** nt pocket money; ~**nlampe** f (electric) torch, flashlight (US); ~**nmesser** nt penknife; ~**nspieler** m conjurer; ~**ntuch** nt handkerchief.
Tasse ['tasə] f -, -n cup.
Tast- ['tast] cpd: ~**atur** [-a'tu:r] f keyboard; ~**e** f -, -n push-button control; (an Schreibmaschine) key; t~**en** vt feel, touch; vi feel, grope; vr feel one's way; ~**sinn** m sense of touch.
Tat [ta:t] f -, -en act, deed, action; **in der** ~ indeed, as a matter of fact; ~**bestand** m facts pl of the case; t~**enlos** a inactive.
Tät- ['tɛ:t] cpd: ~**er(in** f) m -s, - perpetrator, culprit; ~**erschaft** f guilt; t~**ig** a active; **in einer Firma t~ig sein** work for a firm; T~**igkeit** f activity;

(Beruf) occupation; t~**lich** a violent; ~**lichkeit** f violence; pl blows pl.
tätowieren [tɛto'vi:rən] vt tattoo.
Tat- cpd: ~**sache** f fact; t~**sächlich** a actual; ad really.
Tatze ['tatsə] f -, -n paw.
Tau [tau] nt -(e)s, -e rope; m -(e)s dew.
taub [taup] a deaf; Nuß hollow; T~**heit** f deafness; ~**stumm** a deaf-and-dumb.
Taube ['taubə] f -, -n dove; pigeon; ~**nschlag** m dovecote.
Tauch- ['taux] cpd: t~**en** vt dip; vi dive; (Naut) submerge; ~**er** m -s, - diver; ~**eranzug** m diving suit; ~**sieder** m -s, - portable immersion heater.
tauen ['tauən] vti, v impers thaw.
Tauf- ['tauf] cpd: ~**becken** nt font; ~**e** f -, -n baptism; t~**en** vt christen, baptize; ~**name** m Christian name; ~**pate** m godfather; ~**patin** f godmother; ~**schein** m certificate of baptism.
Taug- ['taug] cpd: t~**en** vi be of use; t~**en für** do or be good for; **nicht** t~**en** be no good or useless; ~**enichts** m -es, -e good-for-nothing; t~**lich** ['tauklıç] a suitable; (Mil) fit (for service); ~**lichkeit** f suitability; fitness.
Taumel ['tauməl] m -s dizziness; (fig) frenzy; t~**ig** a giddy, reeling; t~**n** vi reel, stagger.
Tausch [tauʃ] m -(e)s, -e exchange; t~**en** vt exchange, swap; ~**handel** m barter.
täuschen ['tɔyʃən] vt deceive; vi be deceptive; vr be wrong; ~**d** a deceptive.
Täuschung f deception; (optisch) illusion.
tausend ['tauzənt] num (a) thousand; T~**füßler** m -s, - centipede; millipede.
Tau- cpd: ~**tropfen** m dew drop; ~**wetter** nt thaw; ~**ziehen** nt -s, - tug-of-war.
Taxi ['taksi] nt -(s), -(s) taxi; ~**fahrer** m taxi driver.
Tech- ['tɛç] cpd: ~**nik** f technology; (Methode, Kunstfertigkeit) technique; ~**niker** m -s, - technician; t~**nisch** a technical; ~**nolo'gie** f technology; t~**no'logisch** a technological.
Tee [te:] m -s, -s tea; ~**kanne** f teapot; ~**löffel** m teaspoon.
Teer [te:r] m -(e)s, -e tar; t~**en** vt tar.
Tee- cpd: ~**sieb** nt tea strainer; ~**wagen** m tea trolley.
Teich [taıç] m -(e)s, -e pond.
Teig [taık] m -(e)s, -e dough; t~**ig** a doughy; ~**waren** pl pasta sing.
Teil [taıl] m or nt -(e)s, -e part; (An—) share; (Bestand—) component; **zum** ~ partly; t~**bar** a divisible; ~**betrag** m instalment; ~**chen** nt (atomic) particle; t~**en** vtr divide; (mit jdm) share; t~**haben** vi irreg share (an +dat in); ~**haber** m -s, - partner; ~**kaskoversicherung** f third party, fire and theft insurance; ~**nahme** f -, -n participation; (Mitleid) sympathy; t~**nahmslos** a disinterested, apathetic; t~**nehmen** vi irreg take part (an +dat in); ~**nehmer** m -s, - participant; t~**s** ad partly; ~**ung** f division; t~**weise** ad partially, in part;

~**zahlung** *f* payment by instalments.

Teint [tɛ̃:] *m* -s, -s complexion.

Telefon [tele'fo:n] *nt* -s, -e telephone; ~**amt** *nt* telephone exchange; ~**anruf** *m*, ~**at** [telefo'na:t] *nt* -(e)s, -e (tele)phone .call; ~**buch** *nt* telephone directory; t~**ieren** [telefo'ni:rən] *vi* telephone; t~**isch** [-ɪʃ] *a* telephone; *Benachrichtigung* by telephone; ~**ist(in f)** [telefo'nɪst(ɪn)] *m* telephonist; ~**nummer** *f* (tele)phone number; ~**verbindung** *f* telephone connection; ~**zelle** *f* telephone kiosk, callbox; ~**zentrale** *f* telephone exchange.

Telegraf [tele'gra:f] *m* -en, -en telegraph; ~**enleitung** *f* telegraph line; ~**enmast** *m* telegraph pole; ~**ie** [-'fi:] *f* telegraphy; t~**ieren** [-'fi:rən] *vti* telegraph, wire; t~**isch** *a* telegraphic.

Telegramm [tele'gram] *nt* -s, -e telegram, cable; ~**adresse** *f* telegraphic address; ~**formular** *nt* telegram form.

Tele- *cpd*: ~**graph** = ~**graf**; ~**kolleg** ['telekolek] *nt* university of the air; ~**objektiv** ['te:le'ɔpjɛkti:f] *nt* telephoto lens; ~**pathie** [telepa'ti:] *f* telepathy; t~**pathisch** [tele'pa:tɪʃ] *a* telepathic; ~**phon** = ~**fon**; ~**skop** [tele'sko:p] *nt* -s, -e telescope.

Teller ['tɛlər] *m* -s, - plate.

Tempel ['tɛmpəl] *m* -s, - temple.

Temperafarbe ['tɛmpərafarbə] *f* distemper.

Temperament [tɛmpera'mɛnt] *nt* temperament; (*Schwung*) vivacity, liveliness; t~**los** a spiritless; t~**voll** a high-spirited, lively.

Temperatur [tɛmpera'tu:r] *f* temperature.

Tempo ['tɛmpo] *nt* -s, -s speed, pace; *pl* **Tempi** (*Mus*) tempo; ~**!** get a move on!; t~**rär** [-'rɛ:r] *a* temporary; ~**taschentuch** `*` *nt* paper handkerchief.

Tendenz [tɛn'dɛnts] *f* tendency; (*Absicht*) intention; t~**iös** [-i'ø:s] *a* biased, tendentious.

tendieren [tɛn'di:rən] *vi* show a tendency, incline (*zu* to(wards)).

Tenne ['tɛnə] *f* -, -n threshing floor.

Tennis ['tɛnɪs] *nt* - tennis; ~**platz** *m* tennis court; ~**schläger** *m* tennis racket; ~**spieler(in f)** *m* tennis player.

Tenor [te'no:r] *m* -s, ⁺e tenor.

Teppich ['tɛpɪç] *m* -s, -e carpet; ~**boden** *m* wall-to-wall carpeting; ~**kehrmaschine** *f* carpet sweeper; ~**klopfer** *m* carpet beater.

Termin [tɛr'mi:n] *m* -s, -e (*Zeitpunkt*) date; (*Frist*) time limit, deadline; (*Arzt—etc*) appointment; ~**kalender** *m* diary, appointments book; ~**ologie** [-olo'gi:] *f* terminology.

Termite [tɛr'mi:tə] *f* -, -n termite.

Terpentin [tɛrpɛn'ti:n] *nt* -s, -e turpentine, turps *sing*.

Terrasse [tɛ'rasə] *f* -, -n terrace.

Terrine [tɛ'ri:nə] *f* tureen.

territorial [tɛritori'a:l] *a* territorial.

Territorium [tɛri'to:rium] *nt* territory.

Terror ['tɛrɔr] *m* -s terror; reign of terror; t~**isieren** [tɛrori'zi:rən] *vt* terrorize;

~**ismus** [-'rɪsmʊs] *m* terrorism; ~**ist** [-'rɪst] *m* terrorist.

Terz [tɛrts] *f* -, -en (*Mus*) third; ~**ett** [tɛr'tsɛt] *nt* -(e)s, -e trio.

Tesafilm ® ['te:zafɪlm] *m* sellotape ®.

Testament [tɛsta'mɛnt] *nt* will, testament; (*Rel*) Testament; t~**arisch** [-'ta:rɪʃ] *a* testamentary; ~**svollstrecker** *m* executor (of a will).

Test- [tɛst] *cpd*: ~**at** [tɛs'ta:t] *nt* -(e)s, -e certificate; ~**ator** [tɛs'ta:tər] *m* testator; ~**bild** *nt* (*TV*) test card; t~**en** *vt* test.

Tetanus ['te:tanʊs] *m* - tetanus; ~**impfung** *f* (anti-)tetanus injection.

teuer ['tɔyər] *a* dear, expensive; T~**ung** *f* increase in prices; T~**ungszulage** *f* cost of living bonus.

Teufel ['tɔyfəl] *m* -s, - devil; ~**ei** [-'laı] *f* devilry; ~**saustreibung** *f* exorcism.

teuflisch ['tɔyflɪʃ] *a* fiendish, diabolical.

Text [tɛkst] *m* -(e)s, -e text; (*Lieder—*) words *pl*; t~**en** *vi* write the words.

textil [tɛks'ti:l] *a* textile; T~**ien** *pl* textiles *pl*; T~**industrie** *f* textile industry; ~**waren** *pl* textiles *pl*.

Theater [te'a:tər] *nt* -s, - theatre; (*col*) fuss; ~ **spielen** (*lit*, *fig*) playact; ~**besucher** *m* playgoer; ~**kasse** *f* box office; ~**stück** *nt* (stage-)play.

theatralisch [tea'tra:lɪʃ] *a* theatrical.

Theke ['te:kə] *f* -, -n (*Schanktisch*) bar; (*Ladentisch*) counter.

Thema ['te:ma] *nt* -s, **Themen** or -ta theme, topic, subject.

Theo- [teo] *cpd*: ~**loge** [-'lo:gə] *m* -n, -n theologian; ~**logie** [-lo'gi:] *f* theology; t~**logisch** [-'lo:gɪʃ] *a* theological; ~**retiker** [-'re:tikər] *m* -s, - theorist; t~**retisch** [-'re:tɪʃ] *a* theoretical; ~**rie** [-'ri:] *f* theory.

Thera- [tera] *cpd*: ~**peut** [-'pɔyt] *m* -en, -en therapist; t~**peutisch** [-'pɔytɪʃ] *a* therapeutic; ~**pie** [-'pi:] *f* therapy.

Therm- *cpd*: ~**albad** [tɛrm'a:lba:t] *nt* thermal bath; thermal spa; ~**ometer** [tɛrmo'me:tər] *nt* -s, - thermometer; ~**osflasche** ['tɛrmɔsflaʃə] *f* Thermos ® flask; ~**ostat** [tɛrmo'sta:t] *m* -(e)s or -en, -e(n) thermostat.

These ['te:zə] *f* -, -n thesis.

Thrombose [trɔm'bo:zə] *f* -, -n thrombosis.

Thron [tro:n] *m* -(e)s, -e throne; ~**besteigung** *f* accession (to the throne); ~**erbe** *m* heir to the throne; ~**folge** *f* succession (to the throne).

Thunfisch ['tu:nfɪʃ] *m* tuna.

Thymian ['ty:mia:n] *m* -s, -e thyme.

Tick [tɪk] *m* -(e)s, -s tic; (*Eigenart*) quirk; (*Fimmel*) craze; t~**en** *vi* tick.

tief [ti:f] *a* deep; (*tiefsinnig*) profound; *Ausschnitt*, *Ton* low; T~ *nt* -s, -s (*Met*) depression; T~**druck** *m* low pressure; T~**e** *f* -, -n depth; T~**ebene** *f* plain; T~**enpsychologie** *f* depth psychology; T~**enschärfe** *f* (*Phot*) depth of focus; ~**ernst** *a* very grave or solemn; T~**gang** *m* (*Naut*) draught; (*geistig*) depth; ~**gekühlt** *a* frozen; ~**greifend** *a* far-reaching; T~**kühlfach** *nt* deep-freeze compartment; T~**kühltruhe** f deep-freeze, freezer; T~**land** nt lowlands pl; T~**punkt** m low point; (fig) low ebb; T~**schlag** m (Boxen, fig) blow below the belt; ~**schürfend** a profound; T~**see** f deep sea; T~**sinn** m profundity; ~**sinnig** a profound; melancholy; T~**stand** m low level; ~**stapeln** vi be overmodest; T~**start** m (Sport) crouch start; T~**stwert** m minimum or lowest value.

Tiegel ['ti:gəl] m -s, - saucepan; (Chem) crucible.

Tier [ti:r] nt ~(e)s, -e animal; ~**arzt** m vet(erinary surgeon); ~**garten** m zoo(logical gardens pl); t~**isch** a animal; (lit, fig) brutish; (fig) Ernst etc deadly; ~**kreis** m zodiac; ~**kunde** f zoology; t~**liebend** a fond of animals; ~**quälerei** [-kvɛ:lə'raɪ] f cruelty to animals; ~**schutzverein** m society for the prevention of cruelty to animals.

Tiger ['ti:gər] m -s, - tiger; ~**in** f tigress.

tilgen ['tɪlgən] vt erase, expunge; Sünden expiate; Schulden pay off.

Tilgung f erasing, blotting out; expiation; repayment.

Tinktur [tɪŋk'tu:r] f tincture.

Tinte ['tɪntə] f -, -n ink; ~**nfaß** nt inkwell; ~**nfisch** m cuttlefish; ~**nfleck** m ink stain, blot; ~**nstift** m copying or indelible pencil.

tippen ['tɪpən] vti tap, touch; (col: schreiben) type; (col: raten) tip (auf jdn sb); (im Lotto etc) bet (on).

Tipp- [tɪp] cpd: ~**fehler** m (col) typing error; ~**se** f -, -n (col) typist; t~**topp** a (col) tip-top; ~**zettel** m (pools) coupon.

Tisch [tɪʃ] m ~(e)s, -e table; bei ~ at table; vor/nach ~ before/ after eating; unter den ~ fallen (fig) be dropped; ~**decke** f tablecloth; ~**ler** m -s, - carpenter, joiner; ~**le'rei** f joiner's workshop; (Arbeit) carpentry, joinery; t~**lern** vi do carpentry etc; ~**rede** f after-dinner speech; ~**tennis** nt table tennis.

Titel ['ti:təl] m -s, - title; ~**anwärter** m (Sport) challenger; ~**bild** nt cover (picture); (von Buch) frontispiece; ~**rolle** f title role; ~**seite** f cover; (Buch—) title page; ~**verteidiger** m defending champion, title holder.

titulieren [titu'li:rən] vt entitle; (anreden) address.

Toast [to:st] m ~(e)s, -s or -e toast; ~**er** m -s, - toaster.

tob- ['to:b] cpd: ~**en** vi rage; (Kinder) romp about; T~**sucht** f raving madness; ~**süchtig** a maniacal; ~**suchtsanfall** m maniacal fit.

Tochter ['tɔxtər] f -, " daughter.

Tod [to:t] m ~(e)s, -e death; t~**ernst** a (col) deadly serious; ad in dead earnest; ~**esangst** ['to:dəsaŋst] f mortal fear; ~**esanzeige** f obituary (notice); ~**esfall** m death; ~**eskampf** m throes pl of death; ~**esstoß** m death-blow; ~**esstrafe** f death penalty; ~**estag** m anniversary of death; ~**esursache** f cause of death; ~**esurteil** nt death sentence;

~**esverachtung** f utter disgust; t~**krank** a dangerously ill.

tödlich ['tø:tlɪç] a deadly, fatal.

tod- cpd: ~**müde** a dead tired; ~**schick** a (col) smart, classy; ~**sicher** a (col) absolutely or dead certain; T~**sünde** f deadly sin.

Toilette [toa'lɛtə] f toilet, lavatory; (Frisiertisch) dressing table; (Kleidung) outfit; ~**nartikel** pl toiletries pl, toilet articles pl; ~**npapier** nt toilet paper; ~**ntisch** m dressing table.

toi, toi, toi ['tɔy, 'tɔy, 'tɔy] interj touch wood.

tolerant [tole'rant] a tolerant.

Toleranz [tole'rants] f tolerance.

tolerieren [tole'ri:rən] vt tolerate.

toll [tɔl] a mad; Treiben wild; (col) terrific; ~**en** vi romp; T~**heit** f madness, wildness; T~**kirsche** f deadly nightshade; ~**kühn** a daring; T~**wut** f rabies.

Tölpel ['tœlpəl] m -s, - oaf, clod.

Tomate [to'ma:tə] f -, -n tomato; ~**nmark** nt tomato puree.

Ton [to:n] m ~(e)s, -e (Erde) clay; pl "e (Laut) sound; (Mus) note; (Redeweise) tone; (Farb—, Nuance) shade; (Betonung) stress; ~**abnehmer** m pick-up; t~**angebend** a leading; ~**art** f (musical) key; ~**band** nt tape; ~**bandgerät** nt tape recorder.

tönen ['tø:nən] vi sound; vt shade; Haare tint.

tönern ['tø:nərn] a clay.

Ton- cpd: ~**fall** m intonation; ~**film** m sound film; t~**haltig** a clayey; ~**höhe** f pitch; ~**ika** f -, **-iken** (Mus); ~**ikum** nt -s, **-ika** (Med) tonic; ~**künstler** m musician; ~**leiter** f (Mus) scale; t~**los** a soundless.

Tonne ['tɔnə] f -, -n barrel; (Maß) ton.

Ton- cpd: ~**spur** f soundtrack; ~**taube** f clay pigeon; ~**waren** pl pottery, earthenware.

Topf [tɔpf] m ~(e)s, "e pot; ~**blume** f pot plant.

Töpfer ['tœpfər] m -s, - potter; ~**ei** [-'raɪ] f piece of pottery; potter's workshop; ~**scheibe** f potter's wheel.

topographisch [topo'gra:fɪʃ] a topographic.

topp [tɔp] interj O.K.

Tor [to:r] m -en, -en fool; nt ~(e)s, -e gate; (Sport) goal; ~**bogen** m archway.

Torf [tɔrf] m ~(e)s peat; ~**stechen** nt peat-cutting.

Tor- cpd: ~**heit** f foolishness; foolish deed; ~**hüter** m -s, - goalkeeper.

töricht ['tø:rɪçt] a foolish.

torkeln ['tɔrkəln] vi stagger, reel.

torpedieren [tɔrpe'di:rən] vt (lit, fig) torpedo.

Torpedo [tɔr'pe:do] m -s, -s torpedo.

Torte ['tɔrtə] f -, -n cake; (Obst—) flan, tart.

Tortur [tɔr'tu:r] f ordeal.

Tor- cpd: ~**verhältnis** nt goal average; ~**wart** m ~(e)s, -e goalkeeper.

tosen ['to:zən] vi roar.

tot [to:t] a dead; einen ~**en Punkt haben** be at one's lowest.

total [to'ta:l] *a* total; ~**itär** [totali'tɛːr] *a* totalitarian; **T~schaden** *m* (*Aut*) complete write-off.

tot- *cpd*: ~**arbeiten** *vr* work oneself to death; ~**ärgern** *vr* (*col*) get really annoyed.

töten ['tøːtən] *vti* kill.

Tot- *cpd*: ~**enbett** *nt* death bed; **t~enblaß** *a* deathly pale, white as a sheet; ~**engräber** *m* -**s**, - gravedigger; ~**enhemd** *nt* shroud; ~**enkopf** *m* skull; ~**enschein** *m* death certificate; ~**enstille** *f* deathly silence; ~**entanz** *m* danse macabre; ~**e(r)** *mf* dead person; **t~fahren** *vt irreg* run over; **t~geboren** *a* stillborn; **t~lachen** *vr* (*col*) laugh one's head off.

Toto ['to:to] *m or nt* -**s**, -**s** pools *pl*; ~**schein** *m* pools coupon.

tot- *cpd*: ~**sagen** *vt*: **jdn** ~**sagen** say that sb is dead; ~**schlagen** *vt irreg* (*lit, fig*) kill; **T~schläger** *m* killer; (*Waffe*) cosh; ~**schweigen** *vt irreg* hush up; ~**stellen** *vr* pretend to be dead; ~**treten** *vt irreg* trample to death.

Tötung ['tøːtʊŋ] *f* killing.

Toupet [tu'pe:] *nt* -**s**, -**s** toupee.

toupieren [tu'piːrən] *vt* back-comb.

Tour [tuːr] *f* -, -**en** tour, trip; (*Umdrehung*) revolution; (*Verhaltensart*) way; **in einer** ~ incessantly; ~**enzahl** *f* number of revolutions; ~**enzähler** *m* rev counter; ~**ismus** [tu'rɪsmʊs] *m* tourism; ~**ist** [tu'rɪst] *m* tourist; ~**istenklasse** *f* tourist class; ~**nee** [tʊr'neː] *f* -, -**n** (*Theat etc*) tour; **auf** ~**nee gehen** go on tour.

Trab [traːp] *m* -(**e**)**s** trot; ~**ant** [tra'bant] *m* satellite; ~**antenstadt** *f* satellite town; **t~en** *vi* trot.

Tracht [traxt] *f* -, -**en** (*Kleidung*) costume, dress; **eine** ~ **Prügel** a sound thrashing; **t~en** *vi* strive (*nach for*), endeavour; **jdm nach dem Leben t~en** seek to kill sb.

trächtig ['trɛçtɪç] *a Tier* pregnant; (*fig*) rich, fertile.

Tradition [traditsi'o:n] *f* tradition; **t~ell** [-'nɛl] *a* traditional.

Trag- [traːg] *cpd*: ~**bahre** *f* stretcher; **t~bar** *a Gerät* portable; *Kleidung* wearable; (*erträglich*) bearable.

träge ['trɛːgə] *a* sluggish, slow; (*Phys*) inert.

tragen ['traːgən] *irreg vt* carry; *Kleidung, Brille* wear; *Namen, Früchte* bear; (*erdulden*) endure; **sich mit einem Gedanken** ~ have an idea in mind; *vi* (*schwanger sein*) be pregnant; (*Eis*) hold; **zum T~ kommen** have an effect.

Träger ['trɛːgər] *m* -**s**, - carrier; wearer; bearer; (*Ordens—*) holder; (*an Kleidung*) (shoulder) strap; (*Körperschaft etc*) sponsor; ~**rakete** *f* launch vehicle; ~**rock** *m* skirt with shoulder straps.

Trag- [traːk] *cpd*: ~**fähigkeit** *f* load-carrying capacity; ~**fläche** *f* (*Aviat*) wing; ~**flügelboot** *nt* hydrofoil.

Trägheit ['trɛːkhait] *f* laziness; (*Phys*) inertia.

Tragi- ['traːgi] *cpd*: ~**k** *f* tragedy; **t~komisch** *a* tragi-comic; **t~sch** *a* tragic.

Tragödie [tra'gø:diə] *f* tragedy.

Trag- ['traːk] *cpd*: ~**weite** *f* range; (*fig*) scope; ~**werk** *nt* wing assembly.

Train- [trɛːn] *cpd*: ~**er** *m* -**s**, - (*Sport*) trainer, coach; (*Fußball*) manager; **t~ieren** [trɛ'niːrən] *vti* train; *Mensch auch* coach; *Übung* practise; **Fußball t~ieren** do football practise; ~**ing** *nt* -**s**, -**s** training; ~**ingsanzug** *m* track suit.

Traktor ['traktɔr] *m* tractor.

trällern ['trɛlərn] *vti* trill, sing.

trampeln ['trampəln] *vti* trample, stamp.

trampen ['trampən] *vi* hitch-hike.

Tran [traːn] *m* -(**e**)**s**, -**e** train oil, blubber.

tranchieren [trã'ʃiːrən] *vt* carve.

Tranchierbesteck [trã'ʃi:rbəʃtɛk] *nt* (pair of) carvers.

Träne ['trɛːnə] *f* -, -**n** tear; **t~n** *vi* water; ~**ngas** *nt* teargas.

Tränke ['trɛŋkə] *f* -, -**n** watering place; **t~n** *vt* (*naß machen*) soak; *Tiere* water.

Trans- *cpd*: ~**formator** [transfɔr'ma:tɔr] *m* transformer; ~**istor** [tran'zistɔr] *m* transistor; **t~itiv** ['tranzitiːf] *a* transitive; **t~parent** [transpa'rɛnt] *a* transparent; ~**parent** *nt* -(**e**)**s**, -**e** (*Bild*) transparency; (*Spruchband*) banner; **t~pirieren** [transpi'riːrən] *vi* perspire; ~**plantation** [transplantatsi'o:n] *f* transplantation; (*Haut—*) graft(ing); ~**port** [trans'pɔrt] *m* -(**e**)**s**, -**e** transport; **t~portieren** [transpɔr'tiːrən] *vt* transport; ~**portkosten** *pl* transport charges *pl*, carriage; ~**portmittel** *nt* means of transportation; ~**portunternehmen** *nt* carrier.

Trapez [tra'pe:ts] *nt* -**es**, -**e** trapeze; (*Math*) trapezium.

Traube ['traubə] *f* -, -**n** grape; bunch (of grapes); ~**nlese** *f* vintage; ~**nzucker** *m* glucose.

trauen ['trauən] *vi*: **jdm/etw** ~ trust sb/sth; *vr* dare; *vt* marry.

Trauer ['trauər] *f* - sorrow; (*für Verstorbenen*) mourning; ~**fall** *m* death, bereavement; ~**marsch** *m* funeral march; **t~n** *vi* mourn (*um for*); ~**rand** *m* black border; ~**spiel** *nt* tragedy.

Traufe ['traufə] *f* -, -**n** eaves *pl*.

träufeln ['trɔyfəln] *vti* drip.

traulich ['traulɪç] *a* cosy, intimate.

Traum [traum] *m* -(**e**)**s**, **Träume** dream; ~**a** *nt* -**s**, -**men** trauma; ~**bild** *nt* vision.

träum- ['trɔym] *cpd*: **t~en** *vti* dream; **T~er** *m* -**s**, - dreamer; **T~e'rei** *f* dreaming; ~**erisch** *a* dreamy.

traumhaft *a* dreamlike; (*fig*) wonderful.

traurig ['traurɪç] *a* sad; **T~keit** *f* sadness.

Trau- ['trau] *cpd*: ~**ring** *m* wedding ring; ~**schein** *m* marriage certificate; ~**ung** *f* wedding ceremony; ~**zeuge** *m* witness (to a marriage).

treffen ['trɛfən] *irreg vti* strike, hit; (*Bemerkung*) hurt; (*begegnen*) meet; *Entscheidung etc* make; *Maßnahmen* take; **er hat es gut getroffen** he did well; ~ **auf** (+ *acc*) come across, meet with; *vr* meet; **es traf sich, daß...** it so happened that...; **es trifft sich gut** it's convenient; **wie es so trifft** as these things happen;

T~ *nt* -s, - meeting; ~d *a* pertinent, apposite.

Treff- *cpd*: ~er *m* -s, - hit; (*Tor*) goal; (*Los*) winner; t~lich *a* excellent; ~punkt *m* meeting place.

Treib- ['traib] *cpd*: ~eis *nt* drift ice; t~en *irreg vt* drive; *Studien etc* pursue; *Sport* do, go in for; *Unsinn* ~en fool around; *vi* (*Schiff etc*) drift; (*Pflanzen*) sprout; (*Cook*: *aufgehen*) rise; (*Tee, Kaffee*) be diuretic; ~en *nt* -s activity; ~haus *nt* hothouse; ~stoff *m* fuel.

trenn- [trɛn] *cpd*: ~ab *ad* downstairs; ~en *vt* separate; (*teilen*) divide; *vr* separate; sich ~en von part with; T~schärfe *f* (*Rad*) selectivity; T~ung *f* separation; T~wand *f* partition (wall).

Trepp- [trɛp] *cpd*: t~ab *ad* downstairs; t~auf *ad* upstairs; ~e *f* -, -n stair(case); ~engeländer *nt* banister; ~enhaus *nt* staircase.

Tresor [treˈzoːr] *m* -s, -e safe.

treten ['treːtən] *irreg vi* step; (*Tränen, Schweiß*) appear; ~ nach kick at; ~ in (+*acc*) step in(to); in Verbindung ~ get in contact; in Erscheinung ~ appear; *vt* (*mit Fußtritt*) kick; (*nieder-*) tread, trample.

treu [trɔy] *a* faithful, true; T~e *f* - loyalty, faithfulness; T~händer *m* -s, - trustee; T~handgesellschaft *f* trust company; ~herzig *a* innocent; ~lich *ad* faithfully; ~los *a* faithless.

Tribüne [triˈbyːnə] *f* -, -n grandstand; (*Redner-*) platform.

Tribut [triˈbuːt] *nt* -(e)s, -e tribute.

Trichter ['trɪçtər] *m* -s, - funnel; (in *Boden*) crater.

Trick [trɪk] *m* -s, -e *or* -s trick; ~film *m* cartoon.

Trieb [triːp] *m* -(e)s, -e urge, drive; (*Neigung*) inclination; (*an Baum etc*) shoot; ~feder *f* (*fig*) motivating force; t~haft *a* impulsive; ~kraft *f* (*fig*) drive; ~täter *m* sex offender; ~wagen *m* (*Rail*) diesel railcar; ~werk *nt* engine.

triefen ['triːfən] *vi* drip.

triftig ['trɪftɪç] *a* good, convincing.

Trigonometrie [trigonomeˈtriː] *f* trigonometry.

Trikot [triˈkoː] *nt* -s, -s vest; (*Sport*) shirt; *m* -s, -s (*Gewebe*) tricot.

Triller ['trɪlər] *m* -s, - (*Mus*) trill; t~n *vi* trill, warble; ~pfeife *f* whistle.

Trimester [triˈmɛstər] *nt* -s, - term.

trink- ['trɪŋk] *cpd*: ~bar *a* drinkable; ~en *vti irreg* drink; T~er *m* -s, - drinker; T~geld *nt* tip; T~halm *m* (drinking) straw; T~spruch *m* toast; T~wasser *nt* drinking water.

trippeln ['trɪpəln] *vi* toddle.

Tripper ['trɪpər] *m* -s, - gonorrhoea.

Tritt [trɪt] *m* -(e)s, -e step; (*Fuß-*) kick; ~brett *nt* (*Rail*) step; (*Aut*) running-board.

Triumph [triˈʊmf] *m* -(e)s, -e triumph; ~bogen *m* triumphal arch; t~ieren [-ˈfiːrən] *vi* triumph; (*jubeln*) exult.

trivial [triviˈaːl] *a* trivial.

trocken ['trɔkən] *a* dry; T~dock *nt* dry dock; T~element *nt* dry cell; T~haube

f hair-dryer; T~heit *f* dryness; ~legen *vt* Sumpf drain; *Kind* put a clean nappy on; T~milch *f* dried milk.

trocknen ['trɔknən] *vti* dry.

Troddel ['trɔdəl] *f* -, -n tassel.

Trödel ['trøːdəl] *m* -s (*col*) junk; t~n *vi* (*col*) dawdle.

Trödler ['trøːdlər] *m* -s, - secondhand dealer.

Trog [troːk] -(e)s, ⸚e trough.

Trommel ['trɔməl] *f* -, -n drum; ~fell *nt* eardrum; t~n *vti* drum; ~revolver *m* revolver; ~waschmaschine *f* tumble-action washing machine.

Trommler ['trɔmlər] *m* -s, - drummer.

Trompete [trɔmˈpeːtə] *f* -, -n trumpet; ~r *m* -s, - trumpeter.

Tropen ['troːpən] *pl* tropics *pl*; t~beständig *a* suitable for the tropics; ~helm *m* topee, sun helmet.

Tropf [trɔpf] *m* -(e)s, ⸚e (*col*) rogue; armer ~ poor devil.

tröpfeln ['trœpfəln] *vi* drop, trickle.

Tropfen ['trɔpfən] *m* -s, - drop; t~ *vti* drip; *v impers*: es tropft a few raindrops are falling; t~weise *ad* in drops.

Tropfsteinhöhle *f* stalactite cave.

tropisch ['troːpɪʃ] *a* tropical.

Trost [troːst] *m* -es consolation, comfort; t~bedürftig *a* in need of consolation.

tröst- ['trøːst] *cpd*: ~en *vt* console, comfort; T~er(in *f*) *m* -s, - comfort(er); ~lich *a* comforting.

trost- *cpd*: ~los *a* bleak; *Verhältnisse* wretched; T~preis *m* consolation prize; ~reich *a* comforting.

Tröstung ['trøːstʊŋ] *f* comfort; consolation.

Trott [trɔt] *m* -(e)s, -e trot; (*Routine*) routine; ~el *m* -s, - (*col*) fool, dope; t~en *vi* trot; ~oir [trɔtoˈaːr] *nt* -s, -s *or* -e pavement, sidewalk (US).

Trotz [trɔts] *m* -es pigheadedness; etw aus ~ tun do sth just to show them; jdm zum ~ in defiance of sb; t~ *prep* +*gen or dat* in spite of; ~alter *nt* obstinate phase; t~dem *ad* nevertheless; *cj* although; t~ig *a* defiant, pig-headed; ~kopf *m* obstinate child; ~reaktion *f* fit of pique.

trüb [tryːp] *a* dull; *Flüssigkeit, Glas* cloudy; (*fig*) gloomy; ~en ['tryːbən] *vt* cloud; *vr* become clouded; T~heit *f* dullness; cloudiness; gloom; T~sal *f* -, -e distress; ~selig *a* sad, melancholy; T~sinn *m* depression; ~sinnig *a* depressed, gloomy.

trudeln ['truːdəln] *vi* (*Aviat*) (go into a) spin.

Trüffel ['tryfəl] *f* -, -n truffle.

trüg- ['tryːg] *cpd*: ~en *vt irreg* deceive; *vi* be deceptive; ~erisch *a* deceptive.

Trugschluß ['truːkʃlʊs] *m* false conclusion.

Truhe ['truːə] *f* -, -n chest.

Trümmer ['trymər] *pl* wreckage; (*Bau-*) ruins *pl*; ~haufen *m* heap of rubble.

Trumpf ['trʊmpf] *m* -(e)s, ⸚e (*lit, fig*) trump; t~en *vti* trump.

Trunk [trʊŋk] *m* -(e)s, ⸚e drink; t~en *a* intoxicated; ~enbold *m* -(e)s, -e drunkard; ~enheit *f* intoxication;

~enheit am Steuer drunken driving; **~sucht** *f* alcoholism.

Trupp [trup] *m* **-s, -s** troop; **~e** *f* **-, -n** troop; *(Waffengattung)* force; *(Schauspiel—)* troupe; **~en** *pl* troops *pl*; **~enführer** *m* (military) commander; **~enteil** *m* unit; **~enübungsplatz** *m* training area.

Truthahn ['tru:tha:n] *m* turkey.

Tube ['tu:bə] *f* **-, -n** tube.

Tuberkulose [tuberku'lo:zə] *f* **-, -n** tuberculosis.

Tuch [tu:x] *nt* **-(e)s, ̈er** cloth; *(Hals—)* scarf; *(Kopf—)* headscarf; *(Hand—)* towel.

tüchtig ['tʏçtɪç] *a* efficient, (cap)able; *(col: kräftig)* good, sound; **T~keit** *f* efficiency, ability.

Tücke ['tʏkə] *f* **-, -n** *(Arglist)* malice; *(Trick)* trick; *(Schwierigkeit)* difficulty, problem; **seine ~n haben** be temperamental.

tückisch ['tʏkɪʃ] *a* treacherous; *(böswillig)* malicious.

Tugend ['tu:gənt] *f* **-, -en** virtue; **t~haft** *a* virtuous.

Tüll [tʏl] *m* **-s, -e** tulle; **~e** *f* **-, -n** spout.

Tulpe ['tulpə] *f* **-, -n** tulip.

tummeln ['tuməln] *vr* romp, gambol; *(sich beeilen)* hurry.

Tumor ['tu:mɔr] *m* **-s, -e** tumour.

Tümpel ['tʏmpəl] *m* **-s, -** pool, pond.

Tumult [tu'mult] *m* **-(e)s, -e** tumult.

tun [tu:n] *irreg vt (machen)* do; *(legen)* put; **jdm etw ~** *(antun)* do sth to sb; **etw tut es auch** sth will do; **das tut nichts** that doesn't matter; **das tut nichts zur Sache** that's neither here nor there; *vi* act; **so ~, als ob** act as if; *vr:* **es tut sich etwas/viel** something/a lot is happening.

Tünche ['tʏnçə] *f* **-, -n** whitewash; **t~n** *vt* whitewash.

Tunke ['tuŋkə] *f* **-, -n** sauce; **t~n** *vt* dip, dunk.

tunlichst ['tu:nlıçst] *ad* if at all possible; **~ bald** as soon as possible.

Tunnel ['tunəl] *m* **-s, -s** *or* **-** tunnel.

Tüpfel ['tʏfəl] *m* **-s, -** dot, spot; **~chen** *nt* (small) dot; **t~n** *vt* dot, spot.

tupfen ['tupfən] *vti* dab; *(mit Farbe)* dot; **T~** *m* **-s, -** dot, spot.

Tür [ty:r] *f* **-, -en** door.

Turbine [tur'bi:nə] *f* turbine.

Türkis [tʏr'ki:s] *m* **-es, -e** turquoise; **t~** *a* turquoise.

Turm [turm] *m* **-(e)s, ̈e** tower; *(Kirch—)* steeple; *(Sprung—)* diving platform; *(Schach)* castle, rook.

Türm- ['tʏrm] *cpd:* **~chen** *nt* turret; **t~en** *vr* tower up; *vt* heap up; *vi (col)* scarper, bolt.

Turn- ['turn] *cpd:* **t~en** *vi* do gymnastic exercises; *vt* perform; **~en** *nt* **-s** gymnastics; *(Sch)* physical education, P.E.; **~er(in** *f)* *m* **-s, -** gymnast; **~halle** *f* gym(nasium); **~hose** *f* gym shorts *pl*.

Turnier [tur'ni:r] *nt* **-s, -e** tournament.

Turnus ['turnus] *m* **-, -se** rota; **im ~** in rotation.

Turn- *cpd:* **~verein** *m* gymnastics club; **~zeug** *nt* gym things *pl*.

Tusche ['tuʃə] *f* **-, -n** Indian ink.

tuscheln ['tuʃəln] *vti* whisper.

Tuschkasten *m* paintbox.

Tüte ['ty:tə] *f* **-, -n** bag.

tuten ['tu:tən] *vi (Aut)* hoot.

TÜV [tʏf] *m* MOT.

Typ [ty:p] *m* **-s, -en** type; **~e** *f* **-, -n** *(Print)* type.

Typhus ['ty:fus] *m* **-** typhoid (fever).

typisch ['ty:pıʃ] *a* typical *(für* of).

Tyrann [ty'ran] *m* **-en, -en** tyrant; **~ei** [-'nai] *f* tyranny; **t~isch** *a* tyrannical; **t~i'sieren** *vt* tyrannize.

U

U, u [u:] *nt* U, u.

U-Bahn ['u:ba:n] *f* underground, tube.

übel ['y:bəl] *a* bad; *(moralisch auch)* wicked; **jdm ist ~** sb feels sick; **Ü~** *nt* **-s, -** evil; *(Krankheit)* disease; **~gelaunt** *a* bad-tempered, ill-humoured; **Ü~keit** *f* nausea; **~nehmen** *vt irreg:* **jdm eine Bemerkung** *etc* **~nehmen** be offended at sb's remark *etc*; **Ü~stand** *m* bad state of affairs, abuse; **~wollend** *a* malevolent.

üben ['y:bən] *vti* exercise, practise.

über ['y:bər] *prep* **+dat** *or* **acc** over; *(hoch — auch)* above; *(quer — auch)* across; *(Route)* via; *(betreffend)* about; *ad* over; **den ganzen Tag ~** all day long; **jdm in etw** *(dat)* **~ sein** *(col)* be superior to sb in sth; **~ und ~** all over; **~all** [y:bər'al] *ad* everywhere.

überanstrengen [y:bər'anʃtrɛŋən] *vtr insep* overexert (o.s.).

überantworten [y:bər'antvɔrtən] *vt insep* hand over, deliver (up).

überarbeiten [y:bər'arbaɪtən] *vt insep* revise, rework; *vr* overwork (o.s.).

überaus ['y:bər'aus] *ad* exceedingly.

überbelichten ['y:bərbəlıçtən] *vt (Phot)* overexpose.

über'bieten *vt irreg insep* outbid; *(übertreffen)* surpass; *Rekord* break.

Überbleibsel ['y:bərblaıpsəl] *nt* **-s, -** residue, remainder.

Überblick ['y:bərblık] *m* view; *(fig) (Darstellung)* survey, overview; *(Fähigkeit)* overall view, grasp *(über* +acc of); **ü~en** [-'blıkən] *vt insep* survey.

überbring- [y:bər'brıŋ] *cpd:* **~en** *vt irreg insep* deliver, hand over; **Ü~er** *m* **-s, -** bearer; **Ü~ung** *f* delivery.

überbrücken [y:bər'brʏkən] *vt insep* bridge (over).

über'dauern *vt insep* outlast.

über'denken *vt irreg insep* think over.

überdies [y:bər'di:s] *ad* besides.

überdimensional ['y:bərdimenziona:l] *a* oversize.

Überdruß ['y:bərdrus] *m* **-sses** weariness; **bis zum ~** *ad* nauseam.

überdrüssig ['y:bərdrʏsıç] *a* tired, sick *(gen* of).

übereifrig ['y:bəraıfrıç] *a* overkeen, overzealous.

übereilen [y:bər'aılən] *vt insep* hurry.

übereilt *a* (over)hasty, premature.

überein- [y:bər"aɪn] *cpd:* **~ander** [y:bər'aɪ'nandər] *a* one upon the other; **sprechen** about each other; **~anderschlagen** *vt irreg* fold, cross; **~kommen** *vi irreg* agree; **Ü~kunft** *f* -, **-künfte** agreement; **~stimmen** *vi* agree; **Ü~stimmung** *f* agreement.

überempfindlich ['y:bərɛmpfɪntlɪç] *a* hypersensitive.

überfahren ['y:bərfa:rən] *irreg vt* take across; *vi* (go a)cross; [-'fa:rən] *vt insep* (Aut) run over; (fig) walk all over.

Überfahrt ['y:bərfa:rt] *f* crossing.

Überfall ['y:bərfal] *m* (Bank~, Mil) raid; (auf jdn) assault; **ü~en** [-'falən] *vt irreg insep* attack; Bank raid; (besuchen) surprise.

überfällig ['y:bərfɛlɪç] *a* overdue.

über'fliegen *vt irreg insep* fly over, overfly; Buch skim through.

Überfluß ['y:bərflʊs] *m* (super)abundance, excess (an +dat of).

überflüssig ['y:bərflʏsɪç] *a* superfluous.

über'fordern *vt insep* demand too much of; Kräfte etc overtax.

über'führen *vt insep* Leiche etc transport; Täter have convicted (gen of).

Über'führung *f* transport; conviction; (Brücke) bridge, overpass.

Übergabe ['y:bərga:bə] *f* handing over; (Mil) surrender.

Übergang ['y:bərgaŋ] *m* crossing; (Wandel, Überleitung) transition; **~serscheinung** *f* transitory phenomenon; **~slösung** *f* provisional solution, stopgap; **~sstadium** *nt* state of transition; **~szeit** *f* transitional period.

über'geben *irreg insep vt* hand over; (Mil) surrender; **dem Verkehr ~** open to traffic; *vr* be sick.

übergehen ['y:bərge:ən] *irreg vi* (Besitz) pass; (zum Feind etc) go over, defect; (überleiten) go on (zu to); (sich verwandeln) turn (in +acc into); [-'ge:ən] *vt insep* pass over, omit.

Übergewicht ['y:bərgəvɪçt] *nt* excess weight; (fig) preponderance.

überglücklich ['y:bərglʏklɪç] *a* overjoyed.

übergroß ['y:bərgro:s] *a* outsize, huge.

überhaben ['y:bərha:bən] *vt irreg* (col) be fed up with.

überhandnehmen [y:bər'hantne:mən] *vi irreg* gain the ascendancy.

überhängen ['y:bərhɛŋən] *vi irreg* overhang.

überhaupt [y:bər'haupt] *ad* at all; (im allgemeinen) in general; (besonders) especially; **~ nicht** not at all.

überheblich [y:bər'he:plɪç] *a* arrogant; **Ü~keit** *f* arrogance.

über'holen *vt insep* overtake; (Tech) overhaul.

überholt *a* out-of-date, obsolete.

über'hören *vt insep* not hear; (absichtlich) ignore.

überirdisch ['y:bər'ɪrdɪʃ] *a* supernatural, unearthly.

überkompensieren ['y:bərkɔmpɛnzi:rən] *vt insep* overcompensate for.

über'laden *vt irreg insep* overload; *a* (fig) cluttered.

über'lassen *irreg insep vt:* **jdm etw ~** leave sth to sb; *vr:* **sich etw** (dat) **~** give o.s. over to sth.

über'lasten *vt insep* overload; Mensch overtax.

überlaufen ['y:bərlaufən] *irreg vi* (Flüssigkeit) flow over; (zum Feind etc) go over, defect; [-'laufən] *insep v.* (Schauer etc) come over; **~ sein** be inundated or besieged.

Überläufer ['y:bərlɔyfər] *m* -s, - deserter.

über'leben *vt insep* survive; **Ü~de(r)** *mf* survivor.

über'legen *vt insep* consider; *a* superior; **Ü~heit** *f* superiority.

Überlegung *f* consideration, deliberation.

über'liefern *vt insep* hand down, transmit.

Überlieferung *f* tradition.

überlisten [y:bər'lɪstən] *vt insep* outwit.

überm ['y:bərm] = **über dem**.

Übermacht ['y:bərmaxt] *f* superior force, superiority.

übermächtig ['y:bərmɛçtɪç] *a* superior (in strength); Gefühl etc overwhelming.

übermannen [y:bər'manən] *vt insep* overcome.

Übermaß ['y:bərma:s] *nt* excess (an +dat of).

übermäßig ['y:bərmɛ:sɪç] *a* excessive.

Übermensch ['y:bərmɛnʃ] *m* superman; **ü~lich** *a* superhuman.

übermitteln [y:bər'mɪtəln] *vt insep* convey.

übermorgen ['y:bərmɔrgən] *ad* the day after tomorrow.

Übermüdung [y:bər'my:dʊŋ] *f* fatigue, overtiredness.

Übermut ['y:bərmu:t] *m* exuberance.

übermütig ['y:bərmy:tɪç] *a* exuberant, high-spirited; **~ werden** get overconfident.

übernachten [y:bər'naxtən] *vi insep* spend the night (bei jdm at sb's place).

übernächtigt [y:bər'nɛçtɪçt] *a* tired, sleepy.

Übernahme ['y:bərna:mə] *f* -, -n taking over or on, acceptance.

über'nehmen *irreg insep vt* take on, accept; Amt, Geschäft take over; *vr* take on too much.

über'prüfen *vt insep* examine, check.

Überprüfung *f* examination.

überqueren [y:bər'kve:rən] *vt insep* cross.

überragen [y:bər'ra:gən] *vt insep* tower above; (fig) surpass; ['y:bərra:gən] *vi* project, stick out.

überraschen [y:bər'raʃən] *vt insep* surprise.

Überraschung *f* surprise.

überreden [y:bər're:dən] *vt insep* persuade.

überreich ['y:bərraɪç] *a* very/too rich; **~en** [-'raɪçən] *vt insep* present, hand over; **~lich** *a, ad* (more than) ample.

überreizt [y:bər'raɪtst] *a* overwrought.

Überreste ['y:bɔrrɛstə] *pl* remains *pl*, remnants *pl*.

überrumpeln [y:bər'rumpəln] *vt insep* take by surprise.

überrunden [y:bər'rundən] *vt insep* lap.

übers ['y:bərs] = **über das.**

übersättigen [y:bər'zɛtigən] *vt insep* satiate.

Überschall- ['y:bərʃal] *cpd:* ~**flugzeug** *nt* supersonic jet; ~**geschwindigkeit** *f* supersonic speed.

über'schätzen *vtr insep* overestimate.

überschäumen [y:bər'ʃɔymən] *vi* froth over; *(fig)* bubble over.

Überschlag ['y:bərʃla:k] *m (Fin)* estimate; *(Sport)* somersault; **ü~en** [-'ʃla:gən] *irreg insep vt (berechnen)* estimate; *(auslassen) Seite* omit; *vr* somersault; *(Stimme)* crack; *(Aviat)* loop the loop; *a* lukewarm, tepid; ['y:bərʃla:gən] *irreg vt Beine* cross; *vi (Wellen)* break over; *(Funken)* flash over.

überschnappen ['y:bərʃnapən] *vi (Stimme)* crack; *(col: Mensch)* flip one's lid.

über'schneiden *vr irreg insep (lit, fig)* overlap; *(Linien)* intersect.

über'schreiben *vt irreg insep* provide with a heading; **jdm etw** ~ transfer *or* make over sth to sb.

über'schreiten *vt irreg insep* cross over; *(fig)* exceed; *(verletzen)* transgress.

Überschrift ['y:bərʃrift] *f* heading, title.

Überschuß ['y:bərʃus] *m* surplus *(an +dat* of).

überschüssig ['y:bərʃysiç] *a* surplus, excess.

über'schütten *vt insep* **jdn/etw mit etw** ~ *(lit)* pour sth over sb/sth; **jdn mit etw** ~ *(fig)* shower sb with sth.

Überschwang ['y:bərʃvaŋ] *m* exuberance, excess.

überschwemmen [y:bər'ʃvɛmən] *vt insep* flood.

Überschwemmung *f* flood.

überschwenglich [y:bər'ʃvɛŋliç] *a* effusive; **Ü~keit** *f* effusion.

Übersee ['y:bərze:] *f* **nach/in** ~ overseas; **ü~isch** *a* overseas.

über'sehen *vt irreg insep* look (out) over; *(fig) Folgen* see, get an overall view of; *(nicht beachten)* overlook.

über'senden *vt irreg insep* send, forward.

übersetz- *cpd* ~**en** [y:bər'zɛtsən] *vt insep* translate; ['y:bərzɛtsən] *vi* cross; **Ü~er(in** *f)* [-'zɛtsər(ın)] *m* -**s,** - translator; **Ü~ung** [-'zɛtsuŋ] *f* translation; *(Tech)* gear ratio.

Übersicht ['y:bərzıçt] *f* overall view; *(Darstellung)* survey; **ü~lich** *a* clear; *Gelände* open; ~**lichkeit** *f* clarity, lucidity.

übersiedeln ['y:bərzi:dəln] *or* [y:bər'zi:dəln] *vi sep or insep* move.

über'spannen *vt insep (zu sehr spannen)* overstretch; *(überdecken)* cover.

überspannt *a* eccentric; *Idee* wild, crazy; **Ü~keit** *f* eccentricity.

überspitzt [y:bər'ʃpitst] *a* exaggerated.

über'springen *vt irreg insep* jump over; *(fig)* skip.

übersprudeln ['y:bərʃpru:dəln] *vi* bubble over.

überstehen [y:bər'ʃte:ən] *irreg vt insep* overcome, get over; *Winter etc* survive, get through; ['y:bərʃte:ən] *vi* project.

über'stimmen *vt insep* outvote.

Überstunden ['y:bərʃtundən] *pl* overtime.

über'stürzen *insep vt* rush; *vr* follow (one another) in rapid succession.

überstürzt *a* (over)hasty.

übertölpeln [y:bər'tœlpəln] *vt insep* dupe.

über'tönen *vt insep* drown (out).

Übertrag ['y:bərtra:k] *m* ~**(e)s, -träge** *(Comm)* amount brought forward; **ü~bar** [-'tra:kba:r] *a* transferable; *(Med)* infectious; **ü~en** [-'tra:gən] *irreg insep vt* transfer *(auf +acc* to); *(Rad)* broadcast; *(übersetzen)* render; *Krankheit* transmit; **jdm etw ü~en** assign sth to sb; *vr* spread *(auf +acc* to); *a* figurative; ~**ung** [-'tra:guŋ] *f* transfer(ence); *(Rad)* broadcast; rendering; transmission.

über'treffen *vt irreg insep* surpass.

über'treiben *vt irreg insep* exaggerate.

Übertreibung *f* exaggeration.

übertreten [y:bər'tre:tən] *irreg vt insep* cross; *Gebot etc* break; ['y:bərtre:tən] *vi (über Linie, Gebiet)* step over; *(Sport)* overstep; *(in andere Partei)* go over *(in +acc* to); *(zu anderem Glauben)* be converted.

Über'tretung *f* violation, transgression.

übertrieben [y:bər'tri:bən] *a* exaggerated, excessive.

übertrumpfen [y:bər'trumpfən] *vt insep* outdo; *(Cards)* overtrump.

übervölkert [y:bər'fœlkərt] *a* overpopulated.

übervoll ['y:bərfɔl] *a* overfull.

übervorteilen [y:bər'fɔrtailən] *vt insep* dupe, cheat.

über'wachen *vt insep* supervise; *Verdächtigen* keep under surveillance.

Überwachung *f* supervision; surveillance.

überwältigen [y:bər'vɛltigən] *vt insep* overpower; ~**d** *a* overwhelming.

überweisen [y:bər'vaizən] *vt irreg insep* transfer.

Überweisung *f* transfer.

über'wiegen *vi irreg insep* predominate; ~**d** *a* predominant.

über'winden *irreg insep vt* overcome; *vr* make an effort, bring oneself (to do sth).

Überwindung *f* effort, strength of mind.

Überwurf ['y:bərvurf] *m* wrap, shawl.

Überzahl ['y:bərtsa:l] *f* superiority, superior numbers *pl*; **in der** ~ **sein** outnumber sb, be numerically superior.

überzählig ['y:bərtsɛ:liç] *a* surplus.

über'zeugen *vt insep* convince; ~**d** *a* convincing.

Überzeugung *f* conviction; ~**skraft** *f* power of persuasion.

überziehen ['y:bərtsi:ən] *irreg vt* put on [-'tsi:ən] *vt insep* cover; *Konto* overdraw.

Überzug ['y:bərtsu:k] *m* cover; *(Belag)* coating.

üblich ['y:pliç] *a* usual.

U-Boot ['u:bo:t] *nt* submarine.

übrig ['y:brɪç] *a* remaining; **für jdn etwas ~ haben** (*col*) be fond of sb; **die ~en** ['y:brɪgən] the others; **das ~e** the rest; **im ~en besides; ~bleiben** *vi irreg* remain, be left (over); **~ens** *ad* besides; (*nebenbei bemerkt*) by the way; **~lassen** *vt irreg* leave (over).

Übung ['y:bʊŋ] *f* practice; (*Turn-, Aufgabe etc*) exercise; **~ macht den Meister** practice makes perfect.

Ufer ['u:fər] *nt* **-s, -** bank; (*Meeres—*) shore; **~befestigung** *f* embankment.

Uhr [u:r] *f* **-, -en** clock; (*Armband—*) watch; **wieviel ~ ist es?** what time is it?; **1 ~ 1** o'clock; **20 ~ 8** o'clock, 20.00 (twenty hundred) hours; **~band** *nt* watch strap; **~(en)gehäuse** *nt* clock/ watch case; **~kette** *f* watch chain; **~macher** *m* **-s, -** watchmaker; **~werk** *nt* clockwork; works of a watch; **~zeiger** *m* hand; **~zeigersinn** *m*: **im ~zeigersinn** clockwise; **entgegen dem ~zeigersinn** anticlockwise; **~zeit** *f* time (of day).

Uhu ['u:hu] *m* **-s, -s** eagle owl.

UKW [u:ka:'ve:] *abbr* VHF.

Ulk [ʊlk] *m* **-s, -e** lark; **u~ig** *a* funny.

Ulme ['ʊlmə] *f* **-, -n** elm.

Ultimatum [ʊlti'ma:tʊm] *nt* **-s, Ultimaten** ultimatum.

Ultra- *cpd*: **~kurzwellen** [ultra'kʊrtsvɛlən] *pl* very high frequency; **u~violett** [ultra] *a* ultraviolet.

um [ʊm] *prep +acc* (a)round; (*zeitlich*) at; (*mit Größenangabe*) by; (*für*) for; **er schlug ~ sich** he hit about him; **Stunde ~ Stunde** hour after hour; **Auge ~ Auge** an eye for an eye; **~ vieles (besser)** (better) by far; **~ nichts besser** not in the least better; **~ so besser** so much the better; **~ ... willen** for the sake of; *cj* (*damit*) (in order) to; **zu klug, ~ zu ...** too clever to ...; *ad* (*ungefähr*) about.

umadressieren ['ʊmadrɛsi:rən] *vt* readdress.

umänder- ['ʊm'ɛndər] *cpd*: **~n** *vt* alter; **U~ung** *f* alteration.

umarbeiten ['ʊm'arbaɪtn] *vt* remodel; *Buch etc* revise, rework.

umarmen [ʊm'armən] *vt insep* embrace.

Umbau ['ʊmbau] *m* **-(e)s, -e** *or* **-ten** reconstruction, alteration(s); **u~en** *vt* rebuild, reconstruct.

umbenennen ['ʊmbənɛnən] *vt irreg* rename.

umbiegen ['ʊmbi:gən] *vt irreg* bend (over).

umbilden ['ʊmbɪldən] *vt* reorganize; (*Pol*) *Kabinett* reshuffle.

umbinden ['ʊmbɪndən] *vt irreg Krawatte etc* put on; [-'bɪndən] *vt irreg insep* tie (sth) round.

umblättern ['ʊmblɛtərn] *vt* turn over.

umblicken ['ʊmblɪkən] *vr* look around.

umbringen ['ʊmbrɪŋən] *vt irreg* kill.

Umbruch ['ʊmbrʊx] *m* radical change; (*Print*) make-up.

umbuchen ['ʊmbu:xən] *vti* change one's reservation/flight *etc*.

umdenken ['ʊmdɛŋkən] *vi irreg* adjust one's views.

um'drängen *vt insep* crowd round.

umdrehen ['ʊmdre:ən] *vtr* turn (round); *Hals* wring.

Um'drehung *f* revolution; rotation.

umeinander [ʊm'aɪ'nandər] *ad* round one another; (*für einander*) for one another.

umfahren ['ʊmfa:rən] *vt irreg* run over; [-'fa:rən] *insep* drive/sail round.

umfallen ['ʊmfalən] *vi irreg* fall down *or* over.

Umfang ['ʊmfaŋ] *m* extent; (*von Buch*) size; (*Reichweite*) range; (*Fläche*) area; (*Math*) circumference; **u~reich** *a* extensive; *Buch etc* voluminous.

um'fassen *vt insep* embrace; (*umgeben*) surround; (*enthalten*) include; **~d** *a* comprehensive, extensive.

Umfrage ['ʊmfra:gə] *f* poll.

umfüllen ['ʊmfylən] *vt* transfer; *Wein* decant.

umfunktionieren ['ʊmfʊŋktsioni:rən] *vt* convert, transform.

Umgang ['ʊmgaŋ] *m* company; (*mit jdm*) dealings *pl*; (*Behandlung*) way of behaving.

umgänglich ['ʊmgɛŋlɪç] *a* sociable.

Umgangs- *cpd*: **~formen** *pl* manners *pl*; **~sprache** *f* colloquial language.

umgeb- [ʊm'ge:b] *cpd*: **~en** *vt irreg insep* surround; **U~ung** *f* surroundings *pl*; (*Milieu*) environment; (*Personen*) people in one's circle.

umgehen ['ʊmge:ən] *irreg vi* go (a)round; **im Schlosse ~** haunt the castle; **mit jdm grob etc ~** treat sb roughly *etc*; **mit Geld sparsam ~** be careful with one's money; [-'ge:ən] *vt insep* bypass; (*Mil*) outflank; *Gesetz etc* circumvent; (*vermeiden*) avoid; **'~d** *a* immediate.

Um'gehung *f* bypassing; outflanking; circumvention; avoidance; **~sstraße** *f* bypass.

umgekehrt ['ʊmgəke:rt] *a* reverse(d); (*gegenteilig*) opposite; *ad* the other way around; **und ~** and vice versa.

umgraben ['ʊmgra:bən] *vt irreg* dig up.

umgruppieren ['ʊmgrupi:rən] *vt* regroup.

Umhang ['ʊmhaŋ] *m* wrap, cape.

umhängen ['ʊmhɛŋən] *vt Bild* hang somewhere else; **jdm etw ~** put sth on sb.

umhauen ['ʊmhauən] *vt* fell; (*fig*) bowl over.

umher [ʊm'he:r] *ad* about, around; **~gehen** *vi irreg* walk about; **~reisen** *vi* travel about; **~schweifen** *vi* roam about; **~ziehen** *vi irreg* wander from place to place.

umhinkönnen [ʊm'hɪnkœnən] *vi irreg* **ich kann nicht umhin, das zu tun** I can't help doing it.

umhören [ʊm'hø:rən] *vr* ask around.

Umkehr ['ʊmke:r] *f* **-** turning back; (*Änderung*) change; **u~en** *vi* turn back; *vt* turn round, reverse; *Tasche etc* turn inside out; *Gefäß etc* turn upside down.

umkippen ['ʊmkɪpən] *vt* tip over; *vi* overturn; (*fig: Meinung ändern*) change one's mind; (*col: Mensch*) keel over.

Umkleideraum ['ʊmklaɪdəraum] *m* changing *or* dressing room.

umkommen ['ʊmkɔmən] *vi irreg* die, perish; *(Lebensmittel)* go bad.

Umkreis ['ʊmkraɪs] *m* neighbourhood; *(Math)* circumcircle; **im ~ von** within a radius of; **u~en** [ʊm'kraɪzən] *vt insep* circle (round); *(Satellit)* orbit.

umladen ['ʊmla:dən] *vt irreg* transfer, reload.

Umlage ['ʊmla:gə] *f* share of the costs.

Umlauf ['ʊmlaʊf] *m* *(Geld—)* circulation; *(von Gestirn)* revolution; *(Schreiben)* circular; **~bahn** *f* orbit.

Umlaut ['ʊmlaʊt] *m* umlaut.

umlegen ['ʊmle:gən] *vt* put on; *(verlegen)* move, shift; *Kosten* share out; *(umkippen)* tip over; *(col: töten)* bump off.

umleiten ['ʊmlaɪtən] *vt* divert.

Umleitung *f* diversion.

umlernen ['ʊmlɛrnən] *vi* learn something new; adjust one's views.

umliegend ['ʊmli:gənt] *a* surrounding.

Umnachtung [ʊm'naxtʊŋ] *f* (mental) derangement.

um'rahmen *vt insep* frame.

um'randen *vt insep* border, edge.

umrechnen ['ʊmrɛçnən] *vt* convert.

Umrechnung *f* conversion; **~skurs** *m* rate of exchange.

um'reißen *vt irreg insep* outline, sketch.

um'ringen *vt insep* surround.

Umriß ['ʊmrɪs] *m* outline.

umrühren ['ʊmry:rən] *vti* stir.

ums [ʊms] = **um das.**

umsatteln ['ʊmzatəln] *vi (col)* change one's occupation; switch.

Umsatz ['ʊmzats] *m* turnover.

umschalten ['ʊmʃaltən] *vt* switch.

Umschau ['ʊmʃaʊ] *f* look(ing) round; **~ halten nach** look around for; **u~en** *vr* look round.

Umschlag ['ʊmʃla:k] *m* cover; *(Buch—auch)* jacket; *(Med)* compress; *(Brief—)* envelope; *(Wechsel)* change; *(von Hose)* turn-up; **u~en** ['ʊmʃla:gən] *irreg vi* change; *(Naut)* capsize; *vt* knock over; *Ärmel* turn up; *Seite* turn over; *Waren* transfer; **~platz** *m (Comm)* distribution centre.

umschreiben *vt irreg* ['ʊmʃraɪbən] *(neu—)* rewrite; *(übertragen)* transfer *(auf +acc* to); [-'ʃraɪbən] *insep* paraphrase; *(abgrenzen)* circumscribe, define.

umschulen ['ʊmʃu:lən] *vt* retrain; *Kind* send to another school.

umschwärmen [ʊm'ʃvɛrmən] *vt insep* swarm round; *(fig)* surround, idolize.

Umschweife ['ʊmʃvaɪfə] *pl:* **ohne ~** without beating about the bush, straight out.

Umschwung ['ʊmʃvʊŋ] *m* change (around), revolution.

umsehen ['ʊmze:ən] *vr irreg* look around *or* about; *(suchen)* look out *(nach* for).

umseitig ['ʊmzaɪtɪç] *ad* overleaf.

Umsicht ['ʊmzɪçt] *f* prudence, caution; **u~ig** *a* cautious, prudent.

umsonst [ʊm'zɔnst] *ad* in vain; *(gratis)* for nothing.

umspringen ['ʊmʃprɪŋən] *vi irreg* change; *(Wind auch)* veer; **mit jdm ~** treat sb badly.

Umstand ['ʊmʃtant] *m* circumstance; **Umstände** *pl (fig: Schwierigkeiten)* fuss; **in anderen Umständen sein** be pregnant; **Umstände machen** go to a lot of trouble; **unter Umständen** possibly; **mildernde Umstände** *(Jur)* extenuating circumstances.

umständlich ['ʊmʃtɛntlɪç] *a,ad Methode* cumbersome, complicated; *Ausdrucksweise, Erklärung auch* long-winded; *Mensch* ponderous.

Umstands- *cpd:* **~kleid** *nt* maternity dress; **~wort** *nt* adverb.

Umstehende(n) ['ʊmʃte:əndə(n)] *pl* bystanders *pl.*

Umsteig- ['ʊmʃtaɪg] *cpd:* **~ekarte** *f* transfer ticket; **u~en** *vi irreg* (Rail) change.

umstellen ['ʊmʃtɛlən] *vt (an anderen Ort)* change round, rearrange; *(Tech)* convert; *vr* adapt o.s. *(auf +acc* to); [ʊm'ʃtɛlən] *vt insep* surround.

Umstellung ['ʊmʃtɛlʊŋ] *f* change; *(Umgewöhnung)* adjustment; *(Tech)* conversion.

umstimmen ['ʊmʃtɪmən] *vt (Mus)* retune; **jdn ~** make sb change his mind.

umstoßen ['ʊmʃto:sən] *vt irreg (lit)* overturn; *Plan etc* change, upset.

umstritten [ʊm'ʃtrɪtən] *a* disputed.

Umsturz ['ʊmʃtʊrts] *m* overthrow.

umstürzen ['ʊmʃtʏrtsən] *vt (umwerfen)* overturn; *vi* collapse, fall down; *Wagen* overturn.

umstürzlerisch *a* revolutionary.

Umtausch ['ʊmtaʊʃ] *m* exchange; **u~en** *vt* exchange.

Umtriebe [ʊm'tri:bə] *pl* machinations *pl,* intrigues *pl.*

umtun ['ʊmtu:n] *vr irreg* see; **sich nach etw ~** look for sth.

umwandeln ['ʊmvandəln] *vt* change, convert; *(Elec)* transform.

umwechseln ['ʊmvɛksəln] *vt* change.

Umweg ['ʊmve:k] *m* detour, roundabout way.

Umwelt ['ʊmvɛlt] *f* environment; **~verschmutzung** *f* environmental pollution.

umwenden ['ʊmvɛndən] *vtr irreg* turn (round).

um'werben *vt irreg insep* court, woo.

umwerfen ['ʊmvɛrfən] *vt irreg (lit)* upset, overturn; *Mantel* throw on; *(fig: erschüttern)* upset, throw.

umziehen ['ʊmtsi:ən] *irreg vtr* change; *vi* move.

umzingeln [ʊm'tsɪŋəln] *vt insep* surround, encircle.

Umzug ['ʊmtsu:k] *m* procession; *(Wohnungs—)* move, removal.

unab- ['ʊn'ap] *cpd:* **~'änderlich** *a* irreversible, unalterable; **~hängig** *a* independent; **U~hängigkeit** *f* independence; **~kömmlich** *a* indispensable; **zur Zeit ~kömmlich** not free at the moment; **~lässig** *a* incessant, constant; **~sehbar** *a* immeasurable; *Folgen* unforeseeable; *Kosten* incalculable; ~**sichtlich** a unintentional; ~'**wendbar** a inevitable.

unachtsam ['ʊn'axtza:m] a careless; U~**keit** f carelessness.

unan- ['ʊn'an] cpd: ~'**fechtbar** a indisputable; ~**gebracht** a uncalled-for; ~**gemessen** a inadequate; ~**genehm** a unpleasant; U~**nehmlichkeit** f inconvenience; pl trouble; ~**sehnlich** a unsightly; ~**ständig** a indecent, improper; U~**ständigkeit** f indecency, impropriety.

unappetitlich ['ʊn'apeti:tlɪç] a unsavoury.

Unart ['ʊn'a:rt] f bad manners pl; *(Angewohnheit)* bad habit; **u~ig** a naughty, badly behaved.

unauf- ['ʊn'aʊf] cpd: ~**fällig** a unobtrusive; *Kleidung* inconspicuous; ~'**findbar** a undiscoverable, not to be found; ~**gefordert** a unasked; ad spontaneously; ~**haltsam** a irresistible; ~'**hörlich** a incessant, continuous; ~**merksam** a inattentive; ~**richtig** a insincere.

unaus- ['ʊn'aʊs] cpd: ~'**bleiblich** a inevitable, unavoidable; ~**geglichen** a volatile; ~'**sprechlich** a inexpressible; ~'**stehlich** a intolerable; ~'**weichlich** a inescapable, ineluctable.

unbändig ['ʊbɛndɪç] a extreme, excessive.

unbarmherzig ['ʊnbarmhɛrtsɪç] a pitiless, merciless.

unbeabsichtigt ['ʊnbə'apzɪçtɪçt] a unintentional.

unbeachtet ['ʊnbə'axtət] a unnoticed, ignored.

unbedenklich ['ʊnbədɛŋklɪç] a unhesitating; *Plan* unobjectionable; ad without hesitation.

unbedeutend ['ʊnbədɔytənt] a insignificant, unimportant; *Fehler* slight.

unbedingt ['ʊnbədɪŋt] a unconditional; ad absolutely; **mußt du ~ gehen?** do you really have to go?

unbefangen ['ʊnbəfaŋən] a impartial, unprejudiced; *(ohne Hemmungen)* uninhibited; U~**heit** f impartiality; uninhibitedness.

unbefriedig- ['ʊnbəfri:dɪg] cpd: ~**end** a unsatisfactory; ~t [-dɪçt] a unsatisfied, dissatisfied.

unbefugt ['ʊnbəfu:kt] a unauthorized.

unbegabt ['ʊnbəga:pt] a untalented.

unbegreiflich ['ʊnbə'graɪflɪç] a inconceivable.

unbegrenzt ['ʊnbəgrɛntst] a unlimited.

unbegründet ['ʊnbəgryndət] a unfounded.

Unbehag- ['ʊnbəha:g] cpd: ~**en** nt discomfort; **u~lich** [-lɪç] a uncomfortable; *Gefühl* uneasy.

unbeholfen ['ʊnbəhɔlfən] a awkward, clumsy; U~**heit** f awkwardness, clumsiness.

unbeirrt ['ʊnbə'ɪrt] a imperturbable.

unbekannt ['ʊnbəkant] a unknown.

unbekümmert ['ʊnbəkymərt] a unconcerned.

unbeliebt ['ʊnbəli:pt] a unpopular; U~**heit** f unpopularity.

unbequem ['ʊnbəkve:m] a *Stuhl*

uncomfortable; *Mensch* bothersome; *Regelung* inconvenient.

unberech- cpd: ~**enbar** [ʊnbə'rɛçənba:r] a incalculable; *Mensch, Verhalten* unpredictable; ~**tigt** ['ʊnbərɛçtɪçt] a unjustified; *(nicht erlaubt)* unauthorized.

unberufen [ʊnbə'ru:fən] interj touch wood.

unberührt ['ʊnbəry:rt] a untouched, intact; **sie ist noch ~** she is still a virgin.

unbescheiden ['ʊnbəʃaɪdən] a presumptuous.

unbeschreiblich [ʊnbə'ʃraɪplɪç] a indescribable.

unbesonnen ['ʊnbəzɔnən] a unwise, rash, imprudent.

unbeständig ['ʊnbəʃtɛndɪç] a *Mensch* inconstant; *Wetter* unsettled; *Lage* unstable.

unbestechlich [ʊnbə'ʃtɛçlɪç] a incorruptible.

unbestimmt ['ʊnbəʃtɪmt] a indefinite; *Zukunft auch* uncertain; U~**heit** f vagueness.

unbeteiligt [ʊnbə'taɪlɪçt] a unconcerned, indifferent.

unbeugsam ['ʊnbɔykza:m] a inflexible, stubborn; *Wille auch* unbending.

unbewacht ['ʊnbəvaxt] a unguarded, unwatched.

unbeweglich ['ʊnbəve:klɪç] a immovable.

unbewußt ['ʊnbəvʊst] a unconscious.

unbrauchbar ['ʊnbraʊxba:r] a *Arbeit* useless; *Gerät auch* unusable; U~**keit** f uselessness.

und [ʊnt] cj and; ~ **so weiter** and so on.

Undank ['ʊdaŋk] m ingratitude; **u~bar** a ungrateful; ~**barkeit** f ingratitude.

undefinierbar [ʊndefi'ni:rba:r] a indefinable.

undenkbar [ʊn'dɛŋkba:r] a inconceivable.

undeutlich ['ʊndɔytlɪç] a indistinct.

undicht ['ʊndɪçt] a leaky.

Unding ['ʊndɪŋ] nt absurdity.

unduldsam ['ʊndʊldsa:m] a intolerant.

undurch- ['ʊndʊrç] cpd: ~**führbar** [-'fy:rba:r] a impracticable; ~**lässig** [-lɛsɪç] a waterproof, impermeable; ~**sichtig** [-zɪçtɪç] a opaque; *(fig)* obscure.

uneben ['ʊn'e:bən] a uneven.

unehelich ['ʊn'e:əlɪç] a illegitimate.

uneigennützig ['ʊn'aɪgənnytsɪç] a unselfish.

uneinig ['ʊn'aɪnɪç] a divided; ~ **sein** disagree; U~**keit** f discord, dissension.

uneins ['ʊn'aɪns] a at variance, at odds.

unempfindlich ['ʊn'ɛmpfɪntlɪç] a insensitive; U~**keit** f insensitivity.

unendlich [ʊn'ɛntlɪç] a infinite; U~**keit** f infinity.

unent- ['ʊn'ɛnt] cpd: ~**behrlich** [-'be:rlɪç] a indispensable; ~**geltlich** [-gɛltlɪç] a free (of charge); ~**schieden** [-ʃi:dən] a undecided; ~**schieden enden** *(Sport)* end in a draw; ~**schlossen** [-ʃlɔsən] a undecided; irresolute; ~**wegt** ['-ve:kt] a unswerving; *(unaufhörlich)* incessant.

uner- ['ʊn'er] cpd: ~**bittlich** [-bɪtlɪç] a unyielding, inexorable; ~**fahren** [-fa:rən] a inexperienced; ~**freulich** [-frɔylɪç] a unpleasant; **~gründlich** [-'gryntlıç] *a* unfathomable; **~heblich** [-he:plıç] *a* unimportant; **~hört** [-hø:rt] *a* unheard-of; *Bitte* outrageous; **~läßlich** [-'lɛslıç] *a* indispensable; **~laubt** [-laupt] *a* unauthorized; **~meßlich** [-'mɛslıç] *a* immeasurable, immense; **~müdlich** [-'my:tlıç] *a* indefatigable; **~sättlich** [-'zɛtlıç] *a* insatiable; **~schöpflich** [-'fœpflıç] *a* inexhaustible; **~schütterlich** [-'fytərlıç] *a* unshakeable; **~schwinglich** [-'fvıŋlıç] *a Preis* exorbitant; too expensive; **~träglich** [-'trɛ:klıç] *a* unbearable; *Frechheit* insufferable; **~wartet** [-vartət] *a* unexpected; **~wünscht** [-vynʃt] *a* undesirable, unwelcome; **~zogen** [-tso:gən] *a* ill-bred, rude.

unfähig ['unfɛ:ıç] *a* incapable (*zu* of); incompetent; **U~keit** *f* incapacity; incompetence.

unfair ['unfɛ:r] *a* unfair.

Unfall ['unfal] *m* accident; **~flucht** *f* hit-and-run (driving); **~stelle** *f* scene of the accident; **~versicherung** *f* accident insurance.

unfaßbar [un'fasba:r] *a* inconceivable.

unfehlbar [un'fe:lba:r] *a* infallible; *ad* inevitably; **U~keit** *f* infallibility.

unflätig ['unflɛ:tıç] *a* rude.

unfolgsam ['unfɔlkza:m] *a* disobedient.

unfrankiert ['unfraŋki:rt] *a* unfranked.

unfrei ['unfraı] *a* not free, unfree; **~willig** *a* involuntary, against one's will.

unfreundlich ['unfrɔyntlıç] *a* unfriendly; **U~keit** *f* unfriendliness.

Unfriede(n) ['unfri:də(n)] *m* dissension, strife.

unfruchtbar ['unfruxtba:r] *a* infertile; *Gespräche* unfruitful; **U~keit** *f* infertility; unfruitfulness.

Unfug ['unfu:k] *m* -s (*Benehmen*) mischief; (*Unsinn*) nonsense; **grober ~** (*Jur*) gross misconduct; malicious damage.

ungeachtet ['ungə'axtət] *prep* +*gen* notwithstanding.

ungeahnt ['ungə'a:nt] *a* unsuspected, undreamt-of.

ungebeten ['ungəbe:tən] *a* uninvited.

ungebildet ['ungəbıldət] *a* uneducated; uncultured.

ungebräuchlich ['ungəbrɔyçlıç] *a* unusual, uncommon.

ungedeckt ['ungədɛkt] *a Scheck* uncovered.

Ungeduld ['ungədult] *f* impatience; **u~ig** [-dıç] *a* impatient.

ungeeignet ['ungə'aıgnət] *a* unsuitable.

ungefähr ['ungəfɛ:r] *a* rough, approximate; **das kommt nicht von ~** that's hardly surprising; **~lich** *a* not dangerous, harmless.

ungehalten ['ungəhaltən] *a* indignant.

ungeheuer ['ungəhɔyər] *a* huge; *ad* (*col*) enormously; **U~** *nt* -s, - monster; **~lich** [-'hɔyərlıç] *a* monstrous.

ungehobelt ['ungəho:bəlt] *a* (*fig*) uncouth.

ungehörig ['ungəhø:rıç] *a* impertinent, improper; **U~keit** *f* impertinence.

ungehorsam ['ungəho:rza:m] *a* disobedient; **U~** *m* disobedience.

ungeklärt ['ungəklɛ:rt] *a* not cleared up; *Rätsel* unsolved; *Abwasser* untreated.

ungeladen ['ungəla:dən] *a* not loaded; (*Elec*) uncharged; *Gast* uninvited.

ungelegen ['ungəle:gən] *a* inconvenient.

ungelernt ['ungəlɛrnt] *a* unskilled.

ungelogen ['ungəlo:gən] *ad* really, honestly.

ungemein ['ungəmaın] *a* uncommon.

ungemütlich ['ungəmy:tlıç] *a* uncomfortable; *Person* disagreeable.

ungenau ['ungənau] *a* inaccurate; **U~igkeit** *f* inaccuracy.

ungeniert ['unʒeni:rt] *a* free and easy, unceremonious; *ad* without embarrassment, freely.

ungenießbar ['ungəni:sba:r] *a* inedible; undrinkable; (*col*) unbearable.

ungenügend ['ungəny:gənt] *a* insufficient, inadequate.

ungepflegt ['ungəpfle:kt] *a Garten etc* untended; *Person* unkempt; *Hände* neglected.

ungerade ['ungəra:də] *a* uneven, odd.

ungerecht ['ungəreçt] *a* unjust; **~fertigt** *a* unjustified; **U~igkeit** *f* injustice, unfairness.

ungern ['ungɛrn] *ad* unwillingly, reluctantly.

ungeschehen ['ungəfe:ən] *a*: **~ machen** undo.

Ungeschick- ['ungəfık] *cpd*: **~lichkeit** *f* clumsiness; **u~t** *a* awkward, clumsy.

ungeschminkt ['ungəfmıŋkt] *a* without make-up; (*fig*) unvarnished.

ungesetzlich ['ungəzetslıç] *a* illegal.

ungestempelt ['ungəftempəlt] *a Briefmarke* unfranked, uncancelled.

ungestört ['ungəftø:rt] *a* undisturbed.

ungestraft ['ungəftra:ft] *ad* with impunity.

ungestüm ['ungəfty:m] *a* impetuous; tempestuous; **U~** *nt* -(e)s impetuosity; passion.

ungesund ['ungəzunt] *a* unhealthy.

ungetrübt ['ungətry:pt] *a* clear; (*fig*) untroubled; *Freude* unalloyed.

Ungetüm ['ungəty:m] *nt* -(e)s, -e monster.

ungewiß ['ungəvıs] *a* uncertain; **U~heit** *f* uncertainty.

ungewöhnlich ['ungəvø:nlıç] *a* unusual.

ungewohnt ['ungəvo:nt] *a* unaccustomed.

Ungeziefer ['ungətsi:fər] *nt* -s vermin.

ungezogen ['ungətso:gən] *a* rude, impertinent; **U~heit** *f* rudeness, impertinence.

ungezwungen ['ungətsvuŋən] *a* natural, unconstrained.

ungläubig ['unglɔybıç] *a* unbelieving; **ein ~er Thomas** a doubting Thomas; **die U~en** the infidel(s).

unglaub- *cpd*: **~lich** [un'glauplıç] *a* incredible; **~würdig** ['unglaupvyrdıç] *a* untrustworthy, unreliable; *Geschichte* improbable.

ungleich ['unglaıç] *a* dissimilar; unequal; *ad* incomparably; **~artig** *a* different; **U~heit** *f* dissimilarity; inequality.

Unglück ['ungγk] *nt* -(e)s, -e misfortune; (*Pech*) bad luck; (*—sfall*) calamity, disaster; *(Verkehrs—)* accident; **u~lich** *a* unhappy; *(erfolglos)* unlucky; *(unerfreulich)* unfortunate; **u~licherweise** [-'waɪz] *ad* unfortunately; **u~selig** *a* calamitous; *Person* unfortunate; **~sfall** *m* accident, calamity.

ungültig ['ʊngʏltɪç] *a* invalid; **U~keit** *f* invalidity.

ungünstig ['ʊngʏnstɪç] *a* unfavourable.

ungut ['ʊngu:t] *a Gefühl* uneasy; **nichts für** ~ no offence.

unhaltbar ['ʊnhaltbaːr] *a* untenable.

Unheil ['ʊnhaɪl] *nt* evil; *(Unglück)* misfortune; ~ **anrichten** cause mischief; **u~bar** *a* incurable; **u~bringend** *a* fatal, fateful; **u~voll** *a* disastrous.

unheimlich ['ʊnhaɪmlɪç] *a* weird, uncanny; *ad (col)* tremendously.

unhöflich ['ʊnhø:flɪç] *a* impolite; **U~keit** *f* impoliteness.

unhygienisch ['ʊnhygi'e:nɪʃ] *a* unhygienic.

Uni ['ʊni] *f* -, -s university; **u~** [y'ni:] *a* self-coloured.

Uniform [uni'fɔrm] *f* uniform; **u~iert** [-'miːrt] *a* uniformed.

uninteressant ['ʊn'ɪntɛresant] *a* uninteresting.

Universität [univɛrzi'tɛ:t] *f* university.

unkenntlich ['ʊnkɛntlɪç] *a* unrecognizable.

Unkenntnis ['ʊnkɛntnɪs] *f* ignorance.

unklar ['ʊnklaːr] *a* unclear; **im ~en sein über** *(+acc)* be in the dark about; **U~heit** *f* unclarity; *(Unentschiedenheit)* uncertainty.

unklug ['ʊnkluːk] *a* unwise.

Unkosten ['ʊnkɔstən] *pl* expense(s).

Unkraut ['ʊnkraut] *nt* weed; weeds *pl.*

unlängst ['ʊnlɛŋst] *ad* not long ago.

unlauter ['ʊnlautɐ] *a* unfair.

unleserlich ['ʊnle:zɐlɪç] *a* illegible.

unlogisch ['ʊnlo:gɪʃ] *a* illogical.

unlösbar [ʊn'lø:sbaːr], **unlöslich** [ʊn'lø:slɪç] *a* insoluble.

Unlust ['ʊnlust] *f* lack of enthusiasm; **u~ig** *a* unenthusiastic.

unmäßig ['ʊnmɛ:sɪç] *a* immoderate.

Unmenge ['ʊnmɛŋə] *f* tremendous number, hundreds *pl.*

Unmensch ['ʊnmɛnʃ] *m* ogre, brute; **u~lich** *a* inhuman, brutal; *(ungeheuer)* awful.

unmerklich [ʊn'mɛrklɪç] *a* imperceptible.

unmißverständlich ['ʊnmɪsfɛrʃtɛntlɪç] *a* unmistakable.

unmittelbar ['ʊnmɪtəlbaːr] *a* immediate.

unmöbliert ['ʊnmøbliːrt] *a* unfurnished.

unmöglich ['ʊnmø:klɪç] *a* impossible; **U~keit** *f* impossibility.

unmoralisch ['ʊnmoraːlɪʃ] *a* immoral.

Unmut ['ʊnmuːt] *m* ill humour.

unnachgiebig ['ʊnna:xgiːbɪç] *a* unyielding.

unnahbar [ʊn'naːbaːr] *a* unapproachable.

unnötig ['ʊnnø:tɪç] *a* unnecessary; **~erweise** *ad* unnecessarily.

unnütz ['ʊnnʏts] *a* useless.

unordentlich ['ʊn'ɔrdəntlɪç] *a* untidy.

Unordnung ['ʊn'ɔrdnʊŋ] *f* disorder.

unparteiisch ['ʊnpartaiɪʃ] *a* impartial; **U~e(r)** *m* umpire; *(Fußball)* referee.

unpassend ['ʊnpasənt] *a* inappropriate; *Zeit* inopportune.

unpäßlich ['ʊnpɛslɪç] *a* unwell.

unpersönlich ['ʊnpɛrzø:nlɪç] *a* impersonal.

unpolitisch ['ʊnpoli:tɪʃ] *a* apolitical.

unpraktisch ['ʊnpraktɪʃ] *a* unpractical.

unproduktiv ['ʊnprodukti:f] *a* unproductive.

unproportioniert ['ʊnprɔpɔrtsioni:rt] *a* out of proportion.

unpünktlich ['ʊnpʏnktlɪç] *a* unpunctual.

unrationell ['ʊnratsionɛl] *a* inefficient.

unrecht ['ʊnrɛçt] *a* wrong; **U~** *nt* wrong; **zu U~** wrongly; **U~ haben, im U~ sein** be wrong; **~mäßig** *a* unlawful, illegal.

unregelmäßig ['ʊnre:gəlmɛsɪç] *a* irregular; **U~keit** *f* irregularity.

unreif ['ʊnraɪf] *a Obst* unripe; *(fig)* immature.

unrentabel ['ʊnrɛnta:bəl] *a* unprofitable.

unrichtig ['ʊnrɪçtɪç] *a* incorrect, wrong.

Unruh ['ʊnru:] *f* -, -en *(von Uhr)* balance; **~e** *f* -, -en unrest; **~estifter** *m* troublemaker; **u~ig** *a* restless.

uns [ʊns] *pron acc, dat of* wir us; ourselves.

unsachlich ['ʊnzaxlɪç] *a* not to the point, irrelevant; *(persönlich)* personal.

unsagbar [ʊn'za:kbaːr], **unsäglich** [ʊn'zɛ:klɪç] *a* indescribable.

unsanft ['ʊnzanft] *a* rough.

unsauber ['ʊnzaubɐ] *a* unclean, dirty; *(fig)* crooked; *(Mus)* fuzzy.

unschädlich ['ʊnʃɛ:tlɪç] *a* harmless; **jdn/etw ~ machen** render sb/sth harmless.

unscharf ['ʊnʃarf] *a* indistinct; *Bild etc* out of focus, blurred.

unscheinbar ['ʊnʃaɪnbaːr] *a* insignificant; *Aussehen, Haus etc.* unprepossessing.

unschlagbar [ʊn'ʃla:kbaːr] *a* invincible.

unschlüssig ['ʊnʃlʏsɪç] *a* undecided.

Unschuld ['ʊnʃʊlt] *f* innocence; **u~ig** [-dɪç] *a* innocent.

unselbständig ['ʊnzɛlpʃtɛndɪç] *a* dependent, over-reliant on others.

unser ['ʊnzɐ] *pron* our; *gen of* wir of us; **~e(r,s)** ours; **~einer, ~eins, ~esgleichen** *pron* people like us; **~erseits** *ad* on our part; **~twegen, ~twillen** *ad (für uns)* for our sake; *(wegen uns)* on our account; **~ige** *pron*: **der/die/das ~ige** ours.

unsicher ['ʊnzɪçɐ] *a* uncertain; *Mensch* insecure; **U~heit** *f* uncertainty; insecurity.

unsichtbar ['ʊnzɪçtbaːr] *a* invisible; **U~keit** *f* invisibility.

Unsinn ['ʊnzɪn] *m* nonsense; **u~ig** *a* nonsensical.

Unsitte ['ʊnzɪtə] *f* deplorable habit.

unsittlich ['ʊnzɪtlɪç] *a* indecent; **U~keit** *f* indecency.

unsportlich ['ʊnʃpɔrtlɪç] *a* not sporty; unfit; *Verhalten* unsporting.

unsre ['unzrə] = **unsere.**

unsrige ['unzrɪgə] = **unserige.**

unsterblich ['unʃtɛrplɪç] a immortal; U~**keit** f immortality.

Unstimmigkeit ['unʃtɪmɪçkaɪt] f inconsistency; (Streit) disagreement.

unsympathisch ['unzʏmpa:tɪʃ] a unpleasant; **er ist mir ~** I don't like him.

untätig ['unte:tɪç] a idle.

untauglich [un'tauklɪç] a unsuitable; (Mil) unfit; U~**keit** f unsuitability; unfitness.

unteilbar [un'taɪlba:r] a indivisible.

unten ['untən] ad below; (im Haus) downstairs; (an der Treppe etc) at the bottom; **nach ~** down; **~ am Berg** etc at the bottom of the mountain etc; **ich bin bei ihm ~ durch** (col) he's through with me.

unter ['untər] prep +acc or dat under, below; (bei Menschen) among; (während) during; ad under.

Unter- ['untər] cpd: **~abteilung** f subdivision; **~arm** m forearm.

unterbe- ['untərbə] cpd: **~lichten** vt (Phot) underexpose; U~**wußtsein** nt subconscious; **~zahlt** a underpaid.

unterbieten [untər'bi:tən] vt irreg insep (Comm) undercut; Rekord lower, reduce.

unterbinden [untər'bɪndən] vt irreg insep stop, call a halt to.

Unterbodenschutz [untər'bo:dənʃuts] m (Aut) underseal.

unterbrech- [untər'brɛç] cpd: **~en** vt irreg insep interrupt; U~**ung** f interruption.

unterbringen ['untərbrɪŋən] vt irreg (in Koffer) stow; (in Zeitung) place; Person (in Hotel etc) accommodate, put up; (beruflich) fix up (auf, in with).

unterdessen [untər'dɛsən] ad meanwhile.

Unterdruck ['untərdruk] m low pressure.

unterdrücken [untər'drʏkən] vt insep suppress; Leute oppress.

untere(r,s) ['untərə(r,z)] a lower.

untereinander [untər'aɪ'nandər] ad with each other; among themselves etc.

unterentwickelt ['untər'ɛntvɪkəlt] a underdeveloped.

unterernährt ['untər'ɛrnɛ:rt] a undernourished, underfed.

Unterernährung f malnutrition.

Unter'führung f subway, underpass.

Untergang ['untərgaŋ] m (down-)fall, decline; (Naut) sinking; (von Gestirn) setting.

unter'geben a subordinate.

untergehen ['untərge:ən] vi irreg go down; (Sonne auch) set; (Staat) fall; (Volk) perish; (Welt) come to an end; (im Lärm) be drowned.

Untergeschoß ['untərgəʃɔs] nt basement.

unter'gliedern vt insep subdivide.

Untergrund ['untərgrunt] m foundation; (Pol) underground; **~bahn** f underground, tube, subway (US); **~bewegung** f underground (movement).

unterhalb ['untərhalp] prep +gen, ad below; **~ von** below.

Unterhalt ['untərhalt] m maintenance; **u~en** [untər'haltən] irreg insep vt maintain; (belustigen) entertain; vr talk; (sich belustigen) er.joy o.s.; **u~end**, **u~sam** [untər'haltənt] a entertaining; **~ung** f maintenance; (Belustigung) entertainment, amusement; (Gespräch) talk.

Unterhändler ['untərhentlər] m negotiator.

Unterhemd ['untərhɛmt] nt vest, undershirt (US).

Unterhose ['untərho:zə] f underpants pl.

unterirdisch ['untər'ɪrdɪʃ] a underground.

Unterkiefer ['untərki:fər] m lower jaw.

unterkommen ['untərkəmən] vi irreg find shelter; find work; **das ist mir noch nie untergekommen** I've never met with that.

Unterkunft ['untərkunft] f -, **-künfte** accommodation.

Unterlage ['untərla:gə] f foundation; (Beleg) document; (Schreib— etc) pad.

unter'lassen vt irreg insep (versäumen) fail (to do); (sich enthalten) refrain from.

unterlaufen [untər'laufən] vi irreg insep happen; a: **mit Blut ~** suffused with blood; (Augen) bloodshot.

unterlegen [untər'le:gən] vt lay or put under; ['untərle:gən] a inferior (dat to); (besiegt) defeated.

Unterleib ['untərlaip] m abdomen.

unter'liegen vi irreg insep be defeated or overcome (jdm by sb); (unterworfen sein) be subject to.

Untermiete ['untərmi:tə] f: **zur ~ wohnen** be a subtenant or lodger; **~r(in** f) m subtenant, lodger.

unter'nehmen vt irreg insep undertake; U~ nt -s, - undertaking, enterprise (auch Comm); **~d** a enterprising, daring.

Unternehmer [untər'ne:mər] m -s, - entrepreneur, businessman.

Unterprima ['untərpri:ma] f -, **-primen** eighth year of secondary school.

Unterredung [untər're:duŋ] f discussion, talk.

Unterricht ['untərrɪçt] m -(e)s, -e instruction, lessons pl; **u~en** [untər'rɪçtən] insep vt instruct; (Sch) teach; vr inform o.s. (über +acc about).

Unterrock [untərrɔk] m petticoat, slip.

unter'sagen vt insep forbid (jdm etw sb to do sth).

unter'schätzen vt insep underestimate.

unter'scheiden irreg insep vt distinguish; vr differ.

Unter'scheidung f (Unterschied) distinction; (Unterscheiden) differentiation.

Unterschied ['untərʃi:t] m -(e)s, -e difference, distinction; **im ~ zu** as distinct from; **u~lich** a varying, differing; (diskriminierend) discriminatory; **u~slos** ad indiscriminately.

unter'schlagen vt irreg insep embezzle; (verheimlichen) suppress.

Unter'schlagung f embezzlement.

Unterschlupf ['untərʃlupf] m -(e)s, **-schlüpfe** refuge.

unter'schreiben vt irreg insep sign.

Unterschrift ['untərʃrɪft] f signature.

Unterseeboot ['untərze:bo:t] *nt* submarine.

Untersekunda ['untərzekunda] *f* -, -sekunden sixth year of secondary school.

Untersetzer ['untərzɛtsər] *m* tablemat; *(für Gläser)* coaster.

untersetzt [untər'zɛtst] a stocky.

unterste(r,s) ['untərstə(r,z)] a lowest, bottom.

unterstehen [untər'ʃte:ən] *irreg vi insep* be under *(jdm sb)*; *vr* dare; ['untərʃte:ən] *vi* shelter.

unterstellen [untər'ʃtɛlən] *vt insep* subordinate *(dat* to); *(fig)* impute *(jdm etw* sth to sb); ['untərʃtɛlən] *vt Auto* garage, park; *vr* take shelter.

unter'streichen *vt irreg insep (lit, fig)* underline.

Unterstufe ['untərʃtu:fə] *f* lower grade.

unter'stützen *vt insep* support.

Unter'stützung *f* support, assistance.

unter'suchen *vt insep (Med)* examine; *(Polizei)* investigate.

Unter'suchung *f* examination; investigation, inquiry; ~**sausschuß** *m* committee of inquiry; ~**shaft** *f* imprisonment on remand.

Untertan ['untərta:n] *m* -s, -en subject.

untertänig ['untərtɛ:nɪç] a submissive, humble.

Untertasse ['untərtasə] *f* saucer.

untertauchen ['untərtauxən] *vi* dive; *(fig)* disappear, go underground.

Unterteil ['untərtail] *nt or m* lower part, bottom; u~en [untər'tailən] *vt insep* divide up.

Untertertia ['untərtɛrtsia] *f* -, -tertien fourth year of secondary school.

Unterwäsche ['untərvɛʃə] *f* underwear.

unterwegs [untər've:ks] ad on the way.

unter'weisen *vt irreg insep* instruct.

unter'werfen *irreg insep vt* subject; *Volk* subjugate; *vr* submit *(dat* to).

unterwürfig [untər'vyrfɪç] a obsequious, servile.

unter'zeichnen *vt insep* sign.

unter'ziehen *irreg insep vt* subject *(dat* to); *vr.* undergo *(etw (dat)* sth); *(einer Prüfung)* take.

untreu ['untrɔy] a unfaithful; U~**e** *f* unfaithfulness.

untröstlich [un'trø:stlɪç] a inconsolable.

Untugend ['untu:gənt] *f* vice, failing.

unüber- ['un'y:bər] *cpd:* ~**legt** [-le:kt] a ill-considered; ad without thinking; ~**sehbar** ['-ze:ba:r] a incalculable.

unum- [un'um] *cpd:* ~**gänglich** ['-gɛŋlɪç] a indispensable, vital; absolutely necessary; ~**wunden** [-'vundən] a candid; ad straight out.

ununterbrochen ['un'untərbrɔxən] a uninterrupted.

unver- [unfɛr] *cpd:* ~**änderlich** [-'ɛndərlɪç] a unchangeable; ~**antwortlich** [-'antvɔrtlɪç] a irresponsible; *(unentschuldbar)* inexcusable; ~**äußerlich** [-'ɔysərlɪç] a inalienable; ~**besserlich** [-'bɛsərlɪç] a incorrigible; ~**bindlich**

[-'bɪntlɪç] a not binding; *Antwort* curt; ad *(Comm)* without obligation; ~**blümt** [-'bly:mt] a,ad plain(ly), blunt(ly); ~**daulich** ['-daulɪç] a indigestible; ~**dorben** ['-dɔrbən] a unspoilt; ~**einbar** [-'ainba:r] a incompatible; ~**fänglich** ['-fɛŋlɪç] a harmless; ~**froren** ['-fro:rən] a impudent; ~**hofft** ['-hɔft] a unexpected; ~**kennbar** ['-kɛnba:r] a unmistakable; ~**meidlich** [-'maitlɪç] a unavoidable; ~**mutet** ['-mu:tət] a unexpected; ~**nünftig** ['-nynftɪç] a foolish; ~**schämt** ['-ʃɛ:mt] a impudent; U~**schämtheit** *f* impudence, insolence; ~**sehens** ['-ze:əns] ad all of a sudden; ~**sehrt** ['-ze:rt] a uninjured; ~**söhnlich** ['-zø:nlɪç] a irreconcilable; ~**ständlich** ['-ʃtɛntlɪç] a unintelligible; ~**träglich** ['-trɛ:klɪç] a quarrelsome; *Meinungen,* *(Med)* incompatible; ~**wüstlich** [-'vy:stlɪç] a indestructible; *Mensch* irrepressible; ~**zeihlich** [-'tsailɪç] a unpardonable; ~**züglich** [-'tsy:klɪç] a immediate.

unvoll- ['unfɔl] *cpd:* ~**kommen** a imperfect; ~**ständig** a incomplete.

unvor- ['unfo:r] *cpd:* ~**bereitet** a unprepared; ~**eingenommen** a unbiased; ~**hergesehen** [-he:rgəze:ən] a unforeseen; ~**sichtig** [-zɪçtɪç] a careless, imprudent; ~**stellbar** [-'ʃtɛlba:r] a inconceivable; ~**teilhaft** [tailhaft] a disadvantageous.

unwahr ['unva:r] a untrue; ~**haftig** a untruthful; ~**scheinlich** a improbable, unlikely; ad *(col)* incredibly; U~**scheinlichkeit** *f* improbability, unlikelihood.

unweigerlich [un'vaigərlɪç] a unquestioning; ad without fail.

Unwesen ['unve:zən] *nt* nuisance; *(Unfug)* mischief; **sein ~ treiben** wreak havoc; u~**tlich** a inessential, unimportant; u~**tlich besser** marginally better.

Unwetter ['unvɛtər] *nt* thunderstorm.

unwichtig ['unvɪçtɪç] a unimportant.

unwider- [unvi:dər] *cpd:* ~**legbar** [-'le:kba:r] a irrefutable; ~**ruflich** ['-ru:flɪç] a irrevocable; ~**stehlich** [-'ʃte:lɪç] a irresistible.

unwill- ['unvɪl] *cpd:* U~**e(n)** *m* indignation; ~**ig** a indignant; *(widerwillig)* reluctant; ~**kürlich** [-ky:rlɪç] a involuntary; ad instinctively; *lachen* involuntarily.

unwirklich ['unvɪrklɪç] a unreal.

unwirsch ['unvɪrʃ] a cross, surly.

unwirtlich ['unvɪrtlɪç] a inhospitable.

unwirtschaftlich ['unvɪrt-ʃaftlɪç] a uneconomical.

unwissen- ['unvɪsən] *cpd:* ~**d** a ignorant; U~**heit** *f* ignorance; ~**schaftlich** a unscientific.

unwohl ['unvo:l] a unwell, ill; U~**sein** *nt* -s indisposition.

unwürdig ['unvyrdɪç] a unworthy *(jds of* sb).

unzählig [un'tsɛ:lɪç] a innumerable, countless.

unzer- [untsɛr] *cpd:* ~**brechlich** [-'brɛçlɪç] a unbreakable; ~**reißbar**

[-'raɪsbɑ:r] a untearable; ~störbar [-'ʃtö:rbɑ:r] a indestructible; ~trennlich [-'trɛnlɪç] a inseparable.

Unzucht ['ʊntsʊxt] f sexual offence.

unzüchtig ['ʊntsʏçtɪç] a immoral; lewd.

unzu- ['ʊntsu] cpd: ~frieden a dissatisfied; **U~friedenheit** f discontent; ~länglich ['ʊntsu:lɛŋlɪç] a inadequate; ~lässig ['ʊntsu:lɛsɪç] a inadmissible; ~rechnungsfähig ['ʊntsu:rɛçnʊŋsfɛ:ɪç] a irresponsible; ~sammenhängend a disconnected; *Außerung* incoherent; ~treffend ['ʊntsu:-] a incorrect; ~verlässig ['ʊntsu:-] a unreliable.

unzweideutig ['ʊntsvaɪdɔytɪç] *adj* unambiguous.

üppig ['ʏpɪç] *adj Frau* curvaceous; *Busen* full, ample; *Essen* sumptuous, lavish; *Vegetation* luxuriant, lush.

uralt ['u:r'alt] a ancient, very old.

Uran [u'rɑ:n] nt -s uranium.

Ur- ['u:r] in cpds original; ~aufführung f first performance; ~einwohner m original inhabitant; ~eltern pl ancestors pl; ~enkel(in f) m great-grandchild; ~großmutter f great-grandmother; ~großvater m great-grandfather; ~heber m -s, - originator; *(Autor)* author.

Urin [u'ri:n] m -s, -e urine.

ur- cpd: ~komisch a incredibly funny; **U~kunde** f -, -n document, deed; ~kundlich ['u:rkʊntlɪç] a documentary; ~laub m -(e)s, -e holiday(s pl), vacation *(US)*; *(Mil etc)* leave; ~lauber m -s, - holiday-maker, vacationist *(US)*; ~mensch m primitive man.

Urne ['ʊrnə] f -, -n urn.

Ursache ['u:rzaxə] f cause.

Ursprung ['u:rʃprʊŋ] m origin, source; *(von Fluß)* source.

ursprünglich [u:rʃprʏŋlɪç] a, ad original(ly).

Urteil ['ʊrtaɪl] nt -s, -e opinion; *(Jur)* sentence, judgement; **u~en** vi judge; ~sspruch m sentence, verdict.

Ur- cpd: ~wald m jungle; ~zeit f prehistoric times pl.

usw [u:sve:] abbr of **und so weiter** etc.

Utensilien [utɛn'zi:liən] pl utensils pl.

Utopie [uto'pi:] f pipedream.

utopisch [u'to:pɪʃ] a utopian.

V

V, v [faʊ] nt V, v.

vag(e) [va:k, va:gə] a vague.

Vagina [va'gi:na] f -, **Vaginen** vagina.

Vakuum ['va:kuʊm] nt -s, **Vakua** or **Vakuen** vacuum.

Vanille [va'nɪljə] f - vanilla.

Variation [variatsi'o:n] f variation.

variieren [vari'i:rən] vti vary.

Vase ['va:zə] f -, -n vase.

Vater ['fa:tər] m -s, ⸚ father; ~land nt native country; Fatherland; ~landsliebe f patriotism.

väterlich ['fɛ:tərlɪç] a fatherly; ~erseits ad on the father's side.

Vater- cpd: ~schaft f paternity; ~unser nt -s, - Lord's prayer.

Vegetarier(in f) [vege'ta:riər(ɪn)] m -s, - vegetarian.

Veilchen ['faɪlçən] nt violet.

Vene ['ve:nə] f -, -n vein.

Ventil [vɛn'ti:l] nt -s, -e valve; ~ator [vɛnti'la:tɔr] m ventilator.

verab- [fɛr'ap] cpd: ~reden vt agree, arrange; vr arrange to meet *(mit jdm sb)*; **V~redung** f arrangement; *(Treffen)* appointment; ~scheuen vt detest, abhor; ~schieden vt *Gäste* say goodbye to; *(entlassen)* discharge; *Gesetz* pass; vr take one's leave *(von of)*; **V~schiedung** f leave-taking; discharge; passing.

ver- [fɛr] cpd: ~achten vt despise; ~ächtlich [-'ɛçtlɪç] a contemptuous; *(verachtenswert)* contemptible; **jdn ~ächtlich machen** run sb down; **V~achtung** f contempt.

verallgemein- [fɛr'algə'maɪn] cpd: ~ern vt generalize; **V~erung** f generalization.

veralten [fɛr'altən] vi become obsolete or out-of-date.

Veranda [ve'randa] f -, **Veranden** veranda.

veränder- [fɛr'ɛndər] cpd: ~lich a changeable; **V~lichkeit** f variability, instability; ~n vtr change, alter; **V~ung** f change, alteration.

veran- [fɛr'an] cpd: ~lagt a with a ... nature; **V~lagung** f disposition, aptitude; ~lassen vt cause; *Maßnahmen* ~lassen take measures; **sich ~laßt sehen** feel prompted; **V~lassung** f cause; motive; **auf jds V~lassung (hin)** at the instance of sb; ~schaulichen vt illustrate; ~schlagen vt estimate; ~stalten vt organize, arrange; **V~stalter** m -s, - organizer; **V~staltung** f *(Veranstalten)* organizing; *(Veranstaltetes)* event, function.

verantwort- [fɛr'antvɔrt] cpd: ~en vt answer for; vr justify o.s.; ~lich a responsible; **V~ung** f responsibility; ~ungsbewußt a responsible; ~ungslos a irresponsible.

verarbeiten [fɛr'arbaɪtən] vt process; *(geistig)* assimilate; **etw zu etw ~ make** sth into sth.

Verarbeitung f processing; assimilation.

verärgern [fɛr'ɛrgərn] vt annoy.

verausgaben [fɛr'ausga:bən] vr run out of money; *(fig)* exhaust o.s.

veräußern [fɛr'ɔysərn] vt dispose of, sell.

Verb [vɛrp] nt -s, -en verb.

Verband [fɛr'bant] m -(e)s, ⸚e *(Med)* bandage, dressing; *(Bund)* association, society; *(Mil)* unit; ~(s)kasten m medicine chest, first-aid box; ~stoff m, ~zeug nt bandage, dressing material.

verbannen [fɛr'banən] vt banish.

Verbannung f exile.

verbergen [fɛr'bɛrgən] vtr irreg hide *(vor +dat from)*.

verbessern [fɛr'bɛsərn] vtr improve; *(berichtigen)* correct (o.s.).

Verbesserung f improvement; correction.

verbeugen [fɛr'bɔygən] *vr* bow.
Verbeugung *f* bow.
ver'biegen *vi irreg* bend.
ver'bieten *vt irreg* forbid (*jdm etw* sb to do sth).
ver'binden *irreg vt* connect; *(kombinieren)* combine; *(Med)* bandage; **jdm die Augen** ~ blindfold sb; *vr* combine *(auch Chem)*, join.
verbindlich [fɛr'bɪntlɪç] *a* binding; *(freundlich)* friendly: **V~keit** *f* obligation; *(Höflichkeit)* civility.
Ver'bindung *f* connection; *(Zusammensetzung)* combination; *(Chem)* compound; *(Univ)* club.
verbissen [fɛr'bɪsən] *a* grim, dogged; **V~heit** *f* grimness, doggedness.
ver'bitten *vr irreg*: **sich** *(dat)* **etw** ~ not tolerate sth, not stand for sth.
verbittern [fɛr'bɪtərn] *vt* embitter; **vi** get bitter.
verblassen [fɛr'blasən] *vi* fade.
Verbleib [fɛ'blaɪp] *m* -**(e)s** whereabouts; **v~en** [fɛr'blaɪbən] *vi irreg* remain.
Verblendung [fɛr'blɛnduŋ] *f (fig)* delusion.
verblöden [fɛr'blø:dən] *vi* get stupid.
verblüffen [fɛr'blʏfən] *vt* stagger, amaze.
Verblüffung *f* stupefaction.
ver'blühen *vi* wither, fade.
ver'bluten *vi* bleed to death.
verborgen [fɛr'bɔrgən] *a* hidden.
Verbot [fɛr'bo:t] *nt* -**(e)s**, -**e** prohibition, ban; **v~en** *a* forbidden; **Rauchen v~en!** no smoking; **v~enerweise** *ad* though it is forbidden; **~sschild** *nt* prohibitory sign.
Verbrauch [fɛr'braux] *m* -**(e)s** consumption; **v~en** *vt* use up; **~er** *m* -**s**, - consumer; **v~t** *a* used up, finished; *Luft* stale; *Mensch* worn-out.
Verbrechen [fɛr'brɛçən] *nt* -**s**, - crime; **v~** *vt irreg* perpetrate.
Verbrecher [fɛr'brɛçər] *m* -**s**, - criminal; **v~isch** *a* criminal; **~tum** *nt* -**s** criminality.
ver'breiten *vtr* spread; **sich über etw** *(acc)* ~ expound on sth.
verbreitern [fɛr'braɪtərn] *vt* broaden.
Verbreitung *f* spread(ing), propagation.
verbrenn- [fɛr'brɛn] *cpd*: **~bar** *a* combustible; **~en** *vt irreg* burn; *Leiche* cremate; **V~ung** *f* burning; *(in Motor)* combustion; *(von Leiche)* cremation; **V~ungsmotor** *m* internal combustion engine.
ver'bringen *vt irreg* spend.
Verbrüderung [fɛr'bry:duŋ] *f* fraternization.
verbrühen [fɛr'bry:ən] *vt* scald.
verbuchen [fɛr'bu:xən] *vt (Fin)* register; *Erfolg* enjoy; *Mißerfolg* suffer.
verbunden [fɛr'bundən] *a* connected; **jdm** ~ **sein** be obliged *or* indebted to sb; **falsch** ~ *(Tel)* wrong number; **V~heit** *f* bond, relationship.
verbünden [fɛr'bʏndən] *vr* ally o.s.
Verbündete(r) [fɛr'bʏndətə(r)] *mf* ally.
ver'bürgen *vr*: **sich** ~ **für** vouch for.
ver'büßen *vt*: **eine Strafe** ~ serve a sentence.

verchromt [fɛr'kro:mt] *a* chromium-plated.
Verdacht [fɛr'daxt] *m* -**(e)s** suspicion.
verdächtig [fɛr'dɛçtɪç] *a* suspicious, suspect; **~en** [fɛr'dɛçtɪgən] *vt* suspect.
verdammen [fɛr'damən] *vt* damn, condemn.
Verdammnis [fɛr'damnɪs] *f* -, -**se** perdition, damnation.
ver'dampfen *vi* vaporize, evaporate.
ver'danken *vt*: **jdm etw** ~ owe sb sth.
verdauen [fɛr'dauən] *vt (lit, fig)* digest.
verdaulich [fɛr'daulɪç] *a* digestible; **das ist schwer** ~ that is hard to digest.
Verdauung *f* digestion.
Verdeck [fɛr'dɛk] *nt* -**(e)s**, -**e** *(Aut)* hood; *(Naut)* deck; **v~en** *vt* cover (up); *(verbergen)* hide.
ver'denken *vt irreg*: **jdm etw** ~ blame sb for sth, hold sth against sb.
Verderb- [fɛr'dɛrp] *cpd*: **~en** [fɛr'dɛrbən] *nt* -**s** ruin; **v~en** *irreg vt* spoil; *(schädigen)* ruin; *(moralisch)* corrupt; **es mit jdm v~en** get into sb's bad books; *vi (Essen)* spoil, rot; *(Mensch)* go to the bad; **v~lich** *a Einfluß* pernicious; *Lebensmittel* perishable; **v~t** *a* depraved; **~theit** *f* depravity.
verdeutlichen [fɛr'dɔytlɪçən] *vt* make clear.
ver'dichten *vtr* condense.
ver'dienen *vt* earn; *(moralisch)* deserve.
Ver'dienst [fɛr'di:nst] *m* -**(e)s** earnings *pl*; *nt* -**(e)s**, -**e** merit; *(Leistung)* service *(um* to).
verdient [fɛr'di:nt] *a* well-earned; *Person* deserving of esteem; **sich um etw** ~ **machen** do a lot for sth.
verdoppeln [fɛr'dɔpəln] *vt* double.
Verdopp(e)lung *f* doubling.
verdorben [fɛr'dɔrbən] *a* spoilt; *(geschädigt)* ruined; *(moralisch)* corrupt.
verdrängen [fɛr'drɛŋən] *vt* oust, displace *(auch Phys)*; *(Psych)* repress.
Verdrängung *f* displacement; *(Psych)* repression.
ver'drehen *vt (lit, fig)* twist; *Augen* roll; **jdm den Kopf** ~ *(fig)* turn sb's head.
verdreifachen [fɛr'draɪfaxən] *vt* treble.
verdrießlich [fɛr'dri:slɪç] *a* peevish, annoyed.
verdrossen [fɛr'drɔsən] *a* cross, sulky.
ver'drücken *vt (col)* put away, eat; *vr (col)* disappear.
Verdruß [fɛr'drus] *m* -**sses**, -**sse** annoyance, worry.
ver'duften *vi* evaporate; *vir (col)* disappear.
verdummen [fɛr'dumən] *vt* make stupid; *vi* grow stupid.
verdunkeln [fɛr'duŋkəln] *vtr* darken; *(fig)* obscure.
Verdunk(e)lung *f* blackout; *(fig)* obscuring.
verdünnen [fɛr'dʏnən] *vt* dilute.
verdunsten [fɛr'dunstən] *vi* evaporate.
verdursten [fɛr'durstən] *vi* die of thirst.
verdutzt [fɛr'dutst] *a* nonplussed, taken aback.
verehr- [fɛr''e:r] *cpd*: **~en** *vt* venerate,

worship (auch Rel); jdm etw ~ en present sb with sth; V~er(in f) m -s, - admirer, worshipper (auch Rel); ~t a esteemed; V~ung f respect; (Rel) worship.

vereidigen [fɛr'aɪdɪgən] vt put on oath.

Vereidigung f swearing in.

Verein [fɛr'aɪn] m -(e)s, -e club, association; v~bar a compatible; v~baren [-baːrən] vt agree upon; ~barung f agreement; v~fachen [-faxən] vt simplify; v~heitlichen vt standardize; v~igen [-ɪgən] vtr unite; ~igung f union; (Verein) association; v~samen [-zaːmən] vi become lonely; v~t a united; ~zelt a isolated.

vereisen [fɛr'aɪzən] vi freeze, ice over; vt (Med) freeze.

vereiteln [fɛr'aɪtəln] vt frustrate.

ver'eitern vi suppurate, fester.

verengen [fɛr'ɛŋən] vr narrow.

vererb- [fɛr'ɛrb] cpd: ~en vt bequeath; (Biol) transmit; vr be hereditary; ~lich [fɛr'ɛrplɪç] a hereditary; V~ung f bequeathing; (Biol) transmission; (Lehre) heredity.

verewigen [fɛr'eːvɪgən] vt immortalize; vr (col) leave one's name.

ver'fahren irreg vi act; ~ mit deal with; vr get lost; a tangled; V~ nt -s, - procedure; (Tech) process; (Jur) proceedings pl.

Verfall [fɛr'fal] m -(e)s decline; (von Haus) dilapidation; (Fin) expiry; v~en vi irreg decline; (Haus) be falling down; (Fin) lapse; v~en in (+acc) lapse into; v~en auf (+acc) hit upon; einem Laster v~en sein be addicted to a vice.

verfänglich [fɛr'fɛŋlɪç] a awkward, tricky.

ver'färben vr change colour.

Verfasser(in f) [fɛr'fasər(ɪn)] m -s, - author, writer.

Verfassung f constitution (auch Pol); ~sgericht nt constitutional court; v~smäßig a constitutional; v~swidrig a unconstitutional.

ver'faulen vi rot.

ver'fechten vt irreg advocate; defend.

Verfechter [fɛr'fɛçtər] m -s, - champion; defender.

ver'fehlen vt miss; etw für verfehlt halten regard sth as mistaken.

verfeinern [fɛr'faɪnərn] vt refine.

ver'fliegen vi irreg evaporate; (Zeit) pass, fly.

verflossen [fɛr'flɔsən] a past, former.

ver'fluchen vt curse.

verflüchtigen [fɛr'flyçtɪgən] vr vaporize, evaporate; (Geruch) fade.

verflüssigen [fɛr'flysɪgən] vr become liquid.

verfolg- [fɛr'fɔlg] cpd: ~en vt pursue; (gerichtlich) prosecute; (grausam, esp Pol) persecute; V~er m -s, - pursuer; V~ung f pursuit; prosecution; persecution; V~ungswahn m persecution mania.

verfremden [fɛr'frɛmdən] vt alienate, distance.

verfrüht [fɛr'fryːt] a premature.

verfüg- [fɛr'fyːg] cpd: ~bar a available; ~en vt direct, order; vr proceed; vi: ~en über (+acc) have at one's disposal; V~ung f direction, order; zur V~ung at one's disposal; jdm zur V~ung stehen be available to sb.

verführ- [fɛr'fyːr] cpd: ~en vt tempt; (sexuell) seduce; V~er m tempter; seducer; ~erisch a seductive; V~ung f seduction; (Versuchung) temptation.

ver'gammeln vi (col) go to seed; (Nahrung) go off.

vergangen [fɛr'gaŋən] a past; V~heit f past.

vergänglich [fɛr'gɛŋlɪç] a transitory; V~keit f transitoriness, impermanence.

vergasen [fɛr'gaːzən] vt gasify; (töten) gas.

Vergaser m -s, - (Aut) carburettor.

vergeb- [fɛr'geːb] cpd: ~en vt irreg forgive (jdm etw sb for sth); (weggeben) give away; ~en sein be occupied; (col: Mädchen) be spoken for; ~ens ad in vain; ~lich [fɛr'geːplɪç] ad in vain; a vain, futile; V~ung f forgiveness.

vergegenwärtigen [fɛr'geːgənvɛrtɪgən] vr: sich (dat) etw ~ recall or visualize sth.

ver'gehen irreg vi pass by or away; jdm vergeht etw sb loses sth; vr commit an offence (gegen etw against sth); sich an jdm ~ (sexually) assault sb; V~ nt -s, - offence.

ver'gelten vt irreg pay back (jdm etw sb for sth), repay.

Ver'geltung f retaliation, reprisal; ~sschlag m (Mil) reprisal.

vergessen [fɛr'gɛsən] vt irreg forget; V~heit f oblivion.

vergeßlich [fɛr'gɛslɪç] a forgetful; V~heit f forgetfulness.

vergeuden [fɛr'gɔydən] vt squander, waste.

vergewaltigen [fɛrgə'valtɪgən] vt rape; (fig) violate.

Vergewaltigung f rape.

vergewissern [fɛrgə'vɪsərn] vr make sure.

ver'gießen vt irreg shed.

vergiften [fɛr'gɪftən] vt poison.

Vergiftung f poisoning.

Vergißmeinnicht [fɛr'gɪsmaɪnnɪçt] nt -(e)s, -e forget-me-not.

verglasen [fɛr'glaːzən] vt glaze.

Vergleich [fɛr'glaɪç] m -(e)s, -e comparison; (Jur) settlement; im ~ mit or zu compared with or to; v~bar a comparable; v~en irreg vt compare; vr reach a settlement.

vergnügen [fɛr'gnyːgən] vr enjoy or amuse o.s.; V~ nt -s, - pleasure; viel V~! enjoy yourself!

vergnügt [fɛr'gnyːkt] a cheerful.

Vergnügung f pleasure, amusement; ~spark m amusement park; v~ssüchtig a pleasure-loving.

vergolden [fɛr'gɔldən] vt gild.

ver'gönnen vt grant.

vergöttern [fɛr'gœtərn] vt idolize.

ver'graben vt bury.

ver'greifen *vr irreg:* **sich an jdm** ~ lay hands on sb; **sich an etw** ~ misappropriate sth; **sich im Ton** ~ say the wrong thing.

vergriffen [fɛr'grɪfən] *a Buch* out of print; *Ware* out of stock.

vergrößern [fɛr'grøːsərn] *vt* enlarge; *(mengenmäßig)* increase; *(Lupe)* magnify.

Vergrößerung *f* enlargement; increase; magnification; ~**sglas** *nt* magnifying glass.

Vergünstigung [fɛr'gynstɪgʊŋ] *f* concession, privilege.

vergüten [fɛr'gyːtən] *vt:* **jdm etw** ~ compensate sb for sth.

Vergütung *f* compensation.

verhaften [fɛr'haftən] *vt* arrest.

Verhaftete(r) *mf* prisoner.

Verhaftung *f* arrest; ~**sbefehl** *m* warrant (for arrest).

ver'hallen *vi* die away.

ver'halten *irreg vr* be, stand; *(sich benehmen)* behave; *(Math)* be in proportion to; *vt* hold *or* keep back; *Schritt* check; **V~** *nt* **-s** behaviour; **V~sforschung** *f* behavioural science; **V~smaßregel** *f* rule of conduct.

Verhältnis [fɛr'hɛltnɪs] *nt* **-ses, -se** relationship; *(Math)* proportion, ratio; *pl (Umstände)* conditions *pl;* **über seine ~se leben** live beyond one's means; **v~mäßig** *a,ad* relative(ly), comparative(ly).

verhandeln [fɛr'handəln] *vi* negotiate *(über etw (acc)* sth); *(Jur)* hold proceedings; *vt* discuss; *(Jur)* hear.

Verhandlung *f* negotiation; *(Jur)* proceedings *pl.*

ver'hängen *vt (fig)* impose, inflict.

Verhängnis [fɛr'hɛŋnɪs] *nt* **-ses, -se** fate, doom; **jdm zum** ~ **werden** be sb's undoing; **v~voll** *a* fatal, disastrous.

verharmlosen [fɛr'harmloːzən] *vt* make light of, play down.

verharren [fɛr'harən] *vi* remain; *(hartnäckig)* persist.

verhärten [fɛr'hɛrtən] *vr* harden.

verhaßt [fɛr'hast] *a* odious, hateful.

verheerend [fɛr'heːrənt] *a* disastrous, devastating.

verhehlen [fɛr'heːlən] *vt* conceal.

ver'heilen *vi* heal.

verheimlichen [fɛr'haɪmlɪçən] *vt* keep secret *(jdm* from sb).

verheiratet [fɛr'haɪraːtət] *a* married.

ver'heißen *vt irreg:* **jdm etw** ~ promise sb sth.

ver'helfen *vi irreg:* **jdm** ~ **zu** help sb to get.

verherrlichen [fɛr'hɛrlɪçən] *vt* glorify.

ver'hexen *vt* bewitch; **es ist wie verhext** it's jinxed.

ver'hindern *vt* prevent; **verhindert sein** be unable to make it.

Ver'hinderung *f* prevention.

verhöhnen [fɛr'høːnən] *vt* mock, sneer at.

Verhör [fɛr'høːr] *nt* **-(e)s, -e** interrogation; *(gerichtlich)* (cross-)examination;

v~en *vt* interrogate; (cross-)examine; *vr* misunderstand, mishear.

ver'hungern *vi* starve, die of hunger.

ver'hüten *vt* prevent, avert.

Ver'hütung *f* prevention; ~**smittel** *nt* contraceptive.

verirren [fɛr'ɪrən] *vr* go astray.

ver'jagen *vt* drive away *or* out.

verjüngen [fɛr'jyŋən] *vt* rejuvenate; *vr* taper.

verkalken [fɛr'kalkən] *vi* calcify; *(col)* become senile.

verkalkulieren [fɛrkalku'liːrən] *vr* miscalculate.

verkannt [fɛr'kant] *a* unappreciated.

Verkauf [fɛr'kauf] *m* sale; **v~en** *vt* sell.

Verkäufer(in *f***)** [fɛr'kɔyfər(ɪn)] *m* **-s, -** seller; salesman; *(in Laden)* shop assistant.

verkäuflich [fɛr'kɔyflɪç] *a* saleable.

Verkehr [fɛr'keːr] *m* **-s, -e** traffic; *(Umgang, esp sexuell)* intercourse; *(Umlauf)* circulation; **v~en** *vi (Fahrzeug)* ply, run; *(besuchen)* visit regularly *(bei jdm* sb); **v~en mit** associate with; *vtr* turn, transform; ~**sampel** *f* traffic lights *pl;* ~**sdelikt** *nt* traffic offence; ~**sinsel** *f* traffic island; ~**sstockung** *f* traffic jam, stoppage; ~**sunfall** *m* traffic accident; **v~swidrig** *a* contrary to traffic regulations; ~**szeichen** *nt* traffic sign; **v~t** *a* wrong; *(umgekehrt)* the wrong way round.

ver'kennen *vt irreg* misjudge, not appreciate.

ver'klagen *vt* take to court.

verklären [fɛr'klɛːrən] *vt* transfigure; **verklärt lächeln** smile radiantly.

ver'kleben *vt* glue up, stick; *vi* stick together.

verkleiden [fɛr'klaɪdən] *vtr* disguise (o.s.), dress up.

Verkleidung *f* disguise; *(Archit)* wainscoting.

verkleinern [fɛr'klaɪnərn] *vt* make smaller, reduce in size.

verklemmt [fɛr'klɛmt] *a (fig)* inhibited.

ver'klingen *vi irreg* die away.

ver'kneifen *vt (col)* : **sich** *(dat)* **etw** ~ *Lachen* stifle; *Schmerz* hide; *(sich versagen)* do without.

verknüpfen [fɛr'knypfən] *vt* tie (up), knot; *(fig)* connect.

Verknüpfung *f* connection.

verkohlen [fɛr'koːlən] *vti* carbonize; *vt (col)* fool.

ver'kommen *vi irreg* deteriorate, decay; *(Mensch)* go downhill, come down in the world; *a (moralisch)* dissolute, depraved; **V~heit** *f* depravity.

verkörpern [fɛr'kœrpərn] *vt* embody, personify.

verköstigen [fɛr'kœstɪgən] *vt* feed.

verkraften [fɛr'kraftən] *vt* cope with.

ver'kriechen *vr irreg* creep away, creep into a corner.

verkrümmt [fɛr'krymt] *a* crooked.

Verkrümmung *f* bend, warp; *(Anat)* curvature.

verkrüppelt [fɛr'krypəlt] *a* crippled.

verkrustet [fɛr'krustət] *a* encrusted.

ver'kühlen vr get a chill.

ver'kümmern vi waste away.

verkünden [fɛr'kʏndən] vt proclaim; Urteil pronounce.

verkürzen [fɛr'kʏrtsən] vt shorten; Wort abbreviate; sich (dat) die Zeit ~ while away the time.

Verkürzung f shortening; abbreviation.

ver'laden vt irreg load.

Verlag [fɛr'laːk] m -(e)s, -e publishing firm.

verlangen [fɛr'laŋən] vt demand; desire; ~ Sie Herrn X ask for Mr X; vi ~ nach ask for, desire; V~ nt -s, - desire (nach for); auf jds V~ (hin) at sb's request.

verlängern [fɛr'lɛŋərn] vt extend; (länger machen) lengthen.

Verlängerung f extension; (Sport) extra time; ~sschnur f extension cable.

verlangsamen [fɛr'laŋzaːmən] vtr decelerate, slow down.

Verlaß [fɛr'las] m: auf ihn/das ist kein ~ he/it cannot be relied upon.

ver'lassen irreg vt leave; vr depend (auf +acc on); a desolate; Mensch abandoned; V~heit f loneliness.

verläßlich [fɛr'lɛslɪç] a reliable.

Verlauf [fɛr'lauf] m course; v~en irreg vi (zeitlich) pass; (Farben) run; vr get lost; (Menschenmenge) disperse.

ver'lauten vi: etw ~ lassen disclose sth; wie verlautet as reported.

ver'leben vt spend.

verlebt [fɛr'leːpt] a dissipated, worn out.

ver'legen vt move; (verlieren) mislay; (abspielen lassen) Handlung set (nach in); Buch publish; vr: sich auf etw (acc) ~ take up or to sth; a embarrassed; nicht ~ um never at a loss for; V~heit f embarrassment; (Situation) difficulty, scrape.

Verleger [fɛr'leːgər] m -s, - publisher.

Verleih [fɛr'lai] m -(e)s, -e hire service; v~en vt irreg lend; Kraft, Anschein confer, bestow; Preis, Medaille award; ~ung f lending; bestowal; award.

ver'leiten vt lead astray; ~ zu talk into, tempt into.

ver'lernen vt forget, unlearn.

ver'lesen irreg vt read out; (aussondern) sort out; vr make a mistake in reading.

verletz- [fɛr'lɛts] cpd: ~bar a vulnerable; ~en vt (lit, fig) injure, hurt; Gesetz etc violate; ~end a (fig) Worte hurtful; ~lich a vulnerable, sensitive; V~te(r) mf injured person; V~ung f injury; (Verstoß) violation, infringement.

verleugnen [fɛr'lɔygnən] vt deny; Menschen disown.

Verleugnung f denial.

verleumd- [fɛr'lɔymd] cpd: ~en vt slander; ~erisch a slanderous; V~ung f slander, libel.

ver'lieben vr fall in love (in jdn with sb).

verliebt [fɛr'liːpt] a in love; V~heit f being in love.

verlieren [fɛr'liːrən] irreg vti lose; vr get lost; (verschwinden) disappear.

verlob- [fɛr'loːb] cpd: ~en vr get engaged

(mit to); V~te(r) [fɛr'loːptə(r)] mf fiancé(e); V~ung f engagement.

ver'locken vt entice, lure.

Ver'lockung f temptation, attraction.

verlogen [fɛr'loːgən] a untruthful; V~heit f untruthfulness.

verloren [fɛr'loːrən] a lost; Eier poached; der ~e Sohn the prodigal son; etw ~ geben give sth up for lost; ~gehen vi irreg get lost.

verlosen [fɛr'loːzən] vt raffle, draw lots for.

Verlosung f raffle, lottery.

verlottern [fɛr'lɔtərn], verludern [fɛr'luːdərn] vi (col) go to the dogs.

Verlust [fɛr'lʊst] m -(e)s, -e loss; (Mil) casualty.

ver'machen vt bequeath, leave.

Vermächtnis [fɛr'mɛçtnɪs] nt -ses, -se legacy.

vermählen [fɛr'mɛːlən] vr marry.

Vermählung f wedding, marriage.

vermehren [fɛr'meːrən] vtr multiply; (Menge) increase.

Vermehrung f multiplying; increase.

ver'meiden vt irreg avoid.

vermeintlich [fɛr'maintlɪç] a supposed.

vermengen [fɛr'mɛŋən] vtr mix; (fig) mix up, confuse.

Vermerk [fɛr'mɛrk] m -(e)s, -e note; (in Ausweis) endorsement; v~en vt note.

ver'messen irreg vt survey; vr (falsch messen) measure incorrectly; a presumptuous, bold; V~heit f presumptuousness; recklessness.

Ver'messung f survey(ing).

ver'mieten vt let, rent (out); Auto hire out, rent.

Ver'mieter(in f) m -s, - landlord/ landlady.

Ver'mietung f letting, renting (out); (von Autos) hiring (out).

vermindern [fɛr'mɪndərn] vtr lessen, decrease; Preise reduce.

Verminderung f reduction.

ver'mischen vtr mix, blend.

vermissen [fɛr'mɪsən] vt miss.

vermißt [fɛr'mɪst] a missing.

vermitteln [fɛr'mɪtəln] vi mediate; vt Gespräch connect; jdm etw ~ help sb to obtain sth.

Vermittler [fɛr'mɪtlər] m -s, - (Schlichter) agent, mediator.

Vermittlung f procurement; (Stellen~) agency; (Tel) exchange; (Schlichtung) mediation.

ver'mögen vt irreg be capable of; ~ zu be able to; V~ nt -s, - wealth; (Fähigkeit) ability; ein V~ kosten cost a fortune; ~d a wealthy.

vermuten [fɛr'muːtən] vt suppose, guess; (argwöhnen) suspect.

vermutlich a supposed, presumed; ad probably.

Vermutung f supposition; suspicion.

vernachlässigen [fɛr'naːxlɛsɪgən] vt neglect.

vernarben [fɛr'narbən] vi heal up.

ver'nehmen vt irreg perceive, hear;

(erfahren) learn; *(Jur)* (cross-)examine; **dem V~ nach** from what I/we *etc* hear.

vernehmlich [fɛr'neːmlɪç] *a* audible.

Vernehmung *f* (cross-)examination; **v~sfähig** *a* in a condition to be (cross-)examined.

verneigen [fɛr'naɪɡn] *vr* bow.

verneinen [fɛr'naɪnən] *vt* Frage answer in the negative; *(ablehnen)* deny; *(Gram)* negate; **~d** *a* negative.

Verneinung *f* negation.

vernichten [fɛr'nɪçtn] *vt* annihilate, destroy; **~d** *a (fig)* crushing; *Blick* withering; *Kritik* scathing.

Vernichtung *f* destruction, annihilation.

verniedlichen [fɛr'niːdlɪçən] *vt* play down.

Vernunft [fɛr'nʊnft] *f* - reason, understanding.

vernünftig [fɛr'nʏnftɪç] *a* sensible, reasonable.

veröden [fɛr'øːdən] *vi* become desolate; *vt (Med)* remove.

veröffentlichen [fɛr'œfəntlɪçən] *vt* publish.

Veröffentlichung *f* publication.

verordnen [fɛr'ɔrdnən] *vt (Med)* prescribe.

Verordnung *f* order, decree; *(Med)* prescription.

ver'pachten *vt* lease (out).

ver'packen *vt* pack.

Ver'packung *f*, **~smaterial** *nt* packing, wrapping.

ver'passen *vt* miss; **jdm eine Ohrfeige ~** *(col)* give sb a clip round the ear.

verpesten [fɛr'pɛstən] *vt* pollute.

ver'pflanzen *vt* transplant.

Ver'pflanzung *f* transplant(ing).

ver'pflegen *vt* feed, cater for.

Ver'pflegung *f* feeding, catering; *(Kost)* food; *(in Hotel)* board.

verpflichten [fɛr'pflɪçtn] *vt* oblige, bind; *(anstellen)* engage; *vr* undertake; *(Mil)* sign on; *vi* carry obligations; **jdm zu Dank verpflichtet sein** be obliged to sb.

Verpflichtung *f* obligation, duty.

ver'pfuschen *vt (col)* bungle, make a mess of.

verplempern [fɛr'plɛmpərn] *vt (col)* waste.

verpönt [fɛr'pøːnt] *a* disapproved (of), taboo.

verprassen [fɛr'prasən] *vt* squander.

ver'prügeln *vt (col)* beat up, do over.

Verputz [fɛr'pʊts] *m* plaster, roughcast; **v~en** *vt* plaster; *(col) Essen* put away.

verquollen [fɛr'kvɔlən] *a* swollen; *Holz* warped.

verrammeln [fɛr'raməln] *vt* barricade.

Verrat [fɛr'raːt] *m* **-(e)s** treachery; *(Pol)* treason; **v~en** *irreg vt* betray; *Geheimnis* divulge; *vr* give o.s. away.

Verräter [fɛr'rɛːtər] *m* **-s**, - traitor; **~in** *f* traitress; **v~isch** *a* treacherous.

ver'rechnen *vt*: **~ mit** set off against; *vr* miscalculate.

Verrechnungsscheck [fɛr'rɛçnʊŋsʃɛk] *m* crossed cheque.

verregnet [fɛr're:gnət] *a* spoilt by rain, rainy.

ver'reisen *vi* go away (on a journey).

ver'reißen *vt irreg* pull to pieces.

verrenken [fɛr'rɛŋkən] *vt* contort; *(Med)* dislocate; **sich** *(dat)* **den Knöchel ~** sprain one's ankle.

Verrenkung *f* contortion; *(Med)* dislocation, sprain.

ver'richten *vt* do, perform.

verriegeln [fɛr'riːɡəln] *vt* bolt up, lock.

verringern [fɛr'rɪŋərn] *vt* reduce; *vr* diminish.

Verringerung *f* reduction; lessening.

ver'rinnen *vi irreg* run out or away; *(Zeit)* elapse.

ver'rosten *vi* rust.

verrotten [fɛr'rɔtən] *vi* rot.

ver'rücken *vt* move, shift.

verrückt [fɛr'rʏkt] *a* crazy, mad; **V~e(r)** *mf* lunatic; **V~heit** *f* madness, lunacy.

Verruf [fɛr'ruːf] *m*: **in ~ geraten/bringen** fall/bring into disrepute; **v~en** *a* notorious, disreputable.

Vers [fɛrs] *m* **-es, -e** verse.

ver'sagen *vt*: **jdm/sich** *(dat)* **etw ~** deny sb/o.s. sth; *vi* fail; **V~ nt -s** failure.

Versager [fɛr'zaːɡər] *m* **-s**, - failure.

ver'salzen *vt irreg* put too much salt in; *(fig)* spoil.

ver'sammeln *vtr* assemble, gather.

Ver'sammlung *f* meeting, gathering.

Versand [fɛr'zant] *m* **-(e)s** forwarding; dispatch; *(—abteilung)* dispatch department; **~haus** *nt* mail-order firm.

versäumen [fɛr'zɔʏmən] *vt* miss; *(unterlassen)* neglect, fail.

Versäumnis *f* **-, -se** neglect; omission.

ver'schaffen *vt*: **jdm/sich etw ~** get or procure sth for sb/o.s. **verschämt** [fɛr'ʃɛːmt] *a* bashful.

verschandeln [fɛr'ʃandəln] *vt (col)* spoil.

verschanzen [fɛr'ʃantsən] *vr*: **sich hinter etw** *(dat)* **~** dig in behind sth; *(fig)* take refuge behind.

verschärfen [fɛr'ʃɛrfən] *vtr* intensify; *Lage* aggravate.

ver'schätzen *vr* be out in one's reckoning.

ver'schenken *vt* give away.

verscherzen [fɛr'ʃɛrtsən] *vt*: **sich** *(dat)* **etw ~** lose sth, throw away sth.

verscheuchen [fɛr'ʃɔʏçən] *vt* frighten away.

ver'schicken *vt* send off; *Sträfling* transport, deport.

ver'schieben *vt irreg* shift; *(Rail)* shunt; *Termin* postpone; *(Comm)* push.

Ver'schiebung *f* shift, displacement; shunting; postponement.

verschieden [fɛr'ʃiːdən] *a* different; *(pl: mehrere)* various; **sie sind ~ groß** they are of different sizes; **~e** *pl* various people/things *pl*; **~es** *pron* various things *pl*; **etwas V~es** something different; **~artig** *a* various, of different kinds; **zwei so ~artige ...** two such differing ...; **V~heit** *f* difference; **~tlich** *ad* several times.

verschlafen [fɛr'ʃlaːfən] *irreg vt* sleep through; *(fig: versäumen)* miss; *vir* oversleep; *a* sleepy.

Verschlag [fɛr'ʃlaːk] *m* shed; **v~en** [fɛr'ʃlaːgən] *vt irreg* board up; *(Tennis)* hit out of play; *Buchseite* lose; **jdm den Atem v~en** take sb's breath away; **an einen Ort v~en werden** wind up in a place; *a* cunning.

verschlampen [fɛr'ʃlampən] *vi* fall into neglect; *vt* lose, mislay.

verschlechtern [fɛr'ʃlɛçtərn] *vt* make worse; *vr* deteriorate, get worse.

Verschlechterung *f* deterioration.

Verschleierung [fɛr'ʃlaiərʊŋ] *f* veiling; *(fig)* concealment; *(Mil)* screening; **~staktik** *f* smoke-screen tactics *pl.*

Verschleiß [fɛr'ʃlais] *m* **-es, -e** wear and tear; *(Aus)* retail trade; **v~en** *irreg vt* wear out; retail; *vir* wear out.

ver'schleppen *vt* carry off, abduct; *(zeitlich)* drag out, delay.

ver'schleudern *vt* squander; *(Comm)* sell dirt-cheap.

verschließ- [fɛr'ʃliːs] *cpd:* **~bar** *a* lockable; **~en** *irreg vt* close; lock; *vr* **sich einer Sache ~en** close one's mind to sth.

verschlimmern [fɛr'ʃlimərn] *vt* make worse, aggravate; *vr* get worse, deteriorate.

Verschlimmerung *f* deterioration.

verschlingen [fɛr'ʃliŋən] *vt irreg* devour, swallow up; *Fäden* twist.

verschlossen [fɛr'ʃlɔsən] *a* locked; *(fig)* reserved; **V~heit** *f* reserve.

ver'schlucken *vt* swallow; *vr* choke.

Verschluß [fɛr'ʃlʊs] *m* lock; *(von Kleid etc)* fastener; *(Phot)* shutter; *(Stöpsel)* plug; **unter ~ halten** keep under lock and key.

verschlüsseln [fɛr'ʃlʏsəln] *vt* encode.

verschmähen [fɛr'ʃmɛːən] *vt* disdain, scorn.

ver'schmelzen *vti irreg* merge, blend.

ver'schmerzen [fɛr'ʃmɛrtsən] *vt* get over.

verschmutzen [fɛr'ʃmʊtsən] *vt* soil; *Umwelt* pollute.

verschneit [fɛr'ʃnait] *a* snowed up, covered in snow.

verschnüren [fɛr'ʃnyːrən] *vt* tie up.

verschollen [fɛr'ʃɔlən] *a* lost, missing.

ver'schonen *vt* spare *(jdn mit etw* sth sth).

verschönern [fɛr'ʃøːnərn] *vt* decorate; *(verbessern)* improve.

verschränken [fɛr'ʃrɛŋkən] *vt* cross, fold.

ver'schreiben *irreg vt Papier* use up; *(Med)* prescribe; *vr* make a mistake (in writing); **sich einer Sache ~** devote oneself to sth.

verschrien [fɛr'ʃriːən] *a* notorious.

verschroben [fɛr'ʃroːbən] *a* eccentric, odd.

verschrotten [fɛr'ʃrɔtən] *vt* scrap.

verschüchtert [fɛr'ʃʏçtərt] *a* subdued, intimidated.

verschuld- [fɛr'ʃʊld] *cpd:* **~en** *vt* be guilty of; **V~en** *nt* **-s** fault, guilt; **~et** *a* in debt; **V~ung** *f* fault; *(Geld)* debts *pl.*

ver'schütten *vt* spill; *(zuschütten)* fill; *(unter Trümmer)* bury.

ver'schweigen *vt irreg* keep secret; **jdm etw ~** keep sth from sb.

verschwend- [fɛr'ʃvɛnd] *cpd:* **~en** *vt* squander; **V~er** *m* **-s, -** spendthrift; **~erisch** *a* wasteful, extravagant; **V~ung** *f* waste; extravagance.

verschwiegen [fɛr'ʃviːgən] *a* discreet; *Ort* secluded; **V~heit** *f* discretion; seclusion.

ver'schwimmen *vi irreg* grow hazy, become blurred.

ver'schwinden *vi irreg* disappear, vanish; **V~** *nt* **-s** disappearance.

ver'schwitzen *vt* stain with sweat; *(col)* forget.

verschwommen [fɛr'ʃvɔmən] *a* hazy, vague.

verschwör- [fɛr'ʃvøːr] *cpd:* **~en** *vr irreg* plot, conspire; **V~er** *m* **-s, -** conspirator; **V~ung** *f* conspiracy, plot.

ver'sehen *irreg vt* supply, provide; *Pflicht* carry out; *Amt* fill; *Haushalt* keep; *vr (fig)* make a mistake; **ehe er (es) sich ~ hatte ... before he knew it ...**; **V~** *nt* **-s, -** oversight; **aus V~** by mistake; **~tlich** *ad* by mistake.

Versehrte(r) [fɛr'zeːrtə(r)] *mf* disabled person.

ver'senden *vt irreg* forward, dispatch.

ver'senken *vt* sink; *vr* become engrossed *(in +acc* in).

versessen [fɛr'zɛsən] *a:* **~ auf** *(+acc)* mad about.

ver'setzen *vt* transfer; *(verpfänden)* pawn; *(col)* stand up; **jdm einen Tritt/Schlag ~** kick/hit sb; **etw mit etw ~** mix sth with sth; **jdn in gute Laune ~** put sb in a good mood; *vr:* **sich in jdn** *or* **in jds Lage ~** put o.s. in sb's place.

Ver'setzung *f* transfer.

verseuchen [fɛr'zɔyçən] *vt* contaminate.

versichern [fɛr'ziçərn] *vt* assure; *(mit Geld)* insure; *vr* **sich ~** *(+gen)* make sure of.

Versicherung *f* assurance; insurance; **~spolice** *f* insurance policy.

versiegeln [fɛr'ziːgəln] *vt* seal (up).

ver'siegen *vi* dry up.

ver'sinken *vi irreg* sink.

versöhnen [fɛr'zøːnən] *vt* reconcile; *vr* become reconciled.

Versöhnung *f* reconciliation.

ver'sorgen *vt* provide, supply *(mit* with); *Familie etc* look after; *vr* look after o.s.

Ver'sorgung *f* provision; *(Unterhalt)* maintenance; *(Alters- etc)* benefit, assistance.

verspäten [fɛr'ʃpɛːtən] *vr* be late.

Verspätung *f* delay; **~ haben** be late.

ver'sperren *vt* bar, obstruct.

Ver'sperrung *f* barrier.

ver'spielen *vti* lose.

verspielt [fɛr'ʃpiːlt] *a* playful; **bei jdm ~ haben** be in sb's bad books.

ver'spotten *vt* ridicule, scoff at.

ver'sprechen *irreg vt* promise; **sich** *(dat)* **etw von etw ~** expect sth from sth; **V~** *nt* **-s, -** promise.

verstaatlichen [fɛr'ʃtaːtlɪçən] *vt* nationalize.

Verstand [fɛr'ʃtant] *m* intelligence; mind; **den ~ verlieren** go out of one's mind; **über jds ~ gehen** go beyond sb; **v~esmäßig** *a* rational; intellectual.

verständig [fɛr'ʃtɛndɪç] *a* sensible; **~en** [fɛr'ʃtɛndɪgən] *vt* inform; *vr* communicate; *(sich einigen)* come to an understanding; **V~keit** *f* good sense; **V~ung** *f* communication; *(Benachrichtigung)* informing; *(Einigung)* agreement.

verständ- [fɛr'ʃtɛnt] *cpd:* **~lich** *a* understandable, comprehensible; **V~lichkeit** *f* clarity, intelligibility; **V~nis** *nt* **-ses, -se** understanding; **~nislos** *a* uncomprehending; **~nisvoll** *a* understanding, sympathetic.

verstärk- [fɛr'ʃtɛrk] *cpd:* **~en** *vt* strengthen; *Ton* amplify; *(erhöhen)* intensify; *vr* intensify; **V~er** *m* **-s, -** amplifier; **V~ung** *f* strengthening; *(Hilfe)* reinforcements *pl*; *(von Ton)* amplification.

verstauchen [fɛr'ʃtauxən] *vt* sprain.

verstauen [fɛr'ʃtauən] *vt* stow away.

Versteck [fɛr'ʃtɛk] *nt* **-(e)s, -e** hiding (place); *vr* **~en** *vtr* hide; **~spiel** *nt* hide-and-seek; **v~t** *a* hidden.

ver'stehen *irreg vt* understand; *vr* get on.

versteifen [fɛr'ʃtaifən] *vt* stiffen, brace; *vr (fig)* insist *(auf +acc* on).

versteigern [fɛr'ʃtaigərn] *vt* auction.

Versteigerung *f* auction.

verstell- [fɛr'ʃtɛl] *cpd:* **~bar** *a* adjustable, variable; **~en** *vt* move, shift; *Uhr* adjust; *(versperren)* block; *(fig)* disguise; *vr* pretend, put on an act; **V~ung** *f* pretence.

verstiegen [fɛr'ʃtiːgən] *a* exaggerated.

verstimmt [fɛr'ʃtɪmt] *a* out of tune; *(fig)* cross, put out.

verstockt [fɛr'ʃtɔkt] *a* stubborn; **V~heit** *f* stubbornness.

verstohlen [fɛr'ʃtoːlən] *a* stealthy.

ver'stopfen *vt* block, stop up; *(Med)* constipate.

Ver'stopfung *f* obstruction; *(Med)* constipation.

verstorben [fɛr'ʃtɔrbən] *a* deceased, late.

verstört [fɛr'ʃtøːrt] *a Mensch* distraught.

Verstoß [fɛr'ʃtoːs] *m* infringement, violation *(gegen* of); **v~en** *irreg vt* disown, reject; *vi:* **v~en gegen** offend against.

ver'streichen *irreg vt* spread; *vi* elapse.

ver'streuen *vt* scatter (about).

ver'stricken *vt (fig)* entangle, ensnare; *vr* get entangled *(in +acc* in).

verstümmeln [fɛr'ʃtyməln] *vt* maim, mutilate *(auch fig)*.

verstummen [fɛr'ʃtumən] *vi* go silent; *(Lärm)* die away.

Versuch [fɛr'zuːx] *m* **-(e)s, -e** attempt; *(Sci)* experiment; **v~en** *vt* try; *(verlocken)* tempt; *vr:* **sich an etw** *(dat)* **v~en** try one's hand at sth; **~skaninchen** *nt* guinea-pig; **v~sweise** *ad* tentatively; **~ung** *f* temptation.

versunken [fɛr'zʊŋkən] *a* sunken; **~ sein in** *(+acc)* be absorbed or engrossed in.

versüßen [fɛr'zyːsən] *vt:* **jdm etw ~** *(fig)* make sth more pleasant for sb.

vertagen [fɛr'taːgən] *vti* adjourn.

Vertagung *f* adjournment.

ver'tauschen *vt* exchange; *(versehentlich)* mix up.

verteidig- [fɛr'taidɪg] *cpd:* **~en** *vt* defend; **V~er** *m* **-s, -** defender; *(Jur)* defence counsel; **V~ung** *f* defence.

ver'teilen *vt* distribute; *Rollen* assign; *Salbe* spread.

Verteilung *f* distribution, allotment.

verteufelt [fɛr'tɔyfəlt] *a,ad (col)* awful(ly), devilish(ly).

vertiefen [fɛr'tiːfən] *vt* deepen; *vr:* **sich in etw** *(acc)* **~** become engrossed or absorbed in sth.

Vertiefung *f* depression.

vertikal [vɛrti'kaːl] *a* vertical.

vertilgen [fɛr'tɪlgən] *vt* exterminate; *(col)* eat up, consume.

vertippen [fɛr'tɪpən] *vr* make a typing mistake.

vertonen [fɛr'toːnən] *vt* set to music.

Vertrag [fɛr'traːk] *m* **-(e)s, ²e** contract, agreement; *(Pol)* treaty; **v~en** [fɛr'traːgən] *irreg vt* tolerate, stand; *vr* get along; *(sich aussöhnen)* become reconciled; **v~lich** *a* contractual.

verträglich [fɛr'trɛːklɪç] *a* good-natured, sociable; *Speisen* easily digested; *(Med)* easily tolerated; **V~keit** *f* sociability; good nature; digestibility.

Vertrags- *cpd:* **~bruch** *m* breach of contract; **v~brüchig** *a* in breach of contract; **v~mäßig** *a,ad* stipulated, according to contract; **~partner** *m* party to a contract; **~spieler** *m* *(Sport)* contract professional; **v~widrig** *a* contrary to contract.

vertrauen [fɛr'trauən] *vi* trust *(jdm* sb); **~ auf** *(+acc)* rely on; **V~** *nt* **-s** confidence; **~erweckend** *a* inspiring trust; **~sselig** *a* too trustful; **~svoll** *a* trustful; **~swürdig** *a* trustworthy.

vertraulich [fɛr'traulɪç] *a* familiar; *(geheim)* confidential; **V~keit** *f* familiarity; confidentiality.

vertraut [fɛr'traut] *a* familiar; **V~e(r)** *mf* confidant, close friend; **V~heit** *f* familiarity.

ver'treiben *vt irreg* drive away; *(aus Land)* expel; *(Comm)* sell; *Zeit* pass.

Ver'treibung *f* expulsion.

vertret- [fɛr'treːt] *cpd:* **~en** *vt irreg* represent; *Ansicht* hold, advocate; **sich** *(dat)* **die Beine ~en** stretch one's legs; **V~er** *m* **-s, -** representative; *(Verfechter)* advocate; **V~ung** *f* representation; advocacy.

Vertrieb [fɛr'triːp] *m* **-(e)s, -e** marketing.

ver'trocknen *vi* dry up.

ver'trödeln *vt (col)* fritter away.

ver'trösten *vt* put off.

vertun [fɛr'tuːn] *irreg vt (col)* waste; *vr* make a mistake.

vertuschen [fɛr'tuʃən] *vt* hush or cover up.

verübeln [fɛr'yːbəln] *vt:* **jdm etw ~** be cross or offended with sb on account of sth.

verüben [fɛr'yːbən] *vt* commit.

verun- [fɛr'ʊn] *cpd:* **~glimpfen**

[-glɪmpfən] vt disparage; ~**glücken** [-glʏkən] vi have an accident; **tödlich** ~**glücken** be killed in an accident; ~**reinigen** vt soil; Umwelt pollute; ~**sichern** vt rattle; ~**stalten** [-ʃtaltən] vt disfigure; Gebäude etc deface; ~**treuen** [-trɔyən] vt embezzle.

verur- [fɛr'uːr] cpd: ~**sachen** [-zaxən] vt cause; ~**teilen** [-taɪlən] vt condemn; **V~teilung** f condemnation; (Jur) sentence.

verviel- [fɛr'fiːl] cpd: ~**fachen** [-faxən] vt multiply; ~**fältigen** [—fɛltɪgən] vt duplicate, copy; **V~fältigung** f duplication, copying.

vervoll- [fɛr'fɔl] cpd: ~**kommnen** [-kɔmnən] vt perfect; ~**ständigen** [-ʃtɛndɪgən] vt complete.

ver'wackeln vt Photo blur.

ver'wählen vr (Tel) dial the wrong number.

verwahr- [fɛr'vaːr] ~**en** vt keep, lock away; vr protest; ~**losen** [-loːzən] vi become neglected; (moralisch) go to the bad; ~**lost** [-loːst] a neglected; wayward.

verwaist [fɛr'vaɪst] a orphaned.

verwalt- [fɛr'valt] cpd: ~**en** vt manage; administer; **V~er** m -s, - manager; (Vermögens—) trustee; **V~ung** f administration; management; **V~ungsbezirk** m administrative district.

ver'wandeln vtr change, transform.

Ver'wandlung f change, transformation.

verwandt [fɛr'vant] a related (mit to); **V~e(r)** mf relative, relation; **V~schaft** f relationship; (Menschen) relations pl.

ver'warnen vt caution.

Ver'warnung f caution.

ver'waschen a faded; (fig) vague.

verwässern [fɛr'vɛsərn] vt dilute, water down.

ver'wechseln vt confuse (mit with); mistake (mit for); **zum V~ ähnlich** as like as two peas.

Ver'wechslung f confusion, mixing up.

verwegen [fɛr'veːgən] a daring, bold; **V~heit** f daring, audacity, boldness.

Verwehung [fɛr'veːʊŋ] f snow-/ sanddrift.

verweichlich- [fɛr'vaɪçlɪç] cpd: ~**en** vt mollycoddle; ~**t** a effeminate, soft.

ver'weigern vt refuse (jdm etw sb sth); **den Gehorsam/die Aussage ~ refuse** to obey/testify.

Ver'weigerung f refusal.

verweilen [fɛr'vaɪlən] vi stay; (fig) dwell (bei on).

Verweis [fɛr'vaɪs] m -es, -e reprimand, rebuke; (Hinweis) reference; **v~en** [fɛr'vaɪzən] vt irreg refer; **jdm etw v~en** (tadeln) scold sb for sth; **jdn von der Schule v~en** expel sb (from school); **jdn des Landes v~en** deport or expel sb; ~**ung** f reference; (Tadel) reprimand; (Landes—) deportation.

ver'welken vi fade.

ver'wenden irreg vi use; Mühe, Zeit, Arbeit spend; vr intercede.

Ver'wendung f use.

ver'werfen vt irreg reject.

verwerflich [fɛr'vɛrflɪç] a reprehensible.

ver'werten vt utilize.

Ver'wertung f utilization.

verwesen [fɛr've:zən] vi decay.

Verwesung f decomposition.

ver'wickeln vt tangle (up); (fig) involve (in +acc in); vr get tangled (up); **sich ~ in** (+acc) (fig) get involved in.

Verwicklung f complication, entanglement.

verwildern [fɛr'vɪldərn] vi run wild.

ver'winden vt irreg get over.

verwirklichen [fɛr'vɪrklɪçən] vt realize, put into effect.

Verwirklichung f realization.

verwirren [fɛr'vɪrən] vt tangle (up); (fig) confuse.

Verwirrung f confusion.

verwittern [fɛr'vɪtərn] vi weather.

verwitwet [fɛr'vɪtvət] a widowed.

verwöhnen [fɛr'vøːnən] vt spoil.

Verwöhnung f spoiling, pampering.

verworfen [fɛr'vɔrfən] a depraved; **V~heit** f depravity.

verworren [fɛr'vɔrən] a confused.

verwund- cpd ~**bar** [fɛr'vʊntbaːr] a vulnerable; ~**en** [fɛr'vʊndən] vt wound; ~**erlich** [fɛr'vʊndərlɪç] a surprising; **V~erung** [fɛr'vʊndərʊŋ] f astonishment; **V~ete(r)** mf injured (person); **V~ung** f wound, injury.

ver'wünschen vt curse.

verwüsten [fɛr'vy:stən] vt devastate.

Verwüstung f devastation.

verzagen [fɛr'tsaːgən] vi despair.

ver'zählen vr miscount.

verzehren [fɛr'tseːrən] vt consume.

ver'zeichnen vt list; Niederlage, Verlust register.

Verzeichnis [fɛr'tsaɪçnɪs] nt **-ses, -se** list, catalogue; (in Buch) index.

verzeih- [fɛr'tsaɪ] cpd: ~**en** vti irreg forgive (jdm etw sb for sth); ~**lich** a pardonable; **V~ung** f forgiveness, pardon; **V~ung!** sorry!, excuse me!

ver'zerren vt distort.

Verzicht [fɛr'tsɪçt] m -(e)s, -e renunciation (auf +acc of); **v~en** vi forgo, give up (auf etw (acc) sth).

ver'ziehen irreg vi move; vt put out of shape; Kind spoil; Pflanzen thin out; **das Gesicht ~** pull a face; vr go out of shape; (Gesicht) contort; (verschwinden) disappear.

verzieren [fɛr'tsiːrən] vt decorate, ornament.

verzinsen [fɛr'tsɪnzən] vt pay interest on.

ver'zögern vt delay.

Ver'zögerung f delay, time-lag; ~**staktik** f delaying tactics pl.

verzollen [fɛr'tsɔlən] vt declare, pay duty on.

verzück- [fɛr'tsʏk] cpd: ~**en** vt send into ecstasies, enrapture; ~**t** a enraptured; **V~ung** f ecstasy.

verzweif- [fɛr'tsvaɪf] cpd: ~**eln** vi despair; ~**elt** a desperate; **V~lung** f despair.

verzweigen [fɛr'tsvaɪgən] vr branch out.

verzwickt [fɛr'tsvɪkt] a (col) awkward, complicated.

Veto ['ve:to] nt -s, -s veto.

Vetter ['fɛtər] m -s, -n cousin; ~**wirtschaft** f nepotism.

vibrieren [vi'bri:rən] vi vibrate.

Vieh [fi:] nt -(e)s cattle pl; v~**isch** a bestial.

viel [fi:l] a a lot of, much; ~**e** pl a lot of, many; ad a lot, much; ~ **zuwenig** much too little; ~**erlei** a a great variety of; ~**es** a a lot; ~**fach** a,ad many times; auf ~**fachen Wunsch** at the request of many people; V~**falt** f- variety; ~**fältig** a varied, many-sided.

vielleicht [fi'laɪçt] ad perhaps.

viel- cpd: ~**mal(s)** ad many times; **danke** ~**mals** many thanks; ~**mehr** ad rather, on the contrary; ~**sagend** a significant; ~**seitig** a many-sided; ~**versprechend** a promising.

vier [fi:r] num four; V~**eck** nt -(e)s, -e four-sided figure; (gleichseitig) square; ~**eckig** a four-sided; square; V~**takt-motor** m four-stroke engine; ~**te(r,s)** ['fi:rtə(r,z)] a fourth; ~**teilen** vt quarter; V~**tel** ['fɪrtəl] nt -s, - quarter; ~**teljährlich** a quarterly; V~**einote** f crotchet; V~**elstunde** f [fɪrtəl'ʃtundə] f quarter of an hour; ~**zehn** ['fɪrtse:n] num fourteen; **in** ~**zehn Tagen** in a fortnight; ~**zehntägig** a fortnightly; ~**zig** ['fɪrtsɪç] num forty.

Vikar [vi'ka:r] m -s, -e curate.

Villa ['vɪla] f-, **Villen** villa.

Villenviertel ['vɪlənfɪrtəl] nt (prosperous) residential area.

violett [vio'lɛt] a violet.

Violin- [vio'li:n] cpd: ~**bogen** m violin bow; ~**e** f -, -n violin; ~**konzert** nt violin concerto; ~**schlüssel** m treble clef.

Virus ['vi:rʊs] m or nt -, **Viren** virus.

Visier [vi'zi:r] nt -s, -e gunsight; (am Helm) visor.

Visite [vi'zi:tə] f-, -n (Med) visit; ~**nkarte** f visiting card.

visuell [vizu'ɛl] a visual.

Visum ['vi:zum] nt -s, **Visa** or **Visen** visa.

vital [vi'ta:l] a lively, full of life, vital.

Vitamin [vita'mi:n] nt -s, -e vitamin.

Vogel ['fo:gəl] m -s, ̈ - bird; **einen** ~ **haben** (col) have bats in the belfry; **jdm den** ~ **zeigen** (col) tap one's forehead (to indicate that one thinks sb stupid); ~**bauer** nt birdcage; ~**beerbaum** m rowan tree; ~**schau** f bird's-eye view; ~**scheuche** f -, -n scarecrow.

Vokab- cpd: ~**el** [vo'ka:bəl] f -, -n word; ~**ular** [vokabu'la:r] nt -s, -e vocabulary.

Vokal [vo'ka:l] m -s, -e vowel.

Volk [fɔlk] nt -(e)s, ̈ -er people; nation.

Völker- ['fœlkər] cpd: ~**bund** m League of Nations; ~**recht** nt international law; v~**rechtlich** a according to international law; ~**verständigung** f international understanding; ~**wanderung** f migration.

Volks- cpd: ~**abstimmung** f referendum; ~**hochschule** f adult education classes pl; ~**lied** nt folksong; ~**republik** f

people's republic; ~**schule** f elementary school; ~**tanz** m folk dance; v~**tümlich** ['fɔlksty:mlɪç] a popular; ~**wirtschaft** f economics.

voll [fɔl] a full; ~ **und ganz** completely; **jdn für** ~ **nehmen** (col) take sb seriously; ~ **auf** [fɔl'aʊf] ad amply; ~**blütig** a full-blooded; ~'**bringen** vt irreg insep accomplish; ~'**enden** vt insep finish, complete; ~**ends** ['fɔlɛnts] ad completely; V~'**endung** f completion; ~**er** a fuller; (+gen) full of; V~**eyball** ['vɔlibal] m volleyball; V~**gas** nt: **mit** V~**gas** at full throttle; ~**gas geben** step on it.

völlig ['fœlɪç] a,ad complete(ly).

voll- cpd: ~**jährig** a of age; V~**kaskoversicherung** f fully comprehensive insurance; ~'**kommen** a perfect; V~'**kommenheit** f perfection; V~**kornbrot** nt wholemeal bread; ~**machen** vt fill (up); V~**macht** f -, -en authority, full powers pl; V~**mond** m full moon; V~**pension** f full board; ~**ständig** a complete; ~'**strecken** vt insep execute; ~**tanken** vti fill up; ~**zählig** a complete; in full number; ~'**ziehen** vt irreg insep carry out; vr happen; V~'**zug** m execution.

Volt [vɔlt] nt - or -(e)s, - volt.

Volumen [vo'lu:mən] nt -s, - or **Volumina** volume.

vom [fɔm] = **von dem**.

von [fɔn] prep +dat from; (statt Genitiv, bestehend aus) of; (im Passiv) by; **ein Freund** ~ **mir** a friend of mine; ~ **mir aus** (col) OK by me; ~ **wegen** no way!; ~**einander** ad from each other; ~**statten** [fɔn'ʃtatən] ad: ~**statten gehen** proceed, go.

vor [fo:r] prep +dat or acc before; (räumlich) in front of; ~ **Wut/Liebe** with rage/love; ~ **2 Tagen** 2 days ago; ~ **allem** above all; V~**abend** m evening before, eve.

voran [fo'ran] ad before, ahead; ~**gehen** vi irreg go ahead; **einer Sache** (dat) ~**gehen** precede sth; ~**gehend** a previous; ~**kommen** vi irreg come along, make progress.

Vor- ['fo:r] cpd: ~**anschlag** m estimate; ~**arbeiter** m foreman.

voraus [fo'raʊs] ad ahead; (zeitlich) in advance; **jdm** ~ **sein** be ahead of sb; **im** ~ in advance; ~**bezahlen** vt pay in advance; ~**gehen** vi irreg go (on) ahead; (fig) precede; ~**haben** vt irreg: **jdm etw** ~**haben** have the edge on sb in sth; V~**sage** f -, -n prediction; ~**sagen** vt predict; ~**sehen** vt irreg foresee; ~**setzen** vt assume; ~**gesetzt, daß ... provided that ...; ~**setzung** f requirement, prerequisite; V~**sicht** f foresight; **aller** V~**sicht nach** in all probability; **in der** V~**sicht, daß ... anticipating that ...; ~**sichtlich** ad probably.

vorbauen ['fo:rbaʊən] vt build up in front; vi take precautions (dat against).

Vorbehalt ['fo:rbəhalt] m -(e)s, -e reservation, proviso; v~**en** vt irreg:

sich/jdm etw v~en reserve sth (to o.s.)/to sb; v~ los a,ad unconditional(ly).

vorbei [fɔr'baɪ] ad by, past; ~**gehen** vi irreg pass by, go past.

vorbe- cpd: ~**lastet** ['fo:rbəlastət] a (fig) handicapped; ~**reiten** ['fo:rbəraɪtən] vt prepare; **V~reitung** f preparation; ~**straft** ['fo:rbəʃtraft] a previously convicted, with a record.

vorbeugen ['fo:rbɔʏgən] vtr lean forward; vi prevent (einer Sache (dat) sth); ~**d** a preventive.

Vorbeugung f prevention; **zur ~ gegen** for the prevention of.

Vorbild ['fo:rbɪlt] nt model; **sich** (dat) **jdn zum ~ nehmen** model o.s. on sb; **v~lich** a model, ideal.

vorbringen ['fo:rbrɪŋən] vt irreg advance, state; (col: nach vorne) bring to the front.

Vorder- ['fɔrdər] cpd: ~**achse** f front axle; ~**ansicht** f front view; **v~e(r,s)** a front; ~**grund** m foreground; **v~hand** ad for the present; ~**mann** m, pl -**männer** man in front; **jdn auf ~mann bringen** (col) tell sb to pull his socks up; ~**seite** f front (side); **v~ste(r,s)** a front.

vordrängen ['fo:rdrɛŋən] vt push to the front.

vorehelich ['fo:r'e:əlɪç] a premarital.

voreilig ['fo:r'aɪlɪç] a hasty, rash.

voreingenommen ['fo:r'aɪngənɔmən] a biased; **V~heit** f bias.

vorenthalten ['fo:r'ɛnthaltən] vt irreg: **jdm etw ~** withhold sth from sb.

vorerst [fo:r'e:rst] ad for the moment or present.

Vorfahr ['fo:rfa:r] m -en, -en ancestor; **v~en** vi irreg drive (on) ahead; (vors Haus etc) drive up; ~**t** f (Aut) right of way; ~**t achten!** give way!; ~**tsregel** f right of way; ~**tsschild** nt give way sign.

Vorfall ['fo:rfal] m incident; **v~en** vi irreg occur.

vorfinden ['fo:rfɪndən] vt irreg find.

vorführen ['fo:rfy:rən] vt show, display; **dem Gericht ~** bring before the court.

Vorgabe ['fo:rga:bə] f (Sport) start, handicap.

Vorgang ['fo:rgaŋ] m course of events; (esp Sci) process; **der ~ von etw** how sth happens.

Vorgänger(in f) ['fo:rgɛŋər(ɪn)] m -s, - predecessor.

vorgeben ['fo:rge:bən] vt irreg pretend, use as a pretext; (Sport) give an advantage or a start of.

vorge- ['fo:rgə] cpd: ~**faßt** [-fast] a preconceived; ~**fertigt** [-fɛrtɪçt] a prefabricated; **V~fühl** [-fy:l] nt presentiment, anticipation.

vorgehen ['fo:rge:ən] vi irreg (voraus) go (on) ahead; (nach vorn) go up front; (handeln) act, proceed; (Uhr) be fast; (Vorrang haben) take precedence; (passieren) go on; ~ nt -s, - action.

Vorgeschmack ['fo:rgəʃmak] m foretaste.

Vorgesetzte(r) ['fo:rgəzɛtstə(r)] mf superior.

vorgestern ['fo:rgɛstərn] ad the day before yesterday.

vorgreifen ['fo:rgraɪfən] vi irreg anticipate, forestall.

vorhaben ['fo:rha:bən] vt irreg intend; **hast du schon was vor?** have you got anything on?; **V~** nt -s, - intention.

vorhalten ['fo:rhaltən] irreg vt hold or put up; (fig) reproach (jdm etw sb for sth); vi last.

Vorhaltung f reproach.

vorhanden [fo:r'handən] a existing, extant; (erhältlich) available; **V~sein** nt -s existence, presence.

Vorhang ['fo:rhaŋ] m curtain.

Vorhängeschloß ['fo:rhɛŋəʃlɔs] nt padlock.

Vorhaut ['fo:rhaut] f (Med) foreskin.

vorher [fo:r'he:r] ad before(hand); ~**bestimmen** vt Schicksal preordain; ~**gehen** vi irreg precede; ~**ig** [fo:r'he:rɪç] a previous.

Vorherrschaft ['fo:rhɛrʃaft] f predominance, supremacy.

vorherrschen ['fo:rhɛrʃən] vi predominate.

vorher- [fo:r'he:r] cpd: **V~sage** f -, -n forecast; ~**sagen** vt forecast, predict; ~**sehbar** a predictable; ~**sehen** vt irreg foresee.

vorhin [fo:r'hɪn] ad not long ago, just now; ~**ein** ['fo:rhɪnaɪn] ad: **im ~ein** beforehand.

vorig ['fo:rɪç] a previous, last.

vorjährig ['fo:rjɛ:rɪç] a of the previous year; last year's.

Vorkehrung ['fo:rke:ruŋ] f precaution.

vorkommen ['fo:rkɔmən] vi irreg come forward; (geschehen, sich finden) occur; (scheinen) seem (to be); **sich** (dat) **dumm** etc ~ feel stupid etc; **V~** nt -s, - occurrence.

Vorkommnis ['fo:rkɔmnɪs] nt -ses, -se occurrence.

Vorkriegs- ['fo:rkri:ks] in cpds prewar.

Vorladung ['fo:rla:duŋ] f summons.

Vorlage ['fo:rla:gə] f model, pattern; (Gesetzes~) bill; (Sport) pass.

vorlassen ['fo:rlasən] vt irreg admit; (vorgehen lassen) allow to go in front.

vorläufig ['fo:rlɔʏfɪç] a temporary, provisional.

vorlaut ['fo:rlaut] a impertinent, cheeky.

Vorleg- ['fo:rle:g] cpd: **v~en** vt put in front; (fig) produce, submit; **jdm etw v~en** put sth before sb; ~**er** m -s, - mat.

vorlesen ['fo:rle:zən] vt irreg read (out).

Vorlesung f (Univ) lecture.

vorletzte(r, s) ['fo:rlɛtstə(r,s)] a last but one.

Vorliebe ['fo:rli:bə] f preference, partiality.

vorliebnehmen [fo:r'li:pne:mən] vi irreg: ~ **mit** make do with.

vorliegen ['fo:rli:gən] vi irreg be (here); **etw liegt jdm vor** sb has sth; ~**d** a present, at issue.

vormachen ['fo:rmaxən] vt: **jdm etw ~** show sb how to do sth; (fig) fool sb; have sb on.

Vormachtstellung ['fo:rmaxtʃtcluŋ] *f* supremacy, hegemony.

Vormarsch ['fo:rmarʃ] *m* advance.

vormerken ['fo:rmɛrkən] *vt* book.

Vormittag ['fo:rmɪta:k] *m* morning; **v~s** *ad* in the morning, before noon.

Vormund ['fo:rmunt] *m* -(e)s, -e or -münder guardian.

vorn(e) ['fɔrn(ə)] *ad* in front; **von ~ anfangen** start at the beginning; **nach ~** to the front.

Vorname ['fo:rna:mə] *m* first or Christian name.

vornan [fɔrn''an] *ad* at the front.

vornehm ['fo:rne:m] *a* distinguished; refined; elegant; **~ tun** *vt irreg* (fig) carry out; **sich** (dat) etw **~en** start on sth; (beschließen) decide to do sth; **sich** (dat) **jdn ~en** tell sb off; **~lich** *ad* chiefly, specially.

vornherein ['fɔrnhɛraɪn] *ad:* **von ~** from the start.

Vorort ['fo:r'ɔrt] *m* suburb; **~zug** *m* commuter train.

Vorrang ['fo:rraŋ] *m* precedence, priority; **v~ig** *a* of prime importance, primary.

Vorrat ['fo:rra:t] *m* stock, supply; **~skammer** *f* pantry.

vorrätig ['fo:rrɛ:tɪç] *a* in stock.

Vorrecht ['fo:rrɛçt] *nt* privilege.

Vorrichtung ['fo:rrɪçtuŋ] *f* device, contrivance.

vorrücken ['fo:rrykən] *vi* advance; *vt* move forward.

vorsagen ['fo:rza:gən] *vt* recite, say out loud; (Sch: zuflüstern) tell secretly, prompt.

Vorsatz ['fo:rzats] *m* intention; (Jur) intent; **einen ~ fassen** make a resolution.

vorsätzlich ['fo:rzɛtslɪç] *a,ad* intentional(ly); (Jur) premeditated.

Vorschau ['fo:rʃau] *f* (Rad, TV) (programme) preview; (Film) trailer.

vorschieben ['fo:rʃi:bən] *vt irreg* push forward; (vor etw) push across; (fig) put forward as an excuse; **jdn ~** use sb as a front.

Vorschlag ['fo:rʃla:k] *m* suggestion, proposal; **v~en** *vt irreg* suggest, propose.

vorschnell ['fo:rʃnɛl] *ad* hastily, too quickly.

vorschreiben ['fo:rʃraɪbən] *vt irreg* prescribe, specify.

Vorschrift ['fo:rʃrɪft] *f* regulation(s); rule(s); (Anweisungen) instruction(s); **Dienst nach ~** work-to-rule; **v~smäßig** *a* as per regulations/instructions.

Vorschuß ['fo:rʃus] *m* advance.

vorschweben ['fo:rʃve:bən] *vi:* **jdm schwebt etw vor** sb has sth in mind.

vorsehen ['fo:rze:ən] *irreg vt* provide for, plan; *vr* take care, be careful; *vi* be visible.

Vorsehung *f* providence.

vorsetzen ['fo:rzɛtsən] *vt* move forward; (vor etw) put in front of; (anbieten) offer.

Vorsicht ['fo:rzɪçt] *f* caution, care; **~!** look out!, take care!; (auf Schildern) caution!, danger!; **~, Stufe!** mind the step!; **v~ig** *a* cautious, careful; **v~shalber** *ad* just in case.

Vorsilbe ['fo:rzɪlbə] *f* prefix.

Vorsitz ['fo:rzɪts] *m* chair(manship); **~ende(r)** *mf* chairman/-woman.

Vorsorge ['fo:rzɔrgə] *f* precaution(s), provision(s); **v~n** *vi:* **v~en für** make provision(s) for.

vorsorglich ['fo:rzɔrklɪç] *ad* as a precaution.

Vorspeise ['fo:rʃpaɪzə] *f* hors d'oeuvre, appetizer.

Vorspiel ['fo:rʃpi:l] *nt* prelude.

vorsprechen ['fo:rʃprɛçən] *irreg vt* say out loud, recite; *vi:* **bei jdm ~** call on sb.

Vorsprung ['fo:rʃpruŋ] *m* projecrion, ledge; (fig) advantage, start.

Vorstadt ['fo:rʃtat] *f* suburbs *pl.*

Vorstand ['fo:rʃtant] *m* executive committee; (Comm) board (of directors); (Person) director, head.

vorstehen ['fo:rʃte:ən] *vi irreg* project; etw (dat) **~** (fig) be the head of sth.

vorstell- ['fo:rʃtɛl] *cpd:* **~bar** *a* conceivable; **~en** *vt* put forward; (vor etw) put in front; (bekannt machen) introduce; (darstellen) represent; **sich** (dat) etw **~en** imagine sth; **V~ung** *f* (Bekanntmachen) introduction; (Theat etc) performance; (Gedanke) idea, thought.

Vorstoß ['fo:rʃto:s] *m* advance; **v~en** *vti irreg* push forward.

Vorstrafe ['fo:rʃtra:fə] *f* previous conviction.

vorstrecken [fo:rʃtrɛkən] *vt* stretch out; Geld advance.

Vorstufe ['fo:rʃtu:fə] *f* first step(s).

Vortag ['fo:rtak] *m* day before (einer Sache sth).

vortäuschen ['fo:rtɔyʃən] *vt* feign, pretend.

Vorteil ['fortaɪl] *m* -s, -e advantage (gegenüber over); **im ~ sein** have the advantage; **v~haft** *a* advantageous.

Vortrag ['fo:rtra:k] *m* -(e)s, Vorträge talk, lecture; (~sart) delivery, rendering; (Comm) balance carried forward; **v~en** *vt irreg* carry forward (auch Comm); (fig) recite; Rede deliver; Lied perform; Meinung etc express.

vortrefflich [fo:rtrɛflɪç] *a* excellent.

vortreten [fo:rtre:tən] *vi irreg* step forward; (Augen etc) protrude.

vorüber [fo:ry:bər] *ad* past, over; **~gehen** *vi irreg* pass (by); **~gehen an** (+dat) (fig) pass over; **~gehend** *a* temporary, passing.

Vorurteil ['fo:r'urtaɪl] *nt* prejudice; **v~sfrei, v~slos** *a* unprejudiced, openminded.

Vorverkauf ['fo:rfɛrkauf] *m* advance booking.

Vorwahl ['fo:rva:l] *f* preliminary election; (Tel) dialling code.

Vorwand ['fo:rvant] *m* -(e)s, Vorwände pretext.

vorwärts ['fo:rvɛrts] *ad* forward; **V~gang** *m* (Aut etc) forward gear; **~gehen** *vi irreg* progress; **~kommen** *vi irreg* get on, make progress.

vorweg [fo:rvɛk] *ad* in advance; **V~nahme** *f* -, -n anticipation;

~**nehmen** *vt irreg* anticipate.
vorweisen ['fo:rvaɪzən] *vt irreg* show, produce.
vorwerfen ['fo:rverfən] *vt irreg*: **jdm etw** ~ reproach sb for sth, accuse sb of sth; **sich** (*dat*) **nichts vorzuwerfen haben** have nothing to reproach o.s. with.
vorwiegend ['fo:rvi:gənt] *a,ad* predominant(ly).
Vorwitz ['fo:rvɪts] *m* cheek; **v~ig** *a* saucy, cheeky.
Vorwort ['fo:rvɔrt] *nt* -(e)s, -e preface.
Vorwurf ['fo:rvʊrf] *m* reproach; **jdm/sich Vorwürfe machen** reproach sb/o.s.; **v~svoll** *a* reproachful.
vorzeigen ['fo:rtsaɪgən] *vt* show, produce.
vorzeitig ['fo:rtsaɪtɪç] *a* premature.
vorziehen ['fo:rtsi:ən] *vt irreg* pull forward; *Gardinen* draw; (*lieber haben*) prefer.
Vorzug ['fo:rtsu:k] *m* preference; (*gute Eigenschaft*) merit, good quality; (*Vorteil*) advantage; (*Rail*) relief train.
vorzüglich [fo:r'tsy:klɪç] *a* excellent, first-rate.
vulgär [vʊl'gɛ:r] *a* vulgar.
Vulkan [vʊl'ka:n] *m* -s, -e volcano; **v~i-'sieren** *vt* vulcanize.

W

W, w [ve:] *nt* W, w.
Waage ['va:gə] *f* -, -n scales *pl*; (*Astrol*) Libra; **w~recht** *a* horizontal.
wabb(e)lig ['vab(ə)lɪç] *a* wobbly.
Wabe ['va:bə] *f*-, -n honeycomb.
wach [vax] *a* awake; (*fig*) alert; **W~e** *f* -, -n guard, watch; **W~e halten** keep watch; **W~e stehen** stand guard; **~en** *vi* be awake; (*W~e halten*) guard.
Wacholder [va'xɔldər] *m* -s, - juniper.
Wachs [vaks] *nt* -es, -e wax.
wachsam ['vaxza:m] *a* watchful, vigilant, alert; **W~keit** *f* vigilance.
Wachs- *cpd*: **w~en** *vi irreg* grow; *vt Skier* wax; **~tuch** *nt* oilcloth; **~tum** *nt* -s growth.
Wächter ['veçtər] *m* -s, - guard, warder, keeper; (*Parkplatz~*) attendant.
Wacht- [vaxt] *cpd*: **~meister** *m* officer; **~posten** *m* guard, sentry.
wackel- ['vakəl] *cpd*: **~ig** *a* shaky, wobbly; **W~kontakt** *m* loose connection; **~n** *vi* shake; (*fig: Position*) be shaky.
wacker ['vakər] *a* valiant, stout; *ad* well, bravely.
Wade ['va:də] *f*-, -n (*Anat*) calf.
Waffe ['vafə] *f* -, -n weapon; **~l** *f* -, -n waffle; wafer; **~nschein** *m* gun licence; **~nstillstand** *m* armistice, truce.
Wagemut ['va:gəmu:t] *m* daring.
wagen ['va:gən] *vt* venture, dare.
Wagen ['va:gən] *m* -s, - vehicle; (*Auto*) car; (*Rail*) carriage; (*Pferde~*) cart; **~führer** *m* driver; **~heber** *m* -s, - jack.
Waggon [va'gõ:] *m* -s, -s carriage; (*Güter~*) goods van, freight truck (*US*).
waghalsig ['va:khalzɪç] *a* foolhardy.
Wagnis ['va:knɪs] *nt* -ses, -se risk.
Wahl ['va:l] *f* -, -en choice; (*Pol*) election;

zweite ~ seconds *pl*; **w~berechtigt** *a* entitled to vote.
wähl- ['vɛ:l] *cpd*: **~bar** *a* eligible; **~en** *vti* choose; (*Pol*) elect, vote (for); (*Tel*) dial; **W~er(in** *f*) *m* -s, voter; **~erisch** *a* fastidious, particular; **W~erschaft** *f* electorate.
Wahl- *cpd*: **~fach** *nt* optional subject; **~gang** *m* ballot; **~kabine** *f* polling booth; **~kampf** *m* election campaign; **~kreis** *m* constituency; **~liste** *f* electoral register; **~lokal** *nt* polling station; **w~los** *ad* at random; **~recht** *nt* franchise; **~spruch** *m* motto; **~urne** *f* ballot box.
Wahn [va:n] *m* -(e)s delusion; folly; **~sinn** *m* madness; **w~sinnig** *a* insane, mad; *ad* (*col*) incredibly.
wahr [va:r] *a* true; **~en** *vt* maintain, keep.
während ['vɛ:rən] *vi* last; **~d** *prep* +*gen* during; *cj* while; **~ddessen** [vɛ:rənt'dɛsən] *ad* meanwhile.
wahr- *cpd*: **~haben** *vt irreg*: **etw nicht ~haben wollen** refuse to admit sth; **~haft** *ad* (*tatsächlich*) truly; **~haftig** [va:r'haftɪç] *a* true, real; *ad* really; **W~heit** *f* truth; **~nehmen** *vt irreg* perceive, observe; **W~nehmung** *f* perception; **~sagen** *vi* prophesy, tell fortunes; **W~sager(in** *f*) *m* -s, - fortune teller; **~scheinlich** [va:r'faɪnlɪç] *a* probable; *ad* probably; **W~scheinlichkeit** *f* probability; **aller W~scheinlichkeit nach** in all probabilty; **W~zeichen** *nt* emblem.
Währung ['vɛ:rʊŋ] *f* currency.
Waise ['vaɪzə] *f* -, -n orphan; **~nhaus** *nt* orphanage; **~nkind** *nt* orphan.
Wald [valt] *m* -(e)s, -er wood(s); (*groß*) forest; **w~ig** ['valdɪç] *a* wooded.
Wäldchen ['vɛltçən] *nt* copse, grove.
Wal(fisch) ['va:l(fɪʃ)] *m* -(e)s, -e whale.
Wall [val] *m* -(e)s, -e embankment; (*Bollwerk*) rampart; **w~fahren** *vi irreg* insep go on a pilgrimage; **~fahrer(in** *f*) *m* pilgrim; **~fahrt** *f* pilgrimage.
Wal- ['val] *cpd*: **~nuß** *f* walnut; **~roß** *nt* walrus.
Walze ['valtsə] *f* -, -n (*Gerät*) cylinder; (*Fahrzeug*) roller; **w~n** *vt* roll (out).
wälzen ['vɛltsən] *vt* roll (over); *Bücher* hunt through; *Probleme* deliberate on; *vr* wallow; (*vor Schmerzen*) roll about; (*im Bett*) toss and turn.
Walzer ['valtsər] *m* -s, - waltz.
Wälzer ['vɛltsər] *m* -s, - (*col*) tome.
Wand [vant] *f* -, -e wall; (*Trenn~*) partition; (*Berg~*) precipice.
Wandel ['vandəl] *m* -s change; **w~bar** *a* changeable, variable; **w~n** *vtr* change; *vi* (*gehen*) walk.
Wander- ['vandər] *cpd*: **~bühne** *f* travelling theatre; **~er** *m* -s, - hiker, rambler; **w~n** *vi* hike; (*Blick*) wander; (*Gedanken*) stray; **~preis** *m* challenge trophy; **~schaft** *f* travelling; **~ung** *f* walking tour, hike.
Wand- *cpd*: **~lung** *f* change, transformation; (*Rel*) transubstantiation; **~schirm** *m* (folding) screen; **~schrank**

m cupboard; **~teppich** *m* tapestry; **~verkleidung** *f* wainscoting.

Wange ['vaŋə] *f* -, -n cheek.

wankelmütig [vaŋkəlmy:tɪç] *a* vacillating, inconstant.

wanken ['vankən] *vi* stagger; *(fig)* waver.

wann [van] *ad* when.

Wanne ['vanə] *f* -, -n tub.

Wanze ['vantsə] *f* -, -n bug.

Wappen ['vapən] *nt* -s, - coat of arms, crest; **~kunde** *f* heraldry.

Ware ['va:rə] *f* -, -n ware; **~nhaus** *nt* department store; **~nlager** *nt* stock, store; **~nprobe** *f* sample; **~nzeichen** *nt* trademark.

warm [varm] *a* warm; *Essen* hot.

Wärm- ['vɛrm] *cpd*: **~e** *f* -, -n warmth; **w~en** *vtr* warm, heat; **~flasche** *f* hot-water bottle.

warm- *cpd*: **~herzig** *a* warm-hearted; **~laufen** *vi irreg (Aut)* warm up; **W~-'wassertank** *m* hot-water tank.

warnen ['varnən] *vt* warn.

Warnung *f* warning.

warten ['vartən] *vi* wait *(auf +acc* for); **auf sich ~ lassen** take a long time.

Wärter(in *f*) ['vɛrtər(ɪn)] *m* -s, - attendant.

Warte- *cpd*: **~saal** *m (Rail)*, **~zimmer** *nt* waiting room.

Wartung *f* servicing; service.

warum [va'rum] *ad* why.

Warze [vartsə] *f* -, -n wart.

was [vas] *pron* what; *(col: etwas)* something.

Wasch- ['vaʃ] *cpd*: **w~bar** *a* washable; **~becken** *nt* washbasin; **w~echt** *a* colourfast; *(fig)* genuine.

Wäsche ['vɛʃə] *f* -, -n wash(ing); *(Bett—)* linen; *(Unter—)* underclothing; **~klammer** *f* clothes peg, clothespin *(US)*; **~leine** *f* washing line.

waschen ['vaʃən] *irreg vti* wash; *vr* (have a) wash; **sich** *(dat)* **die Hände ~** wash one's hands; **~ und legen** Haare shampoo and set.

Wäsche- *cpd*: **~'rei** *f* laundry; **~schleuder** *f* spin-drier.

Wasch- *cpd*: **~küche** *f* laundry room; **~lappen** *m* face flannel, washcloth *(US)*; *(col)* sissy; **~maschine** *f* washing machine; **~mittel** *nt*, **~pulver** *nt* detergent, washing powder; **~tisch** *m* washhand basin.

Wasser ['vasər] *nt* -s, - water; **w~dicht** *a* watertight, waterproof; **~fall** *m* waterfall; **~farbe** *f* watercolour; **w~gekühlt** *a (Aut)* water-cooled; **~hahn** *m* tap, faucet *(US)*.

wässerig ['vɛsərɪç] *a* watery.

Wasser- *cpd*: **~kraftwerk** *nt* hydro-electric power station; **~leitung** *f* water pipe; **~ mann** *n (Astrol)* Aquarius; **w~n** *vi* land on the water.

wässern ['vɛsərn] *vti* water.

Wasser- *cpd*: **w~scheu** *a* afraid of the water; **~schi** *nt* water-skiing; **~stand** *m* water level; **~stoff** *m* hydrogen; **~stoff-bombe** *f* hydrogen bomb; **~waage** *f*

spirit level; **~welle** *f* shampoo and set; **~zeichen** *nt* watermark.

waten ['va:tən] *vi* wade.

watscheln ['va:tʃəln] *vi* waddle.

Watt [vat] *nt* -(e)s, -en mud flats *pl*; *nt* -s, - *(Elec)* watt; **~e** *f* -, -n cotton wool, absorbent cotton *(US)*; **w~ieren** [va'ti:rən] *vt* pad.

Web- ['ve:b] *cpd*: **w~en** *vt irreg* weave; **~er** *m* -s, - weaver; **~e'rei** *f (Betrieb)* weaving mill; **~stuhl** *m* loom.

Wechsel ['vɛksəl] *m* -s, - change; *(Comm)* bill of exchange; **~beziehung** *f* correlation; **~geld** *nt* change; **w~haft** *a Wetter* variable; **~jahre** *pl* change of life; **~kurs** *m* rate of exchange; **w~n** *vt* change; *Blicke* exchange; *vi* change; vary; *(Geld —)* have change; **~strom** *m* alternating current; **~wirkung** *f* interaction.

wecken ['vɛkən] *vt* wake (up); call.

Wecker ['vɛkər] *m* -s, - alarm clock.

wedeln ['ve:dəln] *vi (mit Schwanz)* wag; *(mit Fächer)* fan; *(Ski)* wedeln.

weder ['ve:dər] *cj* neither; **~ ... noch ...** neither ... nor ...

weg [vɛk] *ad* away, off; **über etw** *(acc)* **~ sein** be over sth; **er war schon ~** he had already left; **Finger ~!** hands off!; **W~** ['ve:k] *m* -(e)s, -e way; *(Pfad)* path; *(Route)* route; **sich auf den W~ machen** be on one's way; **jdm aus dem W~ gehen** keep out of sb's way; **W~bereiter** *m* -s, - pioneer; **~blasen** *vt irreg* blow away; **~bleiben** *vi irreg* stay away.

wegen ['ve:gən] *prep +gen or (col)* dat because of.

weg- ['vɛk] *cpd*: **~fahren** *vi irreg* drive away; leave; **~fallen** *vi irreg* be left out; *(Ferien, Bezahlung)* be cancelled; *(aufhören)* cease; **~gehen** *vi irreg* go away; leave; **~jagen** *vt* chase away; **~lassen** *vt irreg* leave out; **~laufen** *vi irreg* run away *or* off; **~legen** *vt* put aside; **~machen** *vt (col)* get rid of; **~müssen** *vi irreg (col)* have to go; **~nehmen** *vt irreg* take away; **~räumen** *vt* clear away; **~schaffen** *vt* clear away; **~schnappen** *vt* snatch away *(jdm etw* sth from sb); **~tun** *vt irreg* put away; **W~weiser** ['ve:gvaɪzər] *m* -s, - road sign, signpost; **~werfen** *vt irreg* throw away; **~werfend** *a* disparaging; **~ziehen** *vi irreg* move away.

weh [ve:] *a* sore; **~ tun** hurt, be sore; **jdm/sich ~ tun** hurt sb/o.s.; **~(e)** *interj* **~(e), wenn du ...** woe betide you if ...; **o ~! oh dear!; W~e** *f* -, -n drift; **~en** *vti* blow; *(Fahnen)* flutter; **W~en** *pl (Med)* labour pains *pl*; **~klagen** *vi insep* wail; **~leidig** *a* whiny, whining; **W~mut** *f* - melancholy; **~mütig** *a* melancholy.

Wehr [ve:r] *nt* -(e)s, -e weir; *f*: **sich zur ~ setzen** defend o.s.; **~dienst** *m* military service; **w~en** *vr* defend o.s.; **w~los** *a* defenceless; **~macht** *f* armed forces *pl*; **~pflicht** *f* compulsory military service; **w~pflichtig** *a* liable for military service.

Weib [vaɪp] *nt* -(e)s, -er woman, female; wife; **~chen** *nt* female; **w~isch** ['vaɪbɪʃ] a sissyish; w~lich a feminine.

weich [vaiç] a soft; W~e f -, -n (Rail) points pl; ~en vi irreg yield, give away; W~ensteller m -s, - pointsman; W~heit f softness; ~lich a soft, namby-pamby; W~ling m weakling.

Weide ['vaidə] f -, -n (Baum) willow; (Gras) pasture; w~n vi graze; vr: **sich an etw** (dat) w~n delight in sth.

weidlich ['vaitliç] ad thoroughly.

weigern ['vaigərn] vr refuse.

Weigerung ['vaigəruŋ] f refusal.

Weih- ['vai] cpd: ~e f -, -n consecration; (Priester—) ordination; w~en vt consecrate; ordain; ~er m -s, - pond; ~nacht f -, ~nachten nt - Christmas; w~nachtlich a Christmas; ~nachts-abend m Christmas Eve; ~nachtslied nt Christmas carol; ~nachtsmann m Father Christmas, Santa Claus; zweiter ~nachtstag m Boxing Day; ~rauch m incense; ~wasser nt holy water.

weil [vail] cj because.

Weile ['vailə] f - while, short time.

Wein [vain] m -(e)s, -e wine; (Pflanze) vine; ~bau m cultivation of vines; ~beere f grape; ~berg m vineyard; ~bergschnecke f snail; ~brand m brandy; w~en vti cry; **das ist zum ~en** it's enough to make you cry or weep; w~erlich a tearful; ~geist m spirits of wine; ~lese f vintage; ~rebe f vine; ~stein m tartar; ~stock m vine; ~traube f grape.

weise ['vaizə] a wise; W~(r) mf wise old man/woman, sage.

Weise ['vaizə] f -, -n manner, way; (Lied) tune; **auf diese ~** in this way; w~n vt irreg show.

Weisheit ['vaishait] f wisdom; ~szahn m wisdom tooth.

weiß [vais] a white; W~brot nt white bread; ~en vt whitewash; W~glut f (Tech) incandescence; **jdn bis zur W~glut bringen** (fig) make sb see red; W~kohl m (white) cabbage; W~wein m white wine.

Weisung ['vaizuŋ] f instruction.

weit [vait] a wide; Begriff broad; Reise, Wurf long; **wie ~ ist es . . .?** how far is it . . .?; **in ~er Ferne** in the far distance; **das geht zu ~** that's going too far; ad far; **~aus** ad by far; ~blickend a far-seeing; W~e f -, -n width; (Raum) space; (von Entfernung) distance; ~en vtr widen.

weiter ['vaitər] a wider; broader; farther (away); (zusätzlich) further; **ohne ~es** without further ado; just like that; ad further; ~ **nichts/niemand** nothing/nobody else; ~arbeiten vi go on working; ~bilden vr continue one's studies; ~empfehlen vt irreg recommend (to others); W~fahrt f continuation of the journey; ~gehen vi irreg go on; ~hin ad: **etw ~hin tun** go on doing sth; ~leiten vt pass on; ~machen vti continue; ~reisen vi continue one's journey.

weit- cpd: ~gehend a considerable; ad largely; ~läufig a Gebäude spacious; Erklärung lengthy; Verwandter distant;

~schweifig a long-winded; ~sichtig a (lit) long-sighted; (fig) far-sighted; W~sprung m long jump; ~verbreitet a widespread; W~winkelobjektiv nt (Phot) wide-angle lens.

Weizen ['vaitsən] m -s, - wheat.

welch [velç] pron: ~ **ein(e) . . . what a . . .;** ~e indef pron (col: einige) some; ~e(r,s) rel pron (für Personen) who; (für Sachen) which; interrog pron (adjektivisch) which; (substantivisch) which one.

welk [velk] a withered; ~en vi wither.

Well- [vel] cpd: ~blech nt corrugated iron; ~e f -, -n wave; (Tech) shaft; ~enbereich m waveband; ~enbrecher m -s, - breakwater; ~enlänge f (lit, fig) wavelength; ~enlinie f wavy line; ~ensittich m budgerigar; ~pappe f corrugated cardboard.

Welt [velt] f -, -en world; ~all nt universe; ~anschauung f philosophy of life; w~berühmt a world-famous; w~fremd a unworldly; ~krieg m world war; w~lich a worldly; (nicht kirchlich) secular; ~macht f world power; w~männisch a sophisticated; ~meister m world champion; ~raum m space; ~reise f trip round the world; ~stadt f metropolis; w~weit a world-wide; ~wunder nt wonder of the world.

wem [ve:m] pron (dat) to whom.

wen [ve:n] pron (acc) whom.

Wende ['vendə] f -, -n turn; (Veränderung) change; ~kreis m (Geog) tropic; (Aut) turning circle; ~ltreppe f spiral staircase; w~n vtir irreg turn; **sich an jdn w~n** go/come to sb; ~punkt m turning point.

Wendung f turn; (Rede—) idiom.

wenig ['ve:niç] a,ad little; ~e ['ve:nigə] pl few pl; W~keit f trifle; **meine W~keit** yours truly, little me; ~ste(r,s) a least; ~stens ad at least.

wenn [ven] cj if; (zeitlich) when; ~ **auch ...** even if . . .; ~ **ich doch . . .** if only I . . .; ~**schon** ad: **na ~schon** so what? ~**schon, dennschon!** if a thing's worth doing, it's worth doing properly.

wer [ve:r] pron who.

Werbe- ['verbə] cpd: ~fernsehen nt commercial television; ~kampagne f advertising campaign; w~n irreg vt win; Mitglied recruit; vi werben; **um jdn/etw w~n** try to win sb/sth; **für jdn/etw w~n** promote sb/sth.

Werbung f advertising; (von Mitgliedern) recruitment; (um jdn/etw) promotion (um of).

Werdegang ['ve:rdəgaŋ] m development; (beruflich) career.

werden ['ve:rdən] vi irreg become; v aux (Futur) shall, will; (Passiv) be; **was ist aus ihm/aus der Sache geworden?** what became of him/it?; **es ist nichts/gut geworden** it came to nothing/turned out well; **mir wird kalt** I'm getting cold; **das muß anders ~** that will have to change; **zu Eis ~** turn to ice.

werfen ['verfən] vt irreg throw.

Werft [verft] f -, -en shipyard, dockyard.

Werk [vɛrk] nt -(e)s, -e work; (Tätigkeit) job; (Fabrik, Mechanismus) works pl; ans ~ gehen set to work; ~statt f -, -stätten workshop; (Aut) garage; ~student m self-supporting student; ~tag m working day; w~tags ad on working days; w~tägig a working; ~zeug nt tool; ~zeugschrank m tool chest.

Wermut ['ve:rmu:t] m -(e)s wormwood; (Wein) vermouth.

Wert [ve:rt] m -(e)s, -e worth; (Fin) value; ~ legen auf (+acc) attach importance to; es hat doch keinen ~ it's useless; w~ a worth; (geschätzt) dear; worthy; das ist nichts/viel w~ it's not worth anything/it's worth a lot; das ist es/er mir w~ it's/he's worth that to me; ~angabe f declaration of value; w~en vt rate; ~gegenstand m article of value; w~los a worthless; ~losigkeit f worthlessness; ~papier nt security; w~voll a valuable; ~zuwachs m appreciation.

Wesen ['ve:zən] nt -s, - (Geschöpf) being; (Natur, Character) nature; w~tlich a significant; (beträchtlich) considerable.

weshalb [vɛsˈhalp] ad why.

Wespe ['vɛspə] f -, -n wasp.

wessen ['vɛsən] pron (gen) whose.

West- [vɛst] cpd: ~e f -, -n waistcoat, vest (US); (Woll-) cardigan; ~en m -s west; w~lich a western; ad to the west; w~wärts ad westwards.

weswegen [vɛsˈve:gən] ad why.

wett [vɛt] a even; W~bewerb m competition; W~e f -, -n bet, wager; W~eifer m rivalry; ~en vt bet.

Wetter ['vɛtər] nt -s, - weather; ~bericht m weather report; ~dienst m meteorological service; ~lage f (weather) situation; ~vorhersage f weather forecast; ~warte f -, -n weather station; w~wendisch a capricious.

Wett- cpd: ~kampf m contest; ~lauf m race; w~laufen vi irreg race; w~machen vt make good; ~spiel nt match; ~streit m contest.

wetzen ['vɛtsən] vt sharpen.

Wicht [vɪçt] m -(e)s, -e titch; (pej) worthless creature; w~ig a important; ~igkeit f importance.

wickeln ['vɪkəln] vt wind; Haare set; Kind change; jdn/etw in etw (acc) ~ wrap sb/sth in sth.

Widder ['vɪdər] m -s, - ram; (Astrol) Aries.

wider ['vi:dər] prep +acc against; ~'fahren vi irreg happen (jdm to sb); ~'legen vt refute.

widerlich ['vi:dərlɪç] a disgusting, repulsive; W~keit f repulsiveness.

wider- ['vi:dər] cpd: ~rechtlich a unlawful; W~rede f contradiction.

Widerruf ['vi:dərru:f] m retraction; countermanding; w~en [vi:dərˈru:fən] vt irreg insep retract; Anordnung revoke; Befehl countermand.

wider'setzen vr insep oppose (jdm/etw sb/sth).

widerspenstig ['vi:dərʃpɛnstɪç] a wilful; W~keit f wilfulness.

widerspiegeln ['vi:dərʃpi:gəln] vt reflect.

wider'sprechen vi irreg insep contradict (jdm sb); ~d a contradictory.

Widerspruch ['vi:dərʃprux] m contradiction; w~slos ad without arguing.

Widerstand ['vi:dərʃtant] m resistance; ~sbewegung f resistance (movement); w~sfähig a resistant, tough; w~slos a unresisting.

wider'stehen vi irreg insep withstand (jdm/etw sb/sth).

Wider- ['vi:dər] cpd: ~streit m conflict; w~wärtig a nasty, horrid; ~wille m aversion (gegen to); w~willig a unwilling, reluctant.

widmen ['vɪtmən] vt dedicate; vtr devote (o.s.).

Widmung f dedication.

widrig ['vi:drɪç] a Umstände adverse; Mensch repulsive.

wie [vi:] ad how; cj ~ ich schon sagte as I said; (so) schön ~ ... as beautiful as ...; ~ du like you; singen ~ ein ... sing like a ...

wieder ['vi:dər] ad again; ~ da sein be back (again); gehst du schon ~? are you off again? ~ ein(e) ... another ...; ~ ... ~ ein(e) ... another ...; W~aufbau [-ˈʔaufbau] m rebuilding; W~aufnahme [-ˈʔaufna:mə] f resumption; ~aufnehmen vt irreg resume; ~bekommen vt irreg get back; ~bringen vt irreg bring back; ~erkennen vt irreg recognize; W~erstattung f reimbursement; W~gabe f reproduction; ~geben vt irreg (zurückgeben) return; Erzählung etc repeat; Gefühle etc convey; ~gutmachen [-ˈgu:tmaxən] vt make up for; Fehler put right; W~'gutmachung f reparation; ~'herstellen vt restore; ~'holen vt insep repeat; W~holung f repetition; W~hören nt : auf W~hören (Tel) goodbye; W~kehr f - return; (von Vorfall) repetition, recurrence; W~kunft f -, -e return; ~sehen vt irreg see again; auf W~sehen goodbye; ~um ad again; (andererseits) on the other hand; ~vereinigen vt reunite; W~wahl f re-election.

Wiege ['vi:gə] f -, -n cradle; w~n vt (schaukeln) rock; vti irreg (Gewicht) weigh; ~nfest nt birthday.

wiehern ['vi:ərn] vi neigh, whinny.

Wiese ['vi:zə] f -, -n meadow; ~l nt -s, - weasel.

wieso [vi:ˈzo:] ad why.

wieviel [vi:ˈfi:l] a how much; ~ Menschen how many people; ~mal ad how often; ~te(r,s) a: zum ~ten Mal? how many times?; den W~ten haben wir? what's the date?; an ~ter Stelle? in what place?; der ~te Besucher war er? how many visitors were there before him?

wieweit [vi:vait] ad to what extent.

wild [vɪlt] a wild; W~ nt -(e)s game; ~ern ['vɪldərn] vi poach; ~fremd a (col) quite strange or unknown; W~heit f wildness; W~leder nt suede; W~nis f -, -se wilderness; W~schwein nt (wild) boar.

Wille ['vɪlə] *m* **-ns, -n** will; **w~n** *prep* +*gen*: **um . . . w~n** for the sake of . . .; **w~nlos** a weak-willed; **w~nsstark** a strong-willed.

will- *cpd*: **~ig** a willing; **~kommen** [vɪl'kɔmən] *a* welcome; **jdn ~kommen heißen** welcome sb; **W~kommen** *nt* **-s,** - welcome; **~kürlich** *a* arbitrary; *Bewegung* voluntary.

wimmeln ['vɪməln] *vi* swarm (*von* with).

wimmern ['vɪmərn] *vi* whimper.

Wimper ['vɪmpər] *f* -, **-n** eyelash.

Wind [vɪnt] *m* **-(e)s, -e** wind; **~beutel** *m* cream puff; (*fig*) windbag; **~e** ['vɪndə] *f* -, **-n** (*Tech*) winch, windlass; (*Bot*) bindweed; **~el** ['vɪndəl] *f* -, **-n** nappy, diaper (*US*); **w~en** ['vɪndən] *vi impers* be windy; *irreg vt* wind; *Kranz* weave; (*ent—*) twist; *vr* wind; (*Person*) writhe; **~hose** *f* whirlwind; **~hund** *m* greyhound; (*Mensch*) fly-by-night; **w~ig** ['vɪndɪç] *a* windy; (*fig*) dubious; **~mühle** *f* windmill; **~pocken** *pl* chickenpox; **~schutzscheibe** *f* (*Aut*) windscreen, windshield (*US*); **~stärke** *f* wind force; **~stille** *f* calm; **~stoß** *m* gust of wind.

Wink [vɪŋk] *m* **-(e)s, -e** hint; (*mit Kopf*) nod; (*mit Hand*) wave.

Winkel ['vɪnkəl] *m* **-s,** - (*Math*) angle; (*Gerät*) set square; (*in Raum*) corner.

winken ['vɪŋkən] *vti* wave.

winseln ['vɪnzəln] *vi* whine.

Winter ['vɪntər] *m* **-s,** - winter; **w~lich** a wintry; **~sport** *m* winter sports *pl*.

Winzer ['vɪntsər] *m* **-s,** - vine grower.

winzig ['vɪntsɪç] a tiny.

Wipfel ['vɪpfəl] *m* **-s,** - treetop.

wir [vi:r] *pron* we; **~ alle** all of us, we all.

Wirbel ['vɪrbəl] *m* **-s,** - whirl, swirl; (*Trubel*) hurly-burly; (*Aufsehen*) fuss; (*Anat*) vertebra; **w~n** *vi* whirl, swirl; **~säule** *f* spine; **~tier** *nt* vertebrate; **~wind** *m* whirlwind.

wirken ['vɪrkən] *vi* have an effect; (*erfolgreich sein*) work; (*scheinen*) seem; *vt Wunder* work.

wirklich ['vɪrklɪç] a real; **W~keit** *f* reality.

wirksam ['vɪrkza:m] a effective; **W~keit** *f* effectiveness, efficacy.

Wirkung ['vɪrkuŋ] *f* effect; **w~slos** a ineffective; **w~slos bleiben** have no effect; **w~svoll** a effective.

wirr [vɪr] a confused, wild; **W~en** *pl* disturbances *pl*; **W~warr** [-var] *m* **-s** disorder, chaos.

Wirsing(kohl) ['vɪrzɪŋ(ko:l)] *m* **-s** savoy cabbage.

Wirt [vɪrt] *m* **-(e)s, -e** landlord; **~in** *f* landlady; **~schaft** *f* (*Gaststätte*) pub; (*Haushalt*) housekeeping; (*eines Landes*) economy; (*col: Durcheinander*) mess; **w~schaftlich** a economical; (*Pol*) economic; **~schaftskrise** *f* economic crisis; **~schaftsprüfer** *m* chartered accountant; **~schaftswunder** *nt* economic miracle; **~shaus** *nt* inn.

Wisch [vɪʃ] *m* **-(e)s, -e** scrap of paper; **w~en** *vt* wipe; **~er** *m* **-s,** - (*Aut*) wiper.

wispern ['vɪspərn] *vti* whisper.

Wißbegier(de) ['vɪsbəgi:r(də)] *f* thirst for knowledge; **w~ig** a inquisitive, eager for knowledge.

wissen ['vɪsən] *vt irreg* know; **W~** *nt* **-s** knowledge; **W~schaft** *f* science; **W~schaftler(in** *f*) *m* **-s,** scientist; **~schaftlich** a scientific; **~swert** a worth knowing; **~tlich** a knowing.

wittern ['vɪtərn] *vt* scent; (*fig*) suspect.

Witterung *f* weather; (*Geruch*) scent.

Witwe ['vɪtvə] *f* -, **-n** widow; **~r** *m* **-s,** - widower.

Witz [vɪts] *m* **-(e)s, -e** joke; **~blatt** *nt* comic (paper); **~bold** *m* **-(e)s, -e** joker, wit; **w~eln** *vi* joke; **w~ig** a funny.

wo [vo:] *ad* where; (*col: irgendwo*) somewhere; **im Augenblick, ~ . . .** the moment (that) . . .; **die Zeit, ~ . . .** the time when . . .; *cj* (*wenn*) if; **~anders** [vo:'andərs] *ad* elsewhere; **~bei** [vo:'baɪ] *ad* (*rel*) by/with which; (*interrog*) what . . . in/by/with.

Woche ['vɔxə] *f* -, **-n** week; **~nende** *nt* weekend; **w~nlang** a,ad for weeks; **~nschau** *f* newsreel.

wöchentlich ['vœçəntlɪç] a,ad weekly.

wo- *cpd*: **~durch** [vo:'durç] *ad* (*rel*) through which; (*interrog*) what . . . through; **~für** [vo:'fy:r] *ad* (*rel*) for which; (*interrog*) what . . . for.

Woge ['vo:gə] *f* -, **-n** wave; **w~n** *vi* heave, surge.

wo- *cpd*: **~gegen** [vo:'ge:gən] *ad* (*rel*) against which; (*interrog*) what . . . against; **~her** [vo:'he:r] *ad* where . . . from; **~hin** [vo:'hɪn] *ad* where . . . to.

wohl [vo:l] *ad* well; (*behaglich*) at ease, comfortable; (*vermutlich*) I suppose, probably; (*gewiß*) certainly; **er weiß das ~** he knows that perfectly well; **W~** *nt* **-(e)s** welfare; **zum W~!** cheers!; **~auf** [vo:l'auf] *ad* well; **W~behagen** *nt* comfort; **~behalten** *ad* safe and sound; **W~fahrt** *f* welfare; **~habend** a wealthy; **~ig** a contented, comfortable; **W~klang** *m* melodious sound; **~schmeckend** a delicious; **W~stand** *m* prosperity; **W~standsgesellschaft** *f* affluent society; **W~tat** *f* relief; act of charity; **W~täter(in** *f*) *m* benefactor; **~tätig** a charitable; **~tun** *vi irreg* do good (*jdm* sb); **~verdient** a well-earned, well-deserved; **~weislich** *ad* prudently; **W~wollen** *nt* **-s** good will; **~wollend** a benevolent.

wohn- [vo:n] *cpd*: **~en** *vi* live; **~haft** a resident; **~lich** a comfortable; **W~ort** *m* domicile; **W~sitz** *m* place of residence; **W~ung** *f* house; (*Etagen—*) flat, apartment (*US*); **W~ungsnot** *f* housing shortage; **W~wagen** *m* caravan; **W~zimmer** *nt* living room.

wölben ['vœlbən] *vtr* curve.

Wölbung *f* curve.

Wolf [vɔlf] *m* **-(e)s, ⁼e** wolf.

Wölfin ['vœlfɪn] *f* she-wolf.

Wolke ['vɔlkə] *f* -, **-n** cloud; **~nkratzer** *m* skyscraper.

wolkig ['vɔlkɪç] a cloudy.

Wolle ['vɔlə] *f* -, **-n** wool; **w~n** a woollen.

wollen ['vɔlən] *vti* want.

wollüstig ['vɔlʏstɪç] a lusty, sensual.
wo- cpd: ~**mit** [vo:'mɪt] ad (rel) with
which; (interrog) what . . . with;
~**möglich** [vo:'mø:klɪç] ad probably, I
suppose; ~**nach** [vo:'na:x] ad (rel)
after/for which; (interrog) what . . .
for/after.
Wonne ['vɔnə] f -, -n joy, bliss.
wo- cpd: ~**ran** [vo:'ran] ad (rel) on/at
which; (interrog) what . . . on/at; ~**rauf**
[vo:'rauf] ad (rel) on which; (interrog) what
. . . on; ~**raus** [vo:'raus] ad (rel) from/out
of which; (interrog) what . . . from/out of;
~**rin** [vo:'rɪn] ad (rel) in which; (interrog)
what . . . in.
Wort [vɔrt] nt -(e)s, ˬer, -e word; **jdn**
beim ~ **nehmen** take sb at his word;
w~**brüchig** a not true to one's word.
Wörterbuch ['vœrtərbu:x] nt dictionary.
Wort- cpd: ~**führer** m spokesman;
w~**getreu** a true to one's word; Übersetzung-literal; **w**~**karg** a taciturn; ~**laut** m
wording.
wörtlich ['vœrtlɪç] a literal.
Wort- cpd: **w**~**los** a mute; **w**~**reich** a
wordy, verbose; ~**schatz** m vocabulary;
~**spiel** nt play on words, pun; ~**wechsel**
m dispute.
wo- cpd: ~**rüber** [vo:'ry:bər] ad (rel)
over/about which; (interrog) what . . .
over/about; ~**rum** [vo:'rum] ad (rel)
about/round which; (interrog) what . . .
about/round; ~**runter** [vo:'runtər] ad (rel)
under which; (interrog) what . . . under;
~**von** [vo:'fɔn] ad (rel) from which;
(interrog) what . . . from; ~**vor** [vo:'fɔːr] ad
(rel) in front of/before which; (interrog) in
front of/before what; of what; ~**zu**
[vo:'tsu:] ad (rel) to/for which; (interrog)
what . . . for/to; (warum) why.
Wrack [vrak] nt -(e)s, -s wreck.
wringen ['vrɪŋən] vt irreg wring.
Wucher ['vu:xər] m -s profiteering; ~**er**
m -s, - profiteer; **w**~**isch** a profiteering;
w~**n** vi (Pflanzen) grow wild; ~**ung** f
(Med) growth, tumour.
Wuchs [vu:ks] m -es (Wachstum) growth;
(Statur) build.
Wucht [vuxt] f - force; **w**~**ig** a solid,
massive.
wühlen ['vy:lən] vi scrabble; (Tier) root;
(Maulwurf) burrow; (col: arbeiten) slave
away; vt dig.
Wulst [vulst] -es, ˬe bulge; (an Wunde)
swelling.
wund [vunt] a sore, raw; **W**~**e** ['vundə] f -,
-n wound.
Wunder ['vundər] nt -s, - miracle; **es ist**
kein ~ it's no wonder; **w**~**bar** a wonderful, marvellous; ~**kind** nt infant prodigy;
w~**lich** a odd, peculiar; **w**~**n** vr be
surprised (über +acc at); vt surprise;
w~**schön** a beautiful; **w**~**voll** a
wonderful.
Wundstarrkrampf ['vunt∫tarkrampf] m
tetanus, lockjaw.
Wunsch [vun∫] m -(e)s, ˬe wish.
wünschen ['vʏn∫ən] vt wish; **sich** (dat)
etw ~ want sth, wish for sth; ~**swert** a
desirable.

Würde ['vʏrdə] f -, -n dignity; (Stellung)
honour; ~**nträger** m dignitary; **w**~**voll**
a dignified.
würdig ['vʏrdɪç] a worthy; (würdevoll) dignified; ~**en** ['vʏrdɪgən] vt appreciate; **jdn**
keines Blickes ~**en** not so much as look
at sb.
Wurf [vurf] m -s, ˬe throw; (Junge) litter.
Würfel ['vʏrfəl] m -s, - dice; (Math) cube;
~**becher** m (dice) cup; **w**~**n** vi play
dice; vt dice; ~**spiel** nt game of dice;
~**zucker** m lump sugar.
würgen ['vʏrgən] vti choke.
Wurm [vurm] m -(e)s, ˬer worm; **w**~**en**
vt (col) rile, nettle; ~**fortsatz** m (Med)
appendix; **w**~**ig** a worm-eaten; ~**stichig**
a worm-ridden.
Wurst [vurst] f -, ˬe sausage; **das ist mir**
~ (col) I don't care, I don't give a damn.
Würze ['vʏrtsə] f -, -n seasoning, spice.
Wurzel ['vʊrtsəl] f -, -n root.
würz- ['vʏrts] cpd: ~**en** vt season, spice;
~**ig** a spicy.
wüst [vy:st] a untidy, messy; (ausschweifend) wild; (öde) waste; (col: heftig)
terrible; **W**~**e** f -, -n desert; **W**~**ling** m
rake.
Wut [vu:t] f - rage, fury; ~**anfall** m fit of
rage.
wüten ['vy:tən] vi rage; ~**d** a furious, mad.

X

X,x [ɪks] nt X,x.
X-Beine ['ɪksbaɪnə] pl knock-knees pl.
x-beliebig [ɪksbə'li:bɪç] a any (whatever).
xerokopieren [kseroko'pi:rən] vt xerox,
photocopy.
x-mal ['ɪksma:l] ad any number of times, n
times.
Xylophon [ksylo'fo:n] nt -s, -e xylophone.

Y

Y,y ['ʏpsilɔn] nt Y,y.
Ypsilon nt -(s), -s the letter Y.

Z

Z,z [tsɛt] nt Z,z.
Zacke ['tsakə] f -, -n point; (Berg—) jagged
peak; (Gabel—) prong; (Kamm—) tooth.
zackig ['tsakɪç] a jagged; (col) smart;
Tempo brisk.
zaghaft ['tsa:khaft] a timid; **Z**~**igkeit** f
timidity.
zäh [tsɛ:] a tough; Mensch tenacious; Flüssigkeit thick; (schleppend) sluggish; **Z**~**igkeit**
f toughness; tenacity.
Zahl [tsa:l] f -, -en number; **z**~**bar** a
payable; **z**~**en** vti pay; **z**~**en bitte!** the
bill please!
zählen ['tsɛ:lən] vti count (auf +acc on); ~
zu be numbered among.
Zahl- cpd: **z**~**enmäßig** a numerical; ~**er**
m -s, - payer.
Zähler ['tsɛ:lər] m -s, - (Tech) meter;
(Math) numerator.
Zahl- cpd: **z**~**los** a countless; **z**~**reich** a

numerous; ~**tag** m payday; ~**ung** f payment; z~**ungsfähig** a solvent; ~**wort** nt numeral.

zahm [tsa:m] a tame.

zähmen ['tsɛ:mən] vt tame; (fig) curb.

Zahn [tsa:n] m -(e)s, ꞏ̈e tooth; ~**arzt** m dentist; ~**bürste** f toothbrush; z~**en** vi cut teeth; ~**fäule** f - tooth decay, caries; ~**fleisch** nt gums pl; ~**pasta**, ~**paste** f toothpaste; ~**rad** nt cog(wheel); ~**radbahn** f rack railway; ~**schmelz** m (tooth) enamel; ~**schmerzen** pl toothache; ~**stein** m tartar; ~**stocher** m -s, - toothpick.

Zange ['tsaŋə] f -, -n pliers pl; (Zucker– etc) tongs pl; (Beiß–, Zool) pincers pl; (Med) forceps pl; ~**ngeburt** f forceps delivery.

Zank- [tsaŋk] cpd: ~**apfel** m bone of contention; z~**en** vir quarrel.

zänkisch ['tsɛŋkiʃ] a quarrelsome.

Zäpfchen ['tsɛpfçən] nt (Anat) uvula; (Med) suppository.

Zapfen ['tsapfən] m -s, - plug; (Bot) cone; (Eis–) icicle; z~ vt tap; ~**streich** m (Mil) tattoo.

zappelig ['tsapəliç] a wriggly; (unruhig) fidgety.

zappeln ['tsapəln] vi wriggle; fidget.

zart [tsart] a (weich, leise) soft; Braten etc tender; (fein, schwächlich) delicate; Z~**gefühl** nt tact; Z~**heit** f softness; tenderness; delicacy.

zärtlich ['tsɛ:rtliç] a tender, affectionate; Z~**keit** f tenderness; pl caresses pl.

Zauber ['tsaubər] m -s, - magic; (–bann) spell; ~**ei** [-'rai] f magic; ~**er** m -s, - magician; conjuror; z~**haft** a magical, enchanting; ~**künstler** m conjuror; z~n vi conjure, practise magic; ~**spruch** m (magic) spell.

zaudern ['tsaudərn] vi hesitate.

Zaum [tsaum] m -(e)s, Zäume bridle; etw im ~ **halten** keep sth in check.

Zaun [tsaun] m -(e)s, Zäune fence; vom ~(e) **brechen** (fig) start; ~**könig** m wren; ~**pfahl** m: **ein Wink mit dem** ~ **pfahl** a broad hint.

Zeche ['tsɛçə] f -, -n bill; (Bergbau) mine.

Zecke ['tsɛkə] f -, -n tick.

Zehe ['tse:ə] f -, -n toe; (Knoblauch–) clove.

zehn [tse:n] num ten; ~**te(r,s)** a tenth; Z~**tel** nt -s, - tenth (part).

Zeich- ['tsaiç] cpd: ~**en** nt -s, - sign; z~**nen** vti draw; (kenn–) mark; (unter–) sign; ~**ner** m -s, - artist; **technischer** ~**ner** draughtsman; ~**nung** f drawing; (Markierung) markings pl.

Zeig- ['tsaig] cpd: ~**efinger** m index finger; z~**en** vt show; vi point (auf +acc to, at); vr show o.s.; **es wird sich** z~**en time will tell; es zeigte sich, daß ... it turned out that ...**; ~**er** m -s, - pointer; (Uhr–) hand.

Zeile ['tsailə] f -, -n line; (Häuser–) row; ~**nabstand** m line spacing.

Zeit [tsait] f -, -en time; (Gram) tense; zur ~ **at the moment; sich** (dat) ~ **lassen** take one's time; **von** ~ **zu** ~ from time to time; ~**alter** nt age; z~**gemäß** a in

keeping with the times; ~**genosse** m contemporary; z~**ig** a early; z~'**lebens** ad all one's life; z~**lich** a temporal; ~**lupe** f slow motion; ~**raffer** m -s time-lapse photography; z~**raubend** a time-consuming; ~**raum** m period; ~**rechnung** f time, era; **nach/vor unserer** ~**rechnung** A.D./B.C.; ~**schrift** f periodical; ~**ung** f newspaper; ~**verschwendung** f waste of time; ~**vertreib** m pastime, diversion; z~**weilig** a temporary; z~**weise** ad for a time; ~**wort** nt verb; ~**zeichen** nt (Rad) time signal; ~**zünder** m time fuse.

Zell- ['tsɛl] cpd: ~**e** f -, -n cell; (Telefon–) callbox; ~**kern** m cell, nucleus; ~**stoff** m cellulose; ~**teilung** f cell division.

Zelt [tsɛlt] nt -(e)s, -e tent; ~**bahn** f tarpaulin, groundsheet; z~**en** vi camp.

Zement [tse'mɛnt] m -(e)s, -e cement; z~**ieren** [-'ti:rən] vt cement.

zensieren [tsɛn'zi:rən] vt censor; (Sch) mark.

Zensur [tsɛn'zu:r] f censorship; (Sch) mark.

Zent- cpd: ~**imeter** [tsɛnti'me:tər] m or nt centimetre; ~**ner** [tsɛntnər] m -s, - hundredweight.

zentral [tsɛn'tra:l] a central; Z~**e** f -, -n central office; (Tel) exchange; Z~**heizung** f central heating; ~**isieren** [tsɛntrali'zi:rən] vt centralize.

Zentri- [tsɛntri] cpd: ~**fugalkraft** [-fu'ga:lkraft] f centrifugal force; ~**fuge** [-'fu:gə] f -, -n centrifuge; (für Wäsche) spin-dryer.

Zentrum ['tsɛntrum] nt -s, **Zentren** centre.

Zepter ['tsɛptər] nt -s, - sceptre.

zerbrech- [tsɛr'brɛç] cpd: ~**en** vti irreg break; ~**lich** a fragile.

zerbröckeln [tsɛr'brœkəln] vti crumble (to pieces).

zer'drücken vt squash, crush; Kartoffeln mash.

Zeremonie [tseremo'ni:] f ceremony.

zer'fahren a scatterbrained, distracted.

Zerfall [tsɛr'fal] m decay; z~**en** vi irreg disintegrate, decay; (sich gliedern) fall (in +acc into).

zerfetzen [tsɛr'fɛtsən] vt tear to pieces.

zer'fließen vi irreg dissolve, melt away.

zer'gehen vi irreg melt, dissolve.

zerkleinern [tsɛr'klainərn] vt reduce to small pieces.

zerleg- [tsɛr'le:g] cpd: ~**bar** a able to be dismantled; ~**en** vt take to pieces; Fleisch carve; Satz analyse.

zerlumpt [tsɛr'lumpt] a ragged.

zermalmen [tsɛr'malmən] vt crush.

zermürben [tsɛr'myrbən] vt wear down.

zer'platzen vi burst.

zerquetschen [tsɛr'kvɛtʃən] vt squash.

Zerrbild ['tsɛrbilt] nt caricature, distorted picture.

zer'reden vt Problem flog to death.

zer'reiben vt irreg grind down.

zer'reißen irreg vt tear to pieces; vi tear, rip.

zerren ['tsɛrən] vt drag; vi tug (an +dat at).

zer'rinnen vi irreg melt away.

zerrissen [tsɛr'rısən] a torn, tattered; **Z—heit** f tattered state; (Pol) disunion, discord; (innere —) disintegration.

zerrütten [tsɛr'rʏtən] vt wreck, destroy. **zerrüttet** a wrecked, shattered.

zer'schießen vt irreg shoot to pieces.

zer'schlagen irreg vt shatter, smash; vr fall through.

zerschleißen [tsɛr'ʃlaısən] vti irreg wear out.

zer'schneiden vt irreg cut up.

zer'setzen vtr decompose, dissolve.

zersplittern [tsɛr'ʃplıtərn] vti split (into pieces); (Glas) shatter.

zer'springen vi irreg shatter, burst.

zerstäub- [tsɛr'ʃtɔʏb] cpd: **~en** vt spray; **Z—er** m -s, - atomizer.

zerstör- [tsɛr'ʃtöːr] cpd: **~en** vt destroy; **Z—ung** f destruction.

zer'stoßen vt irreg pound, pulverize.

zer'streiten vr irreg fall out, break up.

zerstreu- [tsɛr'ʃtrɔʏ] cpd: **~en** vtr disperse, scatter; (unterhalten) divert; Zweifel etc dispel; **~t** a scattered; Mensch absent-minded; **Z—theit** f absent-mindedness; **Z—ung** f dispersion; (Ablenkung) diversion.

zerstückeln [tsər'ʃtʏkəln] vt cut into pieces.

zer'teilen vt divide into parts.

zer'treten vt irreg crush underfoot.

zertrümmern [tsɛr'trʏmərn] vt shatter; Gebäude etc demolish.

Zerwürfnis [tsɛr'vʏrfnıs] nt -ses, -se dissension, quarrel.

zerzausen [tsɛr'tsauzən] vt Haare ruffle up, tousle.

zetern ['tseːtərn] vi shout, shriek.

Zettel ['tsɛtəl] m -s, - piece of paper, slip; (Notiz—) note; (Formular) form; **~kasten** m card index (box).

Zeug [tsɔʏk] nt -(e)s, -e (col) stuff; (Ausrüstung) gear; **dummes ~** (stupid) nonsense; **das ~ haben zu** have the makings of; **sich ins ~ legen** put one's shoulder to the wheel.

Zeuge ['tsɔʏgə] m -n, -n, **Zeugin** ['tsɔʏgın] f witness; **z~n** vi bear witness, testify; **es zeugt von . . .** it testifies to . . .; vt Kind father; **~naussage** f evidence; **~nstand** m witness box.

Zeugnis ['tsɔʏgnıs] nt -ses, -se certificate; (Sch) report; (Referenz) reference; (Aussage) evidence, testimony; **~ geben von** be evidence of, testify to.

Zeugung ['tsɔʏgʊŋ] f procreation; **z~sunfähig** a sterile.

Zickzack ['tsıktsak] m -(e)s, -e zigzag.

Ziege ['tsiːgə] f -, -n goat; **~nleder** nt kid.

Ziegel ['tsiːgəl] m -s, - brick; (Dach—) tile; **~ei** [-'laı] f brickworks.

ziehen ['tsiːən] irreg vt draw; (zerren) pull; (Schach etc) move; (züchten) rear; **etw nach sich ~** lead to sth, entail sth; vi draw; (um—, wandern) move; (Rauch, Wolke etc) drift; (reißen) pull; v impers: **es zieht there is a draught, it's draughty;** vr

(Gummi) stretch; (Grenze etc) run; (Gespräche) be drawn out.

Ziehharmonika ['tsiːharmoːnika] f concertina; accordion.

Ziehung ['tsiːʊŋ] f (Los—) drawing.

Ziel [tsiːl] nt -(e)s, -e (einer Reise) destination; (Sport) finish; (Mil) target; (Absicht) goal, aim; **z~en** vi aim (auf +acc at); **~fernrohr** nt telescopic sight; **z~los** a aimless; **~scheibe** f target; **z~strebig** a purposeful.

ziemlich ['tsiːmlıç] a quite a; fair; ad rather; quite a bit.

zieren ['tsiːrən] vr act coy.

Zier- [tsiːr] cpd: **z~lich** a dainty; **~lichkeit** f daintiness; **~strauch** m flowering shrub.

Ziffer ['tsıfər] f -, -n figure, digit; **~blatt** nt dial, clock-face.

zig [tsık] a (col) umpteen.

Zigarette [tsiga'rɛtə] f cigarette; **~nautomat** m cigarette machine; **~nschachtel** f cigarette packet; **~nspitze** f cigarette holder.

Zigarillo [tsiga'rılo] nt or m -s, -s cigarillo.

Zigarre [tsi'garə] f -, -n cigar.

Zigeuner(in f) [tsi'gɔʏnər(ın)] m -s, - gipsy.

Zimmer ['tsımər] nt -s, - room; **~antenne** f indoor aerial; **~decke** f ceiling; **~herr** m lodger; **~lautstärke** f reasonable volume; **~mädchen** nt chambermaid; **~mann** m carpenter; **z~n** vt make, carpenter; **~pflanze** f indoor plant.

zimperlich ['tsımpərlıç] a squeamish; (pinglig) fussy, finicky.

Zimt [tsımt] m -(e)s, -e cinnamon; **~stange** f cinnamon stick.

Zink [tsıŋk] nt -(e)s zinc; **~e** f -, -n (Gabel—) prong; (Kamm—) tooth; **z~en** vt Karten mark; **~salbe** f zinc ointment.

Zinn [tsın] nt -(e)s (Element) tin; (in —waren) pewter; **z~oberrot** [tsı'noːbərrot] a vermilion; **~soldat** m tin soldier; **~waren** pl pewter.

Zins [tsıns] m -es, -en interest; **~eszins** m compound interest; **~fuß** m, **~satz** m rate of interest; **z~los** a interest-free.

Zipfel ['tsıpfəl] m -s, - corner; (spitz) tip; (Hemd—) tail; (Wurst—) end; **~mütze** f stocking cap; nightcap.

zirka ['tsırka] ad (round) about.

Zirkel ['tsırkəl] m -s, - circle; (Math) pair of compasses; **~kasten** m geometry set.

Zirkus ['tsırkʊs] m -, -se circus.

Zirrhose [tsı'roːzə] f -, -n cirrhosis.

zischeln ['tsıʃəln] vti whisper.

zischen ['tsıʃən] vi hiss.

Zitat [tsi'taːt] nt -(e)s, -e quotation, quote.

zitieren [tsi'tiːrən] vt quote.

Zitronat [tsitro'naːt] nt -(e)s, -e candied lemon peel.

Zitrone [tsi'troːnə] f -, -n lemon; **~nlimonade** f lemonade; **~nsaft** m lemon juice; **~nscheibe** f lemon slice.

zittern ['tsıtərn] vi tremble.

Zitze [tsıtsə] f -, -n teat, dug.

zivil [tsi'vi:l] a civil; *Preis* moderate; **Z~** *nt* **-s** plain clothes *pl*; *(Mil)* civilian clothing; **Z~bevölkerung** *f* civilian population; **Z~courage** *f* courage of one's convictions; **Z~isation** [tsivilizatsi'o:n] *f* civilization; **Z~isationserscheinung** *f* phenomenon of civilization; **Z~isationskrankheit** *f* disease peculiar to civilization; **~i'sieren** *vt* civilize; **Z~ist** [tsivi'list] *m* civilian; **Z~recht** *nt* civil law.

Zölibat [tsöli'ba:t] *nt or m* **-(e)s** celibacy.

Zoll [tsɔl] *m* **-(e)s, ¨e** customs *pl*: *(Abgabe)* duty; **~abfertigung** *f* customs clearance; **~amt** *nt* customs office; **~beamte(r)** *m* customs official; **~erklärung** *f* customs declaration; **z~frei** *a* duty-free; **z~pflichtig** *a* liable to duty, dutiable.

Zone ['tso:nə] *f* -, -n zone.

Zoo [tso:] *m* **-s, -s** zoo; **~loge** [tsoo'lo:gə] *m* **-n, -n** zoologist; **~lo'gie** *f* zoology; **z~'logisch** *a* zoological.

Zopf [tsɔpf] *m* **-(e)s, ¨e** plait; pigtail; **alter ~** antiquated custom.

Zorn [tsɔrn] *m* **-(e)s** anger; **z~ig** *a* angry.

Zote [tso:tə] *f* -, -n smutty joke/remark.

zottig ['tsɔtiç] *a* shaggy.

zu [tsu:] *(mit Infinitiv)* to; *prep +dat (bei Richtung, Vorgang)* to; *(bei Orts-, Zeit-, Preisangabe)* at; *(Zweck)* for; **~m Fenster herein** through the window; **~ meiner Zeit** in my time; *ad* too; *(in Richtung)* towards (sb/sth); *a (col)* shut.

zualler- ['tsu:'alər] *cpd:* **~erst** *ad* first of all; **~letzt** *ad* last of all.

Zubehör ['tsu:bəhö:r] *nt* **-(e)s, -e** accessories *pl*.

Zuber ['tsu:bər] *m* **-s, -** tub.

zubereiten ['tsu:bəraitən] *vt* prepare.

zubilligen ['tsu:biligən] *vt* grant.

zubinden ['tsu:bindən] *vt irreg* tie up.

zubleiben ['tsu:blaibən] *vi irreg (col)* stay shut.

zubringen ['tsu:briŋən] *vt irreg* spend; *(col) Tür* get shut.

Zubringer *m* **-s, -** *(Tech)* feeder, conveyor; **~straße** *f* approach or slip road.

Zucht [tsuxt] *f* -, **-en** *(von Tieren)* breed(ing); *(von Pflanzen)* cultivation; *(Rasse)* breed; *(Erziehung)* raising; *(Disziplin)* discipline.

züchten ['tsyçtən] *vt Tiere* breed; *Pflanzen* cultivate, grow.

Züchter *m* **-s, -** breeder; grower.

Zucht- *cpd:* **~haus** *nt* prison, penitentiary *(US)*; **~hengst** *m* stallion, stud.

züchtig ['tsyçtiç] *a* modest, demure; **~en** ['tsyçtigən] *vt* chastise; **Z~ung** *f* chastisement.

zucken ['tsukən] *vi* jerk, twitch; *(Strahl etc)* flicker; *vt* shrug.

zücken ['tsykən] *vt Schwert* draw; *Geldbeutel* pull out.

Zucker ['tsukər] *m* **-s, -** sugar; *(Med)* diabetes; **~dose** *f* sugar bowl; **~guß** *m* icing; **z~krank** *a* diabetic; **z~n** *vt* sugar; **~rohr** *nt* sugar cane; **~rübe** *f* sugar beet.

Zuckung ['tsukuŋ] *f* convulsion, spasm; *(leicht)* twitch.

zudecken ['tsu:dɛkən] *vt* cover (up).

zudem [tsu'de:m] *ad* in addition (to this).

zudrehen ['tsu:dre:ən] *vt* turn off.

zudringlich ['tsu:driŋliç] *a* forward, pushing, obtrusive; **Z~keit** *f* forwardness, obtrusiveness.

zudrücken ['tsu:drykən] *vt* close; **ein Auge ~** turn a blind eye.

zueinander [tsu'ai'nandər] *ad* to one other; *(in Verbverbindung)* together.

zuerkennen ['tsu:'ɛrkɛnən] *vt irreg* award *(jdm etw* sth to sb, sb sth).

zuerst [tsu'e:rst] *ad* first; *(zu Anfang)* at first; **~ einmal** first of all.

Zufahrt ['tsu:fa:rt] *f* approach; **~straße** *f* approach road; *(von Autobahn etc)* slip road.

Zufall ['tsu:fal] *m* chance; *(Ereignis)* coincidence; **durch ~** by accident; **so ein ~** what a coincidence; **z~en** *vi irreg* close, shut itself; *(Anteil, Aufgabe)* fall *(jdm* to sb).

zufällig ['tsu:fɛliç] *a* chance; *ad* by chance; *(in Frage)* by any chance.

Zuflucht ['tsu:fluxt] *f* recourse; *(Ort)* refuge.

Zufluß ['tsu:flus] *m* *(Zufließen)* inflow, influx; *(Geog)* tributary; *(Comm)* supply.

zufolge [tsu'fɔlgə] *prep +dat or gen* judging by; *(laut)* according to.

zufrieden [tsu'fri:dən] *a* content(ed), satisfied; **Z~heit** *f* satisfaction, contentedness; **~stellen** *vt* satisfy.

zufrieren ['tsu:fri:rən] *vi irreg* freeze up or over.

zufügen ['tsu:fy:gən] *vt* add *(dat* to); *Leid etc* cause *(jdm etw* sth to sb).

Zufuhr ['tsu:fu:r] *f* -, **-en** *(Herbeibringen)* supplying; *(Met)* influx; *(Mil)* supplies *pl*.

zuführen ['tsu:fy:rən] *vt (leiten)* bring, conduct; *(transportieren)* convey to; *(versorgen)* supply; *vi:* **auf etw (acc) ~** lead to sth.

Zug [tsu:k] *m* **-(e)s, ¨e** *(Eisenbahn)* train; *(Luft—)* draught; *(Ziehen)* pull(ing); *(Gesichts—)* feature; *(Schach etc)* move; *(Klingel—)* pull; *(Schrift—)* stroke; *(Atem—)* breath; *(Charakter—)* trait; *(an Zigarette)* puff, pull, drag; *(Schluck)* gulp; *(Menschengruppe)* procession; *(von Vögeln)* flight; *(Mil)* platoon; **etw in vollen en genießen** enjoy sth to the full.

Zu- ['tsu:] *cpd:* **~gabe** *f* extra; *(in Konzert etc)* encore; **~gang** *m* access, approach; **z~gänglich** *a* accessible; *Mensch* approachable.

Zug- *cpd:* **~abteil** *nt* train compartment; **~brücke** *f* drawbridge.

zugeben ['tsu:ge:bən] *vt irreg (beifügen)* add, throw in; *(zugestehen)* admit; *(erlauben)* permit.

zugehen ['tsu:ge:ən] *vi irreg (schließen)* shut; *v impers (sich ereignen)* go on, proceed; **auf jdn/etw ~** walk towards sb/sth; **dem Ende ~** be finishing.

Zugehörigkeit ['tsu:gəhö:riçkait] *f* membership *(zu* of), belonging *(zu* to); **~sgefühl** *nt* feeling of belonging.

zugeknöpft ['tsu:gəknœpft] *a (col)* reserved, stand-offish.

Zügel ['tsy:gəl] *m* **-s, -** rein(s); *(fig auch)*

curb; **z~los** a unrestrained, licentious; **~losigkeit** f lack of restraint, licentiousness; **z~n** vt curb; *Pferd* auch rein in.

zuge- ['tsu:gə] cpd: **~sellen** vr join (*jdm* up with); **Z~ständnis** nt **-ses, -se** concession; **~stehen** vt irreg admit; *Rechte* concede (*jdm* to sb).

Zug- cpd: **~führer** m (*Rail*) inspector; (*Mil*) platoon commander; **z~ig** a draughty.

zügig ['tsy:gɪç] a speedy, swift.

Zug- cpd: **~luft** f draught; **~maschine** f traction engine, tractor.

zugreifen ['tsu:graifən] vi irreg seize or grab it; (*helfen*) help; (*beim Essen*) help o.s.

zugrunde [tsu'grundə] ad: **~ gehen** collapse; (*Mensch*) perish; **einer Sache etw ~ legen** base sth on sth; **einer Sache ~ liegen** be based on sth; **~ richten** ruin, destroy.

zugunsten [tsu'gunstən] prep +gen or dat in favour of.

zugute [tsu'gu:tə] ad: **jdm etw ~ halten** concede sth; **jdm ~ kommen** be of assistance to sb.

Zug- cpd: **~verbindung** f train connection; **~vogel** m migratory bird.

zuhalten ['tsu:haltən] irreg vt hold shut; vi: **auf jdn/etw ~** make for sb/sth.

Zuhälter ['tsu:hɛltər] m **-s, -** pimp.

Zuhause [tsu'hausə] nt **-** home.

Zuhilfenahme [tsu'hɪlfənɑːmə] f: **unter ~ von** with the help of.

zuhören ['tsu:hø:rən] vi listen (*dat* to).

Zuhörer m **-s, -** listener; **~schaft** f audience.

zujubeln ['tsu:ju:bəln] vi cheer (*jdm* sb).

zukleben ['tsu:kle:bən] vt paste up.

zuknöpfen ['tsu:knœpfən] vt button up, fasten.

zukommen ['tsu:kɔmən] vi irreg come up (*auf* +acc to); (*sich gehören*) be fitting (*jdm* for sb); (*Recht haben auf*) be entitled to; **jdm etw ~ lassen** give sb sth; **etw auf sich ~ lassen** wait and see.

Zukunft ['tsu:kunft] f **-**, **Zukünfte** future.

zukünftig [tsu:kynftɪç] a future; **mein ~er Mann** my husband to be; ad in future.

Zukunfts- cpd: **~aussichten** pl future prospects pl; **~musik** f (col) wishful thinking; crystal ball gazing; **~roman** m science-fiction novel.

Zulage ['tsu:la:gə] f bonus, allowance.

zulassen ['tsu:lasən] vt irreg (*hereinlassen*) admit; (*erlauben*) permit; *Auto* license; (*col: nicht öffnen*) (keep) shut.

zulässig ['tsu:lɛsɪç] a permissible, permitted.

zulaufen ['tsu:laufən] vi irreg run (*auf* +acc towards); (*Tier*) adopt (*jdm* sb); **spitz ~** come to a point.

zulegen ['tsu:le:gən] vt add; *Geld* put in; *Tempo* accelerate, quicken; (*schließen*) cover over; **sich** (*dat*) **etw ~** (col) get hold of sth.

zuleide [tsu'laidə] a: **jdm etw ~ tun** hurt or harm sb.

zuleiten ['tsu:laitən] vt direct (*dat* to); (*schicken*) send.

zuletzt [tsu'lɛtst] ad finally, at last.

zuliebe [tsu'li:bə] ad: **jdm ~** to please sb.

zum [tsum] = **zu dem**: **~ dritten Mal** for the third time; **~ Scherz** as a joke; **~ Trinken** for drinking.

zumachen ['tsu:maxən] vt shut; *Kleidung* do up, fasten; vi shut; (col) hurry up.

zumal [tsu'ma:l] cj especially (as).

zumeist [tsu'maist] ad mostly.

zumindest [tsu'mɪndəst] ad at least.

zumut- cpd: **~bar** ['tsu:mu:tba:r] a reasonable; **~e wie ist ihm ~e?** how does he feel?; **~en** ['tsu:mu:tən] vt expect, ask (*jdm* of sb); **Z~ung** ['tsu:mu:tuŋ] f unreasonable expectation or demand, impertinence.

zunächst [tsu'nɛ:çst] ad first of all; **~ einmal** to start with.

zunähen ['tsu:nɛ:ən] vt sew up.

Zunahme ['tsu:nɑːmə] f **-**, **-n** increase.

Zuname ['tsu:na:mə] m surname.

Zünd- [tsynd] cpd: **z~en** vi (*Feuer*) light, ignite; (*Motor*) fire; (*begeistern*) fire (with enthusiasm) (*bei jdm* sb); **z~end** a fiery; **~er** m **-s, -** fuse; (*Mil*) detonator; **~holz** ['tsynt-] nt match; **~kerze** f (*Aut*) spark(ing) plug; **~schlüssel** m ignition key; **~schnur** f fuse wire; **~stoff** m fuel; (*fig*) dynamite; **~ung** f ignition.

zunehmen ['tsu:ne:mən] vi irreg increase, grow; (*Mensch*) put on weight.

zuneigen ['tsu:naigən] vi incline, lean; **sich dem Ende ~** draw to a close; **einer Auffassung ~** incline towards a view; **jdm zugeneigt sein** be attracted to sb.

Zuneigung f affection.

Zunft [tsunft] f **-**, **-e** guild.

zünftig ['tsynftɪç] a proper, real; *Handwerk* decent.

Zunge ['tsuŋə] f **-**, **-n** tongue; (*Fisch*) sole; **z~nfertig** a glib.

zunichte [tsu'nɪçtə] ad: **~ machen** ruin, destroy; **~ werden** come to nothing.

zunutze [tsu'nutsə] ad: **sich** (*dat*) **etw ~ machen** make use of sth.

zuoberst [tsu'o:bərst] ad at the top.

zupfen ['tsupfən] vt pull, pick, pluck; *Gitarre* pluck.

zur [tsu:r] = **zu der**.

zurech- ['tsu:rɛç] cpd: **~nungsfähig** a responsible, accountable; **Z~nungsfähigkeit** f responsibility, accountability.

zurecht- [tsu:rɛçt] cpd: **~finden** vr irreg find one's way (about); **~kommen** vi irreg (be able to) deal (*mit* with), manage; **~legen** vt get ready; *Ausrede etc* have ready; **~machen** vt prepare; vr get ready; **~weisen** vt irreg reprimand; **Z~weisung** f reprimand, rebuff.

zureden ['tsu:re:dən] vi persuade, urge (*jdm* sb).

zurichten ['tsu:rɪçtən] vt *Essen* prepare; (*beschädigen*) batter, bash up.

zürnen ['tsyrnən] vi be angry (*jdm* with sb).

zurück [tsu'rʏk] ad back; **~behalten** vt irreg keep back; **~bekommen** vt irreg get back; **~bezahlen** vt repay, pay back; **~bleiben** vi irreg (*Mensch*) remain behind; (*nicht nachkommen*) fall behind, lag; (*Schaden*) remain; ~**bringen** *vt irreg* bring back; ~**drängen** *vt Gefühle* repress; *Feind* push back; ~**drehen** *vt* turn back; ~**erobern** *vt* reconquer; ~**fahren** *irreg vi travel back; (vor Schreck)* recoil, start; *vt* drive back; ~**fallen** *vi irreg* fall back; (*in Laster*) relapse; ~**finden** *vi irreg* find one's way back; ~**fordern** *vt* demand back; ~**führen** *vt* lead back; **etw auf etw** (*acc*) ~**führen** trace sth back to sth; ~**geben** *vt irreg* give back; (*antworten*) retort with; ~**geblieben** *a* retarded; ~**gehen** *vi irreg* go back; (*zeitlich*) date back (*auf +acc* to); (*fallen*) go down, fall; ~**gezogen** *a* retired, withdrawn; ~**halten** *irreg vt* hold back; *Mensch* restrain; (*hindern*) prevent; *vr* (*reserviert sein*) be reserved; (*im Essen*) hold back; ~**haltend** *a* reserved; Z~**haltung** *f* reserve; ~**kehren** *vi* return; ~**kommen** *vi irreg* come back; **auf etw** (*acc*) ~**kommen** return to sth; ~**lassen** *vt irreg* leave behind; ~**legen** *vt* put back; *Geld* put by; (*reservieren*) keep back; *Strecke* cover; ~**nehmen** *vt irreg* take back; ~**rufen** *vti irreg* call back; **etw ins Gedächtnis** ~**rufen** recall sth; ~**schrecken** *vi* shrink (*vor +dat* from); ~**setzen** *vt* put back; (*im Preis*) reduce; (*benachteiligen*) put at a disadvantage; ~**stecken** *vt* put back; *vi* (*fig*) moderate (one's wishes); ~**stellen** *vt* put back, replace; (*aufschieben*) put off, postpone; (*Mil*) turn down; *Interessen* defer; *Ware* keep; ~**stoßen** *vt irreg* repulse; ~**treten** *vi irreg* step back; (*vom Amt*) retire; **gegenüber** *or* **hinter etw** ~**treten** diminish in importance in view of sth; ~**weisen** *vt irreg* turn down; *Mensch* reject; Z~**zahlung** *f* repayment; ~**ziehen** *irreg vt* pull back; *Angebot* withdraw; *vr* retire.

Zuruf ['tsu:ru:f] *m* shout, cry.

Zusage ['tsu:za:gə] *f* ~, -n promise; (*Annahme*) consent; **z**~**n** *vi* promise; *vt* accept; **jdm z**~**n** (*gefallen*) agree with or please sb.

zusammen [tsu'zamən] *ad* together; Z~**arbeit** *f* cooperation; ~**arbeiten** *vi* cooperate; ~**beißen** *vt irreg Zähne* clench; ~**bleiben** *vi irreg* stay together; ~**brechen** *vi irreg* collapse; (*Mensch auch*) break down; ~**bringen** *vt irreg* bring or get together; *Geld* get; *Sätze* put together; Z~**bruch** *m* collapse; ~**fahren** *vi irreg* collide; (*erschrecken*) start; ~**fassen** *vt* summarize; (*vereinigen*) unite; ~**fassend** *a* summarizing; *ad* to summarize; Z~**fassung** *f* summary, résumé; ~**finden** *vir irreg* meet (together); ~**fließen** *vi irreg* flow together, meet; Z~**fluß** *m* confluence; ~**fügen** *vt* join (together), unite; ~**gehören** *vi* belong together; (*Paar*) match; ~**gesetzt** *a* compound, composite; ~**halten** *vi irreg* stick together; Z~**hang** *m* connection; **im/aus dem** Z~**hang** in/out of context; ~**hängen** *vi irreg* be connected or linked; ~**hang(s)los** *a* incoherent, disconnected; ~**klappbar** *a* folding, collapsible;

~**kommen** *vi irreg* meet, assemble; (*sich ereignen*) occur at once or together; Z~**kunft** *f* meeting; ~**laufen** *vi irreg* run or come together; (*Straßen, Flüsse etc*) converge, meet; (*Farben*) run into one another; ~**legen** *vt* put together; (*stapeln*) pile up; (*falten*) fold; (*verbinden*) combine, unite; *Termine, Fest* amalgamate; *Geld* collect; ~**nehmen** *vt irreg* summon up; **alles** ~**genommen** all in all; *vr* pull o.s. together; ~**passen** *vi* go well together, match; ~**prallen** *vi* collide; ~**schlagen** *vt irreg Mensch* beat up; *Dinge* smash up; (*falten*) fold; *Hände* clap; *Hacken* click; ~**schließen** *vtr irreg* join (together); Z~**schluß** *m* amalgamation; ~**schreiben** *vt irreg* write together; *Bericht* put together; ~**schrumpfen** *vi* shrink, shrivel up; Z~**sein** *nt* -s get-together; ~**setzen** *vt* put together; *vr* be composed of; Z~**setzung** *f* composition; ~**stellen** *vt* put together; compile; Z~**stellung** *f* list; (*Vorgang*) compilation; Z~**stoß** *m* collision; ~**stoßen** *vi irreg* collide; ~**treffen** *vi irreg* coincide; *Menschen* meet; Z~**treffen** *nt* meeting; coincidence; ~**wachsen** *vi irreg* grow together; ~**zählen** *vt* add up; ~**ziehen** *irreg vt* (*verengern*) draw together; (*vereinigen*) bring together; (*addieren*) add up; *vr* shrink; (*sich bilden*) form, develop.

Zusatz ['tsu:zats] *m* addition; ~**antrag** *m* (*Pol*) amendment.

zusätzlich ['tsu:zɛtslɪç] *a* additional

zuschauen ['tsu:ʃauən] *vi* watch, look on.

Zuschauer *m* -s, - spectator; *pl* (*Theat*) audience.

zuschicken ['tsu:ʃɪkən] *vt* send, forward (*jdm etw* sth to sb).

zuschließen ['tsu:ʃli:sən] *irreg vt* fire (*dat* at); *Geld* put in; *vi:* ~ **auf** (*+acc*) rush towards.

Zuschlag ['tsu:ʃla:k] *m* extra charge, surcharge; **z**~**en** ['tsu:ʃla:gən] *irreg vt Tür* slam; *Ball* hit (*jdm* to sb); (*bei Auktion*) knock down; *Steine etc* knock into shape; *vi* (*Fenster, Tür*) shut; (*Mensch*) hit, punch; ~**skarte** *f* (*Rail*) surcharge ticket; **z**~**spflichtig** *a* subject to surcharge.

zuschließen ['tsu:ʃli:sən] *irreg vt* lock (up).

zuschmeißen ['tsu:ʃmaisən] *vt irreg* (*col*) slam, bang shut.

zuschneiden ['tsu:ʃnaidən] *vt irreg* cut out *or* to size.

zuschnüren ['tsu:ʃny:rən] *vt* tie up.

zuschrauben ['tsu:ʃraubən] *vt* screw down *or* up.

zuschreiben ['tsu:ʃraibən] *vt irreg* (*fig*) ascribe, attribute; (*Comm*) credit.

Zuschrift ['tsu:ʃrɪft] *f* letter, reply.

zuschulden [tsu:ʃuldən] *ad:* **sich** (*dat*) **etw** ~ **kommen lassen** make o.s. guilty of sth.

Zuschuß ['tsu:ʃus] *m* subsidy, allowance.

zuschütten ['tsu:ʃytən] *vt* fill up.

zusehen ['tsu:ze:ən] *vi irreg* watch (*jdm/etw* sb/sth); (*dafür sorgen*) take care; ~**ds** *ad* visibly.

zusenden ['tsu:zɛndən] *vt irreg* forward, send on (*jdm etw* sth to sb).

zusetzen ['tsu:zɛtsən] vt (beifügen) add; Geld lose; vi: **jdm ~ harass** sb; (Krankheit) take a lot out of sb.

zusichern ['tsu:zɪçərn] vt assure (jdm etw sb of sth).

zusperren ['tsu:ʃpɛrən] vt bar.

zuspielen ['tsu:ʃpiːən] vti pass (jdm to sb).

zuspitzen ['tsu:ʃpɪtsən] vt sharpen; vr (Lage) become critical.

zusprechen ['tsu:ʃprɛçən] irreg vt (zuerkennen) award (jdm etw sb sth, sth to sb); **jdm Trost ~** comfort sb; vi speak (jdm to sb); **dem Essen/Alkohol ~** eat/drink a lot.

Zuspruch ['tsu:ʃprux] m encouragement; (Anklang) appreciation, popularity.

Zustand ['tsu:ʃtant] m state, condition; z~e ['tsu:ʃtandə] ad: z~e bringen vt irreg bring about; z~e kommen vi irreg come about.

zuständig ['tsu:ʃtɛndɪç] a competent, responsible; **Z~keit** f competence, responsibility.

zustehen ['tsu:ʃteːən] vi irreg: **jdm ~** be sb's right.

zustellen ['tsu:ʃtɛlən] vt (verstellen) block; Post etc send.

zustimmen ['tsu:ʃtɪmən] vi agree (dat to). **Zustimmung** f agreement, consent.

zustoßen ['tsu:ʃtoːsən] vi irreg (fig) happen (jdm to sb).

zutage [tsu:ˈtaːgə] ad: **~ bringen** bring to light; **~ treten** come to light.

Zutaten ['tsu:taːtən] pl ingredients pl.

zuteilen ['tsu:taɪlən] vt allocate, assign.

zutiefst [tsu:ˈtiːfst] ad deeply.

zutragen ['tsu:traːgən] irreg vt bring (jdm etw sth to sb); Klatsch tell; vr happen.

zuträglich ['tsu:trɛːklɪç] a beneficial.

zutrau- ['tsu:trau] cpd: **~en** vt credit (jdm etw sb with sth); **Z~en** nt -s trust (zu in); **~lich** a trusting, friendly; **Z~lichkeit** f trust.

zutreffen ['tsu:trɛfən] vi irreg be correct; apply; **Z~des bitte unterstreichen** please underline where applicable.

zutrinken ['tsu:trɪŋkən] vi irreg drink to (jdm to sb).

Zutritt ['tsu:trɪt] m access, admittance.

Zutun ['tsu:tuːn] nt -s assistance; vt irreg add; (schließen) shut.

zuverlässig ['tsu:fɛrlɛsɪç] a reliable; **Z~keit** f reliability.

Zuversicht ['tsu:fɛrzɪçt] f - confidence; z~lich a confident; **~lichkeit** f confidence, hopefulness.

zuviel [tsu:ˈfiːl] ad too much.

zuvor [tsu:ˈfoːr] ad before, previously; **~kommen** vi irreg anticipate (jdm sb), beat (sb) to it; **~kommend** a obliging, courteous.

Zuwachs ['tsu:vaks] m -es increase, growth; (col) addition; z~en vi irreg become overgrown; (Wunde) heal (up).

zuwandern ['tsu:vandərn] vi immigrate.

zuwege [tsu:ˈveːgə] ad: etw ~ bringen accomplish sth; mit etw ~ kommen manage sth; gut ~ sein be (doing) well.

zuweilen [tsu:ˈvaɪlən] ad at times, now and then.

zuweisen ['tsu:vaɪzən] vt irreg assign, allocate (jdm to sb).

zuwenden ['tsu:vɛndən] irreg vt turn (dat towards); **jdm seine Aufmerksamkeit ~** give sb one's attention; vr devote o.s., turn (dat to).

zuwenig [tsu:ˈveːnɪç] ad too little.

zuwerfen ['tsu:vɛrfən] vt irreg throw (jdm to sb).

zuwider [tsu:ˈviːdər] ad: etw ist jdm ~ sb loathes sth, sb finds sth repugnant; prep +dat contrary to; **~handeln** vi act contrary (dat to); **einem Gesetz ~handeln** contravene a law; **Z~handlung** f contravention; **~laufen** vi irreg run counter (dat to).

zuziehen ['tsu:tsiːən] irreg vt (schließen) Vorhang draw, close; (herbeirufen) Experten call in; **sich (dat) etw ~ Krankheit** catch; Zorn incur; vi move in, come.

zuzüglich ['tsu:tsyːklɪç] prep +gen plus, with the addition of.

Zwang [tsvaŋ] m -(e)s, ⁺e compulsion, coercion.

zwängen ['tsvɛŋən] vtr squeeze.

Zwang- cpd: **z~los** a informal; **~losigkeit** f informality; **~sarbeit** f forced labour; (Strafe) hard labour; **~sjacke** f straightjacket; **~slage** f predicament, tight corner; z~släufig a necessary, inevitable; **~smaßnahme** f sanction, coercive measure; z~sweise ad compulsorily.

zwanzig ['tsvantsɪç] num twenty.

zwar [tsva:r] ad to be sure, indeed; **das ist ~...**, **aber ...** that may be ... but ...; **und ~ am Sonntag** on Sunday to be precise; **und ~ so schnell, daß ...** in fact so quickly that ...

Zweck ['tsvɛk] m -(e)s, -e purpose, aim; z~dienlich a practical; expedient; **~e** f -, -n hobnail; (Heft~) drawing pin, thumbtack (US); **~entfremdung** f misuse; z~los a pointless; z~mäßig a suitable, appropriate; **~mäßigkeit** f suitability; z~widrig a unsuitable.

zwei [tsvaɪ] num two; **~deutig** a ambiguous; (unanständig) suggestive; **~erlei** a: **~erlei Stoff** two different kinds of material; **~erlei Meinung** of differing opinions; **~erlei zu tun haben** have two different things to do; **~fach** a double.

Zweifel ['tsvaɪfəl] m -s, - doubt; z~haft a doubtful, dubious; z~los a doubtless; z~n vi doubt (an etw (dat) sth); **~sfall** m: **im ~sfall** in case of doubt.

Zweig [tsvaɪk] m -(e)s, -e branch; **~geschäft** nt (Comm) branch; **~stelle** f branch (office).

zwei- cpd: **Z~heit** f duality; **~hundert** num two hundred; **Z~kampf** m duel; **~mal** ad twice; **~motorig** a twin-engined; **~reihig** a (Anzug) double-breasted; **~schneidig** a (fig) two-edged; **Z~sitzer** m -s, - two-seater; **~sprachig** a bilingual; **~spurig** a (Aut) two-lane; **~stimmig** a for two voices;

Z~taktmotor m two-stroke engine.

zweit- [tsvait] cpd: **~ens** ad secondly; **~größte(r,s)** a second largest; **~klassig** a second-class; **~letzte(r,s)** a last but one, penultimate; **~rangig** a second-rate; Z**~wagen** m second car.

Zwerchfell ['tsverçfɛl] nt diaphragm.

Zwerg [tsvɛrk] m -(e)s, -e dwarf.

Zwetsche ['tsvɛtʃə] f -, -n plum.

Zwickel ['tsvikəl] m -s, - gusset.

zwicken ['tsvikən] vt pinch, nip.

Zwieback ['tsvi:bak] m -(e)s, -e rusk.

Zwiebel ['tsvi:bəl] f -, -n onion; (Blumen—) bulb; z**~artig** a bulbous.

Zwie- ['tsvi:] cpd: **~gespräch** vt dialogue; **~licht** nt twilight; z**~lichtig** a shady, dubious; **~spalt** m conflict, split; z**~spältig** a Gefühle conflicting; Charakter contradictory; **~tracht** f discord, dissension.

Zwilling ['tsviliŋ] m -s, -e twin; pl (Astrol) Gemini.

zwingen ['tsviŋən] vt irreg force; **~nd** a Grund etc compelling.

zwinkern ['tsviŋkərn] vi blink; (absichtlich) wink.

Zwirn [tsvirn] m -(e)s, -e thread.

zwischen ['tsviʃən] prep +acc or dat between; Z**~bemerkung** f (incidental) remark; **~blenden** vt (TV) insert; Z**~ding** nt cross; **~durch** [-'durç] ad in between; (räumlich) here and there; Z**~ergebnis** nt intermediate result; Z**~fall** m incident; Z**~frage** f question; Z**~gas** nt: Z**~gas geben** double-declutch; Z**~handel** m middlemen pl; middleman's trade; Z**~händler** m middleman, agent; Z**~landung** f stop, intermediate landing; **~menschlich** a interpersonal; Z**~raum** m space; Z**~ruf** m interjection, interruption; Z**~spiel** nt interlude; **~staatlich** f interstate; international; Z**~station** f intermediate station; Z**~stecker** m (Elec) adaptor; Z**~wand** f partition; Z**~zeit** f interval; **in der Z~zeit** in the interim, meanwhile.

Zwist [tsvist] m -es, -e dispute, feud.

zwitschern ['tsvitʃərn] vti twitter, chirp.

Zwitter ['tsvitər] m -s, - hermaphrodite.

zwölf [tsvœlf] num twelve.

Zyklus ['tsy:klus] m -, **Zyklen** cycle.

Zylinder [tsi'lindər] m -s, - cylinder; (Hut) top hat; z**~förmig** a cylindrical.

Zyniker ['tsy:nikər] m -s, - cynic.

zynisch ['tsy:niʃ] a cynical.

Zynismus [tsy'nismus] m cynicism.

Zyste ['tsystə] f -, -n cyst.

ENGLISH - GERMAN
ENGLISCH - DEUTSCH

A

A, a [eɪ] n A nt, a nt.

a, an [eɪ, ə; æn, ən] indef art ein/eine/ein. **£1 a metre** 1£ pro or das Meter.

aback [ə'bæk] ad: **to be taken ~** verblüfft sein.

abandon [ə'bændən] vt (give up) aufgeben; (desert) verlassen; n Hingabe f.

abashed [ə'bæʃt] a verlegen.

abate [ə'beɪt] vi nachlassen, sich legen.

abattoir ['æbətwɑ:*] n Schlachthaus nt.

abbey ['æbɪ] n Abtei f.

abbot ['æbət] n Abt m.

abbreviate [ə'bri:vɪeɪt] vt abkürzen.

abbreviation [əbri:vɪ'eɪʃən] n Abkürzung f.

ABC ['eɪbi:'si:] n (lit, fig) Abc nt.

abdicate ['æbdɪkeɪt] vt aufgeben; vi abdanken.

abdication [æbdɪ'keɪʃən] n Abdankung f; (Amts)niederlegung f.

abdomen ['æbdəmən] n Unterleib m.

abdominal [æb'dɒmɪnl] a Unterleibs-.

abduct [æb'dʌkt] vt entführen; **~ion** [æb'dʌkʃən] Entführung f.

aberration [æbə'reɪʃən] n (geistige) Verwirrung f.

abet [ə'bet] vt see **aid** vt.

abeyance [ə'beɪəns] n: **in ~** in der Schwebe; (disuse) außer Kraft.

abhor [əb'hɔ:*] vt verabscheuen.

abhorrent [əb'hɒrənt] a verabscheuungswürdig.

abide [ə'baɪd] vt vertragen, leiden; **~ by** vt sich halten an (+acc).

ability [ə'bɪlɪtɪ] n (power) Fähigkeit f; (skill) Geschicklichkeit f.

abject ['æbdʒekt] a liar übel; poverty größte(r, s); apology zerknirscht.

ablaze [ə'bleɪz] a in Flammen, **~ with lights** hell erleuchtet.

able ['eɪbl] a geschickt, fähig; **to be ~ to do sth** etw tun können; **~-bodied** a kräftig; seaman Voll-; (Mil) wehrfähig.

ably ['eɪblɪ] ad geschickt.

abnormal [æb'nɔ:məl] a regelwidrig, abnorm; **~ity** [æbnɔ:'mælɪtɪ] Regelwidrigkeit f; (Med) krankhafte Erscheinung f.

aboard [ə'bɔ:d] ad, prep an Bord (+gen).

abode [ə'bəʊd] n: **of no fixed ~** ohne festen Wohnsitz.

abolish [ə'bɒlɪʃ] vt abschaffen.

abolition [æbə'lɪʃən] n Abschaffung f.

abominable a, **abominably** ad [ə'bɒmɪnəbl, -blɪ] scheußlich.

aborigine [æbə'rɪdʒɪni:] n Ureinwohner m.

abort [ə'bɔ:t] vt abtreiben; fehlgebären; **~ion** [ə'bɔ:ʃən] Abtreibung f; (miscarriage) Fehlgeburt f; **~ive** a mißlungen.

abound [ə'baʊnd] vi im Überfluß vorhanden sein; **to ~ in** Überfluß haben an (+dat).

about [ə'baʊt] ad (nearby) in der Nähe; (roughly) ungefähr; (around) umher, herum; prep (topic) über (+acc); (place) um, um ... herum; **to be ~ to** im Begriff sein zu; **I was ~ to go out** ich wollte gerade weggehen.

above [ə'bʌv] ad oben; prep über; a obig; **~ all** vor allem; **~board** a offen, ehrlich.

abrasion [ə'breɪʒən] n Abschürfung f.

abrasive [ə'breɪzɪv] n Schleifmittel nt; a Abschleif-; personality zermürbend, aufreibend.

abreast [ə'brest] ad nebeneinander; **to keep ~ of** Schritt halten mit.

abridge [ə'brɪdʒ] vt (ab)kürzen.

abroad [ə'brɔ:d] ad be im Ausland; go ins Ausland.

abrupt [ə'brʌpt] a (sudden) abrupt, jäh; (curt) schroff.

abscess ['æbsɪs] n Geschwür nt.

abscond [əb'skɒnd] vi flüchten, sich davonmachen.

absence ['æbsəns] n Abwesenheit f.

absent ['æbsənt] a abwesend, nicht da; (lost in thought) geistesabwesend; **~ee** [æbsən'ti:] Abwesende(r) m; **~eeism** [æbsən'ti:ɪzəm] Fehlen nt (am Arbeitsplatz/in der Schule); **~-minded** a zerstreut.

absolute ['æbsəlu:t] a absolut; power unumschränkt; rubbish vollkommen, rein; **~ly** ['æbsəlu:tlɪ] ad absolut, vollkommen; **~! ** ganz bestimmt!

absolve [əb'zɒlv] vt entbinden; freisprechen.

absorb [əb'zɔ:b] vt aufsaugen, absorbieren; (fig) ganz in Anspruch nehmen, fesseln; **~ent** a absorbierend; **~ent cotton** (US) Verbandwatte f; **~ing** a aufsaugend; (fig) packend.

abstain [əb'steɪn] vi (in vote) sich enthalten; **to ~ from** (keep from) sich enthalten (+gen).

abstemious [əb'sti:mɪəs] a mäßig, enthaltsam.

abstention [əb'stenʃən] n (in vote) (Stimm)enthaltung f.

abstinence ['æbstɪnəns] n Enthaltsamkeit f.

abstract ['æbstrækt] a abstrakt; n Abriß m; [æb'strækt] vt abstrahieren, aussondern.

abstruse [æb'stru:s] a verworren, abstrus.

absurd [əb'sɜ:d] a absurd; **~ity** Unsinnigkeit f, Absurdität f.

abundance [ə'bʌndəns] n Überfluß m (of an +dat).

abundant [ə'bʌndənt] a reichlich.

abuse [ə'bju:s] n (rude language) Beschimpfung f; (ill usage) Mißbrauch m; (bad practice) (Amts)Mißbrauch m; [ə'bju:z] vt (misuse) mißbrauchen.

abusive [ə'bju:sɪv] a beleidigend, Schimpf-.

abysmal [ə'bɪzməl] a scheußlich; ignorance bodenlos.

abyss [ə'bɪs] n Abgrund m.

academic [ækə'demɪk] a akademisch; (theoretical) theoretisch.

academy [ə'kædəmɪ] n (school) Hochschule f; (society) Akademie f.

accede [æk'si:d] vi: ~ to office antreten; throne besteigen; request zustimmen (+dat).

accelerate [æk'seləreɪt] vi schneller werden; (Aut) Gas geben; vt beschleunigen.

acceleration [ækselə'reɪʃən] n Beschleunigung f.

accelerator [ək'seləreɪtə*] n Gas(pedal) nt.

accent ['æksənt] n Akzent m, Tonfall m; (mark) Akzent m; (stress) Betonung f; ~uate [ək'sentjueɪt] vt betonen.

accept [ək'sept] vt (take) annehmen; (agree to) akzeptieren; ~able a annehmbar; ~ance Annahme f.

access ['ækses] n Zugang m; ~ible [æk'sesɪbl] a (easy to approach) zugänglich; (within reach) (leicht) erreichbar; ~ion [æk'seʃən] (to throne) Besteigung f; (to office) Antritt m.

accessory [æk'sesərɪ] n Zubehörteil nt; accessories pl Zubehör nt; toilet accessories pl Toilettenartikel pl.

accident ['æksɪdənt] n Unfall m; (coincidence) Zufall m; by ~ zufällig; ~al [æksɪ'dentl] a unbeabsichtigt; ~ally [æksɪ'dentəlɪ] ad zufällig; to be ~-prone zu Unfällen neigen.

acclaim [ə'kleɪm] vt zujubeln (+dat); n Beifall m.

acclimatize [ə'klaɪmətaɪz] vt: to become ~d sich gewöhnen (to an +acc), sich akklimatisieren.

accolade [ə'kəleɪd] n Auszeichnung f.

accommodate [ə'kɒmədeɪt] vt unterbringen; (hold) Platz haben für; (oblige) (aus)helfen (+dat).

accommodating [ə'kɒmədeɪtɪŋ] a entgegenkommend.

accommodation [ə'kɒmə'deɪʃən] n Unterkunft f.

accompaniment [ə'kʌmpənɪmənt] n Begleitung f.

accompanist [ə'kʌmpənɪst] n Begleiter m.

accompany [ə'kʌmpənɪ] vt begleiten.

accomplice [ə'kʌmplɪs] n Helfershelfer m, Komplize m.

accomplish [ə'kʌmplɪʃ] vt (fulfil) durchführen; (finish) vollenden; aim erreichen; ~ed a vollendet, ausgezeichnet; ~ment (skill) Fähigkeit f; (completion) Vollendung f; (feat) Leistung f.

accord [ə'kɔ:d] n Übereinstimmung f; of one's own ~ freiwillig; vt gewähren; ~ance: in ~ance with in Übereinstimmung mit; ~ing to nach, laut (+gen); ~ingly ad danach, dementsprechend

accordion [ə'kɔ:dɪən] n Ziehharmonika f,

Akkordeon nt; ~ist Akkordeonspieler m.

accost [ə'kɒst] vt ansprechen.

account [ə'kaunt] n (bill) Rechnung f; (narrative) Bericht m; (report) Rechenschaftsbericht m; (in bank) Konto nt; (importance) Geltung f; on ~ auf Rechnung; of no ~ ohne Bedeutung; on no ~ keinesfalls; on ~ of wegen; to take into ~ berücksichtigen; ~ for vt expenditure Rechenschaft ablegen für; how do you ~ for that? wie erklären Sie (sich) das?; ~able a verantwortlich; ~ancy Buchhaltung f; ~ant Wirtschaftsprüfer(in f) m.

accoutrements [ə'ku:trəmənts] npl Ausrüstung f.

accredited [ə'kredɪtɪd] a beglaubigt, akkreditiert.

accretion [ə'kri:ʃən] n Zunahme f.

accrue [ə'kru:] vi erwachsen, sich ansammeln.

accumulate [ə'kju:mjuleɪt] vt ansammeln; vi sich ansammeln.

accumulation [əkju:mju'leɪʃən] n (act) Aufhäufung f; (result) Ansammlung f.

accuracy ['ækjurəsɪ] n Genauigkeit f.

accurate ['ækjurɪt] a genau; ~ly ad genau, richtig.

accursed, accurst [ə'kɜ:st] a verflucht.

accusation [ækju:'zeɪʃən] n Anklage f, Beschuldigung f.

accusative [ə'kju:zətɪv] n Akkusativ m, vierte(r) Fall m.

accuse [ə'kju:z] vt anklagen, beschuldigen; ~d Angeklagte(r) mf.

accustom [ə'kʌstəm] vt gewöhnen (to an +acc); ~ed a gewohnt.

ace [eɪs] n As nt; (col) As nt, Kanone f.

ache [eɪk] n Schmerz m; vi (be sore) schmerzen, weh tun; I ~ all over mir tut es überall weh.

achieve [ə'tʃi:v] vt zustande bringen; aim erreichen; ~ment Leistung f; (act) Erreichen nt.

acid ['æsɪd] n Säure f; a sauer, scharf; ~ity [ə'sɪdɪtɪ] Säuregehalt m; ~ test (fig) Nagelprobe f.

acknowledge [ək'nɒlɪdʒ] vt receipt bestätigen; (admit) zugeben; ~ment Anerkennung f; (letter) Empfangsbestätigung f.

acne ['æknɪ] n Akne f.

acorn ['eɪkɔ:n] n Eichel f.

acoustic [ə'ku:stɪk] a akustisch; ~s pl Akustik f.

acquaint [ə'kweɪnt] vt vertraut machen; ~ance (person) Bekannte(r) m; (knowledge) Kenntnis f.

acquiesce [ækwɪ'es] vi sich abfinden (in mit).

acquire [ə'kwaɪə*] vt erwerben.

acquisition [ækwɪ'zɪʃən] n Errungenschaft f; (act) Erwerb m.

acquisitive [ə'kwɪzɪtɪv] a gewinnsüchtig.

acquit [ə'kwɪt] vt (free) freisprechen; to ~ o.s. sich bewähren; ~tal Freispruch m.

acre ['eɪkə*] n Morgen m; ~age Fläche f.

acrimonious [ækrɪ'məunɪəs] a bitter.

acrobat ['ækrəbæt] n Akrobat m.

acrobatics [ækrə'bætıks] *npl* akrobatische Kunststücke *pl*.

across [ə'krɒs] *prep* über (+*acc*); **he lives ~ the river** er wohnt auf der anderen Seite des Flusses; *ad* hinüber, herüber; **ten metres ~** zehn Meter breit; **he lives ~ from us** er wohnt uns gegenüber; **~-the-board** *a* pauschal.

act [ækt] *n* (*deed*) Tat *f*; (*Jur*) Gesetz *nt*; (*Theat*) Akt *m*; (*Theat: turn*) Nummer *f*; *vi* (*take action*) handeln; (*behave*) sich verhalten; (*pretend*) vorgeben; (*Theat*) spielen; *vt* (*in play*) spielen; **~ing** *a* stellvertretend; *n* Schauspielkunst *f*; (*performance*) Aufführung *f*.

action ['ækʃən] *n* (*deed*) Tat *f*; Handlung *f*; (*motion*) Bewegung *f*; (*way of working*) Funktionieren *nt*; (*battle*) Einsatz *m*, Gefecht *nt*; (*lawsuit*) Klage *f*, Prozeß *m*; to **take ~** etwas unternehmen.

activate ['æktıveıt] *vt* in Betrieb setzen, aktivieren.

active ['æktıv] *a* (*brisk*) rege, tatkräftig; (*working*) aktiv; (*Gram*) aktiv, Tätigkeits-; **~ly** *ad* aktiv, tätig.

activist ['æktıvıst] *n* Aktivist *m*.

activity [æk'tıvıtı] *n* Aktivität *f*; (*doings*) Unternehmungen *pl*; (*occupation*) Tätigkeit *f*.

actor ['æktə*] *n* Schauspieler *m*.

actress ['æktrıs] *n* Schauspielerin *f*.

actual ['æktjuəl] *a* wirklich; **~ly** *ad* tatsächlich; **~ly no** eigentlich nicht.

acumen ['ækjumen] *n* Scharfsinn *m*.

acupuncture ['ækjupʌŋktʃə*] *n* Akupunktur *f*.

acute [ə'kju:t] *a* (*severe*) heftig, akut; (*keen*) scharfsinnig; **~ly** *ad* akut, scharf.

ad [æd] *n abbr of* **advertisement**.

adage ['ædıdʒ] *n* Sprichwort *nt*.

Adam ['ædəm] *n* Adam *m*; **~'s apple** Adamsapfel *m*.

adamant ['ædəmənt] *a* eisern; hartnäckig.

adapt [ə'dæpt] *vt* anpassen; *vi* sich anpassen (*to an* +*acc*); **~able** *a* anpassungsfähig; **~ation** [ædæp'teıʃən] (*Theat etc*) Bearbeitung *f*; (*adjustment*) Anpassung *f*; **~er** (*Elec*) Zwischenstecker *m*.

add [æd] *vt* (*join*) hinzufügen; *numbers* addieren; **~ up** *vi* (*make sense*) stimmen; **~ up to** *vt* ausmachen.

addendum [ə'dendəm] *n* Zusatz *m*.

adder ['ædə*] *n* Kreuzotter *f*, Natter *f*.

addict ['ædıkt] *n* Süchtige(r) *mf*; **~ed** *a* [ə'dıktıd] **~ed to** -süchtig; **~ion** [ə'dıkʃən] Sucht *f*.

adding machine ['ædıŋməʃi:n] *n* Addiermaschine *f*.

addition [ə'dıʃən] *n* Anhang *m*, Addition *f*; (*Math*) Addition *f*, Zusammenzählen *nt*; **in ~** zusätzlich, außerdem; **~al** *a* zusätzlich, weiter.

additive ['ædıtıv] *n* Zusatz *m*.

addled ['ædld] *a* faul, schlecht; (*fig*) verwirrt.

address [ə'dres] *n* Adresse *f*; (*speech*) Ansprache *f*; **form of ~** Anredeform *f*; *vt letter* adressieren; (*speak to*) ansprechen; (*make speech to*) eine Ansprache halten

an (+*acc*); **~ee** [ædre'si:] Empfänger(in *f*) *m*, Adressat *m*.

adenoids ['ædənɔıdz] *npl* Polypen *pl*.

adept ['ædept] *a* geschickt; **to be ~ at** gut sein in (+*dat*).

adequacy ['ædıkwəsı] *n* Angemessenheit *f*.

adequate ['ædıkwıt] *a* angemessen; **~ly** *ad* hinreichend.

adhere [əd'hıə*] *vi*: **~ to** (*lit*) haften an (+*dat*); (*fig*) festhalten an (+*dat*).

adhesion [əd'hi:ʒən] *n* Festhaften *nt*; (*Phys*) Adhäsion *f*.

adhesive [əd'hi:zıv] *a* klebend; Kleb(e)-; *n* Klebstoff *m*.

adieu [ə'dju:] *n* Adieu *nt*, Lebewohl *nt*.

adjacent [ə'dʒeısənt] *n* benachbart.

adjective ['ædʒəktıv] *n* Adjektiv *nt*, Eigenschaftswort *nt*.

adjoining [ə'dʒɔınıŋ] *a* benachbart, Neben-.

adjourn [ə'dʒ3:n] *vt* vertagen; *vi* abbrechen.

adjudicate [ə'dʒu:dıkeıt] *vti* entscheiden, ein Urteil fällen.

adjudication [ədʒu:dı'keıʃən] *n* Entscheidung *f*.

adjudicator [ə'dʒu:dıkeıtə*] *n* Schiedsrichter *m*, Preisrichter *m*.

adjust [ə'dʒʌst] *vt* (*alter*) anpassen; (*put right*) regulieren, richtig stellen; **~able** *a* verstellbar; **~ment** (*rearrangement*) Anpassung *f*; (*settlement*) Schlichtung *f*.

adjutant ['ædʒətənt] *n* Adjutant *m*.

ad-lib [æd'lıb] *vi* improvisieren; *n* Improvisation *f*; *a, ad* improvisiert.

administer [æd'mınıstə*] *vt* (*manage*) verwalten; (*dispense*) ausüben; *justice* sprechen; *medicine* geben.

administration [ədmınıs'treıʃən] *n* Verwaltung *f*; (*Pol*) Regierung *f*.

administrative [əd'mınıstrətıv] *a* Verwaltungs-.

administrator [əd'mınıstreıtə*] *n* Verwaltungsbeamte(r) *m*.

admirable ['ædmərəbl] *a* bewundernswert.

admiral ['ædmərəl] *n* Admiral *m*; **A~ty** Admiralität *f*.

admiration [ædmı'reıʃən] *n* Bewunderung *f*.

admire [əd'maıə*] *vt* (*respect*) bewundern; (*love*) verehren; **~r** Bewunderer *m*.

admission [əd'mıʃən] *n* (*entrance*) Einlaß *m*; (*fee*) Eintritt(spreis) *m*; (*confession*) Geständnis *nt*.

admit [əd'mıt] *vt* (*let in*) einlassen; (*confess*) gestehen; (*accept*) anerkennen; **~tance** Zulassung *f*; **~tedly** *ad* zugegebenermaßen.

ado [ə'du:] *n*: **without more ~** ohne weitere Umstände.

adolescence [ædə'lesns] *n* Jugendalter *nt*.

adolescent [ædə'lesnt] *a* heranwachsend, jugendlich; *n* Jugendliche(r) *mf*.

adopt [ə'dɒpt] *vt child* adoptieren; *idea* übernehmen; **~ion** [ə'dɒpʃən] (*of child*) Adoption *f*; (*of idea*) Übernahme *f*.

adorable [ə'dɔ:rəbl] *a* anbetungswürdig; (*likeable*) entzückend.

adoration [ædo'reɪʃən] *n* Anbetung *f*; Verehrung *f*.

adore [ə'dɔː] *vt* anbeten; verehren.

adoring [ə'dɔːrɪŋ] *a* verehrend.

adorn [ə'dɔːn] *vt* schmücken.

adornment [ə'dɔːnmənt] *n* Schmuck *m*, Verzierung *f*.

adrenalin [ə'drenəlɪn] *n* Adrenalin *nt*.

adrift [ə'drɪft] *ad* Wind und Wellen preisgegeben.

adroit [ə'drɔɪt] *a* gewandt.

adulation [ædju'leɪʃən] *n* Lobhudelei *f*.

adult [ˈædʌlt] *a* erwachsen; *n* Erwachsene(r) *mf*.

adulterate [ə'dʌltəreɪt] *vt* verfälschen, mischen.

adultery [ə'dʌltərɪ] *n* Ehebruch *m*.

advance [əd'vɑːns] *n* (*progress*) Vorrücken *nt*; (*money*) Vorschuß *m*; *vt* (*move forward*) vorrücken; *money* vorschießen; *argument* vorbringen; *vi* vorwärtsgehen; in ~ im voraus; **in** ~ **of** vor (+*dat*); ~ **booking** Vorbestellung *f*, Vorverkauf *m*; ~**d** *a* (*ahead*) vorgerückt; (*modern*) fortgeschritten; *study* für Fortgeschrittene; ~**ment** Förderung *f*; (*promotion*) Beförderung *f*.

advantage [əd'vɑːntɪdʒ] *n* Vorteil *m*; ~**ous** [ædvən'teɪdʒəs] *a* vorteilhaft; **to have an** ~ **over sb** jdm gegenüber im Vorteil sein; **to be of** ~ von Nutzen sein; **to take** ~ **of** (*misuse*) ausnutzen; (*profit from*) Nutzen ziehen aus.

advent [ˈædvent] *n* Ankunft *f*; **A**~ Advent *m*.

adventure [əd'ventʃə] *n* Abenteuer *nt*.

adventurous [əd'ventʃərəs] *a* abenteuerlich, waghalsig.

adverb [ˈædvɜːb] *n* Adverb *nt*, Umstandswort *nt*.

adversary [ˈædvəsərɪ] *n* Gegner *m*.

adverse [ˈædvɜːs] *a* widrig.

adversity [əd'vɜːsɪtɪ] *n* Widrigkeit *f*, Mißgeschick *nt*.

advert [ˈædvɜːt] *n* Anzeige *f*; ~**ise** *vt* anzeigen; *vi* annoncieren; ~**isement** [əd'vɜːtɪsmənt] Anzeige *f*, Annonce *f*, Inserat *nt*; ~**ising** Werbung *f*; ~**ising campaign** Werbekampagne *f*.

advice [əd'vaɪs] *n* Rat(schlag) *m*.

advisable [əd'vaɪzəbl] *a* ratsam.

advise [əd'vaɪz] *vt* raten (+*dat*); ~**r** Berater *m*.

advisory [əd'vaɪzərɪ] *a* beratend, Beratungs-.

advocate [ˈædvəkeɪt] *vt* vertreten.

aegis [ˈiːdʒɪs] *n*: **under the** ~ **of** unter der Schirmherrschaft von.

aerial [ˈɛərɪəl] *n* Antenne *f*; *a* Luft-.

aero- [ˈɛərəʊ] *pref* Luft-.

aeroplane [ˈɛərəpleɪn] *n* Flugzeug *nt*.

aerosol [ˈɛərəsɒl] *n* Aerosol *nt*; Sprühdose *f*.

aesthetic [ɪs'θetɪk] *a* ästhetisch; ~**s** Ästhetik *f*.

afar [ə'fɑː] *ad*: **from** ~ aus der Ferne.

affable [ˈæfəbl] *a* umgänglich.

affair [ə'fɛə] *n* (*concern*) Angelegenheit *f*;

(*event*) Ereignis *nt*; (*love* —) (Liebes)verhältnis *nt*.

affect [ə'fekt] *vt* (*influence*) (ein)wirken auf (+*acc*); (*move deeply*) bewegen; **this change doesn't** ~ **us** diese Änderung betrifft uns nicht; ~**ation** [æfek'teɪʃən] Affektiertheit *f*, Verstellung *f*; ~**ed** *a* affektiert, gekünstelt; ~**ion** [ə'fekʃən] Zuneigung *f*; ~**ionate** [ə'fekʃənɪt] *a* liebevoll, lieb; ~**ionately** [ə'fekʃənɪtlɪ] *ad* liebevoll; ~**ionately yours** herzlichst Dein.

affiliated [ə'fɪlɪeɪtɪd] *a* angeschlossen (*to dat*).

affinity [ə'fɪnɪtɪ] *n* (*attraction*) gegenseitige Anziehung *f*; (*relationship*) Verwandtschaft *f*.

affirmation [æfə'meɪʃən] *n* Behauptung *f*.

affirmative [ə'fɜːmətɪv] *a* bestätigend; *n*: **in the** ~ (*Gram*) nicht verneint; **to answer in the** ~ mit Ja antworten.

affix [ə'fɪks] *vt* aufkleben, anheften.

afflict [ə'flɪkt] *vt* quälen, heimsuchen; ~**ion** [ə'flɪkʃən] Kummer *m*; (*illness*) Leiden *nt*.

affluence [ˈæfluəns] *n* (*wealth*) Wohlstand *m*.

affluent [ˈæfluənt] *a* wohlhabend, Wohlstands-.

afford [ə'fɔːd] *vt* (sich) leisten, erschwingen; (*yield*) bieten, einbringen.

affront [ə'frʌnt] *n* Beleidigung *f*; ~**ed** *a* beleidigt.

afield [ə'fiːld] *ad*: **far** ~ weit fort.

afloat [ə'fləʊt] *a*: **to be** ~ schwimmen.

afoot [ə'fʊt] *ad* im Gang.

aforesaid [ə'fɔːsed] *a* obengenannt.

afraid [ə'freɪd] *a* ängstlich; **to be** ~ **of** Angst haben vor (+*dat*); **to be** ~ **to** sich scheuen; **I am** ~ **I have...** ich habe leider...; **I'm** ~ **so/not** leider/leider nicht.

afresh [ə'freʃ] *ad* von neuem.

aft [ɑːft] *ad* achtern.

after [ˈɑːftə] *prep* nach; (*following, seeking*) hinter ... (*dat*) ... her; (*in imitation*) nach, im Stil von; *ad*: **soon** ~ bald danach; ~ **all** letzten Endes; ~**effects** *pl* Nachwirkungen *pl*; ~**life** Leben *nt* nach dem Tode; ~**math** Auswirkungen *pl*; ~**noon** Nachmittag *m*; **good** ~**noon!** guten Tag!; ~**shave** (**lotion**) Rasierwasser *nt*; ~**thought** nachträgliche(r) Einfall *m*; ~**wards** *ad* danach, nachher.

again [ə'gen] *ad* wieder, noch einmal; (*besides*) außerdem, ferner; ~ **and** ~ immer wieder.

against [ə'genst] *prep* gegen.

age [eɪdʒ] *n* (*of person*) Alter *nt*; (*in history*) Zeitalter *nt*; *vi* altern, alt werden; *vt* älter machen; **to come of** ~ mündig werden; ~**d** *a* ... Jahre alt, -jährig; [ˈeɪdʒɪd] (*elderly*) betagt; **the** ~**d** die Bejahrten *pl*; ~ **group** Altersgruppe *f*, Jahrgang *m*; ~**less** *a* zeitlos; ~ **limit** Altersgrenze *f*.

agency [ˈeɪdʒənsɪ] *n* Agentur *f*; Vermittlung *f*; (*Chem*) Wirkung *f*.

agenda [ə'dʒendə] *n* Tagesordnung *f*.

agent [ˈeɪdʒənt] *n* (*Comm*) Vertreter *m*; (*spy*) Agent *m*.

aggravate ['ægrəveɪt] vt (make worse) verschlimmern; (irritate) reizen.

aggravating ['ægrəveɪtɪŋ] a verschlimmernd; ärgerlich.

aggravation [ægrə'veɪʃən] n Verschlimmerung f, Verärgerung f.

aggregate ['ægrɪgɪt] n Summe f.

aggression [ə'greʃən] n Aggression f.

aggressive a, **~ly** ad [ə'gresɪv, -lɪ] aggressiv; **~ness** Aggressivität f.

aggrieved [ə'griːvd] a bedrückt, verletzt.

aghast [ə'gɑːst] a entsetzt.

agile ['ædʒaɪl] a flink; agil; mind rege.

agitate ['ædʒɪteɪt] vt rütteln; vi agitieren; **~d** a aufgeregt.

agitator ['ædʒɪteɪtə°] n Agitator m; (pej) Hetzer m.

agnostic [æg'nɒstɪk] n Agnostiker (in f) m.

ago [ə'gəʊ] ad: **two days ~** vor zwei Tagen; **not long ~** vor kurzem; **it's so long ~** es ist schon so lange her.

agog [ə'gɒg] a, ad gespannt.

agonized ['ægənaɪzd] a gequält.

agonizing ['ægənaɪzɪŋ] a quälend.

agony ['ægənɪ] n Qual f.

agree [ə'griː] vt date vereinbaren; vi (have same opinion, correspond) übereinstimmen (with mit); (consent) zustimmen; to ~ to do sth sich bereit erklären, etw zu tun; **garlic doesn't ~ with me** Knoblauch vertrage ich nicht; **I ~** einverstanden, ich stimme zu; **to ~ on sth** sich auf etw (acc) einigen; **~able** a (pleasing) liebenswürdig; (willing to consent) einverstanden; **~ably** ad angenehm; **~d** a vereinbart; **~ment** (agreeing) Übereinstimmung f; (contract) Vereinbarung f, Vertrag m.

agricultural [ægrɪ'kʌltʃərəl] a landwirtschaftlich, Landwirtschafts-.

agriculture ['ægrɪkʌltʃə°] n Landwirtschaft f.

aground [ə'graʊnd] a, ad auf Grund.

ahead [ə'hed] ad vorwärts; **to be ~** voraus sein.

ahoy [ə'hɔɪ] interj ahoi!

aid [eɪd] n (assistance) Hilfe f, Unterstützung f; (person) Hilfe f; (thing) Hilfsmittel nt; vt unterstützen, helfen (+dat); **~ and abet** vti Beihilfe leisten (sb jdm).

aide [eɪd] n (person) Gehilfe m; (Mil) Adjutant m.

ailing ['eɪlɪŋ] a kränkelnd.

ailment ['eɪlmənt] n Leiden nt.

aim [eɪm] vt gun, camera richten auf (+acc); **that was ~ed at you** das war auf dich gemünzt; vi (with gun) zielen; (intend) beabsichtigen; **to ~ at sth** etw anstreben; n (intention) Absicht f, Ziel nt; (pointing) Zielen nt, Richten nt; **to take ~** zielen; **~less** a, **~lessly** ad ziellos.

air [eə°] n Luft f, Atmosphäre f; (manner) Miene f, Anschein m; (Mus) Melodie f; vt lüften; (fig) an die Öffentlichkeit bringen; **~bed** Luftmatratze f, **~-conditioned** a mit Klimaanlage; **~-conditioning** Klimaanlage f; **~craft** Flugzeug nt, Maschine f; **~craft carrier** Flugzeugträger m; **~ force** Luftwaffe f; **~gun** Luftgewehr nt; **~ hostess**

Stewardeß f; **~lly** ad leichtfertig; **~ letter** Luftpost(leicht)brief m; **~line** Luftverkehrsgesellschaft f; **~liner** Verkehrsflugzeug nt; **~lock** Luftblase f; by **~ mail** mit Luftpost; **~port** Flughafen m, Flugplatz m; **~ raid** Luftangriff m; **~sick** a luftkrank; **~strip** Landestreifen m; **~tight** a luftdicht; **~y** a luftig; manner leichtfertig.

aisle [aɪl] n Gang m.

ajar [ə'dʒɑː°] ad angelehnt; ein Spalt offen.

alabaster ['æləbɑːstə°] n Alabaster m.

à la carte [æla'kɑːt] a nach der (Speise)karte, à la carte.

alacrity [ə'lækrɪtɪ] n Bereitwilligkeit f.

alarm [ə'lɑːm] n (warning) Alarm m; (bell etc) Alarmanlage f; vt erschrecken; **~ clock** Wecker m; **~ing** a beängstigend; **~ist** Bangemacher m.

alas [ə'læs] interj ach.

album ['ælbəm] n Album nt.

alcohol ['ælkəhɒl] n Alkohol m; **~ic** [ælkə'hɒlɪk] a drink alkoholisch; n Alkoholiker(in f) m; **~ism** Alkoholismus m.

alcove ['ælkəʊv] n Alkoven m.

alderman ['ɔːldəmən] n Stadtrat m.

ale [eɪl] n Ale nt.

alert [ə'lɜːt] a wachsam; n Alarm m; **~ness** Wachsamkeit f.

algebra ['ældʒɪbrə] n Algebra f.

alias ['eɪlɪəs] ad alias; n Deckname m.

alibi ['ælɪbaɪ] n Alibi nt.

alien ['eɪlɪən] n Ausländer m; (foreign) ausländisch; (strange) fremd; **~ate** vt entfremden; **~ation** [eɪlɪə'neɪʃən] Entfremdung f.

alight [ə'laɪt] a, ad brennend; (of building) in Flammen; vi (descend) aussteigen; (bird) sich setzen.

align [ə'laɪn] vt ausrichten; **~ment** Ausrichtung f; Gruppierung f.

alike [ə'laɪk] a gleich, ähnlich; ad gleich, ebenso.

alimony ['ælɪmənɪ] n Unterhalt m, Alimente pl.

alive [ə'laɪv] a (living) lebend; (lively) lebendig, aufgeweckt; (full of) voll (with von), wimmelnd (with von).

alkali ['ælkəlaɪ] n Alkali nt.

all [ɔːl] a (every one of) alle; n (the whole) alles, das Ganze; **~ of the books** alle Bücher; ad (completely) vollkommen, ganz; **it's ~ mine** das gehört alles mir; **it's ~ over** es ist alles aus or vorbei; **~ around** the edge rund um den Rand; **~ at once** auf einmal; **~ but** alle(s) außer; (almost) fast; **~ in** ~ alles in allem; **~ over town** in der ganzen Stadt; **~ right** okay, in Ordnung; **not at ~** ganz und gar nicht; (don't mention it) bitte.

allay [ə'leɪ] vt fears beschwichtigen.

allegation [ælɪ'geɪʃən] n Behauptung f.

allege [ə'ledʒ] vt (declare) behaupten; (falsely) vorgeben; **~dly** [ə'ledʒɪdlɪ] ad angeblich.

allegiance [ə'liːdʒəns] n Treue f, Ergebenheit f.

allegory ['ælɪgərɪ] n Allegorie f.

all-embracing ['ɔːlɪm'breɪsɪŋ] a allumfassend.

allergic [ə'lɜːdʒɪk] a allergisch (*to* gegen).

allergy ['ælədʒɪ] n Allergie f.

alleviate [ə'liːvɪeɪt] vt erleichtern, lindern.

alleviation [əliːvɪ'eɪʃən] n Erleichterung f.

alley ['ælɪ] n Gasse f, Durchgang m.

alliance [ə'laɪəns] n Bund m, Allianz f.

allied ['ælaɪd] a vereinigt; *powers* alliiert; verwandt (*to* mit).

alligator ['ælɪgeɪtə*] n Alligator m.

all-important ['ɔːlɪm'pɔːtənt] a äußerst wichtig.

all-in ['ɔːlɪn] a, ad *charge* alles inbegriffen, Gesamt-; (*exhausted*) erledigt, kaputt.

alliteration [əlɪtə'reɪʃən] n Alliteration f, Stabreim m.

all-night ['ɔːl'naɪt] a *café*, *cinema* die ganze Nacht geöffnet, Nacht-.

allocate ['æləkeɪt] vt zuweisen, zuteilen.

allocation [ælə'keɪʃən] n Zuteilung f.

allot [ə'lɒt] vt zuteilen; ~**ment** (*share*) Anteil m; (*plot*) Schrebergarten m.

all-out ['ɔːl'aʊt] a, ad total.

allow [ə'laʊ] vt (*permit*) erlauben, gestatten (*sb* jdm); (*grant*) bewilligen; (*deduct*) abziehen; ~ **for** vt berücksichtigen, einplanen; ~**ance** Beihilfe f; to make ~ances for berücksichtigen.

alloy ['ælɔɪ] n Metallegierung f.

all-round ['ɔːl'raʊnd] a *sportsman* allseitig, Allround-.

all-rounder ['ɔːl'raʊndə*] n (*Sport*) vielseitige(r) Sportler; (*general*) Allerweltskerl m.

all-time ['ɔːl'taɪm] a *record*, *high* ... aller Zeiten, Höchst-.

allude [ə'luːd] vi hinweisen, anspielen (*to* auf +acc).

alluring [ə'ljʊərɪŋ] a verlockend.

allusion [ə'luːʒən] n Anspielung f, Andeutung f.

alluvium [ə'luːvɪəm] n Schwemmland nt.

ally ['ælaɪ] n Verbündete(r) mf; (*Pol*) Alliierte(r) m.

almanac ['ɔːlmənæk] n Kalender m.

almighty [ɔːl'maɪtɪ] a allmächtig; the A~ der Allmächtige.

almond ['ɑːmənd] n Mandel f.

almost ['ɔːlməʊst] ad fast, beinahe.

alms [ɑːmz] n Almosen nt.

alone [ə'ləʊn] a, ad allein.

along [ə'lɒŋ] prep entlang, längs; ad (*onward*) vorwärts, weiter; ~ **with** zusammen mit; ~**side** ad *walk* nebenher; *come* nebendran; *be* daneben; prep (*walk*, *compared with*) neben (+dat); (*come*) neben (+acc); (*be*) entlang, neben (+dat); (*of ship*) längsseits (+gen); ~ **the river** den Fluß entlang; **I knew all ~** ich wußte die ganze Zeit.

aloof [ə'luːf] a zurückhaltend; ad fern; ~**ness** Zurückhaltung f, Sich-Fernhalten nt.

aloud [ə'laʊd] ad laut.

alphabet ['ælfəbet] n Alphabet nt; ~**ical** [ælfə'betɪkl] a alphabetisch.

alpine ['ælpaɪn] a alpin, Alpen-.

already [ɔːl'redɪ] ad schon, bereits.

also ['ɔːlsəʊ] ad auch, außerdem.

altar ['ɔːltə*] n Altar m.

alter ['ɔːltə*] vti ändern; *dress* umändern; ~**ation** [ɔːltə'reɪʃən] Änderung f, Umänderung f; (*to building*) Umbau m.

alternate [ɒl'tɜːnɪt] a abwechselnd; [ɒltə'neɪt] vi abwechseln (*with* mit); ~**ly** ad abwechselnd, wechselweise.

alternative [ɒl'tɜːnətɪv] a andere(r, s); n (Aus)wahl f, Alternative f; what's the ~? welche Alternative gibt es?; we have no ~ uns bleibt keine andere Wahl; ~**ly** ad im anderen Falle.

although [ɔːl'ðəʊ] cj obwohl, wenn auch.

altitude ['æltɪtjuːd] n Höhe f.

alto ['æltəʊ] n Alt m.

altogether [ɔːltə'geðə*] ad (*on the whole*) im ganzen genommen; (*entirely*) ganz und gar.

altruistic [æltrʊ'ɪstɪk] a uneigennützig, altruistisch.

aluminium [æljʊ'mɪnɪəm], (*US*) **aluminum** [ə'luːmɪnəm] n Aluminium nt.

always ['ɔːlweɪz] ad immer; **it was ~ that** way es war schon immer so.

amalgam [ə'mælgəm] n Amalgam nt; (*fig*) Mischung f.

amalgamate [ə'mælgəmeɪt] vi (*combine*) sich vereinigen; vt (*mix*) amalgamieren.

amalgamation [əmælgə'meɪʃən] n Verschmelzung f, Zusammenschluß m.

amass [ə'mæs] vt anhäufen.

amateur ['æmətə*] n Amateur m; (*pej*) Amateur m, Bastler m, Stümper m; a Amateur-, Bastler-; ~**ish** a (*pej*) dilettantisch, stümperhaft.

amaze [ə'meɪz] vt erstaunen, in Staunen versetzen; ~**ment** höchste(s) (Er)staunen nt.

amazing [ə'meɪzɪŋ] a höchst erstaunlich.

ambassador [æm'bæsədə*] n Botschafter m.

amber ['æmbə*] n Bernstein m.

ambidextrous [æmbɪ'dekstrəs] a beidhändig.

ambiguity [æmbɪ'gjuːɪtɪ] n Zweideutigkeit f, Unklarheit f.

ambiguous [æm'bɪgjʊəs] a zweideutig; (*not clear*) unklar.

ambition [æm'bɪʃən] n Ehrgeiz m.

ambitious [æm'bɪʃəs] a ehrgeizig.

ambivalent [æm'bɪvələnt] n *attitude* zwiespältig.

amble ['æmbl] vi schlendern.

ambulance ['æmbjʊləns] n Krankenwagen m.

ambush ['æmbʊʃ] n Hinterhalt m; vt aus dem Hinterhalt angreifen, überfallen.

ameliorate [ə'miːlɪəreɪt] vt verbessern.

amelioration [əmiːlɪə'reɪʃən] n Verbesserung f.

amen ['ɑː'men] interj amen.

amenable [ə'miːnəbl] a gefügig; (*to reason*) zugänglich (*to* dat); (*to flattery*) empfänglich (*to* für); (*to law*) unterworfen (*to* dat).

amend [ə'mend] vt *law etc* abändern, ergänzen; to make ~s etw wiedergutmachen; ~**ment** Abänderung f.

amenity [ə'miːnɪtɪ] n (*moderne*) Einrichtung f.

Americanize [ə'merɪkənaɪz] vt amerikanisieren.

amethyst ['æmɪθɪst] n Amethyst m.

amiable ['eɪmɪəbl] a liebenswürdig, sympathisch.

amicable ['æmɪkəbl] a freundschaftlich; settlement gütlich.

amid(st) [ə'mɪd(st)] prep mitten in or unter (+dat).

amiss [ə'mɪs] a verkehrt, nicht richtig; ad to take sth ~ etw übelnehmen.

ammeter ['æmɪtə*] n (Aut) Amperemeter m.

ammunition [æmju'nɪʃən] n Munition f.

amnesia [æm'niːzɪə] n Gedächtnisverlust m.

amnesty ['æmnɪstɪ] n Amnestie f.

amock [ə'mɒk] ad see **amuck**.

amoeba [ə'miːbə] n Amöbe f.

among(st) [ə'mʌŋ(st)] prep unter.

amoral [æ'mɒrəl] a unmoralisch.

amorous ['æmərəs] a verliebt.

amorphous [ə'mɔːfəs] a formlos, gestaltlos.

amount [ə'maunt] n (of money) Betrag m; (of time, energy) Aufwand m (of an +dat); (of water, sand) Menge f; no ~ of ... kein(e) ...; vi: ~ to (total) sich belaufen auf (+acc); this ~s to treachery das kommt Verrat gleich; it ~s to the same es läuft aufs gleiche hinaus; he won't ~ to much aus ihm wird nie was.

amp [æmp] n, **ampere** ['æmpɛə*] n Ampere m.

amphibious [æm'fɪbɪəs] a amphibisch, Amphibien-.

amphitheatre ['æmfɪθɪətə*] n Amphitheater nt.

ample ['æmpl] a portion reichlich; dress weit, groß; ~ time genügend Zeit.

amplifier ['æmplɪfaɪə*] n Verstärker m.

amply ['æmplɪ] ad reichlich.

amputate ['æmpjuteɪt] vt amputieren, abnehmen.

amuck [ə'mʌk] ad: to run ~ Amok laufen.

amuse [ə'mjuːz] vt (entertain) unterhalten; (make smile) belustigen; (occupy) unterhalten; I'm not ~d das find' ich gar nicht lustig; if that ~s you wann es dir Spaß macht; ~ment (feeling) Unterhaltung f; (recreation) Zeitvertreib m.

amusing [ə'mjuːzɪŋ] a amüsant, unterhaltend.

an [æn, ən] indef art ein(e).

anaemia [ə'niːmɪə] n Anämie f.

anaemic [ə'niːmɪk] a blutarm.

anaesthetic [ænɪs'θetɪk] n Betäubungsmittel nt; **under** ~ unter Narkose.

anagram ['ænəgræm] n Anagramm nt.

analgesic [ænæl'dʒiːsɪk] n schmerzlindernde(s) Mittel nt.

analogous [ə'næləgəs] a analog.

analogy [ə'nælədʒɪ] n Analogie f.

analyse ['ænəlaɪz] vt analysieren.

analysis [ə'næləsɪs] n Analyse f.

analytic [ænə'lɪtɪk] a analytisch.

anarchist ['ænəkɪst] n Anarchist(in f) m.

anarchy ['ænəkɪ] n Anarchie f.

anathema [ə'næθɪmə] n (fig) Greuel nt.

anatomical [ænə'tɒmɪkəl] a anatomisch.

anatomy [ə'nætəmɪ] n (structure) anatomische(r) Aufbau m; (study) Anatomie f.

ancestor ['ænsestə*] n Vorfahr m.

ancestral [æn'sestrəl] n angestammt, Ahnen-.

ancestry ['ænsɪstrɪ] n Abstammung f; Vorfahren pl.

anchor ['æŋkə*] n Anker m; vi ankern, vor Anker liegen; vt verankern; ~age Ankerplatz m.

anchovy ['æntʃəvɪ] n Sardelle f.

ancient ['eɪnʃənt] a alt; car etc uralt.

and [ænd, ənd, ən] cj und.

anecdote ['ænɪkdəut] n Anekdote f.

anemia [ə'niːmɪə] n (US) = **anaemia**.

anemone [ə'neməni] n Anemone f.

anesthetic [ænɪs'θetɪk] n (US) = **anaesthetic**.

anew [ə'njuː] ad von neuem.

angel ['eɪndʒəl] n Engel m; ~ic [æn'dʒelɪk] a engelhaft.

anger ['æŋgə*] n Zorn m; vt ärgern.

angina [æn'dʒaɪnə] n Angina f, Halsentzündung f.

angle ['æŋgl] n Winkel m; (point of view) Standpunkt m; at an ~ nicht gerade; vt stellen; to ~ for aussein auf (+acc); ~r Angler m.

Anglican ['æŋglɪkən] a anglikanisch; n Anglikaner(in f) m.

anglicize ['æŋglɪsaɪz] vt anglisieren.

angling ['æŋglɪŋ] n Angeln nt.

Anglo- ['æŋgləu] pref Anglo-.

angrily ['æŋgrɪlɪ] ad ärgerlich, böse.

angry ['æŋgrɪ] a ärgerlich, ungehalten, böse; wound entzündet.

anguish ['æŋgwɪʃ] n Qual f.

angular ['æŋgjulə*] a eckig, winkelförmig; face kantig.

animal ['ænɪməl] n Tier nt; (living creature) Lebewesen nt; a tierisch, animalisch.

animate ['ænɪmeɪt] vt beleben; ['ænɪmət] a lebhaft; ~d a lebendig; film Zeichentrick-.

animation [ænɪ'meɪʃən] n Lebhaftigkeit f.

animosity [ænɪ'mɒsɪtɪ] n Feindseligkeit f, Abneigung f.

aniseed ['ænɪsiːd] n Anis m.

ankle ['æŋkl] n (Fuß)knöchel m.

annex ['æneks] n Anbau m; [ə'neks] vt anfügen; (Pol) annektieren, angliedern.

annihilate [ə'naɪəleɪt] vt vernichten.

anniversary [ænɪ'vɜːsərɪ] n Jahrestag m.

annotate ['ænəteɪt] vt kommentieren.

announce [ə'nauns] vt ankündigen, anzeigen; ~ment Ankündigung f; (official) Bekanntmachung f; ~r Ansager(in f) m.

annoy [ə'nɔɪ] vt ärgern; ~ance Ärgernis nt, Störung f; ~ing a ärgerlich; person lästig.

annual ['ænjuəl] a jährlich; salary Jahres-; n (plant) einjährige Pflanze f; (book) Jahrbuch nt; ~ly ad jährlich.

annuity [ə'njuːɪtɪ] n Jahresrente f.

annul [ə'nʌl] vt aufheben, annullieren; ~ment Aufhebung f, Annullierung f.

anoint [ə'nɔɪnt] vt salben.
anomalous [ə'nɒmələs] a unregelmäßig, anomal.
anomaly [ə'nɒməlɪ] n Abweichung f von der Regel.
anon [ə'nɒn] a = **anonymous.**
anonymity [ænə'nɪmɪtɪ] n Anonymität f.
anonymous [ə'nɒnɪməs] a anonym.
anorak ['ænəræk] n Anorak m, Windjacke f.
another [ə'nʌðə*] a, pron (different) ein(e) andere(r, s); (additional) noch eine(r, s).
answer ['ɑːnsə*] n Antwort f; vi antworten; (on phone) sich melden; vt person antworten (+dat); letter, question beantworten; telephone gehen an (+acc), abnehmen; door öffnen; ~able a beantwortbar; (responsible) verantwortlich, haftbar; ~ back vi frech sein; to ~ for sth für etw verantwortlich sein; to ~ to the name of auf den Namen ... hören.
ant [ænt] n Ameise f.
antagonism [æn'tægənɪzəm] n Antagonismus m.
antagonist [æn'tægənɪst] n Gegner m, Antagonist m; ~ic [æntægə'nɪstɪk] a feindselig.
antagonize [æn'tægənaɪz] vt reizen.
anteater ['æntiːtə*] n Ameisenbär m.
antecedent [æntɪ'siːdənt] n Vorhergehende(s) nt; ~s pl Vorleben nt, Vorgeschichte f.
antelope ['æntɪləʊp] n Antilope f.
antenatal [æntɪ'neɪtl] a vor der Geburt.
antenna [æn'tenə] n (Biol) Fühler m; (Rad) Antenne f.
anteroom ['æntɪrʊm] n Vorzimmer nt.
anthem ['ænθəm] n Hymne f.
anthology [æn'θɒlədʒɪ] n Gedichtsammlung f, Anthologie f.
anthropologist [ænθrə'pɒlədʒɪst] n Anthropologe m.
anthropology [ænθrə'pɒlədʒɪ] n Anthropologie f.
anti- ['æntɪ] pref Gegen-, Anti-.
anti-aircraft ['æntɪ'ɛəkrɑːft] a Flugabwehr-.
antibiotic ['æntɪbaɪ'ɒtɪk] n Antibiotikum nt.
anticipate [æn'tɪsɪpeɪt] vt (expect) trouble, question erwarten, rechnen mit; (look forward to) sich freuen auf (+acc); (do first) vorwegnehmen; (foresee) ahnen, vorhersehen.
anticipation [æntɪsɪ'peɪʃən] n Erwartung f; (foreshadowing) Vorwegnahme f; that was good ~ das war gut vorausgesehen.
anticlimax ['æntɪ'klaɪmæks] n Ernüchterung f.
anticlockwise ['æntɪ'klɒkwaɪz] a entgegen dem Uhrzeigersinn.
antics ['æntɪks] npl Possen pl.
anticyclone ['æntɪ'saɪkləʊn] n Hoch nt, Hochdruckgebiet nt.
antidote ['æntɪdəʊt] n Gegenmittel nt.
antifreeze ['æntɪfriːz] n Frostschutzmittel nt.
antipathy [æn'tɪpəθɪ] n Abneigung f, Antipathie f.

antiquarian [æntɪ'kwɛərɪən] a altertümlich; n Antiquitätensammler m.
antiquated ['æntɪkweɪtɪd] a antiquiert.
antique [æn'tiːk] n Antiquität f; a antik; (old-fashioned) altmodisch.
antiquity [æn'tɪkwɪtɪ] n Antike f, Altertum nt.
antiseptic [æntɪ'septɪk] n Antiseptikum nt; a antiseptisch.
antisocial [æntɪ'səʊʃl] a person ungesellig; law unsozial.
antithesis [æn'tɪθɪsɪs] n Gegensatz m, Antithese f.
antlers ['æntləz] npl Geweih nt.
anus ['eɪnəs] n After m.
anvil ['ænvɪl] n Amboß m.
anxiety [æŋ'zaɪətɪ] n Angst f; (worry) Sorge f.
anxious ['æŋkʃəs] a ängstlich; (worried) besorgt; ~ly ad besorgt; to be ~ to do sth etw unbedingt tun wollen.
any ['enɪ] a: take ~ one nimm irgendein(e,n,s)!; do you want ~ apples? willst du Apfel (haben)?; do you want ~? willst du welche?; not ~ keine; ad: ~ faster schneller; ~body pron irgend jemand; (everybody) jedermann; ~how ad sowieso, ohnehin; (carelessly) einfach so; ~one pron = ~body; ~thing pron irgend etwas; ~time ad jederzeit; ~way ad sowieso, ohnehin; ~way, let's stop na ja or sei's drum, hören wir auf; ~where ad irgendwo; (everywhere) überall.
apace [ə'peɪs] ad rasch.
apart [ə'pɑːt] ad (parted) auseinander; (away) beiseite, abseits; ~ from außer.
apartheid [ə'pɑːteɪt] n Apartheid f.
apartment [ə'pɑːtmənt] n (US) Wohnung f; ~s pl (möblierte Miet)wohnung f.
apathetic [æpə'θetɪk] a teilnahmslos, apathisch.
apathy ['æpəθɪ] n Teilnahmslosigkeit f, Apathie f.
ape [eɪp] n (Menschen)affe m; vt nachahmen.
aperitif [ə'perɪtɪv] n Aperitif m.
aperture ['æpətjʊə*] n Öffnung f; (Phot) Blende f.
apex ['eɪpeks] n Spitze f, Scheitelpunkt m.
aphorism ['æfərɪzəm] n Aphorismus m.
aphrodisiac [æfrəʊ'dɪzɪæk] n Aphrodisiakum nt.
apiece [ə'piːs] ad pro Stück; (per person) pro Kopf.
aplomb [ə'plɒm] n selbstbewußte(s) Auftreten nt.
apocryphal [ə'pɒkrɪfəl] a apokryph, unecht.
apologetic [əpɒlə'dʒetɪk] a entschuldigend; to be ~ sich sehr entschuldigen.
apologize [ə'pɒlədʒaɪz] vi sich entschuldigen.
apology [ə'pɒlədʒɪ] n Entschuldigung f.
apoplexy ['æpəpleksɪ] n Schlaganfall m.
apostle [ə'pɒsl] n Apostel m; (pioneer) Vorkämpfer m.
apostrophe [ə'pɒstrəfɪ] n Apostroph m.

appal [ə'pɔːl] vt erschrecken; ~ling a schrecklich.

apparatus ['æpəreɪtəs] n Apparat m, Gerät nt.

apparent [ə'pærənt] a offenbar; ~ly ad anscheinend.

apparition [æpə'rɪʃən] n (ghost) Erscheinung f, Geist m; (appearance) Erscheinen nt.

appeal [ə'piːl] vi dringend ersuchen; dringend bitten (for um); sich wenden (to an +acc); (to public) appellieren (to an +acc); (Jur) Berufung einlegen (n Aufruf m; (Jur) Berufung f; ~ing a ansprechend.

appear [ə'pɪə*] vi (come into sight) erscheinen; (be seen) auftauchen; (seem) scheinen; ~ance (coming into sight) Erscheinen nt; (outward show) Äußere(s) nt; to put in or make an ~ance sich zeigen.

appease [ə'piːz] vt beschwichtigen.

appendage [ə'pendɪdʒ] n Anhang m, Anhängsel nt.

appendicitis [əpendɪ'saɪtɪs] n Blinddarmentzündung f.

appendix [ə'pendɪks] n (in book) Anhang m; (Med) Blinddarm m.

appetite ['æpɪtaɪt] n Appetit m; (fig) Lust f.

appetizing ['æpɪtaɪzɪŋ] a appetitanregend.

applaud [ə'plɔːd] vti Beifall klatschen (+dat), applaudieren.

applause [ə'plɔːz] n Beifall m, Applaus m.

apple ['æpl] n Apfel m; ~ tree Apfelbaum m.

appliance [ə'plaɪəns] n Gerät nt.

applicable [ə'plɪkəbl] a anwendbar; (in forms) zutreffend.

applicant ['æplɪkənt] n Bewerber(in f) m.

application [æplɪ'keɪʃən] n (request) Antrag m; (for job) Bewerbung f; (putting into practice) Anwendung f; (hard work) Fleiß m.

applied [ə'plaɪd] a angewandt.

apply [ə'plaɪ] vi (ask) sich wenden (to an +acc), sich melden; (be suitable) zutreffen; vt (place on) auflegen; cream auftragen; (put into practice) anwenden; (devote o.s.) sich widmen (+dat).

appoint [ə'pɔɪnt] vt (to office) ernennen, berufen; (settle) festsetzen; ~ment (meeting) Verabredung f; (at hairdresser etc) Bestellung f; (in business) Termin m; (choice for a position) Ernennung f; (Univ) Berufung f.

apportion [ə'pɔːʃən] vt zuteilen.

appreciable [ə'priːʃəbl] a (perceptible) merklich; (able to be estimated) abschätzbar.

appreciate [ə'priːʃeɪt] vt (value) zu schätzen wissen; (understand) einsehen; vi (increase in value) im Wert steigen.

appreciation [əpriːʃɪ'eɪʃən] n Wertschätzung f; (Comm) Wertzuwachs m.

appreciative [ə'priːʃɪətɪv] a (showing thanks) dankbar; (showing liking) anerkennend.

apprehend [æprɪ'hend] vt (arrest) festnehmen; (understand) erfassen.

apprehension [æprɪ'henʃən] n Angst f.

apprehensive [æprɪ'hensɪv] a furchtsam.

apprentice [ə'prentɪs] n Lehrling m; ~ship Lehrzeit f.

approach [ə'prəʊtʃ] vi sich nähern; vt herantreten an (+acc); problem herangehen an (+acc); n Annäherung f; (to problem) Ansatz m; (path) Zugang m, Zufahrt f; ~able a zugänglich.

approbation [æprə'beɪʃən] n Billigung f.

appropriate [ə'prəʊprɪeɪt] vt (take for o.s.) sich aneignen; (set apart) bereitstellen; [ə'prəʊprɪət] a angemessen; remark angebracht; ~ly [ə'prəʊprɪətlɪ] ad passend.

approval [ə'pruːvəl] n (show of satisfaction) Beifall m; (permission) Billigung f; (Comm) on ~ bei Gefallen.

approve [ə'pruːv] vti billigen (of acc); I don't ~ of it/him ich halte nichts davon/von ihm.

approximate [ə'prɒksɪmɪt] a annähernd, ungefähr; [ə'prɒksɪmeɪt] vt nahekommen (+dat); ~ly ad rund, ungefähr.

approximation [əprɒksɪ'meɪʃən] n Annäherung f.

apricot ['eɪprɪkɒt] n Aprikose f.

April ['eɪprəl] n April m.

apron ['eɪprən] n Schürze f.

apt [æpt] a (suitable) passend; (able) begabt; (likely) geneigt.

aptitude ['æptɪtjuːd] n Begabung f.

aqualung ['ækwəlʌŋ] n Unterwasseratmungsgerät nt.

aquarium [ə'kweərɪəm] n Aquarium nt.

Aquarius [ə'kweərɪəs] n Wassermann m.

aquatic [ə'kwætɪk] a Wasser-.

aqueduct ['ækwɪdʌkt] n Aquädukt nt.

arable ['ærəbl] a bebaubar, Kultur-.

arbiter ['ɑːbɪtə*] n (Schieds)richter m.

arbitrary ['ɑːbɪtrərɪ] a willkürlich.

arbitrate ['ɑːbɪtreɪt] vti schlichten.

arbitration [ɑːbɪ'treɪʃən] n Schlichtung f; to go to ~ vor ein Schiedsgericht gehen.

arbitrator ['ɑːbɪtreɪtə*] n Schiedsrichter m, Schlichter m.

arc [ɑːk] n Bogen m.

arcade [ɑː'keɪd] n Säulengang m.

arch [ɑːtʃ] n Bogen m; vt überwölben; back krumm machen; vi sich wölben; a durchtrieben; ~ enemy Erzfeind m.

archaeologist [ɑːkɪ'ɒlədʒɪst] n Archäologe m.

archaeology [ɑːkɪ'ɒlədʒɪ] n Archäologie f.

archaic [ɑː'keɪɪk] a altertümlich.

archbishop ['ɑːtʃ'bɪʃəp] n Erzbischof m.

archer ['ɑːtʃə*] n Bogenschütze m; ~y Bogenschießen nt.

archipelago [ɑːkɪ'pelɪgəʊ] n Archipel m; (sea) Inselmeer nt.

architect ['ɑːkɪtekt] n Architekt(in f) m; ~ural [ɑːkɪ'tektʃərəl] a architektonisch; ~ure Architektur f.

archives ['ɑːkaɪvz] npl Archiv nt.

archivist ['ɑːkɪvɪst] n Archivar m.

archway ['ɑːtʃweɪ] n Bogen m.

ardent ['ɑːdənt] a glühend.

ardour ['ɑːdə*] n Eifer m.

arduous ['ɑːdjuːəs] a mühsam.

are [ɑː*] see be.

area ['ɛərɪə] n Fläche f; (of land) Gebiet nt;

(part of sth) Teil *m*, Abschnitt *m*.

arena [ə'riːnɔ] *n* Arena *f*.

aren't [ɑːnt] = **are not**.

arguable ['ɑːgjuɔbl] *a* *(doubtful)* diskutabel; *(possible)* **it's ~ that . . .** man könnte argumentieren daß ...

argue ['ɑːgjuː] *vt case* vertreten; *vi* diskutieren; *(angrily)* streiten; **don't ~!** keine Widerrede!; **to ~ with sb** sich mit jdm streiten.

argument ['ɑːgjumənt] *n* *(theory)* Argument *nt*; *(reasoning)* Argumentation *f*; *(row)* Auseinandersetzung *f*, Streit *m*; **~ative** [ɑːgju'mentɔtɪv] *a* streitlustig; **to have an ~** sich streiten.

aria ['ɑːrɪɔ] *n* Arie *f*.

arid ['ærɪd] *a* trocken; **~ ity** [ɔ'rɪdɪtɪ] *n* Dürre *f*.

Aries ['εɔriːz] *n* Widder *m*.

arise [ɔ'raɪz] *vi irreg* aufsteigen; *(get up)* aufstehen; *(difficulties etc)* entstehen; *(case)* vorkommen; **to ~ out of sth** herrühren von etw.

aristocracy [ærɪs'tɒkrɔsɪ] *n* Adel *m*, Aristokratie *f*.

aristocrat ['ærɪstɔkræt] *n* Adlige(r) *mf*, Aristokrat(in *f*) *m*; **~ic** [ærɪstɔ'krætɪk] *a* adlig, aristokratisch.

arithmetic [ɔ'rɪθmɔtɪk] *n* Rechnen *nt*, Arithmetik *f*.

ark [ɑːk] *n*: **Noah's A~** die Arche Noah.

arm [ɑːm] *n* Arm *m*; *(branch of military service)* Zweig *m*; *vt* bewaffnen; **~s** *pl* *(weapons)* Waffen *pl*; **~chair** Lehnstuhl *m*; **~ed** *a forces* Streit-, bewaffnet; *robbery* bewaffnet; **~ful** Armvoll *m*.

armistice ['ɑːmɪstɪs] *n* Waffenstillstand *m*.

armour ['ɑːmə*] *n* *(knight's)* Rüstung *f*; *(Mil)* Panzerplatte *f*; **~y** Waffenlager *nt*; *(factory)* Waffenfabrik *f*.

armpit ['ɑːmpɪt] *n* Achselhöhle *f*.

army ['ɑːmɪ] *n* Armee *f*, Heer *nt*; *(host)* Heer *m*.

aroma [ɔ'rəumɔ] *n* Duft *m*, Aroma *nt*; **~tic** [ærɔ'mætɪk] *a* aromatisch, würzig.

around [ɔ'raund] *ad* ringsherum; *(almost)* ungefähr; *prep* um . . . herum; **is he ~?** ist er hier?

arouse [ɔ'rauz] *vt* wecken.

arrange [ɔ'reɪndʒ] *vt time, meeting* festsetzen; *holidays* festlegen; *flowers, hair, objects* anordnen; **I ~d to meet him** ich habe mit ihm ausgemacht, ihn zu treffen; **it's all ~d** es ist alles arrangiert; **~ment** *(order)* Reihenfolge *f*; *(agreement)* Übereinkommen *nt*; *(plan)* Vereinbarung *f*.

array [ɔ'reɪ] *n* Aufstellung *f*.

arrears [ɔ'rɪɔz] *npl* *(of debts)* Rückstand *m*; *(of work)* Unerledigte(s) *nt*; **in ~** im Rückstand.

arrest [ɔ'rest] *vt person* verhaften; *(stop)* aufhalten; *n* Verhaftung *f*; **under ~** in Haft; **you're under ~** Sie sind verhaftet.

arrival [ɔ'raɪvɔl] *n* Ankunft *f*.

arrive [ɔ'raɪv] *vi* ankommen *(at* in +*dat*, *bei)*; **to ~ at a decision** zu einer Entscheidung kommen.

arrogance ['ærɔgɔns] *n* Überheblichkeit *f*, Arroganz *f*.

arrogant ['ærɔgɔnt] *a* anmaßend, arrogant.

arrow ['ærɔu] *n* Pfeil *m*.

arse [ɑːs] *n* *(col)* Arsch *m*.

arsenal ['ɑːsɪnl] *n* Waffenlager *nt*, Zeughaus *nt*.

arsenic ['ɑːsnɪk] *n* Arsen *nt*.

arson ['ɑːsn] *n* Brandstiftung *f*.

art [ɑːt] *n* Kunst *f*; **~s** *pl* Geisteswissenschaften *pl*; **~ gallery** Kunstgalerie *f*.

artery ['ɑːtɔrɪ] *n* Schlagader *f*, Arterie *f*.

artful ['ɑːtful] *a* verschlagen.

arthritis [ɑː'θraɪtɪs] *n* Arthritis *f*.

artichoke ['ɑːtɪtʃɔuk] *n* Artischocke *f*.

article ['ɑːtɪkl] *n* *(Press, Gram)* Artikel *m*; *(thing)* Gegenstand *m*, Artikel *m*; *(clause)* Abschnitt *m*, Paragraph *m*.

articulate [ɑː'tɪkjulɪt] *a* *(able to express o.s.)* redegewandt; *(speaking clearly)* deutlich, verständlich; **to be ~** sich gut ausdrücken können; [ɑː'tɪkjuleɪt] *vt (connect)* zusammenfügen, gliedern; **~d vehicle** Sattelschlepper *m*.

artifice ['ɑːtɪfɪs] *n* *(skill)* Kunstgriff *m*; *(trick)* Kniff *m*, List *f*.

artificial [ɑːtɪ'fɪʃɔl] *a* künstlich, Kunst-; **~ respiration** künstliche Atmung *f*.

artillery [ɑː'tɪlɔrɪ] *n* Artillerie *f*.

artisan ['ɑːtɪzæn] *n* gelernte(r) Handwerker *m*.

artist ['ɑːtɪst] *n* Künstler(in *f*) *m*; **~ic** [ɑː'tɪstɪk] *a* künstlerisch; **~ry** künstlerische(s) Können *nt*.

artless ['ɑːtlɪs] *a* ungekünstelt; *character* arglos.

arty ['ɑːtɪ] *a*: **to be ~** auf Kunst machen.

as [æz] *ad, cj (since)* da, weil; *(while)* als; *(like)* wie; *(in role of)* als; **~ soon ~ he comes** sobald er kommt; **~ big ~** so groß wie; **~ well** auch; **~ well ~** und auch; **~ for him** was ihn anbetrifft; **~ if, ~ though** als ob; **~ it were** sozusagen; **old ~ he was** so alt er auch war.

asbestos [æz'bestɔs] *n* Asbest *m*.

ascend [ɔ'send] *vi* aufsteigen; *vt* besteigen; **~ancy** Oberhand *f*.

ascension [ɔ'senʃɔn] *n* *(Eccl)* Himmelfahrt *f*.

ascent [ɔ'sent] *n* Aufstieg *m*; Besteigung *f*.

ascertain [æsɔ'teɪn] *vt* feststellen.

ascetic [ɔ'setɪk] *a* asketisch.

ascribe [ɔs'kraɪb] *vt* zuschreiben *(to dat)*.

ash [æʃ] *n (dust)* Asche *f*; *(tree)* Esche *f*.

ashamed [ɔ'feɪmd] *a* beschämt.

ashen [æʃɔn] *a (pale)* aschfahl.

ashore [ɔ'fɔː*] *ad* an Land.

ashtray ['æʃtreɪ] *n* Aschenbecher *m*.

aside [ɔ'saɪd] *ad* beiseite; **~ from** *(US)* abgesehen von; *n* beiseite gesprochene Worte *pl*.

ask [ɑːsk] *vti* fragen; *permission* bitten um; **~ him his name** frage ihn nach seinem Namen; **he ~ed to see you** er wollte dich sehen; **you ~ed for that!** da bist du selbst schuld.

askance [ɔs'kɑːns] *ad*: **to look ~ at s.o.** jdn schief ansehen.

askew [ɔs'kjuː] *ad* schief.

asleep [ə'sli:p] a, ad: **to be** ~ schlafen; **to fall** ~ einschlafen.

asp [æsp] n Espe f.

asparagus [əs'pærəgəs] n Spargel m.

aspect ['æspekt] n (appearance) Aussehen nt; Aspekt m.

asphalt ['æsfælt] n Asphalt m.

asphyxiate [əs'fıksıeıt] vt ersticken.

asphyxiation [əsfıksı'eıʃən] n Erstickung f.

aspirate ['æspərıt] n Hauchlaut m.

aspiration [æspə'reıʃən] n Trachten nt; **to have** ~**s towards sth** etw anstreben.

aspire [əs'paıə•] vi streben (to nach).

aspirin ['æsprın] n Aspirin nt.

ass [æs] n (lit, fig) Esel m.

assailant [ə'seılənt] n Angreifer m.

assassin [ə'sæsın] n Attentäter(in f) m; ~**ate** vt ermorden; ~**ation** [əsæsı'neıʃən] Ermordung f.

assault [ə'sɔ:lt] n Angriff m; vt überfallen; **woman** herfallen über (+acc).

assemble [ə'sembl] vt versammeln; **parts** zusammensetzen; vi sich versammeln.

assembly [ə'semblı] n (meeting) Versammlung f; (construction) Zusammensetzung f, Montage f; ~ **line** Fließband nt.

assent [ə'sent] n Zustimmung f; vi zustimmen (to dat).

assert [ə'sɜ:t] vt erklären; ~**ion** [ə'sɜ:ʃən] Behauptung f; ~**ive** a selbstsicher.

assess [ə'ses] vt schätzen; ~**ment** Bewertung f, Einschätzung f; ~**or** Steuerberater m.

asset ['æset] n Vorteil m, Wert m; ~**s** pl Vermögen nt; (estate) Nachlaß m.

assiduous [ə'sıdjuəs] a fleißig, aufmerksam.

assign [ə'saın] vt zuweisen.

assignment [ə'saınmənt] n Aufgabe f, Auftrag m.

assimilate [ə'sımıleıt] vt sich aneignen, aufnehmen.

assimilation [əsımı'leıʃən] n Assimilierung f, Aufnahme f.

assist [ə'sıst] vt beistehen (+dat); ~**ance** Unterstützung f, Hilfe f; ~**ant** Assistent(in f) m, Mitarbeiter(in f) m; (in shop) Verkäufer(in f) m.

assizes [ə'saızız] npl Landgericht nt.

associate [ə'səuʃııt] n (partner) Kollege m, Teilhaber m; (member) außerordentliche(s) Mitglied nt; [ə'səuʃıeıt] vt verbinden (with mit); vi (keep company) verkehren (with mit).

association [əsəusı'eıʃən] a Verband m, Verein m; (Psych) Assoziation f; (link) Verbindung f; ~ **football** (Brit) Fußball nt.

assorted [ə'sɔ:tıd] a gemischt, verschieden.

assortment [ə'sɔ:tmənt] n Sammlung f; (Comm) Sortiment nt (of von), Auswahl f (of an +dat).

assume [ə'sju:m] vt (take for granted) annehmen; (put on) annehmen, sich geben; ~**d name** Deckname m.

assumption [ə'sʌmpʃən] n Annahme f.

assurance [ə'ʃuərəns] n (firm statement) Versicherung f; (confidence) Selbstsicherheit f; (insurance) (Lebens)versicherung f.

assure [ə'ʃuə•] vt (make sure) sicherstellen; (convince) versichern (+dat); **life** versichern.

assuredly [ə'ʃuərıdlı] ad sicherlich.

asterisk ['æstərısk] n Sternchen nt.

astern [əs'tɜ:n] ad achtern.

asthma ['æsmə] n Asthma nt; ~**tic** [æs'mætık] a asthmatisch; n Asthmatiker(in f) m.

astir [ə'stɜ:•] ad in Bewegung.

astonish [əs'tonıʃ] vt erstaunen; ~**ing** a erstaunlich; ~**ment** Erstaunen nt.

astound [əs'taund] vt verblüffen; ~**ing** a verblüffend.

astray [əs'treı] ad in die Irre; auf Abwege; a irregehend.

astride [əs'traıd] ad rittlings; prep rittlings auf.

astringent [əs'trındʒənt] a (Med) zusammenziehend; (severe) streng.

astrologer [əs'trolədʒə•] n Astrologe m, Astrologin f.

astrology [əs'trolədʒı] n Astrologie f.

astronaut ['æstrənɔ:t] n Astronaut(in f) m.

astronomer [əs'tronəmə•] n Astronom m.

astronomical [æstrə'nomıkəl] a astronomisch; **numbers** astronomisch; **success** riesig.

astronomy [əs'tronəmı] n Astronomie f.

astute [əs'tju:t] a scharfsinnig; schlau, gerissen.

asunder [ə'sʌndə•] ad entzwei.

asylum [ə'saıləm] n (home) Heim nt; (refuge) Asyl nt.

at [æt] prep ~ **home** zuhause; ~ **John's** bei John; ~ **table** bei Tisch; ~ **school** in der Schule; ~ **Easter** an Ostern; ~ **2 o'clock** um 2 Uhr; ~ **(the age of) 16** mit 16; ~ **£5** zu 5 Pfund; ~ **20 mph** mit 20 Meilen pro Stunde; ~ **that** darauf; (also) dazu.

ate [et, eıt] pt of **eat**.

atheism ['eıθıızəm] n Atheismus m.

atheist ['eıθııst] n Atheist(in f) m.

athlete ['æθli:t] n Athlet m, Sportler m.

athletic [æθ'letık] a sportlich, athletisch; ~**s** pl Leichtathletik f.

atlas ['ætləs] n Atlas m.

atmosphere ['ætməsfıə•] n Atmosphäre f.

atoll ['ætol] n Atoll nt.

atom ['ætəm] n Atom nt; (fig) bißchen nt; ~**ic** [ə'tomık] a atomar, Atom-; ~**(ic) bomb** Atombombe f; ~**ic power** Atomkraft f; ~**izer** Zerstäuber m.

atone [ə'təun] vi sühnen (for acc).

atrocious [ə'trəuʃəs] a gräßlich.

atrocity [ə'trosıtı] n Scheußlichkeit f; (deed) Greueltat f.

attach [ə'tætʃ] vt (fasten) befestigen; **importance** etc legen (to auf +acc), beimessen (to dat); **to be** ~**ed to sb/sth** an jdm/etw hängen; ~**é** [ə'tæʃeı] Attaché m.

attack [ə'tæk] vti angreifen; n Angriff m; (Med) Anfall m.

attain [ə'teın] vt erreichen; ~**ment** Erreichung f; ~**ments** pl Kenntnisse pl.

attempt [ə'tempt] n Versuch m; vti versuchen.

attend [ə'tend] vt (go to) teilnehmen (an +dat); lectures besuchen; vi (pay attention) aufmerksam sein; to ~ to needs nachkommen (+dat); person sich kümmern um; ~**ance** (presence) Anwesenheit f; (people present) Besucherzahl f; good ~ance gute Teilnahme; ~**ant** n (companion) Begleiter(in f) m; Gesellschafter(in f) m; (in car park etc) Wächter(in f) m; (servant) Bediente(r) mf; a begleitend; (fig) herrisch.

attention [ə'tenʃən] n Aufmerksamkeit f; (care) Fürsorge f; (for machine etc) Pflege f.

attentive a, ~**ly** ad [ə'tentiv, -li] aufmerksam.

attenuate [ə'tenjueit] vt verdünnen.

attest [ə'test] vt bestätigen; to ~ to sich verbürgen für.

attic ['ætik] n Dachstube f, Mansarde f.

attire [ə'taiə*] n Gewand nt.

attitude ['ætitju:d] n (position) Haltung f; (mental) Einstellung f.

attorney [ə'tə:ni] n (solicitor) Rechtsanwalt m; (representative) Bevollmächtigte(r) mf; **A~ General** Justizminister m.

attract [ə'trækt] vt anziehen; attention erregen; employees anlocken; ~**ion** [ə'trækʃən] n Anziehungskraft f; (thing) Attraktion f; ~**ive** a attraktiv; **the idea** ~**s me** ich finde die Idee attraktiv.

attribute ['ætribju:t] n Eigenschaft f, Attribut nt; [ə'tribju:t] vt zuschreiben (to dat).

attrition [ə'triʃən] n Verschleiß m; **war of** ~ Zermürbungskrieg m.

aubergine ['əubəʒi:n] n Aubergine f.

auburn ['ɔ:bən] a kastanienbraun.

auction ['ɔ:kʃən] n Versteigerung f, Auktion f; vt versteigern; ~**eer** [ɔ:kʃə'niə*] Versteigerer m.

audacious [ɔ:'deiʃəs] a (daring) verwegen; (shameless) unverfroren.

audacity [ɔ:'dæsiti] n (boldness) Wagemut m; (impudence) Unverfrorenheit f.

audible ['ɔ:dibl] a hörbar.

audience ['ɔ:diəns] n Zuhörer pl, Zuschauer pl; (with king etc) Audienz f.

audit ['ɔ:dit] n Bücherrevision f; vt prüfen.

audition [ɔ:'diʃən] n Probe f.

auditorium [ɔ:di'tɔ:riəm] n Zuschauerraum m.

augment [ɔ:g'ment] vt vermehren; vi zunehmen.

augur ['ɔ:gə*] vti bedeuten, voraussagen; **this** ~**s well** das ist ein gutes Omen; ~**y** ['ɔ:gjuri] Vorbedeutung f, Omen nt.

August ['ɔ:gəst] n August m.

august [ɔ:'gʌst] a erhaben.

aunt [ɑ:nt] n Tante f; ~**y**, ~**ie** Tantchen nt.

au pair ['əu' pɛə*] n (also ~ **girl**) Au-pair-Mädchen nt.

aura ['ɔ:rə] n Nimbus m.

auspices ['ɔ:spisiz] npl: **under the** ~ **of** unter der Schirmherrschaft von.

auspicious [ɔ:s'piʃəs] a günstig; verheißungsvoll.

austere [ɒs'tiə*] a streng; room nüchtern.

austerity [ɒs'teriti] n Strenge f; (Pol) wirtschaftliche Einschränkung f.

authentic [ɔ:'θentik] a echt, authentisch; ~**ate** vt beglaubigen; ~**ity** [ɔ:θen'tisiti] n Echtheit f.

author ['ɔ:θə*] n Autor m, Schriftsteller m; (beginner) Urheber m, Schöpfer m.

authoritarian [ɔ:θɒri'tɛəriən] a autoritär.

authoritative [ɔ:'θɒritətiv] a account maßgeblich; manner herrisch.

authority [ɔ:'θɒriti] n (power) Autorität f; (expert) Autorität f, Fachmann m; **the authorities** pl die Behörden pl.

authorize ['ɔ:θəraiz] vt bevollmächtigen; (permit) genehmigen.

auto ['ɔ:təu] n (US) Auto nt, Wagen m.

autobiographical [ɔ:təbaiə'græfikəl] a autobiographisch.

autobiography [ɔ:təbai'ɒgrəfi] n Autobiographie f.

autocracy [ɔ:'tɒkrəsi] n Autokratie f.

autocratic [ɔ:tə'krætik] a autokratisch.

autograph ['ɔ:təgrɑ:f] n (of celebrity) Autogramm nt; vt mit Autogramm versehen.

automate ['ɔ:təmeit] vt automatisieren, auf Automation umstellen.

automatic [ɔ:tə'mætik] a automatisch; n Selbstladepistole f; (car) Automatik m; ~**ally** ad automatisch.

automation [ɔ:tə'meiʃən] n Automation f.

automaton [ɔ:'tɒmətən] n Automat m, Roboter m.

automobile ['ɔ:təməbi:l] n (US) Auto(mobil) nt.

autonomous [ɔ:'tɒnəməs] a autonom.

autonomy [ɔ:'tɒnəmi] n Autonomie f, Selbstbestimmung f.

autopsy ['ɔ:tɒpsi] n Autopsie f.

autumn ['ɔ:təm] n Herbst m.

auxiliary [ɔ:g'ziliəri] a Hilfs-; n Hilfskraft f; (Gram) Hilfsverb nt.

avail [ə'veil] vt: ~ **o.s. of sth** sich einer Sache bedienen; n: **to no** ~ nutzlos; ~**ability** [əveilə'biliti] Erhältlichkeit f, Vorhandensein nt; ~**able** erhältlich; zur Verfügung stehend; person erreichbar, abkömmlich.

avalanche ['ævəlɑ:nʃ] n Lawine f.

avant-garde ['ævã'gɑ:d] a avantgardistisch; n Avantgarde f.

avarice ['ævəris] n Habsucht f, Geiz m.

avaricious [ævə'riʃəs] a geizig, habsüchtig.

avenge [ə'vendʒ] vt rächen, sühnen.

avenue ['ævənju:] n Allee f.

average ['ævəridʒ] n Durchschnitt m; a durchschnittlich, Durchschnitts-; vt figures den Durchschnitt nehmen von; (perform) durchschnittlich leisten; (in car etc) im Schnitt fahren; **on** ~ durchschnittlich, im Durchschnitt.

averse [ə'və:s] a: **to be** ~ **to** eine Abneigung haben gegen.

aversion [ə'və:ʃən] n Abneigung f.

avert [ə'və:t] vt (turn away) abkehren; (prevent) abwehren.

aviary ['eiviəri] n Vogelhaus nt.

aviation [eɪvɪ'eɪʃən] n Luftfahrt f, Flugwesen nt.

aviator ['eɪvɪeɪtə*] n Flieger m.

avid ['ævɪd] a gierig (for auf +acc); ~**ly** ad gierig.

avocado [ævə'kɑːdəʊ] n (also ~ pear) Avocado(birne) f.

avoid [ə'vɔɪd] vt vermeiden; ~**able** a vermeidbar; ~**ance** Vermeidung f.

avowal [ə'vaʊəl] n Erklärung f.

await [ə'weɪt] vt erwarten, entgegensehen (+dat).

awake [ə'weɪk] a wach; irreg vi aufwachen; vt (auf)wecken; ~**ning** Erwachen nt.

award [ə'wɔːd] n (judgment) Urteil nt; (prize) Preis m; vt zuerkennen.

aware [ə'wɛə*] a bewußt; **to be** ~ **sich bewußt sein** (of gen); ~**ness** Bewußtsein nt.

awash [ə'wɒʃ] a überflutet.

away [ə'weɪ] ad weg, fort.

awe [ɔː] n Ehrfurcht f; ~**-inspiring, ~some** a ehrfurchtgebietend; ~**-struck** a von Ehrfurcht ergriffen.

awful ['ɔːful] a (very bad) furchtbar; ~**ly** ad furchtbar, sehr.

awhile [ə'waɪl] ad eine kleine Weile, ein bißchen.

awkward ['ɔːkwəd] a (clumsy) ungeschickt, linkisch; (embarrassing) peinlich; ~**ness** Ungeschicklichkeit f.

awning ['ɔːnɪŋ] n Markise f.

awry [ə'raɪ] ad, a schief; **to go** ~ (person) fehlgehen; (plans) schiefgehen.

ax (US), **axe** [æks] n Axt f, Beil nt; vt (to end suddenly) streichen.

axiom ['æksɪəm] n Grundsatz m, Axiom nt; ~**atic** [æksɪə'mætɪk] a axiomatisch.

axis ['æksɪs] n Achse f.

axle ['æksl] n Achse f.

ay(e) [aɪ] interj (yes) ja; **the** ~**es** pl die Jastimmen pl.

azure ['eɪʒə*] a himmelblau.

B

B, b [biː] n B nt, b nt.

babble ['bæbl] vi schwätzen; (stream) murmeln; n Geschwätz nt.

babe [beɪb] n Baby nt.

baboon [bə'buːn] n Pavian m.

baby ['beɪbɪ] n Baby nt, Säugling m; ~**carriage** (US) Kinderwagen m; ~**ish** a kindisch; ~**-sit** vi irreg Kinder hüten, babysitten; ~**-sitter** Babysitter m.

bachelor ['bætʃələ*] n Junggeselle m; B~ **of Arts** Bakkalaureus m der philosophischen Fakultät; B~ **of Science** Bakkalaureus m der Naturwissenschaften.

back [bæk] n (of person, horse) Rücken m; (of house) Rückseite f; (of train) Ende nt; (Ftbl) Verteidiger m; vt (support) unterstützen; (wager) wetten auf (+acc); car rückwärts fahren; vi (go backwards) rückwärts gehen or fahren; a hinter(e, s); ad zurück; (to the rear) nach hinten; ~ **down** vi zurückstecken; ~ **out** vi sich zurückziehen; kneifen (col); ~**biting** Verleumdung f; ~**bone** Rückgrat nt;

(support) Rückhalt m; ~**cloth** Hintergrund m; ~**er** Förderer m; ~**fire** vi (plan) fehlschlagen; (Tech) fehlzünden; ~**ground** Hintergrund m; (information) Hintergrund m, Umstände pl; (person's education) Vorbildung f; ~**hand** (Sport) Rückhand f, a Rückhand-; ~**handed** a shot Rückhand-; compliment zweifelhaft; ~**ing** (support) Unterstützung f; ~**lash** (Tech) tote(r) Gang m; (fig) Gegenschlag m; ~**log** (of work) Rückstand m; ~**number** (Press) alte Nummer f; ~**pay** (Gehalts-, Lohn)nachzahlung f; ~**side** (col) Hintern m; ~**stroke** Rückenschwimmen nt; ~**ward** a (less developed) zurückgeblieben; (primitive) rückständig; ~**wardness** (of child) Unterentwicklung f; (of country) Rückständigkeit f; ~**wards** ad (in reverse) rückwärts; (towards the past) zurück, rückwärts; ~**water** (fig) Kaff nt; cultural ~**water** tiefste Provinz f; ~**yard** Hinterhof m.

bacon ['beɪkən] n Schinkenspeck m.

bacteria [bæk'tɪərɪə] npl Bakterien pl.

bad [bæd] a schlecht, schlimm.

badge [bædʒ] n Abzeichen nt.

badger ['bædʒə*] n Dachs m; vt plagen.

badly ['bædlɪ] ad schlecht, schlimm; ~ **off:** he is ~ off es geht ihm schlecht.

badminton ['bædmɪntən] n Federballspiel nt.

bad-tempered ['bæd'tempəd] a schlecht gelaunt.

baffle ['bæfl] vt (puzzle) verblüffen.

bag [bæg] n (sack) Beutel m; (paper) Tüte f; (hand-) Tasche f; (suitcase) Koffer m; (booty) Jagdbeute f; (col: old woman) alte Schachtel f; vi sich bauschen; vt (put in sack) in einen Sack stecken; (hunting) erlegen; ~**ful** Sackvoll m; ~**gage** ['bægɪdʒ] Gepäck nt; ~**gy** a bauschig, sackartig; ~**pipes** pl Dudelsack m.

bail [beɪl] n (money) Kaution f; vt prisoner gegen Kaution freilassen; (also ~ **out**) boat ausschöpfen; see **bale**.

bailiff ['beɪlɪf] n Gerichtsvollzieher(in f) m.

bait [beɪt] n Köder m; vt mit einem Köder versehen; (fig) ködern.

bake [beɪk] vti backen; ~**r** Bäcker m; ~**ry** Bäckerei f; ~**r's dozen** dreizehn.

baking ['beɪkɪŋ] n Backen nt; ~ **powder** Backpulver nt.

balance ['bæləns] n (scales) Waage f; (equilibrium) Gleichgewicht nt; (Fin: state of account) Saldo m; (difference) Bilanz f; (amount remaining) Restbetrag m; vt (weigh) wägen; (make equal) ausgleichen; ~**d** a ausgeglichen; ~ **sheet** Bilanz f, Rechnungsabschluß m.

balcony ['bælkənɪ] n Balkon m.

bald [bɔːld] a kahl; statement knapp.

bale [beɪl] n Ballen m; **to** ~ **or bail out** (from a plane) abspringen.

baleful ['beɪlful] a (sad) unglückselig; (evil) böse.

balk [bɔːk] vt (hinder) vereiteln; vi scheuen (at vor +dat).

ball [bɔːl] n Ball m.

ballad ['bæləd] n Ballade f.

ballast ['bæləst] n Ballast m.

ball bearing ['bɔːl'bɛərɪŋ] n Kugellager nt.

ballerina [bælə'riːnə] n Ballerina f.

ballet ['bæleɪ] n Ballett nt.

ballistics [bə'lɪstɪks] n Ballistik f.

balloon [bə'luːn] n (Luft)ballon m.

ballot ['bælət] n (geheime) Abstimmung f.

ball-point (pen) ['bɔːlpɔɪnt('pen)] n Kugelschreiber m.

ballroom ['bɔːlrum] n Tanzsaal m.

balmy ['bɑːmɪ] a lindernd; mild.

balsa ['bɔːlsə] n (also ~ **wood**) Balsaholz nt.

balustrade [bæləs'treɪd] n Brüstung f.

bamboo [bæm'buː] n Bambus m.

bamboozle [bæm'buːzl] vt übers Ohr hauen.

ban [bæn] n Verbot nt; vt verbieten.

banal [bə'nɑːl] a banal.

banana [bə'nɑːnə] n Banane f.

band [bænd] n Band nt; (group) Gruppe f; (of criminals) Bande f; (Mus) Kapelle f, Band f; vi (+together) sich zusammentun; ~**age** Verband m; (elastic) Bandage f.

bandit ['bændɪt] n Bandit m.

bandy ['bændɪ] vt wechseln; ~(-**legged**) a o-beinig.

bang [bæŋ] n (explosion) Knall m; (blow) Hieb m; vti knallen.

bangle ['bæŋgl] n Armspange f.

banish ['bænɪʃ] vt verbannen.

banister(s) ['bænɪstə*(z)] n(pl) (Treppen)geländer nt.

banjo ['bændʒəʊ] n Banjo nt.

bank [bæŋk] n (raised ground) Erdwall m; (of lake etc) Ufer nt; (Fin) Bank f; vt (tilt: Aviat) in die Kurve bringen; money einzahlen; **to** ~ **on sth** mit etw rechnen; ~ **account** Bankkonto nt; (employee) Bankbeamte(r) m; ~ **holiday** gesetzliche(r) Feiertag m; ~**ing** Bankwesen nt, Bankgeschäft nt; ~**note** Banknote f; ~**rupt** n Zahlungsunfähige(r) mf; vt bankrott machen; **to go** ~**rupt** Pleite machen; ~**ruptcy** Bankrott m.

banner ['bænə*] n Banner nt.

banns [bænz] npl Aufgebot nt.

banquet ['bæŋkwɪt] n Bankett nt, Festessen nt.

banter ['bæntə*] n Neckerei f.

baptism ['bæptɪzəm] n Taufe f.

baptize [bæp'taɪz] vt taufen.

bar [bɑː*] n (rod) Stange f; (obstacle) Hindernis nt; (of chocolate) Tafel f; (of soap) Stück nt; (for food, drink) Buffet nt, Bar f; (pub) Wirtschaft f; (Mus) Takt(strich) m; vt (fasten) verriegeln; (hinder) versperren; (exclude) ausschließen; **the B~: to be called to the B~** als Anwalt zugelassen werden; ~ **none** ohne Ausnahme.

barbarian [bɑː'bɛərɪən] n Barbar(in f) m.

barbaric [bɑː'bærɪk] a primitiv, unkultiviert.

barbarity [bɑː'bærɪtɪ] n Grausamkeit f.

barbarous ['bɑːbərəs] a grausam, barbarisch.

barbecue ['bɑːbɪkjuː] n Barbecue nt.

barbed wire ['bɑːbd'waɪə*] n Stacheldraht m.

barber ['bɑːbə*] n Herrenfriseur m.

barbiturate [bɑː'bɪtjʊrɪt] n Barbiturat nt, Schlafmittel nt.

bare [bɛə*] a nackt; trees, country kahl; (mere) bloß; vt entblößen; ~**back** ad ungesattelt; ~**faced** a unverfroren; ~**foot** a barfuß; ~**headed** a mit bloßem Kopf; ~**ly** ad kaum, knapp; ~**ness** Nacktheit f; Kahlheit f.

bargain ['bɑːgɪn] n (sth cheap) günstiger Kauf; (agreement) (written) Kaufvertrag m; (oral) Geschäft nt; **into the** ~ obendrein; ~ **for** vt rechnen mit.

barge [bɑːdʒ] n Lastkahn m; ~ **in** vi hereinplatzen.

baritone ['bærɪtəʊn] n Bariton m.

bark [bɑːk] n (of tree) Rinde f; (of dog) Bellen nt; vi (dog) bellen.

barley ['bɑːlɪ] n Gerste f.

barmaid ['bɑːmeɪd] n Bardame f.

barman ['bɑːmən] n Barkellner m.

barn [bɑːn] n Scheune f.

barnacle ['bɑːnəkl] n Entenmuschel f.

barometer [bə'rɒmɪtə*] n Barometer nt.

baron ['bærən] n Baron m; ~**ess** Baronin f; ~**ial** [bə'rəʊnɪəl] a freiherrlich.

baroque [bə'rɒk] a barock.

barracks ['bærəks] npl Kaserne f.

barrage ['bærɑːʒ] n (gunfire) Sperrfeuer nt; (dam) Staudamm m; Talsperre f.

barrel ['bærəl] n Faß nt; (of gun) Lauf m; ~ **organ** Drehorgel f.

barren ['bærən] a unfruchtbar.

barricade [bærɪ'keɪd] n Barrikade f; vt verbarrikadieren.

barrier ['bærɪə*] n (obstruction) Hindernis nt; (fence) Schranke f.

barrister ['bærɪstə*] n (Brit) Rechtsanwalt m.

barrow ['bærəʊ] n (cart) Schubkarren m.

bartender ['bɑːtendə*] n (US) Barmann or -kellner m.

barter ['bɑːtə*] n Tauschhandel m; vi Tauschhandel treiben.

base [beɪs] n (bottom) Boden m, Basis f; (Mil) Stützpunkt m; vt gründen; **to be** ~**d on** basieren auf (+dat); a (low) gemein; ~**ball** Baseball m; ~**less** a grundlos; ~**ment** Kellergeschoß nt.

bash [bæʃ] vt (col) (heftig) schlagen.

bashful ['bæʃful] a schüchtern.

basic ['beɪsɪk] a grundlegend; ~**ally** ad im Grunde.

basin ['beɪsn] n (dish) Schüssel f; (for washing, also valley) Becken nt; (dock) (Trocken)becken nt.

basis ['beɪsɪs] n Basis f, Grundlage f.

bask [bɑːsk] vi sich sonnen.

basket ['bɑːskɪt] n Korb m; ~**ball** Basketball m.

bass [beɪs] n (Mus, also instrument) Baß m; (voice) Baßstimme f; ~ **clef** Baßschlüssel m.

bassoon [bə'suːn] n Fagott nt.

bastard ['bɑːstəd] n Bastard m; Arschloch nt.

baste [beɪst] vt meat mit Fett begießen.

bastion ['bæstɪən] n (lit, fig) Bollwerk nt.

bat [bæt] n (Sport) Schlagholz nt; Schläger

m; (Zool) Fledermaus f; vt: he didn't ~ an eyelid er hat nicht mit der Wimper gezuckt; off one's own ~ auf eigene Faust.

batch [bætʃ] n (of letters) Stoß m; (of samples) Satz m.

bated ['beɪtɪd] a: with ~ breath mit verhaltenem Atem.

bath [bɑːθ] n Bad nt; (tub) Badewanne f; vt baden; ~s [bɑːðz] pl (Schwimm)bad nt; ~chair Rollstuhl m.

bathe [beɪð] vti baden; ~r Badende(r) mf.

bathing ['beɪðɪŋ] n Baden nt; ~ cap Badekappe f; ~ costume Badeanzug m.

bathmat ['bɑːθmæt] n Badevorleger m.

bathroom ['bɑːðrum] n Bad(ezimmer) nt.

baths [bɑːðz] npl see **bath**.

bath towel ['bɑːθtauəl] n Badetuch nt.

batman ['bætmən] n (Offiziers)bursche m.

baton ['bætən] n (of police) Gummiknüppel m; (Mus) Taktstock m.

battalion [bə'tælɪən] n Bataillon nt.

batter ['bætə*] vt verprügeln; n Schlagteig m; (for cake) Biskuitteig m.

battery ['bætərɪ] n (Elec) Batterie f; (Mil) Geschützbatterie f.

battle ['bætl] n Schlacht f; (small) Gefecht nt; vi kämpfen; ~-axe (col) Xanthippe f; ~field Schlachtfeld nt; ~ments pl Zinnen pl; ~ship Schlachtschiff nt.

batty ['bætɪ] a (col) plemplem.

bauble ['bɔːbl] n Spielzeug nt.

bawdy ['bɔːdɪ] a unflätig.

bawl [bɔːl] vi brüllen; to ~ sb out jdn zur Schnecke machen.

bay [beɪ] n (of sea) Bucht f; at ~ gestellt, in die Enge getrieben; to keep at ~ unter Kontrolle halten.

bayonet ['beɪənet] n Bajonett nt.

bay window ['beɪ'wɪndəu] n Erkerfenster nt.

bazaar [bə'zɑː*] n Basar m.

bazooka [bə'zuːkə] n Panzerfaust f.

be [biː] vi irreg sein; (become, for passive) werden; (be situated) liegen, sein; the book is 40p das Buch kostet 40p; he wants to ~ a teacher er will Lehrer werden; how long have you been here? wie lange sind Sie schon da?; have you been to Rome? warst du schon einmal in Rom?, bist du schon einmal in Rom gewesen?; his name is on the list sein Name steht auf der Liste; there is/are es gibt.

beach [biːtʃ] n Strand m; vt ship auf den Strand setzen; ~wear Strandkleidung f.

beacon ['biːkən] n (signal) Leuchtfeuer nt; (traffic ~) Bake f.

bead [biːd] n Perle f; (drop) Tropfen m.

beak [biːk] n Schnabel m.

beaker ['biːkə*] n Becher m.

beam [biːm] n (of wood) Balken m; (of light) Strahl m; (smile) strahlende(s) Lächeln nt; vi strahlen.

bean [biːn] n Bohne f.

bear [bɛə*] vt irreg weight, crops tragen; (tolerate) ertragen; young gebären; n Bär m; ~-able a erträglich; to ~ on relevant sein für.

beard [bɪəd] n Bart m; ~ed a bärtig.

bearer ['bɛərə*] n Träger m.

bearing ['bɛərɪŋ] n (posture) Haltung f; (relevance) Relevanz f; (relation) Bedeutung f; (Tech) Kugellager nt; ~s pl (direction) Orientierung f.

bearskin ['bɛəskɪn] n Bärenfellmütze f.

beast [biːst] n Tier nt, Vieh nt; (person) Bestie f; (nasty person) Biest nt; ~ly ad viehisch; (col) scheußlich; ~ of burden Lasttier nt.

beat [biːt] n (stroke) Schlag m; (pulsation) (Herz)schlag m; (police round) Runde f; Revier nt; (Mus) Takt m; Beat m; vt irreg schlagen; to ~ about the bush wie die Katze um den heißen Brei herumgehen; to ~ time den Takt schlagen; ~ off vt abschlagen; ~ up vt zusammenschlagen; ~en track gebahnte(r) Weg m; (fig) herkömmliche Art und Weise; off the ~en track abgelegen; ~er (for eggs, cream) Schneebesen m.

beautiful ['bjuːtɪful] a schön; ~ly ad ausgezeichnet.

beautify ['bjuːtɪfaɪ] vt verschönern.

beauty ['bjuːtɪ] n Schönheit f.

beaver ['biːvə*] n Biber m.

becalm [bɪ'kɑːz] vt: to be ~ed eine Flaute haben.

because [bɪ'kɒz] ad, cj weil; prep: ~ of wegen (+gen or (col) dat).

beckon ['bekən] vti ein Zeichen geben (sb jdm).

become [bɪ'kʌm] vt irreg werden; (clothes) stehen (+dat).

becoming [bɪ'kʌmɪŋ] a (suitable) schicklich; clothes kleidsam.

bed [bed] n Bett nt; (of river) Flußbett nt; (foundation) Schicht f; (in garden) Beet nt; ~ and breakfast Übernachtung f mit Frühstück; ~clothes pl Bettwäsche f; ~ding Bettzeug nt.

bedeck [bɪ'dek] vt schmücken.

bedlam ['bedləm] n (uproar) tolle(s) Durcheinander nt.

bedraggled [bɪ'drægld] a ramponiert.

bedridden ['bedrɪdn] a bettlägerig.

bedroom ['bedrum] n Schlafzimmer nt.

bedside ['bedsaɪd] n: at the ~ am Bett.

bed-sitter ['bed'sɪtə*] n Einzimmerwohnung f, möblierte(s) Zimmer nt.

bedtime ['bedtaɪm] n Schlafenszeit f.

bee [biː] n Biene f.

beech [biːtʃ] n Buche f.

beef [biːf] n Rindfleisch nt.

beehive ['biːhaɪv] n Bienenstock m.

beeline ['biːlaɪn] n: to make a ~ for schnurstracks zugehen auf (+acc).

beer [bɪə*] n Bier nt.

beetle ['biːtl] n Käfer m.

beetroot ['biːtruːt] n rote Bete f.

befall [bɪ'fɔːl] irreg vi sich ereignen; vt zustoßen (+dat).

befit [bɪ'fɪt] vt sich schicken für.

before [bɪ'fɔː*] prep vor; cj bevor; ad (of time) zuvor; früher; I've done it ~ das hab' ich schon mal getan.

befriend [bɪ'frend] vt sich (jds) annehmen.

beg [beg] vti (implore) dringend bitten;

alms betteln; **~gar** Bettler(in *f*) *m.*

begin [bɪ'gɪn] *vti irreg* anfangen, beginnen; (*found*) gründen; **to ~ with** zunächst (einmal); **~ner** Anfänger *m;* **~ning** Anfang *m.*

begrudge [bɪ'grʌdʒ] *vt* (be)neiden; **to ~ sb sth** jdm etw mißgönnen.

behalf [bɪ'hɑːf] *n:* **on or in** (*US*) **~ of** im Namen (+*gen*); **on my ~** für mich.

behave [bɪ'heɪv] *vi* sich benehmen.

behaviour, (*US*) **behavior** [bɪ'heɪvjə*] *n* Benehmen *nt.*

behead [bɪ'hed] *vt* enthaupten.

behind [bɪ'haɪnd] *prep* hinter; *ad* (*late*) im Rückstand; (*in the rear*) hinten; *n* (*col*) Hinterteil *nt.*

behold [bɪ'həʊld] *vt irreg* (*old*) erblicken.

beige [beɪʒ] *a* beige.

being ['biːɪŋ] *n* (*existence*) (Da)sein *nt;* (*person*) Wesen *nt.*

belch [beltʃ] *n* Rülpsen *nt; vi* rülpsen; *vt smoke* ausspeien.

belfry ['belfrɪ] *n* Glockenturm *m.*

belie [bɪ'laɪ] *vt* Lügen strafen (+*acc*).

belief [bɪ'liːf] *n* Glaube *m* (*in an* +*acc*); (*conviction*) Überzeugung *f.*

believable [bɪ'liːvəbl] *a* glaubhaft.

believe [bɪ'liːv] *vt* glauben (+*dat*); (*think*) glauben, meinen, denken; *vi* (*have faith*) glauben; **~r** Gläubige(r) *mf.*

belittle [bɪ'lɪtl] *vt* herabsetzen.

bell [bel] *n* Glocke *f.*

belligerent [bɪ'lɪdʒərənt] *a person* streitsüchtig; *country* kriegsführend.

bellow ['beləʊ] *vti* brüllen; *n* Gebrüll *nt.*

bellows ['beləʊz] *npl* (*Tech*) Gebläse *nt;* (*for fire*) Blasebalg *m.*

belly ['belɪ] *n* Bauch *m; vi* sich ausbauchen.

belong [bɪ'lɒŋ] *vi* gehören (*to sb* jdm); (*to club*) angehören (+*dat*); **it does not ~ here** es gehört nicht hierher; **~ings** *pl* Habe *f.*

beloved [bɪ'lʌvɪd] *a* innig geliebt; *n* Geliebte(r) *mf.*

below [bɪ'ləʊ] *prep* unter; *ad* unten.

belt [belt] *n* (*band*) Riemen *m;* (*round waist*) Gürtel *m; vt* (*fasten*) mit Riemen befestigen; (*col: beat*) schlagen; *vi* (*col: go fast*) rasen.

bench [bentʃ] *n* (*seat*) Bank *f;* (*workshop*) Werkbank *f;* (*judge's seat*) Richterbank *f;* (*judges*) Richterstand *m.*

bend [bend] *vt irreg* (*curve*) biegen; (*stoop*) beugen; *n* Biegung *f;* (*in road*) Kurve *f.*

beneath [bɪ'niːθ] *prep* unter; *ad* darunter.

benefactor ['benɪfæktə*] *n* Wohltäter(in *f*) *m.*

beneficial [benɪ'fɪʃl] *a* vorteilhaft; (*to health*) heilsam.

beneficiary [benɪ'fɪʃərɪ] *n* Nutznießer(in *f*) *m.*

benefit ['benɪfɪt] *n* (*advantage*) Nutzen *m; vt* fördern; *vi* Nutzen ziehen (*from* aus).

benevolence [bɪ'nevələns] *n* Wohlwollen *nt.*

benevolent [bɪ'nevələnt] *a* wohlwollend.

benign [bɪ'naɪn] *a person* gütig; *climate* mild.

bent [bent] *n* (*inclination*) Neigung *f; a* (*col:*

dishonest) unehrlich; **to be ~ on** versessen sein auf (+*acc*).

bequeath [bɪ'kwiːð] *vt* vermachen.

bequest [bɪ'kwest] *n* Vermächtnis *nt.*

bereaved [bɪ'riːvd] *n* (*person*) Hinterbliebene(r) *mf.*

bereavement [bɪ'riːvmənt] *n* schmerzliche(r) Verlust *m.*

beret ['bereɪ] *n* Baskenmütze *f.*

berry ['berɪ] *n* Beere *f.*

berserk [bə'sɜːk] *a:* **to go ~** wild werden.

berth [bɜːθ] *n* (*for ship*) Ankerplatz *m;* (*in ship*) Koje *f;* (*in train*) Bett *nt; vt* am Kai festmachen; *vi* anlegen.

beseech [bɪ'siːtʃ] *vt irreg* anflehen.

beset [bɪ'set] *vt irreg* bedrängen.

beside [bɪ'saɪd] *prep* neben, bei; (*except*) außer; **to be ~ o.s.** außer sich sein (*with* vor +*dat*).

besides [bɪ'saɪdz] *prep* außer, neben; *ad* zudem, überdies.

besiege [bɪ'siːdʒ] *vt* (*Mil*) belagern; (*surround*) umlagern, bedrängen.

besmirch [bɪ'smɜːtʃ] *vt* besudeln.

bespectacled [bɪ'spektɪkld] *a* bebrillt.

bespoke tailor [bɪ'spəʊk'teɪlə*] *n* Maßschneider *m.*

best [best] *a* beste(r, s); *ad* am besten; **at ~** höchstens; **to make the ~ of it** das Beste daraus machen; **for the ~** zum Besten; **~ man** Trauzeuge *m.*

bestial ['bestɪəl] *a* bestialisch.

bestow [bɪ'stəʊ] *vt* verleihen.

bestseller ['best'selə*] *n* Bestseller *m,* meistgekaufte(s) Buch *nt.*

bet [bet] *n* Wette *f; vti irreg* wetten.

betray [bɪ'treɪ] *vt* verraten; **~al** Verrat *m.*

better ['betə*] *a, ad* besser; *vt* verbessern; *n:* **to get the ~ of sb** jdn überwinden; **he thought ~ of it** er hat sich eines Besseren besonnen; **you had ~ leave** Sie gehen jetzt wohl besser; **~ off** *a* (*richer*) wohlhabender.

betting ['betɪŋ] *n* Wetten *nt;* **~ shop** Wettbüro *nt.*

between [bɪ'twiːn] *prep* zwischen; (*among*) unter; *ad* dazwischen.

bevel ['bevəl] *n* Abschrägung *f.*

beverage ['bevərɪdʒ] *n* Getränk *nt.*

beware [bɪ'weə*] *vt* sich hüten vor (+*dat*); **'~ of the dog'** 'Vorsicht, bissiger Hund!'

bewildered [bɪ'wɪldəd] *a* verwirrt.

bewildering [bɪ'wɪldərɪŋ] *a* verwirrend.

bewitching [bɪ'wɪtʃɪŋ] *a* bestrickend.

beyond [bɪ'jɒnd] *prep* (*place*) jenseits (+*gen*); (*time*) über . . . hinaus; (*out of reach*) außerhalb (+*gen*); **it's ~ me** das geht über meinen Horizont; *ad* darüber hinaus.

bias ['baɪəs] *n* (*slant*) Neigung *f;* (*prejudice*) Vorurteil *nt;* **~(s)ed** *a* voreingenommen.

bib [bɪb] *n* Latz *m.*

Bible ['baɪbl] *n* Bibel *f.*

biblical ['bɪblɪkəl] *a* biblisch.

bibliography [bɪblɪ'ɒgrəfɪ] *n* Bibliographie *f.*

bicentenary [baɪsen'tiːnərɪ] *n* Zweihundertjahrfeier *f.*

biceps ['baɪseps] *npl* Bizeps *m.*

bicker ['bɪkə°] vi zanken; ~ing Gezänk nt, Gekeife nt.

bicycle ['baɪsɪkl] n Fahrrad nt.

bid [bɪd] n (offer) Gebot nt; (attempt) Versuch m; vt irreg (offer) bieten; to ~ farewell Lebewohl sagen; ~der (person) Steigerer m; ~ding (command) Geheiß nt.

bide [baɪd] vt: ~ one's time abwarten.

big [bɪg] a groß.

bigamy ['bɪgəmɪ] n Bigamie f.

bigheaded ['bɪg'hedɪd] a eingebildet.

bigot ['bɪgət] n Frömmler m; ~ed a bigott; ~ry Bigotterie f.

bigwig ['bɪgwɪg] n (col) hohe(s) Tier nt.

bike [baɪk] n Rad nt.

bikini [bɪ'kiːnɪ] n Bikini m.

bilateral [baɪ'lætərəl] a bilateral.

bile [baɪl] n (Biol) Galle(nflüssigkeit) f.

bilge [bɪldʒ] n (water) Bilgenwasser nt.

bilingual [baɪ'lɪŋwəl] a zweisprachig.

bilious ['bɪlɪəs] a (sick) gallenkrank; (peevish) verstimmt.

bill [bɪl] n (account) Rechnung f; (Pol) Gesetzentwurf m; (US Fin) Geldschein m; ~ of exchange Wechsel m.

billet ['bɪlɪt] n Quartier nt.

billfold ['bɪlfəʊld] n (US) Geldscheintasche f.

billiards ['bɪlɪədz] n Billard nt.

billion ['bɪlɪən] n Billion f; (US) Milliarde f.

billy goat ['bɪlɪgəʊt] n Ziegenbock m.

bin [bɪn] n Kasten m; (dust-) (Abfall)eimer m.

bind [baɪnd] vt irreg (tie) binden; (tie together) zusammenbinden; (oblige) verpflichten; ~ing (Buch)einband m; a verbindlich.

binge [bɪndʒ] n (col) Sauferei f.

bingo ['bɪŋgəʊ] n Bingo nt.

binoculars [bɪ'nɒkjʊləz] npl Fernglas nt.

biochemistry ['baɪəʊ'kemɪstrɪ] n Biochemie f.

biographer [baɪ'ɒgrəfə°] n Biograph m.

biographic(al) [baɪəʊ'græfɪk(l)] a biographisch.

biography [baɪ'ɒgrəfɪ] n Biographie f.

biological [baɪə'lɒdʒɪkl] a biologisch.

biologist [baɪ'ɒlədʒɪst] n Biologe m.

biology [baɪ'ɒlədʒɪ] n Biologie f.

biped ['baɪped] n Zweifüßler m.

birch [bɜːtʃ] n Birke f.

bird [bɜːd] n Vogel m; (col: girl) Mädchen nt; ~'s-eye view Vogelschau f.

birth [bɜːθ] n Geburt f; of good ~ aus gutem Hause; ~ certificate Geburtsurkunde f; ~ control Geburtenkontrolle f; ~day Geburtstag m; ~place Geburtsort m; ~ rate Geburtenrate f.

biscuit ['bɪskɪt] n Keks m.

bisect [baɪ'sekt] vt halbieren.

bishop ['bɪʃəp] n Bischof m.

bit [bɪt] n bißchen, Stückchen nt; (horse's) Gebiß nt; a ~ tired etwas müde.

bitch [bɪtʃ] n (dog) Hündin f; (unpleasant woman) Weibsstück nt.

bite [baɪt] vti irreg beißen; n Biß m; (mouthful) Bissen m; ~ to eat Happen m.

biting ['baɪtɪŋ] a beißend.

bitter ['bɪtə°] a bitter; memory etc schmerzlich; person verbittert; n (beer) dunkles Bier; to the ~ end bis zum bitteren Ende; ~ness Bitterkeit f; ~sweet bittersüß.

bivouac ['bɪvʊæk] n Biwak nt.

bizarre [bɪ'zɑː°] a bizarr.

blab [blæb] vi klatschen; vt ausplaudern.

black [blæk] a schwarz; night finster; vt schwärzen; shoes wichsen; eye blau schlagen; (industry) boykottieren; ~ and blue grün und blau; ~berry Brombeere f; ~bird Amsel f; ~board (Wand)tafel f; ~currant schwarze Johannisbeere f; ~guard ['blægɑːd] Schuft m; ~leg Streikbrecher(in f) m; ~list schwarze Liste f; ~mail Erpressung f; vt erpressen; ~mailer Erpresser(in f) m; ~ market Schwarzmarkt m; ~ness Schwärze f; ~out Verdunklung f; (Med) to have a ~out bewußtlos werden; ~ sheep schwarze(s) Schaf nt; ~smith Schmied m.

bladder ['blædə°] n Blase f.

blade [bleɪd] n (of weapon) Klinge f; (of grass) Halm m; (of oar) Ruderblatt nt.

blame [bleɪm] n Tadel m, Schuld f; vt tadeln, Vorwürfe machen (+dat) he is to ~ er ist daran schuld; ~less a untadelig.

blanch [blɑːntʃ] vi bleich werden.

blancmange [blə'mɒnʒ] n Pudding m.

bland [blænd] a mild.

blank [blæŋk] a leer, unbeschrieben; look verdutzt; cheque Blanko-; verse Blank-; n (space) Lücke f; Zwischenraum m; (cartridge) Platzpatrone f.

blanket ['blæŋkɪt] n (Woll)decke f.

blankly ['blæŋklɪ] ad leer; look verdutzt.

blare [blɛə°] vti (radio) plärren; (horn) tuten; (Mus) schmettern; n Geplärr nt; Getute nt; Schmettern nt.

blasé ['blɑːzeɪ] a blasiert.

blaspheme [blæs'fiːm] vi (Gott) lästern.

blasphemous ['blæsfɪməs] a lästernd, lästerlich.

blasphemy ['blæsfəmɪ] n (Gottes)lästerung f, Blasphemie f.

blast [blɑːst] n Explosion f; (of wind) Windstoß m; vt (blow up) sprengen; ~! (col) verflixt!; ~ furnace Hochofen m; ~-off (Space) (Raketen)abschuß m.

blatant ['bleɪtənt] a offenkundig.

blaze [bleɪz] n (fire) lodernde(s) Feuer nt; vi lodern; vt: ~ a trail Bahn brechen.

blazer ['bleɪzə°] n Klubjacke f, Blazer m.

bleach [bliːtʃ] n Bleichmittel nt; vt bleichen.

bleak [bliːk] a kahl, rauh; future trostlos.

bleary-eyed ['blɪərɪaɪd] a triefäugig; (on waking up) mit verschlafenen Augen.

bleat [bliːt] n (of sheep) Blöken nt; (of goat) Meckern nt; vi blöken; meckern.

bleed [bliːd] irreg vi bluten; vt (draw blood) Blut abnehmen; to ~ to death verbluten.

bleeding ['bliːdɪŋ] a blutend.

blemish ['blemɪʃ] n Makel m; vt verunstalten.

blench [blentʃ] vi zurückschrecken; see **blanch**.

blend [blend] n Mischung f; vt mischen; vi sich mischen.

bless [bles] vt segnen; (give thanks) preisen; (make happy) glücklich machen; ~ you! Gesundheit!; ~ing Segen m; (at table) Tischgebet nt; (happiness) Wohltat f; Segen m; (good wish) Glück nt.

blight [blaɪt] n (Bot) Mehltau m; (fig) schädliche(r) Einfluß m; vt zunichte machen.

blimey ['blaɪmɪ] interj (Brit col) verflucht.

blind [blaɪnd] a blind; corner unübersichtlich; n (for window) Rouleau nt; vt blenden; ~ alley Sackgasse f; ~fold Augenbinde f; a mit verbundenen Augen; vt die Augen verbinden (sb jdm); ~ly a blind; (fig) blindlings; ~ness Blindheit f; ~ spot (Aut) toter Winkel m; (fig) schwache(r) Punkt m.

blink [blɪŋk] vti blinzeln; ~ers pl Scheuklappen pl.

bliss [blɪs] n (Glück)seligkeit f; ~fully ad glückselig.

blister ['blɪstə*] n Blase f; vt Blasen werfen auf (+dat); vi Blasen werfen.

blithe [blaɪð] a munter; ~ly ad fröhlich.

blitz [blɪts] n Luftkrieg m; vt bombardieren.

blizzard ['blɪzəd] n Schneesturm m.

bloated ['bləʊtɪd] a aufgedunsen; (col: full) nudelsatt.

blob [blɒb] n Klümpchen nt.

bloc [blɒk] n (Pol) Block m.

block [blɒk] n (of wood) Block m, Klotz m; (of houses) Häuserblock m; vt hemmen; ~ade [blɒˈkeɪd] Blockade f; vt blockieren; ~age Verstopfung f.

bloke [bləʊk] n (col) Kerl m, Typ m.

blonde [blɒnd] a blond; n Blondine f.

blood [blʌd] n Blut nt; ~ donor Blutspender m; ~ group Blutgruppe f; ~less a blutleer; ~ poisoning Blutvergiftung f; ~ pressure Blutdruck m; ~shed Blutvergießen nt; ~shot a blutunterlaufen; ~stained a blutbefleckt; ~stream Blut n, Blutkreislauf m; ~thirsty a blutrünstig; ~ transfusion Blutübertragung f; ~y a (col) verdammt, saumäßig; (lit) blutig; ~y-minded a stur.

bloom [bluːm] n Blüte f; (freshness) Glanz m; vi blühen; in ~ in Blüte.

blossom ['blɒsəm] n Blüte f; vi blühen.

blot [blɒt] n Klecks m; vt beklecksen; (ab)löschen; ~ out vt auslöschen.

blotchy ['blɒtʃɪ] a fleckig.

blotting paper ['blɒtɪŋpeɪpə*] n Löschpapier nt.

blouse [blaʊz] n Bluse f.

blow [bləʊ] n Schlag m; irreg vt blasen; vi (wind) wehen; to ~ one's top (vor Wut) explodieren; ~ over vi vorübergehen; ~ up vi explodieren; vt sprengen; ~lamp Lötlampe f; ~out (Aut) geplatzte(r) Reifen m; ~up (Phot) Vergrößerung f; ~y a windig.

blubber ['blʌbə*] n Walfischspeck m.

bludgeon ['blʌdʒən] vt (fig) zwingen.

blue [bluː] a blau; (col: unhappy) niedergeschlagen; (obscene) pornographisch; joke anzüglich; to have the ~s traurig

sein; ~bell Glockenblume f; ~-blooded a blaublütig; ~bottle Schmeißfliege f; ~print (fig) Entwurf m; ~s pl (Mus) Blues m.

bluff [blʌf] vt bluffen, täuschen; n (deception) Bluff m; a gutmütig und derb.

bluish ['bluːɪʃ] a bläulich.

blunder ['blʌndə*] n grobe(r) Fehler m, Schnitzer m; vi einen groben Fehler machen.

blunt [blʌnt] a knife stumpf; talk unverblümt; vt abstumpfen; ~ly ad frei heraus; ~ness Stumpfheit f; (fig) Plumpheit f.

blur [blɜː*] n Fleck m; vi verschwimmen; vt verschwommen machen.

blurb [blɜːb] n Waschzettel m.

blurt [blɜːt] vt: ~ out herausplatzen mit.

blush [blʌʃ] vi erröten; n (Scham)röte f; ~ing a errötend.

bluster ['blʌstə*] vi (wind) brausen; (person) darauf lospoltern, schwadronieren; ~y a sehr windig.

boa ['bəʊə] n Boa f.

boar [bɔː*] n Keiler m, Eber m.

board [bɔːd] n (of wood) Brett nt; (of card) Pappe f; (committee) Ausschuß m; (of firm) Aufsichtsrat m; (Sch) Direktorium nt; vt train einsteigen in (+acc); ship an Bord gehen (+gen); ~ and lodging Unterkunft f und Verpflegung; to go by the ~ flachfallen, über Bord gehen; ~ up vt mit Brettern vernageln; ~er Kostgänger m; (Sch) Internatsschüler(in f) m; ~ing house Pension f; ~ing school Internat nt; ~ room Sitzungszimmer nt.

boast [bəʊst] vi prahlen; n Großtuerei f; Prahlerei f; ~ful a prahlerisch; ~fulness Überheblichkeit f.

boat [bəʊt] n Boot nt; (ship) Schiff nt; ~er (hat) Kreissäge f; ~ing Bootfahren nt; ~swain ['bəʊsn] = bosun; ~ train Zug m mit Schiffsanschluß.

bob [bɒb] vi sich auf und nieder bewegen.

bobbin ['bɒbɪn] n Spule f.

bobsleigh ['bɒbsleɪ] n Bob m.

bodice ['bɒdɪs] n Mieder nt.

-bodied ['bɒdɪd] a -gebaut.

bodily ['bɒdɪlɪ] a, ad körperlich.

body ['bɒdɪ] n Körper m; (dead) Leiche f; (group) Mannschaft f; (Aut) Karosserie f; (trunk) Rumpf m; in a ~ in einer Gruppe; the main ~ of the work der Hauptanteil der Arbeit; ~guard Leibwache f; ~work Karosserie f.

bog [bɒg] n Sumpf m; vi: to get ~ged down sich festfahren.

bogey ['bəʊgɪ] n Schreckgespenst nt.

boggle ['bɒgl] vi stutzen.

bogus ['bəʊgəs] a unecht, Schein-.

boil [bɔɪl] vti kochen; n (Med) Geschwür nt; to come to the ~ zu kochen anfangen; ~er Boiler m; ~ing point Siedepunkt m.

boisterous ['bɔɪstərəs] a ungestüm.

bold [bəʊld] a (fearless) unerschrocken; handwriting fest und klar; ~ly ad keck; ~ness Kühnheit f; (cheekiness) Dreistigkeit f.

bollard ['bɒləd] n (Naut) Poller m; (on road) Pfosten m.

bolster ['bəʊlstə*] n Polster nt; ~ **up** vt unterstützen.

bolt [bəʊlt] n Bolzen m; (lock) Riegel m; vt verriegeln; (swallow) verschlingen; vi (horse) durchgehen.

bomb [bɒm] n Bombe f; vt bombardieren; ~**ard** [bɒmˈbɑːd] vt bombardieren; ~**ardment** [bɒmˈbɑːdmənt] Beschießung f; ~**er** Bomber m; ~**ing** Bombenangriff m; ~**shell** (fig) Bombe f.

bombastic [bɒmˈbæstɪk] a bombastisch.

bona fide ['bəʊnəˈfaɪdɪ] a echt.

bond [bɒnd] n (link) Band nt; (Fin) Schuldverschreibung f.

bone [bəʊn] n Knochen m; (of fish) Gräte f; (piece of ~) Knochensplitter m; ~ **of contention** Zankapfel m; vt die Knochen herausnehmen (+dat); fish entgräten; ~-**dry** a knochentrocken; ~**r** (US col) Schnitzer m.

bonfire ['bɒnfaɪə*] n Feuer nt im Freien.

bonnet ['bɒnɪt] n Haube f; (for baby) Häubchen nt; (Brit Aut) Motorhaube f.

bonny ['bɒnɪ] a (Scot) hübsch.

bonus ['bəʊnəs] n Bonus m; (annual ~) Prämie f.

bony ['bəʊnɪ] a knochig, knochendürr.

boo [buː] vt auspfeifen.

book [bʊk] n Buch nt; vt ticket etc vorbestellen; person verwarnen; ~**able** a im Vorverkauf erhältlich; ~**case** Bücherregal nt, Bücherschrank m; ~**ing office** (Rail) Fahrkartenschalter m; (Theat) Vorverkaufsstelle f; ~**keeping** Buchhaltung f; ~**let** Broschüre f; ~**maker** Buchmacher m; ~**seller** Buchhändler m; ~**shop** Buchhandlung f, ~**stall** Bücherstand m; (Rail) Bahnhofsbuchhandlung f; ~**worm** Bücherwurm m.

boom [buːm] n (noise) Dröhnen nt; (busy period) Hochkonjunktur f; vi dröhnen.

boomerang ['buːmərəŋ] n Bumerang m.

boon [buːn] n Wohltat f, Segen m.

boorish ['bʊərɪʃ] a grob.

boost [buːst] n Auftrieb m; (fig) Reklame f; vt Auftrieb geben.

boot [buːt] n Stiefel m; (Brit Aut) Kofferraum m; vt (kick) einen Fußtritt geben; to ~ (in addition) obendrein.

booty ['buːtɪ] n Beute f.

booze [buːz] n (col) Alkohol m, Schnaps m; vi saufen.

border ['bɔːdə*] n Grenze f; (edge) Kante f; (in garden) (Blumen)rabatte f; ~ **on** vt grenzen an (+acc); ~**line** Grenze f.

bore [bɔː*] vt bohren; (weary) langweilen; n (person) langweilige(r) Mensch m; (thing) langweilige Sache f; (of gun) Kaliber nt; ~**dom** Langeweile f.

boring ['bɔːrɪŋ] a langweilig.

born [bɔːn] to be ~ geboren werden.

borough ['bʌrə] n Stadt(gemeinde) f, Stadtbezirk m.

borrow ['bɒrəʊ] vt borgen; ~**ing** (Fin) Anleihe f.

bosom ['bʊzəm] n Busen m.

boss [bɒs] n Chef m, Boß m; vt: ~ **around** herumkommandieren; ~**y** a herrisch.

bosun ['bəʊsn] n Bootsmann m.

botanical [bəˈtænɪkəl] a botanisch.

botanist ['bɒtənɪst] n Botaniker(in f) m.

botany ['bɒtənɪ] n Botanik f.

botch [bɒtʃ] vt verpfuschen.

both [bəʊθ] a beide(s); ~ (**of**) **the books** beide Bücher; **I like them** ~ ich mag (sie) beide; pron beide(s); ad: ~ **X and Y** sowohl X wie or als auch Y.

bother ['bɒðə*] vt (pester) quälen; vi (fuss) sich aufregen; (take trouble) sich Mühe machen; n Mühe f, Umstand m.

bottle ['bɒtl] n Flasche f; vt (in Flaschen) abfüllen; ~**neck** (lit, fig) Engpaß m.

bottom ['bɒtəm] n Boden m; (of person) Hintern m; (riverbed) Flußbett nt; at ~ im Grunde; a unterste(r, s); ~**less** a bodenlos.

bough [baʊ] n Zweig m, Ast m.

boulder ['bəʊldə*] n Felsbrocken m.

bounce [baʊns] vi (ball) hochspringen; (person) herumhüpfen; (cheque) platzen; vt (auf)springen lassen; n (rebound) Aufprall m; ~**r** Rausschmeißer m.

bound [baʊnd] n Grenze f; (leap) Sprung m; vi (spring, leap) (auf)springen; a gebunden, verpflichtet; **out of** ~**s** Zutritt verboten; to be ~ **to do sth** verpflichtet sein, etw zu tun, etw tun müssen; **it's** ~ **to happen** es muß so kommen; to be ~ **for . . . nach** . . . fahren; ~**ary** Grenze f, Grenzlinie f; ~**less** a grenzenlos.

bouquet [bʊˈkeɪ] n Strauß m; (of wine) Blume f.

bourgeois ['bʊəʒwɑː] a kleinbürgerlich, bourgeois.

bout [baʊt] n (of illness) Anfall m; (of contest) Kampf m.

bow[1] [bəʊ] n (ribbon) Schleife f; (weapon, Mus) Bogen m.

bow[2] [baʊ] vi sich verbeugen; (submit) sich beugen (+dat); n Verbeugung f; (of ship) Bug m.

bowels ['baʊəlz] npl Darm m; (centre) Innere nt.

bowl [bəʊl] n (basin) Schüssel f; (of pipe) (Pfeifen)kopf m; (wooden ball) (Holz)kugel f; vti (die Kugel) rollen; ~**s** pl (game) Bowls-Spiel nt.

bow-legged ['bəʊlegɪd] a o-beinig.

bowler ['bəʊlə*] n Werfer m; (hat) Melone f.

bowling ['bəʊlɪŋ] n Kegeln nt; ~ **alley** Kegelbahn f; ~ **green** Rasen m zum Bowling-Spiel.

bow tie ['bəʊ'taɪ] n Fliege f.

box [bɒks] n Schachtel f; (bigger) Kasten m; (Theat) Loge f; vt einpacken; to ~ **sb's ears** jdm eine Ohrfeige geben; vi boxen; ~**er** Boxer m; ~ **in** vt einpferchen; ~**ing** (Sport) Boxen nt; **B**~**ing Day** zweiter Weihnachtsfeiertag; ~**ing ring** Boxring m; ~ **office** (Theater)kasse f; ~**room** Rumpelkammer f.

boy [bɔɪ] n Junge m; ~ **scout** Pfadfinder m.

boycott ['bɔɪkɒt] n Boykott m; vt boykottieren.

boyfriend ['bɔɪfrend] n Freund m.

boyish ['bɔɪɪʃ] a jungenhaft.

bra [brɑː] n BH m.

brace [breɪs] n (Tech) Stütze f; (Med)
Klammer f; vt stützen; ~s pl Hosenträger
pl.

bracelet ['breɪslɪt] n Armband nt.

bracing ['breɪsɪŋ] a kräftigend.

bracken ['brækən] n Farnkraut nt.

bracket ['brækɪt] n Halter m, Klammer f;
(in punctuation) Klammer f; (group)
Gruppe f; vt einklammern; (fig) in
dieselbe Gruppe einordnen.

brag [bræg] vi sich rühmen.

braid [breɪd] n (hair) Flechte f; (trim)
Borte f.

Braille [breɪl] n Blindenschrift f.

brain [breɪn] n (Anat) Gehirn nt; (intellect)
Intelligenz f, Verstand m; (person)
kluge(r) Kopf m; ~s pl Verstand m;
~less a dumm; ~storm verrückte(r)
Einfall m; ~wash vt Gehirnwäsche f vor-
nehmen bei; ~wave gute(r) Einfall m,
Geistesblitz m; ~y gescheit.

braise [breɪz] vt schmoren.

brake [breɪk] n Bremse f; vti bremsen.

branch [brɑːntʃ] n Ast m; (division) Zweig
m; vi (road) sich verzweigen.

brand [brænd] n (Comm) Marke f, Sorte f;
(on cattle) Brandmal nt; vt brandmarken;
(Comm) eine Schutzmarke geben (+dat).

brandish ['brændɪʃ] vt (drohend)
schwingen.

brand-new ['brænd'njuː] a funkel-
nagelneu.

brandy ['brændɪ] n Weinbrand m, Kognak
m.

brash [bræʃ] a unverschämt.

brass [brɑːs] n Messing nt; ~ band
Blaskapelle f.

brassière ['bræsɪə*] n Büstenhalter m.

brat [bræt] n ungezogene(s) Kind nt, Gör
nt.

bravado [brə'vɑːdəʊ] n Tollkühnheit f.

brave [breɪv] a tapfer; n indianische(r)
Krieger m; vt die Stirn bieten (+dat); ~ly
ad tapfer; ~ry ['breɪvərɪ] Tapferkeit f.

bravo ['brɑː'vəʊ] interj bravo!

brawl [brɔːl] n Rauferei f; vi Krawall
machen.

brawn [brɔːn] n (Anat) Muskeln pl;
(strength) Muskelkraft f; ~y muskulös,
stämmig.

bray [breɪ] n Eselsschrei m; vi schreien.

brazen ['breɪzn] a (shameless) unverschämt; vt: ~ it out sich mit Lügen
und Betrügen durchsetzen.

brazier ['breɪzɪə*] n (of workmen)
offene(r) Kohlenofen m.

breach [briːtʃ] n (gap) Lücke f; (Mil)
Durchbruch m; (of discipline) Verstoß m
(gegen die Disziplin); (of faith) Ver-
trauensbruch m; vt durchbrechen; ~ of
the peace öffentliche Ruhestörung f.

bread [bred] n Brot nt; ~ and butter
Butterbrot nt; ~crumbs pl Brotkrumen
pl; (Cook) Paniermehl nt; to be on the
~line sich gerade so durchschlagen;
~winner Ernährer m.

breadth [bredθ] n Breite f.

break [breɪk] irreg vt (destroy) (ab- or
zer)brechen; promise brechen, nicht ein-

halten; vi (fall apart) auseinanderbrechen;
(collapse) zusammenbrechen; (of dawn)
anbrechen; n (gap) Lücke f; (chance)
Chance f, Gelegenheit f; (fracture) Bruch
m; (rest) Pause f; ~ down vi (car) eine
Panne haben; (person) zusammenbrechen;
to ~ free or loose sich losreißen; ~ in
vt animal abrichten; horse zureiten; vi
(burglar) einbrechen; ~ out vi ausbrechen; ~ up vi zerbrechen; (fig) sich
zerstreuen; (Sch) in die Ferien gehen; vt
brechen; ~able a zerbrechlich; ~age
Bruch m, Beschädigung f; ~down (Tech)
Panne f; (of nerves) Zusammenbruch m;
~er Brecher m; ~fast ['brekfəst] Frühstück nt; ~through Durchbruch m;
~water Wellenbrecher m.

breast [brest] n Brust f; ~ stroke Brust-
schwimmen nt.

breath [breθ] n Atem m; out of ~ außer
Atem; under one's ~ flüsternd.

breathalize ['breθəlaɪz] vt blasen lassen.

breathe [briːð] vti atmen; ~r Verschnauf-
pause f.

breathless ['breθlɪs] a atemlos.

breath-taking ['breθteɪkɪŋ] a atem-
beraubend.

breed [briːd] irreg vi sich vermehren; vt
züchten; n (race) Rasse f, Zucht f; ~er
(person) Züchter m; ~ing Züchtung f; (upbringing) Erziehung f; (education) Bildung
f.

breeze [briːz] n Brise f.

breezy ['briːzɪ] a windig; manner munter.

brevity ['brevɪtɪ] n Kürze f.

brew [bruː] vt brauen; plot anzetteln; vi
(storm) sich zusammenziehen; ~ery
Brauerei f.

bribe ['braɪb] n Bestechungsgeld nt or
-geschenk nt; vt bestechen; ~ry
['braɪbərɪ] Bestechung f.

bric-à-brac ['brɪkəbræk] n Nippes pl.

brick [brɪk] n Backstein m; ~layer
Maurer m; ~work Mauerwerk nt;
~works Ziegelei f.

bridal ['braɪdl] a Braut-, bräutlich.

bride [braɪd] n Braut f; ~groom
Bräutigam m; ~smaid Brautjungfer f.

bridge [brɪdʒ] n Brücke f; (Naut)
Kommandobrücke f; (Cards) Bridge nt;
(Anat) Nasenrücken m; vt eine Brücke
schlagen über (+acc); (fig) überbrücken.

bridle ['braɪdl] n Zaum m; vt (fig) zügeln;
horse aufzäumen; ~ path Saumpfad m.

brief [briːf] a kurz; n (Jur) Akten pl; vt
instruieren; ~s pl Schlüpfer m, Slip m;
~case Aktentasche f; ~ing (genaue)
Anweisung f; ~ly ad kurz; ~ness Kürze
f.

brigade [brɪ'geɪd] n Brigade f.

brigadier [brɪgə'dɪə*] n Brigadegeneral m.

bright [braɪt] a hell; (cheerful) heiter; idea
klug; ~en up vt aufhellen; person aufheitern; vi sich aufheitern; ~ly ad hell;
heiter.

brilliance ['brɪljəns] n Glanz m; (of
person) Scharfsinn m.

brilliant a ~ly ad ['brɪlɪənt, -lɪ] glänzend.

brim [brɪm] n Rand m; vi voll sein; ~ful a
übervoll.

brine [braɪn] *n* Salzwasser *nt.*

bring [brɪŋ] *vt irreg* bringen; ~ **about** *vt* zustande bringen; ~ **off** *vt* davontragen; **success** erzielen; ~ **round** *or* **to** *vt* wieder zu sich bringen; ~ **up** *vt* aufziehen; **question** zur Sprache bringen.

brisk [brɪsk] *a* lebhaft.

bristle ['brɪsl] *n* Borste *f*; *vi* sich sträuben; **bristling with** strotzend vor (+*dat*).

brittle ['brɪtl] *a* spröde.

broach [brəʊtʃ] *vt subject* anschneiden.

broad [brɔːd] *a* breit; *hint* deutlich; *daylight* hellicht; (*general*) allgemein; *accent* stark; ~**cast** *n* Rundfunkübertragung *f*; *vti irreg* übertragen, senden; ~**casting** *n* Rundfunk *m*; ~**en** *vt* erweitern; *vi* sich erweitern; ~**ly** *ad* allgemein gesagt; ~**-minded** *a* tolerant.

brocade [brə'keɪd] *n* Brokat *m.*

broccoli ['brɒkəlɪ] *n* Spargelkohl *m*, Brokkoli *pl.*

brochure ['brəʊʃʊə*] *n* Broschüre *f.*

broiler ['brɔɪlə*] *n* Bratrost *m.*

broke [brəʊk] *a* (*col*) pleite.

broken-hearted ['brəʊkən'hɑːtɪd] *a* untröstlich.

broker ['brəʊkə*] *n* Makler *m.*

bronchitis [brɒŋ'kaɪtɪs] *n* Bronchitis *f.*

bronze [brɒnz] *n* Bronze *f*; ~**d** *a* sonnengebräunt.

brooch [brəʊtʃ] *n* Brosche *f.*

brood [bruːd] *n* Brut *f*; *vi* brüten; ~**y** *a* brütend.

brook [brʊk] *n* Bach *m.*

broom [bruːm] *n* Besen *m*; ~**stick** Besenstiel *m.*

broth [brɒθ] *n* Suppe *f*, Fleischbrühe *f.*

brothel ['brɒθl] *n* Bordell *nt.*

brother ['brʌðə*] *n* Bruder *m*; ~**hood** Bruderschaft *f*; ~**-in-law** Schwager *m*; ~**ly** *a* brüderlich.

brow [braʊ] *n* (*eyebrow*) (Augen)braue *f*; (*forehead*) Stirn *f*; (*of hill*) Bergkuppe *f*; ~**beat** *vt irreg* einschüchtern.

brown [braʊn] *a* braun; *n* Braun *nt*; *vt* bräunen; ~**ie** Wichtel *m*; ~ **paper** Packpapier *nt.*

browse [braʊz] *vi* (*in books*) blättern; (*in shop*) schmökern, herumschauen.

bruise [bruːz] *n* Bluterguß *m*, blaue(r) Fleck *m*; *vti* einen blauen Fleck geben/bekommen.

brunette [bruː'net] *n* Brünette *f.*

brunt [brʌnt] *n* volle Wucht *f.*

brush [brʌʃ] *n* Bürste *f*; (*for sweeping*) Handbesen *m*; (*for painting*) Pinsel *m*; (*fight*) kurze(r) Kampf *m*; (*Mil*) Scharmützel *nt*; (*fig*) Auseinandersetzung *f*; *vt* (*clean*) bürsten; (*sweep*) fegen; (*touch*) streifen; **give sb the** ~**-off** (*col*) jdm eine Abfuhr erteilen; ~ **aside** *vt* abtun; ~ **wood** Gestrüpp *nt.*

brusque [bruːsk] *a* schroff.

Brussels sprout ['brʌslz'spraʊt] *n* Rosenkohl *m.*

brutal ['bruːtl] *a* brutal; ~**ity** [bruː'tælɪtɪ] *n* Brutalität *f.*

brute [bruːt] *n* (*person*) Scheusal *nt*; ~

force rohe Kraft; (*violence*) nackte Gewalt *nt.*

brutish ['bruːtɪʃ] *a* tierisch.

bubble ['bʌbl] *n* (Luft)blase *f*; *vi* sprudeln; (*with joy*) übersprudeln.

buck [bʌk] *n* Bock *m*; (*US col*) Dollar *m*; *vi* bocken; ~ **up** *vi* (*col*) sich zusammenreißen.

bucket ['bʌkɪt] *n* Eimer *m.*

buckle ['bʌkl] *n* Schnalle *f*; *vt* (*an- or zusammen*)schnallen; *vi* (*bend*) sich verziehen.

bud [bʌd] *n* Knospe *f*; *vi* knospen, keimen.

Buddhism ['bʊdɪzəm] *n* Buddhismus *m.*

Buddhist ['bʊdɪst] *n* Buddhist(in *f*) *m*; *a* buddhistisch.

budding ['bʌdɪŋ] *a* angehend.

buddy ['bʌdɪ] *n* (*col*) Kumpel *m.*

budge [bʌdʒ] *vti* (sich) von der Stelle rühren.

budgerigar ['bʌdʒərɪgɑː*] *n* Wellensittich *m.*

budget ['bʌdʒɪt] *n* Budget *nt*; (*Pol*) Haushalt *m*; *vi* haushalten.

budgie ['bʌdʒɪ] *n* = **budgerigar.**

buff [bʌf] *a colour* lederfarben; *n* (*enthusiast*) Fan *m.*

buffalo ['bʌfələʊ] *n* Büffel *m.*

buffer ['bʌfə*] *n* Puffer *m.*

buffet ['bʌfɪt] *n* (*blow*) Schlag *m*; ['bʊfeɪ] (*bar*) Imbißraum *m*, Erfrischungsraum *m*; (*food*) (kaltes) Büffet *nt*; *vt* ['bʌfɪt] (herum)stoßen.

buffoon [bʌ'fuːn] *n* Hanswurst *m.*

bug [bʌg] *n* (*lit, fig*) Wanze *f*; *vt* verwanzen; ~**bear** Schreckgespenst *nt.*

bugle ['bjuːgl] *n* Jagd-, Bügelhorn *nt.*

build [bɪld] *vt irreg* bauen; *n* Körperbau *m*; ~**er** *n* Bauunternehmer *m*; ~**ing** Gebäude *nt*; ~**ing society** Baugenossenschaft *f*; ~**-up** Aufbau *m*; (*publicity*) Reklame *f.*

built [bɪlt]: **well-**~ *a person* gut gebaut; ~**-in** *a cupboard* eingebaut; ~**-up area** Wohngebiet *nt.*

bulb [bʌlb] *n* (*Bot*) (Blumen)zwiebel *f*; (*Elec*) Glühlampe *f*, Birne *f*; ~**ous** *a* knollig.

bulge [bʌldʒ] *n* (Aus)bauchung *f*; *vi* sich (aus)bauchen.

bulk [bʌlk] *n* Größe *f*, Masse *f*; (*greater part*) Großteil *m*; ~**head** Schott *nt*; ~**y** *a* (sehr) umfangreich; *goods* sperrig.

bull [bʊl] *n* (*animal*) Bulle *m*; (*cattle*) Stier *m*; (*papal*) Bulle *f*; ~**dog** Bulldogge *f.*

bulldoze ['bʊldəʊz] *vt* planieren; (*fig*) durchboxen; ~**r** Planierraupe *f*, Bulldozer *m.*

bullet ['bʊlɪt] *n* Kugel *f.*

bulletin ['bʊlɪtɪn] *n* Bulletin *nt*, Bekanntmachung *f.*

bullfight ['bʊlfaɪt] *n* Stierkampf *m.*

bullion ['bʊlɪən] *n* Barren *m.*

bullock ['bʊlək] *n* Ochse *m.*

bull's-eye ['bʊlzaɪ] *n* das Schwarze *nt.*

bully ['bʊlɪ] *n* Raufbold *m*; *vt* einschüchtern.

bum [bʌm] *n* (*col: backside*) Hintern *m*; (*tramp*) Landstreicher *m*; (*nasty person*) fieser Kerl m; ~ **around** vi herumgammeln.

bumblebee ['bʌmblbi:] n Hummel f.

bump [bʌmp] n (blow) Stoß m; (swelling) Beule f; vti stoßen, prallen; ~er (Brit Aut) Stoßstange f; a edition dick; harvest Rekord-.

bumptious ['bʌmpʃəs] a aufgeblasen.

bumpy ['bʌmpɪ] a holprig.

bun [bʌn] n Korinthenbrötchen nt.

bunch [bʌntʃ] n (of flowers) Strauß m; (of keys) Bund m; (of people) Haufen m.

bundle ['bʌndl] n Bündel nt; vt bündeln; ~ off vt fortschicken.

bung [bʌŋ] n Spund m; vt (col: throw) schleudern.

bungalow ['bʌŋgələu] n einstöckige(s) Haus nt, Bungalow m.

bungle ['bʌŋgl] vt verpfuschen.

bunion ['bʌnɪən] n entzündete(r) Fußballen m.

bunk [bʌŋk] n Schlafkoje f; ~ bed Etagenbett nt.

bunker ['bʌŋkə*] n (coal store) Kohlenbunker m; (golf) Sandloch nt.

bunny ['bʌnɪ] n Häschen nt.

Bunsen burner ['bʌnsn 'bɜːnə*] n Bunsenbrenner m.

bunting ['bʌntɪŋ] n Fahnentuch nt.

buoy [bɔɪ] n Boje f; (lifebuoy) Rettungsboje f; ~ancy Schwimmkraft f; ~ant a (floating) schwimmend; (fig) heiter; ~ up vt Auftrieb geben (+dat).

burden ['bɜːdn] n (weight) Ladung f, Last f; (fig) Bürde f; vt belasten.

bureau ['bjuərəu] n (desk) Sekretär m; (for information etc) Büro nt.

bureaucracy [bjuə'rɒkrəsɪ] n Bürokratie f.

bureaucrat ['bjuərəkræt] n Bürokrat(in f) m; ~ic [bjuərə'krætɪk] a bürokratisch.

burglar ['bɜːglə*] n Einbrecher m; ~ alarm Einbruchssicherung f; ~ize vt (US) einbrechen in (+acc); ~y Einbruch m.

burgle ['bɜːgl] vt einbrechen in (+acc).

burial ['berɪəl] n Beerdigung f; ~ ground Friedhof m.

burlesque [bɜː'lesk] n Burleske f.

burly ['bɜːlɪ] a stämmig.

burn [bɜːn] irreg vt verbrennen; vi brennen; n Brandwunde f; to ~ one's fingers sich die Finger verbrennen; ~ing question brennende Frage f.

burnish ['bɜːnɪʃ] vt polieren.

burrow ['bʌrəu] n (of fox) Bau m; (of rabbit) Höhle f; vi sich eingraben; vt eingraben.

bursar ['bɜːsə*] n Kassenverwalter m, Quästor m.

burst [bɜːst] irreg vt zerbrechen; vi platzen; (into tears) ausbrechen; n Explosion f; (outbreak) Ausbruch m; (in pipe) Bruch(stelle f) m.

bury ['berɪ] vt vergraben; (in grave) beerdigen; to ~ the hatchet das Kriegsbeil begraben.

bus [bʌs] n (Auto)bus m, Omnibus m.

bush [buʃ] n Busch m.

bushel ['buʃl] n Scheffel m.

bushy ['buʃɪ] a buschig.

busily ['bɪzɪlɪ] ad geschäftig.

business ['bɪznɪs] n Geschäft nt; (concern) Angelegenheit f; it's none of your ~ es geht dich nichts an; to mean ~ es ernst meinen; ~man Geschäftsmann m.

bus-stop ['bʌsstɒp] n Bushaltestelle f.

bust [bʌst] n Büste f; a (broken) kaputt-(gegangen); business pleite; to go ~ pleite machen.

bustle ['bʌsl] n Getriebe nt; vi hasten.

bustling ['bʌslɪŋ] a geschäftig.

bust-up ['bʌstʌp] n (col) Krach m.

busy ['bɪzɪ] a beschäftigt; road belebt; vt: ~ o.s. sich beschäftigen; ~body Übereifrige(r) mf.

but [bʌt, bət] cj aber; not this ~ that nicht dies, sondern das; (only) nur; (except) außer.

butane ['bju:teɪn] n Butan nt.

butcher ['butʃə*] n Metzger m; (murderer) Schlächter m; vt schlachten; (kill) abschlachten.

butler ['bʌtlə*] n Butler m.

butt [bʌt] n (cask) große(s) Faß nt; (target) Zielscheibe f; (thick end) dicke(s) Ende nt; (of gun) Kolben m; (of cigarette) Stummel m; vt (mit dem Kopf) stoßen.

butter ['bʌtə*] n Butter f; vt buttern; ~fly Schmetterling m.

buttocks ['bʌtəks] npl Gesäß nt.

button ['bʌtn] n Knopf m; vti zuknöpfen; ~hole Knopfloch nt; Blume f im Knopfloch; vt rankriegen.

buttress ['bʌtrɪs] n Strebepfeiler m; Stützbogen m.

buxom ['bʌksəm] a drall.

buy [baɪ] vt irreg kaufen; ~ up vt aufkaufen; ~er Käufer(in f) m.

buzz [bʌz] n Summen nt; vi summen.

buzzard ['bʌzəd] n Bussard m.

buzzer ['bʌzə*] n Summer m.

by [baɪ] prep (near) bei; (via) über (+acc); (past) an (+dat) . . . vorbei; (before) bis; ~ day/night tags/nachts; ~ train/bus mit dem Zug/Bus; done ~ sb/sth von jdm/durch etw gemacht; ~ oneself allein; ~ and large im großen und ganzen; ~-election Nachwahl f; ~gone a vergangen; n: let ~gones be ~gones laß(t) das Vergangene vergangen sein; ~(e)-law Verordnung f; ~pass Umgehungsstraße f; ~product Nebenprodukt nt; ~stander Zuschauer m; ~word Inbegriff m.

C

C, c [si:] n C nt, c nt.

cab [kæb] n Taxi nt; (of train) Führerstand m; (of truck) Führersitz m.

cabaret ['kæbəreɪ] n Kabarett nt.

cabbage ['kæbɪdʒ] n Kohl(kopf) m.

cabin ['kæbɪn] n Hütte f; (Naut) Kajüte f; (Aviat) Kabine f; ~ cruiser Motorjacht f.

cabinet ['kæbɪnɪt] n Schrank m; (for china) Vitrine f; (Pol) Kabinett nt; ~maker Kunsttischler m.

cable ['keɪbl] n Drahtseil nt, Tau nt; (Tel)

(Leitungs)kabel nt; (telegram) Kabel nt; vti kabeln, telegraphieren; ~-car Seilbahn f; ~gram (Übersee)telegramm nt; ~ railway (Draht)seilbahn f.

cache [kæʃ] n Versteck nt; (for ammunition) geheimes Munitionslager nt; (for food) geheimes Proviantlager nt; (supplies of ammunition) Munitionsvorrat m; (supplies of food) Lebensmittelvorrat m.

cackle ['kækl] n Gegacker nt; vi gacken.

cactus ['kæktəs] n Kaktus m, Kaktee f.

caddie ['kædɪ] n Golfjunge m.

caddy ['kædɪ] n Teedose f.

cadence ['keɪdəns] n Tonfall m; (Mus) Kadenz f.

cadet [kə'det] n Kadett m.

cadge [kædʒ] vt schmarotzen, nassauern.

Caesarean [si:'zɛərɪən] a: ~ (section) Kaiserschnitt m.

café ['kæfɪ] n Café nt, Restaurant nt.

cafeteria [kæfɪ'tɪərɪə] n Selbstbedienungsrestaurant nt.

caffein(e) ['kæfi:n] n Koffein nt.

cage [keɪdʒ] n Käfig m; vt einsperren.

cagey ['keɪdʒɪ] a geheimnistuerisch, zurückhaltend.

cajole [kə'dʒəʊl] vt überreden.

cake [keɪk] n Kuchen m; (of soap) Stück nt; ~d verkrustet.

calamine ['kæləmaɪn] n Galmei m.

calamitous [kə'læmɪtəs] a katastrophal, unglückselig.

calamity [kə'læmɪtɪ] n Unglück nt, (Schicksals)schlag m.

calcium ['kælsɪəm] n Kalzium nt.

calculate ['kælkjuleɪt] vt berechnen, kalkulieren.

calculating ['kælkjuleɪtɪŋ] a berechnend.

calculation [kælkju'leɪʃən] n Berechnung f.

calculator ['kælkjuleɪtə*] Rechner m.

calculus ['kælkjuləs] n Rechenart f.

calendar ['kælɪndə*] n Kalender m.

calf [kɑːf] n Kalb nt; (leather) Kalbsleder nt; (Anat) Wade f.

calibre, (US) caliber ['kælɪbə*] n Kaliber nt.

call [kɔːl] vt rufen; (summon) herbeirufen; (name) nennen; (meeting) einberufen; (awaken) wecken; (Tel) anrufen; vi (for help) rufen, schreien; (visit) vorbeikommen; n (shout) Schrei m, Ruf m; (visit) Besuch m; (Tel) Anruf m; on ~ in Bereitschaft; ~box Fernsprechzelle f; ~er Besucher(in f) m; (Tel) Anrufer m; ~ girl Call-Girl nt; ~ing (vocation) Berufung f; to be ~ed heißen; ~ for vt rufen (nach); (fetch) abholen; (fig: require) erfordern, verlangen; ~ off vt meeting absagen; ~ on vt besuchen, aufsuchen; (request) fragen; ~ up vt (Mil) einziehen, einberufen.

callous a, ~ly ad ['kæləs, -lɪ] herzlos; ~ness Herzlosigkeit f.

callow ['kæləʊ] a unerfahren, noch nicht flügge.

calm [kɑːm] n Stille f, Ruhe f; (Naut) Flaute f; vt beruhigen; a still, ruhig; person gelassen; ~ly ad ruhig, still; ~ness Stille

f, Ruhe f; (mental) Gelassenheit f; ~ down vi sich beruhigen; vt beruhigen, besänftigen.

calorie ['kælərɪ] n Kalorie f, Wärmeeinheit f.

calve [kɑːv] vi kalben.

camber ['kæmbə*] n Wölbung f.

camel ['kæməl] n Kamel nt.

cameo ['kæmɪəʊ] n Kamee f.

camera ['kæmərə] n Fotoapparat m, Kamera f; in ~ unter Ausschluß der Öffentlichkeit; ~man Kameramann m.

camomile ['kæməmaɪl] n: ~ tea Kamillentee m.

camouflage ['kæməflɑːʒ] n Tarnung f; vt tarnen; (fig) verschleiern, bemänteln.

camp [kæmp] n Lager nt, Camp nt; (Mil) Feldlager nt; (permanent) Kaserne f; (camping place) Zeltplatz m; vi zelten, campen.

campaign [kæm'peɪn] n Kampagne f; (Mil) Feldzug m; vi (Mil) Krieg führen; (participate) in den Krieg ziehen; (fig) werben, Propaganda machen; (Pol) den Wahlkampf führen; electoral ~ Wahlkampf m.

campbed ['kæmp'bed] n Campingbett nt.

camper ['kæmpə*] n Zeltende(r) mf, Camper m.

camping ['kæmpɪŋ] n: to go ~ zelten, Camping machen.

campsite ['kæmpsaɪt] n Zeltplatz m, Campingplatz m.

campus ['kæmpəs] n (Sch) Schulgelände nt; (Univ) Universitätsgelände nt, Campus m.

can [kæn] v aux irreg (be able) können, fähig sein; (be allowed) dürfen, können; n Büchse f, Dose f; (for water) Kanne f; vt konservieren, in Büchsen einmachen.

canal [kə'næl] n Kanal m.

canary [kə'nɛərɪ] n Kanarienvogel m; a hellgelb.

cancel ['kænsəl] vt (delete) durchstreichen; (Math) kürzen; arrangement aufheben; meeting absagen; treaty annullieren; stamp entwerten; ~lation [kænsə'leɪʃən] n Aufhebung f; Absage f; Annullierung f; Entwertung f.

cancer ['kænsə*] n (also Astrol C~) Krebs m.

candid ['kændɪd] a offen, ehrlich; ~ly ad ehrlich.

candidate ['kændɪdeɪt] n Bewerber(in f) m; (Pol) Kandidat(in f) m.

candle ['kændl] n Kerze f; ~light Kerzenlicht nt; ~stick Kerzenleuchter m.

candour ['kændə*] n Offenheit f.

candy ['kændɪ] n Kandis(zucker) m; (US) Bonbons pl.

cane [keɪn] n (Bot) Rohr nt; (for walking, Sch) Stock m; vt schlagen.

canister ['kænɪstə*] n Blechdose f.

cannabis ['kænəbɪs] n Hanf m, Haschisch nt.

canned [kænd] a Büchsen-, eingemacht.

cannibal ['kænɪbəl] n Menschenfresser m; ~ism Kannibalismus m.

cannon ['kænən] n Kanone f.

cannot ['kænɒt] = **can not**.

canny ['kænɪ] a (shrewd) schlau, erfahren; (cautious) umsichtig, vorsichtig.

canoe [kə'nuː] n Paddelboot nt, Kanu nt; ~**ing** Kanufahren nt; ~**ist** Kanufahrer(in f) m.

canon ['kænən] n Domherr m; (in church law) Kanon m; (standard) Grundsatz m.

canonize ['kænənaɪz] vt heiligsprechen.

can opener ['kænəupnə*] n Büchsenöffner m.

canopy ['kænəpɪ] n Baldachin m.

can't [kænt] = **can not**.

cantankerous [kæn'tæŋkərəs] a zänkisch, mürrisch.

canteen [kæn'tiːn] n (in factory) Kantine f, (case of cutlery) Besteckkasten m.

canter ['kæntə*] n Kanter m, kurzer leichter Galopp m; vi in kurzem Galopp reiten.

cantilever ['kæntɪliːvə*] n Träger m, Ausleger m.

canvas ['kænvəs] n Segeltuch nt, Zeltstoff m; (sail) Segel nt; (for painting) Leinwand f; (painting) Ölgemälde nt; **under** ~ (people) in Zelten; (boat) unter Segel.

canvass ['kænvəs] vt werben; ~**er** Wahlwerber(in f) m.

canyon ['kænjən] n Felsenschlucht f.

cap [kæp] n Kappe f, Mütze f; (lid) (Verschluß)kappe f, Deckel m; vt verschließen; (surpass) übertreffen.

capability [keɪpə'bɪlɪtɪ] n Fähigkeit f.

capable ['keɪpəbl] a fähig; **to be** ~ **of sth** zu etw fähig or imstande sein.

capacity [kə'pæsɪtɪ] n Fassungsvermögen nt; (ability) Fähigkeit f; (position) Eigenschaft f.

cape [keɪp] n (garment) Cape nt, Umhang m; (Geog) Kap nt.

caper ['keɪpə*] n Kaper f.

capital ['kæpɪtl] n (— city) Hauptstadt f; (Fin) Kapital nt; (— letter) Großbuchstabe m; ~**ism** Kapitalismus m; ~**ist** a kapitalistisch; n Kapitalist(in f) m; ~ **punishment** Todesstrafe f.

capitulate [kə'pɪtjuleɪt] vi kapitulieren.

capitulation [kəpɪtju'leɪʃən] n Kapitulation f.

capricious [kə'prɪʃəs] a launisch.

Capricorn ['kæprɪkɔːn] n Steinbock m.

capsize [kæp'saɪz] vti kentern.

capstan ['kæpstən] n Ankerwinde f, Poller m.

capsule ['kæpsjuːl] n Kapsel f.

captain ['kæptɪn] n Führer m; (Naut) Kapitän m; (Mil) Hauptmann m; (Sport) (Mannschafts)kapitän m; vt anführen.

caption ['kæpʃən] n Unterschrift f, Text m.

captivate ['kæptɪveɪt] vt fesseln.

captive ['kæptɪv] n Gefangene(r) mf; a gefangen(gehalten).

captivity [kæp'tɪvɪtɪ] n Gefangenschaft f.

capture ['kæptʃə*] vt fassen, gefangennehmen; n Gefangennahme f.

car [kɑː*] n Auto nt, Wagen m.

carafe [kə'ræf] n Karaffe f.

caramel ['kærəməl] n Karamelle f.

carat ['kærət] n Karat nt.

caravan ['kærəvæn] n Wohnwagen m; (in desert) Karawane f.

caraway ['kærəweɪ] n: ~ **seed** Kümmel m.

carbohydrate [kɑːbəu'haɪdreɪt] n Kohlenhydrat nt.

carbon ['kɑːbən] n Kohlenstoff m; (— paper) Kohlepapier nt; ~ **copy** Durchschlag m.

carburettor ['kɑːbjuretə*] n Vergaser m.

carcass ['kɑːkəs] n Kadaver m.

card [kɑːd] n Karte f; ~**board** Pappe f; ~**board box** Pappschachtel f; ~ **game** Kartenspiel nt.

cardiac ['kɑːdɪæk] a Herz-.

cardigan ['kɑːdɪgən] n Strickjacke f.

cardinal ['kɑːdɪnl] a: ~ **number** Kardinalzahl f.

care [kɛə*] n Sorge f, Mühe f; (charge) Obhut f, Fürsorge f; vi: **I don't** ~ es ist mir egal; **to** ~ **about sb/sth** sich kümmern um jdn/etw; **to take** ~ (watch) vorsichtig sein; (take pains) darauf achten; **take** ~ **of** vt sorgen für; ~ **for** vt (look after) sorgen für; (like) mögen, gern haben.

career [kə'rɪə*] n Karriere f, Laufbahn f; vi rasen.

carefree ['kɛəfriː] a sorgenfrei.

careful a, ~**ly** ad ['kɛəful, -fəlɪ] sorgfältig.

careless a, ~**ly** ad ['kɛəlɪs, -lɪ] unvorsichtig; ~**ness** Unachtsamkeit f; (neglect) Nachlässigkeit f.

caress [kə'res] n Liebkosung f; vt liebkosen.

caretaker ['kɛəteɪkə*] n Hausmeister m.

car-ferry ['kɑːferɪ] n Autofähre f.

cargo ['kɑːgəu] n Kargo m, Schiffsladung f.

caricature ['kærɪkətjuə*] n Karikatur f; vt karikieren.

carnage ['kɑːnɪdʒ] n Blutbad nt.

carnal ['kɑːnl] a fleischlich, sinnlich.

carnation [kɑː'neɪʃən] n Nelke f.

carnival ['kɑːnɪvəl] n Karneval m, Fastnacht f, Fasching m.

carnivorous [kɑː'nɪvərəs] a fleischfressend.

carol ['kærl] n (Weihnachts)lied nt.

carp [kɑːp] n (fish) Karpfen m; ~ **at** vt herumnörgeln an (+dat).

car park ['kɑːpɑːk] n Parkplatz m; Parkhaus nt.

carpenter ['kɑːpɪntə*] n Zimmermann m.

carpentry ['kɑːpɪntrɪ] n Zimmerei f.

carpet ['kɑːpɪt] n Teppich m; vt mit einem Teppich auslegen.

carping ['kɑːpɪŋ] a (critical) krittelnd, Mecker-.

carriage ['kærɪdʒ] n Wagen m; (of goods) Beförderung f; (bearing) Haltung f; ~**way** (on road) Fahrbahn f.

carrier ['kærɪə*] n Träger(in f) m; (Comm) Spediteur m; ~ **bag** Tragetasche m; ~ **pigeon** Brieftaube f.

carrion ['kærɪən] n Aas nt.

carrot ['kærət] n Möhre f, Mohrrübe f, Karotte f.

carry ['kærɪ] vt tragen; vi weit tragen, reichen; ~**cot** Babytragetasche f; **to be**

carried away (*fig*) hingerissen sein; ~ **on** *vti* fortführen, weitermachen; ~ **out** *vt* orders ausführen.

cart [kɑːt] *n* Wagen *m*, Karren *m*; *vt* schleppen.

cartilage [ˈkɑːtɪlɪdʒ] *n* Knorpel *m*.

cartographer [kɑːˈtɒɡrəfə*] *n* Kartograph(in *f*) *m*.

carton [ˈkɑːtən] *n* (Papp)karton *m*; (*of cigarettes*) Stange *f*.

cartoon [kɑːˈtuːn] *n* (*Press*) Karikatur *f*; (*Cine*) (Zeichen)trickfilm *m*.

cartridge [ˈkɑːtrɪdʒ] *n* (*for gun*) Patrone *f*; (*film*) Rollfilm *m*; (*of record player*) Tonabnehmer *m*.

carve [kɑːv] *vti* wood schnitzen; stone meißeln; meat (vor)schneiden.

carving [ˈkɑːvɪŋ] *n* (*in wood etc*) Schnitzerei *f*; ~ **knife** Tranchiermesser *nt*.

car wash [ˈkɑːwɒʃ] *n* Autowäsche *f*.

cascade [kæsˈkeɪd] *n* Wasserfall *m*; *vi* kaskadenartig herabfallen.

case [keɪs] *n* (*box*) Kasten *m*, Kiste *f*; (*suit*—) Koffer *m*; (*Jur, matter*) Fall *m*; **in** ~ falls, im Falle; **in any** ~ jedenfalls, auf jeden Fall.

cash [kæʃ] *n* (Bar)geld *nt*; *vt* einlösen; ~ **desk** Kasse *f*; ~**ier** [kæˈʃɪə*] Kassierer(in *f*) *m*; ~ **on delivery** per Nachnahme; ~ **register** Registrierkasse *f*.

cashmere [ˈkæʃmɪə*] *n* Kaschmirwolle *f*.

casing [ˈkeɪsɪŋ] *n* Gehäuse *nt*.

casino [kəˈsiːnəʊ] *n* Kasino *nt*.

cask [kɑːsk] *n* Faß *nt*.

casket [ˈkɑːskɪt] *n* Kästchen *nt*; (*US: coffin*) Sarg *m*.

casserole [ˈkæsərəʊl] *n* Kasserole *f*; (*food*) Auflauf *m*.

cassock [ˈkæsək] *n* Soutane *f*, Talar *m*.

cast [kɑːst] *irreg vt* werfen; horns etc verlieren; metal gießen; (*Theat*) besetzen; roles verteilen; *n* (*Theat*) Besetzung *f*; ~ **off** *vi* (*Naut*) losmachen; ~**off clothing** abgelegte Kleidung.

castanets [kæstəˈnets] *npl* Kastagnetten *pl*.

castaway [ˈkɑːstəweɪ] *n* Schiffbrüchige(r) *mf*.

caste [kɑːst] *n* Kaste *f*.

casting [ˈkɑːstɪŋ] *a*: ~ **vote** entscheidende Stimme *f*.

castiron [ˈkɑːstˈaɪən] *n* Gußeisen *nt*; *a* gußeisern; alibi todsicher.

castle [ˈkɑːsl] *n* Burg *f*; Schloß *nt*; (*country mansion*) Landschloß *nt*; (*chess*) Turm *m*.

castor [ˈkɑːstə*] *n* (*wheel*) Laufrolle *f*; ~ **oil** Rizinusöl *nt*; ~ **sugar** Streuzucker *m*.

castrate [kæsˈtreɪt] *vt* kastrieren.

casual [ˈkæʒjʊl] *a* arrangement beiläufig; attitude nachlässig; dress leger; meeting zufällig; ~**ly** *ad* dress zwanglos, leger; remark beiläufig.

casualty [ˈkæʒjʊltɪ] *n* Verletzte(r) *mf*; Tote(r) *mf*; (*department in hospital*) Unfallstation *f*.

cat [kæt] *n* Katze *f*.

catalog (*US*), **catalogue** [ˈkætəlɒg] *n* Katalog *m*; *vt* katalogisieren.

catalyst [ˈkætəlɪst] *n* (*lit, fig*) Katalysator *m*.

catapult [ˈkætəpʌlt] *n* Katapult *nt*; Schleuder *f*.

cataract [ˈkætərækt] *n* Wasserfall *m*; (*Med*) graue(r) Star *m*.

catarrh [kəˈtɑː*] *n* Katarrh *m*.

catastrophe [kəˈtæstrəfɪ] *n* Katastrophe *f*.

catastrophic [kætəsˈtrɒfɪk] *a* katastrophal.

catch [kætʃ] *vt irreg* fangen; train etc nehmen; erreichen; (*surprise*) ertappen; (*understand*) begreifen; *n* (*of lock*) Sperrhaken *m*; (*of fish*) Fang *m*; **to** ~ **a cold** sich erkälten.

catching [ˈkætʃɪŋ] *a* (*Med, fig*) ansteckend.

catch phrase [ˈkætʃfreɪz] *n* Schlagwort *nt*, Slogan *m*.

catchy [ˈkætʃɪ] *a tune* eingängig.

catechism [ˈkætɪkɪzəm] *n* Katechismus *m*.

categorical *a*, ~**ly** *ad* [kætəˈgɒrɪkl, -klɪ] kategorisch.

categorize [ˈkætɪgəraɪz] *vt* kategorisieren.

category [ˈkætɪgərɪ] *n* Kategorie *f*.

cater [ˈkeɪtə*] *vi* versorgen; ~**ing** Gastronomie *f*; Bewirtung *f*; ~ **for** *vt* (*lit*) party ausrichten; (*fig*) eingestellt sein auf (+acc); berücksichtigen.

caterpillar [ˈkætəpɪlə*] *n* Raupe *f*; ~ **track** Gleiskette *f*.

cathedral [kəˈθiːdrəl] *n* Kathedrale *f*, Dom *m*.

Catholic [ˈkæθəlɪk] *a* (*Rel*) katholisch; *n* Katholik(in *f*) *m*; **c**~ vielseitig.

cattle [ˈkætl] *npl* Vieh *nt*.

catty [ˈkætɪ] *a* gehässig.

cauliflower [ˈkɒlɪflaʊə*] *n* Blumenkohl *m*.

cause [kɒz] *n* Ursache *f*; Grund *m*; (*purpose*) Sache *f*; **in a good** ~ zu einem guten Zweck; *vt* verursachen.

causeway [ˈkɒzweɪ] *n* Damm *m*.

caustic [ˈkɒstɪk] *a* ätzend; (*fig*) bissig.

cauterize [ˈkɒtəraɪz] *vt* ätzen, ausbrennen.

caution [ˈkɔːʃən] *n* Vorsicht *f*; (*warning*) Warnung *f*; (*Jur*) Verwarnung *f*; *vt* (ver)warnen.

cautious *a*, ~**ly** *ad* [ˈkɔːʃəs, -lɪ] vorsichtig.

cavalcade [kævəlˈkeɪd] *n* Kavalkade *f*.

cavalier [kævəˈlɪə*] *a* blasiert.

cavalry [ˈkævəlrɪ] *npl* Kavallerie *f*.

cave [keɪv] *n* Höhle *f*; ~**man** Höhlenmensch *m*; ~ **in** *vi* einstürzen.

cavern [ˈkævən] *n* Höhle *f*; ~**ous** *a cheeks* hohl; eyes tiefliegend.

cavil [ˈkævɪl] *vi* kritteln (at an +dat).

cavity [ˈkævɪtɪ] *n* Höhlung *f*; (*in tooth*) Loch *nt*.

cavort [kəˈvɔːt] *vi* umherspringen.

cease [siːs] *vi* aufhören; *vt* beenden; ~**fire** Feuereinstellung *f*; ~**less** *a* unaufhörlich.

cedar [ˈsiːdə*] *n* Zeder *f*.

cede [siːd] *vt* abtreten.

ceiling [ˈsiːlɪŋ] *n* Decke *f*; (*fig*) Höchstgrenze *f*.

celebrate [ˈselɪbreɪt] *vt* feiern; anniversary begehen; *vi* feiern; ~**d** *a* gefeiert.

celebration [selɪˈbreɪʃən] *n* Feier *f*.

celebrity [sɪ'lebrɪtɪ] *n* gefeierte Persönlichkeit *f*.

celery ['selǝrɪ] *n* Sellerie *m or f*.

celestial [sɪ'lestɪǝl] *a* himmlisch.

celibacy ['selɪbǝsɪ] *n* Zölibat *nt or m*.

cell [sel] *n* Zelle *f*; (*Elec*) Element *nt*.

cellar ['selǝ*] *n* Keller *m*.

cellist ['tʃelɪst] *n* Cellist(in *f*) *m*.

cello ['tʃelǝʊ] *n* Cello *nt*.

cellophane ['selǝfeɪn] *n* Cellophan *nt*.

cellular ['seljʊlǝ*] *a* zellenförmig, zellular.

cellulose ['seljʊlǝʊs] *n* Zellulose *f*.

cement [sɪ'ment] *n* Zement *m*; *vt* (*lit*) zementieren; (*fig*) festigen.

cemetery ['semɪtrɪ] *n* Friedhof *m*.

cenotaph ['senǝtɑːf] *n* Ehrenmal *nt*, Zenotaph *m*.

censor ['sensǝ*] *n* Zensor *m*; ~**ship** Zensur *f*.

censure ['senʃǝ*] *vt* rügen.

census ['sensǝs] *n* Volkszählung *f*.

centenary [sen'tiːnǝrɪ] *n* Jahrhundertfeier *f*.

center ['sentǝ*] *n* (*US*) = **centre**.

centigrade ['sentɪgreɪd] *a*: **10 (degrees)** ~ 10 Grad Celsius.

centilitre, (*US*) ~**liter** ['sentɪliːtǝ*] *n* Zentiliter *nt or m*.

centimetre, (*US*) ~**meter** ['sentɪmiːtǝ*] *n* Zentimeter *nt*.

centipede ['sentɪpiːd] *n* Tausendfüßler *m*.

central ['sentrǝl] *a* zentral ; ~ **heating** Zentralheizung *f*; ~**ize** *vt* zentralisieren.

centre ['sentǝ*] *n* Zentrum *nt*; ~ **of gravity** Schwerpunkt *m*; **to** ~ **on** (sich) konzentrieren auf (+*acc*).

century ['sentjʊrɪ] *n* Jahrhundert *nt*.

ceramic [sɪ'ræmɪk] *a* keramisch.

cereal ['sɪǝrɪǝl] *n* (*any grain*) Getreide *nt*; (*at breakfast*) Getreideflocken *pl*.

ceremonial [serɪ'mǝʊnɪǝl] *a* zeremoniell.

ceremony ['serɪmǝnɪ] *n* Feierlichkeiten *pl*, Zeremonie *f*.

certain ['sɜːtǝn] *a* sicher; (*particular*) gewiß; **for** ~ ganz bestimmt; ~**ly** .*ad* sicher, bestimmt; ~**ty** Gewißheit *f*.

certificate [sǝ'tɪfɪkɪt] *n* Bescheinigung *f*; (*Sch etc*) Zeugnis *nt*.

certify ['sɜːtɪfaɪ] *vti* bescheinigen.

cessation [se'seɪʃǝn] *n* Einstellung *f*, Ende *nt*.

chafe [tʃeɪf] *vti* (wund)reiben, scheuern.

chaffinch ['tʃæfɪntʃ] *n* Buchfink *m*.

chain [tʃeɪn] *n* Kette *f*; *vt* (*also* ~ **up**) anketten; mit Ketten fesseln; ~ **reaction** Kettenreaktion *f*; ~ **smoker** Kettenraucher(in *f*) *m*; ~ **store** Kettenladen *m*.

chair [tʃɛǝ*] *n* Stuhl *m*; (*arm*—) Sessel *m*; (*Univ*) Lehrstuhl *m*; *vt*: **to** ~ **a meeting** in einer Versammlung den Vorsitz führen; ~**lift** Sessellift *m*; ~**man** Vorsitzende(r) *m*; (*of firm*) Präsident *m*.

chalet ['ʃæleɪ] *n* Chalet *nt*.

chalice ['tʃælɪs] *n* (Abendmahls)kelch *m*.

chalk ['tʃɔːk] *n* Kreide *f*.

challenge ['tʃælɪndʒ] *n* Herausforderung *f*; *vt* auffordern; (*contest*) bestreiten; ~**r** Herausforderer *m*.

challenging ['tʃælɪndʒɪŋ] *a* *statement* herausfordernd; *work* anspruchsvoll.

chamber ['tʃeɪmbǝ*] *n* Kammer *f*; ~ **of commerce** Handelskammer *f*; ~**maid** Zimmermädchen *nt*; ~ **music** Kammermusik *f*; ~**pot** Nachttopf *m*.

chameleon [kǝ'miːlɪǝn] *n* Chamäleon *nt*.

chamois ['ʃæmwɑː] *n* Gemse *f*; ~ **leather** ['ʃæmɪ'leðǝ*] Sämischleder *m*.

champagne [ʃæm'peɪn] *n* Champagner *m*, Sekt *m*.

champion ['tʃæmpɪǝn] *n* (*Sport*) Sieger(in *f*) *m*, Meister *m*; (*of cause*) Verfechter(in *f*) *m*; ~**ship** Meisterschaft *f*.

chance [tʃɑːns] *n* (*luck, fate*) Zufall *m*; (*possibility*) Möglichkeit *f*; (*opportunity*) Gelegenheit *f*, Chance *f*; (*risk*) Risiko *nt*; *a* zufällig; *vt*: **to** ~ **it** es darauf ankommen lassen; **by** ~ zufällig; **to take a** ~ ein Risiko eingehen; **no** ~ keine Chance.

chancel ['tʃɑːnsǝl] *n* Altarraum *m*, Chor *m*.

chancellor ['tʃɑːnsǝlǝ*] *n* Kanzler *m*; **C**~ **of the Exchequer** Schatzkanzler *m*.

chancy ['tʃɑːnsɪ] *a* (*col*) riskant.

chandelier [ʃændɪ'lɪǝ*] *n* Kronleuchter *m*.

change [tʃeɪndʒ] *vt* verandern; *money* wechseln; *vi* sich verändern; (*trains*) umsteigen; (*colour etc*) sich verwandeln; (*clothes*) sich umziehen; *n* Veränderung *f*; (*money*) Wechselgeld *nt*; (*coins*) Kleingeld *nt*; ~**able** *a weather* wechselhaft; ~**over** Umstellung *f*, Wechsel *m*.

changing ['tʃeɪndʒɪŋ] *a* veränderlich; ~**room** Umkleideraum *m*.

channel ['tʃænl] *n* (*stream*) Bachbett *nt*; (*Naut*) Straße *f*, Meerenge *f*; (*Rad, TV*) Kanal *m*; (*fig*) Weg *m*; *vt* (hindurch)leiten, lenken; **through official** ~**s** durch die Instanzen; **the (English) C**~ der Armelkanal; **C**~ **Islands** Kanalinseln *pl*.

chant [tʃɑːnt] *n* liturgischer Gesang *m*; Sprechgesang *m*, Sprechchor *m*; *vt* intonieren.

chaos ['keɪɒs] *n* Chaos *nt*, Durcheinander *nt*.

chaotic [keɪ'ɒtɪk] *a* chaotisch.

chap [tʃæp] *n* (*col*) Bursche *m*, Kerl *m*; *vt* *skin* rissig machen; *vi* (*hands etc*) aufspringen.

chapel ['tʃæpǝl] *n* Kapelle *f*.

chaperon ['ʃæpǝrǝʊn] *n* Anstandsdame *f*; *vt* begleiten.

chaplain ['tʃæplɪn] *n* Geistliche(r) *m*, Pfarrer *m*, Kaplan *m*.

chapter ['tʃæptǝ*] *n* Kapitel *nt*.

char [tʃɑː*] *vt* (*burn*) verkohlen; *vi* (*cleaner*) putzen gehen.

character ['kærɪktǝ*] *n* Charakter *m*, Wesen *nt*; (*Liter*) Figur *f*, Gestalt *f*; (*Theat*) Person *f*, Rolle *f*; (*peculiar person*) Original *nt*; (*in writing*) Schriftzeichen *nt*; ~**istic** [kærɪktǝ'rɪstɪk] *a* charakteristisch, bezeichnend (*of* für); *n* Kennzeichen *nt*, Eigenschaft *f*; ~**ize** *vt* charakterisieren, kennzeichnen.

charade [ʃǝ'rɑːd] *n* Scharade *f*.

charcoal ['tʃɑːkǝʊl] *n* Holzkohle *f*.

charge [tʃɑːdʒ] *n* (*cost*) Preis *m*; (*Jur*) Anklage *f*; (*of gun*) Ladung *f*; (*attack*) Angriff *m*; *vt gun, battery* laden; *price* verlangen; (*Mil*) angreifen; *vi* (*rush*) angreifen, (an)stürmen; **to be in ~ of** verantwortlich sein f; **to take ~** (die Verantwortung) übernehmen.

chariot ['tʃæriət] n (Streit)wagen m.

charitable ['tʃæritəbl] a wohltätig; (lenient) nachsichtig.

charity ['tʃæriti] n (institution) Wohlfahrtseinrichtung f, Hilfswerk nt; (attitude) Nächstenliebe f, Wohltätigkeit f.

charlady ['tʃɑːleɪdi] n Reinemachefrau f, Putzfrau f.

charlatan ['ʃɑːlətən] n Scharlatan m, Schwindler(in f) m.

charm [tʃɑːm] n Charme m, gewinnende(s) Wesen nt; (in superstition) Amulett nt; Talisman m; vt bezaubern; **~ing** a reizend, liebenswürdig, charmant.

chart [tʃɑːt] n Tabelle f, (Naut) Seekarte f.

charter ['tʃɑːtə°] vt (Naut, Aviat) chartern; n Schutzbrief m; (cost) Schiffsmiete f; **~ flight** Charterflug m; **~ed accountant** Wirtschaftsprüfer(in f) m.

charwoman ['tʃɑːwumən] n Reinemachefrau f, Putzfrau f.

chary ['tʃɛəri] a zurückhaltend (of sth mit etw).

chase [tʃeɪs] vt jagen, verfolgen; n Jagd f.

chasm ['kæzəm] n Kluft f.

chassis ['ʃæsi] n Chassis nt, Fahrgestell nt.

chaste [tʃeɪst] a keusch.

chastity ['tʃæstiti] n Keuschheit f.

chat [tʃæt] vi plaudern, sich (zwanglos) unterhalten; n Plauderei f.

chatter ['tʃætə°] vi schwatzen; (teeth) klappern; n Geschwätz nt; **~box** Quasselstrippe f.

chatty ['tʃæti] a geschwätzig.

chauffeur ['ʃəufə°] n Chauffeur m, Fahrer m.

cheap [tʃiːp] a billig; joke schlecht; (of poor quality) minderwertig; **to ~en o.s.** sich herablassen; **~ly** a/ad billig.

cheat [tʃiːt] vti betrügen; (Sch) mogeln; n Betrüger(in f) m; **~ing** Betrug m.

check [tʃek] vt prüfen; (look up, make sure) nachsehen; (control) kontrollieren; (restrain) zügeln; (stop) anhalten; n (examination, restraint) Kontrolle f; (restaurant bill) Rechnung f; (pattern) Karo(muster) nt; (US) = **cheque**; **~ers** (US) Damespiel nt; **~list** Kontroll-liste f; **~mate** Schachmatt nt; **~point** Kontrollpunkt m; **~up** (Nach)prüfung f; (Med) (ärztliche) Untersuchung f.

cheek [tʃiːk] n Backe f, Wange f; (fig) Frechheit f, Unverschämtheit f; **~bone** Backenknochen m; **~y** a frech, übermütig.

cheep [tʃiːp] n Pieps(er) nt.

cheer [tʃiə°] n Beifallsruf m, Hochruf m; **~s!** Prost!; vt zujubeln; (encourage) ermuntern, aufmuntern; vi jauchzen, Hochrufe ausbringen; **~ful** a fröhlich; **~fulness** Fröhlichkeit f, Munterkeit f; **~ing** Applaus m; a aufheiternd; **~io** interj tschüs!; **~less** a prospect trostlos; person verdrießlich; **~ up** vt ermuntern; vi: **~ up!** Kopf hoch!

cheese [tʃiːz] n Käse m; **~board**

(gemischte) Käseplatte f; **~cake** Käsekuchen m.

cheetah ['tʃiːtə] n Gepard m.

chef [ʃef] n Küchenchef m.

chemical ['kemikəl] a chemisch.

chemist ['kemist] n (Med) Apotheker m, Drogist m; (Chem) Chemiker m; **~ry** Chemie f; **~'s (shop)** (Med) Apotheke f, Drogerie f.

cheque [tʃek] n Scheck m; **~book** Scheckbuch nt; **~ card** Scheckkarte f.

chequered ['tʃekəd] a (fig) bewegt.

cherish ['tʃeriʃ] vt person lieben; hope hegen; memory bewahren.

cheroot [ʃə'ruːt] n Zigarillo nt or m.

cherry ['tʃeri] n Kirsche f.

chervil ['tʃɑːvil] n Kerbel m.

chess [tʃes] n Schach nt; **~board** Schachbrett nt; **~man** Schachfigur f; **~player** Schachspieler(in f) m.

chest [tʃest] n Brust f, Brustkasten m; (box) Kiste f, Kasten m; **to get sth off one's ~** seinem Herzen Luft machen; **~ of drawers** Kommode f.

chestnut ['tʃesnʌt] n Kastanie f; **~ (tree)** Kastanienbaum m.

chew [tʃuː] vti kauen; **~ing gum** Kaugummi m.

chic [ʃiːk] a schick, elegant.

chicanery [ʃi'keɪnəri] n Schikane f.

chick [tʃik] n Küken nt; **~en** Huhn nt; (food: roast) Hähnchen nt; **~enpox** Windpocken pl; **~pea** Kichererbse f.

chicory ['tʃikəri] n Zichorie f; (plant) Chicorée f.

chief [tʃiːf] n (Ober)haupt nt; Anführer m; (Comm) Chef m; a höchst, Haupt-; **~ly** ad hauptsächlich.

chieftain ['tʃiːftən] n Häuptling m.

chilblain ['tʃilbleɪn] n Frostbeule f.

child [tʃaɪld] n Kind nt; **~birth** Entbindung f; **~hood** Kindheit f; **~ish** a kindisch; **~like** a kindlich; **~ren** ['tʃildrən] npl of **child**; **~'s play** (fig) Kinderspiel nt.

chill [tʃil] n Kühle f; (Med) Erkältung f; **~y** a kühl, frostig.

chime [tʃaɪm] n Glockenschlag m, Glockenklang m; vi ertönen, (er)klingen.

chimney ['tʃimni] n Schornstein m, Kamin m.

chimpanzee [tʃimpæn'ziː] n Schimpanse m.

chin [tʃin] n Kinn nt.

china ['tʃaɪnə] n Porzellan nt.

chink [tʃiŋk] n (opening) Ritze f, Spalt m; (noise) Klirren nt.

chintz [tʃints] n Kattun m.

chip [tʃip] n (of wood etc) Splitter m; (potato) **~s** pl Pommes frites pl; (US: crisp) Chip m; vt absplittern; **~ in** vi Zwischenbemerkungen machen.

chiropodist [ki'ropədist] n Fußpfleger(in f) m.

chirp [tʃɜːp] n Zwitschern nt; vi zwitschern.

chisel ['tʃizl] n Meißel m.

chit [tʃit] n Notiz f; **~chat** Plauderei f.

chivalrous ['ʃivəlrəs] a ritterlich.

chivalry ['ʃivəlri] n Ritterlichkeit f; (honour) Ritterschaft f.

chive [tʃaɪv] n Schnittlauch m.
chloride ['klɔːraɪd] n Chlorid nt.
chlorine ['klɔːriːn] n Chlor nt.
chock [tʃɒk] n Keil m; ~-**a-block** a vollgepfropft.
chocolate ['tʃɒklɪt] n Schokolade f.
choice [tʃɔɪs] n Wahl f; (of goods) Auswahl f; a auserlesen, Qualitäts-.
choir ['kwaɪə*] n Chor m; ~**boy** Chorknabe m.
choke [tʃəʊk] vi ersticken; vt erdrosseln; (block) (ab)drosseln; n (Aut) Starterklappe f.
cholera ['kɒlərə] n Cholera f.
choose [tʃuːz] vt irreg wählen; (decide) beschließen.
chop [tʃɒp] vt (zer)hacken; wood spalten; vi: to ~ **and change** wechseln n Hieb m; (meat) Kotelett nt; ~**py** a bewegt; ~**sticks** pl (Eß)stäbchen pl.
choral ['kɔːrəl] a Chor-.
chord [kɔːd] n Akkord m; (string) Saite f.
chore [tʃɔː*] n Pflicht f; harte Arbeit f.
choreographer [kɒrɪ'ɒgrəfə*] n Choreograph(in f) m.
chorister ['kɒrɪstə*] n Chorsänger(in f) m.
chortle ['tʃɔːtl] vi glucksen, tief lachen.
chorus ['kɔːrəs] n Chor m; (in song) Refrain m.
chow [tʃaʊ] n (dog) Chow-Chow m.
Christ [kraɪst] n Christus m.
christen ['krɪsn] vt taufen; ~**ing** Taufe f.
Christian ['krɪstɪən] a christlich; n Christ(in f) m; ~ **name** Vorname m; ~**ity** [krɪstɪ'ænɪtɪ] Christentum nt.
Christmas ['krɪsməs] n Weihnachten pl; ~ **card** Weihnachtskarte f; ~ **tree** Weihnachtsbaum m.
chrome [krəʊm] n = **chromium plating**.
chromium ['krəʊmɪəm] n Chrom nt; ~ **plating** Verchromung f.
chronic ['krɒnɪk] a (Med) chronisch; (terrible) scheußlich.
chronicle ['krɒnɪkl] n Chronik f.
chronological [krɒnə'lɒdʒɪkəl] a chronologisch.
chrysalis ['krɪsəlɪs] n (Insekten)puppe f.
chrysanthemum [krɪs'ænθɪməm] n Chrysantheme f.
chubby ['tʃʌbɪ] a child pausbäckig; adult rundlich.
chuck [tʃʌk] vt werfen; n (Tech) Spannvorrichtung f.
chuckle ['tʃʌkl] vi in sich hineinlachen.
chum [tʃʌm] n (child) Spielkamerad m; (adult) Kumpel m.
chunk [tʃʌŋk] n Klumpen m; (of food) Brocken m.
church [tʃɜːtʃ] n Kirche f; (clergy) Geistlichkeit f; ~**yard** Kirchhof m.
churlish ['tʃɜːlɪʃ] a grob.
churn [tʃɜːn] n Butterfaß nt; (for transport) (große) Milchkanne f; ~ **out** vt (col) produzieren.
chute [ʃuːt] n Rutsche f.
cicada [sɪ'kɑːdə] n Zikade f.
cider ['saɪdə*] n Apfelwein m.
cigar [sɪ'gɑː*] n Zigarre f; ~**ette** [sɪgə'ret]

Zigarette f; ~**ette case** Zigarettenetui nt; ~**ette end** Zigarettenstummel m; ~**ette holder** Zigarettenspitze f.
cinch [sɪntʃ] n (col) klare(r) Fall m; (easy) Kinderspiel nt.
cinder ['sɪndə*] n Zinder m.
Cinderella [sɪndə'relə] n Aschenbrödel nt.
cine ['sɪnɪ] n: ~-**camera** Filmkamera f; ~ **film** Schmalfilm m.
cinema ['sɪnəmə] n Kino nt.
cine-projector [sɪnɪprə'dʒektə*] n Filmvorführapparat m.
cinnamon ['sɪnəmən] n Zimt m.
cipher ['saɪfə*] n (code) Chiffre f; (numeral) Ziffer f.
circle ['sɜːkl] n Kreis m; vi kreisen; vt umkreisen; (attacking) umzingeln.
circuit ['sɜːkɪt] n Umlauf m; (Elec) Stromkreis m; ~**ous** [sɜː'kjuːɪtəs] a weitschweifig.
circular ['sɜːkjulə*] a (kreis)rund, kreisförmig; n Rundschreiben nt.
circularize ['sɜːkjuləraɪz] vt (inform) benachrichtigen; letter herumschicken.
circulate ['sɜːkjuleɪt] vi zirkulieren; vt in Umlauf setzen.
circulation [sɜːkju'leɪʃən] n (of blood) Kreislauf m; (of newspaper) Auflage f; (of money) Umlauf m.
circumcise ['sɜːkəmsaɪz] vt beschneiden.
circumference [sə'kʌmfərəns] n (Kreis)umfang m.
circumspect ['sɜːkəmspekt] a umsichtig.
circumstances ['sɜːkəmstənsəz] npl (facts connected with sth) Umstände pl; (financial condition) Verhältnisse pl.
circumvent [sɜːkəm'vent] vt umgehen.
circus ['sɜːkəs] n Zirkus m.
cissy ['sɪsɪ] n Weichling m.
cistern ['sɪstən] n Zisterne f; (of W.C.) Spülkasten m.
citation [saɪ'teɪʃən] n Zitat nt.
cite [saɪt] vt zitieren, anführen.
citizen ['sɪtɪzn] n Bürger(in f) m; (of nation) Staatsangehörige(r) mf; ~**ship** Staatsangehörigkeit f.
citrus ['sɪtrəs] adj: ~ **fruit** Zitrusfrucht f.
city ['sɪtɪ] n Großstadt f; (centre) Zentrum nt, City f.
civic ['sɪvɪk] a städtisch, Bürger-.
civil ['sɪvɪl] a (of town) Bürger-; (of state) staatsbürgerlich; (not military) zivil; (polite) höflich; ~ **engineer** Bauingenieur m; ~ **engineering** Hoch- und Tiefbau m; ~**ian** [sɪ'vɪlɪən] n Zivilperson f; a zivil, Zivil-; ~**ization** [sɪvɪlaɪ'zeɪʃən] n Zivilisation f, Kultur f; ~**ized** a zivilisiert; Kultur-; ~ **law** bürgerliche(s) Recht, Zivilrecht nt; ~ **rights** pl Bürgerrechte pl; ~ **servant** Staatsbeamte(r) m; ~ **service** Staatsdienst m; ~ **war** Bürgerkrieg m.
clad [klæd] a gekleidet; ~ **in** gehüllt in (+acc).
claim [kleɪm] vt beanspruchen; (have opinion) behaupten; n (demand) Forderung f; (right) Anspruch m; Behauptung f; ~**ant** Antragsteller(in f) m.

clairvoyant [klɛə'vɔɪənt] n Hellseher(in f) m; a hellseherisch.

clam [klæm] n Venusmuschel f.

clamber ['klæmbə°] vi kraxeln.

clammy ['klæmɪ] a feucht(kalt); klamm.

clamorous ['klæmərəs] a lärmend, laut.

clamp [klæmp] n Schraubzwinge f; vt einspannen.

clan [klæn] n Sippe f, Clan m.

clang [klæŋ] n Klang m; Scheppern nt; vi klingen; scheppern.

clap [klæp] vi klatschen; vt Beifall klatschen (+dat); **~ping** (Beifall)-klatschen nt.

claret ['klærɪt] n rote(r) Bordeaux(wein) m.

clarification [klærɪfɪ'keɪʃən] n Erklärung f.

clarify ['klærɪfaɪ] vt klären, erklären.

clarinet [klærɪ'net] n Klarinette f.

clarity ['klærɪtɪ] n Klarheit f.

clash [klæʃ] n (fig) Konflikt m, Widerstreit m; (sound) Knall m; vi zusammenprallen; (colours) sich beißen; (argue) sich streiten.

clasp [klɑːsp] n Klammer f, Haken m; (on belt) Schnalle f; vt umklammern.

class [klɑːs] n Klasse f, vt einordnen, einstufen; **~-conscious** a klassenbewußt.

classic ['klæsɪk] n Klassiker(in f) m; a (traditional) klassisch; **~al** a klassisch.

classification [klæsɪfɪ'keɪʃən] n Klassifizierung f; Einteilung f.

classify ['klæsɪfaɪ] vt klassifizieren, einteilen.

classroom ['klɑːsrʊm] n Klassenzimmer nt.

classy ['klɑːsɪ] a (col) todschick.

clatter ['klætə°] n Klappern nt, Rasseln nt; (of feet) Getrappel nt; vi klappern, rasseln; (feet) trappeln.

clause [klɔːz] n (Jur) Klausel f; (Gram) Satz(teil) m, Satzglied nt.

claustrophobia [klɒstrə'fəʊbɪə] n Platzangst f, Klaustrophobie f.

claw [klɔː] n Kralle f; vt (zer)kratzen.

clay [kleɪ] n Lehm m; (for pots) Ton m.

clean [kliːn] a sauber; (fig) schuldlos; shape ebenmäßig; cut glatt; vt saubermachen, reinigen, putzen; **~er** (person) Putzfrau f; (for grease etc) Scheuerpulver nt; **~ers** pl Chemische Reinigung f. **~ing** Reinigen nt, Säubern nt; **~liness** ['klenlɪnɪs] Sauberkeit f, Reinlichkeit f; **~ly** ad reinlich; **~se** [klenz] vt reinigen, säubern; **~-shaven** a glattrasiert; **~-up** Reinigung f; **~ out** vt gründlich putzen; **~ up** vt aufräumen.

clear ['klɪə°] a water klar; glass durchsichtig; sound deutlich, klar, hell; meaning genau, klar; (certain) klar, sicher; road frei; **to stand ~ of** sth etw frei halten; vt road etc freimachen; vi (become clear) klarwerden; **~ance** ['klɪərns] (removal) Räumung f; (free space) Lichtung f; (permission) Freigabe f; **~-cut** a scharf umrissen; case eindeutig; **~ing** Lichtung f; **~ly** ad klar, deutlich, zweifellos; **~way** (Brit) (Straße f mit) Halteverbot nt; **~ up** vi (weather) sich aufklären; vt reinigen, säubern; (solve) aufklären.

clef [klef] n Notenschlüssel m.

clench [klentʃ] vt teeth zusammenbeißen; fist ballen.

clergy ['klɜːdʒɪ] n Geistliche(n) pl; **~man** Geistliche(r) m.

clerical ['klerɪkəl] a (office)Schreib-, Büro-; (Eccl) geistlich, Pfarr(er)-; **~ error** Schreibfehler m.

clerk [klɑːk, US klɜːk] n (in office) Büroangestellte(r) mf; (US: salesman) Verkäufer(in f) m.

clever a, **~ly** ad ['klevə°, -əlɪ] klug, geschickt, gescheit.

cliché ['kliːʃeɪ] n Klischee nt.

click [klɪk] vi klicken; n Klicken nt; (of door) Zuklinken nt.

client ['klaɪənt] n Klient(in f) m; **~ele** [kliːɑːn'tel] Kundschaft f.

cliff [klɪf] n Klippe f.

climate ['klaɪmɪt] n Klima nt.

climatic [klaɪ'mætɪk] a klimatisch.

climax ['klaɪmæks] n Höhepunkt m.

climb [klaɪm] vt besteigen; vi steigen, klettern; n Aufstieg m; **~er** Bergsteiger m, Kletterer m; (fig) Streber m; **~ing** Bergsteigen nt, Klettern nt.

clinch [klɪntʃ] vt (decide) entscheiden; deal festmachen; n (boxing) Clinch m.

cling [klɪŋ] vi irreg anhaften, anhängen.

clinic ['klɪnɪk] n Klinik f; **~al** a klinisch.

clink [klɪŋk] n (of coins) Klimpern nt; (of glasses) Klirren nt; (col: prison) Knast m; vi klimpern; vt klimpern mit; glasses anstoßen.

clip [klɪp] n Spange f; paper **~** (Büro-, Heft)klammer f; vt papers heften; hair, hedge stutzen; **~pers** pl (instrument) (for hedge) Heckenschere f; (for hair) Haarschneidemaschine f.

clique [kliːk] n Clique f, Gruppe f.

cloak [kləʊk] n lose(r) Mantel m, Umhang m; **~room** (for coats) Garderobe f; (W.C.) Toilette f.

clobber ['klɒbə°] n (col) Klamotten pl; vt schlagen.

clock [klɒk] n Uhr f; **~wise** ad im Uhrzeigersinn; **~work** Uhrwerk nt; like **~work** wie am Schnürchen.

clog [klɒg] n Holzschuh m; vt verstopfen.

cloister ['klɔɪstə°] n Kreuzgang m.

close [kləʊs] a nahe; march geschlossen; thorough genau, gründlich; weather schwül; ad knapp; **~ly** ad gedrängt, dicht; **~ to** prep in der Nähe (+gen); **I had a ~ shave** das war knapp; **~-up** Nahaufnahme f.

close [kləʊz] vt schließen, abschließen; vi sich schließen; n (end) Ende nt, Schluß m; **to ~ with sb** jdn angreifen; **~ down** vt Geschäft aufgeben; vi einstellen; **~d** a road gesperrt; shop etc geschlossen; **~d shop** Gewerkschaftszwang m.

closet ['klɒzɪt] n Abstellraum m, Schrank m.

closure ['kləʊʒə°] n Schließung f.

clot [klɒt] n Klumpen m; (of blood) Blutgerinnsel nt; (fool) Blödmann m; vi gerinnen.

cloth [klɒθ] n (material) Stoff m, Tuch nt;

(for washing etc) Lappen m, Tuch nt.

clothe [kləʊð] vt kleiden, bekleiden; ~s pl Kleider pl, Kleidung f; see **bedclothes**; ~s **brush** Kleiderbürste f; ~s **line** Wäscheleine f; ~s **peg** Wäscheklammer f.

clothing ['kləʊðɪŋ] n = **clothes**.

cloud [klaʊd] n Wolke f; ~**burst** Wolkenbruch m; ~**y** a wolkig, bewölkt.

clout [klaʊt] (col) n Schlag m; vt hauen.

clove [kləʊv] n Gewürznelke f; ~ **of garlic** Knoblauchzehe f.

clover ['kləʊvə°] n Klee m; ~**leaf** Kleeblatt nt.

clown [klaʊn] n Clown m, Hanswurst m; vi kaspern, sich albern benehmen.

cloy [klɔɪ] vi: **it** ~s **es** übersättigt einen.

club [klʌb] n Knüppel m; (society) Klub m; (golf) Golfschläger m; (Cards) Kreuz nt; vt prügeln; ~ **together** vi (with money etc) zusammenlegen; ~**house** Klubhaus m.

cluck [klʌk] vi glucken.

clue [klu:] n Anhaltspunkt m, Fingerzeig m, Spur f; **he hasn't a** ~ er hat keine Ahnung.

clump [klʌmp] n Gebüsch nt.

clumsy ['klʌmzɪ] a person ungelenk, unbeholfen; object, shape unförmig.

cluster ['klʌstə°] n Traube f; (of trees etc) Gruppe f; ~ **round** vi sich scharen um; umschwärmen.

clutch [klʌtʃ] n feste(r) Griff m; (Aut) Kupplung f; vt sich festklammern an (+dat); book an sich klammern.

clutter ['klʌtə°] vt vollpropfen; desk etc übersäen; n Unordnung f.

coach [kəʊtʃ] n Omnibus m, (Überland)bus m; (old) Kutsche f; (Rail) (Personen)wagen m; (trainer) Trainer m; (Sch) Nachhilfeunterricht geben (+dat); (Sport) trainieren.

coagulate [kəʊˈægjʊleɪt] vi gerinnen.

coal [kəʊl] n Kohle f.

coalesce [kəʊəˈles] vi sich verbinden.

coal face ['kəʊlfeɪs] n (Abbau)sohle f, Streb m; **at the** ~ vor Ort.

coalfield ['kəʊlfiːld] n Kohlengebiet nt.

coalition [kəʊəˈlɪʃən] n Zusammenschluß m; (Pol) Koalition f.

coalmine ['kəʊlmaɪn] n Kohlenbergwerk nt; ~**r** Bergarbeiter m.

coarse [kɔ:s] a (lit) grob; (fig) ordinär.

coast [kəʊst] n Küste f; ~**al** a Küsten-; ~**er** Küstenfahrer m; ~**guard** Küstenwache f; ~**line** Küste(nlinie) f.

coat [kəʊt] n Mantel m; (on animals) Fell nt, Pelz m; (of paint) Schicht f; vt überstreichen; (cover) bedecken; ~ **of arms** Wappen nt; ~**hanger** Kleiderbügel m; ~**ing** Schicht f, Überzug m; (of paint) Schicht f.

coax [kəʊks] vt beschwatzen.

cobble(stone)s ['kɒbl(stəʊn)z] npl Pflastersteine pl.

cobra ['kəʊbrə] n Kobra f.

cobweb ['kɒbweb] n Spinnennetz nt.

cocaine [kəˈkeɪn] n Kokain nt.

cock [kɒk] n Hahn m; vt ears spitzen; gun den Hahn spannen; ~**erel** junge(r) Hahn

m; ~-**eyed** a (fig) verrückt.

cockle ['kɒkl] n Herzmuschel f.

cockney ['kɒknɪ] n echte(r) Londoner m.

cockpit ['kɒkpɪt] n (Aviat) Pilotenkanzel f.

cockroach ['kɒkrəʊtʃ] n Küchenschabe f.

cocktail ['kɒkteɪl] n Cocktail m; ~ **cabinet** Hausbar f; ~ **party** Cocktailparty f; ~ **shaker** Mixbecher m.

cocoa ['kəʊkəʊ] n Kakao m.

coconut ['kəʊkənʌt] n Kokosnuß f.

cocoon [kəˈkuːn] n Puppe f, Kokon m.

cod [kɒd] n Kabeljau m.

code [kəʊd] n Kode m; (Jur) Kodex m; **in** ~ verschlüsselt, in Kode.

codeine ['kəʊdiːn] n Kodein nt.

codify ['kəʊdɪfaɪ] vt message verschlüsseln; (Jur) kodifizieren.

coeducational [kəʊedjʊˈkeɪʃənl] a koedukativ, gemischt.

coerce [kəʊˈɜːs] vt nötigen, zwingen.

coercion [kəʊˈɜːʃən] n Zwang m, Nötigung f.

coexistence [kəʊɪɡˈzɪstəns] n Koexistenz f.

coffee ['kɒfɪ] n Kaffee m; ~ **bar** Kaffeeausschank m, Café nt.

coffin ['kɒfɪn] n Sarg m.

cog [kɒg] n (Rad)zahn m.

cogent ['kəʊdʒənt] a triftig, überzeugend, zwingend.

cognac ['kɒnjæk] n Kognak m.

coherent [kəʊˈhɪərnt] a zusammenhängend, einheitlich.

coil [kɔɪl] n Rolle f; (Elec) Spule f; vt aufrollen, aufwickeln.

coin [kɔɪn] n Münze f; vt prägen; ~**age** (word) Prägung f.

coincide [kəʊɪnˈsaɪd] vi (happen together) zusammenfallen; (agree) übereinstimmen; ~**nce** [kəʊˈɪnsɪdəns] Zufall m; **by a strange** ~**nce** merkwürdigerweise; ~**ntal** [kəʊɪnsɪˈdentl] a zufällig.

coke [kəʊk] n Koks m.

colander ['kʌləndə°] n Durchschlag m.

cold [kəʊld] a kalt; **I'm** ~ mir ist kalt, ich friere; n Kälte f; (illness) Erkältung f; **to have** ~ **feet** (fig) kalte Füße haben, Angst haben; **to give sb the** ~ **shoulder** jdm die kalte Schulter zeigen; ~**ly** ad kalt; (fig) gefühllos; ~ **sore** Erkältungsbläschen nt.

coleslaw ['kəʊlslɔ:] n Krautsalat m.

colic ['kɒlɪk] n Kolik f.

collaborate [kəˈlæbəreɪt] vi zusammenarbeiten.

collaboration [kəlæbəˈreɪʃən] n Zusammenarbeit f; (Pol) Kollaboration f.

collaborator [kəˈlæbəreɪtə°] n Mitarbeiter m; (Pol) Kollaborateur m.

collage [kɒˈlɑ:ʒ] n Collage f.

collapse [kəˈlæps] vi (people) zusammenbrechen; (things) einstürzen; n Zusammenbruch m, Einsturz m.

collapsible [kəˈlæpsəbl] a zusammenklappbar, Klapp-.

collar ['kɒlə°] n Kragen m; ~**bone** Schlüsselbein nt.

collate [kɒˈleɪt] vt zusammenstellen und vergleichen.

colleague ['kɒliːg] n Kollege m, Kollegin f.

collect [kə'lekt] vt sammeln; (fetch) abholen; vi sich sammeln; ~ **call** (US) R-Gespräch nt; ~ **ed** a gefaßt; ~**ion** [kə'lekʃən] Sammlung f; (Eccl) Kollekte f; ~**ive** a gemeinsam; (Pol) kollektiv; ~ **or** Sammler m; (tax —or) (Steuer)einnehmer m.

college ['kɒlɪdʒ] n (Univ) College nt; (Tech) Fach-, Berufsschule f.

collide [kə'laɪd] vi zusammenstoßen, kollidieren, im Widerspruch stehen (with zu).

collie ['kɒlɪ] n schottische(r) Schäferhund m, Collie m.

colliery ['kɒlɪərɪ] n (Kohlen)bergwerk nt, Zeche f.

collision [kə'lɪʒən] n Zusammenstoß m; (of opinions) Konflikt m.

colloquial [kə'ləʊkwɪəl] a umgangssprachlich.

collusion [kə'lu:ʒən] n geheime(s) Einverständnis nt, Zusammenspiel nt.

colon ['kəʊlɒn] n Doppelpunkt m.

colonel ['kɜ:nl] n Oberst m.

colonial [kə'ləʊnɪəl] a Kolonial-.

colonize ['kɒlənaɪz] vt kolonisieren.

colonnade [kɒlə'neɪd] n Säulengang m.

colony ['kɒlənɪ] n Kolonie f.

color ['kʌlə*] (US) = colour.

Colorado beetle [kɒlə'rɑ:dəʊ 'bi:tl] n Kartoffelkäfer m.

colossal [kə'lɒsl] a kolossal, riesig.

colour ['kʌlə*] n Farbe f; off ~ nicht wohl; vt (lit, fig) färben; vi sich verfärben; ~**s** pl Fahne f; ~ **bar** Rassenschranke f; ~**blind** a farbenblind; ~**ed** a farbig; ~**ed** (wo)man Farbige(r) mf; ~ **film** Farbfilm m; ~**ful** a bunt; ~ **scheme** Farbgebung f; ~ **television** Farbfernsehen nt.

colt [kəʊlt] n Fohlen nt.

column ['kɒləm] n Säule f; (Mil) Kolonne f; (of print) Spalte f; ~**ist** ['kɒləmnɪst] Kolumnist m.

coma ['kəʊmə] n Koma nt.

comb [kəʊm] n Kamm m; vt kämmen; (search) durchkämmen.

combat ['kɒmbæt] n Kampf m; vt bekämpfen.

combination [kɒmbɪ'neɪʃən] n Verbindung f, Kombination f.

combine [kəm'baɪn] vt verbinden; vi sich vereinigen; ['kɒmbaɪn] n (Comm) Konzern m, Verband m; ~ **harvester** Mähdrescher m.

combustible [kəm'bʌstɪbl] a brennbar, leicht entzündlich.

combustion [kəm'bʌstʃən] n Verbrennung f.

come [kʌm] irreg vi kommen; (reach) ankommen, gelangen; ~ **about** vi geschehen; ~ **across** vt (find) stoßen auf (+acc); ~ **away** vi (person) weggehen; (handle etc) abgehen; ~ **by** vi vorbeikommen; vt (find) zu etw kommen; ~ **down** vi (price) fallen; ~ **forward** vi (volunteer) sich melden; **where do you ~ from?** wo kommen Sie her?; **I ~ from London** ich komme aus London; ~ **in for**

vt abkriegen; ~ **into** vi eintreten in (+acc); (inherit) erben; ~ **of** vi: **what came of it?** was ist daraus geworden?; ~ **off** vi (handle) abgehen; (happen) stattfinden; (succeed) klappen; ~ **off it!** laß den Quatsch!; ~ **on** vi (progress) vorankommen; **how's the book coming on?** was macht das Buch?; ~ **on!** komm!; (hurry) beeil dich!; (encouraging) los!; ~ **out** vi herauskommen; ~ **out with** vt herausrücken mit; ~ **round** vi (visit) vorbeikommen; (Med) wieder zu sich kommen; ~ **to** vi (Med) wieder zu sich kommen; (bill) sich belaufen auf; ~ **up** vi hochkommen; (problem) auftauchen ~ **upon** vt stoßen auf (+acc); ~ **up to** vi (approach) zukommen auf (+acc); (water) reichen bis; (expectation) entsprechen (+dat); **to ~ up with sth** sich etw einfallen lassen; ~**back** Wiederauftreten nt, Comeback nt.

comedian [kə'mi:dɪən] n Komiker m.

comedown ['kʌmdaʊn] n Abstieg m.

comedy ['kɒmədɪ] n Komödie f.

comet ['kɒmɪt] n Komet m.

comfort ['kʌmfət] n Bequemlichkeit f; (of body) Behaglichkeit f; (of mind) Trost m; vt trösten; ~**s** pl Annehmlichkeiten pl; ~**able** a bequem, gemütlich; ~ **station** (US) öffentliche Toilette f.

comic ['kɒmɪk] n Comic(heft) nt; (comedian) Komiker m; a (also ~**al**) komisch, humoristisch.

coming ['kʌmɪŋ] n Kommen nt, Ankunft f.

comma ['kɒmə] n Komma nt.

command [kə'mɑ:nd] n Befehl m; (control) Führung f; (Mil) Kommando nt, (Ober)befehl m; vt befehlen (+dat); (Mil) kommandieren, befehligen; (be able to get) verfügen über (+acc); vi befehlen; ~**eer** [kɒmən'dɪə*] vt (Mil) requirieren; ~**er** [kə'mɑ:ndə*] Befehlshaber m, Kommandant m; ~**ing officer** Kommandeur m; ~**ment** Gebot nt; ~**o** (Mitglied einer) Kommandotruppe f.

commemorate [kə'meməreɪt] vt gedenken (+gen).

commemoration [kəmemə'reɪʃən] n: in ~ **of** zum Gedächtnis or Andenken an (+acc).

commemorative [kə'memərətɪv] a Gedächtnis-, Gedenk-.

commence [kə'mens] vti beginnen; ~**ment** Beginn m.

commend [kə'mend] vt (recommend) empfehlen; (praise) loben; ~**able** a empfehlenswert, lobenswert; ~**ation** [kɒmen'deɪʃən] Empfehlung f; (Sch) Lob nt.

commensurate [kə'mensjurɪt] a vergleichbar, entsprechend (with dat).

comment ['kɒment] n (remark) Bemerkung f; (note) Anmerkung f; (opinion) Stellungnahme f; vi etw sagen (on zu); sich äußern (on zu); ~**ary** ['kɒməntrɪ] Kommentar m; Erläuterungen pl; ~**ator** ['kɒmenteɪtə*] Kommentator m.

commerce ['kɒmɜ:s] n Handel m.

commercial [kə'mɜ:ʃəl] a kommerziell, geschäftlich; training kaufmännisch; n (TV) Fernsehwerbung f; ~**ize** vt kommerzialisieren; ~ **television** Werbefernsehen *nt*; ~ **vehicle** Lieferwagen *m*.

commiserate [kə'mɪzəreɪt] *vi* Mitleid haben.

commission [kə'mɪʃən] *n* Auftrag *m*; (*fee*) Provision *f*; (*Mil*) Offizierspatent *nt*; (*of offence*) Begehen *nt*; (*reporting body*) Kommission *f*; *vt* bevollmächtigen, beauftragen; **out of** ~ außer Betrieb; ~**aire** [kəmɪʃ'nɛə*] Portier *m*; ~**er** (Regierungs)bevollmächtigte(r) *m*.

commit [kə'mɪt] *vt crime* begehen; (*undertake*) sich verpflichten; (*entrust*) übergeben, anvertrauen; **I don't want to** ~ **myself** ich will mich nicht festlegen; ~**ment** Verpflichtung *f*.

committee [kə'mɪtɪ] *n* Ausschuß *m*, Komitee *nt*.

commodious [kə'məʊdɪəs] *a* geräumig.

commodity [kə'mɒdɪtɪ] *n* Ware *f*; (Handels-, Gebrauchs)artikel *m*.

commodore ['kɒmədɔ:*] *n* Flotillenadmiral *m*.

common ['kɒmən] *a cause* gemeinsam; (*public*) öffentlich, allgemein; *experience* allgemein, alltäglich; (*pej*) gewöhnlich; (*widespread*) üblich, häufig, gewöhnlich; *n* Gemeindeland *nt*; öffentliche Anlage *f*; ~**ly** *ad* im allgemeinen, gewöhnlich; **C**~ **Market** Gemeinsame(r) Markt *m*; ~**place** *a* alltäglich; *n* Gemeinplatz *m*; ~**room** Gemeinschaftsraum *m*; ~**sense** gesunde(r) Menschenverstand *m*; **the C**~**wealth** das Commonwealth.

commotion [kə'məʊʃən] *n* Aufsehen *nt*, Unruhe *f*.

communal ['kɒmjuːnl] *a* Gemeinde-; Gemeinschafts-.

commune ['kɒmjuːn] *n* Kommune *f*; *vi* sich mitteilen (*with dat*), vertraulich verkehren.

communicate [kə'mjuːnɪkeɪt] *vt* (*transmit*) übertragen; *vi* (*be in touch*) in Verbindung stehen; (*make self understood*) sich verständlich machen.

communication [kəmjuːnɪ'keɪʃən] *n* (*message*) Mitteilung *f*; (*Rad, TV etc*) Kommunikationsmittel *nt*; (*making understood*) Kommunikation *f*; ~**s** *pl* (*transport etc*) Verkehrswege *pl*; ~ **cord** Notbremse *f*.

communion [kə'mjuːnɪən] *n* (*group*) Gemeinschaft *f*; (*Rel*) Religionsgemeinschaft *f*; (*Holy*) **C**~ Heilige(s) Abendmahl *nt*, Kommunion *f*.

communiqué [kə'mjuːnɪkeɪ] *n* Kommuniqué *nt*, amtliche Verlautbarung *f*.

communism ['kɒmjʊnɪzəm] *n* Kommunismus *m*.

communist ['kɒmjʊnɪst] *n* Kommunist(in *f*) *m*; *a* kommunistisch.

community [kə'mjuːnɪtɪ] *n* Gemeinschaft *f*; (*public*) Gemeinwesen *nt*; ~ **centre** Gemeinschaftszentrum *nt*; ~ **chest** (*US*) Wohltätigkeitsfonds *m*.

commutation ticket [kɒmjʊ'teɪʃən'tɪkɪt] *n* (*US*) Zeitkarte *f*.

commute [kə'mjuːt] *vi* pendeln; ~**r** Pendler *m*.

compact [kəm'pækt] *a* kompakt, fest,

dicht; ['kɒmpækt] *n* Pakt *m*, Vertrag *m*; (*for make-up*) Puderdose *f*.

companion [kəm'pænɪən] *n* Begleiter(in *f*) *m*; ~**ship** Gesellschaft *f*.

company ['kʌmpənɪ] *n* Gesellschaft *f*; (*Comm also*) Firma *f*; (*Mil*) Kompanie *f*; **to keep sb** ~ jdm Gesellschaft leisten.

comparable ['kɒmpərəbl] *a* vergleichbar.

comparative [kəm'pærətɪv] *a* (*relative*) verhältnismäßig, relativ; (*Gram*) steigernd; ~**ly** *ad* verhältnismäßig.

compare [kəm'pɛə*] *vt* vergleichen; *vi* sich vergleichen lassen.

comparison [kəm'pærɪsn] *n* Vergleich *m*; (*object*) Vergleichsgegenstand *m*; **in** ~ (**with**) im Vergleich (mit *or* zu).

compartment [kəm'pɑːtmənt] *n* (*Rail*) Abteil *nt*; (*in drawer etc*) Fach *nt*.

compass ['kʌmpəs] *n* Kompaß *m*; ~**es** *pl* Zirkel *m*.

compassion [kəm'pæʃən] *n* Mitleid *nt*; ~**ate** *a* mitfühlend.

compatible [kəm'pætɪbl] *a* vereinbar, im Einklang; **we're not** ~ wir vertragen uns nicht.

compel [kəm'pel] *vt* zwingen; ~**ling** *a argument* zwingend.

compendium [kəm'pendɪəm] *n* Kompendium *nt*.

compensate ['kɒmpenseɪt] *vt* entschädigen; **to** ~ **for** Ersatz leisten für, kompensieren.

compensation [kɒmpen'seɪʃən] *n* Entschädigung *f*; (*money*) Schadenersatz *m*; Entschädigung *f*; (*Jur*) Abfindung *f*; (*Psych etc*) Kompensation *f*.

compère ['kɒmpɛə*] *n* Conférencier *m*.

compete [kəm'piːt] *vi* sich bewerben; konkurrieren, sich messen mit.

competence ['kɒmpɪtəns] *n* Fähigkeit *f*; (*Jur*) Zuständigkeit *f*.

competent ['kɒmpɪtənt] *a* kompetent, fähig; (*Jur*) zuständig.

competition [kɒmpɪ'tɪʃən] *n* Wettbewerb *m*; (*Comm*) Konkurrenz *f*.

competitive [kəm'petɪtɪv] *a* Konkurrenz-; (*Comm*) konkurrenzfähig.

competitor [kəm'petɪtə*] *n* Mitbewerber(in *f*) *m*; (*Comm*) Konkurrent(in *f*) *m*; (*Sport*) Teilnehmer(in *f*) *m*.

compile [kəm'paɪl] *vt* zusammenstellen.

complacency [kəm'pleɪsnsɪ] *n* Selbstzufriedenheit *f*, Gleichgültigkeit *f*.

complacent [kəm'pleɪsnt] *a* selbstzufrieden, gleichgültig.

complain [kəm'pleɪn] *vi* sich beklagen, sich beschweren (*about* über +*acc*); ~**t** Beschwerde *f*; (*Med*) Leiden *nt*.

complement ['kɒmplɪmənt] *n* Ergänzung *f*; (*ship's crew etc*) Bemannung *f*; ~**ary** [kɒmplɪ'mentərɪ] *a* Komplementär-, (sich) ergänzend.

complete [kəm'pliːt] *a* vollständig, vollkommen, ganz; *vt* vervollständigen; (*finish*) beenden; ~**ly** *ad* vollständig, ganz.

completion [kəm'pliːʃən] *n* Vervollständigung *f*; (*of building*) Fertigstellung *f*.

complex ['kɒmpleks] *a* kompliziert, verwickelt; *n* Komplex *m*.

complexion [kəm'plekʃən] *n* Gesichtsfarbe f, Teint m; (fig) Anstrich m, Aussehen nt.

complexity [kəm'pleksɪtɪ] n Verwicklung f, Kompliziertheit f.

compliance [kəm'plaɪəns] n Fügsamkeit f, Einwilligung f.

complicate ['komplɪkeɪt] vt komplizieren, verwickeln; ~d a kompliziert, verwickelt.

complication [komplɪ'keɪʃən] a Komplikation f, Erschwerung f.

compliment ['komplɪmənt] n Kompliment nt; ['komplɪment] vt ein Kompliment machen (sb jdm); ~s pl Grüße pl, Empfehlung f; ~ary [komplɪ'mentərɪ] a schmeichelhaft; (free) Frei-, Gratis-.

comply [kəm'plaɪ] vi: ~ with erfüllen (+acc); entsprechen (+dat).

component [kəm'pəʊnənt] a Teil-; n Bestandteil m.

compose [kəm'pəʊz] vt (arrange) zusammensetzen; music komponieren; poetry schreiben; thoughts sammeln; features beherrschen; ~d a ruhig, gefaßt; to be ~d of bestehen aus; ~r Komponist(in f) m.

composite ['kompəzɪt] a zusammengesetzt.

composition [kompə'zɪʃən] n (Mus) Komposition f; (Sch) Aufsatz m; (composing) Zusammensetzung f, Gestaltung f; (structure) Zusammensetzung f, Aufbau m.

compositor [kəm'pozɪtə°] n Schriftsetzer m.

compos mentis ['kompos'mentɪs] a klar im Kopf.

compost ['kompost] n Kompost m; ~ heap Komposthaufen m.

composure [kəm'pəʊʒə°] n Gelassenheit f, Fassung f.

compound ['kompaʊnd] n (Chem) Verbindung f; (mixture) Gemisch nt; (enclosure) eingezäunte(s) Gelände nt; (Ling) Kompositum nt; a zusammengesetzt; ~ fracture komplizierte(r) Bruch m; ~ interest Zinseszinsen pl.

comprehend [komprɪ'hend] vt begreifen; (include) umfassen, einschließen.

comprehension [komprɪ'henʃən] n Fassungskraft f, Verständnis nt.

comprehensive [komprɪ'hensɪv] a umfassend; ~ school Gesamtschule f.

compress [kəm'pres] vt zusammendrücken, komprimieren; ['kompres] n (Med) Kompresse f, Umschlag m; ~ion [kəm'preʃən] Komprimieren f.

comprise [kəm'praɪz] vt (also be ~d of) umfassen, bestehen aus.

compromise ['komprəmaɪz] n Kompromiß m, Verständigung f; vt reputation kompromittieren; vi einen Kompromiß schließen.

compulsion [kəm'pʌlʃən] n Zwang m.

compulsive [kəm'pʌlsɪv] a Gewohnheits-.

compulsory [kəm'pʌlsərɪ] a (obligatory) obligatorisch, Pflicht-.

computer [kəm'pjuːtə°] n Computer m, Rechner m.

comrade ['komrɪd] n Kamerad m; (Pol) Genosse m; ~ship Kameradschaft f.

concave ['kon'keɪv] a konkav, hohlgeschliffen.

conceal [kən'siːl] vt secret verschweigen; to ~ o.s. sich verbergen.

concede [kən'siːd] vt (grant) gewähren; point zugeben; vi (admit) zugeben.

conceit [kən'siːt] n Eitelkeit f, Einbildung f; ~ed a eitel, eingebildet.

conceivable [kən'siːvəbl] a vorstellbar.

conceive [kən'siːv] vt idea ausdenken; imagine sich vorstellen; vti baby empfangen.

concentrate ['konsəntreɪt] vi sich konzentrieren (on auf +acc); vt (gather) konzentrieren.

concentration [konsən'treɪʃən] n Konzentration f; ~ camp Konzentrationslager nt, KZ nt.

concentric [kon'sentrɪk] a konzentrisch.

concept ['konsept] n Begriff m; ~ion [kən'sepʃən] (idea) Vorstellung f; (Physiol) Empfängnis f.

concern [kən'sɜːn] n (affair) Angelegenheit f; (Comm) Unternehmen nt, Konzern m; (worry) Sorge f, Unruhe f; vt (interest) angehen; (be about) handeln von; (have connection with) betreffen; ~ed a (anxious) besorgt; ~ing prep betreffend, hinsichtlich (+gen).

concert ['konsət] n Konzert nt; in ~ (with) im Einverständnis (mit); ~ed [kən'sɜːtɪd] a gemeinsam; (Fin) konzertiert; ~ hall Konzerthalle f.

concertina [konsə'tiːnə] n Handharmonika f.

concerto [kən'tʃɜːtəʊ] n Konzert nt.

concession [kən'seʃən] n (yielding) Zugeständnis nt; (right to do sth) Genehmigung f.

conciliation [kənsɪlɪ'eɪʃən] n Versöhnung f; (official) Schlichtung f.

conciliatory [kən'sɪlɪətrɪ] a vermittelnd; versöhnlich.

concise [kən'saɪs] a knapp, gedrängt.

conclave ['konkleɪv] n Konklave nt.

conclude [kən'kluːd] vt (end) beenden; treaty (ab)schließen; (decide) schließen, folgern; vi (finish) schließen.

conclusion [kən'kluːʒən] n (Ab)schluß m; in ~ zum Schluß, schließlich.

conclusive [kən'kluːsɪv] a überzeugend, schlüssig; ~ly ad endgültig.

concoct [kən'kokt] vt zusammenbrauen.

concord ['konkɔːd] n Eintracht f.

concourse ['konkɔːs] n (Bahnhofs)halle f, Vorplatz m.

concrete ['konkriːt] n Beton m; a konkret.

concur [kən'kɜː] vi übereinstimmen.

concurrently [kən'kʌrəntlɪ] ad gleichzeitig.

concussion [kən'kʌʃən] n (Gehirn)erschütterung f.

condemn [kən'dem] vt verdammen; (Jur) verurteilen; building abbruchreif erklären; ~ation [kondem'neɪʃən] Verurteilung f; (of object) Verwerfung f.

condensation [konden'seɪʃən] n Kondensation f.

condense [kən'dens] vi (Chem) konden-

sieren; *vt* *(fig)* zusammendrängen; ~**d milk** Kondensmilch *f.*
condescend [kɔndɪ'send] *vi* sich herablassen; ~**ing** *a* herablassend.
condition [kən'dɪʃən] *n* (*state*) Zustand *m*, Verfassung *f*; (*presupposition*) Bedingung *f*; *vt* hair *etc* behandeln; (*regulate*) regeln; **on** ~ **that** ... unter der Bedingung, daß ...; ~**ed to** gewöhnt an (+*acc*); ~**ed reflex** bedingter Reflex; ~**s** *pl* (*circumstances, weather*) Verhältnisse *f*; ~**al** *a* bedingt; (*Gram*) Bedingungs-.
condolences [kən'dəulənsɪz] *npl* Beileid *nt.*
condone [kən'dəun] *vt* gutheißen.
conducive [kən'dju:sɪv] *a* dienlich (*to dat*).
conduct ['kɔndʌkt] *n* (*behaviour*) Verhalten *nt*; (*management*) Führung *f*; [kən'dʌkt] *vt* führen, leiten; (*Mus*) dirigieren; ~**ed tour** Führung *f*; ~**or** [kən'dʌktə*] (*of orchestra*) Dirigent *m*; (*in bus*) Schaffner *m*; ~**ress** [kən'dʌktrɪs] (*in bus*) Schaffnerin *f.*
conduit ['kɔndɪt] *n* (*water*) Rohrleitung *f*; (*Elec*) Isolierrohr *nt.*
cone [kəun] *n* (*Math*) Kegel *m*; (*for ice cream*) (*Waffel*)tüte *f*; (*fir*) Tannenzapfen *m.*
confectioner [kən'fekʃənə*] *n* Konditor *m*; ~**'s (shop)** Konditorei *f*; ~**y** (*cakes*) Konfekt *nt*, Konditorwaren *pl*; (*sweets*) Süßigkeiten *pl.*
confederation [kɔnfedə'reɪʃən] *n* Bund *m.*
confer [kən'fɜ:*] *vt* *degree* verleihen; *vi* (*discuss*) konferieren, verhandeln; ~**ence** ['kɔnfərəns] Konferenz *f.*
confess [kən'fes] *vti* gestehen; (*Eccl*) beichten; ~**ion** [kən'feʃən] Geständnis *nt*; (*Eccl*) Beichte *f*; ~**ional** [kən'feʃənl] Beichtstuhl *m*; ~**or** (*Eccl*) Beichtvater *m.*
confetti [kən'fetɪ] *n* Konfetti *nt.*
confide [kən'faɪd] *vi*: ~ **in** (sich) anvertrauen (+*dat*); (*trust*) vertrauen (+*dat*); ~**nce** ['kɔnfɪdəns] Vertrauen *nt*; (*assurance*) Selbstvertrauen *nt*; (*secret*) vertrauliche Mitteilung *f*, Geheimnis *nt*; ~**nce trick** ['kɔnfɪdənstrɪk] Schwindel *m.*
confident ['kɔnfɪdənt] *a* (*sure*) überzeugt; sicher; (*self-assured*) selbstsicher; ~**ial** [kɔnfɪ'denʃəl] *a* (*secret*) vertraulich, geheim; (*trusted*) Vertrauens-.
confine [kən'faɪn] *vt* (*limit*) begrenzen, einschränken; (*lock up*) einsperren; ~**s** ['kɔnfaɪnz] *pl* Grenze *f*; ~**d** *a* space eng, begrenzt; ~**ment** (*of room*) Beengtheit *f*; (*in prison*) Haft *f*; (*Med*) Wochenbett *nt.*
confirm [kən'fɜ:m] *vt* bestätigen; ~**ation** [kɔnfə'meɪʃən] Bestätigung *f*; (*Rel*) Konfirmation *f*; ~**ed** *a* unverbesserlich, hartnäckig; *bachelor* eingefleischt.
confiscate ['kɔnfɪskeɪt] *vt* beschlagnahmen, konfiszieren.
confiscation [kɔnfɪs'keɪʃən] *n* Beschlagnahme *f.*
conflagration [kɔnflə'greɪʃən] *n* Feuersbrunst *f.*
conflict ['kɔnflɪkt] *n* Kampf *m*; (*of words, opinions*) Konflikt *m*, Streit *m*; [kən'flɪkt] *vi* im Widerspruch stehen; ~**ing** [kən'flɪktɪŋ] *a* gegensätzlich; *testimony* sich widersprechend.

conform [kən'fɔ:m] *vi* sich anpassen (*to dat*); (*to rules*) sich fügen (*to dat*); (*to general trends*) sich richten (*to nach*); ~**ist** Konformist(in *f*) *m.*
confront [kən'frʌnt] *vt* *enemy* entgegentreten (+*dat*); *sb with sth* konfrontieren; *sb with sb* gegenüberstellen (*with dat*); ~**ation** [kɔnfrən'teɪʃən] Gegenüberstellung *f*; (*quarrel*) Konfrontation *f.*
confuse [kən'fju:z] *vt* verwirren; (*sth with sth*) verwechseln.
confusing [kən'fju:zɪŋ] *a* verwirrend.
confusion [kən'fju:ʒən] *n* (*disorder*) Verwirrung *f*; (*tumult*) Aufruhr *m*; (*embarrassment*) Bestürzung *f.*
congeal [kən'dʒi:l] *vi* (*freeze*) gefrieren; (*clot*) gerinnen.
congenial [kən'dʒi:nɪəl] *a* (*agreeable*) angenehm.
congenital [kən'dʒenɪtəl] *a* angeboren.
conger eel ['kɔŋgər'i:l] *n* Meeraal *m.*
congested [kən'dʒestɪd] *a* überfüllt.
congestion [kən'dʒestʃən] *n* Stauung *f*, Stau *m.*
conglomeration [kɔnglɔmə'reɪʃən] *n* Anhäufung *f.*
congratulate [kən'grætjuleɪt] *vt* beglückwünschen (*on zu*).
congratulations [kən'grætju'leɪʃənz] *npl* Glückwünsche *pl*; ~! gratuliere!, herzlichen Glückwunsch!
congregate ['kɔngrɪgeɪt] *vi* sich versammeln.
congregation [kɔngrɪ'geɪʃən] *n* Gemeinde *f.*
congress ['kɔngres] *n* Kongreß *m*; ~**ional** [kən'greʃənl] *a* Kongreß-; ~**man** (*US*) Mitglied *nt* des amerikanischen Repräsentantenhauses.
conical ['kɔnɪkəl] *a* kegelförmig, konisch.
conifer ['kɔnɪfə*] *n* Nadelbaum *m*; ~**ous** [kə'nɪfərəs] *a* zapfentragend.
conjecture [kən'dʒektʃə*] *n* Vermutung *f*; *vti* vermuten.
conjugal ['kɔndʒugəl] *a* ehelich.
conjunction [kən'dʒʌŋkʃən] *n* Verbindung *f*; (*Gram*) Konjunktion *f*, Verbindungswort *nt.*
conjunctivitis [kəndʒʌŋktɪ'vaɪtɪs] *n* Bindehautentzündung *f.*
conjure ['kʌndʒə*] *vti* zaubern; ~ **up** *vt* heraufbeschwören; ~**r** Zauberer *m*; (*entertainer*) Zauberkünstler(in *f*) *m.*
conjuring ['kʌndʒərɪŋ] *n*: ~ **trick** Zauberkunststück *nt.*
conk [kɔŋk]: ~ **out** *vi* (*col*) stehenbleiben, streiken.
connect [kə'nekt] *vt* verbinden; *train* koppeln; ~**ion** [kə'nekʃən] Verbindung *f*; (*relation*) Zusammenhang *m*; **in** ~**ion with** in Verbindung mit.
connexion [kə'nekʃən] *n* = **connection.**
connoisseur [kɔnɪ'sɜ:*] *n* Kenner *m.*
connotation [kɔnə'teɪʃən] *n* Konnotation *f.*
conquer ['kɔŋkə*] *vt* (*overcome*) überwinden, besiegen; (*Mil*) besiegen; *vi* siegen; ~**or** Eroberer *m.*
conquest ['kɔŋkwest] *n* Eroberung *f.*
conscience ['kɔnʃəns] *n* Gewissen *nt.*

conscientious [kɒnʃɪ'enʃəs] a gewissenhaft; ~ **objector** Wehrdienstverweigerer m (aus Gewissensgründen).

conscious ['kɒnʃəs] a bewußt; (Med) bei Bewußtsein; ~**ness** Bewußtsein nt.

conscript ['kɒnskrɪpt] n Wehrpflichtige(r) m; ~**ion** [kən'skrɪpʃən] Wehrpflicht f.

consecrate ['kɒnsɪkreɪt] vt weihen.

consecutive [kən'sekjʊtɪv] a aufeinanderfolgend.

consensus [kən'sensəs] n allgemeine Übereinstimmung f.

consent [kən'sent] n Zustimmung f; vi zustimmen (to dat).

consequence ['kɒnsɪkwəns] n (importance) Bedeutung f, Konsequenz f; (result, effect) Wirkung f.

consequently ['kɒnsɪkwəntlɪ] ad folglich.

conservation [kɒnsə'veɪʃən] n Erhaltung f, Schutz m.

conservative [kən'sɜːvətɪv] a konservativ; (cautious) mäßig, vorsichtig; C~ a party konservativ; n Konservative(r) mf.

conservatory [kən'sɜːvətrɪ] n (greenhouse) Gewächshaus nt; (room) Wintergarten m.

conserve [kən'sɜːv] vt erhalten.

consider [kən'sɪdə*] vt überlegen; (take into account) in Betracht ziehen; (regard) halten für; ~**able** a beträchtlich; ~**ate** a rücksichtsvoll, aufmerksam; ~**ation** [kənsɪdə'reɪʃən] Rücksicht(nahme) f; (thought) Erwägung f; (reward) Entgelt nt; ~**ing** prep in Anbetracht (+gen); cj da; on no ~**ation** unter keinen Umständen.

consign [kən'saɪn] vt übergeben; ~**ment** (of goods) Sendung f, Lieferung f.

consist [kən'sɪst] vi bestehen (of aus).

consistency [kən'sɪstənsɪ] n (of material) Festigkeit f, (of argument) Folgerichtigkeit f; (of person) Konsequenz f.

consistent [kən'sɪstənt] a gleichbleibend, stetig; argument folgerichtig; she's not ~ sie ist nicht konsequent.

consolation [kɒnsə'leɪʃən] n Trost m; ~ **prize** Trostpreis m.

console [kən'səʊl] vt trösten.

consolidate [kən'sɒlɪdeɪt] vt festigen.

consommé [kən'sɒmeɪ] n Fleischbrühe f.

consonant ['kɒnsənənt] n Konsonant m, Mitlaut m.

consortium [kən'sɔːtɪəm] n Gruppe f, Konsortium nt.

conspicuous [kən'spɪkjʊəs] a (prominent) auffallend; (visible) deutlich, sichtbar.

conspiracy [kən'spɪrəsɪ] n Verschwörung f, Komplott nt.

conspire [kən'spaɪə*] vi sich verschwören.

constable ['kʌnstəbl] n Polizist(in f) m.

constabulary [kən'stæbjʊlərɪ] n Polizei f.

constancy ['kɒnstənsɪ] n Beständigkeit f, Treue f.

constant ['kɒnstənt] a dauernd; ~**ly** ad (continually) andauernd; (faithfully) treu, unwandelbar.

constellation [kɒnstə'leɪʃən] n (temporary) Konstellation f; (permanent) Sternbild nt.

consternation [kɒnstə'neɪʃən] n (dismay) Bestürzung f.

constipated ['kɒnstɪpeɪtəd] a verstopft.

constipation [kɒnstɪ'peɪʃən] n Verstopfung f.

constituency [kən'stɪtjʊənsɪ] n Wahlkreis m.

constituent [kən'stɪtjʊənt] n (person) Wähler m; (part) Bestandteil m.

constitute ['kɒnstɪtjuːt] vt ausmachen.

constitution [kɒnstɪ'tjuːʃən] n Verfassung f; ~**al** a Verfassungs-; monarchy konstitutionell.

constrain [kən'streɪn] vt zwingen; ~**t** Zwang m; (Psych) Befangenheit f.

constrict [kən'strɪkt] vt zusammenziehen; ~**ion** [kən'strɪkʃən] Zusammenziehung f; (of chest) Zusammenschnürung f, Beklemmung f.

construct [kən'strʌkt] vt bauen; ~**ion** [kən'strʌkʃən] (action) (Er)bauen nt, Konstruktion f; (building) Bau m; under ~**ion** im Bau befindlich; ~**ive** a konstruktiv.

construe [kən'struː] vt (interpret) deuten.

consul ['kɒnsl] n Konsul m; ~**ate** ['kɒnsjʊlət] Konsulat nt.

consult [kən'sʌlt] vt um Rat fragen; doctor konsultieren; book nachschlagen in (+dat); ~**ant** (Med) Facharzt m; (other specialist) Gutachter m; ~**ation** [kɒnsəl'teɪʃən] Beratung f; (Med) Konsultation f; ~**ing room** Sprechzimmer nt.

consume [kən'sjuːm] vt verbrauchen; food verzehren, konsumieren; ~**r** Verbraucher m.

consummate ['kɒnsʌmeɪt] vt vollenden; marriage vollziehen.

consumption [kən'sʌmpʃən] n Verbrauch m; (of food) Konsum m.

contact ['kɒntækt] n (touch) Berührung f; (connection) Verbindung f; (person) Kontakt m, Beziehung f; vt sich in Verbindung setzen mit; ~ **lenses** pl Kontaktlinsen pl.

contagious [kən'teɪdʒəs] a ansteckend.

contain [kən'teɪn] vt enthalten; to ~ o.s. sich zügeln; ~**er** Behälter m; (transport) Container m.

contaminate [kən'tæmɪneɪt] vt verunreinigen; (germs) infizieren.

contamination [kəntæmɪ'neɪʃən] n Verunreinigung f.

contemplate ['kɒntəmpleɪt] vt (nachdenklich) betrachten; (think about) überdenken; (plan) vorhaben.

contemplation [kɒntem'pleɪʃən] n Betrachtung f; (Rel) Meditation f.

contemporary [kən'tempərərɪ] a zeitgenössisch; n Zeitgenosse m.

contempt [kən'tempt] n Verachtung f; ~**ible** a verächtlich, nichtswürdig; ~**uous** a voller Verachtung (of für).

contend [kən'tend] vt (fight) kämpfen (um); (argue) behaupten; ~**er** (for post) Bewerber(in f) m; (Sport) Wettkämpfer(in f) m.

content [kən'tent] a zufrieden; vt befriedigen; [kɒntent] n (also ~s) Inhalt m; ~**ed** a zufrieden.

contention [kən'tenʃən] n (dispute) Streit

m; (*argument*) Behauptung f.

contentment [kən'tentmənt] n Zufriedenheit f.

contest ['kɒntest] n (Wett)kampf m; [kən'test] vt (*dispute*) bestreiten; (*Pol*) kandidieren (*in dat*); ~ant [kən'testənt] Bewerber(in f) m.

context ['kɒntekst] n Zusammenhang m.

continent ['kɒntɪnənt] n Kontinent m, Festland nt; the C~ das europäische Festland, der Kontinent; ~al [kɒntɪ'nentl] a kontinental; n Bewohner(in f) m des Kontinents.

contingency [kən'tɪndʒənsɪ] n Möglichkeit f.

contingent [kən'tɪndʒənt] n (*Mil*) Kontingent nt; a abhängig (*upon* von).

continual [kən'tɪnjʊəl] a (*endless*) fortwährend; (*repeated*) immer wiederkehrend; ~ly ad immer wieder.

continuation [kəntɪnjʊ'eɪʃən] n Verlängerung f; Fortsetzung f.

continue [kən'tɪnjuː] vi (*go on*) anhalten; (*last*) fortbestehen; **shall we** ~? wollen wir weitermachen?; **if this** ~s wenn das so weitergeht; **the rain** ~d es regnete weiter; vt fortsetzen; **to** ~ **doing sth** fortfahren, etw zu tun.

continuity [kɒntɪ'njuːɪtɪ] n Kontinuität nt; (*wholeness*) Zusammenhang m.

continuous [kən'tɪnjʊəs] a ununterbrochen.

contort [kən'tɔːt] vt verdrehen; ~ion [kən'tɔːʃən] Verzerrung f; ~ionist [kən'tɔːʃənɪst] Schlangenmensch m.

contour ['kɒntʊə*] n Umriß m; (*height*) Höhenlinie f.

contraband ['kɒntrəbænd] n Schmuggelware f.

contraception [kɒntrə'sepʃən] n Empfängnisverhütung f.

contraceptive [kɒntrə'septɪv] n empfängnisverhütende(s) Mittel nt; a empfängnisverhütend.

contract ['kɒntrækt] n (*agreement*) Vertrag m, Kontrakt m; [kən'trækt] vi (*to do sth*) sich vertraglich verpflichten; (*muscle*) sich zusammenziehen; (*become smaller*) schrumpfen; ~ion [kən'trækʃən] (*shortening*) Verkürzung f; ~or [kən'træktə*] Unternehmer m; (*supplier*) Lieferant m.

contradict [kɒntrə'dɪkt] vt widersprechen (+dat); ~ion [kɒntrə'dɪkʃən] Widerspruch m.

contralto [kən'træltəʊ] n (tiefe) Altstimme f.

contraption [kən'træpʃən] n (col) komische Konstruktion f, komische(s) Ding nt.

contrary ['kɒntrərɪ] a entgegengesetzt; *wind* ungünstig, Gegen-; (*obstinate*) widerspenstig, eigensinnig; n Gegenteil nt; **on the** ~ im Gegenteil.

contrast ['kɒntrɑːst] n Kontrast m; [kən'trɑːst] vt entgegensetzen; ~ing [kən'trɑːstɪŋ] a Kontrast-.

contravene [kɒntrə'viːn] vt verstoßen gegen.

contribute [kən'trɪbjuːt] vti beitragen; *money* spenden.

contribution [kɒntrɪ'bjuːʃən] n Beitrag m.

contributor [kən'trɪbjʊtə*] n Beitragende(r) mf.

contrite ['kɒntraɪt] a zerknirscht.

contrivance [kən'traɪvəns] n Vorrichtung f, Kniff m, Erfindung f.

contrive [kən'traɪv] vt zustande bringen; **to** ~ **to do sth** es schaffen, etw zu tun.

control [kən'trəʊl] vt (*direct, test*) kontrollieren; n Kontrolle f; (*business*) Leitung f; ~s pl (*of vehicle*) Steuerung f; (*of engine*) Schalttafel f; ~ **point** Kontrollstelle f; **out of** ~ außer Kontrolle; **under** ~ unter Kontrolle.

controversial [kɒntrə'vɜːʃəl] a umstritten, kontrovers.

controversy ['kɒntrəvɜːsɪ] n Meinungsstreit m, Kontroverse f.

convalesce [kɒnvə'les] vi gesund werden; ~nce Genesung f; ~nt a auf dem Wege der Besserung; n Genesende(r) mf.

convector [kən'vektə*] n Heizlüfter m.

convene [kən'viːn] vt zusammenrufen; vi sich versammeln.

convenience [kən'viːnɪəns] n Annehmlichkeit f; (*thing*) bequeme Einrichtung f; see **public**.

convenient [kən'viːnɪənt] a günstig.

convent ['kɒnvənt] n Kloster nt.

convention [kən'venʃən] n Versammlung f; (*Pol*) Übereinkunft f; (*custom*) Konvention f; ~al a herkömmlich, konventionell.

converge [kən'vɜːdʒ] vi zusammenlaufen.

conversant [kən'vɜːsənt] a vertraut; (*in learning*) bewandert (*with* in +dat).

conversation [kɒnvə'seɪʃən] n Unterhaltung f; ~al a Unterhaltungs-.

converse [kən'vɜːs] vi sich unterhalten; ['kɒnvɜːs] a gegenteilig; ~ly [kɒn'vɜːslɪ] ad umgekehrt.

conversion [kən'vɜːʃən] n Umwandlung f; (*esp Rel*) Bekehrung f; ~ **table** Umrechnungstabelle f.

convert [kən'vɜːt] vt (*change*) umwandeln; (*Rel*) bekehren; ['kɒnvɜːt] n Bekehrte(r) mf, Konvertit(in f) m; ~ible (*Aut*) Kabriolett nt; a umwandelbar; (*Fin*) konvertierbar.

convex ['kɒn'veks] a konvex.

convey [kən'veɪ] vt (*carry*) befördern; *feelings* vermitteln; ~or belt Fließband nt.

convict [kən'vɪkt] vt verurteilen; ['kɒnvɪkt] n Häftling m; ~ion [kən'vɪkʃən] (*verdict*) Verurteilung f; (*belief*) Überzeugung f.

convince [kən'vɪns] vt überzeugen.

convincing [kən'vɪnsɪŋ] a überzeugend.

convivial [kən'vɪvɪəl] a festlich, froh.

convoy ['kɒnvɔɪ] n (*of vehicles*) Kolonne f; (*protected*) Konvoi m.

convulse [kən'vʌls] vt zusammenzucken lassen; **to be** ~d **with laughter** sich vor Lachen krümmen.

convulsion [kən'vʌlʃən] n (*esp Med*) Zuckung f, Krampf m.

coo [kuː] vi (*dove*) gurren.

cook [kʊk] vti kochen; n Koch m, Köchin f.

~book Kochbuch *nt*; ~er Herd *m*; ~ery Kochkunst *f*; ~ery book = ~book; ~ie (*US*) Plätzchen *nt*; ~ing Kochen *nt*.

cool [ku:l] *a* kühl; *vti* (ab)kühlen; ~ down *vti* (*fig*) (sich) beruhigen; ~ing-tower Kühlturm *m*; ~ness Kühle *f*; (*of temperament*) kühle(r) Kopf.

coop [ku:p] *n* Hühnerstall *m*; *vt*: ~ up (*fig*) einpferchen.

co-op ['kəʊp] *n* = cooperative.

cooperate [kəʊ'ɒpəreɪt] *vi* zusammenarbeiten.

cooperation [kəʊɒpə'reɪʃən] *n* Zusammenarbeit *f*.

cooperative [kəʊ'ɒpərətɪv] *a* hilfsbereit; (*Comm*) genossenschaftlich; *n* (*of farmers*) Genossenschaft *f*; (~ *store*) Konsumladen *m*.

coordinate [kəʊ'ɔ:dɪneɪt] *vt* koordinieren.

coordination [kəʊɔ:dɪ'neɪʃən] *n* Koordination *f*.

coot [ku:t] *n* Wasserhuhn *nt*.

cop [kɒp] *n* (*col*) Polyp *m*, Bulle *m*.

cope [kəʊp] *vi* fertig werden, schaffen (*with acc*).

co-pilot ['kəʊ'paɪlət] *n* Kopilot *m*.

copious ['kəʊpɪəs] *a* reichhaltig.

copper ['kɒpə*] *n* Kupfer *nt*; Kupfermünze *f*; (*col: policeman*) Polyp *m*, Bulle *m*.

coppice ['kɒpɪs], copse [kɒps] *n* Unterholz *nt*.

copulate ['kɒpjʊleɪt] *vi* sich paaren.

copy ['kɒpɪ] *n* (*imitation*) Nachahmung *f*; (*of book etc*) Exemplar *nt*; (*of newspaper*) Nummer *f*; *vt* kopieren, abschreiben; ~cat Nachäffer *m*; ~right Copyright *nt*; ~right reserved alle Rechte vorbehalten, Nachdruck verboten.

coral ['kɒrəl] *n* Koralle *f*; ~ reef Korallenriff *nt*.

cord [kɔ:d] *n* Schnur *f*, Kordel *f*; *see* vocal.

cordial ['kɔ:dɪəl] *a* herzlich; *n* Fruchtsaft *m*; ~ly herzlich.

cordon ['kɔ:dn] *n* Absperrkette *f*.

corduroy ['kɔ:dərɔɪ] *n* Kord(samt) *m*.

core [kɔ:*] *n* Kern *m*; *vt* entkernen.

cork [kɔ:k] *n* (*bark*) Korkrinde *f*; (*stopper*) Korken *m*; ~age Korkengeld *nt*; ~screw Korkenzieher *m*.

corm [kɔ:m] *n* Knolle *f*.

cormorant ['kɔ:mərənt] *n* Kormoran *m*.

corn [kɔ:n] *n* Getreide *nt*, Korn *nt*; (*US: maize*) Mais *m*; (*on foot*) Hühnerauge *nt*.

cornea ['kɔ:nɪə] *n* Hornhaut *f*.

corned beef ['kɔ:nd'bi:f] *n* Corned Beef *nt*.

corner ['kɔ:nə*] *n* Ecke *f*; (*nook*) Winkel *m*; (*on road*) Kurve *f*; *vt* in die Enge treiben; *vi* (*Aut*) in die Kurve gehen; ~ flag Eckfahne *f*; ~ kick Eckball *m*; ~stone Eckstein *m*.

cornet ['kɔ:nɪt] *n* (*Mus*) Kornett *nt*; (*for ice cream*) Eistüte *f*.

cornflour ['kɔ:nflaʊə*] *n* Maizena ® *nt*, Maismehl *nt*.

cornice ['kɔ:nɪs] *n* Gesims *nt*.

cornstarch ['kɔ:nstɑ:tʃ] *n* (*US*) = cornflour.

cornucopia [kɔ:nju'kəʊpɪə] *n* Füllhorn *nt*.

corny ['kɔ:nɪ] *a* (*joke*) blöd(e).

corollary [kə'rɒlərɪ] *n* Folgesatz *m*.

coronary ['kɒrənərɪ] *a* (*Med*) Koronar-; ~ Herzinfarkt *m*; ~ thrombosis Koronarthrombose *f*.

coronation [kɒrə'neɪʃən] *n* Krönung *f*.

coroner ['kɒrənə*] *n* Untersuchungsrichter *m* und Leichenbeschauer *m*.

coronet ['kɒrənɪt] *n* Adelskrone *f*.

corporal ['kɔ:pərəl] *n* Obergefreite(r) *m*; *a*: ~ punishment Prügelstrafe *f*.

corporate ['kɔ:pərɪt] *a* gemeinschaftlich, korporativ.

corporation [kɔ:pə'reɪʃən] *n* Gemeinde *f*, Stadt *f*; (*esp business*) Körperschaft *f*, Aktiengesellschaft *f*.

corps [kɔ:*] *n* (Armee)korps *nt*.

corpse [kɔ:ps] *n* Leiche *f*.

corpulent ['kɔ:pjʊlənt] *a* korpulent.

Corpus Christi ['kɔ:pəs'krɪstɪ] *n* Fronleichnamsfest *nt*.

corpuscle ['kɔ:pʌsl] *n* Blutkörperchen *nt*.

corral [kə'rɑ:l] *n* Pferch *m*, Korral *m*.

correct [kə'rekt] *a* (*accurate*) richtig; (*proper*) korrekt; *vt* mistake berichtigen; pupil tadeln; ~ion [kə'rekʃən] Berichtigung *f*; ~ly richtig; korrekt.

correlate ['kɒrɪleɪt] *vt* aufeinander beziehen; *vi* korrelieren.

correlation [kɒrɪ'leɪʃən] *n* Wechselbeziehung *f*.

correspond [kɒrɪs'pɒnd] *vi* übereinstimmen; (*exchange letters*) korrespondieren; ~ence (*similarity*) Entsprechung *f*; Briefwechsel *m*, Korrespondenz *f*; ~ence course Fernkurs *m*; ~ent (*Press*) Berichterstatter *m*; ~ing *a* entsprechend, gemäß (*to dat*).

corridor ['kɒrɪdɔ:*] *n* Gang *m*.

corroborate [kə'rɒbəreɪt] *vt* bestätigen, erhärten.

corroboration [kərɒbə'reɪʃən] *n* Bekräftigung *f*.

corrode [kə'rəʊd] *vt* zerfressen; *vi* rosten.

corrosion [kə'rəʊʒən] *n* Rost *m*, Korrosion *f*.

corrugated ['kɒrəgeɪtɪd] *a* gewellt; ~ cardboard Wellpappe *f*; ~ iron Wellblech *nt*.

corrupt [kə'rʌpt] *a* korrupt; *vt* verderben; (*bribe*) bestechen; ~ion [kə'rʌpʃən] (*of society*) Verdorbenheit *f*; (*bribery*) Bestechung *f*.

corset ['kɔ:sɪt] *n* Korsett *nt*.

cortège [kɔ:'te:ʒ] *n* Zug *m*; (*of funeral*) Leichenzug *m*.

cortisone ['kɔ:tɪzəʊn] *n* Kortison *nt*.

cosh [kɒʃ] *n* Totschläger *m*; *vt* über den Schädel hauen.

cosignatory ['kəʊ'sɪgnətərɪ] *n* Mitunterzeichner(in *f*) *m*.

cosine ['kəʊsaɪn] *n* Kosinus *m*.

cosiness ['kəʊzɪnɪs] *n* Gemütlichkeit *f*.

cosmetic [kɒz'metɪk] *n* Schönheitsmittel *nt*, kosmetische(s) Mittel *nt*; *a* kosmetisch.

cosmic ['kɒzmɪk] *a* kosmisch.

cosmonaut ['kɒzmənɔ:t] *n* Kosmonaut(in *f*) *m*.

cosmopolitan [kɒzmə'pɒlɪtən] a international; *city* Welt-.

cosmos ['kɒzmɒs] n Weltall nt, Kosmos m.

cost [kɒst] n Kosten pl, Preis m; vt irreg kosten; it ~ him his life/job es kostete ihm sein Leben/seine Stelle; **at all** ~s um jeden Preis; ~ **of living** Lebenshaltungskosten pl.

co-star ['kəʊstɑː*] n zweite(r) or weitere(r) Hauptdarsteller(in f) m.

costing ['kɒstɪŋ] n Kostenberechnung f.

costly ['kɒstlɪ] a kostspielig.

cost price ['kɒst'praɪs] n Selbstkostenpreis m.

costume ['kɒstjuːm] n Kostüm nt; (fancy dress) Maskenkostüm nt; (for bathing) Badeanzug m; ~ **jewellery** Modeschmuck m.

cosy ['kəʊzɪ] a behaglich, gemütlich.

cot [kɒt] n Kinderbett(chen) nt.

cottage ['kɒtɪdʒ] n kleine(s) Haus nt (auf dem Land); ~ **cheese** Hüttenkäse m.

cotton ['kɒtn] n (material) Baumwollstoff m; a dress etc Baumwoll-, Kattun-; ~ **wool** Watte f.

couch [kaʊtʃ] n Couch f; vt (in Worte) fassen, formulieren.

cougar ['kuːgə*] n Puma m.

cough [kɒf] vi husten; n Husten m; ~ **drop** Hustenbonbon nt.

could [kʊd] pt of **can**; ~**n't** = **could not**.

council ['kaʊnsl] n (of town) Stadtrat m; ~ **estate/house** Siedlung f/Haus nt des sozialen Wohnungsbaus; ~**lor** ['kaʊnsɪlə*] Stadtrat m.

counsel ['kaʊnsl] n (barrister) Anwalt m, Rechtsbeistand m; (advice) Rat(schlag) m; ~**lor** Berater m.

count [kaʊnt] vti zählen; vi (be important) zählen, gelten; n (reckoning) Abrechnung f; (nobleman) Graf m; ~**down** Countdown m; ~ **on** vt zählen auf (+acc); ~ **up** vt zusammenzählen.

counter ['kaʊntə*] n (in shop) Ladentisch m; (in café) Tresen m, Theke f; (in bank, post office) Schalter m; vt entgegnen; ad entgegen; ~**act** [kaʊntə'rækt] vt entgegenwirken (+dat); ~**attack** Gegenangriff m; ~**balance** vt aufwiegen; ~**clockwise** ad entgegen dem Uhrzeigersinn; ~**espionage** Spionageabwehr f; ~**felt** Fälschung f, vt fälschen; a gefälscht, unecht; ~**foil** (Kontroll)abschnitt m; ~**part** (object) Gegenstück nt; (person) Gegenüber nt.

countess ['kaʊntɪs] n Gräfin f.

countless ['kaʊntlɪs] a zahllos, unzählig.

countrified ['kʌntrɪfaɪd] a ländlich.

country ['kʌntrɪ] n Land nt; **in the** ~ auf dem Land(e); ~ **dancing** Volkstanztanzen nt; ~ **house** Landhaus nt; ~**man** (national) Landsmann m; (rural) Bauer m; ~**side** Landschaft f.

county ['kaʊntɪ] n Landkreis m; (Brit) Grafschaft f; ~ **town** Kreisstadt f.

coup [kuː] n Coup m; ~ **d'état** Staatsstreich m, Putsch m.

coupé [kuː'peɪ] n (Aut) Coupé nt.

couple ['kʌpl] n Paar nt; **a** ~ **of** ein paar; vt koppeln.

couplet ['kʌplɪt] n Reimpaar nt.

coupling ['kʌplɪŋ] n Kupplung f.

coupon ['kuːpɒn] n Gutschein m.

courage ['kʌrɪdʒ] n Mut m; ~**ous** [kə'reɪdʒəs] a mutig.

courier ['kʊrɪə*] n (for holiday) Reiseleiter m; (messenger) Kurier m, Eilbote m.

course [kɔːs] n (race) Strecke f, Bahn f; (of stream) Lauf m; (of action) Richtung f; (of lectures) Vortragsreihe f; (of study) Studiengang m; **summer** ~ Sommerkurs m; (Naut) Kurs m; (in meal) Gang m; **of** ~ natürlich; **in the** ~ **of** im Laufe (+gen); **in due** ~ zu gegebener Zeit; see **golf**.

court [kɔːt] n (royal) Hof m; (Jur) Gericht nt; vt gehen mit; see **tennis**.

courteous ['kɜːtɪəs] a höflich, zuvorkommend.

courtesan [kɔːtɪ'zæn] n Kurtisane f.

courtesy ['kɜːtəsɪ] n Höflichkeit f.

courthouse ['kɔːthaʊs] n (US) Gerichtsgebäude nt.

courtier ['kɔːtɪə*] n Höfling m.

court-martial ['kɔːt'mɑːʃəl] n Kriegsgericht nt; vt vor ein Kriegsgericht stellen.

courtroom ['kɔːtrʊm] n Gerichtssaal m.

courtyard ['kɔːtjɑːd] n Hof m.

cousin ['kʌzn] n Cousin m, Vetter m; Kusine f.

cove [kəʊv] n kleine Bucht f.

covenant ['kʌvənənt] n feierliche(s) Abkommen nt.

cover ['kʌvə*] vt (spread over) bedecken; (shield) abschirmen; (include) sich erstrecken über (+acc); (protect) decken; n (lid) Deckel m; (for bed) Decke f; (Mil) Bedeckung f; ~**age** ['kʌvrɪdʒ] (Press) (reports) Berichterstattung f; (distribution) Verbreitung f; ~ **charge** Bedienungsgeld nt; ~**ing** Bedeckung f; ~**ing letter** Begleitbrief m.

covet ['kʌvɪt] vt begehren.

covetous ['kʌvɪtəs] a begehrlich.

cow [kaʊ] n Kuh f.

coward ['kaʊəd] n Feigling m; ~**ice** ['kaʊədɪs] Feigheit f; ~**ly** a feige.

cowboy ['kaʊbɔɪ] n Cowboy m.

cower ['kaʊə*] vi kauern; (movement) sich kauern.

co-worker ['kəʊ'wɜːkə*] n Mitarbeiter(in f) m.

cowshed ['kaʊʃed] n Kuhstall m.

coxswain ['kɒksn] n (abbr **cox**) Steuermann m.

coy [kɔɪ] a schüchtern; girl spröde.

coyote [kɔɪ'əʊtɪ] n Präriewolf m.

crab [kræb] n Krebs m; ~**apple** Holzapfel m.

crack [kræk] n Riß m, Sprung m; (noise) Knall m; vt (break) springen lassen; joke reißen; vi (noise) krachen, knallen; a erstklassig; troops Elite-; ~**er** (firework) Knallkörper m, Kracher m; (biscuit) Keks m; (Christmas —) Knallbonbon m; ~ **up** vi (fig) zusammenbrechen.

crackle ['krækl] vi knistern; (fire) prasseln.

crackling ['kræklɪŋ] n Knistern n; (rind) Kruste f (des Schweinebratens).

cradle ['kreidl] n Wiege f.

craft [kraːft] n (skill) (Hand- or Kunst)fertigkeit f; (trade) Handwerk nt; (cunning) Verschlagenheit f; (Naut) Fahrzeug nt, Schiff nt; ~**sman** gelernte(r) Handwerker m; ~**smanship** (quality) handwerkliche Ausführung f; (ability) handwerkliche(s) Können nt; ~**y** a schlau, gerieben.

crag [kræg] n Klippe f; ~**gy** a schroff, felsig.

cram [kræm] vt vollstopfen; (col) (teach) einpauken; vi (learn) pauken.

cramp [kræmp] n Krampf m; vt (hinder) einengen, hemmen.

crampon ['kræmpən] n Steigeisen nt.

cranberry ['krænbəri] n Preiselbeere f.

crane [krein] n (machine) Kran m; (bird) Kranich m.

cranium ['kreiniəm] n Schädel m.

crank [kræŋk] n (lever) Kurbel f; (person) Spinner m; vt ankurbeln; ~**shaft** Kurbelwelle f.

cranky ['kræŋki] a verschroben.

cranny ['kræni] n Ritze f.

crap [kræp] n (col) Mist m, Scheiße f.

craps [kræps] n (US) Würfelspiel nt.

crash [kræʃ] n (noise) Krachen nt; (with cars) Zusammenstoß m; (with plane) Absturz m; vi stürzen; (cars) zusammenstoßen; (plane) abstürzen; (economy) zusammenbrechen; (noise) knallen; a course Schnell-; ~ **helmet** Sturzhelm m; ~ **landing** Bruchlandung f.

crass [kræs] a kraß.

crate [kreit] n (lit, fig) Kiste f.

crater ['kreitə*] n Krater m.

cravat(e) [krə'væt] n Krawatte f.

crave [kreiv] vi verlangen (for nach).

craving ['kreiviŋ] n Verlangen nt.

crawl [krɔːl] vi kriechen; (baby) krabbeln; n Kriechen nt; (swim) Kraul nt.

crayon ['kreiən] n Buntstift m.

craze [kreiz] n Fimmel m.

crazy ['kreizi] a (foolish) verrückt; (insane) wahnsinnig; (eager for) versessen (auf +acc); ~ **paving** Mosaikpflaster nt.

creak [kriːk] n Knarren nt; vi quietschen, knarren.

cream [kriːm] n (from milk) Rahm m, Sahne f; (polish, cosmetic) Creme f; (colour) Cremefarbe f; (fig: people) Elite f; ~ **cake** (small) Sahnetörtchen nt; (big) Sahnekuchen m; ~ **cheese** Rahmquark m; ~**ery** Molkerei f; ~**y** a sahnig.

crease [kriːs] n Falte f; vt falten; (untidy) zerknittern.

create [kriː'eit] vt erschaffen; (cause) verursachen.

creation [kriː'eiʃən] n Schöpfung f.

creative [kriː'eitiv] a schöpferisch, kreativ.

creator [kriː'eitə*] n Schöpfer m.

creature ['kriːtʃə*] n Geschöpf nt.

credence ['kriːdəns] n Glauben m.

credentials [kri'denʃəlz] npl Beglaubigungsschreiben nt.

credibility [kredi'biliti] n Glaubwürdigkeit f.

credible ['kredibl] a (person) glaubwürdig; (story) glaubhaft.

credit ['kredit] n (Comm) Kredit m; Guthaben nt; vt Glauben schenken (+dat); **to sb's** ~ zu jds Ehre; ~**s** pl (of film) die Mitwirkenden; ~**able** a rühmlich; ~ **card** Kreditkarte f; ~**or** Gläubiger m.

credulity [kri'djuːliti] n Leichtgläubigkeit f.

creed [kriːd] n Glaubensbekenntnis nt.

creek [kriːk] n (inlet) kleine Bucht f; (US: river) kleine(r) Wasserlauf m.

creep [kriːp] vi irreg kriechen; ~**er** Kletterpflanze f; ~**y** a (frightening) gruselig.

cremate [kri'meit] vt einäschern.

cremation [kri'meiʃən] n Einäscherung f.

crematorium [kremə'tɔːriəm] n Krematorium nt.

creosote ['kriːəsəut] n Kreosot nt.

crepe [kreip] n Krepp m; ~ **bandage** Elastikbinde f.

crescent ['kresnt] n (of moon) Halbmond m.

cress [kres] n Kresse f.

crest [krest] n (of cock) Kamm m; (of wave) Wellenkamm m; (coat of arms) Wappen nt; ~**fallen** a niedergeschlagen.

cretin ['kretin] n Idiot m.

crevasse [kri'væs] n Gletscherspalte f.

crevice ['krevis] n Riß m; (in rock) Felsspalte f.

crew [kruː] n Besatzung f, Mannschaft f; ~**cut** Bürstenschnitt m; ~**neck** runde(r) Ausschnitt m.

crib [krib] n (bed) Krippe f; (translation) wortwörtliche Übersetzung f, Klatsche f.

crick [krik] n Muskelkrampf m.

cricket ['krikit] n (insect) Grille f; (game) Kricket nt; ~**er** Kricketspieler m.

crime [kraim] n Verbrechen nt.

criminal ['kriminl] n Verbrecher m; a kriminell, strafbar.

crimp [krimp] vt hair drehen.

crimson ['krimzn] n Karmesin nt; a leuchtend rot.

cringe [krindʒ] vi sich ducken.

crinkle ['kriŋkl] vt zerknittern; vi knittern.

crinkly ['kriŋkli] a hair kraus.

cripple ['kripl] n Krüppel m; vt lahmlegen; (Med) lähmen, verkrüppeln.

crisis ['kraisis] n Krise f.

crisp [krisp] a knusprig; n Chip m.

criss-cross ['kriskrɔs] a gekreuzt, Kreuz-.

criterion [krai'tiəriən] n Kriterium nt.

critic ['kritik] n Kritiker(in f) m; ~**al** a kritisch; ~**ally** ad kritisch; ill gefährlich; ~**ism** ['kritisizəm] Kritik f; ~**ize** ['kritisaiz] vt kritisieren; (comment) beurteilen.

croak [krəuk] vi krächzen; (frog) quaken; n Krächzen nt; Quaken nt.

crochet ['krəuʃei] n Häkelei f.

crockery ['krɔkəri] n Geschirr nt.

crocodile ['krɔkədail] n Krokodil nt.

crocus ['krəukəs] n Krokus m.

croft [krɔft] n kleine(s) Pachtgut nt; ~**er** Kleinbauer m.

crony ['krəuni] n (col) Kumpel m.

crook [kruk] n (criminal) Gauner m, Schwindler m; (stick) Hirtenstab m; ~ed ['krukɪd] a krumm.

crop [krɒp] n (harvest) Ernte f; (col: series) Haufen m; ~ up vi auftauchen; (thing) passieren.

croquet ['krəʊkeɪ] n Krocket nt.

croquette [krɔ'ket] n Krokette f.

cross [krɒs] n Kreuz nt; (Biol) Kreuzung f; vt road überqueren; legs übereinander legen; (write) einen Querstrich ziehen; (Biol) kreuzen; cheque als Verrechnungsscheck kennzeichnen; a (annoyed) ärgerlich, böse; ~bar Querstange f; ~breed Kreuzung f; ~-country (race) Geländelauf m; ~-examination Kreuzverhör nt; ~-examine vt ins Kreuzverhör nehmen; ~-eyed a: to be ~-eyed schielen; ~ing (crossroads) (Straßen)kreuzung f; (of ship) Überfahrt f; (for pedestrians) Fußgängerüberweg m; ~ out vt streichen; to be at ~ purposes von verschiedenen Dingen reden; ~reference Querverweis m; ~roads Straßenkreuzung f; (fig) Scheideweg m; ~section Querschnitt m; ~wind Seitenwind m; ~word (puzzle) Kreuzworträtsel nt.

crotch [krɒtʃ] n Zwickel m; (Anat) Unterleib nt.

crotchet ['krɒtʃɪt] n Viertelnote f.

crotchety ['krɒtʃɪtɪ] a person launenhaft.

crouch [krautʃ] vi hocken.

crouton ['kru:tɔ̃ŋ] n geröstete(r) Brotwürfel m.

crow [krəʊ] n Krähen nt; vi krähen.

crowbar ['krəʊba:ʳ] n Stemmeisen nt.

crowd [kraud] n Menge f, Gedränge nt; vt (fill) überfüllen; vi drängen; ~ed a überfüllt.

crown [kraun] n Krone f; (of head, hat) Kopf m; vt krönen; ~ jewels pl Kronjuwelen pl; ~ prince Kronprinz m.

crow's-nest ['krəʊznest] n Krähennest nt, Ausguck m.

crucial ['kru:ʃəl] a entscheidend.

crucifix ['kru:sɪfɪks] n Kruzifix nt; ~ion [kru:sɪ'fɪkʃən] Kreuzigung f.

crucify ['kru:sɪfaɪ] vt kreuzigen.

crude [kru:d] a (raw) roh; humour, behaviour grob, unfein; ~ly ad grob; ~ness Roheit f.

crudity ['kru:dɪtɪ] n = **crudeness**.

cruel ['kruəl] a grausam; (distressing) schwer; (hard-hearted) hart, gefühllos; ~ty Grausamkeit f.

cruet ['kru:ɪt] n Gewürzständer m, Menage f.

cruise [kru:z] n Kreuzfahrt f; vi kreuzen; ~r (Mil) Kreuzer m.

cruising-speed ['kru:zɪŋspi:d] n Reisegeschwindigkeit f.

crumb [krʌm] n Krume f; (fig) Bröckchen nt.

crumble ['krʌmbl] vti zerbröckeln.

crumbly ['krʌmblɪ] a krümelig.

crumpet ['krʌmpɪt] n Tee(pfann)kuchen m.

crumple ['krʌmpl] vt zerknittern.

crunch [krʌntʃ] n Knirschen nt; (fig) der entscheidende Punkt; vt knirschen; ~y a knusprig.

crusade [kru:'seɪd] n Kreuzzug m; ~r Kreuzfahrer m.

crush [krʌʃ] n Gedränge nt; vt zerdrücken; (rebellion) unterdrücken, niederwerfen; vi (material) knittern; ~ing a überwältigend.

crust [krʌst] n (of bread) Rinde f, Kruste f; (Med) Schorf m.

crutch [krʌtʃ] n Krücke f; see also **crotch**.

crux [krʌks] n (crucial point) der springende Punkt, Haken m (col).

cry [kraɪ] vi (call) ausrufen; (shout) schreien; (weep) weinen; n (call) Schrei m; ~ing a (fig) himmelschreiend; ~ off vi (plötzlich) absagen.

crypt [krɪpt] n Krypta f.

cryptic ['krɪptɪk] a (secret) geheim; (mysterious) rätselhaft.

crystal ['krɪstl] n Kristall m; (glass) Kristallglas nt; (mineral) Bergkristall m; ~-clear a kristallklar; ~-lize vti (lit) kristallisieren; (fig) klären.

cub [kʌb] n Junge(s) nt; (young Boy Scout) Wölfling m.

cubbyhole ['kʌbɪhəʊl] n Eckchen nt.

cube [kju:b] n Würfel m; (Math) Kubikzahl f.

cubic ['kju:bɪk] a würfelförmig; centimetre etc Kubik-.

cubicle ['kju:bɪkl] n Kabine f.

cubism ['kju:bɪzəm] n Kubismus m.

cuckoo ['kuku:] n Kuckuck m; ~ clock Kuckucksuhr f.

cucumber ['kju:kʌmbəʳ] n Gurke f.

cuddle ['kʌdl] vti herzen, drücken (col); n enge Umarmung f.

cuddly ['kʌdlɪ] a anschmiegsam; teddy zum Drücken.

cudgel ['kʌdʒəl] n Knüppel m.

cue [kju:] n Wink m; (Theat) Stichwort nt; Billardstock m.

cuff [kʌf] n (of shirt, coat etc) Manschette f; Aufschlag m; (US) = **turn-up**; ~link Manschettenknopf m.

cuisine [kwɪ'zi:n] n Kochkunst f, Küche f.

cul-de-sac ['kʌldəsæk] n Sackgasse f.

culinary ['kʌlɪnərɪ] a Koch-.

culminate ['kʌlmɪneɪt] vi gipfeln.

culmination [kʌlmɪ'neɪʃən] n Höhepunkt m.

culpable ['kʌlpəbl] a strafbar, schuldhaft.

culprit ['kʌlprɪt] n Täter m.

cult [kʌlt] n Kult m.

cultivate ['kʌltɪveɪt] vt (Agr) bebauen; mind bilden; ~d a (Agr) bebaut; (cultured) kultiviert.

cultivation [kʌltɪ'veɪʃən] n (Agr) Bebauung f; (of person) Bildung f.

cultural ['kʌltʃərəl] a kulturell, Kultur-.

culture ['kʌltʃəʳ] n (refinement) Kultur f, Bildung f; (of community) Kultur f; ~d a gebildet, kultiviert.

cumbersome ['kʌmbəsəm] a task beschwerlich; object schwer zu handhaben.

cummberbund ['kʌmbəbʌnd] n Kummerbund m.

cumulative ['kju:mjulətɪv] a gehäuft; **to be ~** sich häufen.

cunning ['kʌnɪŋ] n Verschlagenheit f; a schlau.

cup [kʌp] n Tasse f; (prize) Pokal m; **~board** ['kʌbəd] Schrank m; **~ final** Meisterschaftsspiel nt; **~ful** Tasse(voll) f.

cupola ['kju:pələ] n Kuppel f.

curable ['kjuərəbl] a heilbar.

curator [kjuˈreɪtə*] n Kustos m.

curb [kɜ:b] vt zügeln; n Zaum m; (on spending etc) Einschränkung f.

cure [kjuə*] n Heilmittel nt; (process) Heilverfahren nt; **there's no ~ for ...** es gibt kein Mittel gegen ...; vt heilen.

curfew ['kɜ:fju:] n Ausgangssperre f, Sperrstunde f.

curiosity [kjuərɪ'ɒsɪtɪ] n Neugier f; (for knowledge) Wißbegierde f; (object) Merkwürdigkeit f.

curious ['kjuərɪəs] a neugierig; (strange) seltsam; **~ly** ad besonders.

curl [kɜ:l] n Locke f; vti locken; **~er** Lockenwickler m.

curlew ['kɜ:lju:] n Brachvogel m.

curly ['kɜ:lɪ] a lockig.

currant ['kʌrənt] n Korinthe f; Johannisbeere f.

currency ['kʌrənsɪ] n Währung f; (of ideas) Geläufigkeit f.

current ['kʌrənt] n Strömung f; a expression gängig, üblich; issue neueste; **~ account** Girokonto nt; **~ affairs** pl Zeitgeschehen nt; **~ly** ad zur Zeit.

curriculum [kə'rɪkjuləm] n Lehrplan m; **~ vitae** Lebenslauf m.

curry ['kʌrɪ] n Currygericht nt; **~ powder** Curry(pulver) nt.

curse [kɜ:s] vi (swear) fluchen (at auf +acc); vt (insult) verwünschen; n Fluch m.

cursory ['kɜ:sərɪ] a flüchtig.

curt [kɜ:t] a schroff.

curtail [kɜ:'teɪl] vt abkürzen; rights einschränken.

curtain ['kɜ:tn] n Vorhang m, Gardine f; (Theat) Vorhang m.

curtsy ['kɜ:tsɪ] n Knicks m; vi knicksen.

cushion ['kuʃən] n Kissen nt; vt polstern.

custard ['kʌstəd] n Vanillesoße f.

custodian [kʌs'təudɪən] n Kustos m, Verwalter(in f) m.

custody ['kʌstədɪ] n Aufsicht f; (police) Polizeigewahrsam m.

custom ['kʌstəm] n (tradition) Brauch m; (business dealing) Kundschaft f; **~s** (taxes) Einfuhrzoll m; **C~s** Zollamt nt; **~ary** a üblich; **~er** Kunde m, Kundin f; **~-made** a speziell angefertigt; **C~s officer** Zollbeamte(r) mf.

cut [kʌt] vt irreg schneiden; wages kürzen; prices heruntersetzen; **I ~ my hand** ich habe mir in die Hand geschnitten; n Schnitt m; (wound) Schnittwunde f; (in book, income etc) Kürzung f; (share) Anteil m.

cute [kju:t] a reizend, niedlich.

cuticle ['kju:tɪkl] n (on nail) Nagelhaut f.

cutlery ['kʌtlərɪ] n Besteck nt.

cutlet ['kʌtlɪt] n (pork) Kotelett nt; (veal) Schnitzel nt.

cutout ['kʌtaut] n (Elec) Sicherung f.

cut-price ['kʌtpraɪs] a verbilligt.

cutting ['kʌtɪŋ] a schneidend; n (from paper) Ausschnitt m.

cyanide ['saɪənaɪd] n Zyankali nt.

cybernetics [saɪbə'netɪks] n Kybernetik f.

cyclamen ['sɪkləmən] n Alpenveilchen nt.

cycle ['saɪkl] n Fahrrad nt; (series) Reihe f; (of songs) Zyklus m; vi radfahren.

cycling ['saɪklɪŋ] n Radfahren nt; (Sport) Radsport m.

cyclist ['saɪklɪst] n Radfahrer(in f) m.

cyclone ['saɪkləun] n Zyklon m.

cygnet ['sɪgnɪt] n junge(r) Schwan m.

cylinder ['sɪlɪndə*] n Zylinder m; (Tech) Walze f; **~ block** Zylinderblock m; **~ capacity** Zylindervolumen nt, Zylinderinhalt m; **~ head** Zylinderkopf m.

cymbals ['sɪmbəlz] npl Becken nt.

cynic ['sɪnɪk] n Zyniker(in f) m; **~al** a zynisch; **~ism** Zynismus m.

cypress ['saɪprɪs] n Zypresse f.

cyst [sɪst] n Zyste f.

czar [zɑ:*] n Zar m; **~ina** [zɑ:'ri:nə] Zarin f.

D

D, d [di:] n D nt, d nt.

dab [dæb] vt wound, paint betupfen; n (little bit) bißchen nt; (of paint) Tupfer m; (smear) Klecks m.

dabble ['dæbl] vi (splash) plätschern; (fig) **to ~ in sth** in etw (dat) machen.

dachshund ['dækshund] n Dackel m.

dad(dy) [dæd, -ɪ] n Papa m, Vati m; **daddy-long-legs** Weberknecht m.

daffodil ['dæfədɪl] n Osterglocke f.

daft [dɑ:ft] a (col) blöd(e), doof.

dagger ['dægə*] n Dolch m.

dahlia ['deɪlɪə] n Dahlie f.

daily ['deɪlɪ] a täglich; n (Press) Tageszeitung f; (woman) Haushaltshilfe f.

dainty ['deɪntɪ] a zierlich; (attractive) reizend.

dairy ['dɛərɪ] n (shop) Milchgeschäft nt; (on farm) Molkerei f; a Milch-.

daisy ['deɪzɪ] n Gänseblümchen nt.

dally ['dælɪ] vi tändeln.

dam [dæm] n (Stau)damm m; vt stauen.

damage ['dæmɪdʒ] n Schaden m; vt beschädigen; **~s** (Jur) Schaden(s)ersatz m.

dame [deɪm] n Dame f; (col) Weibsbild nt.

damn [dæm] vt verdammen, verwünschen; a (col) verdammt; **~ it!** verflucht!; **~ing** a vernichtend.

damp [dæmp] a feucht; n Feuchtigkeit f; vt (also **~en**) befeuchten; (discourage) dämpfen; **~ness** Feuchtigkeit f.

damson ['dæmzən] n Damaszenerpflaume f.

dance [dɑ:ns] n Tanz m; (party) Tanz(abend) m; vi tanzen; **~ hall** Tanzlokal nt; **~r** Tänzer m.

dancing ['dɑ:nsɪŋ] n Tanzen nt.

dandelion ['dændɪlaɪən] n Löwenzahn m.

dandruff ['dændrəf] n (Kopf)schuppen pl.

dandy ['dændɪ] n Dandy m.

danger ['deɪndʒə°] n Gefahr f; ~! (sign) Achtung!; **in ~** in Gefahr; **on the ~-list** in Lebensgefahr; ~**ous** a, ~**ously** ad gefährlich.

dangle ['dæŋgl] vi baumeln; vt herabhängen lassen.

dapper ['dæpə°] a elegant.

dare [dɛə°] vt herausfordern; vi: ~ (to) do sth es wagen, etw zu tun; **I ~ say** ich würde sagen.

daring ['dɛərɪŋ] a (audacious) verwegen; (bold) wagemutig; dress gewagt; n Mut m.

dark [dɑːk] a dunkel; (fig) düster, trübe; (deep colour) dunkel-; n Dunkelheit f; **after ~** nach Anbruch der Dunkelheit; **D~ Ages** (finsteres) Mittelalter nt; ~**en** vti verdunkeln; ~**ness** Finsternis nt; ~**room** Dunkelkammer f.

darling ['dɑːlɪŋ] n Liebling m; a lieb.

darn [dɑːn] n Gestopfte(s) nt; vt stopfen.

dart [dɑːt] n (leap) Satz m; (weapon) Pfeil m; vi sausen; ~**s** (game) Pfeilwerfen nt; ~**board** Zielscheibe f.

dash [dæʃ] n Sprung m; (mark) (Gedanken)strich m; vt (lit) schmeißen; vi stürzen; ~**board** Armaturenbrett nt; ~**ing** a schneidig.

data ['deɪtə] npl Einzelheiten pl, Daten pl; ~ **processing** Datenverarbeitung f.

date [deɪt] n Datum nt; (for meeting etc) Termin m; (with person) Verabredung f; (fruit) Dattel f; vt letter etc datieren; person gehen mit; ~**d** a altmodisch; ~-**line** Datumsgrenze f.

dative ['deɪtɪv] n Dativ m; a Dativ-.

daub [dɔːb] vt beschmieren; paint schmieren.

daughter ['dɔːtə°] n Tochter f; ~-**in-law** Schwiegertochter f.

daunt [dɔːnt] vt entmutigen.

davenport ['dævnpɔːt] n Sekretär m; (US: sofa) Sofa nt.

dawdle ['dɔːdl] vi trödeln.

dawn [dɔːn] n Morgendämmerung f; vi dämmern; (fig) dämmern (on dat).

day [deɪ] n Tag m; (daylight) Tageslicht nt; ~ **by** ~ Tag für Tag, täglich; **one** ~ eines Tages; ~**break** Tagesanbruch m; ~**dream** n Wachtraum m, Träumerei f; vi irreg (mit offenen Augen) träumen; ~**light** Tageslicht nt; ~**time** Tageszeit f.

daze [deɪz] vt betäuben; n Betäubung f; ~**d** a benommen.

dazzle ['dæzl] vt blenden; n Blenden nt.

deacon ['diːkən] n Diakon m; Kirchenvorsteher m.

dead [dɛd] a tot, gestorben; (without feeling) gefühllos; (without movement) leer, verlassen; ~ **centre** genau in der Mitte; ad völlig; **the** ~ pl die Toten pl; ~**en** vt pain abtöten; sound ersticken; ~ **end** Sackgasse f; ~ **heat** tote(s) Rennen nt; ~-**line** Frist(ablauf) m, Stichtag m; ~-**lock** Stillstand m; ~**ly** a tödlich; ~-**pan** a undurchdringlich.

deaf [dɛf] a taub; ~-**aid** Hörgerät nt; ~**en** vt taub machen; ~**ening** a ohrenbetäubend; ~**ness** Taubheit f; ~-**mute** Taubstumme(r) m.

deal [diːl] n Geschäft nt; vti irreg austeilen; **a great ~ of** sehr viel; to ~ **with** person behandeln; department sich befassen mit; ~**er** (Comm) Händler m; (Cards) Kartengeber m; ~**ings** pl (Fin) Geschäfte pl; (relations) Beziehungen pl, Geschäftsverkehr m.

dean [diːn] n (Protestant) Superintendent m; (Catholic) Dechant m; (Univ) Dekan m.

dear [dɪə°] a lieb; (expensive) teuer; n Liebling m; ~ **me!** du liebe Zeit!; **D~ Sir** Sehr geehrter Herr!; **D~ John** Lieber John!; ~**ly** ad love herzlich; pay teuer.

dearth [dɜːθ] n Mangel m (of an + dat).

death [dɛθ] n Tod m; (end) Ende nt; (statistic) Sterbefall m; ~-**bed** Sterbebett nt; ~ **certificate** Totenschein m; ~ **duties** (Brit) Erbschaftssteuer f; ~**ly** a totenähnlich, Toten-; ~ **penalty** Todesstrafe f; ~ **rate** Sterblichkeitsziffer f.

debar [dɪˈbɑː°] vt ausschließen.

debase [dɪˈbeɪs] vt entwerten.

debatable [dɪˈbeɪtəbl] a anfechtbar.

debate [dɪˈbeɪt] n Debatte f, Diskussion f; vt debattieren, diskutieren; (consider) überlegen.

debauched [dɪˈbɔːtʃt] a ausschweifend.

debauchery [dɪˈbɔːtʃərɪ] n Ausschweifungen pl.

debit ['dɛbɪt] n Schuldposten m; vt belasten.

debris ['dɛbriː] n Trümmer pl.

debt [dɛt] n Schuld f; to be in ~ verschuldet sein; ~**or** Schuldner m.

début ['deɪbuː] n Debüt nt.

decade ['dɛkeɪd] n Jahrzehnt nt.

decadence ['dɛkədəns] n Verfall m, Dekadenz f.

decadent ['dɛkədənt] a dekadent.

decanter [dɪˈkæntə°] n Karaffe f.

decarbonize [diːˈkɑːbənaɪz] vt entkohlen.

decay [dɪˈkeɪ] n Verfall m; vi verfallen; teeth, meat etc faulen; leaves etc verrotten.

decease [dɪˈsiːs] n Hinscheiden nt; ~**d** verstorben.

deceit [dɪˈsiːt] n Betrug m; ~**ful** a falsch.

deceive [dɪˈsiːv] vt täuschen.

decelerate [diːˈseləreɪt] vti (sich) verlangsamen, die Geschwindigkeit verringern.

December [dɪˈsembə°] n Dezember m.

decency ['diːsənsɪ] n Anstand m.

decent [diːsənt] a (respectable) anständig; (pleasant) annehmbar.

decentralization [diːsentrəlaɪˈzeɪʃən] n Dezentralisierung f.

deception [dɪˈsepʃən] n Betrug m.

deceptive [dɪˈseptɪv] a täuschend, irreführend.

decibel ['desɪbel] n Dezibel nt.

decide [dɪˈsaɪd] vt entscheiden; vi sich entscheiden; to ~ **on sth** etw beschließen; ~**d** a bestimmt, entschieden; ~**dly** ad entschieden.

deciduous [dɪˈsɪdjʊəs] a jedes Jahr abfallend, Laub-.

decimal ['desɪməl] a dezimal; n Dezimalzahl f; ~ **point** Komma nt (eines

Dezimalbruches); ~ **system** Dezimalsystem nt.

decimate ['desɪmeɪt] vt dezimieren.

decipher [dɪ'saɪfə*] vt entziffern.

decision [dɪ'sɪʒən] n Entscheidung f, Entschluß m.

decisive [dɪ'saɪsɪv] a entscheidend, ausschlaggebend.

deck [dek] n (Naut) Deck nt; (of cards) Pack m; ~**chair** Liegestuhl m; ~**hand** Matrose m.

declaration [deklə'reɪʃən] n Erklärung f.

declare [dɪ'klɛə*] vt (state) behaupten; war erklären; (Customs) verzollen.

decline [dɪ'klaɪn] n (decay) Verfall m; (lessening) Rückgang m, Niedergang m; vt invitation ausschlagen, ablehnen; vi (of strength) nachlassen; (say no) ablehnen.

declutch ['diː'klʌtʃ] vi auskuppeln.

decode ['diː'kəʊd] vt entschlüsseln.

decompose [diːkəm'pəʊz] vi (sich) zersetzen.

decomposition [diːkɔmpə'zɪʃən] n Zersetzung f.

decontaminate [diːkən'tæmɪneɪt] vt entgiften.

décor ['deɪkɔː*] n Ausstattung f.

decorate ['dekəreɪt] vt room tapezieren; streichen; (adorn) (aus)schmücken; cake verzieren; (honour) auszeichnen.

decoration [dekə'reɪʃən] n (of house) (Wand)dekoration f; (medal) Orden m.

decorative [dekərətɪv] a dekorativ, Schmuck-.

decorator ['dekəreɪtə*] n Maler m, Anstreicher m.

decorum [dɪ'kɔːrəm] n Anstand m.

decoy ['diːkɔɪ] n (lit, fig) Lockvogel m.

decrease [diː'kriːs] n Abnahme f; vt vermindern; vi abnehmen.

decree [dɪ'kriː] n Verfügung f, Erlaß m.

decrepit [dɪ'krepɪt] a hinfällig.

dedicate ['dedɪkeɪt] vt (to God) weihen; book widmen.

dedication [dedɪ'keɪʃən] n (devotion) Ergebenheit f.

deduce [dɪ'djuːs] vt ableiten, schließen (from aus).

deduct [dɪ'dʌkt] vt abziehen; ~**ion** [dɪ'dʌkʃən] (of money) Abzug m; (conclusion) (Schluß)folgerung f.

deed [diːd] n Tat f; (document) Urkunde f.

deep [diːp] a tief; ~**en** vt vertiefen; ~**freeze** Tiefkühlung f; ~**seated** a tiefsitzend; ~**set** a tiefliegend.

deer [dɪə*] n Reh nt; (with antlers) Hirsch m.

deface [dɪ'feɪs] vt entstellen.

defamation [defə'meɪʃən] n Verleumdung f.

default [dɪ'fɔːlt] n Versäumnis nt; vi versäumen; **by** ~ durch Nichterscheinen nt; ~**er** Schuldner m, Zahlungsunfähige(r) m.

defeat [dɪ'fiːt] n (overthrow) Vernichtung f; (battle) Niederlage f; vt schlagen, zu Fall bringen; ~**ist** a defätistisch.

defect ['diːfekt] n Defekt m, Fehler m; [dɪ'fekt] vi überlaufen; ~**ive** [dɪ'fektɪv] a fehlerhaft, schadhaft.

defence [dɪ'fens] n (Mil, Sport) Verteidigung f; (excuse) Rechtfertigung f; ~**less** a wehrlos.

defend [dɪ'fend] vt verteidigen; ~**ant** Angeklagte(r) m; ~**er** Verteidiger m.

defensive [dɪ'fensɪv] a defensiv, Schutz-.

defer [dɪ'fɜː*] vt verschieben; ~**ence** ['defərəns] Hochachtung f, Rücksichtnahme f; ~**ential** [defə'renʃəl] a ehrerbietig.

defiance [dɪ'faɪəns] n Trotz m, Unnachgiebigkeit f; **in** ~ **of the order** dem Befehl zum Trotz.

defiant [dɪ'faɪənt] a trotzig, unnachgiebig.

deficiency [dɪ'fɪʃənsɪ] n Unzulänglichkeit f, Mangel m.

deficient [dɪ'fɪʃənt] a unzureichend.

deficit ['defɪsɪt] n Defizit nt, Fehlbetrag m.

defile [dɪ'faɪl] vt beschmutzen; n ['dɪ:faɪl] Schlucht f.

define [dɪ'faɪn] vt bestimmen; (explain) definieren.

definite ['defɪnɪt] a bestimmt; (clear) klar, eindeutig; ~**ly** ad bestimmt.

definition [defɪ'nɪʃən] n Definition f; (Phot) Schärfe f.

definitive [dɪ'fɪnɪtɪv] a definitiv, endgültig.

deflate [diː'fleɪt] vt die Luft ablassen aus.

deflation [diː'fleɪʃən] n (Fin) Deflation f.

deflect [dɪ'flekt] vt ablenken.

deform [dɪ'fɔːm] vt deformieren, entstellen; ~**ed** a deformiert; ~**ity** Verunstaltung f, Mißbildung f.

defraud [dɪ'frɔːd] vt betrügen.

defray [dɪ'freɪ] vt bestreiten.

defrost [diː'frɔst] vt fridge abtauen; food auftauen.

deft [deft] a geschickt.

defunct [dɪ'fʌŋkt] a verstorben.

defy [dɪ'faɪ] vt (challenge) sich widersetzen (+dat); (resist) trotzen (+dat), sich stellen gegen.

degenerate [dɪ'dʒenəreɪt] vi degenerieren; [dɪ'dʒenərɪt] a degeneriert.

degradation [degrə'deɪʃən] n Erniedrigung f.

degrading [dɪ'greɪdɪŋ] a erniedrigend.

degree [dɪ'griː] n Grad m; (Univ) akademische(r) Grad m; **by** ~**s** allmählich; **to take one's** ~ sein Examen machen.

dehydrated [diːhaɪ'dreɪtɪd] a getrocknet, Trocken-.

de-ice [diː'aɪs] vt enteisen, auftauen.

deign [deɪn] vi sich herablassen.

deity ['diːɪtɪ] n Gottheit f.

dejected [dɪ'dʒektɪd] niedergeschlagen.

dejection [dɪ'dʒekʃən] n Niedergeschlagenheit f.

delay [dɪ'leɪ] vt (hold back) aufschieben; **the flight was** ~**ed** die Maschine hatte Verspätung; vi (linger) sich aufhalten, zögern; n Aufschub m, Verzögerung f; **without** ~ unverzüglich; ~**ed** a action verzögert.

delegate ['delɪgɪt] n Delegierte(r) mf, Abgeordnete(r) mf; ['delɪgeɪt] vt delegieren.

delegation [deli'geiʃən] n Abordnung f; (foreign) Delegation f.

delete [di'li:t] vt (aus)streichen.

deliberate [di'libərit] a (intentional) bewußt, überlegt; (slow) bedächtig; [di'libəreit] vi (consider) überlegen; (debate) sich beraten; ~ly ad vorsätzlich.

deliberation [dilibə'reiʃən] n Überlegung f, Beratung f.

delicacy ['delikəsi] n Zartheit f; (weakness) Anfälligkeit f; (tact) Zartgefühl nt; (food) Delikatesse f.

delicate ['delikit] a (fine) fein; (fragile) zart; (situation) heikel; (Med) empfindlich; ~ly ad bedenklich.

delicatessen [delikə'tesn] n Feinkostgeschäft nt.

delicious [di'liʃəs] a köstlich, lecker, delikat.

delight [di'lait] n Wonne f; vt entzücken; ~ful a entzückend, herrlich.

delinquency [di'liŋkwənsi] n Straffälligkeit f, Delinquenz f.

delinquent [di'liŋkwənt] n Straffällige(r) mf; a straffällig.

delirious [di'liriəs] a irre, im Fieberwahn.

delirium [di'liriəm] n Fieberwahn m, Delirium nt.

deliver [di'livə*] vt goods (ab)liefern; letter bringen, zustellen; verdict aussprechen; speech halten; ~y (Ab)lieferung f; (of letter) Zustellung f; (of speech) Vortragsweise f; ~y van Lieferwagen m.

delouse [di:'laus] vt entlausen.

delta ['deltə] n Delta nt.

delude [di'lu:d] vt täuschen.

deluge ['delju:dʒ] n Überschwemmung f; (fig) Flut f; vt (fig) überfluten.

delusion [di'lu:ʒən] n (Selbst)täuschung f.

de luxe [di'lʌks] a Luxus-.

demand [di'ma:nd] vt verlangen; n (request) Verlangen nt; (Comm) Nachfrage f; in ~ begehrt, gesucht; on ~ auf Verlangen; ~ing a anspruchsvoll.

demarcation [di:ma:'keiʃən] n Abgrenzung f.

demeanour [di'mi:nə*] n Benehmen nt.

demented [di'mentid] a wahnsinnig.

demi- ['demi] pref halb-.

demise [di'maiz] n Ableben nt.

demobilization [di:məubilai'zeiʃən] n Demobilisierung f.

democracy [di'mokrəsi] n Demokratie f.

democrat ['deməkræt] n Demokrat m; ~ic a, ~ically ad [demə'krætik, -li] demokratisch.

demolish [di'moliʃ] vt (lit) abreißen; (destroy) zerstören; (fig) vernichten.

demolition [demə'liʃən] n Abbruch m.

demon ['di:mən] n Dämon m.

demonstrate ['demənstreit] vti demonstrieren.

demonstration [demən'streiʃən] n Demonstration f; (proof) Beweisführung f.

demonstrative [di'monstrətiv] a demonstrativ.

demonstrator ['demənstreitə*] n (Pol) Demonstrant(in f) m.

demoralize [di'morəlaiz] vt demoralisieren.

demote [di'məut] vt degradieren.

demure [di'mjuə*] a ernst.

den [den] n (of animal) Höhle f, Bau m; Bude f; ~ of vice Lasterhöhle f.

denationalize [di:'næʃnəlaiz] vt reprivatisieren.

denial [di'naiəl] n Leugnung f; official ~ Dementi nt.

denigrate ['denigreit] vt verunglimpfen.

denim ['denim] a Denim-; ~s pl Denim-Jeans.

denomination [dinomi'neiʃən] n (Eccl) Bekenntnis nt; (type) Klasse f; (Fin) Wert m.

denominator [di'nomineitə*] n Nenner; common ~ gemeinsame(r) Nenner m.

denote [di'nəut] vt bedeuten.

denounce [di'nauns] vt brandmarken.

dense [dens] a dicht, dick; (stupid) schwer von Begriff; ~ly ad dicht.

density ['densiti] n Dichte f.

dent [dent] n Delle f; vt einbeulen.

dental ['dentl] a Zahn-; ~ surgeon = dentist.

dentifrice ['dentifris] n Zahnputzmittel nt.

dentist ['dentist] n Zahnarzt m /-ärztin f; ~ry Zahnmedizin f.

denture ['dentʃə*] n künstliche(s) Gebiß nt.

denude [di'nju:d] vt entblößen.

deny [di'nai] vt leugnen; rumour widersprechen (+dat); knowledge verleugnen; help abschlagen; to ~ o.s. sth sich etw versagen.

deodorant [di:'əudərənt] n Desodorans nt.

depart [di'pa:t] vi abfahren.

department [di'pa:tmənt] n (Comm) Abteilung f, Sparte f; (Univ, Sch) Fachbereich m; (Pol) Ministerium nt, Ressort nt; ~al [di:pa:t'mentl] a Fach-; ~ store Warenhaus nt.

departure [di'pa:tʃə*] n (of person) Weggang m; (on journey) Abreise f; (of train) Abfahrt f; (of plane) Abflug m; new ~ Neuerung f.

depend [di'pend] vi: it ~s es kommt darauf an; ~ on vt abhängen von; parents etc angewiesen sein auf (+acc); ~able a zuverlässig; ~ence Abhängigkeit f; ~ent n (person) Familienangehörige(r) mf; a bedingt (on durch).

depict [di'pikt] vt schildern.

depleted [di'pli:tid] a aufgebraucht.

deplorable [di'plo:rəbl] a bedauerlich.

deplore [di'plo:*] vt mißbilligen.

deploy [di'ploi] vt einsetzen.

depopulation ['di:popju'leiʃən] n Entvölkerung f.

deport [di'po:t] vt deportieren; ~ation [di:po:'teiʃən] Abschiebung f; ~ation order Ausweisung f; ~ment Betragen nt.

depose [di'pəuz] vt absetzen.

deposit [di'pozit] n (in bank) Guthaben nt; (down payment) Anzahlung f; (security) Kaution f; (Chem) Niederschlag m; vt (in bank) deponieren; (put down) niederlegen;

~ **account** Sparkonto *nt*; ~**or** Kontoinhaber *m*.

depot ['depəʊ] *n* Depot *nt*.

deprave [dɪ'preɪv] *vt* (moralisch) verderben; ~**d** a verworfen.

depravity [dɪ'prævɪtɪ] *n* Verworfenheit *f*.

deprecate ['deprɪkeɪt] *vt* mißbilligen.

depreciate [dɪ'priːʃɪeɪt] *vi* im Wert sinken.

depreciation [dɪpriːʃɪ'eɪʃən] *n* Wertminderung *f*.

depress [dɪ'pres] *vt* (*press down*) niederdrücken; (*in mood*) deprimieren; ~**ed** a person niedergeschlagen, deprimiert; ~**ed area** Notstandsgebiet *nt*; ~**ing** a deprimierend; ~**ion** [dɪ'preʃən] (*mood*) Depression *f*; (*in trade*) Wirtschaftskrise *f*; (*hollow*) Vertiefung *f*; (*Met*) Tief(druckgebiet) *nt*.

deprivation [deprɪ'veɪʃən] *n* Entbehrung *f*, Not *f*.

deprive [dɪ'praɪv] *vt* berauben (*of* +*gen*); ~**d** a child sozial benachteiligt; area unterentwickelt.

depth [depθ] *n* Tiefe *f*; **in the** ~**s of despair** in tiefster Verzweiflung; **to be out of one's** ~ den Boden unter den Füßen verloren haben; ~ **charge** Wasserbombe *f*.

deputation [depjʊ'teɪʃən] *n* Abordnung *f*.

deputize ['depjʊtaɪz] *vi* vertreten (*for* +*acc*).

deputy ['depjʊtɪ] a stellvertretend; (*Stell*)vertreter *m*.

derail [dɪ'reɪl] *vt* entgleisen lassen; **to be** ~**ed** entgleisen; ~**ment** Entgleisung *f*.

deranged [dɪ'reɪndʒd] a irr, verrückt.

derby ['dɑːbɪ] *n* (*US*) Melone *f*.

derelict ['derɪlɪkt] a verlassen; building baufällig.

deride [dɪ'raɪd] *vt* auslachen.

derision [dɪ'rɪʒən] *n* Hohn *m*, Spott *m*.

derisory [dɪ'raɪsərɪ] a spöttisch.

derivation [derɪ'veɪʃən] *n* Ableitung *f*.

derivative [dɪ'rɪvətɪv] *n* Abgeleitete(s) *nt*; a abgeleitet.

derive [dɪ'raɪv] *vt* (*get*) gewinnen; (*deduce*) ableiten; *vi* (*come from*) abstammen.

dermatitis [dɜːmə'taɪtɪs] *n* Hautentzündung *f*.

derogatory [dɪ'rɒgətərɪ] a geringschätzig.

derrick ['derɪk] *n* Drehkran *m*.

desalination [diːsælɪ'neɪʃən] *n* Entsalzung *f*.

descend [dɪ'send] *vti* hinuntersteigen; **to** ~ **from** abstammen von; ~**ant** Nachkomme *m*.

descent [dɪ'sent] *n* (*coming down*) Abstieg *m*; (*origin*) Abstammung *f*.

describe [dɪs'kraɪb] *vt* beschreiben.

description [dɪs'krɪpʃən] *n* Beschreibung *f*; (*sort*) Art *f*.

descriptive [dɪs'krɪptɪv] a beschreibend; word anschaulich.

desecrate ['desɪkreɪt] *vt* schänden.

desegregation [diːsegrə'geɪʃən] *n* Aufhebung *f* der Rassentrennung.

desert[1] ['dezət] *n* Wüste *f*.

desert[2] [dɪ'zɜːt] *vt* verlassen; (*temporarily*) im Stich lassen; *vi* (*Mil*) desertieren; ~**er** Deserteur *m*; ~**ion** [dɪ'zɜːʃən] (*of wife*) böswillige(s) Verlassen *nt*; (*Mil*) Fahnenflucht *f*.

deserve [dɪ'zɜːv] *vt* verdienen.

deserving [dɪ'zɜːvɪŋ] a person würdig; action verdienstvoll.

design [dɪ'zaɪn] *n* (*plan*) Entwurf *m*; (*drawing*) Zeichnung *f*; (*planning*) Gestaltung *f*, Design *nt*; *vt* entwerfen; (*intend*) bezwecken; **to have** ~**s on sb/sth** es auf jdn/etw abgesehen haben.

designate ['dezɪgneɪt] *vt* bestimmen; ['dezɪgnɪt] a designiert.

designation [dezɪg'neɪʃən] *n* Bezeichnung *f*.

designer [dɪ'zaɪnə*] *n* Designer *m*; (*Theat*) Bühnenbildner(in *f*) *m*.

desirability [dɪzaɪərə'bɪlɪtɪ] *n* Erwünschtheit *f*.

desirable [dɪ'zaɪərəbl] *n* wünschenswert; woman begehrenswert.

desire [dɪ'zaɪə*] *n* Wunsch *m*, Verlangen *nt*; *vt* (*lust*) begehren, wünschen; (*ask for*) verlangen, wollen.

desirous [dɪ'zaɪərəs] a begierig (*of* auf +*acc*).

desist [dɪ'zɪst] *vi* Abstand nehmen, aufhören.

desk [desk] *n* Schreibtisch *m*.

desolate ['desəlɪt] a öde; (*sad*) trostlos.

desolation [desə'leɪʃən] *n* Trostlosigkeit *f*.

despair [dɪs'pɛə*] *n* Verzweiflung *f*; *vi* verzweifeln (*of an* +*dat*).

despatch [dɪs'pætʃ] = **dispatch**.

desperate ['despərɪt] a verzweifelt; situation hoffnungslos; **to be** ~ **for sth** etw unbedingt brauchen; ~**ly** ad verzweifelt.

desperation [despə'reɪʃən] *n* Verzweiflung *f*.

despicable [dɪs'pɪkəbl] a abscheulich.

despise [dɪs'paɪz] *vt* verachten.

despite [dɪs'paɪt] prep trotz (+*gen*).

despondent [dɪs'pɒndənt] a mutlos.

dessert [dɪ'zɜːt] *n* Nachtisch *m*; ~**spoon** Dessertlöffel *m*.

destination [destɪ'neɪʃən] *n* (*of person*) (Reise)ziel *nt*; (*of goods*) Bestimmungsort *m*.

destine ['destɪn] *vt* (*set apart*) bestimmen.

destiny ['destɪnɪ] *n* Schicksal *nt*.

destitute ['destɪtjuːt] a notleidend.

destitution [destɪtjuː'ʃən] *n* Elend *f*.

destroy [dɪs'trɔɪ] *vt* zerstören; ~**er** (*Naut*) Zerstörer *m*.

destruction [dɪs'trʌkʃən] *n* Zerstörung *f*.

destructive [dɪs'trʌktɪv] a zerstörend.

detach [dɪ'tætʃ] *vt* loslösen; ~**able** a abtrennbar; ~**ed** a attitude distanziert, objektiv; house Einzel-; ~**ment** (*Mil*) Abteilung *f*, Sonderkommando *nt*; (*fig*) Abstand *m*, Unvoreingenommenheit *f*.

detail ['diːteɪl] *n* Einzelheit *f*, Detail *nt*; (*minor part*) unwichtige Einzelheit *f*; *vt* (*relate*) ausführlich berichten; (*appoint*) abkommandieren; **in** ~ ausführlichst, bis ins kleinste.

detain [dɪ'teɪn] vt aufhalten; (imprison) in Haft halten.

detect [dɪ'tekt] vt entdecken; ~ion [dɪ'tekʃən] Aufdeckung f; ~ive Detektiv m; ~ive story Krimi(nalgeschichte f) m; ~or Detektor m.

détente ['deɪtɑ:nt] n Entspannung f.

detention [dɪ'tenʃən] n Haft f; (Sch) Nachsitzen nt.

deter [dɪ'tɜ:*] vt abschrecken.

detergent [dɪ'tɜ:dʒənt] n Waschmittel nt; Reinigungsmittel nt.

deteriorate [dɪ'tɪərɪəreɪt] vi sich verschlechtern.

deterioration [dɪtɪərɪə'reɪʃən] n Verschlechterung f.

determination [dɪtɜ:mɪ'neɪʃən] n Entschlossenheit f.

determine [dɪ'tɜ:mɪn] vt bestimmen; ~d a entschlossen.

deterrent [dɪ'terənt] n Abschreckungsmittel nt; a abschreckend.

detest [dɪ'test] vt verabscheuen; ~able a abscheulich.

dethrone [di:'θrəʊn] vt entthronen.

detonate ['detəneɪt] vt detonieren.

detonator ['detəneɪtə*] n Sprengkapsel f.

detour ['deɪtʊə*] n Umweg m; (on road sign) Umleitung f.

detract [dɪ'trækt] vi schmälern (from acc).

detriment ['detrɪmənt] n: to the ~ of zum Schaden (+gen); ~al [detrɪ'mentl] a schädlich.

deuce [dju:s] n (tennis) Einstand m.

devaluation [dɪvælju'eɪʃən] n Abwertung f.

devalue ['di:'vælju:] vt abwerten.

devastate ['devəsteɪt] vt verwüsten.

devastating ['devəsteɪtɪŋ] a verheerend.

develop [dɪ'veləp] vt entwickeln; resources erschließen; vi sich entwickeln; ~er (Phot) Entwickler m; (of land) Bauunternehmer m; ~ing a country Entwicklungs-; ~ment Entwicklung f.

deviant ['di:vɪənt] a abweichend; n Abweichler m.

deviate ['di:vɪeɪt] vi abweichen.

deviation [di:vɪ'eɪʃən] n Abweichung f.

device [dɪ'vaɪs] n Vorrichtung f, Gerät nt.

devil ['devl] n Teufel m; ~ish a teuflisch.

devious ['di:vɪəs] a route gewunden; means krumm; person verschlagen.

devise [dɪ'vaɪz] vt entwickeln.

devoid [dɪ'vɔɪd] a: ~ of ohne, bar (+gen).

devolution [di:və'lu:ʃən] n Dezentralisierung f.

devote [dɪ'vəʊt] vt widmen (to dat); ~d a ergeben; ~e [devəʊ'ti:] Anhänger(in f) m, Verehrer(in f) m.

devotion [dɪ'vəʊʃən] n (piety) Andacht f; (loyalty) Ergebenheit f, Hingabe f.

devour [dɪ'vaʊə*] vt verschlingen.

devout [dɪ'vaʊt] a andächtig.

dew [dju:] n Tau m.

dexterity [deks'terɪtɪ] n Geschicklichkeit f.

diabetes [daɪə'bi:ti:z] n Zuckerkrankheit f.

diabetic [daɪə'betɪk] a zuckerkrank; n Diabetiker m.

diagnose ['daɪəgnəʊz] vt (Med) diagnostizieren; feststellen.

diagnosis [daɪəg'nəʊsɪs] n Diagnose f.

diagonal [daɪ'ægənl] a diagonal, schräg; n Diagonale f.

diagram ['daɪəgræm] n Diagramm nt, Schaubild nt.

dial ['daɪəl] n (Tel) Wählscheibe f; (of clock) Zifferblatt nt; vt wählen; ~ling tone Amtszeichen nt.

dialect ['daɪəlekt] n Dialekt m.

dialogue ['daɪəlɒg] n Gespräch nt; (Liter) Dialog m.

diameter [daɪ'æmɪtə*] n Durchmesser m.

diametrically [daɪə'metrɪkəl] ad: ~ opposed to genau entgegengesetzt (+dat).

diamond ['daɪəmənd] n Diamant m; (Cards) Karo nt.

diaper ['daɪəpə*] n (US) Windel f.

diaphragm ['daɪəfræm] n Zwerchfell nt.

diarrhoea [daɪə'rɪ:ə] n Durchfall m.

diary ['daɪərɪ] n Taschenkalender m; (account) Tagebuch nt.

dice [daɪs] n Würfel pl; vt (Cook) in Würfel schneiden.

dicey ['daɪsɪ] a (col) riskant.

dichotomy [dɪ'kɒtəmɪ] n Kluft f.

dictate [dɪk'teɪt] vt diktieren; (of circumstances) gebieten; ['dɪkteɪt] n Mahnung f, Gebot nt.

dictation [dɪk'teɪʃən] n Diktat nt.

dictator [dɪk'teɪtə*] n Diktator m.

dictatorship [dɪk'teɪtəʃɪp] n Diktatur f.

diction ['dɪkʃən] n Ausdrucksweise f.

dictionary ['dɪkʃənrɪ] n Wörterbuch nt.

diddle ['dɪdl] vt (col) übers Ohr hauen.

didn't ['dɪdənt] = did not.

die [daɪ] vi sterben; (end) aufhören; ~ away vi schwächer werden; ~ down vi nachlassen; ~ out vi aussterben; (fig) nachlassen.

diesel ['di:zəl] ~ engine Dieselmotor m.

diet ['daɪət] n Nahrung f, Kost f; (special food) Diät f; (slimming) Abmagerungskur f; vi eine Abmagerungskur machen.

differ ['dɪfə*] vi sich unterscheiden; (disagree) anderer Meinung sein; we ~ wir sind unterschiedlicher Meinung; ~ence Unterschied m; (disagreement) (Meinungs)unterschied m; ~ent a verschieden; that's ~ent das ist anders; ~ential [dɪfə'renʃəl] (Aut) Differentialgetriebe nt; (in wages) Lohnstufe f; ~entiate [dɪfə'renʃɪeɪt] vti unterscheiden; ~ently ad verschieden, unterschiedlich.

difficult ['dɪfɪkəlt] a schwierig; ~y Schwierigkeit f; with ~y nur schwer.

diffidence ['dɪfɪdəns] n mangelnde(s) Selbstvertrauen nt.

diffident ['dɪfɪdənt] a schüchtern.

diffuse [dɪ'fju:s] a langatmig; [dɪ'fju:z] vt verbreiten.

dig [dɪg] vti irreg hole graben; garden (um)graben; claws senken; n (prod) Stoß m; ~ in vi (Mil) sich eingraben; (to food) sich hermachen über (+acc); in! greif zu!; ~ up vt ausgraben; (fig) aufgabeln.

digest [daɪ'dʒest] vt (lit, fig) verdauen;

['daɪdʒest] n Auslese f; ~**ible** a verdaulich; ~**ion** Verdauung f.

digit ['dɪdʒɪt] n einstellige Zahl f; (Anat) Finger m; Zehe f; ~**al** computer Einzahlencomputer m.

dignified ['dɪgnɪfaɪd] a würdevoll.

dignify ['dɪgnɪfaɪ] vt Würde verleihen (+dat).

dignitary ['dɪgnɪtərɪ] n Würdenträger m.

dignity ['dɪgnɪtɪ] n Würde f.

digress [daɪ'gres] vi abschweifen; ~**ion** [daɪ'greʃən] Abschweifung f.

digs [dɪgz] npl (Brit col) Bude f.

dilapidated [dɪ'læpɪdeɪtɪd] a baufällig.

dilate [daɪ'leɪt] vti (sich) weiten.

dilatory ['dɪlətərɪ] a hinhaltend.

dilemma [daɪ'lemə] n Dilemma nt.

dilettante [dɪlɪ'tæntɪ] n Dilettant m.

diligence ['dɪlɪdʒəns] n Fleiß m.

diligent ['dɪlɪdʒənt] a fleißig.

dill [dɪl] n Dill m.

dilly-dally ['dɪlɪdælɪ] vi (col) herumtrödeln.

dilute [daɪ'luːt] vt verdünnen; a verdünnt.

dim [dɪm] a trübe, matt; (stupid) schwer von Begriff; **to take a** ~ **view of sth** etw mißbilligen; vt verdunkeln.

dime [daɪm] n (US) Zehncentstück nt.

dimension [dɪ'menʃən] n Dimension f; ~**s** pl Maße pl.

diminish [dɪ'mɪnɪʃ] vti verringern.

diminutive [dɪ'mɪnjutɪv] a winzig; n Verkleinerungsform f.

dimly ['dɪmlɪ] ad trübe.

dimple ['dɪmpl] n Grübchen nt.

dim-witted ['dɪm'wɪtɪd] a (col) dämlich.

din [dɪn] n Getöse nt.

dine [daɪn] vi speisen; ~**r** Tischgast m; (Rail) Speisewagen m.

dinghy ['dɪŋgɪ] n kleine(s) Ruderboot nt; Dinghy nt.

dingy ['dɪndʒɪ] a armselig.

dining car ['daɪnɪŋkɑː*] n Speisewagen m.

dining room ['daɪnɪŋrʊm] n Eßzimmer nt; (in hotel) Speisezimmer nt.

dinner ['dɪnə*] n Mittagessen nt, Abendessen nt; (public) Festessen nt; ~ **jacket** Smoking m; ~ **party** Tischgesellschaft f; ~ **time** Tischzeit f.

dinosaur ['daɪnəsɔː*] n Dinosaurier m.

diocese ['daɪəsɪs] n Diözese f, Sprengel m.

dip [dɪp] n (hollow) Senkung f; (bathe) kurze(s) Bad(en) nt; vt eintauchen; (Aut) abblenden; vi (slope) sich senken, abfallen.

diphtheria [dɪf'θɪərɪə] n Diphterie f.

diphthong ['dɪfθɒŋ] n Diphthong m.

diploma [dɪ'pləʊmə] n Urkunde f, Diplom nt.

diplomat ['dɪpləmæt] n Diplomat(in f) m; ~**ic** [dɪplə'mætɪk] a diplomatisch; ~**ic corps** diplomatische(s) Korps nt.

dipstick ['dɪpstɪk] n Ölmeßstab m.

dire [daɪə*] a schrecklich.

direct [daɪ'rekt] a direkt; vt leiten; film die Regie führen (+gen); jury anweisen; (aim) richten, lenken; (tell way) den Weg erklären (+dat); (order) anweisen; ~ **current** Gleichstrom m; ~ **hit** Volltreffer m; ~**ion** [dɪ'rekʃən] Führung f,

Leitung f; (course) Richtung f; (Cine) Regie f; ~**ions** pl (for use) Gebrauchsanleitung f; (orders) Anweisungen pl; ~**ional** [dɪ'rekʃənl] a Richt-; ~**ive** Direktive f; ~**ly** ad (in straight line) gerade, direkt; (at once) unmittelbar, sofort; ~**or** Direktor m, Leiter m; (of film) Regisseur m; ~**ory** Adreßbuch nt; (Tel) Telefonbuch nt.

dirt [dɜːt] n Schmutz m, Dreck m; ~ **road** unbefestigte Straße; ~**y** a schmutzig, dreckig; gemein; vt beschmutzen; ~ **cheap** a spottbillig.

disability [dɪsə'bɪlɪtɪ] n Körperbehinderung f.

disabled [dɪs'eɪbld] a körperbehindert.

disabuse [dɪsə'bjuːz] vt befreien.

disadvantage [dɪsəd'vɑːntɪdʒ] n Nachteil m; ~**ous** [dɪsædvɑːn'teɪdʒəs] a ungünstig.

disagree [dɪsə'griː] vi nicht übereinstimmen; (quarrel) (sich) streiten; (food) nicht bekommen (with dat); ~**able** a person widerlich; task unangenehm; ~**ment** (between persons) Streit m; (between things) Widerspruch m.

disallow [dɪsə'laʊ] vt nicht zulassen.

disappear [dɪsə'pɪə*] vi verschwinden; ~**ance** Verschwinden nt.

disappoint [dɪsə'pɔɪnt] vt enttäuschen; ~**ing** a enttäuschend; ~**ment** Enttäuschung f.

disapproval [dɪsə'pruːvəl] n Mißbilligung f.

disapprove [dɪsə'pruːv] vi mißbilligen (of acc); **she** ~**s** sie mißbilligt es.

disarm [dɪs'ɑːm] vt entwaffnen; (Pol) abrüsten; ~**ament** Abrüstung f.

disaster [dɪ'zɑːstə*] n Unglück nt; Katastrophe f.

disastrous [dɪ'zɑːstrəs] a verhängnisvoll.

disband [dɪs'bænd] vt auflösen.

disbelief ['dɪsbə'liːf] n Ungläubigkeit f.

disc [dɪsk] n Scheibe f; (record) (Schall)-platte f.

discard ['dɪskɑːd] vt ablegen.

disc brake ['dɪsk breɪk] n Scheibenbremse f.

discern [dɪ'sɜːn] vt unterscheiden (können), erkennen; ~**ing** a scharfsinnig.

discharge [dɪs'tʃɑːdʒ] vt ship entladen; duties nachkommen (+dat); (dismiss) entlassen; gun abschießen; n (of ship) Entladung f; [dɪs'tʃɑːdʒ] (Med) Ausfluß m.

disciple [dɪ'saɪpl] n Jünger m.

disciplinary ['dɪsɪplɪnərɪ] a disziplinarisch.

discipline ['dɪsɪplɪn] n Disziplin f; vt (train) schulen; (punish) bestrafen.

disc jockey ['dɪsk dʒɒkɪ] n Diskjockey m.

disclaim [dɪs'kleɪm] vt nicht anerkennen; (Pol) dementieren.

disclose [dɪs'kləʊz] vt enthüllen.

disclosure [dɪs'kləʊʒə*] n Enthüllung f.

disco ['dɪskəʊ] n abbr of **discotheque**.

discoloured [dɪs'kʌləd] a verfärbt, verschossen.

discomfort [dɪs'kʌmfət] n Unbehagen nt; (embarrassment) Verlegenheit f.

disconcert [dɪskən'sɜːt] vt aus der

Fassung bringen; (*puzzle*) verstimmen.

disconnect ['dɪskə'nekt] *vt* abtrennen.

discontent ['dɪskən'tent] *n* Unzufriedenheit *f*; ~**ed** *a* unzufrieden.

discontinue ['dɪskən'tɪnjuː] *vt* einstellen; *vi* aufhören.

discord ['dɪskɔːd] *n* Zwietracht *f*; (*noise*) Dissonanz *f*; ~**ant** [dɪs'kɔːdənt] *a* uneinig; *noise* mißtönend.

discotheque ['dɪskəʊtek] *n* Diskothek *f*.

discount ['dɪskaʊnt] *n* Rabatt *m*; [dɪs'kaʊnt] *vt* außer acht lassen.

discourage [dɪs'kʌrɪdʒ] *vt* entmutigen; (*prevent*) abraten, abhalten.

discouraging [dɪs'kʌrɪdʒɪŋ] *a* entmutigend.

discourteous [dɪs'kɜːtɪəs] *a* unhöflich.

discover [dɪs'kʌvə*] *vt* entdecken; ~**y** Entdeckung *f*.

discredit [dɪs'kredɪt] *vt* in Verruf bringen.

discreet *a*, ~**ly** *ad* [dɪs'kriːt, -lɪ] taktvoll, diskret.

discrepancy [dɪs'krepənsɪ] *n* Unstimmigkeit *f*, Diskrepanz *f*.

discretion [dɪs'kreʃən] *n* Takt *m*, Diskretion *f*; (*decision*) Gutdünken *nt*; **to leave sth to sb's** ~ etw jds Gutdünken überlassen.

discriminate [dɪs'krɪmɪneɪt] *vi* unterscheiden; **to** ~ **against** diskriminieren.

discriminating [dɪs'krɪmɪneɪtɪŋ] *a* klug; *taste* anspruchsvoll.

discrimination [dɪskrɪmɪ'neɪʃən] *n* Urteilsvermögen *nt*; (*pej*) Diskriminierung *f*.

discus ['dɪskəs] *n* Diskus *m*.

discuss [dɪs'kʌs] *vt* diskutieren, besprechen; ~**ion** [dɪs'kʌʃən] Diskussion *f*, Besprechung *f*.

disdain [dɪs'deɪn] *vt* verachten, für unter seiner Würde halten; *n* Verachtung *f*; ~**ful** *a* geringschätzig.

disease [dɪ'ziːz] *n* Krankheit *f*; ~**d** *a* erkrankt.

disembark [dɪsɪm'bɑːk] *vt* aussteigen lassen; *vi* von Bord gehen.

disenchanted ['dɪsɪn'tʃɑːntɪd] *a* desillusioniert.

disengage [dɪsɪn'geɪdʒ] *vt* (*Aut*) auskuppeln.

disentangle ['dɪsɪn'tæŋgl] *vt* entwirren.

disfavour [dɪs'feɪvə*] *n* Ungunst *f*.

disfigure [dɪs'fɪgə*] *vt* entstellen.

disgrace [dɪs'greɪs] *n* Schande *f*; (*thing*) Schandfleck *m*; *vt* Schande bringen über (+*acc*); (*less strong*) blamieren; ~**ful** *a* schändlich, unerhört; **it's** ~**ful** es ist eine Schande.

disgruntled [dɪs'grʌntld] *a* verärgert.

disguise [dɪs'gaɪz] *vt* verkleiden; *feelings* verhehlen; *voice* verstellen; *n* Verkleidung *f*; **in** ~ verkleidet, maskiert.

disgust [dɪs'gʌst] *n* Abscheu *f*; *vt* anwidern; ~**ing** *a* abscheulich; (*terrible*) gemein.

dish [dɪʃ] *n* Schüssel *f*; (*food*) Gericht *nt*; ~ **up** *vt* auftischen; ~ **cloth** Spüllappen *m*.

dishearten [dɪs'hɑːtn] *vt* entmutigen.

dishevelled [dɪ'ʃevəld] *a hair* zerzaust; *clothing* ungepflegt.

dishonest [dɪs'ɒnɪst] *a* unehrlich; ~**y** Unehrlichkeit *f*.

dishonour [dɪs'ɒnə*] *n* Unehre *f*; *vt cheque* nicht einlösen; ~**able** *a* unehrenhaft.

dishwasher ['dɪʃwɒʃə*] *n* Geschirrspülmaschine *f*.

disillusion [dɪsɪ'luːʒən] *vt* enttäuschen, desillusionieren.

disinfect [dɪsɪn'fekt] *vt* desinfizieren; ~**ant** Desinfektionsmittel *nt*.

disingenuous [dɪsɪn'dʒenjʊəs] *a* unehrlich.

disinherit ['dɪsɪn'herɪt] *vt* enterben.

disintegrate [dɪs'ɪntɪgreɪt] *vi* sich auflösen.

disinterested [dɪs'ɪntrɪstɪd] *a* uneigennützig; (*col*) uninteressiert.

disjointed [dɪs'dʒɔɪntɪd] *a* unzusammenhängend.

disk [dɪsk] *n* = **disc**.

dislike [dɪs'laɪk] *n* Abneigung *f*; *vt* nicht leiden können.

dislocate ['dɪsləʊkeɪt] *vt* auskugeln; (*upset*) in Verwirrung bringen.

dislodge [dɪs'lɒdʒ] *vt* verschieben; (*Mil*) aus der Stellung werfen.

disloyal ['dɪs'lɔɪəl] *a* treulos.

dismal ['dɪzməl] *a* trostlos, trübe.

dismantle [dɪs'mæntl] *vt* demontieren.

dismay [dɪs'meɪ] *n* Bestürzung *f*; *vt* bestürzen.

dismiss [dɪs'mɪs] *vt employee* entlassen; *idea* von sich weisen; (*send away*) wegschicken; (*Jur*) *complaint* abweisen; ~**al** Entlassung *f*.

disobedience [dɪsə'biːdɪəns] *n* Ungehorsam *m*.

disobedient [dɪsə'biːdɪənt] *a* ungehorsam.

disobey ['dɪsə'beɪ] *vt* nicht gehorchen (+*dat*).

disorder [dɪs'ɔːdə*] *n* (*confusion*) Verwirrung *f*; (*commotion*) Aufruhr *m*; (*Med*) Erkrankung *f*.

disorderly [dɪs'ɔːdəlɪ] *a* (*untidy*) unordentlich; (*unruly*) ordnungswidrig.

disorganized [dɪs'ɔːgənaɪzd] *a* unordentlich.

disown [dɪs'əʊn] *vt son* verstoßen; **I** ~ **you** ich will nichts mehr mit dir zu tun haben.

disparaging [dɪs'pærɪdʒɪŋ] *a* geringschätzig.

disparity [dɪs'pærɪtɪ] *n* Verschiedenheit *f*.

dispassionate [dɪs'pæʃnɪt] *a* gelassen, unparteiisch.

dispatch [dɪs'pætʃ] *vt goods* abschicken, abfertigen; *n* Absendung *f*; (*esp Mil*) Meldung *f*.

dispel [dɪs'pel] *vt* zerstreuen.

dispensable [dɪs'pensəbl] *a* entbehrlich.

dispensary [dɪs'pensərɪ] *n* Apotheke *f*.

dispensation [dɪspen'seɪʃən] *n* (*Eccl*) Befreiung *f*.

dispense [dɪs'pens] ~ **with** *vt* verzichten auf (+*acc*); ~**r** (*container*) Spender *m*.

dispensing [dɪs'pensɪŋ] *a*: ~ **chemist** Apotheker *m*.

dispersal [dɪs'pɜːsəl] *n* Zerstreuung *f*.

disperse [dɪs'pɜːs] *vt* zerstreuen; *vi* sich verteilen.

dispirited [dɪsˈpɪrɪtɪd] a niedergeschlagen.
displace [dɪsˈpleɪs] vt verschieben; ~d a:
~ **person** Verschleppte(r) mf.
display [dɪsˈpleɪ] n (of goods) Auslage f; (of
feeling) Zurschaustellung f; (Mil) Entfaltung f; vt zeigen, entfalten.
displease [dɪsˈpliːz] vt mißfallen (+dat).
displeasure [dɪsˈpleʒə*] n Mißfallen nt.
disposable [dɪsˈpəʊzəbl] a container etc
Wegwerf-.
disposal [dɪsˈpəʊzəl] n (of property)
Verkauf m; (throwing away) Beseitigung f;
to be at one's ~ einem zur Verfügung
stehen.
dispose [dɪsˈpəʊz]: ~ **of** vt loswerden.
disposed [dɪsˈpəʊzd] a geneigt.
disposition [dɪspəˈzɪʃən] n Wesen nt, Natur
f.
disproportionate [dɪsprəˈpɔːʃnɪt] a unver-
hältnismäßig.
disprove [dɪsˈpruːv] vt widerlegen.
dispute [dɪsˈpjuːt] n Streit m; vt bestreiten.
disqualification [dɪskwɒlɪfɪˈkeɪʃən] n Dis-
qualifizierung f.
disqualify [dɪsˈkwɒlɪfaɪ] vt disquali-
fizieren.
disquiet [dɪsˈkwaɪət] n Unruhe f.
disregard [dɪsrɪˈɡɑːd] vt nicht (be)achten.
disreputable [dɪsˈrepjʊtəbl] a verrufen.
disrepute [dɪsrɪˈpjuːt] n Verruf m.
disrespectful [dɪsrɪsˈpektful] a respektlos.
disrupt [dɪsˈrʌpt] vt stören; programme
unterbrechen; ~**ion** [dɪsˈrʌpʃən] Störung f,
Unterbrechung f.
dissatisfaction [ˈdɪssætɪsˈfækʃən] n
Unzufriedenheit f.
dissatisfied [ˈdɪsˈsætɪsfaɪd] a unzufrieden.
dissect [dɪˈsekt] vt zerlegen, sezieren.
disseminate [dɪˈsemɪneɪt] vt verbreiten.
dissent [dɪˈsent] n abweichende Meinung
f; vi nicht übereinstimmen.
dissident [ˈdɪsɪdənt] a andersdenkend; n
Dissident m.
dissimilar [ˈdɪˈsɪmɪlə*] a unähnlich (to
dat).
dissipate [ˈdɪsɪpeɪt] vt (waste) verschwenden; (scatter) zerstreuen; ~**d** a
ausschweifend.
dissipation [dɪsɪˈpeɪʃən] n Ausschweifung
f.
dissociate [dɪˈsəʊʃɪeɪt] vt trennen.
dissolute [ˈdɪsəluːt] a liederlich.
dissolve [dɪˈzɒlv] vt auflösen; vi sich
auflösen.
dissuade [dɪˈsweɪd] vt abraten (+dat).
distance [ˈdɪstəns] n Entfernung f; **in the**
~ **in der Ferne.**
distant [ˈdɪstənt] a entfernt, fern; (with
time) fern; (formal) distanziert.
distaste [ˈdɪsˈteɪst] n Abneigung f; ~**ful** a
widerlich.
distemper [dɪsˈtempə*] n (paint)
Temperafarbe f; (Med) Staupe f.
distend [dɪsˈtend] vti (sich) ausdehnen.
distil [dɪsˈtɪl] vt destillieren; ~**lery**
Brennerei f.
distinct [dɪsˈtɪŋkt] a (separate) getrennt;
(clear) klar, deutlich; ~**ion** [dɪsˈtɪŋkʃən]

Unterscheidung f; (eminence) Berühmtheit f; (in exam) Auszeichnung f; ~**ive** a
bezeichnend; ~**ly** ad deutlich.
distinguish [dɪsˈtɪŋgwɪʃ] vt unterscheiden;
~**ed** a (eminent) berühmt; ~**ing** a unter-
scheidend, bezeichnend.
distort [dɪsˈtɔːt] vt verdrehen; (misrepresent) entstellen; ~**ion** [dɪsˈtɔːʃən]
Verzerrung f.
distract [dɪsˈtrækt] vt ablenken; (bewilder)
verwirren; ~**ing** a verwirrend; ~**ion**
[dɪsˈtrækʃən] Zerstreutheit f; (distress)
Raserei f; (diversion) Zerstreuung f.
distraught [dɪsˈtrɔːt] a bestürzt.
distress [dɪsˈtres] n Not f; (suffering) Qual
f; vt quälen; ~**ing** a erschütternd; ~
signal Notsignal nt.
distribute [dɪsˈtrɪbjuːt] vt verteilen.
distribution [dɪstrɪˈbjuːʃən] n Verteilung f.
distributor [dɪsˈtrɪbjutə*] n Verteiler m.
district [ˈdɪstrɪkt] n (of country) Kreis m;
(of town) Bezirk m; ~ **attorney** (US)
Oberstaatsanwalt m; ~ **nurse** (Brit)
Kreiskrankenschwester f.
distrust [dɪsˈtrʌst] n Mißtrauen nt; vt
mißtrauen (+dat).
disturb [dɪsˈtɜːb] vt stören; (agitate)
erregen; ~**ance** Störung f; ~**ing** a
beunruhigend.
disuse [ˈdɪsˈjuːs] n Nichtgebrauch m; **to
fail into** ~ außer Gebrauch kommen.
disused [ˈdɪsˈjuːzd] a aufgegeben, außer
Gebrauch.
ditch [dɪtʃ] n Graben m; vt im Stich lassen.
dither [ˈdɪðə*] vi verdattert sein.
ditto [ˈdɪtəʊ] n dito, ebenfalls.
divan [dɪˈvæn] n Liegesofa nt.
dive [daɪv] n (into water) Kopfsprung m;
(Aviat) Sturzflug m; vi tauchen; ~**r**
Taucher m.
diverge [daɪˈvɜːdʒ] vi auseinandergehen.
diverse [daɪˈvɜːs] a verschieden.
diversification [daɪvɜːsɪfɪˈkeɪʃən] n Ver-
zweigung f.
diversify [daɪˈvɜːsɪfaɪ] vt (ver)ändern; vi
variieren.
diversion [daɪˈvɜːʃən] n Ablenkung f;
(traffic) Umleitung f.
diversity [daɪˈvɜːsɪti] n Verschiedenheit f;
(variety) Mannigfaltigkeit f.
divert [daɪˈvɜːt] vt ablenken; traffic
umleiten.
divide [dɪˈvaɪd] vt teilen; vi sich teilen.
dividend [ˈdɪvɪdend] n Dividende f; (fig)
Gewinn m.
divine [dɪˈvaɪn] a göttlich; vt erraten.
diving board [ˈdaɪvɪŋbɔːd] n Sprungbrett
nt.
divinity [dɪˈvɪnɪti] n Gottheit f, Gott m;
(subject) Religion f.
divisible [dɪˈvɪzəbl] a teilbar.
division [dɪˈvɪʒən] n Teilung f; (Math)
Division f, Teilung f; (Mil) Division f;
(part) Teil m, Abteilung f; (in opinion)
Uneinigkeit f.
divorce [dɪˈvɔːs] n (Ehe)scheidung f; vt
scheiden; ~**d** a geschieden; **to get** ~**d**
sich scheiden lassen; ~**e** [dɪvɔːˈsiː]
Geschiedene(r) mf.

divulge [daɪˈvʌldʒ] vt preisgeben.
dizziness [ˈdɪzɪnəs] n Schwindelgefühl nt.
dizzy [ˈdɪzɪ] a schwindlig.
do [duː] irreg vt tun, machen; vi (proceed) vorangehen; (be suitable) passen; (be enough) genügen; n (party) Party f; how ~ you ~? guten Tag! etc.
docile [ˈdəʊsaɪl] a gefügig; dog gutmütig.
dock [dɒk] n Dock nt; (Jur) Anklagebank f; vi ins Dock gehen; ~er Hafenarbeiter m.
docket [ˈdɒkɪt] n Inhaltsvermerk m.
dockyard [ˈdɒkjɑːd] n Werft f.
doctor [ˈdɒktə*] n Arzt m, Ärztin f; (Univ) Doktor m.
doctrinaire [dɒktrɪˈnɛə*] a doktrinär.
doctrine [ˈdɒktrɪn] n Doktrin f.
document [ˈdɒkjʊmənt] n Dokument nt; ~ary [dɒkjʊˈmentərɪ] Dokumentarbericht m; (film) Dokumentarfilm m; a dokumentarisch; ~ation [dɒkjʊmenˈteɪʃən] dokumentarische(r) Nachweis m.
doddering [ˈdɒdərɪŋ], **doddery** [ˈdɒdərɪ] a zittrig.
dodge [dɒdʒ] n Kniff m; vt umgehen; ausweichen (+dat); vi umgehen.
dodo [ˈdəʊdəʊ] n Dronte f: as dead as the ~ von Anno dazumal.
dog [dɒg] n Hund m; ~ biscuit Hundekuchen m; ~ collar Hundehalsband nt; (Eccl) Kragen m des Geistlichen; ~-eared a mit Eselsohren; ~-fish Hundsfisch m; ~ food Hundefutter nt.
dogged [ˈdɒgɪd] a hartnäckig.
dogma [ˈdɒgmə] n Dogma nt; ~tic [dɒgˈmætɪk] a dogmatisch.
doings [ˈduːɪŋz] npl (activities) Treiben nt.
do-it-yourself [ˈduːɪtjəˈself] n Do-it-yourself nt; a zum Selbermachen.
doldrums [ˈdɒldrəmz] npl: to be in the ~ Flaute haben; (person) deprimiert sein.
dole [dəʊl] n (Brit) Stempelgeld nt; to be on the ~ stempeln gehen; ~ out vt ausgeben, austeilen.
doleful [ˈdəʊlfʊl] a traurig.
doll [dɒl] n Puppe f; vt: ~ o.s. up sich aufdonnern.
dollar [ˈdɒlə*] n Dollar m.
dollop [ˈdɒləp] n Brocken m.
dolphin [ˈdɒlfɪn] n Delphin m, Tümmler m.
domain [dəʊˈmeɪn] n Sphäre f, Bereich m.
dome [dəʊm] n Kuppel f.
domestic [dəˈmestɪk] a häuslich; (within country) Innen-, Binnen-; animal Haus-; ~ated a person häuslich; animal zahm.
domicile [ˈdɒmɪsaɪl] n (ständiger) Wohnsitz m.
dominant [ˈdɒmɪnənt] a vorherrschend.
dominate [ˈdɒmɪneɪt] vt beherrschen.
domination [dɒmɪˈneɪʃən] n (Vor)herrschaft f.
domineering [dɒmɪˈnɪərɪŋ] a herrisch, überheblich.
dominion [dəˈmɪnɪən] n (rule) Regierungsgewalt f; (land) Staatsgebiet nt mit Selbstverwaltung.
dominoes [ˈdɒmɪnəʊz] n Domino(spiel) nt.
don [dɒn] n akademische(r) Lehrer m.
donate [dəʊˈneɪt] vt (blood, little money) spenden; (lot of money) stiften.

donation [dəʊˈneɪʃən] n Spende f.
donkey [ˈdɒŋkɪ] n Esel m.
donor [ˈdəʊnə*] n Spender m.
don't [dəʊnt] = **do not**.
doom [duːm] n böse(s) Geschick nt; (downfall) Verderben nt; vt: to be ~ed zum Untergang verurteilt sein.
door [dɔː*] n Tür f; ~bell Türklingel f; ~-handle Türklinke f; ~man Türsteher m; ~mat Fußmatte f; ~step Türstufe f; ~way Türöffnung f.
dope [dəʊp] n (drug) Aufputschmittel nt.
dopey [ˈdəʊpɪ] a (col) bekloppt.
dormant [ˈdɔːmənt] a schlafend, latent.
dormitory [ˈdɔːmɪtrɪ] n Schlafsaal m.
dormouse [ˈdɔːmaʊs] n Haselmaus f.
dosage [ˈdəʊsɪdʒ] n Dosierung f.
dose [dəʊs] n Dosis f; vt dosieren.
dossier [ˈdɒsɪeɪ] n Dossier m, Aktenbündel nt.
dot [dɒt] n Punkt m; on the ~ pünktlich.
dote [dəʊt]: ~ on vt vernarrt sein in (+acc).
double [ˈdʌbl] a, ad doppelt; n Doppelgänger m; vt verdoppeln; (fold) zusammenfalten; vi (in amount) sich verdoppeln; at the ~ im Laufschritt; ~s (tennis) Doppel nt; ~ bass Kontrabaß m; ~ bed Doppelbett nt; ~-breasted a zweireihig; ~cross n Betrug m; vt hintergehen; ~decker Doppeldecker m; ~room Doppelzimmer nt.
doubly [ˈdʌblɪ] ad doppelt.
doubt [daʊt] n Zweifel m; vi zweifeln; vt bezweifeln; without ~ zweifellos; ~ful a zweifelhaft, fraglich; ~less ad ohne Zweifel, sicherlich.
dough [dəʊ] n Teig m; ~nut Krapfen m, Pfannkuchen m.
dove [dʌv] n Taube f; ~tail n Schwalbenschwanz m, Zinke f; vt verzahnen, verzinken.
dowdy [ˈdaʊdɪ] a unmodern, schlampig.
down [daʊn] n (fluff) Flaum m; (hill) Hügel m; ad unten; (motion) herunter; hinunter; prep he came ~ the street er kam die Straße herunter; to go ~ the street die Straße hinuntergehen; he lives ~ the street er wohnt unten an der Straße; ~ niederschlagen; ~ with X! nieder mit X!; ~-and-out a abgerissen; n Tramp m; ~-at-heel a schäbig; ~cast a niedergeschlagen; ~fall Sturz m; ~-hearted a niedergeschlagen, mutlos; ~hill ad bergab; ~pour Platzregen m; ~right a völlig ausgesprochen; ~stairs ad unten; (motion) nach unten; a untere(r, s); ~stream ad flußabwärts; ~town ad in die/der Innenstadt; a (US) im Geschäftsviertel, City-; ~ward a sinkend, Abwärts-; ~wards ad abwärts, nach unten.
dowry [ˈdaʊrɪ] n Mitgift f.
doze [dəʊz] vi dösen; n Schläfchen nt, Nickerchen nt.
dozen [ˈdʌzn] n Dutzend nt.
drab [dræb] a düster, eintönig.
draft [drɑːft] n Skizze f, Entwurf m; (Fin) Wechsel m; (US Mil) Einberufung f; vt skizzieren.
drag [dræg] vt schleifen, schleppen; river

mit einem Schleppnetz absuchen; *vi* sich (dahin)schleppen; *n* (*bore*) etwas Blödes; (*hindrance*) Klotz *m* am Bein; **in ~** als Tunte; **~ on** *vi* sich in die Länge ziehen.

dragon ['drægən] *n* Drache *m*; **~fly** Libelle *f*.

drain [dreɪn] *n* (*lit*) Abfluß *m*; (*ditch*) Abflußgraben *m*; (*fig: burden*) Belastung *f*; *vt* ableiten; (*exhaust*) erschöpfen; *vi* (*of water*) abfließen; **~age** Kanalisation *f*; **~pipe** Abflußrohr *nt*.

drama ['drɑːmə] *n* (*lit, fig*) Drama *nt*; **~tic** [drə'mætɪk] *a* dramatisch; **~tist** Dramatiker *m*.

drape [dreɪp] *vt* drapieren; *npl*: **~s** (*US*) Vorhänge *pl*; **~r** Tuchhändler *m*.

drastic ['dræstɪk] *a* drastisch.

draught [drɑːft] *n* Zug *m*; (*Naut*) Tiefgang *m*; **~s** Damespiel *nt*; (*beer*) **on ~** vom Faß; **~board** Zeichenbrett *nt*; **~sman** technische(r) Zeichner *m*; **~y** a zugig.

draw [drɔː] *irreg vt* ziehen; *crowd* anlocken; *picture* zeichnen; *money* abheben; *water* schöpfen; *vi* (*Sport*) unentschieden spielen; *n* (*Sport*) Unentschieden *nt*; (*lottery*) Ziehung *f*; **to ~ to a close** (*speech*) zu Ende kommen; (*year*) zu Ende gehen; **~ out** *vi* (*train*) ausfahren; (*lengthen*) sich hinziehen; *vt money* abheben; **~ up** *vi* (*stop*) halten; *vt document* aufsetzen; **~back** (*disadvantage*) Nachteil *m*; (*obstacle*) Haken *m*; **~bridge** Zugbrücke *f*; **~er** Schublade *f*; **~ing** Zeichnung *f*; Zeichnen *nt*; **~ing pin** Reißzwecke *f*; **~ing room** Salon *m*.

drawl [drɔːl] *n* schleppende Sprechweise *f*; *vi* gedehnt sprechen.

drawn [drɔːn] *a game* unentschieden; *face* besorgt.

dread [dred] *n* Furcht *f*, Grauen *nt*; *vt* fürchten; sich grauen vor (+*dat*); **~ful** a furchtbar.

dream [driːm] *n* Traum *m*; (*fancy*) Wunschtraum *m*; *vti irreg* träumen (*about* von); *a house etc* Traum-; **~er** Träumer *m*; **~ world** Traumwelt *f*; **~y** a verträumt.

dreary ['drɪərɪ] *a* trostlos, öde.

dredge [dredʒ] *vt* ausbaggern; (*with flour etc*) mit Mehl *etc* bestreuen; **~r** Baggerschiff *nt*; (*for flour etc*) (Mehl *etc*)streuer *m*.

dregs [dregz] *npl* Bodensatz *m*; (*fig*) Abschaum *m*.

drench [drentʃ] *vt* durchnässen.

dress [dres] *n* Kleidung *f*; (*garment*) Kleid *nt*; *vt* anziehen; (*Med*) verbinden; (*Agr*) düngen; *food* anrichten; **to get ~ed** sich anziehen; **~ up** *vi* sich fein machen; **~ circle** erste(r) Rang *m*; **~er** (*furniture*) Anrichte *f*, Geschirrschrank *m*; **she's a smart ~er** sie zieht sich elegant an; **~ing** (*Med*) Verband *m*; (*Cook*) Soße *f*; **~ing gown** Morgenrock *m*; **~ing room** (*Theat*) Garderobe *f*, (*Sport*) Umkleideraum *m*; **~ing table** Toilettentisch *m*; **~maker** Schneiderin *f*; **~making** Schneidern *nt*; **~ rehearsal** Generalprobe *f*; **~ shirt** Frackhemd *nt*.

dribble ['drɪbl] *vi* tröpfeln; *vt* sabbern.

drift [drɪft] *n* Trift *f*, Strömung *f*; (*snow—*) Schneewehe *f*; (*fig*) Richtung *f*; *vi* getrieben werden; (*aimlessly*) sich treiben lassen; **~wood** Treibholz *nt*.

drill [drɪl] *n* Bohrer *m*; (*Mil*) Drill *m*; *vt* bohren; (*Mil*) ausbilden; *vi* (*Mil*) exerzieren; bohren (*for nach*); **~ing** Bohren *nt*; (*hole*) Bohrloch *nt*; (*Mil*) Exerzieren *nt*.

drink [drɪŋk] *n* Getränk *nt*; (*spirits*) Drink *m*; *vti irreg* trinken; **~able** *a* trinkbar; **~er** Trinker *m*; **~ing water** Trinkwasser *nt*.

drip [drɪp] *n* Tropfen *m*; (*dripping*) Tröpfeln *nt*; *vi* tropfen; **~-dry** a bügelfrei; **~ping** Bratenfett *nt*; **~ping wet** a triefend.

drive [draɪv] *n* Fahrt *f*; (*road*) Einfahrt *f*; (*campaign*) Aktion *f*; (*energy*) Schwung *m*, Tatkraft *f*; (*Sport*) Schlag *m*; *irreg vt car* fahren; *animals* treiben; *nail* einschlagen; *ball* schlagen; (*power*) antreiben; (*force*) treiben; *vi* fahren; **to ~ sb mad** jdn verrückt machen; **what are you driving at?** worauf willst du hinaus?; **~-in** a Drive-in-.

drivel ['drɪvl] *n* Faselei *f*.

driver ['draɪvə] *n* Fahrer *m*; **~'s license** (*US*) Führerschein *m*.

driving ['draɪvɪŋ] *a rain* stürmisch; **~ instructor** Fahrlehrer *m*; **~ lesson** Fahrstunde *f*; **~ licence** (*Brit*) Führerschein *m*; **~ school** Fahrschule *f*; **~ test** Fahrprüfung *f*.

drizzle ['drɪzl] *n* Nieselregen *m*; *vi* nieseln.

droll [drəʊl] *a* drollig.

dromedary ['drɒmɪdərɪ] *n* Dromedar *nt*.

drone [drəʊn] *n* (*sound*) Brummen *nt*; (*bee*) Drohne *f*.

drool [druːl] *vi* sabbern.

droop [druːp] *vi* (*schlaff*) herabhängen.

drop [drɒp] *n* (*of liquid*) Tropfen *m*; (*fall*) Fall *m*; *vt* fallen lassen; (*lower*) senken; (*abandon*) fallenlassen; *vi* (*fall*) herunterfallen; **~ off** *vi* (*sleep*) einschlafen; **~ out** *vi* (*withdraw*) ausscheiden; **~out** Ausgeflippte(r) *mf*, Drop-out *mf*.

dross [drɒs] *n* Unrat *m*.

drought [draʊt] *n* Dürre *f*.

drove [drəʊv] *n* (*crowd*) Herde *f*.

drown [draʊn] *vt* ertränken; *sound* übertönen; *vi* ertrinken.

drowsy ['draʊzɪ] *a* schläfrig.

drudge [drʌdʒ] *n* Kuli *m*; **~ry** ['drʌdʒərɪ] Plackerei *f*.

drug [drʌg] *n* (*Med*) Arznei *f*; (*narcotic*) Rauschgift *nt*; *vt* betäuben; **~ addict** Rauschgiftsüchtige(r) *mf*; **~gist** (*US*) Drogist *m*; **~store** (*US*) Drogerie *f*.

drum [drʌm] *n* Trommel *f*; **~mer** Trommler *m*.

drunk [drʌŋk] *a* betrunken; *n* Betrunkene(r) *m*; Trinker(in *f*) *m*; **~ard** Trunkenbold *m*; **~en** a betrunken; **~enness** Betrunkenheit *f*.

dry [draɪ] *a* trocken; *vt* (ab)trocknen; *vi* trocknen, trocken werden; **~ up** *vi* austrocknen; (*dishes*) abtrocknen; **~clean** *vt* chemisch reinigen; **~cleaning** chemische Reinigung *f*; **~er** Trockner *m*;

~**ness** Trockenheit f; ~ **rot** Hausschwamm m.

dual ['djuəl] a doppelt; ~ **carriageway** zweispurige Fahrbahn f; ~ **nationality** doppelte Staatsangehörigkeit f; ~**-purpose** a Mehrzweck-.

dubbed [dʌbd] a film synchronisiert.

dubious ['dju:bɪəs] a zweifelhaft.

duchess ['dʌtʃɪs] n Herzogin f.

duck [dʌk] n Ente f; vt (ein)tauchen; vi sich ducken; ~**ling** Entchen nt.

duct [dʌkt] n Röhre f.

dud [dʌd] n Niete f; a wertlos, miserabel; cheque ungedeckt.

due [dju:] a fällig; (fitting) angemessen; **the train is** ~ der Zug soll ankommen; n Gebühr f; (right) Recht nt; ad south etc genau, gerade; ~ **to** infolge (+gen), wegen (+gen).

duel ['djuəl] n Duell nt.

duet [dju:'et] n Duett nt.

duke [dju:k] n Herzog m.

dull [dʌl] a colour, weather trübe; (stupid) schwer von Begriff; (boring) langweilig; vt (soften, weaken) abstumpfen.

duly ['dju:lɪ] ad ordnungsgemäß, richtig; (on time) pünktlich.

dumb [dʌm] a (lit) stumm; (col: stupid) doof, blöde.

dummy ['dʌmɪ] n Schneiderpuppe f; (substitute) Attrappe f; (teat) Schnuller m; a Schein-.

dump [dʌmp] n Abfallhaufen m; (Mil) Stapelplatz m; (col: place) Nest nt; vt abladen, auskippen; ~**ing** (Comm) Schleuderexport m; (of rubbish) Schuttabladen nt.

dumpling ['dʌmplɪŋ] n Kloß m, Knödel m.

dunce [dʌns] n Dummkopf m.

dune [dju:n] n Düne f.

dung [dʌŋ] n Mist m; (Agr) Dünger m.

dungarees [dʌŋgə'ri:z] npl Arbeitsanzug m, Arbeitskleidung f.

dungeon ['dʌndʒən] n Kerker m.

dupe [dju:p] n Gefoppte(r) m; vt hintergehen, anführen.

duplicate ['dju:plɪkɪt] a doppelt; n Duplikat nt; ['dju:plɪkeɪt] vt verdoppeln; (make copies) kopieren; **in** ~ in doppelter Ausführung.

duplicator ['dju:plɪkeɪtə*] n Vervielfältigungsapparat m.

durability [djuərə'bɪlɪtɪ] n Haltbarkeit f.

durable ['djuərəbl] a haltbar.

duration [djuə'reɪʃən] n Dauer f.

during ['djuərɪŋ] prep während (+gen).

dusk [dʌsk] n Abenddämmerung f.

dust [dʌst] n Staub m; vt abstauben; (sprinkle) bestäuben; ~**bin** (Brit) Mülleimer m; ~**er** Staubtuch nt; ~**man** (Brit) Müllmann m; ~ **storm** Staubsturm m; ~**y** a staubig.

dutiable ['dju:tɪəbl] a zollpflichtig.

duty ['dju:tɪ] n Pflicht f; (job) Aufgabe f; (tax) Einfuhrzoll m; **on** ~ im Dienst, diensthabend; ~**-free** a zollfrei; ~**-free articles** zollfreie Waren pl.

dwarf [dwɔ:f] n Zwerg m.

dwell [dwel] vi irreg wohnen; ~ **on** vt ver

weilen bei; ~**ing** Wohnung f.

dwindle ['dwɪndl] vi schwinden.

dye [daɪ] n Farbstoff m; vt färben.

dying ['daɪɪŋ] a person sterbend; moments letzt.

dynamic [daɪ'næmɪk] a dynamisch; ~**s** Dynamik f.

dynamite ['daɪnəmaɪt] n Dynamit nt.

dynamo ['daɪnəməʊ] n Dynamo m.

dynasty ['dɪnəstɪ] n Dynastie f.

dysentery ['dɪsntrɪ] n Ruhr f.

dyspepsia [dɪs'pepsɪə] n Verdauungsstörung f.

E

E, e [i:] n E nt, e nt.

each [i:tʃ] a jeder/jede/jedes; pron (ein) jeder/(eine) jede/(ein) jedes; ~ **other** einander, sich.

eager a, ~**ly** ad ['i:gə*, -lɪ] eifrig; ~**ness** Eifer m; Ungeduld f.

eagle ['i:gl] n Adler m.

ear [ɪə*] n Ohr nt; (of corn) Ähre f; ~**ache** Ohrenschmerzen pl; ~**drum** Trommelfell nt.

earl [ɜ:l] n Graf m.

early ['ɜ:lɪ] a, ad früh; **you're** ~ du bist früh dran.

earmark ['ɪəmɑ:k] vt vorsehen.

earn [ɜ:n] vt verdienen.

earnest ['ɜ:nɪst] a ernst; **in** ~ im Ernst.

earnings ['ɜ:nɪŋz] npl Verdienst m.

earphones ['ɪəfəʊnz] npl Kopfhörer pl.

earplug ['ɪəplʌg] n Ohropax ® nt.

earring ['ɪərɪŋ] n Ohrring m.

earshot ['ɪəʃɒt] n Hörweite f.

earth [ɜ:θ] n Erde f; (Elec) Erdung f; vt erden; ~**enware** Steingut nt; ~**quake** Erdbeben nt.

earthy ['ɜ:θɪ] a roh; (sensual) sinnlich.

earwig ['ɪəwɪg] n Ohrwurm m.

ease [i:z] n (simplicity) Leichtigkeit f; (social) Ungezwungenheit f; vt pain lindern; burden erleichtern; **at** ~ ungezwungen; (Mil) rührt euch!; **to feel at** ~ sich wohl fühlen; ~ **off** or **up** vi nachlassen.

easel ['i:zl] n Staffelei f.

easily ['i:zɪlɪ] ad leicht.

east [i:st] n Osten m; a östlich; ad nach Osten.

Easter ['i:stə*] n Ostern nt.

eastern ['i:stən] a östlich; orientalisch.

eastward(s) ['i:stwəd(z)] ad ostwärts.

easy ['i:zɪ] a task einfach; life bequem; manner ungezwungen, natürlich; ad leicht.

eat [i:t] vt irreg essen; (animals) fressen; (destroy) (zer)fressen; ~ **away** vt (corrode) zerfressen; ~**able** a genießbar.

eaves [i:vz] npl (überstehender) Dachrand m.

eavesdrop ['i:vzdrɒp] vi horchen, lauschen; **to** ~ **on sb** jdn belauschen.

ebb [eb] n Ebbe f; vi ebben.

ebony ['ebənɪ] n Ebenholz nt.

ebullient [ɪ'bʌlɪənt] a sprudelnd, temperamentvoll.

eccentric [ɪk'sentrɪk] a exzentrisch, über

spannt; *n* exzentrische(r) Mensch *m*.

ecclesiastical [ɪkliːzɪˈæstɪkəl] *a* kirchlich, geistlich.

echo [ˈekəʊ] *n* Echo *nt*; *vt* zurückwerfen; (*fig*) nachbeten; *vi* widerhallen.

eclipse [ɪˈklɪps] *n* Verfinsterung *f*, Finsternis *f*; *vt* verfinstern.

ecology [ɪˈkɒlədʒɪ] *n* Ökologie *f*.

economic [iːkəˈnɒmɪk] *a* (volks)wirtschaftlich, ökonomisch; **~al** *a* wirtschaftlich; *person* sparsam; **~s** Volkswirtschaft *f*.

economist [ɪˈkɒnəmɪst] *n* Volkswirt-(schaftler) *m*.

economize [ɪˈkɒnəmaɪz] *vi* sparen (*on* an +*dat*).

economy [ɪˈkɒnəmɪ] *n* (*thrift*) Sparsamkeit *f*; (*of country*) Wirtschaft *f*.

ecstasy [ˈekstəsɪ] *n* Ekstase *f*.

ecstatic [eksˈtætɪk] *a* hingerissen.

ecumenical [iːkjuːˈmenɪkəl] *a* ökumenisch.

eczema [ˈeksɪmə] *n* Ekzem *nt*.

Eden [ˈiːdn] *n* (Garten *m*) Eden *nt*.

edge [edʒ] *n* Rand *m*; (*of knife*) Schneide *f*; **on ~** nervös; (*nerves*) überreizt.

edging [ˈedʒɪŋ] *n* Einfassung *f*.

edgy [ˈedʒɪ] *a* nervös.

edible [ˈedɪbl] *a* eßbar.

edict [ˈiːdɪkt] *n* Erlaß *m*.

edifice [ˈedɪfɪs] *n* Gebäude *nt*.

edit [ˈedɪt] *vt* edieren, redigieren; **~ion** [ɪˈdɪʃən] Ausgabe *f*; **~or** (*of newspaper*) Redakteur *m*; (*of book*) Lektor *m*; **~orial** [edɪˈtɔːrɪəl] *a* Redaktions-; *n* Leitartikel *m*.

educate [ˈedjʊkeɪt] *vt* erziehen, (aus)bilden.

education [edjʊˈkeɪʃən] *n* (*teaching*) Unterricht *m*; (*system*) Schulwesen *nt*; (*schooling*) Erziehung *f*; Bildung *f*; **~al** *a* pädagogisch.

eel [iːl] *n* Aal *m*.

eerie [ˈɪərɪ] *a* unheimlich.

efface [ɪˈfeɪs] *vt* auslöschen.

effect [ɪˈfekt] *n* Wirkung *f*; *vt* bewirken; **in ~** in der Tat; **~s** *pl* (*sound, visual*) Effekte *pl*; **~ive** *a* wirksam, effektiv.

effeminate [ɪˈfemɪnɪt] *a* weibisch.

effervescent [efəˈvesnt] *a* (*lit, fig*) sprudelnd.

efficiency [ɪˈfɪʃənsɪ] *n* Leistungsfähigkeit *f*.

efficient *a*, **~ly** *ad* [ɪˈfɪʃənt, -lɪ] tüchtig; (*Tech*) leistungsfähig; *method* wirksam.

effigy [ˈefɪdʒɪ] *n* Abbild *nt*.

effort [ˈefət] *n* Anstrengung *f*; **to make an ~** sich anstrengen; **~less** *a* mühelos.

effrontery [ɪˈfrʌntərɪ] *n* Unverfrorenheit *f*.

egalitarian [ɪgælɪˈtɛərɪən] *a* Gleichheits-, egalitär.

egg [eg] *n* Ei *nt*; **~ on** *vt* anstacheln; **~cup** Eierbecher *m*; **~plant** Aubergine *f*; **~shell** Eierschale *f*.

ego [ˈiːgəʊ] *n* Ich *nt*, Selbst *nt*.

egotism [ˈegəʊtɪzəm] *n* Ichbezogenheit *f*.

egotist [ˈegəʊtɪst] *n* Egozentriker *m*.

eiderdown [ˈaɪdədaʊn] *n* Daunendecke *f*.

eight [eɪt] *num* acht; **~een** *num* achtzehn; **~h** [eɪtθ] *a* achte(r,s); *n* Achtel *nt*; **~y** *num* achtzig.

either [ˈaɪðə*] *cj* **~ ... or** entweder ... oder;

pron **~ of the two** eine(r,s) von beiden; **I don't want ~** ich will keins von beiden; **a on ~ side** auf beiden Seiten; *ad* **I don't ~** ich auch nicht.

eject [ɪˈdʒekt] *vt* ausstoßen, vertreiben; **~or seat** Schleudersitz *m*.

elaborate [ɪˈlæbərɪt] *a* sorgfältig ausgearbeitet, ausführlich; [ɪˈlæbəreɪt] *vt* sorgfältig ausarbeiten; **~ly** *ad* genau, ausführlich.

elaboration [ɪlæbəˈreɪʃən] *n* Ausarbeitung *f*.

elapse [ɪˈlæps] *vi* vergehen.

elastic [ɪˈlæstɪk] *n* Gummiband *nt*; *a* elastisch; **~ band** Gummiband *nt*.

elated [ɪˈleɪtɪd] *a* froh, in gehobener Stimmung.

elation [ɪˈleɪʃən] *n* gehobene Stimmung *f*.

elbow [ˈelbəʊ] *n* Ellbogen *m*.

elder [ˈeldə*] *a* älter; *n* Ältere(r) *mf*; **~ly** *a* ältere(r,s).

elect [ɪˈlekt] *vt* wählen; *a* zukünftig; **~ion** Wahl *f*; **~ioneering** [ɪlekʃəˈnɪərɪŋ] Wahlpropaganda *f*; **~or** Wähler *m*; **~oral** *a* Wahl-; **~orate** Wähler *pl*, Wählerschaft *f*.

electric [ɪˈlektrɪk] *a* elektrisch, Elektro-; **~al** *a* elektrisch; **~ blanket** Heizdecke *f*; **~ chair** elektrische(r) Stuhl *m*; **~ cooker** Elektroherd *m*; **~ current** elektrische(r) Strom *m*; **~ fire** elektrische(r) Heizofen *m*; **~ian** [ɪlekˈtrɪʃən] Elektriker *m*; **~ity** [ɪlekˈtrɪsɪtɪ] Elektrizität *f*.

electrification [ɪlektrɪfɪˈkeɪʃən] *n* Elektrifizierung *f*.

electrify [ɪˈlektrɪfaɪ] *vt* elektrifizieren; (*fig*) elektrisieren.

electro- [ɪˈlektrəʊ] *pref* Elektro-.

electrocute [ɪˈlektrəkjuːt] *vt* elektrisieren; durch elektrischen Strom töten.

electrode [ɪˈlektrəʊd] *n* Elektrode *f*.

electron [ɪˈlektrɒn] *n* Elektron *nt*.

electronic [ɪlekˈtrɒnɪk] *a* elektronisch, Elektronen-; **~s** Elektronik *f*.

elegance [ˈelɪgəns] *n* Eleganz *f*.

elegant [ˈelɪgənt] *a* elegant.

elegy [ˈelɪdʒɪ] *n* Elegie *f*.

element [ˈelɪmənt] *n* Element *nt*; (*fig*) Körnchen *nt*; **~ary** [elɪˈmentərɪ] *a* einfach; (*primary*) grundlegend, Anfangs-.

elephant [ˈelɪfənt] *n* Elefant *m*.

elevate [ˈelɪveɪt] *vt* emporheben.

elevation [elɪˈveɪʃən] *n* (*height*) Erhebung *f*; (*of style*) Niveau *nt*; (*Archit*) (Quer)schnitt *m*.

elevator [ˈelɪveɪtə*] *n* (*US*) Fahrstuhl *m*, Aufzug *m*.

eleven [ɪˈlevn] *num* elf; *n* (*team*) Elf *f*.

elf [elf] *n* Elfe *f*.

elicit [ɪˈlɪsɪt] *vt* herausbekommen.

eligible [ˈelɪdʒəbl] *a* wählbar; **he's not ~** er kommt nicht in Frage; **to be ~ for a pension/competition** pensions-/teilnahmeberechtigt sein; **~ bachelor** gute Partie *f*.

eliminate [ɪˈlɪmɪneɪt] *vt* ausschalten; beseitigen.

elimination [ɪlɪmɪˈneɪʃən] *n* Ausschaltung *f*; Beseitigung *f*.

elite [eɪˈliːt] *n* Elite *f*.

elm [elm] *n* Ulme *f*.

elocution [elə'kjuːʃən] n Sprecherziehung f; (clarity) Artikulation f.

elongated ['iːlɒŋgeitid] a verlängert.

elope [i'ləup] vi entlaufen; ~ment Entlaufen nt.

eloquence ['eləkwəns] n Beredsamkeit f.

eloquent a, ~ly ad ['eləkwənt, -li] redegewandt.

else [els] ad sonst; ~where ad anderswo, woanders; who ~? wer sonst?; sb ~ jd anders; or ~ sonst.

elucidate [i'luːsideit] vt erläutern.

elude [i'luːd] vt entgehen (+dat).

elusive [i'luːsiv] a schwer faßbar.

emaciated [i'meisieitid] a abgezehrt.

emanate ['eməneit] vi ausströmen (from aus).

emancipate [i'mænsipeit] vt emanzipieren; slave freilassen.

emancipation [imænsi'peiʃən] n Emanzipation f; Freilassung f.

embalm [im'baːm] vt einbalsamieren.

embankment [im'bæŋkmənt] n (of river) Uferböschung f; (of road) Straßendamm m.

embargo [im'baːgəu] n Embargo nt.

embark [im'baːk] vi sich einschiffen; ~ on vt unternehmen; ~ation [embaː'keiʃən] Einschiffung f.

embarrass [im'bærəs] vt in Verlegenheit bringen; ~ed a verlegen; ~ing a peinlich; ~ment Verlegenheit f.

embassy ['embəsi] n Botschaft f.

embed [im'bed] vt einbetten.

embellish [im'beliʃ] vt verschönern.

embers ['embəz] npl Glut(asche) f.

embezzle [im'bezl] vt unterschlagen; ~ment Unterschlagung f.

embitter [im'bitə*] vt verbittern.

emblem ['embləm] n Emblem nt, Abzeichen nt.

embodiment [im'bɒdimənt] n Verkörperung f.

embody [im'bɒdi] vt ideas verkörpern; new features (in sich) vereinigen.

emboss [im'bɒs] vt prägen.

embrace [im'breis] vt umarmen; (include) einschließen; n Umarmung f.

embroider [im'brɔidə*] vt (be)sticken; story ausschmücken; ~y Stickerei f.

embryo ['embriəu] n (lit) Embryo m; (fig) Keim m.

emerald ['emərəld] n Smaragd m; a smaragdgrün.

emerge [i'məːdʒ] vi auftauchen; (truth) herauskommen; ~nce Erscheinen nt; ~ncy n Notfall m; a action Not-; ~ncy exit Notausgang m.

emery ['eməri] n: ~ paper Schmirgelpapier nt.

emetic [i'metik] n Brechmittel nt.

emigrant ['emigrənt] n Auswanderer m, Emigrant m; a Auswanderungs-.

emigrate ['emigreit] vi auswandern, emigrieren.

emigration [emi'greiʃən] n Auswanderung f, Emigration f.

eminence ['eminəns] n hohe(r) Rang m; E~ Eminenz f.

eminent ['eminənt] a bedeutend.

emission [i'miʃən] n (of gases) Ausströmen nt.

emit [i'mit] vt von sich (dat) geben.

emotion [i'məuʃən] n Emotion f, Gefühl nt; ~al a person emotional; scene ergreifend; ~ally ad gefühlsmäßig; behave emotional; sing ergreifend.

emotive [i'məutiv] a gefühlsbetont.

emperor ['empərə*] n Kaiser m.

emphasis ['emfəsis] n (Ling) Betonung f; (fig) Nachdruck m.

emphasize ['emfəsaiz] vt betonen.

emphatic a, ~ally ad [im'fætik, -əli] nachdrücklich; to be ~ about sth etw nachdrücklich betonen.

empire ['empaiə*] n Reich nt.

empirical [em'pirikəl] a empirisch.

employ [im'plɔi] vt (hire) anstellen; (use) verwenden; ~ee [emplɔi'iː] Angestellte(r) mf; ~er Arbeitgeber(in f) m; ~ment Beschäftigung f; in ~ment beschäftigt.

empress ['empris] n Kaiserin f.

emptiness ['emptinis] n Leere f.

empty ['empti] a leer; vt contents leeren; container ausleeren; ~-handed a mit leeren Händen.

emu ['iːmjuː] n Emu m.

emulate ['emjuleit] vt nacheifern (+dat).

enable [i'neibl] vt ermöglichen; it ~s us to . . . das ermöglicht es uns, zu . . .

enamel [i'næml] n Email nt; (of teeth) (Zahn)schmelz m.

enamoured [i'næməd] a verliebt sein (of in +dat).

encase [in'keis] vt einschließen; (Tech) verschalen.

enchant [in'tʃaːnt] vt bezaubern; ~ing a entzückend.

encircle [in'səːkl] vt umringen.

enclose [in'kləuz] vt einschließen; (in letter) beilegen (in, with dat); ~d (in letter) beiliegend, anbei.

enclosure [in'kləuʒə*] n Einfriedung f; (in letter) Anlage f.

encore ['ɒŋkɔː*] n Zugabe f; ~! da capo!

encounter [in'kauntə*] n Begegnung f; (Mil) Zusammenstoß m; vt treffen; resistance stoßen auf (+acc).

encourage [in'kʌridʒ] vt ermutigen; ~ment Ermutigung f, Förderung f.

encouraging [in'kʌridʒiŋ] a ermutigend, vielversprechend.

encroach [in'krəutʃ] vi eindringen ((up)on in +acc), überschreiten ((up)on acc).

encyclop(a)edia [ensaiklə'piːdiə] n Konversationslexikon nt.

end [end] n Ende nt, Schluß m; (purpose) Zweck m; a End-; vt beenden; vi zu Ende gehen; ~ up vi landen.

endanger [in'deindʒə*] vt gefährden.

endeavour [in'devə*] n Bestrebung f; vi sich bemühen.

ending ['endiŋ] n Ende nt.

endless ['endlis] a endlos; plain unendlich.

endorse [in'dɔːs] vt unterzeichnen; (approve) unterstützen; ~ment Bestätigung f; (of document) Unterzeichnung f; (on licence) Eintrag m.

endow [ɪn'dau] *vt*: ~ **sb with sth** jdm etw verleihen; (*with money*) jdm etw stiften.

end product ['endprɔdʌkt] *n* Endprodukt *nt*.

endurable [ɪn'djuərəbl] *a* erträglich.

endurance [ɪn'djuərəns] *n* Ausdauer *f*; (*suffering*) Ertragen *nt*.

endure [ɪn'djuə*] *vt* ertragen; *vi* (*last*) (fort)dauern.

enemy ['enɪmɪ] *n* Feind *m*; *a* feindlich.

energetic [enə'dʒetɪk] *a* tatkräftig.

energy ['enədʒɪ] *n* (*of person*) Energie *f*, Tatkraft *f*; (*Phys*) Energie *f*.

enervating ['enɜːveɪtɪ] *a* nervenaufreibend.

enforce [ɪn'fɔːs] *vt* durchsetzen; *obedience* erzwingen.

engage [ɪn'geɪdʒ] *vt* (*employ*) einstellen; (*in conversation*) verwickeln; (*Mil*) angreifen; (*Tech*) einrasten lassen, einschalten; ~d *a* verlobt; (*Tel, toilet*) besetzt; (*busy*) beschäftigt, unabkömmlich; **to get** ~d sich verloben; ~**ment** (*appointment*) Verabredung *f*; (*to marry*) Verlobung *f*; (*Mil*) Gefecht *nt*; ~**ment ring** Verlobungsring *m*.

engaging [ɪn'geɪdʒɪ] *a* gewinnend.

engender [ɪn'dʒendə*] *vt* hervorrufen.

engine ['endʒɪn] *n* (*Aut*) Motor *m*; (*Rail*) Lokomotive *f*; ~**er** [endʒɪ'nɪə*] Ingenieur *m*; (*US Rail*) Lokomotivführer *m*; ~**ering** [endʒɪ'nɪərɪ] Technik *f*; Maschinenbau *m*; ~ **failure,** ~ **trouble** Maschinenschaden *m*; (*Aut*) Motorschaden *m*.

engrave [ɪn'greɪv] *vt* (*carve*) einschneiden; (*fig*) tief einprägen; (*print*) gravieren.

engraving [ɪn'greɪvɪ] *n* Stich *m*.

engrossed [ɪn'grəust] *a* vertieft.

engulf [ɪn'gʌlf] *vt* verschlingen.

enhance [ɪn'hɑːns] *vt* steigern, heben.

enigma [ɪ'nɪgmə] *n* Rätsel *nt*; ~**tic** [enɪg'mætɪk] *a* rätselhaft.

enjoy [ɪn'dʒɔɪ] *vt* genießen; *privilege* besitzen; ~**able** *a* erfreulich; ~**ment** Genuß *m*, Freude *f*.

enlarge [ɪn'lɑːdʒ] *vt* erweitern; (*Phot*) vergrößern; **to** ~ **on sth** etw weiter ausführen; ~**ment** Vergrößerung *f*.

enlighten [ɪn'laɪtn] *vt* aufklären; ~**ment** Aufklärung *f*.

enlist [ɪn'lɪst] *vt* gewinnen; *vi* (*Mil*) sich melden.

enmity ['enmɪtɪ] *n* Feindschaft *f*.

enormity [ɪ'nɔːmɪtɪ] *n* Ungeheuerlichkeit *f*.

enormous *a*, ~**ly** *ad* [ɪ'nɔːməs, -lɪ] ungeheuer.

enough [ɪ'nʌf] *a* genug; *ad* genug, genügend; ~**!** genug!; **that's** ~**!** das reicht!

enquire [ɪn'kwaɪə*] = **inquire.**

enrich [ɪn'rɪtʃ] *vt* bereichern.

enrol [ɪn'rəul] *vt* (*Mil*) anwerben; *vi* (*register*) sich anmelden; ~**ment** (*for course*) Anmeldung *f*; (*Univ*) Einschreibung *f*.

en route [ã:n'ruːt] *ad* unterwegs.

ensign ['ensaɪn] *n* (*Naut*) Flagge *f*; (*Mil*) Fähnrich *m*.

enslave [ɪn'sleɪv] *vt* versklaven.

ensue [ɪn'sjuː] *vi* folgen, sich ergeben.

ensuing [ɪn'sjuːɪ] *a* (nach)folgend.

ensure [ɪn'ʃuə*] *vt* garantieren.

entail [ɪn'teɪl] *vt* mit sich bringen.

enter ['entə*] *vt* eintreten in (+*dat*), betreten; *club* beitreten (+*dat*); (*in book*) eintragen; *vi* hereinkommen, hineingehen; ~ **for** *vt* sich beteiligen an (+*dat*); ~ **into** *vt* *agreement* eingehen; *argument* sich einlassen auf (+*acc*); ~ **upon** *vt* beginnen.

enterprise ['entəpraɪz] *n* (*in person*) Initiative *f*, Unternehmungsgeist *m*; (*Comm*) Unternehmen *nt*, Betrieb *m*.

enterprising ['entəpraɪzɪ] *a* unternehmungslustig.

entertain [entə'teɪn] *vt* *guest* bewirten; (*amuse*) unterhalten; ~**er** Unterhaltungskünstler(in *f*) *m*; ~**ing** *a* unterhaltend, amüsant; ~**ment** (*amusement*) Unterhaltung *f*; (*show*) Veranstaltung *f*.

enthralled [ɪn'θrɔːld] *a* gefesselt.

enthusiasm [ɪn'θuːzɪæzəm] *n* Begeisterung *f*.

enthusiast [ɪn'θuːzɪæst] *n* Enthusiast *m*, Schwärmer(in *f*) *m*; ~**ic** [ɪnθuːzɪ'æstɪk] *a* begeistert.

entice [ɪn'taɪs] *vt* verleiten, locken.

entire [ɪn'taɪə*] *a* ganz; ~**ly** *ad* ganz, völlig; ~**ty** [ɪn'taɪərətɪ]: **in its** ~**ty** in seiner Gesamtheit.

entitle [ɪn'taɪtl] *vt* (*allow*) berechtigen; (*name*) betiteln.

entity ['entɪtɪ] *n* Ding *nt*, Wesen *nt*.

entrance ['entrəns] *n* Eingang *m*; (*entering*) Eintritt *m*; [ɪn'trɑːns] *vt* hinreißen; ~ **examination** Aufnahmeprüfung *f*; ~ **fee** Eintrittsgeld *nt*.

entrancing [ɪn'trɑːnsɪ] *a* bezaubernd.

entrant ['entrənt] *n* (*for exam*) Kandidat *m*; (*into job*) Anfänger *m*; (*Mil*) Rekrut *m*; (*in race*) Teilnehmer *m*.

entreat [ɪn'triːt] *vt* anflehen, beschwören; ~**y** flehende Bitte *f*, Beschwörung *f*.

entrée ['ɒntreɪ] *n* Zwischengang *m*.

entrenched [ɪn'trentʃt] *a* (*fig*) verwurzelt.

entrust [ɪn'trʌst] *vt* anvertrauen (*sb with sth* jdm etw).

entry ['entrɪ] *n* Eingang *m*; (*Theat*) Auftritt *m*; (*in account*) Eintragung *f*; (*in dictionary*) Eintrag *m*; '**no** ~' 'Eintritt verboten'; (*for cars*) 'Einfahrt verboten'; ~ **form** Anmeldeformular *nt*.

enunciate [ɪ'nʌnsɪeɪt] *vt* (deutlich) aussprechen.

envelop [ɪn'veləp] *vt* einhüllen; ~**e** ['envələup] *n* Umschlag *m*.

enviable ['envɪəbl] *a* beneidenswert.

envious ['envɪəs] *a* neidisch.

environment [ɪn'vaɪərənmənt] *n* Umgebung *f*, (*ecology*) Umwelt *f*; ~**al** [ɪnvaɪərən'mentl] *a* Umwelt-.

envisage [ɪn'vɪzɪdʒ] *vt* sich (*dat*) vorstellen; (*plan*) ins Auge fassen.

envoy ['envɔɪ] *n* Gesandte(r) *mf*.

envy ['envɪ] *n* Neid *m*; (*object*) Gegenstand *m* des Neides; *vt* beneiden (*sb sth* jdn um etw).

enzyme ['enzaɪm] n Enzym nt.
ephemeral [ɪ'femərəl] a kurzlebig, vorübergehend.
epic ['epɪk] n Epos nt; (film) Großfilm m; a episch; (fig) heldenhaft.
epidemic [epɪ'demɪk] n Epidemie f.
epigram ['epɪgræm] n Epigramm nt.
epilepsy ['epɪlepsɪ] n Epilepsie f.
epileptic [epɪ'leptɪk] a epileptisch; n Epileptiker(in f) m.
epilogue ['epɪlɒg] n (of drama) Epilog m; (of book) Nachwort nt.
episode ['epɪsəʊd] n (incident) Vorfall m; (story) Episode f.
epistle [ɪ'pɪsl] n Brief m.
epitaph ['epɪtɑːf] n Grab(in)schrift f.
epitome [ɪ'pɪtəmɪ] n Inbegriff m.
epitomize [ɪ'pɪtəmaɪz] vt verkörpern.
epoch ['iːpɒk] n Epoche f.
equable ['ekwəbl] a ausgeglichen.
equal ['iːkwl] a gleich; ~ to the task der Aufgabe gewachsen; ~ n Gleichgestellte(r) mf; vt gleichkommen (+dat); two times two ~s four zwei mal zwei ist (gleich) vier; without ~ ohne seinesgleichen; ~ity [ɪ'kwɒlɪtɪ] Gleichheit f; (equal rights) Gleichberechtigung f; ~ize vt gleichmachen; vi (Sport) ausgleichen; ~izer (Sport) Ausgleich(streffer) m; ~ly ad gleich; ~s sign Gleichheitszeichen nt.
equanimity [ekwə'nɪmɪtɪ] n Gleichmut m.
equate [ɪ'kweɪt] vt gleichsetzen.
equation [ɪ'kweɪʒən] n Gleichung f.
equator [ɪ'kweɪtə*] n Äquator m; ~ial [ekwə'tɔːrɪəl] a Äquator-.
equilibrium [iːkwɪ'lɪbrɪəm] n Gleichgewicht nt.
equinox ['iːkwɪnɒks] n Tag- und Nachtgleiche f.
equip [ɪ'kwɪp] vt ausrüsten; ~ment Ausrüstung f; (Tech) Gerät nt.
equitable ['ekwɪtəbl] a gerecht, billig.
equity ['ekwɪtɪ] n Billigkeit f, Gerechtigkeit f.
equivalent [ɪ'kwɪvələnt] a gleichwertig (to dat), entsprechend (to dat); n (amount) gleiche Menge f; (in money) Gegenwert m; Äquivalent nt.
equivocal [ɪ'kwɪvəkəl] a zweideutig; (suspect) fragwürdig.
era ['ɪərə] n Epoche f, Ära f.
eradicate [ɪ'rædɪkeɪt] vt ausrotten.
erase [ɪ'reɪz] vt ausradieren; tape löschen; ~r Radiergummi m.
erect [ɪ'rekt] a aufrecht; vt errichten; ~ion Errichtung f; (Physiol) Erektion f.
ermine ['ɜːmɪn] n Hermelin(pelz) m.
erode [ɪ'rəʊd] vt zerfressen; land auswaschen.
erosion [ɪ'rəʊʒən] n Auswaschen nt, Erosion f.
erotic [ɪ'rɒtɪk] a erotisch; ~ism [ɪ'rɒtɪsɪzəm] Erotik f.
err [ɜː*] vi sich irren.
errand ['erənd] n Besorgung f, ~ boy Laufbursche m.
erratic [ɪ'rætɪk] a sprunghaft; driving unausgeglichen.
erroneous [ɪ'rəʊnɪəs] a irrig, irrtümlich.

error ['erə*] n Fehler m.
erudite ['erʊdaɪt] a gelehrt.
erudition [erʊ'dɪʃən] n Gelehrsamkeit f.
erupt [ɪ'rʌpt] vi ausbrechen; ~ion Ausbruch m.
escalate ['eskəleɪt] vt steigern; vi sich steigern.
escalator ['eskəleɪtə*] n Rolltreppe f.
escapade [eskə'peɪd] n Eskapade f, Streich m.
escape [ɪs'keɪp] n Flucht f; (of gas) Entweichen nt; vti entkommen (+dat); (prisoners) fliehen; (leak) entweichen; to ~ notice unbemerkt bleiben; the word ~s me das Wort ist mir entfallen.
escapism [ɪs'keɪpɪzəm] n Flucht f (vor der Wirklichkeit).
escort ['eskɔːt] n (person accompanying) Begleiter m; (guard) Eskorte f; [ɪs'kɔːt] vt lady begleiten; (Mil) eskortieren.
especially [ɪs'peʃəlɪ] ad besonders.
espionage ['espɪənɑːʒ] n Spionage f.
esplanade ['espləneɪd] n Esplanade f, Promenade f.
Esquire [ɪs'kwaɪə*] n (in address) J. Brown, Esq Herrn J. Brown.
essay ['eseɪ] n Aufsatz m; (Liter) Essay m.
essence ['esəns] n (quality) Wesen nt; (extract) Essenz f, Extrakt m.
essential [ɪ'senʃəl] a (necessary) unentbehrlich; (basic) wesentlich; n Hauptbestandteil m, Allernötigste(s) nt; ~ly ad in der Hauptsache, eigentlich.
establish [ɪs'tæblɪʃ] vt (set up) gründen, einrichten; (prove) nachweisen; ~ment (setting up) Einrichtung f; (business) Unternehmen nt; the E~ment das Establishment.
estate [ɪs'teɪt] n Gut nt; (housing ~) Siedlung f; (will) Nachlaß m; ~ agent Grundstücksmakler m; ~ car (Brit) Kombiwagen m.
esteem [ɪs'tiːm] n Wertschätzung f.
estimate ['estɪmət] n (opinion) Meinung f; (of price) (Kosten)voranschlag m; ['estɪmeɪt] vt schätzen.
estimation [estɪ'meɪʃən] n Einschätzung f; (esteem) Achtung f.
estuary ['estjʊərɪ] n Mündung f.
etching ['etʃɪŋ] n Kupferstich m.
eternal a, ~ly ad [ɪ'tɜːnl, -nəlɪ] ewig.
eternity [ɪ'tɜːnɪtɪ] n Ewigkeit f.
ether ['iːθə*] n (Med) Äther m.
ethical ['eθɪkəl] a ethisch.
ethics ['eθɪks] npl Ethik f.
ethnic ['eθnɪk] a Volks-, ethnisch.
etiquette ['etɪket] n Etikette f.
Eucharist ['juːkərɪst] n heilige(s) Abendmahl nt.
eulogy ['juːlədʒɪ] n Lobrede f.
eunuch ['juːnək] n Eunuch m.
euphemism ['juːfɪmɪzəm] n Euphemismus m.
euphoria [juː'fɔːrɪə] n Taumel m, Euphorie f.
euthanasia [juːθə'neɪzɪə] n Euthanasie f.
evacuate [ɪ'vækjʊeɪt] vt place räumen; people evakuieren; (Med) entleeren.

evacuation [ɪvækju'eɪʃən] n Evakuierung f; Räumung f; Entleerung f.

evade [ɪ'veɪd] vt (escape) entkommen (+dat); (avoid) meiden; duty sich entziehen (+dat).

evaluate [ɪ'væljueɪt] vt bewerten; information auswerten.

evangelical [i:væn'dʒelɪkəl] a evangelisch.

evangelist [ɪ'vændʒəlɪst] n Evangelist m.

evaporate [ɪ'væpəreɪt] vi verdampfen; vt verdampfen lassen; ~d milk Kondensmilch f.

evaporation [ɪvæpə'reɪʃən] n Verdunstung f.

evasion [ɪ'veɪʒən] n Umgehung f; (excuse) Ausflucht f.

evasive [ɪ'veɪzɪv] a ausweichend.

even ['i:vən] a eben; gleichmäßig; score etc unentschieden; number gerade; vt (einebnen, glätten; ad ~ you selbst or sogar du; he ~ said . . . er hat sogar gesagt . . .; ~ as he spoke (gerade) da er sprach; ~ if sogar or selbst wenn, wenn auch; ~ so dennoch; ~ out or up vi sich ausgleichen; vt ausgleichen; get ~ sich revanchieren.

evening ['i:vnɪŋ] n Abend m; in the ~ abends, am Abend; ~ class Abendschule f; ~ dress (man's) Gesellschaftsanzug m; (woman's) Abendkleid nt.

evenly ['i:vənlɪ] ad gleichmäßig.

evensong ['i:vənsɒŋ] n (Rel) Abendandacht f.

event [ɪ'vent] n (happening) Ereignis nt; (Sport) Disziplin f; (horses) Rennen nt; in the ~ nach der nächste Wettkampf; in the ~ of im Falle (+gen); ~ful a ereignisreich.

eventual [ɪ'ventʃuəl] a (final) schließlich; ~ity [ɪventʃu'ælɪtɪ] Möglichkeit f; ~ly ad (at last) am Ende; (given time) schließlich.

ever ['evə'] ad (always) immer; (at any time) je(mals); ~ so big sehr groß; ~ so many sehr viele; ~green a immergrün; n Immergrün nt; ~-lasting a immerwährend.

every ['evrɪ] a jeder/jede/jedes; ~ day jeden Tag; ~ other day jeden zweiten Tag; ~body pron jeder, alle pl; ~day a (daily) täglich; (commonplace) alltäglich, Alltags-; ~one = ~body; ~ so often hin und wieder; ~thing pron alles; ~where ad überall.

evict [ɪ'vɪkt] vt ausweisen; ~ion Ausweisung f.

evidence ['evɪdəns] n (sign) Spur f; (proof) Beweis m; (testimony) Aussage f; in ~ (obvious) zu sehen.

evident ['evɪdənt] a augenscheinlich; ~ly ad offensichtlich.

evil ['i:vl] a böse, übel; n Übel nt; Unheil nt; (sin) Böse(s) nt.

evocative [ɪ'vɒkətɪv] a to be ~ of sth an etw (acc) erinnern.

evoke [ɪ'vəuk] vt hervorrufen.

evolution [i:və'lu:ʃən] n Entwicklung f; (of life) Evolution f.

evolve [ɪ'vɒlv] vt entwickeln; vi sich entwickeln.

ewe [ju:] n Mutterschaf nt.

ex- [eks] a Ex-, Alt-, ehemalig.

exact a, ~ly ad [ɪg'zækt, -lɪ] genau; vt (demand) verlangen; (compel) erzwingen; money, fine einziehen; punishment vollziehen; ~ing a anspruchsvoll; ~itude Genauigkeit f; ~ness Genauigkeit f, Richtigkeit f.

exaggerate [ɪg'zædʒəreɪt] vti übertreiben; ~d a übertrieben.

exaggeration [ɪgzædʒə'reɪʃən] n Übertreibung f.

exalt [ɪg'zɔ:lt] vt (praise) verherrlichen.

exam [ɪg'zæm] n Prüfung f.

examination [ɪgzæmɪ'neɪʃən] n Untersuchung f; (Sch, Univ) Prüfung f, Examen nt; (customs) Kontrolle f.

examine [ɪg'zæmɪn] vt untersuchen; (Sch) prüfen; (consider) erwägen; ~r Prüfer m.

example [ɪg'zɑ:mpl] n Beispiel nt; for ~ zum Beispiel.

exasperate [ɪg'zɑ:spəreɪt] vt zum Verzweifeln bringen.

exasperating [ɪg'zɑ:spəreɪtɪŋ] a ärgerlich, zum Verzweifeln bringend.

exasperation [ɪgzɑ:spə'reɪʃən] n Verzweiflung f.

excavate ['ekskəveɪt] vt (hollow out) aushöhlen; (unearth) ausgraben.

excavation [ekskə'veɪʃən] n Ausgrabung f.

excavator ['ekskəveɪtə'] n Bagger m.

exceed [ɪk'si:d] vt überschreiten; hopes übertreffen; ~ingly ad in höchstem Maße.

excel [ɪk'sel] vi sich auszeichnen; vt übertreffen; ~lence ['eksələns] Vortrefflichkeit f; His E~lency ['eksələnsɪ] Seine Exzellenz f; ~lent ['eksələnt] a ausgezeichnet.

except [ɪk'sept] prep (also ~ for) außer (+dat); vt ausnehmen; ~ing prep = except; ~ion [ɪk'sepʃən] Ausnahme f; to take ~ion to Anstoß nehmen an (+dat); ~ional a, ~ionally ad [ɪk'sepʃənl, -nəlɪ] außergewöhnlich.

excerpt ['eksɜ:pt] n Auszug m.

excess [ɪk'ses] n Übermaß nt (of an +dat); Exzeß m; a money Nach-; baggage Mehr-; ~es pl Ausschweifungen pl, Exzesse pl; (violent) Ausschreitungen pl; ~ weight (of thing) Mehrgewicht nt; (of person) Übergewicht nt; ~ive a, ~ively ad übermäßig.

exchange [ɪks'tʃeɪndʒ] n Austausch m; (Fin) Wechselstube f; (Tel) Vermittlung f, Zentrale f; (Post Office) (Fernsprech)amt nt; vt goods tauschen; greetings austauschen; money, blows wechseln; see rate.

exchequer [ɪks'tʃekə'] n Schatzamt nt.

excisable ['eksaɪzbl] a (verbrauchs)-steuerpflichtig.

excise ['eksaɪz] n Verbrauchssteuer f; [ek'saɪz] vt (Med) herausschneiden.

excitable [ɪk'saɪtəbl] a erregbar, nervös.

excite [ɪk'saɪt] vt erregen; ~d a aufgeregt; to get ~d sich aufregen; ~ment Aufgeregtheit f, Erregung f.

exciting [ɪk'saɪtɪŋ] a aufregend; book, film spannend.

exclaim [ɪks'kleɪm] vi ausrufen.

exclamation [eksklə'meɪʃən] n Ausruf m;

~ **mark** Ausrufezeichen *nt.*
exclude [ɪksˈkluːd] *vt* ausschließen.
exclusion [ɪksˈkluːʒən] *n* Ausschluß *m.*
exclusive [ɪksˈkluːsɪv] *a* (*select*) exklusiv; (*sole*) ausschließlich, Allein-; ~ **of** exklusive (+*gen*); ~**ly** *ad* nur, ausschließlich.
excommunicate [ekskəˈmjuːnɪkeɪt] *vt* exkommunizieren.
excrement [ˈekskrɪmənt] *n* Kot *m.*
excruciating [ɪksˈkruːʃɪeɪtɪŋ] *a* qualvoll.
excursion [ɪksˈkɜːʃən] *n* Ausflug *m.*
excusable [ɪksˈkjuːzəbl] *a* entschuldbar.
excuse [ɪksˈkjuːs] *n* Entschuldigung *f*; [ɪksˈkjuːz] *vt* entschuldigen; ~ **me!** entschuldigen Sie!
execute [ˈeksɪkjuːt] *vt* (*carry out*) ausführen; (*kill*) hinrichten.
execution [eksɪˈkjuːʃən] *n* Ausführung *f*; (*killing*) Hinrichtung *f*; ~ **er** Scharfrichter *m.*
executive [ɪgˈzekjutɪv] *n* (*Comm*) leitende(r) Angestellte(r) *m*, Geschäftsführer *m*; (*Pol*) Exekutive *f*; *a* Exekutiv-, ausführend.
executor [ɪgˈzekjutə*] *n* Testamentsvollstrecker *m.*
exemplary [ɪgˈzemplərɪ] *a* musterhaft.
exemplify [ɪgˈzemplɪfaɪ] *vt* veranschaulichen.
exempt [ɪgˈzempt] *a* befreit; *vt* befreien; ~**ion** [ɪgˈzempʃən] Befreiung *f.*
exercise [ˈeksəsaɪz] *n* Übung *f*; *vt power* ausüben; *muscle, patience* üben; *dog* ausführen; ~ **book** (Schul)heft *nt.*
exert [ɪgˈzɜːt] *vt influence* ausüben; ~ **o.s.** sich anstrengen; ~**ion** Anstrengung *f.*
exhaust [ɪgˈzɔːst] *n* (*fumes*) Abgase *pl*; (*pipe*) Auspuffrohr *nt*; *vt* (*weary*) ermüden; (*use up*) erschöpfen; ~**ed** *a* erschöpft; ~**ing** *a* anstrengend; ~**ion** Erschöpfung *f*; ~**ive** *a* erschöpfend.
exhibit [ɪgˈzɪbɪt] *n* (*Art*) Ausstellungsstück *nt*; (*Jur*) Beweisstück *nt*; *vt* ausstellen; ~**ion** [eksɪˈbɪʃən] (*Art*) Ausstellung *f*; (*of temper etc*) Zurschaustellung *f*; ~**ionist** [eksɪˈbɪʃənɪst] Exhibitionist *m*; ~**or** Aussteller *m.*
exhilarating [ɪgˈzɪləreɪtɪŋ] *a* erhebend.
exhilaration [ɪgzɪləˈreɪʃən] *n* erhebende(s) Gefühl *nt.*
exhort [ɪgˈzɔːt] *vt* ermahnen; beschwören.
exile [ˈeksaɪl] *n* Exil *nt*; (*person*) im Exil Lebende(r) *mf*; *vt* verbannen; **in** ~ im Exil.
exist [ɪgˈzɪst] *vi* existieren; (*live*) leben; ~**ence** Existenz *f*; (*way of life*) Leben *nt*, Existenz *f*; ~**ing** *a* vorhanden, bestehend.
exit [ˈeksɪt] *n* Ausgang *m*; (*Theat*) Abgang *m.*
exonerate [ɪgˈzɒnəreɪt] *vt* entlasten.
exorbitant [ɪgˈzɔːbɪtənt] *a* übermäßig; *price* Phantasie-.
exotic [ɪgˈzɒtɪk] *a* exotisch.
expand [ɪksˈpænd] *vt* (*spread*) ausspannen; *operations* ausdehnen; *vi* sich ausdehnen.
expanse [ɪksˈpæns] *n* weite Fläche *f*, Weite *f.*
expansion [ɪksˈpænʃən] *n* Erweiterung *f.*

expatriate [eksˈpætrɪeɪt] *a* Exil-; *n* im Exil Lebende(r) *mf*; *vt* ausbürgern.
expect [ɪksˈpekt] *vt* erwarten; (*suppose*) annehmen; *vi*: **to be** ~**ing** ein Kind erwarten; ~**ant** *a* (*hopeful*) erwartungsvoll; *mother* werdend; ~**ation** [ekspekˈteɪʃən] (*hope*) Hoffnung *f*; ~**ations** *pl* Erwartungen *pl*; (*prospects*) Aussicht *f.*
expedience [ɪksˈpiːdɪəns], **expediency** [ɪksˈpiːdɪənsɪ] *n* Zweckdienlichkeit *f.*
expedient [ɪksˈpiːdɪənt] *a* zweckdienlich; *n* (Hilfs)mittel *nt.*
expedite [ˈekspɪdaɪt] *vt* beschleunigen.
expedition [ekspɪˈdɪʃən] *n* Expedition *f.*
expel [ɪksˈpel] *vt* ausweisen; *student* (ver)weisen.
expend [ɪksˈpend] *vt money* ausgeben; *effort* aufwenden; ~**able** *a* entbehrlich; ~**iture** Kosten *pl*, Ausgaben *pl.*
expense [ɪksˈpens] *n* (*cost*) Auslage *f*, Ausgabe *f*; (*high cost*) Aufwand *m*; ~**s** *pl* Spesen *pl*; **at the** ~ **of** auf Kosten von; ~ **account** Spesenkonto *nt.*
expensive [ɪksˈpensɪv] *a* teuer.
experience [ɪksˈpɪərɪəns] *n* (*incident*) Erlebnis *nt*; (*practice*) Erfahrung *f*; *vt* erfahren, erleben; *hardship* durchmachen; ~**d** *a* erfahren.
experiment [ɪksˈperɪmənt] *n* Versuch *m*, Experiment *m*; [ɪksˈperɪment] *vi* experimentieren; ~**al** [ɪksperɪˈmentl] *a* versuchsweise, experimentell.
expert [ˈekspɜːt] *n* Fachmann *m*; (*official*) Sachverständige(r) *m*; *a* erfahren; (*practised*) gewandt; ~**ise** [ekspɜːˈtiːz] Sachkenntnis *f.*
expiration [ekspaɪəˈreɪʃən] *n* (*breathing*) Ausatmen *nt*; (*fig*) Ablauf *m.*
expire [ɪksˈpaɪə*] *vi* (*end*) ablaufen; (*die*) sterben; (*ticket*) verfallen.
expiry [ɪksˈpaɪərɪ] *n* Ablauf *m.*
explain [ɪksˈpleɪn] *vt* (*make clear*) erklären; (*account for*) begründen; ~ **away** *vt* wegerklären.
explanation [ekspləˈneɪʃən] *n* Erklärung *f.*
explanatory [ɪksˈplænətərɪ] *a* erklärend.
explicable [eksˈplɪkəbl] *a* erklärlich.
explicit [ɪksˈplɪsɪt] *a* (*clear*) ausdrücklich; (*outspoken*) deutlich; ~**ly** *ad* deutlich.
explode [ɪksˈpləʊd] *vi* explodieren; *vt bomb* zur Explosion bringen; *theory* platzen lassen.
exploit [ˈeksplɔɪt] *n* (Helden)tat *f*, [ɪksˈplɔɪt] *vt* ausbeuten; ~**ation** [eksplɔɪˈteɪʃən] Ausbeutung *f.*
exploration [eksplɔːˈreɪʃən] *n* Erforschung *f.*
exploratory [eksˈplɔːrətərɪ] *a* sondierend, Probe-.
explore [ɪksˈplɔː*] *vt* (*travel*) erforschen; (*search*) untersuchen; ~**r** Forschungsreisende(r) *m*, Erforscher(in *f*) *m.*
explosion [ɪksˈpləʊʒən] *n* (*lit*) Explosion *f*; (*fig*) Ausbruch *m.*
explosive [ɪksˈpləʊzɪv] *a* explosiv, Spreng-; *n* Sprengstoff *m.*
exponent [eksˈpəʊnənt] *n* Exponent *m.*
export [eksˈpɔːt] *vt* exportieren; [ˈekspɔːt] *n* Export *m*; *a trade* Export-; ~**ation**

[ekspɔː'teɪʃən] Ausfuhr f; ~**er** Exporteur m.

expose [ɪks'pəʊz] vt (to danger etc) aussetzen (to dat); imposter entlarven; lie aufdecken.

exposé [eks'pəʊzeɪ] n (of scandal) Enthüllung f.

exposed [ɪks'pəʊzd] a position exponiert.

exposure [ɪks'pəʊʒə°] m (Med) Unterkühlung f; (Phot) Belichtung f; ~ **meter** Belichtungsmesser m.

expound [ɪks'paʊnd] vt entwickeln.

express [ɪks'pres] a ausdrücklich; (speedy) Expreß-, Eil-; n (Rail) Zug m; vt ausdrücken; **to ~ o.s.** sich ausdrücken; ~**ion** [ɪks'preʃən] (phrase) Ausdruck m; (look) (Gesichts)ausdruck m; ~**ive** a ausdrucksvoll; ~**ly** ad ausdrücklich, extra.

expropriate [eks'prəʊprɪeɪt] vt enteignen.

expulsion [ɪks'pʌlʃən] n Ausweisung f.

exquisite [eks'kwɪzɪt] a erlesen; ~**ly** ad ausgezeichnet.

extend [ɪks'tend] vt visit etc verlängern; building vergrößern, ausbauen; hand ausstrecken; welcome bieten.

extension [ɪks'tenʃən] n Erweiterung f; (of building) Anbau m; (Tel) Nebenanschluß m, Apparat m.

extensive [ɪks'tensɪv] a knowledge umfassend; use weitgehend.

extent [ɪks'tent] n Ausdehnung f; (fig) Ausmaß nt.

extenuating [ɪks'tenjueɪtɪŋ] a mildernd.

exterior [eks'tɪərɪə°] a äußere(r,s), Außen-; n Äußere(s) nt.

exterminate [eks'tɜːmɪneɪt] vt ausrotten.

extermination [ekstɜːmɪ'neɪʃən] n Ausrottung f.

external [eks'tɜːnl] a äußere(r,s), Außen-; ~**ly** ad äußerlich.

extinct [ɪks'tɪŋkt] a ausgestorben; ~**ion** [ɪks'tɪŋkʃən] Aussterben nt.

extinguish [ɪks'tɪŋgwɪʃ] vt (aus)löschen; ~**er** Löschgerät nt.

extort [ɪks'tɔːt] vt erpressen (sth from sb jdn um etw); ~**ion** [ɪks'tɔːʃən] Erpressung f; ~**ionate** [ɪks'tɔːʃənɪt] a überhöht, erpresserisch.

extra [ˈekstrə] a zusätzlich; ad besonders; n (work) Sonderarbeit f; (benefit) Sonderleistung f; (charge) Zuschlag m; (Theat) Statist m.

extract [ɪks'trækt] vt (heraus)ziehen; (select) auswählen; [ˈekstrækt] n (from book etc) Auszug m; (Cook) Extrakt m; ~**ion** (Heraus)ziehen nt; (origin) Abstammung f.

extradite [ˈekstrədaɪt] vt ausliefern.

extradition [ekstrə'dɪʃən] n Auslieferung f.

extraneous [eks'treɪnɪəs] a unwesentlich; influence äußere(r,s).

extraordinary [ɪks'trɔːdnrɪ] a außerordentlich; (amazing) erstaunlich.

extravagance [ɪks'trævəgəns] n Verschwendung f; (lack of restraint) Zügellosigkeit f, (an —) Extravaganz f.

extravagant [ɪks'trævəgənt] a extravagant.

extreme [ɪks'triːm] a edge äußerste(r,s), hinterste(r,s); cold äußerste(r,s); behaviour

außergewöhnlich, übertrieben; n Extrem nt, das Äußerste; ~**s** pl (excesses) Ausschreitungen pl; (opposites) Extreme pl; ~**ly** ad äußerst, höchst.

extremist [ɪks'triːmɪst] a extremistisch; n Extremist(in f) m.

extremity [ɪks'tremɪtɪ] n (end) Spitze f, äußerste(s) Ende nt; (hardship) bitterste Not f; (Anat) Hand f; Fuß m.

extricate [ˈekstrɪkeɪt] vt losmachen, befreien.

extrovert [ˈekstrəʊvɜːt] n Extravertierte(r) m f; a extravertiert.

exuberance [ɪg'zuːbərəns] n Überschwang m.

exuberant [ɪg'zuːbərənt] a ausgelassen.

exude [ɪg'zjuːd] vt absondern; vi sich absondern.

exult [ɪg'zʌlt] vi frohlocken; ~**ation** [egzʌl'teɪʃən] Jubel m.

eye [aɪ] n Auge nt; (of needle) Öhr nt; vt betrachten; (up and down) mustern; **to keep an ~ on** aufpassen auf (+acc); **in the ~s of** in den Augen (+gen); **up to the ~s in** bis zum Hals in; ~**ball** Augapfel m; ~**bath** Augenbad nt; ~**brow** Augenbraue f; ~**lash** Augenwimper f; ~**lid** Augenlid nt; **that was an ~opener** das hat mir die Augen geöffnet; ~**shadow** Lidschatten m; ~**sight** Sehkraft f; ~**sore** Schandfleck m; ~**wash** (lit) Augenwasser nt; (fig) Schwindel m; Quatsch m; ~ **witness** Augenzeuge m.

F

F,f [ef] n F nt, f nt.

fable [ˈfeɪbl] n Fabel f.

fabric [ˈfæbrɪk] n Stoff m, Gewebe nt; (fig) Gefüge nt.

fabricate [ˈfæbrɪkeɪt] vt fabrizieren.

fabulous [ˈfæbjʊləs] a (imaginary) legendär, sagenhaft; (unbelievable) unglaublich; (wonderful) fabelhaft, unglaublich.

façade [fə'sɑːd] n (lit, fig) Fassade f.

face [feɪs] n Gesicht nt; (grimace) Grimasse f; (surface) Oberfläche f; (of clock) Zifferblatt nt; vt (point towards) liegen nach; situation sich gegenübersehen (+dat); difficulty mutig entgegentreten (+dat); **in the ~ of** angesichts (+gen); **to ~ up to sth** einer Sache ins Auge sehen; ~ **cream** Gesichtscreme f; ~ **powder** (Gesichts)puder m.

facet [ˈfæsɪt] n Seite f, Aspekt m; (of gem) Kristallfläche f, Schliff m.

facetious [fə'siːʃəs] a schalkhaft; (humorous) witzig; ~**ly** ad spaßhaft, witzig.

face to face [feɪstə'feɪs] ad Auge in Auge, direkt.

face value [ˈfeɪs 'væljuː] n Nennwert m; (fig) **to take sth at its ~** etw für bare Münze nehmen.

facial [ˈfeɪʃəl] a Gesichts-.

facile [ˈfæsaɪl] a oberflächlich; (US: easy) leicht.

facilitate [fə'sɪlɪteɪt] vt erleichtern.

facility [fə'sɪlɪtɪ] n (ease) Leichtigkeit f;

(skill) Gewandtheit f; **facilities** pl Einrichtungen pl.

facing ['feısıŋ] a zugekehrt; prep gegenüber.

facsimile [fæk'sımılı] n Faksimile nt.

fact [fækt] n Tatsache f; **in** ~ in der Tat.

faction ['fækʃən] n Splittergruppe f.

factor ['fæktə*] n Faktor m.

factory ['fæktərı] n Fabrik f.

factual ['fæktjʊəl] a Tatsachen-, sachlich.

faculty ['fækəltı] n Fähigkeit f; *(Univ)* Fakultät f; *(US: teaching staff)* Lehrpersonal nt.

fade [feıd] vi *(lose colour)* verschießen, verblassen; *(grow dim)* nachlassen, schwinden; *(sound, memory)* schwächer werden; *(wither)* verwelken; vt material verblassen lassen; ~ d a verwelkt; colour verblichen; **to** ~ **in/out** *(Cine)* ein-/ausblenden.

fag [fæg] n Plackerei f; *(col: cigarette)* Kippe f; ~ **ged** a *(exhausted)* erschöpft.

Fahrenheit ['færənhaıt] n Fahrenheit.

fail [feıl] vt exam nicht bestehen; student durchfallen lassen; *(courage)* verlassen; *(memory)* im Stich lassen; vi *(supplies)* zu Ende gehen; *(student)* durchfallen; *(eyesight)* nachlassen; *(light)* schwächer werden; *(crop)* fehlschlagen; *(remedy)* nicht wirken; ~ **to do sth** *(neglect)* es unterlassen, etw zu tun; *(be unable)* es nicht schaffen, etw zu tun; **without** ~ ganz bestimmt, unbedingt; ~ **ing** this falls nicht, sonst; ~ **ure** *(person)* Versager m; *(act)* Versagen nt; *(Tech)* Defekt m.

faint [feınt] a schwach, matt; n Ohnmacht f; vi ohnmächtig werden; ~ **hearted** a mutlos, kleinmütig; ~ **ly** ad schwach; ~ **ness** Schwäche f; *(Med)* Schwächegefühl nt.

fair [fɛə*] a schön; hair blond; skin hell; weather schön, trocken; *(just)* gerecht, fair; *(not very good)* leidlich, mittelmäßig; conditions günstig, gut; *(sizeable)* ansehnlich; ad play ehrlich, fair; n *(Comm)* Messe f; *(fun* ~) Jahrmarkt m; ~ **ly** ad *(honestly)* gerecht, fair; *(rather)* ziemlich; ~ **ness** Schönheit f; *(of hair)* Blondheit f; *(of game)* Ehrlichkeit f, Fairneß f; ~ **way** *(Naut)* Fahrrinne f.

fairy ['fɛərı] n Fee f; ~ **land** Märchenland nt; ~ **tale** Märchen nt.

faith [feıθ] n Glaube m; *(trust)* Vertrauen nt; *(sect)* Bekenntnis nt, Religion f; ~ **ful** a, ~ **fully** ad treu; **yours** ~ **fully** hochachtungsvoll.

fake [feık] n *(thing)* Fälschung f; *(person)* Schwindler m; a vorgetäuscht; vt fälschen.

falcon ['fɔːlkən] n Falke m.

fall [fɔːl] n Fall m, Sturz m; *(decrease)* Fallen nt; *(of snow)* Schnee)fall m; *(US: autumn)* Herbst m; vi irreg *(lit, fig)* fallen; *(night)* hereinbrechen; ~ **s** pl *(waterfall)* Fälle pl; ~ **back on** vt in Reserve haben; ~ **down** vi *(person)* hinfallen; *(building)* einstürzen; ~ **flat** vi *(lit)* platt hinfallen; *(joke)* nicht ankommen; **the plan fell flat** aus dem Plan wurde nichts; ~ **for** vt trick

hereinfallen auf *(+acc)*; person sich verknallen in *(+acc*); ~ **off** vi herunterfallen *(von)*; *(diminish)* sich vermindern; ~ **out** vi sich streiten; ~ **through** vi *(plan)* ins Wasser fallen.

fallacy ['fæləsı] n Trugschluß m.

fallible ['fæləbl] a fehlbar.

fallout ['fɔːlaʊt] n radioaktive(r) Niederschlag m.

fallow ['fæləʊ] a brach(liegend).

false [fɔːls] a falsch; *(artificial)* gefälscht, künstlich; **under** ~ **pretences** unter Vorspiegelung falscher Tatsachen; ~ **alarm** Fehlalarm m; ~ **ly** ad fälschlicherweise; ~ **teeth** pl Gebiß nt.

falter ['fɔːltə*] vi schwanken; *(in speech)* stocken.

fame [feım] n Ruhm m.

familiar [fə'mılıə*] a vertraut, bekannt; *(intimate)* familiär; **to be** ~ **with** vertraut sein mit, gut kennen; ~ **ity** [fəmılı'ærıtı] Vertrautheit f; ~ **ize** vt vertraut machen.

family ['fæmılı] n Familie f; *(relations)* Verwandtschaft f; ~ **allowance** Kindergeld nt; ~ **business** Familienunternehmen nt; ~ **doctor** Hausarzt m; ~ **life** Familienleben nt; ~ **planning** Geburtenkontrolle f.

famine ['fæmın] n Hungersnot f.

famished ['fæmıʃt] a ausgehungert.

famous ['feıməs] a berühmt.

fan [fæn] n *(folding)* Fächer m; *(Elec)* Ventilator m; *(admirer)* begeisterte(r) Anhänger m; Fan m; vt fächeln; ~ **out** vi sich (fächerförmig) ausbreiten.

fanatic [fə'nætık] n Fanatiker(in f) m; ~ **al** a fanatisch.

fan belt ['fænbelt] n Keilriemen m.

fancied ['fænsıd] a beliebt, populär.

fanciful ['fænsıful] a *(odd)* seltsam; *(imaginative)* phantasievoll.

fancy ['fænsı] n *(liking)* Neigung f; *(imagination)* Phantasie f, Einbildung f; a schick, ausgefallen; vt *(like)* gern haben, wollen; *(imagine)* sich einbilden; **(just)** ~ **(that)!** stellen Sie sich (das nur) vor!; ~ **dress** Verkleidung f, Maskenkostüm m; ~ **dress ball** Maskenball m.

fanfare ['fænfɛə*] n Fanfare f.

fang [fæŋ] n Fangzahn m; *(snake's)* Giftzahn m.

fanlight ['fænlaıt] n Oberlicht nt.

fantastic [fæn'tæstık] a phantastisch.

fantasy ['fæntəzı] n Phantasie f.

far [fɑː*] a weit; ad weit entfernt; *(very much)* weitaus, (sehr) viel; ~ **away**, ~ **off** weit weg; **by** ~ bei weitem; **so** ~ soweit; bis jetzt; ~ **away** a weit entfernt; **the F** ~ **East** der Ferne Osten.

farce [fɑːs] n Schwank m, Posse f; *(fig)* Farce f.

farcical ['fɑːsıkəl] a possenhaft; *(fig)* lächerlich.

fare [fɛə*] n Fahrpreis m; Fahrgeld nt; *(food)* Kost f, vi: **he is faring well** es ergeht ihm gut; ~ **well** Abschied(sgruß) m; interj lebe wohl!; a Abschieds-.

far-fetched ['fɑː'fetʃt] a weit hergeholt.

farm [fɑːm] n Bauernhof m, Farm f; vt

bewirtschaften; *vi* Landwirt *m* sein; ~**er**
Bauer *m*, Landwirt *m*; ~**hand** Landarbeiter *m*; ~**house** Bauernhaus *nt*; ~**ing**
Landwirtschaft *f*; ~**land** Ackerland *nt*;
~**yard** Hof *m*.

far-reaching ['fɑː'riːtʃɪŋ] *a* weitgehend.
far-sighted ['fɑː'saɪtɪd] *a* weitblickend.
fart [fɑːt] *n* (*col*) Furz *m*; *vi* (*col*) furzen.
farther ['fɑːðə*] *a*, *ad* weiter.
farthest ['fɑːðɪst] *a* weiteste(r,s),
fernste(r,s); *ad* am weitesten.
fascinate ['fæsɪneɪt] *vt* faszinieren,
bezaubern.
fascinating ['fæsɪneɪtɪŋ] *a* faszinierend,
spannend.
fascination [fæsɪ'neɪʃən] *n* Faszination *f*,
Zauber *m*.
fascism ['fæʃɪzəm] *n* Faschismus *m*.
fascist ['fæʃɪst] *n* Faschist *m*; *a*
faschistisch.
fashion ['fæʃən] *n* (*of clothes*) Mode *f*;
(*manner*) Art *f* (und Weise *f*); *vt* machen,
gestalten; **in** ~ in Mode; **out of** ~ unmodisch; ~**able** *a* *clothes* modern,
modisch; *place* elegant; ~ **show** Mode(n)-
schau *f*.
fast [fɑːst] *a* schnell; (*firm*) fest; *dye*
waschecht; **to be** ~ (*clock*) vorgehen; *ad*
schnell; (*firmly*) fest; *n* Fasten *nt*; *vi* fasten.
fasten ['fɑːsn] *vt* (*attach*) befestigen; *seat
belt* festmachen; (*with rope*) zuschnüren; *vi*
sich schließen lassen; ~**er**, ~**ing**
Verschluß *m*.
fastidious [fæs'tɪdɪəs] *a* wählerisch.
fat [fæt] *a* dick, fett; *n* (*on person*) Fett *nt*,
Speck *m* (*col*); (*on meat*) Fett *nt*; (*for cooking*) (Braten)fett *nt*.
fatal ['feɪtl] *a* tödlich; (*disastrous*) verhängnisvoll; ~**ism** Fatalismus *m*,
Schicksalsglaube *m*; ~**ity** [fə'tælɪtɪ] (*road
death etc*) Todesopfer *nt*; ~**ly** *ad* tödlich.
fate [feɪt] *n* Schicksal *nt*; ~**ful** *a* (*prophetic*) schicksalsschwer; (*important*)
schicksalhaft.
father ['fɑːðə*] *n* Vater *m*; (*Rel*) Pater *m*;
~-**in-law** Schwiegervater *m*; ~**ly** *a*
väterlich.
fathom ['fæðəm] *n* Klafter *m*; *vt* ausloten;
(*fig*) ergründen.
fatigue [fə'tiːg] *n* Ermüdung *f*; *vt* ermüden.
fatness ['fætnɪs] *n* Dicke *f*.
fatten ['fætn] *vt* dick machen; *animals*
mästen; *vi* dick werden.
fatty ['fætɪ] *a* *food* fettig.
fatuous ['fætjuəs] *a* albern, affig.
faucet ['fɔːsɪt] *n* (*US*) Wasserhahn *m*.
fault [fɔːlt] *n* (*defect*) Defekt *m*; (*Elec*)
Störung *f*; (*blame*) Fehler *m*, Schuld *f*;
(*Geog*) Verwerfung *f*; **it's your** ~ du bist
daran schuld; **at** ~ schuldig, im Unrecht;
vt: ~ **sth** etwas an etw (*dat*) auszusetzen
haben; ~**less** *a* fehlerfrei, tadellos; ~**y** *a*
fehlerhaft, defekt.
fauna ['fɔːnə] *n* Fauna *f*.
favour, (*US*) **favor** ['feɪvə*] *n* (*approval*)
Wohlwollen *nt*; (*kindness*) Gefallen *m*; *vt*
(*prefer*) vorziehen; **in** ~ **of** für; zugunsten
(+*gen*); ~**able** *a*, ~**ably** *ad* günstig; ~**ite**
['feɪvərɪt] *a* Lieblings-; *n* Günstling *m*;
(*child*) Liebling *m*; (*Sport*) Favorit *m*;

~**itism** (*Sch*) Bevorzugung *f*; (*Pol*)
Günstlingswirtschaft *f*.
fawn [fɔːn] *a* rehbraun; *n* (*colour*)
Rehbraun *nt*; (*animal*) (Reh)kitz *nt*.
fawning ['fɔːnɪŋ] *a* kriecherisch.
fear [fɪə*] *n* Furcht *f*; *vt* fürchten; **no** ~!
keine Angst!; ~**ful** *a* (*timid*) furchtsam;
(*terrible*) fürchterlich; ~**less** *a*, ~**lessly**
ad furchtlos; ~**lessness** Furchtlosigkeit *f*.
feasibility [fiːzə'bɪlɪtɪ] *n* Durchführbarkeit
f.
feasible ['fiːzəbl] *a* durchführbar, machbar.
feast [fiːst] *n* Festmahl *nt*; (*Rel*) Kirchenfest *nt*; *vi* sich gütlich tun (**on an** +*dat*); ~
day kirchliche(r) Feiertag *m*.
feat [fiːt] *n* Leistung *f*.
feather ['feðə*] *n* Feder *f*.
feature ['fiːtʃə*] *n* (*Gesichts*)zug *m*;
(*important part*) Grundzug *m*; (*Cine, Press*)
Feature *nt*; *vt* darstellen; (*advertising etc*)
groß herausbringen; **featuring X** mit X;
vi vorkommen; ~ **film** Spielfilm *m*;
~**less** *a* nichtssagend.
February ['februərɪ] *n* Februar *m*.
federal ['fedərəl] *a* Bundes-.
federation [fedə'reɪʃən] *n* (*society*)
Verband *m*; (*of states*) Staatenbund *m*.
fed-up [fed'ʌp] *a*: **to be** ~ **with sth** etw
satt haben; **I'm** ~ ich habe die Nase voll.
fee [fiː] *n* Gebühr *f*.
feeble ['fiːbl] *a* *person* schwach; *excuse*
lahm; ~-**minded** *a* geistesschwach.
feed [fiːd] *n* (*for baby*) Essen *nt*; (*for
animals*) Futter *nt*; *vt* *irreg* füttern;
(*support*) ernähren; **to** ~ **on** leben von,
fressen; ~**back** (*Tech*) Rückkopplung *f*;
(*information*) Feedback *nt*.
feel [fiːl] *n*: **it has a soft** ~ es fühlt sich
weich an; **to get the** ~ **of sth** sich an etw
(*acc*) gewöhnen; *irreg* *vt* (*sense*) fühlen;
(*touch*) anfassen; (*think*) meinen; *vi*
(*person*) sich fühlen; (*thing*) sich anfühlen;
I ~ **cold** mir ist kalt; **I** ~ **like a cup of
tea** ich habe Lust auf eine Tasse Tee;
~**er** Fühler *m*; ~**ing** Gefühl *nt*; (*opinion*)
Meinung *f*.
feet [fiːt] *npl of* **foot.**
feign [feɪn] *vt* vortäuschen; ~**ed** *a* vorgetäuscht, Schein-.
feint [feɪnt] *n* Täuschungsmanöver *nt*.
feline ['fiːlaɪn] *a* Katzen-, katzenartig.
fell [fel] *vt* *tree* fällen; *n* (*hill*) kahle(r) Berg
m; *a*: **with one** ~ **swoop** mit einem
Schlag; auf einen Streich.
fellow ['feləu] *n* (*companion*) Gefährte *m*,
Kamerad *m*; (*man*) Kerl *m*; ~ **citizen**
Mitbürger(in *f*) *m*; ~ **countryman**
Landsmann *m*; ~ **feeling** Mitgefühl *nt*;
~ **men** *pl* Mitmenschen *pl*; ~**ship**
(*group*) Körperschaft *f*; (*friendliness*)
Gemeinschaft *f*, Kameradschaft *f*; (*scholarship*) Forschungsstipendium *nt*; ~
worker Mitarbeiter(in *f*) *m*.
felony ['felənɪ] *n* schwere(s) Verbrechen
nt.
felt [felt] *n* Filz *m*.
female ['fiːmeɪl] *n* (*of animals*) Weibchen
nt; *a* weiblich.

feminine ['femɪnɪn] a (Gram) weiblich; qualities fraulich.

femininity [femɪ'nɪnɪtɪ] n Weiblichkeit f; (quality) Fraulichkeit f.

feminist ['femɪnɪst] n Feminist(in f) m.

fence [fens] n Zaun m; (crook) Hehler m; vi fechten; ~ **in** vt einzäunen; ~ **off** vt absperren.

fencing ['fensɪŋ] n Zaun m; (Sport) Fechten nt.

fend [fend] vi: ~ **for o.s.** sich (allein) durchschlagen.

fender ['fendə*] n Kaminvorsetzer m; (US Aut) Kotflügel m.

ferment [fə'ment] vi (Chem) gären; ['fɜːment] n (excitement) Unruhe f; ~**ation** [fɜːmen'teɪʃən] Gärung f.

fern [fɜːn] n Farn m.

ferocious [fə'rəʊʃəs] a wild, grausam; ~**ly** ad wild.

ferocity [fə'rɒsɪtɪ] n Wildheit f, Grimmigkeit f.

ferry ['ferɪ] n Fähre f; vt übersetzen.

fertile ['fɜːtaɪl] a fruchtbar.

fertility [fə'tɪlɪtɪ] n Fruchtbarkeit f.

fertilization [fɜːtɪlaɪ'zeɪʃən] n Befruchtung f.

fertilize ['fɜːtɪlaɪz] vt (Agr) düngen; (Biol) befruchten; ~**r** (Kunst)dünger m.

fervent ['fɜːvənt] a admirer glühend; hope innig.

festival ['festɪvəl] n (Rel etc) Fest nt; (Art, Mus) Festspiele pl; Festival nt.

festive ['festɪv] a festlich; **the ~ season** (Christmas) die Festzeit f.

festivity [fes'tɪvɪtɪ] n Festlichkeit f.

fetch [fetʃ] vt holen; (in sale) einbringen, erzielen.

fetching ['fetʃɪŋ] a einnehmend, reizend.

fête [feɪt] n Fest nt.

fetish ['fiːtɪʃ] n Fetisch m.

fetters ['fetəz] npl (lit, fig) Fesseln pl.

fetus ['fiːtəs] n (US) = **foetus**.

feud [fjuːd] n Fehde f; vi sich befehden; ~**al** a lehnsherrlich, Feudal-; ~**alism** Lehenswesen nt, Feudalismus m.

fever ['fiːvə*] n Fieber nt; ~**ish** a (Med) fiebrig, Fieber-; (fig) fieberhaft; ~**ishly** ad (fig) fieberhaft.

few [fjuː] a wenig; pron wenige; a ~ a, pron einige; ~**er** weniger; ~**est** wenigste(r,s); **a good** ~ ziemlich viele.

fiancé [fɪ'ɑːnseɪ] n Verlobte(r) m; ~**e** Verlobte f.

fiasco [fɪ'æskəʊ] n Fiasko nt, Reinfall m.

fib [fɪb] n Flunkerei f; vi flunkern.

fibre, (US) **fiber** ['faɪbə*] n Faser f, Fiber f; (material) Faserstoff m; ~**glass** Glaswolle f.

fickle ['fɪkl] a unbeständig, wankelmütig; ~**ness** Unbeständigkeit f, Wankelmut m.

fiction ['fɪkʃən] n (novels) Romanliteratur f; (story) Erdichtung f; ~**al** a erfunden.

fictitious [fɪk'tɪʃəs] a erfunden, fingiert.

fiddle ['fɪdl] n Geige f, Fiedel f; (trick) Schwindelei f; vt accounts frisieren; ~ **with** vi herumfummeln an (+dat); ~**r** Geiger m.

fidelity [fɪ'delɪtɪ] n Treue f.

fidget ['fɪdʒɪt] vi zappeln; n Zappelphilipp m; ~**y** a nervös, zappelig.

field [fiːld] n Feld nt; (range) Gebiet nt; ~ **day** (gala) Paradetag m; ~ **marshal** Feldmarschall m; ~**work** (Mil) Schanze f; (Univ) Feldforschung f.

fiend [fiːnd] n Teufel m; (beast) Unhold m; Fanatiker(in f) m; ~**ish** a teuflisch.

fierce a, ~**ly** ad [fɪəs, -lɪ] wild; ~**ness** Wildheit f.

fiery ['faɪərɪ] a glühend; (blazing) brennend; (hot-tempered) hitzig, heftig.

fifteen [fɪf'tiːn] num fünfzehn.

fifth [fɪfθ] a fünfte(r,s); n Fünftel nt.

fifty ['fɪftɪ] num fünfzig; ~-~ halbe halbe, fifty fifty (col).

fig [fɪg] n Feige f.

fight [faɪt] n Kampf m; (brawl) Schlägerei f; (argument) Streit m; irreg vt kämpfen gegen; sich schlagen mit; (fig) bekämpfen; vi kämpfen; sich schlagen; streiten; ~**er** Kämpfer(in f) m; (plane) Jagdflugzeug nt; ~**ing** Kämpfen nt; (war) Kampfhandlungen pl.

figment ['fɪgmənt] n ~ **of imagination** reine Einbildung f.

figurative ['fɪgərətɪv] a bildlich.

figure ['fɪgə*] n Form f; (of person) Figur f; (person) Gestalt f; (illustration) Zeichnung f; (number) Ziffer f; vt (US: imagine) glauben; vi (appear) eine Rolle spielen, erscheinen; (US: make sense) stimmen; ~ **out** vt verstehen, herausbekommen; ~**head** (Naut, fig) Galionsfigur f; ~ **skating** Eiskunstlauf m.

filament ['fɪləmənt] n Faden m; (Elec) Glühfaden m.

file [faɪl] n (tool) Feile f; (dossier) Akte f; (folder) Aktenordner m; (row) Reihe f; vt metal, nails feilen; papers abheften; claim einreichen; vi: ~ **in/out** hintereinander hereinkommen/hinausgehen; **in single** ~ einer hinter dem anderen.

filing ['faɪlɪŋ] n Feilen nt; ~**s** pl Feilspäne pl; ~ **cabinet** Aktenschrank m.

fill [fɪl] vt füllen; (occupy) ausfüllen; (satisfy) sättigen; n: **to eat one's** ~ sich richtig satt essen; **to have had one's** ~ genug haben; **to** ~ **the bill** (fig) allen Anforderungen genügen; ~ **in** vt hole (auf)füllen; form ausfüllen; ~ **up** vt container auffüllen; form ausfüllen.

fillet ['fɪlɪt] n Filet nt; vt als Filet herrichten.

filling ['fɪlɪŋ] n (Cook) Füllung f; (for tooth) (Zahn)plombe f; ~ **station** Tankstelle f.

fillip ['fɪlɪp] n Anstoß m, Auftrieb m.

film [fɪlm] n Film m; (layer) Häutchen nt, Film m; vt scene filmen; ~ **star** Filmstar m; ~**strip** Filmstreifen m.

filter ['fɪltə*] n Filter m; (for traffic) Verkehrsfilter m; vt filtern; vi durchsickern; ~ **tip** Filter m, Filtermundstück nt; ~-**tipped cigarette** Filterzigarette f.

filth [fɪlθ] n (lit) Dreck m; (fig) Unflat m; ~**y** a dreckig; (behaviour) gemein; weather scheußlich.

fin [fɪn] n Flosse f.

final ['faɪnl] a letzte(r,s); End-; (conclusive) endgültig; n (Ftbl etc) Endspiel nt; ~**s** pl

(*Univ*) Abschlußexamen *nt*; (*Sport*) Schlußrunde *f*; ~**e** [fɪˈnɑːlɪ] (*Theat*) Schlußszene *f*; (*Mus*) Finale *nt*; ~**ist** (*Sport*) Schlußrundenteilnehmer *m*; ~**ize** *vt* endgültige Form geben (+*dat*); abschließen; ~**ly** *ad* (*lastly*) zuletzt; (*eventually*) endlich; (*irrevocably*) endgültig.

finance [faɪˈnæns] *n* Finanzwesen *nt*; ~**s** *pl* Finanzen *pl*; (*income*) Einkünfte *pl*; *vt* finanzieren.

financial [faɪˈnænʃəl] *a* Finanz-; finanziell; ~**ly** *ad* finanziell.

financier [faɪˈnænsɪə*] *n* Finanzier *m*.

find [faɪnd] *irreg vt* finden; *vi* (*realize*) erkennen; *n* Fund *m*; to ~ **sb guilty** jdn für schuldig erklären; to ~ **out** herausfinden; ~**ings** *pl* (*Jur*) Ermittlungsergebnis *nt*; (*of report*) Feststellung *f*, Befund *m*.

fine [faɪn] *a* fein; (*thin*) dünn, fein; (*good*) gut; *clothes* elegant; *weather* schön; *ad* (*well*) gut; (*small*) klein; *n* (*Jur*) Geldstrafe *f*; *vt* (*Jur*) mit einer Geldstrafe belegen; to **cut it** ~ (*fig*) knapp rechnen; ~ **arts** *pl* die schönen Künste *pl*; ~**ness** *n* Feinheit *f*; ~**ry** [ˈfaɪnərɪ] Putz *m*; ~**sse** [fɪˈnes] Finesse *f*.

finger [ˈfɪŋgə*] *n* Finger *m*; *vt* befühlen; ~**nail** Fingernagel *m*; ~**print** Fingerabdruck *m*; ~**stall** Fingerling *m*; ~**tip** Fingerspitze *f*; to **have sth at one's ~ tips** etw parat haben.

finicky [ˈfɪnɪkɪ] *a* pingelig.

finish [ˈfɪnɪʃ] *n* Ende *nt*; (*Sport*) Ziel *nt*; (*of object*) Verarbeitung *f*; (*of paint*) Oberflächenwirkung *f*; *vt* beenden; *book* zu Ende lesen; to **be** ~**ed with sth** fertig sein mit etw; *vi* aufhören; (*Sport*) ans Ziel kommen; ~**ing line** Ziellinie *f*; ~**ing school** Mädchenpensionat *nt*.

finite [ˈfaɪnaɪt] *a* endlich, begrenzt; (*Gram*) finit.

fiord [fjɔːd] *n* Fjord *m*.

fir [fɜː*] *n* Tanne *f*, Fichte *f*.

fire [faɪə*] *n* (*lit, fig*) Feuer *nt*; (*damaging*) Brand *m*, Feuer *nt*; to **set** ~ to sth etw in Brand stecken; to **be on** ~ brennen; *vt* (*Aut*) zünden; *gun* abfeuern; (*fig*) *imagination* entzünden; (*dismiss*) hinauswerfen; *vi* (*Aut*) zünden; to ~ **at sb** auf jdn schießen; ~ **away!** schieß los!; ~ **alarm** Feueralarm *m*; ~**arm** Schußwaffe *f*; ~ **brigade** Feuerwehr *f*; ~ **engine** Feuerwehrauto *nt*; ~ **escape** Feuerleiter *f*; ~ **extinguisher** Löschgerät *nt*; ~**man** Feuerwehrmann *m*; ~**place** offene(r) Kamin *m*; ~**proof** *a* feuerfest; ~**side** Kamin *m*; ~ **station** Feuerwehrwache *f*; ~**wood** Brennholz *nt*; ~**works** *pl* Feuerwerk *nt*.

firing [ˈfaɪərɪŋ] *n* Schießen *nt*; ~ **squad** Exekutionskommando *nt*.

firm *a*, ~**ly** *ad* [fɜːm,-lɪ] fest; (*determined*) entschlossen; *n* Firma *f*; ~**ness** Festigkeit *f*; Entschlossenheit *f*.

first [fɜːst] *a* erste(r,s); *ad* zuerst; *arrive* als erste(r); *happen* zum erstenmal; *n* (*person: in race*) Erste(r) *mf*; (*Univ*) Eins *f*; (*Aut*) erste(r) Gang *m*; **at** ~ zuerst, anfangs; ~

of all zu allererst; ~ **aid** Erste Hilfe *f*; ~-**aid kit** Verbandskasten *m*; ~-**class** *a* erstklassig; (*travel*) erste(r) Klasse; ~-**hand** *a* aus erster Hand; ~ **lady** (*US*) First Lady *f*; ~**ly** *ad* erstens; ~ **name** Vorname *m*; ~ **night** Premiere *f*; Erstaufführung *f*; ~-**rate** *a* erstklassig.

fiscal [ˈfɪskəl] *a* fiskalisch, Finanz-.

fish [fɪʃ] *n* Fisch *m*; *vt river* angeln in (+*dat*); *sea* fischen in (+*dat*); *vi* fischen; angeln; ~ **out** *vt* herausfischen; to **go** ~**ing** angeln gehen; (*in sea*) fischen gehen; ~**erman** Fischer *m*; ~**ery** Fischgrund *m*; ~ **finger** Fischstäbchen *nt*; ~ **hook** Angelhaken *m*; ~**ing boat** Fischerboot *nt*; ~**ing line** Angelschnur *f*; ~**ing rod** Angel(rute) *f*; ~**ing tackle** Angelzeug *nt*; ~ **market** Fischmarkt *m*; ~**monger** Fischhändler *m*; ~ **slice** Fischvorlegemesser *nt*; ~**y** *a* (*col: suspicious*) faul.

fission [ˈfɪʃən] *n* Spaltung *f*.

fissure [ˈfɪʃə*] *n* Riß *m*.

fist [fɪst] *n* Faust *f*.

fit [fɪt] *a* (*Med*) gesund; (*Sport*) in Form, fit; (*suitable*) geeignet; *vt* passen (+*dat*); (*insert, attach*) einsetzen; *vi* (*correspond*) passen (zu); (*clothes*) passen; (*in space, gap*) hineinpassen; *n* (*of clothes*) Sitz *m*; (*Med, of anger*) Anfall *m*; (*of laughter*) Krampf *m*; ~ **in** *vi* sich einfügen; (*fig*) passen; ~ **out** *vt*, ~ **up** *vt* ausstatten; ~**fully, by** ~**s and starts** *move* ruckweise; *work* unregelmäßig; ~**ment** Einrichtungsgegenstand *m*; ~**ness** (*suitability*) Eignung *f*; (*Med*) Gesundheit *f*; (*Sport*) Fitneß *f*; ~**ter** (*Tech*) Monteur *m*; ~**ting** *a* passend; *n* (*of dress*) Anprobe *f*; (*piece of equipment*) (Ersatz)teil *nt*; ~**tings** *pl* Zubehör *nt*.

five [faɪv] *num* fünf; ~**r** (*Brit*) Fünf-Pfund-Note *f*.

fix [fɪks] *vt* befestigen; (*settle*) festsetzen; (*repair*) richten, reparieren; *drink* zurechtmachen; *n*: **in a** ~ in der Klemme; ~**ed** *a* repariert; *time* abgemacht; **it was** ~**ed** (*dishonest*) das war Schiebung; ~**ture** [ˈfɪkstʃə*] Installationsteil *m*; (*Sport*) Spiel *nt*.

fizz [fɪz] *n* Sprudeln *nt*; *vi* sprudeln.

fizzle [ˈfɪzl] *vi* zischen; ~ **out** *vi* verpuffen.

fizzy [ˈfɪzɪ] *a* Sprudel-, sprudelnd.

fjord [fjɔːd] *n* = **fiord**.

flabbergasted [ˈflæbəgɑːstɪd] *a* (*col*) platt.

flabby [ˈflæbɪ] *a* wabbelig.

flag [flæg] *n* Fahne *f*; *vi* (*strength*) nachlassen; (*spirit*) erlahmen; ~ **down** *vt* stoppen, abwinken.

flagon [ˈflægən] *n* bauchige (Wein)flasche *f*; Krug *m*.

flagpole [ˈflægpəʊl] *n* Fahnenstange *f*.

flagrant [ˈfleɪgrənt] *a* offenkundig; *offence* schamlos; *violation* flagrant.

flagstone [ˈflægstəʊn] *n* Steinplatte *f*.

flair [flɛə*] *n* (*talent*) Talent *nt*; (*of style*) Schick *m*.

flake [fleɪk] *n* (*of snow*) Flocke *f*; (*of rust*) Schuppe *f*; *vi* (*also* ~ **off**) abblättern.

flamboyant [flæmˈbɔɪənt] *a* extravagant; *colours* brillant; *gesture* großartig.

flame [fleɪm] n Flamme f.

flaming ['fleɪmɪŋ] a (col) verdammt; row irre.

flamingo [flə'mɪŋgəʊ] n Flamingo m.

flan [flæn] n Obsttorte f.

flank [flæŋk] n Flanke f; vt flankieren.

flannel ['flænl] n Flanell m; (face —) Waschlappen m; (col) Geschwafel nt; ~s pl Flanellhose f.

flap [flæp] n Klappe f; (col: crisis) (helle) Aufregung f; vt wings schlagen mit; vi lose herabhängen; flattern; (col: panic) sich aufregen.

flare [flɛə*] n (signal) Leuchtsignal nt; (in skirt etc) Weite f; ~ up vi aufflammen; (fig) aufbrausen; (revolt) (plötzlich) ausbrechen.

flared [flɛəd] a trousers ausgestellt.

flash [flæʃ] n Blitz m; (news —) Kurzmeldung f; (Phot) Blitzlicht nt; vt aufleuchten lassen; message durchgeben; vi aufleuchten; **in a** ~ im Nu; **to** ~ **by** or **past** vorbeirasen; ~**back** Rückblende f; ~ **bulb** Blitzlichtbirne f; ~**er** (Aut) Blinker m.

flashy ['flæʃɪ] a (pej) knallig.

flask [flɑːsk] n Reiseflasche f; (Chem) Kolben m; (vacuum —) Thermosflasche f.

flat [flæt] a flach; (dull) matt; (Mus) erniedrigt; beer schal; tyre platt; **A** ~ as; ad (Mus) zu tief; n (rooms) Wohnung f; (Mus) b nt; (Aut) Reifenpanne f, Platte(r) m; ~ **broke** a (col) völlig pleite; ~**footed** a plattfüßig; ~**ly** ad glatt; ~**ness** Flachheit f; ~**ten** vt (also ~ten out) platt machen, (ein)ebnen.

flatter ['flætə*] vt schmeicheln (+dat); ~**er** Schmeichler(in f) m; ~**ing** a schmeichelhaft; ~**y** Schmeichelei f.

flatulence ['flætjʊləns] n Blähungen pl.

flaunt [flɔːnt] vt prunken mit.

flavour, (US) **flavor** ['fleɪvə*] n Geschmack m; vt würzen; ~**ing** Würze f.

flaw [flɔː] n Fehler m; (in argument) schwache(r) Punkt m; ~**less** a einwandfrei.

flax [flæks] n Flachs m; ~**en** a flachsfarben.

flea [fliː] n Floh m.

flee [fliː] irreg vi fliehen; vt fliehen vor (+dat); country fliehen aus.

fleece [fliːs] n Schaffell nt, Vlies nt; vt (col) schröpfen.

fleet [fliːt] n Flotte f.

fleeting [fliːtɪŋ] a flüchtig.

flesh [fleʃ] n Fleisch nt; (of fruit) Fruchtfleisch nt; ~ **wound** Fleischwunde f.

flex [fleks] n (Leitungs)kabel nt; vt beugen, biegen; ~**ibility** [fleksɪ'bɪlɪtɪ] Biegsamkeit f; (fig) Flexibilität f; ~**ible** a biegsam; plans flexibel.

flick [flɪk] n Schnippen nt; (blow) leichte(r) Schlag m; vt leicht schlagen; ~ **through** vt durchblättern; **to** ~ **sth off** etw wegschnippen.

flicker ['flɪkə*] n Flackern nt; (of emotion) Funken m; vi flackern.

flier ['flaɪə*] n Flieger m.

flight [flaɪt] n Fliegen nt; (journey) Flug m; (fleeing) Flucht f; ~ **of stairs** Treppe f;

to take ~ die Flucht ergreifen; **to put to** ~ in die Flucht schlagen; ~ **deck** Flugdeck nt; ~**y** a flatterhaft.

flimsy ['flɪmzɪ] a nicht stabil, windig; (thin) hauchdünn; excuse fadenscheinig.

flinch [flɪntʃ] vi zurückschrecken (away from vor +dat).

fling [flɪŋ] vt irreg schleudern.

flint [flɪnt] n (in lighter) Feuerstein m.

flip [flɪp] vt werfen; **he** ~**ped the lid off** er klappte den Deckel auf.

flippancy ['flɪpənsɪ] n Leichtfertigkeit f.

flippant ['flɪpənt] a schnippisch; **to be** ~ **about sth** etw nicht ernst nehmen.

flirt [flɜːt] vi flirten; n kokette(s) Mädchen nt; **he/she is a** ~ er/sie flirtet gern; ~**ation** [flɜː'teɪʃən] Flirt m.

flit [flɪt] vi flitzen.

float [fləʊt] n (Fishing) Schwimmer m; (esp in procession) Plattformwagen m; vi schwimmen; (in air) schweben; vt schwimmen lassen; (Comm) gründen; currency floaten; ~**ing** a (lit) schwimmend; (fig) votes unentschieden.

flock [flɒk] n (of sheep, Rel) Herde f; (of birds) Schwarm m; (of people) Schar f.

flog [flɒg] vt prügeln; peitschen; (col: sell) verkaufen.

flood [flʌd] n Überschwemmung f; (fig) Flut f; **the F~** die Sintflut f; **to be in** ~ Hochwasser haben; vt (lit, fig) überschwemmen; ~**ing** Überschwemmung f; ~**light** n Flutlicht nt; vt anstrahlen; ~**lighting** Beleuchtung f.

floor [flɔː*] n (of building) Fußboden m; (storey) Stock m; vt person zu Boden schlagen; **ground** ~ (Brit), **first** ~ (US) Erdgeschoß nt; **first** ~ (Brit), **second** ~ (US) erste(r) Stock m; ~**board** Diele f; ~ **show** Kabarettvorstellung f; ~**walker** (Comm) Abteilungsaufseher m.

flop [flɒp] n Plumps m; (failure) Reinfall m; vi (fail) durchfallen; **the project** ~**ped** aus dem Plan wurde nichts.

floppy ['flɒpɪ] a hängend; ~ **hat** Schlapphut m.

flora ['flɔːrə] n Flora f; ~**l** a Blumen-.

florid ['flɒrɪd] a style blumig.

florist ['flɒrɪst] n Blumenhändler(in f) m; ~'**s (shop)** Blumengeschäft nt.

flotsam ['flɒtsəm] n Strandgut nt.

flounce [flaʊns] n (on dress) Besatz m; vi: ~ **in/out** hinein-/hinausstürmen.

flounder ['flaʊndə*] vi herumstrampeln; (fig) ins Schleudern kommen.

flour ['flaʊə*] n Mehl nt.

flourish ['flʌrɪʃ] vi blühen; gedeihen; vt (wave) schwingen; n (waving) Schwingen nt; (of trumpets) Tusch m, Fanfare f; ~**ing** a blühend.

flout [flaʊt] vt mißachten, sich hinwegsetzen über (+acc).

flow [fləʊ] n Fließen nt; (of sea) Flut f; vi fließen.

flower ['flaʊə*] n Blume f; vi blühen; ~**bed** Blumenbeet nt; ~**pot** Blumentopf m; ~**y** a style blumenreich.

flowing ['fləʊɪŋ] a fließend; hair wallend; style flüssig.

flu [fluː] n Grippe f.

fluctuate ['flʌktjʊeɪt] vi schwanken.

fluctuation [flʌktjʊ'eɪʃən] n Schwankung f.

fluency ['fluːənsɪ] n Flüssigkeit f; **his ~ in English** seine Fähigkeit, fließend Englisch zu sprechen.

fluent a **~ly** ad ['fluːənt,-lɪ] speech flüssig; **to be ~ in German** fließend Deutsch sprechen.

fluff [flʌf] n Fussel f; **~y** a flaumig; pastry flockig.

fluid ['fluːɪd] n Flüssigkeit f; a (lit) flüssig; (fig) plans veränderbar.

fluke [fluːk] n (col) Dusel m.

fluorescent [flʊə'resnt] a fluoreszierend, Leucht-.

fluoride ['flʊəraɪd] n Fluorid nt.

flurry ['flʌrɪ] n (of activity) Aufregung f; (of snow) Gestöber nt.

flush [flʌʃ] n Erröten nt; (of excitement) Glühen nt; (Cards) Sequenz f; vt (aus)spülen; vi erröten; a glatt; **~ed** a rot.

fluster ['flʌstə*] n Verwirrung f; **~ed** a verwirrt.

flute [fluːt] n Querflöte f.

fluted ['fluːtɪd] a gerillt.

flutter ['flʌtə*] n (of wings) Flattern nt; (of excitement) Beben nt; vi flattern; (person) rotieren.

flux [flʌks] n: **in a state of ~** im Fluß.

fly [flaɪ] n (insect) Fliege f; (on trousers, also **flies**) (Hosen)schlitz m; irreg vt fliegen; (flee) fliehen; (flag) wehen; **~ open** vi auffliegen; **let ~** vti (shoot) losschießen; (verbally) loswettern; insults loslassen; **~ing** n Fliegen nt; **with ~ing colours** mit fliegenden Fahnen; **~ing saucer** fliegende Untertasse f; **~ing start** que(r) Start m; **~ing visit** Stippvisite f; **~over** (Brit) Überführung f; **~paper** Fliegenfänger m; **~past** Luftparade f; **~sheet** (for tent) Regendach nt; **~swatter** Fliegenwedel m; **~wheel** Schwungrad nt.

foal [fəʊl] n Fohlen nt.

foam [fəʊm] n Schaum m; (plastic etc) Schaumgummi m; vi schäumen.

fob [fɒb] n: **~ off** vt andrehen (sb with sth jdm etw); (with promise) abspeisen.

focal ['fəʊkəl] a im Brennpunkt (stehend), Brennpunkt-.

focus ['fəʊkəs] n Brennpunkt m; (fig) Mittelpunkt m; vt attention konzentrieren; camera scharf einstellen; vi sich konzentrieren (on auf +acc); **in ~** scharf eingestellt; **out of ~** unscharf (eingestellt).

fodder ['fɒdə*] n Futter nt.

foe [fəʊ] n (liter) Feind m, Gegner m.

foetus ['fiːtəs] n Fötus m.

fog [fɒg] n Nebel m; vt issue verunklären, verwirren; **~gy** a neblig, trüb.

foible ['fɔɪbl] n Schwäche f, Faible nt.

foil [fɔɪl] vt vereiteln; n (metal, also fig) Folie f; (fencing) Florett nt.

fold [fəʊld] n (bend, crease) Falte f; (Agr) Pferch m; (for sheep) Pferch m; vt falten; **~ up** vt map etc zusammenfalten; vi (business) eingehen; **~er** (pamphlet) Broschüre f; (portfolio) Schnellhefter m; **~ing** a chair etc zusammenklappbar, Klapp-.

foliage ['fəʊlɪdʒ] n Laubwerk nt.

folio ['fəʊlɪəʊ] n Foliant m.

folk [fəʊk] n Volk nt; a Volks-; **~s** pl Leute pl; **~lore** (study) Volkskunde f; (tradition) Folklore f; **~song** Volkslied nt; (modern) Folksong m.

follow ['fɒləʊ] vt folgen (+dat); (obey) befolgen; fashion mitmachen; profession nachgehen (+dat); (understand) folgen können (+dat); vi folgen; (result) sich ergeben; **as ~s** wie im folgenden; **~ up** vt (weiter) verfolgen; **~er** Anhänger(in f) m; **~ing** a folgend; n Folgende(s) nt; (people) Gefolgschaft f.

folly ['fɒlɪ] n Torheit f.

fond [fɒnd] a: **to be ~ of** gern haben; **~ly** ad (with love) liebevoll; (foolishly) törichterweise; **~ness** Vorliebe f; (for people) Liebe f.

font [fɒnt] n Taufbecken nt.

food [fuːd] n Essen nt, Nahrung f; (for animals) Futter nt; **~ mixer** Küchenmixer m; **~poisoning** Lebensmittelvergiftung f; **~stuffs** pl Lebensmittel pl.

fool [fuːl] n Narr m, Närrin f; (jester) (Hof)narr m, Hanswurst m; (food) Mus nt; vt (deceive) hereinlegen; vi (behave like a ~) (herum)albern; **~hardy** a tollkühn; **~ish** a, **~ishly** ad dumm; albern; **~ishness** Dummheit f; **~proof** a idiotensicher.

foot [fʊt] n Fuß m; (of animal) Pfote f; **to put one's ~ in it** ins Fettnäpfchen treten; **on ~** zu Fuß; vt bill bezahlen; **~ball** Fußball m; **~baller** Fußballer m; **~brake** Fußbremse f; **~bridge** Fußgängerbrücke f; **~hills** pl Ausläufer pl; **~hold** Halt m; Stütze f; **~ing** (lit) Halt m; (fig) Verhältnis nt; **to get a ~ing in society** in der Gesellschaft Fuß fassen; **to be on a good ~ing with sb** mit jdm auf gutem Fuß stehen; **~light** Rampenlicht nt; **~man** Bediente(r) m; **~-and-mouth** (disease) Maul- und Klauenseuche f; **~note** Fußnote f; **~path** Fußweg m; **~rest** Fußstütze f; **~sore** a fußkrank; **~step** Schritt m; **in his father's ~steps** in den Fußstapfen seines Vaters; **~wear** Schuhzeug nt.

fop [fɒp] n Geck m.

for [fɔː*] prep für; cj denn; **what ~?** wozu?

forage ['fɒrɪdʒ] n (Vieh)futter nt; vi nach Nahrung suchen.

foray ['fɒreɪ] n Raubzug m.

forbearing [fɔ'bɛərɪŋ] a geduldig.

forbid [fə'bɪd] vt irreg verbieten; **~den** a verboten; **~ding** a einschüchternd, abschreckend.

force [fɔːs] n Kraft f, Stärke f; (compulsion) Zwang m; (Mil) Truppen pl; vt zwingen; lock aufbrechen; plant hochzüchten; **in ~** rule gültig; group in großer Stärke; **the F~s** pl die Armee; **~d** a smile gezwungen; landing Not-; **~ful** a speech kraftvoll; personality resolut.

forceps ['fɔːseps] npl Zange f.

forcible ['fɔːsəbl] a (convincing) wirksam, überzeugend; (violent) gewaltsam.

forcibly ['fɔːsəblɪ] ad unter Zwang, zwangsweise.

ford [fɔːd] n Furt f; vt durchwaten.

fore   **258**   **fragile**

fore [fɔː*] a vorder, Vorder-; n: **to the ~** in den Vordergrund.
forearm ['fɔːrɑːm] n Unterarm m.
foreboding [fɔː'bəʊdɪŋ] n Vorahnung f.
forecast ['fɔːkɑːst] n Vorhersage f; vt irreg voraussagen.
forecourt ['fɔːkɔːt] n (of garage) Vorplatz m.
forefathers ['fɔːfɑːðəz] npl Vorfahren pl.
forefinger ['fɔːfɪŋgə*] n Zeigefinger m.
forefront ['fɔːfrʌnt] n Spitze f.
forego [fɔː'gəʊ] vt irreg verzichten auf (+acc); **~ing** a vorangehend; **~ne con-clusion** ausgemachte Sache.
foreground ['fɔːgraʊnd] n Vordergrund m.
forehead ['fɔrɪd] n Stirn f.
foreign ['fɔrɪn] a Auslands-; country, accent ausländisch; trade Außen-; body Fremd-; **~er** Ausländer(in f) m; **~ exchange** Devisen pl; **~ minister** Außenminister m.
foreman ['fɔːmən] n Vorarbeiter m.
foremost ['fɔːməʊst] a erste(r,s).
forensic [fə'rensɪk] a gerichtsmedizinisch.
forerunner ['fɔːrʌnə*] n Vorläufer m.
foresee [fɔː'siː] vt irreg vorhersehen; **~able** a absehbar.
foreshore ['fɔːʃɔː*] n Küste f, Küstenland nt.
foresight ['fɔːsaɪt] n Voraussicht f.
forest ['fɔrɪst] n Wald m.
forestall [fɔː'stɔːl] vt zuvorkommen (+dat).
forestry ['fɔrɪstrɪ] n Forstwirtschaft f.
foretaste ['fɔːteɪst] n Vorgeschmack m.
foretell [fɔː'tel] vt irreg vorhersagen.
forever [fə'revə*] ad für immer.
forewarn [fɔː'wɔːn] vt vorherwarnen.
foreword ['fɔːwɜːd] n Vorwort nt.
forfeit ['fɔːfɪt] n Einbuße f; vt verwirken.
forge [fɔːdʒ] n Schmiede f; vt fälschen; iron schmieden; **~ ahead** vi Fortschritte machen; **~r** Fälscher m; **~ry** Fälschung f.
forget [fə'get] vti irreg vergessen; **~ful** a vergeßlich; **~fulness** Vergeßlichkeit f.
forgive [fə'gɪv] vt irreg verzeihen (sb for sth jdm etw).
forgiveness [fə'gɪvnəs] n Verzeihung f.
forgo [fɔː'gəʊ] see **forego.**
fork [fɔːk] n Gabel f; (in road) Gabelung f; vi (road) sich gabeln; **~ out** vti (col: pay) blechen; **~ed** a gegabelt; lightning zick-zackförmig.
forlorn [fə'lɔːn] a person verlassen; hope vergeblich.
form [fɔːm] n Form f; (type) Art f; (figure) Gestalt f; (Sch) Klasse f; (bench) (Schul)-bank f; (document) Formular nt; vt formen; (be part of) bilden.
formal ['fɔːməl] a förmlich, formell; occasion offiziell; **~ity** [fɔː'mælɪtɪ] Förm-lichkeit f; (of occasion) offizielle(r) Charakter m; **~ities** pl Formalitäten pl; **~ly** ad (ceremoniously) formell; (officially) offiziell.
format ['fɔːmæt] n Format nt.
formation [fɔː'meɪʃən] n Bildung f, Gestal-tung f; (Aviat) Formation f.

formative ['fɔːmətɪv] a years formend.
former ['fɔːmə*] a früher; (opposite of latter) erstere(r,s); **~ly** ad früher.
Formica * [fɔː'maɪkə] n Resopal * nt.
formidable ['fɔːmɪdəbl] a furchtbar; gewaltig.
formula ['fɔːmjʊlə] n Formel f; **~te** ['fɔːmjʊleɪt] vt formulieren.
forsake [fə'seɪk] vt irreg im Stich lassen, verlassen; habit aufgeben.
fort [fɔːt] n Feste f, Fort nt.
forte ['fɔːtɪ] n Stärke f, starke Seite f.
forth [fɔːθ] ad: **and so ~** und so weiter; **~coming** a kommend; character entgegenkommend; **~right** a offen, gerade heraus.
fortification [fɔːtɪfɪ'keɪʃən] n Befestigung f.
fortify ['fɔːtɪfaɪ] vt (ver)stärken; (protect) befestigen.
fortitude ['fɔːtɪtjuːd] n Seelenstärke f, Mut m.
fortnight ['fɔːtnaɪt] n zwei Wochen pl, vierzehn Tage pl; **~ly** a zweiwöchentlich; ad alle vierzehn Tage.
fortress ['fɔːtrɪs] n Festung f.
fortuitous [fɔː'tjuːɪtəs] a zufällig.
fortunate ['fɔːtʃənɪt] a glücklich; **~ly** ad glücklicherweise, zum Glück.
fortune ['fɔːtʃən] n Glück nt; (money) Ver-mögen nt; **~teller** Wahrsager(in f) m.
forty ['fɔːtɪ] num vierzig.
forum ['fɔːrəm] n Forum nt.
forward ['fɔːwəd] a vordere(r,s); movement vorwärts; person vorlaut; planning Voraus-; ad vorwärts; n (Sport) Stürmer m; vt (send) schicken; (help) fördern; **~s** ad vorwärts.
fossil ['fɔsl] n Fossil nt, Versteinerung f.
foster ['fɔstə*] vt talent fördern; **~ child** Pflegekind nt; **~ mother** Pflegemutter f.
foul [faʊl] a schmutzig; language gemein; weather schlecht; n (Sport) Foul nt; vt mechanism blockieren; (Sport) foulen.
found [faʊnd] vt (establish) gründen; **~ation** [faʊn'deɪʃən] (act) Gründung f; (fig) Fundament nt; **~ations** pl Fundament nt.
founder ['faʊndə*] n Gründer(in f) m; vi sinken.
foundry ['faʊndrɪ] n Gießerei f, Eisenhütte f.
fount [faʊnt] n (liter) Quell m; **~ain** (Spring)brunnen m; **~ain pen** Füllfederhalter m.
four [fɔː*] num vier; **~on all ~s** auf allen vieren; **~some** Quartett nt; **~teen** num vierzehn; **~th** a vierte(r,s).
fowl [faʊl] n Huhn nt; (food) Geflügel nt.
fox [fɔks] n Fuchs m; **~ed** a verblüfft; **~hunting** Fuchsjagd f; **~trot** Foxtrott m.
foyer ['fɔɪeɪ] n Foyer nt, Vorhalle f.
fracas ['frækɑː] n Radau m.
fraction ['frækʃən] n (Math) Bruch m; (part) Bruchteil m.
fracture ['fræktʃə*] n (Med) Bruch m; vt brechen.
fragile ['frædʒaɪl] a zerbrechlich.

fragment ['frægmənt] n Bruchstück nt, Fragment nt; (small part) Stück nt, Splitter m; ~**ary** [fræg'mentərı] a bruchstückhaft, fragmentarisch.

fragrance ['freɪgrəns] n Duft m.

fragrant ['freɪgrənt] a duftend.

frail [freɪl] a schwach, gebrechlich.

frame [freɪm] n Rahmen m; (body) Gestalt f; vt einrahmen; (make) gestalten, machen; (col: incriminate) to ~ sb jdm etw anhängen; ~ **of mind** Verfassung f; ~**work** Rahmen m; (of society) Gefüge nt.

franchise ['fræntʃaɪz] n (aktives) Wahlrecht nt.

frank [fræŋk] a offen; ~**furter** Saitenwürstchen nt; ~**ly** ad offen gesagt; ~**ness** Offenheit f.

frankincense ['fræŋkınsens] n Weihrauch m.

frantic ['fræntık] a effort verzweifelt; ~ **with worry** außer sich vor Sorge; ~**ally** ad außer sich; verzweifelt.

fraternal [frə'tɜːnl] a brüderlich.

fraternity [frə'tɜːnıtı] n (club) Vereinigung f; (spirit) Brüderlichkeit f; (US Sch) Studentenverbindung f.

fraternization [frætənaı'zeıʃən] n Verbrüderung f.

fraternize ['frætənaız] vi fraternisieren.

fraud [frɔːd] n (trickery) Betrug m; (trick) Schwindel m, Trick m; (person) Schwindler(in f) m.

fraudulent ['frɔːdjʊlənt] a betrügerisch.

fraught [frɔːt] a voller (with gen).

fray [freı] n Rauferei f, vti ausfransen.

freak [friːk] n Monstrosität f; (crazy person) Irre(r) mf; (storm etc) Ausnahmeerscheinung f; a storm, conditions anormal; animal monströs; ~ **out** vi (col) durchdrehen.

freckle ['frekl] n Sommersprosse f; ~**d** a sommersprossig.

free [friː] a frei; (loose) lose; (liberal) freigebig; **to get sth** ~ etw umsonst bekommen; **you're** ~ **to ...** es steht dir frei zu ... ; vt (set free) befreien; (unblock) freimachen; ~**dom** Freiheit f, ~**-for-all** allgemeine(r) Wettbewerb m; (fight) allgemeine(s) Handgemenge nt; ~ **kick** Freistoß m; ~**lance** a frei; artist freischaffend; ~**ly** ad frei; lose; (generously) reichlich; admit offen; ~**mason** Freimaurer m; ~**masonry** Freimaurerei f; ~ **trade** Freihandel m; ~**way** (US) Autobahn f; ~**wheel** vi im Freilauf fahren.

freesia ['friːzjə] n Freesie f.

freeze [friːz] irreg vi gefrieren; (feel cold) frieren; vt (lit, fig) einfrieren; n (fig, Fin) Stopp m; ~**r** Tiefkühltruhe f; (in fridge) Gefrierfach nt.

freezing ['friːzıŋ] a eisig; (— cold) eiskalt; ~ **point** Gefrierpunkt m.

freight [freıt] n (goods) Fracht f; (money charged) Fracht(gebühr) f; ~ **car** (US) Güterwagen m; ~**er** (Naut) Frachtschiff nt.

French [frentʃ] a: ~ **fried potatoes** pl Pommes frites pl; ~ **window** Verandatür f; see appendix.

frenzy ['frenzı] n Raserei f, wilde Aufregung f.

frequency ['friːkwənsı] n Häufigkeit f; (Phys) Frequenz f.

frequent a, ~**ly** ad ['friːkwənt,-lı] häufig; [frı'kwent] vt (regelmäßig) besuchen.

fresco ['freskəʊ] n Fresko nt.

fresh [freʃ] a frisch; (new) neu; (cheeky) frech; ~**en** (also ~**en up**) vi (sich) auffrischen; (person) sich frisch machen; vt auffrischen; ~**ly** ad gerade; ~**ness** Frische f; ~**water** a fish Süßwasser-.

fret [fret] vi sich (dat) Sorgen machen (about über + acc).

friar ['fraıə*] n Klosterbruder m.

friction ['frıkʃən] n (lit, fig) Reibung f.

Friday ['fraıdeı] n Freitag m; see good.

fridge [frıdʒ] n Kühlschrank m.

fried [fraıd] a gebraten.

friend [frend] n Bekannte(r) mf; (more intimate) Freund(in f) m; ~**liness** Freundlichkeit f; ~**ly** a freundlich; relations freundschaftlich; ~**ship** Freundschaft f.

frieze [friːz] n Fries m.

frigate ['frıgıt] n Fregatte f.

fright [fraıt] n Schrecken m; **you look a** ~ (col) du siehst unmöglich aus!; ~**en** vt erschrecken; **to be ~ened** Angst haben; ~**ening** a schrecklich; ängstigend; ~**ful** a, ~**fully** ad (col) schrecklich, furchtbar.

frigid ['frıdʒıd] a kalt, eisig; woman frigide; ~**ity** [frı'dʒıdıtı] Kälte f; Frigidität f.

frill [frıl] n Rüsche f.

fringe [frındʒ] n Besatz m; (hair) Pony m; (fig) äußere(r) Rand m, Peripherie f.

frisky ['frıskı] a lebendig, ausgelassen.

fritter ['frıtə*] : ~ **away** vt vertun, verplempern.

frivolity [frı'volıtı] n Leichtfertigkeit f, Frivolität f.

frivolous ['frıvələs] a frivol, leichtsinnig.

frizzy ['frızı] a kraus.

fro [frəʊ] see to.

frock [frok] n Kleid nt.

frog [frog] n Frosch m; ~**man** Froschmann m.

frolic ['frolık] n lustige(r) Streich m; vi ausgelassen sein.

from [from] prep von; (place) aus; (judging by) nach; (because of) wegen (+gen).

front [frʌnt] n Vorderseite f; (of house) Fassade f; (promenade) Strandpromenade f; (Mil, Pol, Met) Front f; (fig: appearances) Fassade f; a (forward) vordere(r,s), Vorder-; (first) vorderste(r,s); page erste(r,s); door Eingangs-, Haus-; **in** ~ **ad** vorne; **in** ~ **of** prep vor; ~**age** Vorderfront f; ~**al** a frontal, Vorder-; ~ **er** [frʌntıə*] Grenze f; ~ **room** (Brit) Vorderzimmer nt, Wohnzimmer nt; ~**-wheel drive** Vorderradantrieb m.

frost [frost] n Frost m; ~**bite** Erfrierung f; ~**ed** a glass Milch-; ~**y** a frostig.

froth [froθ] n Schaum m; ~**y** a schaumig.

frown [fraʊn] n Stirnrunzeln nt; vi die Stirn runzeln.

frozen ['frəʊzn] a food gefroren; (Fin) assets festgelegt.

frugal ['fruːgəl] a sparsam, bescheiden.

fruit [fru:t] n (particular) Frucht f; **I like ~** ich esse gern Obst; **~erer** Obsthändler m; **~ful** a fruchtbar; **~ion** [fru:ˈiʃən] Verwirklichung f; **to come to ~ion** in Erfüllung gehen; **~ machine** Spielautomat m; **~ salad** Obstsalat m.

frustrate [frʌsˈtreit] vt vereiteln; **~d** a gehemmt; (Psych) frustriert.

frustration [frʌsˈtreiʃən] n Behinderung f; Frustration f.

fry [frai] vt braten; **small ~** pl kleine Leute pl; (children) Kleine(n) pl; **~ing pan** Bratpfanne f.

fuchsia [ˈfju:ʃə] n Fuchsie f.

fuddy-duddy [ˈfʌdɪdʌdɪ] n altmodische(r) Kauz m.

fudge [fʌdʒ] n Karamellen pl.

fuel [fjʊəl] n Treibstoff m; (for heating) Brennstoff m; (for cigarette lighter) Benzin nt; **~ oil** (diesel fuel) Heizöl nt; **~ tank** Tank m.

fugitive [ˈfju:dʒɪtɪv] n Flüchtling m; (from prison) Flüchtige(r) mf.

fulfil [fʊlˈfɪl] vt duty erfüllen; promise einhalten; **~ment** Erfüllung f, Einhaltung f.

full [fʊl] a box, bottle, price voll; person (satisfied) satt; member, power, employment, moon Voll-; (complete) vollständig, Voll-; speed höchste(r, s); skirt weit; **in ~** vollständig, ungekürzt; **~back** Verteidiger m; **~ness** Fülle f; **~ stop** Punkt m; **~-time** a job Ganztags-; ad work hauptberuflich; **~y** ad völlig; **~y-fledged** a (lit, fig) flügge; **a ~y-fledged teacher** ein vollausgebildeter Lehrer.

fumble [ˈfʌmbl] vi herumfummeln (with, at an +dat).

fume [fju:m] vi rauchen, qualmen; (fig) wütend sein, kochen (col); **~s** pl Abgase pl; Qualm m.

fumigate [ˈfju:mɪgeɪt] vt ausräuchern.

fun [fʌn] n Spaß m; **to make ~ of** sich lustig machen über (+acc).

function [ˈfʌŋkʃən] n Funktion f; (occasion) Veranstaltung f, Feier f; vi funktionieren; **~al** a funktionell, praktisch.

fund [fʌnd] n (money) Geldmittel pl, Fonds m; (store) Schatz m, Vorrat m.

fundamental [fʌndəˈmentl] a fundamental, grundlegend; **~s** pl Grundbegriffe pl; **~ly** ad im Grunde.

funeral [ˈfju:nərəl] n Beerdigung f; a Beerdigungs-.

fungus [ˈfʌŋgəs] n, pl **fungi** or **funguses** Pilz m.

funicular [fju:ˈnɪkjʊlə*] n (Draht)seilbahn f.

funnel [ˈfʌnl] n Trichter m; (Naut) Schornstein m.

funnily [ˈfʌnɪlɪ] ad komisch; **~ enough** merkwürdigerweise.

funny [ˈfʌnɪ] a komisch; **~ bone** Musikantenknochen m.

fur [fɜ:*] n Pelz m; **~ coat** Pelzmantel m.

furious a, **~ly** ad [ˈfjʊərɪəs, -lɪ] wütend; attempt heftig.

furlong [ˈfɜ:lɒŋ] n = 220 yards.

furlough [ˈfɜ:ləʊ] n (US) Urlaub m.

furnace [ˈfɜ:nɪs] n (Brenn)ofen m.

furnish [ˈfɜ:nɪʃ] vt einrichten, möblieren;

(supply) versehen; **~ings** pl Einrichtung f.

furniture [ˈfɜ:nɪtʃə*] n Möbel pl.

furrow [ˈfʌrəʊ] n Furche f.

furry [ˈfɜ:rɪ] a pelzartig; tongue pelzig; animal Pelz-.

further [ˈfɜ:ðə*] comp of **far**; a weitere(r,s); ad weiter; vt fördern; **~ education** Weiterbildung f; Erwachsenenbildung f; **~more** ad ferner.

furthest [ˈfɜ:ðɪst] superl of **far**.

furtive a, **~ly** ad [ˈfɜ:tɪv, -lɪ] verstohlen.

fury [ˈfjʊərɪ] n Wut f, Zorn m.

fuse [fju:z] n (Elec) Sicherung f; (of bomb) Zünder m; vt verschmelzen; vi (Elec) durchbrennen; **~ box** Sicherungskasten m.

fuselage [ˈfju:zəlɑ:ʒ] n Flugzeugrumpf m.

fusion [ˈfju:ʒən] n Verschmelzung f.

fuss [fʌs] n Theater nt; **~y** a (difficult) heikel; (attentive to detail) kleinlich.

futile [ˈfju:taɪl] a zwecklos, sinnlos.

futility [fju:ˈtɪlɪtɪ] n Zwecklosigkeit f.

future [ˈfju:tʃə*] a zukünftig; n Zukunft f; **in (the) ~** in Zukunft, zukünftig.

futuristic [fju:tʃəˈrɪstɪk] a futuristisch.

fuze [fju:z] (US) = **fuse**.

fuzzy [ˈfʌzɪ] a (indistinct) verschwommen; hair kraus.

G

G, g [dʒi:] n G nt, g nt.

gabble [ˈgæbl] vi plappern.

gable [ˈgeɪbl] n Giebel m.

gadget [ˈgædʒɪt] n Vorrichtung f; **~ry** Kinkerlitzchen pl.

gaffe [gæf] n Fauxpas m.

gag [gæg] n Knebel m; (Theat) Gag m; vt knebeln; (Pol) mundtot machen.

gaiety [ˈgeɪɪtɪ] n Fröhlichkeit f.

gaily [ˈgeɪlɪ] ad lustig, fröhlich.

gain [geɪn] vt (obtain) erhalten; (win) gewinnen; vi (improve) gewinnen (in an +dat); (make progress) Vorsprung gewinnen; (clock) vorgehen; n Gewinn m; **~ful employment** Erwerbstätigkeit f.

gala [ˈgɑ:lə] n Fest nt.

galaxy [ˈgæləksɪ] n Sternsystem nt.

gale [geɪl] n Sturm m.

gallant [ˈgælənt] a tapfer, ritterlich; (polite) galant; **~ry** Tapferkeit f, Ritterlichkeit f; Galanterie f.

gall-bladder [ˈgɔ:lblædə*] n Gallenblase f.

gallery [ˈgælərɪ] n Galerie f.

galley [ˈgælɪ] n (ship's kitchen) Kombüse f; (ship) Galeere f.

gallon [ˈgælən] n Gallone f.

gallop [ˈgæləp] n Galopp m; vi galoppieren.

gallows [ˈgæləʊz] npl Galgen m.

gallstone [ˈgɔ:lstəʊn] n Gallenstein m.

gamble [ˈgæmbl] vi (um Geld) spielen; vt (risk) aufs Spiel setzen; n Risiko nt; **~r** Spieler(in f) m.

gambling [ˈgæmblɪŋ] n Glücksspiel nt.

game [geɪm] n Spiel nt; (hunting) Wild nt; a bereit (for zu); (brave) mutig; **~keeper** Wildhüter m.

gammon [ˈgæmən] n geräucherte(r) Schinken m.

gander ['gændə*] n Gänserich m.
gang [gæŋ] n (of criminals, youths) Bande f; (of workmen) Kolonne f.
gangrene ['gæŋgri:n] n Brand m.
gangster ['gæŋstə*] n Gangster m.
gangway ['gæŋwei] n (Naut) Laufplanke f.
gaol [dʒeil] n = **jail**.
gap [gæp] n (hole) Lücke f; (space) Zwischenraum n.
gape [geip] vi glotzen.
gaping ['geipiŋ] a wound klaffend; hole gähnend.
garage ['gæra:ʒ] n Garage f; (for repair) (Auto)reparaturwerkstatt f; (for petrol) Tankstelle f; vt einstellen.
garbage ['ga:bidʒ] n Abfall m; ~ **can** (US) Mülltonne f.
garbled ['ga:bld] a story verdreht.
garden ['ga:dn] n Garten m; vi gärtnern; ~ **er** Gärtner(in f) m; ~ **ing** Gärtnern nt; ~ **party** Gartenfest nt.
gargle ['ga:gl] vi gurgeln; n Gurgelmittel nt.
gargoyle ['ga:gɔil] n Wasserspeier m.
garish ['gɛəriʃ] a grell.
garland ['ga:lənd] n Girlande f.
garlic ['ga:lik] n Knoblauch m.
garment ['ga:mənt] n Kleidungsstück nt.
garnish ['ga:niʃ] vt food garnieren; n Garnierung f.
garret ['gærit] n Dachkammer f, Mansarde f.
garrison ['gærisən] n Garnison f; vt besetzen.
garrulous ['gæruləs] a geschwätzig.
garter ['ga:tə*] n Strumpfband nt.
gas [gæs] n Gas nt; (Med) Betäubungsmittel nt; (esp US: petrol) Benzin nt; to step on the ~ Gas geben; vt vergasen; ~ **cooker** Gasherd m; ~ **cylinder** Gasflasche f; ~ **fire** Gasofen m, Gasheizung f.
gash [gæʃ] n klaffende Wunde f; vt tief verwunden.
gasket ['gæskit] n Dichtungsring m.
gasmask ['gæsma:sk] n Gasmaske f.
gas meter ['gæsmi:tə*] n Gaszähler m.
gasoline ['gæsəli:n] n (US) Benzin nt.
gasp [ga:sp] vi keuchen; (in astonishment) tief Luft holen; n Keuchen nt.
gas ring ['gæsriŋ] n Gasring m.
gas station ['gæssteiʃən] n (US) Tankstelle f.
gas stove ['gæs'stəuv] n Gaskocher m.
gassy ['gæsi] a drink sprudelnd.
gastric ['gæstrik] a Magen-; ~ **ulcer** Magengeschwür nt.
gastronomy [gæs'trɔnəmi] n Kochkunst f.
gate [geit] n Tor nt; (barrier) Schranke f; ~ **crash** vt party platzen in (+acc); ~ **way** Toreingang m.
gather ['gæðə*] vt people versammeln; things sammeln; vi (understand) annehmen; (deduce) schließen (from aus); (assemble) sich versammeln; ~ **ing** Versammlung f.
gauche [gəuʃ] a linkisch.
gaudy ['gɔ:di] a schreiend.
gauge [geidʒ] n Normalmaß nt; (Rail) Spurweite f; (dial) Anzeiger m; (measure)

Maß nt; vt (lit) (ab)messen; (fig) abschätzen.
gaunt [gɔ:nt] a hager.
gauntlet ['gɔ:ntlit] n (knight's) Fehdehandschuh m; Handschuh m.
gauze [gɔ:z] n Mull m, Gaze f.
gawk [gɔ:k] vi dumm (an)glotzen (at acc).
gay [gei] a lustig; (coloured) bunt; (col) schwul.
gaze [geiz] n Blick m; vi (an)blicken (at acc).
gazelle [gə'zel] n Gazelle f.
gazetteer [gæzi'tiə*] n geographische(s) Lexikon nt.
gear [giə*] n Getriebe nt; (equipment) Ausrüstung f; (Aut) Gang m; to be out of/in ~ aus-/eingekuppelt sein; ~ **box** Getriebe(gehäuse) nt; ~ **-lever**, ~ **shift** (US) Schalthebel m.
geese [gi:s] pl of **goose**.
gelatin(e) ['dʒeləti:n] n Gelatine f.
gem [dʒem] n Edelstein m; (fig) Juwel nt.
Gemini ['dʒemini:] n Zwillinge pl.
gen [dʒen] n (col: information) Infos pl (on über +acc).
gender ['dʒendə*] n (Gram) Geschlecht nt.
gene [dʒi:n] n Gen nt.
general ['dʒenərəl] n General m; a allgemein; ~ **election** allgemeine Wahlen pl; ~ **ization** Verallgemeinerung f; ~ **ize** vi verallgemeinern; ~ **ly** ad allgemein, im allgemeinen.
generate ['dʒenəreit] vt erzeugen.
generation [dʒenə'reiʃən] n Generation f; (act) Erzeugung f.
generator ['dʒenəreitə*] n Generator m.
generosity [dʒenə'rɔsiti] n Großzügigkeit f.
generous a, ~ **ly** ad ['dʒenərəs, -li] (noble-minded) hochherzig; (giving freely) großzügig.
genetics [dʒi'netiks] n Genetik f, Vererbungslehre f.
genial ['dʒi:niəl] a freundlich, jovial.
genitals ['dʒenitlz] npl Geschlechtsteile pl, Genitalien pl.
genitive ['dʒenitiv] n Genitiv m, Wesfall m.
genius ['dʒi:niəs] n Genie nt.
genocide ['dʒenəusaid] n Völkermord m.
genteel [dʒen'ti:l] a (polite) wohlanständig; (affected) affektiert.
gentile ['dʒentail] n Nichtjude m.
gentle ['dʒentl] a sanft, zart; ~ **man** Herr m; (polite) Gentleman m; ~ **ness** Zartheit f, Milde f.
gently ['dʒentli] ad zart, sanft.
gentry ['dʒentri] n Landadel m.
gents [dʒents] n: '**G~**' (lavatory) 'Herren'.
genuine ['dʒenjuin] a echt, wahr; ~ **ly** ad wirklich, echt.
geographer [dʒi'ɔgrəfə*] n Geograph(in f) m.
geographical [dʒiə'græfikəl] a geographisch.
geography [dʒi'ɔgrəfi] n Geographie f, Erdkunde f.
geological [dʒiəu'lɔdʒikəl] a geologisch.
geologist [dʒi'ɔlədʒist] n Geologe m, Geologin f.

geology [dʒɪˈɒlədʒɪ] n Geologie f.

geometric(al) [dʒɪəˈmetrɪk(əl)] a geometrisch.

geometry [dʒɪˈɒmɪtrɪ] n Geometrie f.

geranium [dʒɪˈreɪnɪəm] n Geranie f.

germ [dʒɜːm] n Keim m; (Med) Bazillus m.

germination [dʒɜːmɪˈneɪʃən] n Keimen nt.

gesticulate [dʒesˈtɪkjuleɪt] vi gestikulieren.

gesticulation [dʒestɪkjuˈleɪʃən] n Gesten pl, Gestikulieren nt.

gesture [ˈdʒestʃəʳ] n Geste f.

get [get] vt irreg (receive) bekommen, kriegen; (become) werden; (go, travel) kommen; (arrive) ankommen; **to ~ sb to do sth** jdn dazu bringen, etw zu tun, jdn etw machen lassen; **~ along** vi (people) (gut) zurechtkommen; (depart) sich (acc) auf den Weg machen; **~ at** vt facts herausbekommen; **to ~ at sb** (nag) an jdm herumnörgeln; **~ away** vi (leave) sich (acc) davonmachen; (escape) entkommen (from dat); **~ away with you!** laß den Quatsch!; **~ down** vi (her)untergehen; vt (depress) fertigmachen; **~ in** vi (train) ankommen; (arrive home) heimkommen; **~ off** vi (from train etc) aussteigen (aus); (from horse) absteigen (von); **~ on** vi (progress) vorankommen; (be friends) auskommen; (age) alt werden; vt train etc einsteigen (in +acc); horse aufsteigen (auf +acc); **~ out** vi (of house) herauskommen; (of vehicle) aussteigen; vt (take out) herausholen; **~ over** vt illness sich (acc) erholen von; surprise verkraften; news fassen; loss sich abfinden mit; **I couldn't ~ over her** ich konnte mich nicht vergessen; **~ up** vi aufstehen; **~ away** Flucht f.

geyser [ˈgiːzəʳ] n Geiser m; (heater) Durchlauferhitzer m.

ghastly [ˈgɑːstlɪ] a (horrible) gräßlich; (pale) totenbleich.

gherkin [ˈgɜːkɪn] n Gewürzgurke f.

ghetto [ˈgetəu] n G(h)etto nt.

ghost [gəust] n Gespenst nt, Geist m; **~ly** a gespenstisch; **~ story** Gespenstergeschichte f.

giant [ˈdʒaɪənt] n Riese m; a riesig, Riesen-.

gibberish [ˈdʒɪbərɪʃ] n dumme(s) Geschwätz nt.

gibe [dʒaɪb] n spöttische Bemerkung f.

giblets [ˈdʒɪblɪts] npl Geflügelinnereien pl.

giddiness [ˈgɪdɪnəs] n Schwindelgefühl nt.

giddy [ˈgɪdɪ] a schwindlig; (frivolous) leichtsinnig.

gift [gɪft] n Geschenk nt; (ability) Begabung f; **~ed** a begabt.

gigantic [dʒaɪˈgæntɪk] a riesenhaft, ungeheuer groß.

giggle [ˈgɪgl] vi kichern; n Gekicher nt.

gild [gɪld] vt vergolden.

gill¹ [dʒɪl] n (1/4 pint) Viertelpinte f.

gill² [gɪl] n (of fish) Kieme f.

gilt [gɪlt] n Vergoldung f; a vergoldet.

gimlet [ˈgɪmlɪt] n Handbohrer m.

gimmick [ˈgɪmɪk] n (for sales, publicity) Gag m; **it's so ~y** es ist alles nur ein Gag.

gin [dʒɪn] n Gin m.

ginger [ˈdʒɪndʒəʳ] n Ingwer m; **~ ale**, **~ beer** Ingwerbier nt; **~bread** Pfefferkuchen m; **~-haired** a rothaarig.

gingerly [ˈdʒɪndʒəlɪ] ad behutsam.

gipsy [ˈdʒɪpsɪ] n Zigeuner(in f) m.

giraffe [dʒɪˈrɑːf] n Giraffe f.

girder [ˈgɜːdəʳ] n (steel) Eisenträger m; (wood) Tragebalken m.

girdle [ˈgɜːdl] n (woman's) Hüftgürtel m; vt umgürten.

girl [gɜːl] n Mädchen nt; **~friend** Freundin f; **~ish** a mädchenhaft.

girth [gɜːθ] n (measure) Umfang m; (strap) Sattelgurt m.

gist [dʒɪst] n Wesentliche(s) nt, Quintessenz f.

give [gɪv] irreg vt geben; vi (break) nachgeben; **~ away** vi (give free) verschenken; (betray) verraten; **~ back** vt zurückgeben; **~ in** vi (yield) aufgeben; (agree) nachgeben; vt (hand in) abgeben; **~ up** vti aufgeben; **~ way** vi (traffic) Vorfahrt lassen; (to feelings) nachgeben (+dat).

glacier [ˈglæsɪəʳ] n Gletscher m.

glad [glæd] a froh; **I was ~ to hear ...** ich habe mich gefreut, zu hören . . .; **~den** vt erfreuen.

gladiator [ˈglædɪeɪtəʳ] n Gladiator m.

gladioli [glædɪˈəulaɪ] npl Gladiolen pl.

gladly [ˈglædlɪ] ad gern(e).

glamorous [ˈglæmərəs] a bezaubernd; life reizvoll.

glamour [ˈglæməʳ] n Zauber m, Reiz m.

glance [glɑːns] n flüchtige(r) Blick m; vi schnell (hin)blicken (at auf +acc); **~ off** vi (fly off) abprallen von.

glancing [ˈglɑːnsɪŋ] a blow abprallend, Streif-.

gland [glænd] n Drüse f; **~ular fever** Drüsenentzündung f.

glare [glɛəʳ] n (light) grelle(s) Licht nt; (stare) wilde(r) Blick m; vi grell scheinen; (angrily) böse ansehen (at acc).

glaring [ˈglɛərɪŋ] a injustice schreiend; mistake kraß.

glass [glɑːs] n Glas nt; (mirror) Spiegel m; **~es** pl Brille f; **~house** Gewächshaus nt; **~ware** Glaswaren pl; **~y** a glasig.

glaze [gleɪz] vt verglasen; (finish with a ~) glasieren; n Glasur f.

glazier [ˈgleɪzɪəʳ] n Glaser m.

gleam [gliːm] n Schimmer m; vi schimmern; **~ing** a schimmernd.

glee [gliː] n Frohsinn m; **~ful** a fröhlich.

glen [glen] n Bergtal nt.

glib [glɪb] a (rede)gewandt; (superficial) oberflächlich; **~ly** ad glatt.

glide [glaɪd] vi gleiten; n Gleiten nt; (Aviat) Segelflug m; **~r** (Aviat) Segelflugzeug nt.

gliding [ˈglaɪdɪŋ] n Segelfliegen nt.

glimmer [ˈglɪməʳ] n Schimmer m; **~ of hope** Hoffnungsschimmer m.

glimpse [glɪmps] n flüchtige(r) Blick m; vt flüchtig erblicken.

glint [glɪnt] n Glitzern nt; vi glitzern.

glisten [ˈglɪsn] vi glänzen.

glitter ['glɪtə*] vi funkeln; n Funkeln nt; ~ing a glitzernd.

gloat over ['gləʊtəʊvə*] vt sich weiden an (+dat).

global ['gləʊbl] a global.

globe [gləʊb] n Erdball m; (sphere) Globus m; ~-trotter Weltenbummler(in f) m, Globetrotter(in f) m.

gloom [glu:m] n (also ~iness) (darkness) Dunkel nt, Dunkelheit f; (depression) düstere Stimmung f; ~ily ad, ~y a düster.

glorification [glɔ:rɪfɪˈkeɪʃən] n Verherrlichung f.

glorify ['glɔ:rɪfaɪ] vt verherrlichen; just a glorified cafe nur ein besseres Café.

glorious ['glɔ:rɪəs] a glorreich; (splendid) prächtig.

glory ['glɔ:rɪ] n Herrlichkeit f; (praise) Ruhm m; to ~ in sich sonnen in (+dat).

gloss [glɒs] n (shine) Glanz m; ~ paint Ölfarbe f; ~ over vt übertünchen.

glossary ['glɒsərɪ] n Glossar nt.

glossy ['glɒsɪ] a surface glänzend.

glove [glʌv] n Handschuh m.

glow [gləʊ] vi glühen, leuchten; n (heat) Glühen nt; (colour) Röte f; (feeling) Wärme f.

glower ['glaʊə*] vi: ~ at finster anblicken.

glucose ['glu:kəʊs] n Traubenzucker m.

glue [glu:] n Klebstoff m, Leim m; vt leimen, kleben.

glum [glʌm] a bedrückt.

glut [glʌt] n Überfluß m; vt überladen.

glutton ['glʌtn] n Vielfraß m; (fig) Unersättliche(r) mf; ~ous a gierig; ~y Völlerei f; Unersättlichkeit f.

glycerin(e) ['glɪsəri:n] n Glyzerin nt.

gnarled [nɑ:ld] a knorrig.

gnat [næt] n Stechmücke f.

gnaw [nɔ:] vt nagen an (+dat).

gnome [nəʊm] n Gnom m.

go [gəʊ] vi irreg gehen; (travel) reisen, fahren; (depart: train) (ab)fahren; (money) ausgeben; (vision) verschwinden; (smell) verfliegen; (disappear) (fort)gehen; (be sold) kosten; (at auction) weggehen; (work) gehen, funktionieren; (fit, suit) passen (with zu); (become) werden; (break etc) nachgeben; n (energy) Schwung m; (attempt) Versuch m; can I have another ~? darf ich noch mal?; ~ ahead vi (proceed) weitergehen; ~ along with vt (agree to support) zustimmen (+dat), unterstützen; ~ away vi (depart) weggehen; ~ back vi (return) zurückgehen; ~ back on vt promise nicht halten; ~ by vi (years, time) vergehen; ~ down vi (sun) untergehen; ~ for vt (fetch) holen (gehen); (like) mögen; (attack) sich stürzen auf (+acc); ~ in vi hineingehen; ~ into vt (enter) hineingehen in (+acc); (study) sich befassen mit; ~ off vi (depart) weggehen; (lights) ausgehen; (milk etc) sauer werden; (explode) losgehen; vt (dislike) nicht mehr mögen; ~ on vi (continue) weitergehen; (col: complain) meckern; (lights) angehen; to ~ on with sth mit etw weitermachen; ~ out vi

(fire, light) ausgehen; (of house) hinausgehen; ~ over vt (examine, check) durchgehen; ~ up vi (price) steigen; ~ without vt sich behelfen ohne; food entbehren.

goad [gəʊd] vt anstacheln; n Treibstock m.

go-ahead ['gəʊəhed] a zielstrebig; (progressive) fortschrittlich; n grünes Licht nt.

goal [gəʊl] n Ziel nt; (Sport) Tor nt; ~keeper Torwart m; ~-post Torpfosten m.

goat [gəʊt] n Ziege f.

gobble ['gɒbl] vt hinunterschlingen.

go-between ['gəʊbɪtwi:n] n Mittelsmann m.

goblet ['gɒblɪt] n Kelch(glas nt) m.

goblin ['gɒblɪn] n Kobold m.

god [gɒd] n Gott m; ~child Patenkind nt; ~dess Göttin f; ~father Pate m; ~forsaken a gottverlassen; ~mother Patin f; ~send Geschenk nt des Himmels.

goggle ['gɒgl] vi (stare) glotzen; to ~ at anglotzen; ~s pl Schutzbrille f.

going ['gəʊɪŋ] n (condition of ground) Straßenzustand m; (horse-racing) Bahn f; it's hard ~ es ist schwierig; a rate gängig; concern gutgehend; ~s-on pl Vorgänge pl.

gold [gəʊld] n Gold nt; ~en a golden, Gold-; ~fish Goldfisch m; ~ mine Goldgrube f.

golf [gɒlf] n Golf nt; ~ club (society) Golfklub m; (stick) Golfschläger m; ~ course Golfplatz m; ~er Golfspieler(in f) m.

gondola ['gɒndələ] n Gondel f.

gong [gɒŋ] n Gong m.

good [gʊd] n (benefit) Wohl nt; (moral excellence) Güte f; a gut; (suitable) passend; ~s pl Ware(n pl) f, Güter pl; a ~ deal of ziemlich viel; a ~ many ziemlich viele; ~bye! auf Wiedersehen!; G~ Friday Karfreitag m; ~-looking a gutaussehend; ~ morning! guten Morgen!; ~ness Güte f; (virtue) Tugend f; ~will (favour) Wohlwollen nt; (Comm) Firmenansehen nt.

goose [gu:s] n Gans f; ~berry [gʊzbərɪ] Stachelbeere f; ~flesh, ~ pimples pl Gänsehaut f.

gore [gɔ:*] vt durchbohren; aufspießen; n Blut nt.

gorge [gɔ:dʒ] n Schlucht f; vti (sich voll)fressen.

gorgeous ['gɔ:dʒəs] a prächtig; person bildhübsch.

gorilla [gəˈrɪlə] n Gorilla m.

gorse [gɔ:s] n Stechginster m.

gory ['gɔ:rɪ] a blutig.

go-slow ['gəʊ'sləʊ] n Bummelstreik m.

gospel ['gɒspəl] n Evangelium nt.

gossamer ['gɒsəmə*] n Spinnfäden pl.

gossip ['gɒsɪp] n Klatsch m; (person) Klatschbase f; vi klatschen.

goulash ['gu:læʃ] n Gulasch nt or m.

gout [gaʊt] n Gicht f.

govern ['gʌvən] vt regieren; verwalten; (Gram) bestimmen; ~ess Gouvernante f; ~ing a leitend; (fig) bestimmend; ~ment Regierung f; a Regierungs-; ~or Gouverneur m.

gown [gaun] n Gewand nt; (Univ) Robe f.
grab [græb] vt packen; an sich reißen; n plötzliche(r) Griff m; (crane) Greifer m.
grace [greɪs] n Anmut f; (favour) Güte f, Gefälligkeit f; (blessing) Gnade f; (prayer) Tischgebet nt; (Comm) Zahlungsfrist f; vt (adorn) zieren; (honour) auszeichnen; **5 days'** ~ 5 Tage Aufschub m; ~**ful** a ~**fully** ad anmutig, graziös.
gracious ['greɪʃəs] a gnädig; (kind, courteous) wohlwollend, freundlich.
gradation [grə'deɪʃən] n (Ab)stufung f.
grade [greɪd] n Grad m; (slope) Gefälle nt; **to make the** ~ es schaffen; vt (classify) einstufen; ~ **crossing** (US) Bahnübergang m.
gradient ['greɪdɪənt] n Steigung f; Gefälle nt.
gradual a, ~**ly** ad ['grædjuəl,-lɪ] allmählich.
graduate ['grædjuɪt] n: **to be a** ~ das Staatsexamen haben; ['grædjueɪt] vi das Staatsexamen machen or bestehen.
graduation [grædju'eɪʃən] n Erlangung f eines akademischen Grades.
graft [grɑːft] n (on plant) Pfropfreis nt; (hard work) Schufterei f; (Med) Verpflanzung f; (unfair self-advancement) Schiebung f; vt propfen; (fig) aufpfropfen; (Med) verpflanzen.
grain [greɪn] n Korn nt, Getreide nt; (particle) Körnchen nt, Korn nt; (in wood) Maserung f.
grammar ['græmə*] n Grammatik f.
grammatical [grə'mætɪkəl] a grammatisch.
gram(me) [græm] n Gramm nt.
gramophone ['græməfəun] n Grammophon nt.
granary ['grænərɪ] n Kornspeicher m.
grand [grænd] a großartig; ~**daughter** Enkelin f; ~**eur** ['grændjə*] Erhabenheit f; ~**father** Großvater m; ~**iose** a (imposing) großartig; (pompous) schwülstig; ~**mother** Großmutter f; ~ **piano** Flügel m; ~**son** Enkel m; ~**stand** Haupttribüne f; ~ **total** Gesamtsumme f.
granite ['grænɪt] n Granit m.
granny ['grænɪ] n Oma f.
grant [grɑːnt] vt gewähren; (allow) zugeben; n Unterstützung f; (Univ) Stipendium nt; **to take sb/sth for** ~**ed** jdn/etw als selbstverständlich (an)nehmen.
granulated ['grænjuleɪtɪd] a sugar raffiniert.
granule ['grænjuːl] n Körnchen nt.
grape [greɪp] n (Wein)traube f; ~**fruit** Pampelmuse f, Grapefruit f; ~ **juice** Traubensaft m.
graph [grɑːf] n Schaubild nt; ~**ic** a (descriptive) anschaulich, lebendig; drawing graphisch.
grapple ['græpl] vi sich raufen; ~ **with** (lit, fig) kämpfen mit.
grasp [grɑːsp] vt ergreifen; (understand) begreifen; n Griff m; (possession) Gewalt f; (of subject) Beherrschung f; ~**ing** a habgierig.
grass [grɑːs] n Gras nt; ~**hopper** Heuschrecke f; ~**land** Weideland nt; ~

roots pl (fig) Basis f; ~ **snake** Ringelnatter f; ~**y** a grasig, Gras-.
grate [greɪt] n Feuerrost m, Kamin m; vi kratzen; (sound) knirschen; (on nerves) zerren (on an +dat); vt cheese reiben.
grateful a, ~**ly** ad ['greɪtful, -flɪ] dankbar.
grater ['greɪtə*] n (in kitchen) Reibe f.
gratification [grætɪfɪ'keɪʃən] n Befriedigung f.
gratify ['grætɪfaɪ] vt befriedigen.
gratifying ['grætɪfaɪɪŋ] a erfreulich.
grating ['greɪtɪŋ] n (iron bars) Gitter nt; a noise knirschend.
gratitude ['grætɪtjuːd] n Dankbarkeit f.
gratuitous [grə'tjuːɪtəs] a (uncalled-for) grundlos, überflüssig; (given free) unentgeltlich, gratis.
gratuity [grə'tjuːɪtɪ] n (Geld)geschenk nt; (Comm) Gratifikation f.
grave [greɪv] n Grab nt; a (serious) ernst, schwerwiegend; (solemn) ernst, feierlich; ~**digger** Totengräber m.
gravel ['grævəl] n Kies m.
gravely ['greɪvlɪ] ad schwer, ernstlich.
gravestone ['greɪvstəun] n Grabstein m.
graveyard ['greɪvjɑːd] n Friedhof m.
gravitate ['grævɪteɪt] vi streben; (fig) tendieren.
gravity ['grævɪtɪ] n Schwerkraft f; (seriousness) Schwere f, Ernst m.
gravy ['greɪvɪ] n (Braten)soße f.
gray [greɪ] a = grey.
graze [greɪz] vi grasen; vt (touch) streifen; (Med) abschürfen; n (Med) Abschürfung f.
grease [griːs] n (fat) Fett nt; (lubricant) Schmiere f; vt (ab)schmieren; einfetten; ~ **gun** Schmierspritze f; ~**proof** a paper Butterbrot-.
greasy ['griːsɪ] a fettig.
great [greɪt] a groß; (important) groß, bedeutend; (distinguished) groß, hochstehend; (col: good) prima; ~**grandfather** Urgroßvater m; ~**grandmother** Urgroßmutter f; ~**ly** ad sehr; ~**ness** Größe f.
greed [griːd] n (also ~**iness**) Gier f (for nach); (meanness) Geiz m; ~**ily** ad gierig; ~**y** a gefräßig, gierig; ~**y for money** geldgierig.
green [griːn] a grün; n (village ~) Dorfwiese f; ~**grocer** Obst- und Gemüsehändler m; ~**house** Gewächshaus nt; ~**ish** a grünlich; ~ **light** (lit, fig) grüne(s) Licht nt.
greet [griːt] vt grüßen; ~**ing** Gruß m, Begrüßung f.
gregarious [grɪ'gɛərɪəs] a gesellig.
grenade [grɪ'neɪd] n Granate f.
grey [greɪ] a grau; ~**haired** a grauhaarig; ~**hound** Windhund m; ~**ish** a gräulich.
grid [grɪd] n Gitter nt; (Elec) Leitungsnetz nt; (on map) Gitternetz nt; ~**iron** Bratrost m.
grief [griːf] n Gram m, Kummer m.
grievance ['griːvəns] n Beschwerde f.
grieve [griːv] vi sich grämen; vt betrüben.
grill [grɪl] n (on cooker) Grill m; vt grillen;

(*question*) in die Mangel nehmen.
grille [grɪl] *n* (*on car etc*) (Kühler)gitter *nt*.
grim [grɪm] *a* grimmig; *situation* düster.
grimace [grɪ'meɪs] *n* Grimasse *f*; *vi* Grimassen schneiden.
grime [graɪm] *n* Schmutz *m*.
grimly ['grɪmlɪ] *ad* grimmig, finster.
grimy ['graɪmɪ] *a* schmutzig.
grin [grɪn] *n* Grinsen *nt*; *vi* grinsen.
grind [graɪnd] *vt irreg* mahlen; (*sharpen*) schleifen; *teeth* knirschen mit; *n* (*bore*) Plackerei *f*.
grip [grɪp] *n* Griff *m*; (*mastery*) Griff *m*, Gewalt *f*; (*suitcase*) kleine(r) Handkoffer *m*; *vt* packen.
gripes [graɪps] *npl* (*bowel pains*) Bauchschmerzen *pl*, Bauchweh *nt*.
gripping ['grɪpɪŋ] *a* (*exciting*) spannend.
grisly ['grɪzlɪ] *a* gräßlich.
gristle ['grɪsl] *n* Knorpel *m*.
grit [grɪt] *n* Splitt *m*; (*courage*) Mut *m*, Mumm *m*; *vt teeth* knirschen mit; *road* (mit Splitt be)streuen.
groan [grəʊn] *n* Stöhnen *nt*; *vi* stöhnen.
grocer ['grəʊsə*] *n* Lebensmittelhändler *m*; ~**ies** *pl* Lebensmittel *pl*.
grog [grɒg] *n* Grog *m*.
groggy ['grɒgɪ] *a* benommen; (*boxing*) angeschlagen.
groin [grɔɪn] *n* Leistengegend *f*.
groom [gru:m] *n* Bräutigam *m*; (*for horses*) Pferdeknecht *m*; *to* ~ **o.s.** (*of man*) sich zurechtmachen, sich pflegen; (*well*) ~**ed** gepflegt; *to* ~ **sb for a career** jdn auf eine Laufbahn vorbereiten.
groove [gru:v] *n* Rille *f*, Furche *f*.
grope [grəʊp] *vi* tasten.
gross [grəʊs] *a* (*coarse*) dick, plump; (*bad*) grob, schwer; (*Comm*) brutto; Gesamt-; *n* Gros *nt*; ~**ly** *ad* höchst, ungeheuerlich.
grotesque [grəʊ'tesk] *a* grotesk.
grotto ['grɒtəʊ] *n* Grotte *f*.
ground [graʊnd] *n* Boden *m*, Erde *f*; (*land*) Grundbesitz *m*; (*reason*) Grund *m*; ~**s** *pl* (*dregs*) Bodensatz *m*; (*around house*) (Garten)anlagen *pl*; *vt* (*run ashore*) auf Strand setzen; *aircraft* stillegen; (*instruct*) die Anfangsgründe beibringen (+*dat*); *vi* (*run ashore*) stranden, auflaufen; ~ **floor** (*Brit*) Erdgeschoß *nt*, Parterre *nt*; ~**ing** (*instruction*) Anfangsunterricht *m*; ~**sheet** Zeltboden *m*; ~**work** Grundlage *f*.
group [gru:p] *n* Gruppe *f*; *vti* (sich) gruppieren.
grouse [graʊs] *n* (*bird*) schottische(s) Moorhuhn *nt*; (*complaint*) Nörgelei *f*; *vi* (*complain*) meckern.
grove [grəʊv] *n* Gehölz *nt*, Hain *m*.
grovel ['grɒvl] *vi* auf dem Bauch kriechen; (*fig*) kriechen.
grow [grəʊ] *irreg vi* wachsen, größer werden; (*grass*) wachsen; (*become*) werden; **it** ~**s on you** man gewöhnt sich daran; *vt* (*raise*) anbauen, ziehen; ~ **up** *vi* aufwachsen; (*mature*) erwachsen werden; ~**er** Züchter *m*; ~**ing** *a* wachsend; (*fig*) zunehmend.
growl [graʊl] *vi* knurren; *n* Knurren *nt*.

grown-up ['grəʊn'ʌp] *a* erwachsen; *n* Erwachsene(r) *mf*.
growth [grəʊθ] *n* Wachstum *nt*, Wachsen *nt*; (*increase*) Anwachsen *nt*, Zunahme *f*; (*of beard etc*) Wuchs *m*.
grub [grʌb] *n* Made *f*, Larve *f*; (*col: food*) Futter *nt*; ~**by** *a* schmutzig, schmuddelig.
grudge [grʌdʒ] *n* Groll *m*; *vt* misgönnen (*sb sth* jdm etw); *to* **bear sb a** ~ einen Groll gegen jdn hegen.
grudging ['grʌdʒɪŋ] *a* neidisch; (*unwilling*) widerwillig.
gruelling ['grʊəlɪŋ] *a climb, race* mörderisch.
gruesome ['gru:səm] *a* grauenhaft.
gruff [grʌf] *a* barsch.
grumble ['grʌmbl] *vi* murren, schimpfen; *n* Brummen *nt*, Murren *nt*.
grumpy ['grʌmpɪ] *a* verdrießlich.
grunt [grʌnt] *vi* grunzen; *n* Grunzen *nt*.
guarantee [gærən'ti:] *n* (*promise to pay*) Gewähr *f*; (*promise to replace*) Garantie *f*; *vt* gewährleisten; garantieren.
guarantor [gærən'tɔ:*] *n* Gewährsmann *m*, Bürge *m*.
guard [gɑ:d] *n* (*defence*) Bewachung *f*; (*sentry*) Wache *f*; (*Rail*) Zugbegleiter *m*; *to* **be on** ~ Wache stehen; *to* **be on one's** ~ aufpassen; *vt* bewachen, beschützen; ~**ed** *a* vorsichtig, zurückhaltend; ~**ian** Vormund *m*; (*keeper*) Hüter *m*; ~**'s van** (*Brit Rail*) Dienstwagen *m*.
guerrilla [gə'rɪlə] *n* Guerilla(kämpfer) *m*; ~ **warfare** Guerillakrieg *m*.
guess [ges] *vti* (er)raten, schätzen; *n* Vermutung *f*; ~**work** Raterei *f*; **good** ~ gut geraten.
guest [gest] *n* Gast *m*; ~-**house** Pension *f*; ~ **room** Gastzimmer *nt*.
guffaw [gʌ'fɔ:] *n* schallende(s) Gelächter *nt*; *vi* schallend lachen.
guidance ['gaɪdəns] *n* (*control*) Leitung *f*; (*advice*) Rat *m*, Beratung *f*.
guide [gaɪd] *n* Führer *m*; *vt* führen; **girl** ~ Pfadfinderin *f*; ~**book** Reiseführer *m*; ~**d missile** Fernlenkgeschoß *nt*; ~**lines** *pl* Richtlinien *pl*.
guild [gɪld] *n* (*Hist*) Gilde *f*; (*society*) Vereinigung *f*; ~**hall** (*Brit*) Stadthalle *f*.
guile [gaɪl] *n* Arglist *f*; ~**less** *a* arglos.
guillotine [gɪlə'ti:n] *n* Guillotine *f*.
guilt [gɪlt] *n* Schuld *f*; ~**y** *a* schuldig.
guise [gaɪz] *n* (*appearance*) Verkleidung *f*; **in the** ~ **of** (*things*) in der Form (+*gen*); (*people*) gekleidet als.
guitar [gɪ'tɑ:*] *n* Gitarre *f*; ~**ist** Gitarrist(in *f*) *m*.
gulf [gʌlf] *n* Golf *m*; (*fig*) Abgrund *m*.
gull [gʌl] *n* Möwe *f*.
gullet ['gʌlɪt] *n* Schlund *m*.
gullible ['gʌlɪbl] *a* leichtgläubig.
gully ['gʌlɪ] *n* (Wasser)rinne *f*; (*gorge*) Schlucht *f*.
gulp [gʌlp] *vi* hinunterschlucken; (*gasp*) schlucken; *n* große(r) Schluck *m*.
gum [gʌm] *n* (*around teeth*) Zahnfleisch *nt*; (*glue*) Klebstoff *m*; (*chewing* —) Kaugummi *m*; *vt* gummieren, kleben; ~**boots** *pl* Gummistiefel *pl*.

gumption ['gʌmpʃən] n (col) Mumm m.

gum tree ['gʌmtri:] n Gummibaum m; **up a ~** (col) in der Klemme.

gun [gʌn] n Schußwaffe f; **~fire** Geschützfeuer nt; **~ man** bewaffnete(r) Verbrecher m; **~ner** Kanonier m, Artillerist m; **~powder** Schießpulver nt; **~shot** Schuß m; **~ down** vt niederknallen.

gurgle ['gɜ:gl] n Gluckern nt; vi gluckern.

gush [gʌʃ] n Strom m, Erguß m; vi (rush out) hervorströmen; (fig) schwärmen.

gusset ['gʌsɪt] n Keil m, Zwickel m.

gust [gʌst] n Windstoß m, Bö f.

gusto ['gʌstəʊ] n Genuß m, Lust f.

gut [gʌt] n (Anat) Gedärme pl; (string) Darm m; **~s** pl (fig) Schneid m.

gutter ['gʌtə⁎] n Dachrinne f; (in street) Gosse f.

guttural ['gʌtərəl] a guttural, Kehl-.

guy [gaɪ] n (rope) Halteseil nt; (man) Typ m, Kerl m.

guzzle ['gʌzl] vti (drink) saufen; (eat) fressen.

gym(nasium) [dʒɪm'neɪzɪəm] n Turnhalle f.

gymnast ['dʒɪmnæst] n Turner(in f) m; **~ics** [dʒɪm'næstɪks] Turnen nt, Gymnastik f.

gyn(a)ecologist [gaɪnɪ'kɒlədʒɪst] n Frauenarzt m/-ärztin f, Gynäkologe m, Gynäkologin f.

gyn(a)ecology [gaɪnɪ'kɒlədʒɪ] n Gynäkologie f, Frauenheilkunde f.

gypsy ['dʒɪpsɪ] n = **gipsy**.

gyrate [dʒaɪ'reɪt] vi kreisen.

H

H, h [eɪtʃ] n H nt, h nt.

haberdashery [hæbə'dæʃərɪ] n Kurzwaren pl.

habit ['hæbɪt] n (An)gewohnheit f; (monk's) Habit nt or m.

habitable ['hæbɪtəbl] a bewohnbar.

habitat ['hæbɪtæt] n Lebensraum m.

habitation [hæbɪ'teɪʃən] n Bewohnen nt; (place) Wohnung f.

habitual [hə'bɪtjʊəl] a üblich, gewohnheitsmäßig; **~ly** ad gewöhnlich.

hack [hæk] vt hacken; n Hieb m; (writer) Schreiberling m.

hackney cab ['hæknɪˈkæb] n Taxi nt.

hackneyed ['hæknɪd] a abgedroschen.

haddock ['hædək] n Schellfisch m.

hadn't ['hædnt] = **had not**.

haemorrhage, (US) **hemo~** ['hemərɪdʒ] n Blutung f.

haemorrhoids, (US) **hemo~** ['hemərɔɪdz] Hämorrhoiden pl.

haggard ['hægəd] a abgekämpft.

haggle ['hægl] vi feilschen.

haggling ['hæglɪŋ] n Feilschen nt.

hail [heɪl] n Hagel m; vt umjubeln; **to ~ sb as emperor** jdn zum Kaiser ausrufen; vi hageln; **~storm** Hagelschauer m.

hair [hɛə⁎] n Haar nt, Haare pl; (one ~) Haar nt; **~brush** Haarbürste f; **~cut** Haarschnitt m; **to get a ~cut** sich (dat) die Haare schneiden lassen; **~do** Frisur f;

~dresser Friseur m, Friseuse f; **~drier** Trockenhaube f; (hand) Fön m; **~net** Haarnetz nt; **~ oil** Haaröl nt; **~piece** (lady's) Haarteil nt; (man's) Toupet nt; **~pin** (lit) Haarnadel f; **~pin bend** Haarnadelkurve f; **~raising** a haarsträubend; **~'s breadth** Haaresbreite f; **~ style** Frisur f; **~y** a haarig.

hake [heɪk] n Seehecht m.

half [hɑ:f] n Hälfte f; a halb; ad halb, zur Hälfte; **~back** Läufer m; **~breed, ~caste** Mischling m; **~hearted** a lustlos, unlustig; **~hour** halbe Stunde f; **~penny** ['heɪpnɪ] halbe(r) Penny m; **~price** halbe(r) Preis m; **~time** Halbzeit f; **~way** ad halbwegs, auf halbem Wege.

halibut ['hælɪbət] n Heilbutt m.

hall [hɔ:l] n Saal m; (entrance ~) Hausflur m; (building) Halle f.

hallmark ['hɔ:lmɑ:k] n (lit, fig) Stempel m.

hallo [hʌ'ləʊ] see **hello**.

hallucination [həluːsɪ'neɪʃən] n Halluzination f.

halo ['heɪləʊ] n (of saint) Heiligenschein m; (of moon) Hof m.

halt [hɔ:lt] n Halt m; vti anhalten.

halve [hɑ:v] vt halbieren.

ham [hæm] n Schinken m; **~ sandwich** Schinkenbrötchen nt; **~burger** Frikadelle f.

hamlet ['hæmlɪt] n Weiler m.

hammer ['hæmə⁎] n Hammer m; vt hämmern.

hammock ['hæmək] n Hängematte f.

hamper ['hæmpə⁎] vt (be)hindern; n Picknickkorb m; Geschenkkorb m.

hand [hænd] n Hand f; (of clock) (Uhr)zeiger m; (worker) Arbeiter m; vt (pass) geben; **to give sb a ~** jdm helfen; **at first ~** aus erster Hand; **to ~** zur Hand; **in ~** (under control) in fester Hand, unter Kontrolle; (being done) im Gange; (extra) übrig; **~bag** Handtasche f; **~ball** Handball m; **~book** Handbuch nt; **~brake** Handbremse f; **~ cream** Handcreme f; **~cuffs** pl Handschellen pl; **~ful** Handvoll f; (col: person) Plage f.

handicap ['hændɪkæp] n Handikap nt; vt benachteiligen.

handicraft ['hændɪkrɑːft] n Kunsthandwerk nt.

handkerchief ['hæŋkətʃɪf] n Taschentuch nt.

handle ['hændl] n (of door etc) Klinke f; (of cup etc) Henkel m; (for winding) Kurbel f; vt (touch) anfassen; (deal with) things sich befassen mit; people umgehen mit; **~bars** pl Lenkstange f.

hand-luggage ['hændlʌgɪdʒ] n Handgepäck nt.

handmade ['hændmeɪd] a handgefertigt.

handshake ['hændʃeɪk] n Händedruck m.

handsome ['hænsəm] a gutaussehend; (generous) großzügig.

handwriting ['hændraɪtɪŋ] n Handschrift f.

handy ['hændɪ] a praktisch; shops leicht erreichbar.

handyman ['hændɪmən] n Mädchen nt für

alles; (*do-it-yourself*) Bastler *m*; (*general* —) Gelegenheitsarbeiter *m*.

hang [hæŋ] *irreg vt* aufhängen; (*execute*) hängen; **to ~ sth on sth** etw an etw (*acc*) hängen; *vi* (*droop*) hängen; **~ about** *vi* sich herumtreiben.

hangar ['hæŋə*] *n* Hangar *m*, Flugzeughalle *f*.

hanger ['hæŋə*] *n* Kleiderbügel *m*.

hanger-on ['hæŋər'ɒn] *n* Anhänger(in *f*) *m*.

hangover ['hæŋəʊvə*] *n* Kater *m*.

hank [hæŋk] *n* Strang *m*.

hanker ['hæŋkə*] *vi* sich sehnen (*for, after* nach).

haphazard ['hæp'hæzəd] *a* wahllos, zufällig.

happen ['hæpən] *vi* sich ereignen, passieren; **~ing** *n* Ereignis *nt*; (*Art*) Happening *nt*.

happily ['hæpɪlɪ] *ad* glücklich; (*fortunately*) glücklicherweise.

happiness ['hæpɪnɪs] *n* Glück *nt*.

happy ['hæpɪ] *a* glücklich; **~-lucky** *a* sorglos.

harass ['hærəs] *vt* bedrängen, plagen.

harbour, (*US*) **harbor** ['hɑ:bə*] *n* Hafen *m*.

hard [hɑ:d] *a* (*firm*) hart, fest; (*difficult*) schwer, schwierig; (*physically*) schwer; (*harsh*) hart(herzig), gefühllos; *ad work* hart; *try* sehr; *push, hit* fest; **~ by** (*close*) dicht *or* nahe an(+*dat*); **he took it ~** er hat es schwer genommen; **~-back** *n* kartonierte Ausgabe; **~-boiled** *a* hartgekocht; **~en** *vt* erhärten; (*fig*) verhärten; *vi* hart werden; (*fig*) sich verhärten; **~-hearted** *a* hartherzig; **~ly** *ad* kaum; **~ship** Not *f*; (*injustice*) Unrecht *nt*; **~-up** *a* knapp bei Kasse; **~ware** Eisenwaren *pl*.

hardy ['hɑ:dɪ] *a* (*strong*) widerstandsfähig; (*brave*) verwegen.

hare [hεə*] *n* Hase *m*.

harem [hɑ:'ri:m] *n* Harem *m*.

harm [hɑ:m] *n* Schaden *m*; Leid *nt*; *vt* schaden (+*dat*); **it won't do any ~** es kann nicht schaden; **~ful** *a* schädlich; **~less** *a* harmlos, unschädlich.

harmonica [hɑ:'mɒnɪkə] *n* Mundharmonika *f*.

harmonious [hɑ:'məʊnɪəs] *a* harmonisch.

harmonize ['hɑ:mənaɪz] *vt* abstimmen; *vi* harmonieren.

harmony ['hɑ:mənɪ] *n* Harmonie *f*; (*fig also*) Einklang *m*.

harness ['hɑ:nɪs] *n* Geschirr *nt*; *vt horse* anschirren; (*fig*) nutzbar machen.

harp [hɑ:p] *n* Harfe *f*; **to ~ on about sth** auf etw (*dat*) herumreiten; **~ist** Harfenspieler(in *f*) *m*.

harpoon [hɑ:'pu:n] *n* Harpune *f*.

harrow ['hærəʊ] *n* Egge *f*; *vt* eggen.

harrowing ['hærəʊɪŋ] *a* nervenaufreibend.

harsh [hɑ:ʃ] *a* (*rough*) rauh, grob; (*severe*) schroff, streng; **~ly** *ad* rauh, barsch; **~ness** Härte *f*.

harvest ['hɑ:vɪst] *n* Ernte *f*; (*time*) Erntezeit *f*; *vt* ernten.

harvester ['hɑ:vɪstə*] *n* Mähbinder *m*.

hash [hæʃ] *vt* kleinhacken; *n* (*mess*) Kuddelmuddel *m*; (*meat cooked*) Haschee *nt*; (*raw*) Gehackte(s) *nt*.

hashish ['hæʃɪʃ] *n* Haschisch *nt*.

haste [heɪst] *n* (*speed*) Eile *f*; (*hurry*) Hast *f*; **~n** ['heɪsn] *vt* beschleunigen; *vi* eilen, sich beeilen.

hasty *a*, **hastily** *ad* [heɪstɪ, -lɪ] hastig; (*rash*) vorschnell.

hat [hæt] *n* Hut *m*.

hatbox ['hætbɒks] *n* Hutschachtel *f*.

hatch [hætʃ] *n* (*Naut*) Luke *f*; (*in house*) Durchreiche *f*; *vi* brüten; (*young*) ausschlüpfen; *vt brood* ausbrüten; *plot* aushecken.

hatchet ['hætʃɪt] *n* Beil *nt*.

hate [heɪt] *vt* hassen; **I ~ queuing** ich stehe nicht gern Schlange; *n* Haß *m*; **~ful** *a* verhaßt.

hatred ['heɪtrɪd] *n* Haß *m*; (*dislike*) Abneigung *f*.

hat trick ['hættrɪk] *n* Hattrick *m*.

haughty *a*, **haughtily** *ad* [hɔ:tɪ, -lɪ] hochnäsig, überheblich.

haul [hɔ:l] *vt* ziehen, schleppen; *n* (*pull*) Zug *m*; (*catch*) Fang *m*; **~age** Transport *m*; (*Comm*) Spedition *f*; **~ier** Transportunternehmer *m*, Spediteur *m*.

haunch [hɔ:ntʃ] *n* Lende *f*; **to sit on one's ~es** hocken.

haunt [hɔ:nt] *vt* (*ghost*) spuken in (+*dat*), umgehen in (+*dat*); (*memory*) verfolgen; *pub* häufig besuchen; **the castle is ~ed** in dem Schloß spukt es; *n* Lieblingsplatz *m*.

have [hæv] *vt irreg* haben; (*at meal*) essen, trinken; (*col: trick*) hereinlegen; **to ~ sth done** etw machen lassen; **to ~ to do sth** etw tun müssen; **to ~ sb on** jdn auf den Arm nehmen.

haven ['heɪvn] *n* Hafen *m*; (*fig*) Zufluchtsort *m*.

haversack ['hævəsæk] *n* Rucksack *m*.

havoc ['hævək] *n* Verwüstung *f*.

hawk [hɔ:k] *n* Habicht *m*.

hay [heɪ] *n* Heu *nt*; **~ fever** Heuschnupfen *m*; **~stack** Heuschober *m*.

haywire ['heɪwaɪə*] *a* (*col*) durcheinander.

hazard ['hæzəd] *n* (*chance*) Zufall *m*; (*danger*) Wagnis *nt*, Risiko *nt*; *vt* aufs Spiel setzen; **~ous** *a* gefährlich, riskant.

haze [heɪz] *n* Dunst *m*; (*fig*) Unklarheit *f*.

hazelnut ['heɪzlnʌt] *n* Haselnuß *f*.

hazy ['heɪzɪ] *a* (*misty*) dunstig, diesig; (*vague*) verschwommen.

he [hi:] *pron* er.

head [hed] *n* Kopf *m*; (*top*) Spitze *f*; (*leader*) Leiter *m*; *a* Kopf-; (*leading*) Ober-; *vt* (an)führen, leiten; **~ for** Richtung nehmen auf (+*acc*), zugehen auf (+*acc*); **~ache** Kopfschmerzen *pl*, Kopfweh *nt*; **~ing** Überschrift *f*; **~lamp** Scheinwerfer *m*; **~land** Landspitze *f*; **~light = ~lamp**; **~line** Schlagzeile *f*; **~long** *ad* kopfüber; **~master** (*of primary school*) Rektor *m*; (*of secondary school*) Direktor *m*; **~mistress** Rektorin *f*; Direktorin *f*; **~-on** *a* Frontal-; **~quarters** *pl* Zentrale *f*; (*Mil*) Hauptquartier *nt*; **~rest**

Kopfstütze f; ~**room** (of bridges etc)
lichte Höhe f; Platz m für den Kopf; ~**s**
(on coin) Kopf m, Wappen nt; ~**scarf**
Kopftuch nt; ~**strong** a eigenwillig; ~
waiter Oberkellner m; ~**way** Fahrt f
(voraus); (fig) Fortschritte pl; ~**wind**
Gegenwind m; ~**y** a (rash) hitzig; (intoxi-
cating) stark, berauschend.

heal [hi:l] vt heilen; vi verheilen.

health [helθ] n Gesundheit f; **your** ~!
prost!; ~**y** a gesund.

heap [hi:p] n Haufen m; vt häufen.

hear [hɪə°] irreg vt hören; (listen to)
anhören; vi hören; ~**ing** Gehör nt; (Jur)
Verhandlung f; (of witnesses) Vernehmung
f; to give sb a ~**ing** jdn anhören; ~**ing
aid** Hörapparat m; ~**say** Hörensagen nt.

hearse [hɜːs] n Leichenwagen m.

heart [hɑːt] n Herz nt; (centre also) Zentrum nt; (courage) Mut m; **by** ~ auswendig; **the** ~ **of the matter** der Kern
des Problems; ~ **attack** Herzanfall m;
~**beat** Herzschlag m; ~**breaking** a
herzzerbrechend; ~**broken** a (ganz)
gebrochen; ~**burn** Sodbrennen nt; ~
failure Herzschlag m; ~**felt** a aufrichtig.

hearth [hɑːθ] n Herd m.

heartily [ˈhɑːtɪlɪ] ad herzlich; eat herzhaft.

heartless [ˈhɑːtlɪs] a herzlos.

hearty [ˈhɑːtɪ] a kräftig; (friendly) freundlich.

heat [hi:t] n Hitze f; (of food, water etc)
Wärme f; (Sport) Ausscheidungsrunde f;
(excitement) Feuer nt; **in the** ~ **of the
moment** in der Hitze des Gefechts; vt
house heizen; substance heiß machen,
erhitzen; ~ **up** vi warm werden; vt aufwärmen; ~**ed** a erhitzt; (fig) hitzig; ~**er**
m (Heiz)ofen m.

heath [hi:θ] n (Brit) Heide f.

heathen [ˈhiːðən] n Heide m; a heidnisch,
Heiden-.

heather [ˈheðə°] n Heidekraut nt, Erika f.

heating [ˈhiːtɪŋ] n Heizung f.

heatstroke [ˈhiːtstrəuk] n Hitzschlag m.

heatwave [ˈhiːtweɪv] n Hitzewelle f.

heave [hi:v] vt hochheben; sigh ausstoßen;
vi wogen; (breast) sich heben; n Heben nt.

heaven [ˈhevn] n Himmel m; (bliss) (der
siebte) Himmel m; ~**ly** a himmlisch; ~**ly
body** Himmelskörper m.

heavy a, **heavily** ad [ˈhevɪ, -lɪ] schwer.

heckle [ˈhekl] vt unterbrechen; vi da-
zwischenrufen, störende Fragen stellen.

hectic [ˈhektɪk] a hektisch.

he'd [hi:d] = **he had; he would**.

hedge [hedʒ] n Hecke f; vt einzäunen; to
~ **one's bets** sich absichern; vi (fig) ausweichen.

hedgehog [ˈhedʒhɒg] n Igel m.

heed [hi:d] vt beachten; n Beachtung f;
~**ful** a achtsam; ~**less** a achtlos.

heel [hi:l] n Ferse f; (of shoe) Absatz m; vt
shoes mit Absätzen versehen.

hefty [ˈheftɪ] a person stämmig; portion
reichlich; bite kräftig; weight schwer.

heifer [ˈhefə°] n Färse f.

height [haɪt] n (of person) Größe f; (of
object) Höhe f; (high place) Gipfel m; ~**en**
vt erhöhen.

heir [ɛə°] n Erbe m; ~**ess** [ˈɛərɪs] Erbin f;
~**loom** Erbstück nt.

helicopter [ˈhelɪkɒptə°] n Hubschrauber
m.

hell [hel] n Hölle f; interj verdammt!

he'll [hi:l] = **he will, he shall**.

hellish [ˈhelɪʃ] a höllisch, verteufelt.

hello [hʌˈləu] interj (greeting) Hallo; (surprise) hallo, he.

helm [helm] n Ruder nt, Steuer nt.

helmet [ˈhelmɪt] n Helm m.

helmsman [ˈhelmzmən] n Steuermann m.

help [help] n Hilfe f; vt helfen (+dat); I
can't ~ it ich kann nichts dafür; I
couldn't ~ laughing ich mußte lachen;
~ **yourself** bedienen Sie sich;
~**er** Helfer m; ~**ful** a hilfreich; ~**ing**
Portion f; ~**less** a hilflos.

hem [hem] n Saum m; ~ **in** vt einschließen; (fig) einengen.

hemisphere [ˈhemɪsfɪə°] n Halbkugel f;
Hemisphäre f.

hemline [ˈhemlaɪn] n Rocklänge f.

hemp [hemp] n Hanf m.

hen [hen] n Henne f.

hence [hens] ad von jetzt an; (therefore)
daher.

henchman [ˈhentʃmən] n Anhänger m,
Gefolgsmann m.

henpecked [ˈhenpekt] a: to be ~ unter
dem Pantoffel stehen; ~ **husband**
Pantoffelheld m.

her [hɜː°] pron (acc) sie; (dat) ihr; a ihr.

herald [ˈherəld] n Herold m; (fig) (Vor)-
bote m; vt verkünden, anzeigen.

heraldry [ˈherəldrɪ] n Wappenkunde f.

herb [hɜːb] n Kraut n.

herd [hɜːd] n Herde f.

here [hɪə°] ad hier; (to this place) hierher;
~**after** ad hernach, künftig; n Jenseits nt;
~**by** ad hiermit.

hereditary [hɪˈredɪtərɪ] a erblich.

heredity [hɪˈredɪtɪ] n Vererbung f.

heresy [ˈherəsɪ] n Ketzerei f.

heretic [ˈheratɪk] n Ketzer m; ~**al**
[hɪˈretɪkəl] a ketzerisch.

herewith [ˈhɪəˈwɪð] ad hiermit; (Comm)
anbei.

heritage [ˈherɪtɪdʒ] n Erbe nt.

hermetically [hɜːˈmetɪkəlɪ] ad luftdicht,
hermetisch.

hermit [ˈhɜːmɪt] n Einsiedler m.

hernia [ˈhɜːnɪə] n Bruch m.

hero [ˈhɪərəu] n Held m; ~**ic** [hɪˈrəuɪk] a
heroisch.

heroin [ˈherəuɪn] n Heroin nt.

heroine [ˈherəuɪn] n Heldin f.

heroism [ˈherəuɪzəm] n Heldentum nt.

heron [ˈherən] n Reiher m.

herring [ˈherɪŋ] n Hering m.

hers [hɜːz] pron ihre(r,s).

herself [hɜːˈself] pron sich (selbst);
(emphatic) selbst; **she's not** ~ mit ihr ist
etwas los or nicht in Ordnung.

he's [hi:z] = **he is, he has**.

hesitant [ˈhezɪtənt] a zögernd; speech
stockend.

hesitate [ˈhezɪteɪt] vi zögern; (feel doubtful)
unschlüssig sein.

hesitation [hezɪ'teɪʃən] n Zögern nt, Schwanken nt.

het up [het'ʌp] a (col) aufgeregt.

hew [hju:] vt irreg hauen, hacken.

hexagon ['heksəgən] n Sechseck nt; ~al [hek'sægənəl] a sechseckig.

heyday ['heɪdeɪ] n Blüte f, Höhepunkt m.

hi [haɪ] interj he, hallo.

hibernate ['haɪbəneɪt] vi Winterschlaf halten.

hibernation [haɪbə'neɪʃən] n Winterschlaf m.

hiccough, hiccup ['hɪkʌp] vi den Schluckauf haben; ~s pl Schluckauf m.

hide [haɪd] n (skin) Haut f, Fell nt; irreg vt verstecken; (keep secret) verbergen; vi sich verstecken; ~-and-seek Versteckspiel nt.

hideous ['hɪdɪəs] a abscheulich; ~ly ad scheußlich.

hiding ['haɪdɪŋ] n (beating) Tracht f Prügel; to be in ~ sich versteckt halten; ~ place Versteck nt.

hierarchy ['haɪərɑːkɪ] n Hierarchie f.

high [haɪ] a hoch; importance groß; spirits Hoch-; wind stark; living extravagant, üppig; ad hoch; ~brow n Intellektuelle(r) mf; a (betont) intellektuell; (pej) hochgestochen; ~chair Hochstuhl m, Sitzer m; ~-handed a eigenmächtig; ~-heeled a hochhackig; ~jack = hijack; ~-level a meeting wichtig, Spitzen-; ~light (fig) Höhepunkt m; ~ly ad in hohem Maße, höchst; praise in hohen Tönen; ~ly strung a überempfindlich, reizbar; H~ Mass Hochamt nt; ~ness Höhe f; H~ness Hoheit f; ~-pitched a voice hoch, schrill, hell; ~ school Oberschule f; ~-speed a Schnell-; ~ tide Flut f; ~way Landstraße f.

hijack ['haɪdʒæk] vt hijacken, entführen.

hike [haɪk] vi wandern; n Wanderung f; ~r Wanderer m.

hiking ['haɪkɪŋ] n Wandern nt.

hilarious [hɪ'leərɪəs] a lustig; zum Schreien komisch.

hilarity [hɪ'lærɪtɪ] n Lustigkeit f.

hill [hɪl] n Berg m; ~side (Berg)hang m; ~top Bergspitze f; ~y a hügelig.

hilt [hɪlt] n Heft nt; up to the ~ ganz und gar.

him [hɪm] pron (acc) ihn; (dat) ihm.

himself [hɪm'self] pron sich (selbst); (emphatic) selbst; he's not ~ mit ihm ist etwas los or nicht in Ordnung.

hind [haɪnd] a hinter, Hinter-; n Hirschkuh f.

hinder ['hɪndə*] vt (stop) hindern; (delay) behindern.

hindrance ['hɪndrəns] n (delay) Behinderung f; (obstacle) Hindernis nt.

hinge [hɪndʒ] n Scharnier nt; (on door) Türangel f; mit Scharnieren versehen; vi (fig) abhängen (on von).

hint [hɪnt] n Tip m, Andeutung f; (trace) Anflug m; vi andeuten (at acc), anspielen (at auf +acc).

hip [hɪp] n Hüfte f.

hippopotamus [hɪpə'pɒtəməs] n Nilpferd nt.

hire ['haɪə*] vt worker anstellen; car mieten; n Miete f; for ~ taxi frei; to have for ~ verleihen; ~ purchase Teilzahlungskauf m.

his [hɪz] poss a sein; poss pron seine(r,s).

hiss [hɪs] vi zischen; n Zischen nt.

historian [hɪs'tɔːrɪən] n Geschichtsschreiber m; Historiker m.

historic [hɪs'tɒrɪk] a historisch.

historical [hɪs'tɒrɪkəl] a historisch, geschichtlich.

history ['hɪstərɪ] n Geschichte f; (personal) Entwicklung f, Werdegang m.

hit [hɪt] vt irreg schlagen; (injure) treffen, verletzen; n (blow) Schlag m, Stoß m; (success) Erfolg m, Treffer m; (Mus) Hit m.

hitch [hɪtʃ] vt festbinden; (pull up) hochziehen; n (loop) Knoten m; (difficulty) Schwierigkeit f, Haken m.

hitch-hike ['hɪtʃhaɪk] vi trampen, per Anhalter fahren; ~r Tramper m.

hitherto ['hɪðə'tuː] ad bislang.

hive [haɪv] n Bienenkorb m.

hoard [hɔːd] n Schatz m; vt horten, hamstern.

hoarding ['hɔːdɪŋ] n Bretterzaun m; (for advertising) Reklamewand f.

hoarfrost ['hɔː'frɒst] n (Rauh)reif m.

hoarse [hɔːs] a heiser, rauh.

hoax [həʊks] n Streich m.

hobble ['hɒbl] vi humpeln.

hobby ['hɒbɪ] n Steckenpferd nt, Hobby nt.

hobo ['həʊbəʊ] n (US) Tippelbruder m.

hock [hɒk] n (wine) weiße(r) Rheinwein m.

hockey ['hɒkɪ] n Hockey nt.

hoe [həʊ] n Hacke f; vt hacken.

hog [hɒg] n Schlachtschwein nt; vt mit Beschlag belegen.

hoist [hɔɪst] n Winde f; vt hochziehen.

hold [həʊld] irreg vt halten; (keep) behalten; (contain) enthalten; (be able to contain) fassen; (keep back) zurück(be)halten; breath anhalten; meeting abhalten; vi (withstand pressure) standhalten, aushalten; n (grasp) Halt m; (claim) Anspruch m; (Naut) Schiffsraum m; ~ back vt zurückhalten; ~ down vt niederhalten; job behalten; ~ out vt hinhalten, bieten; vi aushalten; ~ up vt (delay) aufhalten; (rob) überfallen; ~all Reisetasche f; ~er Behälter m; ~ing (share) (Aktien)anteil m; ~up (in traffic) Stockung f; (robbery) Überfall m.

hole [həʊl] n Loch nt; vt durchlöchern.

holiday ['hɒlɪdeɪ] n (day) Feiertag m; freie(r) Tag m; (vacation) Urlaub m; (Sch) Ferien pl; ~-maker Feriengast m, Urlauber(in f) m.

holiness ['həʊlɪnɪs] n Heiligkeit f.

hollow ['hɒləʊ] a hohl; (fig) leer; n Vertiefung f; (in rock) Höhle f; ~ out vt aushöhlen.

holly ['hɒlɪ] n Stechpalme f.

holster ['həʊlstə*] n Pistolenhalfter m.

holy ['həʊlɪ] a heilig; (religious) fromm.

homage ['hɒmɪdʒ] n Huldigung f; to pay ~ to huldigen (+dat).

home [həʊm] n Heim nt, Zuhause nt; (insti-

tution) Heim *nt*, Anstalt *f*; a einheimisch; (*Pol*) inner; ad heim, nach Hause; at ~ zu Hause; ~**coming** Heimkehr *f*; ~**less** a obdachlos; ~**ly** a häuslich; (*US: ugly*) unscheinbar; ~**made** a selbstgemacht; ~**sick** a: to be ~**sick** Heimweh haben; ~**ward(s)** a heimwärts; ~**work** Hausaufgaben *pl*.

homicide ['hɒmɪsaɪd] *n* (*US*) Totschlag *m*, Mord *m*.

homoeopathy [həʊmɪ'ɒpəθɪ] *n* Homöopathie *f*.

homogeneous [hɒmə'dʒiːnɪəs] a homogen, gleichartig.

homosexual ['hɒməʊ'seksjʊəl] a homosexuell; *n* Homosexuelle(r) *m*.

hone [həʊn] *n* Schleifstein *m*; *vt* feinschleifen.

honest ['ɒnɪst] a ehrlich; (*upright*) aufrichtig; ~**ly** ad ehrlich; ~**y** Ehrlichkeit *f*.

honey ['hʌnɪ] *n* Honig *m*; ~**comb** Honigwabe *f*; ~**moon** Flitterwochen *pl*, Hochzeitsreise *f*.

honk [hɒŋk] *n* (*Aut*) Hupensignal *nt*; *vi* hupen.

honorary ['ɒnərərɪ] a Ehren-.

honour, (*US*) **honor** ['ɒnə*] *vt* ehren; *cheque* einlösen; *debts* begleichen; *contract* einhalten; *n* (*respect*) Ehre *f*, (*reputation*) Ansehen *nt*, gute(r) Ruf *m*; (*sense of right*) Ehrgefühl *nt*; ~**s** *pl* (*titles*) Auszeichnungen *pl*; ~**able** a ehrenwert, rechtschaffen; *intention* ehrenhaft.

hood [hʊd] *n* Kapuze *f*; (*Aut*) Verdeck *nt*; (*US Aut*) Kühlerhaube *f*; ~**wink** *vt* reinlegen.

hoof [huːf] *n* Huf *m*.

hook [hʊk] *n* Haken *m*; *vt* einhaken; ~-**up** Gemeinschaftssendung *f*.

hooligan ['huːlɪgən] *n* Rowdy *m*.

hoop [huːp] *n* Reifen *m*.

hoot [huːt] *vi* (*Aut*) hupen; to ~ **with laughter** schallend lachen; *n* (*shout*) Johlen *nt*; (*Aut*) Hupen *nt*; ~**er** (*Naut*) Dampfpfeife *f*; (*Aut*) (Auto)hupe *f*.

hop[1] [hɒp] *vi* hüpfen, hopsen; *n* (*jump*) Hopser *m*.

hop[2] [hɒp] *n* (*Bot*) Hopfen *m*.

hope [həʊp] *vi* hoffen; I ~ **that** ... hoffentlich ...; *n* Hoffnung *f*; ~**ful** a hoffnungsvoll; (*promising*) vielversprechend; ~**less** a hoffnungslos; (*useless*) unmöglich.

horde [hɔːd] *n* Horde *f*.

horizon [hə'raɪzn] *n* Horizont *m*; ~**tal** [hɒrɪ'zɒntl] a horizontal.

hormone ['hɔːməʊn] *n* Hormon *nt*.

horn [hɔːn] *n* Horn *nt*; (*Aut*) Hupe *f*; ~**ed** a gehörnt, Horn-.

hornet ['hɔːnɪt] *n* Hornisse *f*.

horny ['hɔːnɪ] a schwielig; (*US*) scharf.

horoscope ['hɒrəskəʊp] *n* Horoskop *nt*.

horrible a, **horribly** ad ['hɒrɪbl, -blɪ] fürchterlich.

horrid a, ~**ly** ad ['hɒrɪd, -lɪ] abscheulich, scheußlich.

horrify ['hɒrɪfaɪ] *vt* entsetzen.

horror ['hɒrə*] *n* Schrecken *m*; (*great dislike*) Abscheu *m* (*of* vor +*dat*).

hors d'oeuvre [ɔː'dɜːvr] *n* Vorspeise *f*.

horse [hɔːs] *n* Pferd *nt*; **on** ~**back** berittten; ~ **chestnut** Roßkastanie *f*; ~**drawn** a von Pferden gezogen, Pferde-; ~**power** Pferdestärke *f*, PS *nt*; ~**racing** Pferderennen *nt*; ~**shoe** Hufeisen *nt*.

horsy ['hɔːsɪ] a pferdenärrisch.

horticulture ['hɔːtɪkʌltʃə*] *n* Gartenbau *m*.

hose(pipe) ['həʊz(paɪp)] *n* Schlauch *m*.

hosiery ['həʊzɪərɪ] *n* Strumpfwaren *pl*.

hospitable [hɒs'pɪtəbl] a gastfreundlich.

hospital ['hɒspɪtl] *n* Krankenhaus *nt*.

hospitality [hɒspɪ'tælɪtɪ] *n* Gastlichkeit *f*, Gastfreundschaft *f*.

host [həʊst] *n* Gastgeber *m*; (*innkeeper*) (Gast)wirt *m*; (*large number*) Heerschar *f*; (*Eccl*) Hostie *f*.

hostage ['hɒstɪdʒ] *n* Geisel *f*.

hostel ['hɒstəl] *n* Herberge *f*.

hostess ['həʊstes] *n* Gastgeberin *f*.

hostile ['hɒstaɪl] a feindlich.

hostility [hɒs'tɪlɪtɪ] *n* Feindschaft *f*; **hostilities** *pl* Feindseligkeiten *pl*.

hot [hɒt] a heiß; *drink, food, water* warm; (*spiced*) scharf; (*angry*) hitzig; ~ **air** (*col*) Gewäsch *nt*; ~**bed** (*lit*) Mistbeet *nt*; (*fig*) Nährboden *m*; ~-**blooded** a heißblütig; ~ **dog** heiße(s) Würstchen *nt*.

hotel [həʊ'tel] *n* Hotel *nt*; ~**ier** Hotelier *m*.

hotheaded ['hɒt'hedɪd] a hitzig, aufbrausend.

hothouse ['hɒthaʊs] *n* (*lit, fig*) Treibhaus *nt*.

hot line ['hɒtlaɪn] *n* (*Pol*) heiße(r) Draht *m*.

hotly ['hɒtlɪ] ad *argue* hitzig; *pursue* dicht.

hot news ['hɒt'njuːz] *n* das Neueste vom Neuen.

hotplate ['hɒtpleɪt] *n* Kochplatte *f*.

hot-water bottle [hɒt'wɔːtəbɒtl] *n* Wärmflasche *f*.

hound [haʊnd] *n* Jagdhund *m*; *vt* jagen, hetzen.

hour ['aʊə*] *n* Stunde *f*; (*time of day*) (Tages)zeit *f*; ~**ly** a stündlich.

house [haʊs] *n* Haus *nt*; [haʊz] *vt* (*accommodate*) unterbringen; (*shelter*) aufnehmen; ~**boat** Hausboot *nt*; ~**breaking** Einbruch *m*; ~**hold** Haushalt *m*; ~**keeper** Haushälterin *f*; ~**keeping** Haushaltung *f*; ~**wife** Hausfrau *f*; ~**work** Hausarbeit *f*.

housing ['haʊzɪŋ] *n* (*act*) Unterbringung *f*; (*houses*) Wohnungen *pl*; (*Pol*) Wohnungsbau *m*; (*covering*) Gehäuse *nt*; ~ **estate** (Wohn)siedlung *f*.

hovel ['hɒvəl] *n* elende Hütte *f*; Loch *nt*.

hover ['hɒvə*] *vi* (*bird*) schweben; (*person*) wartend herumstehen; ~**craft** Luftkissenfahrzeug *nt*.

how [haʊ] ad wie; ~ **many** wie viele; ~ **much** wieviel; ~**ever** ad (*but*) (je)doch, aber; ~**ever you phrase it** wie Sie es auch ausdrücken.

howl [haʊl] *n* Heulen *nt*; *vi* heulen.

howler ['haʊlə*] *n* grobe(r) Schnitzer *m*.

hub [hʌb] *n* Radnabe *f*; (*of the world*) Mittelpunkt *m*; (*of commerce*) Zentrum *nt*.

hubbub ['hʌbʌb] *n* Tumult *m*.

hub cap ['hʌbkæp] n Radkappe f.
huddle ['hʌdl] vi sich zusammendrängen; n Grüppchen nt.
hue [hju:] n Färbung f, Farbton m; ~ **and cry** Zetergeschrei nt.
huff [hʌf] n Eingeschnapptsein nt; **to go into a** ~ einschnappen.
hug [hʌg] vt umarmen; (fig) sich dicht halten an (+acc); n Umarmung f.
huge [hju:dʒ] a groß, riesig.
hulk [hʌlk] n (ship) abgetakelte(s) Schiff nt; (person) Koloß m; ~**ing** a ungeschlacht.
hull [hʌl] n Schiffsrumpf m.
hullo [hʌ'ləu] see **hello.**
hum [hʌm] vi summen; (bumblebee) brummen; vt summen; n Summen nt.
human ['hju:mən] a menschlich; n (also ~ **being**) Mensch m.
humane [hju:'meɪn] a human.
humanity [hju:'mænɪtɪ] n Menschheit f; (kindliness) Menschlichkeit f.
humble ['hʌmbl] a demütig; (modest) bescheiden; vt demütigen.
humbly ['hʌmblɪ] ad demütig.
humdrum ['hʌmdrʌm] a eintönig, langweilig.
humid ['hju:mɪd] a feucht; ~**ity** [hju:'mɪdɪtɪ] Feuchtigkeit f.
humiliate [hju:'mɪlɪeɪt] vt demütigen.
humiliation [hju:mɪlɪ'eɪʃən] n Demütigung f.
humility [hju:'mɪlɪtɪ] n Demut f.
humorist ['hju:mərɪst] n Humorist m.
humorous ['hju:mərəs] a humorvoll, komisch.
humour, (US) **humor** ['hju:mə*] n (fun) Humor m; (mood) Stimmung f; vt nachgeben (+dat); bei Stimmung halten.
hump [hʌmp] n Buckel m.
hunch [hʌntʃ] n (presentiment) (Vor)-ahnung f; vt shoulders hochziehen; ~**back** Bucklige(r) m.
hundred ['hʌndrɪd] num, a, n hundert; ~**weight** Zentner m.
hunger ['hʌŋgə*] n Hunger m; (fig) Verlangen nt (for nach); vi hungern.
hungry a, **hungrily** ad ['hʌŋgrɪ, -lɪ] hungrig; **to be** ~ Hunger haben.
hunt [hʌnt] vt jagen; (search) suchen (for acc); vi jagen; n Jagd f; ~**er** Jäger m; ~**ing** Jagen nt, Jagd f.
hurdle ['hɜ:dl] n (lit, fig) Hürde f.
hurl [hɜ:l] vt schleudern.
hurrah [hu'rɑ:], **hurray** [hu'reɪ] n Hurra nt.
hurricane ['hʌrɪkən] n Orkan m.
hurried ['hʌrɪd] a eilig; (hasty) übereilt; ~**ly** ad übereilt, hastig.
hurry ['hʌrɪ] n Eile f; **to be in a** ~ es eilig haben; vi sich beeilen; ~**!** mach schnell!; vt (an)treiben; job übereilen.
hurt [hɜ:t] irreg vt weh tun (+dat); (injure, fig) verletzen; vi weh tun; ~**ful** a schädlich; remark verletzend.
hurtle ['hɜ:tl] vt schleudern; vi sausen.
husband ['hʌzbənd] n (Ehe)mann m, Gatte m.

hush [hʌʃ] n Stille f; vt zur Ruhe bringen; vi still sein; ~ interj pst, still.
husk [hʌsk] n Spelze f.
husky ['hʌskɪ] a voice rauh; figure stämmig; n Eskimohund m.
hustle ['hʌsl] vt (push) stoßen; (hurry) antreiben, drängen; n (Hoch)betrieb m; ~ **and bustle** Geschäftigkeit f.
hut [hʌt] n Hütte f.
hutch [hʌtʃ] n (Kaninchen)stall m.
hyacinth ['haɪəsɪnθ] n Hyazinthe f.
hybrid ['haɪbrɪd] n Kreuzung f; a Misch-.
hydrant ['haɪdrənt] n Hydrant m.
hydraulic [haɪ'drɒlɪk] a hydraulisch.
hydroelectric ['haɪdrəʊ'lektrɪk] a hydroelektrisch.
hydrofoil ['haɪdrəʊfɔɪl] n Tragflügel m; Tragflügelboot nt.
hydrogen ['haɪdrɪdʒən] n Wasserstoff m.
hyena [haɪ'i:nə] n Hyäne f.
hygiene ['haɪdʒi:n] n Hygiene f.
hygienic [haɪ'dʒi:nɪk] a hygienisch.
hymn [hɪm] n Kirchenlied nt.
hyphen ['haɪfən] n Bindestrich m; Trennungszeichen nt.
hypnosis [hɪp'nəʊsɪs] n Hypnose f.
hypnotism ['hɪpnətɪzəm] n Hypnotismus m.
hypnotist ['hɪpnətɪst] n Hypnotiseur m.
hypnotize ['hɪpnətaɪz] vt hypnotisieren.
hypochondriac [haɪpəʊ'kondrɪæk] n eingebildete(r) Kranke(r) mf.
hypocrisy [hɪ'pokrɪsɪ] n Heuchelei f, Scheinheiligkeit f.
hypocrite ['hɪpəkrɪt] n Heuchler m, Scheinheilige(r) m f.
hypocritical [hɪpə'krɪtɪkəl] a scheinheilig, heuchlerisch.
hypothesis [haɪ'pɒθɪsɪs] n Hypothese f.
hypothetic(al) [haɪpəʊ'θetɪk(əl)] a hypothetisch.
hysteria [hɪs'tɪərɪə] n Hysterie f.
hysterical [hɪs'terɪkəl] a hysterisch.
hysterics [hɪs'terɪks] npl hysterische(r) Anfall m.

I

I, i [aɪ] n I nt, i nt; **I** pron ich.
ice [aɪs] n Eis nt; vt (Cook) mit Zuckerguß überziehen; vi (also ~ **up**) vereisen; ~-**axe** Eispickel m; ~**berg** Eisberg m; ~**box** (US) Kühlschrank m; ~-**cream** Eis nt; ~-**cold** a eiskalt; ~-**cube** Eiswürfel m; ~ **hockey** Eishockey nt; ~**rink** (Kunst)eisbahn f.
icicle ['aɪsɪkl] n Eiszapfen m.
icing ['aɪsɪŋ] n (on cake) Zuckerguß m; (on window) Vereisung f.
icon ['aɪkɒn] n Ikone f.
icy ['aɪsɪ] a (slippery) vereist; (cold) eisig.
I'd [aɪd] = **I would; I had.**
idea [aɪ'dɪə] n Idee f; no ~ keine Ahnung; **my** ~ **of a holiday** wie ich mir einen Urlaub vorstelle.
ideal [aɪ'dɪəl] n Ideal nt; a ideal; ~**ism** Idealismus m; ~**ist** Idealist m; ~**ly** ad ideal(erweise).

identical [aɪ'dentɪkəl] a identisch; *twins* eineiig.

identification [aɪdentɪfɪ'keɪʃən] n Identifizierung f.

identify [aɪ'dentɪfaɪ] vt identifizieren; (*regard as the same*) gleichsetzen.

identity [aɪ'dentɪtɪ] n Identität f; ~ **card** Personalausweis m; ~ **papers** pl (Ausweis)papiere pl.

ideology [aɪdɪ'ɒlədʒɪ] n Ideologie f.

idiocy ['ɪdɪəsɪ] n Idiotie f.

idiom ['ɪdɪəm] n (*expression*) Redewendung f; (*dialect*) Idiom nt.

idiosyncrasy [ɪdɪə'sɪŋkrəsɪ] n Eigenart f.

idiot ['ɪdɪət] n Idiot(in f) m; ~**ic** [ɪdɪ'ɒtɪk] a idiotisch.

idle ['aɪdl] a (*doing nothing*) untätig, müßig; (*lazy*) faul; (*useless*) vergeblich, nutzlos; *machine* still(stehend); *threat, talk* leer; ~**ness** Müßiggang m; Faulheit f; ~**r** Faulenzer m.

idol ['aɪdl] n Idol nt; ~**ize** vt vergöttern.

idyllic [ɪ'dɪlɪk] a idyllisch.

if [ɪf] cj wenn, falls; (*whether*) ob; ~ **only ... wenn ...** doch nur; ~ **not** falls nicht.

igloo ['ɪgluː] n Iglu m or nt.

ignite [ɪg'naɪt] vt (an)zünden.

ignition [ɪg'nɪʃən] n Zündung f; ~ **key** (*Aut*) Zündschlüssel m.

ignoramus [ɪgnə'reɪməs] n Ignorant m.

ignorance ['ɪgnərəns] n Unwissenheit f, Ignoranz f.

ignorant ['ɪgnərənt] a unwissend.

ignore [ɪg'nɔː*] vt ignorieren.

ikon ['aɪkɒn] n = **icon**.

I'll [aɪl] = **I will, I shall**.

ill [ɪl] a krank; (*evil*) schlecht, böse; n Übel nt; ~**-advised** a schlecht beraten, unklug; ~**-at-ease** a unbehaglich.

illegal a, ~**ly** ad [ɪ'liːgəl, -ɪ] illegal.

illegible [ɪ'ledʒəbl] a unleserlich.

illegitimate [ɪlɪ'dʒɪtɪmət] a unzulässig; *child* unehelich.

ill-fated [ɪl'feɪtɪd] a unselig.

ill-feeling [ɪl'fiːlɪŋ] n Verstimmung f.

illicit [ɪ'lɪsɪt] a verboten.

illiterate [ɪ'lɪtərət] a ungebildet.

ill-mannered [ɪl'mænəd] a ungehobelt.

illness ['ɪlnəs] n Krankheit f.

illogical [ɪ'lɒdʒɪkəl] a unlogisch.

ill-treat [ɪl'triːt] vt mißhandeln.

illuminate [ɪ'luːmɪneɪt] vt beleuchten.

illumination [ɪluːmɪ'neɪʃən] n Beleuchtung f.

illusion [ɪ'luːʒən] n Illusion f.

illusive [ɪ'luːsɪv], **illusory** [ɪ'luːsərɪ] a illusorisch, trügerisch.

illustrate ['ɪləstreɪt] vt *book* illustrieren; (*explain*) veranschaulichen.

illustration [ɪlə'streɪʃən] n Illustration f; (*explanation*) Veranschaulichung f.

illustrious [ɪ'lʌstrɪəs] a berühmt.

ill will ['ɪl'wɪl] n Groll m.

I'm [aɪm] = **I am**.

image ['ɪmɪdʒ] n Bild nt; (*likeness*) Abbild nt; (*public* —) Image nt; ~**ry** Symbolik f.

imaginable [ɪ'mædʒɪnəbl] a vorstellbar.

imaginary [ɪ'mædʒɪnərɪ] a eingebildet; *world* Phantasie-.

imagination [ɪmædʒɪ'neɪʃən] n Einbildung f; (*creative*) Phantasie f.

imaginative [ɪ'mædʒɪnətɪv] a phantasiereich, einfallsreich.

imagine [ɪ'mædʒɪn] vt sich vorstellen; (*wrongly*) sich einbilden.

imbalance [ɪm'bæləns] n Unausgeglichenheit f.

imbecile ['ɪmbəsiːl] n Schwachsinnige(r) mf.

imbue [ɪm'bjuː] vt durchdringen.

imitate ['ɪmɪteɪt] vt nachmachen, imitieren.

imitation [ɪmɪ'teɪʃən] n Nachahmung f, Imitation f.

imitator ['ɪmɪteɪtə*] n Nachahmer m.

immaculate [ɪ'mækjʊlɪt] a makellos; *dress* tadellos; (*Eccl*) unbefleckt.

immaterial [ɪmə'tɪərɪəl] a unwesentlich.

immature [ɪmə'tjʊə*] a unreif.

immaturity [ɪmə'tjʊərɪtɪ] n Unreife f.

immediate [ɪ'miːdɪət] a (*instant*) sofortig; (*near*) unmittelbar; *relatives* nächste(r, s) *needs* dringlich; ~**ly** ad sofort; (*in position*) unmittelbar.

immense [ɪ'mens] a unermeßlich; ~**ly** ad ungeheuerlich; *grateful* unheimlich.

immerse [ɪ'mɜːs] vt eintauchen.

immersion heater [ɪ'mɜːʃənhiːtə*] n Heißwassergerät nt.

immigrant ['ɪmɪgrənt] n Einwanderer m.

immigration [ɪmɪ'greɪʃən] n Einwanderung f.

imminent ['ɪmɪnənt] a bevorstehend; *danger* drohend.

immobilize [ɪ'məʊbɪlaɪz] vt lähmen.

immoderate [ɪ'mɒdərət] a maßlos, übertrieben.

immoral [ɪ'mɒrəl] a unmoralisch; (*sexually*) unsittlich; ~**ity** [ɪmə'rælɪtɪ] Verderbtheit f.

immortal [ɪ'mɔːtl] a unsterblich; n Unsterbliche(r) mf; ~**ity** [ɪmɔː'tælɪtɪ] Unsterblichkeit f; (*of book etc*) Unvergänglichkeit f; ~**ize** vt unsterblich machen.

immune [ɪ'mjuːn] a (*secure*) geschützt (*from* gegen), sicher (*from* vor +dat); (*Med*) immun.

immunity [ɪ'mjuːnɪtɪ] n (*Med, Jur*) Immunität f; (*fig*) Freiheit f.

immunization [ɪmjʊnaɪ'zeɪʃən] n Immunisierung f.

immunize ['ɪmjʊnaɪz] vt immunisieren.

impact ['ɪmpækt] n (*lit*) Aufprall m; (*force*) Wucht f; (*fig*) Wirkung f.

impair [ɪm'peə*] vt beeinträchtigen.

impale [ɪm'peɪl] vt aufspießen.

impartial [ɪm'pɑːʃəl] a unparteiisch; ~**ity** [ɪmpɑːʃɪ'ælɪtɪ] Unparteilichkeit f.

impassable [ɪm'pɑːsəbl] a unpassierbar.

impassioned [ɪm'pæʃnd] a leidenschaftlich.

impatience [ɪm'peɪʃəns] n Ungeduld f.

impatient a, ~**ly** ad [ɪm'peɪʃənt, -lɪ] ungeduldig; **to be** ~ **to do sth** es nicht erwarten können, etw zu tun.

impeccable [ɪm'pekəbl] a tadellos.
impede [ɪm'piːd] vt (be)hindern.
impediment [ɪm'pedɪmənt] n Hindernis nt; (in speech) Sprachfehler m.
impending [ɪm'pendɪŋ] a bevorstehend.
impenetrable [ɪm'penɪtrəbl] a (lit, fig) undurchdringlich; forest unwegsam; theory undurchsichtig; mystery unerforschlich.
imperative [ɪm'perətɪv] a (necessary) unbedingt erforderlich; n (Gram) Imperativ m, Befehlsform f.
imperceptible [ɪmpə'septəbl] a nicht wahrnehmbar.
imperfect [ɪm'pɜːfɪkt] a (faulty) fehlerhaft; (incomplete) unvollständig; ~ion [ɪmpə'fekʃən] Unvollkommenheit f; (fault) Fehler m; (faultiness) Fehlerhaftigkeit f.
imperial [ɪm'pɪərɪəl] a kaiserlich; ~ism Imperialismus m.
imperil [ɪm'perɪl] vt gefährden.
impersonal [ɪm'pɜːsnl] a unpersönlich.
impersonate [ɪm'pɜːsəneɪt] vt sich ausgeben als; (for amusement) imitieren.
impersonation [ɪmpɜːsə'neɪʃən] n Verkörperung f; (Theat) Imitation f.
impertinence [ɪm'pɜːtɪnəns] n Unverschämtheit f.
impertinent [ɪm'pɜːtɪnənt] a unverschämt, frech.
imperturbable [ɪmpə'tɜːbəbl] a unerschütterlich, gelassen.
impervious [ɪm'pɜːvɪəs] a undurchlässig; (fig) unempfänglich (to für).
impetuous [ɪm'petjʊəs] a heftig, ungestüm.
impetus ['ɪmpɪtəs] n Triebkraft f; (fig) Auftrieb m.
impinge [ɪm'pɪndʒ]: ~ on vt beeinträchtigen; (light) fallen auf (+acc).
implausible [ɪm'plɔːzəbl] a unglaubwürdig, nicht überzeugend.
implement ['ɪmplɪmənt] n Werkzeug nt, Gerät nt; ['ɪmplɪment] vt ausführen.
implicate ['ɪmplɪkeɪt] vt verwickeln, hineinziehen.
implication [ɪmplɪ'keɪʃən] n (meaning) Bedeutung f; (effect) Auswirkung f; (hint) Andeutung f; (in crime) Verwicklung f; by ~ folglich.
implicit [ɪm'plɪsɪt] a (suggested) unausgesprochen; (utter) vorbehaltlos.
implore [ɪm'plɔː*] vt anflehen.
imply [ɪm'plaɪ] vt (hint) andeuten; (be evidence for) schließen lassen auf (+acc); what does that ~? was bedeutet das?
impolite [ɪmpəl'aɪt] a unhöflich.
impolitic [ɪm'pɒlɪtɪk] a undiplomatisch.
imponderable [ɪm'pɒndərəbl] a unwägbar.
import [ɪm'pɔːt] vt einführen, importieren; ['ɪmpɔːt] n Einfuhr f, Import m; (meaning) Bedeutung f, Tragweite f.
importance [ɪm'pɔːtəns] n Bedeutung f; (influence) Einfluß m.
important [ɪm'pɔːtənt] a wichtig; (influential) bedeutend, einflußreich.
import duty ['ɪmpɔːtdjuːtɪ] n Einfuhrzoll m.

imported [ɪm'pɔːtɪd] a eingeführt, importiert.
importer [ɪm'pɔːtə*] n Importeur m.
import licence ['ɪmpɔːtlaɪsəns] n Einfuhrgenehmigung f.
impose [ɪm'pəʊz] vti auferlegen (on dat); penalty, sanctions verhängen (on gegen); to ~ (o.s.) on sb sich jdm aufdrängen; to ~ on sb's kindness jds Liebenswürdigkeit ausnützen.
imposing [ɪm'pəʊzɪŋ] a eindrucksvoll.
imposition [ɪmpə'zɪʃən] n (of burden, fine) Auferlegung f; (Sch) Strafarbeit f.
impossibility [ɪmpɒsə'bɪlɪtɪ] n Unmöglichkeit f.
impossible a, **impossibly** ad [ɪm'pɒsəbl, -blɪ] unmöglich.
impostor [ɪm'pɒstə*] n Betrüger m; Hochstapler m.
impotence ['ɪmpətəns] n Impotenz f.
impotent ['ɪmpətənt] a machtlos; (sexually) impotent.
impound [ɪm'paʊnd] vt beschlagnahmen.
impoverished [ɪm'pɒvərɪʃt] a verarmt.
impracticable [ɪm'præktɪkəbl] a undurchführbar.
impractical [ɪm'præktɪkəl] a unpraktisch.
imprecise [ɪmprə'saɪs] a ungenau.
impregnable [ɪm'pregnəbl] a castle uneinnehmbar.
impregnate ['ɪmpregneɪt] vt (saturate) sättigen; (fertilize) befruchten; (fig) durchdringen.
impresario [ɪmpre'sɑːrɪəʊ] n Impresario m.
impress [ɪm'pres] vt (influence) beeindrucken; (imprint) (auf)drücken; to ~ sth on sb jdm etw einschärfen; ~ion Eindruck m; (on wax, footprint) Abdruck m; (of stamp) Aufdruck m; (of book) Auflage f; (take-off) Nachahmung f; I was under the ~ion ich hatte den Eindruck; ~ionable a leicht zu beeindrucken(d); ~ionist Impressionist m; ~ive a eindrucksvoll.
imprison [ɪm'prɪzn] vt ins Gefängnis schicken; ~ment Inhaftierung f; Gefangenschaft f; 3 years' ~ment eine Gefängnisstrafe von 3 Jahren.
improbable [ɪm'prɒbəbl] a unwahrscheinlich.
impromptu [ɪm'prɒmptjuː] a, ad aus dem Stegreif, improvisiert.
improper [ɪm'prɒpə*] a (indecent) unanständig; (wrong) unrichtig, falsch; (unsuitable) unpassend.
impropriety [ɪmprə'praɪətɪ] n Ungehörigkeit f.
improve [ɪm'pruːv] vt verbessern; vi besser werden; ~ment (Ver)besserung f; (of appearance) Verschönerung f.
improvisation [ɪmprəvaɪ'zeɪʃən] n Improvisation f.
improvise ['ɪmprəvaɪz] vti improvisieren.
imprudence [ɪm'pruːdəns] n Unklugheit f.
imprudent [ɪm'pruːdənt] a unklug.
impudent ['ɪmpjʊdənt] a unverschämt.
impulse ['ɪmpʌls] n (desire) Drang m; (driving force) Antrieb m, Impuls m; my first ~ was to... ich wollte zuerst...

impulsive [ɪm'pʌlsɪv] a impulsiv.
impunity [ɪm'pju:nɪtɪ] n Straflosigkeit f.
impure [ɪm'pjuə*] a (dirty) unrein; (mixed) gemischt; (bad) schmutzig, unanständig.
impurity [ɪm'pjuərɪtɪ] n Unreinheit f; (Tech) Verunreinigung f.
in [ɪn] prep in; (made of) aus; ~ Dickens/a child bei Dickens/einem Kind; ~ him you'll have ... an ihm hast du ...; ~ doing this he has ... dadurch, daß er das tat, hat er ...; ~ saying that I mean ... wenn ich das sage, meine ich ...; I haven't seen him ~ years ich habe ihn seit Jahren nicht mehr gesehen; 15 pence ~ the £ 15 Pence per Pfund; blind ~ the left eye auf dem linken Auge or links blind; ~ itself an sich; ~ that, ~ so or as far as insofern als; ad hinein; to be ~ zuhause sein; (train) da sein; (in fashion) in (Mode) sein; to have it ~ for sb es auf jdn abgesehen haben; ~s and outs pl Einzelheiten pl; to know the ~s and outs sich auskennen.
inability [ɪnə'bɪlɪtɪ] n Unfähigkeit f.
inaccessible [ɪnæk'sesəbl] a unzugänglich.
inaccuracy [ɪn'ækjurəsɪ] n Ungenauigkeit f.
inaccurate [ɪn'ækjurɪt] a ungenau; (wrong) unrichtig.
inaction [ɪn'ækʃən] n Untätigkeit f.
inactive [ɪn'æktɪv] a untätig.
inactivity [ɪnæk'tɪvɪtɪ] n Untätigkeit f.
inadequacy [ɪn'ædɪkwəsɪ] n Unzulänglichkeit f; (of punishment) Unangemessenheit f.
inadequate [ɪn'ædɪkwət] a unzulänglich; punishment unangemessen.
inadvertently [ɪnəd'vɜ:təntlɪ] ad unabsichtlich.
inadvisable [ɪnəd'vaɪzəbl] a nicht ratsam.
inane [ɪ'neɪn] a dumm, albern.
inanimate [ɪn'ænɪmət] a leblos.
inapplicable [ɪnə'plɪkəbl] a unzutreffend.
inappropriate [ɪnə'prəuprɪət] a clothing ungeeignet; remark unangebracht.
inapt [ɪn'æpt] a unpassend; (clumsy) ungeschickt; ~itude Untauglichkeit f.
inarticulate [ɪnɑ:'tɪkjulət] a unklar; to be ~ sich nicht ausdrücken können.
inartistic [ɪnɑ:'tɪstɪk] a unkünstlerisch.
inasmuch as [ɪnəz'mʌtʃəz] ad da, weil; (in so far as) soweit.
inattention [ɪnə'tenʃən] n Unaufmerksamkeit f.
inattentive [ɪnə'tentɪv] a unaufmerksam.
inaudible [ɪn'ɔ:dəbl] a unhörbar.
inaugural [ɪ'nɔ:gjurəl] a Eröffnungs-; (Univ) Antritts-.
inaugurate [ɪ'nɔ:gjureɪt] vt (open) einweihen; (admit to office) (feierlich) einführen.
inauguration [ɪnɔ:gju'reɪʃən] n Eröffnung f; (feierliche) Amtseinführung f.
inborn [ɪn'bɔ:n] a angeboren.
inbred [ɪn'bred] a quality angeboren; they are ~ bei ihnen herrscht Inzucht.
inbreeding [ɪn'bri:dɪŋ] n Inzucht f.
incalculable [ɪn'kælkjuləbl] a person

unberechenbar; consequences unabsehbar.
incapability [ɪnkeɪpə'bɪlɪtɪ] n Unfähigkeit f.
incapable [ɪn'keɪpəbl] a unfähig (of doing sth etw zu tun); (not able) nicht einsatzfähig.
incapacitate [ɪnkə'pæsɪteɪt] vt untauglich machen; ~d behindert; machine nicht gebrauchsfähig.
incapacity [ɪnkə'pæsɪtɪ] n Unfähigkeit f.
incarcerate [ɪn'kɑ:səreɪt] vt einkerkern.
incarnate [ɪn'kɑ:nɪt] a menschgeworden; (fig) leibhaftig.
incarnation [ɪnkɑ:'neɪʃən] n (Eccl) Menschwerdung f; (fig) Inbegriff m.
incendiary [ɪn'sendɪərɪ] a brandstifterisch, Brand-; (fig) aufrührerisch; n Brandstifter m; (bomb) Brandbombe f.
incense ['ɪnsens] n Weihrauch m; [ɪn'sens] vt erzürnen.
incentive [ɪn'sentɪv] n Anreiz m.
incessant a, ~ly ad [ɪn'sesnt, -lɪ] unaufhörlich.
incest ['ɪnsest] n Inzest m.
inch [ɪntʃ] n Zoll m.
incidence ['ɪnsɪdəns] n Auftreten nt; (of crime) Quote f.
incident ['ɪnsɪdənt] n Vorfall m; (disturbance) Zwischenfall m; ~al [ɪnsɪ'dentl] a music Begleit-; expenses Neben-; (unplanned) zufällig; (unimportant) nebensächlich; remark beiläufig; ~al to sth mit etw verbunden; ~ally [ɪnsɪ'dentəlɪ] ad (by chance) nebenbei; (by the way) nebenbei bemerkt, übrigens.
incinerator [ɪn'sɪnəreɪtə*] n Verbrennungsofen m.
incision [ɪn'sɪʒən] n Einschnitt m.
incisive [ɪn'saɪsɪv] a style treffend; person scharfsinnig.
incite [ɪn'saɪt] vt anstacheln.
inclement [ɪn'klemənt] a weather rauh.
inclination [ɪnklɪ'neɪʃən] n Neigung f.
incline ['ɪnklaɪn] n Abhang m; [ɪn'klaɪn] vt neigen; (fig) veranlassen; to be ~d to do sth Lust haben, etw zu tun; (have tendency) dazu neigen, etw zu tun; vi sich neigen.
include [ɪn'klu:d] vt einschließen; (on list, in group) aufnehmen.
including [ɪn'klu:dɪŋ] prep: ~ X X inbegriffen.
inclusion [ɪn'klu:ʒən] n Aufnahme f, Einbeziehung f.
inclusive [ɪn'klu:sɪv] a einschließlich; (Comm) inklusive.
incognito [ɪnkɒg'ni:təu] ad inkognito.
incoherent [ɪnkəu'hɪərənt] a zusammenhanglos.
income ['ɪnkʌm] n Einkommen nt; (from business) Einkünfte pl; ~ tax Lohnsteuer f; (of self-employed) Einkommensteuer f.
incoming ['ɪnkʌmɪŋ] a ankommend; (succeeding) folgend; mail eingehend; tide steigend.
incomparable [ɪn'kɒmpərəbl] a unvergleichlich.
incompatible [ɪnkəm'pætəbl] a unvereinbar; people unverträglich.

incompetence [ɪn'kɒmpɪtəns] *n* Unfähigkeit *f*.

incompetent [ɪn'kɒmpɪtənt] *a* unfähig; (*not qualified*) nicht berechtigt.

incomplete [ɪnkəm'pliːt] *a* unvollständig.

incomprehensible [ɪnkɒmprɪ'hensəbl] *a* unverständlich.

inconceivable [ɪnkən'siːvəbl] *a* unvorstellbar.

inconclusive [ɪnkən'kluːsɪv] *a* nicht schlüssig.

incongruity [ɪnkɒŋ'gruːɪtɪ] *n* Seltsamkeit *f*; (*of remark etc*) Unangebrachtsein *nt*.

incongruous [ɪn'kɒŋgruəs] *a* seltsam; *remark* unangebracht.

inconsequential [ɪnkɒnsɪ'kwenʃəl] *a* belanglos.

inconsiderable [ɪnkən'sɪdərəbl] *a* unerheblich.

inconsiderate [ɪnkən'ʃɪdərət] *a* rücksichtslos; (*hasty*) unüberlegt.

inconsistency [ɪnkən'sɪstənsɪ] *n* innere(r) Widerspruch *m*; (*state*) Unbeständigkeit *f*.

inconsistent [ɪnkən'sɪstənt] *a* unvereinbar; *behaviour* inkonsequent; *action, speech* widersprüchlich; *person, work* unbeständig.

inconspicuous [ɪnkən'spɪkjuəs] *a* unauffällig.

inconstancy [ɪn'kɒnstənsɪ] *n* Unbeständigkeit *f*.

inconstant [ɪn'kɒnstənt] *a* unbeständig.

incontinence [ɪn'kɒntɪnəns] *n* (*Med*) Unfähigkeit *f*, Stuhl und Harn zurückzuhalten; (*fig*) Zügellosigkeit *f*.

incontinent [ɪn'kɒntɪnənt] *a* (*Med*) nicht fähig, Stuhl und Harn zurückzuhalten; (*fig*) zügellos.

inconvenience [ɪnkən'viːnɪəns] *n* Unbequemlichkeit *f*; (*trouble to others*) Unannehmlichkeiten *pl*.

inconvenient [ɪnkən'viːnɪənt] *a* ungelegen; *journey* unbequem.

incorporate [ɪn'kɔːpəreɪt] *vt* (*include*) aufnehmen; (*unite*) vereinigen.

incorporated [ɪn'kɔːpəreɪtɪd] *a* eingetragen; (*US*) GmbH.

incorrect [ɪnkə'rekt] *a* unrichtig; *behaviour* inkorrekt.

incorrigible [ɪn'kɒrɪdʒəbl] *a* unverbesserlich.

incorruptible [ɪnkə'rʌptəbl] *a* unzerstörbar; *person* unbestechlich.

increase ['ɪnkriːs] *n* Zunahme *f*, Erhöhung *f*; (*pay —*) Gehaltserhöhung *f*; (*in size*) Vergrößerung *f*; [ɪn'kriːs] *vt* erhöhen; *wealth, rage* vermehren; *business* erweitern; *vi* zunehmen; (*prices*) steigen; (*in size*) größer werden; (*in number*) sich vermehren.

increasingly [ɪn'kriːsɪŋlɪ] *ad* zunehmend.

incredible *a*, **incredibly** *ad* [ɪn'kredəbl, -blɪ] unglaublich.

incredulity [ɪnkrɪ'djuːlɪtɪ] *n* Ungläubigkeit *f*.

incredulous [ɪn'kredjuləs] *a* ungläubig.

increment ['ɪnkrɪmənt] *n* Zulage *f*.

incriminate [ɪn'krɪmɪneɪt] *vt* belasten.

incubation [ɪnkjʊ'beɪʃən] *n* Ausbrüten *nt*; *~ period* Inkubationszeit *f*.

incubator ['ɪnkjʊbeɪtə*] *n* Brutkasten *m*.

incur [ɪn'kɜː*] *vt* sich zuziehen; *debts* machen.

incurable [ɪn'kjʊərəbl] *a* unheilbar; (*fig*) unverbesserlich.

incursion [ɪn'kɜːʃən] *n* (feindlicher) Einfall *m*.

indebted [ɪn'detɪd] *a* (*obliged*) verpflichtet (*to sb* jdm); (*owing*) verschuldet.

indecency [ɪn'diːsnsɪ] *n* Unanständigkeit *f*.

indecent [ɪn'diːsnt] *a* unanständig.

indecision [ɪndɪ'sɪʒən] *n* Unschlüssigkeit *f*.

indecisive [ɪndɪ'saɪsɪv] *a* *battle* nicht entscheidend; *result* unentschieden; *person* unentschlossen.

indeed [ɪn'diːd] *ad* tatsächlich, in der Tat.

indefinable [ɪndɪ'faɪnəbl] *a* undefinierbar; (*vague*) unbestimmt.

indefinite [ɪn'defɪnɪt] *a* unbestimmt; *~ly ad* auf unbestimmte Zeit; *wait* unbegrenzt lange.

indelible [ɪn'deləbl] *a* unauslöschlich; *~ pencil* Tintenstift *m*.

indemnify [ɪn'demnɪfaɪ] *vt* entschädigen; (*safeguard*) versichern.

indentation [ɪnden'teɪʃən] *n* Einbuchtung *f*; (*Print*) Einrückung *f*.

independence [ɪndɪ'pendəns] *n* Unabhängigkeit *f*.

independent [ɪndɪ'pendənt] *a* (*free*) unabhängig; (*unconnected*) unabhängig *v* von.

indescribable [ɪndɪs'kraɪbəbl] *a* unbeschreiblich.

index ['ɪndeks] *n* Index *m* (*also Eccl*), Verzeichnis *nt*; *~ finger* Zeigefinger *m*.

indicate ['ɪndɪkeɪt] *vt* anzeigen; (*hint*) andeuten.

indication [ɪndɪ'keɪʃən] *n* Anzeichen *nt*; (*information*) Angabe *f*.

indicative [ɪn'dɪkətɪv] *n* (*Gram*) Indikativ *m*.

indicator ['ɪndɪkeɪtə*] *n* (*sign*) (An)zeichen *nt*; (*Aut*) Richtungsanzeiger *m*.

indict [ɪn'daɪt] *vt* anklagen; *~able a person* strafrechtlich verfolgbar; *offence* strafbar; *~ment* Anklage *f*.

indifference [ɪn'dɪfrəns] *n* (*lack of interest*) Gleichgültigkeit *f*; (*unimportance*) Unwichtigkeit *f*.

indifferent [ɪn'dɪfrənt] *a* (*not caring*) gleichgültig; (*unimportant*) unwichtig; (*mediocre*) mäßig.

indigenous [ɪn'dɪdʒɪnəs] *a* einheimisch; *a plant ~ to X* eine in X vorkommende Pflanze.

indigestible [ɪndɪ'dʒestəbl] *a* unverdaulich.

indigestion [ɪndɪ'dʒestʃən] *n* Verdauungsstörung *f*; verdorbene(r) Magen *m*.

indignant [ɪn'dɪgnənt] *a* ungehalten, entrüstet.

indignation [ɪndɪg'neɪʃən] *n* Entrüstung *f*.

indignity [ɪn'dɪgnɪtɪ] *n* Demütigung *f*.

indigo ['ɪndɪgəʊ] *n* Indigo *m or nt*; *a* indigoblau.

indirect *a*, *~ly ad* [ɪndɪ'rekt, -lɪ] indirekt; *answer* nicht direkt; *by ~ means* auf Umwegen.

indiscernible [ɪndɪˈsɜːnəbl] *a* nicht wahrnehmbar.

indiscreet [ɪndɪsˈkriːt] *a* (*insensitive*) unbedacht; (*improper*) taktlos; (*telling secrets*) indiskret.

indiscretion [ɪndɪsˈkreʃən] *n* Taktlosigkeit *f*; Indiskretion *f*.

indiscriminate [ɪndɪsˈkrɪmɪnət] *a* wahllos; kritiklos.

indispensable [ɪndɪsˈpensəbl] *a* unentbehrlich.

indisposed [ɪndɪsˈpəʊzd] *a* unpäßlich.

indisposition [ɪndɪspəˈzɪʃən] *n* Unpäßlichkeit *f*.

indisputable [ɪndɪsˈpjuːtəbl] *a* unbestreitbar; *evidence* unanfechtbar.

indistinct [ɪndɪsˈtɪŋkt] *a* undeutlich.

indistinguishable [ɪndɪsˈtɪŋgwɪʃəbl] *a* nicht unterscheidbar; *difference* unmerklich.

individual [ɪndɪˈvɪdjʊəl] *n* Einzelne(r) *mf*, Individuum *nt*; *a* individuell; *case* Einzel-; (*of, for one person*) eigen, individuell; (*characteristic*) eigentümlich; **~ist** Individualist *m*; **~ity** [ɪndɪvɪdjʊˈælɪtɪ] Individualität *f*; **~ly** *ad* einzeln, individuell.

indoctrinate [ɪnˈdɒktrɪneɪt] *vt* indoktrinieren.

indoctrination [ɪndɒktrɪˈneɪʃən] *n* Indoktrination *f*.

indolence [ˈɪndələns] *n* Trägheit *f*.

indolent [ˈɪndələnt] *a* träge.

indoor [ˈɪndɔː*] *a* Haus-; Zimmer-; Innen-; (*Sport*) Hallen-; **~s** *ad* drinnen, im Haus; **to go ~s** hinein *or* ins Haus gehen.

indubitable [ɪnˈdjuːbɪtəbl] *a* unzweifelhaft.

indubitably [ɪnˈdjuːbɪtəblɪ] *ad* zweifellos.

induce [ɪnˈdjuːs] *vt* dazu bewegen, veranlassen; *reaction* herbeiführen; **~ment** Veranlassung *f*; (*incentive*) Anreiz *m*.

induct [ɪnˈdʌkt] *vt* in sein Amt einführen.

indulge [ɪnˈdʌldʒ] *vt* (*give way*) nachgeben (+*dat*); (*gratify*) frönen (+*dat*); **to ~ o.s. in sth** sich (*dat*) etw gönnen; *vi* frönen (*in dat*), sich gönnen (*in acc*); **~nce** Nachsicht *f*; (*enjoyment*) (übermäßiger) Genuß *m*; **~nt** *a* nachsichtig; (*pej*) nachgiebig.

industrial [ɪnˈdʌstrɪəl] *a* Industrie-, industriell; *dispute, injury* Arbeits-; **~ist** Industrielle(r) *mf*; **~ize** *vt* industrialisieren.

industrious [ɪnˈdʌstrɪəs] *a* fleißig.

industry [ˈɪndəstrɪ] *n* Industrie *f*; (*diligence*) Fleiß *m*; **hotel ~** Hotelgewerbe *nt*.

inebriated [ɪˈniːbrɪeɪtɪd] *a* betrunken, berauscht.

inedible [ɪnˈedɪbl] *a* ungenießbar.

ineffective [ɪnɪˈfektɪv], **ineffectual** [ɪnɪˈfektjʊəl] *a* unwirksam, wirkungslos; *person* untauglich.

inefficiency [ɪnɪˈfɪʃənsɪ] *n* Ineffizienz *f*.

inefficient [ɪnɪˈfɪʃənt] *a* ineffizient; (*ineffective*) unwirksam.

inelegant [ɪnˈelɪgənt] *a* unelegant.

ineligible [ɪnˈelɪdʒəbl] *a* nicht berechtigt; *candidate* nicht wählbar.

ineluctable [ɪnɪˈlʌktəbl] *a* unausweichlich.

inept [ɪˈnept] *a* *remark* unpassend; *person* ungeeignet.

inequality [ɪnɪˈkwɒlɪtɪ] *n* Ungleichheit *f*.

ineradicable [ɪnɪˈrædɪkəbl] *a* unausrottbar; *mistake* unabänderlich; *guilt* tiefsitzend.

inert [ɪˈnɜːt] *a* träge; (*Chem*) inaktiv; (*motionless*) unbeweglich.

inertia [ɪˈnɜːʃə] *n* Trägheit *f*.

inescapable [ɪnɪsˈkeɪpəbl] *a* unvermeidbar.

inessential [ɪnɪˈsenʃəl] *a* unwesentlich.

inestimable [ɪnˈestɪməbl] *a* unschätzbar.

inevitability [ɪnevɪtəˈbɪlɪtɪ] *n* Unvermeidlichkeit *f*.

inevitable [ɪnˈevɪtəbl] *a* unvermeidlich.

inexact [ɪnɪgˈzækt] *a* ungenau.

inexcusable [ɪnɪksˈkjuːzəbl] *a* unverzeihlich.

inexhaustible [ɪnɪgˈzɔːstəbl] *a* *wealth* unerschöpflich; *talker* unermüdlich; *curiosity* unstillbar.

inexorable [ɪnˈeksərəbl] *a* unerbittlich.

inexpensive [ɪnɪksˈpensɪv] *a* preiswert.

inexperience [ɪnɪksˈpɪərɪəns] *n* Unerfahrenheit *f*; **~d** *a* unerfahren.

inexplicable [ɪnɪksˈplɪkəbl] *a* unerklärlich.

inexpressible [ɪnɪksˈpresəbl] *a* *pain, joy* unbeschreiblich; *thoughts* nicht ausdrückbar.

inextricable [ɪnɪksˈtrɪkəbl] *a* un(auf)lösbar.

infallibility [ɪnfæləˈbɪlɪtɪ] *n* Unfehlbarkeit *f*.

infallible [ɪnˈfæləbl] *a* unfehlbar.

infamous [ˈɪnfəməs] *a* *place* verrufen; *deed* schändlich; *person* niederträchtig.

infamy [ˈɪnfəmɪ] *n* Verruftheit *f*; Niedertracht *f*; (*disgrace*) Schande *f*.

infancy [ˈɪnfənsɪ] *n* frühe Kindheit *f*; (*fig*) Anfangsstadium *nt*.

infant [ˈɪnfənt] *n* kleine(s) Kind *nt*, Säugling *m*; **~ile** *a* kindisch, infantil; **~ school** Vorschule *f*.

infantry [ˈɪnfəntrɪ] *n* Infanterie *f*; **~man** Infanterist *m*.

infatuated [ɪnˈfætjʊeɪtɪd] *a* vernarrt; **to become ~ with** sich vernarren in (+*acc*).

infatuation [ɪnfætjʊˈeɪʃən] *n* Vernarrtheit *f* (*with in* +*acc*).

infect [ɪnˈfekt] *vt* anstecken (*also fig*), infizieren; **~ion** Ansteckung *f*, Infektion *f*; **~ious** [ɪnˈfekʃəs] *a* ansteckend.

infer [ɪnˈfɜː*] *vt* schließen; **~ence** [ˈɪnfərəns] *a* Schlußfolgerung *f*.

inferior [ɪnˈfɪərɪə*] *a* *rank* untergeordnet, niedriger; *quality* minderwertig; *n* Untergebene(r) *m*; **~ity** [ɪnfɪərɪˈɒrɪtɪ] Minderwertigkeit *f*; (*in rank*) untergeordnete Stellung *f*; **~ity complex** Minderwertigkeitskomplex *m*.

infernal [ɪnˈfɜːnl] *a* höllisch.

inferno [ɪnˈfɜːnəʊ] *n* Hölle *f*, Inferno *nt*.

infertile [ɪnˈfɜːtaɪl] *a* unfruchtbar.

infertility [ɪnfɜːˈtɪlɪtɪ] *n* Unfruchtbarkeit *f*.

infest [ɪnˈfest] *vt* plagen, heimsuchen; **to be ~ed with** wimmeln von.

infidel ['ınfıdəl] n Ungläubige(r) mf.

infidelity [ınfı'delıtı] n Untreue f.

in-fighting ['ınfaıtıŋ] n Nahkampf m.

infiltrate ['ınfıltreıt] vt infiltrieren; spies einschleusen; (liquid) durchdringen; vi (Mil, liquid) einsickern; (Pol) unterwandern (into acc).

infinite ['ınfınıt] a unendlich.

infinitive [ın'fınıtıv] n Infinitiv m, Nennform f.

infinity [ın'fınıtı] n Unendlichkeit f.

infirm [ın'fɜːm] a schwach, gebrechlich; (irresolute) willensschwach.

infirmary [ın'fɜːmərı] n Krankenhaus nt.

infirmity [ın'fɜːmıtı] n Schwäche f, Gebrechlichkeit f.

inflame [ın'fleım] vt (Med) entzünden; person reizen; anger erregen.

inflammable [ın'flæməbl] a feuergefährlich.

inflammation [ınflə'meıʃən] n Entzündung f.

inflate [ın'fleıt] vt aufblasen; tyre aufpumpen; prices hochtreiben.

inflation [ın'fleıʃən] n Inflation f, ~ary a increase inflationistisch; situation inflationär.

inflexible [ın'fleksəbl] a person nicht flexibel; opinion starr; thing unbiegsam.

inflict [ın'flıkt] vt zufügen (sth on sb jdm etw); punishment auferlegen (on dat); wound beibringen (on dat); ~ion [ın'flıkʃən] Zufügung f; Auferlegung f; (suffering) Heimsuchung f.

inflow ['ınfləu] n Einfließen nt, Zustrom m.

influence ['ınfluəns] n Einfluß m; vt beeinflussen.

influential [ınflu'enʃəl] a einflußreich.

influenza [ınflu'enzə] n Grippe f.

influx ['ınflʌks] n (of water) Einfluß m; (of people) Zustrom m; (of ideas) Eindringen nt.

inform [ın'fɔːm] vt informieren; to keep sb ~ed jdn auf dem laufenden halten.

informal [ın'fɔːməl] a zwanglos; ~ity [ınfɔː'mælıtı] Ungezwungenheit f.

information [ınfə'meıʃən] n Auskunft f, Information f.

informative [ın'fɔːmətıv] a informativ; person mitteilsam.

informer [ın'fɔːmə°] n Denunziant(in f) m.

infra-red [ınfrə'red] a infrarot.

infrequent [ın'friːkwənt] a selten.

infringe [ın'frındʒ] vt law verstoßen gegen; ~ upon vt verletzen; ~ment Verstoß m, Verletzung f.

infuriate [ın'fjuərıeıt] vt wütend machen.

infuriating [ın'fjuərıeıtıŋ] a ärgerlich.

ingenious [ın'dʒiːnıəs] a genial; thing raffiniert.

ingenuity [ındʒı'njuːıtı] n Findigkeit f, Genialität f, Raffiniertheit f.

ingot ['ıŋgət] n Barren m.

ingratiate [ın'greıʃıeıt] vt einschmeicheln (o.s. with sb sich bei jdm).

ingratitude [ın'grætıtjuːd] n Undankbarkeit f.

ingredient [ın'griːdıənt] n Bestandteil m; (Cook) Zutat f.

inhabit [ın'hæbıt] vt bewohnen; ~ant Bewohner(in f) m; (of island, town) Einwohner(in f) m.

inhale [ın'heıl] vt einatmen; (Med, cigarettes) inhalieren.

inherent [ın'hıərənt] a innewohnend (in dat).

inherit [ın'herıt] vt erben; ~ance Erbe nt, Erbschaft f.

inhibit [ın'hıbıt] vt hemmen; (restrain) hindern; ~ion [ınhı'bıʃən] Hemmung f.

inhospitable [ınhɒs'pıtəbl] a person ungastlich; country unwirtlich.

inhuman [ın'hjuːmən] a unmenschlich.

inimitable [ı'nımıtəbl] a unnachahmlich.

iniquity [ı'nıkwıtı] n Ungerechtigkeit f.

initial [ı'nıʃəl] a anfänglich, Anfangs-; n Anfangsbuchstabe m, Initiale f; vt abzeichnen; (Pol) paraphieren; ~ly a anfangs.

initiate [ı'nıʃıeıt] vt einführen; negotiations einleiten; (instruct) einweihen.

initiation [ınıʃı'eıʃən] n Einführung f; Einleitung f.

initiative [ı'nıʃıtıv] n Initiative f.

inject [ın'dʒekt] vt einspritzen; (fig) einflößen; ~ion Spritze f, Injektion f.

injure ['ındʒə°] vt verletzen; (fig) schaden (+dat).

injury ['ındʒərı] n Verletzung f.

injustice [ın'dʒʌstıs] n Ungerechtigkeit f.

ink [ıŋk] n Tinte f.

inkling ['ıŋklıŋ] n (dunkle) Ahnung f.

inlaid ['ın'leıd] a eingelegt, Einlege-.

inland ['ınlænd] a Binnen-; (domestic) Inlands-; ad landeinwärts; ~ revenue (Brit) Fiskus m.

in-law ['ınlɔː] n angeheiratete(r) Verwandte(r) mf.

inlet ['ınlet] n Öffnung f, Einlaß m; (bay) kleine Bucht f.

inmate ['ınmeıt] n Insasse m.

inn [ın] n Gasthaus nt, Wirtshaus nt.

innate [ı'neıt] a angeboren, eigen (+dat).

inner ['ınə°] a inner, Innen-; (fig) verborgen, innerste(r,s).

innocence ['ınəsns] n Unschuld f; (ignorance) Unkenntnis f.

innocent ['ınəsnt] a unschuldig.

innocuous [ı'nɒkjuəs] a harmlos.

innovation [ınəu'veıʃən] n Neuerung f.

innuendo [ınju'endəu] n (versteckte) Anspielung f.

innumerable [ı'njuːmərəbl] a unzählig.

inoculation [ınɒkju'leıʃən] n Impfung f.

inopportune [ın'ɒpətjuːn] a remark unangebracht; visit ungelegen.

inordinately [ı'nɔːdınıtlı] ad unmäßig.

inorganic [ınɔː'gænık] a unorganisch; (Chem) anorganisch.

in-patient ['ınpeıʃənt] n stationäre(r) Patient(in f) m.

input ['ınput] n (Elec) (Auf)ladung f; (Tech) zugeführte Menge f; (labour) angewandte Arbeitsleistung f; (money) Investitionssumme f.

inquest ['ınkwest] n gerichtliche Untersuchung f.

inquire [ın'kwaıə°] vi sich erkundigen; vt

price sich erkundigen nach; ~ **into** *vt* untersuchen.

inquiring [ɪn'kwaɪərɪŋ] *a mind* wissensdurstig.

inquiry [ɪn'kwaɪərɪ] *n (question)* Erkundigung *f*, Nachfrage *f*; (*investigation*) Untersuchung *f*; ~ **office** Auskunft(sbüro *nt*) *f*.

inquisitive [ɪn'kwɪzɪtɪv] *a* neugierig; *look* forschend.

inroad ['ɪnrəʊd] *n (Mil)* Einfall *m*; (*fig*) Eingriff *m*.

insane [ɪn'seɪn] *a* wahnsinnig; (*Med*) geisteskrank.

insanitary [ɪn'sænɪtərɪ] *a* unhygienisch, gesundheitsschädlich.

insanity [ɪn'sænɪtɪ] *n* Wahnsinn *m*.

insatiable [ɪn'seɪʃəbl] *a* unersättlich.

inscription [ɪn'skrɪpʃən] *n (on stone)* Inschrift *f*; (*in book*) Widmung *f*.

inscrutable [ɪn'skruːtəbl] *a* unergründlich.

insect ['ɪnsekt] *n* Insekt *nt*; ~**icide** [ɪn'sektɪsaɪd] *a* Insektenvertilgungsmittel *nt*.

insecure [ɪnsɪ'kjʊə*] *a person* unsicher; *thing* nicht fest *or* sicher.

insecurity [ɪnsɪ'kjʊərɪtɪ] *n* Unsicherheit *f*.

insensible [ɪn'sensɪbl] *a* gefühllos; (*unconscious*) bewußtlos; (*imperceptible*) unmerklich; ~ **of** *or* **to sth** unempfänglich für etw.

insensitive [ɪn'sensɪtɪv] *a (to pain)* unempfindlich; (*without feelings*) gefühllos.

inseparable [ɪn'sepərəbl] *a people* unzertrennlich; *word* untrennbar.

insert [ɪn'sɜːt] *vt* einfügen; *coin* einwerfen; (*stick into*) hineinstecken; *advert* aufgeben; ['ɪnsɜːt] *n* Beifügung *f*; (*in book*) Einlage *f*; (*in magazine*) Beilage *f*; ~**ion** Einfügung *f*; (*Press*) Inserat *nt*.

inshore ['ɪn'ʃɔː*] *a* Küsten-; ['ɪn'ʃɔː*] *ad* an der Küste.

inside [ɪn'saɪd] *n* Innenseite *f*, Innere(s) *nt*; *a* innere(r,s), Innen-; *ad (place)* innen; (*direction*) nach innen, hinein; *prep (place)* in (+*dat*); (*direction*) in (+*acc*) ... hinein; (*time*) innerhalb (+*gen*); ~ **forward** (*Sport*) Halbstürmer *m*; ~ **out** *ad* linksherum; *know* in- und auswendig; ~**r** Eingeweihte(r) *mf*; (*member*) Mitglied *nt*.

insidious [ɪn'sɪdɪəs] *a* heimtückisch.

insight ['ɪnsaɪt] *n* Einsicht *f*; Einblick *m* (*into* in +*acc*).

insignificant [ɪnsɪg'nɪfɪkənt] *a* unbedeutend.

insincere [ɪnsɪn'sɪə*] *a* unaufrichtig, falsch.

insincerity [ɪnsɪn'serɪtɪ] *n* Unaufrichtigkeit *f*.

insinuate [ɪn'sɪnjʊeɪt] *vt (hint)* andeuten; **to** ~ **o.s. into sth** sich in etw (*acc*) einschleichen.

insinuation [ɪnsɪnjʊ'eɪʃən] *n* Anspielung *f*.

insipid [ɪn'sɪpɪd] *a* fad(e).

insist [ɪn'sɪst] *vi* bestehen (*on* auf +*acc*); ~**ence** Bestehen *nt*; ~**ent** *a* hartnäckig; (*urgent*) dringend.

insolence ['ɪnsələns] *n* Frechheit *f*.

insolent ['ɪnsələnt] *a* frech.

insoluble [ɪn'sɒljʊbl] *a* unlösbar; (*Chem*) unlöslich.

insolvent [ɪn'sɒlvənt] *a* zahlungsunfähig.

insomnia [ɪn'sɒmnɪə] *n* Schlaflosigkeit *f*.

inspect [ɪn'spekt] *vt* besichtigen, prüfen; (*officially*) inspizieren; ~**ion** Besichtigung *f*, Inspektion *f*; ~**or** (*official*) Aufsichtsbeamte(r) *m*, Inspektor *m*; (*police*) Polizeikommissar *m*; (*Rail*) Kontrolleur *m*.

inspiration [ɪnspɪ'reɪʃən] *n* Inspiration *f*.

inspire [ɪn'spaɪə*] *vt respect* einflößen (*in dat*); *hope* wecken (*in* in +*dat*); *person* inspirieren; **to** ~ **sb to do sth** jdn dazu anregen, etw zu tun; ~**d** *a* begabt, einfallsreich.

inspiring [ɪn'spaɪərɪŋ] *a* begeisternd.

instability [ɪnstə'bɪlɪtɪ] *n* Unbeständigkeit *f*, Labilität *f*.

install [ɪn'stɔːl] *vt (put in)* einbauen, installieren; *telephone* anschließen; (*establish*) einsetzen; ~**ation** [ɪnstə'leɪʃən] (*of person*) (Amts)einsetzung *f*; (*of machinery*) Einbau *m*, Installierung *f*; (*machines etc*) Anlage *f*.

instalment, (*US*) **installment** [ɪn'stɔːlmənt] *n* Rate *f*; (*of story*) Fortsetzung *f*; **to pay in** ~**s** auf Raten zahlen.

instance ['ɪnstəns] *n* Fall *m*; (*example*) Beispiel *nt*; **for** ~ zum Beispiel.

instant ['ɪnstənt] *n* Augenblick *m*; *a* augenblicklich, sofortig; ~ **coffee** Pulverkaffee *m*; ~**ly** *ad* sofort.

instead [ɪn'sted] *ad* stattdessen; ~ **of** *prep* anstatt (+*gen*).

instigation [ɪnstɪ'geɪʃən] *n* Veranlassung *f*; (*of crime etc*) Anstiftung *f*.

instil [ɪn'stɪl] *vt (fig)* beibringen (*in sb* jdm).

instinct ['ɪnstɪŋkt] *n* Instinkt *m*; ~**ive** *a*, ~**ively** *ad* [ɪn'stɪŋktɪv, -lɪ] instinktiv.

institute ['ɪnstɪtjuːt] *n* Institut *nt*; (*society also*) Gesellschaft *f*; *vt* einführen; *search* einleiten.

institution [ɪnstɪ'tjuːʃən] *n (custom)* Einrichtung *f*, Brauch *m*; (*society*) Institution *f*; (*home*) Anstalt *f*; (*beginning*) Einführung *f*, Einleitung *f*.

instruct [ɪn'strʌkt] *vt* anweisen; (*officially*) instruieren; ~**ion** [ɪn'strʌkʃən] Unterricht *m*; ~**ions** *pl* Anweisungen *pl*; (*for use*) Gebrauchsanweisung *f*; ~**ive** *a* lehrreich; ~**or** Lehrer *m*; (*Mil*) Ausbilder *m*.

instrument ['ɪnstrəmənt] *n (tool)* Instrument *nt*, Werkzeug *nt*; (*Mus*) (Musik)-instrument *nt*; ~**al** [ɪnstru'mentl] *a (Mus)* Instrumental-; (*helpful*) behilflich (*in* bei); ~**alist** [ɪnstru'mentəlɪst] Instrumentalist *m*; ~ **panel** Armaturenbrett *nt*.

insubordinate [ɪnsə'bɔːdənət] *a* aufsässig, widersetzlich.

insubordination ['ɪnsəbɔːdɪ'neɪʃən] *n* Gehorsamsverweigerung *f*.

insufferable [ɪn'sʌfərəbl] *a* unerträglich.

insufficient *a*, ~**ly** *ad* [ɪnsə'fɪʃənt, -lɪ] ungenügend.

insular ['ɪnsjələ*] *a (fig)* engstirnig; ~**ity** [ɪnsjʊ'lærɪtɪ] (*fig*) Engstirnigkeit *f*.

insulate ['ɪnsjʊleɪt] *vt (Elec)* isolieren; (*fig*) abschirmen (*from* vor +*dat*).

insulating tape ['ɪnsjʊleɪtɪŋteɪp] *n* Isolierband *nt*.

insulation [ɪnsju'leɪʃən] *n* Isolierung *f*.

insulator ['ɪnsjʊleɪtə°] *n* Isolator *m*.

insulin ['ɪnsjʊlɪn] *n* Insulin *nt*.

insult ['ɪnsʌlt] *n* Beleidigung *f*; [ɪn'sʌlt] *vt* beleidigen; ~**ing** [ɪn'sʌltɪŋ] *a* beleidigend.

insuperable [ɪn'suːpərəbl] *a* unüberwindlich.

insurance [ɪn'ʃʊərəns] *n* Versicherung *f*; ~ **agent** Versicherungsvertreter *m*; ~ **policy** Versicherungspolice *f.*

insure [ɪn'ʃʊə°] *vt* versichern.

insurmountable [ɪnsə'maʊntəbl] *a* unüberwindlich.

insurrection [ɪnsə'rekʃən] *n* Aufstand *m*.

intact [ɪn'tækt] *a* intakt, unangetastet, ganz.

intake ['ɪnteɪk] *n* (*place*) Einlaßöffnung *f*; (*act*) Aufnahme *f*; (*amount*) aufgenommene Menge *f*; (*Sch*) Neuaufnahme *f.*

intangible [ɪn'tændʒəbl] *a* unfaßbar; *thing* nicht greifbar.

integer ['ɪntɪdʒə°] *n* ganze Zahl *f.*

integral ['ɪntɪgrəl] *a* (*essential*) wesentlich; (*complete*) vollständig; (*Math*) Integral-.

integrate ['ɪntɪgreɪt] *vt* vereinigen; *people* eingliedern, integrieren.

integration [ɪntɪ'greɪʃən] *n* Eingliederung *f*, Integration *f.*

integrity [ɪn'tegrɪtɪ] *n* (*honesty*) Redlichkeit *f*, Integrität *f.*

intellect ['ɪntɪlekt] *n* Intellekt *m*; ~**ual** [ɪntɪ'lektjʊəl] *a* geistig, intellektuell; *n* Intellektuelle(r) *mf.*

intelligence [ɪn'telɪdʒəns] *n* (*understanding*) Intelligenz *f*; (*news*) Information *f*; (*Mil*) Geheimdienst *m.*

intelligent [ɪn'telɪdʒənt] *a* intelligent; *beings* vernunftbegabt; ~**ly** *ad* klug; *write, speak* verständlich.

intelligible [ɪn'telɪdʒəbl] *a* verständlich.

intemperate [ɪn'tempərət] *a* unmäßig.

intend [ɪn'tend] *vt* beabsichtigen; *that was ~ed for you* das war für dich gedacht.

intense [ɪn'tens] *a* stark, intensiv; *person* ernsthaft; ~**ly** *ad* äußerst; *study* intensiv.

intensify [ɪn'tensɪfaɪ] *vt* verstärken, intensivieren.

intensity [ɪn'tensɪtɪ] *n* Intensität *f*, Stärke *f.*

intensive *a*, ~**ly** *ad* [ɪn'tensɪv, -lɪ] intensiv.

intent [ɪn'tent] *n* Absicht *f*; **to all ~s and purposes** praktisch; ~**ly** *ad* aufmerksam; *look* forschend; **to be ~ on doing sth** fest entschlossen sein, etw zu tun.

intention [ɪn'tenʃən] *n* Absicht *f*; **with good ~s** mit guten Vorsätzen; ~**al** *a*, ~**ally** *ad* absichtlich.

inter [ɪn'tɜː°] *vt* beerdigen.

inter- ['ɪntə°] *pref* zwischen-, Zwischen-.

interact [ɪntər'ækt] *vi* aufeinander einwirken; ~**ion** *n* Wechselwirkung *f.*

intercede [ɪntə'siːd] *vi* sich verwenden; (*in argument*) vermitteln.

intercept [ɪntə'sept] *vt* abfangen; ~**ion** *n* Abfangen *nt.*

interchange ['ɪntə'tʃeɪndʒ] *n* (*exchange*) Austausch *m*; (*on roads*) Verkehrskreuz *nt*; [ɪntə'tʃeɪndʒ] *vt* austauschen; ~**able** [ɪntə'tʃeɪndʒəbl] *a* austauschbar.

intercom ['ɪntəkom] *n* (Gegen)sprechanlage *f.*

interconnect [ɪntəkə'nekt] *vt* miteinander verbinden; *vi* miteinander verbunden sein; (*roads*) zusammenführen.

intercontinental ['ɪntəkɒntɪ'nentl] *a* interkontinental.

intercourse ['ɪntəkɔːs] *n* (*exchange*) Verkehr *m*, Beziehungen *pl*; (*sexual*) Geschlechtsverkehr *m.*

interdependence [ɪntədɪ'pendəns] *n* gegenseitige Abhängigkeit *f.*

interest ['ɪntrest] *n* Interesse *nt*; (*Fin*) Zinsen *pl*; (*Comm: share*) Anteil *m*; (*group*) Interessengruppe *f*; **to be of ~** von Interesse sein; *vt* interessieren; ~**ed** *a* (*having claims*) beteiligt; (*attentive*) interessiert; **to be ~ed in** sich interessieren für; ~**ing** *a* interessant.

interfere [ɪntə'fɪə°] *vi* (*meddle*) sich einmischen (*with* in + *acc*) stören (*with acc*); (*with an object*) sich zu schaffen machen (*with an* + *dat*); ~**nce** *f*; (*TV*) Störung *f.*

interim ['ɪntərɪm] *a* vorläufig; *n*: **in the ~** inzwischen.

interior [ɪn'tɪərɪə°] *n* Innere(s) *nt*; *a* innere(r,s), Innen-.

interjection [ɪntə'dʒekʃən] *n* Ausruf *m*; (*Gram*) Interjektion *f.*

interlock [ɪntə'lɒk] *vi* ineinandergreifen; *vt* zusammenschließen, verzahnen.

interloper ['ɪntələʊpə°] *n* Eindringling *m.*

interlude ['ɪntəluːd] *n* Pause *f*; (*in entertainment*) Zwischenspiel *nt.*

intermarriage [ɪntə'mærɪdʒ] *n* Mischehe *f.*

intermarry [ɪntə'mærɪ] *vi* untereinander heiraten.

intermediary [ɪntə'miːdɪərɪ] *n* Vermittler *m.*

intermediate [ɪntə'miːdɪət] *a* Zwischen-, Mittel-.

interminable [ɪn'tɜːmɪnəbl] *a* endlos.

intermission [ɪntə'mɪʃən] *n* Pause *f.*

intermittent [ɪntə'mɪtənt] *a* periodisch, stoßweise; ~**ly** *ad* mit Unterbrechungen.

intern [ɪn'tɜːn] *vt* internieren; ['ɪntɜːn] *n* (*US*) Assistenzarzt *m*/-ärztin *f.*

internal [ɪn'tɜːnl] *a* (*inside*) innere(r,s); (*domestic*) Inlands-; ~**ly** *ad* innen; (*Med*) innerlich; intern; ~ **revenue** (*US*) Sozialprodukt *nt.*

international [ɪntə'næʃnəl] *a* international; *n* (*Sport*) Nationalspieler *m*; (*match*) internationale(s) Spiel *nt.*

internment [ɪn'tɜːnmənt] *n* Internierung *f.*

interplanetary [ɪntə'plænɪtərɪ] *a* interplanetar.

interplay ['ɪntəpleɪ] *n* Wechselspiel *nt.*

Interpol ['ɪntəpɒl] *n* Interpol *f.*

interpret [ɪn'tɜːprɪt] *vt* (*explain*) auslegen, interpretieren; (*translate*) verdolmetschen; (*represent*) darstellen; ~**ation** Deutung *f*, Interpretation *f*; (*translation*)

Dolmetschen *nt*; ~ **er** Dolmetscher(in *f*) *m*.

interrelated [ɪntərɪ'leɪtɪd] *a* unter-einander zusammenhängend.

interrogate [ɪn'terəgeɪt] *vt* befragen; (*Jur*) verhören.

interrogation [ɪntərə'geɪʃən] *n* Verhör *nt*.

interrogative [ɪntə'rɒgətɪv] *a* fragend, Frage-.

interrogator [ɪn'terəgeɪtə*] *n* Vernehmungsbeamte(r) *m*.

interrupt [ɪntə'rʌpt] *vt* unterbrechen; ~ **ion** Unterbrechung *f*.

intersect [ɪntə'sekt] *vt* (durch)schneiden; *vi* sich schneiden; ~ **ion** (*of roads*) Kreuzung *f*; (*of lines*) Schnittpunkt *m*.

intersperse [ɪntə'spɜːs] *vt* (*scatter*) verstreuen; to ~ **sth with sth** etw mit etw durchsetzen.

intertwine [ɪntə'twaɪn] *vti* (sich) verflechten.

interval ['ɪntəvəl] *n* Abstand *m*; (*break*) Pause *f*; (*Mus*) Intervall *nt*; **at** ~ **s** hier und da; (*time*) dann und wann.

intervene [ɪntə'viːn] *vi* dazwischenliegen; (*act*) einschreiten (*in* gegen), eingreifen (*in* in +*acc*).

intervening [ɪntə'viːnɪŋ] *a* dazwischenliegend.

intervention [ɪntə'venʃən] *n* Eingreifen *nt*, Intervention *f*.

interview ['ɪntəvjuː] *n* (*Press etc*) Interview *nt*; (*for job*) Vorstellungsgespräch *nt*; *vt* interviewen; ~ **er** Interviewer *m*.

intestate [ɪn'testeɪt] *a* ohne Hinterlassung eines Testaments.

intestinal [ɪn'testɪnl] *a* Darm-.

intestine [ɪn'testɪn] *n* Darm *m*; ~ **s** *pl* Eingeweide *nt*.

intimacy ['ɪntɪməsɪ] *n* vertraute(r) Umgang *m*, Intimität *f*.

intimate ['ɪntɪmət] *a* (*inmost*) innerste(r,s); *knowledge* eingehend; (*familiar*) vertraut; *friends* eng; ['ɪntɪmeɪt] *vt* andeuten; ~ **ly** *ad* vertraut, eng.

intimidate [ɪn'tɪmɪdeɪt] *vt* einschüchtern.

intimidation [ɪntɪmɪ'deɪʃən] *n* Einschüchterung *f*.

into ['ɪntu] *prep* (*motion*) in (+*acc*) . . . hinein; **5** ~ **25** 25 durch 5.

intolerable [ɪn'tɒlərəbl] *a* unerträglich.

intolerance [ɪn'tɒlərəns] *n* Intoleranz *f*.

intolerant [ɪn'tɒlərənt] *a* intolerant.

intonation [ɪntə'neɪʃən] *n* Intonation *f*.

intoxicate [ɪn'tɒksɪkeɪt] *vt* betrunken machen; (*fig*) berauschen; ~ **d** *a* betrunken; (*fig*) trunken.

intoxication [ɪntɒksɪ'keɪʃən] *n* Rausch *m*.

intractable [ɪn'træktəbl] *a* schwer zu handhaben(d); *problem* schwer lösbar.

intransigent [ɪn'trænsɪdʒənt] *a* unnachgiebig.

intransitive [ɪn'trænsɪtɪv] *a* intransitiv.

intravenous [ɪntrə'viːnəs] *a* intravenös.

intrepid [ɪn'trepɪd] *a* unerschrocken.

intricacy ['ɪntrɪkəsɪ] *n* Kompliziertheit *f*.

intricate ['ɪntrɪkət] *a* kompliziert.

intrigue [ɪn'triːg] *n* Intrige *f*; *vt* faszinieren.

intriguing [ɪn'triːgɪŋ] *a* faszinierend.

intrinsic [ɪn'trɪnsɪk] *a* innere(r,s); *difference* wesentlich.

introduce [ɪntrə'djuːs] *vt person* vorstellen (*to sb* jdm); *sth* new einführen; *subject* anschneiden; **to** ~ **sb to sth** jdn in etw (*acc*) einführen.

introduction [ɪntrə'dʌkʃən] *n* Einführung *f*; (*to book*) Einleitung *f*.

introductory [ɪntrə'dʌktərɪ] *a* Einführungs-, Vor-.

introspective [ɪntrəʊ'spektɪv] *a* nach innen gekehrt.

introvert ['ɪntrəʊvɜːt] *n* Introvertierte(r) *mf*; *a* introvertiert.

intrude [ɪn'truːd] *vi* stören (*on* acc); ~ **r** Eindringling *m*.

intrusion [ɪn'truːʒən] *n* Störung *f*; (*coming into*) Eindringen *nt*.

intrusive [ɪn'truːsɪv] *a* aufdringlich.

intuition [ɪn'tjuːɪʃən] *n* Intuition *f*.

intuitive *a*, ~ **ly** *ad* [ɪn'tjuːɪtɪv, -lɪ] intuitiv.

inundate ['ɪnʌndeɪt] *vt* (*lit, fig*) überschwemmen.

invade [ɪn'veɪd] *vt* einfallen in (+*acc*); ~ **r** Eindringling *m*.

invalid ['ɪnvəlɪd] *n* (*disabled*) Kranke(r) *mf*; Invalide *m*; *a* (*ill*) krank; (*disabled*) invalide; [ɪn'vælɪd] (*not valid*) ungültig; ~ **ate** [ɪn'vælɪdeɪt] *vt passport* (für) ungültig erklären; (*fig*) entkräften.

invaluable [ɪn'væljuəbl] *a* unschätzbar.

invariable [ɪn'vɛərɪəbl] *a* unveränderlich.

invariably [ɪn'vɛərɪəblɪ] *ad* ausnahmslos.

invasion [ɪn'veɪʒən] *n* Invasion *f*, Einfall *m*.

invective [ɪn'vektɪv] *n* Beschimpfung *f*.

invent [ɪn'vent] *vt* erfinden; ~ **ion** [ɪn'venʃən] Erfindung *f*; ~ **ive** *a* erfinderisch; ~ **iveness** Erfindungsgabe *f*; ~ **or** Erfinder *m*.

inventory ['ɪnvəntrɪ] *n* (Bestands)-verzeichnis *nt*, Inventar *nt*.

inverse ['ɪnvɜːs] *n* Umkehrung *f*; *a*, ~ **ly** [ɪn'vɜːs, -lɪ] *ad* umgekehrt.

invert [ɪn'vɜːt] *vt* umdrehen; ~ **ed commas** *pl* Anführungsstriche *pl*.

invertebrate [ɪn'vɜːtɪbrət] *n* wirbellose(s) Tier *nt*.

invest [ɪn'vest] *vt* (*Fin*) anlegen, investieren; (*endue*) ausstatten.

investigate [ɪn'vestɪgeɪt] *vt* untersuchen.

investigation [ɪnvestɪ'geɪʃən] *n* Untersuchung *f*.

investigator [ɪn'vestɪgeɪtə*] *n* Untersuchungsbeamte(r) *m*.

investiture [ɪn'vestɪtʃə*] *n* Amtseinsetzung *f*.

investment [ɪn'vestmənt] *n* Investition *f*.

investor [ɪn'vestə*] *n* (Geld)anleger *m*.

inveterate [ɪn'vetərət] *a* unverbesserlich.

invigorating [ɪn'vɪgəreɪtɪŋ] *a* stärkend.

invincible [ɪn'vɪnsəbl] *a* unbesiegbar.

inviolate [ɪn'vaɪələt] *a* unverletzt.

invisible [ɪn'vɪzəbl] *a* unsichtbar; *ink* Geheim-.

invitation [ɪnvɪ'teɪʃən] *n* Einladung *f*.

invite [ɪn'vaɪt] *vt* einladen; *criticism, discussion* herausfordern.

inviting [ɪn'vaɪtɪŋ] *a* einladend.

invoice ['ınvɔıs] *n* Rechnung *f*, Lieferschein *m*; *vt goods* in Rechnung stellen (*sth for sb* jdm etw *acc*).

invoke [ın'vəuk] *vt* anrufen.

involuntary *a*, **involuntarily** *ad* [ın'vɔləntərı, -lı] (*unwilling*) unfreiwillig; (*unintentional*) unabsichtlich.

involve [ın'vɔlv] *vt* (*entangle*) verwickeln; (*entail*) mit sich bringen; ~**d** a verwickelt; **the person** ~**d** die betreffende Person; ~**ment** Verwicklung *f*, (*fig*) unangreifbar.

invulnerable [ın'vʌlnərəbl] *a* unverwundbar; (*fig*) unangreifbar.

inward ['ınwəd] *a* innere(r,s); *curve* Innen-; ~(**s**) *ad* nach innen; ~**ly** *ad* im Innern.

iodine ['aıədi:n] *n* Jod *nt*.

iota [aı'əutə] *n* (*fig*) bißchen *nt*.

irascible [ı'ræsıbl] a reizbar.

irate [aı'reıt] a zornig.

iris ['aıərıs] *n* Iris *f*.

irk [ɜːk] *vt* verdrießen.

irksome ['ɜːksəm] a lästig.

iron ['aıən] *n* Eisen *nt*; (*for ironing*) Bügeleisen *nt*; (*golf club*) Golfschläger *m*, Metallschläger *m*; *a* eisern; *vt* bügeln; ~**s** *pl* (*chains*) Hand-/Fußschellen *pl*; ~ **out** *vt* (*lit, fig*) ausbügeln; *differences* ausgleichen; **I~ Curtain** Eiserne(r) Vorhang *m*.

ironic(al) [aı'rɔnık(əl)] *a* ironisch; *coincidence etc* witzig; ~**ally** *ad* ironisch; witzigerweise.

ironing ['aıənıŋ] *n* Bügeln *nt*; (*laundry*) Bügelwäsche *f*; ~ **board** Bügelbrett *nt*.

ironmonger ['aıənmʌŋgə*] *n* Eisenwarenhändler *m*; ~'**s** (**shop**) Eisenwarenhandlung *f*.

iron ore ['aıənɔː*] *n* Eisenerz *nt*.

ironworks ['aıənwɜːks] *n* Eisenhütte *f*.

irony ['aıərənı] *n* Ironie *f*; **the ~ of it was** ... das Witzige daran war ...

irrational [ı'ræʃənl] *a* unvernünftig, irrational.

irreconcilable [ırekən'saıləbl] *a* unvereinbar.

irredeemable [ırı'di:məbl] *a* (*Comm*) *money* nicht einlösbar; *loan* unkündbar; (*fig*) rettungslos.

irrefutable [ırı'fju:təbl] *a* unwiderlegbar.

irregular [ı'regjulə*] *a* unregelmäßig; *shape* ungleich(mäßig); (*fig*) unüblich; *behaviour* ungehörig; ~**ity** [ıregju'lærıtı] Unregelmäßigkeit *f*; Ungleichmäßigkeit *f*; (*fig*) Vergehen *nt*.

irrelevance [ı'reləvəns] *n* Belanglosigkeit *f*.

irrelevant [ı'reləvənt] *a* belanglos, irrelevant.

irreligious [ırı'lıdʒəs] *a* ungläubig.

irreparable [ı'repərəbl] *a* nicht gutzumachen(d).

irreplaceable [ırı'pleısəbl] *a* unersetzlich.

irrepressible [ırı'presəbl] *a* nicht zu unterdrücken(d); *joy* unbändig.

irreproachable [ırı'prəutʃəbl] *a* untadelig.

irresistible [ırı'zıstəbl] *a* unwiderstehlich.

irresolute [ı'rezəlu:t] *a* unentschlossen.

irrespective [ırı'spektıv] : ~ **of** *prep* ungeachtet (+*gen*).

irresponsibility ['ırıspɔnsə'bılıtı] *n* Verantwortungslosigkeit *f*.

irresponsible [ırıs'pɔnsəbl] *a* verantwortungslos.

irretrievably [ırı'tri:vəblı] *ad* unwiederbringlich; *lost* unrettbar.

irreverence [ı'revərəns] *n* Mißachtung *f*.

irreverent [ı'revərənt] *a* respektlos.

irrevocable [ı'revəkəbl] *a* unwiderrufbar.

irrigate ['ırıgeıt] *vt* bewässern.

irrigation [ırı'geıʃən] *n* Bewässerung *f*.

irritability [ırıtə'bılıtı] *n* Reizbarkeit *f*.

irritable ['ırıtəbl] *a* reizbar.

irritant ['ırıtənt] *n* Reizmittel *nt*.

irritate ['ırıteıt] *vt* irritieren, reizen (*also Med*).

irritating ['ırıteıtıŋ] *a* irritierend, aufreizend.

irritation [ırı'teıʃən] *n* (*anger*) Ärger *m*; (*Med*) Reizung *f*.

is [ız] *see* **be**.

Islam ['ızlɑːm] *n* Islam *m*.

island ['aılənd] *n* Insel *f*; ~**er** Inselbewohner(in *f*) *m*.

isle [aıl] *n* (kleine) Insel *f*.

isn't ['ıznt] = **is not**.

isobar ['aısəubɑː*] *n* Isobare *f*.

isolate ['aısəuleıt] *vt* isolieren; ~**d** *a* isoliert; *case* Einzel-.

isolation [aısəu'leıʃən] *n* Isolierung *f*; **to treat sth in ~** etw vereinzelt *or* isoliert behandeln.

isolationism [aısəu'leıʃənızəm] *n* Isolationismus *m*.

isotope ['aısətəup] *n* Isotop *nt*.

issue ['ıʃu:] *n* (*matter*) Problem *nt*, Frage *f*; (*outcome*) Resultat *nt*, Ausgang *m*; (*of newspaper, shares*) Ausgabe *f*; (*offspring*) Nachkommenschaft *f*; (*of river*) Mündung *f*; **that's not at** ~ das steht nicht zur Debatte; **to make an ~ out of sth** ein Theater machen wegen etw (*dat*); *vt* ausgeben; *warrant* erlassen; *documents* ausstellen; *orders* erteilen; *books* herausgeben; *verdict* aussprechen; **to ~ sb with sth** etw (*acc*) an jdn ausgeben.

isthmus ['ısməs] *n* Landenge *f*.

it [ıt] *pron* (*nom, acc*) es; (*dat*) ihm.

italic [ı'tælık] *a* kursiv; ~**s** *pl* Kursivschrift *f*; **in** ~**s** kursiv gedruckt.

itch [ıtʃ] *n* Juckreiz *m*; (*fig*) brennende(s) Verlangen *nt*; *vi* jucken; **to be** ~**ing to do sth** darauf brennen, etw zu tun; ~**ing** Jucken *nt*; ~**y** a juckend.

it'd ['ıtd] = **it would**; **it had**.

item ['aıtəm] *n* Gegenstand *m*; (*on list*) Posten *m*; (*in programme*) Nummer *f*; (*in agenda*) (Programm)punkt *m*; (*in newspaper*) (Zeitungs)notiz *f*; ~**ize** *vt* verzeichnen.

itinerant [ı'tınərənt] *a person* umherreisend.

itinerary [aı'tınərərı] *n* Reiseroute *f*; (*records*) Reisebericht *m*.

it'll ['ıtl] = **it will**, **it shall**.

its [ıts] *poss a* (*masculine, neuter*) sein; (*feminine*) ihr; *poss pron* seine(r,s); ihre(r,s).

it's [ıts] = **it is**; **it has**.

itself [ɪt'self] *pron* sich (selbst); (*emphatic*) selbst.

I've [aɪv] = **I have**.

ivory ['aɪvərɪ] *n* Elfenbein *nt*; ~ **tower** (*fig*) Elfenbeinturm *m*.

ivy ['aɪvɪ] *n* Efeu *nt*.

J

J, j [dʒeɪ] *n* J *nt*, j *nt*.

jab [dʒæb] *vti* (hinein)stechen; *n* Stich *m*, Stoß *m*; (*col*) Spritze *f*.

jabber ['dʒæbə*] *vi* plappern.

jack [dʒæk] *n* (Wagen)heber *m*; (*Cards*) Bube *m*; ~ **up** *vt* aufbocken.

jackdaw ['dʒækdɔ:] *n* Dohle *f*.

jacket ['dʒækɪt] *n* Jacke *f*, Jackett *nt*; (*of book*) Schutzumschlag *m*; (*Tech*) Ummantelung *f*.

jack-knife ['dʒæknaɪf] *n* Klappmesser *nt*; *vi* (*truck*) sich zusammenschieben.

jackpot ['dʒækpɒt] *n* Haupttreffer *m*.

jade [dʒeɪd] *n* (*stone*) Jade *m*.

jaded ['dʒeɪdɪd] *a* ermattet.

jagged ['dʒægɪd] *a* zackig; *blade* schartig.

jail [dʒeɪl] *n* Gefängnis *nt*; *vt* einsperren; ~**break** Gefängnisausbruch *m*; ~**er** Gefängniswärter *m*.

jam [dʒæm] *n* Marmelade *f*; (*crowd*) Gedränge *nt*; (*col: trouble*) Klemme *f*; *see* **traffic**; *vt people* zusammendrängen; (*wedge*) einklemmen; (*cram*) hineinzwängen; (*obstruct*) blockieren; **to ~ on the brakes** auf die Bremse treten.

jamboree [dʒæmbə'ri:] *n* (Pfadfinder)-treffen *nt*.

jangle ['dʒæŋgl] *vti* klimpern; (*bells*) bimmeln.

janitor ['dʒænɪtə*] *n* Hausmeister *m*.

January ['dʒænjʊərɪ] *n* Januar *m*.

jar [dʒɑ:*] *n* Glas *nt*; *vi* kreischen; (*colours etc*) nicht harmonieren.

jargon ['dʒɑ:gən] *n* Fachsprache *f*, Jargon *m*.

jarring ['dʒɑ:rɪŋ] *a sound* kreischend; *colour* unharmonisch.

jasmin(e) ['dʒæzmɪn] *n* Jasmin *m*.

jaundice ['dʒɔ:ndɪs] *n* Gelbsucht *f*; ~**d** *a* (*fig*) mißgünstig.

jaunt [dʒɔ:nt] *n* Spritztour *f*; ~**y** *a* (*lively*) munter; (*brisk*) flott; *attitude* unbekümmert.

javelin ['dʒævlɪn] *n* Speer *m*.

jaw [dʒɔ:] *n* Kiefer *m*; ~**s** *pl* (*fig*) Rachen *m*.

jaywalker ['dʒeɪwɔ:kə*] *n* unvorsichtige(r) Fußgänger *m*, Verkehrssünder *m*.

jazz [dʒæz] *n* Jazz *m*; ~ **up** *vt* (*Mus*) verjazzen; (*enliven*) aufpolieren; ~ **band** Jazzkapelle *f*; ~**y** *a colour* schreiend, auffallend.

jealous ['dʒeləs] *a* (*envious*) mißgünstig; *husband* eifersüchtig; (*watchful*) bedacht (*of auf* +acc); ~**ly** *ad* mißgünstig; eifersüchtig; sorgsam; ~**y** Mißgunst *f*; Eifersucht *f*.

jeans [dʒi:nz] *npl* Jeans *pl*.

jeep [dʒi:p] *n* Jeep *m*.

jeer [dʒɪə*] *vi* höhnisch lachen (*at über* +acc), verspotten (*at sb* jdn); *n* Hohn *m*; (*remark*) höhnische Bemerkung *f*; ~**ing** *a* höhnisch.

jelly ['dʒelɪ] *n* Gelee *nt*; (*on meat*) Gallert *nt*; (*dessert*) Grütze *f*; ~**fish** Qualle *f*.

jemmy ['dʒemɪ] *n* Brecheisen *nt*.

jeopardize ['dʒepədaɪz] *vt* gefährden.

jeopardy ['dʒepədɪ] *n* Gefahr *f*.

jerk [dʒɜ:k] *n* Ruck *m*; (*col: idiot*) Trottel *m*; *vt* ruckartig bewegen; *vi* sich ruckartig bewegen; (*muscles*) zucken.

jerkin ['dʒɜːkɪn] *n* Wams *nt*.

jerky ['dʒɜ:kɪ] *a movement* ruckartig; *writing* zitterig; *ride* rüttelnd.

jersey ['dʒɜ:zɪ] *n* Pullover *m*.

jest [dʒest] *n* Scherz *m*; **in** ~ im Spaß; *vi* spaßen.

jet [dʒet] *n* (*stream: of water etc*) Strahl *m*; (*spout*) Düse *f*; (*Aviat*) Düsenflugzeug *nt*; ~-**black** *a* rabenschwarz; ~ **engine** Düsenmotor *m*.

jetsam ['dʒetsəm] *n* Strandgut *nt*.

jettison ['dʒetɪsn] *vt* über Bord werfen.

jetty ['dʒetɪ] *n* Landesteg *m*, Mole *f*.

Jew [dʒu:] *n* Jude *m*.

jewel ['dʒu:əl] *n* (*lit, fig*) Juwel *nt*; (*stone*) Edelstein *m*; ~(**l**)**er** Juwelier *m*; ~(**l**)**er's** (**shop**) Schmuckwarengeschäft *nt*, Juwelier *m*; ~(**le**)**ry** Schmuck *m*, Juwelen *pl*.

Jewess ['dʒu:ɪs] *n* Jüdin *f*.

Jewish ['dʒu:ɪʃ] *a* jüdisch.

jib [dʒɪb] *n* (*Naut*) Klüver *m*; *vi* sich scheuen (*at vor* +dat).

jibe [dʒaɪb] *n* spöttische Bemerkung *f*.

jiffy ['dʒɪfɪ] *n* (*col*) **in a** ~ sofort.

jigsaw (puzzle) ['dʒɪgsɔ:(pʌzl)] *n* Puzzle-(spiel) *nt*.

jilt [dʒɪlt] *vt* den Laufpaß geben (+dat).

jingle ['dʒɪŋgl] *n* (*advertisement*) Werbesong *m*; (*verse*) Reim *m*; *vti* klimpern; (*bells*) bimmeln.

jinx [dʒɪŋks] *n* Fluch *m*; **to put a** ~ **on sth** etw verhexen.

jitters ['dʒɪtəz] *npl* (*col*) **to get the** ~ einen Bammel kriegen.

jittery ['dʒɪtərɪ] *a* (*col*) nervös.

jiujitsu [dʒu:'dʒɪtsu:] *n* Jiu-Jitsu *nt*.

job [dʒɒb] *n* (*piece of work*) Arbeit *f*; (*occupation*) Stellung *f*, Arbeit *f*; (*duty*) Aufgabe *f*; (*difficulty*) Mühe *f*; **what's your** ~? was machen Sie von Beruf?; **it's a good** ~ **he** ... es ist ein Glück, daß er ...; **just the** ~ genau das Richtige; ~**bing** *a* (*in factory*) Akkord-; (*freelance*) Gelegenheits-; ~**less** *a* arbeitslos.

jockey ['dʒɒkɪ] *n* Jockei *m*; *vi*: **to** ~ **for position** sich in eine gute Position drängeln.

jocular ['dʒɒkjʊlə*] *a* scherzhaft, witzig.

jodhpurs ['dʒɒdpɜ:z] *npl* Reithose *f*.

jog [dʒɒg] *vt* (an)stoßen; *vi* (*run*) einen Dauerlauf machen.

john [dʒɒn] *n* (*US col*) Klo *nt*.

join [dʒɔɪn] *vt* (*put together*) verbinden (*to mit*); *club* beitreten (+dat); *person* sich anschließen (+dat); *vi* (*unite*) sich vereinigen; (*bones*) zusammenwachsen; *n*

Verbindungsstelle f, Naht f; ~ **in** vi mitmachen; ~ **up** vi (Mil) zur Armee gehen; ~**er** Schreiner m; ~**ery** Schreinerei f; ~**t** n (Tech) Fuge f; (of bones) Gelenk nt; (of meat) Braten m; (col: place) Lokal nt; a, ~**tly** ad gemeinsam.

joist [dʒɔɪst] n Träger m.

joke [dʒəʊk] n Witz m; **it's no** ~ es ist nicht zum Lachen; vi spaßen, Witze machen; **you must be joking** das ist doch wohl nicht dein Ernst; ~**r** Witzbold m; (Cards) Joker m.

joking [dʒəʊkɪŋ] a scherzhaft; ~**ly** ad zum Spaß; talk im Spaß, scherzhaft.

jollity [dʒɒlɪtɪ] n Fröhlichkeit f.

jolly [dʒɒlɪ] a lustig, vergnügt; ad (col) ganz schön; ~ **good!** prima!; to ~ sb **along** jdn ermuntern.

jolt [dʒəʊlt] n (shock) Schock m; (jerk) Stoß m, Rütteln nt; vt (push) stoßen; (shake) durchschütteln; (fig) aufrütteln; vi holpern.

jostle [dʒɒsl] vt anrempeln.

jot [dʒɒt] n: **not one** ~ kein Jota nt; ~ **down** vt schnell aufschreiben, notieren; ~**ter** Notizbuch nt; (Sch) Schulheft nt.

journal [dʒɜːnl] n (diary) Tagebuch nt; (magazine) Zeitschrift f; ~**ese** [dʒɜːnəˈliːz] Zeitungsstil m; ~**ism** Journalismus m; ~**ist** Journalist(in f) m.

journey [dʒɜːnɪ] n Reise f.

jovial [dʒəʊvɪəl] a jovial.

joy [dʒɔɪ] n Freude f, ~**ful** a freudig; (gladdening) erfreulich; ~**fully** ad freudig; ~**ous** a freudig; ~ **ride** Schwarzfahrt f; ~**stick** Steuerknüppel m.

jubilant [dʒuːbɪlənt] a triumphierend.

jubilation [dʒuːbɪˈleɪʃən] n Jubel m.

jubilee [dʒuːbɪliː] n Jubiläum nt.

judge [dʒʌdʒ] n Richter m; (fig) Kenner m; vt (Jur) person die Verhandlung führen über (+acc); case verhandeln; (assess) beurteilen; (criticize) verurteilen; vi ein Urteil abgeben; **as far as I can** ~ soweit ich das beurteilen kann; **judging by sth** nach etw zu urteilen; ~**ment** (Jur) Urteil nt; (Eccl) Gericht nt; (opinion) Ansicht f; (ability) Urteilsvermögen nt.

judicial [dʒuːˈdɪʃl] a gerichtlich, Justiz-.

judicious [dʒuːˈdɪʃəs] a weis(e).

judo [dʒuːdəʊ] n Judo nt.

jug [dʒʌg] n Krug m.

juggernaut [dʒʌgənɔːt] n (truck) Fernlastwagen m.

juggle [dʒʌgl] vi jonglieren; vt facts verdrehen; figures frisieren; ~**r** Jongleur m.

jugular [dʒʌgjʊlə*] a vein Hals-.

juice [dʒuːs] n Saft m.

juiciness [dʒuːsɪnɪs] n Saftigkeit f.

juicy [dʒuːsɪ] a (lit, fig) saftig; story schlüpfrig.

jukebox [dʒuːkbɒks] n Musikautomat m.

July [dʒuːˈlaɪ] n Juli m.

jumble [dʒʌmbl] n Durcheinander nt; vt (also ~ **up**) durcheinanderwerfen; facts durcheinanderbringen; ~ **sale** (Brit) Basar m, Flohmarkt m.

jumbo (jet) [dʒʌmbəʊ(dʒet)] n Jumbo(-Jet) m.

jump [dʒʌmp] vi springen; (nervously) zusammenzucken; **to** ~ **to conclusions** voreilige Schlüsse ziehen; vt überspringen; **to** ~ **the gun** (fig) voreilig handeln; **to** ~ **the queue** sich vordrängeln; n Sprung m; **to give sb a** ~ jdn erschrecken; ~**ed-up** a (col) eingebildet; ~**er** Pullover m; ~**y** a nervös.

junction [dʒʌŋkʃən] n (of roads) (Straßen)kreuzung f; (Rail) Knotenpunkt m.

juncture [dʒʌŋktʃə*] n: **at this** ~ in diesem Augenblick.

June [dʒuːn] n Juni m.

jungle [dʒʌŋgl] n Dschungel m, Urwald m.

junior [dʒuːnɪə*] a (younger) jünger; (after name) junior; (Sport) Junioren-; (lower position) untergeordnet; (for young people) Junioren-; n Jüngere(r) m.

junk [dʒʌŋk] n (rubbish) Plunder m; (ship) Dschunke f; ~**shop** Ramschladen m.

junta [dʒʌntə] n Junta f.

jurisdiction [dʒʊərɪsˈdɪkʃən] n Gerichtsbarkeit f; (range of authority) Zuständigkeit(sbereich m) f.

jurisprudence [dʒʊərɪsˈpruːdəns] n Rechtswissenschaft f, Jura no art.

juror [dʒʊərə*] n Geschworene(r) mf; Schöffe m, Schöffin f; (in competition) Preisrichter m.

jury [dʒʊərɪ] n (court) Geschworene pl; (in competition) Jury f, Preisgericht nt; ~**man** = juror.

just [dʒʌst] a gerecht; ad (recently, now) gerade, eben; (barely) gerade noch; (exactly) genau, gerade; (only) nur, bloß; (a small distance) gleich; (absolutely) einfach; ~ **as I arrived** gerade als ich ankam; ~ **as nice** genauso nett; ~ **as well** um so besser; ~ **about** so etwa; ~ **now** soeben, gerade; **not** ~ **now** nicht im Moment; ~ **try** versuch es bloß or mal.

justice [dʒʌstɪs] n (fairness) Gerechtigkeit f; (magistrate) Richter m; ~ **of the peace** Friedensrichter m.

justifiable [dʒʌstɪfaɪəbl] a berechtigt.

justifiably [dʒʌstɪfaɪəblɪ] ad berechtigterweise, zu Recht.

justification [dʒʌstɪfɪˈkeɪʃən] n Rechtfertigung f.

justify [dʒʌstɪfaɪ] vt rechtfertigen.

justly [dʒʌstlɪ] ad say mit Recht; condemn gerecht.

justness [dʒʌstnəs] n Gerechtigkeit f.

jut [dʒʌt] vi (also ~ **out**) herausragen, vorstehen.

juvenile [dʒuːvənaɪl] a (young) jugendlich; (for the young) Jugend-; n Jugendliche(r) mf; ~ **delinquency** Jugendkriminalität f; ~ **delinquent** jugendliche(r) Straftäter(in f) m.

juxtapose [dʒʌkstəpəʊz] vt nebeneinanderstellen.

juxtaposition [dʒʌkstəpəˈzɪʃən] n Nebeneinanderstellung f.

K

K, k [keɪ] n K nt, k nt.

kaleidoscope [kə'laɪdəskəup] n Kaleidoskop nt.

kangaroo [kæŋgə'ru:] n Känguruh nt.

kayak ['kaɪæk] n Kajak m or nt.

keel [ki:l] n Kiel m; **on an even ~** (fig) im Lot.

keen [ki:n] a eifrig, begeistert; intelligence, wind, blade scharf; sight, hearing gut; price günstig; **~ly** ad leidenschaftlich; (sharply) scharf; **~ness** Schärfe f; (eagerness) Begeisterung f.

keep [ki:p] irreg vt (retain) behalten; (have) haben; animals, one's word halten; (support) versorgen; (maintain in state) halten; (preserve) aufbewahren; (restrain) abhalten; vi (continue in direction) sich halten; (food) sich halten; (remain: quiet etc) sein, bleiben; **it ~s happening** es passiert immer wieder; n Unterhalt m; (tower) Burgfried m; **~ back** vt fernhalten; secret verschweigen; **~ on** vi: **~ on doing sth** etw immer weiter tun; vt anbehalten; hat aufbehalten; **~ out** vt draußen lassen, nicht hereinlassen; **'~ out!'** 'Eintritt verboten!'; **~ up** vi Schritt halten; vt aufrechterhalten; (continue) weitermachen; **~ing** (care) Obhut f; **in ~ing (with)** in Übereinstimmung (mit).

keg [keg] n Faß nt.

kennel ['kenl] n Hundehütte f.

kerb(stone) ['kɜːbstəun] n Bordstein m.

kernel ['kɜːnl] n Kern m.

kerosene ['kerəsi:n] n Kerosin nt.

kestrel ['kestrəl] n Turmfalke m.

ketchup ['ketʃəp] n Ketchup nt or m.

kettle ['ketl] n Kessel m; **~drum** Pauke f.

key [ki:] n Schlüssel m; (solution, answers) Schlüssel m, Lösung f; (of piano, typewriter) Taste f; (Mus) Tonart f; (explanatory note) Zeichenerklärung f; a position etc Schlüssel-; **~board** (of piano, typewriter) Tastatur f; **~hole** Schlüsselloch nt; **~note** Grundton m; **~ ring** Schlüsselring m.

khaki ['kɑːkɪ] n K(h)aki nt; a k(h)aki-(farben).

kick [kɪk] vt einen Fußtritt geben (+dat), treten; vi treten; (baby) strampeln; (horse) ausschlagen; n (Fuß)tritt m; (thrill) Spaß m; **~ around** vt person herumstoßen; **~ off** vi (Sport) anstoßen; **~ up** vt (col) schlagen; **~-off** (Sport) Anstoß m.

kid [kɪd] n (child) Kind nt; (goat) Zicklein nt; (leather) Glacéleder nt; vt auf den Arm nehmen; vi Witze machen.

kidnap ['kɪdnæp] vt entführen, kidnappen; **~per** Kidnapper m, Entführer m; **~ping** Entführung f, Kidnapping nt.

kidney ['kɪdnɪ] n Niere f.

kill [kɪl] vt töten, umbringen; chances ruinieren; vi töten; n Tötung f; (hunting) (Jagd)beute f; **~er** Mörder m.

kiln [kɪln] n Brennofen m.

kilo ['ki:ləu] n Kilo nt; **~gram(me)** Kilogramm nt; **~metre**, (US) **~meter** Kilometer m; **~watt** Kilowatt nt.

kilt [kɪlt] n Schottenrock m.

kimono [kɪ'məunəu] n Kimono m.

kin [kɪn] n Verwandtschaft f, Verwandte(n) pl.

kind [kaɪnd] a freundlich, gütig; n Art f; a **~ of** eine Art von; **(two) of a ~** (zwei) von der gleichen Art; **in ~** auf dieselbe Art; (in goods) in Naturalien.

kindergarten ['kɪndəgɑːtn] n Kindergarten m.

kind-hearted ['kaɪnd'hɑːtɪd] a gutherzig.

kindle ['kɪndl] vt (set on fire) anzünden; (rouse) reizen, (er)wecken.

kindliness ['kaɪndlɪnəs] n Freundlichkeit f, Güte f.

kindly ['kaɪndlɪ] a freundlich; ad liebenswürdig(erweise); **would you ~ ...?** wären Sie so freundlich und ...?

kindness ['kaɪndnəs] n Freundlichkeit f.

kindred ['kɪndrɪd] a verwandt; **~ spirit** Gleichgesinnte(r) mf.

kinetic [kɪ'netɪk] a kinetisch.

king [kɪŋ] n König m; **~dom** Königreich nt; **~fisher** Eisvogel m; **~pin** (Tech) Bolzen m; (Aut) Achsschenkelbolzen m; (fig) Stütze f; **~-size** a cigarette Kingsize.

kink [kɪŋk] n Knick m; **~y** a (fig) exzentrisch.

kiosk ['ki:ɒsk] n (Tel) Telefonhäuschen nt.

kipper ['kɪpə*] n Räucherhering m.

kiss [kɪs] n Kuß m; vt küssen; vi: **they ~ed** sie küßten sich.

kit [kɪt] n Ausrüstung f; (tools) Werkzeug nt; **~bag** Seesack m.

kitchen ['kɪtʃɪn] n Küche f; **~ garden** Gemüsegarten m; **~ sink** Spülbecken nt; **~ware** Küchengeschirr nt.

kite [kaɪt] n Drachen m.

kith [kɪθ] n: **~ and kin** Blutsverwandte pl; **with ~ and kin** mit Kind und Kegel.

kitten ['kɪtn] n Kätzchen n.

kitty ['kɪtɪ] n (money) (gemeinsame) Kasse f.

kleptomaniac [kleptəu'meɪnɪæk] n Kleptomane m, Kleptomanin f.

knack [næk] n Dreh m, Trick m.

knapsack ['næpsæk] n Rucksack m; (Mil) Tornister m.

knave [neɪv] n (old) Schurke m.

knead [ni:d] vt kneten.

knee [ni:] n Knie nt; **~cap** Kniescheibe f; **~-deep** a knietief.

kneel [ni:l] vi irreg knien.

knell [nel] n Grabgeläute nt.

knickers ['nɪkəz] npl Schlüpfer m.

knife [naɪf] n Messer nt; vt erstechen.

knight [naɪt] n Ritter m; (chess) Springer m, Pferd nt; **~hood** Ritterwürde f.

knit [nɪt] vti stricken; vi (bones) zusammenwachsen; (people) harmonieren; **~ting** (occupation) Stricken nt; (work) Strickzeug nt; **~ting machine** Strickmaschine f, **~ting needle** Stricknadel f; **~wear** Strickwaren pl.

knob [nɒb] n Knauf m; (on instrument) Knopf m; (of butter etc) kleine(s) Stück nt.

knock [nɒk] vt schlagen; (criticize) heruntermachen; vi klopfen; (knees) zittern; n Schlag m; (on door) Klopfen nt;

~ **off** vt (do quickly) hinhauen; (col: steal) klauen; vi (finish) Feierabend machen; ~ **out** vt ausschlagen; (boxing) k.o. schlagen; ~**er** (on door) Türklopfer m; ~**-kneed** a x-beinig; ~**out** (lit) K.o.-Schlag m; (fig) Sensation f.

knot [nɒt] n Knoten m; (in wood) Astloch nt; (group) Knäuel nt or m; vt (ver)knoten; ~**ted** a verknotet.

knotty ['nɒtɪ] a knorrig; problem kompliziert.

know [nəʊ] vti irreg wissen; (be able to) können; (be acquainted with) kennen; (recognize) erkennen; **to ~ how to do sth** wissen, wie man etw macht, etw tun können; **you ~** nicht (wahr); **to be well ~n** bekannt sein; ~**-all** Alleswisser m; ~**-how** Kenntnis f, Know-how nt; ~**ing** a schlau; look, smile wissend; ~**ingly** ad wissend; (intentionally) wissentlich.

knowledge ['nɒlɪdʒ] n Wissen nt, Kenntnis f; ~**able** a informiert.

knuckle ['nʌkl] n Fingerknöchel m.

kudos ['kjuːdɒs] n Ehre f.

L

L, l [el] n L nt, l nt.

lab [læb] n (col) Labor nt.

label ['leɪbl] n Etikett nt, Schild nt; vt mit einer Aufschrift versehen, etikettieren.

laboratory [lə'bɒrətərɪ] n Laboratorium nt.

laborious a, ~**ly** ad [lə'bɔːrɪəs, -lɪ] mühsam.

labour, (US) **labor** ['leɪbə*] n Arbeit f; (workmen) Arbeitskräfte pl; (Med) Wehen pl; a (Pol) Labour-; **hard ~** Zwangsarbeit f; ~**er** Arbeiter m; ~**-saving** a arbeitssparend.

laburnum [lə'bɜːnəm] n Goldregen m.

labyrinth ['læbɪrɪnθ] n (lit, fig) Labyrinth nt.

lace [leɪs] n (fabric) Spitze f; (of shoe) Schnürsenkel m; (braid) Litze f; vt (also ~ up) (zu)schnüren.

lacerate ['læsəreɪt] vt zerschneiden, tief verwunden.

lack [læk] vt nicht haben; **sb ~s sth** jdm fehlt etw (nom); vi: **to be ~ing** fehlen; **sb is ~ing in sth** es fehlt jdm an etw (dat); n Mangel m; **for ~ of** aus Mangel an (+dat).

lackadaisical [lækə'deɪzɪkəl] a lasch.

lackey ['lækɪ] n Lakei m.

lacklustre, (US) **lackluster** ['læklʌstə*] a glanzlos, matt.

laconic [lə'kɒnɪk] a lakonisch.

lacquer ['lækə*] n Lack m.

lacrosse [lə'krɒs] n Lacrosse nt.

lacy ['leɪsɪ] a spitzenartig, Spitzen-.

lad [læd] n (boy) Junge m; (young man) Bursche m.

ladder ['lædə*] n (lit) Leiter f; (fig) Stufenleiter f; (Brit: in stocking) Laufmasche f; vt Laufmaschen bekommen in (+dat).

laden ['leɪdn] a beladen, voll.

ladle ['leɪdl] n Schöpfkelle f.

lady ['leɪdɪ] n Dame f; (title) Lady f; **'Ladies'** (lavatory) 'Damen'; ~ **bird**, (US)

~**bug** Marienkäfer m; ~**-in-waiting** Hofdame f; ~**-like** a damenhaft, vornehm.

lag [læg] n (delay) Verzug m; (time —) Zeitabstand m; vi (also ~ **behind**) zurückbleiben; vt pipes verkleiden.

lager ['lɑːgə*] n Lagerbier nt, helles Bier nt.

lagging ['lægɪŋ] n Isolierung f.

lagoon [lə'guːn] n Lagune f.

laid [leɪd]: **to be ~ up** ans Bett gefesselt sein.

lair [lɛə*] n Lager nt.

laissez-faire ['leɪsɪ'fɛə*] n Laisser-faire nt.

laity ['leɪɪtɪ] n Laien pl.

lake [leɪk] n See m.

lamb [læm] n Lamm nt; (meat) Lammfleisch nt; ~ **chop** Lammkotelett nt; ~**'s wool** Lammwolle f.

lame [leɪm] a lahm; person also gelähmt; excuse faul.

lament [lə'ment] n Klage f; vt beklagen; ~**able** ['læməntəbl] a bedauerlich; (bad) erbärmlich; ~**ation** [læmən'teɪʃən] Wehklage f.

laminated ['læmɪneɪtɪd] a beschichtet.

lamp [læmp] n Lampe f; (in street) Straßenlaterne f; ~**post** Laternenpfahl m; ~**shade** Lampenschirm m.

lance [lɑːns] n Lanze f; vt (Med) aufschneiden; ~ **corporal** Obergefreite(r) m.

lancet ['lɑːnsɪt] n Lanzette f.

land [lænd] n Land nt; vi (from ship) an Land gehen; (Aviat, end up) landen; vt (obtain) gewinnen, kriegen; passengers absetzen; goods abladen; troops, space probe landen; ~**ed** a Land-; ~**ing** Landung f; (on stairs) (Treppen)absatz m; ~**ing craft** Landungsboot nt; ~**ing stage** Landesteg m; ~**ing strip** Landebahn f; ~**lady** (Haus)wirtin f; ~**locked** a landumschlossen, Binnen-; ~**lord** (of house) Hauswirt m, Besitzer m; (of pub) Gastwirt m; (of land) Grundbesitzer m; ~**lubber** Landratte f; ~**mark** Wahrzeichen nt; (fig) Meilenstein m; ~**owner** Grundbesitzer m; ~**scape** Landschaft f; ~**slide** (Geog) Erdrutsch m; (Pol) überwältigende(r) Sieg m.

lane [leɪn] n (in town) Gasse f; (in country) Weg m; Sträßchen nt; (of motorway) Fahrbahn f, Spur f; (Sport) Bahn f.

language ['læŋgwɪdʒ] n Sprache f; (style) Ausdrucksweise f.

languid ['læŋgwɪd] a schlaff, matt.

languish ['læŋgwɪʃ] vi schmachten; (pine) sich sehnen (for nach).

languor ['læŋgə*] n Mattigkeit f.

languorous ['læŋgərəs] a schlaff, träge.

lank [læŋk] a dürr; ~**y** a schlacksig.

lantern ['læntən] n Laterne f.

lanyard ['lænjəd] n (Naut) Taljereep nt; (Mil) Kordel f.

lap [læp] n Schoß m; (Sport) Runde f; vt auflecken; vi (water) plätschern; ~**dog** Schoßhund m.

lapel [lə'pel] n Rockaufschlag m, Revers nt or m.

lapse [læps] n (mistake) Irrtum m; (moral) Fehltritt m; (time) Zeitspanne f.

larceny ['lɑːsənɪ] *n* Diebstahl *m*.
lard [lɑːd] *n* Schweineschmalz *nt*.
larder ['lɑːdə°] *n* Speisekammer *f*.
large [lɑːdʒ] *a* groß; **at ~** auf freiem Fuß; **by and ~** im großen und ganzen; **~ly** *ad* zum größten Teil; **~-scale** *a* groß angelegt, Groß-; **~sse** [lɑː'ʒes] Freigebigkeit *f*.
lark [lɑːk] *n (bird)* Lerche *f; (joke)* Jux *m;* **~ about** *vi (col)* herumalbern.
larva ['lɑːvə] *n* Larve *f*.
laryngitis [lærɪn'dʒaɪtɪs] *n* Kehlkopfentzündung *f*.
larynx ['lærɪŋks] *n* Kehlkopf *m*.
lascivious *a,* **~ly** *ad* [lə'sɪvɪəs, -lɪ] wollüstig.
lash [læʃ] *n* Peitschenhieb *m; vt (beat against)* schlagen an (+*acc*); *(rain)* schlagen gegen; *(whip)* peitschen; *(bind)* festbinden; **~ out** *vi (with fists)* um sich schlagen; *(spend money)* sich in Unkosten stürzen; *vt money etc* springen lassen; **~ing** *(beating)* Tracht *f* Prügel; *(tie)* Schleife *f;* **~ings of** *(col)* massenhaft.
lass [læs] *n* Mädchen *nt*.
lassitude ['læsɪtjuːd] *n* Abgespanntheit *f*.
lasso [læ'suː] *n* Lasso *nt; vt* mit einem Lasso fangen.
last [lɑːst] *a* letzte(r, s); *ad* zuletzt; *(last time)* das letztemal; *n (person)* Letzte(r) *mf; (thing)* Letzte(s) *nt; (for shoe)* (Schuh)leisten *m; vi (continue)* dauern; *(remain good)* sich halten; *(money)* ausreichen; **at ~** endlich; **~ night** gestern abend; **~ing** *a* dauerhaft, haltbar; *shame etc* andauernd; **~-minute** *a* in letzter Minute.
latch [lætʃ] *n* Riegel *m;* **~key** Hausschlüssel *m*.
late [leɪt] *a* spät; zu spät; *(recent)* jüngste(r, s); *(former)* frühere(r,s); *(dead)* verstorben; *ad* spät; *(after proper time)* zu spät; **to be ~** zu spät kommen; **of ~** in letzter Zeit; **~ in the day** *(lit)* spät; *(fig)* reichlich spät; **~comer** Nachzügler *m;* **~ly** *ad* in letzter Zeit.
lateness ['leɪtnəs] *n (of person)* Zuspätkommen *nt; (of train)* Verspätung *f;* **~ of the hour** die vorgerückte Stunde.
latent ['leɪtənt] *a* latent.
lateral ['lætərəl] *a* seitlich.
latest ['leɪtɪst] *n (news)* Neu(e)ste(s) *nt;* **at the ~** spätestens.
latex ['leɪteks] *n* Milchsaft *m*.
lath [læθ] *n* Latte *f,* Leiste *f*.
lathe [leɪð] *n* Drehbank *f*.
lather ['lɑːðə°] *n* (Seifen)schaum *m; vt* einschäumen; *vi* schäumen.
latitude ['lætɪtjuːd] *n (Geog)* Breite *f; (freedom)* Spielraum *m*.
latrine [lə'triːn] *n* Latrine *f*.
latter ['lætə°] *a (second of two)* letztere; *(coming at end)* letzte(r, s), später; **~ly** *ad* in letzter Zeit; **~-day** *a* modern.
lattice work ['lætɪswɜːk] *n* Lattenwerk *nt,* Gitterwerk *nt*.
laudable ['lɔːdəbl] *a* löblich.
laugh [lɑːf] *n* Lachen *nt; vi* lachen; **~ at** *vt* lachen über (+*acc*); **~ off** *vt* lachend abtun; **~able** *a* lachhaft; **~ing** *a* lachend;

~ing stock Zielscheibe *f* des Spottes; **~ter** Lachen *nt,* Gelächter *nt*.
launch [lɔːntʃ] *n (of ship)* Stapellauf *m; (of rocket)* Raketenabschuß *m; (boat)* Barkasse *f; (pleasure boat)* Vergnügungsboot *nt; vt (set afloat)* vom Stapel laufen lassen; *rocket* (ab)schießen; *(set going)* in Gang setzen, starten; **~ing** Stapellauf *m;* **~(ing) pad** Abschußrampe *f*.
launder ['lɔːndə°] *vt* waschen und bügeln; **~ette** [lɔːndə'ret] Waschsalon *m*.
laundry ['lɔːndrɪ] *n (place)* Wäscherei *f; (clothes)* Wäsche *f*.
laureate ['lɔːrɪət] *a see* poet.
laurel ['lɒrəl] *n* Lorbeer *m*.
lava ['lɑːvə] *n* Lava *f*.
lavatory ['lævətrɪ] *n* Toilette *f*.
lavender ['lævɪndə°] *n* Lavendel *m*.
lavish ['lævɪʃ] *n (extravagant)* verschwenderisch; *(generous)* großzügig; *vt money* verschwenden *(on* auf +*acc); attentions, gifts* überschütten mit *(on* sb jdn);* **~ly** *ad* verschwenderisch.
law [lɔː] *n* Gesetz *nt; (system)* Recht *nt; (of game etc)* Regel *f; (as studies)* Jura *no art;* **~-abiding** *a* gesetzestreu; **~breaker** Gesetzesübertreter *m;* **~ court** Gerichtshof *m;* **~ful** *a* gesetzlich, rechtmäßig; **~fully** *ad* rechtmäßig; **~less** *a* gesetzlos.
lawn [lɔːn] *n* Rasen *m;* **~ mower** Rasenmäher *m;* **~ tennis** Rasentennis *m*.
law school ['lɔːskuːl] *n* Rechtsakademie *f*.
law student ['lɔːstjuːdənt] *n* Jurastudent *m*.
lawsuit ['lɔːsuːt] *n* Prozeß *m*.
lawyer ['lɔːjə°] *n* Rechtsanwalt *m* Rechtsanwältin *f*.
lax [læks] *a* lax.
laxative ['læksətɪv] *n* Abführmittel *nt*.
laxity ['læksɪtɪ] *n* Laxheit *f*.
lay [leɪ] *a* Laien-; *vt irreg (place)* legen; *table* decken; *fire* anrichten; *egg* legen; *trap* stellen; *money* wetten; **~ aside** *vt* zurücklegen; **~ by** *vt (set aside)* beiseite legen; **~ down** *vt* hinlegen; *rules* vorschreiben; *arms* strecken; **~ off** *vt workers* (vorübergehend) entlassen; **~ on** *vt* auftragen; *concert etc* veranstalten; **~ out** *vt* (her)auslegen; *money* ausgeben; *corpse* aufbahren; **~ up** *vt (store)* aufspeichern; *supplies* anlegen; *(save)* zurücklegen; **~about** Faulenzer *m;* **~-by** Parkbucht *f; (bigger)* Rastplatz *m;* **~er** Schicht *f;* **~ette** [leɪ'et] Babyausstattung *f;* **~man** Laie *m;* **~out** Anlage *f; (Art)* Layout *nt*.
laze [leɪz] *vi* faulenzen.
lazily ['leɪzɪlɪ] *ad* träge, faul.
laziness ['leɪzɪnəs] *n* Faulheit *f*.
lazy ['leɪzɪ] *a* faul; *(slow-moving)* träge.
lead¹ [led] *n* Blei *nt; (of pencil)* (Blei-stift)mine *f;* *a* bleiern, Blei-.
lead² [liːd] *n (front position)* Führung *f; (distance, time ahead)* Vorsprung *f; (example)* Vorbild *nt; (clue)* Tip *m; (of police)* Spur *f; (Theat)* Hauptrolle *f; (dog's)* Leine *f, irreg vt (guide)* führen; *group etc* leiten; *vi (be first)* führen; **~ astray** *vt* irreführen; **~ away** *vt* wegführen; *prisoner* abführen; **~ back** *vi* zurück-

führen; ~ **on** vt anführen; ~ **to** vt (street) (hin)führen nach; (result in) führen zu; ~ **up to** vt (drive) führen zu; (speaker etc) hinführen auf (+ acc); ~**er** Führer m, Leiter m; (of party) Vorsitzende(r) m; (Press) Leitartikel m; ~**ership** (office) Leitung f; (quality) Führerschaft f; ~**ing** a führend; ~**ing lady** (Theat) Hauptdarstellerin f; ~**ing light** (person) führende(r) Geist m; ~**ing man** (Theat) Hauptdarsteller m.

leaf [liːf] n Blatt nt; (of table) Ausziehplatte; ~**let** Blättchen nt; (advertisement) Prospekt m; (pamphlet) Flugblatt nt; (for information) Merkblatt nt; ~**y** a belaubt.

league [liːg] n (union) Bund m, Liga f; (Sport) Liga f, Tabelle f; (measure) 3 englische Meilen.

leak [liːk] n undichte Stelle f; (in ship) Leck nt; vi liquid etc durchlassen; vi (pipe etc) undicht sein; (liquid etc) auslaufen; ~ **out** vi (liquid etc) auslaufen; (information) durchsickern.

leaky ['liːkɪ] a undicht.

lean [liːn] a mager; n Magere(s) nt; irreg vi sich neigen; **to** ~ **against sth** an etw (dat) angelehnt sein; sich an etw (acc) anlehnen; vt (an)lehnen; ~ **back** vi sich zurücklehnen; ~ **forward** vi sich vorbeugen; ~ **on** vi sich stützen auf (+acc); ~ **over** vi sich hinüberbeugen; ~ **towards** vt neigen zu; ~**ing** Neigung f; ~-**to** Anbau m.

leap [liːp] n Sprung m; vi irreg springen; **by** ~**s and bounds** schnell; ~**frog** Bockspringen nt; ~ **year** Schaltjahr nt.

learn [lɜːn] vti irreg lernen; (find out) erfahren, hören; ~**ed** ['lɜːnɪd] a gelehrt; ~**er** Anfänger(in f) m; (Aut) Fahrschüler(in f) m; ~**ing** Gelehrsamkeit f.

lease [liːs] n (of property) Mietvertrag m; (of land) Pachtvertrag m; vt mieten; pachten.

leash [liːʃ] n Leine f.

least [liːst] a kleinste(r, s); (slightest) geringste(r, s); n Mindeste(s) nt; **at** ~ zumindest; **not in the** ~! durchaus nicht!

leather ['leðə*] n Leder nt; a ledern, Leder-; ~**y** a zäh, ledern.

leave [liːv] irreg vt verlassen; (— behind) zurücklassen; (forget) vergessen; (allow to remain) lassen; (after death) hinterlassen; (entrust) überlassen (to sb jdm); **to be left** (remain) übrigbleiben; vi weggehen, wegfahren; (for journey) abreisen; (bus, train) abfahren; n Erlaubnis f; (Mil) Urlaub m; **on** ~ auf Urlaub; **to take one's** ~ **of** Abschied nehmen von; ~ **off** vi aufhören; ~ **out** vt auslassen.

lecherous ['letʃərəs] a lüstern.

lectern ['lektɜːn] n Lesepult nt.

lecture ['lektʃə*] n Vortrag m; (Univ) Vorlesung f; vi einen Vortrag halten; (Univ) lesen; ~**r** Vortragende(r) mf; (Univ) Dozent(in f) m.

ledge [ledʒ] n Leiste f, (window —) Sims m or nt; (of mountain) (Fels)vorsprung m.

ledger ['ledʒə*] n Hauptbuch nt.

lee [liː] n Windschatten m; (Naut) Lee f.

leech [liːtʃ] n Blutegel m.

leek [liːk] n Lauch m.

leer [lɪə*] n schiefe(r) Blick m; vi schielen (at nach).

leeway ['liːweɪ] n (fig) Rückstand m; (freedom) Spielraum m.

left [left] a linke(r, s); ad links; nach links; n (side) linke Seite f; **the L**~ (Pol) die Linke f; ~-**hand drive** Linkssteuerung f; ~-**handed** a linkshändig; ~-**hand side** linke Seite f; ~-**luggage (office)** Gepäckaufbewahrung f; ~-**overs** pl Reste pl, Überbleibsel pl; ~ **wing** linke(r) Flügel m; ~-**wing** a linke(r, s).

leg [leg] n Bein nt; (of meat) Keule f, (stage) Etappe f.

legacy ['legəsɪ] n Erbe nt, Erbschaft f.

legal ['liːgəl] a gesetzlich, rechtlich; (allowed) legal, rechtsgültig; **to take** ~ **action** prozessieren; ~**ize** vt legalisieren; ~**ly** ad gesetzlich; legal; ~ **tender** gesetzliche(s) Zahlungsmittel nt.

legation [lɪ'geɪʃən] n Gesandtschaft f.

legend ['ledʒənd] n Legende f; ~**ary** a legendär.

-**legged** ['legɪd] a -beinig.

leggings ['legɪŋz] npl (hohe) Gamaschen pl; (for baby) Gamaschenhose f.

legibility [ledʒɪ'bɪlɪtɪ] n Leserlichkeit f.

legible a, **legibly** ad ['ledʒəbl, -blɪ] leserlich.

legion ['liːdʒən] n Legion f.

legislate ['ledʒɪsleɪt] vi Gesetze geben.

legislation [ledʒɪs'leɪʃən] n Gesetzgebung f.

legislative ['ledʒɪslətɪv] a gesetzgebend.

legislator ['ledʒɪsleɪtə*] n Gesetzgeber m.

legislature ['ledʒɪslətʃə*] n Legislative f.

legitimacy [lɪ'dʒɪtɪməsɪ] n Rechtmäßigkeit f; (of birth) Ehelichkeit f.

legitimate [lɪ'dʒɪtɪmət] a rechtmäßig, legitim; child ehelich.

legroom ['legrum] n Platz m für die Beine.

leisure ['leʒə*] n Freizeit f; a Freizeit-; **to be at** ~ Zeit haben; ~**ly** a gemächlich.

lemming ['lemɪŋ] n Lemming m.

lemon ['lemən] n Zitrone f; (colour) Zitronengelb nt; ~**ade** [lemə'neɪd] Limonade f.

lend [lend] vt irreg leihen; **to** ~ **sb sth** jdm etw leihen; **it** ~**s itself to** es eignet sich zu; ~**er** Verleiher m; ~**ing library** Leihbibliothek f.

length [leŋθ] n Länge f; (section of road, pipe etc) Strecke f; (of material) Stück nt; ~ **of time** Zeitdauer f; **at** ~ (lengthily) ausführlich; (at last) schließlich; ~**en** vt verlängern; vi länger werden; ~**ways** ad längs; ~**y** a sehr lang; langatmig.

leniency ['liːnɪənsɪ] n Nachsicht f.

lenient ['liːnɪənt] a nachsichtig; ~**ly** ad milde.

lens [lenz] n Linse f; (Phot) Objektiv nt.

Lent [lent] n Fastenzeit f.

lentil ['lentɪl] n Linse f.

Leo ['liːəʊ] n Löwe m.

leopard ['lepəd] n Leopard m.

leotard ['liːətɑːd] n Trikot nt, Gymnastikanzug m.

leper ['lepə*] n Leprakranke(r) mf.

leprosy ['leprəsɪ] n Lepra f.

lesbian ['lezbɪən] a lesbisch; n Lesbierin f.
less [les] a, ad, n weniger.
lessen ['lesn] vi abnehmen; vt verringern, verkleinern.
lesser ['lesə*] a kleiner, geringer.
lesson ['lesn] n (Sch) Stunde f; (unit of study) Lektion f; (fig) Lehre f; (Eccl) Lesung f; ~s start at 9 der Unterricht beginnt um 9.
lest [lest] cj damit ... nicht.
let [let] n: without ~ or hindrance völlig unbehindert; vt irreg lassen; (lease) vermieten; ~'s go! gehen wir!; ~ down vt hinunterlassen; (disappoint) enttäuschen; ~ go vi loslassen; vt things loslassen; person gehen lassen; ~ off vt gun abfeuern; steam ablassen; (forgive) laufen lassen; ~ out vt herauslassen; scream fahren lassen; ~ up vi nachlassen; (stop) aufhören; ~-down Enttäuschung f.
lethal ['li:θl] a tödlich.
lethargic [le'θɑ:dʒɪk] a lethargisch, träge.
lethargy ['leθədʒɪ] n Lethargie f, Teilnahmslosigkeit f.
letter ['letə*] n (of alphabet) Buchstabe m; (message) Brief m; ~s pl (literature) (schöne) Literatur f; ~box Briefkasten m; ~ing Beschriftung f.
lettuce ['letɪs] n (Kopf)salat m.
let-up ['letʌp] n (col) Nachlassen nt.
leukaemia, (US) **leukemia** [lu:'ki:mɪə] n Leukämie f.
level ['levl] a ground eben; (at same height) auf gleicher Höhe; (equal) gleich gut; head kühl; to do one's ~ best sein möglichstes tun; ad auf gleicher Höhe; to draw ~ with gleichziehen mit; n (instrument) Wasserwaage f; (altitude) Höhe f; (flat place) ebene Fläche f; (position on scale) Niveau nt; (amount, degree) Grad m; talks on a high ~ Gespräche auf hoher Ebene; profits keep on the same ~ Gewinne halten sich auf dem gleichen Stand; on the moral ~ aus moralischer Sicht; on the ~ (lit) auf gleicher Höhe; (fig: honest) erhlich; vt ground einebnen; building abreißen; town dem Erdboden gleichmachen; blow versetzen (at sb jdm); remark richten (at gegen); ~ off or out vi flach or eben werden; (fig) sich ausgleichen; (plane) horizontal fliegen; vt ground planieren; differences ausgleichen; ~ crossing Bahnübergang m; ~-headed a vernünftig.
lever ['li:və*], (US) ['levə*] n Hebel m; (fig) Druckmittel nt; vt (hoch)stemmen; ~age Hebelkraft f; (fig) Einfluß m.
levity ['levɪtɪ] n Leichtfertigkeit f.
levy ['levɪ] n (of taxes) Erhebung f; (tax) Abgaben pl; (Mil) Aushebung f; vt erheben; (Mil) ausheben.
lewd [lu:d] a unzüchtig, unanständig.
liability [laɪə'bɪlɪtɪ] n (burden) Belastung f; (duty) Pflicht f; (debt) Verpflichtung f; (proneness) Anfälligkeit f; (responsibility) Haftung f.
liable ['laɪəbl] a (responsible) haftbar; (prone) anfällig; to be ~ for etw (dat) unterliegen; it's ~ to happen es kann leicht vorkommen.
liaison [li:'eɪzɒn] n Verbindung f.

liar ['laɪə*] n Lügner m.
libel ['laɪbl] n Verleumdung f; vt verleumden; ~(l)ous a verleumderisch.
liberal ['lɪbərəl] a (generous) großzügig; (open-minded) aufgeschlossen; (Pol) liberal; n liberal denkende(r) Mensch m; L~ (Pol) Liberale(r) mf; ~ly ad (abundantly) reichlich.
liberate ['lɪbəreɪt] vt befreien.
liberation [lɪbə'reɪʃən] n Befreiung f.
liberty ['lɪbətɪ] n Freiheit f; (permission) Erlaubnis f; to be at ~ to do sth etw tun dürfen; to take liberties with sich (dat) Freiheiten herausnehmen gegenüber
Libra ['li:brə] n Waage f.
librarian [laɪbrɛərɪən] n Bibliothekar(in f) m.
library ['laɪbrərɪ] n Bibliothek f; (lending ~) Bücherei f.
libretto [lɪ'bretəʊ] n Libretto nt.
lice [laɪs] npl of louse.
licence, (US) **license** ['laɪsəns] n (permit) Erlaubnis f, amtliche Zulassung f; (driving ~) Führerschein m; (excess) Zügellosigkeit f; ~ plate (US Aut) Nummernschild nt.
license ['laɪsəns] vt genehmigen, konzessionieren; ~e [laɪsən'si:] Konzessionsinhaber m.
licentious [laɪ'senʃəs] a ausschweifend.
lichen ['laɪkən] n Flechte f.
lick [lɪk] vt lecken; vi (flames) züngeln; n Lecken nt; (small amount) Spur f.
licorice ['lɪkərɪs] n Lakritze f.
lid [lɪd] n Deckel m; (eye~) Lid nt.
lido ['li:dəʊ] n Freibad nt.
lie [laɪ] n Lüge f; vi lügen; irreg (rest, be situated) liegen; (put o.s. in position) sich legen; to ~ idle stillstehen; ~ detector Lügendetektor m.
lieu [lu:] n: in ~ of anstatt (+gen).
lieutenant [lef'tenənt], (US) [lu:'tenənt] n Leutnant m.
life [laɪf] n Leben nt; (story) Lebensgeschichte f; (energy) Lebendigkeit f; ~assurance Lebensversicherung f; ~belt Rettungsring m; ~boat Rettungsboot f; ~guard Badewärter m; Rettungsschwimmer m; ~jacket Schwimmweste f; ~less a (dead) leblos, tot; (dull) langweilig; ~like a lebenswahr, naturgetreu; ~line (lit) Rettungsleine f; (fig) Rettungsanker m; ~long a lebenslang; ~ preserver Totschläger m; ~raft Rettungsfloß nt; ~-sized a in Lebensgröße; ~ span Lebensspanne f; ~time Lebenszeit f.
lift [lɪft] vt hochheben; vi sich heben; n (raising) (Hoch)heben nt; (elevator) Aufzug m, Lift m; to give sb a ~ jdn mitnehmen; ~-off Abheben nt (vom Boden).
ligament ['lɪgəmənt] n Sehne f, Band nt.
light [laɪt] n Licht nt; (lamp) Lampe f; (flame) Feuer nt; ~s pl (Aut) Beleuchtung f; in the ~ of angesichts (+gen); vt irreg beleuchten; lamp anmachen; fire, cigarette anzünden; (brighten) erleuchten, erhellen; a (bright) hell, licht; (pale) hell-; (not heavy, easy) leicht; punishment mild; taxes niedrig; touch leicht; ~ up vi (lamp) angehen; (face) aufleuchten; vt (illuminate)

beleuchten; *lights* anmachen; ~ **bulb** Glühbirne *f*; ~**en** *vi* *(brighten)* hell werden; *(lightning)* blitzen; *vt* *(give light to)* erhellen; *hair* aufhellen; *gloom* aufheitern; *(make less heavy)* leichter machen; *(fig)* erleichtern; ~**er** *(cigarette —)* Feuerzeug *nt*; *(boat)* Leichter *m*; ~**-headed** *a* *(thoughtless)* leichtsinnig; *(giddy)* schwindlig; ~**-hearted** *a* leichtherzig, fröhlich; ~**house** Leuchturm *m*; ~**ing** Beleuchtung *f*; ~**ing-up time** Zeit *f* des Einschaltens der Straßen-/Auto-beleuchtung; ~**ly** *ad* leicht; *(irresponsibly)* leichtfertig; ~ **meter** *(Phot)* Belichtungs-messer *m*; ~**ness** *(of weight)* Leichtigkeit *f*; *(of colour)* Helle *f*; *(light)* Helligkeit *f*; ~**ning** Blitz *m*; ~**ning conductor** Blitz-ableiter *m*; ~**weight** *a suit* leicht; ~**weight boxer** Leichtgewicht *nt*; ~**year** Lichtjahr *nt*.

lignite ['lignait] *n* Lignit *m*.

like [laik] *vt* mögen, gernhaben; **would you ~ ...?** hatten Sie gern ...?; **would you ~ to ...?** möchten Sie gern...?; *prep* wie; **what's it/he ~?** wie ist es/er?; **that's just ~ him** das sieht ihm ähnlich; ~ **that/this** so; *a (similar)* ähnlich; *(equal)* gleich; ~ Gleiche(s) *nt*; ~**able** *a* sympathisch; ~**lihood** Wahrschein-lichkeit *f*; ~**ly** *a (probable)* wahrschein-lich; *(suitable)* geeignet; *ad* wahrscheinlich; ~**-minded** *a* gleichgesinnt; ~**n** *vt* vergleichen *(to mit)*; ~**wise** *ad* ebenfalls.

liking ['laikiŋ] *n* Zuneigung *f*; *(taste for)* Vorliebe *f*.

lilac ['lailək] *n* Flieder *m*.

lilting [liltiŋ] *a accent* singend; *tune* munter.

lily ['lili] *n* Lilie *f*; ~ **of the valley** Mai-glöckchen *nt*.

limb [lim] *n* Glied *nt*.

limber ['limbə•]: ~ **up** *vi* sich auflockern; *(fig)* sich vorbereiten.

limbo ['limbəu] *n*: **to be in ~** *(fig)* in der Schwebe sein.

lime [laim] *n (tree)* Linde *f*; *(fruit)* Limone *f*; *(substance)* Kalk *m*; ~ **juice** Limonensaft *m*; ~ **light** *(fig)* Rampenlicht *nt*.

limerick ['limərik] *n* Limerick *m*.

limestone ['laimstəun] *n* Kalkstein *m*.

limit ['limit] *n* Grenze *f*; *(col)* Höhe *f*; *vt* begrenzen, einschränken; ~**ation** Grenzen *pl*, Einschränkung *f*; ~**ed** *a* beschränkt; ~**ed company** Gesellschaft *f* mit beschränkter Haftung, GmBH *f*.

limousine ['liməzi:n] *n* Limousine *f*.

limp [limp] *n* Hinken *nt*; *vi* hinken; *a (without firmness)* schlaff.

limpet ['limpit] *n (lit)* Napfschnecke *f*; *(fig)* Klette *f*.

limpid ['limpid] *a* klar.

limply ['limpli] *ad* schlaff.

line [lain] *n* Linie *f*; *(rope)* Leine *f*, Schnur *f*; *(on face)* Falte *f*; *(row)* Reihe *f*; *(of hills)* Kette *f*; *(US: queue)* Schlange *f*; *(company)* Linie *f*, Gesellschaft *f*; *(Rail)* Strecke *f*; *(pl)* Geleise *pl*; *(Tel)* Leitung *f*; *(written)* Zeile *f*; *(direction)* Richtung *f*; *(fig: business)* Branche *f*; Beruf *m*; *(range of items)* Kollek-tion *f*; **it's a bad ~** *(Tel)* die Verbindung

ist schlecht; **hold the ~** bleiben Sie am Apparat; **in ~ with** in Übereinstimmung mit; *vt coat* füttern; *(border)* säumen; ~ **up** *vi* sich aufstellen; *vt* aufstellen; *(prepare)* sorgen für; *support* mobilisieren; *surprise* planen.

linear ['liniə•] *a* gerade; *(measure)* Längen-.

linen ['linin] *n* Leinen *nt*; *(sheets etc)* Wäsche *f*.

liner ['lainə•] *n* Überseedampfer *m*.

linesman ['lainzmən] *n (Sport)* Linien-richter *m*.

line-up ['lainʌp] *n* Aufstellung *f*.

linger ['liŋgə•] *vi (remain long)* verweilen; *(taste)* (zurück)bleiben; *(delay)* zögern, verharren.

lingerie ['lænʒəri:] *n* Damenunterwäsche *f*.

lingering ['liŋgəriŋ] *a lang*; *doubt* zurück-bleibend; *disease* langwierig; *taste* nach-haltend; *look* lang.

lingo ['liŋgəu] *n (col)* Sprache *f*.

linguist ['liŋgwist] *n* Sprachkundige(r) *mf*; *(Univ)* Sprachwissenschaftler(in *f*) *m*.

linguistic [liŋ'gwistik] *a* sprachlich; sprachwissenschaftlich; ~**s** Sprach-wissenschaft *f*, Linguistik *f*.

liniment ['linimənt] *n* Einreibemittel *nt*.

lining ['lainiŋ] *n (of clothes)* Futter *nt*.

link [liŋk] *n* Glied *nt*; *(connection)* Ver-bindung *f*; *vt* verbinden; ~**s** *pl* Golfplatz *m*; ~**-up** *(Tel)* Verbindung *f*; *(of spaceships)* Kopplung *f*.

lino ['lainəu] *n*, **linoleum** [li'nəuliəm] *n* Linoleum *nt*.

linseed oil ['linsi:d'ɔil] *n* Leinöl *nt*.

lint [lint] *n* Verbandstoff *m*.

lintel ['lintl] *n (Archit)* Sturz *m*.

lion ['laiən] *n* Löwe *m*; ~**ess** Löwin *f*.

lip [lip] *n* Lippe *f*; *(of jug)* Tülle *f*, Schnabel *m*; ~**read** *vi irreg* von den Lippen ablesen; **to pay ~ service (to)** ein Lippenbekenntnis ablegen (zu); ~**stick** Lippenstift *m*.

liquefy ['likwifai] *vt* verflüssigen.

liqueur [li'kjuə•] *n* Likör *m*.

liquid ['likwid] *n* Flüßigkeit *f*; *a* flüssig; ~**ate** *vt* liquidieren; ~**ation** Liquidation *f*.

liquor ['likə•] *n* Alkohol *m*, Spirituosen *pl*.

lisp [lisp] *n* Lispeln *nt*; *vti* lispeln.

list [list] *n* Liste *f*, Verzeichnis *nt*; *(of ship)* Schlagseite *f*; *vt (write down)* eine Liste machen von; *(verbally)* aufzählen; *vi (ship)* Schlagseite haben.

listen ['lisn] *vi* hören, horchen; ~ **to** *vt* zuhören (+ Dat); hören (+ Dat); ~**er** *(Rad)* Hörer *m*.

listless *a*, ~**ly** *ad* ['listləs, -li] lustlos, teil-nahmslos; ~**ness** Lustlosigkeit *f*, Teil-nahmslosigkeit *f*.

litany ['litəni] *n* Litanei *f*.

literacy ['litərəsi] *n* Fähigkeit *f* zu lesen und zu schreiben.

literal ['litərəl] *a* eigentlich, buchstäblich; *translation* wortwörtlich; ~**ly** *ad* wörtlich, buchstäblich.

literary ['litərəri] *a* literarisch, Literatur-.

literate ['lɪtərət] a des Lesens und Schreibens kundig.

literature ['lɪtrɪtʃə*] n Literatur f.

lithograph ['lɪθəʊgrɑːf] n Lithographie f.

litigate ['lɪtɪgeɪt] vi prozessieren.

litmus ['lɪtməs] n: ~ paper Lackmuspapier nt.

litre, (US) liter ['liːtə*] n Liter m.

litter ['lɪtə*] n (rubbish) Abfall m; (of animals) Wurf m; vt in Unordnung bringen; to be ~ed with übersät sein mit.

little ['lɪtl] a klein; (unimportant) unbedeutend; ad n wenig; a ~ ein bißchen; the ~ das wenige.

liturgy ['lɪtədʒɪ] n Liturgie f.

live¹ [lɪv] vi leben; (last) fortleben; (dwell) wohnen; vt life führen; ~ down vt Gras wachsen lassen über (+acc); I'll never ~ it down das wird man mir nie vergessen; ~ on vi weiterleben; ~ on sth von etw leben; ~ up to vt standards gerecht werden (+dat); principles anstreben; hopes entsprechen (+dat).

live² [laɪv] a lebendig; (burning) glühend; (Mil) scharf; (Elec) geladen; broadcast live.

livelihood ['laɪvlɪhʊd] n Lebensunterhalt m.

liveliness ['laɪvlɪnəs] n Lebendigkeit f.

lively ['laɪvlɪ] a lebhaft, lebendig.

liver ['lɪvə*] n (Anat) Leber f; ~ish a (bad-tempered) gallig.

livery ['lɪvərɪ] n Livree f.

livestock ['laɪvstɒk] n Vieh nt, Viehbestand m.

livid ['lɪvɪd] a (lit) bläulich; (furious) fuchsteufelswild.

living ['lɪvɪŋ] n (Lebens)unterhalt m; a lebendig; language etc lebend; wage ausreichend; ~ room Wohnzimmer nt.

lizard ['lɪzəd] n Eidechse f.

llama ['lɑːmə] n Lama nt.

load [ləʊd] n (burden) Last f; (amount) Ladung f, Fuhre f; ~s of (col) massenhaft; vt (be)laden; (fig) überhäufen; camera Film einlegen in (+acc); gun laden.

loaf [ləʊf] n Brot nt, Laib m; vi herumlungern, faulenzen.

loam [ləʊm] n Lehmboden m.

loan [ləʊn] n Leihgabe f; (Fin) Darlehen nt; vt leihen; on ~ geliehen.

loathe [ləʊð] vt verabscheuen.

loathing ['ləʊðɪŋ] n Abscheu f.

lobby ['lɒbɪ] n Vorhalle f; (Pol) Lobby f; vt politisch beeinflussen (wollen).

lobe [ləʊb] n Ohrläppchen nt.

lobster ['lɒbstə*] n Hummer m.

local ['ləʊkəl] a ortsansässig, hiesig, Orts-; anaesthetic örtlich; n (pub) Stammwirtschaft f; the ~s pl die Ortsansässigen pl; ~ colour Lokalkolorit nt; ~ity [ləʊˈkælɪtɪ] Ort m; ~ly ad örtlich, am Ort.

locate [ləʊˈkeɪt] vt ausfindig machen; (establish) errichten.

location [ləʊˈkeɪʃən] n Platz m, Lage f; on ~ (Cine) auf Außenaufnahme.

loch [lɒx] n (Scot) See m.

lock [lɒk] n Schloß nt; (Naut) Schleuse f; (of hair) Locke f; vt (fasten) (ver)schließen; vi

(door etc) sich schließen (lassen); (wheels) blockieren.

locker ['lɒkə*] n Spind m.

locket ['lɒkɪt] n Medaillon nt.

locomotive [ləʊkəˈməʊtɪv] n Lokomotive f.

locust ['ləʊkəst] n Heuschrecke f.

lodge [lɒdʒ] n (gatehouse) Pförtnerhaus nt; (freemasons') Loge f; vi (in Untermiete) wohnen (with bei); (get stuck) stecken(bleiben); vt protest einreichen; ~r (Unter)mieter m.

lodgings ['lɒdʒɪŋz] n (Miet)wohnung f; Zimmer nt.

loft [lɒft] n (Dach)boden m.

lofty ['lɒftɪ] a hoch(ragend); (proud) hochmütig.

log [lɒg] n Klotz m; (Naut) Log nt.

logarithm ['lɒgərɪðəm] n Logarithmus m.

logbook ['lɒgbʊk] n Bordbuch nt, Logbuch nt; (for lorry) Fahrtenschreiber m; (Aut) Kraft-fahrzeugbrief m.

loggerheads ['lɒgəhedz] n: to be at ~ sich in den Haaren liegen.

logic ['lɒdʒɪk] n Logik f; ~al a logisch; ~ally ad logisch(erweise).

logistics [lɒˈdʒɪstɪks] npl Logistik f.

loin [lɔɪn] n Lende f.

loiter ['lɔɪtə*] vi herumstehen, sich herumtreiben.

loll [lɒl] vi sich rekeln.

lollipop ['lɒlɪpɒp] n (Dauer)lutscher m.

lone [ləʊn] a einsam.

loneliness ['ləʊnlɪnəs] n Einsamkeit f.

lonely ['ləʊnlɪ] a einsam.

long [lɒŋ] a lang; distance weit; ad lange; two-day-~ zwei Tage lang; vi sich sehnen (for nach); ~ ago vor langer Zeit; before ~ bald; as ~ as solange; in the ~ run the Dauer; ~-distance a Fern-; ~-haired a langhaarig; ~hand Langschrift f; ~ing Verlangen nt, Sehnsucht f; a sehnsüchtig; ~ish a ziemlich lang; ~itude Längengrad m; ~ jump Weitsprung m; ~-lost a längst verloren geglaubt; ~-playing record Langspielplatte f; ~-range a Langstrecken-, Fern-; ~-sighted a weitsichtig; ~-standing a alt, seit langer Zeit bestehend; ~-suffering a schwer geprüft; ~-term a langfristig; ~ wave Langwelle f; ~-winded a langatmig.

loo [luː] n (col) Klo nt.

loofah ['luːfə*] n (plant) Luffa f; (sponge) Luffa(schwamm) m.

look [lʊk] vi schauen, blicken; (seem) aussehen; (face) liegen nach, gerichtet sein nach; n Blick m; ~s pl Aussehen nt; ~ after vt (care for) sorgen für; (watch) aufpassen auf (+acc); ~ down on vt (fig) herabsehen auf (+acc); ~ for vt (seek) suchen (nach); (expect) erwarten; ~ forward to vt sich freuen auf (+acc); ~ out for vt Ausschau halten nach; (be careful) achtgeben auf (+acc); ~ out (take care of) achtgeben auf (+acc); (rely on) sich verlassen auf (+acc); ~ up vi aufblicken; (improve) sich bessern; vt word nachschlagen; person besuchen; ~ up to vt aufsehen zu; ~-out (watch) Ausschau f;

(person) Wachposten m; *(place)* Ausguck m; *(prospect)* Aussichten pl.

loom [lu:m] n Webstuhl m; vi sich abzeichnen.

loop [lu:p] n Schlaufe f, Schleife f; vt schlingen; ~hole *(fig)* Hintertürchen nt.

loose [lu:s] a lose, locker; *(free)* frei; *(inexact)* unpräzise; vt lösen, losbinden; to be at a ~ end nicht wissen, was man tun soll; ~ly ad locker, lose; ~ly speaking grob gesagt; ~n vt lockern, losmachen; ~ness Lockerheit f.

loot [lu:t] n Beute f; vt plündern; ~ing Plünderung f.

lop [lɔp]: ~ off vt abhacken.

lop-sided ['lɔp'saɪdɪd] a schief.

lord [lɔ:d] n *(ruler)* Herr m, Gebieter m; *(Brit, title)* Lord m; the L~ *(Gott)* der Herr m; ~ly a vornehm; *(proud)* stolz.

lore [lɔ:*] n Überlieferung f.

lorry ['lɔrɪ] n Lastwagen m.

lose [lu:z] irreg vt verlieren; chance verpassen; ~ out on zu kurz kommen bei; vi verlieren; ~r Verlierer m.

losing ['lu:zɪŋ] a Verlierer-; *(Comm)* verlustbringend.

loss [lɔs] n Verlust m; at a ~ *(Comm)* mit Verlust; *(unable)* außerstande; I am at a ~ for words mir fehlen die Worte.

lost [lɔst] a verloren; ~ cause aussichtslose Sache f; ~ property Fundsachen pl.

lot [lɔt] n *(quantity)* Menge f; *(fate, at auction)* Los nt; *(col: people, things)* Haufen m; the ~ alles; *(people)* alle; a ~ of viel; pl viele; ~s of massenhaft, viel(e).

lotion ['lɔuʃən] n Lotion f.

lottery ['lɔtərɪ] n Lotterie f.

loud [laud] a laut; *(showy)* schreiend; ad laut; ~ly ad laut; ~ness Lautheit f; ~speaker Lautsprecher m.

lounge [laundʒ] n *(in hotel)* Gesellschaftsraum m; *(in house)* Wohnzimmer nt; *(on ship)* Salon m; vi sich herumlümmeln; ~suit Straßenanzug m.

louse [laus] n Laus f.

lousy ['lauzɪ] a *(lit)* verlaust; *(fig)* lausig, miserabel.

lout [laut] n Lümmel m.

lovable ['lʌvəbl] a liebenswert.

love [lʌv] n Liebe f; *(person)* Liebling m, Schatz m; *(Sport)* null; vt person lieben; activity gerne mögen; to ~ to do sth etw (sehr) gerne tun; to make ~ sich lieben; to make ~ to/with sb jdn lieben; ~affair (Liebes)verhältnis nt; ~ letter Liebesbrief m; ~ life Liebesleben nt; ~ly a schön; person, object also entzückend, reizend; ~-making Liebe f; ~r Liebhaber m; Geliebte f; *(of books etc)* Liebhaber m; the ~rs die Liebenden, das Liebespaar; ~song Liebeslied nt.

loving ['lʌvɪŋ] a liebend, liebevoll; ~ly ad liebevoll.

low [lɔu] a niedrig; rank niedere(r, s); level, note, neckline tief; intelligence, density gering; *(vulgar)* ordinär; *(not loud)* leise; *(depressed)* gedrückt; ad *(not high)* niedrig; *(not loudly)* leise; n *(low point)* Tiefstand m;

(Met) Tief nt; ~-cut a dress tiefausgeschnitten.

lower ['lɔuə*] vt herunterlassen; eyes, gun senken; *(reduce)* herabsetzen, senken.

lowly ['lɔulɪ] a bescheiden.

loyal ['lɔɪəl] a *(true)* treu; *(to king)* loyal, treu; ~ly ad treu; loyal; ~ty Treue f; Loyalität f.

lozenge ['lɔzɪndʒ] n Pastille f.

lubricant ['lu:brɪkənt] n Schmiermittel nt.

lubricate ['lu:brɪkeɪt] vt (ab)schmieren, ölen.

lubrication [lu:brɪ'keɪʃən] n (Ein- or Ab)schmierung f.

lucid ['lu:sɪd] a klar; *(sane)* bei klarem Verstand; moment licht; ~ity [lu:'sɪdɪtɪ] Klarheit f; ~ly ad klar.

luck [lʌk] n Glück nt; bad ~ Pech nt; ~ily ad glücklicherweise, zum Glück; ~y a glücklich, Glücks-; to be ~ Glück haben.

lucrative ['lu:krətɪv] a einträglich.

ludicrous ['lu:dɪkrəs] a grotesk.

ludo ['lu:dəu] n Mensch ärgere dich nicht nt.

lug [lʌg] vt schleppen.

luggage ['lʌgɪdʒ] n Gepäck nt; ~ rack Gepäcknetz nt.

lugubrious [lu:'gu:brɪəs] a traurig.

lukewarm ['lu:kwɔ:m] a lauwarm; *(indifferent)* lau.

lull [lʌl] n Flaute f; vt einlullen; *(calm)* beruhigen; ~aby ['lʌləbaɪ] Schlaflied nt.

lumbago [lʌm'beɪgəu] n Hexenschuß m.

lumber ['lʌmbə*] n Plunder m; *(wood)* Holz nt; ~jack Holzfäller m.

luminous ['lu:mɪnəs] a leuchtend, Leucht-.

lump [lʌmp] n Klumpen m; *(Med)* Schwellung f; *(in breast)* Knoten m; *(of sugar)* Stück nt; vt zusammentun; *(judge together)* in einen Topf werfen; ~ sum Pauschalsumme f; ~y klumpig; to go ~y klumpen.

lunacy ['lu:nəsɪ] n Irrsinn m.

lunar ['lu:nə*] a Mond-.

lunatic ['lu:nətɪk] n Wahnsinnige(r) mf; a wahnsinnig, irr.

lunch [lʌntʃ] n *(also* ~eon [-ən]*)* Mittagessen nt; ~ hour Mittagspause f; ~time Mittagszeit f; ~eon meat Frühstücksfleisch nt.

lung [lʌŋ] n Lunge f; ~ cancer Lungenkrebs m.

lunge [lʌndʒ] vi (los)stürzen; n Taumeln nt; *(Naut)* plötzliche(s) Schlingern nt.

lupin ['lu:pɪn] n Lupine f.

lurch [lɔ:tʃ] vi taumeln; *(Naut)* schlingern; n Taumeln nt; *(Naut)* plötzliche(s) Schlingern nt.

lure [ljuə*] n Köder m; *(fig)* Lockung f; vt (ver)locken.

lurid ['ljuərɪd] a *(shocking)* grausig, widerlich; colour grell.

lurk [lɔ:k] vi lauern.

luscious ['lʌʃəs] a köstlich; colour satt.

lush [lʌʃ] a satt; vegetation üppig.

lust [lʌst] n sinnliche Begierde f *(for nach)*; *(sensation)* Wollust f; *(greed)* Gier f; vi gieren *(after nach)*; ~ful a wollüstig, lüstern.

lustre, *(US)* **luster** ['lʌstə*] n Glanz m.

lusty ['lʌstɪ] a gesund und munter; *old person* rüstig.

lute [luːt] n Laute f.

luxuriant [lʌg'zjuərɪənt] a üppig.

luxurious [lʌg'zjuərɪəs] a luxuriös, Luxus-.

luxury ['lʌkʃərɪ] n Luxus m; **the little luxuries** die kleinen Genüsse.

lying ['laɪɪŋ] n Lügen nt; a verlogen.

lynch [lɪntʃ] vt lynchen.

lynx [lɪŋks] n Luchs m.

lyre ['laɪə*] n Leier f.

lyric ['lɪrɪk] n Lyrik f; (pl: words for song) (Lied)text m; a lyrisch; **~al** a lyrisch, gefühlvoll.

M

M, m [em] n M nt, m nt.

mac [mæk] n (Brit col) Regenmantel m.

macabre [mə'kɑːbr] a makaber.

macaroni [mækə'rəʊnɪ] n Makkaroni pl.

mace [meɪs] n Amtsstab m; (spice) Muskat m.

machine [mə'ʃiːn] n Maschine f; vt dress etc mit der Maschine nähen; maschinell herstellen/bearbeiten; **~gun** Maschinengewehr nt; **~ry** [mə'ʃiːnərɪ] Maschinerie f, Maschinen pl; **~ tool** Werkzeugmaschine f.

machinist [mə'ʃiːnɪst] n Maschinist m.

mackerel ['mækrəl] n Makrele f.

mackintosh ['mækɪntɒʃ] n Regenmantel m.

macro- ['mækrəʊ] pref Makro-, makro-.

mad [mæd] a verrückt; dog tollwütig; (angry) wütend; **~ about** (fond of) verrückt nach, versessen auf (+acc).

madam ['mædəm] n gnädige Frau f.

madden ['mædn] vt verrückt machen; (make angry) ärgern; **~ing** a ärgerlich.

made-to-measure ['meɪdtə'meʒə*] a Maß-.

made-up ['meɪd'ʌp] a story erfunden.

madly ['mædlɪ] ad wahnsinnig.

madman ['mædmən] n Verrückte(r) m, Irre(r) m.

madness ['mædnəs] n Wahnsinn m.

Madonna [mə'dɒnə] n Madonna f.

madrigal ['mædrɪgəl] n Madrigal nt.

magazine ['mægəziːn] n Zeitschrift f; (in gun) Magazin nt.

maggot ['mægət] n Made f.

magic ['mædʒɪk] n Zauberei f, Magie f; (fig) Zauber m; a magisch, Zauber-; **~al** a magisch; **~ian** [mə'dʒɪʃən] Zauberer m.

magistrate ['mædʒɪstreɪt] n (Friedens)richter m.

magnanimity [mægnə'nɪmɪtɪ] n Großmut f.

magnanimous [mæg'nænɪməs] a großmütig.

magnate ['mægneɪt] n Magnat m.

magnet ['mægnɪt] n Magnet m; **~ic** [mæg'netɪk] a magnetisch; (fig) anziehend, unwiderstehlich; **~ism** Magnetismus m; (fig) Ausstrahlungskraft f.

magnification [mægnɪfɪ'keɪʃən] n Vergrößerung f.

magnificence [mæg'nɪfɪsəns] n Großartigkeit f.

magnificent a, **~ly** ad [mæg'nɪfɪsənt, -lɪ] großartig.

magnify ['mægnɪfaɪ] vt vergrößern; **~ing glass** Vergrößerungsglas nt, Lupe f.

magnitude ['mægnɪtjuːd] n (size) Größe f; (importance) Ausmaß nt.

magnolia [mæg'nəʊlɪə] n Magnolie f.

magpie ['mægpaɪ] n Elster f.

maharajah [mɑːhə'rɑːdʒə] n Maharadscha m.

mahogany [mə'hɒgənɪ] n Mahagoni nt; a Mahagoni-.

maid [meɪd] n Dienstmädchen nt; **old ~** alte Jungfer f; **~en** (liter) Maid f; a flight, speech Jungfern-; **~en name** Mädchenname m.

mail [meɪl] n Post f; vt aufgeben; **~ box** (US) Briefkasten m; **~ing list** Anschreibeliste f; **~ order** Bestellung f durch die Post; **~ order firm** Versandhaus nt.

maim [meɪm] vt verstümmeln.

main [meɪn] a hauptsächlich, Haupt-; n (pipe) Hauptleitung f; **in the ~** im großen und ganzen; **~land** Festland nt; **~ road** Hauptstraße f; **~stay** (fig) Hauptstütze f.

maintain [meɪn'teɪn] vt machine, roads instand halten; (support) unterhalten; (keep up) aufrechterhalten; (claim) behaupten; innocence beteuern.

maintenance ['meɪntənəns] n (Tech) Wartung f; (of family) Unterhalt m.

maisonette [meɪzə'net] n kleine(s) Eigenheim nt; Wohnung f.

maize [meɪz] n Mais m.

majestic [mə'dʒestɪk] a majestätisch.

majesty ['mædʒɪstɪ] n Majestät f.

major ['meɪdʒə*] n Major m; a (Mus) Dur; (more important) Haupt-; (bigger) größer.

majority [mə'dʒɒrɪtɪ] n Mehrheit f; (Jur) Volljährigkeit f.

make [meɪk] vt irreg machen; (appoint) ernennen (zu); (cause to do sth) veranlassen; (reach) erreichen; (in time) schaffen; (earn) verdienen; **to ~ sth happen** etw geschehen lassen; n Marke f, Fabrikat nt; **~ for** vi gehen/fahren nach; **~ out** vi zurechtkommen; vt (write out) ausstellen; (understand) verstehen; (pretend) (so) tun (als ob); **~ up** vt (make) machen, herstellen; face schminken; quarrel beilegen; story etc erfinden; vi sich versöhnen; **~ up for** vt wiedergutmachen; (Comm) vergüten; **~-believe** n it's **~-believe** es ist nicht wirklich; a Phantasie-, ersonnen; **~r** (Comm) Hersteller m; **~shift** a behelfsmäßig, Not-; **~-up** Schminke f, Make-up nt.

making ['meɪkɪŋ] n: **in the ~** im Entstehen; **to have the ~s of** das Zeug haben zu.

maladjusted ['mælə'dʒʌstɪd] a fehlangepaßt, umweltgestört.

malaise [mæ'leɪz] n Unbehagen nt.

malaria [mə'lɛərɪə] n Malaria f.

male [meɪl] n Mann m; (animal) Männchen nt; a männlich.

malevolence [mə'levələns] n Böswilligkeit f.

malevolent [mə'levələnt] a übelwollend.

malfunction [mæl'fʌŋkʃən] vi versagen, nicht funktionieren.

malice ['mælɪs] n Bosheit f.

malicious a, **~ly** ad [mə'lɪʃəs, -lɪ] böswillig, gehässig.

malign [mə'laɪn] vt verleumden.

malignant [mə'lɪgnənt] a bösartig.

malinger [mə'lɪŋgə*] vi simulieren; **~er** Drückeberger m, Simulant m.

malleable ['mælɪəbl] a formbar.

mallet ['mælɪt] n Holzhammer m.

malnutrition ['mælnjuː'trɪʃən] n Unterernährung f.

malpractice ['mæl'præktɪs] n Amtsvergehen nt.

malt [mɔːlt] n Malz nt.

maltreat [mæl'triːt] vt mißhandeln.

mammal ['mæməl] n Säugetier nt.

mammoth ['mæməθ] a Mammut-, Riesen-.

man [mæn] n, pl **men** Mann m; (human race) der Mensch, die Menschen pl; vt bemannen.

manage ['mænɪdʒ] vi zurechtkommen; vt (control) führen, leiten; (cope with) fertigwerden mit; **to ~ to do sth** etw schaffen; **~able** a person, animal lenksam, fügsam; object handlich; **~ment** (control) Führung f, Leitung f; (directors) Management nt; **~r** Geschäftsführer m, (Betriebs)leiter m; **~ress** ['mænɪdʒə'res] Geschäftsführerin f; **~rial** [mænə'dʒɪərɪəl] a leitend; problem etc Management-.

managing ['mænɪdʒɪŋ] a: **~ director** Betriebsleiter m.

mandarin ['mændərɪn] n (fruit) Mandarine f; (Chinese official) Mandarin m.

mandate ['mændeɪt] n Mandat nt.

mandatory ['mændətərɪ] a obligatorisch.

mandolin(e) ['mændəlɪn] n Mandoline f.

mane [meɪn] n Mähne f.

maneuver [mə'nuːvə*] (US) = manoeuvre.

manful a, **~ly** ad ['mænful, -fəlɪ] beherzt, mannhaft.

mangle ['mæŋgl] vt verstümmeln.

mango ['mæŋgəʊ] n Mango(pflaume) f.

mangrove ['mæŋgrəʊv] n Mangrove f.

mangy ['meɪndʒɪ] a dog räudig.

manhandle ['mænhændl] vt grob behandeln.

manhole ['mænhəʊl] n (Straßen)schacht m.

manhood ['mænhʊd] n Mannesalter nt; (manliness) Männlichkeit f.

man-hour ['mæn'aʊə*] n Arbeitsstunde f.

manhunt ['mænhʌnt] n Fahndung f.

mania ['meɪnɪə] n (craze) Sucht f, Manie f; (madness) Wahn(sinn) m; **~c** ['meɪnɪæk] Wahnsinnige(r) mf, Verrückte(r) mf.

manicure ['mænɪkjʊə*] n Maniküre f; vt maniküren; **~ set** Necessaire nt.

manifest ['mænɪfest] vt offenbaren; a offenkundig; **~ation** (showing) Ausdruck m, Bekundung f; (sign) Anzeichen nt; **~ly** ad offenkundig; **~o** [mænɪ'festəʊ] Manifest nt.

manipulate [mə'nɪpjuleɪt] vt handhaben; (fig) manipulieren.

manipulation [mənɪpju'leɪʃən] n Manipulation f.

mankind [mæn'kaɪnd] n Menschheit f.

manliness ['mænlɪnəs] n Männlichkeit f.

manly ['mænlɪ] a männlich; mannhaft.

man-made ['mæn'meɪd] a fibre künstlich.

manner ['mænə*] n Art f, Weise f; (style) Stil m; **in such a ~** so; **in a ~ of speaking** sozusagen; **~s** pl Manieren pl; **~ism** (of person) Angewohnheit f; (of style) Manieriertheit f.

manoeuvrable [mə'nuːvrəbl] a manövrierfähig.

manoeuvre [mə'nuːvə*] vti manövrieren; n (Mil) Feldzug m; (general) Manöver nt, Schachzug m; **~s** pl Truppenübungen pl, Manöver nt.

manor ['mænə*] n Landgut nt; **~ house** Herrenhaus nt.

manpower ['mænpaʊə*] n Arbeitskräfte pl.

manservant ['mænsɜːvənt] n Diener m.

mansion ['mænʃən] n Herrenhaus nt, Landhaus nt.

manslaughter ['mænslɔːtə*] n Totschlag m.

mantelpiece ['mæntlpiːs] n Kaminsims m.

mantle ['mæntl] n (cloak) lange(r) Umhang m.

manual ['mænjʊəl] a manuell, Hand-; n Handbuch nt.

manufacture [mænju'fæktʃə*] vt herstellen; n Herstellung f; **~r** Hersteller m.

manure [mə'njʊə*] n Dünger m.

manuscript ['mænjuskrɪpt] n Manuskript nt.

many ['menɪ] a viele; **as ~ as 20** sage und schreibe 20; **a good soldier** so mancher gute Soldat; **~'s the time** oft.

map [mæp] n (Land)karte f; (of town) Stadtplan m; vt eine Karte machen von; **~ out** vt (fig) ausarbeiten.

maple ['meɪpl] n Ahorn m.

mar [mɑː*] vt verderben, beeinträchtigen.

marathon ['mærəθən] n (Sport) Marathonlauf m; (fig) Marathon m.

marauder [mə'rɔːdə*] n Plünderer m.

marble ['mɑːbl] n Marmor m; (for game) Murmel f.

March [mɑːtʃ] n März m.

march [mɑːtʃ] vi marschieren; n Marsch m; **~-past** Vorbeimarsch m.

mare [meə*] n Stute f; **~'s nest** Windei nt.

margarine [mɑːdʒə'riːn] n Margarine f.

margin ['mɑːdʒɪn] n Rand m; (extra amount) Spielraum m; (Comm) Spanne f; **~al** a note Rand-; difference etc geringfügig; **~ally** ad nur wenig.

marigold ['mærɪgəʊld] n Ringelblume f.

marijuana [mærɪ'hwɑːnə] n Marihuana nt.

marina [mə'riːnə] n Yachthafen m.

marine [mə'riːn] a Meeres-, See-; n (Mil) Marineinfanterist m; (fleet) Marine f; **~r** ['mærɪnə*] Seemann m.

marionette [mærɪə'net] n Marionette f.

marital ['mærɪtl] a ehelich, Ehe-.

maritime ['mærɪtaɪm] a See-.

marjoram ['mɑːdʒərəm] n Majoran m.

mark [mɑːk] n *(coin)* Mark f; *(spot)* Fleck m; *(scar)* Kratzer m; *(sign)* Zeichen nt; *(target)* Ziel nt; *(Sch)* Note f; **quick off the ~** blitzschnell; **on your ~s** auf die Plätze; vt *(make mark)* Flecken/Kratzer machen auf *(+acc)*; *(indicate)* markieren, bezeichnen; *(note)* sich *(dat)* merken; *exam* korrigieren; **to ~ time** *(lit, fig)* auf der Stelle treten; **~ out** vt bestimmen; *area* abstecken; **~ed** a deutlich; **~edly** ['mɑːkɪdlɪ] ad merklich; **~er** *(in book)* (Lese)zeichen nt; *(on road)* Schild nt.

market ['mɑːkɪt] n Markt m; *(stock —)* Börse f; vt *(Comm: new product)* auf dem Markt bringen; *(sell)* vertreiben; **~ day** Markttag m; **~ garden** *(Brit)* Handelsgärtnerei f; **~ing** Marketing nt; **~ place** Marktplatz m.

marksman ['mɑːksmən] n Scharfschütze m; **~ship** Treffsicherheit f.

marmalade ['mɑːməleɪd] n Orangenmarmelade f.

maroon [mə'ruːn] vt aussetzen; a *(colour)* kastanienbraun.

marquee [mɑː'kiː] n große(s) Zelt nt.

marquess, **marquis** ['mɑːkwɪs] n Marquis m.

marriage ['mærɪdʒ] n Ehe f; *(wedding)* Heirat f; *(fig)* Verbindung f.

married ['mærɪd] a *person* verheiratet; *couple, life* Ehe-.

marrow ['mærəʊ] n (Knochen)mark nt; *(vegetable)* Kürbis m.

marry ['mærɪ] vt *(join)* trauen; *(take as husband, wife)* heiraten; vi *(also* **get married)** heiraten.

marsh [mɑːʃ] n Marsch f, Sumpfland nt.

marshal ['mɑːʃəl] n *(US)* Bezirkspolizeichef m; vt (an)ordnen, arrangieren.

marshy ['mɑːʃɪ] a sumpfig.

martial ['mɑːʃəl] a kriegerisch; **~ law** Kriegsrecht nt.

martyr ['mɑːtə*] n *(lit, fig)* Märtyrer(in f) m; vt zum Märtyrer machen; **~dom** Martyrium nt.

marvel ['mɑːvəl] n Wunder nt; vi sich wundern *(at* über *+acc)*; **~lous**, *(US)* **~ous** a, **~lously**, *(US)* **~ously** ad wunderbar.

Marxism ['mɑːksɪzəm] n Marxismus m.

Marxist ['mɑːksɪst] n Marxist(in f) m.

marzipan [mɑːzɪ'pæn] n Marzipan nt.

mascara [mæs'kɑːrə] n Wimperntusche f.

mascot ['mæskət] n Maskottchen nt.

masculine ['mæskjʊlɪn] a männlich; n Maskulinum nt.

masculinity [mæskjʊ'lɪnɪtɪ] n Männlichkeit f.

mashed [mæʃt] a: **~ potatoes** pl Kartoffelbrei m or -püree nt.

mask [mɑːsk] n *(lit, fig)* Maske f; vt maskieren, verdecken.

masochist ['mæzəʊkɪst] n Masochist(in f) m.

mason ['meɪsn] n *(stone—)* Steinmetz m; *(free—)* Freimaurer m; **~ic** [mə'sɒnɪk] a Freimaurer-; **~ry** Mauerwerk nt.

masquerade [mæskə'reɪd] n Maskerade f; vi sich maskieren, sich verkleiden; **to ~ as** sich ausgeben als.

mass [mæs] n Masse f; *(greater part)* Mehrheit f; *(Rel)* Messe f; **~es of** massenhaft; vt sammeln, anhäufen; vi sich sammeln.

massacre ['mæsəkə*] n Blutbad nt; vt niedermetzeln, massakrieren.

massage ['mæsɑːʒ] n Massage f; vt massieren.

masseur [mæ'sɜː*] n Masseur m.

masseuse mæ'sɜːz] n Masseuse f.

massive ['mæsɪv] a gewaltig, massiv.

mass media ['mæs'miːdɪə] npl Massenmedien pl.

mass-produce ['mæsprə'djuːs] vt serienmäßig herstellen.

mass production ['mæsprə'dʌkʃən] n Serienproduktion f, Massenproduktion f.

mast [mɑːst] n Mast m.

master ['mɑːstə*] n Herr m; *(Naut)* Kapitän m; *(teacher)* Lehrer m; *(artist)* Meister m; vt meistern; *language etc* beherrschen; **~ly** a meisterhaft; **~mind** n Kapazität f; vt geschickt lenken; **M~ of Arts** Magister Artium m; **~piece** Meisterstück nt; *(Art)* Meisterwerk nt; **~ stroke** Glanzstück nt; **~y** Können nt; **to gain ~y over** sb die Oberhand gewinnen über jdn.

masturbate ['mæstəbeɪt] vi masturbieren, onanieren.

masturbation [mæstə'beɪʃən] n Masturbation f, Onanie f.

mat [mæt] n Matte f; *(for table)* Untersetzer m; vi sich verfilzen; vt verfilzen.

match [mætʃ] n Streichholz nt; *(sth corresponding)* Pendant nt; *(Sport)* Wettkampf m; *(ball games)* Spiel nt; **it's a good ~** es paßt gut *(for* zu); **to be a ~ for** sb sich mit jdm messen können; jdm gewachsen sein; **he's a good ~** er ist eine gute Partie; vt *(be alike, suit)* passen zu; *(equal)* gleichkommen *(+dat)*; *(Sport)* antreten lassen; vi zusammenpassen; **~box** Streichholzschachtel f; **~ing** a passend; **~less** a unvergleichlich; **~maker** Kuppler(in f) m.

mate [meɪt] n *(companion)* Kamerad m; *(spouse)* Lebensgefährte m; *(of animal)* Weibchen nt/Männchen nt; *(Naut)* Schiffsoffizier m; vi *(chess)* (schach)matt sein; *(animals)* sich paaren; vt *(chess)* matt setzen.

material [mə'tɪərɪəl] n Material nt; *(for book, cloth)* Material nt, Stoff m; a *(important)* wesentlich; *damage* Sach-; *comforts etc* materiell; **~s** pl Materialien pl; **~istic** a materialistisch; **~ize** vi sich verwirklichen, zustande kommen; **~ly** ad grundlegend.

maternal [mə'tɜːnl] a mütterlich, Mutter-; **~ grandmother** Großmutter mütterlicherseits.

maternity [mə'tɜːnɪtɪ] a Schwangeren-; *dress* Umstands-; *benefit* Wochen-.

matey ['meɪtɪ] a *(Brit col)* kameradschaftlich.

mathematical a, **~ly** ad [mæθə'mætɪkəl, -lɪ] mathematisch.

mathematician [mæθəmə'tɪʃən] n Mathematiker m.

mathematics [mæθə'mætɪks] n Mathematik f.

maths [mæθs] n Mathe f.

matinée ['mætɪneɪ] n Matinee f.

mating ['meɪtɪŋ] n Paarung f; ~ **call** Lockruf m.

matins ['mætɪnz] n (Früh)mette f.

matriarchal [meɪtrɪ'ɑːkl] a matriarchalisch.

matrimonial [mætrɪ'məʊnɪəl] a ehelich, Ehe-.

matrimony ['mætrɪmənɪ] n Ehestand m.

matron ['meɪtrən] n (Med) Oberin f; (Sch) Hausmutter f; ~**ly** a matronenhaft.

matt [mæt] a paint matt.

matter ['mætə°] n (substance) Materie f; (affair) Sache f, Angelegenheit f; (content) Inhalt m; (Med) Eiter m; vi darauf ankommen; **it doesn't** ~ es macht nichts; **no** ~ **how/what** egal wie/was; **what is the** ~? was ist los?; **as a** ~ **of fact** eigentlich; ~-**of-fact** a sachlich, nüchtern.

mattress ['mætrəs] n Matratze f.

mature [mə'tjʊə°] a reif; vi reif werden.

maturity [mə'tjʊərɪtɪ] n Reife f.

maudlin ['mɔːdlɪn] a weinerlich; gefühlsduselig.

maul [mɔːl] vt übel zurichten.

mausoleum [mɔːsə'liːəm] n Mausoleum nt.

mauve [məʊv] a mauve.

mawkish ['mɔːkɪʃ] a kitschig; taste süßlich.

maxi ['mæksɪ] pref Maxi-.

maxim ['mæksɪm] n Maxime f.

maximize ['mæksɪmaɪz] vt maximieren.

maximum ['mæksɪməm] a höchste(r, s), Höchst-, Maximal-; n Höchstgrenze f; Maximum nt.

May [meɪ] n Mai m.

may [meɪ] v aux (be possible) können; (have permission) dürfen; **I** ~ **come** ich komme vielleicht, es kann sein, daß ich komme; **we** ~ **as well go** wir können ruhig gehen; ~ **you be very happy** ich hoffe, ihr seid glücklich; ~**be** ad vielleicht.

Mayday ['meɪdeɪ] n (message) SOS nt.

mayonnaise [meɪə'neɪz] n Mayonnaise f.

mayor [mɛə°] n Bürgermeister m; ~**ess** (wife) (die) Frau f Bürgermeister; (lady —) Bürgermeisterin f.

maypole ['meɪpəʊl] n Maibaum m.

maze [meɪz] n (lit) Irrgarten m; (fig) Wirrwarr nt; **to be in a** ~ (fig) durcheinander sein.

me [miː] pron (acc) mich; (dat) mir; **it's** ~ ich bin's.

meadow ['medəʊ] n Wiese f.

meagre, (US) **meager** ['miːgə°] a dürftig, spärlich.

meal [miːl] n Essen nt, Mahlzeit f; (grain) Schrotmehl nt; **to have a** ~ essen (gehen); ~**time** Essenszeit f; ~**y-mouthed** a: **to be** ~**y-mouthed** d(a)rum herumreden.

mean [miːn] a (stingy) geizig; (spiteful) gemein; (shabby) armselig, schäbig; (average) durchschnittlich, Durchschnitts-; irreg vt (signify) bedeuten; vi (intend) vorhaben, beabsichtigen; (be resolved) entschlossen sein; **he** ~**s well** er meint es gut; **I** ~ **it!** ich meine das ernst!; **do you** ~ **me?** meinen Sie mich?; **it** ~**s nothing to me** es sagt mir nichts; n (average) Durchschnitt m; ~**s** pl Mittel pl; (wealth) Vermögen nt; **by** ~ **of** durch; **by all** ~**s** selbstverständlich; **by no** ~**s** keineswegs.

meander [mɪ'ændə°] vi sich schlängeln.

meaning ['miːnɪŋ] n Bedeutung f; (of life) Sinn m; ~**ful** a bedeutungsvoll; life sinnvoll; ~**less** a sinnlos.

meanness ['miːnnəs] n (stinginess) Geiz m; (spitefulness) Gemeinheit f; (shabbiness) Schäbigkeit f.

meantime ['miːntaɪm] ad, **meanwhile** ['miːnwaɪl] ad inzwischen, mittlerweile; **for the** ~ vorerst.

measles ['miːzlz] n Masern pl; **German** ~ Röteln pl.

measly ['miːzlɪ] a (col) poplig.

measurable ['meʒərəbl] a meßbar.

measure ['meʒə°] n Maß nt; (step) Maßnahme f; **to be a** ~ **of sth** etw erkennen lassen; ~**d** a (slow) gemessen; ~**ment** (way of measuring) Messung f; (amount measured) Maß nt.

meat [miːt] n Fleisch nt; ~**y** a (lit) fleischig; (fig) gehaltvoll.

mechanic [mɪ'kænɪk] n Mechaniker m; ~**s** Mechanik f; ~**al** a mechanisch.

mechanism ['mekənɪzəm] n Mechanismus m.

mechanization [mekənaɪ'zeɪʃən] n Mechanisierung f.

mechanize ['mekənaɪz] vt mechanisieren.

medal ['medl] n Medaille f; (decoration) Orden m; ~**lion** [mɪ'dælɪən] Medaillon nt; ~**list,** (US) ~**ist** Medaillengewinner(in f) m.

meddle ['medl] vi sich einmischen (in in +acc); (tamper) hantieren (with an +dat); ~ **with sb** sich mit jdm einlassen.

media ['miːdɪə] npl Medien pl.

mediate ['miːdɪeɪt] vi vermitteln.

mediation [miːdɪ'eɪʃən] n Vermittlung f.

mediator ['miːdɪeɪtə°] n Vermittler m.

medical ['medɪkəl] a medizinisch; Medizin-; ärztlich; n (ärztliche) Untersuchung f.

medicated ['medɪkeɪtɪd] a medizinisch.

medicinal [me'dɪsɪnl] a medizinisch, Heil-.

medicine ['medsɪn] n Medizin f; (drugs) Arznei f; ~ **chest** Hausapotheke f.

medieval [medɪ'iːvəl] a mittelalterlich.

mediocre [miːdɪ'əʊkə°] a mittelmäßig.

mediocrity [miːdɪ'ɒkrɪtɪ] n Mittelmäßigkeit f; (person also) kleine(r) Geist m.

meditate ['medɪteɪt] vi nachdenken (on über +acc); meditieren (on über +acc).

meditation [medɪ'teɪʃən] n Nachsinnen nt; Meditation f.

medium ['miːdɪəm] a mittlere(r, s), Mittel-, mittel-; n Mitte f; (means) Mittel nt; (person) Medium nt.

medley ['medlɪ] n Gemisch nt.

meek a, ~**ly** ad [miːk, -lɪ] sanft(mütig); (pej) duckmäuserisch.

meet [miːt] irreg vt (encounter) treffen, begegnen (+dat); (by arrangement) sich treffen mit; difficulties stoßen auf (+acc);

(become acquainted with) kennenlernen; *(fetch)* abholen; *(join)* zusammentreffen mit; *(river)* fließen in (+acc); *(satisfy)* entsprechen (+dat); *debt* bezahlen; **pleased to ~ you!** angenehm!; *vi* sich treffen; *(become acquainted)* sich kennenlernen; *(join)* sich treffen; *(rivers)* ineinanderfließen; *(roads)* zusammenlaufen; **~ with** *vt problems* stoßen auf (+acc); *(US: people)* zusammentreffen mit; **~ing** Treffen *nt*; *(business —)* Besprechung *f*, Konferenz *f*; *(discussion)* Sitzung *f*; *(assembly)* Versammlung *f*; **~ing place** Treffpunkt *m*.

megaphone ['megǝfǝun] *n* Megaphon *nt*.

melancholy ['melǝnkǝlı] *n* Melancholie *f*; *a person* melancholisch, schwermütig; *sight, event* traurig.

mellow ['melǝu] *a* mild, weich; *fruit* reif, weich; *(fig)* gesetzt; *vi* reif werden.

melodious [mı'lǝudıǝs] *a* wohlklingend.

melodrama ['melǝudrɑːmǝ] *n* Melodrama *nt*; **~tic** [melǝudrǝ'mætık] *a* melodramatisch.

melody ['melǝdı] *n* Melodie *f*.

melon ['melǝn] *n* Melone *f*.

melt [melt] *vi* schmelzen; *(anger)* verfliegen; *vt* schmelzen; **~ away** *vi* dahinschmelzen; **~ down** *vt* einschmelzen; **~ing point** Schmelzpunkt *m*; **~ing pot** *(fig)* Schmelztiegel *m*; **to be in the ~ing pot** in der Schwebe sein.

member ['membǝ*] *n* Mitglied *nt*; *(of tribe, species)* Angehörige(r) *m*; *(Anat)* Glied *nt*; **~ship** Mitgliedschaft *f*.

membrane ['membreın] *n* Membrane *f*.

memento [mǝ'mentǝu] *n* Andenken *nt*.

memo ['memǝu] *n* Notiz *f*, Mitteilung *f*.

memoirs ['memwɑː*z] *npl* Memoiren *pl*.

memorable ['memǝrǝbl] *a* denkwürdig.

memorandum [memǝ'rændǝm] *n* Notiz *f*, Mitteilung *f*; *(Pol)* Memorandum *nt*.

memorial [mı'mɔːrıǝl] *n* Denkmal *nt*; *a* Gedenk-.

memorize ['memǝraız] *vt* sich einprägen.

memory ['memǝrı] *n* Gedächtnis *nt*; *(of computer)* Speicher *m*; *(sth recalled)* Erinnerung *f*; **in ~ of** zur Erinnerung an (+acc); **from ~** aus dem Kopf.

men [men] *npl of* **man**.

menace ['menıs] *n* Drohung *f*, Gefahr *f*; *vt* bedrohen.

menacing *a*, **~ly** *ad* ['menısıŋ, -lı] drohend.

ménage [me'nɑːʒ] *n* Haushalt *m*.

menagerie [mı'nædʒǝrı] *n* Tierschau *f*.

mend [mend] *vt* reparieren, flicken; *n* ausgebesserte Stelle *f*; **on the ~** auf dem Wege der Besserung.

menial ['miːnıǝl] *a* niedrig, untergeordnet.

meningitis [menın'dʒaıtıs] *n* Hirnhautentzündung *f*, Meningitis *f*.

menopause ['menǝupɔːz] *n* Wechseljahre *pl*, Menopause *f*.

menstrual ['menstruǝl] *a* Monats-, Menstruations-.

menstruate ['menstrueıt] *vi* menstruieren.

menstruation [menstru'eıʃǝn] *n* Menstruation *f*.

mental ['mentl] *a* geistig, Geistes-; *arithmetic* Kopf-; *hospital* Nerven-; *cruelty* seelisch; *(col: abnormal)* verrückt; **~ity** [men'tælıtı] Mentalität *f*; **~ly** *ad* geistig; **~ly ill** geisteskrank.

mentholated ['menθǝleıtıd] *a* Menthol-.

mention ['menʃǝn] *n* Erwähnung *f*; *vt* erwähnen; *names* nennen; **don't ~ it!** bitte (sehr), gern geschehen.

menu ['menjuː] *n* Speisekarte *f*; *(food)* Speisen *pl*.

mercantile ['mɜːkǝntaıl] *a* Handels-.

mercenary ['mɜːsınǝrı] *a person* geldgierig; *(Mil)* Söldner-; *n* Söldner *m*.

merchandise ['mɜːtʃǝndaız] *n* (Handels)ware *f*.

merchant ['mɜːtʃǝnt] *n* Kaufmann *m*; *a* Handels-; **~ navy** Handelsmarine *f*.

merciful ['mɜːsıful] *a* gnädig, barmherzig; **~ly** ['mɜːsıfǝlı] *ad* gnädig; *(fortunately)* glücklicherweise.

merciless *a*, **~ly** *ad* ['mɜːsılǝs, -lı] erbarmunglos.

mercurial [mɜː'kjuǝrıǝl] *a* quecksilbrig, Quecksilber-.

mercury ['mɜːkjurı] *n* Quecksilber *nt*.

mercy ['mɜːsı] *n* Erbarmen *nt*; Gnade *f*; *(blessing)* Segen *m*; **at the ~ of** ausgeliefert (+dat).

mere *a*, **~ly** *ad* [mıǝ*, 'mıǝlı] bloß.

merge [mɜːdʒ] *vt* verbinden; *(Comm)* fusionieren; *vi* verschmelzen; *(roads)* zusammenlaufen; *(Comm)* fusionieren; **to ~ into** übergehen in (+acc); **~r** *(Comm)* Fusion *f*.

meridian [mǝ'rıdıǝn] *n* Meridian *m*.

meringue [mǝ'ræŋ] *n* Baiser *nt*, Schaumgebäck *nt*.

merit ['merıt] *n* Verdienst *nt*; *(advantage)* Vorzug *m*; **to judge on ~** nach Leistung beurteilen; *vt* verdienen.

mermaid ['mɜːmeıd] *n* Wassernixe *f*, Meerjungfrau *f*.

merrily ['merıdʒ] *ad* lustig.

merriment ['merımǝnt] *n* Fröhlichkeit *f*; *(laughter)* Gelächter *nt*.

merry ['merı] *a* fröhlich; *(col)* angeheitert; **~-go-round** Karussell *nt*.

mesh [meʃ] *n* Masche *f*; *vi (gears)* ineinandergreifen.

mesmerize ['mezmǝraız] *vt* hypnotisieren; *(fig)* faszinieren.

mess [mes] *n* Unordnung *f*; *(dirt)* Schmutz *m*; *(trouble)* Schwierigkeiten *pl*; *(Mil)* Messe *f*; **to look a ~** fürchterlich aussehen; **to make a ~ of sth** etw verpfuschen; **~ about** *vi (tinker with)* herummurksen *(with* an +dat); *(play fool)* herumalbern; *(do nothing in particular)* herumgammeln; **~ up** *vt* verpfuschen; *(make untidy)* in Unordnung bringen.

message ['mesıdʒ] *n* Mitteilung *f*, Nachricht *f*; **to get the ~** kapieren.

messenger ['mesındʒǝ*] *n* Bote *m*.

messy ['mesı] *a* schmutzig; *(untidy)* unordentlich.

metabolism [me'tæbǝlızǝm] *n* Stoffwechsel *m*.

metal ['metl] *n* Metall *nt*; **~lic** [mı'tælık] *a*

metallisch; ~**lurgy** [me'tælədʒɪ] Metallurgie f.

metamorphosis [metə'mɔːfəsɪs] n Metamorphose f.

metaphor ['metəfɔː*] n Metapher f; ~**ical** [metə'fɔrɪkəl] a bildlich, metaphorisch.

metaphysics [metə'fɪzɪks] n Metaphysik f.

meteor ['miːtɪə*] n Meteor m; ~**ic** [miːtɪ'ɒrɪk] a meteorisch, Meteor-; ~**ite** Meteorit m; ~**ological** [miːtɪərə'lɒdʒɪkəl] a meteorologisch; ~**ology** [miːtɪə'rɒlədʒɪ] Meteorologie f.

meter ['miːtə*] n Zähler m; (US) = **metre**.

method ['meθəd] n Methode f; ~**ical** [mɪ'θɒdɪkəl] a methodisch; ~**ology** [meθə'dɒlədʒɪ] Methodik f.

methylated spirit ['meθɪleɪtɪd' spɪrɪt] n (also **meths**) (Brenn)spiritus m.

meticulous [mɪ'tɪkjʊləs] a (über)genau.

metre ['miːtə*] n Meter m or nt; (verse) Metrum nt.

metric ['metrɪk] a (also ~**al**) metrisch; ~**ation** Umstellung f auf das Dezimalsystem; ~ **system** Dezimalsystem nt.

metronome ['metrənəʊm] n Metronom nt.

metropolis [me'trɒpəlɪs] n Metropole f.

mettle ['metl] n Mut m.

mezzanine ['mezəniːn] n Hochparterre nt.

miaow [miː'aʊ] vi miauen.

mice [maɪs] npl of **mouse**.

mickey ['mɪkɪ] n: **to take the ~ out of sb** (col) jdn auf den Arm nehmen.

microbe ['maɪkrəʊb] n Mikrobe f.

microfilm ['maɪkrəʊfɪlm] n Mikrofilm m; vt auf Mikrofilm aufnehmen.

microphone ['maɪkrəfəʊn] n Mikrophon nt.

microscope ['maɪkrəskəʊp] n Mikroskop nt.

microscopic [maɪkrə'skɒpɪk] a mikroskopisch.

mid [mɪd] a mitten in (+dat); **in the ~ eighties** Mitte der achtziger Jahre; **in ~ course** mittendrin.

midday ['mɪddeɪ] n Mittag m.

middle ['mɪdl] n Mitte f; (waist) Taille f; **in the ~ of** mitten in (+dat); a mittlere(r, s), Mittel-; ~-**aged** a mittleren Alters; **the M~ Ages** pl das Mittelalter; ~-**class** Mittelstand m or -klasse f; a Mittelstands-, Mittelklassen-; **the M~ East** der Nahe Osten; ~**man** (Comm) Zwischenhändler m; ~ **name** zweiter Vorname m; ~-**of-the-road** a gemäßigt.

middling ['mɪdlɪŋ] a mittelmäßig.

midge [mɪdʒ] n Mücke f.

midget ['mɪdʒɪt] n Liliputaner(in f) m; a Kleinst-.

midnight ['mɪdnaɪt] n Mitternacht f.

midriff ['mɪdrɪf] n Taille f.

midst [mɪdst] n **in the ~ of** persons mitten unter (+dat); things mitten in (+dat); **in our ~** unter uns.

midsummer ['mɪd'sʌmə*] n Hochsommer m; **M~'s Day** Sommersonnenwende f.

midway ['mɪd'weɪ] ad auf halbem Wege; a Mittel-.

midweek ['mɪd'wiːk] a, ad in der Mitte der Woche.

midwife ['mɪdwaɪf] n Hebamme f; ~**ry** ['mɪdwɪfərɪ] Geburtshilfe f.

midwinter ['mɪd'wɪntə*] n tiefste(r) Winter m.

might [maɪt] n Macht f, Kraft f; pt of **may**; **I ~ come** ich komme vielleicht; ~**ily** ad mächtig; ~**n't** = **might not**; ~**y** a, ad mächtig.

migraine ['miːgreɪn] n Migräne f.

migrant ['maɪgrənt] n (bird) Zugvogel m; (worker) Saison- or Wanderarbeiter m; a Wander-; bird Zug-.

migrate [maɪ'greɪt] vi (ab)wandern; (birds) (fort)ziehen.

migration [maɪ'greɪʃən] n Wanderung f, Zug m.

mike [maɪk] n = **microphone**.

mild [maɪld] a mild; medicine, interest leicht; person sanft.

mildew ['mɪldjuː] n (on plants) Mehltau m; (on food) Schimmel m.

mildly ['maɪldlɪ] ad leicht; **to put it ~** gelinde gesagt.

mildness ['maɪldnəs] n Milde f.

mile [maɪl] n Meile f; ~**age** Meilenzahl f; ~**stone** (lit, fig) Meilenstein m.

milieu ['miːljɜː] n Milieu nt.

militant ['mɪlɪtənt] n Militante(r) mf; a militant.

militarism ['mɪlɪtərɪzəm] n Militarismus m.

military ['mɪlɪtərɪ] a militärisch, Militär-, Wehr-; n Militär nt.

militate ['mɪlɪteɪt] vi sprechen; entgegenwirken (against dat).

militia [mɪ'lɪʃə] n Miliz f, Bürgerwehr f.

milk [mɪlk] n Milch f; vt (lit, fig) melken; ~ **chocolate** Milchschokolade f; ~**ing** Melken nt; ~**man** Milchmann m; ~ **shake** Milchmixgetränk nt; **M~y Way** Milchstraße f.

mill [mɪl] n Mühle f; (factory) Fabrik f; vt mahlen; vi (move around) umherlaufen; ~**ed** a gemahlen.

millennium [mɪ'lenɪəm] n Jahrtausend nt.

miller ['mɪlə*] n Müller m.

millet ['mɪlɪt] n Hirse f.

milligram(me) ['mɪlɪgræm] n Milligramm nt.

millilitre, (US) ~**liter** ['mɪlɪliːtə*] n Milliliter m.

millimetre, (US) ~**meter** ['mɪlɪmiːtə*] n Millimeter m.

milliner ['mɪlɪnə*] n Hutmacher(in f) m; ~**y** (hats) Hüte pl, Modewaren pl; (business) Hutgeschäft nt.

million ['mɪljən] n Million f; ~**aire** [mɪljə'nɛə*] Millionär(in f) m.

millwheel ['mɪlwiːl] n Mühlrad nt.

milometer [maɪ'lɒmɪtə*] n Kilometerzähler m.

mime [maɪm] n Pantomime f; (actor) Mime m, Mimin f; vti mimen.

mimic ['mɪmɪk] n Mimiker m; vti nachahmen; ~**ry** ['mɪmɪkrɪ] Nachahmung f; (Biol) Mimikry f.

mince [mɪns] vt (zer)hacken; vi (walk)

trippeln; n (meat) Hackfleisch nt; ~meat
süße Pastetenfüllung f; ~ pie gefüllte
(süße) Pastete f.
mincing ['mɪnsɪŋ] a manner affektiert.
mind [maɪnd] n Verstand m, Geist m;
(opinion) Meinung f; on my ~ auf dem
Herzen; to my ~ meiner Meinung nach;
to be out of one's ~ wahnsinnig sein; to
bear or keep in ~ bedenken, nicht vergessen; to change one's ~ es sich (dat)
anders überlegen; to make up one's ~
sich entschließen; to have sth in ~ an
etw (acc) denken; etw beabsichtigen; to
have a good ~ to do sth große Lust
haben, etw zu tun; vt aufpassen auf (+acc);
(object to) etwas haben gegen; vi etwas
dagegen haben; I don't ~ the rain der
Regen macht mir nichts aus; do you ~ if
I ... macht es Ihnen etwas aus, wenn ich ...;
do you ~! na hören Sie mall; never ~!
macht nichts!; '~ the step' 'Vorsicht
Stufe'; ~ your own business kümmern
Sie sich um Ihre eigenen Angelegen-
heiten; ~ful a achtsam (of auf +acc);
~less a achtlos, dumm.
mine [maɪn] poss pron meine(r, s); n
(coal—) Bergwerk nt; (Mil) Mine f; (source)
Fundgrube f; vt abbauen; (Mil) verminen;
vi Bergbau betreiben; to ~ for sth etw
gewinnen; ~ detector Minensuchgerät
nt; ~field Minenfeld nt; ~er Bergarbeiter m.
mineral ['mɪnərəl] a mineralisch,
Mineral-; n Mineral nt; ~ water Mineralwasser nt.
minesweeper ['maɪnswiːpə*] n Minen-
suchboot nt.
mingle ['mɪŋgl] vt vermischen; vi sich
mischen (with unter +acc).
mingy ['mɪndʒɪ] a (col) knickerig.
mini ['mɪnɪ] pref Mini-, Klein-.
miniature ['mɪnɪtʃə*] a Miniatur-, Klein-; n
Miniatur f; in ~ en miniature.
minibus ['mɪnɪbʌs] n Kleinbus m, Minibus
m.
minicab ['mɪnɪkæb] n Kleintaxi nt.
minim ['mɪnɪm] n halbe Note f.
minimal ['mɪnɪml] a kleinste(r, s),
minimal, Mindest-.
minimize ['mɪnɪmaɪz] vt auf das
Mindestmaß beschränken; (belittle) herabsetzen.
minimum ['mɪnɪməm] n Minimum nt; a
Mindest-.
mining ['maɪnɪŋ] n Bergbau m; a Bergbau-,
Berg-.
minion ['mɪnjən] n (pej) Trabant m.
miniskirt ['mɪnɪskɜːt] n Minirock m.
minister ['mɪnɪstə*] n (Pol) Minister m;
(Eccl) Geistliche(r) m, Pfarrer m; ~ial
[mɪnɪs'tɪərɪəl] a ministeriell, Minister-.
ministry ['mɪnɪstrɪ] n (government body)
Ministerium nt; (Eccl) (office) geistliche(s)
Amt nt; (all ministers) Geistlichkeit f.
mink [mɪŋk] n Nerz m.
minnow ['mɪnəʊ] n Elritze f.
minor ['maɪnə*] a kleiner; (operation) leicht;
problem, poet unbedeutend; (Mus) Moll;
Smith ~ Smith der Jüngere; n (Brit: under

18) Minderjährige(r) mf; ~ity [maɪ'nɒrɪtɪ]
Minderheit f.
minster ['mɪnstə*] n Münster nt,
Kathedrale f.
minstrel ['mɪnstrəl] n (Hist) Spielmann m,
Minnesänger m.
mint [mɪnt] n Minze f; (sweet) Pfefferminz-
bonbon nt; (place) Münzstätte f; a condition
(wie) neu; stamp ungestempelt; ~ sauce
Minzsoße f.
minuet [mɪnju'et] n Menuett nt.
minus ['maɪnəs] n Minuszeichen nt;
(amount) Minusbetrag m; prep minus,
weniger.
minute [maɪ'njuːt] a winzig, sehr klein;
(detailed) minuziös; ['mɪnɪt] n Minute f;
(moment) Augenblick m; ~s pl Protokoll
nt; ~ly [maɪ'njuːtlɪ] ad (in detail) genau.
miracle ['mɪrəkl] n Wunder nt; ~ play
geistliche(s) Drama nt.
miraculous [mɪ'rækjʊləs] a wunderbar;
~ly ad auf wunderbare Weise.
mirage ['mɪrɑːʒ] n Luftspiegelung f, Fata
Morgana f.
mirror ['mɪrə*] n Spiegel m; vt
(wider)spiegeln.
mirth [mɜːθ] n Freude f; Heiterkeit f.
misadventure [mɪsəd'ventʃə*] n Mißgeschick nt, Unfall m.
misanthropist [mɪ'zænθrəpɪst] n
Menschenfeind m.
misapprehension ['mɪsæprɪ'henʃən] n
Mißverständnis nt; to be under the ~
that . . . irrtümlicherweise annehmen,
daß . . .
misappropriate ['mɪsə'prəʊprɪeɪt] vt
funds veruntreuen.
misappropriation ['mɪsəprəʊprɪ'eɪʃən] n
Veruntreuung f.
misbehave ['mɪsbɪ'heɪv] vi sich schlecht
benehmen.
miscalculate ['mɪs'kælkjʊleɪt] vt falsch
berechnen.
miscalculation ['mɪskælkjʊ'leɪʃən] n
Rechenfehler m.
miscarriage ['mɪskærɪdʒ] n (Med)
Fehlgeburt f; ~ of justice Fehlurteil nt.
miscellaneous [mɪsɪ'leɪnɪəs] a verschieden.
miscellany [mɪ'selənɪ] n (bunte) Sammlung f.
mischance [mɪs'tʃɑːns] n Mißgeschick nt.
mischief ['mɪstʃɪf] n Unfug m; (harm)
Schaden m.
mischievous a, ~ly ad ['mɪstʃɪvəs, -lɪ]
person durchtrieben; glance verschmitzt;
rumour bösartig.
misconception ['mɪskən'sepʃən] n fälsch-
liche Annahme f.
misconduct [mɪs'kɒndʌkt] n Vergehen nt.
misconstrue ['mɪskən'struː] vt mißverstehen.
miscount ['mɪs'kaʊnt] vt falsch
(be)rechnen.
misdemeanour, (US) **misdemeanor**
[mɪsdɪ'miːnə*] n Vergehen nt.
misdirect ['mɪsdɪ'rekt] vt person
irreleiten; letter fehlleiten.
miser ['maɪzə*] n Geizhals m.

miserable ['mizərəbl] a (unhappy) unglücklich; headache, weather fürchterlich; (poor) elend; (contemptible) erbärmlich.

miserably ['mizərəbli] ad unglücklich; fail kläglich.

miserly ['maizəli] a geizig.

misery ['mizəri] n Elend nt, Qual f.

misfire ['mis'faiə*] vi (gun) versagen; (engine) fehlzünden; (plan) fehlgehen.

misfit ['misfit] n Außenseiter m.

misfortune [mis'fɔːtʃən] n Unglück nt.

misgiving [mis'givin] n (often pl) Befürchtung f, Bedenken pl.

misguided ['mis'gaidid] a fehlgeleitet; opinions irrig.

mishandle ['mis'hændl] vt falsch handhaben.

mishap ['mishæp] n Unglück nt; (slight) Panne f.

mishear ['mis'hiə*] vt irreg mißverstehen.

misinform ['misin'fɔːm] vt falsch unterrichten.

misinterpret ['misin'tɜːprit] vt falsch auffassen; ~ation ['misintɜːpri'teiʃən] falsche Auslegung f.

misjudge ['mis'dʒʌdʒ] vt falsch beurteilen.

mislay [mis'lei] vt irreg verlegen.

mislead [mis'liːd] vt irreg (deceive) irreführen; ~ing a irreführend.

mismanage ['mis'mænidʒ] vt schlecht verwalten; ~ment Mißwirtschaft f.

misnomer ['mis'nəumə*] n falsche Bezeichnung f.

misogynist [mi'sɔdʒinist] n Weiberfeind m.

misplace ['mis'pleis] vt verlegen.

misprint ['misprint] n Druckfehler m.

mispronounce ['misprə'nauns] vt falsch aussprechen.

misread ['mis'riːd] vt irreg falsch lesen.

misrepresent ['misrepri'zent] vt falsch darstellen.

miss [mis] vt (fail to hit, catch) verfehlen; (not notice) verpassen; (be too late) versäumen, verpassen; (omit) auslassen; (regret the absence of) vermissen; I ~ you du fehlst mir; vi fehlen; n (shot) Fehlschuß m; (failure) Fehlschlag m; (title) Fräulein nt.

missal ['misəl] n Meßbuch nt.

misshapen ['mis'ʃeipən] a mißgestaltet.

missile ['misail] n Geschoß nt, Rakete f.

missing ['misin] a person vermißt; thing fehlend; to be ~ fehlen.

mission ['miʃən] n (work) Auftrag n, Mission f; (people) Delegation f; (Rel) Mission f; ~ary Missionar(in f) m.

misspent ['mis'spent] a youth vergeudet.

mist [mist] n Dunst m, Nebel m; vi (also ~ over, ~ up) sich beschlagen.

mistake [mis'teik] n Fehler m; vt irreg (misunderstand) mißverstehen; (mix up) verwechseln (for mit); ~n a idea falsch; ~n identity Verwechslung f; to be ~n sich irren.

mister ['mistə*] n (abbr Mr) Herr m.

mistletoe ['misltəu] n Mistel f.

mistranslation ['mistræns'leiʃən] n falsche Übersetzung f.

mistreat [mis'triːt] vt schlecht behandeln.

mistress ['mistris] n (teacher) Lehrerin f; (in house) Herrin f; (lover) Geliebte f; (abbr Mrs) Frau f.

mistrust ['mis'trʌst] vt mißtrauen (+dat).

misty ['misti] a neblig.

misunderstand ['misʌndə'stænd] vti irreg mißverstehen, falsch verstehen; ~ing Mißverständnis nt; (disagreement) Meinungsverschiedenheit f.

misunderstood ['misʌndə'stud] a person unverstanden.

misuse ['mis'juːs] n falsche(r) Gebrauch m; ['mis'juːz] vt falsch gebrauchen.

mite [mait] n Milbe f; (fig) bißchen nt.

mitigate ['mitigeit] vt pain lindern; punishment mildern.

mitre, (US) miter ['maitə*] n (Eccl) Mitra f.

mitt(en) ['mit(n)] n Fausthandschuh m.

mix [miks] vt (blend) (ver)mischen; vi (liquids) sich (ver)mischen lassen; (people) (get on) sich vertragen; (associate) Kontakt haben; he ~es well er ist kontaktfreudig; n (mixture) Mischung f; ~ed a gemischt; ~er (for food) Mixer m; ~ture (assortment) Mischung f; (Med) Saft m; ~-up Durcheinander nt, Verwechslung f; ~ up vt (mix) zusammenmischen; (confuse) verwechseln; to be ~ed up in sth in etw (dat) verwickelt sein; ~-ed-up a papers, person durcheinander.

moan [məun] n Stöhnen nt; (complaint) Klage f; vi stöhnen; (complain) maulen; ~ing Stöhnen nt; Gemaule f.

moat [məut] n (Burg)graben m.

mob [mɔb] n Mob m; (the masses) Pöbel m; vt star herfallen über (+acc).

mobile ['məubail] a beweglich; library etc fahrbar; n (decoration) Mobile nt; ~ home Wohnwagen m.

mobility [məu'biliti] n Beweglichkeit f.

moccasin ['mɔkəsin] n Mokassin m.

mock [mɔk] vt verspotten; (defy) trotzen (+dat); a Schein-; ~ery Spott m; (person) Gespött nt; ~ing a tone spöttisch; ~ing bird Spottdrossel f; ~-up Modell nt.

mode [məud] n (Art f und) Weise f.

model ['mɔdl] n Modell nt; (example) Vorbild nt; (in fashion) Mannequin nt; vt (make) formen, modellieren, bilden; (clothes) vorführen; a railway Modell-; (perfect) Muster-; vorbildlich; ~ling, (US) ~ing ['mɔdlin] (~ making) Basteln nt.

moderate ['mɔdərət] a gemäßigt; (fairly good) mittelmäßig; n (Pol) Gemäßigte(r) mf; ['mɔdəreit] vi sich mäßigen; vt mäßigen; ~ly ['mɔdərətli] ad mäßig.

moderation [mɔdə'reiʃən] n Mäßigung f; in ~ mit Maßen.

modern ['mɔdən] a modern; history, languages neuere(r, s); Greek etc Neu-; ~ity [mɔ'dɜːniti] Modernität f; ~ization [mɔdənai'zeiʃən] Modernisierung f; ~ize vt modernisieren.

modest a, ~ly ad ['mɔdist, -li] attitude bescheiden; meal, home einfach; (chaste) schamhaft; ~y Bescheidenheit f; (chastity) Schamgefühl nt.

modicum ['modikəm] n bißchen nt.

modification [modifi'keiʃən] n (Ab)änderung f.

modify ['modifai] vt abändern; (Gram) modifizieren.

modulation [modju'leiʃən] n Modulation f.

module ['modjul] n (Raum)kapsel f.

mohair ['məuhɛə*] n Mohair m; a Mohair-.

moist [moist] a feucht; ~en ['moisn] vt befeuchten; ~ure Feuchtigkeit f; ~urizer Feuchtigkeitscreme f.

molar ['məulə*] n Backenzahn m.

molasses [mə'læsiz] npl Melasse f.

mold [məuld] (US) = **mould.**

mole [məul] n (spot) Leberfleck m; (animal) Maulwurf m; (pier) Mole f.

molecular [mə'lekjulə*] a molekular, Molekular-.

molecule ['molikju:l] n Molekül nt.

molest [məu'lest] vt belästigen.

mollusc ['moləsk] n Molluske f, Weichtier nt.

mollycoddle ['molikodl] vt verhätscheln.

molt [məult] (US) = **moult.**

molten ['məultən] a geschmolzen.

moment ['məumənt] n Moment m, Augenblick m; (importance) Tragweite f; ~ of truth Stunde f der Wahrheit; any ~ jeden Augenblick; ~arily [məumən-'tɛrəli] ad momentan; ~ary a kurz; ~ous [məu'mentəs] a folgenschwer; ~um [məu'mentəm] Schwung m.

monarch ['monək] n Herrscher(in f) m; ~ist Monarchist(in f) m; ~y Monarchie f.

monastery ['monəstri] n Kloster nt.

monastic [mə'næstik] a klösterlich, Kloster-.

Monday ['mʌndei] n Montag m.

monetary ['mʌnitəri] a geldlich, Geld-; (of currency) Währungs-, monetär.

money ['mʌni] n Geld nt; ~ed a vermögend; ~lender Geldverleiher m; ~making a einträglich, lukrativ; n Gelderwerb m; ~ order Postanweisung f.

mongol ['mongəl] n (Med) mongoloide(s) Kind nt; a mongolisch; (Med) mongoloid.

mongoose ['mongu:s] n Mungo m.

mongrel ['mʌngrəl] n Promenadenmischung f; a Misch-.

monitor ['monitə*] n (Sch) Klassenordner m; (television ~) Monitor m; vt broadcasts abhören; (control) überwachen.

monk [mʌnk] n Mönch m.

monkey ['mʌnki] n Affe m; ~ nut Erdnuß f; ~ wrench (Tech) Engländer m, Franzose m.

mono- ['monəu] pref Mono-.

monochrome ['monəkrəum] a schwarzweiß.

monocle ['monəkl] n Monokel nt.

monogram ['monəgræm] n Monogramm nt.

monolithic [monəu'liθik] a monolithisch.

monologue ['monəlog] n Monolog m.

monopolize [mə'nopəlaiz] vt beherrschen.

monopoly [mə'nopəli] n Monopol nt.

monorail ['monəureil] n Einschienenbahn f.

monosyllabic ['monəusi'læbik] a einsilbig.

monotone ['monətəun] n gleichbleibende(r) Ton(fall) m.

monotonous [mə'notənəs] a eintönig, monoton.

monotony [mə'notəni] n Eintönigkeit f, Monotonie f.

monseigneur [monsen'jɜ:*], **monsignor** [mon'si:njə*] n Monsignore m.

monsoon [mon'su:n] n Monsun m.

monster ['monstə*] n Ungeheuer nt; (person) Scheusal nt; a (col) Riesen-.

monstrosity [mons'trositi] n Ungeheuerlichkeit f; (thing) Monstrosität f.

monstrous ['monstrəs] a (shocking) gräßlich, ungeheuerlich; (huge) riesig.

montage [mon'ta:ʒ] n Montage f.

month [mʌnθ] n Monat m; ~ly a monatlich, Monats-; ad einmal im Monat; n (magazine) Monatsschrift f.

monument ['monjumənt] n Denkmal nt; ~al [monju'mentl] a (huge) gewaltig; ignorance ungeheuer.

moo [mu:] vi muhen.

mood [mu:d] n Stimmung f, Laune f; to be in the ~ for aufgelegt sein zu; I am not in the ~ for laughing mir ist nicht zum Lachen zumute; ~ily ad launisch; ~iness Launenhaftigkeit f; ~y a launisch.

moon [mu:n] n Mond m; ~beam Mondstrahl m; ~less a mondlos; ~light Mondlicht nt; ~lit a mondhell; ~shot Mondflug m.

moor [muə*] n Heide f, Hochmoor nt; vt ship festmachen, verankern; vi anlegen; ~ings pl Liegeplatz m; ~land Heidemoor nt.

moose [mu:s] n Elch m.

moot [mu:t] vt aufwerfen; a: ~ point strittige(r) Punkt m.

mop [mop] n Mop m; vt (auf)wischen; ~ of hair Mähne f.

mope [məup] vi Trübsal blasen.

moped ['məuped] n (Brit) Moped nt.

moping ['məupiŋ] a trübselig.

moquette [mo'ket] n Plüschgewebe nt.

moral ['morəl] a moralisch; values sittlich; (virtuous) tugendhaft; n Moral f; ~s pl Moral f; ~e [mo'ra:l] Moral f, Stimmung f; ~ity [mə'ræliti] Sittlichkeit f; ~ly ad moralisch.

morass [mə'ræs] n Sumpf m.

morbid ['mo:bid] a morbid, krankhaft; jokes makaber.

more [mo:*] a, n, pron, ad mehr; ~ or less mehr oder weniger; ~ than ever mehr denn je; a few ~ noch ein paar; ~ beautiful schöner; ~over ad überdies.

morgue [mo:g] n Leichenschauhaus nt.

moribund ['moribʌnd] a aussterbend.

morning ['mo:niŋ] n Morgen m; a morgendlich, Morgen-, Früh-; in the ~ am Morgen; ~ sickness (Schwangerschafts)erbrechen nt.

moron ['mo:ron] n Schwachsinnige(r) m; ~ic [mə'ronik] a schwachsinnig.

morose [mɔ'rəus] a mürrisch.
morphine ['mɔ:fi:n] n Morphium nt.
Morse [mɔ:s] n (also ~ **code**) Morse-
alphabet nt.
morsel ['mɔ:sl] n Stückchen nt, bißchen nt.
mortal ['mɔ:tl] a sterblich; (deadly) tödlich;
(very great) Todes-; n (human being)
Sterbliche(r) mf; ~**ity** [mɔ:'tæliti]
Sterblichkeit f; (death rate) Sterblichkeitsziffer f; ~**ly** ad tödlich.
mortar ['mɔ:tə*] n (for building) Mörtel m;
(bowl) Mörser m; (Mil) Granatwerfer m.
mortgage ['mɔ:gidʒ] n Hypothek f; vt eine
Hypothek aufnehmen (+acc).
mortification [mɔ:tifi'keiʃən] n
Beschämung f.
mortified ['mɔ:tifaid] a: I was ~ es war
mir schrecklich peinlich.
mortuary ['mɔ:tjuəri] n Leichenhalle f.
mosaic [məu'zeiik] n Mosaik nt.
mosque [mɔsk] n Moschee f.
mosquito [mɔs'ki:təu] n Moskito m.
moss [mɔs] n Moos nt; ~y a bemoost.
most [məust] a meiste(r, s); ~ **men** die
meisten Männer; ad am meisten; (very)
höchst; n das meiste, der größte Teil;
(people) die meisten; ~ **of the time**
meistens, die meiste Zeit; ~ **of the**
winter fast den ganzen Winter über; **the**
~ **beautiful** der/die/das Schönste; **at**
the (very) ~ allerhöchstens; **to make**
the ~ **of** das Beste machen aus; ~**ly** ad
größtenteils.
motel [məu'tel] n Motel nt.
moth [mɔθ] n Nachtfalter m; (wool-eating)
Motte f; ~**ball** Mottenkugel f; ~-**eaten** a
mottenzerfressen.
mother ['mʌðə*] n Mutter f; vt bemuttern;
a tongue Mutter-; country Heimat-; ~**hood**
Mutterschaft f; ~-**in-law** Schwieger-
mutter f; ~**ly** a mütterlich; ~-**to-be**
werdende Mutter f.
mothproof ['mɔθpru:f] a mottenfest.
motif [məu'ti:f] n Motiv nt.
motion ['məuʃən] n Bewegung f; (in meeting) Antrag m; vti winken (+dat), zu verstehen geben (+dat); ~**less** a regungslos;
~ **picture** Film m.
motivated ['məutiveitid] a motiviert.
motivation [məuti'veiʃən] n Motivierung f.
motive ['məutiv] n Motiv nt, Beweggrund
m; a treibend.
motley ['mɔtli] a bunt.
motor ['məutə*] n Motor m; (car) Auto nt; vi
(im Auto) fahren; a Motor-; ~**bike** Motorrad nt; ~**boat** Motorboot nt; ~**car** Auto
nt; ~**cycle** Motorrad nt; ~**cyclist** Motor-
radfahrer(in f) m; ~ **ist** ['məutərist] Autofahrer(in f)
m; ~ **oil** Motorenöl nt; ~ **racing** Auto-
rennen nt; ~ **scooter** Motorroller m; ~
vehicle Kraftfahrzeug nt; ~**way** (Brit)
Autobahn f.
mottled ['mɔtld] a gesprenkelt.
motto ['mɔtəu] n Motto nt, Wahlspruch m.
mould [məuld] n Form f; (mildew)
Schimmel m; vt (lit, fig) formen; ~**er** vi
(decay) vermodern; ~**ing** Formen nt; ~**y**
a schimmelig.
moult [məult] vi sich mausern.

mound [maund] n (Erd)hügel m.
mount [maunt] n (liter: hill) Berg m; (horse)
Pferd nt; (for jewel etc) Fassung f; vt horse
steigen auf (+acc); (put in setting) fassen;
exhibition veranstalten; attack unternehmen; vi (also ~ **up**) sich häufen; (on
horse) aufsitzen; ~**ain** ['mauntin] Berg m;
~**aineer** [maunti'niə*] Bergsteiger(in f)
m; ~**aineering** Bergsteigen nt; **to go**
~**aineering** klettern gehen; ~**ainous** a
bergig; ~**ainside** Berg(ab)hang m.
mourn [mɔ:n] vt betrauern, beklagen; vi
trauern (for um); ~**er** Trauernde(r) mf;
~**ful** a traurig; ~**ing** (grief) Trauer f; **in**
~**ing** (period etc) in Trauer; (dress) in
Trauerkleidung f.
mouse [maus] n, pl **mice** Maus f; ~**trap**
Mausefalle f.
moustache [məs'tɑ:ʃ] n Schnurrbart m.
mousy ['mausi] a colour mausgrau; person
schüchtern.
mouth [mauθ] n Mund m; (general) Öffnung
f; (of river) Mündung f; (of harbour) Einfahrt f; [mauð] vt words affektiert
sprechen; **down in the** ~ niedergeschlagen; ~**ful** Mundvoll m; ~**organ**
Mundharmonika f; ~**piece** (lit) Mundstück nt; (fig) Sprachrohr nt; ~**wash**
Mundwasser nt; ~**watering** a lecker,
appetitlich.
movable ['mu:vəbl] a beweglich.
move [mu:v] n (movement) Bewegung f; (in
game) Zug m; (step) Schritt m; (of house)
Umzug m; vt bewegen; object rücken;
people transportieren; (in job) versetzen;
(emotionally) bewegen, ergreifen; **to ~ sb**
to do sth jdn veranlassen, etw zu tun; vi
sich bewegen; (change place) gehen;
(vehicle, ship) fahren; (take action) etwas
unternehmen; (go to another house)
umziehen; **to get a ~ on** sich beeilen; **on**
the ~ in Bewegung; **to ~ house**
umziehen; **to ~ closer to or towards sth**
sich etw (dat) nähern; ~ **about** vi sich
hin- und herbewegen; (travel) unterwegs
sein; ~ **away** vi weggehen; ~ **back** vi
zurückgehen; (to the rear) zurückweichen;
~ **forward** vi vorwärtsgehen, sich
vorwärtsbewegen; vt vorschieben; time
vorverlegen; ~ **in** vi (to house) einziehen;
(troops) einrücken; ~ **on** vi weitergehen;
vt weitergehen lassen; ~ **out** vi (of house)
ausziehen; (troops) abziehen; ~ **up** vi aufsteigen; (in job) befördert werden; vt nach
oben bewegen; (in job) befördern; (Sch)
versetzen; ~**ment** Bewegung f; (Mus) Satz
m; (of clock) Uhrwerk nt.
movie ['mu:vi] n Film m; **the** ~**s** (the
cinema) das Kino; ~ **camera** Filmkamera f.
moving ['mu:viŋ] a beweglich; force
treibend; (touching) ergreifend.
mow [məu] vt irreg mähen; ~ **down** vt
(fig) niedermähen; ~**er** (machine) Mähmaschine f; (lawn—) Rasenmäher m.
Mr [mistə*] Herr m.
Mrs ['misiz] Frau f.
Ms [miz] n Frau f.
much [mʌtʃ] a viel; ad sehr; viel; n viel,
eine Menge f; ~ **better** viel besser; ~

the same size so ziemlich gleich groß; **how** ~? wieviel?; **too** ~ zuviel; ~ **to my surprise** zu meiner großen Überraschung; ~ **as I should like to** so gern ich möchte.

muck [mʌk] n (lit) Mist m; (fig) Schmutz m; ~ **about** (col) vi herumlungern; (meddle) herumalbern (with an +dat); vt ~ **sb about** mit jdm treiben, was man will; ~ **up** vt (col: ruin) vermasseln; (dirty) dreckig machen; ~ **y** a (dirty) dreckig.

mucus ['mjuːkəs] n Schleim m.

mud [mʌd] n Schlamm m; (fig) Schmutz m.

muddle ['mʌdl] n Durcheinander nt; vt (also ~ **up**) durcheinanderbringen; ~ **through** vi sich durchwursteln.

muddy ['mʌdɪ] a schlammig.

mudguard ['mʌdgɑːd] n Schutzblech nt.

mudpack ['mʌdpæk] n Moorpackung f.

mud-slinging ['mʌdslɪŋɪŋ] n (col) Verleumdung f.

muff [mʌf] n Muff m.

muffin ['mʌfɪn] n süße(s) Teilchen nt.

muffle ['mʌfl] vt sound dämpfen; (wrap up) einhüllen.

mufti ['mʌftɪ] n: **in** ~ in Zivil.

mug [mʌg] n (cup) Becher m; (col: face) Visage f; (col: fool) Trottel m; vt überfallen und ausrauben; ~ **ging** Überfall m.

muggy ['mʌgɪ] a weather schwül.

mulatto [mjuːˈlætəʊ] n Mulatte m, Mulattin f.

mule [mjuːl] n Maulesel m.

mull [mʌl]: ~ **over** vt nachdenken über (+acc).

mulled [mʌld] a wine Glüh-.

multi- ['mʌltɪ] pref Multi-, multi-.

multicoloured, (US) **multicolored** ['mʌltɪˈkʌləd] a mehrfarbig.

multifarious [mʌltɪˈfɛərɪəs] a mannigfaltig.

multilateral ['mʌltɪˈlætərəl] a multilateral.

multiple ['mʌltɪpl] n Vielfache(s) nt; a mehrfach; (many) mehrere; ~ **sclerosis** multiple Sklerose f; ~ **store** Kaufhauskette f.

multiplication [mʌltɪplɪˈkeɪʃən] n Multiplikation f.

multiply ['mʌltɪplaɪ] vt multiplizieren (by mit); vi (Biol) sich vermehren.

multiracial ['mʌltɪˈreɪʃəl] a gemischtrassig; ~ **policy** Rassenintegration f.

multitude ['mʌltɪtjuːd] n Menge f.

mum[1] [mʌm] a: **to keep** ~ den Mund halten (about über +acc).

mum[2] [mʌm] n (col) Mutti f.

mumble ['mʌmbl] vti murmeln; n Gemurmel nt.

mummy ['mʌmɪ] n (dead body) Mumie f; (col) Mami f.

mumps [mʌmps] n Mumps m.

munch [mʌntʃ] vti mampfen.

mundane ['mʌnˈdeɪn] a weltlich; (fig) profan.

municipal [mjuːˈnɪsɪpəl] a städtisch, Stadt-; ~ **ity** [mjuːnɪsɪˈpælɪtɪ] Stadt f mit Selbstverwaltung.

munificence [mjuːˈnɪfɪsns] n Freigebigkeit f.

munitions [mjuːˈnɪʃənz] npl Munition f.

mural ['mjʊərəl] n Wandgemälde nt.

murder ['mɜːdə] n Mord m; **it was** ~ (fig) es war möderisch; **to get away with** ~ (fig) sich alles erlauben können; vt ermorden; ~ **er** Mörder m; ~ **ess** Mörderin f; ~ **ous** a Mord-; (fig) mörderisch.

murk [mɜːk] n Dunkelheit f ~ **y** a finster.

murmur ['mɜːmə] n Murmeln nt; (of water, wind) Rauschen nt; **without a** ~ ohne zu murren; vti murmeln.

muscle ['mʌsl] n Muskel m.

muscular ['mʌskjʊlə] a Muskel-; (strong) muskulös.

muse [mjuːz] vi (nach)sinnen; **M** ~ Muse f.

museum [mjuːˈzɪəm] n Museum nt.

mushroom ['mʌʃruːm] n Champignon m; Pilz m; vi (fig) emporschießen.

mushy [mʌʃɪ] a breiig; (sentimental) gefühlsduselig.

music ['mjuːzɪk] n Musik f; (printed) Noten pl; ~ **al** a sound melodisch; person musikalisch; n (show) Musical nt; ~ **al box** Spieldose f; ~ **al instrument** Musikinstrument nt; ~ **ally** ad musikalisch; sing melodisch; ~ **hall** (Brit) Varieté nt; ~ **ian** [mjuːˈzɪʃən] Musiker(in f) m.

muslin ['mʌzlɪn] n Musselin m.

mussel ['mʌsl] n Miesmuschel f.

must [mʌst] v aux müssen; (in negation) dürfen; n Muß nt; **the film is a** ~ den Film muß man einfach gesehen haben.

mustache ['mʌstæʃ] (US) = **moustache.**

mustard ['mʌstəd] n Senf m.

muster ['mʌstə] vt (Mil) antreten lassen; courage zusammennehmen.

mustiness ['mʌstɪnəs] n Muffigkeit f.

mustn't ['mʌsnt] = **must not.**

musty ['mʌstɪ] a muffig.

mute [mjuːt] a stumm; n (person) Stumme(r) mf; (Mus) Dämpfer m.

mutilate ['mjuːtɪleɪt] vt verstümmeln.

mutilation [mjuːtɪˈleɪʃən] n Verstümmelung f.

mutinous ['mjuːtɪnəs] a meuterisch.

mutiny ['mjuːtɪnɪ] n Meuterei f; vi meutern.

mutter ['mʌtə] vti murmeln.

mutton ['mʌtn] n Hammelfleisch nt.

mutual ['mjuːtjʊəl] a gegenseitig; beiderseitig; ~ **ly** ad gegenseitig; auf beiden Seiten; für beide Seiten.

muzzle ['mʌzl] n (of animal) Schnauze f; (for animal) Maulkorb m; (of gun) Mündung f; vt einen Maulkorb anlegen (+dat).

my [maɪ] poss a mein.

myopic [maɪˈɒpɪk] a kurzsichtig.

myrrh [mɜː] n Myrrhe f.

myself [maɪˈself] pron mich (acc); mir (dat); (emphatic) selbst; **I'm not** ~ mit mir ist etwas nicht in Ordnung.

mysterious [mɪsˈtɪərɪəs] a geheimnisvoll, mysteriös; ~ **ly** ad auf unerklärliche Weise.

mystery ['mɪstərɪ] n (secret) Geheimnis nt;

(sth difficult) Rätsel *nt;* ~ **play** Mysterienspiel *nt.*

mystic ['mɪstɪk] *n* Mystiker *m; a* mystisch; ~**al** *a* mystisch; ~**ism** ['mɪstɪsɪzəm] Mystizismus *m.*

mystification [mɪstɪfɪ'keɪʃən] *n* Verblüffung *f.*

mystify ['mɪstɪfaɪ] *vt* ein Rätsel sein *(+dat);* verblüffen.

mystique [mɪs'tiːk] *n* geheimnisvolle Natur *f.*

myth [mɪθ] *n* Mythos *m; (fig)* Erfindung *f;* ~**ical** *a* mythisch, Sagen-; ~**ological** [mɪθə'lɒdʒɪkəl] *a* mythologisch; ~**ology** [mɪ'θɒlədʒɪ] Mythologie *f.*

N

N, n [en] *n* N *nt*, n *nt.*

nab [næb] *vt (col)* schnappen.

nadir ['neɪdɪə*] *n* Tiefpunkt *m.*

nag [næg] *n (horse)* Gaul *m; (person)* Nörgler(in *f) m; vti* herumnörgeln *(sb an jdm);* ~**ging** *a doubt* nagend; *n* Nörgelei *f.*

nail [neɪl] *n* Nagel *m; vt* nageln; ~ **down** *vt (lit, fig)* festnageln; ~**brush** Nagelbürste *f;* ~**file** Nagelfeile *f;* ~ **polish** Nagellack *m;* ~ **scissors** *pl* Nagelschere *f.*

naive *a,* ~**ly** *ad* [naɪ'iːv, -lɪ] naiv.

naked ['neɪkɪd] *a* nackt; ~**ness** Nacktheit *f.*

name [neɪm] *n* Name *m; (reputation)* Ruf *m; vt* nennen; *sth new* benennen; *(appoint)* ernennen; **what's your** ~? wie heißen Sie?; **in the** ~ **of** im Namen *(+gen); (for the sake of)* um *(+gen)* willen; ~ **dropping: he's always** ~ **dropping** er wirft immer mit großen Namen um sich; ~**less** *a* namenlos; ~**ly** *ad* nämlich; ~**sake** Namensvetter *m.*

nanny ['nænɪ] *n* Kindermädchen *nt.*

nap [næp] *n (sleep)* Nickerchen *nt; (on cloth)* Strich *m;* **to have a** ~ ein Nickerchen machen.

napalm ['neɪpɑːm] *n* Napalm *nt.*

nape [neɪp] *n* Nacken *m.*

napkin ['næpkɪn] *n (at table)* Serviette *f; (Brit: for baby)* Windel *f.*

nappy ['næpɪ] *n (Brit: for baby)* Windel *f.*

narcissism [nɑː'sɪsɪzəm] *n* Narzißmus *m.*

narcotic [nɑː'kɒtɪk] *n* Betäubungsmittel *nt.*

narrate [nə'reɪt] *vt* erzählen.

narration [nə'reɪʃən] *n* Erzählung *f.*

narrative ['nærətɪv] *n* Erzählung *f; a* erzählend.

narrator [nə'reɪtə*] *n* Erzähler(in *f) m.*

narrow ['nærəʊ] *a* eng, schmal; *(limited)* beschränkt; *vi* sich verengen; **to** ~ **sth down to sth** etw auf etw *(acc)* einschränken; ~**ly** *ad miss* knapp; *escape* mit knapper Not; ~-**minded** *a* engstirnig; ~-**mindedness** Engstirnigkeit *f.*

nasal ['neɪzəl] *a* Nasal-.

nastily ['nɑːstɪlɪ] *ad* böse, schlimm.

nastiness ['nɑːstɪnəs] *n* Ekligkeit *f.*

nasty ['nɑːstɪ] *a* ekelhaft, fies; *business, wound* schlimm; **to turn** ~ gemein werden.

nation ['neɪʃən] *n* Nation *f,* Volk *nt;* ~**al**

['næʃənl] *a* national, National-, Landes-; *n* Staatsangehörige(r) *mf;* ~**al anthem** Nationalhymne *f;* ~**alism** ['næʃnəlɪzəm] Nationalismus *m;* ~**alist** ['næʃnəlɪst] *n* Nationalist(in *f) m; a* nationalistisch; ~**ality** [næʃə'nælɪtɪ] Staatsangehörigkeit *f,* Nationalität *f;* ~**alization** [næʃnəlaɪ'zeɪʃən] Verstaatlichung *f;* ~**alize** ['næʃnəlaɪz] *vt* verstaatlichen; ~**ally** ['næʃnəlɪ] *ad* national, auf Staatsebene; ~-**wide** *a, ad* allgemein, landesweit.

native ['neɪtɪv] *n (born in)* Einheimische(r) *mf; (original inhabitant)* Eingeborene(r) *mf; a (coming from a certain place)* einheimisch; *(of the original inhabitants)* Eingeborenen-; *(belonging by birth)* heimatlich, Heimat-; *(inborn)* angeboren, natürlich; **a** ~ **of Germany** ein gebürtiger Deutscher; ~ **language** Muttersprache *f.*

natter ['nætə*] *vi (col: chat)* quatschen; *n* Gequatsche *nt.*

natural ['nætʃrəl] *a* natürlich; Natur-; *(inborn)* (an)geboren; ~**ist** Naturkundler(in *f) m;* ~**ize** *vt foreigner* einbürgern, naturalisieren; *plant etc* einführen; ~**ly** *ad* natürlich; ~**ness** Natürlichkeit *f.*

nature ['neɪtʃə*] *n* Natur *f;* **by** ~ von Natur (aus).

naught [nɔːt] *n* Null *f.*

naughtily ['nɔːtɪlɪ] *ad* unartig.

naughtiness ['nɔːtɪnəs] *n* Unartigkeit *f.*

naughty ['nɔːtɪ] *a child* unartig, ungezogen; *action* ungehörig.

nausea ['nɔːsɪə] *n (sickness)* Übelkeit *f; (disgust)* Ekel *m;* ~**te** ['nɔːsɪeɪt] *vt* anekeln.

nauseating ['nɔːsɪeɪtɪŋ] *a* ekelerregend; *job* widerlich.

nautical ['nɔːtɪkəl] *a* nautisch; See-; *expression* seemännisch.

naval ['neɪvəl] *a* Marine-, Flotten-.

nave [neɪv] *n* Kirchen(haupt)schiff *nt.*

navel ['neɪvəl] *n* Nabel *m.*

navigable ['nævɪgəbl] *a* schiffbar.

navigate ['nævɪgeɪt] *vt ship etc* steuern; *vi (sail) (zu Schiff)* fahren.

navigation [nævɪ'geɪʃən] *n* Navigation *f.*

navigator ['nævɪgeɪtə*] *n* Steuermann *m; (explorer)* Seefahrer *m; (Aviat)* Navigator *m; (Aut)* Beifahrer(in *f) m.*

navvy ['nævɪ] *n* Straßenarbeiter *m; (on railway)* Streckenarbeiter *m.*

navy ['neɪvɪ] *n* Marine *f,* Flotte *f; (warships etc)* (Kriegs)flotte *f;* ~-**blue** Marineblau *nt; a* marineblau.

nay [neɪ] *ad (old) (no)* nein; *(even)* ja sogar.

neap [niːp] *a:* ~ **tide** Nippflut *f.*

near [nɪə*] *a* nah; **the holidays are** ~ es sind bald Ferien; *ad* in der Nähe; **to come** ~**er** näher kommen; *(time)* näher rücken; *prep (also)* ~ **to** *(space)* in der Nähe *(+gen); (time)* um *(+acc)* ... herum; *vt* sich nähern *(+dat);* ~ **at hand** nicht weit weg; ~**by** nahe (gelegen); *ad* in der Nähe; ~**ly** *ad* fast; **a** ~ **miss** knapp daneben; ~**ness** Nähe *f;* ~**side** *(Aut)* Beifahrerseite *f, a* auf der Beifahrerseite; **a** ~ **thing** knapp.

neat *a,* ~**ly** *ad* ['niːt, -lɪ] *(tidy)* ordentlich; *(clever)* treffend; *solution* sauber; *(pure)*

...dünnt, rein; ~**ness** Ordentlichkeit f, ...aberkeit f.

nebulous ['nebjuləs] a nebelhaft, verschwommen.

necessarily ['nesɪsərɪlɪ] ad unbedingt; notwendigerweise.

necessary ['nesɪsərɪ] a notwendig, nötig.

necessitate [nɪ'sesɪteɪt] vt erforderlich machen.

necessity [nɪ'sesɪtɪ] n (need) Not f; (compulsion) Notwendigkeit f; **in case of** ~ im Notfall; **necessities of life** Bedürfnisse pl des Lebens.

neck [nek] n Hals m; ~ **and** ~ Kopf an Kopf; ~**lace** ['neklɪs] Halskette f; ~**line** Ausschnitt m; ~**tie** (US) Krawatte f.

nectar ['nektə*] n Nektar m.

née [neɪ] a geborene.

need [ni:d] n Bedarf m no pl (for an +dat); Bedürfnis nt (for für); (want) Mangel m; (necessity) Notwendigkeit f; (poverty) Not f; vt brauchen; **to** ~ **to do** tun müssen; **if** ~ **be** wenn nötig; **to be in** ~ **of** brauchen; **there is no** ~ **for you to come** du brauchst nicht zu kommen; **there's no** ~ es ist nicht nötig.

needle ['ni:dl] n Nadel f.

needless a, ~**ly** ad ['ni:dlɪs, -lɪ] unnötig.

needlework ['ni:dlwɜ:k] n Handarbeit f.

needy ['ni:dɪ] a bedürftig.

negation [nɪ'geɪʃən] n Verneinung f.

negative ['negətɪv] n (Phot) Negativ nt; a negativ; answer abschlägig.

neglect [nɪ'glekt] vt (leave undone) versäumen; (take no care of) vernachlässigen; n Vernachlässigung f.

negligée ['neglɪʒeɪ] n Negligé nt.

negligence ['neglɪdʒəns] n Nachlässigkeit f.

negligent a, ~**ly** ad ['neglɪdʒənt, -lɪ] nachlässig, unachtsam.

negligible ['neglɪdʒəbl] a unbedeutend, geringfügig.

negotiable [nɪ'gəʊʃɪəbl] a cheque übertragbar, einlösbar.

negotiate [nɪ'gəʊʃɪeɪt] vi verhandeln; vt treaty abschließen, aushandeln; difficulty überwinden; corner nehmen.

negotiation [nɪgəʊʃɪ'eɪʃən] n Verhandlung f.

negotiator [nɪ'gəʊʃɪeɪtə*] n Unterhändler m.

Negress ['ni:gres] n Negerin f.

Negro ['ni:grəʊ] n Neger m; a Neger-.

neighbour, (US) **neighbor** ['neɪbə*] n Nachbar(in f) m; ~**hood** Nachbarschaft f; Umgebung f; ~**ing** a benachbart, angrenzend; ~**ly** a freundlich.

neither ['naɪðə*] a, pron keine(r, s) (von beiden); cj weder; **he can't do it, and** ~ **can I** er kann es nicht und ich auch nicht.

neo- ['ni:əʊ] pref neo-.

neon ['ni:ɒn] n Neon nt; ~ **light** Neonlicht nt.

nephew ['nefju:] n Neffe m.

nerve [nɜ:v] n Nerv m; (courage) Mut m; (impudence) Frechheit f; ~-**racking** a nervenaufreibend.

nervous ['nɜ:vəs] a (of the nerves) Nerven-;

(timid) nervös, ängstlich; ~ **breakdown** Nervenzusammenbruch m; ~**ly** ad nervös; ~**ness** Nervosität f.

nest [nest] n Nest nt.

nestle ['nesl] vi sich kuscheln; (village) sich schmiegen.

net [net] n Netz nt; a: ~**(t)** netto, Netto-, Rein-; ~**ball** Netzball m.

netting ['netɪŋ] n Netz(werk) nt, Drahtgeflecht nt.

network ['netwɜ:k] n Netz nt.

neurosis [njʊə'rəʊsɪs] n Neurose f.

neurotic [njʊə'rɒtɪk] a neurotisch; n Neurotiker(in f) m.

neuter ['nju:tə*] a (Biol) geschlechtslos; (Gram) sächlich; n (Biol) kastrierte(s) Tier nt; (Gram) Neutrum nt.

neutral ['nju:trəl] a neutral; ~**ity** [nju:'trælɪtɪ] Neutralität f.

never ['nevə*] ad nie(mals); **well I** ~ na so was!; ~-**ending** a endlos; ~**theless** [nevəðə'les] ad trotzdem, dennoch.

new [nju:] a neu; **they are still** ~ **to the work** die Arbeit ist ihnen noch neu; ~ **from** frisch aus or von; ~**born** a neugeboren; ~**comer** Neuankömmling m; ~**ly** ad frisch, neu; ~ **moon** Neumond m; ~**ness** Neuheit f.

news [nju:z] n Nachricht f; (Rad, TV) Nachrichten pl; ~**agent** Zeitungshändler m; ~**flash** Kurzmeldung f; ~**letter** Rundschreiben nt; ~**paper** Zeitung f; ~**reel** Wochenschau f.

New Year ['nju:'jɪə*] n Neujahr nt; ~'**s Day** Neujahrstag m; ~'**s Eve** Silvester(abend m) nt.

next [nekst] a nächste(r, s); ad (after) dann, darauf; (next time) das nächstemal; prep: ~ **to** (gleich) neben (+dat); ~ **to nothing** so gut wie nichts; **to do sth** ~ etw als nächstes tun; **what** ~! was denn noch (alles)?; **the** ~ **day** am nächsten or folgenden Tag; ~ **door** ad nebenan; ~ **year** nächstes Jahr; ~ **of kin** Familienangehörige(r) mf.

nib [nɪb] n Spitze f.

nibble ['nɪbl] vt knabbern an (+dat).

nice [naɪs] a hübsch, nett, schön; (subtle) fein; ~-**looking** a hübsch, gutaussehend; ~**ly** ad gut, fein, nett.

nick [nɪk] n Einkerbung f; **in the** ~ **of time** gerade rechtzeitig.

nickel ['nɪkl] n Nickel nt; (US) Nickel m (5 cents).

nickname ['nɪkneɪm] n Spitzname m.

nicotine ['nɪkəti:n] n Nikotin nt.

niece [ni:s] n Nichte f.

niggardly ['nɪgədlɪ] a schäbig; person geizig.

niggling ['nɪglɪŋ] a pedantisch; doubt, worry quälend; detail kleinlich.

night [naɪt] n Nacht f; (evening) Abend m; **good** ~! gute Nacht!; **at** or **by** ~ nachts; abends; ~**cap** (drink) Schlummertrunk m; ~**club** Nachtlokal nt; ~**dress** Nachthemd nt; ~**fall** Einbruch m der Nacht; ~**ie** (col) Nachthemd nt; ~**ingale** Nachtigall f; ~**life** Nachtleben nt; ~**ly** a, ad jeden Abend; jede Nacht; ~**mare** Alptraum m; ~ **school** Abendschule f;

~time Nacht f; at ~ **time** nachts; ~ **watchman** Nachtwächter m.

nil [nɪl] n Nichts nt, Null f (also Sport).

nimble ['nɪmbl] a behend(e), flink; mind beweglich.

nimbly ['nɪmblɪ] ad flink.

nine [naɪn] n Neun f; a neun; ~**teen** n Neunzehn f; a neunzehn; ~**ty** n Neunzig f; a neunzig.

ninth [naɪnθ] a neunte(r, s); n Neuntel nt.

nip [nɪp] vt kneifen; n Kneifen nt.

nipple ['nɪpl] n Brustwarze f.

nippy ['nɪpɪ] a (col) person flink; car flott; (cold) frisch.

nit [nɪt] n Nisse f.

nitrogen ['naɪtrədʒən] n Stickstoff m.

no [nəʊ] a kein; ad nein; n Nein nt; ~ **further** nicht weiter; ~ **more time** keine Zeit mehr; **in ~ time** schnell.

nobility [nəʊ'bɪlɪtɪ] n Adel m; **the ~ of** this deed diese edle Tat.

noble ['nəʊbl] a rank adlig; (splendid) nobel, edel; n Adlige(r) mf; ~**man** Edelmann m, Adlige(r) m.

nobly ['nəʊblɪ] ad edel, großmütig.

nobody ['nəʊbədɪ] pron niemand, keiner; n Niemand m.

nod [nɒd] vi nicken; ~ **off** einnicken; n Nicken nt.

noise [nɔɪz] n (sound) Geräusch nt; (unpleasant, loud) Lärm m.

noisily ['nɔɪzɪlɪ] ad lärmend, laut.

noisy ['nɔɪzɪ] a laut; crowd lärmend.

nomad ['nəʊmæd] n Nomade m; ~**ic** [nəʊ'mædɪk] a nomadisch.

no-man's land ['nəʊmænzlænd] n (lit, fig) Niemandsland nt.

nominal ['nɒmɪnl] a nominell; (Gram) Nominal-.

nominate ['nɒmɪneɪt] vt (suggest) vorschlagen; (in election) aufstellen; (appoint) ernennen.

nomination [nɒmɪ'neɪʃən] n (election) Nominierung f; (appointment) Ernennung f.

nominee [nɒmɪ'niː] n Kandidat(in f) m.

non- [nɒn] pref Nicht-, un-; ~**alcoholic** a alkoholfrei.

nonchalant ['nɒnʃələnt] a lässig.

nondescript ['nɒndɪskrɪpt] a mittelmäßig.

none [nʌn] a, pron kein(e, r, s); ad: ~ **the wiser** keineswegs klüger; ~ **of your cheek!** sei nicht so frech!

nonentity [nɒ'nentɪtɪ] n Null f (col).

nonetheless ['nʌnðə'les] ad nichtsdestoweniger.

non-fiction ['nɒn'fɪkʃən] n Sachbücher pl.

nonplussed ['nɒn'plʌst] a verdutzt.

nonsense ['nɒnsəns] n Unsinn m.

non-stop ['nɒn'stɒp] a pausenlos, Nonstop-.

noodles ['nuːdlz] npl Nudeln pl.

nook [nʊk] n Winkel m, Eckchen nt.

noon [nuːn] n (12 Uhr) Mittag m.

no one ['nəʊwʌn] pron = **nobody**.

noose [nuːs] n Schlinge f.

norm [nɔːm] n Norm f, Regel f.

normal ['nɔːməl] a normal; ~**ly** ad normal; (usually) normalerweise.

north [nɔːθ] n Norden m; a nördlich, Nord-; ad nördlich, nach or im Norden; ~**east**

Nordosten m; ~**ern** ['nɔːðən] a nördlich, Nord-; ~**ward(s)** ad nach Norden; ~**west** Nordwesten m.

nose [nəʊz] n Nase f; ~**bleed** Nasenbluten nt; ~**dive** Sturzflug m; ~**y** a neugierig.

nostalgia [nɒs'tældʒɪə] n Sehnsucht f, Nostalgie f.

nostalgic [nɒs'tældʒɪk] a wehmütig, nostalgisch.

nostril ['nɒstrɪl] n Nasenloch nt; (of animal) Nüster f.

not [nɒt] ad nicht; **he is ~ an expert** er ist kein Experte; ~ **at all** keineswegs; (don't mention it) gern geschehen.

notable ['nəʊtəbl] a bemerkenswert.

notably ['nəʊtəblɪ] ad (especially) besonders; (noticeably) bemerkenswert.

notch [nɒtʃ] n Kerbe f, Einschnitt m.

note [nəʊt] n (Mus) Note f, Ton m; (short letter) Nachricht f; (Pol) Note f; (comment, attention) Notiz f; (of lecture etc) Aufzeichnung f; (bank—) Schein m; (fame) Ruf m, Ansehen nt; vt (observe) bemerken; (write down) notieren; **to take ~s of** sich Notizen machen über (+acc); ~**book** Notizbuch nt; ~**case** Brieftasche f; ~**d** a bekannt; ~**paper** Briefpapier nt.

nothing ['nʌθɪŋ] n nichts; **for ~** umsonst; **it is ~ to me** es bedeutet mir nichts.

notice ['nəʊtɪs] n (announcement) Anzeige f, Bekanntmachung f; (attention) Beachtung f; (warning) Ankündigung f; (dismissal) Kündigung f; vt bemerken; **to take ~ of** beachten; **to bring sth to sb's ~** jdn auf etw (acc) aufmerksam machen; **take no ~** I kümmere dich nicht darum!; ~**able** a merklich; ~ **board** Anschlagtafel f.

notification [nəʊtɪfɪ'keɪʃən] n Benachrichtigung f.

notify ['nəʊtɪfaɪ] vt benachrichtigen.

notion ['nəʊʃən] n (idea) Vorstellung f, Idee f; (fancy) Lust f.

notorious [nəʊ'tɔːrɪəs] a berüchtigt.

notwithstanding [nɒtwɪð'stændɪŋ] ad trotzdem; prep trotz.

nougat ['nuːgɑː] n weiße(r) Nougat m.

nought [nɔːt] n Null f.

noun [naʊn] n Hauptwort nt, Substantiv nt.

nourish ['nʌrɪʃ] vt nähren; ~**ing** a nahrhaft; ~**ment** Nahrung f.

novel ['nɒvəl] n Roman m; a neu(artig); ~**ist** Schriftsteller(in f) m; ~**ty** Neuheit f.

November [nəʊ'vembə*] n November m.

novice ['nɒvɪs] n Neuling m; (Eccl) Novize m.

now [naʊ] ad jetzt; **right ~** jetzt, gerade; **do it right ~** tun Sie es sofort; ~ **and then**, ~ **and again** ab und zu, manchmal; ~, ~ na, na; ~ ... ~ or **then** bald ... bald, mal ... mal; ~**adays** ad heutzutage.

nowhere ['nəʊwɛə*] ad nirgends.

nozzle ['nɒzl] n Düse f.

nuance ['njuːɑːns] n Nuance f.

nuclear ['njuːklɪə*] a energy etc Atom-, Kern-.

nucleus ['njuːklɪəs] n Kern m.

nude [njuːd] a nackt; n (person) Nackte(r) mf; (Art) Akt m; **in the ~** nackt.

nudge [nʌdʒ] vt leicht anstoßen.

nudist ['nju:dɪst] n Nudist(in f) m.
nudity ['nju:dɪtɪ] n Nacktheit f.
nuisance ['nju:sns] n Ärgernis nt; **that's a** ~ das ist ärgerlich; **he's a** ~ er geht einem auf die Nerven.
null [nʌl] a: ~ **and void** null und nichtig; ~**ify** vt für null und nichtig erklären.
numb [nʌm] a taub, gefühllos; vt betäuben.
number ['nʌmbə*] n Nummer f; (numeral also) Zahl f; (quantity) (An)zahl f; (Gram) Numerus m; (of magazine also) Ausgabe f; vt (give a number to) numerieren; (amount to) sein; **his days are** ~**ed** seine Tage sind gezählt; ~ **plate** (Brit Aut) Nummernschild nt.
numbness ['nʌmnəs] n Gefühllosigkeit f.
numbskull ['nʌmskʌl] n Idiot m.
numeral ['nju:mərəl] n Ziffer f.
numerical [nju:'merɪkəl] a order zahlenmäßig.
numerous ['nju:mərəs] a zahlreich.
nun [nʌn] n Nonne f.
nurse [nɜ:s] n Krankenschwester f; (for children) Kindermädchen nt; vt patient pflegen; doubt etc hegen; ~**ry** (for children) Kinderzimmer nt; (for plants) Gärtnerei f; (for trees) Baumschule f; ~**ry rhyme** Kinderreim m; ~**ry school** Kindergarten m.
nursing ['nɜ:sɪŋ] n (profession) Krankenpflege f; ~ **home** Privatklinik f.
nut [nʌt] n Nuß f; (screw) Schraubenmutter f; (col) Verrückte(r) mf; ~**s** a (col: crazy) verrückt.
nutcase ['nʌtkeɪs] n (col) Verrückte(r) mf.
nutcrackers ['nʌtkrækəz] npl Nußknacker m.
nutmeg ['nʌtmeg] n Muskat(nuß f) m.
nutrient ['nju:trɪənt] n Nährstoff m.
nutrition [nju:'trɪʃən] n Nahrung f.
nutritious [nju:'trɪʃəs] a nahrhaft.
nutshell ['nʌtʃel] n: **in a** ~ in aller Kürze.
nylon ['naɪlɒn] n Nylon nt; a Nylon-.

O

O, o [əʊ] n O nt, o nt; (Tel) Null f; see **oh**.
oaf [əʊf] n Trottel m.
oak [əʊk] n Eiche f; a Eichen(holz)-.
oar [ɔ:*] n Ruder nt.
oasis [əʊ'eɪsɪs] n Oase f.
oath [əʊθ] n (statement) Eid m, Schwur m; (swearword) Fluch m.
oatmeal ['əʊtmi:l] n Haferschrot m.
oats [əʊts] n pl Hafer m; (Cook) Haferflocken pl.
obedience [ə'bi:dɪəns] n Gehorsam m.
obedient [ə'bi:dɪənt] a gehorsam, folgsam.
obelisk ['ɒbɪlɪsk] n Obelisk m.
obesity [əʊ'bi:sɪtɪ] n Korpulenz f, Fettleibigkeit f.
obey [ə'beɪ] vti gehorchen (+dat), folgen (+dat).
obituary [ə'bɪtjʊərɪ] n Nachruf m.
object ['ɒbdʒɪkt] n (thing) Gegenstand m, Objekt nt; (of feeling etc) Gegenstand m; (purpose) Zweck m; (Gram) Objekt nt; [əb'dʒekt] vi dagegen sein, Einwände haben (to gegen); (morally) Anstoß

nehmen (to an +acc); ~**ion** [əb'dʒekʃən] (reason against) Einwand m, Einspruch m; (dislike) Abneigung f; ~**ionable** [əb'dʒekʃnəbl] a nicht einwandfrei; language anstößig; ~**ive** [əb'dʒektɪv] n Ziel nt; a objektiv; ~**ively** [əb'dʒektɪvlɪ] ad objektiv; ~**ivity** [ɒbdʒɪk'tɪvɪtɪ] Objektivität f; ~**or** [əb'dʒektə*] Gegner(in f) m.
obligation [ɒblɪ'geɪʃən] n (duty) Pflicht f; (promise) Verpflichtung f; **no** ~ unverbindlich; **be under an** ~ verpflichtet sein.
obligatory [ɒ'blɪgətərɪ] a bindend, obligatorisch; **it is** ~ **to . . .** es ist Pflicht, zu . . .
oblige [ə'blaɪdʒ] vt (compel) zwingen; (do a favour) einen Gefallen tun (+dat); **you are not** ~**d to do it** Sie sind nicht verpflichtet, es zu tun; **much** ~**d** herzlichen Dank.
obliging [ə'blaɪdʒɪŋ] a entgegenkommend.
oblique [ə'bli:k] a schräg, schief; n Schrägstrich m.
obliterate [ə'blɪtəreɪt] vt auslöschen.
oblivion [ə'blɪvɪən] n Vergessenheit f.
oblivious [ə'blɪvɪəs] a nicht bewußt (of gen); **he was** ~ **of it** er hatte es nicht bemerkt.
oblong ['ɒblɒŋ] n Rechteck nt; a länglich.
obnoxious [əb'nɒkʃəs] a abscheulich, widerlich.
oboe ['əʊbəʊ] n Oboe f.
obscene [əb'si:n] a obszön, unanständig.
obscenity [əb'senɪtɪ] n Obszönität f; **obscenities** Zoten pl.
obscure [əb'skjʊə*] a unklar; (indistinct) undeutlich; (unknown) unbekannt, obskur; (dark) düster; vt verdunkeln; view verbergen; (confuse) verwirren.
obscurity [əb'skjʊərɪtɪ] n Unklarheit f; (being unknown) Verborgenheit f; (darkness) Dunkelheit f.
obsequious [əb'si:kwɪəs] a servil.
observable [əb'zɜ:vəbl] a wahrnehmbar, sichtlich.
observance [əb'zɜ:vəns] n Befolgung f.
observant [əb'zɜ:vənt] a aufmerksam.
observation [ɒbzə'veɪʃən] n (noticing) Beobachtung f; (surveillance) Überwachung f; (remark) Bemerkung f.
observatory [əb'zɜ:vətrɪ] n Sternwarte f, Observatorium nt.
observe [əb'zɜ:v] vt (notice) bemerken; (watch) beobachten; customs einhalten; ~**er** Beobachter(in f) m.
obsess [əb'ses] vt verfolgen, quälen; **to be** ~**ed with an idea** von einem Gedanken besessen sein; ~**ion** [əb'seʃən] Besessenheit f, Wahn m; ~**ive** a krankhaft.
obsolescence [ɒbsə'lesns] n Veralten nt.
obsolescent [ɒbsə'lesnt] a veraltend.
obsolete ['ɒbsəli:t] a überholt, veraltet.
obstacle ['ɒbstəkl] n Hindernis nt; ~ **race** Hindernisrennen nt.
obstetrics [ɒb'stetrɪks] n Geburtshilfe f.
obstinacy ['ɒbstɪnəsɪ] n Hartnäckigkeit f, Sturheit f.
obstinate a, ~**ly** ad ['ɒbstɪnət, -lɪ] hartnäckig, stur.

obstreperous [əb'strepərəs] a aufmüpfig.

obstruct [əb'strʌkt] vt versperren; pipe verstopfen; (hinder) hemmen; ~ion [əb'strʌkʃən] Versperrung f; Verstopfung f; (obstacle) Hindernis nt; ~ive a hemmend.

obtain [əb'teɪn] vt erhalten, bekommen; result erzielen; ~able a erhältlich.

obtrusive [əb'truːsɪv] a aufdringlich.

obtuse [əb'tjuːs] a begriffsstutzig; angle stumpf.

obviate ['obvɪeɪt] vt beseitigen; danger abwenden.

obvious ['obvɪəs] a offenbar, offensichtlich; ~ly ad offensichtlich.

occasion [ə'keɪʒən] n Gelegenheit f; (special event) große(s) Ereignis nt; (reason) Grund m, Anlaß m; on ~ gelegentlich; vt veranlassen; ~al a, ~ally ad gelegentlich; very ~ally sehr selten.

occult [o'kʌlt] n the ~ der Okkultismus; a okkult.

occupant ['okjupənt] n Inhaber(in f) m; (of house etc) Bewohner(in f) m.

occupation [okju'peɪʃən] n (employment) Tätigkeit f, Beruf m; (pastime) Beschäftigung f; (of country) Besetzung f, Okkupation f; ~al a hazard Berufs-; therapy Beschäftigungs-.

occupier ['okjupaɪə*] n Bewohner(in f) m.

occupy ['okjupaɪ] vt (take possession of) besetzen; seat belegen; (live in) bewohnen; position, office bekleiden; position in sb's life einnehmen; time beanspruchen; mind beschäftigen.

occur [ə'kɜː*] vi (happen) vorkommen, geschehen; (appear) vorkommen; (come to mind) einfallen (to dat); ~rence (event) Ereignis nt; (appearing) Auftreten nt.

ocean ['əuʃən] n Ozean m, Meer nt; ~-going a Hochsee-.

ochre ['əukə*] n Ocker m or nt.

o'clock [ə'klok] ad: it is 5 ~ es ist 5 Uhr.

octagonal [ok'tægənl] a achteckig.

octane ['okteɪn] n Oktan nt.

octave ['oktɪv] n Oktave f.

October [ok'təubə*] n Oktober m.

octopus ['oktəpəs] n Krake f; (small) Tintenfisch m.

oculist ['okjulɪst] n Augenarzt m/-ärztin f.

odd [od] a (strange) sonderbar; (not even) ungerade; (the other part missing) einzeln; (about) ungefähr; (surplus) übrig; (casual) Gelegenheits-, zeitweilig; ~ity (strangeness) Merkwürdigkeit f; (queer person) seltsame(r) Kauz m; (thing) Kuriosität f; ~ly ad seltsam; ~ly enough merkwürdigerweise; ~ment Rest m, Einzelstück nt; ~s pl Chancen pl; (betting) Gewinnchancen pl; it makes no ~s es spielt keine Rolle; at ~s uneinig; ~s and ends pl Reste pl; Krimskrams m.

ode [əud] n Ode f.

odious ['əudɪəs] a verhaßt; action abscheulich.

odour, (US) **odor** ['əudə*] n Geruch m; ~less a geruchlos.

of [ov, əv] prep von; (indicating material) aus; the first ~ May der erste Mai; within a month ~ his death einen Monat nach seinem Tod; a girl ~ ten ein zehnjähriges Mädchen; ~ fear ~ God Gottesfurcht f; love ~ money Liebe f zum Geld; the six ~ us wir sechs.

off [of] ad (absent) weg, fort; (switch) aus(geschaltet), ab(geschaltet); (milk) sauer; I'm ~ ich gehe jetzt; the button's ~ der Knopf ist ab; to be well-/badly ~ reich/arm sein; prep von; (distant from) ab(gelegen) von; 3% ~ 3% Nachlaß or Abzug; just ~ Piccadilly gleich bei Piccadilly; I'm ~ smoking ich rauche nicht mehr.

offal ['ofəl] n Innereien pl.

off-colour ['ofkʌlə*] a nicht wohl.

offence, (US) **offense** [ə'fens] n (crime) Vergehen nt, Straftat f; (insult) Beleidigung f.

offend [ə'fend] vt beleidigen; ~er Gesetzesübertreter m; ~ing a verletzend.

offensive [ə'fensɪv] a (unpleasant) übel, abstoßend; weapon Kampf-; remark verletzend; n Angriff m, Offensive f.

offer ['ofə*] n Angebot f; on ~ zum Verkauf angeboten; vt anbieten; reward aussetzen; opinion äußern; resistance leisten; ~ing Gabe f; (collection) Kollekte f.

offhand ['ofhænd] a lässig; ad ohne weiteres.

office ['ofɪs] n Büro nt; (position) Amt nt; (duty) Aufgabe f; (Eccl) Gottesdienst m; ~ block Büro(hoch)haus nt; ~ boy Laufjunge m; ~r (Mil) Offizier m; (public ~) Beamte(r) m im öffentlichen Dienst; ~ work Büroarbeit f; ~ worker Büroangestellte(r) mf.

official [ə'fɪʃəl] a offiziell, amtlich; n Beamte(r) m; (Pol) amtliche(r) Sprecher m; (of club etc) Funktionär m, Offizielle(r) m; ~ly ad offiziell.

officious [ə'fɪʃəs] a aufdringlich.

offing ['ofɪŋ] n: in the ~ in (Aus)sicht.

off-licence ['oflaɪsəns] n Wein- und Spirituosenhandlung f.

off-peak ['ofpiːk] a heating Speicher-; charges verbilligt.

off-season ['ofsiːzn] a außer Saison.

offset ['ofset] vt irreg ausgleichen.

offshore ['ofʃɔː*] ad in einiger Entfernung von der Küste; a küstennah, Küsten-.

offside ['ofsaɪd] a (Sport) im Abseits (stehend); ad abseits; n (Aut) Fahrerseite f.

offspring ['ofsprɪŋ] n Nachkommenschaft f; (one) Sprößling m.

offstage ['ofsteɪdʒ] ad hinter den Kulissen.

off-the-cuff ['ofðəkʌf] a unvorbereitet, aus dem Stegreif.

often ['ofn] ad oft.

ogle ['əugl] vt liebäugeln mit.

oh [əu] interj oh, ach.

oil [oɪl] n Öl nt; vt ölen; ~can Ölkännchen nt; ~field Ölfeld nt; ~-fired a Öl-; ~ level Ölstand m; ~ painting Ölgemälde nt; ~ refinery Ölraffinerie f; ~rig Ölplattform f; ~skins pl Ölzeug nt; ~ tanker (Öl)tanker m; ~ well Ölquelle f; ~y a ölig; (dirty) ölbeschmiert; manners schleimig.

ointment ['oɪntmənt] n Salbe f.

O.K., okay ['əu'keɪ] interj in Ordnung, O.K.;

a in Ordnung; **that's ~ with** *or* **by me** ich bin damit einverstanden; *n* Zustimmung *f*; *vt* genehmigen.

old [əʊld] *a* alt; *(former also)* ehemalig; **in the ~ days** früher; **any ~ thing** irgend etwas; **~ age** Alter *nt*; **~en** *a* (liter) alt, vergangen; **~-fashioned** *a* altmodisch; **~ maid** alte Jungfer *f*.

olive ['ɒlɪv] *n* (fruit) Olive *f*; (colour) Olive *nt*; *a* Oliven-; (coloured) olivenfarbig; **~ branch** Ölzweig *m*; **~ oil** Olivenöl *nt*.

Olympic [əʊ'lɪmpɪk] *a* olympisch; **~ Games, ~s** *pl* Olympische Spiele *pl*.

omelet(te) ['ɒmlət] *n* Omelett *nt*.

omen ['əʊmən] *n* Zeichen *nt*, Omen *nt*.

ominous ['ɒmɪnəs] *a* bedrohlich.

omission [əʊ'mɪʃən] *n* Auslassung *f*; *(neglect)* Versäumnis *nt*.

omit [əʊ'mɪt] *vt* auslassen; *(fail to do)* versäumen.

on [ɒn] *prep* auf; **~ TV** im Fernsehen; **I have it ~ me** ich habe es bei mir; **a ring ~ his finger** ein Ring am Finger; **~ the main road/the bank of the river** an der Hauptstraße/dem Flußufer; **~ foot** zu Fuß; **a lecture ~ Dante** eine Vorlesung über Dante; **~ the left** links; **~ the right** rechts; **~ Sunday** am Sonntag; **~ Sundays** sonntags; **~ hearing this, he left** als er das hörte, ging er; *ad* (slap)auf; **she had nothing ~** sie hatte nichts an; *(no plans)* sie hatte nichts vor; **what's ~ at the cinema?** was läuft im Kino?; **move ~** weitergehen; **go ~** mach weiter; **the light is ~** das Licht ist an; **you're ~** (col) akzeptiert; **it's not ~** (col) das ist nicht drin; **~ and off** hin und wieder.

once [wʌns] *ad* einmal; *cj* wenn ... einmal; **~ you've seen him** wenn du ihn erst einmal gesehen hast; **~ she had seen him** sobald sie ihn gesehen hatte; **at ~** sofort; *(at the same time)* gleichzeitig; **all at ~** plötzlich; **~ more** noch einmal; **more than ~** mehr als einmal; **~ in a while** ab und zu; **~ and for all** ein für allemal; **~ upon a time** es war einmal.

oncoming ['ɒnkʌmɪŋ] *a* traffic Gegen-, entgegenkommend.

one [wʌn] *a* ein; *(only)* einzig; *n* Eins *f*; *pron* eine(r, s); *(people, you)* man; **this ~, that ~** das; dieser/diese/dieses; **~ day** eines Tages; **the blue ~** der/die/das blaue; **which ~** welche(r, s); **he is ~ of us** er ist einer von uns; **~ by ~** einzeln; **~ another** einander; **~-man** *a* Einmann-; **~self** *pron* sich (selber); **~-way** *a* street Einbahn-.

ongoing ['ɒngəʊɪŋ] *a* stattfindend, momentan; *(progressing)* sich entwickelnd.

onion ['ʌnjən] *n* Zwiebel *f*.

onlooker ['ɒnlʊkə*] *n* Zuschauer(in *f*) *m*.

only ['əʊnlɪ] *ad* nur, bloß; *a* einzige(r, s); **~ yesterday** erst gestern; **~ just arrived** gerade erst angekommen.

onset ['ɒnset] *n* (beginning) Beginn *m*.

onshore ['ɒnʃɔ:*] *ad* an Land; *a* Küsten-.

onslaught ['ɒnslɔ:t] *n* Angriff *m*.

onto ['ɒntu] *prep* = **on to**.

onus ['əʊnəs] *n* Last *f*, Pflicht *f*.

onwards [ˌɒnwədz] *ad* (place) voran, vorwärts; **from that day ~** von dem Tag an; **from today ~** ab heute.

onyx ['ɒnɪks] *n* Onyx *m*.

ooze [u:z] *vi* sickern.

opacity [əʊ'pæsɪtɪ] *n* Undurchsichtigkeit *f*.

opal ['əʊpəl] *n* Opal *m*.

opaque [əʊ'peɪk] *a* undurchsichtig.

open ['əʊpən] *a* offen; *(public)* öffentlich; *mind* aufgeschlossen; *sandwich* belegt; **in the ~ (air)** im Freien; **to keep a day ~** einen Tag freihalten; *vt* öffnen, aufmachen; *trial, motorway, account* eröffnen; *vi (begin)* anfangen; *(shop)* aufmachen; *(door, flower)* aufgehen; *(play)* Premiere haben; **~ out** *vt* ausbreiten; *hole, business* erweitern; *vi (person)* aus sich herausgehen; **~ up** *vt route* erschließen; *shop, prospects* eröffnen; **~-air** *a* Frei(luft)-; **~er** Öffner *m*; **~ing** *(hole)* Öffnung *f*, Loch *nt*; *(beginning)* Eröffnung *f*, Anfang *m*; *(good chance)* Gelegenheit *f*; **~ly** *ad* offen; *(publicly)* öffentlich; **~-minded** *a* aufgeschlossen; **~-necked** *a* offen.

opera ['ɒpərə] *n* Oper *f*; **~ glasses** *pl* Opernglas *nt*; **~ house** Opernhaus *nt*.

operate ['ɒpəreɪt] *vt machine* bedienen; *brakes, light* betätigen; *vi (machine)* laufen, in Betrieb sein; *(person)* arbeiten; *(Med)* **to ~ on** operieren.

operatic [ɒpə'rætɪk] *a* Opern-.

operation [ɒpə'reɪʃən] *n (working)* Betrieb *m*, Tätigkeit *f*; *(Med)* Operation *f*; *(undertaking)* Unternehmen *nt*; *(Mil)* Einsatz *m*; **in full ~** in vollem Gang; **to be in ~** *(Jur)* in Kraft sein; *(machine)* in Betrieb sein; **~al** *a* einsatzbereit.

operative ['ɒpərətɪv] *a* wirksam; *law* rechtsgültig; *(Med)* operativ; *n* Mechaniker *m*; Agent *m*.

operator ['ɒpəreɪtə*] *n (of machine)* Arbeiter *m*; *(Tel)* Telefonist(in *f*) *m*; **phone the ~** rufen Sie die Vermittlung *or* das Fernamt an.

operetta [ɒpə'retə] *n* Operette *f*.

opinion [ə'pɪnjən] *n* Meinung *f*; **in my ~** meiner Meinung nach; **a matter of ~** Ansichtssache; **~ated** *a* starrsinnig.

opium ['əʊpɪəm] *n* Opium *nt*.

opponent [ə'pəʊnənt] *n* Gegner *m*.

opportune ['ɒpətju:n] *a* günstig; *remark* passend.

opportunist [ɒpə'tju:nɪst] *n* Opportunist *m*.

opportunity [ɒpə'tju:nɪtɪ] *n* Gelegenheit *f*, Möglichkeit *f*.

oppose [ə'pəʊz] *vt* entgegentreten *(+dat)*; *argument, idea* ablehnen; *plan* bekämpfen; **~d a: to be ~d to sth** gegen etw sein; **as ~d to** im Gegensatz zu.

opposing [ə'pəʊzɪŋ] *a* gegnerisch; *points of view* entgegengesetzt.

opposite ['ɒpəzɪt] *a house* gegenüberliegend; *direction* entgegengesetzt; *ad* gegenüber; *prep* gegenüber; **~ me** mir gegenüber; *n* Gegenteil *nt*; **~ number** *(person)* Pendant *nt*; *(Sport)* Gegenspieler *m*.

opposition [ɒpə'zɪʃən] *n (resistance)* Widerstand *m*; *(Pol)* Opposition *f*; *(contrast)* Gegensatz *m*.

oppress [ə'pres] vt unterdrücken; (heat etc) bedrücken; **~ion** [ə'preʃən] Unterdrückung f; **~ive** a authority, law ungerecht; burden, thought bedrückend; heat drückend.

opt [ɒpt] vi: **~ for sth** sich entscheiden für etw; **to ~ to do sth** sich entscheiden, etw zu tun; **~ out of** vi sich drücken vor (+dat); (of society) ausflippen aus (+dat).

optical ['ɒptɪkəl] a optisch.

optician [ɒp'tɪʃən] n Optiker m.

optimism ['ɒptɪmɪzəm] n Optimismus m.

optimist ['ɒptɪmɪst] n Optimist m; **~ic** ['ɒptɪ'mɪstɪk] a optimistisch.

optimum ['ɒptɪməm] a optimal.

option ['ɒpʃən] n Wahl f; (Comm) Vorkaufsrecht m, Option f; **~al** a freiwillig; subject wahlfrei; **~al extras** Extras auf Wunsch.

opulence ['ɒpjuləns] n Reichtum m.

opulent ['ɒpjulənt] a sehr reich.

opus ['əupəs] n Werk nt, Opus nt.

or [ɔ:*] cj oder; **he could not read ~ write** er konnte weder lesen noch schreiben.

oracle ['ɒrəkl] n Orakel nt.

oral ['ɔ:rəl] a mündlich; n (exam) mündliche Prüfung f, Mündliche(s) nt.

orange ['ɒrɪndʒ] n (fruit) Apfelsine f, Orange f; (colour) Orange nt; a orange.

orang-outang, orang-utan [ɔ:'ræŋu:'tæn] n Orang-Utan m.

oration [ɔ:'reɪʃən] n feierliche Rede f.

orator ['ɒrətə*] n Redner(in f) m.

oratorio [ɒrə'tɔ:rɪəu] n Oratorium nt.

orbit ['ɔ:bɪt] n Umlaufbahn f; **2 ~s 2** Umkreisungen; **to be in ~** (die Erde/den Mond etc) umkreisen; vt umkreisen.

orchard ['ɔ:tʃəd] n Obstgarten m.

orchestra ['ɔ:kɪstrə] n Orchester nt; **~l** [ɔ:'kestrəl] a Orchester-, orchestral; **~te** ['ɔ:kɪstreɪt] vt orchestrieren.

orchid ['ɔ:kɪd] n Orchidee f.

ordain [ɔ:'deɪn] vt (Eccl) weihen; (decide) verfügen.

ordeal [ɔ:'di:l] n schwere Prüfung f, Qual f.

order ['ɔ:də*] n (sequence) Reihenfolge f; (good arrangement) Ordnung f; (command) Befehl m; (Jur) Anordnung f; (peace) Ordnung f, Ruhe f; (condition) Zustand m; (rank) Klasse f; (Comm) Bestellung f; (Eccl, honour) Orden m; **out of ~** außer Betrieb; **in ~ to do sth** um etw zu tun; **in ~ that** damit; **holy ~s** Priesterweihe f; vt (arrange) ordnen; (command) befehlen (sth etw acc, sb jdm); (Comm) bestellen; **~-form** Bestellschein m; **~ly** n (Mil) Offiziersbursche m; (Mil Med) Sanitäter m; (Med) Pfleger m; a (tidy) ordentlich; (well-behaved) ruhig; **~ly officer** diensthabender Offizier.

ordinal ['ɔ:dɪnl] a Ordnungs-, Ordinal-.

ordinarily ['ɔ:dnrɪlɪ] ad gewöhnlich.

ordinary ['ɔ:dnrɪ] a (usual) gewöhnlich, normal; (commonplace) gewöhnlich, alltäglich.

ordination [ɔ:dɪ'neɪʃən] n Priesterweihe f; (Protestant) Ordination f.

ordnance ['ɔ:dnəns] n Artillerie f, Munition f; **~ factory** Munitionsfabrik f.

ore [ɔ:*] n Erz nt.

organ ['ɔ:gən] n (Mus) Orgel f; (Biol, fig) Organ nt; **~ic** [ɔ:'gænɪk] a organisch; **~ism** ['ɔ:gənɪzm] Organismus m; **~ist** Organist(in f) m.

organization [ɔ:gənaɪ'zeɪʃən] n Organisation f; (make-up) Struktur f.

organize ['ɔ:gənaɪz] vt organisieren; **~r** Organisator m, Veranstalter m.

orgasm ['ɔ:gæzəm] n Orgasmus m.

orgy ['ɔ:dʒɪ] n Orgie f.

Orient ['ɔ:rɪənt] n Orient m.

oriental [ɔ:rɪ'entəl] a orientalisch; n Orientale m, Orientalin f.

orientate ['ɔ:rɪenteɪt] vt orientieren.

orifice ['ɒrɪfɪs] n Öffnung f.

origin ['ɒrɪdʒɪn] n Ursprung m; (of the world) Anfang m, Entstehung f.

original [ə'rɪdʒɪnl] a (first) ursprünglich; painting original; idea originell; n Original nt; **~ity** [ərɪdʒɪ'nælɪtɪ] Originalität f; **~ly** ad ursprünglich; originell.

originate [ə'rɪdʒɪneɪt] vi entstehen; **to ~ from** stammen aus; vt ins Leben rufen.

originator [ə'rɪdʒɪneɪtə*] n (of movement) Begründer m; (of invention) Erfinder m.

ornament ['ɔ:nəmənt] n Schmuck m; (on mantelpiece) Nippesfigur f; (fig) Zierde f; **~al** [ɔ:nə'mentl] a schmückend, Zier-; **~ation** Verzierung f.

ornate [ɔ:'neɪt] a reich verziert; style überladen.

ornithologist [ɔ:nɪ'θɒlədʒɪst] n Ornithologe m, Ornithologin f.

ornithology [ɔ:nɪ'θɒlədʒɪ] n Vogelkunde f, Ornithologie f.

orphan ['ɔ:fən] n Waise f, Waisenkind nt; vt zur Waise machen; **~age** Waisenhaus nt.

orthodox ['ɔ:θədɒks] a orthodox.

orthopaedic, (US) orthopedic [ɔ:θəu'pi:dɪk] a orthopädisch.

oscillation [ɒsɪ'leɪʃən] n Schwingung f, Oszillation f.

ostensible a, **ostensibly** ad [ɒs'tensəbl, -blɪ] vorgeblich, angeblich.

ostentation [ɒsten'teɪʃən] n Zurschaustellen nt.

ostentatious [ɒsten'teɪʃəs] a großtuerisch, protzig.

ostracize ['ɒstrəsaɪz] vt ausstoßen.

ostrich ['ɒstrɪtʃ] n Strauß m.

other ['ʌðə*] a andere(r, s); **the ~ day** neulich; **every ~ day** jeden zweiten Tag; **any person ~ than him** alle außer ihm; **there are 6 ~s** da sind noch 6; pron andere(r, s); ad: **~ than** anders als; **~wise** ad (in a different way) anders; (in other ways) sonst, im übrigen; (or else) sonst.

otter ['ɒtə*] n Otter m.

ought [ɔ:t] v aux sollen; **he behaves as he ~** er benimmt sich, wie es sich gehört; **you ~ to do that** Sie sollten das tun; **he ~ to win** er müßte gewinnen; **that ~ to do das** müßte or dürfte reichen.

ounce [auns] n Unze f.

our [auə*] poss a unser; **~s** poss pron unsere(r, s); **~selves** pron uns (selbst); (emphatic) (wir) selbst.

oust [aʊst] *vt* verdrängen.

out [aʊt] *ad* hinaus/heraus; *(not indoors)* draußen; *(not alight)* aus; *(unconscious)* bewußtlos; *(results)* bekanntgegeben; **to eat/go** ~ auswärts essen/ausgehen; **that fashion's** ~ das ist nicht mehr Mode; **the ball was** ~ der Ball war aus; **the flowers are** ~ die Blumen blühen; **he was** ~ **in his calculations** seine Berechnungen waren nicht richtig; **to be** ~ **for sth** auf etw *(acc)* aus sein; ~ **loud** *ad* laut; ~ **of** *prep* aus; *(away from)* außerhalb *(+gen)*; **to be** ~ **of milk** *etc* keine Milch *etc* mehr haben; **made** ~ **of wood** aus Holz gemacht; ~ **of danger** außer Gefahr; ~ **of place** fehl am Platz; ~ **of curiosity** aus Neugier; **nine** ~ **of ten** neun von zehn; ~ **and** ~ durch und durch; ~**-of-bounds** *a* verboten; ~**-of-date** *a* veraltet; ~**-of-doors** *ad* im Freien; ~**-of-the-way** *a (off the general route)* abgelegen; *(unusual)* ungewöhnlich.

outback ['aʊtbæk] *n* Hinterland *nt*.

outboard (motor) ['aʊtbɔːd ('məʊtəᵊ)] *n* Außenbordmotor *m*.

outbreak ['aʊtbreɪk] *n* Ausbruch *m*.

outbuilding ['aʊtbɪldɪŋ] *n* Nebengebäude *nt*.

outburst ['aʊtbɜːst] *n* Ausbruch *m*.

outcast ['aʊtkɑːst] *n* Ausgestoßene(r) *mf*.

outclass [aʊt'klɑːs] *vt* übertreffen.

outcome ['aʊtkʌm] *n* Ergebnis *nt*.

outcry ['aʊtkraɪ] *n* Protest *m*.

outdated ['aʊt'deɪtɪd] *a* veraltet, überholt.

outdo [aʊt'duː] *vt irreg* übertrumpfen.

outdoor ['aʊtdɔːᵊ] *a* Außen-; *(Sport)* im Freien.

outdoors [aʊt'dɔːz] *ad* draußen, im Freien; **to go** ~ ins Freie *or* nach draußen gehen.

outer ['aʊtəᵊ] *a* äußere(r, s); ~ **space** Weltraum *m*.

outfit ['aʊtfɪt] *n* Ausrüstung *f; (set of clothes)* Kleidung *f*; ~**ters** *(for men's clothes)* Herrenausstatter *m*.

outgoings ['aʊtgəʊɪŋz] *npl* Ausgaben *pl*.

outgrow [aʊt'grəʊ] *vt irreg clothes* herauswachsen aus; *habit* ablegen.

outing ['aʊtɪŋ] *n* Ausflug *m*.

outlandish [aʊt'lændɪʃ] *a* eigenartig.

outlaw ['aʊtlɔː] *n* Geächtete(r) *m; vt* ächten; *(thing)* verbieten.

outlay ['aʊtleɪ] *n* Auslage *f*.

outlet ['aʊtlet] *n* Auslaß *m*, Abfluß *m; (Comm)* Absatzmarkt *m; (for emotions)* Ventil *nt*.

outline ['aʊtlaɪn] *n* Umriß *m*.

outlive [aʊt'lɪv] *vt* überleben.

outlook ['aʊtlʊk] *n (lit, fig)* Aussicht *f; (attitude)* Einstellung *f*.

outlying ['aʊtlaɪɪŋ] *a* entlegen; *district* Außen-.

outmoded [aʊt'məʊdɪd] *a* veraltet.

outnumber [aʊt'nʌmbəᵊ] *vt* zahlenmäßig überlegen sein *(+dat)*.

outpatient ['aʊtpeɪʃənt] *n* ambulante(r) Patient(in *f*) *m*.

outpost ['aʊtpəʊst] *n (Mil, fig)* Vorposten *m*.

output ['aʊtpʊt] *n* Leistung *f*, Produktion *f*.

outrage ['aʊtreɪdʒ] *n (cruel deed)* Aus-

schreitung *f*, Verbrechen *nt; (indecency)* Skandal *m; vt morals* verstoßen gegen; *person* empören; ~**ous** [aʊt'reɪdʒəs] *a* unerhört, empörend.

outright ['aʊtraɪt] *ad (at once)* sofort; *(openly)* ohne Umschweife; **to refuse** ~ rundweg ablehnen; *a denial* völlig; *sale* Total-; *winner* unbestritten.

outset ['aʊtset] *n* Beginn *m*.

outside ['aʊt'saɪd] *n* Außenseite *f;* **on the** ~ außen; **at the very** ~ höchstens; *a* äußere(r, s), Außen-; *price* Höchst-; *chance* gering; *ad* außen; **to go** ~ nach draußen *or* hinaus gehen; *prep* außerhalb *(+gen)*; ~**r** Außenseiter(in *f*) *m*.

outsize ['aʊtsaɪz] *a* übergroß.

outskirts ['aʊtskɜːts] *npl* Stadtrand *m*.

outspoken [aʊt'spəʊkən] *a* offen, freimütig.

outstanding [aʊt'stændɪŋ] *a* hervorragend; *debts etc* ausstehend.

outstay [aʊt'steɪ] *vt:* ~ **one's welcome** länger bleiben als erwünscht.

outstretched ['aʊtstretʃt] *a* ausgestreckt.

outward ['aʊtwəd] *a* äußere(r, s); *journey* Hin-; *freight* ausgehend; *ad* nach außen; ~**ly** *ad* äußerlich.

outweigh [aʊt'weɪ] *vt (fig)* überwiegen.

outwit [aʊt'wɪt] *vt* überlisten.

outworn [aʊt'wɔːn] *a expression* abgedroschen.

oval ['əʊvəl] *a* oval; *n* Oval *nt*.

ovary ['əʊvərɪ] *n* Eierstock *m*.

ovation [əʊ'veɪʃən] *n* Beifallssturm *m*.

oven ['ʌvn] *n* Backofen *m*.

over ['əʊvəᵊ] *ad (across)* hinüber/herüber; *(finished)* vorbei; *(left)* übrig; *(again)* wieder, noch einmal; *prep* über; *(in every part of)* in; *pref (excessively)* übermäßig; **famous the world** ~ in der ganzen Welt berühmt; **five times** ~ fünfmal; ~ **the weekend** übers Wochenende; ~ **coffee** bei einer Tasse Kaffee; ~ **the phone** am Telephon; **all** ~ *(everywhere)* überall; *(finished)* vorbei; ~ **and** ~ immer wieder; ~ **and above** über hinaus.

over- ['əʊvəᵊ] *pref* über-.

overact ['əʊvər'ækt] *vi* übertreiben.

overall ['əʊvərɔːl] *n (Brit) (for woman)* Kittelschürze *f; a situation* allgemein; *length* Gesamt-; *ad* insgesamt; ~**s** *pl (for man)* Overall *m*.

overawe [əʊvər'ɔː] *vt (frighten)* einschüchtern; *(make impression)* überwältigen.

overbalance [əʊvə'bæləns] *vi* Übergewicht bekommen.

overbearing [əʊvə'beərɪŋ] *a* aufdringlich.

overboard ['əʊvəbɔːd] *ad* über Bord.

overcast ['əʊvəkɑːst] *a* bedeckt.

overcharge ['əʊvə'tʃɑːdʒ] *vt* zuviel verlangen von.

overcoat ['əʊvəkəʊt] *n* Mantel *m*.

overcome [əʊvə'kʌm] *vt irreg* überwinden; *(sleep, emotion)* übermannen; ~ **by the song** vom Lied gerührt.

overcrowded [əʊvə'kraʊdɪd] *a* überfüllt.

overcrowding [əʊvə'kraʊdɪŋ] *n* Überfüllung *f*.

overdo ['əuvə'du:] vt irreg (cook too much) verkochen; (exaggerate) übertreiben.

overdose ['əuvədəus] n Überdosis f.

overdraft ['əuvədra:ft] n (Konto)überziehung f; **to have an ~** sein Konto überzogen haben.

overdrawn ['əuvə'drɔ:n] a account überzogen.

overdrive ['əuvədraiv] n (Aut) Schnellgang m.

overdue ['əuvə'dju:] a überfällig.

overenthusiastic ['əuvərinθju:zi'æstik] a zu begeistert.

overestimate ['əuvər'estimeit] vt überschätzen.

overexcited ['əuvərik'saitid] a überreizt; children aufgeregt.

overexertion ['əuvərig'zɜ:ʃən] n Überanstrengung f.

overexpose ['əuvəriks'pəuz] vt (Phot) überbelichten.

overflow ['əuvə'fləu] vi überfließen; ['əuvəfləu] n (excess) Überschuß m; (outlet) Überlauf m.

overgrown ['əuvə'grəun] a garden verwildert.

overhaul ['əuvə'hɔ:l] vt car überholen; plans überprüfen; ['əuvəhɔ:l] n Überholung f.

overhead ['əuvəhed] a Hoch-; wire oberirdisch; lighting Decken-; ['əuvə'hed] ad oben; **~s** pl allgemeine Unkosten pl.

overhear ['əuvə'hiə*] vt irreg (mit an)hören.

overjoyed ['əuvə'dʒɔid] a überglücklich.

overland ['əuvəlænd] a Überland-; ['əuvə'pəuə*] ad travel über Land.

overlap ['əuvə'læp] vi sich überschneiden; (objects) sich teilweise decken; ['əuvəlæp] n Überschneidung f.

overload ['əuvə'ləud] vt überladen.

overlook ['əuvə'luk] vt (view from above) überblicken; (not to notice) übersehen; (pardon) hinwegsehen über (+acc).

overlord ['əuvələːd] n Lehnsherr m.

overnight ['əuvə'nait] a journey Nacht-; ad über Nacht; **~ bag** Reisetasche f; **~ stay** Übernachtung f.

overpass ['əuvəpɑːs] n Überführung f.

overpower ['əuvə'pauə*] vt überwältigen; **~ing** a überwältigend.

overrate ['əuvə'reit] vt überschätzen.

override ['əuvə'raid] vt irreg order, decision aufheben; objection übergehen.

overriding ['əuvə'raidiŋ] a Haupt-, vorherrschend.

overrule ['əuvə'ru:l] vt verwerfen; **we were ~d** unser Vorschlag wurde verworfen.

overseas ['əuvə'si:z] a nach/in Übersee, überseeisch, Übersee-.

overseer ['əuvəsiə*] n Aufseher m.

overshadow ['əuvə'ʃædəu] vt überschatten.

overshoot ['əuvə'ʃu:t] vt irreg runway hinausschießen über (+acc).

oversight ['əuvəsait] n (mistake) Versehen nt.

oversimplify ['əuvə'simplifai] vt zu sehr vereinfachen.

oversleep ['əuvə'sli:p] vi irreg verschlafen.

overspill ['əuvəspil] n (Bevölkerungs)Überschuß m.

overstate ['əuvə'steit] vt übertreiben; **~ment** Übertreibung f.

overt [əu'vɜ:t] a offen(kundig).

overtake [əuvə'teik] vti irreg überholen.

overthrow [əuvə'θrəu] vt irreg (Pol) stürzen.

overtime ['əuvətaim] n Überstunden pl.

overtone ['əuvətəun] n (fig) Note f.

overture ['əuvətjuə*] n Ouvertüre f; **~s** pl (fig) Angebot nt.

overturn ['əuvə'tɜ:n] vti umkippen.

overweight ['əuvə'weit] a zu dick, zu schwer.

overwhelm [əuvə'welm] vt überwältigen; **~ing** a überwältigend.

overwork ['əuvə'wɜ:k] n Überarbeitung f; vt überlasten; vi sich überarbeiten.

overwrought ['əuvə'rɔ:t] a überreizt.

owe [əu] vt schulden; **to ~ sth to sb** money jdm etw schulden; favour etc jdm etw verdanken.

owing to ['əuiŋ'tu:] prep wegen (+gen).

owl [aul] n Eule f.

own [əun] vt besitzen; (admit) zugeben; **who ~s that?** wem gehört das?; a eigen; **I have money of my ~** ich habe selbst Geld; n Eigentum nt; **all my ~** mein Eigentum; **on one's ~** allein; **~ up** vi zugeben (to sth etw acc); **~er** Besitzer(in f) m, Eigentümer(in f) m; **~ership** Besitz m.

ox [ɒks] n Ochse m.

oxide ['ɒksaid] n Oxyd nt.

oxtail ['ɒksteil] n: **~ soup** Ochsenschwanzsuppe f.

oxyacetylene ['ɒksiə'setili:n] a Azetylensauerstoff-.

oxygen ['ɒksidʒən] n Sauerstoff m; **~ mask** Sauerstoffmaske f; **~ tent** Sauerstoffzelt m.

oyster ['ɔistə*] n Auster f.

ozone ['əuzəun] n Ozon nt.

P

P, p [pi:] n P nt, p nt.

pa [pɑ:] n (col) Papa m.

pace [peis] n Schritt m; (speed) Geschwindigkeit f, Tempo nt; vi schreiten; **to keep ~ with** Schritt halten mit; **~-maker** Schrittmacher m.

pacification [pæsifi'keiʃən] n Befriedung f.

pacifism ['pæsifizəm] n Pazifismus m.

pacifist ['pæsifist] n Pazifist m.

pacify ['pæsifai] vt befrieden; (calm) beruhigen.

pack [pæk] n Packen m; (of wolves) Rudel nt; (of hounds) Meute f; (of cards) Spiel nt; (gang) Bande f; vti case packen; clothes einpacken; **~age** Paket nt; **~age tour** Pauschalreise; f; **~et** Päckchen nt; **~horse** Packpferd nt; **~ ice** Packeis nt; **~ing** (action) Packen nt; (material) Verpackung f; **~ing case** (Pack)kiste f.

pact [pækt] n Pakt m, Vertrag m.

pad [pæd] n (of paper) (Schreib)block m;

(for inking) Stempelkissen *nt; (padding)* Polster *nt; vt* polstern.

paddle ['pædl] *n* Paddel *nt; vt boat* paddeln; *vi (in sea)* plantschen.

paddling pool ['pædlɪŋ puːl] *n* Plantschbecken *nt.*

paddock ['pædək] *n* Koppel *f.*

paddy ['pædɪ] *n* ~ field Reisfeld *nt.*

padlock ['pædlɒk] *n* Vorhängeschloß *nt.*

padre ['pɑːdrɪ] *n* Militärgeistliche(r) *m.*

paediatrics [piːdɪ'ætrɪks] *n* Kinderheilkunde *f.*

pagan ['peɪgən] *a* heidnisch.

page [peɪdʒ] *n* Seite *f; (person)* Page *m; vt (in hotel etc)* ausrufen lassen.

pageant ['pædʒənt] *n* Festzug *m;* ~ry Gepränge *nt.*

pagoda [pə'gəʊdə] *n* Pagode *f.*

pail [peɪl] *n* Eimer *m.*

pain [peɪn] *n* Schmerz *m,* Schmerzen *pl;* ~s *pl (efforts)* große Mühe *f,* große Anstrengungen *pl;* to be at ~s to do sth sich *(dat)* Mühe geben, etw zu tun; ~ed *a expression* gequält; ~ful *a (physically)* schmerzhaft; *(embarrassing)* peinlich; *(difficult)* mühsam; ~-killing drug schmerzstillende(s) Mittel *nt;* ~less *a* schmerzlos; ~staking *a* gewissenhaft.

paint [peɪnt] *n* Farbe *f, vt* anstreichen; *picture* malen; ~brush Pinsel *m;* ~er Maler *m; (decorator)* Maler *m,* Anstreicher *m;* ~ing *(act)* Malen *nt; (Art)* Malerei *f; (picture)* Bild *nt,* Gemälde *nt.*

pair [peə*] *n* Paar *nt;* ~ of scissors Schere *f;* ~ of trousers Hose *f.*

pajamas *(US)* [pə'dʒɑːməz] *npl* Schlafanzug *m.*

pal [pæl] *n (col)* Kumpel *m; (woman) (gute)* Freundin *f.*

palace ['pæləs] *n* Palast *m,* Schloß *nt.*

palatable ['pælətəbl] *a* schmackhaft.

palate ['pælɪt] *n* Gaumen *m; (taste)* Geschmack *m.*

palaver [pə'lɑːvə*] *n (col)* Theater *nt.*

pale [peɪl] *a face* blaß, bleich; *colour* hell, blaß; ~ness *f* Blässe *f.*

palette ['pælɪt] *n* Palette *f.*

palisade [pælɪ'seɪd] *n* Palisade *f.*

pall [pɔːl] *n* Bahr- or Leichentuch *nt; (of smoke)* (Rauch)wolke *f; vi* jeden Reiz verlieren, verblassen; ~bearer Sargträger *m.*

pallid ['pælɪd] *a* blaß, bleich.

pally ['pælɪ] *a (col)* befreundet.

palm [pɑːm] *n (of hand)* Handfläche *f; (also* ~ tree) Palme *f;* ~ist Handleserin *f;* P~ Sunday Palmsonntag *m.*

palpable ['pælpəbl] *a (lit, fig)* greifbar.

palpably ['pælpəblɪ] *ad* offensichtlich.

palpitation [pælpɪ'teɪʃən] *n* Herzklopfen *nt.*

paltry ['pɔːltrɪ] *a* armselig.

pamper ['pæmpə*] *vt* verhätscheln.

pamphlet ['pæmflət] *n* Broschüre *f.*

pan [pæn] *n* Pfanne *f; vi (Cine)* schwenken.

pan- [pæn] *pref* Pan-, All-.

panacea [pænə'sɪə] *n (fig)* Allheilmittel *nt.*

panache [pə'næʃ] *n* Schwung *m.*

pancake ['pænkeɪk] *n* Pfannkuchen *m.*

panda ['pændə] *n* Panda *m.*

pandemonium [pændɪ'məʊnɪəm] *n* Hölle *f; (noise)* Höllenlärm *m.*

pander ['pændə*] *vi* sich richten *(to* nach*).*

pane [peɪn] *n* (Fenster)scheibe *f.*

panel ['pænl] *n (of wood)* Tafel *f; (TV)* Diskussionsteilnehmer *pl;* ~ing *(US),* ~ling Täfelung *f.*

pang [pæŋ] *n* Stich *m,* Qual *f;* ~s of conscience Gewissensbisse *pl.*

panic ['pænɪk] *n* Panik *f; a* panisch; *vi* von panischem Schrecken erfaßt werden, durchdrehen; don't ~ *(nur)* keine Panik; ~ky *a person* überängstlich.

pannier ['pænɪə*] *n* (Trage)korb *m; (on bike)* Satteltasche *f.*

panorama [pænə'rɑːmə] *n* Rundblick *m,* Panorama *nt.*

panoramic [pænə'ræmɪk] *a* Panorama-.

pansy ['pænzɪ] *n (flower)* Stiefmütterchen *nt; (col)* Schwule(r) *m.*

pant [pænt] *vi* keuchen; *(dog)* hecheln.

pantechnicon [pæn'teknɪkən] *n* Möbelwagen *m.*

panther ['pænθə*] *n* Panther *m.*

panties ['pæntɪz] *npl* (Damen)slip *m.*

pantomime ['pæntəmaɪm] *n* Märchenkomödie *f* um Weihnachten.

pantry ['pæntrɪ] *n* Vorratskammer *f.*

pants [pænts] *npl* Unterhose *f; (trousers)* Hose *f.*

papal ['peɪpəl] *a* päpstlich.

paper ['peɪpə*] *n* Papier *nt; (newspaper)* Zeitung *f; (essay)* Vortrag *m,* Referat *nt; a* Papier-, aus Papier; *vt wall* tapezieren; ~s *pl (identity)* Ausweis(papiere *pl) m;* ~back Taschenbuch *nt;* ~ bag Tüte *f;* ~ clip Büroklammer *f;* ~weight Briefbeschwerer *m;* ~work Schreibarbeit *f.*

papier-mâché ['pæpɪeɪ'mæʃeɪ] *n* Papiermaché *nt.*

paprika ['pæprɪkə] *n* Paprika *m.*

papyrus [pə'paɪərəs] *n* Papyrus *m.*

par [pɑː*] *n (Comm)* Nennwert *m; (Golf)* Par *nt;* on a ~ with ebenbürtig *(+dat);* to be on a ~ with sb sich mit jdm messen können; below ~ unter (jds) Niveau.

parable ['pærəbl] *n* Parabel *f; (Rel)* Gleichnis *nt.*

parachute ['pærəʃuːt] *n* Fallschirm *m; vi* (mit dem Fallschirm) abspringen.

parachutist ['pærəʃuːtɪst] *n* Fallschirmspringer *m.*

parade [pə'reɪd] *n* Parade *f; vt* aufmarschieren lassen; *vi* paradieren, vorbeimarschieren.

paradise ['pærədaɪs] *n* Paradies *nt.*

paradox ['pærədɒks] *n* Paradox *nt;* ~ical [pærə'dɒksɪkəl] *a* paradox, widersinnig; ~ically [pærə'dɒksɪkəlɪ] *ad* paradoxerweise.

paraffin ['pærəfɪn] *n* Paraffin *nt.*

paragraph ['pærəgrɑːf] *n* Absatz *m,* Paragraph *m.*

parallel ['pærəlel] *a* parallel; *n* Parallele *f.*

paralysis [pə'rælɪsɪs] *n* Lähmung *f.*

paralyze ['pærəlaɪz] *vt* lähmen.

paramount ['pærəmaʊnt] *a* höchste(r, s), oberste(r, s).

paranoia [pærə'nɔiə] n Paranoia f.

parapet ['pærəpit] n Brüstung f.

paraphernalia ['pærəfə'neiliə] n Zubehör nt, Utensilien pl.

paraphrase ['pærəfreiz] vt umschreiben.

paraplegic [pærə'pli:dʒik] n Querschnittsgelähmte(r) mf.

parasite ['pærəsait] n (lit, fig) Schmarotzer m, Parasit m.

parasol ['pærəsɔl] n Sonnenschirm m.

paratrooper ['pærətru:pə*] n Fallschirmjäger m.

parcel ['pɑ:sl] n Paket nt; vt (also ~ up) einpacken.

parch [pɑ:tʃ] vt (aus)dörren; I'm ~ed ich bin am Verdursten.

parchment ['pɑ:tʃmənt] n Pergament nt.

pardon ['pɑ:dn] n Verzeihung f; vt (Jur) begnadigen; ~ me!, I beg your ~! verzeihen Sie bitte!; (objection) aber ich bitte Sie!; ~ me? (US), (I beg your) ~? wie bitte?

parent ['pɛərənt] n Elternteil m; ~al [pə'rentl] a elterlich, Eltern-; ~hood Elternschaft f; ~s pl Eltern pl; ~ ship Mutterschiff nt.

parenthesis [pə'renθisis] n Klammer f; (sentence) Parenthese f.

parish ['pæriʃ] n Gemeinde f; ~ioner [pə'riʃənə*] Gemeindemitglied nt.

parity ['pæriti] n (Fin) Umrechnungskurs m, Parität f.

park [pɑ:k] n Park m; vti parken; ~ing Parken nt; 'no ~ing' Parken verboten; ~ing lot (US) Parkplatz m; ~ing meter Parkuhr f; ~ing place Parkplatz m.

parliament ['pɑ:ləmənt] n Parlament nt; ~ary [pɑ:lə'mentəri] a parlamentarisch, Parlaments-.

parlour, (US) parlor ['pɑ:lə*] n Salon m, Wohnzimmer nt.

parlous ['pɑ:ləs] a state schlimm.

parochial [pə'rəukiəl] a Gemeinde-, gemeindlich; (narrow-minded) eng(stirnig), Provinz-.

parody ['pærədi] n Parodie f; vt parodieren.

parole [pə'rəul] n: on ~ (prisoner) auf Bewährung.

parquet ['pɑ:kei] n Parkett(fußboden m) nt.

parrot ['pærət] n Papagei m; ~ fashion ad wie ein Papagei.

parry ['pæri] vt parieren, abwehren.

parsimonious a, ~ly ad [pɑ:si'məuniəs, -li] knauserig.

parsley ['pɑ:sli] n Petersilie f.

parsnip ['pɑ:snip] n Pastinake f, Petersilienwurzel f.

parson ['pɑ:sn] n Pfarrer m.

part [pɑ:t] n (piece) Teil m, Stück nt; (Theat) Rolle f; (of machine) Teil nt; a Teil-; ad = partly; vt trennen; hair scheiteln; vi (people) sich trennen, Abschied nehmen; for my ~ ich für meinen Teil; for the most ~ meistens, größtenteils; ~ with vt hergeben; (renounce) aufgeben; in ~ exchange in Zahlung; ~ial ['pɑ:ʃəl] a (incomplete) teilweise, Teil-; (biased) eingenommen, parteiisch; eclipse partiell; to be ~ial to eine (besondere) Vorliebe haben für; ~ially ['pɑ:ʃəli] ad teilweise, zum Teil.

participate [pɑ:'tisipeit] vi teilnehmen (in an +dat).

participation [pɑ:tisi'peiʃən] n Teilnahme f; (sharing) Beteiligung f.

participle ['pɑ:tisipl] n Partizip nt, Mittelwort nt.

particular [pə'tikjulə*] a bestimmt, speziell; (exact) genau; (fussy) eigen; n Einzelheit f; ~s pl (details) Einzelheiten pl; Personalien pl; ~ly ad besonders.

parting ['pɑ:tiŋ] n (separation) Abschied m, Trennung f; (of hair) Scheitel m; a Abschieds-.

partisan [pɑ:ti'zæn] n Parteigänger m; (guerrilla) Partisan m; a Partei-; Partisanen-.

partition [pɑ:'tiʃən] n (wall) Trennwand f; (division) Teilung f.

partly ['pɑ:tli] ad zum Teil, teilweise.

partner ['pɑ:tnə*] n Partner m; (Comm also) Gesellschafter m, Teilhaber m; vt der Partner sein von; ~ship Partnerschaft f, Gemeinschaft f; (Comm) Teilhaberschaft f.

partridge ['pɑ:tridʒ] n Rebhuhn nt.

part-time ['pɑ:t'taim] a (half-day only) halbtägig, Halbtags-; (part of the week only) nebenberuflich; ad halbtags; nebenberuflich.

party ['pɑ:ti] n (Pol, Jur) Partei f; (group) Gesellschaft f; (celebration) Party f; a dress Gesellschafts-, Party-; politics Partei-.

pass [pɑ:s] vt vorbeikommen an (+dat); (on foot) vorbeigehen an (+dat); vorbeifahren an (+dat); (surpass) übersteigen; (hand on) weitergeben; (approve) gelten lassen, genehmigen; time verbringen; exam bestehen; vi (go by) vorbeigehen, vorbeifahren; (years) vergehen; (be successful) bestehen; n (in mountains) Paß m; (permission) Durchgangs- or Passierschein m; (Sport) Paß m, Abgabe f; (in exam) Bestehen nt; to get a ~ bestehen; ~ away vi (euph) verscheiden; ~ by vi vorbeigehen; vorbeifahren; (years) vergehen; ~ for vi gehalten werden für; ~ out vi (faint) ohnmächtig werden; ~able a road passierbar, befahrbar; (fairly good) passabel, leidlich; ~ably ad leidlich, ziemlich; ~age ['pæsidʒ] (corridor) Gang m, Korridor m; (in book) (Text)stelle f; (voyage) Überfahrt f; ~ageway Passage f, Durchgang m.

passenger ['pæsindʒə*] n Passagier m; (on bus) Fahrgast m; (in aeroplane also) Fluggast m.

passer-by ['pɑ:sə'bai] n Passant(in f) m.

passing ['pɑ:siŋ] n (death) Ableben nt; a car vorbeifahrend; thought, affair momentan; in ~ en passant.

passion ['pæʃən] n Leidenschaft f; ~ate a, ~ately ad leidenschaftlich.

passive ['pæsiv] n Passiv nt; a Passiv-, passiv.

Passover ['pɑ:səuvə*] n Passahfest nt.

passport ['pɑ:spɔ:t] n (Reise)paß m.

password ['pɑ:swɜ:d] n Parole f, Kennwort nt, Losung f.

past [pɑ:st] n Vergangenheit f; ad vorbei; prep **to go ~ sth** an etw (dat) vorbeigehen; **to be ~ 10** (with age) über 10 sein; (with time) nach 10 sein; **a years** vergangen; president etc ehemalig.

paste [peɪst] n (for pastry) Teig m; (fish- etc) Paste f; (glue) Kleister m; vt kleben; (put — on) mit Kleister bestreichen.

pastel ['pæstəl] a colour Pastell-.

pasteurized ['pæstəraɪzd] a pasteurisiert.

pastille ['pæstɪl] n Pastille f.

pastime ['pɑ:staɪm] n Hobby nt, Zeitvertreib m.

pastor ['pɑ:stə*] n Pastor m, Pfarrer m.

pastoral ['pɑ:stərəl] a literature Schäfer-, Pastoral-.

pastry ['peɪstrɪ] n Blätterteig m; (tarts etc) Stückchen pl; Tortengebäck nt.

pasture ['pɑ:stʃə*] n Weide f.

pasty ['pæstɪ] n (Fleisch)pastete f; ['peɪstɪ] a bläßlich, käsig.

pat [pæt] n leichte(r) Schlag m, Klaps m; vt tätscheln.

patch [pætʃ] n Fleck m; vt flicken; **~ of fog** Nebelfeld nt; **a bad ~** eine Pechsträhne; **~work** Patchwork nt; **~y** a (irregular) ungleichmäßig.

pate [peɪt] n Schädel m.

patent ['peɪtənt] n Patent nt; vt patentieren lassen; (by authorities) patentieren; a offenkundig; **~ leather** Lackleder nt; **~ly** ad offensichtlich; **~ medicine** pharmazeutische(s) Präparat nt.

paternal [pə'tɜ:nl] a väterlich; **his ~ grandmother** seine Großmutter väterlicherseits; **~istic** [pətɜ:nə'lɪstɪk] a väterlich, onkelhaft.

paternity [pə'tɜ:nɪtɪ] n Vaterschaft f.

path [pɑ:θ] n Pfad m; Weg m; (of the sun) Bahn f.

pathetic a, **~ally** ad [pə'θetɪk, -lɪ] (very bad) kläglich; **it's ~** es ist zum Weinen.

pathological [pæθə'lɒdʒɪkəl] a krankhaft, pathologisch.

pathologist [pə'θɒlədʒɪst] n Pathologe m.

pathology [pə'θɒlədʒɪ] n Pathologie f.

pathos ['peɪθɒs] n Rührseligkeit f.

pathway ['pɑ:θweɪ] n Pfad m, Weg m.

patience ['peɪʃəns] n Geduld f; (Cards) Patience f.

patient ['peɪʃənt] n Patient(in f) m, Kranke(r) mf; a, **~ly** ad geduldig.

patio ['pætɪəʊ] n Innenhof m; (outside) Terrasse f.

patriotic [pætrɪ'ɒtɪk] a patriotisch.

patriotism ['pætrɪətɪzəm] n Patriotismus m.

patrol [pə'trəʊl] n Patrouille f; (police) Streife f; vt patrouillieren in (+dat); vi (police) die Runde machen; (Mil) patrouillieren; **on ~** (police) auf Streife; **~ car** Streifenwagen m; **~man** (US) (Streifen)polizist m.

patron ['peɪtrən] n (in shop) (Stamm)kunde m; (in hotel) (Stamm)gast m; (supporter) Förderer m; **~age** ['pætrənɪdʒ] Förderung f; Schirmherrschaft f; (Comm) Kundschaft f; **~ize** also ['pætrənaɪz] vt (support) unterstützen; shop besuchen; ['pætrənaɪz] (treat condescendingly) von oben herab behandeln; **~izing** a attitude herablassend; **~ saint** Schutzheilige(r) mf, Schutzpatron(in f) m.

patter ['pætə*] n (sound) (of feet) Trappeln nt; (of rain) Prasseln nt; (sales talk) Art f zu reden, Gerede nt; vi (feet) trappeln; (rain) prasseln.

pattern ['pætən] n Muster nt; (sewing) Schnittmuster nt; (knitting) Strickanleitung f; vt **~ sth on sth** etw nach etw bilden.

paunch [pɔ:ntʃ] n dicke(r) Bauch m, Wanst m.

pauper ['pɔ:pə*] n Arme(r) mf.

pause [pɔ:z] n Pause f; vi innehalten.

pave [peɪv] vt pflastern; **to ~ the way for** den Weg bahnen für; **~ment** (Brit) Bürgersteig m.

pavilion [pə'vɪlɪən] n Pavillon m; (Sport) Klubhaus nt.

paving ['peɪvɪŋ] n Straßenpflaster nt.

paw [pɔ:] n Pfote f; (of big cats) Tatze f, Pranke f; vt (scrape) scharren; (handle) betatschen.

pawn [pɔ:n] n Pfand nt; (chess) Bauer m; vt versetzen, verpfänden; **~broker** Pfandleiher m; **~shop** Pfandhaus nt.

pay [peɪ] n Bezahlung f, Lohn m; **to be in sb's ~** von jdm bezahlt werden; irreg vt bezahlen; **it would ~ you to ...** es würde sich für dich lohnen, zu ...; **to ~ attention** achtgeben (to auf +acc); vi zahlen; (be profitable) sich bezahlt machen; **it doesn't ~** es lohnt sich nicht; **~ for** vt bezahlen für; **~ up** vi bezahlen, seine Schulden begleichen; **~able** a zahlbar, fällig; **~day** Zahltag m; **~ee** [peɪ'i:] Zahlungsempfänger m; **~ing** a einträglich, rentabel; **~load** Nutzlast f; **~ment** Bezahlung f; **~ packet** Lohntüte f; **~roll** Lohnliste f.

pea [pi:] n Erbse f; **~ souper** (col) Suppe f, Waschküche f.

peace [pi:s] n Friede(n) m; **~able** a, **~ably** ad friedlich; **~ful** a friedlich, ruhig; **~-keeping** a Friedens-; **~-keeping role** Vermittlerrolle f; **~ offering** Friedensangebot nt; **~time** Friede(n) m.

peach [pi:tʃ] n Pfirsich m.

peacock ['pi:kɒk] n Pfau m.

peak [pi:k] n Spitze f; (of mountain) Gipfel m; (fig) Höhepunkt m; (of cap) (Mützen)schirm m; **~ period** Stoßzeit f, Hauptzeit f.

peal [pi:l] n (Glocken)läuten nt.

peanut ['pi:nʌt] n Erdnuß f; **~ butter** Erdnußbutter f.

pear [pɛə*] n Birne f.

pearl [pɜ:l] n Perle f.

peasant ['pezənt] n Bauer m.

peat [pi:t] n Torf m.

pebble ['pebl] n Kiesel m.

peck [pek] vti picken; n (with beak) Schnabelhieb m; (kiss) flüchtige(r) Kuß m; **~ish** a (col) ein bißchen hungrig.

peculiar [pɪ'kju:lɪə*] a (odd) seltsam; **~ to** charakteristisch für; **~ity** [pɪkjʊlɪ'ærɪtɪ] (singular quality) Besonderheit f; (strange-

ness) Eigenartigkeit *f;* ~**ly** *ad* seltsam; *(especially)* besonders.

pecuniary [pɪ'kjuːnɪərɪ] *a* Geld-, finanziell, pekuniär.

pedal ['pedl] *n* Pedal *nt; vti (cycle)* fahren, radfahren.

pedant ['pedənt] *n* Pedant *m.*

pedantic [pɪ'dæntɪk] *a* pedantisch.

pedantry ['pedəntrɪ] *n* Pedanterie *f.*

peddle ['pedl] *vt* hausieren gehen mit.

pedestal ['pedɪstl] *n* Sockel *m.*

pedestrian [pɪ'destrɪən] *n* Fußgänger *m; a* Fußgänger-; *(humdrum)* langweilig; ~ **crossing** Fußgängerüberweg *m;* ~ **precinct** Fußgängerzone *f.*

pediatrics [piːdɪ'ætrɪks] *n (US) =* **paediatrics.**

pedigree ['pedɪgriː] *n* Stammbaum *m; a animal* reinrassig, Zucht-.

pee [piː] *vi (col)* pissen, pinkeln.

peek [piːk] *n* flüchtige(r) Blick *m; vi* gucken.

peel [piːl] *n* Schale *f; vt* schälen; *vi (paint etc)* abblättern; *(skin)* sich schälen; ~ **ings** *pl* Schalen *pl.*

peep [piːp] *n (look)* neugierige(r) Blick *m; (sound)* Piepsen *nt; vi (look)* neugierig gucken; ~**hole** Guckloch *nt.*

peer [pɪə*] *vi* spähen; angestrengt schauen *(at* auf *+acc); (peep)* gucken; *n (nobleman)* Peer *m; (equal)* Ebenbürtige(r) *m; his* ~**s** seinesgleichen; ~**age** Peerswürde *f;* ~**less** *a* unvergleichlich.

peeve [piːv] *vt (col)* verärgern; ~**d** *a* ärgerlich; *person* sauer.

peevish ['piːvɪʃ] *a* verdrießlich, brummig; ~**ness** Verdrießlichkeit *f.*

peg [peg] *n* Stift *m; (hook)* Haken *m; (stake)* Pflock *m; clothes* ~ Wäscheklammer *f;* **off the** ~ von der Stange.

pejorative [pɪ'dʒɒrɪtɪv] *a* pejorativ, herabsetzend.

pekinese [piːkɪ'niːz] *n* Pekinese *m.*

pelican ['pelɪkən] *n* Pelikan *m.*

pellet ['pelɪt] *n* Kügelchen *nt.*

pelmet ['pelmɪt] *n* Blende *f,* Schabracke *f.*

pelt [pelt] *vt* bewerfen; *n* Pelz *m,* Fell *nt;* ~ **down** *vi* niederprasseln.

pelvis ['pelvɪs] *n* Becken *nt.*

pen [pen] *n (fountain* ~*)* Federhalter *m; (ball-point)* Kuli *m; (for sheep)* Pferch *m;* **have you got a** ~**?** haben Sie etwas zum Schreiben?

penal ['piːnl] *a* Straf-; ~**ize** *vt (make punishable)* unter Strafe stellen; *(punish)* bestrafen; *(disadvantage)* benachteiligen; ~**ty** ['penlti] Strafe *f; (Ftbl)* Elfmeter *m;* ~**ty area** Strafraum *m;* ~**ty kick** Elfmeter *m.*

penance ['penəns] *n* Buße *f.*

pence [pens] *npl (pl of penny)* Pence *pl.*

penchant ['pãːnʃãːn] *n* Vorliebe *f,* Schwäche *f.*

pencil ['pensl] *n* Bleistift *m;* ~ **sharpener** Bleistiftspitzer *m.*

pendant ['pendənt] *n* Anhänger *m.*

pending ['pendɪŋ] *prep* bis (zu); *a* unentschieden, noch offen.

pendulum ['pendjuləm] *n* Pendel *nt.*

penetrate ['penɪtreɪt] *vt* durchdringen; *(enter into)* eindringen in *(+acc).*

penetrating ['penɪtreɪtɪŋ] *a* durchdringend; *analysis* scharfsinnig.

penetration [penɪ'treɪʃən] *n* Durchdringen *nt;* Eindringen *nt.*

penfriend ['penfrend] *n* Brieffreund(in *f*) *m.*

penguin ['peŋgwɪn] *n* Pinguin *m.*

penicillin [penɪ'sɪlɪn] *n* Penizillin *nt.*

peninsula [pɪ'nɪnsjulə] *n* Halbinsel *f.*

penis ['piːnɪs] *n* Penis *m,* männliche(s) Glied *nt.*

penitence ['penɪtəns] *n* Reue *f.*

penitent ['penɪtənt] *a* reuig; ~**iary** [penɪ'tenʃərɪ] *(US)* Zuchthaus *nt.*

penknife ['pennaɪf] *n* Federmesser *nt.*

pen name ['penneɪm] *n* Pseudonym *nt.*

pennant ['penənt] *n* Wimpel *m; (official* ~*)* Stander *m.*

penniless ['penɪləs] *a* mittellos, ohne einen Pfennig.

penny ['penɪ] *n* Penny *m.*

pension ['penʃən] *n* Rente *f; (for civil servants, executives etc)* Ruhegehalt *nt,* Pension *f;* ~**able** *a person* pensionsberechtigt; *job* mit Renten- or Pensionsanspruch; ~**er** Rentner(in *f*) *m; (civil servant, executive)* Pensionär *m;* ~ **fund** Rentenfonds *m.*

pensive ['pensɪv] *a* nachdenklich.

pentagon ['pentəgən] *n* Fünfeck *nt.*

Pentecost ['pentɪkɒst] *n* Pfingsten *pl or sing.*

penthouse ['penthaus] *n* Dachterrassenwohnung *f.*

pent-up ['pentʌp] *a feelings* angestaut.

penultimate [pɪ'nʌltɪmət] *a* vorletzte(r, s).

people ['piːpl] *n (nation)* Volk *nt; (inhabitants)* Bevölkerung *f; (persons)* Leute *pl;* ~ **think** man glaubt; *vt* besiedeln.

pep [pep] *n (col)* Schwung *m,* Schmiß *m;* ~ **up** *vt* aufmöbeln.

pepper ['pepə*] *n* Pfeffer *m; (vegetable)* Paprika *m; vt (pelt)* bombardieren; ~**mint** *(plant)* Pfefferminze *f; (sweet)* Pfefferminz *nt.*

peptalk ['peptɔːk] *n (col)* Anstachelung *f.*

per [pɜː*] *prep* pro; ~ **annum** pro Jahr; ~ **cent** Prozent *nt.*

perceive [pə'siːv] *vt (realize)* wahrnehmen, spüren; *(understand)* verstehen.

percentage [pə'sentɪdʒ] *n* Prozentsatz *m.*

perceptible [pə'septəbl] *a* merklich, wahrnehmbar.

perception [pə'sepʃən] *n* Wahrnehmung *f; (insight)* Einsicht *f.*

perceptive [pə'septɪv] *a person* aufmerksam; *analysis* tiefgehend.

perch [pɜːtʃ] *n* Stange *f; (fish)* Flußbarsch *m; vi* sitzen, hocken.

percolator ['pɜːkəleɪtə*] *n* Kaffeemaschine *f.*

percussion [pɜː'kʌʃən] *n (Mus)* Schlagzeug *nt.*

peremptory [pə'remptərɪ] *a* schroff.

perennial [pə'renɪəl] *a* wiederkehrend; *(everlasting)* unvergänglich; *n* perennierende Pflanze *f.*

perfect ['pɜːfɪkt] *a* vollkommen; *crime,*

solution perfekt; *(Gram)* vollendet; *n (Gram)* Perfekt *nt;* [pə'fekt] *vt* vervollkommnen; ~**ion** [pə'fekʃən] Vollkommenheit *f;* Perfektion *f;* ~**ionist** [pə'fekʃənɪst] Perfektionist *m;* ~**ly** *ad* vollkommen, perfekt; *(quite)* ganz, einfach.

perforate ['pɜːfəreɪt] *vt* durchlöchern; ~**d** *a* durchlöchert, perforiert.

perforation [pɜːfə'reɪʃən] *n* Perforation *f.*

perform [pə'fɔːm] *vt (carry out)* durch- or ausführen; *task* verrichten; *(Theat)* spielen, geben; *vi (Theat)* auftreten; ~**ance** Durchführung *f; (efficiency)* Leistung *f; (show)* Vorstellung *f;* ~**er** Künstler(in *f) m;* ~**ing** *a animal* dressiert.

perfume ['pɜːfjuːm] *n* Duft *m; (lady's)* Parfüm *nt.*

perfunctory [pə'fʌŋktərɪ] *a* oberflächlich, mechanisch.

perhaps [pə'hæps] *ad* vielleicht.

peril ['perɪl] *n* Gefahr *f;* ~**ous** *a,* ~**ously** *ad* gefährlich.

perimeter [pə'rɪmɪtə*] *n* Peripherie *f; (of circle etc)* Umfang *m.*

period ['pɪərɪəd] *n* Periode *f,* Zeit *f; (Gram)* Punkt *m; (Med)* Periode *f; a costume* historisch; ~**ic(al)** [pɪərɪ'ɒdɪk(əl)] *a* periodisch; ~**ical** *n* Zeitschrift *f;* ~**ically** [pɪərɪ'ɒdɪkəlɪ] *ad* periodisch.

peripheral [pə'rɪfərəl] *a* Rand-, peripher.

periphery [pə'rɪfərɪ] *n* Peripherie *f,* Rand *m.*

periscope ['perɪskəup] *n* Periskop *nt,* Sehrohr *nt.*

perish ['perɪʃ] *vi* umkommen; *(material)* unbrauchbar werden; *(fruit)* verderben; ~ **the thought!** daran wollen wir nicht denken; ~**able** *a fruit* leicht verderblich; ~**ing** *a (col: cold)* eisig.

perjure ['pɜːdʒə*] *vr:* ~ **o.s.** einen Meineid leisten.

perjury ['pɜːdʒərɪ] *n* Meineid *m.*

perk [pɜːk] *n (col: fringe benefit)* Vorteil *m,* Vergünstigung *f;* ~ **up** *vi* munter werden; *vt ears* spitzen; ~**y** *a (cheerful)* keck.

perm [pɜːm] *n* Dauerwelle *f.*

permanence ['pɜːmənəns] *n* Dauer(haftigkeit) *f,* Beständigkeit *f.*

permanent *a,* ~**ly** *ad* ['pɜːmənənt, —lɪ] dauernd, ständig.

permissible [pə'mɪsəbl] *a* zulässig.

permission [pə'mɪʃən] *n* Erlaubnis *f,* Genehmigung *f.*

permissive [pə'mɪsɪv] *a* nachgiebig; *society etc* permissiv.

permit ['pɜːmɪt] *n* Zulassung *f,* Erlaubnis(schein *m) f;* [pə'mɪt] *vt* erlauben, zulassen.

permutation [pɜːmju'teɪʃən] *n* Veränderung *f; (Math)* Permutation *f.*

pernicious [pɜː'nɪʃəs] *a* schädlich.

perpendicular [pɜːpən'dɪkjulə*] *a* senkrecht.

perpetrate ['pɜːpɪtreɪt] *vt* begehen, verüben.

perpetual *a,* ~**ly** *ad* [pə'petjuəl, -ɪ] dauernd, ständig.

perpetuate [pə'petjueɪt] *vt* verewigen, bewahren.

perpetuity [pɜːpɪ'tjuːɪtɪ] *n* Ewigkeit *f.*

perplex [pə'pleks] *vt* verblüffen; ~**ed** *a* verblüfft, perplex; ~**ing** *a* verblüffend; ~**ity** Verblüffung *f.*

persecute ['pɜːsɪkjuːt] *vt* verfolgen.

persecution [pɜːsɪ'kjuːʃən] *n* Verfolgung *f.*

perseverance [pɜːsɪ'vɪərəns] *n* Ausdauer *f.*

persevere [pɜːsɪ'vɪə*] *vi* beharren, durchhalten.

persist [pə'sɪst] *vi (in belief etc)* bleiben *(in* bei*); (rain, smell)* andauern; *(continue)* nicht aufhören; ~**ence** Beharrlichkeit *f;* ~**ent** *a,* ~**ently** *ad* beharrlich; *(unending)* ständig.

person ['pɜːsn] *n* Person *f,* Mensch *m; (Gram)* Person *f;* **on one's** ~ bei sich; **in** ~ persönlich; ~**able** *a* gut aussehend; ~**al** *a* persönlich; *(private)* privat; *(of body)* körperlich, Körper-; ~**ality** [pɜːsə'nælɪtɪ] Persönlichkeit *f;* ~**ally** *ad* persönlich; ~**ification** [pɜːsɒnɪfɪ'keɪʃən] Verkörperung *f;* ~**ify** [pɜː'sɒnɪfaɪ] *vt* verkörpern, personifizieren.

personnel [pɜːsə'nel] *n* Personal *nt; (in factory)* Belegschaft *f;* ~ **manager** Personalchef *m.*

perspective [pə'spektɪv] *n* Perspektive *f.*

Perspex [superscript text] ['pɜːspeks] *n* Plexiglas ® *nt.*

perspicacity [pɜːspɪ'kæsɪtɪ] *n* Scharfsinn *m.*

perspiration [pɜːspə'reɪʃən] *n* Transpiration *f.*

perspire [pəs'paɪə*] *vi* transpirieren.

persuade [pə'sweɪd] *vt* überreden; *(convince)* überzeugen.

persuasion [pə'sweɪʒən] *n* Überredung *f;* Überzeugung *f.*

persuasive *a,* ~**ly** *ad* [pə'sweɪsɪv, -lɪ] überzeugend.

pert [pɜːt] *a* keck.

pertain [pɜː'teɪn] *vt* gehören *(to* zu*).*

pertaining [pɜː'teɪnɪŋ] ~ **to** betreffend *(+acc).*

pertinent ['pɜːtɪnənt] *a* relevant.

perturb [pə'tɜːb] *vt* beunruhigen.

perusal [pə'ruːzəl] *n* Durchsicht *f.*

peruse [pə'ruːz] *vt* lesen.

pervade [pɜː'veɪd] *vt* erfüllen, durchziehen.

pervasive [pɜː'veɪsɪv] *a* durchdringend; *influence etc* allgegenwärtig.

perverse *a,* ~**ly** *ad* [pə'vɜːs, -lɪ] pervers; *(obstinate)* eigensinnig; ~**ness** Perversität *f;* Eigensinn *m.*

perversion [pə'vɜːʃən] *n* Perversion *f; (of justice)* Verdrehung *f.*

perversity [pə'vɜːsɪtɪ] *n* Perversität *f.*

pervert ['pɜːvɜːt] *n* perverse(r) Mensch *m;* [pə'vɜːt] *vt* verdrehen; *(morally)* verderben.

pessimism ['pesɪmɪzəm] *n* Pessimismus *m.*

pessimist ['pesɪmɪst] *n* Pessimist *m;* ~**ic** [pesɪ'mɪstɪk] *a* pessimistisch.

pest [pest] *n* Plage *f; (insect)* Schädling *m; (fig) (person)* Nervensäge *f; (thing)* Plage *f.*

pester ['pestə*] *vt* plagen.

pesticide ['pestɪsaɪd] *n* Insektenvertilgungsmittel *nt.*

pestle ['pesl] *n* Stößel *m.*

pet [pet] n (animal) Haustier nt; (person) Liebling m; vt liebkosen, streicheln.

petal ['petl] n Blütenblatt nt.

peter out ['pi:tə aʊt] vi allmählich zu Ende gehen.

petite [pə'ti:t] a zierlich.

petition [pə'tɪʃn] n Bittschrift f.

petrel ['petrəl] n Sturmvogel m.

petrified ['petrɪfaɪd] a versteinert; person starr (vor Schreck).

petrify ['petrɪfaɪ] vt versteinern; person erstarren lassen.

petrol ['petrəl] n (Brit) Benzin nt, Kraftstoff m; ~**engine** Benzinmotor m; ~**eum** [pɪ'trəʊlɪəm] Petroleum nt; ~ **pump** (in car) Benzinpumpe f; (at garage) Zapfsäule f, Tanksäule f; ~ **station** Tankstelle f; ~ **tank** Benzintank m.

petticoat ['petɪkəʊt] n Petticoat m.

pettifogging ['petɪfɒgɪŋ] a kleinlich.

pettiness ['petɪnəs] n Geringfügigkeit f; (meanness) Kleinlichkeit f.

petty ['petɪ] a (unimportant) geringfügig, unbedeutend; (mean) kleinlich; ~ **cash** Portokasse f; ~ **officer** Maat m.

petulant ['petjʊlənt] a leicht reizbar.

pew [pju:] n Kirchenbank f.

pewter ['pju:tə*] n Zinn nt.

phallic ['fælɪk] a phallisch, Phallus-.

phantom ['fæntəm] n Phantom nt, Geist m.

pharmacist ['fɑ:məsɪst] n Pharmazeut m; (druggist) Apotheker m.

pharmacy ['fɑ:məsɪ] n Pharmazie f; (shop) Apotheke f.

phase [feɪz] n Phase f; ~ **out** vt langsam abbauen; model auslaufen lassen; person absetzen.

pheasant ['feznt] n Fasan m.

phenomenal a, ~**ly** ad [fɪ'nɒmɪnl, -nəlɪ] phänomenal.

phenomenon [fɪ'nɒmɪnən] n Phänomen nt; **common** ~ häufige Erscheinung f.

phial ['faɪəl] n Fläschchen nt, Ampulle f.

philanderer [fɪ'lændərə*] n Schwerenöter m.

philanthropic [fɪlən'θrɒpɪk] a philanthropisch.

philanthropist [fɪ'lænθrəpɪst] n Philanthrop m, Menschenfreund m.

philatelist [fɪ'lætəlɪst] n Briefmarkensammler m, Philatelist m.

philately [fɪ'lætəlɪ] n Briefmarkensammeln nt, Philatelie f.

philosopher [fɪ'lɒsəfə*] n Philosoph m.

philosophical [fɪlə'sɒfɪkəl] a philosophisch.

philosophize [fɪlɒsəfaɪz] vi philosophieren.

philosophy [fɪ'lɒsəfɪ] n Philosophie f; Weltanschauung f.

phlegm [flem] n (Med) Schleim m; (calmness) Gelassenheit f; ~**atic** [fleg'mætɪk] a gelassen.

phobia ['fəʊbɪə] n krankhafte Furcht f, Phobie f.

phoenix ['fi:nɪks] n Phönix m.

phone [fəʊn] n (abbr of **telephone**) n Telefon nt; vti telefonieren, anrufen.

phonetics [fəʊ'netɪks] n Phonetik f,

Laut(bildungs)lehre f; pl Lautschrift f.

phon(e)y ['fəʊnɪ] a (col) unecht; excuse faul; money gefälscht; n (person) Schwindler m; (thing) Fälschung; (pound note) Blüte f.

phonograph ['fəʊnəgrɑ:f] n (US) Grammophon nt.

phonology [fəʊ'nɒlədʒɪ] n Phonologie f, Lautlehre f.

phosphate ['fɒsfeɪt] n Phosphat nt.

phosphorus ['fɒsfərəs] n Phosphor m.

photo ['fəʊtəʊ] n (abbr of **photograph**) Foto nt.

photocopier ['fəʊtəʊ'kɒpɪə*] n Kopiergerät nt.

photocopy ['fəʊtəʊkɒpɪ] n Fotokopie f; vt fotokopieren.

photoelectric ['fəʊtəʊɪ'lektrɪk] a fotoelektrisch.

photo finish ['fəʊtəʊ'fɪnɪʃ] n Zielfotografie f.

photogenic [fəʊtəʊ'dʒenɪk] a fotogen.

photograph ['fəʊtəgrɑ:f] n Fotografie f, Aufnahme f; vt fotografieren, aufnehmen; ~**er** [fə'tɒgrəfə] Fotograf m; ~**ic** ['fəʊtə'græfɪk] a fotografisch; ~**y** [fə'tɒgrəfɪ] Fotografie f, Fotografieren nt; (of film, book) Aufnahmen pl.

photostat ['fəʊtəʊstæt] n Fotokopie f.

phrase [freɪz] n (kurzer) Satz m; (Gram) Phrase f; (expression) Redewendung f, Ausdruck m; vt ausdrücken, formulieren; ~ **book** Sprachführer m.

physical a, ~**ly** ad ['fɪzɪkəl, -ɪ] physikalisch; (bodily) körperlich, physisch; ~ **training** Turnen nt.

physician [fɪ'zɪʃn] n Arzt m.

physicist ['fɪzɪsɪst] n Physiker(in f) m.

physics ['fɪzɪks] n Physik f.

physiology [fɪzɪ'ɒlədʒɪ] n Physiologie f.

physiotherapist [fɪzɪə'θerəpɪst] n Heilgymnast(in f) m.

physiotherapy [fɪzɪə'θerəpɪ] n Heilgymnastik f, Physiotherapie f.

physique [fɪ'zi:k] n Körperbau m; (in health) Konstitution f.

pianist ['pɪənɪst] n Pianist(in f) m.

piano ['pjɑ:nəʊ] n Klavier nt, Piano nt; ~**accordion** Akkordeon nt.

piccolo ['pɪkələʊ] n Pikkoloflöte f.

pick [pɪk] n (tool) Pickel m; (choice) Auswahl f; **the** ~ **of** das Beste von; vt (gather) (auf)lesen, sammeln; fruit pflücken; (choose) aussuchen; (Mus) zupfen; **to** ~ **one's nose** in der Nase bohren; **to** ~ **sb's pocket** jdm bestehlen; **to** ~ **at one's food** im Essen herumstochern; ~ **on** vt person herumhacken auf (+dat); **why** ~ **on me?** warum ich?; ~ **out** vt auswählen; ~ **up** vi (improve) sich erholen; vt (lift up) aufheben; (learn) (schnell) mitbekommen; word aufschnappen; (collect) abholen; girl (sich dat) anlachen; speed gewinnen an (+dat); ~ **axe** Pickel m.

picket ['pɪkɪt] n (stake) Pfahl m, Pflock m; (guard) Posten m; (striker) Streikposten m; vt factory (Streik)posten aufstellen vor (+dat); vi (Streik)posten stehen; ~**ing** Streikwache f; ~ **line** Streikpostenlinie f.

pickle ['pɪkl] n (salty mixture) Pökel m; (col) Klemme f; vt (in Essig) einlegen; einpökeln.

pick-me-up ['pɪkmiːʌp] a Schnäpschen nt.

pickpocket ['pɪkpokɪt] n Taschendieb m.

pickup ['pɪkʌp] n (on record player) Tonabnehmer m; (small truck) Lieferwagen m.

picnic ['pɪknɪk] n Picknick nt; vi picknicken.

pictorial [pɪk'tɔːrɪəl] a in Bildern; n Illustrierte f.

picture ['pɪktʃəʳ] n Bild nt; (likeness also) Abbild nt; (in words also) Darstellung f; **in the ~** (fig) im Bild; vt darstellen; (fig: paint) malen; (visualize) sich (dat) vorstellen; **the ~s** (Brit) Kino nt; **~ book** Bilderbuch nt; **~sque** [pɪktʃə'resk] a malerisch.

piddling ['pɪdlɪŋ] a (col) lumpig; task pingelig.

pidgin ['pɪdʒɪn] a: **~ English** Pidgin-Englisch nt.

pie [paɪ] n (meat) Pastete f; (fruit) Torte f.

piebald ['paɪbɔːld] a gescheckt.

piece [piːs] n Stück nt; **to go to ~s** (work, standard) wertlos werden; **he's gone to ~s** er ist vollkommen fertig; **in ~s** entzwei, kaputt; (taken apart) auseinandergenommen; **a ~ of cake** (col) ein Kinderspiel nt; **~meal** ad stückweise, Stück für Stück; **~work** Akkordarbeit f; **~ together** vt zusammensetzen.

pier [pɪəʳ] n Pier m, Mole f.

pierce [pɪəs] vt durchstechen, durchbohren (also look); durchdringen (also fig).

piercing ['pɪəsɪŋ] a durchdringend; cry also gellend; look also durchbohrend.

piety ['paɪətɪ] n Frömmigkeit f.

pig [pɪg] n Schwein nt.

pigeon ['pɪdʒən] n Taube f; **~hole** (compartment) Ablagefach nt; vt ablegen; idea zu den Akten legen.

piggy bank ['pɪgɪbæŋk] n Sparschwein nt.

pigheaded ['pɪg'hedɪd] a dickköpfig.

piglet ['pɪglət] n Ferkel nt, Schweinchen nt.

pigment ['pɪgmənt] n Farbstoff m, Pigment nt (also Biol); **~ation** [pɪgmən'teɪʃən] Färbung f, Pigmentation f.

pigmy ['pɪgmɪ] n = **pygmy**.

pigskin ['pɪgskɪn] n Schweinsleder nt; a schweinsledern.

pigsty ['pɪgstaɪ] n (lit, fig) Schweinestall m.

pigtail ['pɪgteɪl] n Zopf m.

pike [paɪk] n Pike f; (fish) Hecht m.

pilchard ['pɪltʃəd] n Sardine f.

pile [paɪl] n Haufen m; (of books, wood) Stapel m, Stoß m; (in ground) Pfahl m; (of bridge) Pfeiler m; (on carpet) Flausch m; vti (also **~ up**) sich anhäufen.

piles [paɪlz] n Hämorrhoiden pl.

pile-up ['paɪlʌp] n (Aut) Massenzusammenstoß m.

pilfer ['pɪlfəʳ] vt stehlen, klauen; **~ing** Diebstahl m.

pilgrim ['pɪlgrɪm] n Wallfahrer(in f) m, Pilger(in f) m; **~age** Wallfahrt f, Pilgerfahrt f.

pill [pɪl] n Tablette f, Pille f; **the P~** die (Antibaby)pille.

pillage ['pɪlɪdʒ] vt plündern.

pillar ['pɪləʳ] n Pfeiler m, Säule f (also fig); **~ box** (Brit) Briefkasten m.

pillion ['pɪljən] n Soziussitz m; **~ passenger** Soziusfahrer m.

pillory ['pɪlərɪ] n Pranger m; vt an den Pranger stellen; (fig) anprangern.

pillow ['pɪləʊ] n Kissen nt; **~case** Kissenbezug m.

pilot ['paɪlət] n Pilot m; (Naut) Lotse m; a scheme etc Versuchs-; vt führen; ship lotsen; **~ light** Zündflamme f.

pimp [pɪmp] n Zuhälter m.

pimple ['pɪmpl] n Pickel m.

pimply ['pɪmplɪ] a pick(e)lig.

pin [pɪn] n Nadel f; (sewing) Stecknadel f; (Tech) Stift m, Bolzen m; vt stecken, heften (to an +acc); (keep in one position) pressen, drücken; **~s and needles** Kribbeln nt; **I have ~s and needles in my leg** mein Bein ist (mir) eingeschlafen; **~ down** vt (fig) person festnageln (to auf +acc).

pinafore ['pɪnəfɔːʳ] n Schürze f; **~ dress** Kleiderrock m.

pincers ['pɪnsəz] npl Kneif- or Beißzange f; (Med) Pinzette f.

pinch [pɪntʃ] n Zwicken, Kneifen nt; (of salt) Prise f; vti zwicken, kneifen; (shoe) drücken; vt (col) (steal) klauen; (arrest) schnappen; **at a ~** notfalls, zur Not; **to feel the ~** die Not or es zu spüren bekommen.

pincushion ['pɪnkʊʃən] n Nadelkissen nt.

pine [paɪn] n (also **~ tree**) Kiefer f, Föhre f, Pinie f; vi: **~ for** sich sehnen or verzehren nach; **to ~ away** sich zu Tode sehnen.

pineapple ['paɪnæpl] n Ananas f.

ping [pɪŋ] n Peng nt; Kling nt; **~-pong** Pingpong nt.

pink [pɪŋk] n (plant) Nelke f; (colour) Rosa nt; a rosa inv.

pinnacle ['pɪnəkl] n Spitze f.

pinpoint ['pɪnpɔɪnt] vt festlegen.

pinstripe ['pɪnstraɪp] n Nadelstreifen m.

pint [paɪnt] n Pint nt.

pinup ['pɪnʌp] n Pin-up-girl nt.

pioneer [paɪə'nɪəʳ] n Pionier m; (fig also) Bahnbrecher m.

pious ['paɪəs] a fromm; literature geistlich.

pip [pɪp] n Kern m; (sound) Piepen nt; (on uniform) Stern m; **to give sb the ~** (col) jdn verrückt machen.

pipe [paɪp] n (smoking) Pfeife f; (Mus) Flöte f; (tube) Rohr nt; (in house) (Rohr)leitung f; vti (durch Rohre) leiten; (Mus) blasen; **~ down** vi (be quiet) die Luft anhalten; **~-dream** Luftschloß nt; **~-line** (for oil) Pipeline f; **~r** Pfeifer m; (bagpipes) Dudelsackbläser m; **~ tobacco** Pfeifentabak m.

piping ['paɪpɪŋ] n Leitungsnetz nt; (on cake) Dekoration f; (on uniform) Tresse f; ad: **~ hot** siedend heiß.

piquant ['piːkənt] a pikant.

pique [piːk] n gekränkte(r) Stolz m; **~d** a pikiert.

piracy ['paɪərəsɪ] n Piraterie f, Seeräuberei *f; (plagiarism)* Plagiat *nt.*

pirate ['paɪərɪt] *n* Pirat *m*, Seeräuber *m; (plagiarist)* Plagiator *m;* ~ **radio** Schwarzsender *m; (exterritorial)* Piratensender *m.*

pirouette [pɪrʊ'et] *n* Pirouette *f; vi* pirouettieren, eine Pirouette drehen.

Pisces ['paɪsiːz] *n* Fische *pl.*

pissed [pɪst] *a (col)* blau, besoffen.

pistol ['pɪstl] *n* Pistole *f.*

piston ['pɪstən] *n* Kolben *m.*

pit [pɪt] *n* Grube *f; (Theat)* Parterre *nt; (orchestra —)* Orchestergraben *m; vt (mark with scars)* zerfressen; *(compare)* o.s. messen *(against* mit*); sb/sth* messen *(against an +dat);* **the** ~**s** *pl (motor racing)* die Boxen.

pitch [pɪtʃ] *n* Wurf *m; (of trader)* Stand *m; (Sport)* (Spiel)feld *nt; (slope)* Neigung *f; (degree)* Stufe *f; (Mus)* Tonlage *f; (substance)* Pech *nt;* **perfect** ~ **absolute(s)** Gehör *nt;* **to queer sb's** ~ *(col)* jdm alles verderben; *vt* werfen, schleudern; *(set up)* aufschlagen; *song* anstimmen; ~**ed too high** zu hoch; *vi (fall)* (längelang) hinschlagen; *(Naut)* rollen; ~**black** *a* pechschwarz; ~**ed battle** offene Schlacht *f.*

pitcher ['pɪtʃə*] *n* Krug *m.*

pitchfork ['pɪtʃfɔːk] *n* Heugabel *f.*

piteous ['pɪtɪəs] *a* kläglich, erbärmlich.

pitfall ['pɪtfɔːl] *n (fig)* Falle *f.*

pith [pɪθ] *n* Mark *nt; (of speech)* Kern *m.*

pithead ['pɪthed] *n* Schachtkopf *m.*

pithy ['pɪθɪ] *a* prägnant.

pitiable ['pɪtɪəbl] *a* bedauernswert; *(contemptible)* jämmerlich.

pitiful *a,* ~**ly** *ad* ['pɪtɪfʊl, -fəlɪ] mitleidig; *(deserving pity)* bedauernswert; *(contemptible)* jämmerlich.

pitiless *a,* ~**ly** *ad* ['pɪtɪləs, -lɪ] erbarmungslos.

pittance ['pɪtəns] *n* Hungerlohn *m.*

pity ['pɪtɪ] *n (sympathy)* Mitleid *nt; (shame)* Jammer *m;* **to have or take** ~ **on sb** Mitleid mit jdm haben; **for** ~**'s sake** um Himmels willen; **what a** ~! wie schade!; **it's a** ~ es ist schade; *vt* Mitleid haben mit; **I** ~ **you** du tust mir leid; ~**ing** *a* mitleidig.

pivot ['pɪvət] *n* Drehpunkt *m; (pin)* (Dreh)zapfen *m; (fig)* Angelpunkt *m; vi* sich drehen *(on* um*).*

pixie ['pɪksɪ] *n* Elf(e *f) m.*

placard ['plækɑːd] *n* Plakat *nt*, Anschlag *m; vt* anschlagen.

placate [plə'keɪt] *vt* beschwichtigen, besänftigen.

place [pleɪs] *n* Platz *m; (spot)* Stelle *f; (town etc)* Ort *m; vt* setzen, stellen, legen; *order* aufgeben; *(Sport)* plazieren; *(identify)* unterbringen; **in** ~ am rechten Platz; **out of** ~ nicht am rechten Platz; *(fig)* remark unangebracht; **in** ~ **of** anstelle von; **in the first/second** *etc* ~ erstens/zweitens *etc;* **to give** ~ **to** Platz machen *(+dat);* **to invite sb to one's** ~ jdn zu sich (nach Hause) einladen; **to keep sb in his** ~ jdn in seinen Schranken halten; **to put sb in his** ~ jdn in seine Schranken (ver)weisen; ~ **of worship** Stätte *f* des Gebets; ~ **mat** Platzdeckchen *nt.*

placid ['plæsɪd] *a* gelassen, ruhig; ~**ity** [plə'sɪdɪtɪ] Gelassenheit *f*, Ruhe *f.*

plagiarism ['pleɪdʒɪərɪzəm] *n* Plagiat *nt.*

plagiarist ['pleɪdʒɪərɪst] *n* Plagiator *m.*

plagiarize ['pleɪdʒɪəraɪz] *vt* abschreiben, plagiieren.

plague [pleɪg] *n* Pest *f; (fig)* Plage *f; vt* plagen.

plaice [pleɪs] *n* Scholle *f.*

plaid [plæd] *n* Plaid *nt.*

plain *a,* ~**ly** *ad* [pleɪn, —lɪ] *(clear)* klar, deutlich; *(simple)* einfach, schlicht; *(not beautiful)* einfach, nicht attraktiv; *(honest)* offen; *n* Ebene *f;* **in** ~ **clothes** *(police)* in Zivil(kleidung); **it is** ~ **sailing** das ist ganz einfach; ~**ness** Einfachheit *f.*

plaintiff ['pleɪntɪf] *n* Kläger *m.*

plait [plæt] *n* Zopf *m; vt* flechten.

plan [plæn] *n* Plan *m; vti* planen; *(intend also)* vorhaben; ~ **out** *vt* vorbereiten; **according to** ~ planmäßig.

plane [pleɪn] *n* Ebene *f; (Aviat)* Flugzeug *nt; (tool)* Hobel *m; (tree)* Platane *f; a* eben, flach; *vt* hobeln.

planet ['plænɪt] *n* Planet *m.*

planetarium [plænɪ'tɛərɪəm] *n* Planetarium *nt.*

planetary ['plænɪtərɪ] *a* planetarisch.

plank [plæŋk] *n* Planke *f*, Brett *nt; (Pol)* Programmpunkt *m.*

plankton ['plæŋktən] *n* Plankton *nt.*

planner ['plænə*] *n* Planer *m.*

planning ['plænɪŋ] *n* Planen *nt*, Planung *f.*

plant [plɑːnt] *n* Pflanze *f; (Tech)* (Maschinen)anlage *f; (factory)* Fabrik *f,* Werk *nt; vt* pflanzen; *(set firmly)* stellen.

plantain ['plæntɪn] *n* (Mehl)banane *f.*

plantation [plæn'teɪʃən] *n* Pflanzung *f*, Plantage *f.*

planter ['plɑːntə*] *n* Pflanzer *m.*

plaque [plæk] *n* Gedenktafel *f.*

plasma ['plæzmə] *n* Plasma *nt.*

plaster ['plɑːstə*] *n* Gips *m; (whole surface)* Verputz *m; (Med)* Pflaster *nt; (for fracture:* also ~ **of Paris)** Gipsverband *m;* **in** ~ *(leg etc)* in Gips; *vt* gipsen; *hole* zugipsen; *ceiling* verputzen; *(fig:* with pictures *etc)* bekleben; ~**ed** *a (col)* besoffen; ~**er** Gipser *m.*

plastic ['plæstɪk] *n* Kunststoff *m; a (made of plastic)* Kunststoff-, Plastik-; *(soft)* formbar, plastisch; *(Art)* plastisch, bildend; **p**~**ine** ['plæstɪsiːn] Plastilin *nt;* ~ **surgery** plastische Chirurgie *f;* Schönheitsoperation *f.*

plate [pleɪt] *n* Teller *m; (gold/silver)* vergoldete(s)/versilberte(s) Tafelgeschirr *nt; (flat sheet)* Platte *f; (in book)* (Bild)tafel *f; vt* überziehen, plattieren; **to silver-/gold-**~ versilbern/vergolden.

plateau ['plætəʊ] *n, pl* ~**x** Hochebene *f*, Plateau *nt.*

plateful ['pleɪtfʊl] *n* Teller(voll) *m.*

plate glass ['pleɪt'glɑːs] *n* Tafelglas *nt.*

platform ['plætfɔːm] *n (at meeting)* Plattform *f*, Podium *nt; (stage)* Bühne *f; (Rail)* Bahnsteig *m; (Pol)* Partieprogramm *nt;* ~ **ticket** Bahnsteigkarte *f.*

platinum ['plætɪnəm] *n* Platin *nt.*

platitude ['plætɪtjuːd] n Gemeinplatz m, Platitüde f.

platoon [plə'tuːn] n (Mil) Zug m.

platter ['plætə*] n Platte f.

plausibility [plɔːzə'bɪlɪtɪ] n Plausibilität f.

plausible a, **plausibly** ad ['plɔːzəbl, -blɪ] plausibel, einleuchtend; liar überzeugend.

play [pleɪ] n Spiel m (also Tech); (Theat) (Theater)stück nt, Schauspiel nt; vti spielen; another team spielen gegen; (put sb in a team) einsetzen, spielen lassen; to ~ a joke on sb jdm einen Streich spielen; to ~ sb off against sb else jdn gegen jdn anders ausspielen; to ~ a part in (fig) eine Rolle spielen bei; ~ down vt bagatellisieren, herunterspielen; ~ up vi (cause trouble) frech werden; (bad leg etc) weh tun; vt person plagen; to ~ up to sb jdm flattieren; ~acting Schauspielerei f; ~boy Playboy m; ~er Spieler(in f) m; ~ful a spielerisch, verspielt; ~goer Theaterfreund m; ~ground Spielplatz m; ~group Kindergarten m; ~ing card Spielkarte f; ~ing field Sportplatz m; ~mate Spielkamerad m; ~off (Sport) Entscheidungsspiel nt; ~pen Laufstall m; ~thing Spielzeug nt; ~wright Theaterschriftsteller m.

plea [pliː] n (dringende) Bitte f, Gesuch nt; (Jur) Antwort f des Angeklagten; (excuse) Ausrede f, Vorwand m; (objection) Einrede f; ~ of guilty Geständnis nt.

plead [pliːd] vt poverty zur Entschuldigung anführen; (Jur) sb's case vertreten; vi (beg) dringend bitten (with sb jdn); (Jur) plädieren; to ~ guilty schuldig plädieren.

pleasant a, ~ly ad ['plez.nt, -lɪ] angenehm; freundlich; ~ness Angenehme(s) nt; (of person) angenehme(s) Wesen nt, Freundlichkeit f; ~ry Scherz m.

please [pliːz] vt (be agreeable to) gefallen (+dat); ~! bitte!; ~ yourself! wie du willst!; do what you ~ mach' was du willst; ~d a zufrieden; (glad) erfreut (with über +acc).

pleasing ['pliːzɪŋ] a erfreulich.

pleasurable a, **pleasurably** ad ['pleʒərəbl, -blɪ] angenehm, erfreulich.

pleasure ['pleʒə*] n Vergnügen nt, Freude f; (old: will) Wünsche pl; it's a ~ gern geschehen; they take (no/great) ~ in doing ... es macht ihnen (keinen/ großen) Spaß zu...; ~ ground Vergnügungspark m; ~seeking a vergnügungshungrig; ~ steamer Vergnügungsdampfer m.

pleat [pliːt] n Falte f.

plebeian [plɪ'biːən] n Plebejer(in f) m; a plebejisch.

plebiscite ['plebɪsɪt] n Volksentscheid m, Plebiszit nt.

plebs [plebz] npl Plebs m, Pöbel m.

plectrum ['plektrəm] n Plektron nt.

pledge [pledʒ] n Pfand nt; (promise) Versprechen nt; vt verpfänden; (promise) geloben, versprechen; to take the ~ dem Alkohol abschwören.

plenipotentiary [plenɪpə'tenʃərɪ] m Bevollmächtigter m; a bevollmächtigt; ~ power Vollmacht f.

plentiful ['plentɪful] a reichlich.

plenty ['plentɪ] n Fülle f, Überfluß m; ad (col) ganz schön; ~ of eine Menge, viel; in ~ reichlich, massenhaft; to be ~ genug sein, reichen.

plethora ['pleθərə] n Überfülle f.

pleurisy ['pluərɪsɪ] n Rippenfellentzündung f.

pliability [plaɪə'bɪlɪtɪ] n Biegsamkeit f; (of person) Beeinflußbarkeit f.

pliable ['plaɪəbl] a biegsam; person beeinflußbar.

pliers ['plaɪəz] npl (Kneif)zange f.

plight [plaɪt] n (Not)lage f; (schrecklicher) Zustand m.

plimsolls ['plɪmsəlz] npl Turnschuhe pl.

plinth [plɪnθ] n Säulenplatte f, Plinthe f.

plod [plɒd] vi (work) sich abplagen; (walk) trotten; ~der der Arbeitstier nt; ~ding a schwerfällig.

plonk [plɒŋk] n (col: wine) billige(r) Wein m; vt: ~ sth down etw hinknallen.

plot [plɒt] n Komplott nt, Verschwörung f; (story) Handlung f; (of land) Stück nt Land, Grundstück nt; vt markieren; curve zeichnen; movements nachzeichnen; vi (plan secretly) sich verschwören, ein Komplott schmieden; ~ter Verschwörer m; ~ting Intrigen pl.

plough, (US) **plow** [plau] n Pflug m; vt pflügen; (col) exam candidate durchfallen lassen; ~ back vt (Comm) wieder in das Geschäft stecken; ~ through vt water durchpflügen; book sich kämpfen durch; ~ing Pflügen nt.

ploy [plɔɪ] n Masche f.

pluck [plʌk] vt fruit pflücken; guitar zupfen; goose rupfen; n Mut m; to ~ up courage all seinen Mut zusammennehmen; ~y a beherzt.

plug [plʌg] n Stöpsel m; (Elec) Stecker m; (of tobacco) Pfriem m; (col: publicity) Schleichwerbung f; (Aut) Zündkerze f; vt (zu)stopfen; (col: advertise) Reklame machen für; to ~ in a lamp den Stecker einer Lampe einstecken.

plum [plʌm] n Pflaume f, Zwetschge f; a job etc Bomben-.

plumage ['pluːmɪdʒ] n Gefieder nt.

plumb [plʌm] n Lot nt; out of ~ nicht im Lot; a senkrecht; ad (exactly) genau; vt ausloten; (fig) sondieren; mystery ergründen.

plumber ['plʌmə*] n Klempner m, Installateur m.

plumbing ['plʌmɪŋ] n (craft) Installieren nt; (fittings) Leitungen pl, Installationen pl.

plumbline ['plʌmlaɪn] n Senkblei nt.

plume [pluːm] n Feder f; (of smoke etc) Fahne f; vt (bird) putzen.

plummet ['plʌmɪt] n Senkblei nt; vi (ab)stürzen.

plump [plʌmp] a rundlich, füllig; vi plumpsen, sich fallen lassen; vt plumpsen lassen; to ~ for (col: choose) wählen, sich entscheiden für; ~ness Rundlichkeit f.

plunder ['plʌndə*] n Plünderung f; (loot) Beute f; vt plündern; things rauben.

plunge [plʌndʒ] n Sprung m, Stürzen nt; vt stoßen; vi (sich) stürzen; (ship) rollen; **a room ~d into darkness** ein in Dunkelheit getauchtes Zimmer.

plunging ['plʌndʒɪŋ] a neckline offenherzig.

pluperfect ['plu:'pɜːfɪkt] n Plusquamperfekt nt, Vorvergangenheit f.

plural ['pluərəl] a Plural-, Mehrzahl-; n Plural m, Mehrzahl f; **~istic** [pluərə'lɪstɪk] a pluralistisch.

plus [plʌs] prep plus, und; a Plus-.

plush [plʌʃ] a (also **~y**: col: luxurious) feudal; n Plüsch m.

ply [plaɪ] n as in: **three-~** wood dreischichtig; wool Dreifach-; vt trade (be)treiben; (with questions) zusetzen (+dat); (ship, taxi) befahren; vi (ship, taxi) verkehren; **~wood** Sperrholz nt.

pneumatic [njuː'mætɪk] a pneumatisch; (Tech) Luft-; **~ drill** Preßlufthammer m; **~ tyre** Luftreifen m.

pneumonia [njuː'məʊnɪə] n Lungenentzündung f.

poach [pəʊtʃ] vt (Cook) pochieren; game stehlen; vi (steal) wildern (for nach); **~ed** a egg pochiert, verloren; **~er** Wilddieb m; **~ing** Wildern nt.

pocket ['pɒkɪt] n Tasche f; (of ore) Ader f; (of resistance) Widerstand(s)nest nt; **air ~** Luftloch nt; vt einstecken, in die Tasche stecken; **to be out of ~** kein Geld haben; **~book** Taschenbuch nt; **~ful** Tasche(voll) f; **~ knife** Taschenmesser nt; **~ money** Taschengeld nt.

pockmarked ['pɒkmɑːkt] a face pockennarbig.

pod [pɒd] Hülse f; (of peas also) Schote f.

podgy ['pɒdʒɪ] a pummelig.

poem ['pəʊəm] n Gedicht nt.

poet ['pəʊɪt] n Dichter m, Poet m; **~ic** [pəʊ'etɪk] a poetisch, dichterisch; beauty malerisch, stimmungsvoll; **~ laureate** Hofdichter m; **~ry** Poesie f; (poems) Gedichte pl.

poignant a, **~ly** ad ['pɔɪnjənt, -lɪ] scharf, stechend; (touching) ergreifend, quälend.

point [pɔɪnt] n Punkt m (also in discussion, scoring); (spot also) Stelle f; (sharpened tip) Spitze f; (moment) (Zeit)punkt m, Moment m; (purpose) Zweck m; (idea) Argument nt; (decimal) Dezimalstelle f; (personal characteristic) Seite f; vt zeigen mit; gun richten; vi zeigen; **~s** pl (Rail) Weichen pl; **~ of view** Stand- or Gesichtspunkt m; **what's the ~?** was soll das?; **you have a ~ there** da hast du recht; **three ~ two** drei Komma zwei; **~ out** vt hinweisen auf (+acc); **~ to** vt zeigen auf (+acc); **~-blank** ad (at close range) aus nächster Entfernung; (bluntly) unverblümt; **~ duty** Verkehrsregelungsdienst m; **~ed** a, **~edly** ad spitz, scharf; (fig) gezielt; **~er** Zeigestock m; (on dial) Zeiger m; **~less** a, **~lessly** ad zwecklos, sinnlos; **~lessness** Zwecklosigkeit f, Sinnlosigkeit f.

poise [pɔɪz] n Haltung f; (fig also) Gelassenheit f; vti balancieren; knife, pen bereithalten; o.s. sich bereitmachen; **~d** a beherrscht.

poison ['pɔɪzn] n (lit, fig) Gift nt; vt vergiften; **~ing** Vergiftung f; **~ous** a giftig, Gift-.

poke [pəʊk] vt stoßen; (put) stecken; fire schüren; hole bohren; n Stoß m; **to ~ one's nose into** seine Nase stecken in (+acc); **to ~ fun at sb** sich über jdn lustig machen; **~ about** vi herumstochern; herumwühlen; **~r** Schürhaken m; (Cards) Poker nt; **~r-faced** a undurchdringlich.

poky ['pəʊkɪ] a eng.

polar ['pəʊlə*] a Polar-, polar; **~ bear** Eisbär m; **~ization** [pəʊləraɪ'zeɪʃən] n Polarisation f; **~ize** vt polarisieren; vi sich polarisieren.

pole [pəʊl] n Stange f, Pfosten m; (flag-, telegraph — also) Mast m; (Elec, Geog) Pol m; (Sport) (vaulting —) Stab m; (ski —) Stock m; **~s apart** durch Welten getrennt; **~cat** (US) Skunk m; **~ star** Polarstern m; **~ vault** Stabhochsprung m.

polemic [pə'lemɪk] n Polemik f.

police [pə'liːs] n Polizei f; vt polizeilich überwachen; kontrollieren; **~ car** Polizeiwagen m; **~man** Polizist m; **~ state** Polizeistaat m; **~ station** (Polizei)revier nt, Wache f; **~woman** Polizistin f.

policy ['pɒlɪsɪ] n Politik f; (of business also) Usus m; (insurance) (Versicherungs)police f; (prudence) Klugheit f; (principle) Grundsatz m; **~ decision/statement** Grundsatzentscheidung f/-erklärung f.

polio ['pəʊlɪəʊ] n (spinale) Kinderlähmung f, Polio f.

polish ['pɒlɪʃ] n Politur f; (for floor) Wachs nt; (for shoes) Creme f; (nail —) Lack m; (shine) Glanz m; (of furniture) Politur f; (fig) Schliff m; vt polieren; shoes putzen; (fig) den letzten Schliff geben (+dat), aufpolieren; **~ off** vt (col: work) erledigen; food wegputzen; drink hinunterschütten; **~ up** vt essay aufpolieren; knowledge auffrischen; **~ed** a glänzend (also fig); manners verfeinert.

polite a, **~ly** ad [pə'laɪt, -lɪ] höflich; society fein; **~ness** Höflichkeit f, Feinheit f.

politic ['pɒlɪtɪk] a (prudent) diplomatisch; **~al** a, **~ally** ad [pə'lɪtɪkəl, -ɪ] politisch; **~al science** Politologie f; **~ian** [pɒlɪ'tɪʃən] Politiker m, Staatsmann m; **~s** pl Politik f.

polka ['pɒlkə] n Polka f; **~ dot** Tupfen m.

poll [pəʊl] n Abstimmung f; (in election) Wahl f; (votes cast) Wahlbeteiligung f; (opinion —) Umfrage f; vt votes erhalten, auf sich vereinigen.

pollen ['pɒlən] n Blütenstaub m, Pollen m; **~ count** Pollenkonzentration f.

pollination [pɒlɪ'neɪʃən] n Befruchtung f.

polling booth ['pəʊlɪŋbuːð] n Wahlkabine f.

polling day ['pəʊlɪŋ deɪ] n Wahltag m.

polling station ['pəʊlɪŋ steɪʃən] n Wahllokal nt.

pollute [pə'luːt] vt verschmutzen, verunreinigen.

pollution [pə'luːʃən] n Verschmutzung f.

polo ['pəʊləʊ] n Polo nt.

poly- [pɒlɪ] pref Poly-.

polygamy [pɔ'lɪgəmɪ] n Polygamie f.
polytechnic [pɔlɪ'teknɪk] n technische Hochschule f.
polythene [pɔlɪθiːn] n Plastik nt; ~ **bag** Plastiktüte f.
pomegranate ['pɔməgrænɪt] n Granatapfel m.
pommel ['pʌml] vt mit den Fäusten bearbeiten; n Sattelknopf m.
pomp [pɔmp] n Pomp m, Prunk m.
pompous a, ~**ly** ad ['pɔmpəs, -lɪ] aufgeblasen; language geschwollen.
ponce [pɔns] n (col) (pimp) Louis m; (queer) Schwule m.
pond [pɔnd] n Teich m, Weiher m.
ponder ['pɔndə*] vt nachdenken or nachgrübeln über (+acc); ~**ous** a schwerfällig.
pontiff ['pɔntɪf] n Pontifex m.
pontificate [pɔn'tɪfɪkeɪt] vi (fig) geschwollen reden.
pontoon [pɔn'tuːn] n Ponton m; (Cards) 17-und-4 nt.
pony ['pəʊnɪ] n Pony nt; ~**tail** Pferdeschwanz m.
poodle ['puːdl] n Pudel m.
pooh-pooh [puː'puː] vt die Nase rümpfen über (+acc).
pool [puːl] n (swimming —) Schwimmbad nt; (private) Swimming-pool m; (of spilt liquid, blood) Lache f; (fund) (gemeinsame) Kasse f; (billiards) Poolspiel nt; vt money etc zusammenlegen.
poor [pʊə*] a arm; (not good) schlecht, schwach; the ~ pl die Armen pl; ~**ly** ad schlecht, schwach; dressed ärmlich; a schlecht, elend.
pop [pɔp] n Knall m; (music) Popmusik f; (drink) Limo(nade) f; (US col) Pa m; vt (put) stecken; balloon platzen lassen; vi knallen; ~ **in/out** (person) vorbeikommen/hinausgehen; hinein-/hinausspringen; ~ **concert** Popkonzert nt; ~**corn** Puffmais m.
Pope [pəʊp] n Papst m.
poplar ['pɔplə*] n Pappel f.
poplin ['pɔplɪn] n Popelin m.
poppy ['pɔpɪ] n Mohn m; ~**cock** (col) Quatsch m.
populace ['pɔpjʊlɪs] n Volk nt.
popular ['pɔpjʊlə*] a beliebt, populär; (of the people) volkstümlich, Populär-; (widespread) allgemein; ~**ity** [pɔpjʊ'lærɪtɪ] Beliebtheit f, Popularität f; ~**ize** vt popularisieren; ~**ly** ad allgemein, überall.
populate ['pɔpjʊleɪt] vt bevölkern; town bewohnen.
population [pɔpjʊ'leɪʃən] n Bevölkerung f; (of town) Einwohner pl.
populous ['pɔpjʊləs] a dicht besiedelt.
porcelain ['pɔːslɪn] n Porzellan nt.
porch [pɔːtʃ] n Vorbau m, Veranda f; (in church) Vorhalle f.
porcupine ['pɔːkjʊpaɪn] n Stachelschwein nt.
pore [pɔː*] n Pore f; ~ **over** vt brüten or hocken über (+dat).
pork [pɔːk] n Schweinefleisch nt.
pornography a, ~**ally** ad [pɔːnə'græfɪk, -əlɪ] pornographisch.

pornography [pɔː'nɔgrəfɪ] n Pornographie f.
porous ['pɔːrəs] a porös; skin porig.
porpoise ['pɔːpəs] n Tümmler m.
porridge ['pɔrɪdʒ] n Porridge m, Haferbrei m.
port [pɔːt] n Hafen m; (town) Hafenstadt f; (Naut: left side) Backbord nt; (opening for loads) Luke f; (wine) Portwein m.
portable ['pɔːtəbl] a tragbar; radio Koffer-; typewriter Reise-.
portal ['pɔːtl] n Portal nt.
portcullis [pɔːt'kʌlɪs] n Fallgitter nt.
portend [pɔː'tend] vt anzeigen, hindeuten auf (+acc).
portent ['pɔːtent] n schlimme(s) Vorzeichen nt; ~**ous** [pɔː'tentəs] a schlimm, ominös; (amazing) ungeheuer.
porter ['pɔːtə*] n Pförtner(in f) m; (for luggage) (Gepäck)träger m.
porthole ['pɔːthəʊl] n Bullauge nt.
portico ['pɔːtɪkəʊ] a Säulengang m.
portion ['pɔːʃən] n Teil m, Stück nt; (of food) Portion f.
portly ['pɔːtlɪ] a korpulent, beleibt.
portrait ['pɔːtrɪt] n Porträt nt, Bild(nis) nt.
portray [pɔː'treɪ] vt darstellen; (describe) schildern; ~**al** Darstellung f; Schilderung f.
pose [pəʊz] n Stellung f, Pose f (also affectation); vi posieren, sich in Positur setzen; vt stellen; **to ~ as** sich ausgeben als; ~**r** knifflige Frage f.
posh [pɔʃ] a (col) (piek)fein.
position [pə'zɪʃən] n Stellung f; (place) Position f, Lage f; (job) Stelle f; (attitude) Standpunkt m, Haltung f; **to be in a ~ to do sth** in der Lage sein, etw zu tun; vt aufstellen.
positive a, ~**ly** ad ['pɔzɪtɪv, -lɪ] positiv; (convinced) sicher; (definite) eindeutig.
posse ['pɔsɪ] n (US) Aufgebot nt.
possess [pə'zes] vt besitzen; **what ~ed you to . . .?** was ist in dich gefahren, daß...?; ~**ed** a besessen; ~**ion** [pə'zeʃən] Besitz m; ~**ive** a besitzergreifend, eigensüchtig; (Gram) Possessiv-, besitzanzeigend; ~**ively** ad besitzergreifend, eigensüchtig; ~**or** Besitzer m.
possibility [pɔsə'bɪlɪtɪ] n Möglichkeit f.
possible ['pɔsəbl] a möglich; **if ~** wenn möglich, möglichst; **as big as ~** so groß wie möglich, möglichst groß.
possibly ['pɔsəblɪ] ad möglicherweise, vielleicht; **as soon as I ~ can** sobald ich irgendwie kann.
post [pəʊst] n Post f; (pole) Pfosten m, Pfahl m; (place of duty) Posten m; (job) Stelle f; vt notice anschlagen; letters aufgeben; soldiers aufstellen; ~**age** Postgebühr f, Porto nt; ~**al** a Post-; ~**al order** Postanweisung f; ~**card** Postkarte f; ~**date** vt cheque nachdatieren; ~**er** Plakat nt, Poster m; ~**e restante** Aufbewahrungsstelle f für postlagernde Sendungen; **to send sth ~e restante** etw postlagernd schicken.
posterior [pɔs'tɪərɪə*] n (col) Hintern m.
posterity [pɔs'terɪtɪ] n Nachwelt f; (descendants) Nachkommenschaft f.

postgraduate ['pəust'grædjuɪt] n Weiter-studierender(in f) m.

posthumous a, ~ly ad ['pɒstjuməs, -lɪ] post(h)um.

postman ['pəustmən] n Briefträger m, Postbote m.

postmark ['pəustmɑːk] n Poststempel m.

postmaster ['pəustmɑːstə°] n Postmeister m; P~ General Postminister m.

post-mortem ['pəust'mɔːtəm] n Autopsie f.

post office ['pəustɒfɪs] n Postamt nt, Post f (also organization).

postpone [pə'spəun] vt verschieben, auf-schieben; ~ment Verschiebung f, Aufschub m.

postscript ['pəusskrɪpt] n Nachschrift f, Postskript nt; (in book) Nachwort nt.

postulate ['pɒstjuleɪt] vt voraussetzen; (maintain) behaupten.

postulation [pɒstju'leɪʃən] n Voraus-setzung f, Behauptung f.

posture ['pɒstʃə°] n Haltung f; vi posieren.

postwar ['pəust'wɔː°] a Nachkriegs-.

posy ['pəuzɪ] n Blumenstrauß m.

pot [pɒt] n Topf m; (tea~) Kanne f; (col: marijuana) Hasch m; vt plant eintopfen.

potash ['pɒtæʃ] n Pottasche f.

potato [pə'teɪtəu] n, pl ~es Kartoffel f.

potency ['pəutənsɪ] n Stärke f, Potenz f.

potent ['pəutənt] a stark; argument zwingend.

potentate ['pəutənteɪt] n Machthaber m.

potential [pəu'tenʃəl] a potentiell; he is a ~ virtuoso er hat das Zeug zum Virtuosen; n Potential nt; ~ly ad potentiell.

pothole ['pɒthəul] n Höhle f; (in road) Schlagloch nt; ~r Höhlenforscher m.

potholing ['pɒthəulɪŋ] n: to go ~ Höhlen erforschen.

potion ['pəuʃən] n Trank m.

potluck ['pɒt'lʌk] n: to take ~ with sth etw auf gut Glück nehmen.

potpourri [pəu'puri] n Potpourri nt.

potshot ['pɒtʃɒt] n: to take a ~ at sth auf etw (acc) ballern.

potted ['pɒtɪd] a food eingelegt, eingemacht; plant Topf-; (fig: book, version) konzentriert.

potter ['pɒtə°] n Töpfer m; vi herum-hantieren, herumwursteln; ~y Töpferwaren pl, Steingut nt; (place) Töpferei f.

potty ['pɒtɪ] a (col) verrückt; n Töpfchen nt.

pouch [pautʃ] n Beutel m; (under eyes) Tränensack m; (for tobacco) Tabaksbeutel m.

pouffe [puːf] n Sitzkissen nt.

poultice ['pəultɪs] n Packung f.

poultry ['pəultrɪ] n Geflügel nt; ~ farm Geflügelfarm f.

pounce [pauns] vi sich stürzen (on auf +acc); n Sprung m, Satz m.

pound [paund] n (Fin, weight) Pfund nt; (for cars, animals) Auslösestelle f; (for stray animals) (Tier)asyl nt; vi klopfen, hämmern; vt (zer)stampfen; ~ing starke(s) Klopfen nt, Hämmern nt; (Zer)stampfen nt.

pour [pɔː°] vt gießen, schütten; vi gießen; (crowds etc) strömen; ~ away vt, ~ off vt abgießen; ~ing rain strömende(r) Regen m.

pout [paut] n Schnute f, Schmollmund m; vi eine Schnute ziehen, schmollen.

poverty ['pɒvətɪ] n Armut f; ~-stricken a verarmt, sehr arm.

powder ['paudə°] n Pulver nt; (cosmetic) Puder m; vt pulverisieren; (sprinkle) bestreuen; to ~ one's nose sich (dat) die Nase pudern; ~ room Damentoilette f; ~y a pulverig, Pulver-.

power [pauə°] n Macht f (also Pol); (ability) Fähigkeit f; (strength) Stärke f; (authority) Macht f, Befugnis f; (Math) Potenz f; (Elec) Strom m; vt betreiben, antreiben; ~ cut Stromausfall m; ~ful a person mächtig; engine, government stark; ~less a machtlos; ~ line (Haupt)stromleitung f; ~ point elektrische(r) Anschluß m; ~ station Elektrizitätswerk nt.

powwow ['pauwau] n Besprechung f, vi eine Besprechung abhalten.

practicability [præktɪkə'bɪlɪtɪ] n Durch-führbarkeit f.

practicable ['præktɪkəbl] a durchführbar.

practical ['præktɪkəl] a, ~ly ad ['præktɪkəl, -lɪ] praktisch; ~ joke Streich m.

practice ['præktɪs] n Übung f; (reality) Praxis f; (custom) Brauch m; (in business) Usus m; (doctor's, lawyer's) Praxis f; in ~ (in reality) in der Praxis; out of ~ außer Übung.

practise, (US) practice ['præktɪs] vt üben; profession ausüben; to ~ law/medicine als Rechtsanwalt/Arzt arbeiten; vi (sich) üben; (doctor, lawyer) praktizieren; ~d a erfahren.

practising, (US) practicing ['præktɪsɪŋ] a praktizierend; Christian etc aktiv.

practitioner [præk'tɪʃənə°] n prak-tische(r) Arzt m.

pragmatic [præg'mætɪk] a pragmatisch.

pragmatism ['prægmətɪzəɪn] n Pragmatismus m.

pragmatist ['prægmətɪst] n Pragmatiker m.

prairie ['prɛərɪ] n Prärie f, Steppe f.

praise [preɪz] n Lob nt, Preis m; vt loben; (worship) (lob)preisen, loben; ~worthy a lobenswert.

pram [præm] n Kinderwagen m.

prance [prɑːns] vi (horse) tänzeln; (person) stolzieren; (gaily) herumhüpfen.

prank [præŋk] n Streich m.

prattle ['prætl] vi schwatzen, plappern.

prawn [prɔːn] n Garnele f, Krabbe f.

pray [preɪ] vi beten; ~er [prɛə°] Gebet nt; ~er book Gebetbuch nt.

pre- [priː] pref prä-, vor(her)-.

preach [priːtʃ] vi predigen; ~er Prediger m.

preamble [priː'æmbl] n Einleitung f.

prearrange ['priːə'reɪndʒ] vt vereinbaren, absprechen; ~d a vereinbart; ~ment Vereinbarung f, vorherige Absprache f.

precarious a, ~ly ad [prɪ'kɛərɪəs, -lɪ] prekär, unsicher.

precaution [prɪ'kɔːʃən] n (Vor-sichts)maßnahme f, Vorbeugung f; ~ary *a measure* vorbeugend, Vorsichts-.

precede [prɪ'siːd] *vti* vorausgehen (+*dat*); *(be more important)* an Bedeutung übertreffen; ~**nce** ['presɪdəns] Priorität *f,* Vorrang *m;* **to take** ~**nce over den** Vorrang haben vor (+*dat*); ~**nt** ['presɪdənt] Präzedenzfall *m.*

preceding [prɪ'siːdɪŋ] *a* vorhergehend.

precept ['priːsept] *n* Gebot *nt,* Regel *f.*

precinct ['priːsɪŋkt] *n* Gelände *f; (district)* Bezirk *m; (shopping —)* Einkaufszone *f.*

precious ['preʃəs] *a* kostbar, wertvoll; *(affected)* preziös, geziert.

precipice ['presɪpɪs] *n* Abgrund *m.*

precipitate *a,* ~**ly** *ad* [prɪ'sɪpɪtɪt, -lɪ] überstürzt, übereilt; [prɪ'sɪpɪteɪt] *vt* hinunterstürzen; *events* heraufbeschwören.

precipitation [prɪsɪpɪ'teɪʃən] *n* Niederschlag *m.*

precipitous *a,* ~**ly** *ad* [prɪ'sɪpɪtəs, -lɪ] abschüssig; *action* überstürzt.

précis ['preɪsiː] *n (kurze)* Übersicht *f,* Zusammenfassung *f; (Sch)* Inhaltsangabe *f.*

precise *a,* ~**ly** *ad* [prɪ'saɪs, -lɪ] genau, präzis.

preclude [prɪ'kluːd] *vt* ausschließen; *person* abhalten.

precocious [prɪ'kəʊʃəs] *a* frühreif.

preconceived ['priːkən'siːvd] *a idea* vorgefaßt.

precondition ['priːkən'dɪʃən] *n* Vorbedingung *f,* Voraussetzung *f.*

precursor [priː'kɜːsə°] *n* Vorläufer *m.*

predator ['predətə°] *n* Raubtier *nt;* ~**y** *a* Raub-; räuberisch.

predecessor ['priːdɪsesə°] *n* Vorgänger *m.*

predestination [priːdestɪ'neɪʃən] *n* Vorherbestimmung *f,* Prädestination *f.*

predestine [priː'destɪn] *vt* vorherbestimmen.

predetermine ['priːdɪ'tɜːmɪn] *vt* vorherentscheiden, vorherbestimmen.

predicament [prɪ'dɪkəmənt] *n* mißliche Lage *f;* **to be in a** ~ in der Klemme sitzen.

predicate ['predɪkət] *n* Prädikat *nt,* Satzaussage *f.*

predict [prɪ'dɪkt] *vt* voraussagen; ~**ion** [prɪ'dɪkʃən] Voraussage *f.*

predominance [prɪ'dɒmɪnəns] *n (in power)* Vorherrschaft *f; (fig)* Vorherrschen *nt,* Überwiegen *nt.*

predominant [prɪ'dɒmɪnənt] *a* vorherrschend; *(fig also)* überwiegend; ~**ly** *ad* überwiegend, hauptsächlich.

predominate [prɪ'dɒmɪneɪt] *vi* vorherrschen; *(fig also)* überwiegen.

pre-eminent [priː'emɪnənt] *a* hervorragend, herausragend.

pre-empt [priː'empt] *vt action, decision* vorwegnehmen.

preen [priːn] *vt* putzen; **to** ~ **o.s. on sth** sich *(dat)* etwas auf etw *(acc)* einbilden.

prefab ['priːfæb] *n* Fertighaus *nt.*

prefabricated ['priː'fæbrɪkeɪtɪd] *a* vorgefertigt, Fertig-.

preface ['prefɪs] *n* Vorwort *nt,* Einleitung *f.*

prefect ['priːfekt] *n* Präfekt *m; (Sch)* Aufsichtsschüler(in *f*) *m.*

prefer [prɪ'fɜː°] *vt* vorziehen, lieber mögen; **to** ~ **to do sth** etw lieber tun; ~**able** ['prefərəbl] *a* vorzuziehen(d) *(to dat);* ~**ably** ['prefərəblɪ] *ad* vorzugsweise, am liebsten; ~**ence** ['prefərəns] Präferenz *f,* Vorzug *m;* ~**ential** [prefə'renʃəl] *a* bevorzugt, Vorzugs-.

prefix ['priːfɪks] *n* Vorsilbe *f,* Präfix *nt.*

pregnancy ['pregnənsɪ] *n* Schwangerschaft *f.*

pregnant ['pregnənt] *a* schwanger; ~ **with meaning** *(fig)* bedeutungsschwer or -voll.

prehistoric ['priːhɪs'tɒrɪk] *a* prähistorisch, vorgeschichtlich.

prehistory ['priː'hɪstərɪ] *n* Urgeschichte *f.*

prejudge ['priː'dʒʌdʒ] *vt* vorschnell beurteilen.

prejudice ['predʒʊdɪs] *n* Vorurteil *nt;* Voreingenommenheit *f; (harm)* Schaden *m; vt* beeinträchtigen; ~**d** *a person* voreingenommen.

prelate ['prelət] *n* Prälat *m.*

preliminary [prɪ'lɪmɪnərɪ] *a* einleitend, Vor-; **the preliminaries** *pl* die vorbereitenden Maßnahmen *pl.*

prelude ['preljuːd] *n* Vorspiel *nt; (Mus)* Präludium *nt; (fig also)* Auftakt *m.*

premarital ['priː'mærɪtl] *a* vorehelich.

premature ['premətjʊə°] *a* vorzeitig, verfrüht; *birth* Früh-; *decision* voreilig; ~**ly** *ad* vorzeitig; verfrüht; voreilig.

premeditate [priː'medɪteɪt] *vt* im voraus planen; ~**d** *a* geplant; *murder* vorsätzlich.

premeditation [priːmedɪ'teɪʃən] *n* Planung *f.*

premier ['premɪə°] *a* erste(r, s), oberste(r, s), höchste(r, s); *n* Premier *m.*

premiere [premɪ'ɛə°] *n* Premiere *f,* Uraufführung *f.*

premise ['premɪs] *n* Voraussetzung *f,* Prämisse *f;* ~**s** *pl* Räumlichkeiten *pl; (grounds)* Grundstück *nt.*

premium ['priːmɪəm] *n* Prämie *f;* **to sell at a** ~ mit Gewinn verkaufen.

premonition [premə'nɪʃən] *n* Vorahnung *f.*

preoccupation [priːɒkjʊ'peɪʃən] *n* Sorge *f.*

preoccupied [priː'ɒkjʊpaɪd] *a look* geistesabwesend; **to be** ~ **with sth** mit dem Gedanken an etw *(acc)* beschäftigt sein.

prep [prep] *n (Sch: study)* Hausaufgabe *f.*

prepaid ['priː'peɪd] *a* vorausbezahlt; *letter* frankiert.

preparation ['prepə'reɪʃən] *n* Vorbereitung *f.*

preparatory [prɪ'pærətərɪ] *a* Vor-(bereitungs)-.

prepare [prɪ'pɛə°] *vt* vorbereiten *(for auf +acc); vi* sich vorbereiten; **to be** ~**d to** ... bereit sein zu ...

preponderance [prɪ'pɒndərəns] *n* Übergewicht *nt.*

preposition [prepə'zɪʃən] *n* Präposition *f,* Verhältniswort *nt.*

preposterous [prɪ'pɒstərəs] *a* absurd, widersinnig.

prerequisite ['priː'rekwɪzɪt] n (unerläß-liche) Voraussetzung f.

prerogative [prɪ'rɒgətɪv] n Vorrecht nt, Privileg nt.

presbytery ['prezbɪtərɪ] n (house) Presbyterium nt; (Catholic) Pfarrhaus nt.

prescribe [prɪs'kraɪb] vt vorschreiben, anordnen; (Med) verschreiben.

prescription [prɪs'krɪpʃən] n Vorschrift f; (Med) Rezept nt.

prescriptive [prɪs'krɪptɪv] a normativ.

presence ['prezns] n Gegenwart f, Anwesenheit f; ~ of mind Geistes-gegenwart f.

present ['preznt] a anwesend; (existing) gegenwärtig, augenblicklich; n Gegenwart f; at ~ im Augenblick; Präsens nt (Gram); (gift) Geschenk nt; [prɪ'zent] vt vorlegen; (introduce) vorstellen; (show) zeigen; (give) überreichen; to ~ sb with sth jdm etw überreichen; ~able [prɪ'zentəbl] a präsentabel; ~ation Überreichung f; ~-day a heutig, gegenwärtig, modern; ~ly ad bald; (at present) im Augenblick; ~ participle Partizip nt des Präsens, Mittelwort nt der Gegenwart; ~ tense Präsens nt, Gegenwart f.

preservation [prezə'veɪʃən] n Erhaltung f.

preservative [prɪ'zɜːvətɪv] n Kon-servierungsmittel nt.

preserve [prɪ'zɜːv] vt erhalten, schützen; (food) einmachen, konservieren; n (jam) Eingemachte(s) nt; (hunting) Schutzgebiet nt.

preside [prɪ'zaɪd] vi den Vorsitz haben.

presidency ['prezɪdənsɪ] n (Pol) Präsident-schaft f.

president ['prezɪdənt] n Präsident m; ~ial [prezɪ'denʃəl] a Präsidenten-; election Präsidentschafts-; system Präsidial-.

press [pres] n Presse f; (printing house) Druckerei f; to give the clothes a ~ die Kleider bügeln; vt drücken, pressen; (iron) bügeln; (urge) (be)drängen; vi (push) drücken, pressen; to be ~ed for time unter Zeitdruck stehen; to be ~ed for money/space wenig Geld/Platz haben; to ~ for sth drängen auf etw (acc); ~ on vi vorwärtsdrängen; ~ agency Presse-agentur f; ~ conference Presse-konferenz f; ~ cutting Zeitungsaus-schnitt m; ~ing a dringend; ~-stud Druckknopf m.

pressure ['preʃə*] n Druck m; ~ cooker Schnellkochtopf m; ~ gauge Druck-messer m; ~ group Interessenverband m, Pressure Group f.

pressurized ['preʃəraɪzd] a Druck-.

prestige [pres'tiːʒ] n Ansehen nt, Prestige f.

prestigious [pres'tɪdʒəs] a Prestige-.

presumably [prɪ'zjuːməblɪ] ad vermutlich.

presume [prɪ'zjuːm] vti annehmen; (dare) sich erlauben.

presumption [prɪ'zʌmpʃən] n Annahme f; (impudent behaviour) Anmaßung f.

presumptuous [prɪ'zʌmptjuəs] a anmaßend.

presuppose [priːsə'pəʊz] vt voraussetzen.

presupposition [priːsʌpə'zɪʃən] n Voraus-setzung f.

pretence [prɪ'tens] n Vorgabe f, Vortäuschung f; (false claim) Vorwand m.

pretend [prɪ'tend] vt vorgeben, so tun als ob ...; vi so tun; to ~ to sth Anspruch erheben auf etw (acc).

pretense [prɪ'tens] n (US) = pretence.

pretension [prɪ'tenʃən] n Anspruch m; (impudent claim) Anmaßung f.

pretentious [prɪ'tenʃəs] a angeberisch.

pretext ['priːtekst] n Vorwand m.

prettily ['prɪtɪlɪ] ad hübsch, nett.

pretty ['prɪtɪ] a hübsch, nett; ad (col) ganz schön.

prevail [prɪ'veɪl] vi siegen (against, over über +acc); (custom) vorherrschen; to ~ upon sb to do sth jdn dazu bewegen, etw zu tun; ~ing a vorherrschend.

prevalent ['prevələnt] a vorherrschend.

prevarication [prɪværɪ'keɪʃən] n Ausflucht f.

prevent [prɪ'vent] vt (stop) verhindern, verhüten; to ~ sb from doing sth jdn (daran) hindern, etw zu tun; ~able a verhütbar; ~ative Vorbeugungsmittel nt; ~ion [prɪ'venʃən] Verhütung f, Schutz m (of gegen); ~ive a vorbeugend, Schutz-.

preview ['priːvjuː] n private Vorauf-führung f; (trailer) Vorschau f; vt film privat vorführen.

previous ['priːvɪəs] a früher, vorherig; ~ly ad früher.

prewar ['priː'wɔː*] a Vorkriegs-.

prey [preɪ] n Beute f; ~ on vt Jagd machen auf (+acc); mind nagen an (+dat); bird/beast of ~ Raubvogel m/Raubtier nt.

price [praɪs] n Preis m; (value) Wert m; vt schätzen; (label) auszeichnen; ~less a (lit, fig) unbezahlbar; ~ list Preisliste f; ~y a (col) teuer.

prick [prɪk] n Stich m; vti stechen; to ~ up one's ears die Ohren spitzen.

prickle ['prɪkl] n Stachel m, Dorn m; vi brennen.

prickly ['prɪklɪ] a stachelig; (fig) person reizbar; ~ heat Hitzebläschen pl; ~ pear Feigenkaktus m; (fruit) Kaktusfeige f.

pride [praɪd] n Stolz m; (arrogance) Hoch-mut m; to ~ o.s. on sth auf etw (acc) stolz sein.

priest [priːst] n Priester m; ~ess Priesterin f; ~hood Priesteramt nt.

prig [prɪg] n Selbstgefällige(r) mf.

prim a, ~ly ad [prɪm, -lɪ] prüde.

prima donna ['priːmə 'dɒnə] n Primadonna f.

primarily ['praɪmərɪlɪ] ad vorwiegend, hauptsächlich.

primary ['praɪmərɪ] a Haupt-, Grund-, primär; ~ colour Grundfarbe f; ~ education Grundschul(aus)bildung f; ~ election Vorwahl f; ~ school Grund-schule f, Volksschule f.

primate ['praɪmɪt] n (Eccl) Primas m; (Biol) Primat m.

prime [praɪm] a oberste(r, s), erste(r, s), wichtigste(r, s); (excellent) erstklassig, prima inv; vt vorbereiten; gun laden; n (of

life) beste(s) Alter *nt;* ~ **minister** Premierminister *m,* Ministerpräsident *m;* ~r Elementarlehrbuch *nt,* Fibel *f.*

primeval [praɪ'miːvəl] *a* vorzeitlich; *forests* Ur-.

primitive ['prɪmɪtɪv] *a* primitiv.

primrose ['prɪmrəʊz] *n* (gelbe) Primel *f.*

primula ['prɪmjʊlə] *n* Primel *f.*

primus (stove) " ['praɪməs (stəʊv)] *n* Primuskocher *m.*

prince [prɪns] *n* Prinz *m;* (*ruler*) Fürst *m;* ~**ss** [prɪn'ses] Prinzessin *f;* Fürstin *f.*

principal ['prɪnsəpl] *a* Haupt-; wichtigste(r, s); *n* (*Sch*) (Schul)direktor *m,* Rektor *m;* (*money*) (Grund)kapital *nt;* ~**ity** [prɪnsɪ'pælɪtɪ] Fürstentum *nt;* ~**ly** *ad* hauptsächlich.

principle ['prɪnsəpl] *n* Grundsatz *m,* Prinzip *nt;* **in/on** ~ im/aus Prinzip, prinzipiell.

print [prɪnt] *n* Druck *m;* (*made by feet, fingers*) Abdruck *m;* (*Phot*) Abzug *m;* (*cotton*) Kattun *m; vt* drucken; *name* in Druckbuchstaben schreiben; *Photo* abziehen; ~**ed matter** Drucksache *f;* ~**er** Drucker *m;* ~**ing** Drucken *nt;* (*of photos*) Abziehen *nt;* ~**ing press** Druckerpresse *f;* **is the book still in** ~? wird das Buch noch gedruckt?; **out of** ~ vergriffen.

prior ['praɪə*] *a* früher; ~ **to sth** vor etw (*dat*); ~ **to going abroad, she had . . .** bevor sie ins Ausland ging, hatte sie ...; *n* Prior *m;* ~**ess** Priorin *f;* ~**ity** [praɪ'ɒrɪtɪ] Vorrang *m;* Priorität *f;* ~**y** Kloster *nt.*

prise [praɪz] *vt:* ~ **open** aufbrechen.

prism ['prɪzəm] *n* Prisma *nt.*

prison ['prɪzn] *n* Gefängnis *nt;* ~**er** Gefangene(r) *mf;* ~**er of war** Kriegsgefangene(r) *m;* **to be taken** ~**er in** Gefangenschaft geraten.

prissy ['prɪsɪ] *a* (*col*) etepetete.

pristine ['prɪstiːn] *a* makellos.

privacy ['prɪvəsɪ] *n* Ungestörtheit *f,* Ruhe *f;* Privatleben *nt.*

private ['praɪvɪt] *a* privat, Privat-; (*secret*) vertraulich, geheim; *soldier* einfach; *n* einfache(r) Soldat *m;* **in** ~ privat, unter vier Augen; ~ **eye** Privatdetektiv *m;* ~**ly** *ad* privat; vertraulich, geheim.

privet ['prɪvɪt] *n* Liguster *m.*

privilege ['prɪvɪlɪdʒ] *n* Vorrecht *nt,* Vergünstigung *f,* Privileg *nt;* ~**d** *a* bevorzugt, privilegiert.

privy ['prɪvɪ] *a* geheim, privat; ~ **council** Geheime(r) Staatsrat *m.*

prize [praɪz] *n* Preis *m; a example* erstklassig; *idiot* Voll-; *vt* (hoch)schätzen; ~ **fighting** Preisboxen *nt;* ~ **giving** Preisverteilung *f;* ~ **money** Geldpreis *m;* ~**winner** Preisträger(in *f*) *m;* (*of money*) Gewinner(in *f*) *m.*

pro- [prəʊ] *pref* pro-; *n:* **the** ~**s and cons** *pl* das Für und Wider.

pro [prəʊ] *n* (*professional*) Profi *m.*

probability [prɒbə'bɪlɪtɪ] *n* Wahrscheinlichkeit *f;* **in all** ~ aller Wahrscheinlichkeit nach.

probable *a,* **probably** *ad* ['prɒbəbl, -blɪ] wahrscheinlich.

probation [prə'beɪʃən] *n* Probe(zeit) *f;* (*Jur*) Bewährung *f;* **on** ~ auf Probe; auf Bewährung; ~ **officer** Bewährungshelfer *m;* ~**ary** *a* Probe-; ~**er** (*nurse*) Lernschwester *f;* Pfleger *m* in der Ausbildung; (*Jur*) auf Bewährung freigelassene(r) Gefangene(r) *m.*

probe [prəʊb] *n* Sonde *f;* (*enquiry*) Untersuchung *f; vti* untersuchen, erforschen, sondieren.

probity ['prəʊbɪtɪ] *n* Rechtschaffenheit *f.*

problem ['prɒbləm] *n* Problem *nt;* ~**atic** [prɒblɪ'mætɪk] *a* problematisch.

procedural [prə'siːdjʊrəl] *a* verfahrensmäßig, Verfahrens-.

procedure [prə'siːdʒə*] *n* Verfahren *nt,* Vorgehen *nt.*

proceed [prə'siːd] *vi* (*advance*) vorrücken; (*start*) anfangen; (*carry on*) fortfahren; (*set about*) vorgehen; (*come from*) entstehen (*from aus*); (*Jur*) gerichtlich vorgehen; ~**ings** *pl* Verfahren *nt;* (*record of things*) Sitzungsbericht *m;* ~**s** ['prəʊsiːdz] *pl* Erlös *m,* Gewinn *m.*

process ['prəʊses] *n* Vorgang *m,* Prozeß *m;* (*method also*) Verfahren *nt; vt* bearbeiten; *food* verarbeiten; *film* entwickeln; ~**ing** (*Phot*) Entwickeln *nt.*

procession [prə'seʃən] *n* Prozession *f,* Umzug *m.*

proclaim [prə'kleɪm] *vt* verkünden, proklamieren; **to** ~ **sb king** jdn zum König ausrufen.

proclamation [prɒklə'meɪʃən] *n* Verkündung *f,* Proklamation *f;* Ausrufung *f.*

procrastination [prəʊkræstɪ'neɪʃən] *n* Hinausschieben *nt.*

procreation [prəʊkrɪ'eɪʃən] *n* (Er)zeugung *f.*

procure [prə'kjʊə*] *vt* beschaffen.

prod [prɒd] *vt* stoßen; **to** ~ **sb** (*fig*) bohren; *n* Stoß *m.*

prodigal ['prɒdɪgəl] *a* verschwenderisch (*of mit*); **the** ~ **son** der verlorene Sohn.

prodigious [prə'dɪdʒəs] *a* gewaltig, erstaunlich; (*wonderful*) wunderbar.

prodigy ['prɒdɪdʒɪ] *n* Wunder *nt;* **a child** ~ ein Wunderkind.

produce ['prɒdjuːs] *n* (*Agr*) (Boden)produkte *pl,* (Natur)erzeugnis *nt;* [prə'djuːs] *vt* herstellen, produzieren; (*cause*) hervorrufen; (*farmer*) erzeugen; (*yield*) liefern, bringen; *play* inszenieren; ~**r** Erzeuger *m,* Hersteller *m,* Produzent *m* (*also Cine*).

product ['prɒdʌkt] *n* Produkt *nt,* Erzeugnis *nt;* ~**ion** [prə'dʌkʃən] Produktion *f,* Herstellung *f;* (*thing*) Erzeugnis *nt,* Produkt *nt;* (*Theat*) Inszenierung *f;* ~**ion line** Fließband *nt;* ~**ive** *a* produktiv; (*fertile*) ertragreich, fruchtbar; **to be** ~**ive of** führen zu, erzeugen.

productivity [prɒdʌk'tɪvɪtɪ] *n* Produktivität *f;* (*Comm*) Leistungsfähigkeit *f;* (*fig*) Fruchtbarkeit *f.*

prof [prɒf] *n* (*col*) Professor *m.*

profane [prə'feɪn] *a* weltlich, profan, Profan-.

profess [prə'fes] *vt* bekennen; (*show*)

zeigen; *(claim to be)* vorgeben; ~**ion** [prɔ'feʃən] Beruf *m; (declaration)* Bekenntnis *nt;* ~**ional** [prɔ'feʃənl] Fachmann *m; (Sport)* Berufsspieler(in *f) m;* a Berufs-; *(expert)* fachlich; *player* professionell; ~**ionalism** [prɔ'feʃnəlizəm] *(fachliches)* Können *nt;* Berufssportlertum *nt;* ~**or** Professor *m.*

proficiency [prɔ'fiʃənsi] *n* Fertigkeit *f,* Können *nt.*

proficient [prɔ'fiʃənt] a fähig.

profile ['prəufail] *n* Profil *nt; (fig: report)* Kurzbiographie *f.*

profit ['prɔfit] *n* Gewinn *m,* Profit *m; vi* profitieren *(by, from* von), Nutzen *or* Gewinn ziehen *(by, from* aus); ~**ability** [prɔfitə'biliti] Rentabilität *f;* ~**able** a einträglich, rentabel; ~**ably** ad nützlich; ~**eering** [prɔfi'tiəriŋ] Profitmacherei *f.*

profound [prɔ'faund] a tief; *knowledge* profund; *book, thinker* tiefschürfend; ~**ly** ad zutiefst.

profuse [prɔ'fju:s] a überreich; to be ~ in überschwenglich sein bei; ~**ly** ad überschwenglich; *sweat* reichlich.

profusion [prɔ'fju:ʒən] *n* Überfülle *f,* Überfluß *m (of* an +*dat).*

progeny ['prɔdʒini] *n* Nachkommenschaft *f.*

programme, *(US)* **program** ['prəugræm] *n* Programm *nt; vt* planen; *computer* programmieren.

programming, *(US)* **programing** ['prəugræmiŋ] *n* Programmieren *nt,* Programmierung *f.*

progress ['prəugres] *n* Fortschritt *m;* to be in ~ im Gang sein; to make ~ Fortschritte machen; [prɔ'gres] *vi* fortschreiten, weitergehen; ~**ion** [prɔ'greʃən] Fortschritt *m,* Progression *f; (walking etc)* Fortbewegung *f;* ~**ive** [prɔ'gresiv] a fortschrittlich, progressiv; ~**ively** [prɔ'gresivli] ad zunehmend.

prohibit [prɔ'hibit] *vt* verbieten; ~**ion** [prɔui'biʃən] Verbot *f; (US)* Alkoholverbot *nt,* Prohibition *f;* ~**ive** a *price etc* unerschwinglich.

project ['prɔdʒekt] *n* Projekt *nt;* [prɔ'dʒekt] *vt* vorausplanen; *(Psych)* hineinprojizieren; *film etc* projizieren; *personality, voice* zum Tragen bringen; *vi (stick out)* hervorragen, (her)vorstehen; ~**ile** [prɔ'dʒektail] Geschoß *nt,* Projektil *nt;* ~**ion** [prɔ'dʒekʃən] Projektion *f; (sth prominent)* Vorsprung *m;* ~**or** [prɔ'dʒektə*] Projektor *m,* Vorführgerät *nt.*

proletarian [prəulə'tɛəriən] a proletarisch, Proletarier-; *n* Proletarier(in *f) m.*

proletariat [prəulə'tɛəriət] *n* Proletariat *nt.*

proliferate [prɔ'lifəreit] *vi* sich vermehren.

proliferation [prɔlifə'reiʃən] *n* Vermehrung *f.*

prolific [prɔ'lifik] a fruchtbar; *author etc* produktiv.

prologue ['prəulɔg] *n* Prolog *m; (event)* Vorspiel *nt.*

prolong [prɔ'lɔŋ] *vt* verlängern; ~**ed** a lang.

prom [prɔm] *n abbr of* promenade *and* **promenade concert;** *(US: college ball)* Studentenball *m.*

promenade [prɔmi'nɑ:d] *n* Promenade *f;* ~ **concert** Promenadenkonzert *nt,* Stehkonzert *nt;* ~ **deck** Promenadendeck *nt.*

prominence ['prɔminəns] *n* (große) Bedeutung *f,* Wichtigkeit *f; (sth standing out)* vorspringende(r) Teil *m.*

prominent ['prɔminənt] a bedeutend; *politician* prominent; *(easily seen)* herausragend, auffallend.

promiscuity [prɔmis'kju:iti] *n* Promiskuität *f.*

promiscuous [prɔ'miskjuəs] a lose; *(mixed up)* wild.

promise ['prɔmis] *n* Versprechen *nt; (hope)* Aussicht *f (of* auf + *acc);* to show ~ vielversprechend sein; a writer of ~ ein vielversprechender Schriftsteller; *vti* versprechen; the ~d land das Gelobte Land.

promising ['prɔmisiŋ] a vielversprechend.

promontory ['prɔməntri] *n* Vorsprung *m.*

promote [prɔ'məut] *vt* befördern; *(help on)* fördern, unterstützen; ~**r** *(in sport, entertainment)* Veranstalter *m; (for charity etc)* Organisator *m.*

promotion [prɔ'məuʃən] *n (in rank)* Beförderung *f; (furtherance)* Förderung *f; (Comm)* Werbung *f (of* für).

prompt [prɔmpt] a prompt, schnell; to be ~ to do sth etw sofort tun; ad *(punctually)* genau; at two o'clock ~ punkt zwei Uhr; *vt* veranlassen; *(Theat)* einsagen (+*dat),* soufflieren (+*dat);* ~**er** *(Theat)* Souffleur *m,* Souffleuse *f;* ~**ly** ad sofort; ~**ness** Schnelligkeit *f,* Promptheit *f.*

promulgate ['prɔmʌlgeit] *vt* (öffentlich) bekanntmachen, verkünden; *beliefs* verbreiten.

prone [prəun] a hingestreckt; to be ~ to sth zu etw neigen.

prong [prɔŋ] *n* Zinke *f.*

pronoun ['prəunaun] *n* Pronomen *nt,* Fürwort *nt.*

pronounce [prɔ'nauns] *vt* aussprechen; *(Jur)* verkünden; *vi (give an opinion)* sich äußern *(on* zu); ~**d** a ausgesprochen; ~**ment** Erklärung *f.*

pronto ['prɔntəu] ad *(col)* flix, pronto.

pronunciation [prɔnʌnsi'eiʃən] *n* Aussprache *f.*

proof [pru:f] *n* Beweis *m; (Print)* Korrekturfahne *f; (of alcohol)* Alkoholgehalt *m;* to put to the ~ unter Beweis stellen; a sicher; *alcohol* prozentig; **rain**~ regendicht.

prop [prɔp] *n* Stütze *f (also fig); (Min)* Stempel *m; (Theat)* Requisit *nt; vt (also ~ up)* (ab)stützen.

propaganda [prɔpə'gændə] *n* Propaganda *f.*

propagate ['prɔpəgeit] *vt* fortpflanzen; *news* propagieren, verbreiten.

propagation [prɔpə'geiʃən] *n* Fort-

pflanzung f; (of knowledge also) Verbreitung f.

propel [prə'pel] vt (an)treiben; ~ler Propeller m; ~ling pencil Drehbleistift m.

propensity [prə'pensɪtɪ] n Tendenz f.

proper ['prɒpə*] a richtig; (seemly) schicklich; ~ly ad richtig; ~ly speaking genau genommen; it is not ~ to . . . es schickt sich nicht, zu . . .; ~ noun Eigenname m.

property ['prɒpətɪ] n Eigentum nt, Besitz m, Gut nt; (quality) Eigenschaft f; (land) Grundbesitz m; (Theat) **properties** pl Requisiten pl; ~ owner Grundbesitzer m.

prophecy ['prɒfɪsɪ] n Prophezeiung f.

prophesy ['prɒfɪsaɪ] vt prophezeien, vorhersagen.

prophet ['prɒfɪt] n Prophet m; ~ic [prə'fetɪk] a prophetisch.

proportion [prə'pɔ:ʃən] n Verhältnis nt, Proportion f; (share) Teil m; vt abstimmen (to auf +acc); ~al a, ~ally ad proportional, verhältnismäßig; to be ~al to entsprechen (+dat); ~ate a, ~ately ad verhältnismäßig; ~ed a proportioniert.

proposal [prə'pəʊzl] n Vorschlag m, Antrag m; (of marriage) Heiratsantrag m.

propose [prə'pəʊz] vt vorschlagen; toast ausbringen; vi (offer marriage) einen Heiratsantrag machen; ~r Antragsteller m.

proposition [prɒpə'zɪʃən] n Angebot nt; (Math) Lehrsatz m; (statement) Satz m.

propound [prə'paʊnd] vt theory vorlegen.

proprietary [prə'praɪətərɪ] a Eigentums-; medicine gesetzlich geschützt.

proprietor [prə'praɪətə*] n Besitzer m, Eigentümer m.

props [prɒps] npl Requisiten pl.

propulsion [prə'pʌlʃən] n Antrieb m.

pro-rata [prəʊ'rɑ:tə] ad anteilmäßig.

prosaic [prə'zeɪɪk] a prosaisch, alltäglich.

prose [prəʊz] n Prosa f.

prosecute ['prɒsɪkju:t] vt (strafrechtlich) verfolgen.

prosecution [prɒsɪ'kju:ʃən] n Durchführung f; (Jur) strafrechtliche Verfolgung f; (party) Anklage f; Staatsanwaltschaft f.

prosecutor ['prɒsɪkju:tə*] n Vertreter m der Anklage; Public P~ Staatsanwalt m.

prospect ['prɒspekt] n Aussicht f; [prəs'pekt] vi suchen (for nach); ~ing [prəs'pektɪŋ] (for minerals) Suche f; ~ive [prəs'pektɪv] a möglich; ~or [prəs'pektə*] (Gold)sucher m; ~us [prəs'pektəs] (Werbe)prospekt m.

prosper ['prɒspə*] vi blühen, gedeihen; (person) erfolgreich sein; ~ity [prɒs'perɪtɪ] Wohlstand m; ~ous a wohlhabend, reich; business gutgehend, blühend.

prostitute [prɒstɪtju:t] n Prostituierte f.

prostrate ['prɒstreɪt] a ausgestreckt (liegend); ~ with grief/exhaustion von Schmerz/Erschöpfung übermannt.

protagonist [prəʊ'tægənɪst] n Hauptperson f, Held m.

protect [prə'tekt] vt (be)schützen; ~ion [prə'tekʃən] Schutz m; ~ive a Schutz-,

(be)schützend; ~or (Be)schützer m.

protégé ['prəʊteʒeɪ] n Schützling m.

protein ['prəʊti:n] n Protein nt, Eiweiß nt.

protest ['prəʊtest] n Protest m; [prə'test] vi protestieren (against gegen); to ~ that ... beteuern . . .; P~ant a protestantisch; n Protestant(in f) m.

protocol ['prəʊtəkɒl] n Protokoll nt.

prototype ['prəʊtəʊtaɪp] n Prototyp m.

protracted [prə'træktɪd] a sich hinziehend.

protractor [prə'træktə*] n Winkelmesser m.

protrude [prə'tru:d] vi (her)vorstehen.

protuberance [prə'tju:bərəns] n Auswuchs m.

protuberant [prə'tju:bərənt] a (her)vorstehend.

proud a, ~ly ad [praʊd, -lɪ] stolz (of auf +acc).

prove [pru:v] vt beweisen; vi sich herausstellen, sich zeigen.

proverb ['prɒvɜ:b] n Sprichwort m; ~ial a, ~ially ad [prə'vɜ:bɪəl, -ɪ] sprichwörtlich.

provide [prə'vaɪd] vt versehen; (supply) besorgen; person versorgen; ~ for vt sorgen für, sich kümmern um; emergency Vorkehrungen treffen für; blankets will be ~d Decken werden gestellt; ~d (that) cj vorausgesetzt (daß); P~nce ['prɒvɪdəns] die Vorsehung.

providing [prə'vaɪdɪŋ] cj = **provided (that).**

province ['prɒvɪns] n Provinz f; (division of work) Bereich m; the ~s die Provinz.

provincial [prə'vɪnʃəl] a provinziell, Provinz-; n Provinzler(in f) m.

provision [prə'vɪʒən] n Vorkehrung f, Maßnahme f; (condition) Bestimmung f; ~s pl (food) Vorräte pl, Proviant m; ~al a, ~ally ad vorläufig, provisorisch.

proviso [prə'vaɪzəʊ] n Vorbehalt m, Bedingung f.

provocation [prɒvə'keɪʃən] n Provokation f, Herausforderung f.

provocative [prə'vɒkətɪv] a provokativ, herausfordernd.

provoke [prə'vəʊk] vt provozieren; (cause) hervorrufen.

prow [praʊ] n Bug m; ~ess überragende(s) Können nt; (valour) Tapferkeit f.

prowl [praʊl] vt streets durchstreifen; vi herumstreichen; (animal) schleichen; n: on the ~ umherstreifend; (police) auf der Streife; ~er Eindringling m.

proximity [prɒk'sɪmɪtɪ] n Nähe f.

proxy ['prɒksɪ] n (Stell)vertreter m, Bevollmächtigte(r) m; (document) Vollmacht f; to vote by ~ Briefwahl machen.

prudence ['pru:dəns] n Klugheit f, Umsicht f.

prudent a, ~ly ad ['pru:dənt, -lɪ] klug, umsichtig.

prudish ['pru:dɪʃ] a prüde; ~ness Prüderie f.

prune [pru:n] n Backpflaume f; vt ausputzen; (fig) zurechtstutzen.

pry [praɪ] vi seine Nase stecken (into in +acc).

psalm [sɑːm] n Psalm m.

pseudo ['sjuːdəʊ] a Pseudo-; (false) falsch, unecht; ~nym ['sjuːdənɪm] Pseudonym nt, Deckname m.

psyche ['saɪkɪ] n Psyche f.

psychiatric [saɪkɪ'ætrɪk] a psychiatrisch.

psychiatrist [saɪ'kaɪətrɪst] n Psychiater m.

psychiatry [saɪ'kaɪətrɪ] n Psychiatrie f.

psychic(al) ['saɪkɪk(əl)] a übersinnlich; person paranormal begabt; **you must be** ~ du kannst wohl hellsehen.

psychoanalyse, (US) **psychoanalyze** [saɪkəʊ'ænəlaɪz] vt psychoanalytisch behandeln.

psychoanalysis [saɪkəʊə'næləsɪs] n Psychoanalyse f.

psychoanalyst [saɪkəʊ'ænəlɪst] n Psychoanalytiker(in f) m.

psychological a, **~ly** ad [saɪkə'lɒdʒɪkəl, -lɪ] psychologisch.

psychologist [saɪ'kɒlədʒɪst] n Psychologe m, Psychologin f.

psychology [saɪ'kɒlədʒɪ] n Psychologie f.

psychopath ['saɪkəʊpæθ] n Psychopath(in f) m.

psychosomatic ['saɪkəʊsəʊ'mætɪk] a psychosomatisch.

psychotherapy ['saɪkəʊ'θerəpɪ] n Psychotherapie f.

psychotic [saɪ'kɒtɪk] a psychotisch; n Psychotiker(in f) m.

pub [pʌb] n Wirtschaft f, Kneipe f.

puberty ['pjuːbətɪ] n Pubertät f.

pubic ['pjuːbɪk] a Scham-.

public a, **~ly** ad ['pʌblɪk, -lɪ] öffentlich; n (also general ~) Öffentlichkeit f; **~an** Wirt m; **~ation** [pʌblɪ'keɪʃən] Publikation f, Veröffentlichung f; **~ company** Aktiengesellschaft f; **~ convenience** öffentliche Toiletten pl; **~ house** Lokal nt, Kneipe f; **~ity** [pʌb'lɪsɪtɪ] Publicity f, Werbung f; **~ opinion** öffentliche Meinung f; **~ relations** pl Public Relations pl; **~ school** (Brit) Privatschule f, Internatsschule f; **~-spirited** a mit Gemeinschaftssinn; **to be ~-spirited** Gemeinschaftssinn haben.

publish ['pʌblɪʃ] vt veröffentlichen, publizieren; event bekanntgeben; **~er** Verleger m; **~ing** Herausgabe f, Verlegen nt; (business) Verlagswesen nt.

puce [pjuːs] a violettbraun.

puck [pʌk] n Puck m, Scheibe f.

pucker ['pʌkə*] vt face verziehen; lips kräuseln.

pudding ['pʊdɪŋ] n (course) Nachtisch m; Pudding m.

puddle ['pʌdl] n Pfütze f.

puerile ['pjʊəraɪl] a kindisch.

puff [pʌf] n (of wind etc) Stoß m; (cosmetic) Puderquaste f; vt blasen, pusten; pipe paffen, vi keuchen, schnaufen; (smoke) paffen; **~ed** a (col: out of breath) außer Puste.

puffin ['pʌfɪn] n Papageitaucher m.

puff pastry, (US) **puff paste** ['pʌf'peɪstrɪ, 'pʌf'peɪst] n Blätterteig m.

puffy ['pʌfɪ] a aufgedunsen.

pull [pʊl] n Ruck m; Zug m; (influence) Beziehung f; vt ziehen; trigger abdrücken; vi ziehen; **to ~ a face** ein Gesicht schneiden; **to ~ sb's leg** jdn auf den Arm nehmen; **to ~ to pieces** (lit) in Stücke reißen; (fig) verreißen; **to ~ one's weight** sich in die Riemen legen; **to ~ o.s. together** sich zusammenreißen; **~ apart** vt (break) zerreißen; (dismantle) auseinandernehmen; fighters trennen; **~ down** vt house abreißen; **~ in** vi hineinfahren; (stop) anhalten; (Rail) einfahren; **~ off** vt deal etc abschließen; **~ out** vi (car) herausfahren; (fig: partner) aussteigen; vt herausziehen; **~ round**, **~ through** vi durchkommen; **~ up** vi anhalten.

pulley ['pʊlɪ] n Rolle f, Flaschenzug m.

pullover ['pʊləʊvə*] n Pullover m.

pulp [pʌlp] n Brei m; (of fruit) Fruchtfleisch nt.

pulpit ['pʊlpɪt] n Kanzel f.

pulsate [pʌl'seɪt] vi pulsieren.

pulse [pʌls] n Puls m.

pulverize ['pʌlvəraɪz] vt pulverisieren, in kleine Stücke zerlegen (also fig).

puma ['pjuːmə] n Puma m.

pummel ['pʌml] vt mit den Fäusten bearbeiten.

pump [pʌmp] n Pumpe f; (shoe) leichter (Tanz)schuh m; vt pumpen; **~ up** vt tyre aufpumpen.

pumpkin ['pʌmpkɪn] n Kürbis m.

pun [pʌn] n Wortspiel nt.

punch [pʌntʃ] n (tool) Stanze f; Locher m; (blow) (Faust)schlag m; (drink) Punsch m, Bowle f; vt stanzen; lochen; (strike) schlagen, boxen; **~-drunk** a benommen; **~-up** (col) Keilerei f.

punctual ['pʌŋktjʊəl] a pünktlich; **~ity** [pʌŋktjʊ'ælɪtɪ] Pünktlichkeit f.

punctuate ['pʌŋktjʊeɪt] vt mit Satzzeichen versehen, interpunktieren; (fig) unterbrechen.

punctuation [pʌŋktjʊ'eɪʃən] n Zeichensetzung f, Interpunktion f.

puncture ['pʌŋktʃə*] n Loch nt; (Aut) Reifenpanne f; vt durchbohren.

pundit ['pʌndɪt] n Gelehrte(r) m.

pungent ['pʌndʒənt] a scharf.

punish ['pʌnɪʃ] vt bestrafen; (in boxing etc) übel zurichten; **~able** a strafbar; **~ment** Strafe f; (action) Bestrafung f.

punitive ['pjuːnɪtɪv] a strafend.

punt [pʌnt] n Stechkahn m.

punter ['pʌntə*] n (better) Wetter m.

puny ['pjuːnɪ] a kümmerlich.

pup [pʌp] n = **puppy**.

pupil ['pjuːpl] n Schüler(in f) m; (in eye) Pupille f.

puppet ['pʌpɪt] n Puppe f; Marionette f.

puppy ['pʌpɪ] n junge(r) Hund m.

purchase ['pɜːtʃɪs] n Kauf m, Anschaffung f; (grip) Halt m; vt kaufen, erwerben; **~r** Käufer(in f) m.

pure [pjʊə*] a pur; rein (also fig); **~ly** ['pjuːəlɪ] ad rein; (only) nur; (with a also) rein.

purée ['pjuəreɪ] *n* Püree *nt.*

purgatory ['pɜːgətərɪ] *n* Fegefeuer *nt.*

purge [pɜːdʒ] *n* Säuberung *f (also Pol); (medicine)* Abführmittel *nt; vt* reinigen; *body* entschlacken.

purification [pjuərɪfɪ'keɪʃən] *n* Reinigung *f.*

purify ['pjuərɪfaɪ] *vt* reinigen.

purist ['pjuərɪst] *n* Purist *m.*

puritan ['pjuərɪtən] *n* Puritaner *m;* ~**ical** [pjuərɪ'tænɪkəl] *a* puritanisch.

purity ['pjuərɪtɪ] *n* Reinheit *f.*

purl [pɜːl] *n* linke Masche *f; vt* links stricken.

purple ['pɜːpl] *a* violett; *face* dunkelrot; *n* Violett *nt.*

purpose ['pɜːpəs] *n* Zweck *m,* Ziel *nt; (of person)* Absicht *f; on* ~ absichtlich; ~**ful** *a* zielbewußt, entschlossen; ~**ly** *ad* absichtlich.

purr [pɜː*] *n* Schnurren *nt; vi* schnurren.

purse [pɜːs] *n* Portemonnaie *nt,* Geldbeutel *m; vt lips* zusammenpressen, schürzen.

purser ['pɜːsə*] *n* Zahlmeister *m.*

pursue [pə'sjuː] *vt* verfolgen, nachjagen *(+dat); study* nachgehen *(+dat);* ~**r** *n* Verfolger *m.*

pursuit [pə'sjuːt] *n* Jagd *f (of* nach), Verfolgung *f; (occupation)* Beschäftigung *f.*

purveyor [pɜː'veɪə*] *n* Lieferant *m.*

pus [pʌs] *n* Eiter *m.*

push [puʃ] *n* Stoß *m,* Schub *m; (energy)* Schwung *m; (Mil)* Vorstoß *m; vt* stoßen, schieben; *button* drücken; *idea* durchsetzen; *vi* stoßen, schieben; *at a* ~ zur Not; ~ *aside vt* beiseiteschieben; ~ *off vi (col)* abschieben; ~ *on vi* weitermachen; ~ *through vt* durchdrücken; *policy* durchsetzen; ~ *up vt total* erhöhen; *prices* hochtreiben; ~**chair** (Kinder)sportwagen *m;* ~**ing** *a* aufdringlich; ~**over** *(col)* Kinderspiel *nt;* ~**y** *a (col)* aufdringlich.

puss [pus] *n* Mieze(katze) *f.*

put [put] *vt irreg* setzen, stellen, legen; *(express)* ausdrücken, sagen; *(write)* schreiben; ~ *about vi (turn back)* wenden; *vt (spread)* verbreiten; ~ *across vt (explain)* erklären; ~ *away vt* weglegen; *(store)* beiseitelegen; ~ *back vt* zurückstellen *or* -legen; ~ *by vt* zurücklegen, sparen; ~ *down vt* hinstellen *or* -legen; *(stop)* niederschlagen; *animal* einschläfern; *(in writing)* niederschreiben; ~ *forward vt idea* vorbringen; *clock* vorstellen; ~ *off vt* verlegen, verschieben; *(discourage)* abbringen von; *it* ~ *me off smoking* das hat mir die Lust am Rauchen verdorben; ~ *on vt clothes etc* anziehen; *light etc* anschalten, anmachen; *play etc* aufführen; *brake* anziehen; ~ *out vt hand etc* (her)ausstrecken; *news, rumour* verbreiten; *light etc* ausschalten, ausmachen; ~ *up vt tent* aufstellen; *building* errichten; *price* erhöhen; *person* unterbringen; *to* ~ *up with sich abfinden mit;* **I won't** ~ *up with it* das laß ich mir nicht gefallen.

putrid ['pjuːtrɪd] *a* faul.

putsch [putʃ] *n* Putsch *m.*

putt [pʌt] *vt (golf)* putten, einlochen; *n (golf)* Putten *nt,* leichte(r) Schlag *m;* ~**er** Putter *m.*

putty ['pʌtɪ] *n* Kitt *m; (fig)* Wachs *nt.*

put-up ['putʌp] *a:* ~ *job* abgekartete(s) Spiel *nt.*

puzzle ['pʌzl] *n* Rätsel *nt; (toy)* Geduldspiel *nt; vt* verwirren; *vi* sich den Kopf zerbrechen.

puzzling ['pʌzlɪŋ] *a* rätselhaft, verwirrend.

pygmy ['pɪgmɪ] *n* Pygmäe *m; (fig)* Zwerg *m.*

pyjamas [pɪ'dʒɑːməz] *npl* Schlafanzug *m,* Pyjama *m.*

pylon ['paɪlən] *n* Mast *m.*

pyramid ['pɪrəmɪd] *n* Pyramide *f.*

python ['paɪθən] *n* Pythonschlange *f.*

Q

Q, q [kjuː] *n* Q *nt,* q *nt.*

quack [kwæk] *n* Quacken *nt; (doctor)* Quacksalber *m.*

quad [kwɒd] *abbr of* **quadrangle, quadruple, quadruplet.**

quadrangle ['kwɒdræŋgl] *n (court)* Hof *m; (Math)* Viereck *nt.*

quadruped ['kwɒdruped] *n* Vierfüßler *m.*

quadruple ['kwɒ'druːpl] *a* vierfach; *vi* sich vervierfachen; *vt* vervierfachen.

quadruplet [kwɒ'druːplət] *n* Vierling *m.*

quagmire ['kwæɡmaɪə*] *n* Morast *m.*

quaint [kweɪnt] *a* kurios; malerisch; ~**ly** *ad* kurios; ~**ness** malerischer Anblick *m;* Kuriosität *f.*

quake [kweɪk] *vi* beben, zittern; **Q~r** Quäker *m.*

qualification [kwɒlɪfɪ'keɪʃən] *n* Qualifikation *f; (sth which limits)* Einschränkung *f.*

qualified ['kwɒlɪfaɪd] *a (competent)* qualifiziert; *(limited)* bedingt.

qualify ['kwɒlɪfaɪ] *vt (prepare)* befähigen; *(limit)* einschränken; *vi* sich qualifizieren.

qualitative ['kwɒlɪtətɪv] *a* qualitativ.

quality ['kwɒlɪtɪ] *n* Qualität *f; (characteristic)* Eigenschaft *f; a* Qualitäts-.

qualm [kwɑːm] *n* Bedenken *nt,* Zweifel *m.*

quandary ['kwɒndərɪ] *n* Verlegenheit *f; to be in a* ~ in Verlegenheit sein.

quantitative ['kwɒntɪtətɪv] *a* quantitativ.

quantity ['kwɒntɪtɪ] *n* Menge *f,* Quantität *f.*

quarantine ['kwɒrəntiːn] *n* Quarantäne *f.*

quarrel ['kwɒrəl] *n* Streit *m; vi* sich streiten; ~**some** *a* streitsüchtig.

quarry ['kwɒrɪ] *n* Steinbruch *m; (animal)* Wild *nt; (fig)* Opfer *nt.*

quart [kwɔːt] *n* Quart *nt.*

quarter ['kwɔːtə*] *n* Viertel *nt; (of year)* Quartal *nt,* Vierteljahr *nt; vt (divide)* vierteln, in Viertel teilen; *(Mil)* einquartieren; ~**s** *pl (esp Mil)* Quartier *nt;* ~ *of an hour* Viertelstunde *f;* ~ *past three* viertel nach drei; ~ *to three* dreiviertel drei, viertel vor drei; ~**deck** Achterdeck *nt;* ~ *final* Viertelfinale *nt;* ~**ly** *a* vierteljährlich; ~**master** Quartiermeister *m.*

quartet(te) [kwɔː'tet] *n* Quartett *nt.*

quartz [kwɔːts] *n* Quarz *m.*

quash [kwɒʃ] *vt verdict* aufheben.

quasi [kwɑ:zɪ] ad quasi.
quaver ['kweɪvə*] n (Mus) Achtelnote f; vi (tremble) zittern.
quay [ki:] n Kai m.
queasiness ['kwi:zɪnəs] n Übelkeit f.
queasy ['kwi:zɪ] a übel; **he feels ~** ihm ist übel.
queen [kwi:n] n Königin f; **~ mother** Königinmutter f.
queer [kwɪə*] a seltsam, sonderbar, kurios; **~ fellow** komische(r) Kauz m; n (col: homosexual) Schwule(r) m.
quell [kwel] vt unterdrücken.
quench [kwentʃ] vt thirst löschen, stillen; (extinguish) löschen.
query ['kwɪərɪ] n (question) (An)frage f; (question mark) Fragezeichen nt; vt in Zweifel ziehen, in Frage stellen.
quest [kwest] n Suche f.
question ['kwestʃən] n Frage f; vt (ask) (be)fragen; suspect verhören; (doubt) in Frage stellen, bezweifeln; **beyond ~** ohne Frage; **out of the ~** ausgeschlossen; **~able** a zweifelhaft; **~er** Fragesteller m; **~ing** a fragend; **~ mark** Fragezeichen nt; **~naire** Fragebogen m; (enquiry) Umfrage f.
queue [kju:] n Schlange f; vi (also ~ up) Schlange stehen.
quibble ['kwɪbl] n Spitzfindigkeit f; vi kleinlich sein.
quick a, **~ly** ad [kwɪk, -lɪ] a schnell; n (of nail) Nagelhaut f; (old: the living) die Lebenden; **to the ~** (fig) bis ins Innerste; **~en** vt (hasten) beschleunigen; (stir) anregen; vi sich beschleunigen; **~-fire** a questions etc Schnellfeuer-; **~ness** Schnelligkeit f; (mental) Scharfsinn m; **~sand** Treibsand m; **~step** Quickstep m; **~-witted** a schlagfertig, hell.
quid [kwɪd] n (Brit col: £1) Pfund nt.
quiet ['kwaɪət] a (without noise) leise; (peaceful, calm) still, ruhig; n Stille f, Ruhe f; **~en** (also **~en down**) vi ruhig werden; vt beruhigen; **~ly** ad leise, ruhig; **~ness** Ruhe f, Stille f.
quill [kwɪl] n (of porcupine) Stachel m; (pen) Feder f.
quilt [kwɪlt] n Steppdecke f; **~ing** Füllung f, Wattierung f.
quin [kwɪn] abbr of **quintuplet.**
quince [kwɪns] n Quitte f.
quinine [kwɪ'ni:n] n Chinin nt.
quinsy ['kwɪnzɪ] n Mandelentzündung f.
quintet(te) [kwɪn'tet] n Quintett nt.
quintuplet [kwɪn'tju:plət] n Fünfling m.
quip [kwɪp] n witzige Bemerkung f; vi witzeln.
quirk [kwз:k] n (oddity) Eigenart f.
quit [kwɪt] irreg vt verlassen; vi aufhören.
quite [kwaɪt] ad (completely) ganz, völlig; (fairly) ziemlich; **~ (so)!** richtig!
quits [kwɪts] a quitt.
quiver ['kwɪvə*] vi zittern; n (for arrows) Köcher m.
quiz [kwɪz] n (competition) Quiz nt; (series of questions) Befragung f; vt prüfen; **~zical** a fragend, verdutzt.
quoit [kwɔɪt] n Wurfring m.

quorum ['kwɔ:rəm] n beschlußfähige Anzahl f.
quota ['kwəʊtə] n Anteil m; (Comm) Quote f.
quotation [kwəʊ'teɪʃən] n Zitat nt; (price) Kostenvoranschlag m; **~ marks** pl Anführungszeichen pl.
quote [kwəʊt] n see quotation; vi (from book) zitieren; vt (from book) zitieren; price angeben.
quotient ['kwəʊʃənt] n Quotient m.

R

R, r [ɑ:*] n R nt, r nt.
rabbi ['ræbaɪ] n Rabbiner m; (title) Rabbi m.
rabbit ['ræbɪt] n Kaninchen nt; **~ hutch** Kaninchenstall m.
rabble ['ræbl] n Pöbel m.
rabies ['reɪbi:z] n Tollwut f.
raccoon [rə'ku:n] n Waschbär m.
race [reɪs] n (species) Rasse f; (competition) Rennen nt; (on foot also) Wettlauf m; (rush) Hetze f; vt um die Wette laufen mit; horses laufen lassen; vi (run) rennen; (in contest) am Rennen teilnehmen; **~course** (for horses) Rennbahn f; **~horse** Rennpferd nt; **~ meeting** (for horses) (Pferde)rennen nt; **~ relations** pl Beziehungen pl zwischen den Rassen; **~track** (for cars etc) Rennstrecke f.
racial ['reɪʃəl] a Rassen-; **~ discrimination** Rassendiskriminierung f; **~ism** Rassismus m; **~ist** a rassistisch; n Rassist m.
racing ['reɪsɪŋ] n Rennen nt; **~ car** Rennwagen m; **~ driver** Rennfahrer m.
racism ['reɪsɪzəm] n Rassismus m.
racist ['reɪsɪst] n Rassist m; a rassistisch.
rack [ræk] n Ständer m, Gestell nt; vt (zer)martern; **to go to ~ and ruin** verfallen.
racket ['rækɪt] n (din) Krach m; (scheme) (Schwindel)geschäft nt; (tennis) (Tennis)schläger m.
racquet ['rækɪt] n = **racket** (tennis).
racy ['reɪsɪ] a gewagt; style spritzig.
radar ['reɪdɑ:*] n Radar nt or m.
radiance ['reɪdɪəns] n strahlende(r) Glanz m.
radiant ['reɪdɪənt] a (bright) strahlend; (giving out rays) Strahlungs-.
radiate ['reɪdɪeɪt] vti ausstrahlen; (roads, lines) strahlenförmig wegführen.
radiation [reɪdɪ'eɪʃən] n (Aus)strahlung f.
radiator ['reɪdɪeɪtə*] n (for heating) Heizkörper m; (Aut) Kühler m; **~ cap** Kühlerdeckel m.
radical a, **~ly** ad ['rædɪkəl, -ɪ] radikal.
radio ['reɪdɪəʊ] n Rundfunk m, Radio nt; (set) Radio nt, Radioapparat m; **~active** a radioaktiv; **~activity** Radioaktivität f; **~grapher** [reɪdɪ'ɒɡrəfə*] Röntgenassistent(in f) m; **~graphy** [reɪdɪ'ɒɡrəfɪ] Radiographie f, Röntgenphotographie f; **~logy** [reɪdɪ'ɒlədʒɪ] Strahlenkunde f; **~station** Rundfunkstation f; **~ telephone** Funksprechanlage f; **~ telescope** Radio-

teleskop *nt*; ~**therapist** Radiologie-assistent(in *f*) *m*.

radish ['rædɪʃ] *n* (*big*) Rettich *m*; (*small*) Radieschen *nt*.

radium ['reɪdɪəm] *n* Radium *nt*.

radius ['reɪdɪəs] *n* Radius *m*, Halbkreis *m*; (*area*) Umkreis *m*.

raffia ['ræfɪə] *n* (Raffia)bast *m*.

raffish ['ræfɪʃ] *a* liederlich; *clothes* gewagt.

raffle ['ræfl] *n* Verlosung *f*, Tombola *f*.

raft [rɑːft] *n* Floß *nt*.

rafter ['rɑːftə*] *n* Dachsparren *m*.

rag [ræg] *n* (*cloth*) Lumpen *m*, Lappen *m*; (*col: newspaper*) Käseblatt *nt*; (*Univ: for charity*) studentische Sammelaktion *f*; *vt* auf den Arm nehmen; ~**bag** (*fig*) Sammelsurium *nt*.

rage [reɪdʒ] *n* Wut *f*; (*desire*) Sucht *f*; (*fashion*) große Mode *f*; **to be in a** ~ wütend sein; *vi* wüten, toben.

ragged ['rægɪd] *a* edge gezackt; *clothes* zerlumpt.

raging ['reɪdʒɪŋ] *a* tobend; *thirst* Heiden-.

raid [reɪd] *n* Überfall *m*; (*Mil*) Angriff *m*; (*by police*) Razzia *f*; *vt* überfallen; ~**er** (*person*) (Bank)räuber *m*; (*Naut*) Kaper-schiff *nt*.

rail [reɪl] *n* Schiene *f*, Querstange *f*; (*on stair*) Geländer *nt*; (*of ship*) Reling *f*; (*Rail*) Schiene *f*; **by** ~ per Bahn; ~**ing(s)** Geländer *nt*; ~**road** (*US*), ~**way** (*Brit*) Eisenbahn *f*; ~**road** *or* ~**way station** Bahnhof *m*.

rain [reɪn] *n* Regen *m*; *vti* regnen; **the** ~**s** *pl* die Regenzeit; ~**bow** Regenbogen *m*; ~**coat** Regenmantel *m*; ~**drop** Regen-tropfen *m*; ~**fall** Niederschlag *m*; ~**storm** heftige(r) Regenguß *m*; ~**y** *a* region, season Regen-; day regnerisch, ver-regnet.

raise [reɪz] *n* (*esp US: increase*) (Lohn- or Gehalts- or Preis)erhöhung *f*; *vt* (*lift*) (hoch)heben; (*increase*) erhöhen; question aufwerfen; doubts äußern; funds beschaffen; family großziehen; livestock züchten; (*build*) errichten.

raisin ['reɪzən] *n* Rosine *f*.

rajah ['rɑːdʒə] *n* Radscha *m*.

rake [reɪk] *n* Rechen *m*, Harke *f*; (*person*) Wüstling *m*; *vt* rechen, harken; (*with gun*) (mit Feuer) bestreichen; (*search*) (durch)suchen; **to** ~ **in** *or* **together** zusammenscharren.

rakish ['reɪkɪʃ] *a* verwegen.

rally ['rælɪ] *n* (*Pol etc*) Kundgebung *f*; (*Aut*) Sternfahrt *f*, Rallye *f*; (*improvement*) Erholung *f*; *vt* (*Mil*) sammeln; *vi* Kräfte sammeln; ~ **round** *vti* (sich) scharen um; (*help*) zu Hilfe kommen (+dat).

ram [ræm] *n* Widder *m*; (*instrument*) Ramme *f*; *vt* (*strike*) rammen; (*stuff*) (hinein)stopfen.

ramble ['ræmbl] *n* Wanderung *f*, Ausflug *m*; *vi* (*wander*) umherstreifen; (*talk*) schwafeln; ~**r** Wanderer *m*; (*plant*) Kletterrose *f*.

rambling ['ræmblɪŋ] *a* plant Kletter-; speech weitschweifig; town ausgedehnt.

ramification [ræmɪfɪ'keɪʃən] *n* Verästelung *f*; ~**s** *pl* Tragweite *f*.

ramp [ræmp] *n* Rampe *f*.

rampage [ræm'peɪdʒ] *n*: **to be on the** ~ (*also* ~ *vi*) randalieren.

rampant ['ræmpənt] *a* (*heraldry*) auf-gerichtet; **to be** ~ überhandnehmen.

rampart ['ræmpɑːt] *n* (Schutz)wall *m*.

ramshackle ['ræmʃækl] *a* baufällig.

ranch [rɑːntʃ] *n* Ranch *f*; ~**er** Rancher *m*.

rancid ['rænsɪd] *a* ranzig.

rancour, (*US*) **rancor** ['ræŋkə*] *n* Ver-bitterung *f*, Groll *m*.

random ['rændəm] *a* ziellos, wahllos; *n*: **at** ~ aufs Geratewohl.

randy ['rændɪ] *a* (*Brit*) geil, scharf.

range [reɪndʒ] *n* Reihe *f*; (*of mountains*) Kette *f*; (*Comm*) Sortiment *nt*; (*selection*) (große) Auswahl *f* (*of an* +dat); (*reach*) (Reich)weite *f*; (*of gun*) Schußweite *f*; (*for shooting practice*) Schießplatz *m*; (*stove*) (großer) Herd *m*; *vt* (set in row) anordnen, aufstellen; (*roam*) durchstreifen; *vi* (*extend*) sich erstrecken; **prices ranging from £5 to £10** Preise, die sich zwischen 5£ und 10£ bewegen; ~**r** Förster *m*.

rank [ræŋk] *n* (row) Reihe *f*; (*for taxis*) Stand *m*; (*Mil*) Dienstgrad *m*, Rang *m*; (*social position*) Stand *m*; *vt* einschätzen; *vi* (*have* ~) gehören (*among* zu); *a* (*strong-smelling*) stinkend; (*extreme*) krass; **the** ~**s** *pl* (*Mil*) die Mannschaften *pl*; **the** ~ **and file** (*fig*) die breite Masse.

rankle ['ræŋkl] *vi* nagen.

ransack ['rænsæk] *vt* (*plunder*) plündern; (*search*) durchwühlen.

ransom ['rænsəm] *n* Lösegeld *nt*; **to hold sb to** ~ jdn gegen Lösegeld festhalten.

rant [rænt] *vi* hochtrabend reden; ~**ing** Wortschwall *m*.

rap [ræp] *n* Schlag *m*; *vt* klopfen.

rape [reɪp] *n* Vergewaltigung *f*; *vt* verge-waltigen.

rapid ['ræpɪd] *a* rasch, schnell; ~**s** *pl* Stromschnellen *pl*; ~**ity** [rə'pɪdɪtɪ] Schnelligkeit *f*; ~**ly** *ad* schnell.

rapier ['reɪpɪə*] *n* Florett *nt*.

rapist ['reɪpɪst] *n* Vergewaltiger *m*.

rapport [ræ'pɔː*] *n* gute(s) Verhältnis *nt*.

rapprochement [ræ'proʃmɑːŋ] *n* (Wieder)annäherung *f*.

rapt [ræpt] *a* hingerissen.

rapture ['ræptʃə*] *n* Entzücken *nt*.

rapturous ['ræptʃərəs] *a* applause stürmisch; expression verzückt.

rare [reə*] *a* selten, rar; (*especially good*) vortrefflich; (*underdone*) nicht durch-gebraten; ~**fied** ['reərɪfaɪd] *a* air, atmos-phere dünn; ~**ly** *ad* selten.

rarity ['reərɪtɪ] *n* Seltenheit *f*.

rascal ['rɑːskəl] *n* Schuft *m*; (child) Strick *m*.

rash [ræʃ] *a* übereilt; (*reckless*) unbesonnen; *n* (Haut)ausschlag *m*.

rasher ['ræʃə*] *n* Speckscheibe *f*.

rashly ['ræʃlɪ] *ad* vorschnell, unbesonnen.

rashness ['ræʃnəs] *n* Voreiligkeit *f*; (*reck-lessness*) Unbesonnenheit *f*.

rasp [rɑːsp] *n* Raspel *f*.

raspberry ['rɑːzbərɪ] *n* Himbeere *f*.

rasping ['rɑːspɪŋ] *a* noise kratzend.

rat [ræt] n (animal) Ratte f; (person) Halunke m.

ratable ['reɪtəbl] a: ~ **value** Grundsteuer f.

ratchet ['rætʃɪt] n Sperrad nt.

rate [reɪt] n (proportion) Ziffer f, Rate f; (price) Tarif m, Gebühr f; (speed) Geschwindigkeit f; vt (ein)schätzen; ~s pl (Brit) Grundsteuer f, Gemeindeabgaben pl; **at any** ~ jedenfalls; (at least) wenigstens; **at this** ~ wenn es so weitergeht; ~ **of exchange** (Wechsel)kurs m; ~**payer** Steuerzahler(in f) m; see **first**.

rather ['rɑːðə*] ad (in preference) lieber, eher; (to some extent) ziemlich; ~**!** und ob!

ratification [rætɪfɪ'keɪʃən] n Ratifikation f.

ratify ['rætɪfaɪ] vt bestätigen; (Pol) ratifizieren.

rating ['reɪtɪŋ] n Klasse f; (sailor) Matrose m.

ratio ['reɪʃɪəʊ] n Verhältnis nt.

ration ['ræʃən] n (usually pl) Ration f; vt rationieren.

rational a, ~**ly** ad ['ræʃənl, -nəlɪ] rational, vernünftig; ~**e** [ræʃə'nɑːl] Grundprinzip nt; ~**ization** [ræʃnəlaɪ'zeɪʃən] Rationalisierung f; ~**ize** ['ræʃnəlaɪz] vt rationalisieren.

rationing ['ræʃnɪŋ] n Rationierung f.

rat race ['rætreɪs] n Konkurrenzkampf m.

rattle ['rætl] n (sound) Rattern nt, Rasseln nt; (toy) Rassel f; vi ratteln, klappern; ~**snake** Klapperschlange f.

raucous a, ~**ly** ad ['rɔːkəs, -lɪ] heiser, rauh.

ravage ['rævɪdʒ] vt verheeren; ~**s** pl verheerende Wirkungen pl; **the** ~**s of time** der Zahn der Zeit.

rave [reɪv] vi (talk wildly) phantasieren; (rage) toben.

raven ['reɪvn] n Rabe m.

ravenous ['rævənəs] a heißhungrig; appetite unsättlich.

ravine [rə'viːn] n Schlucht f, Klamm f.

raving ['reɪvɪŋ] a tobend; ~ **mad** total verrückt.

ravioli [rævɪ'əʊlɪ] n Ravioli pl.

ravish ['rævɪʃ] vt (delight) entzücken; (Jur) woman vergewaltigen; ~**ing** a hinreißend.

raw [rɔː] a roh; (tender) wund(gerieben); wound offen; (inexperienced) unerfahren; ~ **material** Rohmaterial nt.

ray [reɪ] n (of light) (Licht)strahl m; (gleam) Schimmer m.

rayon ['reɪɒn] n Kunstseide f, Reyon nt or m.

raze [reɪz] vt dem Erdboden gleichmachen.

razor ['reɪzə*] n Rasierapparat m; ~ **blade** Rasierklinge f.

re- [riː] pref wieder-.

re [riː] prep (Comm) betreffs (+ gen).

reach [riːtʃ] n Reichweite f; (of river) Flußstrecke f; **within** ~ (shops etc) in erreichbarer Weite or Entfernung; vt erreichen; (pass on) reichen, geben; vi (try to get) langen (for nach); (stretch) sich erstrecken; ~ **out** vi die Hand ausstrecken.

react [riː'ækt] vi reagieren; ~**ion** [riː'ækʃən] Reaktion f; ~**ionary** [riː'ækʃənrɪ] a reaktionär; ~**or** Reaktor m.

read [riːd] vti irreg lesen; (aloud) vorlesen; it ~**s as follows** es lautet folgendermaßen; ~**able** a leserlich; (worth ~ing) lesenswert; ~**er** (person) Leser(in f) m; (book) Lesebuch nt; ~**ership** Leserschaft f.

readily ['redɪlɪ] ad (willingly) bereitwillig; (easily) prompt.

readiness ['redɪnəs] n (willingness) Bereitwilligkeit f; (being ready) Bereitschaft f.

reading ['riːdɪŋ] n Lesen nt; (interpretation) Deutung f, Auffassung f; ~ **lamp** Leselampe f; ~ **matter** Lesestoff m, Lektüre f; ~ **room** Lesezimmer nt, Lesesaal m.

readjust ['riːə'dʒʌst] vt wieder in Ordnung bringen; neu einstellen; **to** ~ **(o.s.) to sth** sich wieder anpassen an etw (acc); ~**ment** Wiederanpassung f.

ready ['redɪ] a (prepared) bereit, fertig; (willing) bereit, willens; (in condition to) reif; (quick) schlagfertig; money verfügbar, bar; ad bereit; n: **at the** ~ bereit; ~**-made** a gebrauchsfertig, Fertig-; clothes Konfektions-; ~ **reckoner** Rechentabelle f.

real [rɪəl] a wirklich; (actual) eigentlich; (true) wahr; (not fake) echt; ~ **estate** Grundbesitz m; ~**ism** Realismus m; ~**ist** Realist m; ~**istic** a, ~**istically** ad realistisch; ~**ity** [rɪ'ælɪtɪ] (real existence) Wirklichkeit f, Realität f; (facts) Tatsachen pl; ~**ization** (understanding) Erkenntnis f; (fulfilment) Verwirklichung f; ~**ize** vt (understand) begreifen; (make real) verwirklichen; money einbringen; **I didn't** ~**ize** ... ich wußte nicht, ...; ~**ly** ad wirklich.

realm [relm] n Reich nt.

ream [riːm] n Ries nt.

reap [riːp] vt ernten; ~**er** Mähmaschine f.

reappear ['riːə'pɪə*] vi wieder erscheinen; ~**ance** Wiedererscheinen nt.

reapply ['riːə'plaɪ] vi wiederholt beantragen (for acc); (for job) sich erneut bewerben (for um).

reappoint ['riːə'pɔɪnt] vt wieder anstellen; wiederernennen.

reappraisal ['riːə'preɪzəl] n Neubeurteilung f.

rear [rɪə*] a hintere(r, s), Rück-; n Rückseite f; (last part) Schluß m; vt (bring up) aufziehen; vi (horse) sich aufbäumen; ~**-engined** a mit Heckmotor; ~**guard** Nachhut f.

rearm ['riː'ɑːm] vt wiederbewaffnen; vi wiederaufrüsten; ~**ament** Wiederaufrüstung f.

rearrange ['riːə'reɪndʒ] vt umordnen; plans ändern.

rear-view ['rɪəvjuː] a: ~ **mirror** Rückspiegel m.

reason ['riːzn] n (cause) Grund m; (ability to think) Verstand m; (sensible thoughts) Vernunft f; vi (think) denken; (use arguments) argumentieren; **to** ~ **with sb** mit jdm diskutieren; ~**able** a vernünftig; ~**ably** ad vernünftig; (fairly) ziemlich;

one could ~ably suppose man könnte doch (mit gutem Grund) annehmen; **~ed a argument** durchdacht; **~ing** Urteilen *nt; (argumentation)* Beweisführung *f.*

reassemble ['ri:ə'sembl] *vt* wieder versammeln; *(Tech)* wieder zusammensetzen, wieder zusammenbauen; *vi* sich wieder versammeln.

reassert ['ri:ə'sɔːt] *vt* wieder geltend machen.

reassurance ['ri:ə'ʃuərəns] *n* Beruhigung *f; (confirmation)* nochmalige Versicherung *f.*

reassure ['ri:ə'ʃuə*] *vt* beruhigen; *(confirm)* versichern *(sb* jdm).

reassuring ['ri:ə'ʃuərɪŋ] *a* beruhigend.

reawakening ['ri:ə'weɪknɪŋ] *n* Wiedererwachen *nt.*

rebate ['ri:beɪt] *n* Rabatt *m; (money back)* Rückzahlung *f.*

rebel ['rebl] *n* Rebell *m; a* Rebellen-; **~lion** [rɪ'beliən] rebellion *f,* Aufstand *m;* **~lious** [rɪ'beliəs] *a* rebellisch; *(fig)* widerspenstig.

rebirth ['ri:'bɜːθ] *n* Wiedergeburt *f.*

rebound [rɪ'baund] *vi* zurückprallen; ['ri:baund] *n* Rückprall *m;* **on the ~** *(fig)* als Reaktion.

rebuff [rɪ'bʌf] *n* Abfuhr *f; vt* abblitzen lassen.

rebuild ['ri:'bɪld] *vt irreg* wiederaufbauen; *(fig)* wiederherstellen; **~ing** Wiederaufbau *m.*

rebuke [rɪ'bju:k] *n* Tadel *m; vt* tadeln, rügen.

rebut [rɪ'bʌt] *vt* widerlegen.

recalcitrant [rɪ'kælsɪtrənt] *a* widerspenstig.

recall [rɪ'kɔːl] *vt (call back)* zurückrufen; *(remember)* sich erinnern an *(+acc).*

recant [rɪ'kænt] *vi* (öffentlich) widerrufen.

recap ['ri:kæp] *n* kurze Zusammenfassung *f; vti information* wiederholen.

recapture ['ri:'kæptʃə*] *vt* wieder (ein)fangen.

recede [rɪ'si:d] *vi* zurückweichen.

receding [rɪ'si:dɪŋ] *a:* **~ hair** Stirnglatze *f.*

receipt [rɪ'si:t] *n (document)* Quittung *f; (receiving)* Empfang *m;* **~s** *pl* Einnahmen *pl.*

receive [rɪ'si:v] *vt* erhalten; *visitors etc* empfangen; **~r** *(Tel)* Hörer *m.*

recent ['ri:snt] *a* vor kurzem (geschehen), neuerlich; *(modern)* neu; **~ly** *ad* kürzlich, neulich.

receptacle [rɪ'septəkl] *n* Behälter *m.*

reception [rɪ'sepʃən] *n* Empfang *m; (welcome)* Aufnahme *f; (in hotel)* Rezeption *f;* **~ist** *(in hotel)* Empfangschef *m* /-dame *f; (Med)* Sprechstundenhilfe *f.*

receptive [rɪ'septɪv] *a* aufnahmebereit.

recess [rɪ'ses] *n (break)* Ferien *pl; (hollow)* Nische *f;* **~es** *pl* Winkel *m;* **~ion** [rɪ'seʃən] Rezession *f.*

recharge [rɪ'tʃɑːdʒ] *vt battery* aufladen.

recipe ['resɪpɪ] *n* Rezept *nt.*

recipient [rɪ'sɪpɪənt] *n* Empfänger *m.*

reciprocal [rɪ'sɪprəkəl] *a* gegenseitig; *(mutual)* wechselseitig.

reciprocate [rɪ'sɪprəkeɪt] *vt* erwidern.

recital [rɪ'saɪtl] *n (Mus)* Konzert *nt,* Vortrag *m.*

recitation [resɪ'teɪʃən] *n* Rezitation *f.*

recite [rɪ'saɪt] *vt* vortragen, aufsagen; *(give list of also)* aufzählen.

reckless *a,* **~ly** *ad* ['rekləs, -lɪ] leichtsinnig; *driving* fahrlässig; **~ness** Rücksichtslosigkeit *f.*

reckon ['rekən] *vt (count)* (be- oder er)rechnen; *(consider)* halten für; *vi (suppose)* annehmen; **~ on** *vt* rechnen mit; **~ing** *(calculation)* Rechnen *nt.*

reclaim [rɪ'kleɪm] *vt land* abgewinnen *(from dat); expenses* zurückverlangen.

reclamation [reklə'meɪʃən] *n (of land)* Gewinnung *f.*

recline [rɪ'klaɪn] *vi* sich zurücklehnen.

reclining [rɪ'klaɪnɪŋ] *a* verstellbar, Liege-.

recluse [rɪ'klu:s] *n* Einsiedler *m.*

recognition [rekəg'nɪʃən] *n (recognizing)* Erkennen *nt; (acknowledgement)* Anerkennung *f.*

recognizable ['rekəgnaɪzəbl] *a* erkennbar.

recognize ['rekəgnaɪz] *vt* erkennen; *(Pol, approve)* anerkennen.

recoil [rɪ'kɔɪl] *n* Rückstoß *m; vi (in horror)* zurückschrecken; *(rebound)* zurückprallen.

recollect [rekə'lekt] *vt* sich erinnern an *(+acc);* **~ion** Erinnerung *f.*

recommend [rekə'mend] *vt* empfehlen; **~ation** Empfehlung *f.*

recompense ['rekəmpens] *n (compensation)* Entschädigung *f; (reward)* Belohnung *f; vt* entschädigen; belohnen.

reconcilable ['rekənsaɪləbl] *a* vereinbar.

reconcile ['rekənsaɪl] *vt facts* vereinbaren, in Einklang bringen; *people* versöhnen.

reconciliation [rekənsɪlɪ'eɪʃən] *n* Versöhnung *f.*

reconditioned ['ri:kən'dɪʃənd] *a* überholt, erneuert.

reconnaissance [rɪ'kɒnɪsəns] *n* Aufklärung *f.*

reconnoitre, *(US)* **reconnoiter** [rekə'nɔɪtə*] *vt* erkunden; *vi* aufklären.

reconsider ['ri:kən'sɪdə*] *vti* von neuem erwägen, (es) überdenken.

reconstitute ['ri:'kɒnstɪtju:t] *vt* neu bilden.

reconstruct ['ri:kən'strʌkt] *vt* wiederaufbauen; *crime* nachkonstruieren; **~ion** ['ri:kən'strʌkʃən] Rekonstruktion *f.*

record ['rekɔːd] *n* Aufzeichnung *f; (Mus)* Schallplatte *f; (best performance)* Rekord *m; a time* Rekord-; [rɪ'kɔːd] *vt* aufzeichnen; *(Mus etc)* aufnehmen; **~ card** *(in file)* Karteikarte *f;* **~ed music** Musikaufnahmen *pl;* **~er** [rɪ'kɔːdə*] *(officer)* Protokollführer *m; (Mus)* Blockflöte *f;* **~holder** *(Sport)* Rekordinhaber *m;* **~ing** [rɪ'kɔːdɪŋ] *(Mus)* Aufnahme *f;* **~ library** Schallplattenarchiv *nt;* **~ player** Plattenspieler *m.*

recount ['ri:kaunt] *n* Nachzählung *f; vt (count again)* nachzählen; [rɪ'kaunt] *(tell)* berichten.

recoup [rɪ'ku:p] *vt* wettmachen.

recourse [rɪ'kɔːs] *n* Zuflucht *f.*

recover [rɪˈkʌvə*] vt (get back) zurückerhalten; [ˈriːkʌvə*] quilt etc neu überziehen; vi sich erholen; ~y Wiedererlangung f; (of health) Genesung f.

recreate [ˈriːkrɪˈeɪt] vt wiederherstellen.

recreation [rekrɪˈeɪʃən] n Erholung f; Freizeitbeschäftigung f; ~al a Erholungs-.

recrimination [rɪkrɪmɪˈneɪʃən] n Gegenbeschuldigung f.

recruit [rɪˈkruːt] n Rekrut m; vt rekrutieren; ~ing office Wehrmeldeamt nt; ~ment Rekrutierung f.

rectangle [ˈrektæŋgl] n Rechteck nt.

rectangular [rekˈtæŋgjʊlə*] a rechteckig, rechtwinklig.

rectify [ˈrektɪfaɪ] vt berichtigen.

rectory [ˈrektərɪ] n Pfarrhaus nt.

recuperate [rɪˈkuːpəreɪt] vi sich erholen.

recur [rɪˈkɜː*] vi sich wiederholen; ~rence Wiederholung f; ~rent a wiederkehrend.

red [red] n Rot nt; (Pol) Rote(r) m; a rot; in the ~ in den roten Zahlen; R~ Cross Rote(s) Kreuz nt; ~den vti (sich) röten; (blush) erröten; ~dish a rötlich.

redecorate [ˈriːdekəreɪt] vt renovieren.

redecoration [riːdekəˈreɪʃən] n Renovierung f.

redeem [rɪˈdiːm] vt (Comm) einlösen; (set free) freikaufen; (compensate) retten; to ~ sb from sin jdn von seinen Sünden erlösen.

redeeming [rɪˈdiːmɪŋ] a virtue, feature rettend.

redeploy [ˈriːdɪˈplɔɪ] vt resources umverteilen.

red-haired [ˈredˈhɛəd] a rothaarig.

red-handed [ˈredˈhændɪd] ad auf frischer Tat.

redhead [ˈredhed] n Rothaarige(r) mf.

red herring [ˈredˈherɪŋ] n Ablenkungsmanöver nt.

red-hot [ˈredˈhɒt] a rotglühend; (excited) hitzig; tip heiß.

redirect [ˈriːdaɪˈrekt] vt umleiten.

rediscovery [ˈriːdɪsˈkʌvərɪ] n Wiederentdeckung f.

redistribute [ˈriːdɪsˈtrɪbjuːt] vt neu verteilen.

red-letter day [ˈredˈletədeɪ] n (lit, fig) Festtag m.

redness [ˈrednəs] n Röte f.

redo [ˈriːˈduː] vt irreg nochmals tun or machen.

redolent [ˈredəʊlənt] a: ~ of riechend nach; (fig) erinnernd an (+acc).

redouble [riːˈdʌbl] vt verdoppeln.

red tape [ˈredˈteɪp] n Bürokratismus m.

reduce [rɪˈdjuːs] vt price herabsetzen (to auf +acc); speed, temperature vermindern; photo verkleinern; to ~ sb to tears/silence jdn zum Weinen/Schweigen bringen.

reduction [rɪˈdʌkʃən] n Herabsetzung f; Verminderung f; Verkleinerung f; (amount of money) Nachlaß m.

redundancy [rɪˈdʌndənsɪ] n Überflüssigkeit f; (of workers) Entlassung f.

redundant [rɪˈdʌndənt] a überflüssig;

workers ohne Arbeitsplatz; to be made ~ arbeitslos werden.

reed [riːd] n Schilf nt; (Mus) Rohrblatt nt.

reef [riːf] n Riff nt.

reek [riːk] vi stinken (of nach).

reel [riːl] n Spule f, Rolle f; vt (wind) wickeln, spulen; (stagger) taumeln.

re-election [ˈriːɪˈlekʃən] n Wiederwahl f.

re-engage [ˈriːɪnˈgeɪdʒ] vt wieder einstellen.

re-enter [ˈriːˈentə*] vti wieder eintreten (in +acc).

re-entry [ˈriːˈentrɪ] n Wiedereintritt m.

re-examine [ˈriːɪgˈzæmɪn] vt neu überprüfen.

ref [ref] n (col) Schiri m.

refectory [rɪˈfektərɪ] n (Univ) Mensa f; (Sch) Speisesaal m; (Eccl) Refektorium nt.

refer [rɪˈfɜː*] vt: ~ sb to sb/sth jdn an jdn/etw verweisen; vi: ~ to hinweisen auf (+acc); (to book) nachschlagen in (+dat); (mention) sich beziehen auf (+acc).

referee [refəˈriː] n Schiedsrichter m; (for job) Referenz f; vt schiedsrichtern.

reference [ˈrefrəns] n (mentioning) Hinweis m; (allusion) Anspielung f; (for job) Referenz f; (in book) Verweis m; (number, code) Aktenzeichen nt; Katalognummer f; with ~ to in bezug auf (+acc); ~ book Nachschlagewerk nt.

referendum [refəˈrendəm] n Volksabstimmung f.

refill [ˈriːˈfɪl] vt nachfüllen; [ˈriːfɪl] n Nachfüllung f; (for pen) Ersatzpatrone f; Ersatzmine f.

refine [rɪˈfaɪn] vt (purify) raffinieren, läutern; (fig) bilden, kultivieren; ~d a gebildet, kultiviert; ~ment Bildung f, Kultiviertheit f; ~ry Raffinerie f.

reflect [rɪˈflekt] vt light reflektieren; (fig) (wider)spiegeln, zeigen; vi (meditate) nachdenken (on über +acc); ~ion Reflexion f; (image) Spiegelbild nt; (thought) Überlegung f, Gedanke m; ~or Reflektor m.

reflex [ˈriːfleks] n Reflex m; ~ive [rɪˈfleksɪv] a (Gram) Reflexiv-, rückbezüglich, reflexiv.

reform [rɪˈfɔːm] n Reform f; vt person bessern; the R~ation [refəˈmeɪʃən] die Reformation; ~er Reformer m; (Eccl) Reformator m.

refrain [rɪˈfreɪn] vi unterlassen (from acc).

refresh [rɪˈfreʃ] vt erfrischen; ~er course Wiederholungskurs m; ~ing a erfrischend; ~ments pl Erfrischungen pl.

refrigeration [rɪfrɪdʒəˈreɪʃən] n Kühlung f.

refrigerator [rɪˈfrɪdʒəreɪtə*] n Kühlschrank m.

refuel [ˈriːˈfjʊəl] vti auftanken; ~ling Auftanken nt.

refuge [ˈrefjuːdʒ] n Zuflucht f; ~e [refjʊˈdʒiː] Flüchtling m.

refund [ˈriːfʌnd] n Rückvergütung f; [rɪˈfʌnd] vt zurückerstatten, rückvergüten.

refurbish [ˈriːˈfɜːbɪʃ] vt aufpolieren.

refurnish [ˈriːˈfɜːnɪʃ] vt neu möblieren.

refusal [rɪˈfjuːzəl] n (Ver)weigerung f; (official) abschlägige Antwort f.

refuse ['refjuːs] n Abfall m, Müll m; [rɪ'fjuːz] vt abschlagen; vi sich weigern.

refute [rɪ'fjuːt] vt widerlegen.

regain [rɪ'geɪn] vt wiedergewinnen; consciousness wiedererlangen.

regal ['riːgəl] a königlich; ~ia [rɪ'geɪlɪə] pl Insignien pl; (of mayor etc) Amtsornat m.

regard [rɪ'gɑːd] n Achtung f; vt ansehen; ~s pl Grüße pl; ~ing, as ~s, with ~ to bezüglich (+gen), in bezug auf (+acc); ~less a ohne Rücksicht (of auf +acc); ad unbekümmert, ohne Rücksicht auf die Folgen.

regatta [rɪ'gætə] n Regatta f.

regency ['riːdʒənsɪ] n Regentschaft f.

regent ['riːdʒənt] n Regent m.

régime [reɪ'ʒiːm] n Regime nt.

regiment ['redʒɪmənt] n Regiment nt; ~al [redʒɪ'mentl] a Regiments-; ~ation Reglementierung f.

region ['riːdʒən] n Gegend f, Bereich m; ~al a örtlich, regional.

register ['redʒɪstə*] n Register nt, Verzeichnis nt, Liste f; vt (list) registrieren, eintragen; emotion zeigen; (write down) eintragen; vi (at hotel) sich eintragen; (with police) sich melden (with bei); (make impression) wirken, ankommen; ~ed a design eingetragen; letter Einschreibe-, eingeschrieben.

registrar [redʒɪs'trɑː*] n Standesbeamte(r) m.

registration [redʒɪs'treɪʃən] n (act) Erfassung f, Registrierung f; (number) Autonummer f, polizeiliche(s) Kennzeichen nt.

registry office ['redʒɪstrɪɒfɪs] n Standesamt nt.

regret [rɪ'gret] n Bedauern nt; to have no ~s nichts bedauern; vt bedauern; ~ful a traurig; to be ~ful about sth etw bedauern; ~fully ad mit Bedauern, ungern; ~table a bedauerlich.

regroup ['riːgruːp] vt umgruppieren; vi sich umgruppieren.

regular ['regjulə*] a regelmäßig; (usual) üblich; (fixed by rule) geregelt; (col) regelrecht; n (client etc) Stammkunde m; (Mil) Berufssoldat m; ~ity [regju'lærɪtɪ] Regelmäßigkeit f; ~ly ad regelmäßig.

regulate ['regjuleɪt] vt regeln, regulieren.

regulation [regju'leɪʃən] n (rule) Vorschrift f; (control) Regulierung f; (order) Anordnung f, Regelung f.

rehabilitation ['riːhəbɪlɪ'teɪʃən] n (of criminal) Resozialisierung f.

rehash ['riːhæʃ] vt (col) aufwärmen.

rehearsal [rɪ'hɜːsl] n Probe f.

rehearse [rɪ'hɜːs] vt proben.

reign [reɪn] n Herrschaft f; vi herrschen; ~ing a monarch herrschend; champion gegenwärtig.

reimburse [riːɪm'bɜːs] vt entschädigen, zurückzahlen (sb for sth jdm etw).

rein [reɪn] n Zügel m.

reincarnation ['riːɪnkɑː'neɪʃən] n Wiedergeburt f.

reindeer ['reɪndɪə*] n Ren nt.

reinforce [riːɪn'fɔːs] vt verstärken; ~d a verstärkt; concrete Eisen-; ~ment

Verstärkung f; ~ments pl (Mil) Verstärkungstruppen pl.

reinstate ['riːɪn'steɪt] vt wiedereinsetzen.

reissue ['riː'ɪʃuː] vt neu herausgeben.

reiterate [riː'ɪtəreɪt] vt wiederholen.

reject ['riːdʒekt] n (Comm) Ausschuß(artikel) m; [rɪ'dʒekt] vt ablehnen; (throw away) ausrangieren; ~ion [rɪ'dʒekʃən] Zurückweisung f.

rejoice [rɪ'dʒɔɪs] vi sich freuen.

rejuvenate [rɪ'dʒuːvɪneɪt] vt verjüngen.

rekindle ['riː'kɪndl] vt wieder anfachen.

relapse [rɪ'læps] n Rückfall m.

relate [rɪ'leɪt] vt (tell) berichten, erzählen; (connect) verbinden; ~d a verwandt (to mit).

relating [rɪ'leɪtɪŋ] prep: ~ to bezüglich (+gen).

relation [rɪ'leɪʃən] n Verwandte(r) mf; (connection) Beziehung f; ~ship Verhältnis nt, Beziehung f.

relative ['relətɪv] n Verwandte(r) mf; a relativ, bedingt; ~ly ad verhältnismäßig; ~ pronoun Verhältniswort nt, Relativpronomen nt.

relax [rɪ'læks] vi (slacken) sich lockern; (muscles, person) sich entspannen; (be less strict) freundlicher werden; vt (ease) lockern, entspannen; ~! reg' dich nicht auf!; ~ation [riːlæk'seɪʃən] Entspannung f; ~ed a entspannt, locker; ~ing a entspannend.

relay ['riːleɪ] n (Sport) Staffel f; vt message weiterleiten; (Rad, TV) übertragen.

release [rɪ'liːs] n (freedom) Entlassung f; (Tech) Auslöser m; vt befreien; prisoner entlassen; report, news verlautbaren, bekanntgeben.

relent [rɪ'lent] vi nachgeben; ~less a, ~lessly ad unnachgiebig.

relevance ['reləvəns] n Bedeutung f, Relevanz f.

relevant ['reləvənt] a wichtig, relevant.

reliability [rɪlaɪə'bɪlɪtɪ] n Zuverlässigkeit f.

reliable a, **reliably** ad [rɪ'laɪəbl, -blɪ] zuverlässig.

reliance [rɪ'laɪəns] n Abhängigkeit f (on von).

relic ['relɪk] n (from past) Überbleibsel nt; (Rel) Reliquie f.

relief [rɪ'liːf] n Erleichterung f; (help) Hilfe f, Unterstützung f; (person) Ablösung f; (Art) Relief nt; (distinctness) Hervorhebung f.

relieve [rɪ'liːv] vt (ease) erleichtern; (bring help) entlasten; person ablösen; to ~ sb of sth jdm etw abnehmen.

religion [rɪ'lɪdʒən] n Religion f.

religious [rɪ'lɪdʒəs] a religiös; ~ly ad religiös; (conscientiously) gewissenhaft.

reline ['riː'laɪn] vt brakes neu beschuhen.

relinquish [rɪ'lɪŋkwɪʃ] vt aufgeben.

relish ['relɪʃ] n Würze f, pikante Beigabe f; vt genießen.

relive ['riː'lɪv] vt noch einmal durchleben.

reluctance [rɪ'lʌktəns] n Widerstreben nt, Abneigung f.

reluctant [rɪ'lʌktənt] a widerwillig; ~ly ad ungern.

rely [rɪ'laɪ]: ~ on vt sich verlassen auf (+acc).

remain [rɪ'meɪn] vi (be left) übrigbleiben; (stay) bleiben; ~der Rest m; ~ing a übrig(geblieben); ~s pl Überreste pl; (dead body) sterbliche Überreste pl.

remand [rɪ'mɑːnd] n: on ~ in Untersuchungshaft; vt: ~ in custody in Untersuchungshaft schicken.

remark [rɪ'mɑːk] n Bemerkung f; vt bemerken; ~able a, ~ably ad bemerkenswert.

remarry [rɪ'mærɪ] vi sich wieder verheiraten.

remedial [rɪ'miːdɪəl] a Heil-; teaching Hilfsschul-.

remedy ['remədɪ] n Mittel nt; vt pain abhelfen (+dat); trouble in Ordnung bringen.

remember [rɪ'membə*] vt sich erinnern an (+acc); ~ me to them grüße sie von mir.

remembrance [rɪ'membrəns] n Erinnerung f; (official) Gedenken nt.

remind [rɪ'maɪnd] vt erinnern; ~er Mahnung f.

reminisce [remɪ'nɪs] vi in Erinnerungen schwelgen; ~nces [remɪ'nɪsənsɪz] pl Erinnerungen pl; ~nt a erinnernd (of an +acc), Erinnerungen nachrufend (of an +acc).

remit [rɪ'mɪt] vt money überweisen (to an +acc); ~tance Geldanweisung f.

remnant ['remnənt] n Rest m.

remorse [rɪ'mɔːs] n Gewissensbisse pl; ~ful a reumütig; ~less a, ~lessly ad unbarmherzig.

remote [rɪ'məʊt] a abgelegen, entfernt; (slight) gering; ~ control Fernsteuerung f; ~ly ad entfernt; ~ness Entlegenheit f.

removable [rɪ'muːvəbl] a entfernbar.

removal [rɪ'muːvəl] n Beseitigung f; (of furniture) Umzug m; (from office) Entlassung f; ~ van Möbelwagen m.

remove [rɪ'muːv] vt beseitigen, entfernen; (dismiss) entlassen; ~r (for paint etc) Fleckenentferner m; ~rs pl Möbelspedition f.

remuneration [rɪmjuːnə'reɪʃən] n Vergütung f, Honorar nt.

Renaissance [rə'neɪsɑːns]: the ~ die Renaissance.

rename ['riː'neɪm] vt umbenennen.

rend [rend] vt irreg zerreißen.

render ['rendə*] vt machen; (translate) übersetzen; ~ing (Mus) Wiedergabe f.

rendezvous ['rɒndɪvuː] n Verabredung f, Rendezvous nt.

renegade ['renɪgeɪd] n Überläufer m.

renew [rɪ'njuː] vt erneuern; contract, licence verlängern; (replace) ersetzen; ~al Erneuerung f; Verlängerung f.

renounce [rɪ'naʊns] vt (give up) verzichten auf (+acc); (disown) verstoßen.

renovate [renəʊveɪt] vt renovieren; building restaurieren.

renovation [renəʊ'veɪʃən] n Renovierung f; Restauration f.

renown [rɪ'naʊn] n Ruf m; ~ed a namhaft.

rent [rent] n Miete f; (for land) Pacht f; vt (hold as tenant) mieten; pachten; (let) vermieten; verpachten; car etc mieten; (firm) vermieten; ~al Miete f; Pacht f, Pachtgeld nt.

renunciation [rɪnʌnsɪ'eɪʃən] n Verzicht m (of auf +acc).

reopen ['riː'əʊpən] vt wiedereröffnen.

reorder ['riː'ɔːdə*] vt wieder bestellen.

reorganization ['riːɔːgənaɪ'zeɪʃən] n Neugestaltung f; (Comm etc) Umbildung f.

reorganize ['riː'ɔːgənaɪz] vt umgestalten, reorganisieren.

rep [rep] n (Comm) Vertreter m; (Theat) Repertoire nt.

repair [rɪ'pɛə*] n Reparatur f; in good ~ in gutem Zustand; vt reparieren; damage wiedergutmachen; ~ kit Werkzeugkasten m; ~ man Mechaniker m; ~ shop Reparaturwerkstatt f.

repartee [repɑː'tiː] n Witzeleien pl.

repay [riː'peɪ] vt irreg zurückzahlen; (reward) vergelten; ~ment Rückzahlung f; (fig) Vergelten nt.

repeal [rɪ'piːl] n Aufhebung f; vt aufheben.

repeat [rɪ'piːt] n (Rad, TV) Wiederholung(ssendung) f; vt wiederholen; ~edly ad wiederholt.

repel [rɪ'pel] vt (drive back) zurückschlagen; (disgust) abstoßen; ~lent a abstoßend; n: insect ~lent Insektenmittel nt.

repent [rɪ'pent] vti bereuen; ~ance Reue f.

repercussion [riːpə'kʌʃən] n Auswirkung f; (of rifle) Rückstoß m.

repertoire ['repətwɑː*] n Repertoire nt.

repertory ['repətərɪ] n Repertoire nt.

repetition [repə'tɪʃən] n Wiederholung f.

repetitive [rɪ'petɪtɪv] a sich wiederholend.

rephrase [riː'freɪz] vt anders formulieren.

replace [rɪ'pleɪs] vt ersetzen; (put back) zurückstellen; ~ment Ersatz m.

replenish [rɪ'plenɪʃ] vt (wieder) auffüllen.

replete [rɪ'pliːt] a (zum Platzen) voll.

replica ['replɪkə] n Kopie f.

reply [rɪ'plaɪ] n Antwort f, Erwiderung f; vi antworten, erwidern.

report [rɪ'pɔːt] n Bericht m; (Sch) Zeugnis nt; (of gun) Knall m; vt (tell) berichten; (give information against) melden; (to police) anzeigen; vi (make report) Bericht erstatten; (present o.s.) sich melden; ~er Reporter m.

reprehensible [reprɪ'hensɪbl] a tadelnswert.

represent [reprɪ'zent] vt darstellen, zeigen; (act) darstellen; (speak for) vertreten; ~ation Darstellung f; (being represented) Vertretung f; ~ative n (person) Vertreter m; a räpresentativ.

repress [rɪ'pres] vt unterdrücken; ~ion [rɪ'preʃən] Unterdrückung f; (Psych) Hemmungs-.

reprieve [rɪ'priːv] n Aufschub m; (cancellation) Begnadigung f; (fig) Atempause f nt Gnadenfrist gewähren (+dat); begnadigen.

reprimand ['reprɪmɑːnd] n Verweis m; vt

einen Verweis erteilen *(+dat)*.

reprint [riːˈprɪnt] *n* Neudruck *m*; [ˈriːˈprɪnt] *vt* wieder abdrucken.

reprisal [rɪˈpraɪzəl] *n* Vergeltung *f*.

reproach [rɪˈprəʊtʃ] *n (blame)* Vorwurf *m*, Tadel *m*; *(disgrace)* Schande *f*; **beyond ~** über jeden Vorwurf erhaben; *vt* Vorwürfe machen *(+dat)*, tadeln; **~ful** *a* vorwurfsvoll.

reproduce [riːprəˈdjuːs] *vt* reproduzieren; *vi (have offspring)* sich vermehren.

reproduction [riːprəˈdʌkʃən] *n* Wiedergabe *f*; *(Art, Phot)* Reproduktion *f*; *(breeding)* Fortpflanzung *f*.

reproductive [riːprəˈdʌktɪv] *a* reproduktiv; *(breeding)* Fortpflanzungs-.

reprove [rɪˈpruːv] *vt* tadeln.

reptile [ˈreptaɪl] *n* Reptil *nt*.

republic [rɪˈpʌblɪk] *n* Republik *f*; **~an** *a* republikanisch; *n* Republikaner *m*.

repudiate [rɪˈpjuːdɪeɪt] *vt* zurückweisen, nicht anerkennen.

repugnance [rɪˈpʌgnəns] *n* Widerwille *m*.

repugnant [rɪˈpʌgnənt] *a* widerlich.

repulse [rɪˈpʌls] *vt (drive back)* zurückschlagen; *(reject)* abweisen.

repulsion [rɪˈpʌlʃən] *n* Abscheu *m*.

repulsive [rɪˈpʌlsɪv] *a* abstoßend.

repurchase [ˈriːˈpɜːtʃəs] *vt* zurückkaufen.

reputable [ˈrepjʊtəbl] *a* angesehen.

reputation [repjʊˈteɪʃən] *n* Ruf *m*.

repute [rɪˈpjuːt] *n* hohe(s) Ansehen *nt*; **~d** *a*, **~dly** *ad* angeblich.

request [rɪˈkwest] *n (asking)* Ansuchen *nt*; *(demand)* Wunsch *m*; **at sb's ~** auf jds Wunsch; *vt thing* erbitten; *person* ersuchen.

requiem [ˈrekwɪem] *n* Requiem *nt*.

require [rɪˈkwaɪə*] *vt (need)* brauchen; *(wish)* wünschen; **to be ~d to do sth** etw tun müssen; **~ment** *(condition)* Anforderung *f*; *(need)* Bedarf *m*.

requisite [ˈrekwɪzɪt] *n* Erfordernis *nt*; *a* erforderlich.

requisition [rekwɪˈzɪʃən] *n* Anforderung *f*; *vt* beschlagnahmen; *(order)* anfordern.

reroute [ˈriːˈruːt] *vt* umleiten.

rescind [rɪˈsɪnd] *vt* aufheben.

rescue [ˈreskjuː] *n* Rettung *f*; *vt* retten; **~ party** Rettungsmannschaft *f*; **~r** Retter *m*.

research [rɪˈsɜːtʃ] *n* Forschung *f*; *vi* Forschungen anstellen *(into über +acc)*; *vt* erforschen; **~er** Forscher *m*; **~ work** Forschungsarbeit *f*; **~ worker** wissenschaftliche(r) Mitarbeiter(in *f*) *m*.

resemblance [rɪˈzembləns] *n* Ähnlichkeit *f*.

resemble [rɪˈzembl] *vt* ähneln *(+dat)*.

resent [rɪˈzent] *vt* übelnehmen; **~ful** *a* nachtragend, empfindlich; **~ment** Verstimmung *f*, Unwille *m*.

reservation [rezəˈveɪʃən] *n (of seat)* Reservierung *f*; *(Theat)* Vorbestellung *f*; *(doubt)* Vorbehalt *m*; *(land)* Reservat *nt*.

reserve [rɪˈzɜːv] *n (store)* Vorrat *m*, Reserve *f*; *(manner)* Zurückhaltung *f*; *(game ~)* Naturschutzgebiet *nt*; *(Sport)* Ersatzspieler(in *f*) *m*; *vt* reservieren; *judgement sich (dat)* vor-

behalten; **~s** *pl (Mil)* Reserve *f*; **in ~** in Reserve; **~d** *a* reserviert; **all rights ~d** alle Rechte vorbehalten.

reservist [rɪˈzɜːvɪst] *n* Reservist *m*.

reservoir [ˈrezəvwɑː*] *n* Reservoir *nt*.

reshape [ˈriːˈʃeɪp] *vt* umformen.

reshuffle [ˈriːˈʃʌfl] *vt (Pol)* umbilden.

reside [rɪˈzaɪd] *vi* wohnen, ansässig sein; **~nce** [ˈrezɪdəns] *(house)* Wohnung *f*, Wohnsitz *m*; *(living)* Wohnen *nt*, Aufenthalt *m*; **~nt** [ˈrezɪdənt] *(in house)* Bewohner *m*; *(in area)* Einwohner *m*; *a* wohnhaft, ansässig; **~ntial** [rezɪˈdenʃəl] *a* Wohn-.

residue [ˈrezɪdjuː] *n* Rest *m*; *(Chem)* Rückstand *m*; *(fig)* Bodensatz *m*.

resign [rɪˈzaɪn] *vt* office aufgeben, zurücktreten von; **to be ~ed to sth, to ~ o.s. to sth** sich mit etw abfinden; *vi (from office)* zurücktreten; **~ation** [rezɪgˈneɪʃən] *(resigning)* Aufgabe *f*; *(Pol)* Rücktritt *m*; *(submission)* Resignation *f*; **~ed** *a* resigniert.

resilience [rɪˈzɪlɪəns] *n* Spannkraft *f*, Elastizität *f*; *(of person)* Unverwüstlichkeit *f*.

resilient [rɪˈzɪlɪənt] *a* unverwüstlich.

resin [ˈrezɪn] *n* Harz *nt*.

resist [rɪˈzɪst] *vt* widerstehen *(+dat)*; **~ance** Widerstand *m*; **~ant** *a* widerstandsfähig *(to gegen)*; *(to stains etc)* abstoßend.

resolute *a*, **~ly** *ad* [ˈrezəluːt, -lɪ] entschlossen, resolut.

resolution [rezəˈluːʃən] *n (firmness)* Entschlossenheit *f*; *(intention)* Vorsatz *m*; *(decision)* Beschluß *m*; *(personal)* Entschluß *m*.

resolve [rɪˈzɒlv] *n* Vorsatz *m*, Entschluß *m*; *vt (decide)* beschließen; **it ~d itself** es löste sich; **~d** *a (fest)* entschlossen.

resonant [ˈrezənənt] *a* widerhallend; *voice* volltönend.

resort [rɪˈzɔːt] *n (holiday place)* Erholungsort *m*; *(help)* Zuflucht *f*; *vi* Zuflucht nehmen *(to zu)*; **as a last ~** letzter Ausweg.

resound [rɪˈzaʊnd] *vi* widerhallen; **~ing** *a* nachhallend; *success* groß.

resource [rɪˈsɔːs] *n* Findigkeit *f*; **~s** *pl (of energy)* Energiequellen *pl*; *(of money)* Quellen *pl*; *(of a country etc)* Bodenschätze *pl*; **~ful** *a* findig; **~fulness** Findigkeit *f*.

respect [rɪsˈpekt] *n (esteem)* (Hoch)achtung *f*; *vt* achten, respektieren; **~s** *pl* Grüße *pl*; **with ~ to** in bezug auf *(+acc)*, hinsichtlich *(+gen)*; **in ~ of** in bezug auf *(+acc)*; **in this ~** in dieser Hinsicht; **~ability** [rɪspektəˈbɪlɪtɪ] Anständigkeit *f*, Achtbarkeit *f*; **~able** *a (decent)* angesehen, achtbar; *(fairly good)* leidlich; **~ed** *a* angesehen; **~ful** *a* höflich; **~fully** *ad* ehrerbietig; *(in letter)* mit vorzüglicher Hochachtung; **~ing** *prep* betreffend; **~ive** *a* jeweilig; **~ively** *ad* beziehungsweise.

respiration [respɪˈreɪʃən] *n* Atmung *f*, Atmen *nt*.

respiratory [rɪsˈpɪrətərɪ] *a* Atmungs-.

respite [ˈrespaɪt] *n* Ruhepause *f*; **without ~** ohne Unterlaß.

resplendent [rɪs'plendənt] a strahlend.

respond [rɪs'pɔnd] vi antworten; (react) reagieren (to auf +acc).

response [rɪs'pɔns] n Antwort f; Reaktion f; (to advert etc) Resonanz f.

responsibility [rɪspɔnsə'bɪlɪtɪ] n Verantwortung f.

responsible [rɪs'pɔnsəbl] a verantwortlich; (reliable) verantwortungsvoll.

responsibly [rɪs'pɔnsəblɪ] ad verantwortungsvoll.

responsive [rɪs'pɔnsɪv] a empfänglich.

rest [rest] n Ruhe f; (break) Pause f; (remainder) Rest m; **the ~ of them** die Übrigen; vi sich ausruhen; (be supported) (auf)liegen; (remain) liegen (with bei).

restaurant ['restərɔ̃:ŋ] n Restaurant nt, Gaststätte f; **~ car** Speisewagen m.

rest cure ['restkjuə*] n Erholung f.

restful ['restful] a erholsam, ruhig.

rest home ['resthəum] n Erholungsheim nt.

restitution [restɪ'tju:ʃən] n Rückgabe f, Entschädigung f.

restive ['restɪv] a unruhig; (disobedient) störrisch.

restless ['restləs] a unruhig; **~ly** ad ruhelos; **~ness** Ruhelosigkeit f.

restock ['ri:'stɔk] vt auffüllen.

restoration [restə'reɪʃən] n Wiederherstellung f, Neueinführung f; Wiedereinsetzung f; Rückgabe f; Restauration f; **the R~** die Restauration.

restore [rɪs'tɔ:*] vt order wiederherstellen; customs wieder einführen; person to position wiedereinsetzen; (give back) zurückgeben; paintings restaurieren.

restrain [rɪs'treɪn] vt zurückhalten; curiosity etc beherrschen; **~ed** a style etc gedämpft, verhalten; **~t** (restraining) Einschränkung f; (being restrained) Beschränkung f; (self-control) Zurückhaltung f.

restrict [rɪs'trɪkt] vt einschränken; **~ed** a beschränkt; **~ion** [rɪs'trɪkʃən] Einschränkung f; **~ive** a einschränkend.

rest room ['restrum] n (US) Toilette f.

result [rɪ'zʌlt] n Resultat nt, Folge f; (of exam, game) Ergebnis nt; vi zur Folge haben (in acc); **~ant** a (daraus) entstehend or resultierend.

resume [rɪ'zju:m] vt fortsetzen; (occupy again) wieder einnehmen.

résumé ['reɪzju:meɪ] n Zusammenfassung f.

resumption [rɪ'zʌmpʃən] n Wiederaufnahme f.

resurgence [rɪ'sɜ:dʒəns] n Wiedererwachen nt.

resurrection [rezə'rekʃən] n Auferstehung f.

resuscitate [rɪ'sʌsɪteɪt] vt wiederbeleben.

resuscitation [rɪsʌsɪ'teɪʃən] n Wiederbelebung f.

retail ['ri:teɪl] n Einzelhandel m; a Einzelhandels-, Laden-; ['ri:'teɪl] vt im kleinen verkaufen; vi im Einzelhandel kosten; **~er** ['ri:'teɪlə*] Einzelhändler m, Kleinhändler m; **~ price** Ladenpreis m.

retain [rɪ'teɪn] vt (keep) (zurück)behalten; (pay) unterhalten; **~er** (servant) Gefolgsmann m; (fee) (Honorar)vorschuß m.

retaliate [rɪ'tælɪeɪt] vi zum Vergeltungsschlag ausholen.

retaliation [rɪtælɪ'eɪʃən] n Vergeltung f.

retarded [rɪ'tɑ:dɪd] a zurückgeblieben.

retention [rɪ'tenʃən] n Behalten nt.

retentive [rɪ'tentɪv] a memory gut.

rethink ['ri:'θɪŋk] vt irreg nochmals durchdenken.

reticence ['retɪsəns] n Schweigsamkeit f.

reticent ['retɪsənt] a schweigsam.

retina ['retɪnə] n Netzhaut f.

retinue ['retɪnju:] n Gefolge nt.

retire [rɪ'taɪə*] vi (from work) in den Ruhestand treten; (withdraw) sich zurückziehen; (go to bed) schlafen gehen; **~d** a person pensioniert, im Ruhestand; **~ment** Ruhestand m.

retiring [rɪ'taɪərɪŋ] a zurückhaltend, schüchtern.

retort [rɪ'tɔ:t] n (reply) Erwiderung f; (Sci) Retorte f; vi (scharf) erwidern.

retrace [rɪ'treɪs] vt zurückverfolgen.

retract [rɪ'trækt] vt statement zurücknehmen; claws einziehen; **~able** a aerial ausziehbar.

retrain [rɪ'treɪn] vt umschulen; **~ing** Umschulung f.

retreat [rɪ'tri:t] n Rückzug m; (place) Zufluchtsort m; vi sich zurückziehen.

retrial ['ri:'traɪəl] n Wiederaufnahmeverfahren nt.

retribution [retrɪ'bju:ʃən] n Strafe f.

retrieval [rɪ'tri:vəl] n Wiedergewinnung f.

retrieve [rɪ'tri:v] vt wiederbekommen; (rescue) retten; **~r** Apportierhund m.

retroactive [retrəu'æktɪv] a rückwirkend.

retrograde ['retrəugreɪd] a step Rück-; policy rückschrittlich.

retrospect ['retrəuspekt] n: **in ~** im Rückblick, rückblickend; **~ive** [retrəu'spektɪv] a rückwirkend; rückblickend.

return [rɪ'tɜ:n] n Rückkehr f; (profits) Ertrag m, Gewinn m; (report) amtliche(r) Bericht m; (rail ticket etc) Rückfahrkarte f; (plane) Rückflugkarte f; (bus) Rückfahrschein m; a by **~ of post** postwendend; journey, match Rück-; vi zurückkehren or -kommen; vt zurückgeben, zurücksenden; (pay back) zurückzahlen; (elect) wählen; verdict aussprechen; **~able** a bottle etc mit Pfand.

reunion [ri:'ju:njən] n Wiedervereinigung f; (Sch etc) Treffen nt.

reunite [ri:ju:'naɪt] vt wiedervereinigen.

rev [rev] n Drehzahl f; vti (also **~ up**) (den Motor) auf Touren bringen.

revamp ['ri:'væmp] vt aufpolieren.

reveal [rɪ'vi:l] vt enthüllen; **~ing** a aufschlußreich.

reveille [rɪ'vælɪ] n Wecken nt.

revel ['revl] vi genießen (in acc).

revelation [revə'leɪʃən] n Offenbarung f.

reveller ['revlə*] n Schwelger m.

revelry ['revlrɪ] n Rummel m.

revenge [rɪ'vendʒ] n Rache f; vt rächen; **~ful** a rachsüchtig.

revenue ['revənju:] n Einnahmen pl, Staatseinkünfte pl.

reverberate [rɪ'vɜːbəreɪt] vi widerhallen.

reverberation [rɪvɜːbə'reɪʃən] n Widerhall m.

revere [rɪ'vɪə*] vt (ver)ehren; **~nce** ['revərəns] Ehrfurcht f; ['revərənd] **R~nd** ... Hochwürden ...; **~nt** ['revərənt] a ehrfurchtsvoll.

reverie ['revərɪ] n Träumerei f.

reversal [rɪ'vɜːsəl] n Umkehrung f.

reverse [rɪ'vɜːs] n Rückseite f; (Aut: gear) Rückwärtsgang m; a order, direction entgegengesetzt; vt umkehren; vi (Aut) rückwärts fahren.

reversion [rɪ'vɜːʃən] n Umkehrung f.

revert [rɪ'vɜːt] vi zurückkehren.

review [rɪ'vjuː] n (Mil) Truppenschau f; (of book) Besprechung f, Rezension f; (magazine) Zeitschrift f; **to be under** ~ untersucht werden; vt Rückschau halten auf (+acc); (Mil) mustern; book besprechen, rezensieren; (reexamine) von neuem untersuchen; **~er** n (critic) Rezensent m.

revise [rɪ'vaɪz] vt durchsehen, verbessern; book überarbeiten; (reconsider) ändern, revidieren.

revision [rɪvɪʒən] n Durchsicht f, Prüfung f; (Comm) Revision f; (of book) verbesserte Ausgabe f; (Sch) Wiederholung f.

revisit [riː'vɪzɪt] vt wieder besuchen.

revitalize [riː'vaɪtəlaɪz] vt neu beleben.

revival [rɪ'vaɪvəl] n Wiederbelebung f; (Rel) Erweckung f; (Theat) Wiederaufnahme f.

revive [rɪ'vaɪv] vt wiederbeleben; (fig) wieder auffrischen; vi wiedererwachen; (fig) wieder aufleben.

revoke [rɪ'vəuk] vt aufheben.

revolt [rɪ'vəult] n Aufstand m, Revolte f; vi sich auflehnen; vt entsetzen; **~ing** a widerlich.

revolution [revə'luːʃən] n (turn) Umdrehung f; (change) Umwälzung f; (Pol) Revolution f; **~ary** a revolutionär; n Revolutionär m; **~ize** vt revolutionieren.

revolve [rɪ'vɒlv] vi kreisen; (on own axis) sich drehen; **~r** Revolver m.

revue [rɪ'vjuː] n Revue f.

revulsion [rɪ'vʌlʃən] n (disgust) Ekel m.

reward [rɪ'wɔːd] n Belohnung f; vt belohnen; **~ing** a lohnend.

reword ['riː'wɜːd] vt anders formulieren.

rewrite ['riː'raɪt] vt irreg umarbeiten, neu schreiben.

rhapsody ['ræpsədɪ] n Rhapsodie f; (fig) Schwärmerei f.

rhetoric ['retərɪk] n Rhetorik f, Redekunst f; **~al** [rɪ'tɒrɪkəl] a rhetorisch.

rheumatic [ruː'mætɪk] a rheumatisch.

rheumatism ['ruːmətɪzəm] n Rheumatismus m, Rheuma nt.

rhinoceros [raɪ'nɒsərəs] n Nashorn nt, Rhinozeros nt.

rhododendron [rəudə'dendrən] n Rhododendron m.

rhubarb ['ruːbɑːb] n Rhabarber m.

rhyme [raɪm] n Reim m.

rhythm ['rɪðəm] n Rhythmus m; **~ic(al)** a, **~ically** ad ['rɪðmɪk(l), -l] rhythmisch.

rib [rɪb] n Rippe f; vt (mock) hänseln, aufziehen.

ribald ['rɪbəld] a saftig.

ribbon ['rɪbən] n Band nt.

rice [raɪs] n Reis m; ~ **pudding** Milchreis m.

rich [rɪtʃ] a reich, wohlhabend; (fertile) fruchtbar; (splendid) kostbar; food reichhaltig; **~es** pl Reichtum m, Reichtümer pl; **~ly** ad reich; deserve völlig; **~ness** Reichtum m; (of food) Reichhaltigkeit f; (of colours) Sattheit f.

rick [rɪk] n Schober m.

rickets ['rɪkɪts] n Rachitis f.

rickety ['rɪkɪtɪ] a wack(e)lig.

rickshaw ['rɪkʃɔː] n Riksche f.

ricochet ['rɪkəʃeɪ] n Abprallen nt; (shot) Querschläger m; vi abprallen.

rid [rɪd] vt irreg befreien (of von); **to get ~ of** losweden; **good ~dance!** den/die/das wären wir los!

riddle ['rɪdl] n Rätsel nt; vt (esp passive) durchlöchern.

ride [raɪd] n (in vehicle) Fahrt f; (on horse) Ritt m; irreg vi horse reiten; bicycle fahren; vi fahren; reiten; (ship) vor Anker liegen; **~r** Reiter m; (addition) Zusatz m.

ridge [rɪdʒ] n (of hills) Bergkette f; (top) Grat m, Kamm m; (of roof) Dachfirst m.

ridicule ['rɪdɪkjuːl] n Spott m; vt lächerlich machen.

ridiculous a, **~ly** ad [rɪ'dɪkjuləs, -lɪ] lächerlich.

riding ['raɪdɪŋ] n Reiten nt; **to go** ~ reiten gehen; ~ **habit** Reitkleid nt; ~ **school** Reitschule f.

rife [raɪf] a weit verbreitet.

riffraff ['rɪfræf] n Gesindel nt, Pöbel m.

rifle ['raɪfl] n Gewehr nt; vt berauben; **~range** Schießstand m.

rift [rɪft] n Ritze f, Spalte f; (fig) Bruch m.

rig [rɪg] n (outfit) Takelung f; (fig) Aufmachung f; (oil —) Bohrinsel f; vt election etc manipulieren; **~ging** Takelage f; **~out** vt ausstatten; **~ up** vt zusammenbasteln, konstruieren.

right [raɪt] a (correct, just) richtig, recht; (right side) rechte(r, s); n Recht nt; (not left, Pol) Rechte f; ad (on the right) rechts; (to the right) nach rechts; look, work richtig, recht; (directly) gerade; (exactly) genau; vt in Ordnung bringen, korrigieren; interj gut; ~ **away** sofort; **to be** ~ recht haben; **all** ~! gut!, in Ordnung!, schön!; ~ **now** in diesem Augenblick, eben; **by** ~**s** von Rechts wegen; ~ **to the end** bis ans Ende; **on the** ~ rechts; ~ **angle** Rechteck nt; **~eous** ['raɪtʃəs] a rechtschaffen; **~eousness** Rechtschaffenheit f; **~ful** a rechtmäßig; **~fully** ad rechtmäßig; (justifiably) zu Recht; **~-hand drive:** to have ~-hand drive das Steuer rechts haben; **~-handed** a rechtshändig; **~-hand man** rechte Hand f; **~-hand side** rechte Seite f; **~ly** ad mit Recht; **~-minded** a rechtschaffen; ~ **of way** Vorfahrt f; **~-wing** rechte(r) Flügel m.

rigid ['rɪdʒɪd] a *(stiff)* starr, steif; *(strict)* streng; ~ity [rɪ'dʒɪdɪtɪ] Starrheit f, Steifheit f; Strenge f; ~ly starr, steif; *(fig)* hart, unbeugsam.

rigmarole ['rɪgmərəʊl] n Gewäsch nt.

rigor mortis ['rɪgə'mɔːtɪs] n Totenstarre f.

rigorous a, ~ly ad ['rɪgərəs, -lɪ] streng.

rigour, *(US)* **rigor** ['rɪgə°] n Strenge f, Härte f.

rig-out ['rɪgaut] n *(col)* Aufzug m.

rile [raɪl] vt ärgern.

rim [rɪm] n *(edge)* Rand m; *(of wheel)* Felge f; ~less a randlos; ~med a gerändert.

rind [raɪnd] n Rinde f.

ring [rɪŋ] n Ring m; *(of people)* Kreis m; *(arena)* Ring m, Manege f; *(of telephone)* Klingeln nt, Läuten nt; **to give sb a ~** jdn anrufen; **it has a familiar ~** es klingt bekannt; vti irreg bell läuten; *(also ~ up)* anrufen; ~ **off** vi aufhängen; ~ **binder** Ringbuch nt; ~**leader** Anführer m, Rädelsführer m; ~**lets** pl Ringellocken pl; ~ **road** Umgehungsstraße f.

rink [rɪŋk] n *(ice ~)* Eisbahn f.

rinse [rɪns] n Spülen nt; vt spülen.

riot ['raɪət] n Aufruhr m; vi randalieren; ~**er** Aufrührer m; ~**ous** a, ~**ously** ad aufrührerisch; *(noisy)* lärmend.

rip [rɪp] n Schlitz m, Riß m; vti (zer)reißen.

ripcord ['rɪpkɔːd] n Reißleine f.

ripe [raɪp] a *fruit* reif; *cheese* ausgereift; ~n vti reifen, reif werden (lassen); ~**ness** Reife f.

riposte [rɪ'pɒst] n Nachstoß m; *(fig)* schlagfertige Antwort f.

ripple ['rɪpl] n kleine Welle f; vt kräuseln; vi sich kräuseln.

rise [raɪz] n *(slope)* Steigung f; *(esp in wages)* Erhöhung f; *(growth)* Aufstieg m; vi irreg aufstehen; *(sun)* aufgehen; *(smoke)* aufsteigen; *(mountain)* sich erheben; *(prices)* steigen; *(in revolt)* sich erheben; **to give ~ to** Anlaß geben zu; **to ~ to the occasion** sich der Lage gewachsen zeigen.

risk [rɪsk] n Gefahr f, Risiko nt; vt *(venture)* wagen; *(chance loss of)* riskieren, aufs Spiel setzen; ~**y** a gewagt, gefährlich, riskant.

risqué [ri:skeɪ] a gewagt.

rissole ['rɪsəʊl] n Fleischklößchen nt.

rite [raɪt] n Ritus m; **last ~s** pl Letzte Ölung f.

ritual ['rɪtjʊəl] n Ritual nt; a ritual, Ritual-; *(fig)* rituell.

rival ['raɪvəl] n Rivale m, Konkurrent m; a rivalisierend; vt rivalisieren mit; *(Comm)* konkurrieren mit; ~**ry** Rivalität f, Konkurrenz f.

river ['rɪvə°] n Fluß m, Strom m; ~**bank** Flußufer nt; ~**bed** Flußbett nt; ~**side** n Flußufer nt; a am Ufer gelegen, Ufer-.

rivet ['rɪvɪt] n Niete f; vt *(fasten)* (ver)nieten.

road [rəʊd] n Straße f; ~**block** Straßensperre f; ~**hog** Verkehrsrowdy m; ~**map** Straßenkarte f; ~**side** n Straßenrand m; a an der Landstraße (gelegen); ~ **sign** Straßenschild nt; ~ **user** Verkehrsteilnehmer m; ~**way** Fahrbahn f; ~**worthy** a verkehrssicher.

roam [rəʊm] vi (umher)streifen; vt durchstreifen.

roar [rɔː°] n Brüllen nt, Gebrüll nt; vi brüllen; ~**ing** a *fire* Bomben-, prasselnd; *trade* schwunghaft, Bomben-.

roast [rəʊst] n Braten m; vt braten, rösten, schmoren.

rob [rɒb] vt bestehlen, berauben; *bank* ausrauben; ~**ber** Räuber m; ~**bery** Raub m.

robe [rəʊb] n *(dress)* Gewand nt; *(US)* Hauskleid nt; *(judge's)* Robe f; vt feierlich ankleiden.

robin ['rɒbɪn] n Rotkehlchen nt.

robot ['rəʊbɒt] n Roboter m.

robust [rəʊ'bʌst] a stark, robust.

rock [rɒk] n Felsen m; *(piece)* Stein m; *(bigger)* Fels(brocken) m; *(sweet)* Zuckerstange f; vti wiegen, schaukeln; **on the ~s** *drink* mit Eis(würfeln); *marriage* gescheitert; *ship* aufgelaufen; ~**bottom** *(fig)* Tiefpunkt m; ~ **climber** (Steil)kletterer m; **to go ~ climbing** (steil)klettern gehen; ~**ery** Steingarten m.

rocket ['rɒkɪt] n Rakete f.

rock face ['rɒkfeɪs] n Felswand f.

rocking chair [rɒkɪŋtʃeə°] n Schaukelstuhl m.

rocking horse   ['rɒkɪŋhɔːs]   n Schaukelpferd nt.

rocky ['rɒkɪ] a felsig.

rococo [rəʊ'kəʊkəʊ] a Rokoko-; n Rokoko nt.

rod [rɒd] n *(bar)* Stange f; *(stick)* Rute f.

rodent ['rəʊdənt] n Nagetier nt.

rodeo ['rəʊdɪəʊ] n Rodeo m or nt.

roe [rəʊ] n *(deer)* Reh nt; *(of fish)* Rogen m.

rogue [rəʊg] n Schurke m; *(hum)* Spitzbube m.

roguish ['rəʊgɪʃ] a schurkisch; *hum* schelmisch.

role [rəʊl] n Rolle f.

roll [rəʊl] n Rolle f; *(bread)* Brötchen nt, Semmel f; *(list)* (Namens)liste f, Verzeichnis nt; *(of drum)* Wirbel m; vt *(turn)* rollen, (herum)wälzen; *grass etc* walzen; vi *(swing)* schlingern; *(sound)* (g)rollen; ~ **by** vi *(time)* verfließen; ~ **in** vi *(mail)* hereinkommen; ~ **over** vi sich (herum)drehen; ~ **up** vi *(arrive)* kommen, auftauchen; vt *carpet* aufrollen; ~ **call** Namensaufruf m; ~**ed** a *umbrella* zusammengerollt; ~**er** Rolle f, Walze f; *(road ~er)* Straßenwalze f; ~**er skates** pl Rollschuhe pl.

rollicking ['rɒlɪkɪŋ] a ausgelassen.

rolling ['rəʊlɪŋ] a *landscape* wellig; ~ **pin** Nudel- or Wellholz nt; ~ **stock** Wagenmaterial nt.

Roman [rəʊmən] a römisch; n Römer(in f) m; ~ **Catholic** a römisch-katholisch; n Katholik(in f) m.

romance [rəʊ'mæns] n Romanze f; *(story)* (Liebes)roman m; vi aufschneiden, erfinden; ~r *(storyteller)* Aufschneider m.

romantic [rəʊ'mæntɪk] a romantisch; R~**ism** [rəʊ'mæntɪsɪzəm] Romantik f.

romp [rɒmp] n Tollen nt; vi *(also ~ about)* herumtollen; ~**ers** pl Spielanzug m.

rondo ['rɒndəʊ] n *(Mus)* Rondo nt.

roof [ru:f] n Dach nt; (of mouth) Gaumen nt; vt überdachen, überdecken; ~ing Deckmaterial nt.

rook [ruk] n (bird) Saatkrähe f; (chess) Turm m; vt (cheat) betrügen.

room [rum] n Zimmer nt, Raum m; (space) Platz m; (fig) Spielraum m; ~s pl Wohnung f; ~iness Geräumigkeit f; ~-mate Mitbewohner(in f) m; ~ service Zimmerbedienung f; ~y a geräumig.

roost [ru:st] n Hühnerstange f; vi auf der Stange hocken.

root [ru:t] n (lit, fig) Wurzel f; vt einwurzeln; ~ed a (fig) verwurzelt; ~ about vi (fig) herumwühlen; ~ for vt Stimmung machen für; ~ out vt ausjäten; (fig) ausrotten.

rope [rəup] n Seil nt, Strick m; vt (tie) festschnüren; to ~ sb in jdn gewinnen; ~ off vt absperren; to know the ~s sich auskennen; ~ ladder Strickleiter f.

rosary ['rəuzəri] n Rosenkranz m.

rose [rəuz] n Rose f; a Rosen-, rosenrot.

rosé ['rəuzei] n Rosé m.

rosebed ['rəuzbed] n Rosenbeet nt.

rosebud ['rəuzbʌd] n Rosenknospe f.

rosebush ['rəuzbuʃ] n Rosenstock m, Rosenstrauch m.

rosemary ['rəuzməri] n Rosmarin m.

rosette [rəu'zet] n Rosette f.

roster ['rɒstə*] n Dienstplan m.

rostrum ['rɒstrəm] n Rednerbühne f.

rosy ['rəuzi] a rosig.

rot [rɒt] n Fäulnis f; (nonsense) Quatsch m, Blödsinn m; vti verfaulen (lassen).

rota ['rəutə] n Dienstliste f.

rotary ['rəutəri] a rotierend, sich drehend.

rotate [rəu'teit] vt rotieren lassen; (two or more things in order) turnusmäßig wechseln; vi rotieren.

rotating [rəu'teitiŋ] a rotierend.

rotation [rəu'teiʃən] n Umdrehung f, Rotation f; in ~ der Reihe nach, abwechselnd.

rotor ['rəutə*] n Rotor m.

rotten ['rɒtn] a faul, verfault; (fig) schlecht, gemein.

rotund [rəu'tʌnd] a rund; person rundlich.

rouge [ru:ʒ] n Rouge nt.

rough [rʌf] a (not smooth) rauh; path uneben; (violent) roh, grob; crossing stürmisch; wind rauh; (without comforts) hart, unbequem; (unfinished, makeshift) ·grob; (approximate) ungefähr; n (grass) unebene(r) Boden m; (person) Rowdy m, Rohling m; to ~ it primitiv leben; to play ~ (Sport) hart spielen; to sleep ~ im Freien schlafen; ~ out vt entwerfen, flüchtig skizzieren; ~en vt aufrauhen; ~ly ad grob; (about) ungefähr; ~ness Rauheit f; (of manner) Ungeschliffenheit f.

roulette [ru:'let] n Roulette nt.

round [raund] a rund; figures abgerundet, aufgerundet; ad (in a circle) rundherum; prep um . . . herum; n Runde f; (of ammunition) Magazin nt; (song) Kanon m; theatre in the ~ Rundtheater nt; vt corner biegen um; ~ off vt abrunden; ~ up vt (end) abschließen; figures aufrunden; ~ of

applause Beifall m; ~about n (traffic) Kreisverkehr m; (merry-go-round) Karussell nt; a auf Umwegen; ~ed a gerundet; ~ly ad (fig) gründlich; ~-shouldered a mit abfallenden Schultern; ~sman (general) Austräger m; (milk ~) Milchmann m; ~up Zusammentreiben nt, Sammeln nt.

rouse [rauz] vt (waken) (auf)wecken; (stir up) erregen.

rousing ['rauziŋ] a welcome stürmisch; speech zündend.

rout [raut] n wilde Flucht f; Überwältigung f; vt in die Flucht schlagen.

route [ru:t] n Weg m, Route f.

routine [ru:'ti:n] a Routine f; a Routine-.

rover ['rəuvə*] n Wanderer m.

roving ['rəuviŋ] a reporter im Außendienst.

row [rəu] n (line) Reihe f; vti boat rudern.

row [rau] n (noise) Lärm m, Krach m, Radau m; (dispute) Streit m; (scolding) Krach m; vi sich streiten.

rowboat ['rəubəut] n (US) Ruderboot nt.

rowdy ['raudi] a rüpelhaft; n (person) Rowdy m.

rowing ['rəuiŋ] n Rudern nt; (Sport) Rudersport m; ~ boat Ruderboot nt.

rowlock ['rɒlək] n Rudergabel f.

royal ['rɔiəl] a königlich, Königs-; ~ist n Royalist m; a königstreu; ~ty (family) königliche Familie f; (for invention) Patentgebühr f; (for book) Tantieme f.

rub [rʌb] n (problem) Haken m; to give sb a ~ etw (ab)reiben; vt reiben; ~ off vi (lit, fig) abfärben (on auf +acc); to ~ it in darauf herumreiten.

rubber ['rʌbə*] n Gummi m; (Brit) Radiergummi m; ~ band Gummiband nt; ~ plant Gummibaum m; ~-y a gummiartig, wie Gummi.

rubbish ['rʌbiʃ] n (waste) Abfall m; (nonsense) Blödsinn m, Quatsch m; ~ dump Müllabladeplatz m.

rubble ['rʌbl] n (Stein)schutt m.

ruby ['ru:bi] n Rubin m; a rubinrot.

rucksack ['rʌksæk] n Rucksack m.

rudder ['rʌdə*] n Steuerruder nt.

ruddy ['rʌdi] a (colour) rötlich; (col: bloody) verdammt.

rude, a, ~ly ad [ru:d, -li] unhöflich, unverschämt; shock hart; awakening unsanft; (unrefined, rough) grob; ~ness Unhöflichkeit f, Unverschämtheit f, Grobheit f.

rudiment ['ru:dimənt] n Grundlage f; ~ary [ru:di'mentəri] a rudimentär.

ruff [rʌf] n Halskrause f.

ruffian ['rʌfiən] n Rohling m.

ruffle ['rʌfl] vt kräuseln; durcheinanderbringen.

rug [rʌg] n Brücke f; (in bedroom) Bettvorleger m; (for knees) (Reise)decke f.

rugged ['rʌgid] a coastline zerklüftet; features markig.

ruin ['ru:in] n Ruine f; (downfall) Ruin m; vt ruinieren; ~s pl Trümmer pl; ~ation Zerstörung f, Ruinierung f; ~ous a ruinierend.

rule [ru:l] n Regel f; (government) Herrschaft f. Regierung f; (for measuring) Lineal nt; vti (govern) herrschen über (+acc), regieren; (decide) anordnen, entscheiden; (make lines) linieren; **as a ~** in der Regel; **~d a** a paper liniert; **~r** Lineal nt; Herrscher m.

ruling ['ruːlɪŋ] a party Regierungs-; class herrschend.

rum [rʌm] n Rum m; a (col) komisch.

rumble ['rʌmbl] n Rumpeln nt; (of thunder) Rollen nt; vi rumpeln; grollen.

ruminate ['ruːmɪneɪt] vi grübeln; (cows) wiederkäuen.

rummage ['rʌmɪdʒ] n Durchsuchung f; vi durchstöbern.

rumour, (US) **rumor** ['ruːmə*] n Gerücht nt; vt: **it is ~ed** that man sagt or man munkelt, daß.

rump [rʌmp] n Hinterteil nt; (of fowl) Bürzel m; **~ steak** Rumpsteak nt.

rumpus ['rʌmpəs] n Spektakel m, Krach m.

run [rʌn] n Lauf m; (in car) (Spazier)fahrt f; (series) Serie f, Reihe f; (of play) Spielzeit f; (sudden demand) Ansturm m, starke Nachfrage f; (for animals) Auslauf m; (ski —) (Ski)abfahrt f; (in stocking) Laufmasche f; irreg vt (cause to run) laufen lassen; car, train, bus fahren; (pay for) unterhalten; race, distance laufen, rennen; (manage) leiten, verwalten, führen; knife stoßen; (pass) hand, eye gleiten lassen; vi laufen; (move quickly also) rennen; (bus, train) fahren; (flow) fließen, laufen; (colours) (ab)färben; **on the ~** auf der Flucht; **in the long ~** auf die Dauer; **to ~ riot** Amok laufen; **to ~ a risk** ein Risiko eingehen; **~ about** vi (children) umherspringen; **~ across** vt (find) stoßen auf (+acc); **~ away** vi weglaufen; **~ down** vi (clock) ablaufen; vt (with car) überfahren; (talk against) heruntermachen; **to be ~ down** erschöpft or abgespannt sein; **to ~ for president** für die Präsidentschaft kandidieren; **~ off** vi fortlaufen; **~ out** vi (person) hinausrennen; (liquid) auslaufen; (lease) ablaufen; (money) ausgehen; **he ran out of money/petrol** ihm ging das Geld/Benzin aus; **~ over** vt (in accident) überfahren; (read quickly) überfliegen; **~ through** vt instructions durchgehen; **~ up** vt debt, bill machen; **~ up against** vt difficulties stoßen auf (+acc); **~about** (small car) kleine(r) Flitzer m; **~away a** horse ausgebrochen; person flüchtig.

rung [rʌŋ] n Sprosse f.

runner ['rʌnə*] n Läufer(in f) m; (messenger) Bote m; (for sleigh) Kufe f; **~-up** Zweite(r) mf.

running ['rʌnɪŋ] n (of business) Leitung f; (of machine) Laufen nt, Betrieb m; a water fließend; commentary laufend; **3 days ~** 3 Tage lang or hintereinander.

run-of-the-mill ['rʌnəvðə'mɪl] a gewöhnlich, alltäglich.

runny ['rʌnɪ] a dünn.

runway ['rʌnweɪ] n Startbahn f, Landebahn f, Rollbahn f.

rupture ['rʌptʃə*] n (Med) Bruch m; vt: **o.s.** sich (dat) einen Bruch zuziehen.

rural ['ruərəl] a ländlich, Land-.

ruse [ruːz] n Kniff m, List f.

rush [rʌʃ] n Eile f, Hetze f; (Fin) starke Nachfrage f; vt (carry along) auf dem schnellsten Wege schaffen or transportieren; (attack) losstürmen auf (+acc); **don't ~ me** dräng mich nicht; vi (hurry) eilen, stürzen; **to ~ into sth** etw überstürzen; **~es** pl (Bot) Schilf(rohr) nt; **~ hour** Hauptverkehrszeit f.

rusk [rʌsk] n Zwieback m.

rust [rʌst] n Rost m; vi rosten.

rustic ['rʌstɪk] a bäuerlich, ländlich, Bauern-.

rustle ['rʌsl] n Rauschen nt, Rascheln nt; vi rauschen, rascheln; vt rascheln lassen; cattle stehlen.

rustproof ['rʌstpruːf] a nichtrostend, rostfrei.

rusty ['rʌstɪ] a rostig.

rut [rʌt] n (in track) Radspur f; (of deer) Brunst f; (fig) Trott m.

ruthless a, **~ly** ad ['ruːθləs, -lɪ] erbarmungslos; rücksichtslos; **~ness** Unbarmherzigkeit f; Rücksichtslosigkeit f.

rye [raɪ] n Roggen m; **~ bread** Roggenbrot nt.

S

S, s [es] n S nt, s nt.

sabbath ['sæbəθ] n Sabbat m.

sabbatical [sə'bætɪkəl] a: **~ year** Beurlaubungs- or Forschungsjahr nt.

sabotage ['sæbətɑːʒ] n Sabotage f; vt sabotieren.

sabre, (US) **saber** ['seɪbə*] n Säbel m.

saccharin(e) ['sækərɪn] n Saccharin nt.

sachet ['sæʃeɪ] n (of shampoo) Briefchen nt, Kissen nt.

sack [sæk] n Sack m; **to give sb the ~** (col) jdn hinauswerfen; vt (col) hinauswerfen; (pillage) plündern; **~ful** Sack(voll) m; **~ing** (material) Sackleinen nt; (col) Rausschmiß m.

sacrament ['sækrəmənt] n Sakrament nt.

sacred ['seɪkrɪd] a building, music etc geistlich, Kirchen-; altar, oath heilig.

sacrifice ['sækrɪfaɪs] n Opfer nt; vt (lit, fig) opfern.

sacrilege ['sækrɪlɪdʒ] n Schändung f.

sacrosanct ['sækrəusæŋkt] a sakrosankt.

sad [sæd] a traurig; **~den** vt traurig machen, betrüben.

saddle ['sædl] n Sattel m; vt (burden) aufhalsen (sb with sth jdm etw); **~bag** Satteltasche f.

sadism ['seɪdɪzəm] n Sadismus m.

sadist ['seɪdɪst] n Sadist m; **~ic** [sə'dɪstɪk] a sadistisch.

sadly ['sædlɪ] ad betrübt, beklagenswert; (very) arg.

sadness ['sædnəs] n Traurigkeit f.

safari [sə'fɑːrɪ] n Safari f.

safe [seɪf] a (free from danger) sicher; (careful) vorsichtig; **it's ~ to say** man kann ruhig behaupten; n Safe m, Tresor m, Geldschrank m; **~guard** n Sicherung f; vt sichern, schützen; **~keeping** sichere Verwahrung f; **~ly** ad sicher; arrive wohlbehalten; ~ness Zuverlässigkeit f; ~ty Sicherheit f; ~ty belt Sicherheitsgurt m; ~ty curtain eiserne(r) Vorhang m; ~ty first (slogan) Sicherheit geht vor; ~ty pin Sicherheitsnadel f.

sag [sæg] vi (durch)sacken, sich senken.

saga ['sɑ:gə] n Sage f.

sage [seɪdʒ] n (herb) Salbei m; (man) Weise(r) m.

Sagittarius [sadʒɪ'tɛərɪəs] n Schütze m.

sago ['seɪgəu] n Sago m.

said [sed] a besagt.

sail [seɪl] n Segel nt; (trip) Fahrt f; vt segeln; vi segeln; mit dem Schiff fahren; (begin voyage) (person) abfahren; (ship) auslaufen; (fig: cloud etc) dahinsegeln; ~boat (US) Segelboot nt; ~ing Segeln nt; to go ~ing segeln gehen; ~ing ship Segelschiff nt; ~or Matrose m, Seemann m.

saint [seɪnt] n Heilige(r) mf; ~liness Heiligkeit f; ~ly a heilig, fromm.

sake [seɪk] n: for the ~ of um (+gen) willen; for your ~ um deinetwillen, deinetwegen, wegen dir.

salad ['sæləd] n Salat m; ~ cream gewürzte Mayonnaise f; ~ dressing Salatsoße f; ~ oil Speiseöl nt, Salatöl nt.

salami [sə'lɑ:mɪ] n Salami f.

salaried ['sælərɪd] a: ~ staff Gehaltsempfänger pl.

salary ['sælərɪ] n Gehalt nt.

sale [seɪl] n Verkauf m; (reduced prices) Schlußverkauf m; ~room Verkaufsraum m; ~sman Verkäufer m; (representative) Vertreter m; ~smanship Geschäftstüchtigkeit f; ~swoman Verkäuferin f.

salient ['seɪlɪənt] a hervorspringend, bemerkenswert.

saliva [sə'laɪvə] n Speichel m.

sallow ['sæləu] a fahl; face bleich.

salmon ['sæmən] n Lachs m.

salon ['sælɔ:ŋ] n Salon m.

saloon [sə'lu:n] n (Aut) Limousine f; (ship's lounge) Salon m.

salt [sɔ:lt] n Salz nt; vt (cure) einsalzen; (flavour) salzen; ~cellar Salzfaß nt; ~mine Salzbergwerk nt; ~y a salzig.

salubrious [sə'lu:brɪəs] a gesund; district etc erspriesslich.

salutary ['sæljutərɪ] a gesund, heilsam.

salute [sə'lu:t] n (Mil) Gruß m, Salut m; (with guns) Salutschüsse pl; vt (Mil) salutieren.

salvage ['sælvɪdʒ] n (from ship) Bergung f; (property) Rettung f; vt bergen; retten.

salvation [sæl'veɪʃən] n Rettung f; S~ Army Heilsarmee f.

salver ['sælvə*] n Tablett nt.

salvo ['sælvəu] n Salve f.

same [seɪm] a (similar) gleiche(r,s); (identical) derselbe/dieselbe/ dasselbe; all or just the ~ trotzdem; it's all the ~ to me das ist mir egal; they all look the ~ to me für mich sehen sie alle gleich aus; the ~ to you gleichfalls; at the ~ time zur gleichen Zeit, gleichzeitig; (however) zugleich, andererseits.

sampan ['sæmpæn] n Sampan m.

sample ['sɑ:mpl] n (specimen) Probe f; (example of sth) Muster nt, Probe f; vt probieren.

sanatorium [sænə'tɔ:rɪəm] n Sanatorium nt.

sanctify ['sæŋktɪfaɪ] vt weihen.

sanctimonious [sæŋktɪ'məunɪəs] a scheinheilig.

sanction ['sæŋkʃən] n Sanktion f.

sanctity ['sæŋktɪtɪ] n Heiligkeit f; (fig) Unverletzlichkeit f.

sanctuary ['sæŋktjuərɪ] n Heiligtum nt; (for fugitive) Asyl nt; (refuge) Zufluchtsort m; (for animals) Naturpark m, Schutzgebiet nt.

sand [sænd] n Sand m; vt mit Sand bestreuen; furniture schmirgeln; ~s pl Sand m.

sandal ['sændl] n Sandale f.

sandbag ['sændbæg] n Sandsack m.

sand dune ['sænddju:n] n (Sand)düne f.

sandpaper ['sændpeɪpə*] n Sandpapier nt.

sandpit ['sændpɪt] n Sandkasten m.

sandstone ['sændstəun] n Sandstein m.

sandwich ['sænwɪdʒ] n Sandwich m or nt; vt einklemmen.

sandy ['sændɪ] a sandig, Sand-; (colour) sandfarben; hair rotblond.

sane [seɪn] a geistig gesund or normal; (sensible) vernünftig, gescheit.

sanguine ['sæŋgwɪn] a (hopeful) zuversichtlich.

sanitarium [sænɪ'tɛərɪəm] n (US) = sanatorium.

sanitary ['sænɪtərɪ] a hygienisch (einwandfrei); (against dirt) hygienisch, Gesundheits-; ~ napkin (US), ~ towel (Monats)binde f.

sanitation [sænɪ'teɪʃən] n sanitäre Einrichtungen pl; Gesundheitswesen nt.

sanity ['sænɪtɪ] n geistige Gesundheit f; (good sense) gesunde(r) Verstand m, Vernunft f.

Santa Claus [sæntə'klɔ:z] n Nikolaus m, Weihnachtsmann m.

sap [sæp] n (of plants) Saft m; vt strength schwächen; health untergraben.

sapling ['sæplɪŋ] n junge(r) Baum m.

sapphire ['sæfaɪə*] n Saphir m.

sarcasm ['sɑ:kæzəm] n Sarkasmus m.

sarcastic [sɑ:'kæstɪk] a sarkastisch.

sarcophagus [sɑ:'kɒfəgəs] n Sarkophag m.

sardine [sɑ:'di:n] n Sardine f.

sardonic [sɑ:'dɒnɪk] a zynisch.

sari ['sɑ:rɪ] n Sari m.

sash [sæʃ] n Schärpe f.

Satan ['seɪtn] n Satan m, Teufel m; s~ic [sə'tænɪk] a satanisch, teuflisch.

satchel ['sætʃəl] n (Sch) Schulranzen m, Schulmappe f.

satellite ['sætəlaɪt] n Satellit m; (fig) Trabant m; a Satelliten-.

satin ['sætɪn] n Satin m; a Satin-.

satire ['sætaɪə*] n Satire f.

satirical [sə'tɪrɪkəl] a satirisch.

satirize ['sætəraɪz] vt (durch Satire) verspotten.

satisfaction [sætɪs'fækʃən] n Befriedigung f, Genugtuung f.

satisfactorily [sætɪs'fæktərɪlɪ] *ad* zufriedenstellend.

satisfactory [sætɪs'fæktərɪ] *a* zufriedenstellend, befriedigend.

satisfy ['sætɪsfaɪ] *vt* befriedigen, zufriedenstellen; (*convince*) überzeugen; *conditions* erfüllen; **~ing** *a* befriedigend; *meal* sättigend.

saturate ['sætʃəreɪt] *vt* (durch)tränken.

saturation [sætʃə'reɪʃən] *n* Durchtränkung *f*; (*Chem, fig*) Sättigung *f*.

Saturday ['sætədeɪ] *n* Samstag *m*, Sonnabend *m*.

sauce [sɔːs] *n* Soße *f*, Sauce *f*; **~pan** Kasserolle *f*; **~r** Untertasse *f*.

saucily ['sɔːsɪlɪ] *ad* frech.

sauciness ['sɔːsɪnəs] *n* Frechheit *f*.

saucy ['sɔːsɪ] *a* frech, keck.

sauna ['sɔːnə] *n* Sauna *f*.

saunter ['sɔːntə*] *vi* schlendern; *n* Schlendern *nt*.

sausage ['sɔsɪdʒ] *n* Wurst *f*; **~ roll** Wurst *f* im Schlafrock, Wurstpastete *f*.

savage ['sævɪdʒ] *a* (*fierce*) wild, brutal, grausam; (*uncivilized*) wild, primitiv; *n* Wilde(r) *mf*; *vt* (*animals*) zerfleischen; **~ly** *ad* grausam; **~ry** Roheit *f*, Grausamkeit *f*.

save [seɪv] *vt* retten; *money, electricity etc* sparen; *strength etc* aufsparen; **to ~ you the trouble** um die Mühe zu ersparen; *n* (*Sport*) (Ball)abwehr *f*; *prep, cj* außer, ausgenommen.

saving ['seɪvɪŋ] *a* rettend; *n* Sparen *nt*, Ersparnis *f*; **~s** *pl* Ersparnisse *pl*; **~s bank** Sparkasse *f*.

saviour ['seɪvjə*] *n* Retter *m*; (*Eccl*) Heiland *m*, Erlöser *m*.

savoir-faire ['sævwɑː'fɛə*] *n* Gewandtheit *f*.

savour, (*US*) **savor** ['seɪvə*] *n* Wohlgeschmack *m*; *vt* (*taste*) schmecken; (*fig*) genießen; *vi* schmecken (of nach), riechen (of nach); **~y** *a* schmackhaft; *food* pikant, würzig.

savvy ['sævɪ] *n* (*col*) Grips *m*.

saw [sɔː] *n* (*tool*) Säge *f*; *vti irreg* sägen; **~dust** Sägemehl *nt*; **~mill** Sägewerk *nt*.

saxophone ['sæksəfəʊn] *n* Saxophon *nt*.

say [seɪ] *n* Meinung *f*; (*right*) Mitspracherecht *nt*; **to have no/a ~ in sth** (kein) Mitspracherecht bei etw haben; **let him have his ~** laß ihn doch reden; *vti irreg* sagen; **I couldn't ~** schwer zu sagen; **how old would you ~ he is?** wie alt schätzt du ihn?; **you don't ~!** was du nicht sagst!; **don't ~ you forgot** sag bloß nicht, daß du es vergessen hast; **there are, ~, 50** es sind, sagen wir mal, 50. . .; **that is to ~** das heißt; (*more precisely*) beziehungsweise, mit anderen Worten; **to ~ nothing of . . .** ganz zu schweigen von. . .; **~ing** Sprichwort *nt*; **~-so** (*col*) Ja *nt*, Zustimmung *f*.

scab [skæb] *n* Schorf *m*; (*of sheep*) Räude *f*; (*pej*) Streikbrecher *m*.

scabby ['skæbɪ] *a* *sheep* räudig; *skin* schorfig.

scaffold ['skæfəʊld] *n* (*for execution*) Schafott *nt*; **~ing** (Bau)gerüst *nt*.

scald [skɔːld] *n* Verbrühung *f*; *vt* (*burn*) verbrühen; (*clean*) (ab)brühen; **~ing** *a* brühheiß.

scale [skeɪl] *n* (*of fish*) Schuppe *f*; (*Mus*) Tonleiter *f*; (*dish for measuring*) Waagschale *f*; (*on map, size*) Maßstab *m*; (*gradation*) Skala *f*; *vt* (*climb*) erklimmen; **~s** *pl* (*balance*) Waage *f*; **on a large ~** (*fig*) im großen, in großem Umfang; **~ drawing** maßstabgerechte Zeichnung *f*.

scallop ['skɒləp] *n* Kammuschel *f*.

scalp [skælp] *n* Kopfhaut *f*; *vt* skalpieren.

scalpel ['skælpəl] *n* Skalpell *nt*.

scamp [skæmp] *vt* schlud(e)rig machen, hinschlampen.

scamper ['skæmpə*] *vi* huschen.

scan [skæn] *vt* (*examine*) genau prüfen; (*quickly*) überfliegen; *horizon* absuchen; *poetry* skandieren.

scandal ['skændl] *n* (*disgrace*) Skandal *m*; (*gossip*) böswillige(r) Klatsch *m*; **~ize** *vt* schockieren; **~ous** *a* skandalös, schockierend.

scant [skænt] *a* knapp; **~ily** *ad* knapp, dürftig; **~iness** Knappheit *f*; **~y** knapp, unzureichend.

scapegoat ['skeɪpgəʊt] *n* Sündenbock *m*.

scar [skɑː*] *n* Narbe *f*; *vt* durch Narben entstellen.

scarce ['skɛəs] *a* selten, rar; *goods* knapp; **~ly** *ad* kaum; **~ness** Seltenheit *f*.

scarcity ['skɛəsɪtɪ] *n* Mangel *m*, Knappheit *f*.

scare ['skɛə*] *n* Schrecken *m*, Panik *f*; *vt* erschrecken; ängstigen; **to be ~d** Angst haben; **~crow** Vogelscheuche *f*; **~monger** Bangemacher *m*.

scarf [skɑːf] *n* Schal *m*; (*on head*) Kopftuch *nt*.

scarlet ['skɑːlət] *a* scharlachrot; *n* Scharlachrot *nt*; **~ fever** Scharlach *m*.

scarred ['skɑːd] *a* narbig.

scary ['skɛərɪ] *a* (*col*) schaurig.

scathing ['skeɪðɪŋ] *a* scharf, vernichtend.

scatter ['skætə*] *n* Streuung *f*; *vt* (*sprinkle*) (ver)streuen; (*disperse*) zerstreuen; *vi* sich zerstreuen; **~brained** *a* flatterhaft, schusselig; **~ing of** ein paar.

scavenger ['skævɪndʒə*] *n* (*animal*) Aasfresser *m*.

scene [siːn] *n* (*of happening*) Ort *m*; (*of play, incident*) Szene *f*; (*canvas etc*) Bühnenbild *nt*; (*view*) Anblick *m*; (*argument*) Szene *f*, Auftritt *m*; **on the ~** am Ort, dabei; **behind the ~s** hinter den Kulissen; **~ry** ['siːnərɪ] (*Theat*) Bühnenbild *nt*; (*landscape*) Landschaft *f*.

scenic ['siːnɪk] *a* landschaftlich, Landschafts-.

scent [sent] *n* Parfüm *m*; (*smell*) Duft *m*; (*sense*) Geruchsinn *m*; *vt* parfümieren.

sceptic ['skeptɪk] *n* Skeptiker *m*; **~al** *a* skeptisch; **~ism** ['skeptɪsɪzəm] Skepsis *f*.

sceptre, (*US*) **scepter** ['septə*] *n* Szepter *nt*.

schedule ['ʃedjuːl] *n* (*list*) Liste *f*, Tabelle *f*; (*plan*) Programm *nt*; *vt*: **it is ~d for 2** es soll um 2 abfahren/stattfinden *etc*; **on ~** pünktlich, fahrplanmäßig; **behind ~** mit Verspätung.

scheme   346   scrupulous

scheme [ski:m] *n* Schema *nt*; (*dishonest*) Intrige *f*; (*plan of action*) Plan *m*, Programm *nt*; *vi* sich verschwören, intrigieren; *vt* planen.

scheming ['ski:mɪŋ] *a* intrigierend, ränkevoll.

schism ['skɪzəm] *n* Spaltung *f*; (*Eccl*) Schisma *nt*, Kirchenspaltung *f*.

schizophrenic [skɪtsəʊ'frenɪk] *a* schizophren.

scholar ['skɒlə*] *n* Gelehrte(r) *m*; (*holding scholarship*) Stipendiat *m*; ~**ly** *a* gelehrt; ~**ship** Gelehrsamkeit *f*, Belesenheit *f*; (*grant*) Stipendium *nt*.

school [sku:l] *n* Schule *f*; (*Univ*) Fakultät *f*; *vt* schulen; *dog* trainieren; ~**book** Schulbuch *nt*; ~**boy** Schüler *m*, Schuljunge *m*; ~**days** *pl* (alte) Schulzeit *f*; ~**girl** Schülerin *f*, Schulmädchen *nt*; ~**ing** Schulung *f*, Ausbildung *f*; ~**master** Lehrer *m*; ~**mistress** Lehrerin *f*; ~**room** Klassenzimmer *nt*; ~**teacher** Lehrer(in *f*) *m*.

schooner ['sku:nə*] *n* Schoner *m*; (*glass*) große(s) Sherryglas *nt*.

sciatica [saɪ'ætɪkə] *n* Ischias *m or nt*.

science ['saɪəns] *n* Wissenschaft *f*; (*natural* ~) Naturwissenschaft *f*; ~ **fiction** Science-fiction *f*.

scientific [saɪən'tɪfɪk] *a* wissenschaftlich; (*natural sciences*) naturwissenschaftlich.

scientist ['saɪəntɪst] *n* Wissenschaftler(in *f*) *m*.

scintillating ['sɪntɪleɪtɪŋ] *a* sprühend.

scissors ['sɪzəz] *npl* Schere *f*; **a pair of** ~ eine Schere.

scoff [skɒf] *vt* (*eat*) fressen; *vi* (*mock*) spotten (*at* über +*acc*).

scold [skəʊld] *vt* schimpfen.

scone [skɒn] *n* weiche(s) Teegebäck *nt*.

scoop [sku:p] *n* Schaufel *f*; (*news*) sensationelle Erstmeldung *f*; *vt* (*also* ~ **out** *or* **up**) schaufeln.

scooter ['sku:tə*] *n* Motorroller *m*; (*child's*) Roller *m*.

scope [skəʊp] *n* Ausmaß *nt*; (*opportunity*) (Spiel)raum *m*, Bewegungsfreiheit *f*.

scorch [skɔ:tʃ] *n* Brandstelle *f*; *vt* versengen, verbrennen; ~**er** (*col*) heiße(r) Tag *m*; ~**ing** *a* brennend, glühend.

score [skɔ:*] *n* (*in game*) Punktzahl *f*; (Spiel)ergebnis *nt*; (*Mus*) Partitur *f*; (*line*) Kratzer *m*; (*twenty*) 20, 20 Stück; **on that** ~ in dieser Hinsicht; **what's the** ~? wie steht's?; *vt goal* schießen; *points* machen; (*mark*) einkerben; zerkratzen, einritzen; *vi* (*keep record*) Punkte zählen; ~**board** Anschreibetafel *f*; ~**card** (*Sport*) Punktliste *f*; ~**r** Torschütze *m*; (*recorder*) (Auf)schreiber *m*.

scorn ['skɔːn] *n* Verachtung *f*; *vt* verhöhnen; ~**ful** *a*, ~**fully** *ad* höhnisch, verächtlich.

Scorpio ['skɔːpɪəʊ] *n* Skorpion *m*.

scorpion ['skɔːpɪən] *n* Skorpion *m*.

scotch [skɒtʃ] *vt* (*end*) unterbinden.

scoundrel ['skaʊndrəl] *n* Schurke *m*, Schuft *m*.

scour ['skaʊə*] *vt* (*sea, ch*) absuchen;

(*clean*) schrubben; ~**er** Topfkratzer *m*.

scourge [skɔ:dʒ] *n* (*whip*) Geißel *f*; (*plague*) Qual *f*.

scout [skaʊt] *n* (*Mil*) Späher *m*, Aufklärer *m*; *vi* (*reconnoitre*) auskundschaften; **see boy.**

scowl [skaʊl] *n* finstere(r) Blick *m*; *vi* finster blicken.

scraggy ['skrægɪ] *a* dürr, hager.

scram [skræm] *vi* (*col*) verschwinden, abhauen.

scramble ['skræmbl] *n* (*climb*) Kletterei *f*; (*struggle*) Kampf *m*; *vi* klettern; (*fight*) sich schlagen; ~**d eggs** *pl* Rührei *nt*.

scrap [skræp] *n* (*bit*) Stückchen *nt*; (*fight*) Keilerei *f*; *a* Abfall-; *vt* verwerfen; *vi* (*fight*) streiten, sich prügeln; ~**book** Einklebealbum *nt*; ~**s** *pl* (*waste*) Abfall *m*.

scrape [skreɪp] *n* Kratzen *nt*; (*trouble*) Klemme *f*; *vt* kratzen; *car* zerkratzen; (*clean*) abkratzen; *vi* (*make harsh noise*) kratzen; ~**r** Kratzer *m*.

scrap heap ['skræphi:p] *n* Abfallhaufen *m*; (*for metal*) Schrotthaufen *m*.

scrap iron ['skræp'aɪən] *n* Schrott *m*.

scrappy ['skræpɪ] *a* zusammengestoppelt.

scratch ['skrætʃ] *n* (*wound*) Kratzer *m*, Schramme *f*; **to start from** ~ ganz von vorne anfangen; *a* (*improvised*) zusammengewürfelt; *vt* kratzen; *car* zerkratzen; *vi* (sich) kratzen.

scrawl [skrɔ:l] *n* Gekritzel *nt*; *vti* kritzeln.

scream [skri:m] *n* Schrei *m*; *vi* schreien.

scree ['skri:] *n* Geröll(halde *f*) *nt*.

screech [skri:tʃ] *n* Schrei *m*; *vi* kreischen.

screen [skri:n] *n* (*protective*) Schutzschirm *m*; (*film*) Leinwand *f*; (*TV*) Bildschirm *m*; (*against insects*) Fliegengitter *nt*; (*Eccl*) Lettner *m*; *vt* (*shelter*) (be)schirmen; *film* zeigen, vorführen.

screw [skru:] *n* Schraube *f*; (*Naut*) Schiffsschraube *f*; *vt* (*fasten*) schrauben; (*vulgar*) bumsen; **to** ~ **money out of sb** (*col*) jdm das Geld aus der Tasche ziehen; ~**driver** Schraubenzieher *m*; ~**y** *a* (*col*) verrückt.

scribble ['skrɪbl] *n* Gekritzel *nt*; *vt* kritzeln.

scribe [skraɪb] *n* Schreiber *m*; (*Jewish*) Schriftgelehrte(r) *m*.

script [skrɪpt] *n* (*handwriting*) Handschrift *f*; (*for film*) Drehbuch *nt*; (*Theat*) Manuskript *nt*, Text *m*.

Scripture ['skrɪptʃə*] *n* Heilige Schrift *f*.

scriptwriter ['skrɪptraɪtə*] *n* Textverfasser *m*.

scroll [skrəʊl] *n* Schriftrolle *f*.

scrounge [skraʊndʒ] *vt* schnorren; *n*: **on the** ~ beim Schnorren.

scrub [skrʌb] *n* (*clean*) Schrubben *nt*; (*in countryside*) Gestrüpp *nt*; *vt* (*clean*) schrubben; (*reject*) fallenlassen.

scruff [skrʌf] *n* Genick *nt*, Kragen *m*; ~**y** *a* unordentlich, vergammelt.

scrum(mage) ['skrʌm(ɪdʒ)] *n* Getümmel *nt*.

scruple ['skru:pl] *n* Skrupel *m*, Bedenken *nt*.

scrupulous *a*, ~**ly** *ad* ['skru:pjʊləs, -lɪ] peinlich genau, gewissenhaft.

scrutinize ['skru:tɪnaɪz] vt genau prüfen or untersuchen.

scrutiny ['skru:tɪnɪ] n genaue Untersuchung f.

scuff [skʌf] vt shoes abstoßen.

scuffle ['skʌfl] n Handgemenge nt.

scullery ['skʌlərɪ] n Spülküche f; Abstellraum m.

sculptor ['skʌlptə*] n Bildhauer m.

sculpture ['skʌlptʃə*] n (art) Bildhauerei f; (statue) Skulptur f.

scum [skʌm] n (lit, fig) Abschaum m.

scurrilous ['skʌrɪləs] a unflätig.

scurry ['skʌrɪ] vi huschen.

scurvy ['skɜːvɪ] n Skorbut m.

scuttle ['skʌtl] n Kohleneimer m; vt ship versenken; vi (scamper) (+ away, off) sich davonmachen.

scythe [saɪð] n Sense f.

sea [si:] n Meer nt (also fig), See f; a Meeres-, See-; ~ **bird** Meervogel m; ~**board** Küste f; ~ **breeze** Seewind m; ~**dog** Seebär m; ~**farer** Seefahrer m; ~**faring** a seefahrend; ~**food** Meeresfrüchte pl; ~**front** Strandpromenade f; ~**going** a seetüchtig, Hochsee-; ~**gull** Möwe f.

seal [si:l] n (animal) Robbe f, Seehund m; (stamp, impression) Siegel nt; vt versiegeln.

sea level ['si:levl] n Meeresspiegel m.

sealing wax ['si:lɪŋwæks] n Siegellack m.

sea lion ['si:laɪən] n Seelöwe m.

seam [si:m] n Saum m; (edges joining) Naht f; (layer) Schicht f; (of coal) Flöz nt.

seaman ['si:mən] n Seemann m.

seamless ['si:mlɪs] a nahtlos.

seamy ['si:mɪ] a people, café zwielichtig; life anrüchig; ~ **side** of life dunkle Seite f des Lebens.

seaport ['si:pɔːt] n Seehafen m, Hafenstadt f.

search [sɜːtʃ] n Suche f (for nach); vi suchen; vt (examine) durchsuchen; ~**ing** a look forschend, durchdringend; ~**light** Scheinwerfer m; ~ **party** Suchmannschaft f.

seashore ['si:ʃɔː*] n Meeresküste f.

seasick ['si:sɪk] a seekrank; ~**ness** Seekrankheit f.

seaside ['si:saɪd] n Küste f; at the ~ an der See; to go to the ~ an die See fahren.

season ['si:zn] n Jahreszeit f; (eg Christmas) Zeit f, Saison f; vt (flavour) würzen; ~**al** a Saison-; ~**ing** Gewürz nt, Würze f; ~ **ticket** (Rail) Zeitkarte f; (Theat) Abonnement nt.

seat [si:t] n Sitz m, Platz m; (in Parliament) Sitz m; (part of body) Gesäß nt; (part of garment) Sitzfläche f, Hosenboden m; vt (place) setzen; (have space for) Sitzplätze bieten für; ~ **belt** Sicherheitsgurt m; ~**ing** Anweisen nt von Sitzplätzen.

sea water ['si:wɔːtə*] n Meerwasser nt, Seewasser nt.

seaweed ['si:wi:d] n (See)tang m, Alge f.

seaworthy ['si:wɜːðɪ] a seetüchtig.

secede [sɪ'si:d] vi sich lossagen.

secluded [sɪ'klu:dɪd] a abgelegen, ruhig.

seclusion [sɪ'klu:ʒən] n Zurückgezogenheit f.

second ['sekənd] a zweite(r,s); ad (in ~ position) an zweiter Stelle; (Rail) zweite(r) Klasse; n Sekunde f; (person) Zweite(r) m; (Comm: imperfect) zweite Wahl f; (Sport) Sekundant m; vt (support) unterstützen; ~**ary** a zweitrangig; ~**ary education** Sekundarstufe f; ~**ary school** höhere Schule f, Mittelschule f; ~**er** Unterstützer m; ~**hand** a aus zweiter Hand; car etc gebraucht; ~**ly** ad zweitens; **it is** ~ **nature to him** es ist ihm zur zweiten Natur geworden; ~**rate** a mittelmäßig; **to have** ~ **thoughts** es sich (dat) anders überlegen.

secrecy ['si:krəsɪ] n Geheimhaltung f.

secret ['si:krət] n Geheimnis nt; a geheim, heimlich, Geheim-; **in** ~ geheim, heimlich.

secretarial [sekrə'tɛərɪəl] a Sekretärs-.

secretariat [sekrə'tɛərɪət] n Sekretariat nt.

secretary ['sekrətrɪ] n Sekretär(in f) m; (government) Staatssekretär(in f) m; Minister m.

secretive ['si:krətɪv] a geheimtuerisch.

secretly ['si:krətlɪ] ad heimlich.

sect [sekt] n Sekte f; ~**arian** [sek'tɛərɪən] a (belonging to a sect) Sekten-.

section ['sekʃən] n Teil m, Ausschnitt m; (department) Abteilung f; (of document) Abschnitt m, Paragraph m; ~**al** a (regional) partikularistisch.

sector ['sektə*] n Sektor m.

secular ['sekjulə*] a weltlich, profan.

secure [sɪ'kjuə*] a (safe) sicher; (firmly fixed) fest; vt (make firm) befestigen, sichern; (obtain) sichern; ~**ly** ad sicher, fest.

security [sɪ'kjuərɪtɪ] n Sicherheit f; (pledge) Pfand nt; (document) Sicherheiten pl; (national) ~ Staatssicherheit f; ~ **guard** Sicherheitsbeamte(r) m; see social.

sedate [sɪ'deɪt] a (calm) gelassen; (serious) gesetzt; vt (Med) ein Beruhigungsmittel geben (+dat).

sedation [sɪ'deɪʃən] n (Med) Einfluß m von Beruhigungsmitteln.

sedative ['sedətɪv] n Beruhigungsmittel nt; a beruhigend, einschläfernd.

sedentary ['sedntrɪ] a job sitzend.

sediment ['sedɪmənt] n (Boden)satz m; ~**ary** [sedɪ'mentərɪ] a (Geol) Sediment-.

seduce [sɪ'dju:s] vt verführen.

seduction [sɪ'dʌkʃən] n Verführung f.

seductive [sɪ'dʌktɪv] a verführerisch.

see [si:] irreg vt sehen; (understand) (ein)sehen, erkennen; (find out) sehen, herausfinden; (make sure) dafür sorgen (daß); (accompany) begleiten, bringen; (visit) besuchen; **to** ~ **a doctor** zum Arzt gehen; vi (be aware) sehen; (find out) nachsehen; **I** ~ ach so, ich verstehe; **let me** ~ warte mal; **we'll** ~ werden (mal) sehen; n (Eccl) (R.C.) Bistum nt; (Protestant) Kirchenkreis m; **to** ~ **sth through** etw durchfechten; **to** ~ **through sb/sth** jdn/etw durchschauen; **to** ~ **to it** dafür sorgen; **to** ~ **sb off** jdn zum Zug etc begleiten.

seed [si:d] *n* Samen *m*, (Samen)korn *nt*; *vt* (*Tennis*) plazieren; ~**ling** Setzling *m*; ~**y** a (*ill*) flau, angeschlagen; *clothes* schäbig; *person* zweifelhaft.

seeing ['si:ɪŋ] *cj* da.

seek [si:k] *vt irreg* suchen.

seem [si:m] *vi* scheinen; ~**ingly** *ad* anscheinend; ~**ly** a geziemend.

seep [si:p] *vi* sickern.

seer [sɪə*] *n* Seher *m*.

seesaw ['si:sɔ:] *n* Wippe *f*.

seethe [si:ð] *vi* kochen; (*with crowds*) wimmeln von.

see-through ['si:θru:] a *dress* durchsichtig.

segment ['segmənt] *n* Teil *m*; (*of circle*) Ausschnitt *m*.

segregate ['segrɪgeɪt] *vt* trennen, absondern.

segregation [segrɪ'geɪʃən] *n* Rassentrennung *f*.

seismic ['saɪzmɪk] a seismisch, Erdbeben-.

seize [si:z] *vt* (*grasp*) (er)greifen, packen; *power* ergreifen; (*take legally*) beschlagnahmen; *point* erfassen, begreifen; ~ **up** *vi* (*Tech*) sich festfressen.

seizure ['si:ʒə*] *n* (*illness*) Anfall *m*.

seldom ['seldəm] *ad* selten.

select [sɪ'lekt] a ausgewählt; *vt* auswählen; ~**ion** [sɪ'lekʃən] Auswahl *f*; ~**ive** a *person* wählerisch.

self [self] *n* Selbst *nt*, Ich *nt*; ~-**adhesive** a selbstklebend; ~-**appointed** a selbsternannt; ~-**assurance** Selbstsicherheit *f*; ~-**assured** a selbstbewußt; ~-**coloured**, (*US*) ~-**colored** a einfarbig; ~-**confidence** Selbstvertrauen *nt*, Selbstbewußtsein *nt*; ~-**confident** a selbstsicher; ~-**conscious** a gehemmt, befangen; ~-**contained** a (*complete*) (in sich) geschlossen; *person* verschlossen; ~-**defeating** a: **to be** ~-**defeating** ein Widerspruch in sich sein; ~-**defence** Selbstverteidigung *f*; (*Jur*) Notwehr *f*; ~-**employed** a frei(schaffend); ~-**evident** a offensichtlich; ~-**explanatory** a für sich (selbst) sprechend; ~-**indulgent** a zügellos; ~-**interest** Eigennutz *m*; ~-**ish** a, ~-**ishly** *ad* egoistisch, selbstsüchtig; ~-**ishness** Egoismus *m*, Selbstsucht *f*; ~-**lessly** *ad* selbstlos; ~-**made** a selbstgemacht; ~-**pity** Selbstmitleid *nt*; ~-**portrait** Selbstbildnis *nt*; ~-**propelled** a mit Eigenantrieb; ~-**reliant** a unabhängig; ~-**respect** Selbstachtung *f*; ~-**respecting** a mit Selbstachtung; ~-**righteous** a selbstgerecht; ~-**satisfied** a selbstzufrieden; ~-**service** a Selbstbedienungs-; ~-**sufficient** a selbstgenügsam; ~-**supporting** a (*Fin*) Eigenfinanzierungs-; *person* eigenständig.

sell [sel] *irreg vt* verkaufen; *vi* verkaufen; (*goods*) sich verkaufen (lassen); ~**er** Verkäufer *m*; ~**ing price** Verkaufspreis *m*.

semantic [sɪ'mæntɪk] a semantisch; ~**s** Semantik *f*.

semaphore ['seməfɔ:*] *n* Winkzeichen *pl*.

semi ['semɪ] *n* = ~-**detached house**;

~-**circle** Halbkreis *m*; ~-**colon** Semikolon *nt*; ~-**conscious** a halbbewußt; ~-**detached house** Zweifamilienhaus *nt*, Doppelhaus *nt*; ~-**final** Halbfinale *nt*.

seminar ['seminɑ:*] *n* Seminar *nt*.

semiquaver ['semɪkweɪvə*] *n* Sechzehntel *nt*.

semiskilled ['semɪ'skɪld] a angelernt.

semitone ['semɪtəʊn] *n* Halbton *m*.

semolina [semə'li:nə] *n* Grieß *m*.

senate ['senət] *n* Senat *m*.

senator ['senətə*] *n* Senator *m*.

send [send] *vt irreg* senden, schicken; (*col: inspire*) hinreißen; ~ **away** *vt* wegschicken; ~ **away for** *vt* holen lassen; ~ **back** *vt* zurückschicken; ~ **for** *vt* holen lassen; ~ **off** *vt goods* abschicken; *player* vom Feld schicken; ~ **out** *vt invitation* aussenden; ~ **up** *vt* hinaufsenden; (*col*) verulken; ~**er** Absender *m*; ~-**off** Verabschiedung *f*; ~-**up** (*col*) Verulkung *f*.

senile ['si:naɪl] a senil, Alters-.

senility [sɪ'nɪlɪtɪ] *n* Altersschwachheit *f*.

senior ['si:nɪə*] a (*older*) älter; (*higher rank*) Ober-; *n* (*older person*) Ältere(r) *m*; (*higher ranking*) Rangälteste(r) *m*; ~**ity** [si:nɪ'ɒrɪtɪ] (*of age*) höhere(s) Alter *nt*; (*in rank*) höhere(r) Dienstgrad *m*.

sensation [sen'seɪʃən] *n* Empfindung *f*, Gefühl *nt*; (*excitement*) Sensation *f*, Aufsehen *nt*; ~**al** a sensationell, Sensations-.

sense [sens] *n* Sinn *m*; (*understanding*) Verstand *m*, Vernunft *f*; (*meaning*) Sinn *m*, Bedeutung *f*; (*feeling*) Gefühl *nt*; **to make** ~ Sinn ergeben; *vt* fühlen, spüren; ~**less** a sinnlos; (*unconscious*) besinnungslos; ~**lessly** *ad* (*stupidly*) sinnlos.

sensibility [sensɪ'bɪlɪtɪ] *n* Empfindsamkeit *f*; (*feeling hurt*) Empfindlichkeit *f*.

sensible a, **sensibly** *ad* ['sensəbl, -blɪ] vernünftig.

sensitive ['sensɪtɪv] a empfindlich (*to* gegen); (*easily hurt*) sensibel, feinfühlig; *film* lichtempfindlich.

sensitivity [sensɪ'tɪvɪtɪ] *n* Empfindlichkeit *f*; (*artistic*) Feingefühl *nt*; (*tact*) Feinfühligkeit *f*.

sensual ['sensjʊəl] a sinnlich.

sensuous ['sensjʊəs] a sinnlich, sinnenfreudig.

sentence ['sentəns] *n* Satz *m*; (*Jur*) Strafe *f*; Urteil *nt*; *vt* verurteilen.

sentiment ['sentɪmənt] *n* Gefühl *nt*; (*thought*) Gedanke *m*, Gesinnung *f*; ~**al** [sentɪ'mentl] a sentimental; (*of feelings rather than reason*) gefühlsmäßig; ~**ality** [sentɪmen'tælɪtɪ] Sentimentalität *f*.

sentinel ['sentɪnl] *n* Wachtposten *m*.

sentry ['sentrɪ] *n* (Schild)wache *f*.

separable ['sepərəbl] a (ab)trennbar.

separate ['seprət] a getrennt, separat; ['sepəreɪt] *vt* trennen; *vi* sich trennen; ~**ly** *ad* getrennt.

separation [sepə'reɪʃən] *n* Trennung *f*.

sepia ['si:pɪə] a Sepia-.

September [sep'tembə*] *n* September *m*.

septic ['septɪk] a vereitert, septisch.

sequel ['si:kwəl] *n* Folge *f*.

sequence ['si:kwəns] n (Reihen)folge f.
sequin ['si:kwɪn] n Paillette f.
serenade [serə'neɪd] n Ständchen nt,
Serenade f; vt ein Ständchen bringen
(+dat).
serene a, ~**ly** ad [sə'ri:n, -lɪ] heiter,
gelassen, ruhig.
serenity [sɪ'renɪtɪ] n Heiterkeit f,
Gelassenheit f, Ruhe f.
serf [sɜ:f] n Leibeigene(r) mf.
serge [sɜ:dʒ] n Serge f.
sergeant ['sɑ:dʒənt] n Feldwebel m;
(police) (Polizei)wachtmeister m.
serial ['sɪərɪəl] n Fortsetzungsroman m;
(TV) Fernsehserie f; a number (fort)-
laufend; ~**ize** vt in Fortsetzungen
veröffentlichen/ senden.
series ['sɪərɪz] n Serie f, Reihe f.
serious ['sɪərɪəs] a ernst; injury schwer;
development ernstzunehmend; I'm ~ das
meine ich ernst; ~**ly** ad ernst(haft); hurt
schwer; ~**ness** Ernst m, Ernsthaftigkeit f.
sermon ['sɜ:mən] n Predigt f.
serpent ['sɜ:pənt] n Schlange f.
serrated [se'reɪtɪd] a gezackt; ~ **knife**
Sägemesser nt.
serum ['sɪərəm] n Serum nt.
servant ['sɜ:vənt] n Bedienstete(r) mf,
Diener(in f) m; see civil.
serve [sɜ:v] vt dienen (+dat); guest,
customer bedienen; food servieren; writ
zustellen (on sb jdm); vi dienen, nützen; (at
table) servieren; (tennis) geben, aufschlagen; it ~s him right das geschieht
ihm recht; that'll ~ the purpose das
reicht; that'll ~ as a table das geht als
Tisch; ~ out or up vt food auftragen,
servieren.
service ['sɜ:vɪs] n (help) Dienst m; (trains
etc) Verkehrsverbindungen pl; (hotel)
Service m, Bedienung f; (set of dishes)
Service nt; (Rel) Gottesdienst m; (Mil)
Waffengattung f; (car) Inspektion f; (for
TVs etc) Kundendienst m; (tennis)
Aufschlag m; to be of ~ to sb jdm einen
großen Dienst erweisen; can I be of ~?
kann ich Ihnen behilflich sein?; vt (Aut,
Tech) warten, überholen; the S~s pl
(armed forces) Streitkräfte pl; ~**able** a
brauchbar; ~ **area** (on motorway) Rast-
stätte f; ~ **charge** Bedienung f; ~**man**
(soldier etc) Soldat m; ~ **station** (Groß)-
tankstelle f.
servicing ['sɜ:vɪsɪŋ] n Wartung f.
serviette [sɜ:vɪ'et] n Serviette f.
servile ['sɜ:vaɪl] a sklavisch, unterwürfig.
session ['seʃən] n Sitzung f; (Pol) Sitzungs-
periode f.
set [set] n (collection of things) Satz m, Set
nt; (Rad, TV) Apparat m; (tennis) Satz m;
(group of people) Kreis m; (Cine) Szene f;
(Theat) Bühnenbild nt; a festgelegt;
(ready) bereit; ~ **phrase** feststehende(r)
Ausdruck m; ~ **square** Zeichendreieck
nt; irreg vt (place) setzen, stellen, legen;
(arrange) (an)ordnen; table decken; time,
price festsetzen; alarm, watch stellen; jewels
(ein)fassen; task stellen; exam ausarbeiten;
to ~ one's hair die Haare eindrehen; vi
(sun) untergehen; (become hard) fest

werden; (bone) zusammenwachsen; to ~
on fire anstecken; to ~ free freilassen;
to ~ sth going etw in Gang bringen; to
~ sail losfahren; ~ about vt task
anpacken; ~ aside vt beiseitelegen; ~
back vt zurückwerfen; ~ down vt
absetzen; ~ off vi ausbrechen; vt
(explode) zur Explosion bringen; alarm
losgehen lassen; (show up well) hervorheben; ~ out vi aufbrechen; vt (arrange)
anlegen, arrangieren; (state) darlegen; ~
up vt organization aufziehen; record aufstellen; monument erstellen; ~**back**
Rückschlag m.
settee [se'ti:] n Sofa nt.
setting ['setɪŋ] n (Mus) Vertonung f;
(scenery) Hintergrund m.
settle ['setl] vt beruhigen; (pay)
begleichen, bezahlen; (agree) regeln; vi
(also ~ down) sich einleben; (come to
rest) sich niederlassen; (sink) sich setzen;
(calm down) sich beruhigen; ~**ment**
Regelung f; (payment) Begleichung f;
(colony) Siedlung f, Niederlassung f; ~**r**
Siedler m.
setup ['setʌp] n (arrangement) Aufbau m,
Gliederung f; (situation) Situation f, Lage f.
seven ['sevn] num sieben; ~**teen** num
siebzehn; ~**th** a siebte(r,s); n Siebtel nt;
~**ty** num siebzig.
sever ['sevə°] vt abtrennen.
several ['sevrəl] a mehrere, verschiedene;
pron mehrere.
severance ['sevərəns] n Abtrennung f;
(fig) Abbruch m.
severe [sɪ'vɪə°] a (strict) streng; (serious)
schwer; climate rauh; (plain) streng,
schmucklos; ~**ly** ad (strictly) streng,
strikt; (seriously) schwer, ernstlich.
severity [sɪ'verɪtɪ] n Strenge f; Schwere f;
Ernst m.
sew [səʊ] vti irreg nähen; ~ **up** vt zunähen.
sewage ['sju:ɪdʒ] n Abwässer pl.
sewer ['sjuə°] n (Abwasser)kanal m.
sewing ['səʊɪŋ] n Näharbeit f; ~ **machine**
Nähmaschine f.
sex [seks] n Sex m; (gender) Geschlecht nt;
~ **act** Geschlechtsakt m.
sextant ['sekstənt] n Sextant m.
sextet [seks'tet] n Sextett nt.
sexual ['seksjʊəl] a sexuell, geschlechtlich,
Geschlechts-; ~**ly** ad geschlechtlich,
sexuell.
sexy ['seksɪ] a sexy.
shabbily ['ʃæbɪlɪ] ad schäbig.
shabbiness ['ʃæbɪnəs] n Schäbigkeit f.
shabby ['ʃæbɪ] a (lit, fig) schäbig.
shack [ʃæk] n Hütte f.
shackle ['ʃækl] vt fesseln; ~**s** pl (lit, fig)
Fesseln pl, Ketten pl.
shade [ʃeɪd] n Schatten m; (for lamp)
Lampenschirm m; (colour) Farbton m;
(small quantity) Spur f, Idee f; vt
abschirmen.
shadow ['ʃædəʊ] n Schatten m; vt (follow)
beschatten; a: ~ **cabinet** (Pol) Schatten-
kabinett nt; ~**y** a schattig.
shady ['ʃeɪdɪ] a schattig; (fig) zwielichtig.
shaft [ʃɑ:ft] n (of spear etc) Schaft m; (in

mine) Schacht *m*; (*Tech*) Welle *f*; (*of light*) Strahl *m*.

shaggy ['ʃægɪ] *a* struppig.

shake [ʃeɪk] *irreg vt* schütteln, rütteln; (*shock*) erschüttern; **to ~ hands** die Hand geben (*with dat*); **they shook hands** sie gaben sich die Hand; **to ~ one's head** den Kopf schütteln; *vi* (*move*) schwanken; (*tremble*) zittern, beben; *n* (*jerk*) Schütteln *nt*, Rütteln *nt*; **~ off** *vt* abschütteln; **~ up** *vt* (*lit*) aufschütteln; (*fig*) aufrütteln; **~-up** Aufrüttelung *f*; (*Pol*) Umgruppierung *f*.

shakily ['ʃeɪkɪlɪ] *ad* zitternd, unsicher.

shakiness ['ʃeɪkɪnəs] *n* Wackeligkeit *f*.

shaky ['ʃeɪkɪ] *a* zittrig; (*weak*) unsicher.

shale [ʃeɪl] *n* Schiefer(ton) *m*.

shall [ʃæl] *v aux irreg* werden; (*must*) sollen.

shallow ['ʃæləʊ] *a* flach, seicht (*also fig*); **~s** *pl* flache Stellen *pl*.

sham [ʃæm] *n* Täuschung *f*, Trug *m*, Schein *m*; *a* unecht, falsch.

shambles ['ʃæmblz] *n sing* Durcheinander *nt*.

shame [ʃeɪm] *n* Scham *f*; (*disgrace, pity*) Schande *f*; *vt* beschämen; **what a ~!** wie schade!; **~ on you!** schäm dich!; **~faced** *a* beschämt; **~ful** *a*, **~fully** *ad* schändlich; **~less** *a* schamlos; (*immodest*) unverschämt.

shampoo [ʃæm'puː] *n* Schampoon *nt*; *vt* schampunieren; **~ and set** Waschen *nt* und Legen.

shamrock ['ʃæmrɒk] *n* Kleeblatt *nt*.

shandy ['ʃændɪ] *n* Radlermaß *nt*.

shan't [ʃɑːnt] = **shall not**.

shanty ['ʃæntɪ] *n* (*cabin*) Hütte *f*, Baracke *f*; **~ town** Elendsviertel *nt*.

shape [ʃeɪp] *n* Form *f*, Gestalt *f*; *vt* formen, gestalten; **to take ~** Gestalt annehmen; **~less** *a* formlos; **~ly** *a* wohlgeformt, wohlproportioniert.

share [ʃɛə°] *n* (*An*)teil *m*; (*Fin*) Aktie *f*; *vt* teilen; **~holder** Aktionär *m*.

shark [ʃɑːk] *n* Hai(fisch) *m*; (*swindler*) Gauner *m*.

sharp [ʃɑːp] *a* scharf; *pin* spitz; *person* clever; *child* aufgeweckt; (*unscrupulous*) gerissen, raffiniert; (*Mus*) erhöht; **~ practices** *pl* Machenschaften *pl*; *n* (*Mus*) Kreuz *nt*; *ad* (*Mus*) zu hoch; **nine o'clock ~** Punkt neun; **look ~!** mach schnell!; **~en** *vt* schärfen; *pencil* spitzen; **~ener** Spitzer *m*; **~-eyed** *a* scharfsichtig; **~ness** Schärfe *f*, **~-witted** *a* scharfsinnig, aufgeweckt.

shatter ['ʃætə°] *vt* zerschmettern; (*fig*) zerstören; *vi* zerspringen; **~ed** *a* (*lit, fig*) kaputt; **~ing** *a experience* furchtbar.

shave [ʃeɪv] *n* Rasur *f*, Rasieren *nt*; **to have a ~** sich rasieren (lassen); *vt* rasieren; *vi* sich rasieren; **~n** *a head* geschoren; **~r** (*Elec*) Rasierapparat *m*, Rasierer *m*.

shaving ['ʃeɪvɪŋ] *n* (*action*) Rasieren *nt*; **~s** *pl* (*of wood etc*) Späne *pl*; **~ brush** Rasierpinsel *m*; **~ cream** Rasierkrem *f*; **~ point** Rasiersteckdose *f*; **~ soap** Rasierseife *f*.

shawl [ʃɔːl] *n* Schal *m*, Umhang *m*.

she [ʃiː] *pron* sie; *a* weiblich; **~-bear** Bärenweibchen *nt*.

sheaf [ʃiːf] *n* Garbe *f*.

shear [ʃɪə°] *vt irreg* scheren; **~ off** *vt* abscheren; **~s** *pl* Heckenschere *f*.

sheath [ʃiːθ] *n* Scheide *f*; **~e** [ʃiːð] *vt* einstecken; (*Tech*) verkleiden.

shed [ʃed] *n* Schuppen *m*; (*for animals*) Stall *m*; *vt irreg leaves etc* abwerfen, verlieren; *tears* vergießen.

she'd [ʃiːd] = **she had; she would**.

sheep [ʃiːp] *n* Schaf *nt*; **~dog** Schäferhund *m*; **~ish** *a* verschämt, betreten; **~skin** Schaffell *nt*.

sheer [ʃɪə°] *a* bloß, rein; (*steep*) steil, jäh; (*transparent*) (hauch)dünn, durchsichtig; *ad* (*directly*) direkt.

sheet [ʃiːt] *n* Bettuch *nt*, Bettlaken *nt*; (*of paper*) Blatt *nt*; (*of metal etc*) Platte *f*; (*of ice*) Fläche *f*; **~ lightning** Wetterleuchten *nt*.

sheik(h) [ʃeɪk] *n* Scheich *m*.

shelf [ʃelf] *n* Bord *nt*, Regal *nt*.

she'll [ʃiːl] = **she will; she shall**.

shell [ʃel] *n* Schale *f*; (*sea*—) Muschel *f*; (*explosive*) Granate *f*; (*of building*) Mauern *pl*; *vt peas* schälen; (*fire on*) beschießen; **~fish** Schalentier *nt*; (*as food*) Meeresfrüchte *pl*.

shelter ['ʃeltə°] *n* Schutz *m*; Bunker *m*; *vt* schützen, bedecken; *refugees* aufnehmen; *vi* sich unterstellen; **~ed** *a life* behütet; *spot* geschützt.

shelve [ʃelv] *vt* aufschieben; *vi* abfallen.

shelving ['ʃelvɪŋ] *n* Regale *pl*.

shepherd ['ʃepəd] *n* Schäfer *m*; *vt* treiben, führen; **~ess** Schäferin *f*.

sheriff ['ʃerɪf] *n* Sheriff *m*.

sherry ['ʃerɪ] *n* Sherry *m*.

she's [ʃiːz] = **she is; she has**.

shield [ʃiːld] *n* Schild *m*; (*fig*) Schirm *m*, Schutz *m*; *vt* (be)schirmen; (*Tech*) abschirmen.

shift [ʃɪft] *n* Veränderung *f*, Verschiebung *f*; (*work*) Schicht *f*; *vt* (ver)rücken, verschieben; *office* verlegen; *arm* wegnehmen; *vi* sich verschieben; (*col*) schnell fahren; **~ work** Schichtarbeit *f*; **~y** *a* verschlagen.

shilling ['ʃɪlɪŋ] *n* (*old*) Shilling *m*.

shilly-shally ['ʃɪlɪʃælɪ] *vi* zögern.

shimmer ['ʃɪmə°] *n* Schimmer *m*; *vi* schimmern.

shin [ʃɪn] *n* Schienbein *nt*.

shine [ʃaɪn] *n* Glanz *m*, Schein *m*; *irreg vt* polieren; **to ~ a torch on sb** jdn (mit einer Lampe) anleuchten; *vi* scheinen; (*fig*) glänzen.

shingle ['ʃɪŋgl] *n* Schindel *f*; (*on beach*) Strandkies *m*; **~s** *pl* (*Med*) Gürtelrose *f*.

shining ['ʃaɪnɪŋ] *a light* strahlend.

shiny ['ʃaɪnɪ] *a* glänzend.

ship [ʃɪp] *n* Schiff *nt*; *vt* an Bord bringen, verladen; (*transport as cargo*) verschiffen; **~-building** Schiffbau *m*; **~ canal** Seekanal *m*; **~ment** Verladung *f*; (*goods shipped*) Schiffsladung *f*; **~per** Verschiffer *m*; **~ping** (*act*) Verschiffung *f*; (*ships*) Schiffahrt *f*, **~shape** *a* in Ordnung;

~ wreck Schiffbruch m; (destroyed ship)
Wrack nt; ~ yard Werft f.

shirk [ʃɜːk] vt ausweichen (+dat).

shirt [ʃɜːt] n (Ober)hemd nt; in ~-sleeves
in Hemdsärmeln; ~y a (col) mürrisch.

shiver ['ʃɪvə*] n Schauer m; vi frösteln,
zittern.

shoal [ʃəʊl] n (Fisch)schwarm m.

shock [ʃɒk] n Stoß m, Erschütterung f;
(mental) Schock m; (Elec) Schlag m; vt
erschüttern; (offend) schockieren; ~
absorber Stoßdämpfer m; ~ing a unerhört, schockierend; ~proof a watch
stoßsicher.

shoddiness ['ʃɒdɪnəs] n Schäbigkeit f.

shoddy ['ʃɒdɪ] a schäbig.

shoe [ʃuː] n Schuh m; (of horse) Hufeisen nt;
vt irreg horse beschlagen; ~brush Schuh-
bürste f; ~horn Schuhlöffel m; ~lace
Schnürsenkel m.

shoot [ʃuːt] n (branch) Schößling m; irreg vt
gun abfeuern; goal, arrow schießen; (kill)
erschießen; film drehen, filmen; shot in
the leg ins Bein getroffen; vi (gun, move
quickly) schießen; don't ~! nicht
schießen!; ~ down vt abschießen; ~ing
Schießerei f; ~ing star Sternschnuppe f.

shop [ʃɒp] n Geschäft nt, Laden m; (workshop) Werkstatt f; vi (also go ~ping)
einkaufen gehen; ~ assistant Ver-
käufer(in f) m; ~keeper Geschäfts-
inhaber m; ~lifter Ladendieb m;
~lifting Ladendiebstahl m; ~per
Käufer(in f) m; ~ping Einkaufen nt,
Einkauf m; ~ping bag Einkaufstasche f;
~ping centre, (US) ~ping center Ein-
kaufszentrum   nt;   ~-soiled   a
angeschmutzt; ~ steward Betriebsrat m;
~ window Schaufenster nt; see talk.

shore [ʃɔː*] n Ufer nt; (of sea) Strand m,
Küste f; vt: ~ up abstützen.

short [ʃɔːt] a kurz; person klein; (curt) kurz
angebunden; (measure) zu knapp; to be ~
of zu wenig . . . haben; two ~ zwei zu
wenig; n (Elec: ~circuit) Kurzschluß m;
ad (suddenly) plötzlich; vi (Elec) einen
Kurzschluß haben; to cut ~ abkürzen; to
fall ~ mit einem Kurzschluß haben; for ~ kurz;
~age Knappheit f, Mangel m; ~bread
Mürbegebäck nt, Heidesand m; ~-circuit
Kurzschluß m; vi einen Kurzschluß haben;
~coming Fehler m, Mangel m; ~ cut
Abkürzung f; ~en vt (ab)kürzen; clothes
kürzer machen; ~hand Stenographie f,
Kurzschrift f; ~hand typist Stenotypistin
f; ~list engere Wahl f; ~-lived a kurzlebig; ~ly ad bald; ~ness Kürze f; ~s pl
Shorts   pl;   ~-sighted a   (lit, fig)
kurzsichtig; ~-sightedness Kurzsichtig-
keit f; ~ story Kurzgeschichte f;
~-tempered a leicht aufbrausend;
~-term a effect kurzfristig; ~ wave
(Rad) Kurzwelle f.

shot [ʃɒt] n (from gun) Schuß m; (person)
Schütze m; (try) Versuch m, (injection)
Spritze f; (Phot) Aufnahme f, Schnapp-
schuß m; like a ~ wie der Blitz; ~gun
Schrotflinte f.

should [ʃʊd] v aux: I ~ go now ich sollte
jetzt gehen; I ~ say ich würde sagen; I

~ like to ich möchte gerne, ich würde
gerne.

shoulder ['ʃəʊldə*] n Schulter f; vt rifle
schultern; (fig) auf sich nehmen; ~ blade
Schulterblatt nt.

shouldn't ['ʃʊdnt] = should not.

shout [ʃaʊt] n Schrei m; (call) Ruf m; vt
rufen; vi schreien, laut rufen; to ~ at
anbrüllen; ~ing Geschrei nt.

shove [ʃʌv] n Schubs m, Stoß m; vt
schieben, stoßen, schubsen; ~ off vi
(Naut) abstoßen; (fig col) abhauen.

shovel ['ʃʌvl] n Schaufel f; vt schaufeln.

show [ʃəʊ] n (display) Schau f; (exhibition)
Ausstellung f; (Cine, Theat) Vorstellung f,
Show f; irreg vt zeigen; kindness erweisen;
vi zu sehen sein; to ~ sb in jdn herein-
führen; to ~ sb out jdn hinausbegleiten;
~ off vi (pej) angeben, protzen; vt
(display) ausstellen; ~ up vi (stand out)
sich abheben; (arrive) erscheinen; vt aufzeigen; (unmask) bloßstellen; ~ business
Showbusineß nt; ~down Kraftprobe f,
endgültige Auseinandersetzung f.

shower ['ʃaʊə*] n Schauer m; (of stones)
(Stein)hagel m; (of sparks) (Funken)regen
m; (~ bath) Dusche f; to have a ~
duschen; vt (fig) überschütten; ~proof a
wasserabstoßend;   ~y   a   weather
regnerisch.

showground ['ʃəʊɡraʊnd] n Ausstellungs-
gelände nt.

showing ['ʃəʊɪŋ] n (of film) Vorführung f.

show   jumping   ['ʃəʊdʒʌmpɪŋ]   n
Turnierreiten nt.

showmanship ['ʃəʊmənʃɪp] n Talent nt als
Showman.

show-off ['ʃəʊɒf] n Angeber m.

showpiece ['ʃəʊpiːs] n Paradestück nt.

showroom ['ʃəʊrʊm] n Ausstellungsraum
m.

shrapnel ['ʃræpnl] n Schrapnell nt.

shred [ʃred] n Fetzen m; vt zerfetzen;
(Cook) raspeln; in ~s in Fetzen.

shrewd a, ~ly ad [ʃruːd, -lɪ] scharfsinnig,
clever; ~ness Scharfsinn m.

shriek [ʃriːk] n Schrei m; vti kreischen,
schreien.

shrill [ʃrɪl] a schrill, gellend.

shrimp [ʃrɪmp] n Krabbe f, Garnele f.

shrine [ʃraɪn] n Schrein m.

shrink [ʃrɪŋk] irreg vi schrumpfen,
eingehen; vt einschrumpfen lassen; ~age
Schrumpfung f; ~ away vi zurückschrecken (from vor +dat).

shrivel ['ʃrɪvl] vti (also ~ up) schrumpfen,
schrumpeln.

shroud [ʃraʊd] n Leichentuch nt; vt
umhüllen, (ein)hüllen.

Shrove Tuesday ['ʃrəʊv'tjuːzdeɪ] n Fast-
nachtsdienstag m.

shrub [ʃrʌb] n Busch m, Strauch m; ~bery
Gebüsch nt.

shrug [ʃrʌɡ] n Achselzucken nt; vi die
Achseln zucken; ~ off vt auf die leichte
Schulter nehmen.

shrunken ['ʃrʌŋkən] a eingelaufen.

shudder ['ʃʌdə*] n Schauder m; vi
schaudern.

shuffle ['ʃʌfl] n (Cards) (Karten)mischen

nt; *vt cards* mischen; *vi* (*walk*) schlurfen.
shun [ʃʌn] *vt* scheuen, (ver)meiden.
shunt [ʃʌnt] *vt* rangieren.
shut [ʃʌt] *irreg vt* schließen, zumachen; *vi* sich schließen (lassen); ~ **down** *vti* schließen; ~ **off** *vt supply* abdrehen; ~ **up** *vi* (*keep quiet*) den Mund halten; *vt* (*close*) zuschließen; (*silence*) zum Schweigen bringen; ~ **up!** halt den Mund!; ~**ter** Fensterladen *m*, Rolladen *m*; (*Phot*) Verschluß *m*.
shuttlecock [ʃʌtlkɒk] *n* Federball *m*; Federballspiel *nt*.
shuttle service [ʃʌtlsɜːvɪs] *n* Pendelverkehr *m*.
shy *a*, ~**ly** *ad* [ʃaɪ, -lɪ] schüchtern, scheu; ~**ness** Schüchternheit *f*, Zurückhaltung *f*.
Siamese [saɪəˈmiːz] *a*: ~ **cat** Siamkatze *f*; ~ **twins** *pl* siamesische Zwillinge *pl*.
sick [sɪk] *a* krank; *humour* schwarz; *joke* makaber; **I feel** ~ mir ist schlecht; **I was** ~ ich habe gebrochen; **to be** ~ **of** *sb/sth* jdn/etw satt haben; ~ **bay** (*Schiffs*)lazarett *nt*; ~**bed** Krankenbett *nt*; ~**en** *vt* (*disgust*) krankmachen; *vi* krank werden; ~**ening** *a sight* widerlich; (*annoying*) zum Weinen.
sickle [ˈsɪkl] *n* Sichel *f*.
sick leave [ˈsɪkliːv] *n*: **to be on** ~ krank geschrieben sein.
sick list [ˈsɪklɪst] *n* Krankenliste *f*.
sickly [ˈsɪklɪ] *a* kränklich, blaß; (*causing nausea*) widerlich.
sickness [ˈsɪknəs] *n* Krankheit *f*; (*vomiting*) Übelkeit *f*, Erbrechen *nt*.
sick pay [ˈsɪkpeɪ] *n* Krankengeld *nt*.
side [saɪd] *n* Seite *f*; *a door, entrance* Seiten-, Neben-; **by the** ~ **of** neben; **on all** ~**s** von allen Seiten; **to take** ~**s** (**with**) Partei nehmen (für); *vi*: ~ **with sb** es halten mit jdm; ~**board** Anrichte *f*, Sideboard *nt*; ~**boards**, ~**burns** *pl* Koteletten *pl*; ~ **effect** Nebenwirkung *f*; ~**light** (*Aut*) Parkleuchte *f*, Standlicht *nt*; ~**line** (*Sport*) Seitenlinie *f*; (*fig: hobby*) Nebenbeschäftigung *f*; ~ **road** Nebenstraße *f*; ~ **show** Nebenausstellung *f*; ~**track** *vt* (*fig*) ablenken; ~**walk** (*US*) Bürgersteig *m*; ~**ways** *ad* seitwärts.
siding [ˈsaɪdɪŋ] *n* Nebengleis *nt*.
sidle [ˈsaɪdl] *vi*: ~ **up** sich heranmachen (*to* an +*acc*).
siege [siːdʒ] *n* Belagerung *f*.
siesta [sɪˈestə] *n* Siesta *f*.
sieve [sɪv] *n* Sieb *nt*; *vt* sieben.
sift [sɪft] *vt* sieben; (*fig*) sichten.
sigh [saɪ] *n* Seufzer *m*; *vi* seufzen.
sight [saɪt] *n* (*power of seeing*) Sehvermögen *nt*, Augenlicht *nt*; (*view*) (An)blick *m*; (*scene*) Aussicht *f*, Blick *m*; (*of gun*) Zielvorrichtung *f*, Korn *nt*; ~**s** *pl* (*of city etc*) Sehenswürdigkeiten *pl*; **in** ~ in Sicht; **out of** ~ außer Sicht; ~**seeing** Besuch *m* von Sehenswürdigkeiten; **to go** ~**seeing** Sehenswürdigkeiten besichtigen; ~**seer** Tourist *m*.
sign [saɪn] *n* Zeichen *nt*; (*notice, road* — *etc*) Schild *nt*; *vt* unterschreiben; ~ **out** *vi* sich austragen; ~ **up** *vi* (*Mil*) sich verpflichten; *vt* verpflichten.

signal [ˈsɪɡnl] *n* Signal *nt*; *vt* ein Zeichen geben (+*dat*).
signatory [ˈsɪɡnətrɪ] *n* Signatar *m*.
signature [ˈsɪɡnətʃə*] *n* Unterschrift *f*; ~ **tune** Erkennungsmelodie *f*.
signet ring [ˈsɪɡnətrɪŋ] *n* Siegelring *m*.
significance [sɪɡˈnɪfɪkəns] *n* Bedeutung *f*.
significant [sɪɡˈnɪfɪkənt] *a* (*meaning sth*) bedeutsam; (*important*) bedeutend, wichtig; ~**ly** *ad* bezeichnenderweise.
signify [ˈsɪɡnɪfaɪ] *vt* bedeuten; (*show*) andeuten, zu verstehen geben.
sign language [ˈsaɪnlæŋɡwɪdʒ] *n* Zeichensprache *f*, Fingersprache *f*.
signpost [ˈsaɪnpəʊst] *n* Wegweiser *m*, Schild *nt*.
silence [ˈsaɪləns] *n*. Stille *f*, Ruhe *f*; (*of person*) Schweigen *nt*; *vt* zum Schweigen bringen; ~**r** (*on gun*) Schalldämpfer *m*; (*Aut*) Auspufftopf *m*.
silent [ˈsaɪlənt] *a* still; *person* schweigsam; ~**ly** *ad* schweigend, still.
silhouette [sɪluˈet] *n* Silhouette *f*, Umriß *m*; (*picture*) Schattenbild *nt*; *vt*: **to be** ~**d against** *sth* sich als Silhouette abheben gegen etw.
silk [sɪlk] *n* Seide *f*; *a* seiden, Seiden-; ~**y** *a* seidig.
silliness [ˈsɪlɪnəs] *n* Albernheit *f*, Dummheit *f*.
silly [ˈsɪlɪ] *a* dumm, albern.
silo [ˈsaɪləʊ] *n* Silo *m*.
silt [sɪlt] *n* Schlamm *m*, Schlick *m*.
silver [ˈsɪlvə*] *n* Silber *nt*; *a* silbern, Silber-; ~ **paper** Silberpapier *nt*; ~-**plate** Silber(-geschirr) *nt*; ~-**plated** *a* versilbert; ~**smith** Silberschmied *m*; ~**ware** Silber *nt*; ~**y** *a* silbern.
similar [ˈsɪmɪlə*] *a* ähnlich (*to dat*); ~**ity** [sɪmɪˈlærɪtɪ] Ähnlichkeit *f*; ~**ly** *ad* in ähnlicher Weise.
simile [ˈsɪmɪlɪ] *n* Vergleich *m*.
simmer [ˈsɪmə*] *vti* sieden (lassen).
simple [ˈsɪmpl] *a* einfach; *dress also* schlicht; ~(-**minded**) *a* naiv, einfältig.
simplicity [sɪmˈplɪsɪtɪ] *n* Einfachheit *f*; (*of person*) Einfältigkeit *f*.
simplification [sɪmplɪfɪˈkeɪʃən] *n* Vereinfachung *f*.
simplify [ˈsɪmplɪfaɪ] *vt* vereinfachen.
simply [ˈsɪmplɪ] *ad* einfach; (*only*) bloß, nur.
simulate [ˈsɪmjuleɪt] *vt* simulieren.
simulation [sɪmjuˈleɪʃən] *n* Simulieren *nt*.
simultaneous *a*, ~**ly** *ad* [sɪməlˈteɪnɪəs, -lɪ] gleichzeitig.
sin [sɪn] *n* Sünde *f*; *vi* sündigen.
since [sɪns] *ad* seither; *prep* seit, seitdem; *cj* (*time*) seit; (*because*) da, weil.
sincere [sɪnˈsɪə*] *a* aufrichtig, ehrlich, offen; ~**ly** aufrichtig; **yours** ~**ly** mit freundlichen Grüßen.
sincerity [sɪnˈserɪtɪ] *n* Aufrichtigkeit *f*.
sinecure [ˈsaɪnɪkjuə*] *n* einträgliche(r) Ruheposten *m*.
sinew [ˈsɪnjuː] *n* Sehne *f*; (*of animal*) Flechse *f*.
sinful [ˈsɪnful] *a* sündig, sündhaft.
sing [sɪŋ] *vti irreg* singen.

singe [sɪndʒ] vt versengen.
singer [ˈsɪŋəˀ] n Sänger(in f) m.
singing [ˈsɪŋɪŋ] n Singen nt, Gesang m.
single [ˈsɪŋgl] a (one only) einzig; bed, room
Einzel-, einzeln; (unmarried) ledig; ticket
einfach; (having one part only) einzeln; n
(ticket) einfache Fahrkarte f; ~s (tennis)
Einzel nt; ~ **out** vt aussuchen, auswählen;
~**breasted** a einreihig; **in ~ file**
hintereinander; ~**handed** a allein;
~**minded** a zielstrebig.
singlet [ˈsɪŋglət] n Unterhemd nt.
single [ˈsɪŋglɪ] ad einzeln, allein.
singular [ˈsɪŋgjuləˀ] a (Gram) Singular-;
(odd) merkwürdig, seltsam; n (Gram)
Einzahl f, Singular m; ~**ly** ad besonders,
höchst.
sinister [ˈsɪnɪstəˀ] a (evil) böse; (ghostly)
unheimlich.
sink [sɪŋk] n Spülbecken nt, Ausguß m;
irreg vt ship versenken; (dig) einsenken; vi
sinken; ~ **in** vi (news etc) eingehen
(+dat); ~**ing** a feeling flau.
sinner [ˈsɪnəˀ] n Sünder(in f) m.
sinuous [ˈsɪnjuəs] a gewunden, sich
schlängelnd.
sinus [ˈsaɪnəs] n (Anat) Nasenhöhle f, Sinus
m.
sip [sɪp] n Schlückchen nt; vt nippen an
(+dat).
siphon [ˈsaɪfən] n Siphon(flasche f) m; ~
off vt absaugen; (fig) abschöpfen.
sir [sɜːˀ] n (respect) Herr m; (knight) Sir m;
yes S~ ja(wohl, mein Herr).
siren [ˈsaɪərən] n Sirene f.
sirloin [ˈsɜːlɔɪn] n Lendenstück nt.
sirocco [sɪˈrɒkəu] n Schirokko m.
sissy [ˈsɪsɪ] n = **cissy**.
sister [ˈsɪstəˀ] n Schwester f; (nurse) Ober-
schwester f; (nun) Ordensschwester f;
~**-in-law** Schwägerin f.
sit [sɪt] irreg vi sitzen; (hold session) tagen,
Sitzung halten; vt exam machen; **to ~**
tight abwarten; ~ **down** vi sich
hinsetzen; ~ **up** vi (after lying) sich
aufsetzen; (straight) sich gerade setzen; (at
night) aufbleiben.
site [saɪt] n Platz m; vt plazieren, legen.
sit-in [ˈsɪtɪn] n Sit-in nt.
siting [ˈsaɪtɪŋ] n (location) Platz m, Lage f.
sitting [ˈsɪtɪŋ] n (meeting) Sitzung f,
Tagung f; ~ **room** Wohnzimmer nt.
situated [ˈsɪtjueɪtɪd] a: **to be ~** liegen.
situation [sɪtjuˈeɪʃən] n Situation f, Lage f;
(place) Lage f; (employment) Stelle f.
six [sɪks] num sechs; ~**teen** num sechzehn;
~**th** a sechste(r,s); n Sechstel nt; ~**ty**
num sechzig.
size [saɪz] n Größe f; (of project) Umfang
m; (glue) Kleister m; ~ **up** vt (assess)
abschätzen, einschätzen; ~**able** a ziemlich groß, ansehnlich.
sizzle [ˈsɪzl] n Zischen nt; vi zischen; (Cook)
brutzeln.
skate [skeɪt] n Schlittschuh m; vi
Schlittschuh laufen; ~**r** Schlittschuh-
läufer(in f) m.
skating [ˈskeɪtɪŋ] n Eislauf m; **to go ~**
Eislaufen gehen; ~ **rink** Eisbahn f.

skeleton [ˈskelɪtn] n Skelett nt; (fig) Gerüst
nt; ~ **key** Dietrich m.
skeptic [ˈskeptɪk] n (US) = **sceptic**.
sketch [sketʃ] n Skizze f; (Theat) Sketch m;
vt skizzieren, eine Skizze machen von;
~**book** Skizzenbuch nt; ~**ing** Skizzieren
nt; ~ **pad** Skizzenblock m; ~**y** a skizzen-
haft.
skewer [ˈskjuəˀ] n Fleischspieß m.
ski [skiː] n Ski m, Schi m; vi Ski or Schi
laufen; ~ **boot** Skistiefel m.
skid [skɪd] n (Aut) Schleudern nt; vi
rutschen; (Aut) schleudern.
skidmark [ˈskɪdmɑːk] n Rutschspur f.
skier [ˈskiːəˀ] n Skiläufer(in f) m.
skiing [ˈskiːɪŋ] n: **to go ~** Skilaufen gehen.
ski-jump [ˈskiːdʒʌmp] n Sprungschanze f;
vi Ski springen.
ski-lift [ˈskiːlɪft] n Skilift m.
skilful a, ~**ly** ad [ˈskɪlful, -fəlɪ] geschickt.
skill [skɪl] n Können nt, Geschicklichkeit f;
~**ed** a geschickt; worker Fach-, gelernt.
skim [skɪm] vt liquid abschöpfen; milk
entrahmen; (read) überfliegen; (glide
over) gleiten über (+acc).
skimp [skɪmp] vt (do carelessly) oberflächlich tun; ~**y** a work schlecht gemacht;
dress knapp.
skin [skɪn] n Haut f; (peel) Schale f; vt
abhäuten; schälen; ~**-deep** a oberflächlich; ~ **diving** Schwimmtauchen nt;
~**ny** a dünn; ~**tight** a dress etc hauteng.
skip [skɪp] n Sprung m, Hopser m; vi
hüpfen, springen; (with rope) Seil springen;
vt (pass over) übergehen.
ski pants [ˈskiːpænts] npl Skihosen pl.
skipper [ˈskɪpəˀ] n (Naut) Schiffer m,
Kapitän m; (Sport) Mannschaftskapitän m;
vt führen.
skipping rope [ˈskɪpɪŋrəup] n Hüpfseil nt.
skirmish [ˈskɜːmɪʃ] n Scharmützel nt.
skirt [skɜːt] n Rock m; vt herumgehen um;
(fig) umgehen.
ski run [ˈskiːrʌn] n Skiabfahrt f.
skit [skɪt] n Parodie f.
ski tow [ˈskiːtəu] n Schlepplift m.
skittle [ˈskɪtl] n Kegel m; ~**s** (game)
Kegeln nt.
skive [skaɪv] vi (Brit col) schwänzen.
skulk [skʌlk] vi sich herumdrücken.
skull [skʌl] n Schädel m; ~ **and cross-
bones** Totenkopf m.
skunk [skʌŋk] n Stinktier nt.
sky [skaɪ] n Himmel m ~**-blue** a himmelblau; n Himmelblau nt; ~**light** Dach-
fenster nt, Oberlicht nt; ~**scraper**
Wolkenkratzer m.
slab [slæb] n (of stone) Platte f; (of chocolate) Tafel f.
slack [slæk] a (loose) lose, schlaff, locker;
business flau; (careless) nachlässig, lasch;
vi nachlässig sein; n (in rope etc) durch-
hängende(s) Teil nt; **to take up the ~**
strafziehen; ~**s** pl Hose(n pl) f; ~**en**
(also ~**en off**) vi schlaff/locker werden;
(become slower) nachlassen, stocken; vt
(loosen) lockern; ~**ness** Schlaffheit f.
slag [slæg] n Schlacke f; ~ **heap** Halde f.
slalom [ˈslɑːləm] n Slalom m.

slam [slæm] n Knall m; vt door zuschlagen, zuknallen; (throw down) knallen; vi zuschlagen.

slander ['slɑːndə*] n Verleumdung f; vt verleumden; **~ous** a verleumderisch.

slang [slæŋ] n Slang m; Jargon m.

slant [slɑːnt] n (lit) Schräge f; (fig) Tendenz f, Einstellung f; vt schräg legen; vi schräg liegen; **~ing** a schräg.

slap [slæp] n Schlag m, Klaps m; vt schlagen, einen Klaps geben (+dat); ad (directly) geradewegs; **~dash** a salopp; **~stick** (comedy) Klamauk m; **~-up** a meal erstklassig, prima.

slash [slæʃ] n Hieb m, Schnittwunde f; vt (auf)schlitzen; expenditure radikal kürzen.

slate [sleɪt] n (stone) Schiefer m; (roofing) Dachziegel m; vt (criticize) verreißen.

slaughter ['slɔːtə*] n (of animals) Schlachten nt; (of people) Gemetzel nt; vt schlachten; people niedermetzeln.

slave [sleɪv] n Sklave m Sklavin f; vi schuften, sich schinden; **~ry** Sklaverei f; (work) Schinderei f.

slavish a, **~ly** ad ['sleɪvɪʃ, -lɪ] sklavisch.

slay [sleɪ] vt irreg ermorden.

sleazy ['sliːzɪ] a place schmierig.

sledge ['sledʒ] n Schlitten m; **~hammer** m Schmiedehammer m.

sleek [sliːk] a glatt, glänzend; shape rassig.

sleep [sliːp] n Schlaf m; vi irreg schlafen; **to go to ~** einschlafen; **~ in** vi ausschlafen; (oversleep) verschlafen; **~er** (person) Schläfer m; (Rail) Schlafwagen m; (beam) Schwelle f; **~ily** ad schläfrig; **~iness** Schläfrigkeit f; **~ing bag** Schlafsack m; **~ing car** Schlafwagen m; **~ing pill** Schlaftablette f; **~less** a night schlaflos; **~lessness** Schlaflosigkeit f; **~walker** Schlafwandler m; **~y** schläfrig.

sleet [sliːt] n Schneeregen m.

sleeve [sliːv] n Ärmel m; (of record) Umschlag m; **~less** a garment ärmellos.

sleigh [sleɪ] n Pferdeschlitten m.

sleight [slaɪt] n: **~ of hand** Fingerfertigkeit f.

slender ['slendə*] a schlank; (fig) gering.

slice [slaɪs] n Scheibe f; vt in Scheiben schneiden.

slick [slɪk] a (clever) raffiniert, aalglatt; n Ölteppich m.

slide [slaɪd] n Rutschbahn f; (Phot) Dia-(positiv) nt; (for hair) (Haar-)spange f; (fall in prices) (Preis)rutsch m; vt irreg vt schieben; vi (slip) gleiten, rutschen; **to let things ~** die Dinge schleifen lassen; **~rule** Rechenschieber m.

sliding ['slaɪdɪŋ] a door Schiebe-.

slight [slaɪt] a zierlich; (trivial) geringfügig; (small) leicht, gering; n Kränkung f; vt (offend) kränken; **~ly** ad etwas, ein bißchen.

slim [slɪm] a schlank; book dünn; chance gering; vi eine Schlankheitskur machen.

slime [slaɪm] n Schlamm m; Schleim m.

slimming ['slɪmɪŋ] n Schlankheitskur f.

slimness ['slɪmnəs] n Schlankheit f.

slimy ['slaɪmɪ] a glitschig; (dirty) schlammig; person schmierig.

sling [slɪŋ] n Schlinge f; (weapon) Schleuder f; vt irreg werfen; (hurl) schleudern.

slip [slɪp] n (slipping) Ausgleiten nt, Rutschen nt; (mistake) Flüchtigkeitsfehler m; (petticoat) Unterrock m; (of paper) Zettel m; **to give sb the ~** jdn entwischen; **~ of the tongue** Versprecher m; vt (put) stecken, schieben; **it ~ped my mind** das ist mir entfallen, ich habe es vergessen; vi (lose balance) ausrutschen; (move) gleiten, rutschen; (make mistake) einen Fehler machen; (decline) nachlassen; **to let things ~** die Dinge schleifen lassen; **~ away** vi sich wegstehlen; **~ by** vi (time) verstreichen; **~ in** vt hineingleiten lassen; vi (errors) sich einschleichen; **~ out** vi hinausschlüpfen; **~per** Hausschuh m; **~pery** a glatt; (tricky) aalglatt, gerissen; **~road** Auffahrt f/Ausfahrt f; **~shod** a schlampig; **~stream** Windschatten m; **~-up** Panne f; **~way** Auslaufbahn f.

slit [slɪt] n Schlitz m; vt irreg aufschlitzen.

slither ['slɪðə*] vi schlittern; (snake) sich schlängeln.

slob [slɒb] n (col) Klotz m.

slog [slɒg] n (great effort) Plackerei f; vi (work hard) schuften.

slogan ['slɔːgən] n Schlagwort nt; (Comm) Werbespruch m.

slop [slɒp] vi überschwappen; vt verschütten.

slope [sləup] n Neigung f, Schräge f; (of mountains) (Ab)hang m; vi: **~ down** sich senken; **~ up** ansteigen.

sloping ['sləupɪŋ] a schräg; shoulders abfallend; ground abschüssig.

sloppily ['slɒpɪlɪ] ad schlampig.

sloppiness ['slɒpɪnəs] n Matschigkeit f; (of work) Nachlässigkeit f.

sloppy ['slɒpɪ] a (wet) matschig; (careless) schlampig; (silly) rührselig.

slot [slɒt] n Schlitz m; vt: **~ sth in etw** einlegen; **~ machine** Automat m.

slouch [slautʃ] vi krumm dasitzen or dastehen.

slovenly ['slʌvnlɪ] a schlampig; speech salopp.

slow [sləu] a langsam; **to be ~** (clock) nachgehen; (stupid) begriffsstutzig sein; **~ down** vi langsamer werden; **~ down!** mach langsam!; vt aufhalten, langsamer machen, verlangsamen; **~ up** vi sich verlangsamen, sich verzögern; vt aufhalten, langsamer machen; **~ly** ad langsam; allmählich; **in ~ motion** in Zeitlupe.

sludge [slʌdʒ] n Schlamm m, Matsch m.

slug [slʌg] n Nacktschnecke f; (col: bullet) Kugel f; **~gish** a träge; (Comm) schleppend; **~gishly** ad träge; **~gishness** Langsamkeit f, Trägheit f.

sluice [sluːs] n Schleuse f.

slum [slʌm] n Elendsviertel nt, Slum m.

slumber ['slʌmbə*] n Schlummer m.

slump [slʌmp] n Rückgang m; vi fallen, stürzen.

slur [sləː*] n Undeutlichkeit f; (insult) Verleumdung f; vt (also ~ over) hinweggehen über (+*acc*); ~**red** [slɔ:d] *a pro-nunciation* undeutlich.

slush [slʌʃ] *n* (*snow*) Schneematsch *m*; (*mud*) Schlamm *m*; ~**y** *a* (*lit*) matschig; (*fig: sentimental*) schmalzig.

slut [slʌt] *n* Schlampe *f*.

sly *a*, ~**ly** [slaɪ, -lɪ] *ad* schlau, verschlagen; ~**ness** Schlauheit *f*.

smack [smæk] *n* Klaps *m*; *vt* einen Klaps geben (+*dat*); to ~ **one's lips** schmatzen, sich (*dat*) die Lippen lecken; *vi* ~ **of** riechen nach.

small [smɔ:l] *a* klein; ~ **change** Kleingeld *nt*; ~**holding** Kleinlandbesitz *m*; ~ **hours** *pl* frühe Morgenstunden *pl*; ~**ish** *a* ziemlich klein; ~**ness** Kleinheit *f*; ~**pox** Pocken *pl*; ~**-scale** *a* klein, in kleinem Maßstab; ~ **talk** Konversation *f*, Geplauder *nt*.

smarmy ['smɑ:mɪ] *a* (*col*) schmierig.

smart *a*, ~**ly** *ad* [smɑ:t, -lɪ] (*fashionable*) elegant, schick; (*neat*) adrett; (*clever*) clever; (*quick*) scharf; *vi* brennen, schmerzen; ~**en up** *vi* sich in Schale werfen; *vt* herausputzen; ~**ness** Gescheitheit *f*; Eleganz *f*.

smash [smæʃ] *n* Zusammenstoß *m*; (*tennis*) Schmetterball *m*; *vt* (*break*) zerschmettern; (*destroy*) vernichten; *vi* (*break*) zersplittern, zerspringen; ~**ing** *a* (*col*) toll, großartig.

smattering ['smætərɪŋ] *n* oberflächliche Kenntnis *f*.

smear [smɪə*] *n* Fleck *m*; *vt* beschmieren.

smell [smel] *n* Geruch *m*; (*sense*) Geruchssinn *m*; *vti irreg* riechen (*of* nach); ~**y** *a* übelriechend.

smile [smaɪl] *n* Lächeln *nt*; *vi* lächeln.

smirk [smɜ:k] *n* blöde(s) Grinsen *nt*; *vi* blöde grinsen.

smith [smɪθ] *n* Schmied *m*; ~**y** ['smɪðɪ] Schmiede *f*.

smock [smɒk] *n* Kittel *m*.

smog [smɒg] *n* Smog *m*.

smoke [sməuk] *n* Rauch *m*; *vt* rauchen; *food* räuchern; *vi* rauchen; ~**r** Raucher *m*; (*Rail*) Raucherabteil *nt*; ~ **screen** Rauchwand *f*.

smoking ['sməukɪŋ] *n* Rauchen *nt*; 'no ~' 'Rauchen verboten'.

smoky ['sməukɪ] *a* rauchig; *room* verraucht; *taste* geräuchert.

smolder ['sməuldə*] *vi* (*US*) = **smoulder**.

smooth [smu:ð] *a* glatt; *movement* geschmeidig; *person* glatt, gewandt; *vt* (*also* ~ **out**) glätten, glattstreichen; ~**ly** *ad* glatt, eben; (*fig*) reibungslos; ~**ness** Glätte *f*.

smother ['smʌðə*] *vt* ersticken.

smoulder ['sməuldə*] *vi* glimmen, schwelen.

smudge [smʌdʒ] *n* Schmutzfleck *m*; *vt* beschmieren.

smug [smʌg] *a* selbstgefällig.

smuggle ['smʌgl] *vt* schmuggeln; ~**r** Schmuggler *m*.

smuggling ['smʌglɪŋ] *n* Schmuggel *m*.

smugly ['smʌglɪ] *ad* selbstgefällig.

smugness ['smʌgnəs] *n* Selbstgefälligkeit *f*.

smutty ['smʌtɪ] *a* (*fig: obscene*) obszön, schmutzig.

snack [snæk] *n* Imbiß *m*; ~ **bar** Imbißstube *f*.

snag [snæg] *n* Haken *m*; (*in stocking*) gezogene(r) Faden *m*.

snail [sneɪl] *n* Schnecke *f*.

snake [sneɪk] *n* Schlange *f*.

snap [snæp] *n* Schnappen *nt*; (*photograph*) Schnappschuß *m*; *a decision* schnell; *vt* (*break*) zerbrechen; (*Phot*) knipsen; to ~ **one's fingers** mit den Fingern schnipsen; *vi* (*break*) brechen; (*bite*) schnappen; (*speak*) anfauchen; ~ **out of it!** raff dich auf!; ~ **off** *vt* (*break*) abbrechen; ~ **up** *vt* aufschnappen; ~**py** *a* flott; ~**shot** Schnappschuß *m*.

snare [snɛə*] *n* Schlinge *f*; *vt* mit einer Schlinge fangen.

snarl [snɑ:l] *n* Zähnefletschen *nt*; *vi* (*dog*) knurren; (*engine*) brummen, dröhnen.

snatch [snætʃ] *n* (*grab*) Schnappen *nt*; (*small amount*) Bruchteil *m*; *vt* schnappen, packen.

sneak [sni:k] *vi* schleichen.

sneakers ['sni:kəz] *npl* (*US*) Freizeitschuhe *pl*.

sneer [snɪə*] *n* Hohnlächeln *nt*; *vi* höhnisch grinsen; spötteln.

sneeze [sni:z] *n* Niesen *nt*; *vi* niesen.

snide [snaɪd] *a* (*col: sarcastic*) schneidend.

sniff [snɪf] *n* Schnüffeln *nt*; *vi* schnieben; (*smell*) schnüffeln; *vt* schnuppern.

snigger ['snɪgə*] *n* Kichern *nt*; *vi* hämisch kichern.

snip [snɪp] *n* Schnippel *m*, Schnipsel *m*; *vt* schnippeln.

sniper ['snaɪpə*] *n* Heckenschütze *m*.

snippet ['snɪpɪt] *n* Schnipsel *m*; (*of conversation*) Fetzen *m*.

snivelling ['snɪvlɪŋ] *a* weinerlich.

snob [snɒb] *n* Snob *m*; ~**bery** Snobismus *m*; ~**ish** *a* versnobt; ~**bishness** Versnobtheit *f*, Snobismus *m*.

snooker ['snu:kə*] *n* Snooker *nt*.

snoop [snu:p] *vi*: ~ **about** herumschnüffeln.

snooty ['snu:tɪ] *a* (*col*) hochnäsig; *restaurant* stinkfein.

snooze [snu:z] *n* Nickerchen *nt*; *vi* ein Nickerchen machen, dösen.

snore [snɔ:*] *vi* schnarchen.

snoring ['snɔ:rɪŋ] *n* Schnarchen *nt*.

snorkel ['snɔ:kl] *n* Schnorchel *m*.

snort [snɔ:t] *n* Schnauben *nt*; *vi* schnauben.

snotty ['snɒtɪ] *a* (*col*) rotzig.

snout [snaut] *n* Schnauze *f*; (*of pig*) Rüssel *m*.

snow [snəu] *n* Schnee *m*; *vi* schneien; ~**ball** Schneeball *m*; ~**-blind** *a* schneeblind; ~**bound** *a* eingeschneit; ~**drift** Schneewehe *f*; ~**drop** Schneeglöckchen *nt*; ~**fall** Schneefall *m*; ~**flake** Schneeflocke *f*; ~**line** Schneegrenze *f*; ~**man** Schneemann *m*; ~**plough**, (*US*) ~**plow** Schneepflug *m*; ~**storm** Schneesturm *m*.

snub [snʌb] *vt* schroff abfertigen; *n* Verweis *m*, schroffe Abfertigung *f*; ~**-nosed** stupsnasig.

snuff [snʌf] n Schnupftabak m; ~**box** Schnupftabakdose f.

snug [snʌg] a gemütlich, behaglich.

so [səu] ad so; cj daher, folglich, also; ~ **as to** um zu; **or** ~ so etwa; ~ **long!** (good-bye) tschüß!; ~ **many** so viele; ~ **much** soviel; ~ **that** damit.

soak [səuk] vt durchnässen; (leave in liquid) einweichen; ~ **in** vi einsickern in (+acc); ~**ing** Einweichen nt; ~**ing wet** a klatschnaß.

soap [səup] n Seife f; ~**flakes** pl Seifenflocken pl; ~ **powder** Waschpulver nt; ~**y** a seifig, Seifen-.

soar [sɔː*] vi aufsteigen; (prices) in die Höhe schnellen.

sob [sɒb] n Schluchzen nt; vi schluchzen.

sober [ˈsəubə*] a (lit, fig) nüchtern; ~ **up** vi nüchtern werden; ~**ly** ad nüchtern.

so-called [ˈsəuˈkɔːld] a sogenannt.

soccer [ˈsɒkə*] n Fußball m.

sociability [səufəˈbɪlɪtɪ] n Umgänglichkeit f.

sociable [ˈsəufəbl] a umgänglich, gesellig.

social [ˈsəufəl] a sozial; (friendly, living with others) gesellig; ~**ism** Sozialismus m; ~**ist** Sozialist(in f) m; a sozialistisch; ~**ly** ad gesellschaftlich, privat; ~ **science** Sozialwissenschaft f; ~ **security** Sozialversicherung f; ~ **welfare** Fürsorge f; ~ **work** Sozialarbeit f; ~ **worker** Sozialarbeiter(in f) m.

society [səˈsaɪətɪ] n Gesellschaft f; (fashionable world) die große Welt.

sociological [səusɪəˈlɒdʒɪkəl] a soziologisch.

sociologist [səusɪˈɒlədʒɪst] n Soziologe m, Soziologin f.

sociology [səusɪˈɒlədʒɪ] n Soziologie f.

sock [sɒk] n Socke f; vt (col) schlagen.

socket [ˈsɒkɪt] n (Elec) Steckdose f; (of eye) Augenhöhle f; (Tech) Rohransatz m.

sod [sɒd] n Rasenstück nt; (col) Saukerl m.

soda [ˈsəudə] n Soda f; ~ **water** Mineralwasser nt, Soda(wasser) nt.

sodden [ˈsɒdn] a durchweicht.

sofa [ˈsəufə] n Sofa nt.

soft [sɒft] a weich; (not loud) leise, gedämpft; (kind) weichherzig, gutmütig; (weak) weich, nachgiebig; ~ **drink** alkoholfreie(s) Getränk nt; ~**en** [sɒfn] vt weich machen; blow abschwächen, mildern; vi weich werden; ~**-hearted** a weichherzig; ~**ly** ad sanft; leise; ~**ness** Weichheit f; (fig) Sanftheit f.

soggy [ˈsɒgɪ] a ground sumpfig; bread aufgeweicht.

soil [sɔɪl] n Erde f, Boden m; vt beschmutzen; ~**ed** a beschmutzt, schmutzig.

solace [ˈsɒləs] n Trost m.

solar [ˈsəulə*] a Sonnen-; ~ **system** Sonnensystem nt.

solder [ˈsəuldə*] vt löten; n Lötmetall nt.

soldier [ˈsəuldʒə*] n Soldat m.

sole [səul] n Sohle f; (fish) Seezunge f; vt besohlen; a alleinig, Allein-; ~**ly** ad ausschließlich, nur.

solemn [ˈsɒləm] a feierlich; (serious) feierlich, ernst.

solicitor [səˈlɪsɪtə*] n Rechtsanwalt m.

solid [ˈsɒlɪd] a (hard) fest; (of same material) rein, massiv; (not hollow) massiv, stabil; (without break) voll, ganz; (reliable) solide, zuverlässig; (sensible) solide, gut; (united) eins, einig; meal kräftig; n Feste(s) nt; ~**arity** [sɒlɪˈdærɪtɪ] Solidarität f, Zusammenhalt m; ~ **figure** (Math) Körper m; ~**ify** [səˈlɪdɪfaɪ] vi fest werden, sich verdichten, erstarren; vt fest machen, verdichten; ~**ity** [səˈlɪdɪtɪ] Festigkeit f; ~**ly** ad (fig) behind einmütig; work ununterbrochen.

soliloquy [səˈlɪləkwɪ] n Monolog m.

solitaire [sɒlɪˈtɛə*] n (Cards) Patience f; (gem) Solitär m.

solitary [ˈsɒlɪtərɪ] a einsam, einzeln.

solitude [ˈsɒlɪtjuːd] n Einsamkeit f.

solo [ˈsəuləu] n Solo nt; ~**ist** Soloist(in f) m.

solstice [ˈsɒlstɪs] n Sonnenwende f.

soluble [ˈsɒljubl] a substance löslich; problem (auf)lösbar.

solution [səˈluːʃən] n (lit, fig) Lösung f; (of mystery) Erklärung f.

solve [sɒlv] vt (auf)lösen.

solvent [ˈsɒlvənt] a (Fin) zahlungsfähig.

sombre, (US) **somber** a, ~**ly** ad [ˈsɒmbə*, -əlɪ] düster.

some [sʌm] a people etc einige; water etc etwas; (unspecified) (irgend)ein; (remarkable) toll, enorm; that's ~ **house** das ist vielleicht ein Haus; pron (amount) etwas; (number) einige; ~**body** pron (irgend) jemand; he is ~**body** er ist jemand or wer; ~**day** ad irgendwann; ~**how** ad (in a certain way) irgendwie; (for a certain reason) aus irgendeinem Grunde; ~**one** pron = **somebody**; ~**place** ad (US) = **somewhere**.

somersault [ˈsʌməsɔːlt] n Purzelbaum m; Salto m; vi Purzelbäume schlagen; einen Salto machen.

something [ˈsʌmθɪŋ] pron (irgend) etwas.

sometime [ˈsʌmtaɪm] ad (irgend) einmal; ~**s** ad manchmal, gelegentlich.

somewhat [ˈsʌmwɒt] ad etwas, ein wenig, ein bißchen.

somewhere [ˈsʌmwɛə*] ad irgendwo; (to a place) irgendwohin.

son [sʌn] n Sohn m.

sonata [səˈnɑːtə] n Sonate f.

song [sɒŋ] n Lied nt; ~**writer** Texter m.

sonic [ˈsɒnɪk] a Schall-; ~ **boom** Überschallknall m.

son-in-law [ˈsʌnɪnlɔː] n Schwiegersohn m.

sonnet [ˈsɒnɪt] n Sonett nt.

sonny [ˈsʌnɪ] n (col) Kleine(r) m.

soon [suːn] ad bald; too ~ zu früh; as ~ as possible so bald wie möglich; ~**er** ad (time) eher, früher; (for preference) lieber; no ~**er** kaum.

soot [sut] n Ruß m.

soothe [suːð] vt person beruhigen; pain lindern.

soothing [ˈsuːðɪŋ] a (for person) beruhigend; (for pain) lindernd.

sop [sɒp] n (bribe) Schmiergeld nt.

sophisticated [sə'fɪstɪkeɪtɪd] *a person* kultiviert, weltgewandt; *machinery* differenziert, hochentwickelt; *plan* ausgeklügelt.

sophistication [səfɪstɪ'keɪʃən] *n* Weltgewandtheit *f*, Kultiviertheit *f*; (*Tech*) technische Verfeinerung *f*.

sophomore ['sɒfəmɔː*] *n* (*US*) College-Student *m* im 2. Jahr.

soporific [sɒpə'rɪfɪk] *a* einschläfernd, Schlaf-.

sopping ['sɒpɪŋ] *a* (*very wet*) patschnaß, triefend.

soppy ['sɒpɪ] *a* (*col*) schmalzig.

soprano [sə'prɑːnəʊ] *n* Sopran *m*.

sordid ['sɔːdɪd] *a* (*dirty*) schmutzig; (*mean*) niederträchtig.

sore [sɔː*] *a* schmerzend; *point* wund; **to be ~** weh tun; (*angry*) böse sein; *n* Wunde *f*; **~ly** *ad tempted* stark, sehr; **~ness** Schmerzhaftigkeit *f*, Empfindlichkeit *f*.

sorrow ['sɒrəʊ] *n* Kummer *m*, Leid *nt*; **~ful** *a* sorgenvoll; **~fully** *ad* traurig, betrübt, kummervoll.

sorry ['sɒrɪ] *a* traurig, erbärmlich; (**I'm**) **~** es tut mir leid; **I feel ~ for him** er tut mir leid.

sort [sɔːt] *n* Art *f*, Sorte *f*; *vt* (*also* **~ out**) *papers* sortieren, sichten; *problems* in Ordnung bringen.

so-so ['səʊsəʊ] *ad* so(-so) la-la, mäßig.

soufflé ['suːfleɪ] *n* Auflauf *m*, Soufflé *nt*.

soul [səʊl] *n* Seele *f*; (*music*) Soul *m*; **~-destroying** *a* trostlos; **~ful** *a* seelenvoll; **~less** *a* seelenlos, gefühllos.

sound [saʊnd] *a* (*healthy*) gesund; (*safe*) sicher, solide; (*sensible*) vernünftig; *theory* stichhaltig; (*thorough*) tüchtig, gehörig; *n* (*noise*) Geräusch *nt*, Laut *m*; (*Geog*) Meerenge *f*, Sund *m*; *vt* erschallen lassen; *alarm* (Alarm) schlagen; (*Med*) abhorchen; **to ~ one's horn** hupen; *vi* (*make a sound*) schallen, tönen; (*seem*) klingen; **~ out** *vt opinion* erforschen; *person* auf den Zahn fühlen (+*dat*); **~ barrier** Schallmauer *f*; **~ing** (*Naut etc*) Lotung *f*; **~ly** *ad sleep* fest, tief; *beat* tüchtig; **~proof** *a room* schalldicht; *vt* schalldicht machen; **~-track** Tonstreifen *m*; Filmmusik *f*.

soup [suːp] *n* Suppe *f*; **in the ~** (*col*) in der Tinte; **~-spoon** Suppenlöffel *m*.

sour ['saʊə*] *a* (*lit, fig*) sauer.

source [sɔːs] *n* (*lit, fig*) Quelle *f*.

sourness ['saʊənəs] *n* Säure *f*; (*fig*) Bitterkeit *f*.

south [saʊθ] *n* Süden *m*; *a* Süd-, südlich; *ad* nach Süden, südwärts; **~-east** Südosten *m*; **~erly** ['sʌðəlɪ] *a* südlich; **~ern** ['sʌðən] *a* südlich, südlich; **~ward(s)** *ad* südwärts, nach Süden; **~-west** Südwesten *m*.

souvenir [suːvə'nɪə*] *n* Andenken *nt*, Souvenir *nt*.

sovereign ['sɒvrɪn] *n* (*ruler*) Herrscher *m*; *a* (*independent*) souverän; **~ty** Oberhoheit *f*, Souveränität *f*.

sow [saʊ] *n* Sau *f*; [səʊ] *vt irreg* (*lit, fig*) säen.

soya bean ['sɔɪə'biːn] *n* Sojabohne *f*.

spa [spɑː] *n* (*spring*) Mineralquelle *f*; (*place*) Kurort *m*, Bad *nt*.

space [speɪs] *n* Platz *m*, Raum *m*; (*universe*) Weltraum *m*, All *nt*; (*length of time*) Abstand *m*; **~ out** *vt* Platz lassen zwischen; (*typing*) gesperrt schreiben; **~craft** Raumschiff *nt*; **~man** Raumfahrer *m*.

spacious ['speɪʃəs] *a* geräumig, weit.

spade [speɪd] *n* Spaten *m*; **~s** (*Cards*) Pik *nt*, Schippe *f*; **~work** (*fig*) Vorarbeit *f*.

spaghetti [spə'getɪ] *n* Spaghetti *pl*.

span [spæn] *n* Spanne *f*; Spannweite *f*; *vt* überspannen.

spaniel ['spænjəl] *n* Spaniel *m*.

spank [spæŋk] *vt* verhauen, versohlen.

spanner ['spænə*] *n* Schraubenschlüssel *m*.

spar [spɑː*] *n* (*Naut*) Sparren *m*; *vi* (*boxing*) einen Sparring machen.

spare [speə*] *a* Ersatz-; *n* = **~ part**; *vt lives, feelings* verschonen; *trouble* ersparen; **4 to ~** 4 übrig; **~ part** Ersatzteil *nt*; **~ time** Freizeit *f*.

spark [spɑːk] *n* Funken *m*; **~(ing) plug** Zündkerze *f*.

sparkle ['spɑːkl] *n* Funkeln *nt*, Glitzern *nt*; (*gaiety*) Lebhaftigkeit *f*, Schwung *m*; *vi* funkeln, glitzern.

sparkling ['spɑːklɪŋ] *a* funkelnd, sprühend; *wine* Schaum-; *conversation* spritzig, geistreich.

sparrow ['spærəʊ] *n* Spatz *m*.

sparse *a*, **~ly** *ad* [spɑːs, -lɪ] spärlich, dünn.

spasm ['spæzəm] *n* (*Med*) Krampf *m*; (*fig*) Anfall *m*; **~odic** [spæz'mɒdɪk] *a* krampfartig, spasmodisch; (*fig*) sprunghaft.

spastic ['spæstɪk] *a* spastisch.

spate [speɪt] *n* (*fig*) Flut *f*, Schwall *m*; **in ~** *river* angeschwollen.

spatter ['spætə*] *n* Spritzer *m*; *vt* bespritzen, verspritzen; *vi* spritzen.

spatula ['spætjʊlə] *n* Spatel *m*; (*for building*) Spachtel *f*.

spawn [spɔːn] *vt* laichen.

speak [spiːk] *irreg vt* sprechen, reden; *truth* sagen; *language* sprechen; *vi* sprechen (**to** mit *or* zu); **~ for** *vi* sprechen *or* eintreten für; **~ up** *vi* lauter sprechen; **~er** Sprecher *m*, Redner *m*; **loud~** Lautsprecher *m*; **not to be on ~ing terms** nicht miteinander sprechen.

spear [spɪə*] *n* Speer *m*, Lanze *f*, Spieß *m*; *vt* aufspießen, durchbohren.

spec [spek] *n* (*col*) **on ~** auf gut Glück.

special ['speʃəl] *a* besondere(r,s); speziell; *n* (*Rail*) Sonderzug *m*; **~ist** Spezialist *m*; (*Tech*) Fachmann *m*; (*Med*) Facharzt *m*; **~ity** [speʃɪ'ælɪtɪ] Spezialität *f*; (*study*) Spezialgebiet *nt*; **~ize** *vi* sich spezialisieren (*in* auf +*acc*); **~ly** *ad* besonders; (*explicitly*) extra, ausdrücklich.

species ['spiːʃiːz] *n* Art *f*.

specific [spə'sɪfɪk] *a* spezifisch, eigentümlich, besondere(r,s); **~ally** *ad* genau, spezifisch; **~ations** *pl* [spesɪfɪ'keɪʃənz] genaue Angaben *pl*; (*Tech*) technische Daten *pl*.

specify ['spesɪfaɪ] *vt* genau angeben.

specimen ['spesɪmɪn] n Probe f, Muster nt.

speck [spek] n Fleckchen nt; **~led** a gesprenkelt.

specs [speks] npl (col) Brille f.

spectacle ['spektəkl] n Schauspiel nt; **~s** pl Brille f.

spectacular [spek'tækjulə*] a aufsehenerregend, spektakulär.

spectator [spek'teɪtə*] n Zuschauer m.

spectre, (US) **specter** ['spektə*] n Geist m, Gespenst nt.

spectrum ['spektrəm] n Spektrum nt.

speculate ['spekjuleɪt] vi vermuten, spekulieren (also Fin).

speculation [spekju'leɪʃən] n Vermutung f, Spekulation f (also Fin).

speculative ['spekjulətɪv] a spekulativ.

speech [spiːtʃ] n Sprache f; (address) Rede f, Ansprache f; (manner of speaking) Sprechweise f; **~ day** (Sch) (Jahres)-schlußfeier f; **~less** a sprachlos; **~ therapy** Sprachheilpflege f.

speed [spiːd] n Geschwindigkeit f; (gear) Gang m; vi irreg rasen; (zu) schnell fahren; **~ up** vt beschleunigen; vi schneller werden/fahren; **~boat** Schnellboot nt; **~ily** ad schnell, schleunigst; **~ing** zu schnelles Fahren; **~ limit** Geschwindigkeitsbegrenzung f; **~ometer** [spɪ'dɒmɪtə*] Tachometer m; **~way** (bike racing) Motorradrennstrecke f; **~y** a schnell, zügig.

spell [spel] n (magic) Bann m, Zauber m; (period of time) Zeit f, Zeitlang f, Weile f; **sunny ~s** pl Aufheiterungen pl; **rainy ~s** pl vereinzelte Schauer pl; vt irreg buchstabieren; (imply) bedeuten; **how do you ~ . . .?** wie schreibt man . . .?; **~bound** a (wie) gebannt; **~ing** Buchstabieren nt; **English ~ing** die englische Rechtschreibung.

spend [spend] vt irreg money ausgeben; time verbringen; **~ing money** Taschengeld nt.

spent [spent] a patience erschöpft.

sperm [spɜːm] n (Biol) Samenflüssigkeit f.

spew [spjuː] vt (er)brechen.

sphere [sfɪə*] n (globe) Kugel f; (fig) Sphäre f, Gebiet nt.

spherical ['sferɪkəl] a kugelförmig.

sphinx [sfɪŋks] n Sphinx f.

spice [spaɪs] n Gewürz nt; vt würzen.

spiciness ['spaɪsɪnəs] n Würze f.

spick-and-span ['spɪkən'spæn] a blitzblank.

spicy ['spaɪsɪ] a würzig, pikant (also fig).

spider ['spaɪdə*] n Spinne f; **~y** a writing krakelig.

spike [spaɪk] n Dorn m, Spitze f; **~s** pl Spikes pl.

spill [spɪl] irreg vt verschütten; vi sich ergießen.

spin [spɪn] n Umdrehung f; (trip in car) Spazierfahrt f; (Aviat) (Ab)trudeln nt; (on ball) Drall m; irreg vt thread spinnen; (like top) schnell drehen, (herum)wirbeln; vi sich drehen; **~ out** vt in die Länge ziehen; story ausmalen.

spinach ['spɪnɪtʃ] n Spinat m.

spinal ['spaɪnl] a spinal, Rückgrat-, Rückenmark-; **~ cord** Rückenmark nt.

spindly ['spɪndlɪ] a spindeldürr.

spin-drier ['spɪn'draɪə*] n Wäscheschleuder f.

spin-dry [spɪn'draɪ] vt schleudern.

spine [spaɪn] n Rückgrat nt; (thorn) Stachel m; **~less** a (lit, fig) rückgratlos.

spinet [spɪ'net] n Spinett nt.

spinner ['spɪnə*] n (of thread) Spinner m.

spinning ['spɪnɪŋ] n (of thread) (Faden)-spinnen nt; **~ wheel** Spinnrad nt.

spinster ['spɪnstə*] n unverheiratete Frau f; (pej) alte Jungfer f.

spiral ['spaɪərəl] n Spirale f; a gewunden, spiralförmig, Spiral-; vi sich ringeln; **~ staircase** Wendeltreppe f.

spire ['spaɪə*] n Turm m.

spirit ['spɪrɪt] n Geist m; (humour, mood) Stimmung f; (courage) Mut m; (verve) Elan m; (alcohol) Alkohol m; **~s** pl Spirituosen pl; **in good ~s** gut aufgelegt; **~ed** a beherzt; **~ level** Wasserwaage f; **~ual** a geistig, seelisch; (Rel) geistlich; n Spiritual nt; **~ualism** Spiritismus m.

spit [spɪt] n (for roasting) (Brat)spieß m; (saliva) Spucke f; vi irreg spucken; (rain) sprühen; (make a sound) zischen; (cat) fauchen.

spite [spaɪt] n Gehässigkeit f; vt ärgern, kränken; **in ~ of** trotz (+gen or dat); **~ful** a gehässig.

splash [splæʃ] n Spritzer m; (of colour) (Farb)fleck m; vt bespritzen; vi spritzen; **~down** Wasserlandung f.

spleen [spliːn] n (Anat) Milz f.

splendid a, **~ly** ad ['splendɪd, -lɪ] glänzend, großartig.

splendour, (US) **splendor** ['splendə*] n Pracht f.

splice [splaɪs] vt spleißen.

splint [splɪnt] n Schiene f.

splinter ['splɪntə*] n Splitter m; vi (zer)-splittern.

split [splɪt] n Spalte f; (fig) Spaltung f; (division) Trennung f; irreg vt spalten; vi (divide) reißen; sich spalten; (col: depart) abhauen; **~ up** vi sich trennen; vt aufteilen, teilen; **~ting** a headache rasend, wahnsinnig.

splutter ['splʌtə*] vi spritzen; (person, engine) stottern.

spoil [spɔɪl] irreg vt (ruin) verderben; child verwöhnen, verziehen; vi (food) verderben; **~s** pl Beute f; **~sport** Spielverderber m.

spoke [spəʊk] n Speiche f; **~sman** Sprecher m, Vertreter m.

sponge [spʌndʒ] n Schwamm m; vt mit dem Schwamm abwaschen; vi auf Kosten leben (on gen); **~ bag** Kulturbeutel m; **~ cake** Rührkuchen m; **~r** (col) Schmarotzer m.

spongy ['spʌndʒɪ] a schwammig.

sponsor ['spɒnsə*] n Bürge m; (in advertising) Sponsor m; vt bürgen für; fördern; **~ship** Bürgschaft f; (public) Schirmherrschaft f.

spontaneity [spɒntə'neɪɪtɪ] n Spontanität f.

spontaneous a, **~ly** ad [spon'teɪnɪəs, -lɪ] spontan.

spooky ['spuːkɪ] a (col) gespenstisch.

spool [spuːl] n Spule f, Rolle f.

spoon [spuːn] n Löffel m; **~-feed** vt irreg (lit) mit dem Löffel füttern; (fig) hochpäppeln; **~ful** Löffel(voll) m.

sporadic [spə'rædɪk] a vereinzelt, sporadisch.

sport [spɔːt] n Sport m; (fun) Spaß m; (person) feine(r) Kerl m; **~ing** a (fair) sportlich, fair; **~s car** Sportwagen m; **~(s) coat**, **~(s) jacket** Sportjackett nt; **~sman** Sportler m; (fig) anständige(r) Kerl m; **~smanship** Sportlichkeit f; (fig) Anständigkeit f; **~s page** Sportseite f; **~swear** Sportkleidung f; **~swoman** Sportlerin f; **~y** a sportlich.

spot [spɔt] n Punkt m; (dirty) Fleck(en) m; (place) Stelle f, Platz m; (Med) Pickel m, Pustel f; (small amount) Schluck m, Tropfen m; vt erspähen; mistake bemerken; **~ check** Stichprobe f; **~less** a, **~ly** ad fleckenlos; **~light** Scheinwerferlicht nt; (lamp) Scheinwerfer m; **~ted** a gefleckt; dress gepunktet; **~ty** a face pickelig.

spouse [spauz] n Gatte m/Gattin f.

spout [spaut] n (of pot) Tülle f; (jet) Wasserstrahl m; vi speien, spritzen.

sprain [spreɪn] n Verrenkung f; vt verrenken.

sprawl [sprɔːl] n (of city) Ausbreitung f; vi sich strecken.

spray [spreɪ] n Spray nt; (off sea) Gischt f; (instrument) Zerstäuber m; Spraydose f; (of flowers) Zweig m; vt besprühen, sprayen.

spread [spred] n (extent) Verbreitung f; (of wings) Spannweite f; (col: meal) Schmaus m; (for bread) Aufstrich m; vt irreg ausbreiten; (scatter) verbreiten; butter streichen.

spree [spriː] n lustige(r) Abend m; (shopping) Einkaufsbummel m; **to go out on a ~** einen draufmachen.

sprig [sprɪg] n kleine(r) Zweig m.

sprightly ['spraɪtlɪ] a munter, lebhaft.

spring [sprɪŋ] n (leap) Sprung m; (metal) Feder f; (season) Frühling m; (water) Quelle f; vi irreg (leap) springen; **~ up** vi (problem) entstehen, auftauchen; **~board** Sprungbrett nt; **~clean** vt Frühjahrsputz machen in (+dat); **~-cleaning** Frühjahrsputz m; **~iness** Elastizität f; **~time** Frühling m; **~y** a federnd, elastisch.

sprinkle ['sprɪŋkl] n Prise f; vt salt streuen; liquid sprenkeln.

sprinkling ['sprɪŋklɪŋ] n Spur f, ein bißchen.

sprint [sprɪnt] n Kurzstreckenlauf m; Sprint m; vi sprinten; **~er** Sprinter m, Kurzstreckenläufer m.

sprite [spraɪt] n Elfe f; Kobold m.

sprout [spraut] vi sprießen; n see **Brussels ~.**

spruce [spruːs] n Fichte f; a schmuck, adrett.

spry [spraɪ] a flink, rege.

spud [spʌd] n (col) Kartoffel f.

spur [spɜː*] n Sporn m; (fig) Ansporn m; vt (also ~ on) (fig) anspornen; **on the ~ of the moment** spontan.

spurious ['spjuərɪəs] a falsch, unecht, Pseudo-.

spurn [spɜːn] vt verschmähen.

spurt [spɜːt] n (jet) Strahl m; (acceleration) Spurt m; vt spritzen; vi (jet) steigen; (liquid) schießen; (run) spurten.

spy [spaɪ] n Spion m; vi spionieren; vt erspähen; **to ~ on sb** jdm nachspionieren; **~ing** Spionage f.

squabble ['skwɔbl] n Zank m; vi sich zanken.

squabbling ['skwɔblɪŋ] n Zankerei f.

squad [skwɔd] n (Mil) Abteilung f, (police) Kommando nt.

squadron ['skwɔdrən] n (cavalry) Schwadron f; (Naut) Geschwader nt; (air force) Staffel f.

squalid ['skwɔlɪd] a schmutzig, verkommen.

squall [skwɔːl] n Bö f, Windstoß m; **~y** a weather stürmisch; wind böig.

squalor ['skwɔlə*] n Verwahrlosung f, Schmutz m.

squander ['skwɔndə*] vt verschwenden.

square [skwɛə*] n (Math) Quadrat nt; (open space) Platz m; (instrument) Winkel m; (col: person) Spießer m; a viereckig, quadratisch; (fair) ehrlich, reell; (meal) reichlich; (col) ideas, tastes spießig; ad (exactly) direkt, gerade; vt (arrange) ausmachen, aushandeln; (Math) ins Quadrat erheben; (bribe) schmieren; vi (agree) übereinstimmen; **all ~** quitt; **2 metres ~** 2 Meter im Quadrat; **2 ~ metres** 2 Quadratmeter; **~ly** ad fest, gerade.

squash [skwɔʃ] n (drink) Saft m; vt zerquetschen.

squat [skwɔt] a untersetzt, gedrungen; vi hocken; **~ter** Squatter m, Siedler m ohne Rechtstitel; Hausbesetzer m.

squaw [skwɔː] n Squaw f.

squawk [skwɔːk] n Kreischen nt; vi kreischen.

squeak [skwiːk] n Gequiek(s)e nt; vi quiek(s)en; (spring, door etc) quietschen; **~y** a quiek(s)end; quietschend.

squeal [skwiːl] n schrille(r) Schrei m; (of brakes etc) Quietschen nt; vi schrill schreien.

squeamish ['skwiːmɪʃ] a empfindlich; **that made me ~** davon wurde mir übel; **~ness** Überempfindlichkeit f.

squeeze [skwiːz] n (lit) Pressen nt; (Pol) Geldknappheit f, wirtschaftliche(r) Engpaß m; vt pressen, drücken; orange auspressen; **~ out** vt ausquetschen.

squid [skwɪd] n Tintenfisch m.

squint [skwɪnt] n Schielen nt; vi schielen.

squire ['skwaɪə*] n Gutsherr m.

squirm [skwɜːm] vi sich winden.

squirrel ['skwɪrəl] n Eichhörnchen nt.

squirt [skwɜːt] n Spritzer m, Strahl m; vti spritzen.

stab [stæb] n (blow) Stoß m, Stich m; (col: try) Versuch m; vt erstechen; **~bing** Messerstecherei f.

stability [stə'bılıtı] n Festigkeit f, Stabilität f.

stabilization [steıbəlaı'zeıʃən] n Festigung f, Stabilisierung f.

stabilize ['steıbəlaız] vt festigen, stabilisieren; ~r Stabilisator m.

stable ['steıbl] n Stall m; vt im Stall unterbringen; a fest, stabil; person gefestigt.

staccato [stə'kɑːtəʊ] a stakkato.

stack [stæk] n Stoß m, Stapel m; vt (auf)stapeln.

stadium ['steıdıəm] n Stadion nt.

staff [stɑːf] n (stick, Mil) Stab m; (personnel) Personal nt; (Sch) Lehrkräfte pl; vt (with people) besetzen.

stag [stæg] n Hirsch m.

stage [steıdʒ] n Bühne f; (of journey) Etappe f, (degree) Stufe f; (point) Stadium nt; vt (put on) aufführen; play inszenieren; demonstration veranstalten; in ~s etappenweise; ~ coach Postkutsche f; ~ door Bühneneingang m; ~ manager Spielleiter m, Intendant m.

stagger ['stægə*] vi wanken, taumeln; vt (amaze) verblüffen; hours staffeln; ~ing a unglaublich.

stagnant ['stægnənt] a stagnierend; water stehend.

stagnate [stæg'neıt] vi stagnieren.

stagnation [stæg'neıʃən] n Stillstand m, Stagnation f.

staid [steıd] a gesetzt.

stain [steın] n Fleck m; (colouring for wood) Beize f; vt beflecken, Flecken machen auf (+acc); beizen; ~ed glass window buntes Glasfenster nt; ~less a steel rostfrei, nichtrostend; ~ remover Fleckentferner m.

stair [steə*] n (Treppen)stufe f; ~case Treppenhaus nt, Treppe f; ~s pl Treppe f; ~way Treppenaufgang m.

stake [steık] n (post) Pfahl m, Pfosten m; (money) Einsatz m; vt (bet money) setzen; to be at ~ auf dem Spiel stehen.

stalactite ['stæləktaıt] n Stalaktit m.

stalagmite ['stæləgmaıt] n Stalagmit m.

stale [steıl] a alt; beer schal; bread altbacken; ~mate (chess) Patt nt; (fig) Stillstand m.

stalk [stɔːk] n Stengel m, Stiel m; vt game sich anpirschen an (+acc), jagen; vi (walk) stolzieren.

stall [stɔːl] n (in stable) Stand m, Box f; (in market) (Verkaufs)stand m; vt (Aut) (den Motor) abwürgen; vi (Aut) stehenbleiben; (avoid) Ausflüchte machen, ausweichen; ~s pl (Theat) Parkett nt.

stallion ['stælıən] n Zuchthengst m.

stalwart ['stɔːlwət] a standhaft; n treue(r) Anhänger m.

stamina ['stæmınə] n Durchhaltevermögen nt, Zähigkeit f.

stammer ['stæmə*] n Stottern nt; vti stottern, stammeln.

stamp [stæmp] n Briefmarke f; (with foot) Stampfen nt; (for document) Stempel m; vi stampfen; vt (mark) stempeln; mail frankieren; foot stampfen mit; ~ album Briefmarkenalbum nt; ~ collecting Briefmarkensammeln nt.

stampede [stæm'piːd] n panische Flucht f.

stance [stæns] n (posture) Haltung f, Stellung f; (opinion) Einstellung f.

stand [stænd] n Standort m, Platz m; (for objects) (seats) Gestell nt; (seats) Tribüne f; to make a ~ Widerstand leisten; irreg vi stehen; (rise) aufstehen; (decision) feststehen; to ~ still still stehen; vt setzen, stellen; (endure) aushalten; person ausstehen, leiden können; nonsense dulden; it ~s to reason es ist einleuchtend; ~ by vi (be ready) bereitstehen; vt opinion treu bleiben (+dat); ~ for vt (signify) stehen für; (permit, tolerate) hinnehmen; ~ in for vt einspringen für; ~ out vi (be prominent) hervorstechen; ~ up vi (rise) aufstehen; ~ up for vt sich einsetzen für.

standard ['stændəd] n (measure) Standard m, Norm f; (flag) Standarte f, Fahne f; a size etc Normal-, Durchschnitts-; ~ization Vereinheitlichung f; ~ize vt vereinheitlichen, normen; ~ lamp Stehlampe f; ~ of living Lebensstandard m; ~ time Ortszeit f.

stand-by ['stændbaı] n Reserve f; ~ flight Standby-Flug m.

stand-in ['stændın] n Ersatz(mann) m, Hilfskraft f.

standing ['stændıŋ] a (erect) stehend; (permanent) ständig, dauernd; invitation offen; n (duration) Dauer f; (reputation) Ansehen nt; ~ jump Sprung m aus dem Stand; ~ order (at bank) Dauerauftrag m; ~ orders pl (Mil) Vorschrift; ~ room only nur Stehplatz.

stand-offish ['stænd'ɒfıʃ] a zurückhaltend, sehr reserviert.

standpoint ['stændpɔınt] n Standpunkt m.

standstill ['stændstıl] n: to be at a ~ stillstehen; to come to a ~ zum Stillstand kommen.

stanza ['stænzə] n (verse) Strophe f; (poem) Stanze f.

staple ['steıpl] n (clip) Krampe f; (in paper) Heftklamme f; (article) Haupterzeugnis nt; a Grund-; Haupt-; vt (fest)klammern; ~r Heftmaschine f.

star [stɑː*] n Stern m; (person) Star m; vi die Hauptrolle spielen; vt actor in der Hauptrolle zeigen.

starboard ['stɑːbəd] n Steuerbord nt; a Steuerbord-.

starch [stɑːtʃ] n Stärke f; vt stärken; ~y a stärkehaltig; (formal) steif.

stardom ['stɑːdəm] n Berühmtheit f.

stare [steə*] n starre(r) Blick m; vi starren (at auf +acc); ~ at vt anstarren.

starfish ['stɑːfıʃ] n Seestern m.

staring ['stɑːrıŋ] a eyes starrend.

stark [stɑːk] a öde; ad: ~ naked splitternackt.

starless ['stɑːləs] a sternlos.

starlight ['stɑːlaıt] n Sternenlicht nt.

starling ['stɑːlıŋ] n Star m.

starlit ['stɑːlıt] a sternklar.

starring ['stɑːrıŋ] a mit . . . in der Hauptrolle.

star-studded ['stɑːstʌdıd] a mit Spitzenstars.

starry ['stɑ:rɪ] a Sternen-; **~-eyed** a (*innocent*) blauäugig.

start [stɑ:t] n Beginn m, Anfang m, Start m; (*Sport*) Start m; (*lead*) Vorsprung m; **to give a ~** zusammenfahren; **to give sb a ~** jdn zusammenfahren lassen; vt in Gang setzen, anfangen; car anlassen; vi anfangen; (*car*) anspringen; (*on journey*) aufbrechen; (*Sport*) starten; **~ over** vi (*US*) wieder anfangen; **~ up** vi anfangen; (*startled*) auffahren; vt beginnen; car anlassen; engine starten; **~er** (*Aut*) Anlasser m; (*for race*) Starter m; **~ing handle** Anlaßkurbel f; **~ing point** Ausgangspunkt m.

startle ['stɑ:tl] vt erschrecken.

startling ['stɑ:lɪŋ] a erschreckend.

starvation [stɑ:'veɪʃən] n Verhungern nt; **to die of ~** verhungern.

starve [stɑ:v] vi verhungern; vt verhungern lassen; **to be ~d of affection** unter Mangel an Liebe leiden; **~ out** vt aushungern.

starving ['stɑ:vɪŋ] a (ver)hungernd.

state [steɪt] n (*condition*) Zustand m; (*Pol*) Staat m; (*col: anxiety*) (schreckliche) Verfassung f; vt erklären; facts angeben; **~ control** staatliche Kontrolle f; **~d** a festgesetzt; **~liness** Pracht f, Würde f; **~ly** a würdevoll, erhaben; **~ment** Aussage f; (*Pol*) Erklärung f; **~ secret** Staatsgeheimnis nt; **~sman** Staatsmann m.

static ['stætɪk] n Statik f; a statisch.

station ['steɪʃən] n (*Rail etc*) Bahnhof m; (*police etc*) Station f, Wache f; (*in society*) gesellschaftliche Stellung f; vt aufstellen; **to be ~ed** stationiert sein.

stationary ['steɪʃənərɪ] a stillstehend; car parkend.

stationer ['steɪʃənə*] n Schreibwarenhändler m; **~'s (shop)** Schreibwarengeschäft nt; **~y** Schreibwaren pl.

station master ['steɪʃənmɑ:stə*] n Bahnhofsvorsteher m.

station wagon ['steɪʃənwægən] n Kombiwagen m.

statistic [stə'tɪstɪk] n Statistik f; **~al** a statistisch; **~s** pl Statistik f.

statue ['stætju:] n Statue f.

statuesque [stætju'esk] a statuenhaft.

stature ['stætʃə*] n Wuchs m, Statur f; (*fig*) Größe f.

status ['steɪtəs] n Stellung f, Status m; **the ~ quo** der Status quo; **~ symbol** Statussymbol nt.

statute ['stætju:t] n Gesetz nt.

statutory ['stætjutərɪ] a gesetzlich.

staunch a, **~ly** ad [stɔ:ntʃ, -lɪ] treu, zuverlässig; Catholic standhaft, erz-.

stave [steɪv]: **~ off** vt attack abwehren; threat abwenden.

stay [steɪ] n Aufenthalt m; (*support*) Stütze f; (*for tent*) Schnur f; vi bleiben; (*reside*) wohnen; **to ~** an Ort und Stelle bleiben; **to ~ with friends** bei Freunden untergebracht sein; **to ~ the night** übernachten; **~ behind** vi zurückbleiben; **~ in** vi (*at home*) zu Hause bleiben; **~ on** vi (*continue*) länger bleiben; **~ up** vi (*at night*) aufbleiben.

steadfast ['stedfəst] a standhaft, treu.

steadily ['stedɪlɪ] ad stetig, regelmäßig.

steadiness ['stedɪnəs] n Festigkeit f; (*fig*) Beständigkeit f.

steady ['stedɪ] a (*firm*) fest, stabil; (*regular*) gleichmäßig; (*reliable*) zuverlässig, beständig; hand ruhig; job, boyfriend fest; vt festigen; **to ~ o.s.** sich stützen.

steak [steɪk] n Steak nt; (*fish*) Filet nt.

steal [sti:l] irreg vti stehlen; vi sich stehlen; **~th** ['stelθ] Heimlichkeit f; **~thy** ['stelθɪ] a verstohlen, heimlich.

steam [sti:m] n Dampf m; vt (*Cook*) im Dampfbad erhitzen; vi dampfen; (*ship*) dampfen, fahren; **~ engine** Dampfmaschine f; **~er** Dampfer m; **~roller** Dampfwalze f; **~y** a dampfig.

steel [sti:l] n Stahl m; a Stahl-; (*fig*) stählern; **~works** Stahlwerke pl.

steep [sti:p] a steil; price gepfeffert; vt einweichen.

steeple ['sti:pl] n Kirchturm m; **~chase** Hindernisrennen nt; **~jack** Turmarbeiter m.

steeply ['sti:plɪ] ad steil.

steepness ['sti:pnəs] n Steilheit f.

steer [stɪə*] n Mastochse m; vti steuern; car etc lenken; **~ing** (*Aut*) Steuerung f; **~ing column** Lenksäule f; **~ing wheel** Steuer- or Lenkrad nt.

stellar ['stelə*] a Stern(en)-.

stem [stem] n (*Biol*) Stengel m, Stiel m; (*of glass*) Stiel m; vt aufhalten; **~ from** vi abstammen von.

stench [stentʃ] n Gestank m.

stencil ['stensl] n Schablone f; (*paper*) Matrize f; vt (auf)drucken.

stenographer [ste'nɒgrəfə*] n Stenograph(in f) m.

step [step] n Schritt m; (*stair*) Stufe f; **to take ~s** Schritte unternehmen; vi treten, schreiten; **~s = ~ladder**; **~ down** vi (*fig*) abtreten; **~ up** vt steigern; **~-brother** Stiefbruder m; **~-child** Stiefkind nt; **~-father** Stiefvater m; **~ladder** Trittleiter f; **~-mother** Stiefmutter f.

steppe [step] n Steppe f.

stepping stone ['stepɪŋstəʊn] n Stein m; (*fig*) Sprungbrett nt.

stereo ['steriəʊ] n Stereoanlage f; **~phonic** a stereophonisch; **~type** n Prototyp m; vt stereotypieren; (*fig*) stereotyp machen.

sterile ['steraɪl] a steril, keimfrei; person unfruchtbar; (*after operation*) steril.

sterility [ste'rɪlɪtɪ] n Unfruchtbarkeit f, Sterilität f.

sterilization [sterɪlaɪ'zeɪʃən] n Sterilisation f.

sterilize ['sterɪlaɪz] vt (*make unproductive*) unfruchtbar machen; (*make germfree*) sterilisieren, keimfrei machen.

sterling ['stɜ:lɪŋ] a (*Fin*) Sterling-; silver von Standardwert; character bewährt, gediegen; **£** ~ Pfund Sterling; **~ area** Sterlingblock m.

stern a, **~ly** ad [stɜ:n, -lɪ] streng; n Heck nt, Achterschiff nt; **~ness** Strenge f.

stethoscope ['steθəskəup] n Stethoskop nt, Hörrohr nt.

stevedore ['sti:vədɔ:°] n Schauermann m.

stew [stju:] n Eintopf m; vt: schmoren.

steward ['stju:əd] n Steward m; (in club) Kellner m; (organizer) Verwalter m; ~ess Stewardess f.

stick [stɪk] n Stock m, Stecken m; (of chalk etc) Stück nt; irreg vt (stab) stechen; (fix) stecken; (put) stellen; (gum) (an)kleben; (col: tolerate) vertragen; vi (stop) steckenbleiben; (get stuck) klemmen; (hold fast) kleben, haften; ~ out vi (project) hervorstehen aus; ~ up vi (project) in die Höhe stehen; ~ up for vt (defend) eintreten für; ~er Klebezettel m, Aufkleber m.

stickleback ['stɪklbæk] n Stichling m.

stickler ['stɪklə°] n Pedant m (for in +acc).

stick-up ['stɪkʌp] n (col) (Raub)überfall m.

sticky ['stɪkɪ] a klebrig; atmosphere stickig.

stiff [stɪf] a steif; (difficult) schwierig, hart; paste dick, zäh; drink stark; ~en vt versteifen, (ver)stärken; vi sich versteifen; ~ness Steifheit f.

stifle ['staɪfl] vt yawn etc unterdrücken.

stifling ['staɪflɪŋ] a atmosphere drückend.

stigma ['stɪgmə] n (disgrace) Stigma nt.

stile [staɪl] n Steige f.

still [stɪl] n a still; ad (immer) noch; (anyhow) immerhin; ~born a totgeboren; ~ life Stilleben nt; ~ness Stille f.

stilt [stɪlt] n Stelze f.

stilted ['stɪltɪd] a gestelzt.

stimulant ['stɪmjulənt] n Anregungsmittel nt, Stimulans nt.

stimulate ['stɪmjuleɪt] vt anregen, stimulieren.

stimulating ['stɪmjuleɪtɪŋ] a anregend, stimulierend.

stimulation [stɪmju'leɪʃən] n Anregung f, Stimulation f.

stimulus ['stɪmjuləs] n Anregung f, Reiz m.

sting [stɪŋ] n Stich m; (organ) Stachel m; vti irreg stechen; (on skin) brennen.

stingily ['stɪndʒɪlɪ] ad knickerig, geizig.

stinginess ['stɪndʒɪnəs] n Geiz m.

stinging nettle ['stɪŋɪŋnetl] n Brennessel f.

stingy ['stɪndʒɪ] a geizig, knauserig.

stink [stɪŋk] n Gestank m; vi irreg stinken; ~er m (col) (person) gemeine(r) Hund m; (problem) böse Sache f; ~ing a (fig) widerlich; ~ing rich steinreich.

stint [stɪnt] n Pensum nt; (period) Betätigung f; vt einschränken, knapphalten.

stipend ['staɪpend] n Gehalt nt.

stipulate ['stɪpjuleɪt] vt festsetzen.

stipulation [stɪpju'leɪʃən] n Bedingung f.

stir [stɜ:°] n Bewegung f; (Cook) Rühren nt; (sensation) Aufsehen nt; vt (um)rühren; vi sich rühren; ~ up vt mob aufhetzen; fire entfachen; mixture umrühren; dust aufwirbeln; to ~ things up Ärger machen; ~ring a ergreifend.

stirrup ['stɪrəp] n Steigbügel m.

stitch [stɪtʃ] n (with needle) Stich m; (Med) Faden m; (of knitting) Masche f; (pain) Stich m, Stechen nt; vt nähen.

stoat [stəut] n Wiesel nt.

stock [stɒk] n Vorrat m; (Comm) (Waren)lager nt; (live—) Vieh nt; (Cook) Brühe f; (Fin) Grundkapital nt; a stets vorrätig; (standard) Normal-; vt versehen, versorgen; (in shop) führen; in ~ auf Vorrat; to take ~ Inventur machen; (fig) Bilanz ziehen; to ~ up with Reserven anlegen von; ~ade [stɒ'keɪd] Palisade f; ~broker Börsenmakler m; ~ exchange Börse f.

stocking ['stɒkɪŋ] n Strumpf m.

stockist ['stɒkɪst] n Händler m.

stock market ['stɒkmɑ:kɪt] n Börse f, Effektenmarkt m.

stockpile ['stɒkpaɪl] n Vorrat m; nuclear ~ Kernwaffenvorräte pl; vt aufstapeln.

stocktaking ['stɒkteɪkɪŋ] n Inventur f, Bestandsaufnahme f.

stocky ['stɒkɪ] n untersetzt.

stodgy ['stɒdʒɪ] a füllend, stopfend; (fig) langweilig, trocken.

stoic ['stəuɪk] n Stoiker m; ~al a stoisch; ~ism ['stəuɪsɪzəm] Stoizismus m; (fig) Gelassenheit f.

stoke [stəuk] vt schüren; ~r Heizer m.

stole [stəul] n Stola f; ~n a gestohlen.

stolid ['stɒlɪd] a schwerfällig; silence stur.

stomach ['stʌmək] n Bauch m, Magen m; I have no ~ for it das ist nichts für mich; vt vertragen; ~-ache Magen- or Bauchschmerzen pl.

stone [stəun] n Stein m; (seed) Stein m, Kern m; (weight) Gewichtseinheit f = 6.35 kg; a steinern, Stein-; vt entkernen; (kill) steinigen; ~-cold a eiskalt; ~-deaf a stocktaub; ~mason Steinmetz m; ~work Mauerwerk nt.

stony ['stəunɪ] a steinig.

stool [stu:l] n Hocker m.

stoop [stu:p] vi sich bücken.

stop [stɒp] n Halt m; (bus—) Haltestelle f; (punctuation) Punkt m; vt stoppen, anhalten; (bring to end) aufhören (mit), sein lassen; vi aufhören; (clock) stehenbleiben; (remain) bleiben; to ~ doing sth aufhören, etw zu tun; ~ it! hör auf (damit)!; ~ dead vi plötzlich aufhören, innehalten; ~ in vi (at home) zu Hause bleiben; ~ off vi kurz haltmachen; ~ out vi (of house) ausbleiben; ~ over vi übernachten, über Nacht bleiben; ~ up vi (at night) aufbleiben; vt hole zustopfen, verstopfen; ~-lights pl (Aut) Bremslichter pl; ~over (on journey) Zwischenaufenthalt m; ~page ['stɒpɪdʒ] (An)halten nt; (traffic) Verkehrsstockung f; (strike) Arbeitseinstellung f; ~per Propfen m, Stöpsel m; ~press letzte Meldung f; ~watch Stoppuhr f.

storage ['stɔ:rɪdʒ] n Lagerung f.

store [stɔ:°] n Vorrat m; (place) Lager nt, Warenhaus nt; (large shop) Kaufhaus nt; vt lagern; vt auch sich eindecken mit; ~room Lagerraum m, Vorratsraum m.

storey ['stɔ:rɪ] n (Brit) Stock m, Stockwerk nt.

stork [stɔ:k] n Storch m.

storm [stɔ:m] n (lit, fig) Sturm m; vti stürmen; to take by ~ im Sturm nehmen; ~-**cloud** Gewitterwolke f; ~y a stürmisch.

story ['stɔ:rɪ] n Geschichte f, Erzählung f; (lie) Märchen nt; (US: storey) Stock m, Stockwerk nt; ~**book** Geschichtenbuch nt; ~**teller** Geschichtenerzähler m.

stout [staut] a (bold) mannhaft, tapfer; (too fat) beleibt, korpulent; ~**ness** Festigkeit f; (of body) Korpulenz f.

stove [stəuv] n (Koch)herd m; (for heating) Ofen m.

stow [stəu] vt verstauen; ~**away** blinde(r) Passagier m.

straddle ['strædl] vt horse, fence rittlings sitzen auf (+dat); (fig) überbrücken.

strafe [stra:f] vt beschießen, bombardieren.

straggle ['strægl] vi (branches etc) wuchern; (people) nachhinken; ~**r** Nachzügler m.

straight [streɪt] a gerade; (honest) offen, ehrlich; (in order) in Ordnung; drink pur, unverdünnt; ad (direct) direkt, geradewegs; n (Sport) Gerade f; ~**away** ad sofort, unverzüglich; ~**off** ad sofort; direkt nacheinander; ~ **on** ad geradeaus; ~**en** vt (also ~**en out**) (lit) gerade machen; (fig) in Ordnung bringen, klarstellen; ~**forward** a einfach, unkompliziert.

strain [streɪn] n Belastung f; (streak, trace) Zug m; (of music) Fetzen m; vt überanstrengen; (stretch) anspannen; muscle zerren; (filter) (durch)seihen; **don't ~ yourself** überanstrenge dich nicht; vi (make effort) sich anstrengen; ~**ed** a laugh gezwungen; relations gespannt; ~**er** Sieb nt.

strait [streɪt] n Straße f, Meerenge f; ~**ened** a circumstances beschränkt; ~-**jacket** Zwangsjacke f; ~-**laced** a engherzig, streng.

strand [strænd] n (lit, fig) Faden m; (of hair) Strähne f; **to be ~ed** (lit, fig) gestrandet sein.

strange [streɪndʒ] a fremd; (unusual) merkwürdig, seltsam; ~**ly** ad merkwürdig; fremd; ~**ly enough** merkwürdigerweise; ~**ness** Fremdheit f; ~**r** Fremde(r) mf; **I'm a ~r here** ich bin hier fremd.

strangle ['strængl] vt erdrosseln, erwürgen; ~**hold** (fig) Unklammerung f.

strangulation [strængjʊ'leɪʃən] n Erdrosseln nt.

strap [stræp] n Riemen m; (on clothes) Träger m; vt (fasten) festschnallen; ~**less** a dress trägerlos; ~**ping** a stramm.

stratagem ['strætədʒəm] n (Kriegs)list f.

strategic a, ~**ally** ad [strə'ti:dʒɪk, -əlɪ] strategisch.

strategist ['strætədʒɪst] n Stratege m.

strategy ['strætədʒɪ] n Kriegskunst f; (fig) Strategie f.

stratosphere ['strætəusfɪə°] n Stratosphäre f.

stratum ['strɑ:təm] n Schicht f.

straw [strɔ:] n Stroh nt; (single stalk, drinking —) Strohhalm m; a Stroh-; ~**berry** Erdbeere f.

stray [streɪ] n verirrte(s) Tier nt; vi herumstreunen; a animal verirrt; thought zufällig.

streak ['stri:k] n Streifen m; (in character) Einschlag m; (in hair) Strähne f; ~ **of bad luck** Pechsträhne f; vt streifen; ~**y** a gestreift; bacon durchwachsen.

stream [stri:m] n (brook) Bach m; (fig) Strom m; (flow of liquid) Strom m, Flut f; vi strömen, fluten; ~**er** (pennon) Wimpel m; (of paper) Luftschlange f; ~-**lined** a stromlinienförmig; (effective) rationell.

street [stri:t] n Straße f; ~-**car** (US) Straßenbahn f; ~ **lamp** Straßenlaterne f.

strength [streŋθ] n Stärke f (also fig); Kraft f; ~**en** vt (ver)stärken.

strenuous ['strenjuəs] a anstrengend; ~**ly** ad angestrengt.

stress [stres] n Druck m; (mental) Streß m; (Gram) Betonung f; vt betonen.

stretch [stretʃ] n Stück nt, Strecke f; vt ausdehnen, strecken; vi sich erstrecken; (person) sich strecken; **at a ~** (continuously) ununterbrochen; ~ **out** vi sich ausstrecken; vt ausstrecken; ~**er** Tragbahre f.

stricken ['strɪkən] a person befallen, ergriffen; city, country heimgesucht.

strict [strɪkt] a (exact) genau; (severe) streng; ~**ly** ad streng, genau; ~**ly speaking** streng or genau genommen; ~**ness** Strenge f.

stride [straɪd] n lange(r) Schritt m; vi irreg schreiten.

strident ['straɪdənt] a schneidend, durchdringend.

strife [straɪf] n Streit m.

strike [straɪk] n Streik m, Ausstand m; (discovery) Fund m; (attack) Schlag m; irreg vt (hit) schlagen; treffen; (collide) stoßen gegen; (come to mind) einfallen (+dat); (stand out) auffallen; (find) stoßen auf (+acc), finden; vi (stop work) streiken; (attack) zuschlagen; (clock) schlagen; ~ **down** vt (lay low) niederschlagen; ~ **out** vt (cross out) ausstreichen; ~ **up** vt music anstimmen; friendship schließen; ~ **pay** Streikgeld nt; ~**r** Streikende(r) mf.

striking a, ~**ly** ad ['straɪkɪŋ, -lɪ] auffallend, bemerkenswert.

string [strɪŋ] n Schnur f, Kordel f, Bindfaden m; (row) Reihe f; (Mus) Saite f; ~ **bean** grüne Bohne f.

stringency ['strɪndʒənsɪ] n Schärfe f.

stringent ['strɪndʒənt] a streng, scharf.

strip [strɪp] n Streifen m; vt (uncover) abstreifen, abziehen; clothes ausziehen; (Tech) auseinandernehmen; vi (undress) sich ausziehen; ~-**cartoon** Bildserie f.

stripe [straɪp] n Streifen m; ~**d** a gestreift.

strip light ['strɪplaɪt] n Leuchtröhre f.

stripper ['strɪpə°] n Stripteasetänzerin f.

striptease ['strɪpti:z] n Striptease nt.

strive [straɪv] vi irreg streben (for nach).

stroke [strəuk] n Schlag m, Hieb m; (swim, row) Stoß m; (Tech) Hub m; (Med) Schlaganfall m; (caress) Streicheln nt; vt streicheln; at a ~ mit einem Schlag; **on the ~** of 5 Schlag 5.

stroll [strəul] n Spaziergang m; vi

spazierengehen, schlendern.

strong [strɔŋ] a stark; (firm) fest; **they are 50 ~** sie sind 50 Mann stark; **~hold** Hochburg f; **~ly** ad stark; **~room** Tresor m.

structural ['strʌktʃərəl] a strukturell.

structure ['strʌktʃə*] n Struktur f, Aufbau m; (building) Gebäude nt, Bau m.

struggle ['strʌgl] n Kampf m, Anstrengung f; vi (fight) kämpfen; to **~ to do sth** sich (ab)mühen etw zu tun.

strum [strʌm] vt guitar klimpern auf (+dat).

strung [strʌŋ] see **highly**.

strut [strʌt] n Strebe f, Stütze f; vi stolzieren.

strychnine ['strɪkniːn] n Strychnin f.

stub [stʌb] n Stummel m; (of cigarette) Kippe f.

stubble ['stʌbl] n Stoppel f.

stubbly ['stʌblɪ] a stoppelig, Stoppel-.

stubborn a, **~ly** ad ['stʌbən, -lɪ] stur, hartnäckig; **~ness** Sturheit f, Hartnäckigkeit f.

stubby ['stʌbɪ] a untersetzt.

stucco ['stʌkəu] n Stuck m.

stuck-up ['stʌk'ʌp] a hochnäsig.

stud [stʌd] n (nail) Beschlagnagel m; (button) Kragenknopf m; (number of horses) Stall m; (place) Gestüt nt; **~ded with** übersät mit.

student ['stjuːdənt] n Student(in f) m; (US also) Schüler(in f) m; **fellow ~** Kommilitone m; Kommilitonin f.

studied ['stʌdɪd] a absichtlich.

studio ['stjuːdɪəu] n Studio nt; (for artist) Atelier nt.

studious a, **~ly** ad ['stjuːdɪəs, -lɪ] lernbegierig.

study ['stʌdɪ] n Studium nt; (investigation also) Untersuchung f; (room) Arbeitszimmer nt; (essay etc) Studie f; vt studieren; face erforschen; evidence prüfen; vi studieren; **~ group** Arbeitsgruppe f.

stuff [stʌf] n Stoff m; (col) Zeug nt; **that's hot ~!** das ist Klasse!; vt stopfen, füllen; animal ausstopfen; to **~ o.s.** sich vollstopfen; **~ed full** vollgepfropft; **~iness** Schwüle f, Spießigkeit f; **~ing** Füllung f, **~y** a room schwül; person spießig.

stumble ['stʌmbl] vi stolpern; to **~ on** zufällig stoßen auf (+acc).

stumbling block ['stʌmblɪŋblɒk] n Hindernis nt, Stein m des Anstoßes.

stump [stʌmp] n Stumpf m; vt umwerfen.

stun [stʌn] vt betäuben; (shock) niederschmettern.

stunning ['stʌnɪŋ] a betäubend; news überwältigend, unverhofft; **~ly beautiful** traumhaft schön.

stunt [stʌnt] n Kunststück nt, Trick m; vt verkümmern lassen; **~ed** a verkümmert.

stupefy ['stjuːpɪfaɪ] vt betäuben; (by news) bestürzen; **~ing** a betäubend; bestürzend.

stupendous [stjuːˈpendəs] a erstaunlich, enorm.

stupid a, **~ly** ad ['stjuːpɪd, -lɪ] dumm; **~ity** [stjuːˈpɪdɪtɪ] Dummheit f.

stupor ['stjuːpə*] n Betäubung f.

sturdily ['stɜːdɪlɪ] ad kräftig, stabil.

sturdiness [ˈstɜːdɪnəs] n Robustheit f.

sturdy ['stɜːdɪ] a kräftig, robust.

stutter ['stʌtə*] n Stottern nt; vi stottern.

sty [staɪ] n Schweinestall m.

stye [staɪ] n Gerstenkorn nt.

style [staɪl] n Stil m; (fashion) Mode f; **hair ~** Frisur f; **in ~** mit Stil; vt hair frisieren.

styling ['staɪlɪŋ] n (of car etc) Formgebung f.

stylish a, **~ly** ad ['staɪlɪʃ, -lɪ] modisch, schick, flott.

stylized ['staɪlaɪzd] a stilisiert.

stylus ['staɪləs] n (Grammophon)nadel f.

styptic ['stɪptɪk] a: **~ pencil** blutstillende(r) Stift m.

suave [swɑːv] a zuvorkommend.

sub- [sʌb] pref Unter-.

subconscious ['sʌbˈkɒnʃəs] a unterbewußt; n: **the ~** das Unterbewußte.

subdivide ['sʌbdɪˈvaɪd] vt unterteilen.

subdivision ['sʌbdɪvɪʒən] n Unterteilung f; (department) Unterabteilung f.

subdue [səbˈdjuː] vt unterwerfen; **~d** a lighting gedämpft; person still.

subject ['sʌbdʒɪkt] n (of kingdom) Untertan m; (citizen) Staatsangehörige(r) mf; (topic) Thema nt; (Sch) Fach nt; (Gram) Subjekt nt, Satzgegenstand m; [səbˈdʒekt] vt (subdue) unterwerfen, abhängig machen; (expose) aussetzen; **to be ~ to** unterworfen sein (+dat); (exposed) ausgesetzt sein (+dat); **~ion** [səbˈdʒekʃən] (conquering) Unterwerfung f; (being controlled) Abhängigkeit f; **~ive**, a **~ively** ad [səbˈdʒektɪv, -lɪ] subjektiv; **~ matter** Thema nt.

sub judice [sʌbˈdjuːdɪsɪ] a in gerichtliche(r) Untersuchung.

subjunctive [səbˈdʒʌŋktɪv] n Konjunktiv m, Möglichkeitsform f; a Konjunktiv-, konjunktivisch.

sublet ['sʌbˈlet] vt irreg untervermieten.

sublime [səˈblaɪm] a erhaben.

submarine [sʌbməˈriːn] n Unterseeboot nt, U-Boot nt.

submerge [səbˈmɜːdʒ] vt untertauchen; (flood) überschwemmen; vi untertauchen.

submission [səbˈmɪʃən] n (obedience) Ergebenheit f, Gehorsam m; (claim) Behauptung f; (of plan) Unterbreitung f.

submit [səbˈmɪt] vt behaupten; plan unterbreiten; vi (give in) sich ergeben.

subnormal ['sʌbˈnɔːməl] a minderbegabt.

subordinate [səˈbɔːdɪnət] a untergeordnet; n Untergebene(r) mf.

subpoena [səˈpiːnə] n Vorladung f; vt vorladen.

subscribe [səbˈskraɪb] vi spenden, Geld geben; (to view etc) unterstützen, beipflichten (+dat); (to newspaper) abonnieren (to acc); **~r** (to periodical) Abonnent m; (Tel) Telefonteilnehmer m.

subscription [səbˈskrɪpʃən] n Abonnement nt; (Mitglieds)beitrag m.

subsequent ['sʌbsɪkwənt] a folgend, später; **~ly** ad später.

subside [səb'saɪd] *vi* sich senken; **~nce** [sʌb'saɪdəns] Senkung *f.*

subsidiary [səb'sɪdɪərɪ] *n* Neben-; *n* (*company*) Zweig *m*, Tochtergesellschaft *f.*

subsidize ['sʌbsɪdaɪz] *vt* subventionieren.

subsidy ['sʌbsɪdɪ] *n* Subvention *f.*

subsistence [səb'sɪstəns] *n* Unterhalt *m*; **~ level** Existenzminimum *nt.*

substance ['sʌbstəns] *n* Substanz *f*, Stoff *m*; (*most important part*) Hauptbestandteil *m.*

substandard ['sʌb'stændəd] *a* unterdurchschnittlich.

substantial [səb'stænʃəl] *a* (*strong*) fest, kräftig; (*important*) wesentlich; **~ly** *ad* erheblich.

substantiate [səb'stænʃɪeɪt] *vt* begründen, belegen.

substation ['sʌbsteɪʃən] *n* (*Elec*) Nebenwerk *nt.*

substitute ['sʌbstɪtjuːt] *n* Ersatz *m*; *vt* ersetzen.

substitution [sʌbstɪ'tjuːʃən] *n* Ersetzung *f.*

subterfuge ['sʌbtəfjuːdʒ] *n* Vorwand *m*; Tricks *pl.*

subterranean [sʌbtə'reɪnɪən] *a* unterirdisch.

subtitle ['sʌbtaɪtl] *n* Untertitel *m.*

subtle ['sʌtl] *a* fein; (*sly*) raffiniert; **~ty** subtile Art *f*, Raffinesse *f.*

subtly ['sʌtlɪ] *ad* fein, raffiniert.

subtract [səb'trækt] *vt* abziehen, subtrahieren; **~ion** [səb'trækʃən] Abziehen *nt*, Subtraktion *f.*

subtropical ['sʌb'trɒpɪkəl] *a* subtropisch.

suburb ['sʌbɜːb] *n* Vorort *m*; **~an** [sə'bɜːbən] *a* Vorort(s)-, Stadtrand-; **~ia** [sə'bɜːbɪə] Vorstadt *f.*

subvention [səb'venʃən] *n* (*US*) Unterstützung *f*, Subvention *f.*

subversive [səb'vɜːsɪv] *a* subversiv.

subway ['sʌbweɪ] *n* (*US*) U-Bahn *f*, Untergrundbahn *f*; (*Brit*) Unterführung *f.*

sub-zero ['sʌbzɪərəʊ] *a* unter Null, unter dem Gefrierpunkt.

succeed [sək'siːd] *vi* gelingen (+*dat*), Erfolg haben; **he ~ed** es gelang ihm; *vt* (nach)folgen (+*dat*); **~ing** *a* (nach)folgend.

success [sək'ses] *n* Erfolg *m*; **~ful** *a*, **~fully** *ad* erfolgreich; **~ion** [sək'seʃən] (Aufeinander)folge *f*; (*to throne*) Nachfolge *f*; **~ive** *a* [sək'sesɪv] aufeinanderfolgend; **~or** Nachfolger(in *f*) *m.*

succinct [sək'sɪŋkt] *a* kurz und bündig, knapp.

succulent ['sʌkjʊlənt] *a* saftig.

succumb [sə'kʌm] *vi* zusammenbrechen (*to* unter +*dat*); (*yield*) nachgeben; (*die*) erliegen.

such [sʌtʃ] *a* solche(r, s); **~ a** so ein; **~ a lot** so viel; **~ is life** so ist das Leben; **~ is my wish** das ist mein Wunsch; **~** as wie; *pron* solch; **~ as I have** die, die ich habe; **~-like** *a* derartig; *pron* dergleichen.

suck [sʌk] *vt* saugen; *ice cream etc* lecken; *toffee etc* lutschen; *vi* saugen; **~er** (*col*) Idiot *m*, Dummkopf *m.*

suckle ['sʌkl] *vt* säugen; *child* stillen; *vi* saugen.

suction ['sʌkʃən] *n* Saugen *nt*, Saugkraft *f.*

sudden *a*, **~ly** *ad* ['sʌdn, -lɪ] plötzlich; **all of a ~** ganz plötzlich, auf einmal; **~ness** Plötzlichkeit *f.*

sue [suː] *vt* verklagen.

suède [sweɪd] *n* Wildleder *nt*; *a* Wildleder-.

suet [suɪt] *n* Nierenfett *nt.*

suffer ['sʌfə*] *vt* (er)leiden; (*old: allow*) zulassen, dulden; *vi* leiden; **~er** Leidende(r) *mf*; **~ing** Leiden *nt.*

suffice [sə'faɪs] *vi* genügen.

sufficient *a*, **~ly** *ad* [sə'fɪʃənt, -lɪ] ausreichend.

suffix ['sʌfɪks] *n* Nachsilbe *f.*

suffocate ['sʌfəkeɪt] *vti* ersticken.

suffocation [sʌfə'keɪʃən] *n* Ersticken *nt.*

suffragette [sʌfrə'dʒet] *n* Suffragette *f.*

sugar ['ʃʊgə*] *n* Zucker *m*; *vt* zuckern; **~ beet** Zuckerrübe *f*; **~ cane** Zuckerrohr *nt*; **~y** *a* süß.

suggest [sə'dʒest] *vt* vorschlagen; (*show*) schließen lassen auf (+*acc*); **what does this painting ~ to you?** was drückt das Bild für dich aus?; **~ion** [sə'dʒestʃən] Vorschlag *m*; **~ive** *a* anregend; (*indecent*) zweideutig; **to be ~ive of sth** an etw (*acc*) erinnern.

suicidal [sʊɪ'saɪdl] *a* selbstmörderisch; **that's ~** das ist Selbstmord.

suicide ['sʊɪsaɪd] *n* Selbstmord *m*; **to commit ~** Selbstmord begehen.

suit [suːt] *n* Anzug *m*; (*Cards*) Farbe *f*; *vt* passen (+*dat*); *clothes* stehen (+*dat*); (*adapt*) anpassen; **~ yourself** mach doch, was du willst; **~ability** [suːtə'bɪlɪtɪ] Eignung *f*; **~able** *a* geeignet, passend; **~ably** *ad* passend, angemessen; **~case** (Hand)koffer *m.*

suite [swiːt] *n* (*of rooms*) Zimmerflucht *f*; (*of furniture*) Einrichtung *f*; (*Mus*) Suite *f*; **three-piece ~** Couchgarnitur *f.*

sulfur ['sʌlfə*] *n* (*US*) = **sulphur.**

sulk [sʌlk] *vi* schmollen; **~y** *a* schmollend.

sullen ['sʌlən] *a* (*gloomy*) düster; (*bad-tempered*) mürrisch, verdrossen.

sulphur ['sʌlfə*] *n* Schwefel *m.*

sulphuric [sʌl'fjʊərɪk] *a*: **~ acid** Schwefelsäure *f.*

sultan ['sʌltən] *n* Sultan *m*; **~a** [sʌl'tɑːnə] (*woman*) Sultanin *f*; (*raisin*) Sultanine *f.*

sultry ['sʌltrɪ] *a* schwül.

sum [sʌm] *n* Summe *f*; (*money also*) Betrag *m*; (*arithmetic*) Rechenaufgabe *f*; **~s** *pl* Rechnen *nt*; **~ up** *vti* zusammenfassen; **~marize** *vt* kurz zusammenfassen; **~mary** Zusammenfassung *f*; (*of book etc*) Inhaltsangabe *f.*

summer ['sʌmə*] *n* Sommer *m*; *a* Sommer-; **~house** (*in garden*) Gartenhaus *nt*; **~time** Sommerzeit *f.*

summing-up ['sʌmɪŋ'ʌp] *n* Zusammenfassung *f.*

summit ['sʌmɪt] *n* Gipfel *m*; **~ conference** Gipfelkonferenz *f.*

summon ['sʌmən] *vt* bestellen, kommen lassen; (*Jur*) vorladen; (*gather up*) aufbieten, aufbringen; **~s** (*Jur*) Vorladung *f.*

sump [sʌmp] *n* Ölwanne *f.*

sumptuous ['sʌmptjuəs] a prächtig; **~ness** Pracht f.

sun [sʌn] n Sonne f; **~bathe** vi sich sonnen; **~bathing** Sonnenbaden nt; **~burn** Sonnenbrand m; **to be ~burnt** einen Sonnenbrand haben.

Sunday ['sʌndeɪ] n Sonntag m.

sundial ['sʌndaɪəl] n Sonnenuhr f.

sundown ['sʌndaun] n Sonnenuntergang m.

sundry ['sʌndrɪ] a verschieden; n: **sundries** pl Verschiedene(s) nt; **all and ~** alle.

sunflower ['sʌnflauə*] n Sonnenblume f.

sunglasses ['sʌnglɑːsɪz] npl Sonnenbrille f.

sunken ['sʌŋkən] a versunken; eyes eingesunken.

sunlight ['sʌnlaɪt] n Sonnenlicht nt.

sunlit ['sʌnlɪt] a sonnenbeschienen.

sunny ['sʌnɪ] a sonnig.

sunrise ['sʌnraɪz] n Sonnenaufgang m.

sunset ['sʌnset] n Sonnenuntergang m.

sunshade ['sʌnʃeɪd] n Sonnenschirm m.

sunshine ['sʌnʃaɪn] n Sonnenschein m.

sunspot ['sʌnspɒt] n Sonnenfleck m.

sunstroke ['sʌnstrəuk] n Hitzschlag m.

sun tan ['sʌntæn] n (Sonnen)bräune f; **to get a ~** braun werden.

suntrap ['sʌntræp] n sonnige(r) Platz m.

sunup ['sʌnʌp] n (col) Sonnenaufgang m.

super ['suːpə*] a (col) prima, klasse; Super-, Über-.

superannuation [suːpərænjueɪʃən] n Pension f.

superb a, **~ly** ad [suːˈpɜːb, -lɪ] ausgezeichnet, hervorragend.

supercilious [suːpəˈsɪlɪəs] a herablassend.

superficial a, **~ly** ad [suːpəˈfɪʃl, -lɪ] oberflächlich.

superfluous [suˈpɜːfluəs] a überflüssig.

superhuman [suːpəˈhjuːmən] a effort übermenschlich.

superimpose ['suːpərɪmˈpəuz] vt übereinanderlegen.

superintendent [suːpərɪnˈtendənt] n Polizeichef m.

superior [suˈpɪərɪə*] a (higher) höher(stehend); (better) besser; (proud) überlegen; n Vorgesetzte(r) mf; **~ity** [supɪərɪˈɒrɪtɪ] Überlegenheit f.

superlative [suˈpɜːlətɪv] a höchste(r,s); n (Gram) Superlativ m.

superman ['suːpəmæn] n Übermensch m.

supermarket ['suːpəmɑːkɪt] n Supermarkt m.

supernatural [suːpəˈnætʃərəl] a übernatürlich.

superpower ['suːpəpauə*] n Weltmacht f.

supersede [suːpəˈsiːd] vt ersetzen.

supersonic ['suːpəˈsɒnɪk] a Überschall-.

superstition [suːpəˈstɪʃən] n Aberglaube m.

superstitious [suːpəˈstɪʃəs] a abergläubisch.

supervise ['suːpəvaɪz] vt beaufsichtigen, kontrollieren.

supervision [suːpəˈvɪʒən] n Aufsicht f.

supervisor ['suːpəvaɪzə*] n Aufsichtsperson f; **~y** a Aufsichts-.

supper ['sʌpə*] n Abendessen nt.

supple ['sʌpl] a gelenkig, geschmeidig; wire biegsam.

supplement ['sʌplɪmənt] n Ergänzung f; (in book) Nachtrag m; [sʌplɪˈment] vt ergänzen; **~ary** [sʌplɪˈmentərɪ] a ergänzend, Ergänzungs-, Zusatz-.

supplier [səˈplaɪə*] n Lieferant m.

supply [səˈplaɪ] vt liefern; n Vorrat m; (supplying) Lieferung f; **supplies** pl (food) Vorräte pl; (Mil) Nachschub m; **~ and demand** Angebot nt und Nachfrage.

support [səˈpɔːt] n Unterstützung f; (Tech) Stütze f; vt (hold up) stützen, tragen; (provide for) ernähren; (speak in favour of) befürworten, unterstützen; **~er** Anhänger m; **~ing** a programme Bei-; role Neben-.

suppose [səˈpəuz] vti annehmen, denken, glauben; **I ~ so** ich glaube schon; **~ he comes . . .** angenommen, er kommt . . .; **~dly** [səˈpəuzɪdlɪ] ad angeblich.

supposing [səˈpəuzɪŋ] cj angenommen.

supposition [sʌpəˈzɪʃən] n Voraussetzung f.

suppress [səˈpres] vt unterdrücken; **~ion** [səˈpreʃən] Unterdrückung f; **~or** (Elec) Entstörungselement nt.

supra- ['suːprə] pref Über-.

supremacy [suˈpreməsɪ] n Vorherrschaft f, Oberhoheit f.

supreme a, **~ly** ad [suˈpriːm, -lɪ] oberste(r,s), höchste(r,s).

surcharge ['sɜːtʃɑːdʒ] n Zuschlag m.

sure [ʃuə*] a sicher, gewiß; **to be ~** sicher sein; **to be ~ about sth** sich (dat) einer Sache sicher sein; **we are ~ to win** wir werden ganz sicher gewinnen; ad sicher; **~!** (of course) ganz bestimmt!, natürlich!, klar!; **to make ~ of** sich vergewissern (+gen); **~-footed** a sicher (auf den Füßen); **~ly** ad (certainly) sicherlich, gewiß; **~ly it's wrong** das ist doch wohl falsch; **~ly not!** das ist doch wohl nicht wahr!; **~ty** Sicherheit f; (person) Bürge m.

surf [sɜːf] n Brandung f.

surface ['sɜːfɪs] n Oberfläche f; vt roadway teeren; vi auftauchen; **~ mail** gewöhnliche Post f, Post per Bahn f.

surfboard ['sɜːfbɔːd] n Wellenreiterbrett nt.

surfeit ['sɜːfɪt] n Übermaß nt.

surfing ['sɜːfɪŋ] n Wellenreiten nt, Surfing nt.

surge [sɜːdʒ] n Woge f; vi wogen.

surgeon ['sɜːdʒən] n Chirurg(in f) m.

surgery ['sɜːdʒərɪ] n Praxis f; (room) Sprechzimmer nt; (time) Sprechstunde f; (treatment) operative(r) Eingriff m, Operation f; **he needs ~** er muß operiert werden.

surgical ['sɜːdʒɪkəl] a chirurgisch.

surly ['sɜːlɪ] a verdrießlich, grob.

surmise [sɜːˈmaɪz] vt vermuten.

surmount [sɜːˈmaunt] vt überwinden.

surname ['sɜːneɪm] n Zuname m.

surpass [sɜːˈpɑːs] vt übertreffen.

surplus ['sɜːpləs] n Überschuß m; a überschüssig, Über(schuß)-.

surprise [sə'praiz] n Überraschung f; vt überraschen.

surprising [sə'praiziŋ] a überraschend; **~ly** ad überraschend(erweise).

surrealism [sə'riəlizəm] n Surrealismus m.

surrealist [sə'riəlist] a surrealistisch; n Surrealist m.

surrender [sə'rendə°] n Übergabe f; Kapitulation f; vi sich ergeben, kapitulieren; vt übergeben.

surreptitious a, **~ly** ad [sʌrəp'tiʃəs, -li] verstohlen.

surround [sə'raund] vt umgeben; (come all round) umringen; **~ed by** umgeben von; **~ing** a countryside umliegend; n: **~ings** pl Umgebung f; (environment) Umwelt f.

surveillance [sɜː'veiləns] n Überwachung f.

survey ['sɜːvei] n Übersicht f; [sɜː'vei] vt überblicken; land vermessen; **~ing** [sə'veiiŋ] (of land) (Land)vermessung f; **~or** [sə'veiə°] Land(ver)messer m.

survival [sə'vaivəl] n Überleben nt; (sth from earlier times) Überbleibsel nt.

survive [sə'vaiv] vti überleben.

survivor [sə'vaivə°] n Überlebende(r) mf.

susceptible [sə'septəbl] a empfindlich (to gegen); empfänglich (to für).

suspect ['sʌspekt] n Verdächtige(r) mf; a verdächtig; [səs'pekt] vt verdächtigen; (think) vermuten.

suspend [səs'pend] vt verschieben; (from work) suspendieren; (hang up) aufhängen; (Sport) sperren; n: **~ers** pl Strumpfhalter m; (men's) Sockenhalter m; (US) Hosenträger m.

suspense [səs'pens] n Spannung f.

suspension [səs'penʃən] n (hanging) (Auf-) hängen nt, Aufhängung f; (postponing) Aufschub m; (from work) Suspendierung f; (Sport) Sperrung f; (Aut) Federung f; **~ bridge** Hängebrücke f.

suspicion [səs'piʃən] n Mißtrauen nt; Verdacht m.

suspicious a, **~ly** ad [səs'piʃəs, -li] mißtrauisch; (causing suspicion) verdächtig; **~ness** Mißtrauen nt.

sustain [səs'tein] vt (hold up) stützen, tragen; (maintain) aufrechterhalten; (confirm) bestätigen; (Jur) anerkennen; injury davontragen; **~ed** a effort anhaltend.

sustenance ['sʌstinəns] n Nahrung f.

swab [swɒb] n (Med) Tupfer m; vt decks schrubben; wound abtupfen.

swagger ['swægə°] vi stolzieren; (behave) prahlen, angeben.

swallow ['swɒləʊ] n (bird) Schwalbe f; (of food etc) Schluck m; vt (ver)schlucken; **~ up** vt verschlingen.

swamp [swɒmp] n Sumpf m; vt überschwemmen; **~y** a sumpfig.

swan [swɒn] n Schwan m; **~ song** Schwanengesang m.

swap [swɒp] n Tausch m; vt (ein)tauschen (for gegen); vi tauschen.

swarm [swɔːm] n Schwarm m; vi wimmeln (with von).

swarthy ['swɔːði] a dunkel, braun.

swastika ['swɒstikə] n Hakenkreuz nt.

swat [swɒt] vt totschlagen.

sway [swei] vi schwanken; (branches) schaukeln, sich wiegen; vt schwenken; (influence) beeinflussen.

swear [sweə°] vi irreg (promise) schwören; (curse) fluchen; **to ~ to sth** schwören auf etw (acc); **~word** Fluch m.

sweat [swet] n Schweiß m; vi schwitzen; **~er** Pullover m; **~y** a verschwitzt.

swede [swiːd] n Steckrübe f.

sweep [swiːp] n (cleaning) Kehren nt; (wide curve) Bogen m; (with arm) schwungvolle Bewegung f; (chimney **~**) Schornsteinfeger m; irreg vt fegen, kehren; vi (road) sich dahinziehen; (go quickly) rauschen; **~ away** vt wegfegen; (river) wegspülen; **~ past** vi vorbeisausen; **~ up** vt zusammenkehren; **~ing** a gesture schwungvoll; statement verallgemeinernd; **~stake** Toto nt.

sweet [swiːt] n (course) Nachtisch m; (candy) Bonbon nt; a, **~ly** ad süß; **~corn** Zuckermais m; **~en** vt süßen; (fig) versüßen; **~heart** Liebste(r) mf; **~ness** Süße f; **~ pea** Gartenwicke f; **to have a ~ tooth** ein Leckermaul sein.

swell [swel] n Seegang m; a (col) todschick; irreg vt numbers vermehren; vi (also **~ up**) (an)schwellen; **~ing** Schwellung f.

sweltering ['sweltəriŋ] a drückend.

swerve [swɜːv] vi ausschwenken nt; vti ausscheren, zur Seite schwenken.

swift [swift] n Mauersegler m; a, **~ly** ad geschwind, schnell, rasch; **~ness** Schnelligkeit f.

swig [swig] n Zug m.

swill [swil] n (for pigs) Schweinefutter nt; vt spülen.

swim [swim] n: **to go for a ~** schwimmen gehen; irreg vi schwimmen; **my head is ~ming** mir dreht sich der Kopf; vt (cross) (durch)schwimmen; **~mer** Schwimmer(in f) m; **~ming** Schwimmen nt; **to go ~ming** schwimmen gehen; **~ming baths** pl Schwimmbad nt; **~ming cap** Badehaube f, Badekappe f; **~ming costume** Badeanzug m; **~ming pool** Schwimmbecken nt; (private) Swimming-Pool m; **~suit** Badeanzug m.

swindle ['swindl] n Schwindel m, Betrug m; vt betrügen; **~r** Schwindler m.

swine [swain] n (lit, fig) Schwein nt.

swing [swiŋ] n (child's) Schaukel f; (swinging) Schwingen nt, Schwung m; (Mus) Swing m; irreg vt schwingen, (herum-) schwenken; vi schwingen, pendeln, schaukeln; (turn quickly) schwenken; **in full ~** in vollem Gange; **~ bridge** Drehbrücke f; **~ door** Schwingtür f.

swipe [swaip] n Hieb m; vt (col) (hit) hart schlagen; (steal) klauen.

swirl [swɜːl] n Wirbel m; vi wirbeln.

switch [switʃ] n (Elec) Schalter m; (change) Wechsel m; vti (Elec) schalten; (change) wechseln; **~ off** vt ab- or ausschalten; **~ on** vt an- or einschalten; **~back** Achterbahn f; **~board**

Vermittlung *f*, Zentrale *f*; *(board)* Schaltbrett *nt*.

swivel ['swɪvl] *vti (also* ~ **round)** (sich) drehen.

swollen ['swəʊlən] *a* geschwollen.

swoon [swuːn] *vi (old)* in Ohnmacht fallen.

swoop [swuːp] *n* Sturzflug *m; (esp by police)* Razzia *f; vi (also* ~ **down)** stürzen.

swop [swop] = **swap**.

sword [sɔːd] *n* Schwert *nt;* ~**fish** Schwertfisch *m;* ~**sman** Fechter *m*.

sworn [swɔːn] *a:* ~ **enemies** *pl* Todfeinde *pl*.

sycamore ['sɪkəmɔː*] *n (US)* Platane *f; (Brit)* Bergahorn *m*.

sycophantic [sɪkə'fæntɪk] *a* schmeichlerisch, kriecherisch.

syllable ['sɪləbl] *n* Silbe *f*.

syllabus ['sɪləbəs] *n* Lehrplan *m*.

symbol ['sɪmbəl] *n* Symbol *nt;* ~**ic(al)** [sɪm'bolɪk(əl)] *a* symbolisch; ~**ism** symbolische Bedeutung *f; (Art)* Symbolismus *m;* ~**ize** *vt* versinnbildlichen, symbolisieren.

symmetrical *a,* ~**ly** *ad* [sɪ'metrɪkəl, -ɪ] symmetrisch, gleichmäßig.

symmetry ['sɪmɪtrɪ] *n* Symmetrie *f*.

sympathetic *a,* ~**ally** *ad* [sɪmpə'θetɪk, -əlɪ] mitfühlend.

sympathize ['sɪmpəθaɪz] *vi* sympathisieren; mitfühlen; ~**r** Mitfühlende(r) *mf; (Pol)* Sympathisant *m*.

sympathy ['sɪmpəθɪ] *n* Mitleid *nt*, Mitgefühl *nt; (condolence)* Beileid *nt*.

symphonic [sɪm'fonɪk] *a* sinfonisch.

symphony ['sɪmfənɪ] *n* Sinfonie *f;* ~ **orchestra** Sinfonieorchester *nt*.

symposium [sɪm'pəʊzɪəm] *n* Tagung *f*.

symptom ['sɪmptəm] *n* Symptom *nt*, Anzeichen *nt;* ~**atic** [sɪmptə'mætɪk] *a (fig)* bezeichnend *(of* für).

synagogue ['sɪnəgog] *n* Synagoge *f*.

synchromesh ['sɪŋkrəʊ'meʃ] *n* Synchronschaltung *f*.

synchronize ['sɪŋkrənaɪz] *vt* synchronisieren; *vi* gleichzeitig sein or ablaufen.

syndicate ['sɪndɪkət] *n* Konsortium *nt*, Verband *m*, Ring *m*.

syndrome ['sɪndrəʊm] *n* Syndrom *nt*.

synonym ['sɪnənɪm] *n* Synonym *nt;* ~**ous** [sɪ'nonɪməs] *a* gleichbedeutend.

synopsis [sɪ'nopsɪs] *n* Abriß *m*, Zusammenfassung *f*.

syntactic [sɪn'tæktɪk] *a* syntaktisch.

syntax ['sɪntæks] *n* Syntax *f*.

synthesis ['sɪnθəsɪs] *n* Synthese *f*.

synthetic *a,* ~**ally** *ad* [sɪn'θetɪk, -əlɪ] synthetisch, künstlich.

syphilis ['sɪfɪlɪs] *n* Syphilis *f*.

syphon ['saɪfən] = **siphon**.

syringe [sɪ'rɪndʒ] *n* Spritze *f*.

syrup ['sɪrəp] *n* Sirup *m; (of sugar)* Melasse *f*.

system ['sɪstəm] *n* System *nt;* ~**atic** *a,* ~**atically** *ad* [sɪstə'mætɪk, -əlɪ] systematisch, planmäßig.

T

T, t [tiː] *n* T *nt*, t *nt;* **to a** ~ genau.

ta [taː] *interj (Brit col)* danke.

tab [tæb] *n* Schlaufe *f*, Aufhänger *m; (name* ~) Schild *nt*.

tabby ['tæbɪ] *n (female cat)* (weibliche) Katze *f; a (black-striped)* getigert.

tabernacle ['tæbənækl] *n* Tabernakel *nt* or *m*.

table ['teɪbl] *n* Tisch *m; (list)* Tabelle *f*, Tafel *f;* **to lay sth on the** ~ *(fig)* etw zur Diskussion stellen; *vt (Parl: propose)* vorlegen, einbringen.

tableau ['tæbləʊ] *n* lebende(s) Bild *nt*.

tablecloth ['teɪblklɒθ] *n* Tischtuch *nt*, Tischdecke *f*.

table d'hôte ['tɑːbl'dəʊt] *n* Tagesmenu *nt*.

tablemat ['teɪblmæt] *n* Untersatz *m*.

tablespoon ['teɪblspuːn] *n* Eßlöffel *m;* ~**ful** Eßlöffel(voll) *m*.

tablet ['tæblət] *n (Med)* Tablette *f; (for writing)* Täfelchen *nt; (of paper)* Schreibblock *m; (of soap)* Riegel *m*.

table talk ['teɪbltɔːk] *n* Tischgespräch *nt*.

table tennis ['teɪbltenɪs] *n* Tischtennis *nt*.

table wine ['teɪblwaɪn] *n* Tafelwein *m*.

taboo [tə'buː] *n* Tabu *nt; a* tabu.

tabulate ['tæbjuleɪt] *vt* tabellarisch ordnen.

tacit *a,* ~**ly** *ad* ['tæsɪt, -lɪ] stillschweigend; ~**urn** *a* schweigsam, wortkarg.

tack [tæk] *n (small nail)* Stift *m; (US: thumb*~) Reißzwecke *f; (stitch)* Heftstich *m; (Naut)* Lavieren *nt; (course)* Kurs *m*.

tackle ['tækl] *n (for lifting)* Flaschenzug *m; (Naut)* Takelage *f; (Sport)* Tackling *nt; vt (deal with)* anpacken, in Angriff nehmen; *person* festhalten; *player* angehen; **he couldn't** ~ **it** er hat es nicht bewältigt.

tacky ['tækɪ] *a* klebrig.

tact [tækt] *n* Takt *m;* ~**ful** *a,* ~**fully** *ad* taktvoll.

tactical ['tæktɪkəl] *a* taktisch.

tactics ['tæktɪks] *npl* Taktik *f*.

tactless *a,* ~**ly** *ad* ['tæktləs, -lɪ] taktlos.

tadpole ['tædpəʊl] *n* Kaulquappe *f*.

taffeta ['tæfɪtə] *n* Taft *m*.

taffy ['tæfɪ] *n (US)* Sahnebonbon *nt*.

tag [tæg] *n (label)* Schild *nt*, Anhänger *m; (maker's name)* Etikett *nt; (phrase)* Floskel *f*, Spruch *m;* ~ **along** *vi* mitkommen; ~ **question** Bestätigungsfrage *f*.

tail [teɪl] *n* Schwanz *m; (of list)* Schluß *m; (of comet)* Schweif *m;* ~**s** *(of coin)* Zahl(seite) *f; vt* folgen *(+dat);* ~ **off** *vi* abfallen, schwinden; ~ **end** Schluß *m*, Ende *nt*.

tailor ['teɪlə*] *n* Schneider *m;* ~**ing** Schneidern *nt*, Schneiderarbeit *f;* ~-**made** *a (lit)* maßgeschneidert; *(fig)* wie auf den Leib geschnitten *(for sb* jdm).

tailwind ['teɪlwɪnd] *n* Rückenwind *m*.

tainted ['teɪntɪd] *a* verdorben.

take [teɪk] *vt irreg* nehmen; *prize* entgegennehmen; *trip, exam* machen; *(capture) person* fassen; *town* einnehmen; *disease* bekommen; *(carry to a place)* bringen; (*Math: subtract*) abziehen (*from von*); (*extract*) *quotation* entnehmen (*from dat*); (*get for o.s.*) sich (*dat*) nehmen; (*gain, obtain*) bekommen; (*Fin, Comm*) einnehmen; (*record*) aufnehmen; (*consume*) zu sich nehmen; (*Phot*) aufnehmen, machen; (*put up with*) hinnehmen; (*respond to*) aufnehmen; (*understand, interpret*) auffassen; (*assume*) annehmen; (*contain*) fassen, Platz haben für; (*Gram*) stehen mit; **it ~s 4 hours** man braucht 4 Stunden; **it ~s him 4 hours** er braucht 4 Stunden; **to ~ sth from sb** jdm etw wegnehmen; **to ~ part in** teilnehmen an (+*dat*); **to ~ place** stattfinden; **~ after** *vt* ähnlich sein (+*dat*); **~ back** *vt* (*return*) zurückbringen; (*retract*) zurücknehmen; (*remind*) zurückversetzen (*to in* +*acc*); **~ down** *vt* (*pull down*) abreißen; (*write down*) aufschreiben; **~ in** *vt* (*deceive*) hereinlegen; (*understand*) begreifen; (*include*) einschließen; **~ off** *vi* (*plane*) starten; *vt* (*remove*) wegnehmen, abmachen; *clothing* ausziehen; (*imitate*) nachmachen; **~ on** *vt* (*undertake*) übernehmen; (*engage*) einstellen; (*opponent*) antreten gegen; **~ out** *vt* (*extract*) herausnehmen; (*insurance*) abschließen; *licence* sich (*dat*) geben lassen; *book* ausleihen; (*remove*) entfernen; **to ~ sth out on sb** etw an jdm auslassen; **~ over** *vt* übernehmen; *vi* ablösen (*from acc*); **~ to** *vt* (*like*) mögen; (*adopt as practice*) sich (*dat*) angewöhnen; **~ up** *vt* (*raise*) aufnehmen; *hem* kürzer machen; (*occupy*) in Anspruch nehmen; (*absorb*) aufsaugen; (*engage in*) sich befassen mit; **to ~ sb up on sth** jdn beim Wort nehmen; **to be ~n with** begeistert sein von; **~off** (*Aviat*) Abflug *m*, Start *m*; (*imitation*) Nachahmung *f*; **~over** (*Comm*) Übernahme *f*; **~over bid** Übernahmeangebot *nt*.

takings ['teɪkɪŋz] *npl* (*Comm*) Einnahmen *pl*.

talc [tælk] *n* (*also* **~um powder**) Talkumpuder *m*.

tale [teɪl] *n* Geschichte *f*, Erzählung *f*.

talent ['tælənt] *n* Talent *nt*, Begabung *f*; **~ed** a talentiert, begabt.

talk [tɔ:k] *n* (*conversation*) Gespräch *nt*; (*rumour*) Gerede *nt*; (*speech*) Vortrag *m*; *vi* sprechen, reden; (*gossip*) klatschen, reden; **~ing of** ... da wir gerade von ... sprechen; **~ about impertinence!** so eine Frechheit!; **to ~ sb into doing sth** jdn überreden, etw zu tun; **to ~ shop** fachsimpeln; **~ over** *vt* besprechen; **~ative** a redselig, gesprächig; **~er** Schwätzer *m*.

tall [tɔ:l] a groß; *building* hoch; **~boy** Kommode *f*; **~ness** Größe *f*, Höhe *f*; **~ story** übertriebene Geschichte *f*.

tally ['tælɪ] *n* Abrechnung *f*; *vi* übereinstimmen.

talon ['tælən] *n* Kralle *f*.

tambourine [tæmbə'ri:n] *n* Tamburin *nt*.

tame [teɪm] a zahm; (*fig*) fade, langweilig;

vt zähmen; **~ness** Zahmheit *f*; (*fig*) Langweiligkeit *f*.

tamper ['tæmpə*] **~ with** *vt* herumpfuschen an (+*dat*); *documents* fälschen.

tampon ['tæmpɒn] *n* Tampon *m*.

tan [tæn] *n* (*on skin*) (Sonnen)bräune *f*; (*colour*) Gelbbraun *nt*; a (*colour*) (gelb)braun.

tandem ['tændəm] *n* Tandem *nt*.

tang [tæŋ] *n* Schärfe *f*, scharfe(r) Geschmack *m or* Geruch *m*.

tangent ['tændʒənt] *n* Tangente *f*.

tangerine [tændʒə'ri:n] *n* Mandarine *f*.

tangible ['tændʒəbl] a (*lit*) greifbar; (*real*) handgreiflich.

tangle ['tæŋgl] *n* Durcheinander *nt*; (*trouble*) Schwierigkeiten *pl*; *vt* verwirren.

tango ['tæŋgəʊ] *n* Tango *m*.

tank [tæŋk] *n* (*container*) Tank *m*, Behälter *m*; (*Mil*) Panzer *m*.

tankard ['tæŋkəd] *n* Seidel *nt*, Deckelkrug *m*.

tanker ['tæŋkə*] *n* (*ship*) Tanker *m*; (*vehicle*) Tankwagen *m*.

tankful ['tæŋkfʊl] *n* volle(r) Tank *m*.

tanned [tænd] a *skin* gebräunt, sonnenverbrannt.

tantalizing ['tæntəlaɪzɪŋ] *a* verlockend; (*annoying*) quälend.

tantamount ['tæntəmaʊnt] a gleichbedeutend (*to* mit).

tantrum ['tæntrəm] *n* Wutanfall *m*.

tap [tæp] *n* Hahn *m*; (*gentle blow*) leichte(r) Schlag *m*, Klopfen *nt*; *vt* (*strike*) klopfen; *supply* anzapfen.

tap-dance ['tæpdɑ:ns] *vi* steppen.

tape [teɪp] *n* Band *nt*; (*magnetic*) (Ton)band *nt*; (*adhesive*) Klebstreifen *m*; *vt* (*record*) (auf Band) aufnehmen; **~ measure** Maßband *nt*.

taper ['teɪpə*] *n* (dünne) Wachskerze *f*; *vi* spitz zulaufen.

tape recorder ['teɪprɪkɔ:də*] *n* Tonbandgerät *nt*.

tapered ['teɪpəd], **tapering** ['teɪpərɪŋ] a spitz zulaufend.

tapestry ['tæpɪstrɪ] *n* Wandteppich *m*, Gobelin *m*.

tapioca [tæpɪ'əʊkə] *n* Tapioka *f*.

tappet ['tæpɪt] *n* (*Aut*) Nocke *f*.

tar [tɑ:*] *n* Teer *m*.

tarantula [tə'ræntjʊlə] *n* Tarantel *f*.

tardy ['tɑ:dɪ] a langsam, spät.

target ['tɑ:gɪt] *n* Ziel *nt*; (*board*) Zielscheibe *f*.

tariff ['tærɪf] *n* (*duty paid*) Zoll *m*; (*list*) Tarif *m*.

tarmac ['tɑ:mæk] *n* (*Aviat*) Rollfeld *nt*.

tarn [tɑ:n] *n* Gebirgssee *m*.

tarnish ['tɑ:nɪʃ] *vt* (*lit*) matt machen; (*fig*) beflecken.

tarpaulin [tɑ:'pɔ:lɪn] *n* Plane *f*, Persenning *f*.

tarry ['tærɪ] *vi* (*liter*) bleiben; (*delay*) säumen.

tart [tɑ:t] *n* (*Obst*)torte *f*; (*col*) Nutte *f*; a scharf, sauer; *remark* scharf, spitz.

tartan ['tɑ:tən] *n* schottisch-karierte(r) Stoff *m*; Schottenkaro *nt*.

tartar ['tɑːtə*] n Zahnstein m; ~(e) **sauce** Remouladensoße f.

tartly ['tɑːtlɪ] ad spitz.

task [tɑːsk] n Aufgabe f; (duty) Pflicht f; ~ **force** Sondertrupp m.

tassel ['tæsəl] n Quaste f.

taste [teɪst] n Geschmack m; (sense) Geschmackssinn m; (small quantity) Kostprobe f; (liking) Vorliebe f; vt schmecken; (try) versuchen; vi schmecken (of nach); ~**ful** a, ~**fully** ad geschmackvoll; ~**less** a (insipid) ohne Geschmack, fade; (in bad taste) geschmacklos; ~**lessly** ad geschmacklos.

tastily ['teɪstɪlɪ] ad schmackhaft.

tastiness ['teɪstɪnəs] n Schmackhaftigkeit f.

tasty ['teɪstɪ] a schmackhaft.

tata ['tæ'tɑː] interj (Brit col) tschüß.

tattered ['tætəd] a zerrissen, zerlumpt.

tatters ['tætəz] npl: **in** ~ in Fetzen.

tattoo [tə'tuː] n (Mil) Zapfenstreich m; (on skin) Tätowierung f; vt tätowieren.

tatty ['tætɪ] a (col) schäbig.

taunt [tɔːnt] n höhnische Bemerkung f; vt verhöhnen.

Taurus ['tɔːrəs] n Stier m.

taut [tɔːt] a straff.

tavern ['tævən] n Taverne f.

tawdry ['tɔːdrɪ] a (bunt und) billig.

tawny ['tɔːnɪ] a gelbbraun.

tax [tæks] n Steuer f; vt besteuern; (strain) strapazieren; strength angreifen; ~**ation** [tæk'seɪʃən] Besteuerung f; ~ **collector** Steuereinnehmer m; ~-**free** a steuerfrei.

taxi ['tæksɪ] n Taxi nt; vi (plane) rollen.

taxidermist ['tæksɪdɜːmɪst] n Tierausstopfer m.

taxi driver ['tæksɪ draɪvə*] n Taxifahrer m.

taxi rank ['tæksɪræŋk] n Taxistand m.

taxpayer ['tækspeɪə*] n Steuerzahler m.

tax return ['tæksrɪ'tɜːn] n Steuererklärung f.

tea [tiː] n Tee m; (meal) (frühes) Abendessen nt; ~ **bag** Tee(aufguß)beutel m; ~ **break** Teepause f; ~ **cake** Rosinenbrötchen nt.

teach [tiːtʃ] vti irreg lehren; (Sch also) unterrichten; (show) zeigen, beibringen (sb sth jdm etw); **that'll** ~ **him!** das hat er nun davon!; ~**er** Lehrer(in f) m; ~-**in** Teach-in nt; ~**ing** (teacher's work) Unterricht m, Lehren nt; (doctrine) Lehre f.

tea cosy ['tiːkəʊzɪ] n Teewärmer m.

teacup ['tiːkʌp] n Teetasse f.

teak [tiːk] n Teakbaum m; a Teak(holz)-.

tea leaves ['tiːliːvz] npl Teeblätter pl.

team [tiːm] n (workers) Team nt; (Sport) Mannschaft f; (animals) Gespann nt; ~ **spirit** Gemeinschaftsgeist m; (Sport) Mannschaftsgeist m; ~**work** Zusammenarbeit f, Teamwork nt.

tea party ['tiːpɑːtɪ] n Kaffeeklatsch m.

teapot ['tiːpɒt] n Teekanne f.

tear [tɛə*] n Riß m; irreg vt zerreißen; muscle zerren; **I am torn between ... ich**

schwanke zwischen . . .; vi (zer)reißen; (rush) rasen, sausen.

tear [tɪə*] n Träne f; **in** ~**s** in Tränen (aufgelöst); ~**ful** a weinend; voice weinerlich; ~ **gas** Tränengas nt.

tearing ['tɛərɪŋ] a: **to be in a** ~ **hurry** es schrecklich eilig haben.

tearoom ['tiːrʊm] n Teestube f.

tease [tiːz] n Hänsler m; vt necken, aufziehen; animal quälen; **I was only teasing** ich habe nur Spaß gemacht.

tea set ['tiːset] n Teeservice nt.

teashop ['tiːʃɒp] n Café nt.

teaspoon ['tiːspuːn] n Teelöffel m; ~**ful** Teelöffel(voll) m.

tea strainer ['tiːstreɪnə*] n Teesieb nt.

teat [tiːt] n (of woman) Brustwarze f; (of animal) Zitze f; (of bottle) Sauger m.

tea towel ['tiːtaʊəl] n Küchenhandtuch nt.

tea urn ['tiːɜːn] n Teemaschine f.

technical ['teknɪkəl] a technisch; knowledge, terms Fach-; ~**ity** [teknɪ'kælɪtɪ] technische Einzelheit f; (Jur) Formsache f; ~**ly** ad technisch; speak spezialisiert; (fig) genau genommen.

technician [tek'nɪʃən] n Techniker m.

technique [tek'niːk] n Technik f.

technological [teknə'lɒdʒɪkəl] a technologisch.

technologist [tek'nɒlədʒɪst] n Technologe m.

technology [tek'nɒlədʒɪ] n Technologie f.

teddy (bear) ['tedɪ(bɛə*)] n Teddybär m.

tedious ['tiːdɪəs] a, ~**ly** ad ['tiːdɪəs, -lɪ] langweilig, ermüdend.

tedium ['tiːdɪəm] n Langweiligkeit f.

tee [tiː] n (golf) Abschlagstelle f; (object) Tee nt.

teem [tiːm] vi (swarm) wimmeln (with von); (pour) gießen.

teenage ['tiːneɪdʒ] a fashions etc Teenager-, jugendlich; ~**r** Teenager m, Jugendliche(r) mf.

teens [tiːnz] npl Jugendjahre pl.

teeter ['tiːtə*] vi schwanken.

teeth [tiːθ] npl of tooth.

teethe [tiːð] vi zahnen.

teething ring ['tiːðɪŋrɪŋ] n Beißring m.

teetotal ['tiː'təʊtl] a abstinent; ~**ler**, (US) ~**er** Antialkoholiker m, Abstinenzler m.

telecommunications ['telɪkəmjuːnɪ'keɪʃənz] npl Fernmeldewesen nt.

telegram ['telɪgræm] n Telegramm nt.

telegraph ['telɪgrɑːf] n Telegraph m; ~**ic** [telɪ'græfɪk] a address Telegramm-; ~ **pole** Telegraphenmast m.

telepathic [telɪ'pæθɪk] a telepathisch.

telepathy [tə'lepəθɪ] n Telepathie f, Gedankenübertragung f.

telephone ['telɪfəʊn] n Telefon nt, Fernsprecher m; vi telefonieren; vt anrufen; message telefonisch mitteilen; ~ **booth**, ~ **box** Telefonhäuschen nt, Fernsprechzelle f; ~ **call** Telefongespräch nt, Anruf m; ~ **directory** Telefonbuch nt; ~ **exchange** Telefonvermittlung f, Telefonzentrale f; ~ **number** Telefonnummer f.

telephonist [tə'lefənɪst] n Telefonist(in f) m.

telephoto lens ['telɪ'fəutəu'lenz] n Tele-objektiv nt.

teleprinter ['telɪprɪntə*] n Fernschreiber m.

telescope ['telɪskəup] n Teleskop nt, Fernrohr nt; vt ineinanderschieben.

telescopic [telɪs'kɒpɪk] a teleskopisch; aerial etc ausziehbar.

televiewer ['telɪvjuːə*] n Fernsehteil-nehmer(in f) m.

televise ['telɪvaɪz] vt durch das Fernsehen übertragen.

television ['telɪvɪʒən] n Fernsehen nt; to watch ~ fernsehen; ~ (set) Fern-sehapparat m, Fernseher m; on ~ im Fernsehen.

telex ['teleks] n Telex nt.

tell [tel] irreg vt story erzählen; secret ausplaudern; (say, make known) sagen (sth to sb jdm etw); (distinguish) erkennen (sb by sth jdn an etw dat); (be sure) wissen; (order) sagen, befehlen (sb jdm); to ~ a lie lügen; to ~ sb about sth jdm von etw erzählen; vi (be sure) wissen; (divulge) es verraten; (have effect) sich auswirken; ~ off vt schimpfen; ~ on vt verraten, ver-petzen; ~er Kassenbeamte(r) mf; ~ing verräterisch; blow hart; moment der Wahrheit; ~tale a verräterisch.

telly ['telɪ] n (col) Fernseher m.

temerity [tɪ'merɪtɪ] n (Toll)kühnheit f.

temper ['tempə*] n (disposition) Tempera-ment nt, Gemütsart f; (anger) Gereiztheit f, Zorn m; to be in a (bad) ~ wütend or gereizt sein; vt (tone down) mildern; metal härten; quick ~ed jähzornig, auf-brausend; ~ament Temperament nt, Veranlagung f; ~amental [tempərə'mentl] a (moody) launisch.

temperance ['tempərəns] n Mäßigung f; (abstinence) Enthaltsamkeit f; ~ hotel alkoholfreie(s) Hotel nt.

temperate ['tempərət] a gemäßigt.

temperature ['temprɪtʃə*] n Temperatur f; (Med: high —) Fieber nt.

tempered ['tempəd] a steel gehärtet.

tempest ['tempɪst] n (wilder) Sturm m; ~uous [tem'pestjuəs] a stürmisch; (fig) ungestüm.

template ['templət] n Schablone f.

temple ['templ] n Tempel m; (Anat) Schläfe f.

tempo ['tempəu] n Tempo nt.

temporal ['tempərəl] a (of time) zeitlich; (worldly) irdisch, weltlich.

temporarily ['tempərərɪlɪ] ad zeitweilig, vorübergehend.

temporary ['tempərərɪ] a vorläufig; road, building provisorisch.

tempt [tempt] vt (persuade) verleiten, in Versuchung führen; (attract) reizen, (ver)-locken; ~ation [temp'teɪʃən] Versuchung f, ~ing a person verführerisch; object, situation verlockend.

ten [ten] num zehn.

tenable ['tenəbl] a haltbar; to be ~ (post) vergeben werden.

tenacious a, ~ly ad [tə'neɪʃəs, -lɪ] zäh, hartnäckig.

tenacity [tə'næsɪtɪ] n Zähigkeit f, Hart-näckigkeit f.

tenancy ['tenənsɪ] n Mietverhältnis nt; Pachtverhältnis nt.

tenant ['tenənt] n Mieter m; (of larger property) Pächter m.

tend [tend] vt (look after) sich kümmern um; vi neigen, tendieren (to zu); to ~ to do sth (things) etw gewöhnlich tun; ~ency Tendenz f; (of person also) Neigung f.

tender ['tendə*] a (soft) weich, zart; (delicate) zart; (loving) liebevoll, zärtlich; n (Comm: offer) Kostenanschlag m; ~ize vt weich machen; ~ly ad liebevoll; touch also zart; ~ness Zartheit f; (being loving) Zärtlichkeit f.

tendon ['tendən] n Sehne f.

tenement ['tenəmənt] n Mietshaus nt.

tenet ['tenət] n Lehre f.

tennis ['tenɪs] n Tennis nt; ~ ball Tennis-ball m; ~ court Tennisplatz m; ~ racket Tennisschläger m.

tenor ['tenə*] n (voice) Tenor(stimme f) m; (singer) Tenor m; (meaning) Sinn m, wesentliche(r) Inhalt m.

tense [tens] a angespannt; (stretched tight) gespannt, straff; n Zeitform f; ~ly ad (an)gespannt; ~ness Spannung f; (strain) Angespanntheit f.

tension ['tenʃən] n Spannung f; (strain) (An)gespanntheit f.

tent [tent] n Zelt nt.

tentacle ['tentəkl] n Fühler m; (of sea animals) Fangarm m.

tentative ['tentətɪv] a movement unsicher; offer Probe-; arrangement vorläufig; suggestion unverbindlich; ~ly ad versuchsweise; try, move vorsichtig.

tenterhooks ['tentəhuks] npl: to be on ~ auf die Folter gespannt sein.

tenth [tenθ] a zehnte(r,s); n Zehntel nt.

tent peg ['tentpeg] n Hering m.

tent pole ['tentpəul] n Zeltstange f.

tenuous ['tenjuəs] a fein; air dünn; con-nection, argument schwach.

tenure ['tenjuə*] n (of land) Besitz m; (of office) Amtszeit f.

tepid ['tepɪd] a lauwarm.

term [tɜːm] n (period of time) Zeit(raum m) f; (limit) Frist f; (Sch) Quartal nt; (Univ) Trimester nt; (expression) Aus-druck m; vt (be)nennen; ~s pl (con-ditions) Bedingungen pl; (relationship) Beziehungen pl; to be on good ~s with sb mit jdm gut auskommen; ~inal (Rail, bus —inal; also —inus) Endstation f; (Aviat) Terminal m; a Schluß-; (Med) unheilbar; ~inal cancer Krebs m im Endstadium; ~inate vt beenden; vi enden, aufhören (in auf +dat); ~ination [tɜːmɪ'neɪʃən] Ende nt; (act) Beendigung f; ~inology [tɜːmɪ'nɒlədʒɪ] Terminologie f.

termite ['tɜːmaɪt] n Termite f.

terrace ['terəs] n (of houses) Häuserreihe f; (in garden etc) Terrasse f; ~d a garden terrassenförmig angelegt; house Reihen-.

terracotta ['terə'kɒtə] n Terrakotta f.

terrain [te'reɪn] n Gelände nt, Terrain nt.

terrible ['terəbl] a schrecklich, entsetzlich, fürchterlich.
terribly ['terəbli] ad fürchterlich.
terrier ['terɪə*] n Terrier m.
terrific a. **~ally** ad [tə'rɪfɪk, -lɪ] unwahrscheinlich; **~**! klasse!
terrify ['terɪfaɪ] vt erschrecken; **~ing** a erschreckend, grauenvoll.
territorial [terɪ'tɔːrɪəl] a Gebiets-, territorial; **~ waters** pl Hoheitsgewässer pl.
territory ['terɪtərɪ] n Gebiet nt.
terror ['terə*] n Schrecken m; (Pol) Terror m; **~ism** Terrorismus m; **~ist** Terrorist-(in f) m; **~ize** vt terrorisieren.
terse [tɜːs] a knapp, kurz, bündig.
Terylene * ['terɪliːn] n Terylen(e) nt.
test [test] n Probe f; (examination) Prüfung f; (Psych, Tech) Test m; vt prüfen; (Psych) testen.
testament ['testəmənt] n Testament nt.
test card ['testkɑːd] n (TV) Testbild nt.
test case ['testkeɪs] n (Jur) Präzedenzfall m; (fig) Musterbeispiel nt.
test flight ['testflaɪt] n Probeflug m.
testicle ['testɪkl] n Hoden m.
testify ['testɪfaɪ] vi aussagen; bezeugen (to acc).
testimonial [testɪ'məʊnɪəl] n (of character) Referenz f.
testimony ['testɪmənɪ] n (Jur) Zeugenaussage f; (fig) Zeugnis nt.
test match ['testmætʃ] n (Sport) Länderkampf m.
test paper ['testpeɪpə*] n schriftliche (Klassen)arbeit f.
test pilot ['testpaɪlət] n Testpilot m.
test tube ['testtjuːb] n Reagenzglas nt.
testy ['testɪ] a gereizt; reizbar.
tetanus ['tetənəs] n Wundstarrkrampf m, Tetanus m.
tether ['teðə*] vt anbinden; **to be at the end of one's ~** völlig am Ende sein.
text [tekst] n Text m; (of document) Wortlaut m; **~book** Lehrbuch nt.
textile ['tekstaɪl] n Gewebe nt; **~s** pl Textilien pl.
texture ['tekstʃə*] n Beschaffenheit f, Struktur f.
than [ðæn] prep, cj als.
thank [θæŋk] vt danken (+dat); **you've him to ~ for your success** Sie haben Ihren Erfolg ihm zu verdanken; **~ful** a dankbar; **~fully** ad (luckily) zum Glück; **~less** a undankbar; **~s** pl Dank m; **~s to** dank (+gen); **~ you, ~s** interj danke, dankeschön; **T~sgiving** (US) (Ernte)dankfest nt.
that [ðæt] a der/die/das, jene(r,s); pron das; cj daß; **and ~'s ~** und damit Schluß; **~ is** das heißt; **after ~** danach; **at ~** dazu noch; **~ big** so groß.
thatched [θætʃt] a strohgedeckt.
thaw [θɔː] n Tauwetter nt; vi tauen; (frozen foods, fig: people) auftauen; vt (auf)tauen lassen.
the [ðiː, ðə] def art der/die/das; **to play ~ piano** Klavier spielen; **~ sooner ~ better** je eher desto besser.
theatre, (US) theater ['θɪətə*] n Theater

nt; (for lectures etc) Saal m; (Med) Operationssaal m; **~goer** Theaterbesucher(in f) m.
theatrical [θɪ'ætrɪkəl] a Theater-; **career** Schauspieler-; (showy) theatralisch.
theft [θeft] n Diebstahl m.
their [ðɛə*] poss a ihr; **~s** poss pron ihre(r,s).
them [ðem, ðəm] pron (acc) sie; (dat) ihnen.
theme [θiːm] n Thema nt; (Mus) Motiv nt; **~ song** Titelmusik f.
themselves [ðəm'selvz] pl pron (reflexive) sich (selbst); (emphatic) selbst.
then [ðen] ad (at that time) damals; (next) dann; cj also, folglich; (furthermore) ferner; a damalig; **from ~ on** von da an; **before ~** davor; **by ~** bis dahin; **not till ~** erst dann.
theologian [θɪə'ləʊdʒən] n Theologe m, Theologin f.
theological [θɪə'lɒdʒɪkəl] a theologisch.
theology [θɪ'ɒlədʒɪ] n Theologie f.
theorem ['θɪərəm] n Grundsatz m, Theorem nt.
theoretical a, **~ly** ad [θɪə'retɪkəl, -ɪ] theoretisch.
theorize ['θɪəraɪz] vi theoretisieren.
theory ['θɪərɪ] n Theorie f.
therapeutic(al) [θerə'pjuːtɪk(əl)] a (Med) therapeutisch; erholsam.
therapist ['θerəpɪst] a Therapeut(in f) m.
therapy ['θerəpɪ] n Therapie f, Behandlung f.
there [ðɛə*] ad dort; (to a place) dorthin; interj (see) na also; (to child) (sei) ruhig, na na; **~ are** es sind, es gibt; **~abouts** ad so ungefähr; **~after** [ðɛər'ɑːftə*] ad danach, später; **~by** ad dadurch; **~fore** ad daher, deshalb; **~'s = there is**.
thermal ['θɜːməl] a springs Thermal-; (Phys) thermisch.
thermodynamics ['θɜːməʊdaɪ'næmɪks] n Thermodynamik f.
thermometer [θə'mɒmɪtə*] n Thermometer nt.
thermonuclear ['θɜːməʊ'njuːklɪə*] a thermonuklear.
Thermos ® ['θɜːməs] n Thermosflasche f.
thermostat ['θɜːməstæt] n Thermostat m.
thesaurus [θɪ'sɔːrəs] n Synonymwörterbuch nt.
these [ðiːz] pl pron, a diese.
thesis ['θiːsɪs] n (for discussion) These f; (Univ) Dissertation f, Doktorarbeit f.
they [ðeɪ] pl pron sie; (people in general) man; **~'d = they had; they would; ~'ll = they shall, they will; ~'re = they are; ~'ve = they have**.
thick [θɪk] a dick; forest dicht; liquid dickflüssig; (slow, stupid) dumm, schwer von Begriff; n: **in the ~ of** mitten in (+dat); **~en** vi (fog) dichter werden; vt sauce etc verdicken; **~ness** (of object) Dicke f; Dichte f; Dickflüssigkeit f; (of person) Dummheit f; **~set** a untersetzt; **~skinned** a dickhäutig.
thief [θiːf] n Dieb(in f) m.

thieving [ˈθiːvɪŋ] n Stehlen nt; a diebisch.
thigh [θaɪ] n Oberschenkel m; ~**bone** Oberschenkelknochen m.
thimble [ˈθɪmbl] n Fingerhut m.
thin [θɪn] a dünn; person also mager; (not abundant) spärlich; fog, rain leicht; excuse schwach.
thing [θɪŋ] n Ding nt; (affair) Sache f; my ~s pl meine Sachen pl.
think [θɪŋk] vti irreg denken, denken; (believe) meinen, denken; to ~ of doing sth vorhaben or beabsichtigen, etw zu tun; ~ over or überdenken; ~ up vt sich (dat) ausdenken; ~ing a denkend.
thinly [ˈθɪnlɪ] ad dünn; disguised kaum.
thinness [ˈθɪnnəs] n Dünnheit f; Magerkeit f; Spärlichkeit f.
third [θɜːd] a dritte(r,s); n (person) Dritte(r) mf; (part) Drittel nt; ~**ly** ad drittens; ~ **party insurance** Haftpflichtversicherung f; ~**-rate** a minderwertig.
thirst [θɜːst] n (lit, fig) Durst m; (fig) Verlangen nt; ~**y** a person durstig; work durstig machend; to be ~**y** Durst haben.
thirteen [ˈθɜːˈtiːn] num dreizehn.
thirty [ˈθɜːtɪ] num dreißig.
this [ðɪs] a diese(r,s); pron dies/das; it was ~ long es war so lang.
thistle [ˈθɪsl] n Distel f.
thong [θɒŋ] n (Leder)riemen m.
thorn [θɔːn] n Dorn m, Stachel m; (plant) Dornbusch m; ~**y** a dornig; problem schwierig.
thorough [ˈθʌrə] a gründlich; contempt tief; ~**bred** Vollblut nt; a reinrassig, Vollblut-; ~**fare** Straße f; ~**ly** ad gründlich; (extremely) vollkommen, äußerst; ~**ness** Gründlichkeit f.
those [ðəʊz] pl pron die (da), jene; a die, jene; ~ **who** diejenigen, die.
though [ðəʊ] cj obwohl; ad trotzdem; as ~ als ob.
thought [θɔːt] n (idea) Gedanke m; (opinion) Auffassung f; (thinking) Denken nt, Denkvermögen nt; ~**ful** a (thinking) gedankenvoll, nachdenklich; (kind) rücksichtsvoll, aufmerksam; ~**less** a gedankenlos, unbesonnen; (unkind) rücksichtslos.
thousand [ˈθaʊzənd] num tausend.
thrash [θræʃ] vt (lit) verdreschen; (fig) (vernichtend) schlagen.
thread [θred] n Faden m, Garn nt; (on screw) Gewinde nt; (in story) Faden m, Zusammenhang m; vt needle einfädeln; vi: ~ **one's way** sich hindurchschlängeln; ~**bare** a (lit, fig) fadenscheinig.
threat [θret] n Drohung f; (danger) Bedrohung f, Gefahr f; ~**en** vt bedrohen; vi drohen; to ~**en** sb with sth jdm etw androhen; ~**ening** a drohend; letter Droh-.
three [θriː] num drei; ~**-dimensional** a dreidimensional; ~**fold** a dreifach; ~**-piece suit** dreiteilige(r) Anzug m; ~**-piece suite** dreiteilige Polstergarnitur f; ~**-ply** a wool dreifach; wood dreischichtig; ~**-quarter** [θriːˈkwɔːtə] a dreiviertel; ~**-wheeler** Dreiradwagen m.

thresh [θreʃ] vti dreschen; ~**ing machine** Dreschmaschine f.
threshold [ˈθreʃhəʊld] n Schwelle f.
thrift [θrɪft] n Sparsamkeit f; ~**y** a sparsam.
thrill [θrɪl] n Reiz m, Erregung f; it gave me quite a ~ to . . . es war ein Erlebnis für mich, zu . . .; vt begeistern, packen; vi beben, zittern; ~**er** Krimi m; ~**ing** a spannend, packend; news aufregend.
thrive [θraɪv] vi gedeihen (on bei).
thriving [ˈθraɪvɪŋ] a blühend, gut gedeihend.
throat [θrəʊt] n Hals m, Kehle f.
throb [θrɒb] n Pochen nt, Schlagen nt; (Puls)schlag m; vi klopfen, pochen.
throes [θrəʊz] npl: in the ~ of mitten in (+dat).
thrombosis [θrɒmˈbəʊsɪs] n Thrombose f.
throne [θrəʊn] n Thron m; (Eccl) Stuhl m.
throttle [ˈθrɒtl] n Gashebel m; to open the ~ Gas geben; vt erdrosseln.
through [θruː] prep durch; (time) während (+gen); (because of) aus, durch; ad durch; to put sb ~ (Tel) jdn verbinden (to mit); a ticket, train durchgehend; (finished) fertig; ~**out** [θruːˈaʊt] prep (place) überall in (+dat); (time) während (+gen); ad überall; die ganze Zeit; we're ~ es ist aus zwischen uns.
throw [θrəʊ] n Wurf m; vt irreg werfen; ~ **out** vt hinauswerfen; rubbish wegwerfen; plan verwerfen; ~ **up** vti (vomit) speien; ~**away** a a (disposable) Wegwerf-; bottle Einweg-; ~**-in** Einwurf m.
thru [θruː] (US) = **through**.
thrush [θrʌʃ] n Drossel f.
thrust [θrʌst] n (Tech) Schubkraft f; vti irreg (push) stoßen; (fig) sich drängen; to ~ **oneself on sb** sich jdm aufdrängen; ~**ing** a person aufdringlich, unverfroren.
thud [θʌd] n dumpfe(r) (Auf)schlag m.
thug [θʌg] n Schlägertyp m.
thumb [θʌm] n Daumen m; vt book durchblättern; a well-~**ed book** ein abgegriffenes Buch; to ~ **a lift** per Anhalter fahren (wollen); ~ **index** Daumenregister nt; ~**nail** Daumennagel m; ~**tack** (US) Reißzwecke f.
thump [θʌmp] n (blow) Schlag m; (noise) Bums m; vi hämmern, pochen; vt schlagen auf (+acc).
thunder [ˈθʌndə] n Donner m; vi donnern; vt brüllen; ~**ous** a stürmisch; ~**storm** Gewitter nt, Unwetter nt; ~**struck** a wie vom Donner gerührt; ~**y** a gewitterschwül.
Thursday [ˈθɜːzdeɪ] n Donnerstag m.
thus [ðʌs] ad (in this way) so; (therefore) somit, also, folglich.
thwart [θwɔːt] vt vereiteln, durchkreuzen; person hindern.
thyme [taɪm] n Thymian m.
thyroid [ˈθaɪrɔɪd] n Schilddrüse f.
tiara [tɪˈɑːrə] n Diadem nt; (pope's) Tiara f.
tic [tɪk] n Tick m.
tick [tɪk] n (sound) Ticken nt; (mark) Häkchen nt; in a ~ (col) sofort; vi ticken; vt abhaken.

ticket ['tɪkɪt] n (for travel) Fahrkarte f; (for entrance) (Eintritts)karte f; (price —) Preisschild nt; (luggage —) (Gepäck)-schein m; (raffle —) Los nt; (parking —) Strafzettel m; (permission) Parkschein m; ~ collector Fahrkartenkontrolleur m; ~ holder Karteninhaber m; ~ office (Rail etc) Fahrkartenschalter m; (Theat etc) Kasse f.

ticking-off ['tɪkɪŋ'ɒf] n (col) Anschnauzer m.

tickle ['tɪkl] n Kitzeln nt; vt kitzeln; (amuse) amüsieren; that ~d her fancy das gefiel ihr.

ticklish ['tɪklɪʃ] a (lit, fig) kitzlig.

tidal ['taɪdl] a Flut-, Tide-.

tidbit ['tɪdbɪt] n (US) Leckerbissen m.

tiddlywinks ['tɪdlɪwɪŋks] n Floh-(hüpf)spiel nt.

tide [taɪd] n Gezeiten pl, Ebbe f und Flut; the ~ is in/out es ist Flut/Ebbe.

tidily ['taɪdɪlɪ] ad sauber, ordentlich.

tidiness ['taɪdɪnəs] n Ordnung f.

tidy ['taɪdɪ] a ordentlich; vt aufräumen, in Ordnung bringen.

tie [taɪ] n (necktie) Krawatte f, Schlips m; (sth connecting) Band nt; (Sport) Unentschieden nt; vt (fasten, restrict) binden; knot schnüren, festbinden; vi (Sport) unentschieden spielen; (in competition) punktgleich sein; ~ down vt (lit) festbinden; (fig) binden; ~ up vt (do up) anbinden; parcel verschnüren; boat festmachen; person fesseln; I am ~d up right now ich bin im Moment beschäftigt.

tier [tɪə*] n Reihe f, Rang m; (of cake) Etage f.

tiff [tɪf] n kleine Meinungsverschiedenheit f.

tiger ['taɪgə*] n Tiger m.

tight [taɪt] a (close) eng, knapp; schedule gedrängt; (firm) fest, dicht; screw festsitzend; control streng; (stretched) stramm, (an)gespannt; (col) blau, stramm; ~s pl Strumpfhose f; ~en vt anziehen, anspannen; restrictions verschärfen; vi sich spannen; ~-fisted a knauserig; ~ly ad eng; fest, dicht; stretched straff; ~ness Enge f; Festigkeit f; Straffheit f; (of money) Knappheit f; ~-rope Seil nt.

tile [taɪl] n (in roof) Dachziegel m; (on wall or floor) Fliese f; ~d a roof gedeckt, Ziegel-; floor, wall mit Fliesen belegt.

till [tɪl] n Kasse f; vt bestellen; prep,cj bis; not ~ (in future) nicht vor; (in past) erst.

tiller ['tɪlə*] n Ruderpinne f.

tilt [tɪlt] vt kippen, neigen; vi sich neigen.

timber ['tɪmbə*] n Holz nt; (trees) Baumbestand m.

time [taɪm] n Zeit f; (occasion) Mal nt; (rhythm) Takt m; vt zur rechten Zeit tun, zeitlich einrichten; (Sport) stoppen; I have no ~ for people like him für Leute wie ihn habe ich nichts übrig; in 2 weeks' ~ in 2 Wochen; for the ~ being vorläufig; at all ~s immer; at one ~ früher; at no ~ nie; at ~s manchmal; by the ~ bis; this ~ diesmal, dieses Mal; to have a good ~ viel Spaß haben, sich amüsieren; in ~ (soon enough) rechtzeitig; (after some

time) mit der Zeit; (Mus) im Takt; on ~ pünktlich, rechtzeitig; five ~s fünfmal; local ~ Ortszeit f; what ~ is it? wieviel Uhr ist es?, wie spät ist es?; ~keeper Zeitnehmer m; ~-lag (in travel) Verzögerung f; (difference) Zeitunterschied m; ~less a beauty zeitlos; ~ limit Frist f; ~ly a rechtzeitig; günstig; ~-saving a zeitsparend; ~ switch Zeitschalter m; ~table Fahrplan m; (Sch) Stundenplan m; ~ zone Zeitzone f.

timid ['tɪmɪd] a ängstlich, schüchtern; ~ity [tɪ'mɪdɪtɪ] Ängstlichkeit f; ~ly ad ängstlich.

timing ['taɪmɪŋ] n Wahl f des richtigen Zeitpunkts, Timing nt; (Aut) Einstellung f.

timpani ['tɪmpənɪ] npl Kesselpauken pl.

tin [tɪn] n (metal) Blech nt; (container) Büchse f, Dose f; ~foil Staniolpapier nt.

tinge [tɪndʒ] n (colour) Färbung f; (fig) Anflug m; vt färben, einen Anstrich geben (+dat).

tingle ['tɪŋgl] n Prickeln nt; vi prickeln.

tinker ['tɪŋkə*] n Kesselflicker m; ~ with vt herumpfuschen an (+dat).

tinkle ['tɪŋkl] n Klingeln nt; vi klingeln.

tinned [tɪnd] a food Dosen-, Büchsen-.

tinny ['tɪnɪ] a Blech-, blechern.

tin opener ['tɪnəupnə*] n Dosen- or Büchsenöffner m.

tinsel ['tɪnsəl] n Rauschgold nt; Lametta nt.

tint [tɪnt] n Farbton m; (slight colour) Anflug m; (hair) Tönung f.

tiny ['taɪnɪ] a winzig.

tip [tɪp] n (pointed end) Spitze f; (money) Trinkgeld nt; (hint) Wink m, Tip m; it's on the ~ of my tongue es liegt mir auf der Zunge; vt (slant) kippen; hat antippen; (~ over) umkippen; waiter ein Trinkgeld geben (+dat); ~-off Hinweis m, Tip m; ~ped a cigarette Filter-.

tipple ['tɪpl] n (drink) Schnäpschen nt.

tipsy ['tɪpsɪ] a beschwipst.

tiptoe ['tɪptəu] n: on ~ auf Zehenspitzen.

tiptop ['tɪp'tɒp] a: in ~ condition tipptopp, erstklassig.

tire ['taɪə*] n (US) = tyre; vti ermüden, müde machen/werden; ~d a müde; to be ~d of etw satt haben; ~dness Müdigkeit f; ~less a, ~lessly ad unermüdlich; ~some a lästig.

tiring ['taɪərɪŋ] a ermüdend.

tissue ['tɪʃuː] n Gewebe nt; (paper handkerchief) Papiertaschentuch nt; ~ paper Seidenpapier nt.

tit [tɪt] n (bird) Meise f; (col: breast) Titte f; ~ for tat wie du mir, so ich dir.

titbit ['tɪtbɪt] n Leckerbissen m.

titillate ['tɪtɪleɪt] vt kitzeln.

titillation [tɪtɪ'leɪʃən] n Kitzeln nt.

titivate ['tɪtɪveɪt] vt schniegeln.

title ['taɪtl] n Titel m; (in law) Rechtstitel m, Eigentumsrecht nt; ~ deed Eigentumsurkunde f; ~ role Hauptrolle f.

tittle-tattle ['tɪtltætl] n Klatsch m.

titter ['tɪtə*] vi kichern.

titular ['tɪtjulə*] a Titular-, nominell; possessions Titel-.

to [tuː, tə] prep (towards) zu; (with countries,

towns) nach; (*indir obj*) dat; (*as far as*) bis; (*next to, attached to*) an (+dat); (*per*) pro; cj (*in order to*) um... zu; ad ~ **and fro** hin und her; **to go ~ school/the theatre/bed** in die Schule/ins Theater/ins Bett gehen; **I have never been ~** Germany ich war noch nie in Deutschland; **to give sth ~ sb** jdm etw geben; ~ **this day** bis auf den heutigen Tag; **20 (minutes) ~ 4** 20 (Minuten) vor 4; **superior ~ sth** besser als etw; **they tied him ~ a tree** sie banden ihn an einen Baum.

toad [təud] n Kröte f; ~**stool** Giftpilz m; ~**y** Speichellecker m, Krieecher m; vi kriechen (*to* vor +dat).

toast [təust] n (*bread*) Toast m; (*drinking*) Trinkspruch m; vt trinken auf (+acc); *bread* toasten; (*warm*) wärmen; ~**er** Toaster m; ~**master** Zeremonienmeister m; ~**rack** Toastständer m.

tobacco [tə'bækəu] n Tabak m; ~**nist** [tə'bækənist] Tabakhändler m; ~**nist's (shop)** Tabakladen m.

toboggan [tə'bɒgən] n (Rodel)schlitten m.

today [tə'dei] ad heute; (*at the present time*) heutzutage; n (*day*) heutige(r) Tag m; (*time*) Heute nt, heutige Zeit f.

toddle ['tɒdl] vi watscheln.

toddler ['tɒdlə*] n Kleinkind nt.

toddy ['tɒdi] n (Whisky)grog m.

to-do [tə'du:] n Aufheben nt, Theater nt.

toe [təu] n Zehe f; (*of sock, shoe*) Spitze f; vt: ~ **the line** (*fig*) sich einfügen; ~ **hold** Halt m für die Fußspitzen; ~**nail** Zehennagel m.

toffee ['tɒfi] n Sahnebonbon nt; ~ **apple** kandierte(r) Apfel m.

toga ['təugə] n Toga f.

together [tə'geðə*] ad zusammen; (*at the same time*) gleichzeitig; ~**ness** (*company*) Beisammensein nt; (*feeling*) Zusammengehörigkeitsgefühl nt.

toil [tɔil] n harte Arbeit f, Plackerei f; vi sich abmühen, sich plagen.

toilet ['tɔilət] n Toilette f; a Toiletten-; ~ **bag** Waschbeutel m; ~ **paper** Toilettenpapier nt; ~**ries** ['tɔilətriz] pl Toilettenartikel pl; ~ **roll** Rolle f Toilettenpapier; ~ **soap** Toilettenseife f; ~ **water** Toilettenwasser nt.

token ['təukən] n Zeichen nt; (*gift* ~) Gutschein m.

tolerable ['tɒlərəbl] a (*bearable*) erträglich; (*fairly good*) leidlich.

tolerably ['tɒlərəbli] ad ziemlich, leidlich.

tolerance ['tɒlərəns] n Toleranz f.

tolerant a, ~**ly** ad ['tɒlərənt, -li] tolerant; (*patient*) geduldig.

tolerate ['tɒləreit] vt dulden; *noise* ertragen.

toleration [tɒlə'reiʃən] n Toleranz f.

toll [təul] n Gebühr f; **it took a heavy ~ of human life** es forderte or kostete viele Menschenleben; vi (*bell*) läuten; ~**bridge** gebührenpflichtige Brücke f; ~ **road** gebührenpflichtige Autostraße f.

tomato [tə'mɑ:təu] n, pl ~**es** Tomate f.

tomb [tu:m] n Grab(mal) nt.

tombola [tɒm'bəulə] n Tombola f.

tomboy ['tɒmbɔi] n Wildfang m; **she's a ~** sie ist sehr burschikos.

tombstone ['tu:mstəun] n Grabstein m.

tomcat ['tɒmkæt] n Kater m.

tome [təum] n (*volume*) Band m; (*big book*) Wälzer m.

tomorrow [tə'mɒrəu] n Morgen nt; ad morgen.

ton [tʌn] n Tonne f; ~**s of** (*col*) eine Unmenge von.

tonal ['təunl] a tonal; Klang-.

tone [təun] n Ton m; vi (*harmonize*) passen (zu), harmonisieren (mit); vt eine Färbung geben (+dat); ~ **down** vt *criticism, demands* mäßigen; *colours* abtonen; ~-**deaf** a ohne musikalisches Gehör.

tongs [tɒŋz] npl Zange f; (*curling* ~) Lockenstab m.

tongue [tʌŋ] n Zunge f; (*language*) Sprache f; **with ~ in cheek** ironisch, scherzhaft; ~-**tied** a stumm, sprachlos; ~-**twister** Zungenbrecher m.

tonic ['tɒnik] n (Med) Stärkungsmittel nt; (Mus) Grundton m, Tonika f; ~ **water** Tonic(water) m.

tonight [tə'nait] n heutige(r) Abend m; diese Nacht f; ad heute abend; heute nacht.

tonnage ['tʌnidʒ] n Tonnage f.

tonsil ['tɒnsl] n Mandel f; ~**itis** [tɒnsi'laitis] Mandelentzündung f.

too [tu:] ad zu; (*also*) auch.

tool [tu:l] n (*lit, fig*) Werkzeug nt; ~**box** Werkzeugkasten m; ~**kit** Werkzeug nt.

toot [tu:t] n Hupen nt; vi tuten; (Aut) hupen.

tooth [tu:θ] n, pl **teeth** Zahn m; ~**ache** Zahnschmerzen pl, Zahnweh nt; ~**brush** Zahnbürste f; ~-**paste** Zahnpasta f; ~-**pick** Zahnstocher m; ~ **powder** Zahnpulver nt.

top [tɒp] n Spitze f; (*of mountain*) Gipfel m; (*of tree*) Wipfel m; (*toy*) Kreisel m; (~ *gear*) vierte(r) Gang m; a oberste(r,s); vt *list* an erster Stelle stehen auf (+dat); **to ~ it all, he said ... und er setzte dem noch die Krone auf, indem er sagte ...; **from ~ to toe** von Kopf bis Fuß; ~**coat** Mantel m; ~-**flight** a erstklassig, prima; ~ **hat** Zylinder m; ~-**heavy** a oben schwerer als unten, kopflastig.

topic ['tɒpik] n Thema nt, Gesprächsgegenstand m; ~**al** a aktuell.

topless ['tɒpləs] a *dress* oben ohne.

top-level ['tɒp'levl] a auf höchster Ebene.

topmost ['tɒpməust] a oberste(r,s), höchste(r,s).

topple ['tɒpl] vti stürzen, kippen.

top-secret ['tɒp'si:krət] a streng geheim.

topsy-turvy ['tɒpsi'tз:vi] ad durcheinander; a auf den Kopf gestellt.

torch [tɔ:tʃ] n (Elec) Taschenlampe f; (*with flame*) Fackel f.

torment ['tɔ:ment] n Qual f; [tɔ:'ment] vt (*annoy*) plagen; (*distress*) quälen.

torn [tɔ:n] a hin- und hergerissen.

tornado [tɔ:'neidəu] n Tornado m, Wirbelsturm m.

torpedo [tɔ:'pi:dəu] n Torpedo m.

torpor ['tɔ:pə*] n Erstarrung f.

torrent ['tɔrənt] n Sturzbach m; ~**ial** [tə'renʃəl] a wolkenbruchartig.

torso ['tɔ:səʊ] n Torso m.

tortoise ['tɔ:təs] n Schildkröte f.

tortuous ['tɔ:tjʊəs] a (winding) gewunden; (deceitful) krumm, unehrlich.

torture ['tɔ:tʃə*] n Folter f; vt foltern.

Tory ['tɔ:rɪ] n Tory m; a Tory-, konservativ.

toss [tɒs] vt werfen, schleudern; n (of coin) Hochwerfen nt; to ~ a coin, to ~ up for sth etw mit einer Münze entscheiden.

tot [tɒt] n (small quantity) bißchen nt; (small child) Knirps m.

total ['təʊtl] n Gesamtheit f, Ganze(s) nt; a ganz, gesamt, total; vt (add up) zusammenzählen; (amount to) sich belaufen auf; ~**itarian** [təʊtælɪ'tɛərɪən] a totalitär; ~**ity** [təʊ'tælɪtɪ] Gesamtheit f; ~**ly** ad gänzlich, total.

totem pole ['təʊtəmpəʊl] n Totempfahl m.

totter ['tɒtə*] vi wanken, schwanken, wackeln.

touch [tʌtʃ] n Berührung f; (sense of feeling) Tastsinn m; (small amount) Spur f; (style) Stil m; vt (feel) berühren; (come against) leicht anstoßen; (emotionally) bewegen, rühren; **in** ~ **with** in Verbindung mit; ~ **on** vt topic berühren, erwähnen; ~ **up** vt paint auffrischen; ~**-and-go** a riskant, knapp; ~**down** Landen nt, Niedergehen nt; ~**iness** Empfindlichkeit f, ~**ing** a rührend, ergreifend; ~**line** Seitenlinie f; ~**y** a empfindlich, reizbar.

tough [tʌf] a (strong) zäh, widerstandsfähig; (difficult) schwierig, hart; meat zäh; ~ **luck** Pech nt; n Schläger(typ) m; ~**en** vt zäh machen; (make strong) abhärten; vi zäh werden; ~**ness** Zähigkeit f, Härte f.

toupée ['tu:peɪ] n Toupet nt.

tour ['tʊə*] n Reise f, Tour f, Fahrt f; vi umherreisen; (Theat) auf Tour sein/gehen; ~**ing** Umherreisen nt; (Theat) Tournee f; ~**ism** Fremdenverkehr m, Tourismus m; ~**ist** Tourist(in f); a (class) Touristen-; ad Touristenklasse; ~**ist office** Verkehrsamt nt.

tournament ['tʊənəmənt] n Tournier nt.

tousled ['taʊzld] a zerzaust.

tow [təʊ] n Schleppen f; vt (ab)schleppen.

toward(s) [tə'wɔ:d(z)] prep (with time) gegen; (in direction of) nach; **he walked** ~ **me/the town** er kam auf mich zu/er ging auf die Stadt zu; **my feelings** ~ **him** meine Gefühle ihm gegenüber.

towel ['taʊəl] n Handtuch nt.

tower ['taʊə*] n Turm m; ~ **over** vi (lit, fig) überragen; ~**ing** a hochragend; rage rasend.

town [taʊn] n Stadt f; ~ **clerk** Stadtdirektor m; ~ **hall** Rathaus nt; ~ **planner** Stadtplaner m.

towpath ['taʊpɑ:θ] n Leinpfad m.

towrope ['taʊrəʊp] n Abschlepptau nt.

toxic ['tɒksɪk] a giftig, Gift-.

toy [tɔɪ] n Spielzeug nt; ~ **with** vt spielen mit; ~**shop** Spielwarengeschäft nt.

trace [treɪs] n Spur f; vt (follow a course) nachspüren (+dat); (find out) aufspüren; (copy) zeichnen, durchpausen.

track [træk] n (mark) Spur f; (path) Weg m, Pfad m; (race~—) Rennbahn f; (Rail) Gleis nt; vt verfolgen; to keep ~ of sb jdn im Auge behalten; to keep ~ of an argument einer Argumentation folgen können; to keep ~ of the situation die Lage verfolgen; to make ~s (for) gehen (nach); ~ **down** vt aufspüren; ~**er dog** Spürhund m; ~**less** a pfadlos.

tract [trækt] n (of land) Gebiet nt; (booklet) Abhandlung f, Traktat m.

tractor ['træktə*] n Traktor m.

trade [treɪd] n (commerce) Handel m; (business) Geschäft nt, Gewerbe nt; (people) Geschäftsleute pl; (skilled manual work) Handwerk nt; vi handeln (in mit); vt tauschen; ~ **in** vt in Zahlung geben; ~**mark** Warenzeichen nt; ~ **name** Handelsbezeichnung f; ~**r** Händler m; ~**sman** (shopkeeper) Geschäftsmann m; (workman) Handwerker m; (delivery man) Lieferant m; ~ **union** Gewerkschaft f; ~ **unionist** Gewerkschaftler(in f) m.

trading ['treɪdɪŋ] n Handel m; ~ **estate** Industriegelände nt; ~ **stamp** Rabattmarke f.

tradition [trə'dɪʃən] n Tradition f; ~**al** a traditionell, herkömmlich; ~**ally** ad üblicherweise, schon immer.

traffic ['træfɪk] n Verkehr m; (esp in drugs) Handel m (in mit); ~ **in** esp drugs handeln; ~ **circle** (US) Kreisverkehr m; ~ **jam** Verkehrsstauung f; ~ **lights** pl Verkehrsampeln pl.

tragedy ['trædʒədɪ] n (lit, fig) Tragödie f.

tragic ['trædʒɪk] a tragisch; ~**ally** ad tragisch, auf tragische Weise.

trail [treɪl] n (track) Spur f, Fährte f; (of meteor) Schweif m; (of smoke) Rauchfahne f; (of dust) Staubwolke f; (road) Pfad m, Weg m; vt animal verfolgen; person folgen (+dat); (drag) schleppen; vi (hang loosely) schleifen; (plants) sich ranken; (be behind) hinterherhinken; (Sport) weit zurückliegen; (walk) zuckeln; **on the** ~ auf der Spur; ~ **behind** vi zurückbleiben; ~**er** Anhänger m; (US: caravan) Wohnwagen m; (for film) Vorschau f.

train [treɪn] n Zug m; (of dress) Schleppe f; (series) Folge f, Kette f; vt (teach) person ausbilden; animal abrichten; mind schulen; (Sport) trainieren; (aim) richten (on auf +acc); plant wachsen lassen, ziehen; vi (exercise) trainieren; (study) ausgebildet werden; ~**ed** a eye geschult; person, voice ausgebildet; ~**ee** Anlernling m; Lehrling m; Praktikant(in f) m; ~**er** (Sport) Trainer m; Ausbilder m; ~**ing** (for occupation) Ausbildung f; (Sport) Training nt; **in** ~**ing** im Training; ~**ing college** Pädagogische Hochschule f, Lehrerseminar nt; (for priests) Priesterseminar nt.

traipse [treɪps] vi latschen.

trait [treɪ(t)] n Zug m, Merkmal nt.

traitor ['treɪtə*] n Verräter m.

trajectory [trə'dʒektərɪ] n Flugbahn f.

tram(car) ['træm(kɑ:*)] n Straßenbahn f; ~**line** Straßenbahnschiene f; (route) Straßenbahnlinie f.

tramp [træmp] n Landstreicher m; vi

(*walk heavily*) stampfen, stapfen; (*travel on foot*) wandern; **~le** ['træmpl] *vt* (*nieder*)-trampeln; *vi* (*herum*)trampeln; **~oline** Trampolin *nt*.

trance [trɑːns] *n* Trance *f*.

tranquil ['træŋkwɪl] *a* ruhig, friedlich; **~ity** [træŋ'kwɪlɪtɪ] Ruhe *f*; **~izer** Beruhigungsmittel *nt*.

trans- [trænz] *pref* Trans-.

transact [træn'zækt] *vt* (*durch*)führen, abwickeln; **~ion** Durchführung *f*, Abwicklung *f*; (*piece of business*) Geschäft *nt*, Transaktion *f*.

transatlantic ['trænzət'læntɪk] *a* transatlantisch.

transcend [træn'send] *vt* übersteigen.

transcendent [træn'sendənt] *a* transzendent.

transcript ['trænskrɪpt] *n* Abschrift *f*, Kopie *f*; (*Jur*) Protokoll *nt*; **~ion** [træn'skrɪpʃən] Transkription *f*; (*product*) Abschrift *f*.

transept ['trænsept] *n* Querschiff *nt*.

transfer ['trænsfə*] *n* (*transferring*) Übertragung *f*, (*of business*) Umzug *m*; (*being transferred*) Versetzung *f*; (*design*) Abziehbild *nt*; (*Sport*) Transfer *m*; (*player*) Transferspieler *m*; [træns'fɜː*] *vt business* verlegen; *person* versetzen; *prisoner* überführen; *drawing* übertragen; *money* überweisen; **~able** [træns'fɜːrəbl] *a* übertragbar.

transform [træns'fɔːm] *vt* umwandeln, verändern; **~ation** [trænsfə'meɪʃən] Umwandlung *f*, Veränderung *f*, Verwandlung *f*; **~er** (*Elec*) Transformator *m*.

transfusion [træns'fjuːʒən] *n* Blutübertragung *f*, Transfusion *f*.

transient ['trænzɪənt] *a* kurz(lebig).

transistor [træn'zɪstə*] *n* (*Elec*) Transistor *m*; (*radio*) Transistorradio *nt*.

transit ['trænzɪt] *n*: **in ~** unterwegs, auf dem Transport.

transition [træn'zɪʃən] *n* Übergang *m*; **~al** *a* Übergangs-.

transitive *a*, **~ly** *ad* ['trænzɪtɪv, -lɪ] transitiv.

transitory ['trænzɪtərɪ] *a* vorübergehend.

translate [trænz'leɪt] *vti* übersetzen.

translation [trænz'leɪʃən] *n* Übersetzung *f*.

translator [trænz'leɪtə*] *n* Übersetzer(in *f*) *m*.

transmission [trænz'mɪʃən] *n* (*of information*) Übermittlung *f*; (*Elec, Med, TV*) Übertragung *f*; (*Aut*) Getriebe *nt*; (*process*) Übersetzung *f*.

transmit [trænz'mɪt] *vt message* übermitteln; (*Elec, Med, TV*) übertragen; **~ter** Sender *m*.

transparency [træns'peərənsɪ] *n* Durchsichtigkeit *f*, Transparenz *f*; (*Phot also* [-'pærəns]) Dia(positiv) *nt*.

transparent [træns'pærənt] *a* (*lit*) durchsichtig; (*fig*) offenkundig.

transplant [træns'plɑːnt] *vt* umpflanzen; (*Med*) verpflanzen; (*fig*) *person* verpflanzen; ['trænsplɑːnt] *n* (*Med*) Transplantation *f*; (*organ*) Transplantat *nt*.

transport ['trænspɔːt] *n* Transport *m*, Beförderung *f*; (*vehicle*) fahrbare(r) Untersatz *m*; **means of ~** Transportmittel *nt*; [træns'pɔːt] *vt* befördern; transportieren; **~able** [træns'pɔːtəbl] *a* transportabel; **~ation** [trænspɔː'teɪʃən] Transport *m*, Beförderung *f*; (*means*) Beförderungsmittel *nt*; (*cost*) Transportkosten *pl*.

transverse ['trænzvɜːs] *a* Quer-; *position* horizontal; *engine* querliegend.

transvestite [trænz'vestaɪt] *n* Transvestit *m*.

trap [træp] *n* Falle *f*; (*carriage*) zweirädrige(r) Einspänner *m*; (*col: mouth*) Klappe *f*; *vt* fangen; *person* in eine Falle locken; **the miners were ~ed** die Bergleute waren eingeschlossen; **~door** Falltür *f*.

trapeze [trə'piːz] *n* Trapez *nt*.

trapper ['træpə*] *n* Fallensteller *m*, Trapper *m*.

trappings ['træpɪŋz] *npl* Aufmachung *f*.

trash [træʃ] *n* (*rubbish*) wertlose(s) Zeug *nt*, Plunder *m*; (*nonsense*) Mist *m*, Blech *nt*; **~ can** (*US*) Mülleimer *m*; **~y** *a* wertlos; *novel etc* Schund-.

trauma ['trɔːmə] *n* Trauma *nt*; **~tic** [trɔː'mætɪk] *a* traumatisch.

travel ['trævl] *n* Reisen *nt*; *vi* reisen, eine Reise machen; *vt distance* zurücklegen; *country* bereisen; **~ler,** (*US*) **~er** Reisende(r) *mf*; (*salesman*) Handlungsreisende(r) *m*; **~ler's cheque,** (*US*) **~er's check** Reisescheck *m*; **~ling,** (*US*) **~ing** Reisen *nt*; **~ling bag** Reisetasche *f*; **~ sickness** Reisekrankheit *f*.

traverse [træ'vɜːs] *vt* (*cross*) durchqueren; (*lie across*) überspannen.

travesty ['trævəstɪ] *n* Zerrbild *nt*, Travestie *f*; **a ~ of justice** ein Hohn *m* auf die Gerechtigkeit.

trawler ['trɔːlə*] *n* Fischdampfer *m*, Trawler *m*.

tray [treɪ] *n* (*tea ~*) Tablett *nt*; (*receptacle*) Schale *f*; (*for mail*) Ablage *f*.

treacherous ['tretʃərəs] *a* verräterisch; *memory* unzuverlässig; *road* tückisch.

treachery ['tretʃərɪ] *n* Verrat *m*; (*of road*) tückische(r) Zustand *m*.

treacle ['triːkl] *n* Sirup *m*, Melasse *f*.

tread [tred] *n* Schritt *m*, Tritt *m*; (*of stair*) Stufe *f*; (*on tyre*) Profil *nt*; *vi irreg* treten; (*walk*) gehen; **~ on** *vt* treten auf (+*acc*).

treason ['triːzn] *n* Verrat *m* (*to* an +*dat*).

treasure ['treʒə*] *n* Schatz *m*; *vt* schätzen; **~ hunt** Schatzsuche *f*; **~r** Kassenverwalter *m*, Schatzmeister *m*.

treasury ['treʒərɪ] *n* (*Pol*) Finanzministerium *nt*.

treat [triːt] *n* besondere Freude *f*; (*school ~ etc*) Fest *nt*; (*outing*) Ausflug *m*; *vt* (*deal with*) behandeln; (*entertain*) bewirten; **to ~ sb to sth** jdn zu etw einladen, jdm etw spendieren.

treatise ['triːtɪz] *n* Abhandlung *f*.

treatment ['triːtmənt] *n* Behandlung *f*.

treaty ['triːtɪ] *n* Vertrag *m*.

treble ['trebl] *a* dreifach; *vt* verdreifachen; *n* (*voice*) Sopran *m*; (*music*) Diskant *m*; **~ clef** Violinschlüssel *m*.

tree [triː] *n* Baum *m*; ~**-lined** *a* baumbestanden; ~ **trunk** Baumstamm *m*.

trek [trek] *n* Treck *m*, Zug *m*; *vi* trecken.

trellis ['trelɪs] *n* Gitter *nt*; (*for gardening*) Spalier *nt*.

tremble ['trembl] *vi* zittern; (*ground*) beben.

trembling ['tremblɪŋ] *n* Zittern *nt*; *a* zitternd.

tremendous [trə'mendəs] *a* gewaltig, kolossal; (*col: very good*) prima; ~**ly** *ad* ungeheuer, enorm; (*col*) unheimlich.

tremor ['tremə*] *n* Zittern *nt*; (*of earth*) Beben *nt*.

trench [trentʃ] *n* Graben *m*; (*Mil*) Schützengraben *m*.

trend [trend] *n* Richtung *f*, Tendenz *f*; *vi* sich neigen, tendieren; ~**y** *a* (*col*) modisch.

trepidation [trepɪ'deɪʃən] *n* Beklommenheit *f*.

trespass ['trespəs] *vi* widerrechtlich betreten (*on acc*); '~**ers will be prosecuted**' 'Betreten verboten.'

tress [tres] *n* Locke *f*.

trestle ['tresl] *n* Bock *m*; ~ **table** Klapptisch *m*.

tri- [traɪ] *pref* Drei-, drei-.

trial ['traɪəl] *n* (*Jur*) Prozeß *m*, Verfahren *nt*; (*test*) Versuch *m*, Probe *f*; (*hardship*) Prüfung *f*; **by** ~ **and error** durch Ausprobieren.

triangle ['traɪæŋgl] *n* Dreieck *nt*; (*Mus*) Triangel *f*.

triangular [traɪ'æŋgjulə*] *a* dreieckig.

tribal ['traɪbəl] *a* Stammes-.

tribe [traɪb] *n* Stamm *m*; ~**sman** Stammesangehörige(r) *m*.

tribulation [trɪbju'leɪʃən] *n* Not *f*, Mühsal *f*.

tribunal [traɪ'bjuːnl] *n* Gericht *nt*; (*inquiry*) Untersuchungsausschuß *m*.

tributary ['trɪbjutərɪ] *n* Nebenfluß *m*.

tribute ['trɪbjuːt] *n* (*admiration*) Zeichen *nt* der Hochachtung.

trice [traɪs] *n*: **in a** ~ im Nu.

trick [trɪk] *n* Trick *m*; (*mischief*) Streich *m*; (*habit*) Angewohnheit *f*; (*Cards*) Stich *m*; *vt* überlisten, beschwindeln; ~**ery** Betrügerei *f*, Tricks *pl*.

trickle ['trɪkl] *n* Tröpfeln *nt*; (*small river*) Rinnsal *nt*; *vi* tröpfeln; (*seep*) sickern.

tricky ['trɪkɪ] *a problem* schwierig; *situation* kitzlig.

tricycle ['traɪsɪkl] *n* Dreirad *nt*.

tried [traɪd] *a* erprobt, bewährt.

trier ['traɪə*] *n*: **to be a** ~ sich (*dat*) ernsthaft Mühe geben.

trifle ['traɪfl] *n* Kleinigkeit *f*; (*Cook*) Trifle *m*; *ad*: **a** ~ ein bißchen.

trifling ['traɪflɪŋ] *a* geringfügig.

trigger ['trɪgə*] *n* Drücker *m*; ~ **off** *vt* auslösen.

trigonometry [trɪgə'nɒmətrɪ] *n* Trigonometrie *f*.

trilby ['trɪlbɪ] *n* weiche(r) Filzhut *m*.

trill [trɪl] *n* (*Mus*) Triller *m*.

trilogy ['trɪlədʒɪ] *n* Trilogie *f*.

trim [trɪm] *a* ordentlich, gepflegt; *figure*

schlank; *n* (*gute*) Verfassung *f*; (*embellishment, on car*) Verzierung *f*; **to give sb's hair a** ~ jdm die Haare etwas schneiden; *vt* (*clip*) schneiden; *trees* stutzen; (*decorate*) besetzen; *sails* trimmen; ~**mings** *pl* (*decorations*) Verzierung(en *pl*) *f*; (*extras*) Zubehör *nt*.

Trinity ['trɪnɪtɪ] *n*: **the** ~ die Dreieinigkeit.

trinket ['trɪŋkɪt] *n* kleine(s) Schmuckstück *nt*.

trio ['triːəʊ] *n* Trio *nt*.

trip [trɪp] *n* (*kurze*) Reise *f*; (*outing*) Ausflug *m*; (*stumble*) Stolpern *nt*; *vi* (*walk quickly*) trippeln; (*stumble*) stolpern; ~ **over** *vt* stolpern über (+*acc*); ~ **up** *vi* stolpern; (*fig also*) einen Fehler machen; *vt* zu Fall bringen; (*fig*) hereinlegen.

tripe [traɪp] *n* (*food*) Kutteln *pl*; (*rubbish*) Mist *m*.

triple ['trɪpl] *a* dreifach; ~**ts** ['trɪpləts] *pl* Drillinge *pl*.

triplicate ['trɪplɪkət] *n*: **in** ~ in dreifacher Ausfertigung.

tripod ['traɪpɒd] *n* Dreifuß *m*; (*Phot*) Stativ *nt*.

tripper ['trɪpə*] *n* Ausflügler(in *f*) *m*.

trite [traɪt] *a* banal.

triumph ['traɪʌmf] *n* Triumph *m*; *vi* triumphieren; ~**al** [traɪ'ʌmfəl] *a* triumphal, Sieges-; ~**ant** [traɪ'ʌmfənt] *a* triumphierend; (*victorious*) siegreich; ~**antly** *ad* triumphierend; siegreich.

trivial ['trɪvɪəl] *a* geringfügig, trivial; ~**lity** [trɪvɪ'ælɪtɪ] *n* Trivialität *f*, Nebensächlichkeit *f*.

trolley ['trɒlɪ] *n* Handwagen *m*; (*in shop*) Einkaufswagen; (*for luggage*) Kofferkuli *m*; (*table*) Teewagen *m*; ~ **bus** O(berleitungs)bus *m*.

trollop ['trɒləp] *n* Hure *f*; (*slut*) Schlampe *f*.

trombone [trɒm'bəʊn] *n* Posaune *f*.

troop [truːp] *n* Schar *f*; (*Mil*) Trupp *m*; ~**s** *pl* Truppen *pl*; ~ **in/out** *vi* hinein-/hinausströmen; ~**er** Kavallerist *m*; ~**ship** Truppentransporter *m*.

trophy ['trəʊfɪ] *n* Trophäe *f*.

tropic ['trɒpɪk] *n* Wendekreis *m*; **the** ~**s** *pl* die Tropen *pl*; ~**al** *a* tropisch.

trot [trɒt] *n* Trott *m*; *vi* trotten.

trouble ['trʌbl] *n* (*worry*) Sorge *f*, Kummer *m*; (*in country, industry*) Unruhen *pl*; (*effort*) Umstand *m*, Mühe *f*; *vt* (*disturb*) beunruhigen, stören, belästigen; **to** ~ **to do sth** sich bemühen, etw zu tun; **to make** ~ Schwierigkeiten *or* Unannehmlichkeiten machen; **to have** ~ **with** Ärger haben mit; **to be in** ~ Probleme *or* Ärger haben; ~**d** *a person* beunruhigt; *country* geplagt; ~**-free** *a* sorglos; ~**maker** Unruhestifter *m*; ~**shooter** Vermittler *m*; ~**some** *a* lästig, unangenehm; *child* schwierig.

trough [trɒf] *n* (*vessel*) Trog *m*; (*channel*) Rinne *f*, Kanal *m*; (*Met*) Tief *nt*.

trounce [traʊns] *vt* (*esp Sport*) vernichtend schlagen.

troupe [truːp] *n* Truppe *f*.

trousers ['traʊzəz] *npl* (*lange*) Hose *f*, Hosen *pl*.

trousseau ['tru:səʊ] n Aussteuer f.

trout [traʊt] n Forelle f.

trowel ['traʊəl] n Kelle f.

truant ['truənt] n: to play ~ (die Schule) schwänzen.

truce [tru:s] n Waffenstillstand m.

truck [trʌk] n Lastwagen m, Lastauto nt; (Rail) offene(r) Güterwagen m; (barrow) Gepäckkarren m; to have no ~ with sb nichts zu tun haben wollen mit jdm; ~ driver Lastwagenfahrer m; ~ farm (US) Gemüsegärtnerei f.

truculent ['trʌkjʊlənt] a trotzig.

trudge [trʌdʒ] vi sich (mühselig) dahinschleppen.

true [tru:] a (exact) wahr; (genuine) echt; friend treu.

truffle ['trʌfl] n Trüffel f.

truly ['tru:lɪ] ad (really) wirklich; (exactly) genau; (faithfully) treu; yours ~ Ihr sehr ergebener.

trump [trʌmp] n (Cards) Trumpf m; ~ed-up a erfunden.

trumpet ['trʌmpɪt] n Trompete f; vt ausposaunen; vi trompeten.

truncated [trʌŋ'keɪtɪd] a verstümmelt.

truncheon ['trʌntʃən] n Gummiknüppel m.

trundle ['trʌndl] vt schieben; vi: ~ along (person) dahinschlendern; (vehicle) entlangrollen.

trunk [trʌŋk] n (of tree) (Baum)stamm m; (Anat) Rumpf m; (box) Truhe f, Überseekoffer m; (of elephant) Rüssel m; ~s pl Badehose f; ~ call Ferngespräch nt.

truss [trʌs] n (Med) Bruchband nt.

trust [trʌst] n (confidence) Vertrauen nt; (for property etc) Treuhandvermögen nt; vt (rely on) vertrauen (+dat), sich verlassen auf (+acc); (hope) hoffen; ~ him to break it! er muß es natürlich kaputt machen, typisch!; to ~ sth to sb jdm etw anvertrauen; ~ed a treu; ~ee [trʌs'ti:] Vermögensverwalter m; ~ful a, ~ing a vertrauensvoll; ~worthy a vertrauenswürdig; account glaubwürdig; ~y a treu, zuverlässig.

truth [tru:θ] n Wahrheit f; ~ful a ehrlich; ~fully ad wahrheitsgemäß; ~fulness Ehrlichkeit f; (of statement) Wahrheit f.

try [traɪ] n Versuch m; to have a ~ es versuchen; vt (attempt) versuchen; (test) (aus)probieren; (Jur) person unter Anklage stellen; case verhandeln; (strain) anstrengen; courage, patience auf die Probe stellen; vi (make effort) versuchen, sich bemühen; ~ on vt dress anprobieren; hat aufprobieren; ~ out vt ausprobieren; ~ing a schwierig; ~ing for anstrengend für.

tsar [zɑ:*] n Zar m.

T-shirt ['ti:ʃɜːt] n T-shirt nt.

T-square ['ti:skwɛə*] n Reißschiene f.

tub [tʌb] n Wanne f, Kübel m; (for margarine etc) Becher m.

tuba ['tju:bə] n Tuba f.

tubby ['tʌbɪ] a rundlich, klein und dick.

tube [tju:b] n (pipe) Röhre f, Rohr nt; (for toothpaste etc) Tube f; (in London) U-Bahn f, (Aut: for tyre) Schlauch m; ~less a (Aut) schlauchlos.

tuber ['tju:bə*] n Knolle f.

tuberculosis [tjʊbɜːkjʊ'ləʊsɪs] n Tuberkulose f.

tube station ['tju:bsteɪʃən] n U-Bahnstation f.

tubular ['tju:bjʊlə*] a röhrenförmig.

tuck [tʌk] n (fold) Falte f, Einschlag m; vt (put) stecken; (gather) fälteln, einschlagen; ~ away vt wegstecken; ~ in vt hineinstecken; blanket etc feststecken; person zudecken; vi (eat) hineinhauen, zulangen; ~ up vt child warm zudecken; ~ shop Süßwarenladen m.

Tuesday ['tju:zdeɪ] n Dienstag m.

tuft [tʌft] n Büschel m.

tug [tʌg] n (jerk) Zerren nt, Ruck m; (Naut) Schleppdampfer m; vti zerren, ziehen; boat schleppen; ~-of-war Tauziehen nt.

tuition [tjʊ'ɪʃən] n Unterricht m.

tulip ['tju:lɪp] n Tulpe f.

tumble ['tʌmbl] n (fall) Sturz m; vi (fall) fallen, stürzen; ~ to vt kapieren; ~down a baufällig; ~r (glass) Trinkglas nt, Wasserglas nt; (for drying) Trockenautomat m.

tummy ['tʌmɪ] n (col) Bauch m.

tumour ['tju:mə*] n Tumor m, Geschwulst f.

tumult ['tju:mʌlt] n Tumult m; ~uous [tju:'mʊltjʊəs] a lärmend, turbulent.

tumulus ['tju:mjʊləs] n Grabhügel m.

tuna ['tju:nə] n Thunfisch m.

tundra ['tʌndrə] n Tundra f.

tune [tju:n] n Melodie f; vt (put in tune) stimmen; (Aut) richtig einstellen; to sing in ~/out of ~ richtig/falsch singen; to be out of ~ with nicht harmonieren mit; ~ in vi einstellen (to acc); ~ up vi (Mus) stimmen; ~r (person) (Instrumenten)stimmer m; (radio set) Empfangsgerät nt, Steuergerät nt; (part) Tuner m, Kanalwähler m; ~ful a melodisch.

tungsten ['tʌŋstən] n Wolfram nt.

tunic ['tju:nɪk] n Waffenrock m; (loose garment) lange Bluse f.

tuning ['tju:nɪŋ] n (Rad, Aut) Einstellen nt; (Mus) Stimmen nt.

tunnel ['tʌnl] n Tunnel m, Unterführung f; vi einen Tunnel anlegen.

tunny ['tʌnɪ] n Thunfisch m.

turban ['tɜːbən] n Turban m.

turbid ['tɜːbɪd] a trübe; (fig) verworren.

turbine ['tɜːbaɪn] n Turbine f.

turbot ['tɜːbət] n Steinbutt m.

turbulence ['tɜːbjʊləns] n (Aviat) Turbulenz f.

turbulent ['tɜːbjʊlənt] a stürmisch.

tureen [tjʊri:n] n Terrine f.

turf [tɜːf] n Rasen m; (piece) Sode f.

turgid ['tɜːdʒɪd] a geschwollen.

turkey ['tɜːkɪ] n Puter m, Truthahn m.

turmoil ['tɜːmɔɪl] n Aufruhr m, Tumult m.

turn [tɜːn] n (rotation) (Um)drehung f; (performance) (Programm)nummer f; (Med) Schock m; vt (rotate) drehen; (change position of) umdrehen, wenden; page umblättern; (transform) verwandeln;

(direct) zuwenden; vi (rotate) sich drehen; (change direction) (in car) abbiegen; (wind) drehen; (— round) umdrehen, wenden; (become) werden; (leaves) sich verfärben; (milk) sauer werden; (weather) umschlagen; (become) werden; to make a ~ to the left nach links abbiegen; the ~ of the tide der Gezeitenwechsel; the ~ of the century die Jahrhundertwende; to take a ~ for the worse sich zum Schlechten wenden; it's your ~ du bist dran or an der Reihe; in ~, by ~s abwechselnd; to take ~s sich abwechseln; to do sb a good/bad ~ jdm einen guten/schlechten Dienst erweisen; it gave me quite a ~ daß hat mich schön erschreckt; to ~ sb loose jdn los- or freilassen; ~ back vt umdrehen; person zurückschicken; clock zurückstellen; vi umkehren; ~ down vt (refuse) ablehnen; (fold down) umschlagen; ~ in vi (go to bed) ins Bett gehen; vt (fold inwards) ein- wärts biegen; ~ into vi sich verwandeln in (+acc); ~ off vi abbiegen; vt aus- schalten; tap zudrehen; machine, electricity abstellen; ~ on vt (light) anschalten, ein- schalten; tap aufdrehen; machine anstellen; ~ out vi (prove to be) sich herausstellen, sich erweisen; (people) sich entwickeln; how did the cake ~ out? wie ist der Kuchen geworden?; vt light ausschalten; gas abstellen; (produce) produzieren; ~ to vt sich zuwenden (+dat); ~ up vi auftauchen; (happen) passieren, sich ereignen; vt collar hochklappen, hoch- stellen; nose rümpfen; (increase) radio lauter stellen; heat höher drehen; ~about Kehrtwendung f; ~ed-up a nose Stups-; ~ing (in road) Abzweigung f; ~ing point Wendepunkt m.

turnip ['tɜːnɪp] n Steckrübe f.

turnout ['tɜːnaʊt] n (Besucher)zahl f; (Comm) Produktion f.

turnover ['tɜːnəʊvə°] n Umsatz m; (of staff) Wechsel m; (Cook) Tasche f.

turnpike ['tɜːnpaɪk] n (US) gebühren- pflichtige Straße f.

turnstile ['tɜːnstaɪl] n Drehkreuz nt.

turntable ['tɜːnteɪbl] n (of record-player) Plattenteller m; (Rail) Drehscheibe f.

turn-up ['tɜːnʌp] n (on trousers) Aufschlag m.

turpentine ['tɜːpəntaɪn] n Terpentin nt.

turquoise ['tɜːkwɔɪz] n (gem) Türkis m; (colour) Türkis nt; a türkisfarben.

turret ['tʌrɪt] n Turm m.

turtle ['tɜːtl] n Schildkröte f.

tusk [tʌsk] n Stoßzahn m.

tussle ['tʌsl] n Balgerei f.

tutor ['tjuːtə°] n (teacher) Privatlehrer m; (college instructor) Tutor m; ~ial [tjuːˈtɔːrɪəl] (Univ) Kolloquium nt, Seminarübung f.

tuxedo [tʌkˈsiːdəʊ] n (US) Smoking m.

TV ['tiːˈviː] n Fernseher m; a Fernseh-.

twaddle ['twɒdl] n (col) Gewäsch nt.

twang [twæŋ] n scharfe(r) Ton m; (of voice) Näseln nt; vt zupfen; vi klingen; (talk) näseln.

tweed [twiːd] n Tweed m.

tweezers ['twiːzəz] npl Pinzette f.

twelfth [twelfθ] a zwölfte(r,s); T~ Night Dreikönigsabend m.

twelve [twelv] num a zwölf.

twenty ['twentɪ] num a zwanzig.

twerp [twɜːp] n (col) Knülch m.

twice [twaɪs] ad zweimal; ~ as much doppelt soviel; ~ my age doppelt so alt wie ich.

twig [twɪg] n dünne(r) Zweig m; vt (col) kapieren, merken.

twilight ['twaɪlaɪt] n Dämmerung f, Zwielicht nt.

twill [twɪl] n Köper m.

twin [twɪn] n Zwilling m; a Zwillings-; (very similar) Doppel-.

twine [twaɪn] n Bindfaden m; vi binden.

twinge [twɪndʒ] n stechende(r) Schmerz m, Stechen nt.

twinkle ['twɪŋkl] n Funkeln nt, Blitzen nt; vi funkeln.

twin town ['twɪntaʊn] n Partnerstadt f.

twirl [twɜːl] n Wirbel m; vti (herum)- wirbeln.

twist [twɪst] n (twisting) Biegen nt, Drehung f; (bend) Kurve f; vt (turn) drehen; (make crooked) verbiegen; (distort) verdrehen; vi (wind) sich drehen; (curve) sich winden.

twit [twɪt] n (col) Idiot m.

twitch [twɪtʃ] n Zucken nt; vi zucken.

two [tuː] num a zwei; to break in ~ in zwei Teile brechen; ~ by ~ zu zweit; to be in ~ minds nicht genau wissen; to put ~ and ~ together seine Schlüsse ziehen; ~-door a zweitürig; ~-faced a falsch; ~-fold a, ad zweifach, doppelt; ~-piece a zweiteilig; ~-seater (plane, car) Zweisitzer m; ~some Paar nt; ~-way a traffic Gegen-.

tycoon [taɪˈkuːn] n (Industrie)magnat m.

type [taɪp] n Typ m, Art f; (Print) Type f; vti maschineschreiben, tippen; ~-cast a (Theat, TV) auf eine Rolle festgelegt; ~script maschinegeschriebene(r) Text m; ~writer Schreibmaschine f; ~written a maschinegeschrieben.

typhoid ['taɪfɔɪd] n Typhus m.

typhoon [taɪˈfuːn] n Taifun m.

typhus ['taɪfəs] n Flecktyphus m.

typical a, ~ly ad ['tɪpɪkəl, -klɪ] typisch (of für).

typify ['tɪpɪfaɪ] vt typisch sein für.

typing ['taɪpɪŋ] n Maschineschreiben nt.

typist ['taɪpɪst] n Maschinenschreiber(in f) m, Tippse f (col).

tyranny ['tɪrənɪ] n Tyrannei f, Gewaltherr- schaft f.

tyrant ['taɪrənt] n Tyrann m.

tyre [taɪə°] n Reifen m.

U

U, u [juː] n U nt, u nt.

ubiquitous [juːˈbɪkwɪtəs] adj überall zu finden(d); allgegenwärtig.

udder ['ʌdə°] n Euter nt.

ugh [ɜːh] interj hu.

ugliness ['ʌglɪnəs] n Häßlichkeit f.

ugly [ʌglı] a häßlich; (bad) böse, schlimm.
ukulele [ju:kə'leılı] n Ukulele f.
ulcer ['ʌlsə°] n Geschwür nt.
ulterior [ʌl'tıərıə°] a: ~ **motive** Hintergedanke m.
ultimate ['ʌltımət] a äußerste(r,s), allerletzte(r,s); ~**ly** ad schließlich, letzten Endes.
ultimatum [ʌltı'meıtəm] n Ultimatum nt.
ultra- ['ʌltrə] pref ultra-.
ultraviolet ['ʌltrə'vaıələt] a ultraviolett.
umbilical cord [ʌm'bıklıkl kɔːd] n Nabelschnur f.
umbrage ['ʌmbrıdʒ] n: to take ~ Anstoß nehmen (at an +dat).
umbrella [ʌm'brelə] n Schirm m.
umpire ['ʌmpaıə°] n Schiedsrichter m; vti schiedsrichtern.
umpteen ['ʌmpti:n] num (col) zig.
un- [ʌn] pref un-.
unabashed ['ʌnə'bæʃt] a unerschrocken.
unabated ['ʌnə'beıtıd] a unvermindert.
unable ['ʌn'eıbl] a außerstande; to be ~ to do sth etw nicht tun können.
unaccompanied ['ʌnə'kʌmpanıd] a ohne Begleitung.
unaccountably ['ʌnə'kauntəblı] ad unerklärlich.
unaccustomed ['ʌnə'kʌstəmd] a nicht gewöhnt (to an +acc); (unusual) ungewohnt.
unadulterated ['ʌnə'dʌltəreıtəd] a rein, unverfälscht.
unaided ['ʌn'eıdıd] a selbständig, ohne Hilfe.
unanimity [ju:nə'nımıtı] n Einstimmigkeit f.
unanimous a, ~**ly** ad [ju:'nænıməs, -lı] einmütig; vote einstimmig.
unattached ['ʌnə'tætʃt] a ungebunden.
unattended ['ʌnə'tendıd] a person unbeaufsichtigt; thing unbewacht.
unattractive ['ʌnə'træktıv] a unattraktiv.
unauthorized ['ʌn'ɔːθəraızd] a unbefugt.
unavoidable a, **unavoidably** ad [ʌnə'vɔıdəbl, -blı] unvermeidlich.
unaware ['ʌnə'wcə°] a: to be ~ of sth sich (dat) einer Sache nicht bewußt sein; ~**s** ad unversehens.
unbalanced ['ʌn'bælənst] a unausgeglichen; (mentally) gestört.
unbearable [ʌn'bɛərəbl] a unerträglich.
unbeatable [ʌn'bi:təbl] a unschlagbar.
unbeaten ['ʌn'bi:tn] a ungeschlagen.
unbecoming ['ʌnbı'kʌmıŋ] a dress unkleidsam; behaviour unpassend, unschicklich.
unbeknown ['ʌnbı'nəun] ad ohne jedes Wissen (to gen).
unbelief ['ʌnbı'li:f] n Unglaube m.
unbelievable [ʌnbı'li:vəbl] a unglaublich.
unbend ['ʌn'bend] irreg vt geradebiegen, gerademachen; vi aus sich herausgehen.
unbounded [ʌn'baundıd] a unbegrenzt.
unbreakable ['ʌn'breıkəbl] a unzerbrechlich.
unbridled [ʌn'braıdld] a ungezügelt.
unbroken ['ʌn'brəukən] a period

ununterbrochen; spirit ungebrochen; record unübertroffen.
unburden [ʌn'bɜːdn] vt: ~ o.s. (jdm) sein Herz ausschütten.
unbutton ['ʌn'bʌtn] vt aufknöpfen.
uncalled-for [ʌn'kɔːldfɔː°] a unnötig.
uncanny [ʌn'kænı] a unheimlich.
unceasing [ʌn'si:sıŋ] a unaufhörlich.
uncertain [ʌn'sɜːtn] a unsicher; (doubtful) ungewiß; (unreliable) unbeständig; (vague) undeutlich, vage; ~**ty** Ungewißheit f.
unchanged ['ʌn'tʃeındʒd] a unverändert.
uncharitable [ʌn'tʃærıtəbl] a hartherzig; remark unfreundlich.
uncharted ['ʌn'tʃɑːtıd] a nicht verzeichnet.
unchecked ['ʌn'tʃekt] a ungeprüft; (not stopped) advance ungehindert.
uncivil ['ʌn'sıvıl] a unhöflich, grob.
uncle ['ʌŋkl] n Onkel m.
uncomfortable [ʌn'kʌmfətəbl] a unbequem, ungemütlich.
uncompromising [ʌn'kɒmprəmaızıŋ] a kompromißlos, unnachgiebig.
unconditional ['ʌnkən'dıʃənl] a bedingungslos.
uncongenial ['ʌnkən'dʒi:nıəl] a unangenehm.
unconscious [ʌn'kɒnʃəs] a (Med) bewußtlos; (not aware) nicht bewußt; (not meant) unbeabsichtigt; the ~ das Unbewußte; ~**ly** ad unwissentlich, unbewußt; ~**ness** Bewußtlosigkeit f.
uncontrollable [ʌnkən'trəuləbl] a unkontrollierbar, unbändig.
uncork ['ʌn'kɔːk] vt entkorken.
uncouth [ʌn'ku:θ] a grob, ungehobelt.
uncover [ʌn'kʌvə°] vt aufdecken.
unctuous ['ʌŋktjuəs] a salbungsvoll.
undaunted [ʌn'dɔːntıd] a unerschrocken.
undecided ['ʌndı'saıdıd] a unschlüssig.
undeniable [ʌndı'naıəbl] a unleugbar.
undeniably [ʌndı'naıəblı] ad unbestreitbar.
under ['ʌndə°] prep unter; ad darunter; ~ **repair** in Reparatur; ~**-age** a minderjährig.
undercarriage ['ʌndəkærıdʒ] n Fahrgestell nt.
underclothes ['ʌndəkləuðz] npl Unterwäsche f.
undercoat ['ʌndəkəut] n (paint) Grundierung f.
undercover ['ʌndəkʌvə°] a Geheim-.
undercurrent ['ʌndəkʌrənt] n Unterströmung f.
undercut ['ʌndəkʌt] vt irreg unterbieten.
underdeveloped ['ʌndədı'veləpt] a Entwicklungs-, unterentwickelt.
underdog ['ʌndədɒg] n Unterlegene(r) mf.
underdone ['ʌndə'dʌn] a (Cook) nicht gar, nicht durchgebraten.
underestimate ['ʌndə'estımeıt] vt unterschätzen.
underexposed ['ʌndərıks'pəuzd] a unterbelichtet.
underfed ['ʌndə'fed] a unterernährt.
underfoot ['ʌndə'fut] ad unter den Füßen.
undergo ['ʌndə'gəu] vt irreg experience

durchmachen; *operation, test* sich unterziehen (+*dat*).

undergraduate ['ʌndə'grædjuət] *n* Student(in *f*) *m*.

underground ['ʌndəgraʊnd] *n* Untergrundbahn *f*, U-Bahn *f*; *a press etc* Untergrund-.

undergrowth ['ʌndəgrəʊθ] *n* Gestrüpp *nt*, Unterholz *nt*.

underhand ['ʌndəhænd] *a* hinterhältig.

underlie [ʌndə'laɪ] *vt irreg* (*form the basis of*) zugrundeliegen (+*dat*).

underline [ʌndə'laɪn] *vt* unterstreichen; (*emphasize*) betonen.

underling ['ʌndəlɪŋ] *n* Handlanger *m*.

undermine [ʌndə'maɪn] *vt* unterhöhlen; (*fig*) unterminieren, untergraben.

underneath [ʌndə'niːθ] *ad* darunter; *prep* unter.

underpaid [ʌndə'peɪd] *a* unterbezahlt.

underpants ['ʌndəpænts] *npl* Unterhose *f*.

underpass ['ʌndəpɑːs] *n* Unterführung *f*.

underplay [ʌndə'pleɪ] *vt* herunterspielen.

underprice [ʌndə'praɪs] *vt* zu niedrig ansetzen.

underprivileged [ʌndə'prɪvɪlɪdʒd] *a* benachteiligt, unterprivilegiert.

underrate [ʌndə'reɪt] *vt* unterschätzen.

undershirt ['ʌndəʃɜːt] *n* (*US*) Unterhemd *nt*.

undershorts ['ʌndəʃɔːts] *npl* (*US*) Unterhose *f*.

underside ['ʌndəsaɪd] *n* Unterseite *f*.

underskirt ['ʌndəskɜːt] *n* Unterrock *m*.

understand [ʌndə'stænd] *vt irreg* verstehen; **I ~ that . . .** ich habe gehört, daß . .; **am I to ~ that . . .?** soll das (etwa) heißen, daß . .?; **what do you ~ by that?** was verstehen Sie darunter?; **it is understood that . . .** es wurde vereinbart, daß . .; **to make o.s. understood** sich verständlich machen; **is that understood?** is das klar?; **~able** *a* verständlich; **~ing** Verständnis *nt*; *a* verständnisvoll.

understatement ['ʌndəsteɪtmənt] *n* Untertreibung *f*, Understatement *nt*.

understudy ['ʌndəstʌdɪ] *n* Ersatz(schau)-spieler(in *f*) *m*.

undertake [ʌndə'teɪk] *irreg vt* unternehmen; *vi* (*promise*) sich verpflichten; **~r** Leichenbestatter *m*; **~r's** Beerdigungsinstitut *nt*.

undertaking [ʌndə'teɪkɪŋ] *n* (*enterprise*) Unternehmen *nt*; (*promise*) Verpflichtung *f*.

underwater [ʌndə'wɔːtə*] *ad* unter Wasser; *a* Unterwasser-.

underwear ['ʌndəweə*] *n* Unterwäsche *f*.

underweight [ʌndə'weɪt] *a*: **to be ~** Untergewicht haben.

underworld ['ʌndəwɜːld] *n* (*of crime*) Unterwelt *f*.

underwriter ['ʌndəraɪtə*] *n* Assekurant *m*.

undesirable [ʌndɪ'zaɪərəbl] *a* unerwünscht.

undies ['ʌndɪz] *npl* (*col*) (Damen)unterwäsche *f*.

undiscovered ['ʌndɪs'kʌvəd] *a* unentdeckt.

undisputed ['ʌndɪs'pjuːtɪd] *a* unbestritten.

undistinguished ['ʌndɪs'tɪŋgwɪʃt] *a* unbekannt, nicht ausgezeichnet.

undo ['ʌn'duː] *vt irreg* (*unfasten*) öffnen, aufmachen; *work* zunichte machen; **~ing** Verderben *nt*.

undoubted [ʌn'daʊtɪd] *a* unbezweifelt; **~ly** *ad* zweifellos, ohne Zweifel.

undress ['ʌn'dres] *vti* (sich) ausziehen.

undue ['ʌndjuː] *a* übermäßig.

undulating ['ʌndjuleɪtɪŋ] *a* wellenförmig; *country* wellig.

unduly ['ʌn'djuːlɪ] *ad* übermäßig.

unearth ['ʌn'ɜːθ] *vt* (*dig up*) ausgraben; (*discover*) ans Licht bringen; **~ly** *a* schauerlich.

unease [ʌn'iːz] *n* Unbehagen *nt*; (*public*) Unruhe *f*.

uneasy [ʌn'iːzɪ] *a* (*worried*) unruhig; *feeling* ungut; (*embarrassed*) unbequem; **I feel ~ about it** mir ist nicht wohl dabei.

uneconomic(al) ['ʌniːkə'nɒmɪk(əl)] *a* unwirtschaftlich.

uneducated ['ʌn'edjukeɪtɪd] *a* ungebildet.

unemployed ['ʌnɪm'plɔɪd] *a* arbeitslos; **the ~** die Arbeitslosen *pl*.

unemployment ['ʌnɪm'plɔɪmənt] *n* Arbeitslosigkeit *f*.

unending [ʌn'endɪŋ] *a* endlos.

unenviable ['ʌn'enviəbl] *a* wenig beneidenswert.

unerring ['ʌn'ɜːrɪŋ] *a* unfehlbar.

uneven ['ʌn'iːvən] *a surface* uneben; *quality* ungleichmäßig.

unexploded ['ʌnɪks'pləʊdɪd] *a* nicht explodiert.

unfailing ['ʌn'feɪlɪŋ] *a* nie versagend.

unfair *a*. **~ly** *ad* ['ʌn'fɛə*, -əlɪ] ungerecht, unfair.

unfaithful ['ʌn'feɪθfʊl] *a* untreu.

unfasten ['ʌn'fɑːsn] *vt* öffnen, aufmachen.

unfavourable, (*US*) **unfavorable** ['ʌn'feɪvərəbl] *a* ungünstig.

unfeeling [ʌn'fiːlɪŋ] *a* gefühllos, kalt.

unfinished ['ʌn'fɪnɪʃt] *a* unvollendet.

unfit ['ʌn'fɪt] *a* ungeeignet (*for zu*, für); (*in bad health*) nicht fit.

unflagging [ʌn'flægɪŋ] *a* unermüdlich.

unflappable ['ʌn'flæpəbl] *a* unerschütterlich.

unflinching ['ʌn'flɪntʃɪŋ] *a* unerschrocken.

unfold [ʌn'fəʊld] *vt* entfalten; *paper* auseinanderfalten; *vi* (*develop*) sich entfalten.

unforeseen ['ʌnfɔː'siːn] *a* unvorhergesehen.

unforgivable ['ʌnfə'gɪvəbl] *a* unverzeihlich.

unfortunate [ʌn'fɔːtʃnət] *a* unglücklich, bedauerlich; **~ly** *ad* leider.

unfounded ['ʌn'faʊndɪd] *a* unbegründet.

unfriendly ['ʌn'frendlɪ] *a* unfreundlich.

unfurnished ['ʌn'fɜːnɪʃt] *a* unmöbliert.

ungainly [ʌn'geɪnlɪ] *a* linkisch.

ungodly [ʌn'gɒdlɪ] *a hour* nachtschlafend; *row* heillos.

unguarded ['ʌnˈgɑːdɪd] a moment unbewacht.

unhappiness [ʌnˈhæpɪnəs] n Unglück nt, Unglückseligkeit f.

unhappy [ʌnˈhæpɪ] a unglücklich.

unharmed ['ʌnˈhɑːmd] a wohlbehalten, unversehrt.

unhealthy [ʌnˈhelθɪ] a ungesund.

unheard-of [ʌnˈhɜːdʊv] a unerhört.

unhurt ['ʌnˈhɜːt] a unverletzt.

unicorn ['juːnɪkɔːn] n Einhorn nt.

unidentified ['ʌnaɪˈdentɪfaɪd] a unbekannt, nicht identifiziert.

unification [juːnɪfɪˈkeɪʃən] n Vereinigung f.

uniform ['juːnɪfɔːm] n Uniform f; a einheitlich; ~ity [juːnɪˈfɔːmɪtɪ] Einheitlichkeit f.

unify ['juːnɪfaɪ] vt vereinigen.

unilateral ['juːnɪˈlætərəl] a einseitig.

unimaginable [ʌnɪˈmædʒɪnəbl] a unvorstellbar.

uninjured ['ʌnˈɪndʒəd] a unverletzt.

unintentional ['ʌnɪnˈtenʃənl] a unabsichtlich.

union ['juːnjən] n (uniting) Vereinigung f; (alliance) Bund m, Union f; (trade —) Gewerkschaft f; U~ Jack Union Jack m.

unique [juːˈniːk] a einzig(artig).

unison ['juːnɪzn] n Einstimmigkeit f; in ~ einstimmig.

unit ['juːnɪt] n Einheit f.

unite [juːˈnaɪt] vt vereinigen; vi sich vereinigen; ~d a vereinigt; (together) vereint; U~d Nations Vereinte Nationen pl.

unit trust ['juːnɪtˈtrʌst] n (Brit) Treuhandgesellschaft f.

unity ['juːnɪtɪ] n Einheit f; (agreement) Einigkeit f.

universal a, ~ly ad [juːnɪˈvɜːsəl, -ɪ] allgemein.

universe ['juːnɪvɜːs] n (Welt)all nt, Universum nt.

university [juːnɪˈvɜːsɪtɪ] n Universität f.

unjust ['ʌnˈdʒʌst] a ungerecht.

unjustifiable [ʌnˈdʒʌstɪfaɪəbl] a ungerechtfertigt.

unkempt ['ʌnˈkempt] a ungepflegt, verwahrlost.

unkind [ʌnˈkaɪnd] a unfreundlich.

unknown ['ʌnˈnəʊn] a unbekannt (to dat).

unladen ['ʌnˈleɪdn] a weight Leer-, unbeladen.

unleash ['ʌnˈliːʃ] vt entfesseln.

unleavened ['ʌnˈlevnd] a ungesäuert.

unless [ənˈles] cj wenn nicht, es sei denn ...

unlicensed ['ʌnˈlaɪsənst] a (to sell alcohol) unkonzessioniert.

unlike ['ʌnˈlaɪk] a unähnlich; prep im Gegensatz zu.

unlimited [ʌnˈlɪmɪtɪd] a unbegrenzt.

unload ['ʌnˈləʊd] vt entladen.

unlock ['ʌnˈlɒk] vt aufschließen.

unmannerly [ʌnˈmænəlɪ] a unmanierlich.

unmarried ['ʌnˈmærɪd] a unverheiratet, ledig.

unmask ['ʌnˈmɑːsk] vt demaskieren; (fig) entlarven.

unmistakable ['ʌnmɪsˈteɪkəbl] a unverkennbar.

unmistakably ['ʌnmɪsˈteɪkəblɪ] ad unverwechselbar, unverkennbar.

unmitigated [ʌnˈmɪtɪgeɪtɪd] a ungemildert, ganz.

unnecessary ['ʌnˈnesəsərɪ] a unnötig.

unobtainable ['ʌnəbˈteɪnəbl] a: this number is ~ kein Anschluß unter dieser Nummer.

unoccupied ['ʌnˈɒkjupaɪd] a seat frei.

unopened ['ʌnˈəʊpənd] a ungeöffnet.

unorthodox ['ʌnˈɔːθədɒks] a unorthodox.

unpack ['ʌnˈpæk] vti auspacken.

unpalatable [ʌnˈpælətəbl] a truth bitter.

unparalleled [ʌnˈpærəleld] a beispiellos.

unpleasant [ʌnˈpleznt] a unangenehm.

unplug ['ʌnˈplʌg] vt den Stecker herausziehen von.

unpopular ['ʌnˈpɒpjʊləˈ] a unbeliebt, unpopulär.

unprecedented [ʌnˈpresɪdəntɪd] a noch nie dagewesen; beispiellos.

unqualified [ʌnˈkwɒlɪfaɪd] a success uneingeschränkt, voll; person unqualifiziert.

unravel [ʌnˈrævəl] vt (disentangle) auffasern, entwirren; (solve) lösen.

unreal ['ʌnˈrɪəl] a unwirklich.

unreasonable [ʌnˈriːznəbl] a unvernünftig; demand übertrieben; that's ~ das ist zuviel verlangt.

unrelenting ['ʌnrɪˈlentɪŋ] a unerbittlich.

unrelieved ['ʌnrɪˈliːvd] a monotony ungemildert.

unrepeatable ['ʌnrɪˈpiːtəbl] a nicht zu wiederholen(d).

unrest [ʌnˈrest] n (discontent) Unruhe f; (fighting) Unruhen pl.

unroll ['ʌnˈrəʊl] vt aufrollen.

unruly [ʌnˈruːlɪ] a child undiszipliniert; schwer lenkbar.

unsafe ['ʌnˈseɪf] a nicht sicher.

unsaid ['ʌnˈsed] a: to leave sth ~ etw ungesagt sein lassen.

unsatisfactory ['ʌnsætɪsˈfæktərɪ] a unbefriedigend; unzulänglich.

unsavoury, (US) **unsavory** ['ʌnˈseɪvərɪ] a (fig) widerwärtig.

unscrew ['ʌnˈskruː] vt aufschrauben.

unscrupulous [ʌnˈskruːpjʊləs] a skrupellos.

unselfish ['ʌnˈselfɪ] a selbstlos, uneigennützig.

unsettled ['ʌnˈsetld] a unstet; person rastlos; weather wechselhaft; dispute nicht beigelegt.

unshaven ['ʌnˈʃeɪvn] a unrasiert.

unsightly [ʌnˈsaɪtlɪ] a unansehnlich.

unskilled ['ʌnˈskɪld] a ungelernt.

unsophisticated ['ʌnsəˈfɪstɪkeɪtɪd] a einfach, natürlich.

unsound ['ʌnˈsaʊnd] a ideas anfechtbar.

unspeakable [ʌnˈspiːkəbl] a joy unsagbar; crime scheußlich.

unstuck ['ʌnˈstʌk] a: to come ~ (lit) sich lösen; (fig) ins Wasser fallen.

unsuccessful [ˌʌnsək'sesful] a erfolglos.

unsuitable ['ʌn'suːtəbl] a unpassend.

unsuspecting [ˌʌnsəs'pektɪŋ] a nichts-ahnend.

unswerving [ʌn'swɜːvɪŋ] a loyalty unerschütterlich.

untangle ['ʌn'tæŋgl] vt entwirren.

untapped ['ʌn'tæpt] a resources ungenützt.

unthinkable [ʌn'θɪŋkəbl] a unvorstellbar.

untidy [ʌn'taɪdɪ] a unordentlich.

untie ['ʌn'taɪ] vt aufmachen, aufschnüren.

until [ən'tɪl] prep, cj bis.

untimely [ʌn'taɪmlɪ] a death vorzeitig.

untold ['ʌn'təʊld] a unermeßlich.

untoward [ʌntə'wɔːd] a widrig, ungünstig.

untranslatable ['ʌntræns'leɪtəbl] a unübersetzbar.

untried ['ʌn'traɪd] a plan noch nicht ausprobiert.

unused ['ʌn'juːzd] a unbenutzt.

unusual a, ~ly ad [ʌn'juːʒʊəl, -ɪ] ungewöhnlich.

unveil [ʌn'veɪl] vt enthüllen.

unwary [ʌn'wɛərɪ] a unbedacht(sam).

unwavering [ʌn'weɪvərɪŋ] a standhaft, unerschütterlich.

unwell [ʌn'wel] a unpäßlich.

unwieldy [ʌn'wiːldɪ] a unhandlich, sperrig.

unwilling ['ʌn'wɪlɪŋ] a unwillig.

unwind ['ʌn'waɪnd] irreg vt (lit) abwickeln; vi (relax) sich entspannen.

unwitting [ʌn'wɪtɪŋ] a unwissentlich.

unwrap ['ʌn'ræp] vt aufwickeln, auspacken.

unwritten ['ʌn'rɪtn] a ungeschrieben.

up [ʌp] prep auf; ad nach oben, hinauf; (out of bed) auf; it is ~ to you es liegt bei Ihnen; what is he ~ to? was hat er vor?; he is not ~ to it er kann es nicht (tun); what's ~? was ist los?; ~ to (temporally) bis; ~-and-coming a im Aufstieg; the ~s and downs das Auf und Ab.

upbringing ['ʌpbrɪŋɪŋ] n Erziehung f.

update [ʌp'deɪt] vt auf den neuesten Stand bringen.

upend [ʌp'end] vt auf Kante stellen.

upgrade [ʌp'greɪd] vt höher einstufen.

upheaval [ʌp'hiːvəl] n Umbruch m.

uphill ['ʌp'hɪl] a ansteigend; (fig) mühsam; ad bergauf.

uphold [ʌp'həʊld] vt irreg unterstützen.

upholstery [ʌp'həʊlstərɪ] n Polster nt; Polsterung f.

upkeep ['ʌpkiːp] n Instandhaltung f.

upon [ə'pɒn] prep auf.

upper ['ʌpə°] n (on shoe) Oberleder nt; a obere(r,s), höhere(r,s); the ~ class die Oberschicht; ~-class a vornehm; ~most a oberste(r,s), höchste(r,s).

upright ['ʌpraɪt] a (erect) aufrecht; (honest) aufrecht, rechtschaffen; n Pfosten m.

uprising [ʌp'raɪzɪŋ] n Aufstand m.

uproar ['ʌprɔː°] n Aufruhr m.

uproot [ʌp'ruːt] vt ausreißen; tree ent-wurzeln.

upset ['ʌpset] n Aufregung f; [ʌp'set] vt irreg (overturn) umwerfen; (disturb) aufregen, bestürzen; plans durcheinander-

bringen; ~ting a bestürzend.

upshot ['ʌpʃɒt] n (End)ergebnis nt, Ausgang m.

upside-down ['ʌpsaɪd'daʊn] ad verkehrt herum; (fig) drunter und drüber.

upstairs ['ʌp'stɛəz] ad oben, im oberen Stockwerk; go nach oben; a room obere(r,s), Ober-; n obere(s) Stockwerk nt.

upstart ['ʌpstɑːt] n Emporkömmling m.

upstream ['ʌp'striːm] ad stromaufwärts.

uptake ['ʌpteɪk] n: to be quick on the ~ schnell begreifen; to be slow on the ~ schwer von Begriff sein.

uptight ['ʌp'taɪt] a (col) (nervous) nervös; (inhibited) verklemmt.

up-to-date ['ʌptə'deɪt] a clothes modisch, modern; information neueste(r,s); to bring sth up to date etw auf den neuesten Stand bringen.

upturn ['ʌptɜːn] n (in luck) Aufschwung m.

upward ['ʌpwəd] a nach oben gerichtet; ~(s) ad aufwärts.

uranium [jʊə'reɪnɪəm] n Uran nt.

urban ['ɜːbən] a städtisch, Stadt-.

urbane [ɜː'beɪn] a höflich, weltgewandt.

urchin ['ɜːtʃɪn] n (boy) Schlingel m; (sea —) Seeigel m.

urge [ɜːdʒ] n Drang m; vt drängen, dringen in (+acc); ~ on vt antreiben.

urgency ['ɜːdʒənsɪ] n Dringlichkeit f.

urgent a, ~ly ad ['ɜːdʒənt, -lɪ] dringend.

urinal ['jʊərɪnl] n (Med) Urinflasche f; (public) Pissoir nt.

urinate ['jʊərɪneɪt] vi urinieren, Wasser lassen.

urine ['jʊərɪn] n Urin m, Harn m.

urn [ɜːn] n Urne f; (tea —) Teemaschine f.

us [ʌs] pron uns.

usage ['juːzɪdʒ] n Gebrauch m; (esp Ling) Sprachgebrauch m.

use [juːs] n Verwendung f; (custom) Brauch m, Gewohnheit f; (employment) Gebrauch m; (point) Zweck m; in ~ in Gebrauch; out of ~ außer Gebrauch; it's no ~ es hat keinen Zweck; what's the ~? was soll's?; [juːz] vt gebrauchen; ~d to [juːst] gewöhnt an (+acc); she ~d to live here sie hat früher mal hier gewohnt; ~ up [juːz] vt aufbrauchen, verbrauchen; ~d [juːzd] a car Gebraucht-; ~ful a nützlich; ~fulness Nützlichkeit f; ~less a nutzlos, unnütz; ~lessly ad nutzlos; ~lessness Nutzlosigkeit f; ~r ['juːzə°] Benutzer m.

usher ['ʌʃə°] n Platzanweiser m; ~ette [ʌʃə'ret] Platzanweiserin f.

usual ['juːʒʊəl] a gewöhnlich, üblich; ~ly ad gewöhnlich.

usurp [juː'zɜːp] vt an sich reißen; ~er Usurpator m.

usury ['juːʒʊrɪ] n Wucher m.

utensil [juː'tensl] n Gerät nt, Utensil nt.

uterus ['juːtərəs] n Gebärmutter f, Uterus m.

utilitarian [juːtɪlɪ'tɛərɪən] a Nützlichkeits-.

utility [juː'tɪlɪtɪ] n (usefulness) Nützlichkeit f; (also public —) öffentliche(r) Versorgungsbetrieb m.

utilization [juːtɪlaɪ'zeɪʃən] n Nutzbar-machung f; Benutzung f.

utilize ['ju:tɪlaɪz] vt nutzbar machen; benützen.

utmost ['ʌtməʊst] a äußerste(r,s); n: to do one's ~ sein möglichstes tun.

utter ['ʌtə*] a äußerste(r,s) höchste(r,s), völlig; vt äußern, aussprechen; ~ance Äußerung f; ~ly ad äußerst, absolut, völlig.

U-turn ['ju:'tɜ:n] n (Aut) Kehrtwendung f.

V

V, v [vi:] n V nt, v nt.

vacancy ['veɪkənsɪ] n (job) offene Stelle f; (room) freies Zimmer nt.

vacant ['veɪkənt] a leer; (unoccupied) frei; house leerstehend, unbewohnt; (stupid) (gedanken)leer; '~' (on door) 'frei'.

vacate [və'keɪt] vt seat frei machen; room räumen.

vacation [və'keɪʃən] n Ferien pl, Urlaub m; ~ist (US) Ferienreisende(r) mf.

vaccinate ['væksɪneɪt] vt impfen.

vaccination [væksɪ'neɪʃən] n Impfung f.

vaccine ['væksi:n] n Impfstoff m.

vacuum ['vækjʊm] n luftleere(r) Raum m, Vakuum nt; ~ bottle (US), ~ flask (Brit) Thermosflasche f; ~ cleaner Staubsauger m.

vagary ['veɪgərɪ] n Laune f.

vagina [və'dʒaɪnə] n Scheide f, Vagina f.

vagrant ['veɪgrənt] n Landstreicher m.

vague [veɪg] a unbestimmt, vage; outline verschwommen; (absent-minded) geistesabwesend; ~ly ad unbestimmt, vage; understand, correct ungefähr; ~ness Unbestimmtheit f; Verschwommenheit f.

vain [veɪn] a (worthless) eitel, nichtig; attempt vergeblich; (conceited) eitel, eingebildet; in ~ vergebens, umsonst; ~ly ad vergebens, vergeblich; eitel, eingebildet.

valentine ['væləntaɪn] n Valentinsgruß m.

valiant a, ~ly ad ['væliənt, -lɪ] tapfer.

valid ['vælɪd] a gültig; argument stichhaltig, objection berechtigt; ~ity [və'lɪdɪtɪ] Gültigkeit f; Stichhaltigkeit f.

valise [və'li:z] n Reisetasche f.

valley ['vælɪ] n Tal nt.

valuable ['væljʊəbl] a wertvoll; time kostbar; ~s pl Wertsachen pl.

valuation [væljʊ'eɪʃən] n (Fin) Schätzung f; Beurteilung f.

value ['vælju:] n Wert m; (usefulness) Nutzen m; vt (prize) (hoch)schätzen, werthalten; (estimate) schätzen; ~d a (hoch)geschätzt; ~less a wertlos; ~r Schätzer m.

valve [vælv] n Ventil nt; (Biol) Klappe f; (Rad) Röhre f.

vampire ['væmpaɪə*] n Vampir m.

van [væn] n Lieferwagen m; Kombiwagen m.

vandal ['vændəl] n Vandale m; ~ism mutwillige Beschädigung f, Vandalismus m.

vanilla [və'nɪlə] n Vanille f.

vanish ['vænɪʃ] vi verschwinden.

vanity ['vænɪtɪ] n Eitelkeit f, Einbildung f; ~ case Schminkkoffer m.

vantage ['vɑ:ntɪdʒ] n: ~ point gute(r) Aussichtspunkt m.

vapour, (US) **vapor** ['veɪpə*] n (mist) Dunst m; (gas) Dampf m.

variable ['vɛərɪəbl] a wechselhaft, veränderlich; speed, height regulierbar.

variance ['vɛərɪəns] n: to be at ~ uneinig sein.

variant ['vɛərɪənt] n Variante f.

variation [vɛərɪ'eɪʃən] n Variation f, Veränderung f; (of temperature, prices) Schwankung f.

varicose ['værɪkəʊs] a: ~ veins Krampfadern pl.

varied ['vɛərɪd] a verschieden, unterschiedlich; life abwechslungsreich.

variety [və'raɪətɪ] n (difference) Abwechslung f; (varied collection) Vielfalt f; (Comm) Auswahl f; (sorte) Sorte f, Art f; ~ show Varieté nt.

various ['vɛərɪəs] a verschieden; (several) mehrere.

varnish ['vɑ:nɪʃ] n Lack m; (on pottery) Glasur f; vt lackieren; truth beschönigen

vary ['vɛərɪ] vt (alter) verändern; (give variety to) abwechslungsreicher gestalten; vi sich (ver)ändern; (prices) schwanken; (weather) unterschiedlich sein; to ~ from sth sich von etw unterscheiden; ~ing a unterschiedlich; veränderlich.

vase [vɑ:z] n Vase f.

vast [vɑ:st] a weit, groß, riesig; ~ly ad wesentlich; grateful, amused äußerst; ~ness Unermeßlichkeit f, Weite f.

vat [væt] n große(s) Faß nt.

Vatican ['vætɪkən] n: the ~ der Vatikan.

vaudeville ['vɔːdəvɪl] n (US) Varieté nt.

vault [vɔːlt] n (of roof) Gewölbe nt; (tomb) Gruft f; (in bank) Tresorraum m; (leap) Sprung m; vt überspringen.

vaunted ['vɔːntɪd] a gerühmt, gepriesen.

veal [viːl] n Kalbfleisch nt.

veer [vɪə*] vi sich drehen; (of car) ausscheren.

vegetable ['vedʒətəbl] n Gemüse nt; (plant) Pflanze f.

vegetarian [vedʒɪ'tɛərɪən] n Vegetarier(in f) m; a vegetarisch.

vegetate ['vedʒɪteɪt] vi (dahin)-vegetieren.

vegetation [vedʒɪ'teɪʃən] n Vegetation f.

vehemence ['viːɪməns] n Heftigkeit f.

vehement ['viːɪmənt] a heftig; feelings leidenschaftlich.

vehicle ['viːɪkl] n Fahrzeug nt; (fig) Mittel nt.

vehicular [vɪ'hɪkjʊlə*] a Fahrzeug-; traffic Kraft-.

veil [veɪl] n (lit, fig) Schleier m; vt verschleiern.

vein [veɪn] n Ader f; (Anat) Vene f; (mood) Stimmung f.

velocity [vɪ'lɒsɪtɪ] n Geschwindigkeit f.

velvet ['velvɪt] n Samt m.

vendetta [ven'detə] n Fehde f; (in family) Blutrache f.

vending machine ['vendɪŋməʃiːn] n Automat m.

vendor ['vendɔː°] n Verkäufer m.

veneer [vɔ'nɪɔ°] n (lit) Furnier(holz) nt; (fig) äußere(r) Anstrich m.

venerable ['venɔrəbl] a ehrwürdig.

venereal [vɪ'nɪɔrɪəl] a disease Geschlechts-.

venetian [vɪ'niːʃən] a: ~ **blind** Jalousie f.

vengeance ['vendʒəns] n Rache f; with a ~ gewaltig.

venison ['venɪsn] n Reh(fleisch) nt.

venom ['venəm] n Gift nt; ~**ous** a, ~**ously** ad giftig, gehässig.

vent [vent] n Öffnung f; (in coat) Schlitz m; (fig) Ventil nt; vt emotion abreagieren.

ventilate ['ventɪleɪt] vt belüften; question erörtern.

ventilation [ventɪ'leɪʃən] n (Be)lüftung f, Ventilation f.

ventilator ['ventɪleɪtɔ°] n Ventilator m.

ventriloquist [ven'trɪləkwɪst] n Bauchredner m.

venture ['ventʃɔ°] n Unternehmung f, Projekt nt; vt wagen; life aufs Spiel setzen; vi sich wagen.

venue ['venjuː] n Schauplatz m; Treffpunkt m.

veranda(h) [vɔ'rændə] a Veranda f.

verb [vɜːb] n Zeitwort nt, Verb nt; ~**al** a (spoken) mündlich; translation wörtlich; (of a verb) verbal, Verbal-; ~**ally** ad mündlich; (as a verb) verbal; ~**atim** [vɜː'beɪtɪm] ad Wort für Wort; a wortwörtlich.

verbose [vɜː'bəʊs] a wortreich.

verdict ['vɜːdɪkt] n Urteil nt.

verge [vɜːdʒ] n Rand m; on the ~ of doing sth im Begriff, etw zu tun; vi: ~ **on** grenzen an (+acc).

verger ['vɜːdʒɔ°] n Kirchendiener m, Küster m.

verification [verɪfɪ'keɪʃən] n Bestätigung f; (checking) Überprüfung f; (proof) Beleg m.

verify ['verɪfaɪ] vt (über)prüfen; (confirm) bestätigen; theory beweisen.

vermin ['vɜːmɪn] npl Ungeziefer nt.

vermouth ['vɜːməθ] n Wermut m.

vernacular [vɔ'nækjʊlɔ°] n Landessprache f; (dialect) Dialekt m, Mundart f; (jargon) Fachsprache f.

versatile ['vɜːsətaɪl] a vielseitig.

versatility [vɜːsə'tɪlɪtɪ] n Vielseitigkeit f.

verse [vɜːs] n (poetry) Poesie f; (stanza) Strophe f; (of Bible) Vers m; in ~ in Versform; ~**d** a: ~**d in** bewandert in (+dat), beschlagen in (+dat).

version ['vɜːʃən] n Version f; (of car) Modell nt.

versus ['vɜːsəs] prep gegen.

vertebra ['vɜːtɪbrə] n (Rücken)wirbel m.

vertebrate ['vɜːtɪbrət] a animal Wirbel-.

vertical ['vɜːtɪkəl] a senkrecht, vertikal; ~**ly** ad senkrecht, vertikal.

vertigo ['vɜːtɪgəʊ] n Schwindel m, Schwindelgefühl nt.

verve [vɜːv] n Schwung m.

very ['verɪ] ad sehr; a (extreme) äußerste(r,s); the ~ **book** genau das Buch; at that ~ **moment** gerade or

genau in dem Augenblick; at the ~ latest allerspätestens; the ~ **same day** noch am selben Tag; the ~ **thought** der Gedanke allein, der bloße Gedanke.

vespers ['vespəz] npl Vesper f.

vessel ['vesl] n (ship) Schiff nt; (container) Gefäß nt.

vest [vest] n Unterhemd nt; (US: waistcoat) Weste f; vt: ~ **sb with sth** or **sth in sb** jdm etw verleihen; ~**ed** a: ~**ed interests** pl finanzielle Beteiligung f; (people) finanziell Beteiligte pl; (fig) persönliche(s) Interesse nt.

vestibule ['vestɪbjuːl] n Vorhalle f.

vestige ['vestɪdʒ] n Spur f.

vestry ['vestrɪ] n Sakristei f.

vet [vet] n Tierarzt m/-ärztin f; vt genau prüfen.

veteran ['vetərən] n Veteran m; a altgedient.

veterinary ['vetɪnərɪ] a Veterinär-; ~ **surgeon** Tierarzt m/-ärztin f.

veto ['viːtəʊ] n Veto nt; power of ~ Vetorecht nt; vt sein Veto einlegen gegen.

vex [veks] vt ärgern; ~**ed** a verärgert; ~**ed question** umstrittene Frage f; ~**ing** a ärgerlich.

via ['vaɪə] prep über (+acc).

viability [vaɪə'bɪlɪtɪ] n (of plan, scheme) Durchführbarkeit f; (of company) Rentabilität f; (of life forms) Lebensfähigkeit f.

viable ['vaɪəbl] a plan durchführbar; company rentabel; plant, economy lebensfähig.

viaduct ['vaɪədʌkt] n Viadukt m.

vibrate [vaɪ'breɪt] vi zittern, beben; (machine, string) vibrieren; (notes) schwingen.

vibration [vaɪ'breɪʃən] n Schwingung f; (of machine) Vibrieren nt; (of voice, ground) Beben nt.

vicar ['vɪkə°] n Pfarrer m; ~**age** Pfarrhaus nt.

vice [vaɪs] n (evil) Laster nt; (Tech) Schraubstock m; pref: ~-**chairman** stellvertretende(r) Vorsitzende(r) m; ~-**president** Vizepräsident m; ~ **versa** ad umgekehrt.

vicinity [vɪ'sɪnɪtɪ] n Umgebung f; (closeness) Nähe f.

vicious ['vɪʃəs] a gemein, böse; ~ **circle** Teufelskreis m; ~**ness** Bösartigkeit f, Gemeinheit f.

vicissitudes [vɪ'sɪsɪtjuːdz] npl Wechselfälle pl.

victim ['vɪktɪm] n Opfer nt; ~**ization** [vɪktɪmaɪ'zeɪʃən] Benachteiligung f; ~**ize** vt benachteiligen.

victor ['vɪktə°] n Sieger m.

Victorian [vɪk'tɔːrɪən] a viktorianisch; (fig) (sitten)streng.

victorious [vɪk'tɔːrɪəs] a siegreich.

victory ['vɪktərɪ] n Sieg m.

video ['vɪdɪəʊ] a Fernseh-, Bild-.

vie [vaɪ] vi wetteifern.

view [vjuː] n (sight) Sicht f, Blick m; (scene) Aussicht f; (opinion) Ansicht f, Meinung f; (intention) Absicht f; to have sth in ~ etw beabsichtigen; in ~ of wegen (+gen), angesichts (+gen); vt situation betrachten; house besichtigen; ~er (viewfinder) Sucher m; (Phot: small projector) Gucki m; (TV) Fernsehteilnehmer(in f) m; ~finder Sucher m; ~point Standpunkt m.

vigil ['vɪdʒɪl] n (Nacht)wache f; ~ance Wachsamkeit f; ~ant a wachsam; ~antly ad aufmerksam.

vigorous a, ~ly ad ['vɪgərəs, -lɪ] kräftig; protest energisch, heftig.

vigour, (US) **vigor** ['vɪgə*] n Kraft f, Vitalität f; (of protest) Heftigkeit f.

vile [vaɪl] a (mean) gemein; (foul) abscheulich.

vilify ['vɪlɪfaɪ] vt verleumden.

villa ['vɪlə] n Villa f.

village ['vɪlɪdʒ] n Dorf nt; ~r Dorfbewohner(in f) m.

villain ['vɪlən] n Schurke m, Bösewicht m.

vindicate ['vɪndɪkeɪt] vt rechtfertigen; (clear) rehabilitieren.

vindication [vɪndɪ'keɪʃən] n Rechtfertigung f; Rehabilitation f.

vindictive [vɪn'dɪktɪv] a nachtragend, rachsüchtig.

vine [vaɪn] n Rebstock m, Rebe f.

vinegar ['vɪnɪgə*] n Essig m.

vineyard ['vɪnjəd] n Weinberg m.

vintage ['vɪntɪdʒ] n (of wine) Jahrgang m; ~ car Vorkriegsmodell nt; ~ wine edle(r) Wein m; ~ year besondere(s) Jahr nt.

viola [vɪ'əʊlə] n Bratsche f.

violate ['vaɪəleɪt] vt promise brechen; law übertreten; rights, rule, neutrality verletzen; sanctity, woman schänden.

violation [vaɪə'leɪʃən] n Verletzung f; Übertretung f.

violence ['vaɪələns] n (force) Heftigkeit f; (brutality) Gewalttätigkeit f.

violent a, ~ly ad ['vaɪələnt, -lɪ] (strong) heftig; (brutal) gewalttätig, brutal; contrast kraß; death gewaltsam.

violet ['vaɪələt] n Veilchen nt; a veilchenblau, violett.

violin [vaɪə'lɪn] n Geige f, Violine f.

viper ['vaɪpə*] n Viper f; (fig) Schlange f.

virgin ['vɜːdʒɪn] n Jungfrau f, a jungfräulich, unberührt; ~ity [vɜː'dʒɪnɪtɪ] Unschuld f.

Virgo ['vɜːgəʊ] n Jungfrau f.

virile ['vɪraɪl] a männlich; (fig) kraftvoll.

virility [vɪ'rɪlɪtɪ] n Männlichkeit f.

virtual ['vɜːtjʊəl] a eigentlich; it was a ~ disaster es war geradezu eine Katastrophe; ~ly ad praktisch, fast.

virtue ['vɜːtjuː] n (moral goodness) Tugend f; (good quality) Vorteil m, Vorzug m; by ~ of aufgrund (+gen).

virtuoso [vɜːtjʊ'əʊzəʊ] n Virtuose m.

virtuous ['vɜːtjʊəs] a tugendhaft.

virulence ['vɪrjʊləns] n Bösartigkeit f.

virulent ['vɪrjʊlənt] a (poisonous) bösartig; (bitter) scharf, geharnischt.

virus ['vaɪərəs] n Virus m.

visa ['viːzə] n Visum nt, Sichtvermerk m.

vis-à-vis ['viːzəviː] prep gegenüber.

visibility [vɪzɪ'bɪlɪtɪ] n Sichtbarkeit f; (Met) Sicht(weite) f.

visible ['vɪzəbl] a sichtbar.

visibly ['vɪzəblɪ] ad sichtlich.

vision ['vɪʒən] n (ability) Sehvermögen f; (foresight) Weitblick m; (in dream, image) Vision f; ~ary Hellseher m; (dreamer) Phantast m; a phantastisch.

visit ['vɪzɪt] n Besuch m; vt besuchen; town, country fahren nach; ~ing a professor Gast-; ~ing card Visitenkarte f; ~or (in house) Besucher(in f) m; (in hotel) Gast m; ~or's book Gästebuch m.

visor ['vaɪzə*] n Visier nt; (on cap) Schirm m; (Aut) Blende f.

vista ['vɪstə] n Aussicht f.

visual ['vɪzjʊəl] a Seh-, visuell; ~ aid Anschauungsmaterial nt; ~ize vt (imagine) sich (dat) vorstellen; (expect) erwarten; ~ly ad visuell.

vital ['vaɪtl] a (important) unerläßlich; (necessary for life) Lebens-, lebenswichtig; (lively) vital; ~ity [vaɪ'tælɪtɪ] Vitalität f, Lebendigkeit f; ~ly ad äußerst, ungeheuer.

vitamin ['vɪtəmɪn] n Vitamin nt.

vitiate ['vɪʃɪeɪt] vt verunreinigen; theory etc ungültig machen.

vivacious [vɪ'veɪʃəs] a lebhaft.

vivacity [vɪ'væsɪtɪ] n Lebhaftigkeit f, Lebendigkeit f.

vivid a, ~ly ad ['vɪvɪd, -lɪ] (graphic) lebendig, deutlich; memory lebhaft; (bright) leuchtend.

vivisection [vɪvɪ'sekʃən] n Vivisektion f.

vocabulary [vəʊ'kæbjʊlərɪ] n Wortschatz m, Vokabular nt.

vocal ['vəʊkəl] a Vokal-, Gesang-; (fig) lautstark; ~ cord Stimmband nt; ~ist Sänger(in f) m.

vocation [vəʊ'keɪʃən] n (calling) Berufung f; ~al a Berufs-.

vociferous a, ~ly ad [vəʊ'sɪfərəs, -lɪ] lautstark.

vodka ['vodkə] n Wodka m.

vogue [vəʊg] n Mode f.

voice [vɔɪs] n (lit) Stimme f; (fig) Mitspracherecht nt; (Gram) Aktionsart f; active/passive ~ Aktiv nt/Passiv nt; with one ~ einstimmig; vt äußern; ~d consonant stimmhafte(r) Konsonant m.

void [vɔɪd] n Leere f; a (empty) leer; (lacking) ohne (of acc), bar (of gen); (Jur) ungültig; see null.

volatile ['vɒlətaɪl] a gas flüchtig; person impulsiv; situation brisant.

volcanic [vɒl'kænɪk] a vulkanisch, Vulkan-.

volcano [vɒl'keɪnəʊ] n Vulkan m.

volition [və'lɪʃən] n Wille m; of one's own ~ aus freiem Willen.

volley ['vɒlɪ] n (of guns) Salve f; (of stones) Hagel m; (of words) Schwall m; (tennis) Flugball m; ~ball Volleyball m.

volt [vəʊlt] n Volt nt; ~age (Volt)-spannung f.

volte-face ['vɒlt'fɑːs] n (Kehrt)wendung f.

voluble ['vɒljʊbl] a redselig.

volume ['vɒljuːm] n (book) Band m; (size)

Umfang m; (space) Rauminhalt m, Volumen nt; (of sound) Lautstärke f.

voluntary a, **voluntarily** ad ['vɒləntəri, -lı] freiwillig.

volunteer [vɒlən'tıə*] n Freiwillige(r) mf; vi sich freiwillig melden; vt anbieten.

voluptuous [və'lʌptjuəs] a sinnlich, wollüstig.

vomit ['vɒmɪt] n Erbrochene(s) nt; (act) Erbrechen nt; vt speien; vi sich übergeben.

vote [vəut] n Stimme f; (ballot) Wahl f, Abstimmung f; (result) Wahl- or Abstimmungsergebnis nt; (right to vote) Wahlrecht nt; vti wählen; ~r Wähler(in f) m.

voting ['vəutɪŋ] n Wahl f; low ~ geringe Wahlbeteiligung f.

vouch [vautʃ]: ~ for vt bürgen für.

voucher ['vautʃə*] n Gutschein m.

vow [vau] n Versprechen nt; (Rel) Gelübde nt; vt geloben; vengeance schwören.

vowel ['vauəl] n Vokal m, Selbstlaut m.

voyage ['vɒɪɪdʒ] n Reise f.

vulgar ['vʌlgə*] a (rude) vulgär; (of common people) allgemein, Volks-; ~ity [vʌl'gærɪtɪ] Gewöhnlichkeit f, Vulgarität f.

vulnerability [vʌlnərə'bɪlɪtɪ] n Verletzlichkeit f.

vulnerable ['vʌlnərəbl] a (easily injured) verwundbar; (sensitive) verletzlich.

vulture ['vʌltʃə*] n Geier m.

W

W, w ['dʌbljuː] n W nt, w nt.

wad [wɒd] n (bundle) Bündel nt; (of paper) Stoß m; (of money) Packen m.

wade [weɪd] vi waten.

wafer ['weɪfə*] n Waffel f; (Eccl) Hostie f.

waffle ['wɒfl] n Waffel f; (col: empty talk) Geschwafel nt; vi (col) schwafeln.

waft [wɑːft] vti wehen.

wag [wæg] vt tail wedeln mit; vi (tail) wedeln; her tongue never stops ~ging ihr Mund steht nie still.

wage [weɪdʒ] n (Arbeits)lohn m; vt führen; ~s pl Lohn m; ~ claim Lohnforderung f; ~ earner Lohnempfänger(in f) m; ~ freeze Lohnstopp m.

wager ['weɪdʒə*] n Wette f; vti wetten.

waggle ['wægl] vt tail wedeln mit; vi wedeln.

wag(g)on ['wægən] n (horse-drawn) Fuhrwerk nt; (US Aut) Wagen m; (Brit Rail) Waggon m.

wail [weɪl] n Wehgeschrei nt; vi wehklagen, jammern.

waist [weɪst] n Taille f; ~coat Weste f; ~line Taille f.

wait [weɪt] n Wartezeit f; vi warten (for auf +acc); to ~ for sb to do sth darauf warten, daß jd etw tut; ~ and see! abwarten!; to ~ at table servieren; ~er Kellner m; (as address) Herr Ober m; ~ing list Warteliste f; ~ing room (Med) Wartezimmer nt; (Rail) Wartesaal m; ~ress Kellnerin f; (as address) Fräulein nt.

waive [weɪv] vt verzichten auf (+acc).

wake [weɪk] irreg vt wecken; vi aufwachen; to ~ up to (fig) sich bewußt werden (+gen); n (Naut) Kielwasser nt; (for dead) Totenwache f; in the ~ of unmittelbar nach; ~n vt aufwecken.

walk [wɔːk] n Spaziergang m; (way of walking) Gang m; (route) Weg m; ~s of life pl Sphären pl; to take sb for a ~ mit jdm einen Spaziergang machen; a 10-minute ~ 10 Minuten zu Fuß; vi gehen; (stroll) spazierengehen; (longer) wandern; ~er Spaziergänger m; (hiker) Wanderer m; ~ie-talkie tragbare(s) Sprechfunkgerät nt; ~ing n Gehen nt; Spazieren(gehen) nt; Wandern nt; a Wander-; ~ing stick Spazierstock m; ~out Streik m; ~over (col) leichter Sieg m.

wall [wɔːl] n (inside) Wand f; (outside) Mauer f; ~ed a von Mauern umgeben.

wallet ['wɒlɪt] n Brieftasche f.

wallow ['wɒləu] vi sich wälzen or suhlen.

wallpaper ['wɔːlpeɪpə*] n Tapete f.

walnut ['wɔːlnʌt] n Walnuß f; (tree) Walnußbaum m; (wood) Nußbaumholz nt.

walrus ['wɔːlrəs] n Walroß nt.

waltz [wɔːlts] n Walzer m; vi Walzer tanzen.

wan [wɒn] a bleich.

wand [wɒnd] n Stab m.

wander ['wɒndə*] vi (roam) (herum)wandern; (fig) abschweifen; ~er Wanderer m; ~ing a umherziehend; thoughts abschweifend.

wane [weɪn] vi abnehmen; (fig) schwinden.

want [wɒnt] n (lack) Mangel m (of an +dat); (need) Bedürfnis nt; for ~ of aus Mangel an (+dat); mangels (+gen); vt (need) brauchen; (desire) wollen; (lack) nicht haben; I ~ to go ich will gehen; he ~s confidence ihm fehlt das Selbstvertrauen.

wanton ['wɒntən] a mutwillig, zügellos.

war [wɔː*] n Krieg m.

ward [wɔːd] n (in hospital) Station f; (child) Mündel nt; (of city) Bezirk m; to ~ off abwenden, abwehren.

warden ['wɔːdən] n (guard) Wächter m, Aufseher m; (in youth hostel) Herbergsvater m; (Univ) Heimleiter m.

warder ['wɔːdə*] n Gefängnis-wärter m.

wardrobe ['wɔːdrəub] n Kleiderschrank m; (clothes) Garderobe f.

ware [wɛə*] n Ware f; ~house Lagerhaus nt.

warfare ['wɔːfɛə*] n Krieg m; Kriegsführung f.

warhead ['wɔːhed] n Sprengkopf m.

warily ['wɛərɪlɪ] ad vorsichtig.

warlike ['wɔːlaɪk] a kriegerisch.

warm [wɔːm] a warm; welcome herzlich; vti wärmen; ~ up vt aufwärmen; vi warm werden; ~-hearted a warmherzig; ~ly ad warm; herzlich; ~th Wärme f, Herzlichkeit f.

warn [wɔːn] vt warnen (of, against vor +dat); ~ing Warnung f; without ~ing unerwartet; ~ing light Warnlicht nt.

warp [wɔːp] vt verziehen; ~ed a (lit) wellig; (fig) pervers.

warrant ['worənt] n Haftbefehl m.

warranty ['worənti] n Garantie f.

warrior ['worɪə*] n Krieger m.

warship ['wɔːʃɪp] n Kriegsschiff nt.

wart [wɔːt] n Warze f.

wartime ['wɔːtaɪm] n Kriegszeit f, Krieg m.

wary ['wɛərɪ] a vorsichtig; mißtrauisch.

was [wɒz, wəz] pt of be.

wash [wɒʃ] n Wäsche f; to give sth a ~ etw waschen; **to have a ~** sich waschen; vt waschen; dishes abwaschen; vi sich waschen; (do washing) waschen; ~ **away** vt abwaschen, wegspülen; **~able** a waschbar; ~**basin** Waschbecken nt; ~**er** (Tech) Dichtungsring m; (machine) Wasch- or Spülmaschine f; ~**ing** Wäsche f; ~**ing machine** Waschmaschine f; ~**ing powder** Waschpulver nt; ~**ing-up** Abwasch m; ~ **leather** Waschleder nt; ~**-out** (col) (event) Reinfall m; (person) Niete f; ~**room** Waschraum m.

wasn't ['wɒznt] = was not.

wasp [wɒsp] n Wespe f.

wastage ['weɪstɪdʒ] n Verlust m; **natural** ~ Verschleiß m.

waste [weɪst] n (wasting) Verschwendung f; (what is wasted) Abfall m; ~**s** pl Einöde f; a (useless) überschüssig, Abfall-; vt object verschwenden; time, life vergeuden; vi: ~ **away** verfallen; ~**ful** a, ~**fully** ad verschwenderisch; process aufwendig; ~**land** Ödland nt; ~**paper basket** Papierkorb m.

watch [wɒtʃ] n Wache f; (for time) Uhr f; **to be on the ~** (for sth) (auf etw acc) aufpassen; vt ansehen; (observe) beobachten; (be careful of) aufpassen auf (+acc); (guard) bewachen; to ~ TV fernsehen; to ~ sb doing sth jdm bei etw zuschauen; ~ **it!** paß bloß auf!; vi zusehen; (guard) Wache halten; to ~ **for** sb/sth nach jdm/etw Ausschau halten; ~ **out!** paß auf!; ~**dog** (lit) Wachthund m; (fig) Wächter m; ~**ful** a wachsam; ~**maker** Uhrmacher m; ~ **man** (Nacht-)wächter m; ~ **strap** Uhrarmband nt.

water ['wɔːtə*] n Wasser nt; ~**s** pl Gewässer nt; vt (be)gießen; (river) bewässern; horses tränken; vi (eye) tränen; my mouth is ~**ing** mir läuft das Wasser im Mund zusammen; ~ **down** vt verwässern; ~ **closet** (Wasser)klosett nt; ~**colour,** (US) ~**color** (painting) Aquarell nt; (paint) Wasserfarbe f; ~**cress** (Brunnen)kresse f; ~**fall** Wasserfall m; ~ **hole** Wasserloch nt; ~**ing can** Gießkanne f; ~ **level** Wasserstand m; ~**lily** Seerose f; ~**line** Wasserlinie f; ~**logged** a ground voll Wasser; wood mit Wasser vollgesogen; ~**melon** Wassermelone f; ~ **polo** Wasserball-(spiel) nt; ~**proof** a wasserdicht; ~**shed** Wasserscheide f; ~**-skiing** Wasserschilaufen nt; to go ~**-skiing** wasserschilaufen gehen; ~**tight** a wasserdicht; ~**works** pl Wasserwerk nt; ~**y** a wäss(e)rig.

watt [wɒt] n Watt nt.

wave [weɪv] n Welle f; (with hand) Winken nt; vt (move to and fro) schwenken; hand, flag winken mit; hair wellen; vi (person) winken; (flag) wehen; (hair) sich wellen; to ~ to sb jdm zuwinken; to ~ sb goodbye jdm zum Abschied winken; ~**length** (lit, fig) Wellenlänge f.

waver ['weɪvə*] vi (hesitate) schwanken; (flicker) flackern.

wavy ['weɪvɪ] a wellig.

wax [wæks] n Wachs nt; (sealing ~) Siegellack m; (in ear) Ohrenschmalz nt; vt floor (ein)wachsen; vi (moon) zunehmen; ~**works** pl Wachsfigurenkabinett nt.

way [weɪ] n Weg m; (road also) Straße f; (method) Art und Weise f, Methode f; (direction) Richtung f; (habit) Eigenart f, Gewohnheit f; (distance) Entfernung f; (condition) Zustand m; **a long ~ away** or off weit weg; **to lose one's ~** sich verirren; **to make ~ for sb/sth** jdm/etw Platz machen; **to be in a bad ~** schlecht dransein; **do it this ~** machen Sie es so; give ~ (Aut) Vorfahrt achten!; ~ **of thinking** Meinung f; **to get one's own ~** seinen Willen bekommen; **one ~ or another** irgendwie; **under ~** im Gange; **in a ~** in gewisser Weise; **in the ~** im Wege; **by the ~** übrigens; **by ~ of** (via) über (+acc); (in order to) um . . . zu; (instead of) als; '~ **in'** 'Eingang'; '~ **out'** 'Ausgang'; ~**lay** vt irreg auflauern (+dat); ~**ward** a eigensinnig.

we [wiː] pl pron wir.

weak a, ~**ly** ad [wiːk, -lɪ] schwach; ~**en** vt schwächen, entkräften; vi schwächer werden; nachlassen; ~**ling** Schwächling m; ~**ness** Schwäche f.

wealth [welθ] n Reichtum m; (abundance) Fülle f; ~**y** a reich.

wean [wiːn] vt entwöhnen.

weapon ['wepən] n Waffe f.

wear [wɛə*] n (clothing) Kleidung f; (use) Verschleiß m; irreg vt (have on) tragen; smile etc haben; (use) abnutzen; vi (last) halten; (become old) (sich) verschleißen; (clothes) sich abtragen; ~ **and tear** Abnutzung f, Verschleiß m; ~ **away** vt verbrauchen; vi schwinden; ~ **down** vt people zermürben; ~ **off** vi sich verlieren; ~ **out** vt verschleißen; person erschöpfen; ~**er** Träger(in f) m.

wearily ['wɪərɪlɪ] ad müde.

weariness ['wɪərɪnəs] n Müdigkeit f.

weary ['wɪərɪ] a (tired) müde; (tiring) ermüdend; vt ermüden; vi überdrüssig werden (of gen).

weasel ['wiːzl] n Wiesel nt.

weather ['weðə*] n Wetter nt; vt verwittern lassen; (resist) überstehen; ~**-beaten** a verwittert; skin wettergegerbt; ~**cock** Wetterhahn m; ~ **forecast** Wettervorhersage f.

weave [wiːv] vt irreg weben; to ~ one's way through sth sich durch etw durchschlängeln; ~**r** Weber(in f) m.

weaving ['wiːvɪŋ] n Weben nt, Weberei f.

web [web] n Netz nt; (membrane) Schwimmhaut f; ~**bed a** Schwimm-, schwimmhäutig; ~**bing** Gewebe nt.

wed [wed] vt irreg (old) heiraten.

we'd [wi:d] = we had; we would.
wedding ['wedɪŋ] n Hochzeit f; ~ **day** Hochzeitstag m; ~ **present** Hochzeits- geschenk nt; ~ **ring** Trau- or Ehering m.
wedge [wedʒ] n Keil m; (of cheese etc) Stück nt; vt (fasten) festklemmen; (pack tightly) einkeilen.
Wednesday ['wenzdeɪ] n Mittwoch m.
wee [wi:] a (esp Scot) klein, winzig.
weed [wi:d] n Unkraut nt; vt jäten; ~-**killer** Unkrautvertilgungsmittel nt.
week [wi:k] n Woche f; a ~ **today** heute in einer Woche; ~**day** Wochentag m; ~**end** Wochenende nt; ~**ly** a, ad wöchentlich; wages, magazine Wochen-.
weep [wi:p] vi irreg weinen.
weigh [weɪ] vti wiegen; ~ **down** vt nieder- drücken; ~ **up** vt prüfen, abschätzen; ~**bridge** Brückenwaage f.
weight [weɪt] n Gewicht nt; to **lose/put on** ~ abnehmen/ zunehmen; ~**lessness** Schwerelosigkeit f; ~-**lifter** Gewicht- heber m; ~**y** a (heavy) gewichtig; (impor- tant) schwerwiegend.
weir [wɪə*] n (Stau)wehr nt.
weird [wɪəd] a seltsam.
welcome ['welkəm] n Willkommen nt, Empfang m; vt begrüßen.
welcoming ['welkəmɪŋ] a Begrüßungs-; freundlich.
weld [weld] n Schweißnaht f; vt schweißen; ~**er** Schweißer m; ~**ing** Schweißen nt.
welfare ['welfɛə*] n Wohl nt; (social) Fürsorge f; ~ **state** Wohlfahrtsstaat m.
well [wel] n Brunnen m; (oil —) Quelle f; a (in good health) gesund; **are you** ~? geht es Ihnen gut?; interj nun, na schön; (starting conversation) nun, tja; ~, ~! na, na!; ad gut; ~ **over 40** weit über 40; **it may** ~ **be** es kann wohl sein; **it would be (as)** ~ **to** ... es wäre wohl gut, zu ...; **you did** ~ **(not) to** ... Sie haben gut daran getan, (nicht) zu ...; **very** ~ (O.K.) nun gut.
we'll [wi:l] = we will, we shall.
well-behaved ['welbɪ'heɪvd] a wohlerzogen.
well-being ['welbi:ɪŋ] n Wohl nt, Wohlergehen nt.
well-built ['wel'bɪlt] a kräftig gebaut.
well-developed ['weldɪ'veləpt] a girl gut entwickelt; economy hochentwickelt.
well-earned ['wel'ɜ:nd] a rest wohlverdient.
well-heeled ['wel'hi:ld] a (col: wealthy) gut gepolstert.
wellingtons ['welɪŋtənz] npl Gummistiefel pl.
well-known ['wel'nəʊn] a person weithin bekannt.
well-meaning ['wel'mi:nɪŋ] a person wohlmeinend; action gutgemeint.
well-off ['wel'ɒf] a gut situiert.
well-read ['wel'red] a (sehr) belesen.
well-to-do ['weltə'du:] a wohlhabend.
well-wisher ['welwɪʃə*] n wohl- wollende(r) Freund m, Gönner m.
wench [wentʃ] n (old) Maid f, Dirne f.
went [went] pt of go.

were [wɜ:*] pt pl of be.
we're [wɪə*] = we are.
weren't [wɜ:nt] = were not.
west [west] n Westen m; a West-, westlich; ad westwärts, nach Westen; ~**erly** a westlich; ~**ern** a westlich, West-; n (Cine) Western m; ~**ward(s)** ad westwärts.
wet [wet] a naß; ~ **blanket** (fig) Triefel m; ~**ness** Nässe f, Feuchtigkeit f; '~ **paint**' 'frisch gestrichen'.
we've [wi:v] = we have.
whack [wæk] n Schlag m; vt schlagen.
whale [weɪl] n Wal m.
wharf [wɔ:f] n Kai m.
what [wɒt] pron, interj was; a welche(r,s); ~ **a hat!** was für ein Hut!; ~ **money I had** das Geld, das ich hatte; ~ **about ...?** (suggestion) wie wär's mit ...?; ~ **about it?, so** ~? na und?; **well,** ~ **about him?** was ist mit ihm?; **and** ~ **about me?** und ich?; ~ **for?** wozu?; ~**ever** a: ~**ever he says** egal, was er sagt; **no reason** ~**ever** überhaupt kein Grund.
wheat [wi:t] n Weizen m.
wheel [wi:l] n Rad nt; (steering —) Lenkrad nt; (disc) Scheibe f; vt schieben; vi (revolve) sich drehen; ~**barrow** Schub- karren m; ~**chair** Rollstuhl m.
wheeze [wi:z] n Keuchen nt; vi keuchen.
when [wen] ad interrog wann; ad,cj (with present tense) wenn; (with past tense) als; (with indir question) wann; ~**ever** ad wann immer; immer wenn.
where [wɛə*] ad (place) wo; (direction) wohin; ~ **from** woher; ~**abouts** ['wɛərə'baʊts] ad wo; n Aufenthalt m, Verbleib m; ~**as** [wɛər'æz] cj während, wo ... doch; ~**ever** [wɛər'evə*] ad wo (immer).
whet [wet] vt appetite anregen.
whether ['weðə*] cj ob.
which [wɪtʃ] a (from selection) welche(r,s); rel pron der/die/das; (rel: which fact) was; (interrog) welche(r,s); ~**ever** (book) **he takes** welches (Buch) er auch nimmt.
whiff [wɪf] n Hauch m.
while [waɪl] n Weile f; cj während; **for a** ~ eine Zeitlang.
whim [wɪm] n Laune f.
whimper ['wɪmpə*] n Wimmern nt; vi wimmern.
whimsical ['wɪmzɪkəl] a launisch.
whine [waɪn] n Gewinsel nt, Gejammer nt; vi heulen, winseln.
whip [wɪp] n Peitsche f; (Parl) Einpeitscher m; vt (beat) peitschen; (snatch) reißen; ~-**round** (col) Geld- sammlung f.
whirl [wɜ:l] n Wirbel m; vti (herum)- wirbeln; ~**pool** Wirbel m; ~**wind** Wirbelwind m.
whirr [wɜ:*] vi schwirren, surren.
whisk [wɪsk] n Schneebesen m; vt cream etc schlagen.
whisker ['wɪskə*] n (of animal) Barthaare pl; ~**s** pl (of man) Backenbart m.
whisk(e)y ['wɪskɪ] n Whisky m.
whisper ['wɪspə*] n Flüstern nt; vi flüstern; (leaves) rascheln; vt flüstern, munkeln.

whist [wɪst] n Whist nt.

whistle ['wɪsl] n Pfiff m; (instrument) Pfeife f; vti pfeifen.

white [waɪt] n Weiß nt; (of egg) Eiweiß nt; (of eye) Weiße(s) nt; a weiß; (with fear) blaß; ~collar worker Angestellte(r) m; ~ lie Notlüge f; ~ness Weiß nt; ~wash n (paint) Tünche f; (fig) Ehrenrettung f; vt weißen, tünchen; (fig) reinwaschen.

whiting ['waɪtɪŋ] n Weißfisch m.

Whitsun ['wɪtsn] n Pfingsten nt.

whittle ['wɪtl] vt: ~ away or down stutzen, verringern.

whizz [wɪz] vi sausen, zischen, schwirren; ~ kid (col) Kanone f.

who [huː] pron (interrog) wer; (rel) der/die/das; ~ever [huː'evə*] pron wer immer; jeder, der/jede, die/jedes, das.

whole [həʊl] a ganz; (uninjured) heil; n Ganze(s) nt; the ~ of the year das ganze Jahr; on the ~ im großen und ganzen; ~hearted a rückhaltlos; ~heartedly ad von ganzem Herzen; ~sale Großhandel m; a trade Großhandels-; destruction vollkommen, Massen; ~saler Großhändler m; ~some a bekömmlich, gesund.

wholly ['həʊlɪ] ad ganz, völlig.

whom [huːm] pron (interrog) wen; (rel) den/die/das/die pl.

whooping cough ['huːpɪŋkɒf] n Keuchhusten m.

whopper ['wɒpə*] n (col) Mordsding nt; faustdicke Lüge f.

whopping ['wɒpɪŋ] a (col) kolossal, Riesen-.

whore ['hɔː*] n Hure f.

whose [huːz] pron (interrog) wessen; (rel) dessen/deren/ dessen/deren pl.

why [waɪ] ad warum; interj nanu; that's ~ deshalb.

wick [wɪk] n Docht m.

wicked ['wɪkɪd] a böse; ~ness Bosheit f, Schlechtigkeit f.

wicker ['wɪkə*] n Weidengeflecht nt, Korbgeflecht nt.

wicket ['wɪkɪt] n Tor nt, Dreistab m; (playing pitch) Spielfeld nt.

wide [waɪd] a breit; plain weit; (in firing) daneben; ~ of weitab von; ad weit; daneben; ~angle a lens Weitwinkel-; ~awake a hellwach; ~ly ad weit; known allgemein; ~n vt erweitern; ~ness Breite f, Ausdehnung f; ~open a weit geöffnet; ~spread a weitverbreitet.

widow ['wɪdəʊ] n Witwe f; ~ed a verwitwet; ~er Witwer m.

width [wɪdθ] n Breite f, Weite f.

wield [wiːld] vt schwingen, handhaben.

wife [waɪf] n (Ehe)frau f, Gattin f.

wig [wɪg] n Perücke f.

wiggle ['wɪgl] n Wackeln nt; vt wackeln mit; vi wackeln.

wigwam ['wɪgwæm] n Wigwam m, Indianerzelt nt.

wild [waɪld] a wild; (violent) heftig; plan, idea verrückt; the ~s pl die Wildnis; ~erness ['wɪldənəs] Wildnis f, Wüste f; ~goose chase fruchtlose(s) Unternehmen nt; ~life Tierwelt f; ~ly ad wild, ungestüm; exaggerated irrsinnig.

wilful ['wɪlfʊl] a (intended) vorsätzlich; (obstinate) eigensinnig.

will [wɪl] v aux: he ~ come er wird kommen; I ~ do it! ich werde es tun; (power to choose) Wille m; (wish) Wunsch m, Bestreben nt; (Jur) Testament nt; vt wollen; ~ing a gewillt, bereit; ~ingly ad bereitwillig, gern; ~ingness (Bereit)willigkeit f.

willow ['wɪləʊ] n Weide f.

will power ['wɪl'paʊə*] n Willenskraft f.

wilt [wɪlt] vi (ver)welken.

wily ['waɪlɪ] a gerissen.

win [wɪn] n Sieg m; irreg vt gewinnen; vi (be successful) siegen; to ~ sb over jdn gewinnen, jdn dazu bringen.

wince [wɪns] n Zusammenzucken nt; vi zusammenzucken, zurückfahren.

winch [wɪntʃ] n Winde f.

wind [waɪnd] irreg vt rope winden; bandage wickeln; to ~ one's way sich schlängeln; vi (turn) sich winden; (change direction) wenden; ~ up vt clock aufziehen; debate (ab)schließen.

wind [wɪnd] n Wind m; (Med) Blähungen pl; ~break Windschutz m; ~fall unverhoffte(r) Glücksfall m.

winding ['waɪndɪŋ] a road gewunden, sich schlängelnd.

wind instrument ['wɪndɪnstrumənt] n Blasinstrument nt.

windmill ['wɪndmɪl] n Windmühle f.

window ['wɪndəʊ] n Fenster nt; ~ box Blumenkasten m; ~ cleaner Fensterputzer m; ~ ledge Fenstersims m; ~ pane Fensterscheibe f; ~shopping Schaufensterbummel m; ~sill Fensterbank f.

windpipe ['wɪndpaɪp] n Luftröhre f.

windscreen ['wɪndskriːn], (US) windshield ['wɪndʃiːld] n Windschutzscheibe f; ~ wiper Scheibenwischer m.

windswept ['wɪndswept] a vom Wind gepeitscht; person zersaust.

windy ['wɪndɪ] a windig.

wine [waɪn] n Wein m; ~glass Weinglas nt; ~ list Weinkarte f; ~ merchant Weinhändler m; ~ tasting Weinprobe f; ~ waiter Weinkellner m.

wing [wɪŋ] n Flügel m; (Mil) Gruppe f; ~s pl (Theat) Seitenkulisse f; ~er (Sport) Flügelstürmer m.

wink [wɪŋk] n Zwinkern nt; vi zwinkern, blinzeln; to ~ at sb jdm zublinzeln; forty ~s Nickerchen nt.

winner ['wɪnə*] n Gewinner m; (Sport) Sieger m.

winning ['wɪnɪŋ] a team siegreich, Sieger-; goal entscheidend; n: ~s pl Gewinn m; ~post Ziel nt.

winter ['wɪntə*] n Winter m; a clothes Winter-; vi überwintern; ~ sports pl Wintersport m.

wintry ['wɪntrɪ] a Winter-, winterlich.

wipe [waɪp] n Wischen nt; vt wischen, abwischen; ~ out vt debt löschen; (destroy) auslöschen.

wire ['waɪə*] n Draht m; (telegram) Telegramm nt; vt telegrafieren (sb jdm, sth etw); ~less Radio(apparat m) nt.

wiry ['waɪərɪ] a drahtig.
wisdom ['wɪzdəm] n Weisheit f; (of decision) Klugheit f; ~ **tooth** Weisheitszahn m.
wise [waɪz] a klug, weise; ~**crack** Witzelei f; ~**ly** ad klug, weise.
wish [wɪʃ] n Wunsch m; vt wünschen; he ~es us to do it er möchte, daß wir es tun; with best ~es herzliche Grüße; to ~ sb goodbye jdn verabschieden; to ~ to do sth etw tun wollen; ~**ful thinking** Wunschdenken nt.
wisp [wɪsp] n (Haar)strähne f; (of smoke) Wölkchen nt.
wistful ['wɪstful] a sehnsüchtig.
wit [wɪt] n (also ~s) Verstand m no pl; (amusing ideas) Witz m; (person) Witzbold m; at one's ~s' end mit seinem Latein am Ende; to have one's ~s about one auf dem Posten sein.
witch [wɪtʃ] n Hexe f; ~**craft** Hexerei f.
with [wɪð, wɪθ] prep mit; (in spite of) trotz (+gen or dat); ~ him it's ... bei ihm ist es ...; to stay ~ sb bei jdm wohnen; I have no money ~ me ich habe kein Geld bei mir; shaking ~ fright vor Angst zitternd.
withdraw [wɪð'drɔː] irreg vt zurückziehen; money abheben; remark zurücknehmen; vi sich zurückziehen; ~**al** Zurückziehung f; Abheben nt; Zurücknahme f; ~**al symptoms** pl Entzugserscheinungen pl.
wither ['wɪðə°] vi (ver)welken; ~**ed** a verwelkt, welk.
withhold [wɪð'həʊld] vt irreg vorenthalten (from sb jdm).
within [wɪð'ɪn] prep innerhalb (+gen).
without [wɪð'aʊt] prep ohne; it goes ~ saying es ist selbstverständlich.
withstand [wɪð'stænd] vt irreg widerstehen (+dat).
witness ['wɪtnəs] n Zeuge m; Zeugin f; vt (see) sehen, miterleben; (sign document) beglaubigen; vi aussagen; ~ **box**, (US) ~ **stand** Zeugenstand m.
witticism ['wɪtɪsɪzəm] n witzige Bemerkung f.
witty a, **wittily** ad ['wɪtɪ, -lɪ] witzig, geistreich.
wizard ['wɪzəd] n Zauberer m.
wobble ['wɒbl] vi wackeln.
woe [wəʊ] n Weh nt, Leid nt, Kummer m.
wolf [wʊlf] n Wolf m.
woman ['wʊmən] n, pl **women** Frau f; a ~ **in** f.
womb [wuːm] n Gebärmutter f.
women ['wɪmɪn] npl of **woman**.
wonder ['wʌndə°] n (marvel) Wunder nt; (surprise) Staunen nt, Verwunderung f; vi sich wundern; I ~ **whether** ... ich frage mich, ob ...; ~**ful** a wunderbar, herrlich; ~**fully** ad wunderbar.
won't [wəʊnt] = **will not**.
wood [wʊd] n Holz nt; (forest) Wald m; ~ **carving** Holzschnitzerei f; ~**ed** a bewaldet, waldig, Wald-; ~**en** a (lit, fig) hölzern; ~**pecker** Specht m; ~**wind** Blasinstrumente pl; ~**work** Holzwerk nt; (craft) Holzarbeiten pl; ~**worm** Holzwurm m.

wool [wʊl] n Wolle f; ~**len**, (US) ~**en** a Woll-; ~**ly**, (US) ~**y** a wollig; (fig) schwammig.
word [wɜːd] n Wort nt; (news) Bescheid m; to have a ~ with sb mit jdm reden; to have ~s with sb Worte wechseln mit jdm; by ~ of **mouth** mündlich; vt formulieren; ~**ing** Wortlaut m, Formulierung f.
work [wɜːk] n Arbeit f; (Art, Liter) Werk nt; vi arbeiten; machine funktionieren; (medicine) wirken; (succeed) klappen; ~s (factory) Fabrik f, Werk nt; (of watch) Werk nt; ~ **off** vt debt abarbeiten; anger abreagieren; ~ **on** vi weiterarbeiten; vt (be engaged in) arbeiten an (+dat); (influence) bearbeiten; ~ **out** vi (sum) aufgehen; (plan) klappen; vt problem lösen; plan ausarbeiten; ~ **up to** vt hinarbeiten auf (+acc); to get ~**ed up** sich aufregen; ~**able** a soil bearbeitbar; plan ausführbar; ~**er** Arbeiter(in f) m; ~**ing class** Arbeiterklasse f; ~**ing-class** a Arbeiter-; ~**ing man** Werktätige(r) m; ~**man** Arbeiter m; ~**manship** Arbeit f, Ausführung f; ~**shop** Werkstatt f.
world [wɜːld] n Welt f; (animal — etc) Reich nt; out of this ~ himmlisch; to come into the ~ auf die Welt kommen; to do sb/sth the ~ of good jdm/etw sehr gut tun; to be the ~ to sb jds ein und alles sein; to think the ~ of sb große Stücke auf jdn halten; ~**-famous** a weltberühmt; ~**ly** a weltlich, irdisch; ~**-wide** a weltweit.
worm [wɜːm] n Wurm m.
worn [wɔːn] a clothes abgetragen; ~**-out** a object abgenutzt; person völlig erschöpft.
worried ['wʌrɪd] a besorgt, beunruhigt.
worrier ['wʌrɪə°] n: he is a ~ er macht sich (dat) ewig Sorgen.
worry ['wʌrɪ] n Sorge f, Kummer m; vt quälen, beunruhigen; vi (feel uneasy) sich sorgen, sich (dat) Gedanken machen; ~**ing** a beunruhigend.
worse [wɜːs] a comp of **bad** schlechter, schlimmer; ad comp of **badly** schlimmer, ärger; n Schlimmere(s) nt, Schlechtere(s) nt; ~**n** vt verschlimmern; vi sich verschlechtern.
worship ['wɜːʃɪp] n Anbetung f, Verehrung f; (religious service) Gottesdienst m; (title) Hochwürden m; vt anbeten; ~**per** Gottesdienstbesucher(in f) m.
worst [wɜːst] a superl of **bad** schlimmste(r,s), schlechteste(r,s); ad superl of **badly** am schlimmsten, am ärgsten; n Schlimmste(s) nt, Ärgste(s) nt.
worsted ['wʊstɪd] n Kammgarn nt.
worth [wɜːθ] n Wert m; £10 ~ **of food** Essen für 10 £; a wert; ~ **seeing** sehenswert; it's ~ £10 es ist 10 £ wert; ~**less** a wertlos; person nichtsnutzig; ~**while** a lohnend, der Mühe wert; ad: it's not ~**while going** es lohnt sich nicht, dahin zu gehen; ~**y** ['wɜːðɪ] a (having worth) wertvoll; wert (of gen), würdig (of gen).
would [wʊd] v aux: **she** ~ **come** sie würde kommen; if **you** asked **he** ~

come wenn Sie ihn fragten, würde er kommen; ~ **you like a drink?** möchten Sie etwas trinken?; ~**-be** a angeblich; ~**n't** = ~ **not**.

wound [wu:nd] n (lit, fig) Wunde f; vt verwunden, verletzen (also fig).

wrangle ['ræŋgl] n Streit m; vi sich zanken.

wrap [ræp] n (stole) Umhang m, Schal m; vt (also ~ **up**) einwickeln; **deal** abschließen; ~**per** Umschlag m, Schutzhülle f; ~**ping paper** Einwickelpapier nt.

wreath [ri:θ] n Kranz m.

wreck [rek] n Schiffbruch m; (ship) Wrack nt; (sth ruined) Ruine f, Trümmerhaufen m; a nervous ~ ein Nervenbündel nt; vt zerstören; ~**age** Wrack nt, Trümmer pl.

wren [ren] n Zaunkönig m.

wrench [rentʃ] n (spanner) Schraubenschlüssel m; (twist) Ruck m, heftige Drehung f; vt reißen, zerren.

wrestle ['resl] vi ringen.

wrestling ['reslıŋ] n Ringen nt; ~ **match** Ringkampf m.

wretched ['retʃıd] a hovel elend; (col) verflixt; **I feel** ~ mir ist elend.

wriggle ['rıgl] n Schlängeln nt; vi sich winden.

wring [rıŋ] vt irreg wringen.

wrinkle ['rıŋkl] n Falte f, Runzel f; vt runzeln; vi sich runzeln; (material) knittern.

wrist [rıst] n Handgelenk nt; ~**watch** Armbanduhr f.

writ [rıt] n gerichtliche(r) Befehl m.

write [raıt] vti irreg schreiben; ~ **down** vt niederschreiben, aufschreiben; ~ **off** vt (dismiss) abschreiben; ~ **out** vt essay abschreiben; cheque ausstellen; ~ **up** vt schreiben; ~**-off: it is a off** das kann man abschreiben; ~**r** Verfasser m; (author) Schriftsteller m; ~**-up** Besprechung f.

writing ['raıtıŋ] n (act) Schreiben nt; (hand—) (Hand)schrift f; ~**s** pl Schriften pl, Werke pl; ~ **paper** Schreibpapier nt.

wrong [roŋ] a (incorrect) falsch; (morally) unrecht; (out of order) nicht in Ordnung; **he was** ~ **in doing that** es war nicht recht von ihm, das zu tun; **what's** ~ **with your leg?** was ist mit deinem Bein los?; **to go** ~ (plan) schiefgehen; (person) einen Fehler machen; n Unrecht nt; vt Unrecht tun (+dat); ~**ful** a unrechtmäßig; ~**ly** ad falsch; accuse zu Unrecht.

wrought [rɔ:t] a: ~ **iron** Schmiedeeisen nt.

wry [raı] a schief, krumm; (ironical) trocken; **to make a** ~ **face** das Gesicht verziehen.

X

X, x [eks] n X nt, x nt.

Xmas ['eksməs] n (col) Weihnachten nt.

X-ray ['eks'reı] n Röntgenaufnahme f; vt röntgen.

xylophone ['zaıləfəʊn] n Xylophon nt.

Y

Y, y [waı] n Y nt, y nt.

yacht [jot] n Jacht f; ~**ing** (Sport)segeln nt; ~**sman** Sportsegler m.

Yank [jæŋk] n (col) Ami m.

yap [jæp] vi (dog) kläffen; (people) quasseln.

yard [jɑ:d] n Hof m; (measure) (englische) Elle f, Yard nt, 0,91 m; ~**stick** (fig) Maßstab m.

yarn [jɑ:n] n (thread) Garn nt; (story) (Seemanns)garn nt.

yawn [jɔ:n] n Gähnen nt; vi gähnen.

year ['jıə*] n Jahr nt; ~**ly** a, ad jährlich.

yearn [jɜ:n] vi sich sehnen (for nach); ~**ing** Verlangen nt, Sehnsucht f.

yeast [ji:st] n Hefe f.

yell [jel] n gellende(r) Schrei m; vi laut schreien.

yellow ['jeləʊ] a gelb; n Gelb nt; ~ **fever** Gelbfieber nt.

yelp [jelp] n Gekläff nt; vi kläffen.

yeoman ['jəʊmən] n: **Y~ of the Guard** Leibgardist m.

yes [jes] ad ja; n Ja nt, Jawort nt; ~**man** Jasager m.

yesterday ['jestədeı] ad gestern; n Gestern nt; **the day before** ~ vorgestern.

yet [jet] ad noch; (in question) schon; (up to now) bis jetzt; **and** ~ **again** und wieder or noch einmal; **as** ~ bis jetzt; (in past) bis dahin; cj doch, dennoch.

yew [ju:] n Eibe f.

Yiddish ['jıdıʃ] n Jiddisch nt.

yield [ji:ld] n Ertrag m; vt result, crop hervorbringen; interest, profit abwerfen; (concede) abtreten; vi nachgeben; (Mil) sich ergeben.

yodel ['jəʊdl] vi jodeln.

yoga ['jəʊgə] n Joga m.

yoghurt [jogət] n Joghurt m.

yoke [jəʊk] n (lit, fig) Joch nt.

yolk [jəʊk] n Eidotter m, Eigelb nt.

yonder ['jondə*] ad dort drüben, da drüben; a jene(r, s) dort.

you [ju:] pron (familiar) (sing) (nom) du; (acc) dich; (dat) dir; (pl) (nom) ihr; (acc, dat) euch; (polite) (nom, acc) Sie; (dat) Ihnen; (indef) (nom) man; (acc) einen; (dat) einem.

you'd [ju:d] = **you had; you would**.

you'll [ju:l] = **you will, you shall**.

young [jʌŋ] a jung; npl die Jungen; ~**ish** a ziemlich jung; ~**ster** Junge m, junge(r) Bursche m/junge(s) Mädchen nt.

your ['jɔ:*] poss a (familiar) (sing) dein; (pl) euer, eure pl; (polite) Ihr.

you're ['jʊə*] = **you are**.

yours ['jɔ:z] poss pron (familiar) (sing) deine(r, s); (pl) eure(r, s); (polite) Ihre(r, s).

yourself [jɔ:'self] pron (emphatic) selbst; (familiar) (sing) (acc) dich (selbst); (dat) dir (selbst); (pl) euch (selbst); (polite) sich (selbst); **you're not** ~ mit dir/Ihnen ist etwas nicht in Ordnung.

youth [ju:θ] n Jugend f; (young man)

junge(r) Mann *m*; (*young people*) Jugend *f*;
~ful *a* jugendlich; ~ hostel Jugend-
herberge *f*.

you've [ju:v] = you have.

Z

Z, z [zɛd] *n* Z *nt*, z *nt*.

zany ['zeɪnɪ] *a* komisch.

zeal [zi:l] *n* Eifer *m*; ~ous ['zeləs] *a* eifrig.

zebra ['zi:brə] *n* Zebra *nt*; ~ crossing
['zi:brə'krɒsɪŋ] Zebrastreifen *m*.

zenith ['zenɪθ] *n* Zenit *m*.

zero ['zɪərəʊ] *n* Null *f*; (*on scale*) Nullpunkt
m; ~ hour die Stunde X.

zest [zest] *n* Begeisterung *f*.

zigzag ['zɪgzæg] *n* Zickzack *m*; *vi* im
Zickzack laufen/fahren.

zinc [zɪŋk] *n* Zink *nt*.

Zionism ['zaɪənɪzəm] *n* Zionismus *m*.

zip [zɪp] *n* (*also* ~ fastener, ~per)
Reißverschluß *m*; *vt* (*also* ~ up) den
Reißverschluß zumachen (+*gen*).

zither ['zɪðə°] *n* Zither *f*.

zodiac ['zəʊdɪæk] *n* Tierkreis *m*.

zombie ['zɒmbɪ] *n* Trantüte *f*.

zone [zəʊn] *n* Zone *f*; (*area*) Gebiet *nt*.

zoo [zu:] *n* Zoo *m*; ~logical [zəʊə'lɒdʒɪkəl]
a zoologisch; ~logist [zu:'ɒlədʒɪst]
Zoologe *m*; ~logy [zu:'ɒlədʒɪ] Zoologie *f*.

zoom [zu:m] *vi* (*engine*) surren; (*plane*) aufsteigen; (*move fast*) brausen; (*prices*) hoch-
schnellen; ~ lens Zoomobjektiv *nt*.

Länder, Völker und Sprachen

ich bin Deutscher/Engländer/Albanier I am German/English/Albanian

ein Deutscher/Engländer/Albanier a German/an Englishman/an Albanian; **eine Deutsche/Engländerin/Albanierin** a German (woman/girl)/an English woman/girl/an Albanian (woman/girl)

sprechen Sie Deutsch/Englisch/Albanisch? do you speak German/English/ Albanian?

Adria (die), Adriatische(s) Meer the Adriatic.
Afrika Africa; **Afrikaner(in** f) m African; **afrikanisch** a African.
Ägäis (die), Ägäische(s) Meer the Aegean.
Ägypten Egypt; **Ägypter(in** f) m Egyptian; **ägyptisch** a Egyptian.
Albanien Albania; **Albanier(in** f) m Albanian; **albanisch** a Albanian.
Algerien Algeria; **Algerier(in** f) m Algerian; **algerisch** a Algerian.
Alpen pl (die) the Alps pl.
Amazonas (der) the Amazon.
Amerika America; **Amerikaner(in** f) m American; **amerikanisch** a American.
Anden pl (die) the Andes pl.
Antarktis (die) the Antarctic.
Antillen pl (die) the Antilles pl.
Antwerpen Antwerp.
Arabien Arabia; **Araber** m Arab, Arabian; **arabisch** a Arab, Arabic, Arabian.
Argentinien Argentina, the Argentine; **Argentinier(in** f) m Argentinian; argentinisch a Argentinian.
Ärmelkanal (der) the English Channel.
Armenien Armenia; **Armenier(in** f) m Armenian; **armenisch** a Armenian.
Asien Asia; **Asiat(in** f) m Asian; **asiatisch** a Asian, Asiatic.
Athen Athens; **Athener(in** f) m Athenian; **athenisch** a Athenian.
Äthiopien Ethiopia; **Äthiopier(in** f) m Ethiopian; **äthiopisch** a Ethiopian.
Atlantik (der), Atlantische(r) Ozean the Atlantic (Ocean).
Ätna (der) Mount Etna.
Australien Australia; **Australier(in** f) m Australian; **australisch** a Australian.
Azoren pl (die) the Azores pl.
Balkan (der) the Balkans pl.
Basel Basle.
Bayern Bavaria; **Bayer(in** f) m Bavarian; **bayerisch** a Bavarian.
Belgien Belgium; **Belgier(in** f) m Belgian; **belgisch** a Belgian.
Belgrad Belgrade.
Birma Burma; **Birmane** m, **Birmanin** f Burmese; **Birmanisch** a Burmese.
Biskaya (die) the Bay of Biscay.
Bodensee (der) Lake Constance.
Böhmen Bohemia; **Böhme** m, **Böhmin** f Bohemian; **böhmisch** a Bohemian.
Bolivien Bolivia; **Bolivianer(in** f) m Bolivian; **bolivianisch, bolivisch** a Bolivian.
Brasilien Brazil; **Brasilianer(in** f) m Brazilian; **brasilianisch** a Brazilian.
Braunschweig Brunswick.
Brite m, **Britin** f Briton; **britisch** a British.
Brüssel Brussels.
Bulgarien Bulgaria; **Bulgare** m, **Bulgarin** f Bulgarian, Bulgar; **bulgarisch** a Bulgarian.
Burgund Burgundy; **burgundisch, Burgunder** a Burgundian.
Calais: Straße von Calais (die) the Straits of Dover pl.
Chile Chile; **Chilene** m, **Chilenin** f Chilean; **chilenisch** a Chilean.
China China; **Chinese** m, **Chinesin** f Chinese; **chinesisch** a Chinese.
Dänemark Denmark; **Däne** m, **Dänin** f Dane; **dänisch** a Danish.
Deutsche Demokratische Republik (die) German Democratic Republic, East Germany.
Deutschland Germany; **Deutsche(r)** mf German; **deutsch** a German.
Dolomiten pl (die) the Dolomites pl.
Donau (die) the Danube.
Dünkirchen Dunkirk.

Eismeer (das) the Arctic.
Elfenbeinküste (die) the Ivory Coast.
Elsaß (das) Alsace; **Elsässer(in** *f)* *m* Alsatian; **elsässisch** *a* Alsatian.
Engadin (das) the Engadine.
England England; **Engländer(in** *f)* *m* Englishman/-woman; **englisch** *a* English.
Estland Estonia; **Este** *m*, **Estin** *f* Estonian; **estnisch** *a* Estonian.
Etsch (die) the Adige.
Euphrat (der) the Euphrates.
Eurasien Eurasia.
Europa Europe; **Europäer(in** *f)* *m* European; **europäisch** *a* European.
Ferne(r) Osten (der) the Far East.
Finnland Finland; **Finne** *m*, **Finnin** *f* Finn; **finnisch** *a* Finnish.
Flandern Flanders; **Flame** *m*, **Flämin** *or* **Flamin** *f* Fleming; **flämisch** *a* Flemish.
Florenz Florence; **Florentiner(in** *f)* *m* Florentine; **florentinisch** *a* Florentine.
Frankreich France; **Franzose** *m*, **Französin** *f* Frenchman/-woman; **französisch** *a* French.
Friesland Frisia; **Friese** *m*, **Friesin** *f* Frisian; **friesisch** *a* Frisian.
Genf Geneva.
Genfer See Lake Geneva.
Genua Genoa; **Genuese** *m*, **Genuesin** *f* Genoan; **genuesisch** *a* Genoan.
Griechenland Greece; **Grieche** *m*, **Griechin** *f* Greek; **griechisch** *a* Greek.
Großbritannien Great Britain; **Brite** *m*, **Britin** *f* Briton; **britisch**, **großbritannisch** *a* British.
Guinea Guinea.
Haag (der), **Den Haag** the Hague.
Hannover Hanover; **Hannoveraner(in** *f)* *m* Hanoverian; **Hannoveraner, hannoversch** *a* Hanoverian.
Hebriden *pl* **(die)** the Hebrides *pl*.
Helgoland Heligoland.
Hessen Hesse; **Hesse** *m*, **Hessin** *f* Hessian; **hessisch** *a* Hessian.
Holland Holland; **Holländer(in** *f)* *m* Dutchman/-woman; **holländisch** *a* Dutch.
Iberische Halbinsel (die) the Iberian Peninsula.
Indien India; **Inder(in** *f)* *m*, **Indianer(in** *f)* *m* Indian; **indisch, indianisch** *a* Indian.
Indonesien Indonesia; **Indonesier(in** *f)* *m* Indonesian; **indonesisch** *a* Indonesian.
Irak (auch der) Iraq; **Iraker(in** *f)* *m* Iraqi; **irakisch** *a* Iraqi.
Iran (auch der) Iran; **Iraner(in** *f)* *m* Iranian; **iranisch** *a* Iranian.
Irland Ireland; **Ire** *m*, **Irin** *f* Irishman/-woman; **irisch** *a* Irish.
Island Iceland; **Isländer(in** *f)* *m* Icelander; **isländisch** *a* Icelandic.
Israel Israel; **Israeli** *mf* Israeli; **israelisch** *a* Israeli.
Italien Italy; **Italiener(in** *f)* *m* Italian; **italienisch** *a* Italian.
Japan Japan; **Japaner(in** *f)* *m* Japanese; **japanisch** *a* Japanese.
Jemen (auch der) the Yemen; **Jemenit(in** *f)* *m* Yemeni; **jemenitisch** *a* Yemeni.
Jordanien Jordan; **Jordanier(in** *f)* *m* Jordanian; **jordanisch** *a* Jordanian.
Jugoslawien Yugoslavia; **Jugoslawe** *m*, **Jugoslawin** *f* Yugoslavian; **jugoslawisch** *a* Yugoslavian.
Kanada Canada; **Kanadier(in** *f)* *m* Canadian; **kanadisch** *a* Canadian.
Kanalinseln *pl* **(die)** the Channel Islands *pl*.
Kanarische Inseln *pl* **(die)** the Canary Islands *pl*, the Canaries *pl*.
Kap der Guten Hoffnung (das) the Cape of Good Hope.
Kapstadt Cape Town.
Karibische Inseln *pl* **(die)** the Caribbean Islands *pl*.
Karpaten *pl* **(die)** the Carpathians *pl*.
Kaspische(s) Meer the Caspian Sea.
Kleinasien Asia Minor.
Köln Cologne.
Konstanz Constance.
Kreml (der) the Kremlin.
Kreta Crete; **Kreter(in** *f)* *m* Cretan; **kretisch** *a* Cretan.
Krim (die) the Crimea.
Kroatien Croatia; **Kroate** *m*, **Kroatin** *f* Croatian; **kroatisch** *a* Croatian.
Lappland Lapland; **Lappe** *m*, **Lappin** *f* Laplander; **lappisch** *a* Lapp.
Lateinamerika Latin America.
Lettland Latvia; **Lette** *m*, **Lettin** *f* Latvian; **lettisch** *a* Latvian.
Libanon the Lebanon; **Libanese** *m*, **Libanesin** *f* Lebanese; **libanesisch** *a* Lebanese.
Libyen Libya; **Libyer(in** *f)* *m* Libyan; **libyisch** *a* Libyan.
Lissabon Lisbon.
Litauen Lithuania; **Litauer(in** *f)* *m* Lithuanian; **litauisch** *a* Lithuanian.
Livland Livonia; **Livländer(in** *f)* *m* Livonian; **livländisch** *a* Livonian.
London London; **Londoner(in** *f)* *m* Londoner; **Londoner** *a* London.

Lothringen Lorraine.
Lüneburger Heide (die) the Lüneburg Heath.
Luxemburg Luxembourg.
Maas (die) the Meuse.
Mähren Moravia.
Mailand Milan; **Mailänder(in f)** *m* Milanese; **mailändisch** a Milanese.
Mallorca Majorca.
Mandschurei (die) Manchuria; **Mandschure** *m*, **Mandschurin f** Manchurian; **mandschurisch** a Manchurian.
Marokko Morocco; **Marokkaner(in f)** *m* Moroccan; **marokkanisch** a Moroccan.
Mazedonien Macedonia; **Mazedonier(in f)** *m* Macedonian; **mazedonisch** a Macedonian.
Mittelamerika Central America.
Mitteleuropa Central Europe.
Mittelmeer (das) the Mediterranean.
Moldau (die) Moldavia.
Mongolei (die) Mongolia; **Mongole** *m*, **Mongolin f** Mongol(ian); **mongolisch** a Mongol(ian).
Moskau Moscow; **Moskauer(in f)** *m* Muscovite; **moskauisch** a Muscovite.
München Munich.
Nahe(r) Osten (der) the Near East.
Neapel Naples; **Neapolitaner(in f)** *m* Neapolitan; **neapolitanisch** a Neapolitan.
Neufundland Newfoundland; **Neufundländer(in f)** *m* Newfoundlander; **neufundländisch** a Newfoundland.
Neuguinea New Guinea.
Neuseeland New Zealand; **Neuseeländer(in f)** *m* New Zealander; **neuseeländisch** a New Zealand.
Niederlande pl (die) the Netherlands; **Niederländer(in f)** *m* Dutchman/-woman; **niederländisch** a Dutch.
Niedersachsen Lower Saxony.
Niederrhein Lower Rhine.
Nil (der) the Nile.
Nordirland Northern Ireland.
Nordsee (die) the North Sea.
Norwegen Norway; **Norweger(in f)** *m* Norwegian; **norwegisch** a Norwegian.
Nord-Ostsee-Kanal (der) the Kiel Canal.
Nordrhein-Westfalen North Rhine-Westphalia.
Nürnberg Nuremberg.
Oberbayern Upper Bavaria.
Ostasien Eastern Asia.
Ostende Ostend.
Ostsee (die) the Baltic.
Österreich Austria; **Österreicher(in f)** *m* Austrian; **österreichisch** a Austrian.
Palästina Palestine; **Palästinenser(in f)** *m* Palestinian; **palästinensisch** a Palestinian.
Paris Paris; **Pariser(in f)** *m* Parisian; **Pariser** a Parisian.
Pazifik (der), Pazifische(r) Ozean the Pacific.
Peloponnes (der or die) the Peloponnese.
Persien Persia; **Perser(in f)** *m* Persian; **persisch** a Persian.
Philippinen pl (die) the Philippines pl.
Polen Poland; **Pole** *m*, **Polin f** Pole; **polnisch** a Polish.
Pommern Pomerania; **Pommer(in f)** *m* Pomeranian; **pommerisch** a Pomeranian.
Portugal Portugal; **Portugiese** *m*, **Portugiesin f** Portuguese; **portugiesisch** a Portuguese.
Prag Prague.
Preußen Prussia; **Preuße** *m*, **Preußin f** Prussian; **preußisch** a Prussian.
Pyrenäen pl (die) the Pyrenees pl.
Rhein (der) the Rhine; **rheinisch** a Rhenish.
Rhodesien Rhodesia; **Rhodesier(in f)** *m* Rhodesian; **rhodesisch** a Rhodesian.
Rhodos Rhodes.
Rom Rome; **Römer(in f)** *m* Roman; **römisch** a Roman.
Rote(s) Meer the Red Sea.
Rumänien Ro(u)mania; **Rumäne** *m*, **Rumänin f** Ro(u)manian; **rumänisch** a Ro(u)manian.
Rußland Russia; **Russe** *m*, **Russin f** Russian; **russisch** a Russian.
Saarland the Saar.
Sachsen Saxony; **Sachse** *m*, **Sächsin f** Saxon; **sächsisch** a Saxon.
Sardinien Sardinia; **Sardinier(in f)** *m*, **Sarde** *m*, **Sardin f** Sardinian; **sardinisch, sardisch** a Sardinian.
Schlesien Silesia; **Schlesier(in f)** *m* Silesian; **schlesisch** a Silesian.

Schottland Scotland; **Schotte** m, **Schottin** f Scot, Scotsman/-woman; **schottisch** a Scottish, Scots, Scotch.

Schwaben Swabia; **Schwabe** m, **Schwäbin** f Swabian; **schwäbisch** a Swabian.

Schwarzwald (der) the Black Forest.

Schweden Sweden; **Schwede** m, **Schwedin** f Swede; **schwedisch** a Swedish.

Schweiz (die) Switzerland; **Schweizer(in** f) m Swiss; **schweizerisch** a Swiss.

Serbien Serbia; **Serbe** m, **Serbin** f Serbian; **serbisch** a Serbian.

Sibirien Siberia; **sibirisch** a Siberian.

Sizilien Sicily; **Sizilianer(in** f) m, **Sizilier(in** f) m Sicilian; **sizilisch, sizilianisch** a Sicilian.

Skandinavien Scandinavia; **Skandinavier(in** f) m Scandinavian; **skandinavisch** a Scandinavian.

Slowakei (die) Slovakia; **Slowake** m, **Slowakin** f Slovak; **slowakisch** a Slovak.

Sowjetunion (die) the Soviet Union; **Sowjetbürger(in** f) m Soviet; **sowjetisch** a Soviet.

Spanien Spain; **Spanier(in** f) m Spaniard; **spanisch** a Spanish.

Steiermark Styria; **Steiermärker(in** f) m, **Steirer** m, **Steierin** f Styrian; **steiermärkisch, steirisch** a Styrian.

Stille(r) Ozean the Pacific.

Syrien Syria; **Syrer(in** f) m Syrian; **syrisch** a Syrian.

Teneriffa Tenerife.

Themse (die) the Thames.

Thüringen Thuringia; **Thüringer(in** f) m Thuringian; **thüringisch** a Thuringian.

Tirol the Tyrol; **Tiroler(in** f) m Tyrolean; **tirolisch** a Tyrolean.

Tschechoslowakei (die) Czechoslovakia; **Tscheche** m, **Tschechin** f, **Tschechoslowake** m, **Tschechoslowakin** f Czech, Czechoslovak(ian); **tschechisch, tschechoslowakisch** a Czech, Czechoslovak(ian).

Toscana (die) Tuscany.

Trient Trent.

Tunesien Tunisia; **Tunesier(in** f) m Tunisian; **tunesisch** a Tunisian.

Türkei (die) Turkey; **Türke** m, **Türkin** f Turk; **türkisch** a Turkish.

Ungarn Hungary; **Ungar(in** f) m Hungarian; **ungarisch** a Hungarian.

Venedig Venice; **Venetianer(in** f) m Venetian; **venetianisch** a Venetian.

Vereinigte Staaten pl (die) the United States pl.

Vesuv (der) Vesuvius.

Vierwaldstättersee (der) Lake Lucerne.

Vogesen pl (die) the Vosges pl.

Volksrepublik China (die) the People's Republic of China.

Vorderasien the Near East.

Warschau Warsaw.

Weichsel (die) the Vistula.

Westfalen Westphalia; **Westfale** m, **Westfälin** f Westphalian; **westfälisch** a Westphalian.

Westindien the West Indies; **westindisch** a West Indian.

Wien Vienna; **Wiener(in** f) m Viennese; **Wiener** a Viennese.

Zypern Cyprus; **Zyprer(in** f) m, **Zyprier(in** f) m, **Zypriot(in** f) m Cypriot; **zyprisch, zypriotisch** a Cypriot.

Countries, nationalities and languages

I am German/English/Albanian ich bin Deutscher/Engländer/Albanier

a German/an Englishman/an Albanian ein Deutscher/Engländer/Albanier;
a German (woman/girl)/an English woman/girl/an Albanian (woman/girl) eine Deutsche/Engländerin/Albanierin

do you speak German/English/Albanian? sprechen Sie Deutsch/Englisch/Albanisch?

the Adriatic die Adria.
the Aegean die Ägäis.
Afghanistan Afghanistan nt; **Afghan** n Afghane m, Afghanin f; a afghanisch.
Africa Afrika nt; **African** n Afrikaner(in f) m; a afrikanisch.
Albania Albanien nt; **Albanian** n Albanier(in f) m; a albanisch.

398

Algeria Algerien *nt*; **Algerian** *n* Algerier(in *f*) *m*; a algerisch.
the Alps *pl* die Alpen *pl*.
America Amerika *nt*; **American** *n* Amerikaner(in *f*) *m*; a amerikanisch.
the Andes *pl* die Anden *pl*.
Angola Angola *nt*; **Angolan** *n* Angolaner(in *f*) *m*; a angolanisch.
the Antarctic die Antarktis; **Antarctic** a antarktisch.
Arabia Arabien *nt*; **Arab, Arabian** *n* Araber(in *f*) *m*; a arabisch.
the Arctic die Arktis; **Arctic** a arktisch.
Argentina, the Argentine Argentinien *nt*; **Argentinian** *n* Argentinier(in *f*) *m*; a argentinisch.
Asia Asien *nt*; **Asian** *n* Asiat(in *f*) *m*; a asiatisch.
Asia Minor Kleinasien *nt*.
Athens Athen *nt*.
the Atlantic (Ocean) der Atlantik, der Atlantische Ozean.
Australia Australien *nt*; **Australian** *n* Australier(in *f*) *m*; a australisch.
Austria Österreich *nt*; **Austrian** *n* Österreicher(in *f*) *m*; a österreichisch.
the Baltic die Ostsee.
Bavaria Bayern *nt*; **Bavarian** *n* Bayer(in *f*) *m*; a bay(e)risch.
the Bay of Biscay (der Golf von) Biskaya *f*.
Belgium Belgien *nt*; **Belgian** *n* Belgier(in *f*) *m*; a belgisch.
the Black Forest der Schwarzwald.
Bolivia Bolivien *nt*; **Bolivian** *n* Bolivianer(in *f*) *m*, Bolivier(in *f*) *m*; a boliv(ian)isch.
Brazil Brasilien *nt*; **Brazilian** *n* Brasilianer(in *f*) *m*; a brasilianisch.
Britain Großbritannien *nt*; **Briton** *n* Brite *m*, Britin *f*; **British** a britisch.
Brittany die Bretagne; **Breton** *n* Bretone *m*, Bretonin *f*; a bretonisch.
Brussels Brüssel *nt*.
Bulgaria Bulgarien *nt*; **Bulgarian, Bulgar** *n* Bulgare *m*, Bulgarin *f*; **Bulgarian** a bulgarisch.
Burma Birma *nt*; **Burmese** *n* Birmane *m*, Birmanin *f*; a birmanisch.
California Kalifornien *nt*; **Californian** *n* Kalifornier(in *f*) *m*; a kalifornisch.
Cambodia Kambodscha *nt*; **Cambodian** *n* Kambodschaner(in *f*) *m*; a kambodschanisch.
Canada Kanada *nt*; **Canadian** *n* Kanadier(in *f*) *m*; a kanadisch.
the Canary Islands *pl* die Kanarischen Inseln *pl*.
the Caribbean die Karibik; **Caribbean** a karibisch.
Central America Zentralamerika *nt*.
the Channel Islands *pl* die Kanalinseln *pl*, die Normannischen Inseln *pl*.
Chile Chile *nt*; **Chilean** *n* Chilene *m*, Chilenin *f*; a chilenisch.
China China *nt*; **Chinese** *n* Chinese *m*, Chinesin *f*; a chinesisch.
Cologne Köln *nt*.
Colombia Kolumbien *nt*; **Colombian** *n* Kolumbianer(in *f*) *m*, Kolumbier(in *f*) *m*; a kolumb(ian)isch.
Lake Constance der Bodensee.
Cornish a von/aus Cornwall.
Corsica Korsika *nt*; **Corsican** *n* Korse *m*, Korsin *f*; a korsisch.
Crete Kreta *nt*; **Cretan** *n* Kreter(in *f*) *m*; a kretisch.
Cuba Kuba *nt*; **Cuban** *n* Kubaner(in *f*) *m*; a kubanisch.
Cyprus Zypern *nt*; **Cypriot** *n* Zypriot(in *f*) *m*; a zypriotisch.
Czechoslovakia die Tschechoslowakei; **Czech, Czechoslovak(ian)** *n* Tscheche *m*, Tschechin *f*; a tschechisch.
Denmark Dänemark *nt*; **Dane** *n* Däne *m*, Dänin *f*; **Danish** a dänisch.
Dutch a *see* **Holland**.
East Germany Deutsche Demokratische Republik *f*; **East German** *n* Staatsbürger(in *f*) *m* der Deutschen Demokratischen Republik; **he is an East German** er ist aus der DDR; a der DDR; **East German towns** Städte (in) der DDR.
Ecuador Ecuador *nt*; **Ecuadorian** *n* Ecuadorianer(in *f*) *m*; a ecuadorianisch.
Egypt Ägypten *nt*; **Egyptian** *n* Ägypter(in *f*) *m*; a ägyptisch.
Eire ['eərə] (Republik *f*) Irland *nt*.
England England *nt*; **Englishman/-woman** *n* Engländer(in *f*) *m*; **English** a englisch.
the English Channel der Ärmelkanal.
Ethiopia Äthiopien *nt*; **Ethiopian** *n* Äthiopier(in *f*) *m*; a äthiopisch.
Europe Europa *nt*; **European** *n* Europäer(in *f*) *m*; a europäisch.
Fiji (Islands *pl*) die Fidschiinseln *pl*; **Fijian** *n* Fidschianer(in *f*) *m*; a fidschianisch.
Filipino *n see* **the Philippines**.
Finland Finnland *nt*; **Finn** *n* Finne *m*, Finnin *f*; **Finnish** a finnisch.
Flanders Flandern *nt*; **Fleming** *n* Flame *m*, Flämin *f*; **Flemish** a flämisch.
Florence Florenz *nt*; **Florentine** *n* Florentiner(in *f*) *m*; a florentinisch.

France Frankreich *nt*; **Frenchman/-woman** *n* Franzose *m*, Französin *f*; **French** *a* französisch.

Geneva Genf *nt*; **Lake Geneva** der Genfer See.

Germany Deutschland *nt*; **German** *n* Deutsche(r) *m*, Deutsche *f*; *a* deutsch.

Ghana Ghana *nt*; **Ghanaian** *n* Ghanaer(in *f*) *m*; *a* ghanaisch.

Great Britain Großbritannien *nt*.

Greece Griechenland *nt*; **Greek** *n* Grieche *m*, Griechin *f*; *a* griechisch.

the Hague Den Haag.

Haiti Haiti *nt*; **Haitian** *n* Haitianer(in *f*) *m*, Haitier(in *f*) *m*; *a* haitianisch, haitisch.

Hawaii Hawaii *nt*; **Hawaiian** *n* Hawaiier(in *f*) *m*; *a* hawaiisch.

the Hebrides *pl* die Hebriden *pl*.

the Himalayas *pl* der Himalaja.

Holland Holland *nt*; **Dutchman/-woman** *n* Holländer(in *f*) *m*; **Dutch** *a* holländisch, niederländisch.

Hungary Ungarn *nt*; **Hungarian** *n* Ungar(in *f*) *m*; *a* ungarisch.

Iceland Island *nt*; **Icelander** *n* Isländer(in *f*) *m*; **Icelandic** *a* isländisch.

India Indien *nt*; **Indian** *n* Inder(in *f*) *m*; *a* indisch.

Indonesia Indonesien *nt*; **Indonesian** *n* Indonesier(in *f*) *m*; *a* indonesisch.

Iran (der) Iran; **Iranian** *n* Iraner(in *f*) *m*; *a* iranisch.

Iraq (der) Irak; **Iraqi** *n* Iraker(in *f*) *m*; *a* irakisch.

Ireland Irland *nt*; **Irishman/-woman** *n* Ire *m*, Irin *f*; **Irish** *a* irisch.

Israel Israel *nt*; **Israeli** *n* Israeli *m/f*; *a* israelisch.

Italy Italien *nt*; **Italian** *n* Italiener(in *f*) *m*; *a* italienisch.

Jamaica Jamaika *nt*; **Jamaican** *n* Jamaikaner(in *f*) *m*, Jamaiker(in *f*) *m*; *a* jamaikanisch, jamaikisch.

Japan Japan *nt*; **Japanese** *n* Japaner(in *f*) *m*; *a* japanisch.

Jordan Jordanien *nt*; **Jordanian** *n* Jordanier(in *f*) *m*; *a* jordanisch.

Kenya Kenia *nt*; **Kenyan** *n* Kenianer(in *f*) *m*; *a* kenianisch.

the Kiel Canal der Nord-Ostsee-Kanal.

Korea Korea *nt*; **Korean** *n* Koreaner(in *f*) *m*; *a* koreanisch.

Laos Laos *nt*; **Laotian** *n* Laote *m*, Laotin *f*; *a* laotisch.

Lapland Lappland *nt*; **Lapp** *n* Lappe *m*, Lappin *f*; *a* lappisch.

Latin America Lateinamerika *nt*.

Lebanon (der) Libanon; **Lebanese** *n* Libanese *m*, Libanesin *f*; *a* libanesisch.

Liberia Liberia *nt*; **Liberian** *n* Liberianer(in *f*) *m*; *a* liberianisch.

Libya Libyen *nt*; **Libyan** *n* Libyer(in *f*) *m*; *a* libysch.

Lisbon Lissabon *nt*.

London London *nt*; **Londoner** *n* Londoner(in *f*) *m*; **London** *a* Londoner *inv*.

Luxembourg Luxemburg *nt*; **Luxembourger** *n* Luxemburger(in *f*) *m*.

Majorca Mallorca *nt*; **Majorcan** *n* Bewohner(in *f*) *m* Mallorcas; *a* mallorkinisch.

Malaysia Malaysia *nt*; **Malaysian** *n* Malaysier(in *f*) *m*; *a* malaysisch.

Malta Malta *nt*; **Maltese** *n* Malteser(in *f*) *m*; *a* maltesisch.

the Mediterranean (Sea) das Mittelmeer.

Mexico Mexiko *nt*; **Mexican** *n* Mexikaner(in *f*) *m*; *a* mexikanisch.

Milan Mailand *nt*; **Milanese** *n* Mailänder(in *f*) *m*; *a* mailändisch.

Mongolia die Mongolei; **Mongolian** *n* Mongole *m*, mongolin *f*; *a* mongolisch.

Morocco Marokko *nt*; **Moroccan** *n* Marokkaner(in *f*) *m*; *a* marrokkanisch.

Moscow Moskau *nt*; **Muscovite** *n* Moskauer(in *f*) *m*; *a* moskauisch.

Munich München *nt*.

Naples Neapel *nt*; **Neapolitan** *n* Neapolitaner(in *f*) *m*; *a* neapolitanisch.

the Netherlands *pl* die Niederlande *pl*.

New Zealand Neuseeland *nt*; **New Zealander** *n* Neuseeländer(in *f*) *m*; **New Zealand** *a* neuseeländisch.

Nigeria Nigeria *nt*; **Nigerian** *n* Nigerianer(in *f*) *m*; *a* nigerianisch.

Normandy die Normandie; **Norman** *n* Normanne *m*, Normannin *f*; *a* normannisch.

Northern Ireland Nordirland *nt*.

the North Sea die Nordsee.

Norway Norwegen *nt*; **Norwegian** *n* Norweger(in *f*) *m*; *a* norwegisch.

the Pacific (Ocean) der Pazifik, der Pazifische *or* Stille Ozean.

Pakistan Pakistan *nt*; **Pakistani** *n* Pakistaner(in *f*) *m*; *a* pakistanisch.

Palestine Palästina *nt*; **Palestinian** *n* Palästinenser(in *f*) *m*; *a* palästinensisch.

Paraguay Paraguay *nt*; **Paraguayan** *n* Paraguayer(in *f*) *m*; *a* paraguayisch.

Paris Paris *nt*; **Parisian** *n* Pariser(in *f*) *m*; *a* Pariser *inv*.

the People's Republic of China die Volksrepublik China.

Persia Persien *nt*; **Persian** *n* Perser(in *f*) *m*; *a* persisch.

Peru Peru *nt*; **Peruvian** *n* Peruaner(in *f*) *m*; *a* peruanisch.

the Philippines *pl* die Philippinen *pl*; **Filipino** *n* Philippiner(in *f*) *m*; *a*, **Philippine** *a* philippinisch.

Poland Polen *nt*; **Pole** *n* Pole *m*, Polin *f*; **Polish** *a* polnisch.

Portugal Portugal *nt*; **Portuguese** *n* Portugiese *m*, Portugiesin *f*; a portugiesisch.

Puerto Rico Puerto Rico *nt*; **Puerto-Rican** *n* Puertoricaner(in *f*) *m*; a puertoricanisch.

the Pyrenees *pl* die Pyrenäen *pl*; **Pyrenean** a pyrenäisch.

the Red Sea das Rote Meer.

Rhodes Rhodos *nt*.

Rhodesia Rhodesien *nt*; **Rhodesian** *n* Rhodesier(in *f*) *m*; a rhodesisch.

Rome Rom *nt*; **Roman** *n* Römer(in *f*) *m*; a römisch.

Ro(u)mania Rumänien *nt*; **Ro(u)manian** *n* Rumäne *m*, Rumänin *f*; a rumänisch.

Russia Rußland *nt*; **Russian** *n* Russe *m*, Russin *f*; a russisch.

the Sahara die Sahara.

Sardinia Sardinien *nt*; **Sardinian** *n* Sarde *m*, Sardin *f*; a sardisch.

Saudi Arabia Saudi-Arabien *nt*; **Saudi (Arabian)** *n* Saudiaraber(in *f*) *m*; a saudiarabisch.

Scandinavia Skandinavien *nt*; **Scandinavian** *n* Skandinave *m* Skandinavin *f*; a skandinavisch.

Scotland Schottland *nt*; **Scot, Scotsman/-woman** *n* Schotte *m*, Schottin *f*; **Scottish, Scots, Scotch** a schottisch.

Siberia Sibirien *nt*; **Siberian** *n* Sibirier(in *f*) *m*; a sibirisch.

Sicily Sizilien *nt*; **Sicilian** *n* Sizilianer(in *f*) *m*, Sizilier(in *f*) *m*; a sizilianisch, sizilisch.

South Africa Südafrika *nt*; **South African** *n* Südafrikaner(in *f*) *m*; a südafrikanisch.

the Soviet Union die Sowjetunion.

Spain Spanien *nt*; **Spaniard** *n* Spanier(in *f*) *m*; **Spanish** a spanisch.

Sri Lanka Sri Lanka *nt*; **Sri Lankan** *n* Ceylonese *m*, Ceylonesin *f*; a ceylonesisch.

the Sudan der Sudan; **Sudanese** *n* Sudanese *m*, Sudanesin *f*, Sudaner(in *f*) *m*; a sudanesisch.

the Suez Canal der Suez-Kanal.

Sweden Schweden *nt*; **Swede** *n* Schwede *m*, Schwedin *f*; **Swedish** a schwedisch.

Switzerland die Schweiz; **Swiss** *n* Schweizer(in *f*) *m*; a Schweizer *inv*, schweizerisch.

Syria Syrien *nt*; **Syrian** *n* Syrer(in *f*) *m*, Syrier(in *f*) *m*; a syrisch.

Tahiti Tahiti *nt*; **Tahitian** *n* Tahitianer(in *f*) *m*; a tahitianisch.

Taiwan Taiwan *nt*; **Taiwanese** *n* Taiwanese(r) *m*, Taiwanesin *f*; a taiwanesisch.

Tanzania Tansania *nt*; **Tanzanian** *n* Tansanier(in *f*) *m*; a tansanisch.

Tenerife Teneriffa *nt*.

Thailand Thailand *nt*; **Thai** *n* Thailänder(in *f*) *m*; a thailändisch.

the Thames die Themse.

the Tyrol Tirol *nt*; **Tyrolean** *n* Tiroler(in *f*) *m*; a Tiroler *inv*.

Tunisia Tunesien *nt*; **Tunisian** *n* Tunesier(in *f*) *m*; a tunesisch.

Turkey die Türkei; **Turk** *n* Türke *m*, Türkin *f*; **Turkish** a türkisch.

Uganda Uganda *nt*; **Ugandan** *n* Ugander(in *f*) *m*; a ugandisch.

the United Kingdom das Vereinigte Königreich.

the United States *pl* (**of America**) die Vereinigten Staaten *pl* (von Amerika).

Uruguay Uruguay *nt*; **Uruguayan** *n* Uruguayer(in *f*) *m*; a uruguayisch.

Venezuela Venezuela *nt*; **Venezuelan** *n* Venezolaner(in *f*) *m*; a venezolanisch.

Venice Venedig *nt*; **Venetian** *n* Venezianer(in *f*) *m*; a venezianisch.

Vienna Wien *nt*; **Viennese** *n* Wiener(in *f*) *m*; a wienerisch, Wiener *inv*.

Vietnam Vietnam *nt*; **Vietnamese** *n* Vietnamese *m*, Vietnamesin *f*; a vietnamesisch.

Wales Wales *nt*; **Welshman/-woman** *n* Waliser(in *f*) *m*; **Welsh** a walisisch.

Warsaw Warschau *nt*.

West Germany die Bundesrepublik (Deutschland); **West German** *n* Bundesdeutsche(r) *m*, Bundesdeutsche *f*; a Bundes-, der Bundesrepublik.

the West Indies *pl* Westindien *nt*; **West Indian** *n* Westinder(in *f*) *m*; a westindisch.

the Yemen (der) Jemen; **Yemeni, Yemenite** *n* Jemenit(in *f*) *m*; a jemenitisch.

Yugoslavia Jugoslawien *nt*; **Yugoslav(ian)** *n* Jugoslawe *m*, Jugoslawin *f*; a jugoslawisch.

Zaire Zaire *nt*.

Zambia Sambia *nt*; **Zambian** *n* Sambier(in *f*) *m*; a sambisch.

Deutsche Abkürzungen

Abf.	Abfahrt *departure, dep*
Abk.	Abkürzung *abbreviation, abbr*
Abs.	Absatz *paragraph;* Absender *sender*
Abt.	Abteilung *department, dept*
AG	Aktiengesellschaft *(Brit) (public) limited company, Ltd, (US) corporation, inc*
Ank.	Ankunft *arrival, arr*
Anm.	Anmerkung *note*
b.a.w.	bis auf weiteres *until further notice*
Best. Nr.	Bestellnummer *order number*
Betr.	Betreff, betrifft *re*
Bhf.	Bahnhof *station*
BRD	Bundesrepublik Deutschland *Federal Republic of Germany*
b.w.	bitte wenden *please turn over, pto*
bzgl.	bezüglich *with reference to, re*
bzw.	beziehungsweise *(see text)*
ca.	circa, ungefähr *approximately, approx*
Cie., Co.	Kompanie *company, co*
DDR	Deutsche Demokratische Republik *German Democratic Republic, GDR*
d.h.	das heißt *that is, i.e.*
d.J.	dieses Jahres *of this year*
d.M.	dieses Monats *instant, inst*
DM	Deutsche Mark *German Mark, Deutschmark*
EDV	elektronische Datenverarbeitung *electronic data processing, EDP*
einschl.	einschließlich *inclusive, including, incl*
Einw.	Einwohner *inhabitant*
empf.	empfohlen(er Preis) *recommended (price)*
ev.	evangelisch *Protestant*
evtl.	eventuell *perhaps, possibly*
EWG	Europäische Wirtschaftsgemeinschaft *European Economic Community, EEC*
e. Wz.	eingetragenes Warenzeichen *registered trademark*
Expl.	Exemplar *sample, copy*
Fa.	Firma *firm;* in Briefen: *Messrs*
ff.	folgende Seiten *pages, pp*
Ffm.	Frankfurt am Main
fl. W.	fließendes Wasser *running water*
Forts.	Fortsetzung *continued, cont'd*
geb.	geboren *born;* geborene *née;* gebunden *bound.*
Gebr.	Gebrüder *Brothers, Bros*
ges. gesch.	gesetzlich geschützt *registered*
GmbH	Gesellschaft mit beschränkter Haftung *(Brit) (private) limited company, Ltd, (US) corporation, inc*
Hbf.	Hauptbahnhof *central station*
hl.	heilig *holy*
Hrsg.	Herausgeber *editor, ed*
i.A.	im Auftrag *for;* in Briefen auch: *pp*
Ing.	Ingenieur *engineer*
Inh.	Inhaber *proprietor, prop;* Inhalt *contents*
i.V.	in Vertretung *by proxy, on behalf of;* im Vorjahre *in the last or previous year;* in Vorbereitung *in preparation*
Jh.	Jahrhundert *century, cent*
jr., jun.	junior, der Jüngere *junior, jun, jr*
kath.	katholisch *Catholic, Cath*
kfm.	kaufmännisch *commercial*
Kfz.	*(see text)*
KG	Kommanditgesellschaft *limited partnership*
led.	ledig *single*
Lkw.	*(see text)*

402

lt.	laut *according to*
m. E.	meines Erachtens *in my opinion*
Mehrw. St.	Mehrwertsteuer *value-added tax, VAT*
Mrd.	Milliarde *thousand millions, (US) billion*
n. Chr.	nach Christus *AD*
Nr.	Numero, Nummer *number, no*
NS	Nachschrift *postscript, PS;* nationalsozialistisch *National Socialist*
OHG	Offene Handelsgesellschaft *general partnership*
PKW, Pkw.	*(see text)*
Pl.	Platz *square*
Postf.	Postfach *post-office box, PO box*
PS	Pferdestärken *horsepower, HP;* Nachschrift *postscript, PS*
S.	Seite *page, p*
s.	siehe *see*
sen.	senior, der Ältere *senior, sen, sr*
s.o.	siehe oben *see above*
St.	Stück *piece;* Sankt *Saint, St*
Std., Stde.	Stunde *hour, hr*
stdl.	stündlich *every hour*
Str.	Straße *street, St*
s.u.	siehe unten *see below*
tägl.	täglich *daily, per day*
Tsd.	Tausend *thousand*
u.	und *and*
u.a.	und andere(s) *and others;* unter anderem/anderen *among other things, inter alia/among others*
U.A.w.g.	Um Antwort wird gebeten *an answer is requested;* auf Einladung: *RSVP*
UdSSR	Union der Sozialistischen Sowjetrepubliken *Union of Soviet Socialist Republics, USSR*
u.E.	unseres Erachtens *in our opinion*
USA	Vereinigte Staaten (von Amerika) *United States (of America), USA.*
usf.	und so fort *and so forth, etc*
usw.	und so weiter *etcetera, etc*
u.U.	unter Umständen *possibly*
v. Chr.	vor Christus *BC*
Verf., Vf.	Verfasser *author*
verh.	verheiratet *married*
Verl.	Verlag *publishing firm;* Verleger *publisher*
vgl.	vergleiche *compare, cf, cp*
v.H.	vom Hundert *per cent*
Wz.	Warenzeichnen *registered trademark*
z.B.	zum Beispiel *for example or instance, eg*
z.H(d)	zu Händen *for the attention of*
z.T.	zum Teil *partly*
zw.	zwischen *between; among*
z.Z(t).	zur Zeit *at the time, at present, for the time being*

English abbreviations

AD	after (the birth of) Christ *Anno Domini, nach Christi, A.D., n. Chr.*
AGM	annual general meeting *Jahresvollversammlung*
am	before midday (ante meridiem) *vormittags, vorm.;* 1.00am. *1.00 Uhr*
arr	arrival, arrives *Ankunft, Ank.*
asst	assistant *Assistent, Mitarbeiter*
Ave	avenue *Straße, Str.*
BA	Bachelor of Arts *Bakkalaureus der Philosophischen Fakultät*
B and B	bed and breakfast *Zimmer mit Frühstück,* in catalogue: *Zi. m Fr.,* as sign: *Fremdenzimmer*
BAOR	British Army of the Rhine *(britische) Rheinarmee*
BC	before (the birth of) Christ *vor Christi Geburt, v. Chr.*
BO	body odour *Körpergeruch*
Bros	[brɔs] brothers *Gebrüder, Gebr.*
BSc	Bachelor of Science *Bakkalaureus der Naturwissenschaftlichen Fakultät*

403

Cantab	['kæntæb] Cambridge University (Cantabrigiensis) *Cambridge*
CBI	Confederation of British Industry *Bundesverband der britischen Industrie*
cc	cubic centimetres *Kubikzentimeter, ccm.*
CD	Diplomatic Corps (French: Corps Diplomatique) *Diplomatisches Corps, CD*
CIA	Central Intelligence Agency *CIA*
CID	Criminal Investigation Department *Kriminalpolizei*
cif	cost insurance and freight *Kosten, Versicherung und Fracht einbegriffen*
C-in-C	Commander-in-Chief *Oberkommandierender*
cm	centimetre(s) *Zentimeter, cm*
c/o	care of *bei, c/o*
COD	cash on delivery *gegen Nachnahme*
C of E	Church of England *anglikanische Kirche*
cwt	hundredweight ≈ *Zentner, ztr.*
DA	(*US*) District Attorney *Bezirksstaatsanwalt*
dep	depart(s) *Abfahrt, Abf.*
dept	department *Abteilung, Abt.*
DJ	dinner jacket *Smoking*; disc jockey *Diskjockey*
ed	edited by *herausgegeben, hrsg.*; editor *Herausgeber, Hrsg.*
EEC	European Economic Community *Europäische Wirtschaftsgemeinschaft, EWG*
eg	for example (exempli gratia) *zum Beispiel, z.B.*
ESP	extrasensory perception *übersinnliche Wahrnehmung*
ETA	estimated time of arrival *voraussichtliche Ankunft*
etc	etcetera, and so on *und so weiter, usw., etc.*
FBI	Federal Bureau of Investigation *FBI*
fig	figure, illustration *Abbildung, Abb.*
fob	free on board *frei Schiff*
gbh	grievous bodily harm *schwere Körperverletzung*
GI	(government issue) private in the American Army *amerikanischer Soldat, GI*
govt	government *Regierung*
GP	General Practitioner *praktischer Arzt*
GPO	General Post Office *Britische Post; Hauptpostamt*
HM	His/Her Majesty *Seine/Ihre Majestät*
HMS	His/Her Majesty's Ship *Schiff der Königlichen Marine*
hp	(*Brit*) hire purchase *Abzahlungskauf*; horsepower *Pferdestärke, PS*
HQ	headquarters *Hauptquartier*
hr(s)	hour(s) *Stunde(n), Std.*
HRH	His/Her Royal Highness *Seine/Ihre Hoheit*
ID	identification *Ausweis*
i.e.	that is (id est) *das heißt, d.h.*
IOU	I owe you *Schuldschein*
JP	Justice of the Peace *Friedensrichter*
km	kilometre(s) *Kilometer, km*
kph	kilometres per hour *Stundenkilometer, km/h*
LA	Los Angeles
lb	pound (weight) *Pfund, Pfd.*
LP	long-playing (record), long-player *Langspielplatte, LP*
Ltd	limited (in names of businesses) *Gesellschaft mit beschränkter Haftung, GmbH*
MA	Master of Arts *Magister Artium, M.A.*
max	maximum *maximal, max*
MI5	department of British Intelligence Service (originally Military Intelligence) *Britischer Geheimdienst*
min	minimum *minimal*
MIT	Massachusetts Institute of Technology
mm	millimetre(s) *Millimeter, mm*
mod cons	[mɔd'kɔnz] modern conveniences (cooker, lights, *etc*) *mit allem Komfort*
MOT	Ministry of Transport (used for the roadworthiness test of motor vehicles) *Technischer Überwachungsverein, TÜV*
MP	Member of Parliament *Abgeordneter*; military policeman *Militärpolizist, MP*
mpg	miles per gallon *Meilen pro Gallone, Benzinverbrauch*
mph	miles per hour *Meilen pro Stunde*
Mr	['mɪstə] Mister *Herr*
Mrs	['mɪsɪz] Mistress *Frau*
Ms	[məz] *Frau*

NAAFI	['næfı] (*Brit*) Navy, Army and Air Force Institutes (canteen services) *Kantine*
NATO	['neɪtəʊ] North Atlantic Treaty Organization *Nordatlantikpakt, NATO*
NB	note well (nota bene) *notabene, NB*
NCO	non-commissioned officer *Unteroffizier, Uffz.*
no(s)	number(s) *Nummer(n), Nr.*
o.n.o.	or nearest offer *oder höchstes Angebot*
Oxon	['ɔksɔn] Oxford University (Oxonia) *Oxford*
oz	ounce(s) (onza) *Unze*
p	page *Seite, S.*; (new) pence *Pence, p*
PA	public address (system) *Lautsprecheranlage*
pa	per year (per annum) *pro Jahr, jährlich, jhrl.*
PC	police constable *Polizeibeamter*; Privy Councillor *Mitglied des Geheimen Staatsrats*
PhD	Doctor of Philosophy *Doktor der Philosophie, Dr. phil.*
PM	Prime Minister *Premierminister*
pm	afternoon (post meridiem) *nachmittags, nachm.*; 10.00pm *22.00 Uhr*
pop	population *Einwohner, Einw.*
POW	prisoner of war *Kriegsgefangener*
pp	pages *Seiten, ff.*; pro persona, for *im Auftrag, i.A.*
PRO	public relations officer *PR-Chef*
PS	postscript *Nachschrift, PS*
pto	please turn over *bitte wenden, b.w.*
QC	Queen's Counsel *Anwalt der königlichen Anwaltskammer*
RADA	Royal Academy of Dramatic Art
RAF	Royal Air Force *britische Luftwaffe*
Rd	road *Straße, Str.*
Rev	Reverend *Herr Pfarrer*
RIP	rest in peace (requiescat in pace) *ruhe in Frieden, R.I.P.*
RSVP	please reply (written on invitations, French: répondez s'il vous plaît) *um Antwort wird gebeten, U.A.w.g.*
Rt Hon	Right Honourable *Anrede für Grafen etc, Abgeordnete und Minister*
s.a.e.	stamped addressed envelope *vorfrankierter Umschlag*
SOS	(save our souls) *SOS*
Sq	square (in town) *Platz, Pl.*
ss	steamship *Dampfer*
St	saint *Sankt, St.*; street *Straße, Str.*
st	stone (weight) *6,35 kg*
STD	subscriber trunk dialling *Selbstwählfernverkehr*
TB	tuberculosis *Tuberkulose, TB*
Tel	telephone *Telefon, Tel.*
TUC	Trades Union Congress *Gewerkschaftsbund*
UFO	['juːfəʊ] unidentified flying object *unbekanntes Flugobjekt, Ufo*
UK	United Kingdom *Vereinigtes Königreich*
UN	United Nations *Vereinte Nationen*
USA	United States of America *Vereinigte Staaten von Amerika, USA*; United States Army *Amerikanische Armee*
USAF	United States Air Force *Amerikanische Luftwaffe*
USN	United States Navy *Amerikanische Marine*
USSR	Union of Soviet Socialist Republics *Sowjetunion, UdSSR*
VAT	[*also* væt] value added tax *Mehrwertsteuer, Mehrw.St.*
VD	venereal disease *Geschlechtskrankheit*
VHF	very high frequency *Ultrakurzwelle, UKW*
VIP	very important person *wichtige Persönlichkeit, VIP*
viz	[vɪz] namely (videlicet) *nämlich*
VSO	voluntary service overseas *Entwicklungshilfe*
WASP	(*US*) White Anglo-Saxon Protestant
WC	water closet *Toilette, WC*
ZIP	[zɪp] (*US*) Zone Improvement Plan (postal code) *Postleitzahl, PLZ*

German irregular verbs
* with 'sein'

infinitive	present indicative (2nd, 3rd sing.)	preterite	past participle
aufschrecken*	schrickst auf, schrickt auf	schrak or schreckte auf	aufgeschreckt
ausbedingen	bedingst aus, bedingt aus	bedang or bedingte aus	ausbedungen
backen	bäckst, bäckt	backte or buk	gebacken
befehlen	befiehlst, befiehlt	befahl	befohlen
beginnen	beginnst, beginnt	begann	begonnen
beißen	beißt, beißt	biß	gebissen
bergen*	birgst, birgt	barg	geborgen
bersten*	birst, birst	barst	geborsten
bescheißen*	bescheißt, bescheißt	beschiß	beschissen
bewegen	bewegst, bewegt	bewog	bewogen
biegen	biegst, biegt	bog	gebogen
bieten	bietest, bietet	bot	geboten
binden	bindest, bindet	band	gebunden
bitten	bittest, bittet	bat	gebeten
blasen	bläst, bläst	blies	geblasen
bleiben*	bleibst, bleibt	blieb	geblieben
braten	brätst, brät	briet	gebraten
brechen*	brichst, bricht	brach	gebrochen
brennen	brennst, brennt	brannte	gebrannt
bringen	bringst, bringt	brachte	gebracht
denken	denkst, denkt	dachte	gedacht
dreschen	drisch(e)st, drischt	drasch	gedroschen
dringen*	dringst, dringt	drang	gedrungen
dürfen	darfst, darf	durfte	gedurft
empfehlen	empfiehlst, empfiehlt	empfahl	empfohlen
erbleichen*	erbleichst, erbleicht	erbleichte	erblichen
erlöschen*	erlischst, erlischt	erlosch	erloschen
erschrecken*	erschrickst, erschrickt	erschrak	erschrocken
essen	ißt, ißt	aß	gegessen
fahren*	fährst, fährt	fuhr	gefahren
fallen*	fällst, fällt	fiel	gefallen
fangen	fängst, fängt	fing	gefangen
fechten	fichtst, ficht	focht	gefochten
finden	findest, findet	fand	gefunden
flechten	flichtst, flicht	flocht	geflochten
fliegen*	fliegst, fliegt	flog	geflogen
fliehen*	fliehst, flieht	floh	geflohen
fließen*	fließt, fließt	floß	geflossen
fressen	frißt, frißt	fraß	gefressen
frieren	frierst, friert	fror	gefroren
gären*	gärst, gärt	gor	gegoren
gebären	gebierst, gebiert	gebar	geboren
geben	gibst, gibt	gab	gegeben
gedeihen*	gedeihst, gedeiht	gedieh	gediehen
gehen*	gehst, geht	ging	gegangen
gelingen*	——, gelingt	gelang	gelungen
gelten	giltst, gilt	galt	gegolten
genesen*	gene(se)st, genest	genas	genesen
genießen	genießt, genießt	genoß	genossen
geraten*	gerätst, gerät	geriet	geraten
geschehen*	——, geschieht	geschah	geschehen
gewinnen	gewinnst, gewinnt	gewann	gewonnen
gießen	gießt, gießt	goß	gegossen
gleichen	gleichst, gleicht	glich	geglichen

infinitive	present indicative (2nd, 3rd sing.)	preterite	past participle
gleiten*	gleitest, gleitet	glitt	geglitten
glimmen	glimmst, glimmt	glomm	geglommen
graben	gräbst, gräbt	grub	gegraben
greifen	greifst, greift	griff	gegriffen
haben	hast, hat	hatte	gehabt
halten	hältst, hält	hielt	gehalten
hängen	hängst, hängt	hing	gehangen
hauen	haust, haut	hieb	gehauen
heben	hebst, hebt	hob	gehoben
heißen	heißt, heißt	hieß	geheißen
helfen	hilfst, hilft	half	geholfen
kennen	kennst, kennt	kannte	gekannt
klimmen	klimmst, klimmt	klomm	geklommen
klingen	klingst, klingt	klang	geklungen
kneifen	kneifst, kneift	kniff	gekniffen
kommen*	kommst, kommt	kam	gekommen
können*	kannst, kann	konnte	gekonnt
kriechen*	kriechst, kriecht	kroch	gekrochen
laden	lädst, lädt	lud	geladen
lassen	läßt, läßt	ließ	gelassen
laufen*	läufst, läuft	lief	gelaufen
leiden	leidest, leidet	litt	gelitten
leihen	leihst, leiht	lieh	geliehen
lesen*	liest, liest	las	gelesen
liegen*	liegst, liegt	lag	gelegen
lügen	lügst, lügt	log	gelogen
mahlen	mahlst, mahlt	mahlte	gemahlen
meiden	meidest, meidet	mied	gemieden
melken	milkst, milkt	molk	gemolken
messen	mißt, mißt	maß	gemessen
mißlingen*	——, mißlingt	mißlang	mißlungen
mögen	magst, mag	mochte	gemocht
müssen	mußt, muß	mußte	gemußt
nehmen	nimmst, nimmt	nahm	genommen
nennen	nennst, nennt	nannte	genannt
pfeifen	pfeifst, pfeift	pfiff	gepfiffen
preisen	preist, preist	pries	gepriesen
quellen*	quillst, quillt	quoll	gequollen
raten	rätst, rät	riet	geraten
reiben	reibst, reibt	rieb	gerieben
reißen*	reißt, reißt	riß	gerissen
reiten*	reitest, reitet	ritt	geritten
rennen*	rennst, rennt	rannte	gerannt
riechen	riechst, riecht	roch	gerochen
ringen	ringst, ringt	rang	gerungen
rinnen*	rinnst, rinnt	rann	geronnen
rufen	rufst, ruft	rief	gerufen
salzen	salzt, salzt	salzte	gesalzen
saufen	säufst, säuft	soff	gesoffen
saugen	saugst, saugt	sog	gesogen
schaffen	schaffst, schafft	schuf	geschaffen
schallen	schallst, schallt	scholl	geschollen
scheiden*	scheidest, scheidet	schied	geschieden
scheinen	scheinst, scheint	schien	geschienen
schelten	schiltst, schilt	schalt	gescholten
scheren	scherst, schert	schor	geschoren
schieben	schiebst, schiebt	schob	geschoben
schießen	schießt, schießt	schoß	geschossen
schinden	schindest, schindet	schund	geschunden
schlafen	schläfst, schläft	schlief	geschlafen
schlagen	schlägst, schlägt	schlug	geschlagen
schleichen*	schleichst, schleicht	schlich	geschlichen
schleifen	schleifst, schleift	schliff	geschliffen
schließen	schließt, schließt	schloß	geschlossen
schlingen	schlingst, schlingt	schlang	geschlungen
schmeißen	schmeißt, schmeißt	schmiß	geschmissen
schmelzen*	schmilzt, schmilzt	schmolz	geschmolzen
schneiden	schneidest, schneidet	schnitt	geschnitten
schreiben	schreibst, schreibt	schrieb	geschrieben

infinitive	present indicative (2nd, 3rd sing.)	preterite	past participle
schreien	schreist, schreit	schrie	geschrie(e)n
schreiten	schreitest, schreitet	schritt	geschritten
schweigen	schweigst, schweigt	schwieg	geschwiegen
schwellen*	schwillst, schwillt	schwoll	geschwollen
schwimmen*	schwimmst, schwimmt	schwamm	geschwommen
schwinden*	schwindest, schwindet	schwand	geschwunden
schwingen	schwingst, schwingt	schwang	geschwungen
schwören	schwörst, schwört	schwur	geschworen
sehen	siehst, sieht	sah	gesehen
sein*	bist, ist	war	gewesen
senden	sendest, sendet	sandte	gesandt
singen	singst, singt	sang	gesungen
sinken*	sinkst, sinkt	sank	gesunken
sinnen	sinnst, sinnt	sann	gesonnen
sitzen*	sitzt, sitzt	saß	gesessen
sollen	sollst, soll	sollte	gesollt
speien	speist, speit	spie	gespie(e)n
spinnen	spinnst, spinnt	spann	gesponnen
sprechen	sprichst, spricht	sprach	gesprochen
sprießen*	sprießt, sprießt	sproß	gesprossen
springen*	springst, springt	sprang	gesprungen
stechen	stichst, sticht	stach	gestochen
stecken	steckst, steckt	steckte or stak	gesteckt
stehen	stehst, steht	stand	gestanden
stehlen	stiehlst, stiehlt	stahl	gestohlen
steigen*	steigst, steigt	stieg	gestiegen
sterben*	stirbst, stirbt	starb	gestorben
stinken	stinkst, stinkt	stank	gestunken
stoßen	stößt, stößt	stieß	gestoßen
streichen	streichst, streicht	strich	gestrichen
streiten*	streitest, streitet	stritt	gestritten
tragen	trägst, trägt	trug	getragen
treffen	triffst, trifft	traf	getroffen
treiben*	treibst, treibt	trieb	getrieben
treten*	trittst, tritt	trat	getreten
trinken	trinkst, trinkt	trank	getrunken
trügen	trügst, trügt	trog	getrogen
tun	tust, tut	tat	getan
verderben	verdirbst, verdirbt	verdarb	verdorben
verdrießen	verdrießt, verdrießt	verdroß	verdrossen
vergessen	vergißt, vergißt	vergaß	vergessen
verlieren	verlierst, verliert	verlor	verloren
verschleißen	verschleißt, verschleißt	verschliß	verschlissen
wachsen*	wächst, wächst	wuchs	gewachsen
wägen	wägst, wägt	wog	gewogen
waschen	wäschst, wäscht	wusch	gewaschen
weben	webst, webt	wob	gewoben
weichen*	weichst, weicht	wich	gewichen
weisen	weist, weist	wies	gewiesen
wenden	wendest, wendet	wandte	gewandt
werben	wirbst, wirbt	warb	geworben
werden*	wirst, wird	wurde	geworden
werfen	wirfst, wirft	warf	geworfen
wiegen	wiegst, wiegt	wog	gewogen
winden	windest, windet	wand	gewunden
wissen	weißt, weiß	wußte	gewußt
wollen	willst, will	wollte	gewollt
wringen	wringst, wringt	wrang	gewrungen
zeihen	zeihst, zeiht	zieh	geziehen
ziehen*	ziehst, zieht	zog	gezogen
zwingen	zwingst, zwingt	zwang	gezwungen

English irregular verbs

present	pt	ptp	present	pt	ptp
arise (arising)	arose	arisen	fall	fell	fallen
awake (awaking)	awoke	awaked	feed	fed	fed
be (am, is, are; being)	was, were	been	feel	felt	felt
bear	bore	born(e)	fight	fought	fought
beat	beat	beaten	find	found	found
become (becoming)	became	become	flee	fled	fled
befall	befell	befallen	fling	flung	flung
begin (beginning)	began	begun	fly (flies)	flew	flown
behold	beheld	beheld	forbid (forbidding)	forbade	forbidden
bend	bent	bent	forecast	forecast	forecast
beseech	besought	besought	forego	forewent	foregone
beset (besetting)	beset	beset	foresee	foresaw	foreseen
bet (betting)	bet (also betted)	bet (also betted)	foretell	foretold	foretold
bid (bidding)	bid	bid	forget (forgetting)	forgot	forgotten
bind	bound	bound	forgive (forgiving)	forgave	forgiven
bite (biting)	bit	bitten	forsake (forsaking)	forsook	forsaken
bleed	bled	bled	freeze (freezing)	froze	frozen
blow	blew	blown	get (getting)	got	got, (US) gotten
break	broke	broken	give (giving)	gave	given
breed	bred	bred	go (goes)	went	gone
bring	brought	brought	grind	ground	ground
build	built	built	grow	grew	grown
burn	burnt or burned	burnt (also burned)	hang	hung (also hanged)	hung (also hanged)
burst	burst	burst	have (has; having)	had	had
buy	bought	bought	hear	heard	heard
can	could	(been able)	hide (hiding)	hid	hidden
cast	cast	cast	hit (hitting)	hit	hit
catch	caught	caught	hold	held	held
choose (choosing)	chose	chosen	hurt	hurt	hurt
cling	clung	clung	keep	kept	kept
come (coming)	came	come	kneel	knelt (also kneeled)	knelt (also kneeled)
cost	cost	cost	know	knew	known
creep	crept	crept	lay	laid	laid
cut (cutting)	cut	cut	lead	led	led
deal	dealt	dealt	lean	leant (also leaned)	leant (also leaned)
dig (digging)	dug	dug	leap	leapt (also leaped)	leapt (also leaped)
do (3rd person; he/she/it/does)	did	done	learn	learnt (also learned)	learnt (also learned)
draw	drew	drawn	leave (leaving)	left	left
dream	dreamed (dreamt)	dreamed (dreamt)	lend	lent	lent
drink	drank	drunk	let (letting)	let	let
drive (driving)	drove	driven	lie (lying)	lay	lain
dwell	dwelt	dwelt	light	lit (also lighted)	lit (also lighted)
eat	ate	eaten	lose (losing)	lost	lost

present	pt	ptp	present	pt	ptp
make (making)	made	made	spell	spelt (also spelled)	spelt (also spelled)
may	might	——	spend	spent	spent
mean	meant	meant	spill	spilt (also spilled)	spilt (also spilled)
meet	met	met			
mistake (mistaking)	mistook	mistaken	spin (spinning)	spun	spun
mow	mowed	mown (also mowed)	spit (spitting)	spat	spat
			split (splitting)	split	split
must	(had to)	(had to)	spoil	spoiled (also spoilt)	spoiled (also spoilt)
pay	paid	paid			
put (putting)	put	put	spread	spread	spread
quit (quitting)	quit (also quitted)	quit (also quitted)	spring	sprang	sprung
			stand	stood	stood
read	read	read	steal	stole	stolen
rend	rent	rent	stick	stuck	stuck
rid (ridding)	rid	rid	sting	stung	stung
ride (riding)	rode	ridden	stink	stank	stunk
ring	rang	rung	stride (striding)	strode	stridden
rise (rising)	rose	risen			
run (running)	ran	run	strike (striking)	struck	struck (also stricken)
saw	sawed	sawn			
say	said	said	strive (striving)	strove	striven
see	saw	seen	swear	swore	sworn
seek	sought	sought	sweep	swept	swept
sell	sold	sold	swell	swelled	swollen (also swelled)
send	sent	sent			
set (setting)	set	set	swim (swimming)	swam	swum
shake (shaking)	shook	shaken			
shall	should	——	swing	swung	swung
shear	sheared	shorn (also sheared)	take (taking)	took	taken
			teach	taught	taught
shed (shedding)	shed	shed	tear	tore	torn
shine (shining)	shone	shone	tell	told	told
			think	thought	thought
shoot	shot	shot	throw	threw	thrown
show	showed	shown	thrust	thrust	thrust
shrink	shrank	shrunk	tread	trod	trodden
shut (shutting)	shut	shut	wake (waking)	woke (also waked)	woken (also waked)
sing	sang	sung	waylay	waylaid	waylaid
sink	sank	sunk	wear	wore	worn
sit (sitting)	sat	sat	weave (weaving)	wove (also weaved)	woven (also weaved)
slay	slew	slain			
sleep	slept	slept	wed (wedding)	wedded (also wed)	wedded (also wed)
slide (sliding)	slid	slid			
			weep	wept	wept
sling	slung	slung	win (winning)	won	won
slit (slitting)	slit	slit			
smell	smelt (also smelled)	smelt (also smelled)	wind	wound	wound
			withdraw	withdrew	withdrawn
sow	sowed	sown (also sowed)	withhold	withheld	withheld
			withstand	withstood	withstood
speak	spoke	spoken	wring	wrung	wrung
speed	sped (also speeded)	sped (also speeded)	write (writing)	wrote	written

NOTES TO THE USER OF THIS DICTIONARY

I. Using the dictionary

In using this book, you will either want to check the meaning of a German word you don't know, or find the German for an English word. These two operations are quite different, and so are the problems you may face when using one side of the dictionary or the other. In order to help you, we have tried to explain below the main features of this book.

The 'wordlist' is the alphabetical list of all the items in large bold type, i.e. all the 'headwords'. Each 'entry', or article, is introduced by a headword, and may contain additional 'references' in smaller bold type, such as phrases, derivatives, and compound words. Section 1. below deals with the way references are listed.

The typography distinguishes between three broad categories of text within the dictionary. All items in bold type, large or smaller, are 'source language' references, for which an equivalence in the other language is provided. All items in standard type are translations. Items in italics are information about the words being translated, i.e. either labels, or explanations, or 'signposts' pinpointing the appropriate translation.

1. *Where to look for a word*

1.1 Derivatives

In order to save space, a number of derivatives have been listed within entries, provided this does not break alphabetical order. Thus, **Pensionär, pensionieren** and **Pensionsgast** are listed under the entry for **Pension**, or **caller** and **calling** under **call**. You must remember this when looking for a word you don't find listed as a headword. These derivatives are always listed last within an entry (see also I.2 on entry layout).

1.2 Homographs

There are very few homographs in German (i.e. words spelt exactly the same way, like **Mutter** (mother) and **Mutter** (nut)). As a rule, in order to save space, such words have been treated as one headword only.

When two words differ by an initial capital (i.e. **abkommen** (to get away) and **Abkommen** (agreement)), they are listed under one form only, and the other form is shown within the entry with its intial letter (i.e. **abkommen...; A~...**).

1.3 Umlaut, ß and ck/kk

So-called Umlaut-letters are treated like ordinary a's, o's or u's; thus **Schäfchen** and **Schäfer** come between **Schaf** and **Schaffen**. If two words differ only by the presence of Umlaut dots, the word without the Umlaut comes first; thus **schon** comes before **schön**.

The symbol ß is treated as double s (Eszett [ɛs'tsɛt]), and you will find **Baß** between **basisch** and **Bassin**.

There is no double k in German, except at line breaks, when a word containing the letter 'ck' is split as 'k-k': for instance **Dackel** (dachshund) would be split **Dak-kel**.

1.4 Phrases

Because of the constraints of space, there can be only a limited number of idiomatic phrases in a pocket dictionary like this one. Phrases are sometimes used to illustrate usage (see **agree, level,** and German **versetzen, Spaß**). Other German phrases and idioms are generally given under the noun, or under the first 'key' element (e.g. 'sich köstlich amüsieren' under **köstlich**). English phrases and idioms are listed under the first 'key' element, and verbal phrases with the ten or so basic verbs like **go, set** or **get** are listed under the noun or first other 'key' element.

1.5 Compounds

1.5.1 German compounds

German compounds are often very long, but they are always one-word compounds and are thus easy to find in the wordlist (e.g. **Hausschuh** appears in strict alphabetical order).

In order to save space, consecutive compounds have been listed together under the relevant headword. However, such groups may be interrupted by an extraneous element, such as **hausen** between **Hauseigentümer** and **Hausfrau**.

1.5.2 English compounds

Here there is a problem of where to find a compound because of less predictable spelling than is the case with German: is it **airgun, air-gun** or **air gun**? This is why we choose to list them according to strict alphabetical order. Thus **coal field** and **coalmine** are separated by **coalition**. The entries between **tax** and **technical** will provide a good illustration of the system of listing. It has drawbacks, for instance in that **tax-free** and **taxpayer** are separated by **taxi, taxidermist** and two 'taxi' compounds. However, in a short dictionary used by beginners, it has the merit of simplicity and consistency.

1.5.3 English 'phrasal verbs'

'Phrasal verbs' are verbs like **go off, blow up, cut down** etc. Here you have the advantage of knowing that these words belong together, whereas it will take the foreign user some time before he can identify these verbs immediately. They have been listed under the entry for the basic verb (eg. **go, blow, cut**), grouped alphabetically before any other derivative or compounds - e.g. **pull up** comes before **pulley**. For instance, look up **to back out, to look up** (a word), **to look out.**

1.6 Irregular forms

When looking up a German word, you may not immediately find the form you are looking for, although the word in question has been duly entered in the dictionary. This is possibly because you are looking up an irregular noun or verb form, and these are not always given as entries in their own right.

We have assumed that you know the basics regarding German verb forms, noun plurals and case endings, and you are expected to look up the basic form, i.e. the singular nominative form for a noun, or the infinitive for a verb.

If you come across a German word which you think is a verb and cannot find it in the wordlist, you should refer to the section on verb forms (p. 425) and to the irregular verb tables (p. 406). For instance if you come across **saht**, the section on the verb forms will tell you that it is either a 3rd person singular or a 2nd person plural. However you won't find the verb 'sahen' and you should then scan the irregular verbs list where you will eventually find that 'saht' is a form of sehen (ihr saht,'you pl saw').

Note that a form which contains the letters 'ge-' in initial position or after a prefix is usually a past participle. Quite often in German past participles become adjectives in their own right, for instance **abgegriffen** (well-thumbed) or **abgemacht** (fixed). These are usually listed alphabetically as separate entries. If you cannot find a form like this, check under the infinitive (for instance **abgebrüht** is under **abbrühen**).

2. Entry layout

All entries, however long or complex, are arranged in a very systematic manner. But it may be a little difficult at first to find one's way through an entry like **back**, **round** or **run** because homographs are grouped under the same entry (see 1.2) and the text is run on without any breakdown into paragraphs, in order to save space. Ease of reference comes with practice, but the guidelines below will make it easier for you.

2.1 'Signposting'

If you look up a German word and find a string of quite different English translations, you are unlikely to have much trouble finding out which is the relevant one for your context, because you know what the English words mean, and the context will almost automatically rule out unsuitable translations. It is quite a different matter when you want to find the German for, say, **lock**, in the context 'we got to the lock around lunchtime', and are faced with an entry that reads 'lock: Schloß *nt*; Schleuse *f*; Locke *f.*' You can of course go to the other side and check what each translation means. But this is time-consuming, and it does not always work. This is why we have provided the user with 'signposts' which pinpoint the relevant translation. For instance with **lock**, the entry reads: Schloß *nt*; (*Naut*) Schleuse *f*; (*of hair*) Locke *f.* For the context suggested above, it is now clear that 'Schleuse' is the right word.

2.2 Grammatical categories and meaning categories

Complex entries are first broken down into grammatical categories, e.g.: **lock** *n*; *vt*; *vi*. Be prepared to go through entries like **run** or **back** carefully, and you will find how useful all these 'signposts' are. Each grammatical category is then split where appropriate into the various meanings, e.g.:

> **lock** *n* Schloß *nt*;(*Naut*) Schleuse *f*; (*of hair*) Locke *f*; *vt* (*fasten*) (ver)schließen; *vi* (*door etc*) sich schließen (lassen); (*wheels*) blockieren.

3. *Using the translations*

3.1 Gender

The gender is given after each noun translation. The feminine version is given for words like teacher, research worker etc.: teacher *n* Lehrer(in *f*) *m*. Remember that the German equivalents of his, her or its do not behave like their English counterparts: see the chapter on pronouns for more information.

3.2 Plurals and genitive forms

On the English-German side, no plural forms are given for translations. Plural endings can be found in the table (p. vi) or on the German-English side where plural and genitive forms are shown throughout. The plural form is not given for compounds. For instance, you will have to look up Brief in order to find the plural and genitive forms of Mahnbrief.

3.3 Colloquial language

You should as a rule proceed with great caution when handling foreign language which has a degree of informality. When an English word or phrase has been labelled (*col*), i.e. colloquial, you must assume that the translation belongs to a similar level of informality.

3.4 'Grammatical words'

In a short dictionary such as this one, it is exceedingly difficult to give adequate treatment for words like for, away, whose, which, out, off etc. We have tried to go some way towards providing as much relevant information as possible regarding the most frequent uses of these words. However, for further information use a good monolingual dictionary of German, especially one for foreign learners, and a good modern German grammar.

3.5 Alternative translations

As a rule, translations separated by commas can be regarded as broadly interchangeable for the meaning indicated. Translations separated by a semi-colon are not interchangeable and when in doubt you should consult either a larger bilingual dictionary such as the Collins German dictionary, or a good monolingual German dictionary. You will find, however, that there are very few cases of translations separated by a semi-colon without an intervening 'signpost'.

II Notes on German Grammar

When you are first confronted with German at school, or if you happen to be at a business meeting where you are the only one to speak little or no German, it may seem to you that German is very different from English. On the other hand, when you take a closer look, just comparing the vocabulary for example, German and English actually show quite a lot of similarities.

We have tried here to show some of the main differences especially with the beginner and the dictionary user in mind, without dwelling on subtleties, or on aspects of German that are broadly similar to English. Among the greatest obstacles for the beginner are genders, the cases, verb forms, adjective endings, and, of course, the sounds of German.

1. Nouns

The first thing you will notice about a German noun is the fact that - even when not at the beginning of a sentence - it always starts with a capital letter.

1.1 Genders

Another basic difference is the fact that there are three genders in German, so that instead of 'the fork, the knife, the spoon' and 'a fork, a knife, a spoon' you find 'die Gabel, das Messer, der Löffel' and 'eine Gabel, ein Messer, ein Löffel'. These genders are largely unpredictable, and you just have to learn them as a feature to be remembered with each word. Note also that whenever you refer back to any noun, the pronoun has to have the same gender. This results in the fact that some objects seem to be treated like people, while 'das Mädchen' (the girl) and 'das Kind' (the child) are referred to as if they were things.

Der Löffel ist schön. Er ist sehr alt.	The spoon is nice. It is very old.
Die Tasse ist blau. Sie gehört Ute.	The cup is blue. It belongs to Ute.
Das Mädchen ist nett. Es heißt Anne.	The girl is nice. She is called Anne.

1.2 Cases

One of the problems when learning German is that a noun actually looks different depending on what function it has in the sentence. The form given in dictionaries is the form it takes when it is the subject of the sentence. The noun is then said to be in the 'nominative' case.

With 'der, die, das':

| der Mann/die Mutter/das Kind singt | the man/the mother/the child sings |

| die Männer/die Mütter/die Kinder singen | the men/the mothers/the children sing |

With 'ein, eine':

| ein Mann/eine Mutter/ein Kind singt | a man/a mother/a child sings |

| Männer/Mütter/Kinder singen | men/mothers/children sing |

If the noun moves to another place, for example that of object of the verb, it sometimes changes its ending and article. Perhaps this is a little easier to understand if you think of English pronoun forms like 'me, him, her': it is '*he* sees', but 'I see *him*'. The latter (the object case) is also called the 'accusative' case; here are the accusative forms of the previous German examples:

With 'der, die, das':

| ich sehe den Mann/die Mutter/das Kind | I see the man/the mother/the child |
| ich sehe die Männer/die Mütter/die Kinder | I see the men/the mothers/the children |

With 'ein, eine':

| ich sehe einen Mann/eine Mutter/ein Kind | I see a man/a mother/a child |
| ich sehe Männer/Mütter/Kinder | I see men/mothers/children |

In German there is another 'case' where a noun is linked directly to the verb without the means of a preposition. This is the 'dative' case and usually corresponds to the English 'to' + *noun*, e.g.:

With 'der, die, das':

| ich sage dem Mann/der Mutter/dem Kind | I say to the man/mother/child |

| ich sage den Männern/den Müttern/den Kindern | I say to the men/mothers/children |

With 'ein, eine':

| ich sage einem Mann/einer Mutter/einem Kind | I say to a man/mother/child |

| ich sage Männern/Müttern/Kindern | I say to men/mothers/children |

The fourth function a noun could have in a sentence is to indicate ownership (the child's mother, a friend's car). It is then said to be in the 'genitive' case:

| das Haus des Mannes/der Mutter/des Kindes | the house of the man/mother/child |

| das Haus der Männer/der Mütter/der Kinder | the house of the men/mothers/children |

One exception to this rule are proper names. Here the genitive case is generally quite simply formed with an 's' as in English, but without the apostrophe:

Peters Haus   Peter's house
Italiens Städte   the towns of Italy

1.3 Irregular forms of plurals and genitives

Masculine and neuter nouns take the ending 's' or 'es' in the genitive singular (Mann-Mannes, Kind-Kindes, Mädchen, Mädchens). Nearly all nouns have a slightly different form in the plural, no matter what case they are in (Mann, Männer/Männern; Frau, Frauen; Kind, Kinder/Kindern). It is a good idea to learn these forms together with the word and its gender. There are, however, a few noun endings that always change in the same way. They are listed in the table 'Regular German noun endings' on page vi at the front of the book.

The irregular genitives and plurals are all given on the German/English side of the dictionary. Note: ¨ indicates that an Umlaut is placed over the last vowel sound of the word and the pronunciation is altered slightly. e.g.: 'Mutter, -, ¨' means: nominative singular: die Mutter; genitive singular: der Mutter; plural: die Mütter.

1.4 Prepositions

The form of nouns in German is also affected by prepositions. Some prepositions always require the dative case; others are followed by the noun in the accusative; a few take the genitive.

1. Prepositions with the accusative:
   bis, durch, für, gegen, ohne, um
   entlang (always after the noun: 'die Straße/den Bach entlang')

2. Prepositions with the dative:
   aus, bei, mit, nach, seit, von, zu
   gegenüber (always after the noun: 'dem Haus/der Kirche gegenüber')
   entgegen (always after the noun: 'der Sonne/dem Vater entgegen')

3. Prepositions which take the genitive
   wegen, trotz, während

   You might find that these prepositions - in modern usage - sometimes also take the dative.

There is a fourth group, including some of the most common prepositions, which, depending on meaning, can take either accusative or dative:

4. **an, auf, hinter, in, neben, über, unter, vor, zwischen.** The rule here is that if the preposition indicates *direction* or *movement*, it is followed by the accusative; if it is used to describe a *position* or *state*, it is followed by the dative, thus:

ich gehe in die Stadt   I go into town
ich bin in der Stadt   I am in town

Note: if the prepositions *in, an, zwischen, vor* are used to indicate time, they always take the dative case.

Remember that some prepositions can be combined with the following definite article: bei dem → beim; an dem → am; von dem → vom; zu dem → zum; in dem → im; zu der → zur.

1.5 Articles and related words

Articles change along with the noun. This applies to definite articles *der, die, das* as well as to the indefinite articles *ein, eine*.

There are a few related words that change according to the same patterns. Words that follow the 'der, die, das' pattern are *jeder, dieser, jener, mancher, welcher*.

Words that follow the 'ein, eine' pattern are *kein, mein, dein, sein, ihr, unser, euer, Ihr*.

'der, die, das' Pattern

	masculine	feminine	neuter	plural
Nominative	der	die	das	die
Accusative	den	die	das	die
Genitive	des	der	des	der
Dative	dem	der	dem	den

'ein, eine' Pattern

	masculine	feminine	neuter	plural
Nominative	sein	seine	sein	seine
Accusative	seinen	seine	sein	seine
Genitive	seines	seiner	seines	seiner
Dative	seinem	seiner	seinem	seinen

The use of the article in German is basically similar to its use in English. There are, however, two exceptions:

First, the articles 'a, an' in expressions like 'she is a teacher, he is a postman' are not translated: 'sie ist Lehrerin, er ist Briefträger'.

This only applies to names of professions and crafts, though. Hence: 'his brother is an idiot' = 'sein Bruder ist ein Idiot'.

Secondly, the definite article is often used in German with parts of the body, where English uses the possessive:

| I broke my leg | ich habe mir das Bein gebrochen |
| he trod on my foot | er ist mir auf den Fuß getreten |

2. Adjectives

2.1 Adjective endings

Adjectives can be used in two ways: as the predicate (*this house is old*) or before a noun (*the old house*).
In the first instance, German works just like English. You just take the adjective straight out of the dictionary and put it in your sentence:

the house is old   das Haus ist alt

In the second case, the form of the adjective depends on the preceding article,
i.e. whether it is

a 'der, die, das' word (see 1.5)	das alte Haus	the old house
an 'ein, eine' word (see 1.5)	ein neuer Hut	a new hat
or whether there is no article	frische Luft	fresh air

2.1.1 Following 'der, die, das' words

If the adjective follows the definite article or one of the other 'der' words (see
1.5) it takes one of the following endings, depending on gender and case:

	m	f	nt	pl
Nominative	-e	-e	-e	-en
Accusative	-en	-e	-e	-en
Genitive	-en	-en	-en	-en
Dative	-en	-en	-en	-en

Some examples of the use of adjectives following this pattern:

der junge Mann singt (the young man sings), ich sehe den jungen Mann (I see the
young man), ich helfe dem jungen Mann (I help the young man), das Gesicht des
jungen Mannes (the young man's face), ich sage den jungen Männern (I say to the
young men) etc.

2.1.2 Following 'ein, eine' words

If the indefinite article 'ein, eine' (or any of the related words like 'mein', 'dein',
'sein', 'kein') comes before the adjective, the endings are as listed below.

	m	f	nt	pl
Nominative	-er	-e	-es	-en
Accusative	-en	-e	-es	-en
Genitive	-en	-en	-en	-en
Dative	-en	-en	-en	-en

Here is an illustration of the use of these endings, with the phrase 'mein kleiner
Sohn' (my little son):

mein kleiner Sohn lacht (my little son laughs)
ich höre meinen kleinen Sohn (I hear my little son)
das Gesicht meines kleinen Sohnes (my little son's face)
ich helfe meinem kleinen Sohn (I help my little son)
meine kleinen Söhne lachen (my little sons laugh) etc.

2.1.3 Adjective alone

If the adjective stands on its own, it behaves almost like an article.
In the singular, the forms are:

Nominative:
alter Wein/frische Luft/helles Licht ist gut
old wine/fresh air/bright light is good

Accusative:
ich mag alten Wein/frische Luft/helles Licht
I like old wine/fresh air/bright light

Genitive:
die Vorzüge alt*en* Weines/frisch*er* Luft/hell*en* Lichtes
the advantages of old wine/fresh air/bright light

Dative:
ich gebe den Vorzug alt*em* Wein/frisch*er* Luft/hell*em* Licht
I prefer old wine/fresh air/bright light

In the plural, the forms are:

Nominative
jung*e* Männer/Frauen/Kinder singen
young men/women/children sing

Accusative
ich höre jung*e* Männer/Frauen/Kinder
I hear young men/women/children

Genitive
die Gesichter jung*er* Männer/Frauen/Kinder
the faces of young men/women/children

Dative
ich sage jung*en* Männern/Frauen/Kindern
I say to young men/women/children

2.1.4

One group of adjectives that never change wherever they are found are the adjectives that are derived from town names:

der Kölner Dom, das Frankfurter Würstchen, eine Schwarzwälder Kirschtorte etc.

2.2 Nominalized adjectives

Some adjectives may become nouns in their own right. For instance: **der neue Schüler/Lehrer/Doktor** etc. can become **der Neue** (the newcomer). These adjectives acquire an initial capital letter but retain their adjectival endings (as on pp. 422 to 424). These 'nouns' are shown in the dictionary as follows:

Blinde(r) *mf*, Neue(r) *mf*,

i.e.: der Blinde, ein Blinder/die Blinde, eine Blinde
der Neue, ein Neuer/die Neue, eine Neue

2.3 Comparison of adjectives

The comparison of adjectives is actually one of the few parts of German grammar that is less complicated than its English counterpart. It is always formed in a similar way to the comparison of the word *nice* (*nicer*, *nicest*).

The comparative is formed by adding -er to the adjective; the superlative by adding -st or -est, depending on the ending of the adjective:

billig (cheap)	billiger (cheaper)	billigst (cheapest)
weit (far)	weiter (further)	weitest (furthest)

There are a few exceptions to this rule:

a) adjectives ending in -el and -er lose the -e- in the comparative:

dunkel	dunkler	dunkelst	(dark)
teuer	teurer	teuerst	(expensive)

b) One-syllable adjectives add an Umlaut in the comparative and superlative, where the vowel is 'o', 'a', or 'u' e.g.:

groß	größer	größt	(big)
hoch	höher	höchst	(high)
nah	näher	nächst	(near)

Note: the comparative and superlative forms also take adjectival endings. Hence: der längere Fluß (the longer river), ich sage den besten Schülern (I say to the best pupils).

3. Verbs

3.1 Active Mood Tenses

First of all, don't be disheartened by what looks like a great number of tenses, endings and rules. You will not by any means have to become familiar with all of them at once. At the beginning, you will find that you really need only the present, perfect and imperfect tenses. The following paragraphs will give you patterns for the formation of most tenses for regular verbs. You will see that there are two main 'building principles'. One is a different ending for each person (a different form for "ich, du, wir", etc). The second is the variation in that ending according to tense.

3.1.1 Present tense

The present tense forms are listed below. The basic endings are shown for the verb "spielen". If a *d* or *t* precedes the ending, an *e* is then added in some persons for the sake of pronunciation (see "reden" below).

spielen		reden	
spiel-en	to play	red-en	to speak
ich spiel-e	I play	ich red-e	I speak
du spiel-st	you play	du red-est	you speak
er spiel-t	he plays	er red-et	he speaks
sie spiel-t	she plays	sie red-et	she speaks
es spiel-t	he/she/it plays	es red-et	he/she/it speaks
wir spiel-en	we play	wir red-en	we speak
ihr spiel-t	you play	ihr red-et	you speak
sie spiel-en	they play	sie red-en	they speak
Sie spiel-en	you play	Sie red-en	you speak

Du (singular) and *ihr* (plural) are used to friends, members of the family and children, *Sie* (singular and plural) to people with whom you are not on Christian name terms, e.g.:

'Peter, du sagst....'	'Peter, you say....'
'Herr Maier, Sie sagen....'	'Herr Maier, you say....'
'Maria und Michael, ihr sagt....'	'Maria and Michael, you say....'
'Meine Damen und Herren, Sie sagen....'	'Ladies and Gentlemen, you say....'

The present tense is not only used to describe events that take place in the present, but also largely replaces the future tense. If there is any other indication in a sentence that the action is in the future - a word like 'bald' (soon) or 'morgen' (tomorrow) would be enough - the present tense is used instead of the future.

There is no equivalent of the English progressive '-ing' form. The simple present tense is the only form there is in German.

Verbs that are irregular in the present tense are shown in the table of irregular German verbs (p. 406) The most irregular verb is **sein**, which we give here in full:

ich bin	wir sind
du bist (Sie sind)	ihr seid
er/sie/es ist	sie sind

3.1.2 Imperfect Tense

The forms of the imperfect tense for regular ('weak') verbs are:

spiel-en		red-en	
ich spiel-te	I played	ich red-ete	I spoke
du spiel-test	you played	du red-etest	you spoke
er spiel-te	he played	er red-ete	he spoke
sie spiel-te	she played	sie red-ete	she spoke
es spiel-te	he/she played	es red-ete	he/she spoke
wir spiel-ten	we played	wir red-eten	we spoke
ihr spiel-tet	you played	ihr red-etet	you spoke
sie spiel-ten	they played	sie red-eten	they spoke
Sie spiel-ten	you played	Sie red-eten	you spoke

Both imperfect and perfect tenses (see 3.1.4 below) are used to describe actions and events that take place in the past. There is no basic difference in meaning between the two tenses as there is in English. In German both can often be used to express either the English imperfect or perfect tense. The imperfect tense in German is, however, predominantly used in the written language.

3.1.3 Future and conditional

The future and conditional tenses are formed in a way very similar to English: a form of an auxiliary verb ('werden') + the infinitive.

Future tense

ich werde		I shall	
du wirst		you will	
er wird		he will	
sie wird		she will	
es wird	spielen/reden	he/she will	play/speak
wir werden		we shall	
ihr werdet		you will	
sie werden		they will	
Sie werden		you will (formal)	

Conditional tense

ich würde		I should	
du würdest		you would	
er würde		he would	
sie würde		she would	
es würde	spielen/reden	he/she would	play/speak
wir würden		we should	
ihr würdet		you would	
sie würden		they would	
Sie würden		you would (formal)	

The future tense is only used if there is no other way of telling that the action is in the future. (See above 3.1.1). The conditional is used very much as in English.

3.1.4 Perfect and pluperfect tenses

These are formed very much as in English, i.e. auxiliary verb + past participle.

The difference is that the auxiliary verb which in English is always 'to have' can be either 'haben' or 'sein' in German. Generally, if the verb is describing a movement, like 'laufen' (to run), 'springen' (to jump), 'fahren' (to drive) etc, the auxiliary verb is 'sein'. In all other cases the verb 'haben' is used:

>   ich *habe* gespielt/geredet   I played/spoke
> BUT: ich *bin* gesprungen/gekommen   I jumped/came

These examples also show the different ways of forming the past participle in German. Regular (or so-called "weak") verbs form their past participles by adding *-t* to the root (or *-et* if it already ends in *-t* or *-d*): *spielen - gespielt; reden - geredet.*

"Strong" (or irregular) verbs add *-en* (often with a change of vowel): *singen - gesungen; springen - gesprungen; kommen - gekommen.*
There is no way of predicting the vowel change in strong verbs; they simply have to be learnt along with the verb. A list of such verbs is on page 406.

You will have noticed that the verbs illustrated above take the prefix *ge-* in the past participle. Nearly all verbs do this. The exceptions are those verbs which already have a prefix like *ge-, be-, ent-* etc. and the so-called "separable" verbs, where the *ge-* is inserted between prefix and main verb (see below 3.3).

3.2 Passive mood

The passive is formed as in English, i.e. the past participle is used with an auxiliary verb - "werden" in German, "to be" in English.

e.g.

ich werde gesehen	I am seen
du wirst gesehen	you are seen
ich wurde gesehen	I was seen
du wurdest gesehen	you were seen

It looks slightly more complicated in the future, perfect and pluperfect tenses, but you will normally be able to get along without using them.

e.g.

ich werde gesehen werden	I shall be seen
du wirst gesehen werden	you will be seen
ich bin gesehen worden	I have been seen
ich war gesehen worden	I had been seen
etc.	etc.

Note: the passive construction with "it" as in "it is easily seen" should be translated using an impersonal form:

it is believed	man glaubt
it is easily seen	man sieht leicht

3.3 "Separable" and "inseparable" verbs

In German, some verbs (separable verbs) are composed of a verb and a prefix which can exist as a word in its own right, e.g. auf-tauchen, nach-schlagen. the two elements of such verbs split apart in the present and imperfect tenses and are often found at opposite ends of the sentence:

e.g.: infinitive: weggehen

ich gehe morgen früh weg (I am leaving tomorrow morning)
er ging am Samstag mittag mit Peter weg (he left with Peter on Saturday morning)

The future tense is straightforward in that the verb is re-united with its prefix and the whole infinitive is treated as any other verb in German.

e.g. ich werde mit dir weggehen (I shall leave with you)

In the formation of the past participle, the prefix *ge-* is inserted *between* the two elements of the separable verb:

gehen	ge-gangen
weggehen	weg-ge-gangen

There is another category of verbs, the so-called *in*-separable verbs, which are composed of a prefix and a verb. Here the prefix is not a word that could exist on its own. The prefixes of this group are:

be-	(beantworten	to answer)
emp-	(empfangen	to receive)
ent-	(entscheiden	to decide)
er-	(erleben	to experience)

ge-	(gestehen	to confess)
miß-	(mißbilligen	to disapprove)
ver-	(vergessen	to forget)
zer-	(zerstören	to destroy)

These verbs behave as any other verb in the present and imperfect tense. The past participle, however, is slightly unusual in that it takes no additional prefix ge-.

e.g.: antworten   geantwortet
BUT: beantworten   beantwortet.

3.4 Irregular or "strong" verbs

If you look at the tables of irregular verbs on p. 406, you will find that there are five forms given.

infinitive	2nd singular present tense	3rd singular present tense	3rd singular past tense	past participle
sprechen	sprichst	spricht	sprach	gesprochen

The reasons for giving these forms are the following:

(1) The 2nd and 3rd person (du and er) are the only irregularities in the present tense, and all other persons follow the standard patterns given above (section 3.1.1), e.g.:

ich spreche
du sprichst
er/sie/es spricht
wir sprechen
ihr sprecht
sie sprechen
Sie sprechen

(2) The 3rd person singular in the imperfect tense is the root for the whole imperfect tense, endings being added as shown for the verb "sprechen" below:

ich sprach
du sprachst
er/sie/es sprach
wir sprachen
ihr spracht
sie sprachen
Sie sprachen

(3) The past participle is used unchanged, as with regular verbs, to form the compound tenses and the passive.

3.5 Modal verbs

The modal verbs "dürfen", "können", "wollen", "müssen", "sollen", "mögen" all have irregular forms which are listed in the verb tables. They behave like any other verb in present, imperfect and future tenses. When put into the perfect or pluperfect tense, however, they show an irregularity:

when they are used in connection with a verb, instead of the past participle, they are used in the infinitive:

ich habe gehen wollen	I wanted to go
ich habe reisen müssen	I had to travel
du hast gehen dürfen	you were allowed to go

4. Pronouns

It has already been shown that nouns take different endings and articles depending on their function in the sentence. The same applies to pronouns.

4.1 Personal pronouns

The following table shows the form of the personal pronouns in the nominative, accusative and dative cases:

Nominative		Accusative		Dative	
ich	I	mich	me	mir	to me
du	you	dich	you	dir	to you
er	he	ihn	him	ihm	to him
sie	she	sie	her	ihr	to her
es	it/he/she	es	it/him/her	ihm	to it/him/her
wir	we	uns	us	uns	to us
ihr	you	euch	you	euch	to you
sie	they	sie	them	ihnen	to them
Sie	you	Sie	you	Ihnen	to you

e.g.: ich (*nom*) gab es (*acc*) ihm (*dat*)
 I gave it to him
 wir (*nom*) sagten es (*acc*) ihr (*dat*)
 we said it to her

4.2 Reflexive pronouns

Note that both the accusative and dative forms of the personal pronouns are used for reflexive verbs, which are given in the dictionary as "sich + verb".
e.g. sich waschen
 ich wasche *mich* (I wash myself)
 sich (*dat*) die Hände waschen
 ich wasche *mir* die Hände (I wash my hands)

The reflexive pronouns are as follows:

	accusative	dative
ich	mich	mir
du	dich	dir
er/sie/es	sich	sich
wir	uns	uns
ihr	euch	euch
sie	sich	sich
Sie	sich	sich

4.3 Possessive pronouns

Pronouns that indicate ownership are:

mein	my	unser	our
dein	your	euer	your
sein	his	ihr	their
ihr	her	Ihr	your
sein	its		

Like articles, they take endings depending on the gender, number and case of the following noun. Hence: seine Tante (his aunt), ihr Onkel (her uncle)

As shown above in section 1.5, these endings are the same in the singular as for the article *ein*.

	M	F	N
nominative	-	-e	-
accusative	-en	-e	-
genitive	-es	-er	-es
dative	-em	-er	-em

Hence: mein Lehrer (*nom*) ist hier   my teacher is here
       ich sehe meinen Lehrer (*acc*)   I see my teacher
       das Buch meines Lehrers (*gen*)   my teacher's book
       ich sagte meinem Lehrer (*dat*)   I said to my teacher

In the plural, all genders take the same endings:

nominative	-e
accusative	-e
genitive	-er
dative	-en

Hence: meine Lehrer (*nom*) sind hier   my teachers are here
       ich sehe meine Lehrer (*acc*)   I see my teachers
       die Bücher meiner Lehrer (*gen*) my teachers' books
       ich sagte meinen Lehrern (*dat*) I said to my teachers

5. Sentences

5.1 Inversion

Any sentence which starts with its grammatical subject has the same word order as in English:

Mr. Brown lives in Glasgow
Mr. Brown wohnt in Glasgow

If the sentence, however, starts with any other word, or if a subordinate clause precedes the main clause, the subject and the verb are inverted:

Yesterday we saw the children
Gestern sahen wir die Kinder

When I heard this I came back
Als ich das hörte, kam ich zurück

In the future, perfect and pluperfect tenses, only the conjugated part of the verb changes place with the subject:

Ich werde gewinnen   Bald werde ich gewinnen
I shall win   I shall win soon

Ich habe gelesen   Gestern habe ich gelesen
I read   I read yesterday

5.2 Order of objects

If there is an accusative as well as a dative object in the sentence, the order is: verb + dative object + accusative object.

e.g. ich gebe dem Mann das Buch
     I give the book to the man

However, if one of the objects is a pronoun it *precedes* the noun object, e.g. 'ich gebe es dem Mann'. Where both objects are pronouns the order is usually accusative object + dative object, e.g. 'ich gebe es ihm'.

5.3 Questions

Questions are formed by inversion:

du hast ein Haus in London   you have a house in London
hast du ein Haus in London?   do you have a house in London?

The rules as in 5.1 regarding the position of verbs apply:

er hat ein Buch gekauft   he bought a book
hat er ein Buch gekauft?   did he buy a book?

er wird das Buch kaufen   he will buy the book
wird er das Buch kaufen?   will he buy the book?

The forms of the interrogative pronouns (wer 'who' and was 'what') are listed below:

	person	object
nominative	wer	was
accusative	wen	was
genitive	wessen	wessen
dative	wem	wem

The endings of the interrogative adjective or pronoun welcher, welche, welches ('which' in English) follow the pattern of the definite article as shown in paragraph 1.5. Here are some examples to illustrate the use of the interrogative pronoun:

ich gebe der jungen Frau morgen das neue Buch
'tomorrow I shall give the new book to the young woman'

wer (nom) gibt der jungen Frau morgen das neue Buch? - *Ich.*

wem (dat) gebe ich morgen das neue Buch? - *Der jungen Frau.*

was (acc) gebe ich der jungen Frau morgen? - *Das neue Buch.*

wann gebe ich der jungen Frau das neue Buch? - *Morgen.*

welcher Frau gebe ich morgen das neue Buch? - Der *jungen* Frau.

welches Buch gebe ich der jungen Frau morgen? - Das *neue* Buch.

5.4 Negation

The negative of a statement is most often formed with the word *nicht* placed after the verb or - in the case of compound tenses - after the conjugated part of the verb:

ich singe	ich singe nicht
I sing	I do not sing
ich habe gesungen	ich habe nicht gesungen
I sang	I did not sing
ich werde singen	ich werde nicht singen
I shall sing	I shall not sing

The combination *nicht* + *ein* is never used in German. It is a replaced by the word *kein*, which, as we have shown above (p. 422), is conjugated like *ein*. E.g.:

ich sehe einen Fehler	ich sehe keinen Fehler
I see a mistake	I see no mistake/I don't see a mistake

In the plural:

ich habe Kinder	ich habe keine Kinder
I have children	I have no children

III The sounds of German

Learning to pronounce German well is, as with any foreign language, a matter of adopting different 'speech habits' from those used in speaking English.

A 'foreign accent' results from using the sounds of one's own language to approximate the sounds of the foreign language. This is particularly tempting when the same letter or group of letters represent similar sounds.

German pronunciation is largely regular, so that once you are familiar with the basic rules, you don't have to memorise the pronunciation for each new word you learn.

One of the first things an English speaker will notice about German is that words are hardly ever run into each other. There is a little break - a glottal stop - before each word that starts with a vowel. This means that a German would actually pronounce the two words "it is" separately, rather than like "itis", as an English speaker does.

This minute break occurs, not only between separate words ("ich/antworte", "die/Arbeit" etc.), but also between two words that are linked to form a compound. This is certainly one of the reasons why German sounds so harsh to some ears.

As the table of phonetic symbols on page vi indicates, many letters are pronounced as in English.
The following paragraphs deal with the main differences.

A. *Vowels*

From the table of phonetic symbols on page vi you can see that most vowels have approximate equivalents in English. The two exceptions are the sounds for ö (ó) and ü (y).

ü (y)   Round your lips to say *u* as in "looks" and then try to say *i* as in "bit" instead! There is no j-sound before this vowel, as there is in English "pure".

ö (ó)   To pronounce this vowel, try to say *e* as in "best" with strongly rounded lips.

B. *Consonants*

The main thing to remember is that a soft consonant (b, d, g) "hardens" when it stands at the end of a word or even syllable:

tagen ('ta:gən) but Tag (ta:k)
Stäbe ('ʃtɛbə) but Stab (ʃta:p)

radeln ('ra:dəln) but Rad (ra:t)
End-spiel ('entʃpi:l)
Ab-kommen ('apkɔmən)
Tag-traum ('ta:ktraʊm)

This is so, even when the next syllable starts with a vowel.

Lied-anfang (li:t'anfang)
ab-artig ('apa:rtiç)
schlag-artig ('ʃla:ka:rtiç)

Many consonants are pronounced as in English, and the main differences are listed below:

b	like English b, but like p at the end of words and syllables
c	usually pronounced like German z in front of e, i and like German k in front of a, o, u
d	like English d, but like t at the end of words and syllables
g	always like English g in "garden". Exceptions are words from French, where it is pronounced like the "s" in "leisure"
h	usually like English h in "have". After vowels, its function is simply to lengthen the vowel and it is not pronounced (e.g.: sah)
ch	like the final sound of Scottish loch after a, u, o, au; almost like the "sh" in "should", after ä, ö, ü, eu, ei, e, i, äu
j	usually pronounced like the y in "you"; exceptions are words from English, where it is most often pronounced the English way (e.g. jockey). However, English words that have become truly integrated into German are sometimes pronounced with the y-sound, e.g. "Jazz"
k	like English k in "look"
l	like English l in "London"
qu	always pronounced kv as in "bank vault"
r	this is one of the sounds that is entirely different from English. There are two ways of producing the r-sound in German. The standard one is produced in the throat, almost as if gargling. But there is also a "tongue-tip"-r similar to a rolled English r
s	unlike English, s in front of a vowel is always soft, even at the beginning of a word: e.g. the two s-sounds in Susanne both sound like the s in rose. Note: s at the end of a word or syllable is always hard so the second s in Schiffsanker is hard, though it precedes a vowel
ss	always the s-sound of English "sausage". This also shortens the vowel it follows

ß	pronounced like ss at the end of a word, it does not, however, necessarily shorten the preceding vowel (e.g.: ich muß - short, der Fuß - long). Inside a word it is pronounced like ss and it lengthens the preceding vowel (e.g.: Füße, büßen)
st/sp	at the beginning of a word, always (except for foreign words) pronounced like a combination of "sh" (as in "should") and "t" (as in "teach") or "sh" and "p" (as in "put"). In all other cases like English "st" in "post", or "sp" in "grasp"
sch	always like "sh" in "dash". One exception: if the "s" and the"ch" belong to different syllables: e.g.: Haus, Häus-chen, then they are of course pronounced separately
th	like English t in "tea"
v	usually, this is pronounced like f in "father". The exceptions are mostly words of Latin orgin (Vase, Veranda etc) in which case it is pronounced like English v
w	this sound is always pronounced like English v in "love"
x	always pronounced like English x in "tax"
z	always pronounced like "ts" in "cats"

IV The time, dates and numbers

The time

what time is it?	wie spät ist es?, wieviel Uhr ist es?
it is ...	es ist ...
at what time?	um wieviel Uhr?
at ...	um ...

00.00	Mitternacht, null Uhr
00.10	zehn nach zwölf, null Uhr zehn
00.15	viertel nach zwölf, null Uhr fünfzehn
00.30	halb eins, null Uhr dreißig
00.45	viertel vor eins, null Uhr fünfundvierzig
01.00	ein Uhr (morgens or früh)
01.05	fünf nach eins, ein Uhr fünf
01.10	zehn nach eins (morgens or nachts), ein Uhr zehn
01.15	viertel nach eins, ein Uhr fünfzehn
01.25	fünf vor halb zwei, ein Uhr fünfundzwanzig
01.30	halb zwei, ein Uhr dreißig
01.35	fünf nach halb zwei, ein Uhr fünfunddreißig
01.40	zwanzig vor zwei, zehn nach halb zwei, ein Uhr vierzig
01.45	viertel vor zwei, ein Uhr fünfundvierzig
01.50	zehn vor zwei, ein Uhr fünfzig
01.59	eine Minute vor zwei, ein Uhr neunundfünfzig
12.00	zwölf Uhr (mittags), Mittag
12.30	halb eins (mittags or nachmittags), zwölf Uhr dreißig
13.00	ein Uhr (nachmittags), dreizehn Uhr
13.30	halb zwei (nachmittags), dreizehn Uhr dreißig
19.00	sieben Uhr (abends), neunzehn Uhr
19.30	halb acht (abends), neunzehn Uhr dreißig
23.00	elf Uhr (nachts), dreiundzwanzig Uhr
23.45	viertel vor zwölf (nachts), dreiundzwanzig Uhr fünfundvierzig

in 20 minutes	in zwanzig Minuten
20 minutes ago	vor zwanzig Minuten
wake me up at 7	wecken Sie mich bitte um sieben Uhr
1 hour, 20', 45"	ein Uhr, zwanzig Minuten und fünfundvierzig Sekunden

Dates and numbers

1. The date

what's the date today?	welches Datum ist heute?
it's the ...	heute ist der ...

1st of February	erste Februar
2nd of February	zweite Februar
28th of February	achtundzwanzigste Februar

he's coming on the 7th (of May) er kommt am siebten (Mai)

I was born in 1945
    ich bin neunzehnhundertfünfundvierzig geboren
I was born on the 15th of July 1945
    ich bin am fünfzehnten Juli neunzehnhundertfünfundvierzig geboren

during the sixties	in den sechziger Jahren
in the twentieth century	im zwanzigsten Jahrhundert
in May	im Mai
on Monday (the 15th)	Montag(, den fünfzehnten)
on Mondays	montags
next/last Monday	nächsten/letzten Montag
in 10 days' time	in zehn Tagen

2. Telephone numbers

I would like Bonn 334 22 15
    ich hätte gerne Bonn drei drei vier zwo zwo eins fünf *or*
    dreihundertvierunddreißig zweiundzwanzig fünfzehn
give me Bonn 30 02 02
    geben Sie mir bitte Bonn drei null null zwo null zwo *or* dreißig null zwo null zwo
could you get me Köln 22 00 79, extension 2233
    könnte ich bitte Köln zwo zwo null null sieben neun, Apparat zwo zwo drei drei
    haben?
the Bonn prefix is 0228
    die Vorwahl von Bonn ist null zwo zwo acht

3. Using numbers

he lives at number 10	er wohnt (in) Nummer zehn
it's in chapter 7, on page 7	es steht in Kapitel sieben, auf Seite sieben
he lives on the 7th floor	er wohnt im siebten Stock *or* in der siebten Etage
he came in 7th	er wurde siebter
a share of one seventh	ein Anteil von einem Siebtel
scale 1:25,000	im Maßstab eins zu fünfundzwanzigtausend

Numbers

1	ein(s)	1st	erste(r,s), 1.		
2	zwei	2nd	zweite(r,s), 2.		
3	drei	3rd	dritte(r,s), 3.		
4	vier	4th	vierte(r,s), 4.		
5	fünf	5th	fünfte(r,s), 5.		
6	sechs	6th	sechste(r,s), 6.		
7	sieben	7th	siebte(r,s), 7.		
8	acht	8th	achte(r,s), 8.		
9	neun	9th	neunte(r,s), 9.		
10	zehn	10th	zehnte(r,s), 10.		

11	elf	11th	elfte(r,s)
12	zwölf	12th	zwölfte(r,s)
13	dreizehn	13th	dreizehnte(r,s)
14	vierzehn	14th	vierzehnte(r,s)
15	fünfzehn	15th	fünfzehnte(r,s)
16	sechzehn	16th	sechzehnte(r,s)
17	siebzehn	17th	siebzehnte(r,s)
18	achtzehn	18th	achtzehnte(r,s)
19	neunzehn	19th	neunzehnte(r,s)
20	zwanzig	20th	zwanzigste(r,s)

21	einundzwanzig	21st	einundzwanzigste(r,s)
22	zweiundzwanzig	22nd	zweiundzwanzigste(r,s)
30	dreißig	30th	dreißigste(r,s)
40	vierzig	100th	hundertste(r,s)
50	fünfzig	101st	hunderterste(r,s)
60	sechzig	1,000th	tausendste(r,s)
70	siebzig		
80	achtzig	1/2	ein Halb
90	neunzig	1/3	ein Drittel
		1/4	ein Viertel
100	hundert	1/5	ein Fünftel
101	hunderteins	0.5	null Komma fünf, 0,5
300	dreihundert	10%	zehn Prozent
301	dreihunderteins	100%	hundert Prozent

1,000	tausend, 1.000	$2+2$	zwei plus zwei
1,001	tausend(und)eins, 1.001	$2\div2$	zwei dividiert durch zwei
5,000	fünftausend, 5.000	2×2	zwei mal zwei
1,000,000	eine Million	$2-2=$	zwei minus zwei gleich ...

6^2	sechs zum Quadrat, sechs hoch zwei
6^3	sechs hoch drei
$20m^2$	zwanzig Quadratmeter
$20m^3$	zwanzig Kubikmeter